THE
MAKING OF AMERICANS

The Stein family ca. 1881, East Oakland, California.
(Stein indicated by the X.)

Gertrude Stein

THE
MAKING OF AMERICANS

BEING A HISTORY OF
A FAMILY'S PROGRESS

Foreword by William H. Gass
Introduction by Steven Meyer

Dalkey Archive Press

First published in France by Contact Editions, 1925. First American edition
published by Albert & Charles Boni, 1926. Second American edition
published by Something Else Press, 1966. Third American edition published by
Dalkey Archive Press, 1995.

The frontispiece and the photograph of Gertrude Stein on the back cover are
reproduced courtesy the Yale Collection of American Literature, Beinecke Rare
Book and Manuscript Library, Yale University.

Library of Congress Cataloging-in-Publication Data
Stein, Gertrude, 1874-1946.
The making of Americans : being a history of a family's progress /
Gertrude Stein ; foreword by William H. Gass ;
introduction by Steven Meyer. — 1st Dalkey Archive ed.
p.   cm.
1. Immigrants—United States—Fiction.
2. Family—United States—Fiction.
I. Title.
PS3537.T323M3   1995   813'.52—dc20   95-16357
ISBN 1-56478-088-0

Publication of this volume was made possible in part by grants from the Illinois
Arts Council and the National Endowment for the Arts.

NATIONAL
ENDOWMENT
FOR 🌱 THE
ARTS

Dalkey Archive Press
Illinois State University
Campus Box 4241
Normal, IL 61790-4241

*Printed on permanent/durable acid-free paper and bound in the
United States of America.*

CONTENTS

FOREWORD

by

WILLIAM H. GASS

The computer on which I am writing these words has a function which allows me to examine the layout of the page I am readying for the printer. Since this look at my text is so wide-eyed I cannot read a line, only view the lineup, a magnifying glass which I can draw down out of its shy place in the corner is provided to enlarge and make comprehensible some chosen bit. Because Steven Meyer deals so wonderfully with the development and general themes of *The Making of Americans,* I thought I might take a moment to microscope a single sentence, one which he quotes, since that is convenient, and since it would be my contention that almost any sentence would yield the same results.

It should no longer be necessary to argue Gertrude Stein's importance or insist upon her artistry, but I would like to highlight some of the remarkable aspects of Gertrude Stein's prose; aspects which, if the reader pays attention to them, will slow her pace, but perhaps quicken her sense of the journey. The passage begins: "A man in his living has many things inside him . . ." (149). If we listen to this line, we shall discover how a real artist proceeds. If we look at this line (not merely read it), we shall find out how important looking as well as listening are to the understanding and appreciation of prose.

In one sense Gertrude Stein's style is very plain, and she uses a severely limited vocabulary, but she also insists upon a colorless, somewhat vague language which is almost always oddly phrased—just far enough out of the ordinary to disconcert. If we hear that "a man's gotta do what a man's gotta do," we know that the speaker is using this generalization to refer to himself (unless he is being ironic). Here the narrator is referring to David Hersland, and through him to the rest of us. Earlier the text has distinguished between home life, business life, midlife, and so on, but the categories have been expressed in a progressive way as "business living," "middle living," and "home living." This usage is not customary. So the placement of the phrase "in his living" makes an otherwise straightforward sentence somewhat strange.

She does not write "A man through his living" because that would imply that a man's way of life made him what he is. By emphasizing the preposition "in," Stein suggests submergence and containment. A man's living is larger than he is. "A man in his living has many things inside him . . ." *Amanin,* the music begins. Then the *i*s and the *m*s and the *n*s take over. "*A m an* **in** h *is* l *iv* **in** g h*as man* y th **in** gs **in** s *id* e h **im**." The "in" in "living" and in "things" is not pronounced, but must be seen. The "man" in "man" changes to "men" in "many." "A man in his living has men (ee th ings) inside him." Both the look and the listen of the language matter. The "in" in "inside" and the "in" in "living" look alike but, in terms of sound, go their separate ways.

It is also typical of Gertrude Stein to employ quite colloquial expressions as technical terms. "Does Merriweather have it in him to cross the country?" That is, does he have the gumption. Our selection continues (using a comma where a colon would normally be): "A man in his living has many things inside him, he has in him his important feeling of himself to himself inside him." The schoolteacher would be expected to delete the "in him," because it is redundant, however this "in him" will be followed by ten more, as well as two that are submerged slightly in "inside him," with the total number of "him"s reaching seventeen. One way or another the passage will beat away on **im im im** like a drum.

"A man in his living has many things inside him." *What things?* "He has in him his important feeling of himself to himself inside him." *What's that?* "He has in him the kind of important feeling of himself to himself that makes his kind of man." "In" looks its way out of "kind," which sounds the "I"—kEYEnduh. "Kinda" is the colloquial form. Meanwhile, against the **in im**s, and the narrow slit-shaped vowels, are increasingly placed the open *o*s of "-port-" as well as the look-alike *o*s of "of" and "to" with their *uv oo* music, and the rhyming of "come" and "some" and "from," as here: "this comes sometimes from a mixture in him of all the kinds of natures in him, this comes sometimes from the bottom nature in him, this comes sometimes from the natures in him that are in him that are sometime in him mixed up with the bottom nature in him." You couldn't spell "bot tom" better than it is.

We have shifted from "im" to "om"—that is, *um, I'm.* The function of "sometimes" (as common as "kinda") changes, as the passage moves shrewdly from "himself" to "themselves." "Sometimes in some men this other nature or natures in him are not mixed with the bottom nature in him at any time in his living." The rhetoric has recaptured the opening formula. "Many of such men have the important feeling of themselves inside them coming from the other nature or natures in them not from the bottom nature of them."

The sound shifts throughout follow and reinforce the sense. The sound connections link the language into one melodic line, and the repetitions return us in the manner of the baroque to early elements over which we pass again like swifts in flight.

```
A man                                              in
       his living        has many things          inside him,
    he                   has                       in    him
       his     important feeling of himself to himself   inside him
    he                   has                       in    him
             the kind of
                 important feeling of himself to himself
that makes
       his        kind of man;
       this comes sometimes from a mixture         in    him of all
             the kinds of                  natures in    him,
       this comes sometimes from the bottom nature in    him
       this comes sometimes from the        natures in   him
that are                                           in    him
that are         sometime                          in    him
                       mixed up with
                            the bottom nature      in    him,
              sometimes                            in
              some
men    this                        other nature
                        or     natures             in    him
              are not mixed    with
                            the bottom nature      in    him
             at any time                           in
         his living
                       many of such
men have the
             important feeling of themselves       inside them
         coming             from the other nature
                              or     natures       in    them
                   not from the bottom nature      of    them.
```

In this spindle diagram (so named because we can run our eye, the way one used to be able to thrust a knitting needle through holes punched in IBM cards, down common points of verbal return to see how the sentence revolves), eighteen "in"s and thirteen "him"s line up on the right side, and these "him"s are not the half of it, since four more can be found in the expression "important feeling of himself to himself," giving "him" those seventeen appearances I mentioned, while "nature" has to be satisfied with eight, "sometimes" with five, and "bottom" four. The "his/this" combination is also frequent (eight).

We could easily draw up a phrase diagram, which wouldn't split "in his living" and other grammatical combinations the way the spindle layout does, arranging the groups as the paragraph balances them throughout its length. Assonance, consonance, rnyme, rhythm, repetition, phrase placement, the movement of singulars to plurals, the elaborate colloquial vagueness of reference, the careful distinctions which underlie the meaning, are used together to give emotional weight to the journey—in this case a short passage of analysis, but one which mimics the movement of life itself—a trip which trips over itself, aims at a target reflected in a mirror, returns, redoes, as habits do, when we shave ourselves, or powder our cheeks and comb our hair again, though one more day has passed, because life belongs to the progressive present, it is living, but living is "same after same," it is variations on a theme, a deep theme, made of the mixtures of natures, it is a round, it is fugal, like the ring which Gertrude made to round her roses, and it gives rise to the feeling that, as automatic as habit is, as if it were in charge of each action, and therefore of most of life—our clamorous family of familiar, customary gestures, squalls and bites—it is nevertheless we who run the comb's teeth through our hair, it is we who grimace in the glass, feeling always who we are despite the mechanics of our motions, the repetitions which sum a life: "Some can remember something of some such thing," she writes; however just how does this feeling arise while scraping carrots, preparing dinner, kissing, as always, with puckered lips, so as not to get too intimate—the whore's reserve—how does it happen that we feel we are present in a present our reruns make us absent from? shifting gears, poking in a purse, lighting up, the same creases from the same sheets in the same sleep wrinkling our bare back, so that we recognize even the rare as regular—that's the danger—not even sighing when someone says: your voice sounds better through the mail; and we continue simply to continue, continue to feel a sip's a sip, the same as always, yet just this one, cool and pale, though another, cool and pale will follow, as we've always done, wine at five in a fine glass, because if it didn't arise, if the feeling failed to materialize, we'd be good as dead, a phonograph, rounding on itself silently, making no music, though the needle wears and the grooves deepen and the table's turning slows to let us know that something's happened, something of notably no importance.

In the sentence which follows the one which Steven Meyer and I quote and comment on, another variation on the same words, another teasing of meaning out into the open, another singing of the nearly same song, occurs:

Many men have sometime in their living the important feeling of themselves to themselves inside them, some men have always this feeling inside them, most men have such a feeling more or less in them, perhaps all men and mostly all women have sometime in them a feeling of themselves to themselves inside them; this comes sometimes from a mixture in them of the kind of natures in them, this comes sometimes from the bottom nature of them, this comes sometimes from the natures in them that are mixed up with the bottom natures of them, sometimes in some of them the other nature or natures in them are not mixed with the bottom nature in them, many of such of them have the important feeling of themselves inside them coming from the other natures not from the bottom nature of them.

In the great dirge which concludes *The Making of Americans,* in the surge of life in the ending of it, the answer is given, and we can hear it: consciousness is like the music of the words, for in them, and in their pace, and in their arrangement, their rhetoric, their repetitions, the patterns they lay down, in their prolonged investigation of nuance, of the subtle differences in sameness, in the *in* of "in" itself, lies the wonderful, the saving rainbow of awareness, the presence of force and feeling; but what should anyone expect me to say, except to say "style"—style is consciousness, arising from relation, from the way this syllable connects with that, or cell with cell until the brain bursts into seeing, with sentences whose shape is their understanding, like one which declares, as Stein might: my knowing that I am going, though I go, is never gone, if my going, and my knowing, are strongly sung. She says:

Family living can be existing and any one can come to be a dead one and every one is then a dead one and there are then not any more being living. Any old one can come to be a dead one. Every old one can come to be a dead one. Any family being existing is one having some being then not having come to be a dead one. Any family living can be existing when not every one has come to be a dead one. Every one in a family living having come to be dead ones some are remembering something of some such thing. Some being living not having come to be dead ones can be ones being in a family living. Some being living and having come to be old ones can come then to be dead ones. Some being living and being in a family living and coming then to be old ones can come then to be dead ones. Any one can be certain that some can remember such a thing. Any family living can be one being existing and some can remember something of some such thing. (925)

A routine—a rite, a rigamarole—of this kind is a recognition, a recognition which is one of a kind, though every word is old and overused and done, each perception trite, and each sorrow common. Any and every one of us will die, but only a few, a small sum at any time, can remember—really remember—something of some such thing: when our organs no longer peal, when our words no longer rhyme.

INTRODUCTION

by

Steven Meyer

"I am hard at the Long Book," Gertrude Stein announced to her close friend Carl Van Vechten in June 1925, as she and her companion Alice B. Toklas planted themselves in the French countryside to correct the proofs of *The Making of Americans,* set to be published that fall—a mere fourteen years after it had been completed. "It is long but it ain't bad," she noted. In August, the corrections finished, she wrote to Sherwood Anderson that "it came to 925 pages and has been a pleasure to do and rather strange to do, you see I have not read it all these years." "Lots of people," she added,

will think many strange things in it as to tenses and persons and adjectives and adverbs and divisions are due to the french compositors' errors but they are not it is quite as I worked at it and even when I tried to change it well I didn't really try but I went over it to see if it could go different and I always found myself forced back into its incorrectnesses so there they stand. There are some pretty wonderful sentences in it and we know how fond we both are of sentences.

If "Melanctha," Stein's 1905-6 tale of a young black woman's "wanderings after wisdom," was, as she proposed, "the first definite step away from the nineteenth century and into the twentieth century in literature," *The Making of Americans*—the "monumental work" that she assembled during the next five years—"was the beginning, really the beginning of modern writing." These are pretty strong claims, yet at least with respect to chronological priority, they are indisputable. Among major English-language exemplars of "modern writing," Eliot for instance was still in high school in 1905 and 1906, Joyce had only recently left Dublin for Trieste, Woolf had just moved to Bloomsbury, Pound was finishing—and Lawrence and Moore were just beginning—college, Faulkner was eight years old, and Yeats was still very much a nineteenth-century writer.

Like the United States, which among nations had, according to Stein, "created the twentieth century . . . by the methods of the civil war and the commercial conceptions that followed it," so had she, among writers, introduced the methods and conceptions appropriate to a thoroughgoing twentieth-century literature. However, regarding the features that made her writing so original and at the same time so representative of modernity, she tended to be fairly oblique: as when in *Everybody's Autobiography* (1937) she observed that "The Making of Americans is a very important thing and everybody ought to be *reading at it or it*" (my italics here and throughout). If this suggests, in portmanteau fashion, that reading *The Making of Americans* may require *looking at* or *picking at* or *working at* it—or even *aiming at* a progressively fuller understanding of it—for most readers such "reading at" would feel like an unnatural act, every bit as awkward and "incorrect" as Stein's own phrasing here.

In August 1925 she reported to Van Vechten:

we are almost all done now and it makes me feel well I don't know xactly what it does make me feel but there he is the eldest son, Three Lives being the eldest but a daughter, and ainé as I call him has been a bother, we will hope now that his travaux and all is nicely done that he will make the future easy for his parents, anyway there we are and you are his god father so you're responsible at least for his religion and morals, poor dear ainé.

One might well dispute whether *The Making of Americans* exhibits any religion or morals at all and even whether in the end the "bother" it demands of the reader can be justified. What needs to be shown, then, is how, despite an appearance of "looseness," this eldest son of Stein and Toklas—writer and typewriter respectively, proofreaders together—is indeed "nicely done"; and, this being so, how *The Making of Americans* proceeds to "make the future easy," both for its immediate family and for subsequent readers.

1. THE MAKING OF AMERICANS

Nearly a quarter century before, in September 1902, Stein arrived in England for a visit of five months' duration. With her brother Leo, she spent much of the first month in a cottage in the English countryside, near the home of acquaintances from Florence, Bernard and Mary Berenson. "We have Am[erica] vs. Eng[land] disputes all the time," Leo reported—with the Steins "hold[ing] up the American end" of the discussion against the Berensons and other members of their circle, which included Bertrand Russell, Mary Berenson's brother-in-law. "The general theme is why in the name of all that's reasonable do you think of going back to America?" Shortly after Stein returned to the United States in February—Leo having moved to Paris in the meantime—she began work on her first sustained piece of literary writing, a 35-page narrative entitled "The Making of Americans, Being the History of a Family's Progress," which would serve as the nucleus of the much longer account bearing the same name. (It is included in Stein's *Fernhurst, Q.E.D., and Other Early Writings*.) "It has always seemed to me a rare privilege," the work begins, "this of being an American, a real American and yet one whose tradition it has taken scarcely sixty years to create." "Twenty years ago," the narrator adds, commenting on the period when the story opens, "the fever to be an Anglo Saxon and a gentleman . . . had not [yet] broken over the land."

In a letter from London several months earlier Stein had observed that "though the country is most lovely and the galleries and the book stores all that one could ask for I am not yet enamored of those institutions that have made Englishmen what they are." Like Hawthorne and Henry James before her, she distinguished "individualistic America" from England—and from the "old world" generally—by the relative poverty of its cultural and social institutions. If the narrator of "The Making of Americans" "laud[s] the bourgeois family life at [the] expense if need be of the individual," and argues for "keep[ing] the old world way of being born in a middle class tradition from affectionate honest parents whom you honor for those virtues," this is due not to anti-individualistic prejudice but to the conviction that "a material middle class with its straightened bond of family is the one thing always healthy, human, vital and from which has always sprung the best the world can know." Yet the advantages of "bourgeois family life" become impediments when one "grow[s] old enough to determine [one's own] fortune and relations," only to find that in the United States no socially acceptable alternatives to the values of the "material middle class" exist.

"It takes time," the narrator suggests, "to make queer people[,] time and certainty of place and means. Custom, passion and a feel for mother earth are needed to breed vital singularity in any man *and alas how poor we are in all these three*." As a direct consequence of the impoverished American environment—and the resulting inhospitability to any "strain of singularity" that doesn't "keep within the limits of conventional respectability"—Americans who exhibit traces of "vital singularity" are obliged to "fly to the kindly comfort of an older world accustomed to take all manner of strange forms into its bosom." Although the narrator laments this state of affairs, it remains true that only such cultural impoverishment makes possible the rapid formation of "real Americans," complete with traditionally American family histories, in little more than sixty years.

Stein's narrator regards with dismay exactly those aspects of American culture—"the *thin imagination* and the *superficial sentiment* of American landscape painting"; the "large and splendid canvas completely painted over but painted *full of empty space*" which characterizes both New York and "the home the rich and self made merchant makes [there] to hold his family and himself"; "that certain shade of green[,] *dull without hope*," which "so completely bodies forth the ethically aesthetic aspiration of *the spare American emotion*"—which Stein herself, having completed *The Making of Americans,* would come to defend as a positive resource. Shortly after the outbreak of World War I, for instance, she and Bertrand Russell resumed their earlier dispute concerning the relative merits of America and England. According to the account in *The Autobiography of Alice B. Toklas,* Russell, who had just spent several months teaching at Harvard, criticized "the weaknesses of the american system of education, particularly their neglect of the study of greek," whereupon Stein "replied that of course England which was an island needed Greece which was or might have been an island. At any rate greek was essentially an island culture, while America needed essentially the culture of a continent which was of necessity latin." Subsequently she "grew very eloquent on the disembodied abstract quality of the american character and cited examples, mingling automobiles with Emerson, and all proving that they did not need greek."

Stein's progression from "The Making of Americans" to the completed *Making of Americans* involved an ever-increasing emphasis on the positive nature of "the disembodied quality of the american character," a quality she associated not with the "breeding" or "heredity" or family histories of Americans but with whatever Americans actually made: money, automobiles, works of literature. These products tended to be removed or abstracted from their immediate background, unlike their European counterparts. The title of *The Making of Americans* may consequently be understood in two different but noncontradictory senses, depending on whether one reads it as containing an objective or a subjective genitive: as the process whereby Americans are made (*The making of who? The making of Americans*) or the process whereby Americans make anything (*The what of Americans? The making of Americans*). There is "the half that made me"—as Stein put it in her 1936 lecture "An American and France"—and "the half in which I made what I made." American abstraction is not, however, the product of American family history; rather the form that American family histories generally take, the peculiar "progress" recorded in *The Making of Americans,* is itself the product of American abstraction, an abstraction rooted in what Stein characterized as "the geographical history of America."

"After all," she observed in "An American and France" (in a passage that is repeated almost verbatim from an earlier lecture), "anybody is as their land and air is. Anybody is as the sky is low or high, the air heavy or clear and anybody is as there is wind or no wind there. It is that which makes them and the arts they make and the work they do and the way they eat and the way they drink and the way they learn and everything." The narrator of "The Making of Americans" expressed similar sentiments concerning the "harmony between a people and their land," with the proviso that in the case of Americans the harmony had *yet* to be achieved:

Structure, structure, the earth has been strongly handled in the making of our prospects whether they are the concentrated stony meadows of Northern New

England, the delicate subtle contours of the Connecticut hills or the rich flowing uplands of the middle South that give us an English understanding or the Spanish desert spaces of the West or the bare sun-burned foot-hills of California that make the Western sun-lover feel that to be in Tuscany is to be at home. No it is not for need of strong-featured out of doors that we use the old world, it is for an accomplished harmony between a people and their land, for what understanding have we of the thing we tread, we the children of one generation.

What Stein's narrator fails to recognize is that there may be a distinctively American "feel for mother earth," a feeling for the land and air of the United States as a whole rather than for those parts that resemble, at least geographically, individual European nations. Stein herself came to believe that in the United States space and time were uniquely structured as regions through which Americans wandered without fixed itineraries or set endpoints. By contrast, the English in England, and other European peoples within their own borders, had arrived at relative harmony with the land through centuries, and even millennia, of cultivation. As a result, the aimless wandering that was native to American soil—native, that is, to the entire *land* and not just to particular regions—ran contrary to the feel of English or Italian or Spanish landscapes, every detail and centimeter of which was known, and known to be known. As Stein informed Russell, the United States required "the culture of a continent" in which the intimate geographical knowledge possible on an island or in an enclave was replaced by knowledge which held irrespective of local differences: instead of the specificity of Greek, the "disembodied abstract quality" of Latin.

"The Nineteenth Century was roughly the Englishman's Century," Stein suggested in a 1935 lecture: the typical method of the century was the English one "of 'muddling through,'" "begin[ning] at one end and hop[ing] to come out at the other." If to be born and raised in the nineteenth century was consequently to be "a natural believer in progress"—as Stein acknowledged herself to be—this placed Americans in an especially awkward position. Belief in progress may well have been appropriate for an Englishman, as the product of an island culture, yet it was at odds with American geographical history. For the notion of progress entailed movement directed at some realizable, and desirable, goal. The constitutive form of motion for an American, by contrast, was aimless wandering, and in *The Making of Americans* Stein gradually came to see how such wandering might be regarded positively rather than negatively: from a perspective, that is, which didn't simply prejudge matters by assuming that temporal and spatial movement had to be organized "progressively" in order to be acceptable.

Already in "The Making of Americans" the relation between the open-ended form of American wandering and the closed form of the American family was central to Stein's concerns. "By good fortune while our family are still standing together on the lawn an old peddler comes up the road," her narrator observes. "I say by good fortune for so the picture is complete the picture you must understand if you are to rightly read the story that I mean to tell." Upon seeing the peddler, the paterfamilias is reminded of his own youth, "peddling through the country," and contrasts the education he "gave himself" with "all these modern improvements and all this education business" that his children "think so much of." The distance between "The Making of Americans" and the completed *Making of Americans* is perhaps best measured in these terms. Instead of American wandering being causally or even dialectically related to the American family, no determinate connection still exists between them at the conclusion of *The Making of Americans*. The "history of a[n American] family's progress" differs from that of just any family because it inevitably runs up against "the disembodied abstract quality of the american character." Although this need not put an end to the family, it does put an end to the idea that the family's history can be recorded in the form of a narrative of progress.

2. THE HISTORY OF A FAMILY'S PROGRESS

Despite her distaste for English institutions, it would be some time before Stein fully recognized the inadequacy of narrative—as the prototypically English literary form—for conveying American experience. (She once proposed that English literature from Chaucer on needed "to have in it the emotion that only could come from everything having something that came before and after that thing.") In the summer of 1903 Stein rejoined her brother in Europe and, putting "The Making of Americans" aside, began work on her lesbian roman à clef, *Q.E.D.,* which she had completed by mid-fall. This led to "Fernhurst. The History of Philip Redfern, A Student of the Nature of Woman," probably written in 1904, and then, in 1905 and 1906, the "three histories" published in 1909 as *Three Lives*. Not until she had finished the last of these, "Melanctha"—subtitled "Each One As She May"—did she return to the earlier history and its concern with "family progress," a progress registered emblematically in the names of the four Dehning children, only three of whom make it into the completed work:

The eldest girl now eighteen years of age and born while the old world was still a vital background was named from her maternal grandmother and received Julia in unperverted transmission, the second child though only younger by two years received her Bertha as a modern version of the paternal grandmother's Betty. In the three years before the son was born the first distant mutter of the breaking Anglo Saxon wave had come to them and he was named George with a complete neglect of ancestry and only in his second name of Simon to be slightly held as an initial was there any harking back to sources. In three more years they had another daughter and now there was a call for elegance as well as foreignness and so this child like many of her generation was named Hortense.

Between 1906 and 1908 the focus of the original "Making of Americans" expanded to include a "Western" family, the Herslands—modeled on Stein's own immediate family—in addition to the Dehnings, whom she had modeled on her New York cousins. Although no draft of this intermediate version has survived, Leon Katz has ingeniously reconstructed the general outline of the narrative from the extensive notebooks Stein kept between 1902 and 1911. He proposes that the third and final version of *The Making of Americans*—composed between 1908 and 1911 and reprinted here—contains a "lengthy passage of genuine second-draft text, run[ning] . . . from the conclusion of [Henry] Dehning's sermon to his children on page 11 to the appearance of the 'matchmaker' on page 78." (Actually, material from the first draft is interlaced with new "second-draft text" throughout the first 34 pages of the final version; not until page 35, and the move west, are the parameters set by the 1903 draft breached.) After page 78 *The Making of Americans* changes from what Ulla E. Dydo has called "a fairly conventional nineteenth century novel" into a work of "psychological typology." In the course of this transformation, it progresses, as Stein observed in *The Autobiography of Alice B. Toklas*, "from being a history of a family to being a history of everybody the family knew," as it would later metamorphose into "the history of every kind and of every individual human being," and finally, "in spite of all this," "a hero" would emerge, whose death would bring the book to a close.

One may ask, all the same, just how conventional the novel can have been that Stein resumed writing in early 1906 after having completed the singularly unconventional "Melanctha." No doubt she projected a relatively conventional *narrative* along the lines sketched in her notebooks. Yet surely this does not require that the *history* of family progress which she began anew had to take the form of a conventional nineteenth-century novel, any more than the history of "Melanctha" unfolds in the same order and tempo as does its plot. Nor does the fairly complete plotting of the new *Making of Americans* require one to suppose that in the second draft Stein had already progressed beyond "the appearance of the 'matchmaker' " before her writing shifted course.

The difference between the relatively traditional manner of novelistic storytelling that Stein had aimed for in 1903 and the more open-ended conception she brought to her "family history" several years later is demonstrated by comparing parallel passages in the 1903 draft and in the final version:

1. In [Julia] the mother's type had become something very completely attractive. . . . Julia's reverence for her father's gentleness and justice and her affection for his cheery wholesome person suggested the leavening of a possible self-condemnation and a large part of our family history must be a record of her struggle to live down her mother in her. . . . "Julia is brilliant, attractive and commanding but her younger sister [Bertha] not so striking at first sight is of a nature deeper, finer and more efficient," agreed the suitors and the family friends, for are we

not all slaves to a story-book tradition and can we ever think the brilliant beauty a really good and true one and the quiet, sweet, alluring maiden the very useless member of the family. But this is not the whole of the story either for remember reader that I am not now to take away the character from either one of our young friends; they may still work out the well established tradition or they may try to prove the story-books all wrong. Only keep in mind that futures are uncertain and be well warned in time from the vainglory of sudden judgments.

2. Yes in Julia Dehning the prosperous, good-looking, domineering woman was a very attractive being. . . . Yes Julia Dehning was bright and full of vigor, and with something always a little harsh in her, making underneath her young bright vigorous ardent honest feeling a little of the sense of rasping that was just now in her mother's talking.

And so those who read much in story books surely now can tell what to expect of her, and yet, please reader, remember that this is perhaps not the whole of our story either, neither her father for her, nor the living down her mother who is in her, for I am not ready yet to take away the character from our Julia, for truly she may work out as the story books would have her or we may find all different kinds of things for her, and so reader, please remember, the future is not yet certain for her, and be you well warned reader, from the vain-glory of being sudden in your judgment of her. (15)

In removing all traces of the younger sister from the final version, Stein significantly raises the stakes of her narrator's skepticism toward the "story-book tradition." In the earlier draft the reader is merely warned that the "opposition in resemblance" of the two sisters may not determine their respective roles in the family. Fairy-tale expectations concerning "the brilliant beauty" and "the quiet, sweet, alluring maiden" may prove "vainglorious"; yet this need not diminish the determinative role that "family history" plays in the shaping of character. In the final version, however, the narrator's skepticism extends to "the science of heredity" and its claim that one's character is directly inherited from one's parents. All the subsequent gradations in the "gradual making of *The Making of Americans,*" as Stein titled one of her 1934-35 *Lectures in America,* similarly derive from her narrator's changing conception of just how one may come to know "the whole of anyone from the beginning to the ending" (183), "the whole of [anyone's] story."

In the 1903 "Making of Americans" the narrator thus understands Julia's character as entirely a function of her family history. As such, it is partly a consequence of "the temper" she has been born with (her mother's) and partly a matter of "living down" that temper as a result of her "affection" for her father and her appreciation of the example he sets "for her." If between 1906 and 1908 Stein was already having her narrator suggest that there might be more to the "history of any one" (183) than the story of "the old people in a new world" and "the new people made out of the old" (3), when she began to rewrite the work in 1908 she did so by concentrating on the importance of extrafamilial relations in the formation of character. This new emphasis emerges in the account of the Herslands', and especially Fanny Hersland's, "new living" in Gossols (Oakland). As early as page 57 the narrator observes of Fanny Hersland's family in Bridgepoint (Baltimore) that "they had never any one of them an important feeling of themselves inside them to arise of itself from within them. Such a kind of important feeling [that is, a feeling of self-importance] would not be in them in the way of living it was natural to any one of them to be having," namely, "the family way of good living." "Mrs. Fanny Hersland," the narrator continues, "never would have had such a feeling if she had lived on in Bridgepoint, going on always with the right kind of being."

The thread is picked up again on page 77, when Fanny Hersland's "inner being" is examined more closely:

Mrs. Fanny Hersland had always had in her the beginning of an almost important feeling which she had from being like her mother in her nature, the mother who had had, in her sad trickling arising of itself inside her, an almost important feeling. This beginning of an almost important feeling, had never in Fanny Hissen been very real inside her while she was living in Bridgepoint, for then the strongest thing in her was the family way of being . . . [that is,] the being always a part of the well to do living. . . . It was not marrying that gave her such a feeling. Marrying would never have changed her from her family way of being, it was going to Gossols and leaving the family being and having a for her unnatural way of living that awoke in her a sense inside her of the almost important feeling that was to come to be inside in her.

It is in this context that Mrs. Shilling, "the matchmaker," is introduced. Fanny Hersland's "almost important feeling," we are told,

had its beginning with her knowing, in the hotel where the Herslands were living before they settled down in the ten acre place, it had its beginning with her knowing old Mrs. Shilling and her daughter Sophie Shilling and her other daughter Pauline Shilling. With them there began inside her a sense of individual being, not that it was different in her to her feeling, it was only different in her being. . . . Later it grew stronger in her, this being, that never was different to her in her feeling that she knew inside her, but later it grew stronger in her, a very little by her husband and the power over him she had in her, but mostly with the living that came soon to be all the being there was of her, the living with her servants and governesses and dependents and the for her poor queer kind of people who lived near her [the Herslands' "ten acre place" not being "in the part of Gossols where the other rich people were mostly living" (35)], and the way she had of being a power, of being of them, with them, and always above them, and the feeling they had in them; and all this gave to her the real being of an almost important feeling. (77-78)

In several respects, then, *The Making of Americans* ceases at this point to be an exclusively family history. In the first place, Fanny Hersland begins to acquire a sense of herself as an "individual being" apart from "her family way of being." As a result her "feeling of being important to herself" becomes "realler" (77). (Stein's narrator is careful to distinguish this new state of *being*—in which the feeling becomes more real—from the feeling itself, which Fanny Hersland has always felt, apparently having inherited it from her mother.) Secondly, the individual begins to be defined in relation to extrafamilial acquaintances. In the description of Mrs. Shilling and her daughters there is also the first hint of the vast typology Stein would construct in the following pages. Despite the presence of "something queer" in them—perhaps due, the narrator surmises, to "a hole . . . somewhere inside them"—the Shillings are "like many other ordinary women," with "many millions," for instance, being "made just like" the fat daughter, Sophie (78-79).

Initially, then, an interest in the "kind" of person one may prove to be is subordinated to an interest in family relations and how such relations serve to define one. Stein's narrator thus seeks to understand the "kind of woman" Martha Hersland is in order "to feel what she was doing in arranging a marriage for her brother David" as well as "to see what she had strongly inside her of an important feeling" (71). However, as soon as the narrator begins to focus on David and Fanny Hersland's extrafamilial acquaintances, the concern with kinds becomes more and more central to the account of the family's history. A brief consideration of the "many families of . . . poor queer people living near them"—each family having "in them their own way of living, their own way of going on existing, of having uncertain things in them, of earning their daily living" (112)—quickly becomes a consideration of the "many kinds of men" and "many kinds of women" and "many kinds of ways of mixing them in the children that come out of them" (116).

With the characterization of David Hersland that concludes the first of the two sections featuring "the Hersland parents," the explicit concern with the role of family dynamics in the formation of individual character is left behind. "A man in his living," one is informed,

has many things inside him, he has in him his important feeling of himself to himself inside him, he has in him the kind of important feeling of himself to himself that makes his kind of man; this comes sometimes from a mixture in him of all the kinds of natures in him, this comes sometimes from the bottom nature in him, this comes sometimes from the natures in him that are in him that are sometime in him mixed up with the bottom nature in him, sometimes in some men this other nature or natures in him are not mixed with the bottom nature in him at any time in his living many of such men have the important feeling of themselves inside them coming from the other nature or natures in them not from the bottom nature of them. (149)

The parental "mixture" has become a more general mixing of natures in a gesture that repeats the earlier transformation in Fanny Hersland's "being": the emphasis shifts from a "family way of being" to a sense of self-importance or "individual being." This does not mean, however, that the stress falls wholly on the individual. On the contrary, what concerns Stein's narrator are *kinds* of individuality. It is how one feels one's difference—one's specific form of self-importance—which determines what kind of person one is.

Early in the second section on David and Fanny Hersland, in the course of a meditation on "successful loving" (178), the narrator arrives at a way of characterizing persons in terms of two distinct modes of feeling self-important and hence feeling important relative to others. There are "two kinds of women" (and two kinds of men):

those who have dependent independence in them, [and] those who have in them independent dependence inside them; the ones of the first of them always somehow own the ones they need to love them, the second kind of them have it in them to love only those who need them, such of them have it in them to have power in them over others only when these others have begun already a little to love them, others loving them give to such of them strength in domination. (165)

Of the first kind—who may, like Fanny Hersland, "have it all so peaceably inside them that they have not in them the feeling of being themselves inside them"—"it takes someone around them," someone who needs "to be owned by them," "to make them feel it inside them that they are themselves inside them, to give to them anything of an important feeling." Such newly self-aware persons subsequently express an awareness of self by resisting any person who "makes them own them" (165). Despite being *dependent* on another person for the inauguration of a feeling of self-importance, they nonetheless insist on their *independence:* hence the category "dependent independence." By contrast, the independent dependent person readily conveys an impression of independence—as in the case of David Hersland who "had in him a feeling of being as big as all the world around him" (157)—yet is actually dominated by the need to dominate. For when one's expression of self-importance takes the form of dominance rather than resistance, one becomes dependent on the needs of those whom one seeks to dominate.

All the same, as Stein's narrator acknowledges in a crucial paragraph on page 178, it isn't always easy to demonstrate that "every one is of one kind or the other kind of them the independent dependent or the dependent independent kind of them." Often it is "hard to tell it about them, to describe it how each one is of the kind of them that is in that one. It is hard to tell it about them because the same words can describe all of them the one and the other kind of them." "Sometimes," that is, "resisting comes like attacking, sometimes attacking seems like resisting." In such cases, it "only slowly . . . come[s] to be clear" which is which; only slowly do the differences "come to be clear to every one who listens to the repeating that comes out of them, who sees the repeating that is in them the repeating of the bottom nature in them."

In these lines Stein alludes for the first time in her American-style "history" to the method for investigating character, and understanding "the whole of anyone from the beginning to the ending" (183), which she had been refining since her undergraduate experiments in automatic writing at the Harvard Psychological Laboratory. Indeed, her dualistic typology emerged from the Harvard experiments as well, and already formed the basis of an article she published in the *Psychological Review* in 1898. In that account, Stein divided the subjects who most readily produced automatic writing into two groups. Type I she characterized as "nervous, high-strung, very imaginative, has the capacity to be easily roused and intensely interested. Their attention is strongly and easily held by something that interests them . . . but, on the other hand, they find it hard to concentrate on anything that does not catch the attention and hold the interest." By contrast, individuals of Type II "are distinctly phlegmatic. . . . Their power of concentrated attention is very small. They describe themselves as never being held by their work; they say that their minds wander easily; that they work on after they are tired and just keep pegging away." Roughly speaking, Types I and II correlate with the "independent dependent" and "dependent independent" kinds of *The Making of Americans*.

"I was very much interested," Stein recalled in *Everybody's Autobiography,*

in the way [the subjects] had their nature in them and sitting there while their arm was in the planchette [a device for producing "automatic writing"] and hardly vaguely talking, it was interesting to me to see how I came to feel that I could come sometime to describe every kind there is of men and women and the bottom nature of them and the way it was mixed up with the other natures in them, I kept notes of each one of them and watched the difference between being active and being tired, the way it made some go faster and some go slower and I finally felt and which in The Making of Americans I began to do that one could make diagrams and describe every individual man and woman who ever was or is or will be living.

In "The Gradual Making of The Making of Americans" Stein elaborated further on "the method of writing" which—as she observed in *The Autobiography of Alice B. Toklas*—was "afterwards developed in Three Lives and Making of Americans":

I began to get enormously interested in hearing how everybody said the same thing over and over again with infinite variations but over and over again until finally if you listened with great intensity you could hear it rise and fall and tell all that that there was inside them, not so much by the actual words they said or the thoughts they had but the movement of their thoughts and words.

By the time she began writing the "Martha Hersland" chapter of *The Making of Americans* in mid-1909, the work which had begun as "the history of a family" had fully metamorphosed into "a history of every one." Indeed, the first half of this two-part, 200-page chapter doesn't mention the ostensible subject once and is instead exclusively concerned with Stein's—and her narrator's—methodological problems in knowing and articulating "the being in all men and in all women" (339). The family seems to have been left behind. Yet is this really the case?

3. THE MAKING OF AN AUTHOR

The new chapter opens famously with the sentence, "I am writing for myself and strangers"—famous if only because Stein, in *The Autobiography of Alice B. Toklas,* twice quoted it herself. The narrator continues: "This is the only way that I can do it. Everybody is a real one to me, everybody is like some one else too to me. No one of them that I know can want to know it and so I write for myself and strangers" (289). Although the characterizations of individuals in *The Making of Americans,* other than those drawn from Stein's immediate family, were sufficiently abstract to be in all likelihood unrecognizable, the notebooks where Stein recorded her impressions and worked out her classifications were full of judgments that she knew the subjects would find offensive. To cite just one example: "Alice [Toklas] and Chalfin [an American friend and painter] have not enough brains to content them so they make it up, he with energy (manufactured), with sensitiveness and taste and charlatanism, she with crookedness, melodrama, desire, and prostitution."

If a "love" of "looking and comparing and classifying" compelled Stein, like her narrator, to describe her acquaintances in ways that they could be expected to "dislike"—none of them "ever want[ing] to know it that every one looks like some one else. . . . Mostly every one dislikes to hear it" (289)—the same process of "comparing and classifying" enabled her to transform an unknown and unpredictable world of *strangers* into a more manageable world of *acquaintances.* "I made endless diagrams," Stein recollected in a 1946 interview, "watching people from windows and so on until I could put down every type of human being that could be on the earth." In a 1935 lecture, she described her procedure more precisely:

You start in and you take everyone that you know, and then when you see anybody who has a certain expression or turn of the face that reminds you of some one, you find out where he agree[s] or disagrees with the character, until you build up the whole scheme. I got to the place where I didn't know whether I knew people or not. I made so many charts that when I used to go down the streets of Paris I wondered whether they were people I knew or ones I didn't.

Stein's assumption here that facial characteristics reflect character harkens back to an earlier passage in "The Making of Americans" in which the same link is invoked with respect to the *family* resemblance of the Dehning sisters. "In the eighteenth century that age of manners and of formal morals," Stein's narrator proposes,

it was believed that the temper of a woman was determined by the turn of her features; later, in the beginning nineteenth, the period of inner spiritual illumination it was accepted that the features were moulded by the temper of the soul within; still later in the nineteenth century when the science of heredity had decided that everything proves something different, it was discovered that generalisations must be as complicated as the facts and the problem of interrelation was not to be so simply solved. You reader may subscribe to whichever doctrine pleases you best while I picture for you the opposition in resemblance in the Dehning sisters.

In effect, the "history of every kind and of every individual human being" that Stein was composing six years after she wrote these lines was "a history of a family" writ large, with "kinds" understood as a form of "kin" and "the familiar" an extension of "the family."

This extended family history is not the only history, however, which *The Making of Americans* contains; the work might with equal justification have been called the "Making of an author / being a / History of one woman and many others." Even before she began composing *Three Lives,* Stein jotted down titles for several additional works—among them, the "Making of an author," alternatively referred to as "The Progress of Jane Sands / being the history of one woman and many others." (These titles are listed, together with the original title of *Three Lives*—"Three histories / by Jane Sands"—in a notebook included among the Stein papers in the Yale Collection of American Literature.) Stein ultimately published *Three Lives* under her own name, yet she did so at the risk of having readers confuse the narrator with herself, a risk compounded in *The Making of Americans,* where the narrator isn't just the speaker—"It has always seemed to me a rare privilege, this, of being an American. . . . The old people in a new world, the new people made out of the old, that is the story that I mean to tell" (3)—but is, quite literally, the *writer:*

Bear it in your mind my reader, but truly I never feel it that there ever can be for me any such a creature, no it is this scribbled and dirty and lined paper that is really to be to me always my receiver,—but anyhow reader, bear it in your mind . . . that this that I write down a little each day here on my scraps of paper for you is not just an ordinary kind of novel with a plot and conversations to amuse you, but a record of a decent family progress. (33)

These scraps of paper record "the progress of Jane Sands" as well, the author-narrator who, despite remaining unnamed, is perhaps Stein's most significant creation in what is certainly no ordinary novel. On page 446 "a Sarah Sands" *is* referred to—presumably modeled on Sarah Stein, Stein's sister-in-law—and the narrator subsequently comments on the phenomenon of individuals "yield[ing] to [their] own weakness":

Melanctha put it down to that they wanted it and she gave it but she had no responsibility, it was because she was so game that she did it. Sarah Sands puts her yielding down to unsuspiciousness, that is the reason she yields, she is so easy and that's it. All these things are true as characteristics in each one but they all think that characteristic is the whole of them. It isn't. They all forget their emotion and so it must have been the other person's fault it happened. (447)

The narrator of *The Making of Americans* is as much a creation of Stein's as is Melanctha; and not only is Sarah Sands on a par with Melanctha, both are on speaking terms with the narrator. Readers are likely to forget this, however, and to attribute "characteristics" belonging to Stein to the narrator: for starters, the name "Gertrude Stein" and an existence outside the confines of the writing. Stein, to be sure, isn't just an author; yet she has made an author who is just that, and nothing but that, and the moment one confuses actual author and author-narrator, this remarkable achievement is lost. No doubt many, perhaps all, of the narrator's self-described characteristics and experiences may properly be attributed to Stein. Still, Stein differs from her creation in at least one essential respect: "Jane Sands" has no particular history, no particular family, no particular background. Indeed, in *The Making of Americans,* she has no particular sex.

The narrator's story is twofold: there's the story of the writing—the account of her own "progress" as a writer—and the story she *tells,* an account that ostensibly has nothing to do with the writing but concerns "the making of Americans" and, more generally, the nature of families and, more generally still, the understanding of human existence. The discrepant halves come together in the narrator's embodiment of what Stein would later call "the disembodied abstract quality of the american character"—a characterization certainly not meant to refer to anything like a dematerialized realm of spirit. "To some," one is informed a hundred and fifty pages prior to the close of the dual-track account, "spirituality and idealism have no meaning excepting as meaning completest intensification of any experiencing, any conception of transcending experience has to some not any meaning. To some anything to have meaning must be existing" (779). Such individuals—among whom the narrator counts herself and who would include Stein as well—"have it in them to be certain that everything in a way is made out of real earth the way it was done to make Adam" (544).

The difficulty Stein and her narrator face is how then to account for "what as experience" appears to be "without any condition" (780): an individual's sense of freedom, for instance, or the experience of thought, or even the phenomenon of life. Can these experiential phenomena be understood without either reductively "leav[ing] out something" (779), or, alternatively, falling back on a Bergsonian notion of Vital Spirit or *élan vital,* the idea that "be[ing] a live one" requires something "inspiriting" (583). In other words, does a sense that all "things have really ordinary materially existing being," and consequently have "existing like any dirt in any field or in any road or any place or any garden" (596-97), condemn one to a crude materialism and the necessity of seeing anything as "mov[ing] *against something*"—that is, in relation to a fixed background—in order to be certain that it really exists?

"We in America," Stein observed in her 1934 lecture "Portraits and Repetition," "have tried to make this thing a real thing, [namely,] if the movement, that is any movement is lively enough, perhaps it is possible to know that it is moving even if it is not moving against anything." Something "most intensely alive"—possessing what Stein's narrator calls the "completest intensification of . . . experiencing"—"would exist so completely that it would not be necessary to see it moving against anything to know that it is moving." "This," Stein adds, "is what we mean by life" as distinct from sheer existence, and in her "portrait of the author" in *The Making of Americans* she creates an emblem for such life: a figure abstracted from "family living" and from all but the most general background of "human kinds," who nonetheless avoids being rendered lifeless, bloodless, in the process. The narrator may aptly be contrasted with the "utterly unattached" Cora Douner, "an only child whose parents died just before she entered college," who is "equally detached by her nature from all affairs of the world." Despite a passionate love affair with Martha Hersland's husband—the unfolding of which is recounted in the Farnham episode midway through the book—Miss Douner "never succeed[s] in really touching any [other] human creature." This detachment, conflicting as it does with "her deepest desire," "to partake of all human relations," is "due," the narrator notes, "to an abstracted spirit that could not do what it would" (435-36).

Camerado, Walt Whitman declared in "So Long!," his 1860 valediction "as one disembodied": *this is no book, / Who touches this touches a man.* In a less gendered spirit, the same may be said of the utterly undetached narrator of *The Making of Americans.* A suite of variations played on the narrator's credo of disengagement, "I am writing for myself and strangers," demonstrates this especially graphically:

Often it is very astonishing, it is like seeing something and some one who always has been walking with you and you always have been feeling that one was seeing everything with you and you feel then that they are seeing that thing the way you are seeing it then and you go sometime with that one to a doctor to have that one have their eyes examined and then you find that things you are seeing they cannot see and never have been seeing and it is very astonishing and everything is different and *you know then that you are seeing, you are writing completely only for one and that is yourself then and to every other one it is a different thing.* (430)

Disillusionment in living is the finding out nobody agrees with you not those that are and were fighting with you. Disillusionment in living is the finding out nobody agrees with you not those that are fighting for you. Complete disillusionment is when you realise that no one can for they can't change. The amount they agree is important to you until the amount they do not agree with you is completely realised by you. *Then you say you will write for yourself and strangers, you will be for yourself and strangers and this then makes an old man or an old woman of you.*

This is then one thing, another thing is the perfect joy of finding some one, any one really liking something you are liking, making, doing, being. . . .

It is a very strange feeling . . . you write a book and while you write it you are ashamed for every one must think you are a silly or a crazy one and yet you write it. . . . Then some one says yes to it . . . and then never again can you have completely such a feeling of being afraid and ashamed that you had then. (485)

I am so certain that I am knowing a very great deal about being being in men and in women that it certainly does seem as if something would be missing if not any one could be coming to know from me all of that everything. . . . But then I am remembering that every one being ever in living is pretty well used to this thing that some one has it to have knowing realising something and not any one else even later has that thing and *so then I will go on writing, and not for myself and not for any other one but because it is a thing I certainly can be earnestly doing with sometimes excited feeling and sometimes happy feeling and sometimes longing feeling and sometimes almost indifferent feeling and always with a little dubious feeling.* (708)

Each of these passages varies the terms of the original formulation. In the first, instead of writing for yourself and strangers, "you are writing completely only for one and that is yourself." In the second, you continue to "write for yourself and strangers," yet instead of "mostly every one dislik[ing] to hear . . . that every one looks like some one else," "some one says yes to it." Then with the last passage the original formulation is rejected *in toto:* "I will go on writing, and not for myself and not for any other one."

The initial statement was concerned exclusively with the content of the narrator's observations. Because "mostly every one dislikes" being told that they are cut from a mold, and because the narrator has included all her acquaintances as unknowing subjects in her study of human character, she can only expect strangers actually to want to read the finished work. In the first variant, however, the narrator's attention has shifted from content to the interconnectedness of form and content: to the ways that *how one knows* determines *what one knows*—and what one can know—as well as the ways that this differs from person to person. Of the new perspective, the narrator comments: "You know it then yes but you do not really know it as a continuous knowing in you for then in living always you are feeling that some one else is understanding, feeling seeing something the way you are feeling, seeing, understanding that thing, and always it is a shock to you sometime with every one you are ever knowing" (430).

The second variant, which occurs at the beginning of the "Alfred Hersland and Julia Dehning" chapter, returns to the original perspective, although it is inflected by the intervening material. Complete agreement—in the sense of completely agreeing *about* something—turns out to be impossible precisely because the agreement, or identity, of the *means* is impossible: "no one can [agree] for they can't change." One literally cannot see through another's eyes. "Then," Stein's narrator observes, "you say you will write for yourself and strangers, you will be for yourself and strangers and this then makes an old man or an old woman of you." Here, in putting so disillusioned a spin on the original formulation, the narrator picks up an earlier train of thought. For the reader had been warned at the outset that "to be old to ourselves in our feeling is a losing of ourselves like just dropping off into sleeping. . . . To be ourself like an old man or an old woman to our feeling must be a horrid losing-self sense to be having. It must be a horrid feeling, like the hard leaving of our sense when we are forced into sleeping or the coming to it when we are just waking. It must be a horrid feeling to have such a strong sense of losing" (5). So much for writing for oneself and strangers.

Yet, despite the narrator's incontestably real disillusionment, the original rationale for embracing an apparently inevitable estrangement from one's readers no longer suffices. Someone, it seems, has said "yes," "really lik[ing]" what the narrator is "liking, making, doing, being." For Stein this would have been Alice Toklas, who began typing the work-in-progress around the time Stein wrote this passage in early 1910. "Doing the typing of *The Making of Americans*," Toklas recalled, "was a very happy time for me. Gertrude talked over her work of the day, which I typed the following morning. Frequently these were the characters and incidents of the previous day. It was like living history. I hoped it would go on forever." Toklas's reasons for liking the writing need not have been identical with Stein's; it was enough that she liked it. At this stage in the composition of *The Making of Americans*, then, the narrator's original assertion has come under siege from two opposed directions: on the one hand, from increasing disillusionment, "a horrid losing-self sense"; on the other hand, from increasing contentment, "the perfect joy of finding someone . . . really liking something you are doing."

By the end of the chapter—which like the adjacent chapters is composed of two parts of roughly 100 pages each, in this case allotted to Alfred Hersland and Julia Dehning respectively—the narrator has left the internal division behind along with the intractably divided couple. Instead of conceiving of writing as primarily a means for recording and conveying descriptive knowledge, William James's "knowledge-about," the narrator has come to recognize the impossibility of guaranteeing either the accurate transmission of such knowledge or, supposing it has been received without too much damage, the recipient's "need" for it. "It is like when I was a younger one," the narrator suggests,

I was for years so sorry about things important in something being lost and some one being a dead one by an accident when he was a young one and then later I was certain I would not be using that thing that was lost and would not be reading something if it had been written and if I did not need that thing, very likely not any one would be really needing that thing, and whatever any one is having is plenty good enough unless they want some other thing and perhaps they will find that other thing. (708)

Writing, in sum, is a form of experience, not simply a way of coming to terms with experience.

Apparently, the writing doesn't have to *be* anything aside from the full range of feelings it involves. Yet in the course of the subsequent two-hundred-page "description of being in David Hersland and how men and how women listened to him" (727), the inadequacy of this conclusion becomes clear to the narrator. Like any other human experience, writing cannot be reduced to an aggregation of feelings that exist apart from their expression. Ultimately, even David Hersland's growing "disillusionment" with life serves to confirm the inseparability of experience and expression in "mak[ing] of each one one . . . being living": "certainly the way of experiencing anything and expressing that thing is the being being in each one" (783).

Already in the Alfred Hersland/Julia Dehning chapter, the narrator ceases defining herself wholly as one "loving listening, hearing always all repeating" (292), and starts to identify herself as someone who "likes conversation." Although she "used not to like conversing at all," this changes when she realizes that speech provides "completely successful diversion" and therefore "enough stimulation to keep me completely going on being one going on living" (662). Still, before Stein could realistically portray the narrator's emerging awareness of the connection between expression and "going on being one going on living," she had to familiarize herself more thoroughly with the mechanisms of expression. To this end, she composed the series of word portraits—beginning with "Ada," the double portrait of herself and Toklas, and including celebrated portraits of Matisse and Picasso as well—that interrupted the drafting of the Alfred Hersland/Julia Dehning chapter in late 1910 and early 1911.

In these portraits, and then in the "David Hersland" chapter of *The Making of Americans,* expression, or style, becomes the dominant subject of the writing, no longer just a notable feature of it. "In writing the *Three Lives,*" Stein would recall in 1946, "I was not particularly conscious of the question of style. The style which everybody shouted about surprised me." (The reviewer for the *Boston Morning Herald,* for instance, hailed *Three Lives* as an "extraordinary book," which, "with its strange unconventional English, its haltings, its endless repetitions . . . furnishes hard reading and yet somehow its unfamiliar, almost uncanny, style grips the reader firmly.") Stein had certainly not been unaware of her bravura performance—even predicting to one correspondent shortly after completing

Three Lives that it would "make your hair curl with the complications and tintinabulations [*sic*] of its style." Nonetheless, the public recognition of her "unfamiliar style," just as she was setting out to write the Alfred Hersland/Julia Dehning chapter in early 1910, seems to have triggered a new concern with the ways style functions cognitively, especially in the self-understanding that constitutes anyone's "feeling of being themselves inside them": what Stein's narrator, in describing Martha Hersland, had characterized as the "coming together in them to be a whole one" (382).

4. A SPACE FILLED WITH MOVING

In 1946, after the Second World War had destroyed what was left of the nineteenth century and its faith in progress, Stein contrasted the realism she believed most appropriate to the twentieth century, a "realism of composition," with the nineteenth-century "realism of character." Readers in the nineteenth century, she noted, had "lived and died by . . . the characters in novels"—fictional personages being "more real to the average human being than the people they knew"—but by "the end" of the century, this phenomenon had "died out." Thus in the late novels of Henry James it is "the ensemble" that "lives": "nobody gets excited about the characters." The sense of composition had itself changed; rather than "consist[ing] of a central idea, to which everything else was an accompaniment," much as characters functioned in the nineteenth-century novel, composition was now based on "the idea that . . . one thing was as important as another thing. Each part is as important as the whole." The ensemble not only lives; it lives in every part.

This replacement of "character" by "composition" as the source of life's "realism"—life being "in a way always real," as Stein observed in *Wars I Have Seen* (1945)—was certainly not limited to novels. In her 1935 lecture "How Writing Is Written," Stein suggested that what distinguished twentieth-century experience as such might be summed up as the difference between "conceiv[ing] an automobile as a whole . . . and then creat[ing] it," much as the twentieth century had, or first "see[ing] the parts" and only afterwards "work[ing] towards the automobile through them," as the nineteenth century would have done. It is the difference between conceiving of something "as a whole made up of its parts" and the more mechanistic idea of something consisting of "pieces put together to make a whole."

The nineteenth-century understanding of "character" conforms to the mechanistic notion of "composition" on at least two counts. In the first place, the individual's character is built up piece by piece: this trait from Mother, that trait from Father, one thing from a particular environmental factor, something else from another. Secondly, the combination of living characters is just that, a collection that possesses no life of its own beyond what each character contributes individually. Indeed, *The Making of Americans* may be viewed as an investigation of the relation between these two aspects of nineteenth-century character, as well as of the leap of faith required if one is to attribute the quality of being "a whole one" to any particular individual. How does the enumeration of *characteristics,* which exist yet don't themselves live, yield a *character* who is "felt [to be] alive"? The narrator's inability to resolve the discrepancy between the "two prime elements involved, the element of memory and the other of immediacy"—namely, the discrepancy between having "acquired [one's] knowledge *gradually,*" as Stein puts it in "The Gradual Making of The Making of Americans," and nonetheless possessing a "complete conception . . . of an individual *at one time*"—brings about the need for the paradigm shift that Stein locates, somewhat inexactly, in the transition from the nineteenth to the twentieth centuries.

The narrator's descriptions in *The Making of Americans* of the three Hersland siblings convey a steadily increasing awareness of the inadequacy of the nineteenth-century "realism of character" to account for the emergence of a sense of oneself, or of any other person, as "a whole one." Accordingly, the question of character becomes largely a question of composition. Martha Hersland is unhesitatingly characterized as a singular being, but only in the fairly minimal sense of resembling a single-cell organism: "a mushy mass of independent dependent being with a skin holding it together from flowing away" (384). All that distinguishes her from such a creature is her greater "solidity": "she was all through her of the same concentration, of the same nature, always it was the same being in her" (398). Alfred Hersland, by contrast, gives the impression of being a mere fragment or "piece of being"; yet he too, almost despite himself, has "his own being in him" (521): "He has in him only one kind of being but as I was telling pieces of it get separated off from other pieces of it . . . by-products get disconnected and keep on going in him and things get all disarranged in him" (589). As for the youngest sibling, David Hersland, no comparable spatial configuration will do to represent his extreme self-consciousness. Neither mushy nor fragmentary, he needs to compose himself anew every day to "find the meaning for him of something in each day of living that would make living have meaning for him" (428).

That two intermediate siblings—coming between the youngest Hersland and his two elder siblings—should have "died as little children" (44) is hardly an incidental compositional detail. Like David Hersland's father, who "had always intended to have three children" (743), Stein's own parents "never intended to have more than five"; and had not two of *her* siblings "died in babyhood," Stein suggested in *Everybody's Autobiography,* "I would not have come nor my brother just two years older." "We never talked about this after we had heard of it," she added, "it made us feel funny." It certainly made her sensitive to the role of chance in human life, and in David Hersland (partly modeled on her fellow student at the Harvard Psychological Laboratory, Leon Solomons, whom William James called, after Solomons's early death in 1900, "the keenest intellect we ever had") she created a late-nineteenth-century American rationalist for whom the experience of life's fortuitousness was definitive, and devastating:

he heard this thing when he was still quite a young one and he had it in him then to be certain that being living is a very queer thing, he being one being living and yet it was only because two others had not been ones going on being living. It was to him then that he was certain then that being living was a queer thing. . . . He was in a way then as I was saying needing to be certain that he realised in him every minute in being living needing being being living. (743)

"All three of the Hersland children," Stein's narrator observes early on, "had a passion to be free inside them," especially the youngest one who "always was seeking [to know] what it was inside him that made it right that he should go on with his living" (47-48). For David Hersland, freedom amounts essentially to *negative* freedom: a freedom from necessity, in particular from the need or "will" to live. In the end, "he was not needing being one going on being living" (900). If such freedom translates in part as freedom from the obligations posed by living—obligations which derive from a sense of life as a privilege granted to the fortunate survivor—it also takes the form of freedom from character and from the needs that character, understood as fate, dictates.

"It is hard living down the tempers we are born with," the narrator suggests at the start of *The Making of Americans*. In *The Autobiography of Alice B. Toklas* Stein acknowledged that the passage containing this line was derived from "an old daily theme that she had written when at Radcliffe"; she neglected to mention, however, that her college instructor, upon reading the original theme—"There is nothing we are more intolerant of than our own sins writ large in others"—recommended that she look at Montaigne's *Essays*. There she discovered the anecdote concerning the "angry man drag[ging] his father along the ground" that she later set at the head of *The Making of Americans*. (Montaigne himself had taken the anecdote from Aristotle's *Nichomachean Ethics*.) Unlike Montaigne, who argued that "the hereditary bashing of fathers" has its origins entirely in custom, Stein's narrator, in speaking of "being born with" one's temper or character, presupposes that character is inherited biologically rather than a product of socialization. Nonetheless, it can still be "lived down"—although with difficulty.

In an early note to herself Stein proposed that the "Epilogue of the whole story will be yes I say it is hard living down the tempers we are born with." At this time she was still operating largely within the parameters of a "realism of character": there was nothing more exciting, nothing more real, than questions of temperament or character. By the time she completed the work in 1911, she had fully embraced a "realism of composition." Life was no longer perceived as a set of elements that might just as easily be taken apart as "put together"—much as David Hersland dissects his own life—nor was it located preeminently in human character. Instead it existed whenever a whole was greater than the sum of its parts, whether this occurred in a paragraph or a person or even in a family. Thus in the 19-page "History of a Family's Progress"—the actual epilogue to *The Making of Americans*—"family living" is redefined, so that instead of being a part of an individual that often needs to be "lived down," it is something which the individual is part of and that takes on a life of its own. No less than the individual human being, the family is a living entity; and *The Making of Americans* is "the history of the ending of the existing of the Hersland family" (476) in addition to being the story of the lives and deaths of a dozen or more individuals.

Midway through the Alfred Hersland/Julia Dehning chapter, Stein's narrator explains just what it is that compels her to delineate the "kinds" of human being. Whereas David Hersland is skeptical of life, she is fearful of death: "always to me," she suggests, "to be a dead one is a sombre thing, to be certain that it is existing, always there has been in me the being very much afraid of this thing" (583). Only by "feeling men and women each one as of one kind of them" and knowing "that I can that sometime I will know others like them" (581) is this "sombre feeling" "quiet[ed]" (583). Not religious in any traditional sense, and dubious of any notion of "spirit," the narrator nonetheless expresses a feeling of completion which is religious in the sense that "religion is believing that dead is not dead" (498). The conviction that each individual "is one of a kind of them in men and women and [that] there are always very many of each kind existing" (581) enables her to feel "that to be dead is not [just] to be a dead one," much as the earth is "complete and fructifying" (574) in itself, rather than being, machine-like, "a thing without ending" (521).

The Making of Americans is itself "a complete thing" in two distinct senses. According to the "eternal" sense, "A thing not beginning and not ending is certainly continuing, one completely feeling something is one not having begun to feel anything because to have a beginning means that there will be accumulation and then gradual dying away as ending and this cannot be where a thing is a complete thing" (701). From the perspective of the historical sense, "Some one has done something. It is a completed thing, a quite complete thing. It has a beginning, a middle and an end. It is all done. It is a complete thing. It was done by some one. The one that did that thing began it and went on with it and finished it. It is a complete thing" (860). Insofar as *The Making of Americans* is a "completed" thing—possessing a discernible structure and composed at a particular time—the story of its writing and the story it tells of writing have historical and possibly enduring significance. This makes it "a gentle thing . . . a gently complete thing" (860): readers will have no trouble agreeing that it is complete, even if they may disagree as to its significance. Alternatively, to the extent that Stein, in composing *The Making of Americans,* actually created "a space," as she herself suggested, "filled with moving"—a space in which it not only was possible but remains possible to "add unexpectedly anything"—then there is no telling what readers will find in it. This doesn't make it any less complete. Perhaps it even makes it more complete.

* * *

NOTE ON PUBLICATION HISTORY

As early as September 1911, a month before she completed *The Making of Americans,* Stein sent the first half to the English publisher Grant Richards, who had expressed interest in it on the strength of the reception of *Three Lives.* The next few years Stein doggedly pursued publishers with the help of friends on both sides of the Atlantic, but with no success. After the publication of *Geography and Plays* in 1922, she began once again to look for a publisher, initially with no more luck than before. In 1924, however, Ernest Hemingway persuaded Ford Madox Ford to publish a series of extended excerpts in the *Transatlantic Review;* these appeared in nine of the journal's total run of twelve issues. Finally, in 1925 the American expatriate Robert McAlmon agreed to publish an edition of 500 copies of *The Making of Americans,* which appeared late in the year. One hundred of these were exported for an American edition published by Albert and Charles Boni in 1926. Subsequently, a much shortened version of the work was published by Harcourt, Brace in 1934, based on an abridgment Stein had prepared for French translation.

The present text is a facsimile reprint of the original edition. Aside from the addition of a table of contents—combining the chapter titles of the 1925 edition with, in brackets, the 1934 abridged version's headings for sections originally left untitled—the text is identical with the one that Stein and Toklas proofread during the summer of 1925; hence it is literally authoritative. Typographical errors that escaped their attention—and in a text of this complexity there were bound to be a good many—have not been corrected. (A typical typo is "stregnth," which has been corrected in the quotation from page 165 cited on page xxiii of the introduction.) In addition, there are a number of passages that appear in the manuscript and typescript but not in the printed version. A fully corrected and edited text would be immensely desirable but is not feasible at present. (See the selections from *The Making of Americans* in Ulla E. Dydo's *A Stein Reader* [Northwestern Univ. Press, 1993] for a discussion of the textual problems involved and for samples of a re-edited text.) In the meantime, one must proofread while one reads, taking comfort in an observation Stein attributed to Alice Toklas in *The Autobiography of Alice B. Toklas:* "I always say that you cannot tell what a picture really is or what an object really is until you dust it every day and you cannot tell what a book is until you type it or proof-read it. It then does something to you that only reading it never can do."

THE
MAKING OF AMERICANS

Once an angry man dragged his father along the ground through his own orchard. "Stop !" cried the groaning old man at last, "Stop ! I did not drag my father beyond this tree."

It is hard living down the tempers we are born with. We all begin well, for in our youth there is nothing we are more intolerant of than our own sins writ large in others and we fight them fiercely in ourselves ; but we grow old and we see that these our sins are of all sins the really harmless ones to own, nay that they give a charm to any character, and so our struggle with them dies away.

It has always seemed to me a rare privilege, this, of being an American, a real American, one whose tradition it has taken scarcely sixty years to create. We need only realise our parents, remember our grandparents and know ourselves and our history is complete.

The old people in a new world, the new people made out of the old, that is the story that I mean to tell, for that is what really is and what I really know.

Some of the fathers we must realise so that we can tell our story really, were little boys then, and they came across the water with their parents, the grandparents we need only just remember. Some of these our fathers and our mothers, were not even made then, and the women, the young mothers, our grandmothers we perhaps just have seen once, carried these our fathers and our mothers into the new world inside them, those women of the old world strong to bear them. Some looked very weak and little women, but even these so weak and little, were strong always, to bear many children.

These certain men and women, our grandfathers and grandmothers, with their children born and unborn with them, some whose children were gone ahead to prepare a home to give them ; all countries were full of women who brought with them many children ; but only certain men and women and the children they had in them, to make many generations for them, will fill up this history for us of a family and its progress.

Many kinds of all these women were strong to bear many children.

One was very strong to bear them and then always she was very strong to lead them.

One was strong to bear them and then always she was strong to suffer with them.

One, a little gentle weary woman was strong to bear many children, and then always after she would sadly suffer for them, weeping for the sadness of all sinning, wearying for the rest she knew her death would bring them.

And then there was one sweet good woman, strong just to bear many children, and then she died away and left them, for that was all she knew then to do for them.

And these four women and the husbands they had with them and the children born and unborn in them will make up the history for us of a family and its progress.

Other kinds of men and women and the children they had with them, came at different times to know them ; some, poor things, who never found how they could make a living, some who dreamed while others fought a way to help them, some whose children went to pieces with them, some who thought and thought and then their children rose to greatness through them, and some of all these kinds of men and women and the children they had in them will help to make the history for us of this family and its progress.

These first four women, the grandmothers we need only just remember, mostly never saw each other. It was their children and grandchildren who, later, wandering over the new land, where they were seeking first, just to make a living, and then later, either to grow rich or to gain wisdom, met with one another and were married, and so together they made a family whose progress we are now soon to be watching.

We, living now, are always to ourselves young men and women. When we, living always in such feeling, think back to them who make for us a beginning, it is always as grown and old men and women or as little children that we feel them, these whose lives we have just been thinking. We sometimes talk it long, but really, it is only very little time we feel ourselves ever to have being as old men and women or as children. Such parts of our living are little ever really there to us as present in our feeling. Yes ; we, who are always all our lives, to ourselves grown young men and women, when we think back to them who make for us a beginning, it is always as grown old men and women or as little children that we feel them, such as them whose lives we have just been thinking.

Yes it is easy to think ourselves and our friends, all our lives as young grown men and women, indeed it is hard for us to feel even when we talk it long, that we are old like old men and women or little as a baby or as children. Such parts of our living are never really there to us as present, to our feeling.

Yes we are very little children when we first begin to be to ourselves grown men and women. We say then, yes we are children, but we know then, way inside us, we are not to ourselves real as children, we are grown to ourselves, as young grown men and women. Nay we never know ourselves as other than young and grown men and women. When we know we are no longer to ourselves as children. Very little things we are then and very full of such feeling. No, to be feeling ourselves to be as children is like the state between when we are asleep and when we are just waking, it is never really there to us as present to our feeling.

And so it is to be really old to ourselves in our feeling ; we are weary and are old, and we know it in our working and our thinking, and we talk it long, and we can see it just by looking, and yet we are a very little time really old to ourselves in our feeling, old as old men and old women once were and still are to our feeling. No, no one can be old like that to himself in his feeling. No it must be always as grown and young men and women that we know ourselves and our friends in our feeling. We know it is not so, by our saying, but it must be so always to our feeling. To be old to ourselves in our feeling is a losing of ourselves like just dropping off into sleeping. To be awake, we must have it that we are to ourselves young and grown men and women.

To be ourself like an old man or an old woman to our feeling must be a horrid losing-self sense to be having. It must be a horrid feeling, like the hard leaving of our sense when we are forced into sleeping or the coming to it when we are just waking. It must be a horrid feeling to have such a strong sense of losing, such a feeling as being to ourselves like children or like grown old men and women. Perhaps to some it is a gentle sense of losing some who like themselves to be without a self sense feeling, but certainly it must be always a sense of self losing in each one who finds himself really having a very young or very old self feeling.

Our mothers, fathers, grandmothers and grandfathers, in the histories, and the stories, all the others, they all are always little babies grown old men and women or as children for us. No, old generations and past ages never have grown young men and women in them. So long ago they were, why they must be old grown men and women or as babies or as children. No, them we never can feel as young grown men and women. Such only are ourselves and our friends with whom we have been living.

And so since there is no other way to do with our kind of thinking we will make our elders to be for us the grown old men and women in our stories, or the babies or the children. We will be always, in ourselves, the young grown men and women.

And so now we begin, and with such men and women as we have old or as very little, in us, to our thinking.

One of these four women, the grandmothers old always to us the generation of grandchildren, was a sweet good woman, strong just to bear many children and then she died away and left them for that was all she knew then to do for them.

Like all good older women she had all her life born many children and she had made herself a faithful working woman to her husband who was a good enough ordinary older man.

Her husband lived some years after his wife had died away and left him.

He was just a decent well-meaning faithful good-enough ordinary man. He was honest, and he left that very strongly to his children and he worked hard, but he never came to very much with all his faithful working.

He was just a decent honest good-enough man to do ordinary working. He always was good to his wife and always liked her to be with him, and to have good children, and to help him with her working. He always liked all of his children and he always did all that he could to help them, but they were all soon strong enough to leave him, and now that his wife had died away and left him, he was not really needed much by the world or by his children.

They were good daughters and sons to him, but his sayings and his old ordinary ways of doing had not much importance for them. They were strong, all of them, in their work and in their new way of feeling and full always of their new ways of living. It was alright, he always said it to them, and he thought it so really in him, but it was all too new, it could never be any comfort to him. He had been left out of all life while he was still living. It was all too new for his feeling and his wife was no longer there to stay beside him. He felt it always in him and he sighed and at last he just slowly left off living. "Yes," he would say of his son Henry who was the one who took most care and trouble for him, "Yes, Henry, he is a good man and he knows how to make a living. Yes he is a good boy to me always but he never does anything like I tell him. It aint wrong in him, never I don't say so like that ever for him, only I don't need it any more just to go on like I was living. My wife she did always like I told her, she never knew any way to do it different, and now she is gone peace be with her, and it is all now like it was all over, and I, I got no right now to say do so to my children. I don't ever say it now ever no more to them. What have I got to do with living ? I've got no place to go on now like I was really living. I got nobody now always by me to do things like I tell them. I got nothing to say now anymore to my children. I got all done with what I got to say to them. Well young folks always knows things different, and they got it right not to listen, I got nothing now really to do with their new kinds of ways of living. Anyhow Henry, he knows good how to make a living. He makes money such a way I got no right to say it different to him. He makes money and I never can see how his way he can make it and he is honest and a good man always, with all his making such a good living. And he, has got right always to do like he wants it, and he is good to me always, I can't ever say it any different. He always is good to me, and the others, they come to see me always only now it is all different. My wife she stayed right by me always and the children they always got some new place where they got to go and do it different." And then the old man sighed and then soon too he died away and left them.

Henry Dehning was a grown man and for his day a rich one when his father died away and left them. Truly he had made everything for himself very different ; but it is not as a young man making himself rich that we are now to feel him, he is for us an old grown man telling it all over to his children.

He is a middle aged man now when he talks about it all to his children, middle aged as perhaps sometimes we ourselves are now to our talking, but he, he is grown old man to our thinking. Yes truly this Henry Dehning had made everything for himself to be very different. His ways and his needs and how much money it took now to live to be decent, and all the habits of his daily life, they were all now for him very different.

And it is strange how all forget when they have once made things for themselves to be very different. A man like Dehning never can feel it real to himself, things as they were in his early manhood, now that he has made his life and habits and his feelings all so different. He says it often, as we all do childhood and old age and pain and sleeping, but it can never anymore be really present to his feeling.

Now the common needs in his life are very different. No, not he, nor they all who have made it for themselves to be so different, can remember meekness, nor poor ways, nor self attendance, nor no comforts, all such things are to all of them as indifferent as if they in their own life time themselves had not made it different. It is not their not wanting to remember these things that were so different. Nay they love to remember, and to tell it over, and most often to their children, what they have been and what they have done and how they themselves have made it all to be so different and how well it is for these children that they have had a strong father who knew how to do it so that youngsters could so have it.

Yes, they say it long and often and yet it is never real to them while they are thus talking. No it is not as really present to their thinking as it is to the young ones who never really had the feeling. These have it through their fear, which makes it for them a really present feeling. The old ones have not such a fear and they have it all only like a dim beginning, like the being as babies or as children or as grown old men and women.

And this father Dehning was always very full of such talking. He had made everything for himself and for his children. He was a good and honest man was Henry Dehning. He was strong and rich and good tempered and respected and he showed it in his look, that look that makes young people think older ones are very aged, and he loved to tell it over to his children, how he had made it all for them so they could have it and not have to work to make it different.

"Yes," he would often say to his children, looking at them with that sharp, side-long, shrewd glance that makes fathers so fearful and so aged to their children. Not that he, Dehning, was ever very dreadful to his children, but there is a burr in a man's voice that always makes for terror in his children and there is a sharp, narrow, outward, shut off glance from an old man that will always fill with dread young grown men and women. No it is only by long equal living that their wives know that there is no terror in them, but the young never can be equal enough with them to really rid themselves of such feeling. No, they only really can get rid of such a feeling when they have found in an old man a complete pathetic falling away into a hapless failing. But mostly for all children and young grown men and women there is much terror in an old man's looking.

Not, we repeat, that the Dehnings had much of such a feeling. Their mother had learnt, by perhaps more than equal living that there really was no terror in him and through her they had lost much of such feeling. But always they had something of that dread in them when he would begin talking to them of what had been and what he had done for them. Then it was that he always became very aged to them and he would strongly hold them with his sharp narrow outward kind of looking that, closing him, went very straight into them.

"Yes," he would often say to his children, "Yes I say to you children, you have an easy time of it nowadays doing nothing. Well! What! yes, you think you always have to have everything you can ever think of wanting. Well I guess yes, you have to have your horses and your teachers and your music and your tutors and all kinds of modern improvements and you can't ever do things for yourself, you always have to have somebody there to do it for you ; well, yes you children have an easy time of it nowadays doing nothing. Yes I had it very differently when I was a boy like George here who is just a lazy good for nothing. I didn't have all these new fangled notions. I was already earning my own living and giving myself my own education. What! yes! well I say it to you, you have no idea what an easy time you children all have nowadays just doing nothing. And my poor mother, peace be with her, she never had her own house and all kinds of servants to wait on her like your mother. Yes, well, your mother has everything I can give her, not that she don't deserve everything I can give her, Miss Jenny is the best girl I know and she will always have it as easy as I can make it for her, but you children, you never have done anything yet to make it right that you should always be having everything so easy to you. Yes, I say to you, I don't see with all these modern improvements to always spoil you, you ever will be good to work hard like your father. No all these modern kinds of improvements never can do any good to anybody. Yes, what, well, tell me, you all like to be always explaining to me, tell me exactly what you are going to get from all these your expensive modern kinds of ways of doing. Well I say, just tell me some kind of way so that I can understand you. You know I like to get good value for my money, I always had a name for being pretty good at trading, I say, you know I like to know just what I am getting for my money and you children do certainly cost a great deal of my money, now I say, tell me, I am glad to listen to you, I say you tell me just what you are going to do, to make it good all this money. Well what, what are all these kinds of improvements going to do for you."

The children laughed, "You see you can't tell yet sir," they answered, "it will be different but I guess we will be good for something."

"No you children never will be good for something if I have any right kind of a way to know it," Mr. Dehning answered, and he looked very sharply at them. And this was a cheerful challenge to them for he liked it and they liked it too with him, to fight strongly against him in the everlasting struggle of conscious unproved power in the young against dogmatic pride in having done it, of the old ones.

This father was proud of his children and yet, too, very reproachful in his feeling toward them. His wife from perhaps more than equal living with him never much regarded such a feeling in him, but to the young ones it was new for them however often it came to them, for it always meant a new fighting for the right to their kind of power that they felt strongly inside them.

But always there was a little of the dread in them that comes to even grown young men and women from an old man's sharp looking, for deep down is the fear, perhaps he really knows, his look is so outward from him, he certainly has used it all up the things inside him at which young ones are still always looking. And then comes the strong feeling, no he never has had it inside him the way that gives it a real meaning, and so the young ones are firm to go on with their fighting. And always they stay with their father and listen to him.

His wife from her more than equal living, as it sometimes is in women, has not such a dread of his really knowing when it comes to their ways of living, and then it is really only talking with him for now it is completely his own only way of living, and so she never listens to him, is deaf to him or goes away when he begins this kind of talking. But his children always stay and listen to him. They are ready very strongly to explain their new ways to him. But he does not listen to them, he goes on telling what he has done and what he thinks of them.

"No I say I don't think you children ever will be good for something. No you won't ever know how to make a living, not if all the ways I have seen men make a success in working is any kind of use to tell from. Well, what, what do you know with all your always talking, what do you know about how good hard work is done now ? What is it you know now, when there is nothing you can any of you ever do anyway I ever saw you trying ? No there is too much education business and literary effects in you all for you ever to amount to something, and then you will be always wanting more and so you never will do anything when you have nobody there to always help you. I always tell your mother, she always spoils you wanting you should have all kinds of things that you are never really needing. Not that I have anything to say against your mother's ways of doing. Miss Jenny is the best girl I know, she is too good to you that's all, she spoils all you children the way it always is with a woman giving you all what will never help to make you good for something in any kind of a way to earn a living, what, alright, I say to you, you children have an easy time of it now always doing nothing. Well, what, you think you can do it better with all your literary effects you are all so proud of. Well alright, in a few years now we will see who knows best about you then, I say, you can show me what these new fangled notions and all your modern kinds of improvements and all your education business you and your mamma are now all so fond of can do for you. Yes I say, it is only a few years now and then we all can see how you can do it. No I never had it easy like you children and I had to make it all myself so you could have it different. Yes I am always saying it to you but you think you know it all by yourselves and you never listen to me. Yes it was very different once with me. Yes when I was younger than George here and my brother Adolph was no bigger than my little Hortense, we left home to come and make our way here. We did not have much money so all the family could not come over on the same ship together, and I remember how lonesome Adolph and I were when we went away from home alone together. I remember too while we were waiting in a big bare room for them to give us tickets, I remember we heard some one say our father's name, some man in the same room with us. We did not dare speak to the men near us and we did not know which man it was that knew us, but it made us feel a little better. Yes I say you youngsters have an easy time of it nowadays doing nothing. And that was all years ago and now everything is all very different with me. And my poor mother, peace be with her, she never had a big house and servants to work for her like your mother, and everything she ever wanted I could give her like your mother has now that I can buy it for her. No, my poor mother, peace be with her, it was very different for her. You are named after her Julia but you don't any of you children look much like her. Yes she was a good strong woman was my mother, peace be with her. No you don't any of you ever look much like her and she could do more than all her grandchildren ever can do now all put together. Yes she was a wonderful woman your grandmother, peace be with her. She took care of all us children, we were ten then, and she made our clothes and did her own washing and in between she made peppermint candy for the little ones to sell. She was a wonderful good woman your grandmother, not like you children who never will be good for anything. Yes! I say, I was only a little older than that lazy George here when my poor mother, peace be with her, died away, and we were left there, ten children, and we had to get along without her, and my father, he was an honest and a good man but he never knew much how to make a living, and so he never could help along any of his children. And so what we wanted we had to go out and find out how to get it. And now you children have it very different, you have everything you can ever think you can be needing, and you don't ever show that you can work hard to deserve it. Well you got your literary effect and your new fangled notions and all kinds of education and you all always explain to me how well you know how to do it, I say it will be soon now when I can see what all these new fangled notions and all your kinds of improvements will do for you. See if it can teach you more than we learned working hard and selling candy and anything else we could do to get some money. What, well alright, I say I am good and ready to sit still and watch you to see how you all do it. I am always waiting and if you are any good I will know it. I say I am always watching now to see," and then he went away and left them followed by shouts from them, "Alright sir, you just wait and see."

The young Dehnings had all been born and brought up in the town of Bridgepoint. Their mother too had been born in Bridgepoint. It was there that they had first landed, her father, a harsh man, hard to his wife and to his children but not very good with all his fierceness at knowing how to make a living, and her mother a good gentle wife who never left him, though surely he was not worthy to have her so faithful to him, and she was a good woman who with all her woe was strong to bear many children and always after she was strong to do her best for them and always strong to suffer with them.

And this harsh hard man and his good gentle little wife had many children, and one daughter had long ago married Henry Dehning. It was a happy marriage enough for both of them, their faults and the good things they each had in them made of them a man and wife to very well content all who had to do with them.

All the Dehnings were very fond of Bridgepoint. They had their city and their country house like all the people who were well to do in Bridgepoint.

The Dehnings in the country were simple pleasant people. It was surprising how completely they could shed there the straining luxury and uneasy importance of their city life. Their country house was one of those large commodious wooden double affairs with a wide porch all around and standing well back from the road. In front and at the sides were pleasant lawns and trees and beyond were green open marshes leading down to salt water. In back was a cleared space that spread out into great meadows of stunted oaks no higher than a man's waist, great levels glistening green in the summer and brilliantly red in the autumn stretching away under vast skies, and always here and there was a great tree waving in the wind and wading knee deep in the rough radiant leafy tide.

Yes the Dehnings in the country were simple pleasant people. There they were a contented joyous household. All day the young ones played and bathed and rode and then the family altogether would sail and fish. Yes the Dehnings in the country were simple pleasant people. The Dehning country house was very pleasant too for all young men and boys, the uncles and the cousins of the Dehning family, who all delighted in the friendly freedom of this country home, rare in those days among this kind of people, and so the Dehning house was always full of youth and kindly ways and sport and all altogether there they all always lead a pleasant family life.

The Dehning family itself was made up of the parents and three children. They made a group very satisfying to the eye, prosperous and handsome.

Mr. Dehning was a man successful, strong-featured, gentle tempered, joyous and carrying always his fifty years of life with the good-nature of a cheerful boy. He enjoyed the success that he could boast that he had won, he loved the struggle in which he had always been and always conquered, he was proud of his past and of his present worth, he was proud in his three children and proud that they could teach him things he did not know, he was proud of his wife who was proud of such very different things. "Oh Miss Jenny, she is the best girl I know," he always sang as he came to find her, never content long out of sight of his family when not engrossed by business or cards.

I said that Henry Dehning's wife was proud of such very different things, but that was wrong, she was proud in very different fashion but proud of the same things. She loved his success and the worth with which he conquered and she was not anxious to forget the way that he had come. No she was in her way proud that he himself had done it. She liked his power, and when she ever thought about it she liked the honest way she knew that he had done it. And like him too she was very proud in their three educated children but to her thinking there was very little they could teach her. She knew it all always very well and much better than they could ever know it. But she was very proud of these educated children and she was very proud of her husband Henry Dehning though she knew he always did little things so badly and that he would still always play like a poor man with his fingers and he never would learn not to do it. Yes she was very proud of her husband though he always did little things so badly and she had always to be telling him how a man in his position should know how to do it. She came towards him now when he was through with his talking, and she had one rebuke to him for his always calling her his girl Miss Jenny, and another for the way he had of fidgeting always with his fingers. "Don't do that Henry !," she said to him loudly.

Mrs. Dehning was the quintessence of loud-voiced good-looking prosperity. She was a fair heavy woman, well-looking and firmly compacted and hitting the ground as she walked with the same hard jerk with which she rebuked her husband for his sins. Yes Mrs. Dehning was a woman whose rasping insensibility to gentle courtesy deserved the prejudice one cherished against her, but she was a woman, to do her justice, generous and honest, one whom one might like better the more one saw her less.

Yes it was now all very different for them. It was very pleasant always for Henry Dehning then, to stand and to look about him, yes truly it was now all very different with him. He had his family there about him, a family certain to be a satisfaction to him. They were a group to gratify the feeling of pride in him, they were so prosperous vigorous good-looking, honest, and always respectful to him, and surely they would have later, good hope of winning for themselves all that he could ever wish to them.

Yes it certainly was very different now with him. Could one ever have it real to him that in one life time a man could have it all so different for him, that a man all alone in his single lifetime could make it so that he could have it to be truly all so different in him.

Nay for a man to have it in a single life time all so different for him is more strange than being born and being then a baby and then a child and then a young grown man and then old like a man grown old and then dead and so no more of living, it is more strange because it makes so many lives in this one living. Each one of these lives that he forgets or remembers only as a dim beginning is a whole life to us in our thinking, and so Henry Dehning has had many lives in him to our feeling.

Could one believe it that he was a grown man and he was then living like the man who comes into his place now to do a little selling to the servants in the kitchen. And yet that was one whole full life for him ; and then there was the old world where there had been for him such a very different kind of living. Yes as he stands there talking to his children of the things that are never real now any more to his feeling, a man comes up the walk and slinks back when he sees them and goes sneaking to the kitchen and there he sells little things to the women who buy them out of Irish fun or just to be kind to him, for his things are really not good enough for them, they are things for people poorer than any that work in a kitchen ; and so Mr. Dehning goes on talking to his children and it is all more real to their feeling than it is now to his thinking, for they have it in their fear which young ones always have inside them, and he, he has it only as a dim beginning as being like a baby or an old grown man or woman. Nay how can he ever have it in him to feel it now as really present to him, such things as meekness or poor ways or self attendance or no comforts, it is only a fear that could make such things be now as present to him, and he has no such a fear ever inside him, not for himself ever or even for his children, for he is strong in a sense of always winning. It is they, the children, who, though they too feel a strength inside them and talk about it very often, yet way down deep in them they know they have no way to be really certain ; and always they are brave, good-looking, honest, prosperous children and the father feels strong pride as he looks around him.

The Dehning family was made of this father and mother and three children. Mr. Dehning was very proud of his children and proud of all the things he knew that they could teach him. There were two daughters and a son of them.

Julia Dehning was named after her grandmother, but, as her father often told her, she never looked the least bit like her and yet there was a little in her that made the old world not all lost to her, a little that made one always remember that her grandmother and her father had had always a worn old world to remember.

Yes Julia looked much like her mother. That fair good-loooking prosperous woman had stamped her image on each one of her children, and with her eldest, Julia, the stamp went deep, far deeper than just for the fair good-looking exterior.

Julia Dehning was now just eighteen and she showed in all its vigor, the self-satisfied crude domineering American girlhood that was strong inside her. Perhaps she was born too near to the old world to ever attain quite altogether that crude virginity that makes the American girl safe in all her liberty. Yes the American girl is a crude virgin and she is safe in her freedom.

And now, so thought her mother, and Julia was quite of the same opinion, the time had come for Julia to have a husband and to begin her real important living.

Under Julia's very American face, body, clothes and manner and her vigor of the dominering and crude virgin, there were now and then flashes of passion that lit up an older well hidden tradition. Yes in Julia Dehning the prosperous, good-looking, domineering woman was a very attractive being. Julia irradiated energy and brilliant enjoying, she was vigorous, and like her mother, fair and firmly compacted, and she was full of bright hopes, and strong in the spirit of success that she felt always in her. Julia was much given to hearty joyous laughing and to an ardent honest feeling, and she hit the ground as she walked with the same hard jerking with which her mother Mrs. Dehning always rebuked her husband's sinning. Yes Julia Dehning was bright and full of vigor, and with something always a little harsh in her, making underneath her young bright vigorous ardent honest feeling a little of the sense of rasping that was just now in her mother's talking.

And so those who read much in story books surely now can tell what to expect of her, and yet, please reader, remember that this is perhaps not the whole of our story either, neither her father for her, nor the living down her mother who is in her, for I am not ready yet to take away the character from our Julia, for truly she may work out as the story books would have her or we may find all different kinds of things for her, and so reader, please remember, the future is not yet certain for her, and be you well warned reader, from the vain-glory of being sudden in your judgment of her.

After Julia came the boy George and he was not named after his grandfather. And so it was right that in his name he should not sound as if he were the son of his father, so at least his mother decided for him, and the father, he laughed and let her do the way she liked it. And so the boy was named George and the other was there but hidden as an initial to be only used for signing.

The boy George bade fair to do credit to his christening. George Dehning now about fourteen was strong in sport and washing. He was not foreign in his washing. Oh, no, he was really an american.

It's a great question this question of washing. One never can find any one who can be satisfied with anybody else's washing. I knew a man once who never as far as any one could see ever did any washing, and yet he described another with contempt, why he is a dirty hog sir, he never does any washing. The French tell me it's the Italians who never do any washing, the French and the Italians both find the Spanish a little short in their washing, the English find all the world lax in this business of washing, and the East finds all the West a pig, which never is clean with just the little cold water washing. And so it goes.

Yes it has been said that even a flea has other little fleas to bite him, and so it is with this washing, everybody can find some one to condemn for his lack of washing. Even the man who, when he wants to take a little hut in the country to live in, and they said to him, but there is no water to have there, and he said, what does that matter, in this country one can always have wine for his drinking, he too has others who for him don't think enough about their washing ; and then there is the man who takes the bath-tub out of his house because he don't believe in promiscuous bathing ; and there is the plumber who says, yes I have always got to be fixing bath-tubs for other people to get clean in, and I, I haven't got time enough to wash my hands even ; and then there are the French bohemians, now one never would think of them as extravagantly cleanly beings, and yet in a village in Spain they were an astonishment to all the natives, why do you do so much washing, they all demanded of them, when your skin is so white and clean even when you first begin to clean them ; and then there is the dubious smelly negro woman who tells you about another woman who is as dirty as a dog and as ragged as a spring chicken, and yet some dogs certainly do sometimes do some washing and this woman had certainly not much sign of ever having had such a thing happening ; and then there is the virtuous poor woman who brings her child to the dispensary for a treatment and the doctor says to her, no I won't touch her now anymore until you clean her, and the woman cries out in her indignation, what you think I am poor like a beggar, I got money enough to pay for a doctor, I show you I can hire a real doctor, and she slams the door and rushes out with her daughter. Yes it certainly is very queer in her. All this washing business is certainly most peculiar. Surely it is true that even little fleas have always littler ones to bite them.

And then when we are all through with the pleasant summer and its gorgeous washing, then comes the dreadful question of the winter washing. It's easy enough to wash often when the sun is hot and they are sticky and perspiring and the water in a natural kind of a way is always flowing, but when it comes to be nasty cold as it always is in winter, then it is not any more a pleasure, it is a harsh duty then and hard to follow.

Yes it certainly is all very funny, and so we come back to talk some more about George Dehning, George who in this washing is always strong to do all his duty.

George Dehning was a fair athletic chap, cheery as his father and full of excellent intentions, and though these were almost all lost in their way to their fullfillment, remember, George was only fourteen just then, that time with a boy when he never can have much sense in him, for it nearly always is then with boys that the meekest of them are reckless dare-devil heedless unreflecting fellows, and so reader do not make too much for him of any present weakness in him.

Yes, George Dehning was not at all foreign in his washing but for him, too, the old world was not altogether lost behind him. Sometimes the boy had a way with him, and it would show clear in spite of the fair cheery sporty nature he had in him, a way of looking sleepy and reflecting, and his lids would never be really ever very open, and he would be always only half showing his clear grey eyes that, very often, were bright alive and laughing.

Later such a way of looking could be of great service to him. It would not matter if he never really could have wisdom in him, this look could help him always in his dealings with all men and be of much service too to him with women. He will listen then, and with his veiled eyes it will be as if he were full with thinking, and with himself always well hidden, and so he will be wise ; or for a woman, it will be as if he were always in a dream of them. Wisdom and dreaming, both good things when shown at the right time by a young grown man, who wants to be succeeding, always, in every kind of living.

And so for the moment we leave the sporty cheery well washed George Dehning with his background and his future of wisdom and of dreaming, both now pretty well hidden away in the depths of him.

And then there was the littlest one whose name had been all given without regard to the old world behind them. They called her Hortense for that was both elegant and new then. The father let the mother do as she liked with the naming, he laughed and a little he did not like it in him and then a little he was proud of his Miss Jenny and her way of doing.

And so the littlest was Hortense Dehning. She too had the stamp of the fair prosperous woman who had set her seal so firmly on her children, but little Hortense had perhaps a little more in her of that sweet good woman who had born many children and then had died away and left them for that was all she knew then to do for them.

The little Hortense Dehning was not of much importance yet in the family living. Hortense was ten now and full of adoration for her big sister and yet most of all for her brother. She was not very strong and she could not run after him in his playing, but sometimes he would sit and talk to her about himself and his resolutions and the elaborated purposes that he was always losing. George was always very moral and too he was very hopeful. He always began his to-morrow with himself full of a firm resolution to do all things every minute and to do them all very complicatedly. George felt always he must bring up this little sister for he George was the only one who knew the right ways for her.

And so he preached a great deal to her, and little Hortense was very devout and adored her instructor. There was always a dependent loyal up-gazing sweetness in her.

Being the baby of the family she was much petted by her father and always she was overawed by her brother, who was very careful to be noble to her. She was not just then very much with her mother for she was not at this time very important to her. The mother was so busy with her Julia, to find an important and good husband for her. And so little Hortense was left much to her brother and to the governess they had for her.

For us now as well as for the mother the important matter in the history of the Dehning family is the marrying of Julia. I have said that a strong family likeness bound all the three children firmly to their mother. That fair good-looking prosperous woman had stamped her image on each one of her children, but with only the eldest Julia was the stamp deep, deeper than for the fair good-looking exterior.

All the family had always looked up to Julia. They delighted in her daring and in a kind of heroical sweetness there was in her. They respected in her, her educated ways and her knowing always what was the right way she and all of them should be doing. It was not for nothing she was a crude domineering virgin. And she was strong in the success she knew always that she had inside her, and the family always admired and followed after.

Her father loved her energy and vigor, he loved her happiness and the ardent honest feeling in her. He was always very ready to yield to her, he liked to hear her when she explained to him in her quick decisive manner the new faith she had so strongly in her, the new illusions and the theories and new movements that the spirit of her generation had taught to her. And he laughed at her new fangled notions and her educated literary business and all her modern kinds of improvements as he called them, and he abused them and too the way she had of believing that she knew more than her mother, but always it amused the father to have his bright quick daughter explain all these new ways to him. Mr. Dehning knew well the value of what he had learned by living, but his was a nature generous in its feeling and he was always ready to listen to his children when they could fairly demonstrate their ideas to him.

But Herman Dehning's pride and pleasure in his Julia was all exceeded by the loud voiced satisfaction of the mother to whom this brilliant daughter always seemed as the product of the mother's own exertions. In her it was the vanity and exultation of creation as well as of possesion and she never fairly learned how completely it was the girl who governed all the family life and how very much of this young life was hidden from her knowledge.

Mr. Dehning had never concerned himself very much with the management of the family's way of living and the social life of his wife and children. These things were all always arranged by Mrs. Dehning and he was well content to let her do it though he often grumbled at the foolishness and the expense and at his children always having everything they ever wanted and so being sure to be always good for nothing.

But always he was very proud of his wife and of his children, though, a little, he always felt it was not right, their new fangled ways of doing, and yet, truly, he was very proud of them always, and indeed they were a group to gratify the pride that he had in him, they were so vigorous prosperous and good-looking, and honest, and always respectful to him, and surely they had good hope of later winning for themselves all the happiness and success he could wish them.

Julia Dehning at eighteen had lived through much of the experience that can prepare a girl for womanhood and marriage.

I have said, there were a number of young men and boys connected with the Dehning family, uncles and cousins, generous decent considerate fellows, frank and honest in their friendships, and simple in the fashion of the elder Dehning. With this kindred Julia had always lived as with the members of one family. These men did not supply for her the training and experience that helps to clear the way for an impetuous woman through a world of passions, they only made a sane and moral back-ground on which she in her later life could learn to lean.

With any member of this kindred there would be, in a young and ardent mind, no thought of love or marriage ; nor were the sober business men, young, old, or middle-aged, who came a great deal to the house, attractive to her temper, for Julia was ambitious for passion and position and she needed, too, a strain of romance. No such kind of a man had really come to her and Julia was all ripe for real experience, for even with her well guarded life she had found the sickened sense that comes with learning that some men do wrong. Passionate tempers have greatly this advantage of the unpassionate variety ; you can never guard them with such care but that they find themselves full up with real experience and with the after-taste of disillusion, but vitally as they are always hit they always rise and plunge once more, while their poorly passionate fellows who receive a vital blow never rise to faith again.

Julia as a little girl had had the usual experiences of governess guarded children. She was first the confidant, then the advisor, and last the arranger of the love affairs of her established guardians. Then at her finishing school she became acquainted with that dubious character, the adventuress, the type to be found always in all kinds of places, a character eternally attractive in its mystery and daring, and always able to attach unto itself the most intelligent and honest of its comrades and introduce them to queer vices.

And so Julia Dehning, like all other young girls, learnt many kinds of lessons, and she saw many of the kinds of ways that lead to wisdom, and always her life was healthy vigorous and active. She learnt very well all the things young girls of her class were taught then and she learnt too, in all kinds of ways, all the things girls always can learn, somehow, to be wise in. And so Julia was well prepared now to be a woman. She had singing and piano-playing and sport and all regular school learning, she had good looks, honesty, and brilliant courage, and in her young way a certain kind of wisdom.

Always Julia was a passionate young woman and she had too a heroical kind of sweetness in her way of winning. She was a passionate young woman in the sense that always she was all alive and always all the emotions she had in her being were as intense and present to her feeling as a sensation like a pain is to others who are less alive in their living. And all this time too, Julia Dehning was busily arranging and directing the life and aspirations of her family, for she was strong always in her good right to lead them.

And so Julia Dehning when she was seventeen came out upon the world, and she was filled full with courage and experience and wisdom, and she was well ready now with this energy and wisdom to cope with and conquer all the world and all men and women.

There is nothing more joyous than being healthful young and energetic, and loving movement sunshine and clean air. Combine all this with owning of a horse and courage enough to ride him wildly, and God is good to overflowing to his children. It is pleasant too to have occasionally a sympathetic comrade on such rides. Jameson was a pleasant man of thirty five or thereabouts, a good free rider and an easy talker. Julia knew him first at home and met him usually while riding to the station to meet her father and the city train. They would then either galop home together or go about riding through the glowing meadows of low oaks, racing cheerily along the country roads, and dipping here and there into a pleasant wood that broke the open country into shadow. They met too, occasionally, in riding parties that went in search of new country to discover and explore. It was all very pleasant and unaggressive, but Julia began to notice that Mrs. Jameson frowned on her in anger now, whenever they all met together. Then too Jameson grew gradually less comradely, more intimate, and gross. Julia undestood at last and did not ride with him again.

Such incidents as these are common in the lives of all young women and only are important in those intenser natures that, by their understanding, make each incident into a situation. Such natures suck a full experience from every act, and live so much in what, to others, means so little, for is it not all common and to be expected.

In Julia Dehning all experience had gone to make her wise now in a desire for a master in the art of life, and it came to pass that in Alfred Hersland brought by a cousin to visit at the house she found a man who embodied her ideal in a way to make her heart beat with surprise.

To a bourgeois mind that has within it a little of the fervor for diversity, there can be nothing more attractive than a strain of singularity that yet keeps well within the limits of conventional respectability a singularity that is, so to speak, well dressed and well set up. This is the nearest approach the middle class young woman can ever hope to make to the indifference and distinction of the really noble. When singularity goes further and so gets to be always stronger, there comes to be in it too much real danger for any middle class young woman to follow it farther. Then comes the danger of being mixed by it so that no one just seeing you can know it, and they will take you for the lowest, those who are simply poor or because they have no other way to do it. Surely no young person with any kind of middle class tradition will ever do so, will ever put themselves in the way of such danger, of getting so that no one can tell by just looking that they are not like them who by their nature are always in an ordinary undistinguished degradation. No ! such kind of a danger can never have to a young one of any middle class tradition any kind of an attraction.

Now singularity that is neither crazy, sporty, faddish, or a fashion, or low class with distinction, such a singularity, I say, we have not made enough of yet so that any other one can really know it, it is as yet an unknown product with us. It takes time to make queer people, and to have others who can know it, time and a certainty of place and means. Custom, passion, and a feel for mother earth are needed to breed vital singularity in any man, and alas, how poor we are in all these three.

Brother Singulars, we are misplaced in a generation that knows not Joseph. We flee before the disapproval of our cousins, the courageous condescension of our friends who gallantly sometimes agree to walk the streets with us, from all them who never any way can understand why such ways and not the others are so dear to us, we fly to the kindly comfort of an older world accustomed to take all manner of strange forms into its bosom and we leave our noble order to be known under such forms as Alfred Hersland, a poor thing, and even hardly then our own.

The Herslands were a Western family. David Hersland, the father, had gone out to a Western state to make his money. His wife had been born and brought up in the town of Bridgepoint. Later Mr. Hersland had sent his son Alfred back there to go to college and then to stay on and to study to become a lawyer. Now it was some years later and Alfred Hersland had come again to Bridgepoint, to settle down there to practice law there, and to make for himself his own money.

The Hersland family had not had their money any longer than

the others of this community, but they had taken to culture and to ideas quicker.

Alfred Hersland was well put together to impress a courageous crude young woman, who had an ambition for both passion and position and who needed too to have a strain of romance with them.

Hersland was tall and well dressed and sufficiently good-looking, and he carried himself always with a certain easy dignity and grace. His blond hair, which he wore parted in the middle, a way of doing which at that time showed both courage and conviction, covered a well shaped head. His features were strongly marked, regular and attractive, his expression was pleasing, his talk was always interesting, and his manners were dignified and friendly. His eyes and voice meant knowledge, feeling, and a pleasant mystery.

Julia Dehning threw herself eagerly into this new acquaintance. She no longer wanted that men should bring with them the feel of out of doors, for out of doors with men now was soiled to her sense by the grossness of the Jamesons. Alfred Hersland brought with him the world of art and things, a world to her but vaguely known. He knew that some things made by men are things of beauty, and he spoke this knowledge with interest and conviction.

The time passed quickly by with all this joy of fresh experience and new faith.

Not many months from this first meeting, Julia gave her answer. "Yes, I do care for you," she said, "and you and I will live our lives together, always learning things and doing things, good things they will be for us whatever other people may think or say."

It had been a wonderful time for Julia Dehning these few months of knowing Hersland. She had had, always, stirring within her, a longing for the knowledge of made things, of works of art, of all the wonders that make, she knew, a world, for certain other people. (Twenty years ago, you know, it was still the dark ages in America and lectures on art did not grow on every tongue that had tasted the salt air of the mid-Atlantic. It was a feat then to know about hill towns in Italy, one might have heard of Titian and of Rembrandt but Giorgone and Botticelli were still sacred to the few, one did not then yet have to seek, to find for oneself new painters and new places.) It was a very real desire, this longing for the wisdom of all culture, this that had been always strong in Julia. Of course, mostly, such longing in Julia, took the form of moral idealism, the only form of culture the spare American imagination takes natural refuge in.

Julia Dehning, like all of her kind of people, needed everything, for anything could feed her. It was not strong meat that Hersland offered to her, but her palate was eager, this had the flavour of the dishes she longed to have eaten and to have inside her. To her young crude virgin desire the food he offered to her was plenty real enough to deeply content her.

Of the family about her, it was only Julia who found him worthy to be so important to her. The cousins and the uncles, the men who could make for her the sane and moral background that would give a wholesome middle class condition always to her, they did not like it much that Hersland was now so important for her. They said nothing to her, but they did not like to have him always about with her. He was not their kind and every minute they could know it, and they did not need him, either out in the world in business or at home where they were happy in the rich and solid family comfort they always had had with the Dehnings ; and these men could not find Hersland's knowledge worth much for them, and they did not have it in them that it had a meaning for them that he Hersland had in him, knowledge and a certain kind of feeling that they never could have inside them. What could a pleasant mystery in a man mean to them except only that any man with any sense in him would not ever trust anything real to him.

But they said nothing, any of them, they knew nothing real against him, and, anyhow, it was not business for them to interfere with other people's matters, for after all it was to the Dehnings for them, and it did not in any way really concern any of the others of them. As men they could not feel it in them the right to interfere with a woman who did not as a child or a wife really belong to them.

The boy George and the little sister were too young to think very much about him. The young brother did not feel it in himself much to like him, for young George you may remember was young and heroic, out of doors was not yet in any way soiled for him and he needed that kind of a thing in a man to attract him, but anyhow, Julia liked him and it would be hard for George not to think Julia could judge better about him than any of the other members of the family could have it to know in them.

Mr. Dehning as yet had said nothing   One day he was out walking and his daughter was with him. "Julia hadn't you better be a little careful how much you encourage that young Hersland."

Mr. Dehning, always, in his working, began very far away from a thing he meant later to be firmly attacking. And always in such a far away beginning, he would be looking sharply, out from him, in a side-long, piercing, deprecating, challenging, fashion, the kind of a way he had always of looking when his wife, who, by her more than equal living, as it often is with a woman, had not in any kind of a way any fear in her of him, could be going to rebuke him. And this way he had of looking, always made him an old man to his children, and mostly there was a fear then in them, only now Julia was strong, other things were bright and glowing, and she could not now feel it in him, the old grown man's sharp outward looking that, closing him, went always so straight into them.

And so, now, filled full with her new warm imagining, Julia Dehning had not any kind of a fear from him, the kind of a fear a young grown woman has almost always from an old man's looking.

"Why papa !" she had eagerly quickly demanded of him.

"I say Julia I don't know anything against him. Yes, I say to you Julia I don't know of anything there is against him. I have looked up all the record there is yet of him and I haven't heard anything against him but Julia, I say, somehow I don't quite like him. His family are alright, I know a man who knows all Gossols, and I asked him, he says yes the family are all successful and well appearing, I say Julia I don't say anything against him only I don't altogether trust him. I know all about his father, everybody has heard of David Hersland, he is the richest man they ever had in Gossols, I know too how he made his own money out there, and everybody says he is alright and he made his own money by his own work ; I don't say anything against him, only Julia I think you better be a little careful with him, somehow I don't altogether like him." "Isn't that papa because he plays the piano and parts his hair that way in the middle." Julia was eager in her questioning. The father laughed, "I guess there is some reason in your question Julia, I don't like that kind of thing much in a man, that's right. It's foolish in a man who wants to make a success making a living, it's foolish to do things that make other men feel they don't want to trust him. It's alright if he was just doing nothing, only I never would want you to tie up with a man who didn't know how to take care of himself to make a living, but Hersland has got ambition, he wants to be a lawyer who makes a big success with his living, I know him, and that don't seem to me the kind of a way to make a good beginning, but may be I am wrong, you young ones always think you know everything. Anyhow Julia I think you better be a little careful with him." Mr. Dehning paused, and they walked on a little while and she said nothing.

Henry Dehning had had a long time to learn how to judge the value in a man, the values in them that in their lives concerned him. The more one looked into the quality of him the more one learned respect for the power he had in him and the more wonder one had in them at the gentleness that almost never left him.

Mr. Dehning had a massive face made with a firm unagressive chin, loose masses in the cheeks and a strong curved nose, his eyes were blue and always clear, and set between loose pouches underneath and coarse rough overhanging brows. His strong-skulled rounded head was covered with thinning greyish hair. He was a man of medium height, stocky build and sharply squared shoulders, a man quick in his movements, slow in his judgments, and cheerful in his temper ; a man to understand and to make use of men, slow to anger and tenacious, without heat or bitterness.

His children knew the value of his judgments and the generous quality of his understanding, still he was of the old generation, they of the new, with all his wisdom surely he must fail to see the meanings in the unaccustomed.

"You know Julia" Mr. Dehning went on after a silent interval of walking when they had each been pretty busy with their own thinking, "you know Julia, your mother doesn't like him." "Oh! mamma!" Julia broke out, "you know how mamma is, he talks about love and beauty and mamma thinks it ought to be all wedding dresses and a fine house when it isn't money and business. She would be the same about anybody that I would want."

"Yes Julia, those are your literary notions but a lawyer has got to be a business man now and you like success and money as well as any one. You have always had everything you wanted and you don't want to get along without it. Literary effects and modern improvements are alright for women but with Hersland it ought to be different, it ought to be that he has the kind of sense he needs in his business. I don't say he has't got good sense in him to make a success in him and you want to be careful I say Julia, how far you go with him." "I know papa just what you mean, and that's alright papa, I know it, but you know yourself papa it isn't everything, now, is it. I know papa how you feel about it, you think we young ones are all wrong the way we look at it, but you say yourself papa how different things are nowadays from the way they used to be when you began with it, and surely papa it can't hurt a man to be interesting even if he wants to make a success in his business."

Mr. Dehning shook his head but he did not so carry much conviction to his daughter and on this day they said no more about the matter.

And so Julia began and surely she would win in the struggle. She worked every day and very hard, and slowly she began to bring her father to it. Mrs. Dehning would have to agree if he said she could have it and no one else's opinion in the matter was important.

Time and again Julia would be sure she had succeeded, for her father always listened to her "yes papa I know it, I know what you mean and it's alright, only you know yourself everything nowadays is very different, you know that yourself papa, you know you always say it," and he liked to hear her say it, and he listened with amusement, and he approved when she knew how to do it, when she brought out with great fervor and with much repeating, great arguments against all his objections. He always openly admired the bright way she had then to make clear to him all her theories and convictions, the new faith in her, the new ideas she had of life and business.

And then Julia would be sure she had convinced him, for how could a reasonable man ever resist it, she knew she had good reasons in her.

And each day when their talk was ending and she was saying to him, "you know papa you say yourself now that it's all different, I know what you mean papa, always, I know how you want me to do it, but papa, really, I am not talking without thinking hard about it, you know I listen to you and want to understand it but you know papa, now don't you, that it will be alright and that I am alright just the way you like to have me do it," and then he would have stopped listening to her and his mind would have sort of shut up away from her, and she still held his arm for they had been walking all this time up and down as was their custon every afternoon together, and yet he then himself had quite slipped away from her, and now he would be looking at her with that sharp completed look that, always so full of his own understanding, could not leave it open any way to her to reach inside to him to let in any other kind of a meaning.

And then he would for that time altogether leave her and the last thing he always would say to her, with the quick movement he had when he felt no more time in him then for her. "Alright, yes, well to-morrow is another day Julia I say to-morrow is another day Julia and you think it all over and we will talk about it further, perhaps to-morrow, I say to-morrow is another day Julia. There is your mother there now Julia, you better go in now to her."

It was hard for Julia to have such a kind of resistance fighting against her. It was hard for an impatient and eager temper to endure the kind of a way her father always finished off his long talks with her. It was hard for Julia to have to always begin over every time she started to talk about it with her father. But he was very proud of her, she knew very well his feeling for her, she knew very well too how to win him to agree in the end with her. She loved it in a way the struggle he made each day a new one for her. They loved and admired and respected each other very much this daughter and her father. They understood very well both of them how to please while they were combating with each other. And so each to-morrow they met, and Julia was sturdy and had strong faith in her, and always, her father, a long time each day listened to her.

Hersland could do nothing all this time but wait for Julia to persuade her father. They were both agreed, Hersland and Julia, that any effort on his part to change Mr. Dehning's opinion would only make the fight for Julia so much harder. It was always there that Mr. Dehning did not like young Hersland, and the noblest words and the best acts, never, in any kind of a distrusted person, give any evidence against his condemnation. It is never facts that tell, they are the same when they mean very different things. It is never facts that can make a man feel anything to be made different to him when he has any kind of a judgment in him. Facts can never tell him anything truly about another man in his opinion. It was always there, Mr. Dehning somehow did not trust this man. And so it was only Julia, who by always repeating, perhaps could find a way to change him.

So Julia struggled every day, to have him, arguing discoursing explaining and appealing. She was always winning but it was slow progress like that in very steep and slippery climbing. For every forward movement of three feet she always slipped back two, sometimes all three and often four and five and six and seven. It was long eager steady fighting but the father was slowly understanding that his daughter wanted this thing enough to stand hard by it and with such a feeling and no real fact against the man, such a father was bound to let her some time get married to him.

"I tell you what Julia what I been thinking. When we all get back to town you can tell better whether you do really want him. I say we better leave off all this talking and just wait till we get home now again. I don't say no Julia and I don't say yes to you. When everybody gets back to town and you are busy and running around with your girls and talking and meeting all the other people and the other kinds of young men, you can tell much better then whether all this business is not all just talking with you. I say now Julia we will wait and just see how you feel about it later. I say we will talk it all over when we get home and you are altogether with all your friends there. I say Julia I don't say no to you and I don't say yes yet to you. I say when we get home we will talk it over again all together and then if nothing turns up new against him, and you still want him, I say if then you still want him enough to trust to him and to trust to your own judgment about him, we will see what we can do about him." "Alright papa," Julia said to him, "alright I won't even see Alfy any more till we get back to town then, and papa I won't say another word to you about it. I'll just go and ride around the country and think hard the way you like to have me do it about what we both have said about it."

It was a well meant intention this in Julia of riding by herself around the country and thinking hard about what they had both said about it, but not the certain way to end in a passionate young woman her first intense emo.t on. The wide and glowing meadows of low oaks, the clean clear tingling autumn air, the blaze of color in the bits of woods, the freedom and the rush of rapid motion on the open road, the joy of living in a vital world, the ecstacy of loving and of love, the intensity of feeling in the ardent young, it surely was not so that Julia Dehning could win the sober reason that should judge of men.

And always every day it came and always every day when it was ending it would be the same. "Yes I certainly do care for him and I do know him. And he and I will live our lives together always learning things and doing things, good things they will be for us whatever other people may think or say."

And so at last, filled full with faith and hope and fine new joy she went back to her busy city life, strong in the passion of her eager young imagining.

The home the rich and self made merchant makes to hold his family and himself is always like the city where his fortune has been made. In London it is like that rich and endless dark and gloomy place, in Paris it is filled with pleasant toys, cheery and light and made of gilded decoration and white paint, and in Bridgepoint it was neither gloomy nor yet joyous but like a large and splendid canvas completely painted over but painted full of empty space.

The Dehning city house was of this sort. A nervous restlessness of luxury was through it all. Often the father would complain of the unreasoning extravagance to which his family was addicted but these upraidings had not much result for the rebuke came from conviction and not from any habit of his own.

It was good solid riches in the Dehning house, a parlor full of ornate marbles placed on yellow onyx stands, chairs gold and white of various size and shape, a delicate blue silk brocaded covering on the walls and a ceiling painted pink with angels and cupids all about, a dining room all dark and gold, a living room all rich and gold and red with built-in-couches, glass-covered book-cases and paintings of well washed peasants of the german school, and large and dressed up bedrooms all light and blue and white. (All this was twenty years ago in the dark age, you know, before the passion for the simple line and the toned burlap on the wall and wooden panelling all classic and severe.) Marbles and bronzes and crystal chandeliers and gas logs finished out each room. And always everywhere there were complicated ways to wash, and dressing tables filled full of brushes, sponges, instruments, and ways to make one clean, and to help out all the special doctors in their work.

It was good riches in this house and here it was that Julia Dehning dreamed of other worlds and here each day she grew more firm in her resolve for that free wide and cultured life to which for her young Hersland had the key.

At last it was agreed that these two young people should become engaged, but not be married for a year to come, and if nothing new had then turned up, the father said he would then no longer interfere. And so the marriage now was made for with these kind of people an engagement always meant a marriage excepting only for the gravest cause. And Alfred Hersland and Julia had this time to learn each other's natures and prepare themselves for the event.

When the twelve months had passed away no grave cause had

come to make a reason why this marriage should not be. Julia was twelve months older now, and wiser, and through this wisdom had in general a little more distrusting in her, but never in any kind of a way was she changing about the new world she needed now to content her and she was firm always in her intention to marry Alfred Hersland. She loved him then with all the strength of her eager young imagining, though dimly, somewhere, in her head and heart now there was sometimes a vague dread that comes of ignorance and a beginning wisdom, a distrust she could not then yet seize and look on so that she could really know it, but a distrust that often was there, somewhere in the background, somehow sometimes mixed there to her sense, in with her energy, her new faith, and her feeling.

For a girl like Julia Dehning, all men, excepting those of an outside unknown world, these one read about in books and never really could believe in, for it is a strange feeling one has in one's later living, when one finds the story-books really have truth in them, for one loved the story-books earlier, one loved to read them but one never really believed there was truth in them, and later when one by living has gained a new illusion and a kind of wisdom, and one reads again in them, there it is, the things we have learned since to believe in, there it is and we know then that the man or the woman who wrote them had just the same kind of wisdom in them we have been spending our lives winning, and this shows to any one wise in learning that no young people can learn wisdom from the talking of the older ones around them. If they cannot believe the things they read in the story-books where it is all made life-like, real and interesting for them, how should they ever learn things from older people's talking. Its foolish to expect such things of them. No let them read the story-books we write for them, they don't learn much, to be sure, but more than they can from their fathers', mothers', aunts' and uncles' talking. Yes from their fathers' and their mothers' living they can get some wisdom, yes supply them with a tradition by your lives, you grown men and women, and for the rest let them come to us for their teaching.

But now to come back to Julia Dehning. As I was saying, to a girl like Julia Dehning, all men, excepting those of an outside unknown world, those one reads about in books and never really can believe in, or men like Jameson to whom one never could belong and whom one always knows, now after having once begun with one's living, for what they are whenever one met with them, I say for a girl like Julia Dehning, with the family with which she had all her life been living, to her all men that could be counted as men by her and could be thought of as belonging ever to her, they must be, all, good strong gentle creatures, honest and honorable and honoring. For her to doubt this of all men, of decent men, of men whom she could ever know well or belong to, to doubt this would be for her to recreate the world and make one all from her own head. Surely, of course, she knew it, there were the men one could read of in the books and hear of in the scandal of the daily news, but never could such things be true of men of her own world. For her to think it in herself as real any such a thing would be for her to imagine a vain thing, to recreate the world and make a new one all out of her own head.

No, this was a thought that could not come to her to really think, and so for her the warnings of her father carried no real truth. Of course Alfred Hersland was a good and honest man. All decent men, all men who belonged to her own kind and to whom she could by any chance belong, were good and straight. They had this as they had all simple rights in a sane and simple world. Hersland had besides that he was brillliant, that he knew that there were things of beauty in the world, and that he was in his bearing and appearance a distinguished man. And then over and above all this, he was so freely passionate in his fervent love.

And so the marriage was really to be made. Mrs. Dehning now all reconciled and eager, began the trousseau and the preparation of the house that the young couple were to have as a wedding portion from the elder Dehnings.

In dresses, hats and shoes and gloves and underwear, and jewel ornaments, Julia was very ready to follow her mother in her choice and to agree with her in all variety and richness of trimming in material, but in the furnishing of her own house it must be as she wished, taught as she now had been that there were things of beauty in the world and that decoration should be strange and like old fashions, not be in the new. To have the older things themselves had not yet come to her to know, nor just how old was the best time that they should be. It was queer in its results this mingling of old taste and new desire.

The mother was all disgusted, half-impressed ; she sneered at these new notions to her daughter and bragged of it to all of her acquaintance. She followed Julia about now from store to store, struggling to put in a little her own way, but always she was beaten back and overborne by the eagerness of knowing and the hardness of unconsidering disregard with which her daughter met her words.

The wedding day drew quickly near with all this sharp endeavor of making her new home just what it should be for the life which was to come. Julia thought more of her ideals these days than of her man. Hersland had always, a little, meant more to her as an ideal than as a creature to be known and loved. She had made him, to herself, as she was now making her new house, an unharmonious unreality, a bringing complicated natural tastes to the simplicities of fitness and of decoration of a self-digested older world.

I say again, this was all twenty years ago before the passion for the simple line and toned green burlap on the wall and wooden panelling all classic and severe. But the moral force was making then, as now, in art, all for the simple line, though then it had not come to be, as now alas it is, that natural sense for gilding and all kinds of paint and complicated decoration in design all must be suppressed and thrust away, and so take from us the last small hope that something real might spring from crudity and luxury in ornament. In those days there was still some freedom left to love elaboration in good workmanship and ornate rococoness and complication in design. And all the houses of one's friends and new school rooms and settlements in slums and dining halls and city clubs, had not yet taken on this modern sad resemblance to a college woman's college room.

Julia Dehning's new house was in arrangement a small edition of her mother's. In ways to wash, to help out all the special doctors in their work, in sponges, brushes, running water everywhere, in hygienic ways to air things and keep ones self and everything all clean, this house that Julia was to make fit for her new life which was to come, in this it was very like the old one she had lived in, but always here there were more plunges, douches, showers, ways to get cold water, luxury in freezing, in hardening, than her mother's house had ever afforded to them. In her mother's house there were many ways to get clean but they mostly suggested warm water and a certain comfort, here in the new house was a sterner feeling, it must be a cold world, that one could keep one's soul high and clean in.

All through this new house there were no solid warm substantial riches. There were no silks in curtains, no blue brocade here, no glass chandeliers to make prisms and give tinklings. Here the parlor was covered with modern sombre tapestry, the ceiling all in tone the chairs as near to good colonial as modern imitation can effect, and all about dark aesthetic ornaments from China and Japan. Paintings there were none, only carbon photographs framed close, in dull and wooden frames.

The dining room was without brilliancy, for there can be no brilliance in a real aesthetic aspiration. The chairs were made after some old french fashion, not very certain what, and covered with dull tapestry, copied without life from old designs, the room was all a discreet green with simple oaken wood-work underneath. The living rooms were a prevailing red, that certain shade of red like that certain shade of green, dull, without hope, the shade that so completely bodies forth the ethically aesthetic aspiration of the spare American emotion. Everywhere were carbon photographs upon the walls sadly framed in painted wooden frames. Free couches, open book-cases, and fire places with really burning logs, finished out each room.

These were triumphant days for Julia. Every day she led her

family a new flight and they followed after agape with wonder disapproval and with pride. The mother almost lost all sense of her creation of this original and brilliant daughter, she was almost ready to admit the obedience and defeat she now had in her. Sometimes she still had a little resistance to her but mostly she was swelling inside and to all around her with her admiration and her pride in this new wonderful kind of a daughter.

The father had always been convinced and proud even when he had disapproved the opinions of his daughter. He now took a solid satisfaction in the completeness of accomplishment she now had in her. To her father, to know well what one wanted, and to win it, by patient steady fighting for it, was the best act a man or woman could accomplish, and well had his daughter done it. She had won it, she knew very well what she wanted and she had it. He still shook his head at her new fangled notions, her literary effects, the artistic kind of new improvement, as he called it, that she put into her new house to make it perfect. He did not understand it and he always said it, but he was very proud to see her do it, and he bragged to everybody and made them listen to it, of his daughter and the wonderful new kind of a house she had, and the bright way she knew how to do it.

The little Hortense had always worshipped this wonderful big sister, and the boy George admired too, and followed after.

Altogether these last weeks were brilliant days for Julia.

But always, a little, through all this pride in domination and in the admiration of her family, there was there, somewhere, in the background, to her sense, a vague uncertain kind of feeling as to her understanding and her right. Mostly she had a firm strong feeling in her, but always, a little, there was there, a kind of a doubting somewhere in her. She never in these days did any very real thinking about Hersland as a man to be to her as a husband to control her. But, somehow, a little, he was there in her as an unknown power that might attack her, though she knew very well she had in her a wisdom and experience of life that she could feel strong now always inside her.

A few weeks before the day they were to be married and to begin their new free life together, this vague distrust in Julia became a little sharper. Alfy was talking to her one night about the good life they were to have soon together, about their prospects and his hopes for the future. "I've some good schemes Julia in my head," he said to her, "and I mean to do big things, and with a safe man like your father to back me through now I think I can." Julia somehow was startled though this kind of saying in him was not new to her. "Why what do you mean Alfy?" "Why," he went on, "I want to do some things that have big money and big risks in them and a man as well known as your father for wealth and reliability for a father-in-law will do all that I need. Of course you know Julia," be added very simply enough for her, "you must not talk to him about such things now. You are my wife, my own darling, and you and I will live our lives together always loving and believing in the same good thing."

He said it simply enough to her and he was safe. Julia would not speak of such things now to her father. No torment of doubt, no certainty of misery could bring her to ask questions of her father, now, about the new life she had before her. Hersland was safe, though very simply now, he often made for her that sharp uncertain feeling more dreadful and more clear before her. He was not different in his ways or in his talk to her from the way he always had been with her, but somehow now it had come to her, to see, as dying men are said to see, clearly and freely things as they are and not as she had wished them to be for her.

And then she would remember suddenly what she had really thought he was, and she felt, she knew that all that former thought was truer better judgment than this sudden sight, and so she dulled her momentary clearing mind and hugged her old illusions to her breast.

"Alfy didn't mean it like that," she said over to herself, "he couldn't mean it like that. He only meant that papa would help him along in his career and of course papa will. Oh I know he didn't really mean it like that, he couldn't mean it like that. Anyhow I will ask him what he really meant."

And she asked him and he freely made her understand just what it was he meant. It sounded better then, a little better as he told it to her more at length, but it left her a foreboding sense that perhaps the world had meanings in it that could be hard for her to understand and judge.

But now she had to think that it was all, as it had a little sounded, good and best. She had to think it so else how could she marry him, and how could she not marry him. She had to marry him, and so she had to think it so, and she would think it so, and did.

In a few days more the actual marrying was done and their lives together always doing things and learning things was at last begun.

Bear it in your mind my reader, but truly I never feel it that there ever can be for me any such a creature, no it is this scribbled and dirty and lined paper that is really to be to me always my receiver,—but anyhow reader, bear it in your mind—will there be for me ever any such a creature,—what I have said always before to you, that this that I write down a little each day here on my scraps of paper for you is not just an ordinary kind of novel with a plot and conversations to amuse you, but a record of a decent family progress respectably lived by us and our fathers and our mothers, and our grand-fathers, and grand-mothers, and this is by me carefully a little each day to be written down here ; and so my reader arm yourself in every kind of a way to be patient, and to be eager, for you must always have it now before you to hear much more of these many kinds of decent ordinary people, of old, grown, grand-fathers and grand-mothers, of growing old fathers and growing old mothers, of ourselves who are always to be young grown men and women for us, and then there are still to be others and we must wait and see the younger fathers and young mothers bear them for us, these younger fathers and young mothers who always are ourselves inside us, who are to be always young grown men and women to us. And so listen while I tell you all about us, and wait while I hasten slowly forwards, and love, please, this history of this decent family's progress.

Yes it is a misfortune we have inside us, some few of us, I cannot deny it to you, all you others, it is true the simple interest I take in my family's progress. I have it, this interest in ordinary middle class existence, in simple firm ordinary middle class traditions, in sordid material unaspiring visions, in a repeating, common, decent enough kind of living, with no fine kind of fancy ways inside us, no excitements to surprise us, no new ways of being bad or good to win us.

You see, it is just an ordinary middle class tradition we must use to understand this family's progress. There must be no aspiring thoughts inside us, there must be a feeling always in us of being in a kind of way in business always honest, there must be in a kind of ordinary way always there inside us the sense of decent enough ways of living for us. Yes I am strong to declare that I have it, here in the heart of this high, aspiring, excitement loving people who despise it,—I throw myself open to the public,—I take a simple interest in the ordinary kind of families, histories, I believe in simple middle class monotonous tradition, in a way in honest enough business methods.

Middle-class, middle-class, I know no one of my friends who will admit it, one can find no one among you all to belong to it, I know that here we are to be democratic and aristocratic and not have it, for middle class is sordid material unillusioned unaspiring and always monotonous for it is always there and to be always repeated, and yet I am strong, and I am right, and I know it, and I say it to you and you are to listen to it, yes here in the heart of a people who despise it, that a material middle class who know they are it, with their straightened bond of family to control it, is the one thing always human, vital, and worthy it— worthy that all monotonously shall repeat it,—and from which has always sprung, and all who really look can see it, the very best the world can ever know, and everywhere we always need it.

The Herslands were a western family. David Hersland as a young man had gone far into the new country to make his money. He had

succeeded very well there in making money. He had settled down in
Gossols and had lived there for twenty years and more now.

He had made a big fortune. David Hersland was in some ways
a splendid kind of person.

Mr. Hersland had brought his wife to Gossols with him. He had
married her in Bridgepoint when his fortune was just beginning. His
children had all been born in Gossols to him. They were really western,
all of them, all through them. There were three of them, Martha,
Alfred, David, there had been two others but they had died as little
children. Now Martha, after many changes, was home again with him.
Alfred who had never yet been any trouble to him was gone to Bridgepoint to marry Julia Dehning and then there as a lawyer to win for
himself his own way of living. And the youngest David was soon to
follow Alfred to Bridgepoint, to go to college there and to decide in
him, as his way always had been and no one could ever understand
him, from day to day what life meant to him to make it worth his living.

And so when Alfred Hersland first met Julia Dehning, his family
father mother Martha and David were still living there in Gossols. The
mother was already now a little ailing, the father had no longer his old
strength for living, Martha had come back out of her trouble to them,
Alfred had gone away and left them, David was very soon to follow
him. They had their old place in Gossols to live in but it had not the
beauty and the wonder now it had had all these years for them. Joy
was a little dim inside now for all of them.

For many years it had been full of content, this home they had
always lived in. The Herslands had never had a city house to be
restless around them and to give restlessness inside to them. They
had all these years been in the place they now lived in.

This house they had always lived in was not in the part of Gossols
where the other rich people mostly were living. It was an old place
left over from the days when Gossols was just beginning. It was grounds
about ten acres large, fenced in with just ordinary kind of rail fencing,
it had a not very large wooden house standing on the rising ground in
the center with a winding avenue of eucalyptus, blue gum, leading from
it to the gateway. There was, just around the house, a pleasant garden,
in front were green lawns not very carefully attended and with large
trees in the center whose roots always sucked up for themselves almost
all the moisture, water in this dry western country could not be used
just to keep things green and pretty and so, often, the grass was very
dry in summer, but it was very pleasant then lying there watching the
birds, black in the bright sunlight and sailing, and the firm white summer
clouds breaking away from the horizon and slowly moving. It was
very wonderful there in the summer with the dry heat, and the sun
burning, and the hot earth for sleeping ; and then in the winter with

the rain, and the north wind blowing that would bend the trees and often break them, and the owls in the walls scaring you with their tumbling.

All the rest of the ten acres was for hay and a little vegetable gardening and an orchard with all the kinds of fruit trees that could be got there to do any growing.

In the summer it was good for generous sweating to help the men make the hay into bails for its preserving and it was well for ones growing to eat radishes pulled with the black earth sticking to them and to chew the mustard and find roots with all kinds of funny flavors in them, and to fill ones hat with fruit and sit on the dry ploughed ground and eat and think and sleep and read and dream and never hear them when they would all be calling ; and then when the quail came it was fun to go shooting, and then when the wind and the rain and the ground were ready to help seeds in their growing, it was good fun to help plant them, and the wind would be so strong it would blow the leaves and branches of the trees down around them and you could shout and work and get wet and be all soaking and run out full into the strong wind and let it dry you, in between the gusts of rain that left you soaking.   It was fun all the things that happened all the year there then.

And all around the whole fence that shut these joys in was a hedge of roses, not wild, they had been planted, but now they were very sweet and small and abundant and all the people from that part of Gossols came to pick the leaves to make sweet scented jars and pillows, and always all the Herslands were indignant and they would let loose the dogs to bark and scare them but still the roses grew and always all the people came and took them.   And altogether the Herslands always loved it there in their old home in Gossols.

David Hersland's mother was that good foreign woman who was strong to bear many children and always after was very strong to lead them.   The old woman was a great mountain.   Her back even in her older age was straight, flat, and firmly supporting.   She had it in her to uphold around her, her man, her family, and everybody else whom she saw needing directing.   She was a powerful woman and strong to bear many children and always after she would be strong to lead them.   She had a few weak ways in her toward some of them, mostly toward one of them who had a bad way of eating too much and being weak and loving, and his mother never could be strong to correct him, no she could not be strong to let his brothers try and save him, and so he died a glutton, but the old mother was dead too by then and she did not have the sorrow of seeing what came to him.

Always this strong foreign woman was great and good and directing. She led her family out of the old world into the new one and there they learned through her and by themselves, almost every one of them, how to make for themselves each one a sufficient fortune.

Yes it was she who lead them all out of the old world into the new one. The father was not a man ever to do any such leading. He was a butcher by trade. He was a very gentle creature in his nature. He loved to sit and think and he loved to be important in religion. He was a small man, well enough made, with a nice face, blue eyes, and a little lightish colored beard. He loved his eating and a quiet life, he loved his Martha and his children, and mostly he liked all the world.

It would never come to him to think of a new world. He never wanted to lose anything he ever had had around him. He did not want to go to a new world. He would go,—yes to be sure it would be very nice there, only it was very nice here and here he was important in religion,—and he liked his village and his shop and everything he had known all his life there, and the house they had had ever since he married his good Martha and settled himself to be comfortable together with her,—and now they had their children. Yes, alright, perhaps, maybe she was right, there was no reason, the neighbors had all gotten so rich going to America, there was no reason they shouldn't go and get rich there, alright he would go if his Martha talked about it so much to him, alright, his Martha could fix it anyway she liked it, yes it would be nice to have all of them get rich there. He would go, yes to be sure it would be nice there, but it was very nice here and he had his religion, and he liked his village and his shop and everything he had known all his life here, and the house they had always lived in since he had married his good Martha, and they had settled to be so comfortable there and to stay there, and now they had all those good children. But, yes, alright, perhaps, maybe she was right, there was no reason, the neighbors had all gotten so rich going to America, there was no reason they shouldn't all get rich too there, yes it would be very nice then, to have them all go and get rich there. Alright he would go, they would all go and get rich there, Martha could fix it if she wanted so badly to have it, she would be always talking to him about it. Martha could fix it anyway she liked it, yes it would be nice to have all of them get rich there like the neighbors who were writing all the time how rich they had it, and it would be good for the children to have it, and to send money to some of the old folks who would need it, the way the neighbors always did. Yes the neighbors always were sending money to their father when he needed to have it. Alright they would all go, his Martha could fix it anyway she liked it. If she wanted he would do it.

Martha began then and she soon sold their business and the things on the little farm and in the shop and in their house, and kept only the few things she knew they needed. Her man liked it very well then this being so important and he could use it as he liked to do religion. He liked it very well to see his wife do all this selling. He liked the feeling he had in him when they were all so busy buying and selling all around him, but when the people came to take the things he had been so important about when his wife was selling, then it was a very different feeling he had in him. It was hard for him then the ending. He had liked it very well while they were selling. He had liked the feeling of all the doing and the moving and the being important to all of them and everybody always talking.

It had been very pleasant to him. He never really had to do any deciding, and he had all the emotion and the important feeling, it was just like in religion.

But it was not so pleasant for him when the people came and took the things it had been so pleasant selling. It hurt him to have the things he loved go away from him, and he wanted to give back the money to all of them so that he could keep them. But he knew that that could not be done and he still keep his important feeling that was so pleasant to him ; and then too Martha would not let him. He said nothing to the people when they came to take the things it had been so pleasant selling to them, he was only very slow in giving the things to them. He would lose them so that it was hard to find them but the children and Martha always found them.

Almost everything was sold and the people came and took them. He could not stop them. Now the things did not belong to him any more. Nothing now belonged to him. There was another man in his shop and he acted, in standing there and in selling, just as if it had all always belonged to him. It made poor David Hersland very sad to see him standing there, chopping, talking, selling, wiping his hands on his apron, acting as if it had all always belonged to him, now when there was no place anymore anywhere for Hersland, a place that really belonged to him.

It was too late now, he had done as his Martha had made him. He would have liked to buy back all that they had been selling. It was very hard to keep him moving. It was hard to start him and it was almost harder to keep him going. Now he wanted to settle down again and keep on staying. Perhaps the man who had bought his shop would sell it back to him if they would pay him. "No David," his wife said to him. "We've got to go now, don't talk so foolishly about buying when we just hardly have got through selling. No David, don't you see how the children are all so excited about going. How can you talk so when we have to be working every minute and in two days now we've got to be moving."

Yes it was hard to start him but it was almost harder to keep him going. His Martha worked hard with him to keep him moving. She had to tell it to him very often that now there was no other way for him to be doing. Now they were started they just had to keep going.

Yes it was very hard to keep him moving. It was hard to start him but it was even harder to keep him going. But now it was all done and they were all of them ready to do the last beginning. They were all already to leave the next morning. All the things they had kept had been put in a wagon, the littlest children were to ride on top of them, the rest were to walk beside them until they came to the city by the water where they would find the ship that was to take them to that new world where they were all to make a fortune.

They started very well the next morning, with all the people to say good-by to them and with all the things they needed piled in the wagon, the littlest children set on top of them, the rest of them to walk beside them. The mother was like a great mountain, good and firm and direct-ing, and as always able to uphold around her, her man, her children, and everybody who needed directing, and he was feeling it once more good inside him to be important as if it were in religion, and all the talking and moving and everybody so excited about him. It was very pleasant just then for him, and then the wagon began moving, and some went a little way with them and then they all left them and then it was only the family and the driver of the wagon who were with him and all the pleasant feeling left him.

They went on and on and then suddenly they missed him, the father was not there any longer with them. The mother went back patiently to find him. He was sitting at the first turning, looking at the village below him, at all the things he was leaving, and he simply could not endure it in him.

His wife called to him. He sighed and she came to him. "Don't you want to be going David," she said to him. "If you don't really want to be going you've just got to say David what you want to be doing. I'll never be a woman to make you do anything you are not really wanting. You just say David what it is you are really wanting. I'll do it if you want me really badly to do it. You know I never want you not to do everything just like you really need it. The children, they are all waiting there just for you to say it. David I say you just say it what you want and I do it." He sighed and he looked a little sullen.

"Of course Martha you know I do what I got to do for you and the children. You know I always do what is right for me to do for you and the children. I don't ever think what I am needing, I only just want to do the best I can for you and the children. Can't you see Martha I just came back here to see it. That ain't got nothing to do with what I made up my mind was the right way to do it. I just came here to see I don't forget it. Yes I come now Martha. Sure I always will do it what is right for me to do so you and the children can have it. I never do any other way in it. I go on with you now I got another look to see I don't forget it. I just stopped here to see it. Its just I wanted to see what way it looked so I would get it right not to forget it. Alright Martha I come, you go on, I be with you in a minute. I just look to see I got it fixed right so I don't forget it. Alright Martha I come now. I got it fixed now I can't forget it. Alright we go on now I done what I needed. I came back just to do it. Now we go on to the children and we go on to do it like we said we would do it." And he sighed and he got up and he looked back as he went away from it and she talked about how much the children were going to like it and he began to forget it.

All, the wagon and the driver and the horses and the children, had waited for them to come up to it. Now they went on again, slowly and creaking, as is the way always when a whole family do it. Moving through a country is never done very quickly when a whole family do it.

They had not gone very far yet. They had not been going many hours. They were all having now just coming in them their first tired, the first hot sense of being very tired. This is the hardest time in a day's walking to press through and get over being tired until it comes to the last tired, that last dead tired sense that is so tired. Then you cannot press through to a new strength and to get another tired, you just keep on, that is you keep on when you have learned how you can do it, then you just get hardened to it and know there is no pressing through it, there is no way to win out beyond it, it is just a dreary dull dead tired, and you must learn to know it, and it is always and you must learn to bear it, the dull drag of being almost dead with being tired.

In between these first and last are many little times of tired, many ways of being very tired, but never any like the first hot tired when you begin to learn how to press through it and never any like the last dead tired with no beyond ever to it.

It was this first hot tired they all had in them now just in its beginning, and they were all in their various ways trying to press themselves to go through it, and they were mostly very good about it and not impatient or complaining. They were all now beginning with the dull tired sense of hot trudging when every step has its conscious meaning and all the movement is as if one were lifting each muscle and every part of the skin as a separate action. All the springiness had left them, it was a weary conscious moving the way it always is before one presses through it to the time of steady walking that comes when one does not any longer do it with a conscious sense with each movement. It is not until one has settled to it, the steady walk where one is not conscious of the movement, that you have become really strong to do it, and the whole family were now just coming to it, they were just pressing through their first hot tired.

And now once more the father had done it. The father was no longer with them, once more he had slipped back and they had lost him.

The mother said to the children. "Well you go on, I go back to get him." She felt no anger in her toward him. She just went patiently back to find him.

She told the children to keep on slowly as they were going and she would go back and find him. She walked back looking patiently everywhere for him. She found him before she had gotten back to where she had the last time found him. He had not gotten back yet to where he could see all he was going to leave behind him. She had walked faster than he and had caught him.

She had no impatient feeling in her against him. It was a way he had, she knew it, it was right for him to have it, the kind of a feeling he had about leaving. It was a way he had, she was not impatient with him, he was right to have that kind of a feeling in him. It was right for him to act that way to see about not forgetting. It was only that she knew he would like it and it would be so good for the children that made her want to urge him not to give up now they had made their beginning.

But she was not in any way impatient to him, she had no impatient feeling in her against him. It was just his way and now she would coax him and he would come back with her to the wagon. It was only a way he always had had whenever he had to do a new thing. And so she walked a little with him and began to talk about the children and how nice it would be when they would all get rich and how the children would like it to work and help him, and they sat down and after they had been resting, when they got up again she did not do any discussing, she just started him back toward the wagon, and always she was telling about how good he was to do what was best for her and the children. Soon they came up with the wagon which was still very slowly moving.

It was so hot doing so much walking, she said then to him, he looked a little sick, she thought he ought not to do any more walking, perhaps it would be better if he would get into the wagon and ride a little with the little children. It would be awful if he got sick and nobody to take care of them for he was the only one that could do their talking. And so she coaxed him into the wagon with the children.

They went on and soon it was too far, there was not now any more going back for him. And then he was content, and he had the new city and the ship, and then he was content with the new world around him.

They had, for a little while, a hard time beginning, but on the whole things went very well with them. The sons made money for them, the daughters worked and then got married to men whom they found making money around them. Some did very well then and some not so well, and they all had their troubles as all people have them, and some died, and some lived and were prosperous and had children. One as I was saying died a glutton and spoiling him was the one weak thing the strong mother did to harm any of them.

The old man never made much of a fortune but with the help his children gave him he lived very well and when he died he left his wife a nice little fortune. She lived long and was strong to the last and firmly supporting and her back was straight and firm and always she was like a great mountain, and always she was directing and leading all whom she found needing directing.

She was then very old, and always well, and always working, and then she had a stroke, and then another, and then she died and that was the end of that generation.

There had been born to Martha and David Hersland many sons and daughters. All who lived to be grown up had gotten married and almost all of these were prosperous. One, the glutton, died and left his wife and children to his brothers, he had not made enough money to leave them provided, and his brothers each one in their turn gave the money to support them.

Of the daughters two of them were well married. The third one always lived with her husband but it was her brothers who kept her dressed and gave her children education and then later in their life started them out in their working.

On the whole it was a substantial progress the family had made in wealth, in opportunity, in education, in following out the mother's leading to come to the new world to find for themselves each one a sufficient fortune.

In all of them the father and the mother were variously mixed to make them, but mostly it was the mother who was strongest in them. Some, like the glutton, had in certain ways the important feeling in them that the father had had in religion. Some, like the daughter who had not made much of a success in marrying, had his way of not being very good at keeping on even after they had made the beginning, but mostly all of them had the strength and solid power in them that the mother had it in her to give to all of them. Most of them began and kept on well after they had made a beginning. And so they were mostly very successful in the business of living.

In every one of them the father and mother were very variously mixed up in them. The fourth son, David Hersland, one of the fathers we must soon be realising so that we can understand our own being, was the only one of all of them who had gone to the far west to make his fortune. It is a little hard to see just how the mixture of this father and this mother came to make him. He was in some ways, as I was saying, a very splendid kind of person. He was big and abundant and full of new ways of thinking, and this was all his mother in him, but he had not her patient steadfast working. He was irritable and impatient and uncertain and not always very strong at keeping going, though always he was abundant and forceful and joyous and determined and always powerful in starting. And then too he was in his way important inside to him as his father had been when he felt his religion in him. But all this will show more and more in him as I tell you slowly the history of him.

He had gone as a young man to Gossols to make his fortune. This was the new world in a new world and it took this newest part of this new world to content him. He alone of all the brothers had this restless feeling in him. All the others did very well where the mother had brought them. He alone had needed to go farther to find for himself his life and a sufficient fortune.

As I was saying he had brought his wife to Gossols with him. He had married her in Bridgepoint where one of his sisters had settled with her man who made there a very good living. At this time David though he was quite a young man had already made enough money to support him and a wife and children. This he had done before he had thought to go to Gossols where he was to make his great fortune. And so it was right for his sister at this time to be anxious to arrange a marriage for him. Now the idea of going to the far west was just beginning to work in him. Perhaps marrying might keep him with them, anyway it would be good for him to have a good wife to go to Gossols with him, and so he met little Fanny Hissen. It was arranged by his sister that this young woman should be married to him.

Fanny Hersland all her life was a sweet gentle little woman. Not that she did not have a fierce little temper sometimes in her and one that could be very stubborn, but mostly she was a sweet little gentle mother woman and only would be hurt, not angry, when any bad thing happened to them.

Her mother was one of those four good foreign women the grand-mothers, always old women or as little children to us the generation of grandchildren. These four good foreign women, the grandmothers we need only to be just remembering, had each one a different kind of a foreign man to be a master to them. These four foreign women, the one strong to bear many children and then always after strong to lead them, the steady good one who was patient to bear her many children and then always was patient to suffer with them, the sweet pure one who died as soon as she had born all of them for that was all she knew then to do for them, and the little gentle weeping hopeless one who sorrowed in her having them and always after sorrowed in them, all these four foreign women had very many and very different kinds of children.

The gentle little hopeless one who wept out all the sorrow for her children had many and very little children. She was the mother of the pretty gentle little woman that David Hersland married in Bridgepoint and took out to Gossols with him.

The little weary weeping mother of all these gentle cheery little children had a foreign husband who was not very pleasant to his children. He too was little like his wife and like all his children but there was a great deal in him to cause terror to his wife and children. He was like old David Hersland important in religion. It was very deep inside him and with him it was much harder on his children. His wife too had sorrow in religion, she had sorrow from his being so important in religion and she had sorrow too from her own self in her own religion. But then it was all sorrow and sadness, and always a trickling kind of weeping that she had every moment in her living, and it really was not much worse in religion. It was just a way she had, this trickling weeping, even as when it sometimes did happen she was laughing. She never ever really stopped her sad trickling, to her joy was as it has been said of laughing, it is madness, and of mirth who doeth it, for even in laughter the heart is sorrowful and the end of that mirth is heaviness. It was in her as it was said by the quaker woman. I often think if I could be so fixed as never to laugh or to smile I should be one step better, it fills me with sorrow when I see people so full of laugh.

It was a hard father and a dreary mother that gave the world so many and such pleasant little children. Mostly they were cheerful little children. Perhaps it was that the mother had wept out all the sorrow for them. There was no weeping that she had left over to them. They were mostly all in their later living cheerful hopeful gentle little men and women. They lived without ambition or excitement but they were each in their little circle joyful in the present. They lived and died in mildness and contentment.

It was one of these cheerful gentle little Hissen people that David Hersland married there in Bridgepoint and then took to Gossols with him. And now he with all the mixed up father and strong mother in him and this little gentle cheerful pretty little woman who yet had a fierce little temper that could be very stubborn were to come together and make a life together and to mix up well and then to have many different kinds of children through her.

They had mixed up very well. They had made a good enough success with their living.

They had had five children through her. Two of these had died as little children. Three of them had grown up and were now grown young men and women, and these three are of them who are to be always in this history of us young grown men and women to us, for it is only thus that we can ever feel them to be real inside in us, them who are of the same generation with us.

The mother, little gentle Mrs. Hersland, was very loving in her feeling to all of her children, but they had been always all three, after they had stopped being very little children, too big for her ever to control them. She could not lead them nor could she know what they needed inside them. She could not help them, she could only be hurt not angry when any bad thing happened to them.

She loved them and was very proud of all three of them. Often she wondered as she looked at them, how could they be so perfect and so wonderful and yet all three of them be so different from the others of them that there was hardly anything alike in the three of them.

They were big children and each one of them in his own way was strong to do what they needed to find themselves free inside them. They were big children and she was only a very little mother to them. And they were not very loving children, they were too strong at finding their own way to feel free and important each one to himself inside him. They were to her very good children. She never had any trouble with them. And now she was a little ailing and they were good but then she never had been very important to them.

Now we begin to learn more about the Hersland family and their way of living.

As I was saying the father David Hersland was in some ways a very splendid kind of person but he had some very uncertain things inside him. He too was very proud of his children but it was not easy for them to be free of him. Sometimes he was very angry with them. Sometimes it came to his doing very hard pounding on the table at which they would be sitting and disputing, and ending with the angry word that he was the father, they were his children, they must obey him, he was master and he knew how to make them do as he would have them. Such scenes were very hard on the little gentle mother woman who was all lost in between the angry father and the three big resentful children who knew very well what they needed to have given to them so that they could be free inside them.

This is the way the three Hersland children grew up to be strong each one to be free inside him. They were all big in themselves and in their way of winning. Soon you will learn slowly the history of each one of them, how each one was important to himself in him, and how they won a kind of freedom for themselves each one inside them.

The little mother was not very important to them. They were good enough children in their daily living but they were never very loving to her inside them. They had it too strongly in them to win their own freedom.

They turned to their father, altogether, in their thinking. It was against him inside, and strongly always around them, that they had to do the fighting for their freedom. Now the mother was a little ailing. She was all lost between the father and the three big struggling children.

In their young days the father was proud of his children, proud that they were important each one to himself inside him, proud that they needed to win for themselves their own freedom. Always then he encouraged their disputing, he wanted then that they should fight and win out against him. As I was saying David Hersland the father of these big resentful children was in some ways a splendid kind of person. But now things were going less easily around him. Joy was a little dim inside now for all of them. Now he would often be angry and be given to pounding on the table and loudly declaring, he was the father, they were the children, they must obey else he would know how to make them. And the gentle little mother who every day was giving signs of weakening would sit scared, and afterwards she would be weeping, lost between the father and the three big resentful children.

But this was all when they had become grown young men and women and joy was a little dim inside for all of them.

Now listen to their lives as children, their early struggles each one to find for themselves freedom, the abundant father in them in those days full of joyous beginning, proud of himself and of his children, glad to feel that they were strong all of them to make for themselves their own beginning.

Now I will tell you more of the Hersland ways of living in the old home with the wind and the sun and the rain beating, and the dogs and chickens and the open life, and the hay, and the men working, and the father's way of educating the three children so that they could be strong to make for themselves their own beginning, and the gentle little mother who was not very important to them, who had sometimes a fierce little temper that could be very stubborn but mostly she was only sad, not angry, when any bad thing happened to them, and the three children with the mixed up father and the little unimportant mother in them.

As I was saying Mr. Hersland was big and abundant and always was very full of new ways of thinking. Always he was abundant and joyous and determined and always powerful in starting. Also sometimes he would be irritable and impatient and uncertain. Also he was in his way important inside to him, and all these things came out in his educating of his children.

Truly he loved education. It was to him almost all there is of living. He did not do it with steadfast steady working, things always were a little uncertain with him. One never knew which way it would break out from him the things he was very good at starting and then other things would happen to him and to all the people around who were dependent on him.

It was a very good kind of living the Hersland children had in their beginning, and their freedom in the ten acres where all kinds of things were growing, where they could have all anybody could want of joyous sweating, of rain and wind, of hunting, of cows and dogs and horses, of chopping wood, of making hay, of dreaming, of lying in a hollow all warm with the sun shining while the wind was howling, of knowing all queer poor kinds of people that lived in this part of Gossols where the Herslands were living and where no other rich people were living. And so they grew up with this kind of living, such kind of queer poor, for them, people around them, such uncertain ways of getting education that they had from the father's passion for all kinds of educating, from his strong love of starting and the uncertain things he had inside him.

Altogether it was a good way of living for them who had a passion to be free inside them and this was true of all three of the Hersland children but mostly with Martha the eldest and the only daughter living, and the youngest David who was always searching to decide in him and no one could ever understand him, from day to day what life meant to him to make it worth his living. It was less in Alfred, this love of freedom, in Alfred who was soon now to be marrying Julia Dehning. He had some of it in him but not so strongly inside him as Martha and David and his father had it in them.

Yes I say it again now to all of you, all you who have it a little in them to be free inside them. I say it again to you, we must leave them, we cannot stay where there are none to know it, none who can tell us from the lowest from them who are simply poor or bad because they have no other way to do it. No here there are none who can know it, we must leave ourselves to a poor thing like Alfred Hersland to show it, one who is a little different with it, not with real singularity to be free in it, but it is better with him than to have no one to do it, and so we leave it, and we leave the Alfred Herslands to do it, poor things to represent it, singularity to be free inside with it, poor things and hardly our own in it, but all we can leave behind to show a little how some can begin to do it.

Yes real singularity we have not made enough of yet so that any other one can really know it. I say vital singularity is as yet an unknown product with us, we who in our habits, dress-suit cases, clothes and hats and ways of thinking, walking, making money, talking, having simple lines in decorating, in ways of reforming, all with a metallic clicking like the type-writing which is our only way of thinking, our way of educating, our way of learning, all always the same way of doing, all the way down as far as there is any way down inside to us. We all are the same all through us, we never have it to be free inside us. No brother singulars, it is sad here for us, there is no place in an adolescent world for anything eccentric like us, machine making does not turn out queer things like us, they can never make a world to let us be free each one inside us.

And yet a little I have made it too strong against us in saying Alfred

Hersland was the only one who could in this adolescent world represent us. The father David Hersland we cannot count for us, it was an old world that gave him the stamp to be different from the adolescent world around us. But there is still some hope for us in the younger David who is different from the people all around us, in him who always was seeking to be free inside him, to know it in him, and no one could ever understand him, what it was inside him that made it right that he should go on with his living. He as you shall hear in the history of him, does not really belong to the adolescent metallic world around him, and yet there was not that vital steadfast singularity inside him that custom passion and a feel for mother earth can breed in men. He did not have it really for him, custom, passion, certaintly of place and means of living, stability within himself and around him, a feeling to be really free inside him and strong to be singular in his clothes and in his ways of living.

But now to make again a beginning, to tell of the father David Hersland and the ways he had in him to make himself strong and important inside to him and to prove the right way to educate his children and the singularities the old world had stamped on him.

David Hersland believed in hardening his children. He believed that everyone should make for himself his own beginning, that every one should win for himself his own freedom. This was always strong inside him with all the uncertain ways that he had in him, with all the strong starts and sudden changes in his way of educating the three children who had such different ways in them from the things he meant to give them.

Mostly at first they the children felt this in him in the ways they were ashamed of him in just the simple ways he had of doing in the ordinary every day living.

It is hard on children when the father has queer ways in him. Even when they love him they can never keep themselves from having shame inside them when all the people are looking and wondering and laughing and giving him a name for the queer ways of him.

Mr. Hersland as I have been often saying was in some ways a splendid kind of person, and that was one way one could look at him. In other ways he was an uncertain changeful angry irritable kind of a person with a strong feeling of being important to himself inside him and not always certain to make other men see why he had so much important feeling in him. And then one could think of him, as children when they were young girls and boys felt him, queer in the ways he had of doing things that made them feel a little ashamed to say he was a father to them when other children spoke about him.

These are some of the queer ways he had in him, the ways that made his children feel uncomfortable beside him. They were mostly just simple things in their ordinary living that gave his children this uncomfortable feeling for him.

David Hersland was a big man. He was big in the size of him and in his way of thinking. His eyes were brown and little and sharp and piercing and sometimes dancing with laughing and often angry with irritation. His hands would be quiet a long time and then impatient in their moving. His hair was grey now, his eyebrows long and rough and they could give his eyes a very angry way of looking, and yet one could love him, in a way one was not afraid of him. He never would go so far as his irritation seemed to drive him, and somehow one always knew that of him. He had not so much terror for his children as fathers with more kindness and more steadfast ways of doing. One always had a kind of feeling that what one needed to protect one from him was to stand up strongly against him. He would stop short of where he seemed to be going, anger was there but it would not force him on to the final end of angry acting. All one had to do was to say then to him "Alright but I've got a good right to my opinion. You started us in this way of doing, you have no right to change now and say that its no way for us to be acting." And so each one of the three children, Martha, Alfred and David would each in their own way resist him, and it made a household where there was much fierce talking and much frowning, and then the father would end with pounding on the table and threatening and saying that he was the father they were the children, he was the master, they must obey else he would know the way to make them. And the little unimportant mother would be all lost then in between the angry father and the three big resentful children. But all this was when they were beginning to be grown young men and women. When they were still children there was not any fierceness in the house among them.

And now to come back to the queer ways of him. As I was saying the father was a big man. He liked eating, he liked strange ways of educating his children and he was always changing, and sometimes he was very generous to them and then he would change toward them and it would be hard for them to get even little things that they needed in the position that was given to them by their father's fortune and large way of living.

In the street in his walking, and it was then his children were a little ashamed of him, he always had his hat back on his head so that it always looked as if it were falling, and he would march on, he was a big man and loved walking, with two or three of his children following behind him or with one beside him, and he always forgetting all about them, and everybody would stop short to look at him, accustomed as they were to see him, for he had a way of tossing his head to get freedom and a way of muttering to himself in his thinking and he had always a movement of throwing his body and his shoulders from side to side as he was arguing to himself about things he wanted to be changing, and always he had the important feeling to himself inside him.

And then as I was saying he was a big man and he was very fond of eating, he had had a brother who had died a glutton, and he liked to buy things that looked good to him, and it would always be a very big one, he never liked to undertake anything that was not large in its beginning. The only time in his life that he ever took a little thing was when he chose his wife the little gentle Fanny Hissen who as I have often been saying could only be sad not angry when any bad thing happened to them, but yet she had a fierce little temper in her that could be very stubborn when it was well roused inside her and she sometimes had such a sharp angry feeling at some of the ways her husband had of doing, mostly when it concerned his not giving things she thought they needed to the children. But mostly they lived very well together the father and mother and three children, that is when they were young children, later it was harder for them when the father would get his very angry feeling and the mother was a little ailing and the fierce little temper broke into weakness and helplessness inside her and the three big struggling young grown men and women were seeking each one his own freedom and his own beginning. But now as children it was just the little uncomfortable feeling of being ashamed of the queer ways he had of doing that his children had to endure with him, then he was joyous and it was mostly pleasant enough living with him, and the mother was gentle and pleasant then with them and strong enough to support her little temper that could be very stubborn whenever it arose against him.

But even when he was not doing really queer things there was always a marked character about him. It came from inside him, from the strong ways he had of beginning, from the important feeling he had always inside him from his continual thinking and in a different way from that in which all the other people around about him were thinking, and this thinking somehow marked him even when he was just simply walking and then stopping to talk with somebody or just stopping to ask a question of some stranger or to talk about the weather or other just ordinary enough talking, the kind of thing anybody could be saying, and yet the power of being free inside him made him a marked man even then, and nobody could take him to be an ordinary person or ever forget him.

As he would be walking along with a child beside him or several of them behind him, he would stop and sweep the prospect with his cane and begin talking and somebody near him would come to listen. It was just ordinary talking that he would be doing, about the weather or the country or the fruit and it did not seem to have any deep meaning but it was the power and completeness of the identification of this big man with all creation that forced people to think of him. This man was big as all the world in his beginning, it was nothing in him even if he did not always keep going, he had been as big as all the world once in his feeling and that he never could lose with him.

And so he would stand talking and the unhappy uncomfortable child beside him would keep saying, when he was not afraid to break in on him, "Come on papa all those people are looking." "What !" the father was not listening to him but would keep right on with his talking. The child as much as he dared would twitch or pull at him, "What !" but the father never really heard him and he would go on with the queer ways in him. Slowly his children learned endurance of him. Later in their life they were queer too like him.

Often when he was walking with his children and passed a shop and saw some fruit or cakes or something that pleased him he took it and gave it to his children and they would be most uncomfortable then and say something about not wanting it to him. "What !" and he never listened to them. The children suffered so because they were not sure that the man inside knew that their father would pay him. The father of course always payed for them but there was something in the manner of him that gave one a kind of feeling that he was as big as all the world about him, one included the other in them, the world and him, the earth the sky the people around him the fruit the shops, it was all one and the same, all of it and him, and this kind of a feeling he always gave to them who saw him walking standing thinking talking, that the world was all him, there was no difference in it in him, and the fruit inside or outside him there were no separations of him or from him, and the whole world he lived in always lived inside him.

It was all so simply to him as the world as all him, and it was this that gave him a big freedom and this big important feeling and the big way of beginning and so made a queer man of him, an eccentric from the others around him, and all that stopped it from making a god of him was his way of being impatient inside him and not being very good at keeping going but always making for himself a new beginning.

This large way of him when it made him take up fruit from shops to eat and to give to his children made a very uncomfortable shamed child beside him, and it would be protesting to him, and its father would say, "What", but he never listened to him. The child never did learn that the fruit man would not be worried with him, that they all knew his father and the queer ways of him, and that the father always payed them. The fruit men all knew him and liked the abundant world embracing feeling of him and they liked to see him, but his children never could lose, until they grew up to be queer themselves each one inside him, the uncomfortable feeling that his queer ways gave them.

To him, David Hersland, education was almost the whole of living.

In it was always the making of a new beginning, the having ideas, and often changing. And then there were so many ways of considering the question.

There were so many different ways of seeing the meaning of the various parts that made education. There was the health, the mind, the notion of right living, the learning cooking and all useful things that he knew they should know now to be doing, and then there was his system of hardening so that they would be ready to make each one their own beginning ; and all these needs for them and the many ways to look at them led to many queer things that his children had to endure from him.

Their education was a mixing of hardening, of forcing themselves into a kind of living as if they were poor people and had no one to do things for them, with a way of being very rich, that is having everything the father ever could imagine would do any good to any one of them.

This made a queer mixture in them. They found it a great trouble to them, this past education, when they first began to be young grown men and women. Later in their living they liked it that they had had such a mixing of being rich and poor, together, in them.

As children they all three had loved very well this kind of living. As I was saying they had their ten acres, with a rose hedge to fence their joys in, in that part of Gossols where no other rich people were living. They had all around them, for them, poor people to know in their daily living, and from them they learned their ways which were queer ways for them who had from their father's fortune a very different kind of position to be natural to them.

In Gossols the Herslands could be freer inside them than if the father had remained with his brothers where the mother had brought them and this freedom he used in the education of his children. They never knew any one of them nor the father who was directing it for them just where their learning was coming from or how it would touch them. Mr. Hersland had all kinds of ways of seeing education. He was fondest of all of the idea of hardening but this was difficult for him to keep steadfast in him with his great interest in every kind of new invention, in wanting that his children should always have anything that could do any good to any one of them.

There was joy in them all in their later living that it had been Gossols where they had had their youthful feeling and later when they learned to know other young grown men and women they loved the freedom that they had inside them, that their father had in his queer way won for them.

As I was saying they had ten acres where they had every kind of fruit tree that could be got there to do any growing, and they had cows and dogs and horses and hay making, and the sun in the summer dry and baking, and the wind in the autumn and in the winter the rain beating and then in the spring time the hedge of roses to fence all these joys in.

The mother had always been accustomed to a well to do middle class living, to keeping a good table for her husband and the children, to dressing herself and her children in simple expensive clothing, to have the children get as presents whatever any one of them wanted to have at that time to amuse them. She was a sweet contented little woman who lived in her husband and her children, who could only know well to do middle class living, who never knew what it was her husband and her children were working out inside them and around them. She had strongly inside her the sense of being mistress of the household, the wife of a wealthy and good man and the mother of nice children. When they were little children they liked to cuddle to her when she took them out to visit the rich people who lived in the other part of Gossols. They were all bashful children, living as they did in the part of the town where no rich people were living and so being used to poor queer kind of people and only feeling really at home with them who were not people in the position that their father's fortune and large way of living would naturally make companions for them. And so as little children when they went to visit with their mother in the part of Gossols where other rich people were living, they clung to her or on the sofa where she would be sitting and talking, they climbed behind her, and then too she wore seal-skins and pleasant stuffs for children to rub against and feel as rich things to touch and have near them and so they liked to go with her, and this and the habit of being children with a mother was mostly all of the feeling that they had for her until later when she was ailing and the little stubborn temper in her broke into weakness and helplessness inside her and they had in a way to be good to her.

They always in a way were good to her that is as much as they could remember to think about her, but it was not important inside to any of them to remember about her neither when as children they were near her or when later she was ailing and needed them to be good to her.

She was a little unimportant mother always to them and it was only as a part of the physical home around them that she belonged to them, either when as little children she was mistress of her house and attended to them or later when as weakening she needed to be taken care of by them.

This sweet gentle little mother woman who had sometimes a fierce little temper in her that could be very stubborn when it arose strongly inside her, never knew really in her that she was not important to the children who had come into the world through her. She had a kind of important feeling always inside her. She had a little temper that could make her big husband pay attention to her and she had a power in her in respect to servants and governesses and seamstresses who worked for her. She did not feel it to be important to her what other people felt for her. The life in her family was all of living for her and her children she never thought about in the way of making them feel her.

She had a little pride inside her to make her husband feel her, she had a bigger pride inside her to make her dependents feel her, she had no pride in her to make her children feel her, they were so made of her by having come out into the world through her that they really were apart from her. She did not feel them near her even as little children when they were dependent on her. Later they were so big around her, and she was lost away from them and they never thought about her. But she never felt inside her any anger that they had no deep loving feeling in them for her, all the feeling of pride in her and all the feeling of being important to herself inside her was to make her husband feel her and when she had her little fierce stubborn temper rise inside her, to make him yield to her, or later when the temper broke down into weakness and helplessness inside her to have him then be good to her. All the rest of her feeling herself important to herself inside her had to do with her dependents and the struggles she had with them and they had among themselves and so to feel her.

No she never felt it ever to be very important to her the relation of other rich people of her kind toward her. She had left Bridgepoint and friends and family feeling all behind her. Here in Gossols it was only the house and the ten acre place and those inside it that concerned her.

She knew the value of herself, and their well to do way of living, of her husband, and her nice children, and the simple expensive clothing they wore when they went out visiting to that part of Gossols where the other rich people were living. She could know the value of them and the way other people must feel toward them but these things gave her no strong feeling of being important to them, the other people, who did not come close to her in her daily living. With them it was only a continuing of her well to do living which was the only kind of living it was right to her for anybody to be having. That was there. To have it gave her no important feeling. It was right to have a well to do good husband and nice children and all in simple and expensive clothing, but in the ten acre place in that part of Gossols where no other rich people were living she was cut off from a lively feeling of this right kind of living. Here it was she herself who was important to her feeling, here she was not only a right part of a right way of living, as it had been for her in Bridgepoint in her family in the way the Hissens had always done their living, but she had an individual feeling, not with her children they were completely of her and apart from her as was the right well to do middle class living, it was always there so were her children but they were not important to her feeling. The things that made her important to herself in her feeling was the sometimes controlling her husband by her little temper when it arose to be fierce inside her and the stubborn way it sometimes gave her in acting, and in being mistress and deciding and being above them and yet in their daily living and so interfering with the seamstresses and governesses and servants and all the people they ever had working for them.

Being cut off from the simple rich ordinary way of living never gave her any feeling. It was not being cut off with any sense of losing, it was always there existing, in her and for her, this kind of living and it was not important to her feeling. It was as if one could ever be thinking about the different kinds of air in different parts of the world where one happened to be living, the atmosphere of well to do living was to her as the air she was breathing, it was always there she could not feel it important in her feeling or her thinking, breathing was there, one did not know it as important to one's feeling until one was in some way sick and it stopped or made hard one's breathing, but so long as one was strong and living one went on like everybody else with one's breathing. And so it was with Mrs. Hersland and well to do living, she could not feel it to be important in her feeling whether it was in the rich part of Gossols that they were living, or in Bridgepoint, or in the part of Gossols where no other rich people were living. Always she was of well to do being, with a good rich husband and nice children and when she wanted to have it simple and expensive clothing. The sense of belonging to this kind of living could never give her any kind of important feeling. Her husband David Hersland with the queer nature of him might have an important feeling coming to him from just breathing, that feeling could come to him from the singular nature of him, from his being as big as all the world in his beginning, but to an ordinary gentle little mother woman there could never come such a feeling, this well to do living could only come to be important to her in her feeling if she could ever come to it through a losing, by their money going or by their losing position by some wrong doing, and such a kind of losing it could never come to Mrs. Hersland to ever think of as coming to them.

And so visiting and being, well to do living and her children, these never gave her a strong feeling of being important inside her through them, it was only through her husband and the governess and seamstresses and servants and dependents that she could ever have an individual kind of feeling.

It was queer that her children were to her like well to do living, not important to her feeling.

As I was saying David Hersland had made a decent fortune even before he had left Bridgepoint. He had made enough money to give his wife and children a good position. And so when they first came to

Gossols where he was to make for himself a great fortune they could afford to live in as good a hotel as was then there existing.

Things began very well in their far western living. Martha and Alfred were then very young children. David the youngest had not yet been born to them. Here Mrs. Hersland had been at first a little lonesome.

Mrs. Hersland had left friends and family feeling behind her. Here in Gossols it would have been natural for her to find other people to continue with her the well to do living which was the only right way of being to her.

They lived for a year in that part of Gossols where all the rich people were living.

Here she had her first important feeling. Here she met a Miss Sophie Shilling and her sister Pauline Shilling and their mother old Mrs. Shilling.

Always Mrs. David Hersland had been a right part of a right kind of living. Not that she had not often had strong feeling, not that she did not have dignity in herself and in her family in her feeling, sometimes she had an angry stubborn feeling, sometimes with her sisters or her mother and later when they came together sometimes with Mr. David Hersland who was to be married to her. Sometimes it was a hurt feeling that made her sad not angry when any bad thing happened to her, sometimes it was a hurt feeling that made her a little bitter. All this had been important feeling to her, sometimes it had made a power of her but it did not give to her an important feeling to herself inside her. It was not apart in her from the feeling of herself to her as of the right well to do living that had made her and which was the only right way of being for her.

Old Mrs. Shilling and her daughter Sophie Shilling and her other daughter Pauline Shilling, first gave to her the feeling of being important to herself inside her, important, apart in her, from right being, right acting, and the dignity of decent family living with good eating being the mother of nice children the wife of a good well to do man, and all in simple and expensive clothing.

This family of old Mrs. Shilling and the two daughters with her gave to Mrs. Hersland and the gentle dignity she always had inside her as part of the family she belonged to, gave to her a sense of a new power that was apart in her from the dignity of right being that she had always had around her. It was apart in her this sense of a new kind of power that she had with Mrs. Shilling and the fat daughter Sophie Shilling and the thin pretty dull queer always getting into trouble Pauline Shilling, it was apart in her from the dignity of right living that she had always had inside her. It was the fat daughter Sophie Shilling who was the new kind of friend to her, that gave her the sense of being important to herself inside her. Sophie Shilling made a new kind of friendship for her and it was a new sense that Mrs. Hersland had then inside her, different from all that she had always had in her, different from the right living that had made her.

All the Hissen people had it strongly inside them, the family way of good living. They were all in their natural way of family thinking gentle cheerful little men and women. They lived in their natural way of being, without any strong ambition. It was enough for them to hold to their tradition, the dignity and beauty of right living and right thinking, they never needed to go out to find ambition or excitement in their living, they had excitement and dignity inside them from their family and the gentle pride that made them ; that, sometimes, came in sparkling, sometimes in angry flashes from them but mostly they were hurt not angry when any bad thing happened to them. They lived in their natural way of being without any strong ambition or excitement, they were each in their little circle joyful in the present, they lived and died in mildness and contentment.

They had never any one of them an important feeling of themselves inside them to arise of itself from within them. Such a kind of important feeling would not be in them in the way of living it was natural to any one of them to be having. Mrs. Fanny Hersland never would have had such a feeling if she had lived on in Bridgepoint, going on always with the right kind of being, she would often have had an angry feeling, sometimes with her family, or her husband, or for them when things happened to them to worry them, and sometimes it would be a hurt feeling that would lead to bitter biting talking, sometimes it would be a hurt feeling that would make her sad not angry when any bad thing happened to them and always it would be she who had the feeling and the dignity and the good well to do husband and the simple and expensive clothing, and the nice children and she was the mother of them, but with all this strong feeling, with this being proud or angry or sad or stubborn or happy in her feeling, she would never have that kind of important feeling that she learned to be having in Gossols, first with Sophie Shilling as a beginning and then in Gossols later in the ten acre place where they were always staying cut off from being really a part of the right way of living.

She would have been a part, if she had gone on with her natural living, she would have been a part of the right way of Hissen being ; she could have been in her feeling angry or sad or stubborn or happy, or biting in her talking, or hurt when any bad thing happened to them, she could have all this in her feeling and yet not have that kind of sense of importance to herself inside her that comes with the individual being.

The little religious father who had made them all, all his children, he could not make others not living with him feel him, the little religious father who had made all of his children feel him had such an important feeling inside him, it was his religion gave it to him, it did not arise of itself from within him. It was only being as he felt himself, all there was of religion, could give him such a feeling of being important to himself inside him. He could make all his children feel him, he could in a way make them fearful of him and the religion in him, and all the religion was of him and he was in himself all there was of religion, and so it was that he had the important feeling inside in him, but this did not make any but his children feel him, it did not arise of itself inside him and he could not make any one who did not live with him feel it in him.

The little dreary mother with her trickling kind of weeping that she had every moment in her living, even, as when it sometimes happened, she was laughing, this dreary little trickling woman had with her sadness in religion and in her trickling weeping that kept on always wetting all the sorrow there could be in living, this trickling dreary little Mrs. Hissen, who wept out all the sorrow for her children, had in her an important kind of being that was almost an important feeling, and this almost an important feeling did not come to her as in her husband from religion, it arose up inside in her with her trickling weeping.

Almost it was really an important feeling and it was the having too, such an almost important feeling that made her daughter Mrs. Hersland have really such a feeling when it came to her there in Gossols to have a, for her, not natural way of living, and it first came as a beginning with the old lady Mrs. Shilling and her fat daughter Sophie Shilling and the other daughter Pauline Shilling.

With all the other Hissen men and women there mostly was not such an important feeling inside in them, only with the oldest of them who had religion as the father had inside him, and with her it was as with him, the important feeling did not arise of itself inside her, and only her children could feel it in her, the way of being important that being all there was of religion gave their mother as a power over them in her.

Mostly the Hissen men and women the children of the father and religion and the trickling dreary mother who hardly knew how she came to make them, in all these Hissen little men and women there was never very much of such important feeling. It was only way off there in Gossols, shut off from a lively feeling of well to do living, shut off from her friends and family feeling, that Fanny Hissen, Mrs. Hersland, could find in herself a really important feeling.

All the little Hissen people had very strong family feeling. All together they were important to themselves in their feeling. Not that they did not each one alone have strong feeling and each one of course had in them a different way from all the others of them of being loving or having an angry feeling. They all of course had in them their own individual way of thinking and of doing only they never had inside them each one for himself the real important feeling.

Some of them had often a very angry feeling, some had fierce tempers and sometimes bitter biting ways of talking, some had very stubborn ways inside them, and some had it mostly in them to be only hurt not angry when any bad thing happened to them. Yes they had each one of them their own way of feeling thinking and of doing but they had not any of them inside in them an important feeling of themselves inside them as the father had in religion and as the dreary mother almost had with her continuous way of trickling crying.

Some of the children, as I was saying, had it a little in them. The oldest daughter from her dull stubborn religion that was for her all there really was of living had it in herself and it gave her power over her young children. One, a little younger, Fanny, Mrs. Hersland, had from a, to her, not a natural way of living, and from having had it strongest of them all from the beginning, the almost important feeling that the mother had with her constant trickling, from being cut off from a lively feeling of right being, she had almost before ending a really important feeling. And one next to the youngest of them had a little such a feeling from almost an individual way of thinking, it never really came to a fruition but as with the mother in the constant trickling this one with constant and very nearly an individual kind of thinking had almost a real important feeling.

The Hissen family altogether were, and very really, important to themselves inside them in their feeling. Each one of them had always for himself and all the others of them a dignity and a gentle way of making himself important to the others of them and to every one who ever came to know them. They were all of them, each one in the gentle dignity they all had in them, important to every one who ever came near to them. With some of them, their eyes flashed often with a sharp angry almost fierce feeling, that things happening could arouse within them, often with some of them they would be hurt and then their mouths were drooping. In some of them it was a very stubborn feeling that was the deepest thing inside them after the family way that made all them, and these were the hardest to live with and never to be forgiven when they had been hurt or angry by something some one had done to them. But mostly the Hissen men and women were gentle cheerful little men and women, mostly they lived without ambition or excitement and mostly they were each in their little circle cheerful in the present. Mostly they lived and died in mildness and contentment.

Until they were all really grown men and women, until the women each one found a husband to control them and the men went into a business and were independent of him, until they were in this sense grown men and women, until he died the father always wanted and succeeded in shutting them all up to be always with him. This was not in him from any small feeling inside him but from the important feeling he had in him of being all there was for him of religion and it was his sense of the right way for them to be as children that made him shut them up so and keep them there close to him.

Later when the daughters were married and the sons working were independent of him and had left him, he never in any way wished to interfere with them, with their feeling, their religion, their way of thinking or their doing. When they were with him, they belonged there and he held them shut in with him, when they left him, grown up men and women, it was no longer for him to act upon them, they no longer were his necessary way of living. It was never his children that gave him an important feeling, his power over them when they were shut up with him never gave him any kind of an important feeling. No it was his being all there was of religion that gave him his important feeling, not his wife nor his children nor any power he had from them nor the power he never had had with any one who did not live shut up with him. Nothing in such a way could give him an important feeling. They were his daily living, the necessary right way of doing, they were not important to his feeling, not in themselves nor in any power in him that came from them either as they were or as he made them. Such things could never come to him as an important feeling of himself inside him. It was only being all there was of religion that gave him such an important feeling.

It was queer unless you really could understand him, could really see how the important feeling came to be in him, it was certainly queer to just ordinary thinking to see a man who had been so rigid with his children, keeping them shut up with him, making them live every minute as he would have them, having no power with anyone who did not live so with him, it was queer that when these children came to be grown men and women, that is independent and living away from him, that he never in any way wanted to keep his hold on them. He had for them then as much affection as he ever had had for them, he always went to see them and was open and friendly with them but not in any way had he ever any kind of desire in him to interfere with them or their way of living or their thinking or their doing, no not even with their feeling in religion. They were his children, yes, but not now a part of his necessary living, even when, as he did some years before dying, even when he was living with one of them who with her husband had very different ways of living, of thinking, and of feeling, in religion than he had it in him, even then he never interfered with them who were now independent of him, grown men and women. The only thing that gave him an important feeling was being all there was of religion. When his children were shut in with him they were a part of him, they had to do with his necessary way of being, they had to live in his important feeling, with his being all there was of religion, but when they had left him, when later he even lived with them, they were then no longer a part of him, he was then, all alone, all there was of religion. By that time his wife too had left him, had died away and left him. Always in her living she had never been quite of him, she had been cut off from him, by her having from her constant trickling crying an almost important feeling. And so this old man who was to himself all there was of religion, to whom religion and himself was all there was of living, who had kept his children close shut up with him every minute of their living until they were for him grown up men and women this old man who never had had any power in him for any one who was not shut up with him, this old man had a queer way of being almost perfect in his toleration of things that were all different from his way of thinking and feeling and believing, even with religion, even with his children, now when they were independent of him.

So strong was it in him, this tolerating spirit toward them when they were grown men and women to him, that even when later in their living they sometimes asked him to guide them he would refuse it to them, for they were then apart from him, he was all there was of religion, religion was all there was of being for him ; that made him important to himself inside him. It was not for him to guide them they who were apart from him, they were then as all the world always had been, he had no power over anything not shut up with him, and so he had a tolerant spirit for everything that was not him, for his children now when they were grown up and independent even when as it happened later he was living with some of them.

One of them who had come to be grown up for him was the Fanny Hissen who had married David Hersland the man who was as big as all the world in his beginning and strong to prove this, his feeling, on all who met him, not only on them who were shut up with him, everybody always felt this in him, once he was as big as all the the world around him, he was it, it was in him, there was no difference with it inside him or outside for him ; in his beginning with Fanny Hissen when she first began her living with him she wanted to do as he would have her do in all things. It came to them, in religion, that his ways were not the ways that had been right for her to have when she was living with her family, when they had been all living, shut in with the father who was all there was of religion.

It came one day to a very great division between her husband's way of thinking and feeling in religion and her father's ways as she had learned to have them inside her when she with all her sisters and her brothers were living shut up with him.

She wrote to him and asked him, she said her husband wanted her to go with him and it was not as she had been taught by him her father, she did not feel it wrong to do this thing but she could not do it without asking her father, who had never let his children do any such thing when they were shut in with him. What should she do, she would not make for herself such a decision, she would ask him, was it wrong for her to do this thing, to go with her husband to such a meeting.

The old man replied. "My dear child. There was once a priest, a good man. Once a member of his church came to him and said I have been thinking can I do this thing, can I go to a barber's shop and get shaved on a Sunday morning, is it wrong for me to do this thing. The priest said, yes he must forbid it to him, he must not go to a barber's shop on a Sunday morning and get a man to shave him, it was wrong for him to do this thing, it would be a sin in him. Two Sundays after the man met his priest coming out of a shop shaved all fresh and clean. But how is this, the man said to him, you told me that it was forbidden, you told me, when I asked you, that I should not do this thing, that it would be for me a sin. Ah ! said the priest to him, that was right, I told you I must forbid you to go Sunday morning to a shop and get some one to shave you, that it would be a sin for you to do this thing, but don't you see, I did not do any asking."

Later in the old man's living, when his wife had died away and left him, he came to live with a daughter who had not any kind of an important feeling to herself inside her, neither from a religion to be all her nor from a constant rising up inside her as the dreary mother had it in her to have an almost important feeling to be inside her from the constant trickling of her, the father later came to live with this daughter who had a gentle dignity and good ways in her from the sweet nature of her not from any important feeling in her, and she and the man who was married to her, both, though they had respect in them for the father, and goodness and a delicate feeling to consider all who ever had to do with them, though they were glad to do for him everything he wanted them to be doing yet they had together very different ways of thinking, of feeling, and of living than he had known it to be right to have all his life in his necessary living.

The old father, strong as he always had been in his nature, firm in being for himself all there was of religion, knowing to his dying that religion was all there was of living, yet never in any way was he ever interfering in the living and the feeling and the thinking of his daughter or her husband or any of their children or any of his own children who were there in the same house with him. Now, for him who was no longer leading in a house with others shut up with him, with him who was all there was of religion, for him, now, that they were apart from him being grown men and women to him, even though they were all together every minute with him, although he was up to the last moment of dying as strong as ever in the faith of him, to be himself and to be all there was of religion, yet now it was not for him to ever in any way interfere with any one of them. He never found out anything that was happening, anything that he would not wish to know that any one of them was doing. What a man does not know can never be a worry to him. This was his answer to his children whenever any one of them wanted to explain anything to him or to get him to agree to any new thing in their living.

And so he went on to the last minute of his living, never having had any power in him over any one who was not shut up with him and a necessary part of his living, strong always in his being to himself all that were was of religion, strong in knowing that religion was all there was of being. And so he went on with his living, now never interfering with anybody's living, now that he was himself for himself all there was of living, all there was of religion, and religion always was all there was of living. And so he went on to his dying and through his being so all himself all there was of living and of religion, he was in his old age full of toleration, and slowly in his dying it was a great death that met him. He was himself all there was of him, all there was of religion, and religion was all there was of living for him, and so the dying from old age that came slowly to him all came together to be him. He was religion, death could not rob him, he could lose nothing in his dying, he was all that there was of him, all there was of religion, and religion was all there was of living, and so he, dying of old age, without struggling, met himself by himself in his dying, for religion was everlasting, and so for him there could be no ending, he and religion and living and dying were all one and everything and every one and it was for himself that he was all one, living, dying, being, and religion.

Even his dead wife with her trickling crying that had been to her almost an important feeling of herself inside her, even she had been apart from him, and his children when they were no longer shut up with him were apart from him. All and everything was apart from him, and so he died, and with him died his important feeling, for even in his dying he had no power in him for any one not shut up with him. He was all of power for him for he was for himself all there was of religion. And that was all and he never had had any power in him for anything not shut up with him. And so he died away and left them and his important feeling died inside him.

All of his children had each mixed up in them the father, important to himself in his religion, and the mother, with her almost important feeling, with her constant trickling crying that made her have inside her her almost important feeling. She with the way it came from within her this almost important feeling that she had inside her, could have a power with all who knew her. She was not like her husband with his important feeling giving power only with them like his little chlidren who were shut up with him.

The children had many ways of having the father and the mother mixed up to make them. One of them, as I was saying, the eldest of them, was stubborn and gloomy and hard in her religion and it gave her a power with her children but it was not so perfect to give her her own important feeling as religion had been to her father to give him the important feeling that was all him. In her own being she was not all there was of religion, she as a woman had hard ways that gave her power, not from her religion but from her power as a woman, as any one can have it by using the hard ways everybody has inside them, and so she was less in religion, she had no toleration, she was hard stubborn and gloomy in religion, and always she made it stronger by her power as a woman, and so she had not the greatness in her that her father had who made her, and she had not the almost greatness in her that the mother had arising inside her with the dreary trickling crying that was all her.

And so in each one the father and the mother were variously mixed up in them. Some of them had it in them as an almost important feeling like Fanny Hissen who with this way of having it as a beginning, the almost important feeling that the mother had with her dreary trickling had it brought to a real beginning of a really important feeling, by the knowing old fat Mrs. Shilling and her daughter Sophie Shilling and her other daughter Pauline Shilling, and then in her later living cut off from a lively sense of being part of being which was for her the natural way of living she got it more and more then from her servants and governesses and seamstresses and dependents and the for her poor queer kind of people that she had around her in this later living in that part of Gossols where no other rich people were living, she got it from her power with them, being as she was with them of them, and from her position and her dignity of Hissen living always above them. From those ways that her later living in that part of Gossols away from where the other rich people were living gave to her, in this later living there came to her a kind of importance of herself inside her that was nearly an individual kind of feeling and this was what gave to her family later when she came to pay visits to them out of the far west to them, gave them a sense as if she were almost a princess for them, out of from them, belonging to them, having a different feeling of herself inside her from any other ones of them. Not that this was, in her, in any sense the complete thing of being important to herself inside her, it was only more marked in her than any other of them had found it from the natural way of living it had come to all the rest of them to be leading.

It was not different in her from the rest of them in one important thing. It was mixed up in her with the stubborn feeling that the not having the complete important feeling that the father had from being all there was of religion gave to all of them who had a little of him in them.

All of them, as they had more or less of him in them, had it as a stubborn feeling, for none of them had it as a complete thing as he had had it inside him, and with the eldest of them, as I was saying, she who had most of the religion, with her it was a hard gloomy stubborn feeling and so this eldest one who had as much important feeling as the Fanny who had lived away from them and then had had in her come this for them important thing, this eldest of them although she was a power to all the rest of them by reason of the important feeling they knew inside her for them, was never a princess to them, she had not the gentleness and generous dignity that won them as their other sister had for them she who had had made to her the important feeling of herself inside her by the being away from all of them, away from the natural way of living for them.

Then there were others of them who had all the sweetness in them that had turned to dreary trickling in the mother who had born all them, and one of those who had this sweetness in her dignity and gentleness and generous ways and so was a power to them was the one that the father lived with after his dreary wife had died away and left them.

With these who had sweetness in them, with those who had changed into sweetness the dreary trickling of the mother that had born them, many of them, strongest in them after the sweetness and gentle dignity that made them, had it as the strongest thing inside them to be hurt not angry when any bad thing happened to them, they would be hurt then and their mouths would be drooping. And always all of these, the sweetest of them, had in them some of the stubborness that not being the complete thing as their father had been was sure to put into them.

In some of them the mixing of the trickling and the stubborness inside them came to make an angry feeling that came in flashes from them, in some of them it came to make a suspicious feeling inside them that made it hard for them to trust in women or in men, and always, as I was saying, the father and the dreary mother were very variously mixed up in each one of them

As I was saying, one of them who even more than Fanny Hissen had the almost important feeling that the mother had inside her with her constant trickling crying that was always rising in her, this one came to have it even more in her, came to have it almost really in her by an individual kind of thinking that arose of itself inside her. She had the gentle tenderness in her that made constant dreary trickling in her mother, and it came all from inside her, and she had no stubborn ways in her, she was pure as the sweetest ones of those around her those who had turned to sweetness the dreariness of their mother, and she had not stubborness inside her, she had only from her father the thinking that had made him for himself to be all there was of power. And this one of the Hissen women came very near to winning, came very near to seeing, came very nearly making of herself to herself a really individual being. She was a little not strong enough in keeping going, and so with her it came only to being a very nearly really important feeling of herself to herself inside her. And she was the nearest any of them ever came to winning.

There were very many of them and each one, of course, had his or her own individual way of feeling, thinking, and of doing, and with all of them the father and the mother were variously mixed up in them, and with some of them it was more the father and it made sometimes a stubborn feeling to be the most important thing inside them after the family that made all them and sometimes this the stubborn feeling met in them with the other things they had within them and sometimes then it was a sharp bright angry feeling that was strongest in them after the family way that had made all them, and these then would have a stubborn or an angry feeling when anything happened to any one of them. And then in some of them it was the dreary mother that was strongest in them and they had a sweetness in them and these then would have hurt feelings in them and very often with them then, their mouths would be drooping and these would then be hurt not angry when any bad thing happened to them. And sometimes there was a mixing up of all these ways together in them.

But mostly all of them were cheerful hopeful contented men and women, mostly they lived without ambition or excitement but they were each in their little circle joyful in the present. Mostly they lived and died in mildness and contentment.

David Hersland married Fanny Hissen. He took her out to Gossols with him. He married her in Bridgepoint where her family had always been living. David Hersland had been there visiting a sister who had settled there with her man who was making a very good living. David Hersland was a young man then but already he had made by himself enough money to support himself and a wife and children. And now it had come to him to go west to Gossols where he was to make a great fortune. And so it was right for his sister at this time to arrange a marriage for him. The idea of going to Gossols was just beginning in him. Perhaps marrying might keep him from going, any way it would be good for him to have a good wife to go to Gossols with him.

He met Fanny Hissen and she was pleasing to him. It was arranged by his sister that this young woman was to be married to him. They married soon after the first meeting and then they mixed up their two natures in them and then through them there came the three children, Martha, Alfred, and young David, and these three are of them who are to be always in this history of us young grown men and women to us. In the history of them we will be always ourselves and our friends inside them for so we know them those who are for us always young grown men and women to us even when they are of the age of children or later grown old men and women. Always they are us and we them and so always they are for us young grown men and women.

So now then we begin again this history of us and always we must keep in us the knowledge of the men and women who as parents and grandparents came together and mixed up to make us and we must have always in us a lively sense of these mothers and these fathers, of how they lived and married and then they had us and we came to be inside us in us. We must realise always in us, so that we can know what is us, we must realise inside us their lives and marriages and feelings and how they all slowly came to make us. All things in them must be important to us. And so we must know slowly inside us how they came to be married and so made us, and we must know, so that we can know what we feel inside us, we must know the kind of important feeling in them that made them what they were in their living marrying and thinking, the things that were always inside them, the things that gave each one of them their individual feeling.

In the slow history of three of those who are to be always in this history of us young grown men and women to us, in the slow history of Martha Alfred and young David Hersland, of how they came each one to have their kind of important individual feeling inside them in them, in this slow history of them the thing that we have as a beginning is the history of Fanny Hissen and David Hersland, of their living marrying and their important feeling, and so now we leave the rest of the Hissen living and begin with Fanny and David Hersland and their marrying and then we go on with the important feeling that was always in him and the important feeling and its beginning in her with the new kind of living, and then in her later living how she came to be so strong in this important feeling that when she came back to Bridgepoint to visit the rest of them, the Hissens who had led the for them natural way of living, she was then a kind of princess to them. They did not know, any of them, what it was that made her so different from them. It was only her kind of feeling, rich ways and simple and expensive clothing and far western living could never give them the sense of her being as a princess to them, it was that she had in her, from her way of living that was not the natural way of living for her, it was from this living that had come to her and from the mother who had been begun again inside her that she had come to have a small almost important feeling of herself inside her.

This made her different from the others of them. Only the eldest of them had it as a power in her, an important feeling of herself inside her, and they all could not bear it from her for she had no sweetness toward them in her. But all this history of her will come later. Now David Hersland is to be married to her and she is to leave her family feeling all behind her.

Later there will be more talking of the natural Hissen way of living. Later when the Hersland children have grown to be ready to begin their later living then we will know more of some of them, of some of the Hissen family in the, for them, natural way of living, of what it is in each one of them that makes him different from the others of them, even though they have not ever inside in them a really individual feeling. The mixture in them of the father who was to himself all there was of living and the dreary mother who had almost an important feeling was different in every one of them.

Later Alfred and young David came to know them the gentle cheerful Hissen men and women. Alfred later lived with some of them. When he came to college he stayed with them and later he was there near them when he was married to Julia Dehning. And then young David stayed with some of them and always he was puzzling himself and them and no one of them could help him, but they all were kind and listened to him, he was puzzling in him every day to find out what it was that could make life worth his living. Martha Hersland never came to see them, she had her trouble far from all of them and then she went out of her trouble back to Gossols and so she never saw them.

In American teaching marrying is just loving but that is not enough for marrying. Loving is alright as a beginning but then there is marrying and that is very different. In many towns there are many in each generation, decent well to do men, who keep on in their daily living and never come to any marrying. They all do a little loving. Everybody sometime does a little loving. It takes more for marrying, sometimes it needs a sister of the man to make his marrying, sometimes the mother of the girl who is to be married to him. Mostly it is not the mother of the man nor any sister who has not already then a husband and children who makes marriages for them. Mostly for marrying it takes a sister of the man, one who has already for herself a husband and children or a mother of the girl who is to be married to him. This is not so when they are young, the man and woman, and both are lively in the feeling of loving. It is so when the man has come to be fixed in his way of living, when he finds it pleasant to go on as he is doing. It is then that it is not enough to feel a little loving, it takes then his sister, or the girl herself if she is strong to do the work for winning, or a mother of the girl, to get the man really ripe for marrying.

The American teaching is very well for young people or for poor ones or for those who are strong in a sense of loving, who have a lively sense of wanting, who have strongly the instinct for mating, but for most of them, the well to do, comfortable men and women, it takes more to make a marriage for them, it takes others who are strong to help them, who have strongly inside them the need that all the world keep on going, who have strongly inside them the sense of the right way of living. Mostly those who have a strong sense inside them of the right way of living, of having all the world going on to marrying are the sisters of the men, they who have already then for themselves a man and children, and the mothers of the girls who are to be married to the men, and sometimes it happens that the mother of the man has strongly inside her this sense of right doing, those mothers who are not strong in jealous feeling whose sons are not as lovers to them, and this is the way it happens to almost all the comfortable well to do men and women and the american tradition makes us lie about them and mostly in our writing there are none of these ordinary, good enough, comfortable, well to do men and women.

American teaching says it is all loving but all who know many families of women, all who know comfortable well to do men with a regular way of living know that it is all mostly lying that says it is loving that is strong to make a beginning, they need a sister who has already for herself her own man and children or a girl who is strong to make for herself her own winning or the mother of the girl who is to be married to him. It takes one and sometimes even all three of them and with it a fair amount of loving to make the marrying of well to do men and women. Loving is good but it has to be a very lively sense inside him to make it enough for a well to do man to get married to a woman. Loving is good, and the girl has to be pleasing to him, but it needs coaxing, arranging, flattering teasing, urging, a little good tempered irritated forcing, or else the man will forget all about his loving. It is so easy to forget a little loving. And then he must see her very often and when he is drifting he must be brought back out of his forgetting. And it is right that they should do this for him else how would there be the right kind of marrying, how would there come to be existing the decent, honest enough, comfortable men and women that never get in the american tradition any recognition, but they are always in the world existing these decent well to do men and women with the not very lively sense in them of loving and their easy forgetting, and there are the women, they are always existing, they who have inside them strongly the right feeling of how the world was in its beginning and how it must keep on going. And so there is the right kind of marrying and decent well to do fathers and good mothers are always existing who have a decent loyal feeling of the right kind of loving and they have their children and so they keep on going and we decent respectable well to do comfortable good people are all of them. This business of marrying and loving is very different with the very young, or poor or with quite old men. With all of these loving is strong inside them, they are not so peaceable with their forgetting, they are quicker with marrying than comfortable well to do young men.

They are many families of women and the men find some in each one of them pleasing, and then the men go drifting, doing a little loving and then a little forgetting, and then restarting, until they get so strongly the feeling of loving, if they have the right kind of helping, that they come to have so strongly in them the feeling of loving that then it is an effort for them to begin again with their forgetting, and then they are ripe for marrying, and one of the family of women has him and marrying contents them and they have the right kind of living for them and everything keeps on as it was in the beginning. It is the truth that I have been telling.

David Hersland's sister Martha arranged his marriage for him. She was right to arrange a marriage for him. David had made enough money to support himself and a wife and children. Going to the far west was just beginning to work in him. Perhaps marrying might keep him from going, anyway it would be good for him to have a good wife to go to Gossols with him.

Martha, David Hersland's sister who arranged his marriage for him, had been married five years to a decent good man who had settled in Bridgepoint where he was making for himself a very good living. They had two children.

Martha was one of the two Hersland women who had done very well in marrying. She had an important feeling and this was like the father's feeling in religion, and she was like her mother in her way of keeping on strongly when she had made a beginning, and she always made a beginning whenever it was right for her to do so for her feeling. She was the best one of all of them to arrange a marriage for a brother who needed to have a good wife to go out to Gossols with him.

Martha was very like her father. She was a small good enough looking woman with blue eyes and with a manner that was not very unpleasing. She was like her father because she loved to be important, but with her it was not in religion. She was different from him because she loved to be doing. She loved to be important by the doing of all the things that were right to do to her feeling. One of these things was the marrying her brother so that he would have a good wife to follow him and serve him.

She thought a great deal about it and she did a good deal of talking and at last she decided to choose Fanny Hissen.

Martha, David Hersland's sister, who always did whatever it was right for her to do, to her feeling, was not very unpleasing. In some ways she was quite pleasing, she was so to her husband, to him she was very pleasing. She was not really pleasing to her brother David Hersland, to him she was not appealing nor domineering and it took women of these two kinds to be pleasing to him, but he knew she was a good woman who would always do what was right for her to do to her feeling, and mostly he thought she was right in her feeling and in her way of doing what was right to her feeling and so he was willing that she should choose a wife to content him.

To her husband this Martha was almost always pleasing. He was a big man with strong passion in him and a sentimental feeling and he wanted a wife, not to be domineering, but to hold him with her attraction, and always to be equal to him. He did not want a wife to appeal to him, he would not have one to domineer over him. It was his sentimental feeling that made him not want his wife to be appealing, he wanted to make her an ideal to him. He was a man to be master in his living and so he never would have a wife to domineer over him.

Martha Hersland who was married to him was just right for him. She was the woman to hold him and this one can see from the nature of her as it will come out from her in the history of her as she makes the marriage for her brother.

In some ways Martha was not very pleasing, she was a woman to make a beginning and to keep on going when it was right to do so, to her feeling. When she met with stronger women she would not stop herself from winning, she would not know that she was then losing she only dropped out of that working and made for herself a new beginning. She was not a strong woman, as her mother had been, the mother who was like a mountain, who had it in her to uphold around her, her man, her family, and everybody whom she saw needing directing. Martha was not in such a way a strong woman, she was not in any such way pleasing. She was like her father in her important feeling, but she was stronger than he ever had been, in keeping going, she was fonder of making a beginning, she always liked to be doing, and so she was not very pleasing, in some ways she was very pleasing.

It is this that we must use as a beginning to understand this kind of woman, to feel what she was doing in arranging a marriage for her brother David to content him, to see what she had strongly inside her of an important feeling, to know why she had the right way of doing whatever was right to her feeling in the business of living, to know how her husband could find her so satisfying, to find out how she was pleasing.

Martha was a good woman in doing whatever it was right for her to do, to her feeling. She was fond of doing, good at making a beginning, and almost strong enough to keep on going. It was always all right for her when there was not any strong person resisting, for then she was always strong enough to keep on going and then, though mostly, not altogether winning, she came then near enough to winning to give to her her important feeling. She would not end in any kind of winning if any other one kept up any resisting, then Martha would not know she was losing, she would begin with some other beginning and so she never could lose her important feeling. Her husband listened to her talking, he knew what she did from her telling, she was not strong to be domineering, she was strong enough not to be appealing, she was always attractive to him, she filled up his sentimental feeling, she was an ideal to him with no power to disturb him, she was always pleasing to him.

As I was saying her brother did not find her pleasing but he knew she was a good woman, he felt that she was mostly right in her feeling and in her ways of doing, he was willing that she should choose a wife for him to content him and he was right to let her choose for him.

Martha's husband had a cousin who had once worked for old Mr. Hissen. This cousin and his wife came to know them enough to see them very often. There were not many people who came to know them enough to see them very often. The old man Hissen had his wife and children shut up with him as much and as long as he could keep them. One of them, the eldest girl among them, the one that had most in her, of all of them, of religion, had already come to her marrying. A cousin from another town came to see them and she wanted him and he wanted her to take care of him, and then they made the father consent to their marrying. Perhaps he liked it better that they had no good prospects before them. Marrying should be a sorrow to them, and the mother sorrowed in them, living was all sadness and she knew that it would be so for them. Anyway they were married and they were living happily enough when the wife did not feel too strongly her importance in religion. Now that they were married the old folks did not interfere with them.

This cousin of Martha's husband who had come to see a good deal of them tried to arrange a marriage between his brother and another of the Hissen sisters, one of the pleasantest of them. It was a good chance for her for the brother of the cousin was a very well to do man and he was a good enough man though a very stupid and a dull one. It was a good chance for one of them and this one, one of the pleasant ones of them was willing to meet him but seeing him set her off laughing and every time she saw him again she went on laughing and at last he grew angry and that was the end of her marrying. She never came again to the point of having a man want her to content him.

There were a number of the Hissen women who never came to marrying. Their way of living and with no one except strangers to help them and the eldest daughter not doing very well in her marrying and being gloomy and important in religion and never very strong in pushing or doing things to help them, it came to their being a family of women and three of them, and they were of the pleasant ones among them never came to have a man who wanted any one of them to content him. They lived with their father and later with another one of them who had done very well in marrying and they were all together then gentle cheerful little older women, they were each in their circle cheerful in the present, they lived and died in mildness and contentment.

But now there was a chance for the marrying of another one of them, of Fanny Hissen and she was soon now to meet David Hersland and to see whether she would be pleasing to him, to make a wife to him to content him.

Martha had come to know them well enough to see them fairly often. She was pleasing to the old man Hissen. She was a sensible good woman and always neat in her dressing. She was not afraid of him. She was a patient woman and would listen to the trickling little woman who had always in her sorrowing, who told her often what she thought of living. She was a friend of the eldest daughter of them the one who was married to her cousin. Martha was sure that it was right to do whatever was good in religion. For her it was not religion, for her it was the right way to do in the business of living that was important in her being, but she had a sentiment for religion, she had a respect for the oldest daughter's important feeling. It was alright for both of them for Martha had her important feeling and it was not in religion, it was in the matter of every day living, and so there was no quarrelling between these two women and their kind of important feeling. They each had much respect in them for the other one's way of feeling and right way of doing.

Martha was a neat woman. She was a strong enough woman and always active in doing. She had a kind of sentimental feeling and that made her respect the Hissen religion, she had a hard way of thinking and that made her like the gentleness of all the pleasant Hissen women, she had a kind of a common feeling and that made her respect the old Hissen woman who spent her life in sorrowing, in weeping out the sadness of all living. And yet always Martha had the important feeling, she knew what was the right way to do to keep on living, to help people to marrying, to make the world keep on as it was in the beginning.

Martha was always talking about the Hissen girls and their way of living. She got almost to feel that she was a sister and a mother to them. They did not have in them any such feeling but then the Hissen women all had a pride in them that they did not have any kind of a common feeling in them, even the eldest one who was so unpleasant to the others of them never had any common feeling. Such a thing could never be in any of the Hissen men or women.

To the Hissen women this Martha was always a little common. But they were wrong in their feeling. This Martha was not really inside her even a little common, it was her hard way of thinking that gave the Hissens such a feeling. It was that she did not have in her any fine feeling. All the Hissen men and women had fine feeling. This Martha did not have any fine feeling but she was not common in her feeling. In Martha it was a hard way of thinking that was deceiving.

Any way the Hissen girls who were coming now to be women and who began to feel in them the liking to have men choose them to content them, were very willing to let this Martha do what they could not do themselves with the finer kind of feeling they all had in them. Not that Martha ever had a common match making feeling or ever wanted to do anything except just what it was right for her to do to her feeling. It was not a common or mean feeling that made Martha do what she did for them. It was a strong sense of what was right for her to do in the business of living to make the world go on as it was in the beginning ; it was too, that she had a feeling for the gentle dignity that was the most important thing in all Hissen men and women so that they could not help themselves to win for themselves the things every one needs to have for his living.

And so it came that she chose Fanny Hissen to be the one that should be married to her brother David Hersland who needed now to have a wife to content him, to go to Gossols with him, to help him in his living, to have children for him so that the world could go on as it had from the beginning.

Martha was right to choose Fanny Hissen to content him. As I was saying Martha was not very pleasing to her brother David Hersland who needed a woman to be appealing or a woman to have power, to make her attractive to him. One can see by the feeling that this Martha had for all the Hissen men and women that she was not appealing nor had strongly a power of attracting, and yet she was a good woman, and not very unpleasing, and David was right to let her choose a wife to content him. She could never have any reason to do anything that was not right to her feeling. She had enough of important feeling so that she would not have any jealous feeling to interfere with her right judging, and she had a hard feeling and that gave her a kind of common being that made her have in her a feeling that always would respect the fine being in the Hissen men and women, and yet she never could feel that she was not right to manage for them, for they had the weakness in them from being so fine in the gentle dignity and feeling that made all them, that they could never do for themselves what was necessary, for them to ever be winning what they needed for their living. And so she arranged a marriage for them for marrying David Hersland and Fanny Hissen.

It went very quickly from the beginning for Fanny Hissen was very pleasing to him and David Hersland had nothing common in him for them. He was too big in his feeling and in the way he made any one who saw him feel him ever to give any one, even gentle Hissen men and women any such feeling.

Martha was in a way common to them. David never gave any one of them any such feeling. Martha was not low in her feeling. It was her hard being that gave them such a feeling. She was always considering them in her feeling, she had respect for them and felt in them all the fine things they had inside them but to them she was not sensitive in her feeling, she was always a little common to them always a little low to them, they felt it always inside in them. With her brother David Hersland they never had any such feeling. David never gave any one of them any such feeling. And yet, as I was saying, it was not because Martha was lower in her being that they had always this feeling. The old man Hissen had not such a feeling. Martha was more pleasing to him then than she was to any of the others of them.   To the others of them it was a certain thing inside her that was not so much hard but not sensitive or appealing that made them feel her to be a little common, to their feeling.   David Hersland never gave any of them such a feeling.

It was not because Martha was low in her feeling.   Martha was not low in her feeling, she had no dirty ways inside her in her feeling.   Always she would do what it was right to do to her feeling.   But not having the delicate kind of feeling made her feel things to be right that were right to the Hissen feeling but were not pleasant to them to see anybody doing. As I was saying, the old man Hissen had not any such feeling.   No Martha was not low in her feeling and she was strong to do what was right to her feeling and only in little ways was she unpleasant to the Hissen men and women, though she was never really pleasing to them.   She had not in her any power to impress them or anything appealing to win them.

No Martha was not low in her feeling.   David had things in him that would be very low to them if they knew they were inside him but they never could come to know such things in him.   He was so big in his feeling he could always carry them along inside him, inside him or outside him it was all one, he was in them they were in him and they could never come to any judgment toward him and so they never could come to know any low thing in him.   It was very different with the feeling they always had that Martha was below them Martha had very little of any low or dirty feeling.   She was not delicate in her feeling.   She was a good enough looking woman, not unpleasing, always neat in her dressing and attractive enough like most good enough looking women.   It was mostly never a low feeling she had in her and never toward any one of them but they mostly all always had inside them a certain sense that she was common to them.   David Hersland never gave to any of them any such feeling.   He was as big as all the world in his beginning and low and high and noisy and delicate it was all in him, he was it, they were in him and low things were big in him so that no one could ever feel them in him as low things inside him, no never not even when he was an old man and things were falling down inside him and around him in his being.

The only one who had a feeling that Martha was really pleasing was her husband and she was just right for him.   He only heard what she said to him in anything that she had been concerned in and so he never came to any feeling that she was not a strong woman to win out in the things she always loved to be beginning.   He never could know that she was not strong in winning.   She always did, to herself, whatever it was right for her to do, to her feeling when she met with the beginning of a losing she would not stop herself from winning, she would not know that she was then losing, she only dropped out of that working and made for herself a new beginning.   She was not a strong woman as her mother had been.   Mostly she was not pleasing for she was not strong in winning nor beginning and she had nothing appealing to make her attractive to men or women and so she was not very pleasing, but she was a good enough woman to become a friend of the Hissen men and women, to be satisfying to old Mr. Hissen and to have her brother David Hersland let her choose a wife for him to content him. She was good in doing whatever it was right for her to do, to her feeling. She was fond of doing, good at making a beginning, almost strong enough to keep on going. It was always all right for her when there was not any strong person resisting, for then she was always strong enough to keep on going, and then, though mostly not altogether winning, she would come near enough to winning to keep in her her important feeling. She would not end in any kind of winning if any one kept up any resisting, then Martha would not know she was losing, she would begin with some other beginning, and so she never would lose any important feeling.

To her husband she was altogether pleasing. He had much very soggy passion in him and he had always inside him sentimental feeling so that he wanted a wife, not to be domineering but to hold him so that his passion could have a solid thing to bring it together in him, so that his wife should always be equal to him. He did not want a wife to appeal to him. It was his sentimental feeling that made him not want his wife to be appealing, he wanted to make of her an ideal to him. He was a man to be master in his living and so he never would have a wife to domineer over him, he wanted a wife to be equal to him so that she could harden for him the muddy passion in him, he wanted a wife to be an ideal to him to satisfy his sentimental feeling.

Martha was to him always pleasing. Her husband listened to her talking, he knew what she did from her telling, she was not strong to be domineering, she was strong enough not to be appealing, she was always attractive to him, she filled up his sentimental feeling, she was an ideal to him, with no power to disturb him. She was always pleasing to him.

It is easy to see how to the Hissen men and women Martha was always a little common.

Between the eldest of the Hissen women and Martha there was more of an equal feeling. Martha always did what was right to her feeling. Martha had in her a feeling that it was right to do things in religion. Not that she had in her any feeling in religion. Religion was in her a sentimental kind of feeling. In her what was important to her feeling was the right way to do in the business of living, what was the right way for her to be doing so that she would do what was right to do to her feeling. She had a strong respect for the eldest daughter's important feeling. She had a strong respect for her important feeling in religion. It was alright for both of them. Martha had her important feeling and it was not in religion and each of these two women had much respect in them for the other ones way of feeling and right way of doing.

To all the other Hissen men and women Martha was a good woman, and she was a good friend to them but she was not really pleasing.

To her brother she was not really pleasing but she was a good enough woman for him to choose a wife for him to content him.

Soon now then Fanny Hissen was married to David Hersland and went out to Gossols with him, and now together they were to begin their living, to make children who perhaps would come to have in them a really important feeling of themselves inside them.

David Hersland who was to be the father of them, of the three children who were not yet come into the world through them, had always in him an important feeling, not inside him for it was all of him, everything was of him and he was it and there was not any difference for him between himself and everything existing.

The mother who was to bear the three children, she perhaps would come to an important feeling, she did not have it as a natural thing to have really an important feeling. With her it must come from a, to her, not natural way of living, and it first had its beginning with her friendship with the Shilling women. Then it came to be stronger with the living in Gossols in the ten acre place in the part of Gossols where no other rich people were living, where she was cut off from the rich living which was for her the natural way of being.

Mrs. Fanny Hersland had always had in her the beginning of an almost important feeling which she had from being like her mother in her nature, the mother who had had, in her sad trickling arising of itself inside her, an almost important feeling. This beginning of an almost important feeling, had never in Fanny Hissen been very real inside her while she was living in Bridgepoint, for then the strongest thing in her was the family way of being and that always would have been just so strong in her and it never would have come to her to have any realler feeling of being important to herself inside her if she had not gone to Gossols and left the family way of being behind her. It was only when she left the family way of living, when she went out to Gossols where she was to have none of the being always a part of the well to do living, that it came to her to begin to have this almost important feeling. It was not marrying that gave her such a feeling. Marrying would never have changed her from her family way of being, it was going to Gossols and leaving the family being and having a for her unnatural way of living that awoke in her a sense inside her of the almost important feeling that was to come to be inside in her.

It had its beginning with her knowing, in the hotel where the Herslands were living before they settled down in the ten acre place, it had its beginning with her knowing old Mrs. Shilling and her daughter Sophie Shilling and her other daughter Pauline Shilling. With them there began inside her a sense of individual being, not that it was different in her to her feeling, it was only different in her being.   Now she had no longer in her as the strongest thing inside her the Hissen way of being that was then all her and was the natural way of being to her.   Later it grew stronger in her, this being, that never was different to her in her feeling that she knew inside her, but later it grew stronger in her, a very little by her husband and the power over him she had in her, but mostly with the living that came soon to be all the being there was of her, the living with her servants and governesses and dependents and the for her poor queer kind of people who lived near her, and the way she had of being a power, of being of them, with them, and always above them, and the feeling they had in them ; and all this gave to her the real being of an almost important feeling.

When one just met with them, old heavy flabby Mrs. Shilling and her daughter the fat Sophie Shilling and the other daughter the thinner Pauline Shilling, they were at first meeting and even after longer knowing like many other ordinary women.   Yet always one had a little uncertain feeling that perhaps each one of them had something queer in her.   One could never be very certain with them whether this possible queerness of them was because of something queer inside in all them or that they were queer because something had been left out in each one of them in the making of them or that they had lost something out of them that should have been inside in them, that something had dropped out of each one of them and they had been indolent or stupid or staring each one of them then and they had not noticed such a dropping out of them. Each one of them had perhaps a hole then somewhere inside in them and this may have been that which gave to each one of them the queerness that it was never certain was ever really there in any one of them.   One never was certain with them that there was anything queer about them. Mostly they were just ordinary stupid enough women like millions of them.

The mother was one of those fat heavy women who are all straight down the whole front of them when they are sitting.   When they are walking they are always slowly waddling with heavy breathing.

Many such heavy fat flabby waddling women have something queer about them.   These have big doughy empty heads on top of them.   These heads on them give to one a kind of feeling such as a baby's head gives to one in the first months of its being living, that the head is not well fastened to them, that it will fall off them if one does not hold it together on them.   This kind of a head on them is what gives these fat flabby women the queerness about them that makes strange things of them. They have been living, working, cooking, directing, they have been chosen by a man to content him, they have had children come into the world through them, sometimes strong men and women have been born from inside them, they have made marriages for their children and managed people around them, they have lived and suffered and some of them have had power in them, and they are flabby now with big doughy heads that wobble on them.

It is a queer feeling that one has in them and perhaps it is, that they have something queer in them something that gives to one a strange uncertain feeling with them for their heads are on them as puling babies heads are always on them and it gives to one a queer uncertain feeling to see heads on big women that look loose and wobbly on them.

Old Mrs. Shilling was such a one. It was uncertain always even after a long knowing of her whether the wobbly head on her was all that made a strange thing of her or whether there was something queer inside in her, different from the others of them, different from all of them who always give to one a strange uncertain feeling, all the many fat ones who are made just like her. Perhaps that was all that was queer in her, that which is always queer in all the many fat ones who are made just like her.

The fat daughter Sophie Shilling in the ways one mostly felt her has many millions who are made just like her. The fat daughter Sophie Shilling was a little like her mother but her head was not yet wobbly on her. Sometimes there was something about her that perhaps came from something queer inside her. Mostly she was just an ordinary rather fat young woman and there are many millions made just like her.

As one knew her with her mother and her sister she was an amiable enough good sister and daughter. Mostly one felt that she was a very good sister and a very good daughter. Not that it was a family of women that as far as one could know them were very trying to one another. They seemed to have enough money to live comfortably in the hotel together. They had a poodle dog who was company for the mother. They never quarrelled with each other. They did not have any troubles there at the hotel where they were comfortably living together.

Sophie Shilling and Pauline Shilling were sisterly with one another. Sophie Shilling like most fat sisters was afraid of the thinner. Sometimes it is the thinner who is afraid of the fatter when two daughters are sisterly together but most often it is the fat sister who is afraid of the thinner. It is not so much being older or younger that makes sisters afraid of one another, it is a kind of power that always one has over the other, mostly it is the fat one who is afraid of the other because it would hurt more if pins were stuck into her, not that the thinner is always in any way meaner, sometimes it is the fat one who is afraid who is the meaner, but there is so much more of her, there is so much more unprotected surface to her, somehow, it is that which makes her afraid of the thinner even when the thin one is really never nasty to her. This was true of the sisters Sophie Shilling and Pauline Shilling, the fat one always had fear in her but the thin one never in any way was ever mean or nasty to her. It is this fear that the fat one has in her that often makes the people who know her and see the mother and the sister with her feel that the thin one has mean ways in her. Not that the fat one complains of her but there is a fear in her, and often it is only a fear from there being so much of her, but when others feel the fear in her they are sure it must come from the mean things the thinner one does to her. So it was with Sophie Shilling and they were very sisterly together.

It was a month or so after the Herslands had come to the hotel that Mrs. Hersland began to know Sophie Shilling. She had met her going about in the hotel and sometimes when she was out she met with her and they came in together. They soon were a good deal together. They soon began to call on each other. Mrs. Hersland began to know the mother and the sister Pauline Shilling. Pauline did not take much interest in her. Mostly she and Sophie did not have friends together. The way in which Sophie was afraid of her sister made any one who knew her have an awe of Pauline Shilling, made them have a kind of feeling about her so that they could never be easy with her. Always in them must be a suspicious feeling that there was danger for them in her and they must not be too free when being with her or talking to her. It was the fear in the fat sister that gave to all who knew her a restraint when they were with Pauline Shilling. Not that Sophie ever complained of her, not that Sophie ever knew that she had such a fear in her. It was always there though and affected all who knew her although from their own knowing of her they could see that Pauline Shilling had no mean ways in her. Of course there were people who first knew the thin sister and they never had any such feeling about her. But all who first knew Sophie Shilling never could come to be easy with her sister. Mrs. Hersland first knew Sophie Shilling. It is easy to see how the knowing Sophie Shilling and her mother and the sister Pauline Shilling would awaken in her the always possible almost important feeling that was quiet until then inside her.

Sophie Shilling never meant very much to her. They were very much together and Fanny Hersland always felt for her. She had no affection for her and after she moved away from the hotel she did not very often see her.

The year that they both lived in the hotel they were a great deal together but Sophie did not impress her, she never became really important to her, Mrs. Hersland had not really any affection for her. Mrs. Hersland never came to feel any nearer to the mother, and the sister Pauline Shilling.

Knowing Sophie Shilling and her mother and her sister was really very important to her. They were a problem to her.

Always she had a feeling for Sophie Shilling. Sophie never complained to her and the sister Pauline was always a puzzle to her. She never came to really know inside her that the feeling she had about Pauline Shilling was because of the fear that was always in the fatter sister, a fear that she felt always to be inside Sophie Shilling. Sophie never complained of her sister. She never knew she had such a fear in her. At first Fanny Hersland always felt for her, then slowly she felt that Pauline had no mean ways in her. Pauline was always very pleasant to her, she was always very decent to her mother and her sister Sophie. Perhaps later Mrs. Hersland would have liked it better if she had not first known the sister Sophie but that never really came to be a feeling inside her, even to the end of her knowing her she always felt for her, but, more and more it came to her that she was not sure of what she felt about her or about the mother or the sister Pauline Shilling and so it came to be that there commenced inside her, from the not being certain of the judgment which was natural to her, there came to be inside her a beginning of an almost individual feeling.

The thinner sister Pauline Shilling has not so many millions who are made just like her. There have been always many millions made just like the mother and the fatter sister Sophie Shilling but there have never been so many millions made altogether like the thinner sister Pauline Shilling.

There have been always many millions made just like the mother and the fatter sister Sophie Shilling. That is, there have been always many millions made just like them if they really have nothing queer inside them. Perhaps they have something queer inside them that makes them different from the many millions who have been made just like them.

There have been many millions made just like the mother and the fatter sister Sophie Shilling. That is there are many millions who have been made just like them all excepting the something queer inside them which perhaps made them different inside them from the many millions who have always been made just like them.

Perhaps there was nothing that was really queer inside them. Perhaps it was only from the three of them living together and not meaning much to one another and not meaning very much to any other and so making all together a queer feeling when one felt them together which lasted over to the knowing each one of them. And so one had a feeling that there was something really queer inside them. This was most likely all that they had of queerness in them. They did not have much meaning and the three of them being together and not having much meaning for each other gave one a sense of them that they had something queer inside them. Very likely that was all there was of queerness in them.

The thinner sister Pauline Shilling seemed perhaps to have more of individual being in her. Perhaps that was only because there are not so many millions made just like her as there are many millions made like her mother and her fatter sister. Perhaps that was all the individual being that she had in her.

Perhaps really the queerness of them came from there not being enough in each one of them to fill out the inside in them and so they did not have much meaning or any power or any sense of appealing.

The thinner one had not really any more meaning than the fatter one or than the mother who had born them. She had a more individual seeming because she was a thin one and she was one of them who have not quite so many millions made just like them. But even as a thin one she had not enough inside her to really fill her, to really make her important, not inside her, but to any one who came to be about her, she was not filled out enough inside her to give her any power or make any appeal to any one who came near her. The emptiness in her was different from the emptiness that was inside her fatter sister or her mother.

Pauline Shilling had not any fear in her of any one such as her sister had of her. The fatter sister had this fear in her because she was not all filled up inside her and that gave to her all the unprotected surface that she always had had on her and that made her have a fear in her, not from anything that was ever done to her, but from all the unprotected surface there was of her. She never knew at any time that she had such a fear always inside her and that made it the more deceiving in her, for one always felt it with her but one never really knew it about her.

The thinner sister had not any such a fear in her as the fatter sister had of her and always inside her. This is perhaps why one has a feeling that they are not so many millions made just like her. Perhaps there are as many millions made just like the thinner sister as there are millions made like the fatter sister or the mother.

The many millions made just like the fatter sister or the mother, each one fills up so much more space than a thinner that one gets the feeling that they are commoner, that there are many more millions of them made fatter than there are millions made thinner, and that these the fatter are made more just alike to one another. It is the unprotected surface of these who are made like the fatter sister, that make them seem more completely just like one another than when they are thinner. It is the uncertain head on the many millions made just like the mother that make them seem to be exactly like each other, a great deal more like one another than any of the thinner, alike as these may be to each other.

The vague fear the fatter one almost always has inside her gives a more common quality to her than any other kind of fear she could have in her. The vague fear that comes from all that unprotected surface of her makes it easier to see in her that she is just like all the other millions who have been made just like her all the other millions who have the same kind of fear that she has in her. This fear makes it easier to see a likeness to her than any other kind of fear that she might have had inside her.

The thinner sister Pauline Shilling had a fear in her, she had a fear in her and all the many millions who have been made just like her have the same kind of fear as she has in her, but it is not from the unprotected surface of her, one does not always feel it when one is with her, it has not then the common feeling that can make it so apparent that there are so many made just like her as the fear in her sister makes it to every one that knows her.

The fear the thinner sister had always in her also came from there being not enough inside to fill her, came not from the unprotected surface of the outside of her but from her not being filled out well inside her and so she had the fear in her that always trying to fill up a hole in her without enough to fill it from the being in her without making some other hole inside her, was certain to give to her. This made her without any power, or appeal to any one who was near her.

She was always busy inside in her filling up the hole in her from the rest of her and so making another, for there was not enough inside her ever to entirely fill her. Always she was filling up a hole in her and always she was keeping anything from touching her, everything from coming close to her lest it should push an outside hole into her. She could never feel a power in any other, she could not believe in any other, she could not concern herself with any other, she could never let any other come close to her, she was always there, not filled up inside her, and that was the whole of her, that always gave a fear to her to be inside her, but a kind of fear that did not make a common person of her, as the fear inside her did with the fatter sister Sophie Shilling. It did not make an individual of her because there was never there a whole of her. She did not know that there was not a whole one of her. This incompleteness of her only made a self-defensive instinct in her, and that was all there was to her, comfort and keeping out of danger was all there was of living to her, and so she had no power in her for she had no power of attacking in her, for she was not all together, and it gave her no appeal to any one who came near her because they never could really come close to her, she could not let them touch her lest they should push a hole into her. She could not come near to any other, or believe in any other, and always she must be concerned with herself and the defense of her lest any one should touch her and make a hole into her.

That was all there was of queerness in her and there are many millions who have been made just like her.

Always one was not certain in their judgement of her because she was a good enough woman and always decent to her mother and her sister and pleasant and good enough to every one who came near her. Always there was in her that she would never let any one come very close to her. It was a fear in her. It never came to any one to know it about her for it was always self defensive in her. One felt that they never came close to her and so she was a puzzle to all who knew her, and sometimes they were suspicious of her and sometimes sorry for her. So it was with Fanny Hersland and she never came to know any more about her.

The mother of them was too empty to have any kind of a fear inside her. Her head was like a baby's, wobbly on her. She never could have an abiding fear inside her with such a head on top of her. She was without any fear in her either such a one as her fatter daughter had of another or as her thinner daughter Pauline Shilling had it, lest anything might touch her, that something might make her feel anything inside her.

This was very likely all of queerness that this family of women had in them and it came to be about each one of them because they were three together who had in each of them such an emptiness inside them.

It made a queerness, there being three of them, that every body felt who knew them. Always it was a puzzle to every one, for they were pleasant enough women as one knew them together and each one of them, they never quarrelled with each other, they lived very comfortably there in the hotel together. One never learnt anything about them or against them, nobody gossiped about them, they were plenty of people who knew them and came to see them. Each one of them had their own friends and they always got along very nicely with them, only somehow there was always there this emptiness they had in them. It was a hole that each one had inside in her. It will never be known about them whether they had been made so from the beginning, whether something had been left out in each one of them in the making of them or whether they had lost something out of them that should have been inside in them, something that had perhaps dropped out of each one of them and they had been indolent or fearful or stupid or staring then, each one of them, and they had not noticed such a dropping out of them.

And so one could not come to any certain judgment of them, one could never be sure about them, that they had something queer inside them, or that they were all three of them just like the many millions who have been made just like them.

It is easy to see how this puzzling quality of them would awaken in Mrs. Hersland who was almost always now with them, the always possible almost important feeling that was quiet until then inside her. She always had a feeling for Sophie Shilling but she had no affection for her, Sophie was not in any way important to her, Mrs. Hersland never came to feel any nearer to the mother and the sister Pauline Shilling. She never came to feel certain about them inside her and this not being certain of the kind of judgment which was natural to her, made a beginning inside her of an almost individual feeling, different in her, but not different to her, from the family way of being which had always until then been all there was of living to her.

The only important feeling Mrs. Hersland had in this time of beginning her new living was with the Shillings as I have been saying. After leaving the hotel she never saw much of them. Occasionally she would call on them to show her children. All the Shilling women were always good to them but they were never important to them, there came to be soon very little visiting between them and then very soon there was none. This was the end of the beginning in Mrs. Hersland of the possible almost important feeling.

Always now it kept on growing, a little from her husband and making him do things through her compelling, but mostly from her dependents, the governesses seamstresses servants and the others, the for her poor queer people who soon came to be always around her.

They had lived more than a year in the hotel. David Hersland who was always strong in his beginning commenced then to find the way to his great fortune. Soon he bought the place that was to be for a long time a home to them, in that part of Gossols where no other rich people were living. His children were then very little things or just beginning, his wife had just begun to know some people of the kind it was natural for her to have as friends in her daily living.

Because of the living in the part of Gossols where no other rich people were living she saw them soon only on occasional formal visiting, the children did not then learn to be accustomed to rich well to do kind of people and their living, the mother lost the habit of going to visit with them, she never at all lost the sense of well to do living, she just lost the habit of normal visiting, of being with them the people who were the natural people to have as friends in her daily living. She lived with her husband and her children and her dependents and the for her queer poor people who lived around them in that part of Gossols where no other rich people were living.

Big as all the world in his beginning how could David Hersland have a weak place in him then. The way he did the educating of his three children will make the nature in him become clear to them, will make it clear too to any one who will come to know the nature of them and the education that he gave them.

There were three of them and they all three of them came to have inside them their own kind of important feeling. That came through their being of him and from the education he gave to them which made them uneven in them, being of him and mixed up with the wife who bore them, made them uneven as he was always before them, uneven like the whole world together that he had in him and so it came that he was uneven as the whole world inside him and around him and so it was that there were weak places in him as there are in the big world which was all him. He was all full up inside him but it was not all the same all through him.

He was all full up inside in him and he was a big man and so there was very much in him and of him. He was all full up inside him, there was not much of any way that anything could enter into him.

There was in him the kind of loving that he had for the wife he had chosen to content him and the children who awoke in him a different kind of feeling for each one of them and who were to win through him each one of the three of them a different kind of important feeling each one of them to have inside in them to content them.

The loving David Hersland had in him for his wife was that in some ways she was a flower to him, in some ways just a woman to him. He needed a woman to content him.

The power she had in her sometimes over him was not important to him, that was only a joke to him, what was real in her to him was that sometimes she was a flower to him and mostly she was just a woman to content him.

Often she was not important to him and this will come out in him, in her living there with him in the ten acre place away from the living that was her natural way of being.

David Hersland had his way of needing a woman to content him. Each man has in some ways his own need in a woman to content him, there are many kinds of men and women and each one of them is himself inside him. David Hersland had his way of needing a woman to content him, Henry Dehning had his woman and she filled up his need in him, and then they will come to be old men and it will be easier to see in them then how they need a woman to content them.

There are not so very many kinds of men nor so many kinds of women to content them. One can see this clearer in them when the men are young men, or very old ones, then it comes to be clearer in them that they need a woman to content them a woman to be a certain thing to them and that there are not so many different kinds of them, neither of the men, nor of the women who content them. There are though, all the same, a fair amount of different kinds of them and here we begin with one kind of them, with David Hersland and the kind of man he was inside him and the kind of woman he could find to be contenting to him.

David Hersland and Herman Dehning and the man who was married to David's sister Martha who made his marriage for him were all three of them strong men and all three of them needed women to content them and all three of them were very different each one of them from the others of them.

Now to begin again with David Hersland and the nature he had in him. As I was saying David Hersland was a big man and a man who was all full up inside him and who was very uneven inside him uneven as the world that was all him. He was a big man and there was very much in him and of him. He was all full up inside him. There was not much of any way that anything could enter into him.

A woman had to be a part of the inside in him to content him. She had to have a power in her, to give to him a feeling, or she had to be appealing and so to be a part of the feeling he had inside him. There was not much of any way that anything outside him could enter into him.

A woman to content him could never be outside him, she could never be an ideal to him, she could never have in her a real power for him. With men, outside him, there was for him a need in him to fight with them. A woman could never be for him anything outside him, unless as one who could in a practical way be useful to him as his sister Martha had always been and now she had been useful to him and made a marriage for him, had found a wife for him who was pleasing to him, who had come out with him to Gossols to content him. Such a woman as his sister was for him, was like any other object in the world around him, a thing useful to him or not existing for him, like a chair in his house to sit in or the engine that drew the train the direction in which he needed just then to be going. Such a woman as his sister Martha, as a woman could never be interesting to him, nor any other woman who remained outside him, either when she could be to him an ideal for him or a power in any way over him, not that some women with power in them were not attractive to him, but with such a kind of woman, and he met them often in his living and they had power with him, such a woman always did it for him by entering into him by brilliant seductive managing and so she was a part of him, even though she was apart from him, and so she had power with him. Such a one until he would be an old man and the strength in him was weakening and the things he had in him did not make inside him a completely tight filling and so things outside him could a little more enter into him, until he would come to be an old man and the need in him would come to be more a senile feeling, an old man's need of something to complete him, such a one could never come to be a wife to him, could never be a woman to be his wife and content him. He needed such a woman as his sister Martha had found for him, a woman who was to him, inside him and appealing, whose power over him was never more than a joke to him, who sometimes when a sense for beauty stirred in him was a flower to him, whom he often could forget that she was existing, who never in any big way was resisting, and so she never needed fighting, was always to himself a part of him and inside in him, and so in every kind of way she was contenting to him.

Men outside him awoke in him, a need almost always in him, to fight with them. Women could never give him any such feeling to have inside him. If they had a power in them, he would brush them away from around him, sometimes with men outside him he would in the same way brush them away from before him, but they often then would be stubborn things around him, he could not brush them away from him ; but all women to him, if he needed to brush them away from around him, he could so always rid himself of them. If a woman held her power in him it was because of brilliant seductive managing, and so there would not be aroused in him any desire of fighting nor of brushing her away from him. His wife was different to him, she was appealing there inside him like a tender feeling he had in him. Often she was not important to him, often she was not even existing to him. Sometimes, and this was the rarest thing in him, she filled for him a need to have a sense of beauty in him, then she was like a flower to him, but this did not happen so very often in him. more often she had a kind of power over him that was only a joke to him, mostly in their daily living the power she had in her with him did not to himself touch him, it was her managing to have things for the children, to have her way in small things, sometimes in a big one, but these things never were important to him, and he never knew she felt a power in them, the only power he knew she felt over him was only a joke to him, it could never have any other meaning to him, and that was all there was of the effect she had upon him. Mostly she was pleasing to him, she was a wife who was suited to him, his sister Martha had been right to choose her for him to be married to him, to bear children for him, to go to Gossols with him, to be always, all the years she would be living with him, to be a woman to content him.

He did not need now when he was still a vigorous man and strong in his living, he did not need to have a woman to complete him, he needed a woman only to be pleasing, he needed a woman only to content him. This perhaps would come to be different in him when he would be an old man and weakening, then perhaps a woman who had power in her for him, a power to hold him by seductive managing, such a woman could then fill up in him empty places made by old age and his weakening and his shrinking away from the outside of him, and he would feel it good to him then to be filled up once more inside him; to feel warm with a full feeling ; and so such a woman then could have power with him, he would need such a one then to complete him. Now he was a strong man and vigorous in his living and such a woman could arouse him but he would not need to have her in him and he would, when she was too much with him, for he met her often enough in his living, he would brush her away from before him. His wife Fanny Hersland was the woman for him, the wife who was almost always pleasing to him, the one he wanted to content him, she was for him mostly like a tender feeling in him, she was a good woman to him, and useful to do the daily living with him, with the people around them, and with their three children, she was a good woman in his daily living, the little power she had in her for him was a pleasant joke always to him, the power she had in managing to do things for the children he never noticed as a power she had with him, mostly she was always pleasing to him, sometimes, and this was the rarest thing in him, she filled for him a need in him for pure beauty and then she would be like a flower to him but this came to be more and more rare in him as he grew older and was more filled up with his impatient feeling, then she was hardly enough to content him, always she was like a tender feeling in him but more and more as he was full of impatient feeling, she would be lost to him, mostly she would not then be existing for him, the power which was always a pleasant joke to him then had no more existence for him, a little yet sometimes then she might be a flower to him, always when he felt her then she would be inside him like a tender feeling but mostly then she had no existence for him, she was not enough then to content him, and then she died away and left him, and then the tender feeling was a pain in him, and then she was never any longer an existing thing inside him. More and more he was getting older then and weakening, and shrinking away from the outside of him and more and more then he had not enough even of impatient feeling to completely fill him, and so more and more then he needed to be filled up inside him and she was not then enough to fill him, she had, too, died away and left him, and soon she was not in him any more, not any more as a tender feeling in him, she had soon then not any more any existence in him, soon he needed much more than she had ever been, to fill him up in side in him.

All this will come to be clear in him in his later living, and now there is the beginning, the three children, the ten acre place where they were living, this father and this mother of them and the dependents and the people living there around them.

They were living, the father and the mother and the three children, there had been two other children but they had died in the beginning, they were living then the five of them and the servants and governesses and dependents they had with them, in the ten acre place in that part of Gossols where no other rich people were living. Here they lived a life that was not the natural way of being for them here they had around them only, for them, poor queer kind of people and these came to be for them all the people they had in their daily living. More and more there was no visiting for them with the richer people who were the natural people for them to have as friends around them. The father spent his days with rich men for he had his business with them, he was making his great fortune among them, but more and more his wife lived with the poorer people who were living right around them, more and more his wife in her daily living had all of her being in her relation to the servants seamstresses governesses with whom she was living and she was always of them and always was above them and in the same way she was with them the poor, for her, queer people around them. She was with them and with her husband and her children and these were every day the whole of her daily being, sometimes as I have said, she went visiting with her children dressed in her rich simple clothing, but the children were awkward with the richer living in houses and people different from their daily living and more and more then there was not for any of them any visiting to the part of Gossols where the richer people were living.

Living in this ten acre place in that part of Gossols where no other rich people were living was very joyous for all five of them in the beginning. There was much pleasure in this living by themselves with all the freedom that ten acres could give them, all the freedom that was natural with the living with only, for them, poor queer kind of people around them. There was freedom in such a living, there was an important feeling in it for the mother of them, it was a life to develop in the three children anything of an important feeling that it was possible they could ever come to have inside in them. This with the father's way of educating all three of them made for them, each one of them, an important feeling inside in them that they never could lose in their later living. This education that he gave them came from the feeling he had that education was all there was of living for them, it came to be queer for them because there was in him such a strong way of beginning, because he had strong beliefs in him and often these were changing, because he was like the world which was in his feeling all him he was full up inside in him he was uneven inside in him, because he was already then very full of impatient feeling and more and more in his living he became more full of impatient feeling until when troubles began with him before there was the weakening of old age in him he was all full up with impatient feeling, then that was nearly all that there was in him, that was the end of him before old age began in him and this is the history of him.

It was very joyous for all of them the days of the beginning of their living in the ten acre place which was for many years to be a home to them in that part of Gossols where no other rich people were living. The sun was always shining for them, for years after to all three of the children, Sunday meant sunshine and pleasant lying on the grass with a gentle wind blowing and the grass and flowers smelling, it meant good eating, and pleasant walking, it meant freedom and the joy of mere existing, it meant the pungent smell of cooking, it meant the full satisfied sense of being stuffed up with eating, it meant sunshine and joking, it meant laughing and fooling, it meant warm evenings and running, and in the winter that had its joys too of indoor living and outside the wind would be blowing and the owls in the walls scaring you with their tumbling.

There was freedom and pleasure in this living for all five of them in the beginning, in the ten acre place in that part of Gossols where no other rich people were living, where there were around them only, for them, poor, queer kind of people for all of them to have in their daily living.

There were then the three children, Martha, Alfred and David, there was the father of them and they all three of them more and more had a fear in them of him and all of them more and more mostly were in opposition to him. There was the mother of them and she was never very important to any one of them, she was not as important to any one of them as she was to the father of them for the little power she had in her was always a pleasant joke to him. Then there were the servants, the governesses and the dependents and the people who lived near them, who soon were all that the three of them had as people to be in their daily living.

The occasional visiting to the part of Gossols where the richer people were living had never much of reality to them. It was a kind of a dream world to them between waking and sleeping as one often has it in them when one is not certain whether something has really happened then. Such an in-between existing which is not waking or sleeping was all that such richer living was for the three of them. It never was such an unreal thing for the mother of them. To her rich living was all that there was of real being, she never really knew that she was no longer part of such living. She felt herself always to be of well to do living which was all that there was of being in her thinking. The important feeling of herself inside her which came to her from the living which was not the kind of living that was natural to her to be leading never was conscious to her as being inside her, never was conscious in her as different from the kind of living that had been natural to her. But it did make of her a different creature and this she was inside her though she never came to know it in her.

Visiting with their mother came to be harder for all three of them when they were beginning to be self conscious and a little older. When they were very little ones six years and younger there was a little pleasure in visiting with their mother. Then it began to be harder, they would shrink behind the mother, they got a little pleasure from the smell of fur and silk that they got as they shrank closer to her, they got a little pleasure from the smell of beaver that they had from the best hats they wore when they went with her but that was all there was of pleasure, more and more as they grew older they almost hated the people who lived in that part of Gossols where people were richer, where they were made by them, these children and the mothers of them, where they were made by them to have discomfort by their not knowing how to act when they came together. So more and more they would not go with their mother. More and more the mother lost all interest that she once had in her with the people who were the natural people for her to have in her daily living in the well to do living which was the natural way of being for her. It never came to be in her that she knew it inside her that she was different from the others who were the natural people for her to have around her, she stopped going to visit them for they ceased to have any interest for her but she never knew any of these things inside her. Later when once she went back to Bridgepoint it was this that made a kind of princess of her, gave her a kind of power with the brothers and the sisters who had never left the life that was the natural way of living for her.

The mother never knew it of them that her children were not comfortable with well to do children and the mothers of them because of the living that was not the natural way of living for them.   It never could come to be a real thing to her that she was cut off from the right rich living. This was to her only that her children were shy in meeting other children, her children were never part of her important feeling, they were outside her in their realler being, they were almost all there was of her in their daily living.

Later they were further apart from her, she was a little one and she was lost to herself and they were away from her inside her, then she had a scared feeling in her, then they sometimes would be good to her.   Now when she was younger and the important feeling was beginning to form in her they were of her as if they were still inside her, they were apart from her for they were never any part of the important feeling that was now beginning to come together inside her.

In that part of Gossols where no other richer people were living there was a straggling population, half as if it were in the country that they were living, half with a kind of city feeling.   The Herslands had all of them inside them this half and half feeling.   With the father it was not a half and half feeling.   His country life was just a place to him for resting, sleeping, eating, thinking.   His wife had her half and half feeling.   Here was all there was to her of real every day living, here there was nothing to her of the kind of living that was her natural way of being.   It never could come to her that she was not still part of the right well to do city living.   To the three children it was a half and half being just as it was for all the people they knew, all those who lived near them, they were all country people a little in their actual living it was a small country town of them, they were city people in their feeling.

This mixture in all of them, in all the people who lived around them, in the three children Martha, Alfred and David, in a different way in the mother of them, in a kind of way with her in the servants and the governess who were in the house with them, in his own way in the father of them, made their own life inside them to be different, the children and the people who lived near them, from the mother and the servants and the governesses who lived in the house with them, from the father who all the day lived with the rich men who were the people to have around him in his making his big fortune.

It was then slowly coming to be true of them that the children were more entirely of them, the poorer people who lived around them, than they were of their mother then, than their mother was of them then though they were all that there was of their mother's daily living.   Slowly in the mother the important feeling that later when she went to Bridgepoint where her family had gone on with their natural way of living, made her a kind of princess to them, beautiful and rich to them and apart from them, slowly this important feeling came to be working inside her and in a way in her it was like the important feeling that the governess and other servants had who were around her, it was different from the feeling the children had from their being part of the being that they had in common with the poorer people with whom they were living, different from the father and his beginning, his big fortune, then his impatient feeling and in his old age his weakening and his needing things to fill him.

The children all three of them being a real part of the living of the poorer people who were around them had the same kind of half and half feeling that the people had around them, they had the living that was a country town living, they had the feeling that was a city feeling and only later in their living did they grow away from being of the people who lived there around them. Each one of them had his own way of such changing and this will come out in the character of them as each one of them shows it in them.

As I was saying the mother's half and half feeling was different from the half and half feeling that the children had in them which was the same kind of half and half feeling that the people all had who lived around them, it was different from the feeling her husband had in him.

The being the people around them had in them, the half country town feeling and half city ways they all had in them could never come to be in common with them to the mother of the three children who had the same feeling in them as the people around them had in them. It could never come to the mother of the three of them to feel it to be real inside them the being that was in them that they had in common with the people around them. It would never come to the mother of them to feel this in them, they were her children, they were, to her feeling, inside in her as they had been when she had born them, they were apart from her in their real being, they were a real part of the living around them and they had in them a half and half feeling like the people around them.

To the mother of them they were to the people around them as she was to them, of them and above them in her right well to do city being, it never could come to her to feel that the three children who were to her feeling inside in her as they had been when she bore them were in all their being all in common with the life they were daily leading with all of them who were there around them. Such a thing could never come to be real to her feeling ; it never can come to be real to a governess in her feeling to feel the servant's feeling to be the same as her real feeling from the way she lives in the house with them. The mother to the three children of them could never have it to be real to her feeling what was really in their being that they were like those they had around them in the daily living that was all there was of being in them ; the governess to the servants being in the same house with them she could never feel it to be real to them in their feeling that they feel it to be together with them to them the governess and then with the mistress of them ; the governess to the servants, the servants to the governess who lives in the same house with them, all of them and the mistress of them to the people, the, for them, poor queer kind of people who lived around them. They were for all of them poor queer kind of people who lived in little houses near them. They were many of them. They were different each one of them from all the others of them, the three children knew these differences in them for they were of them, they were together with them, to the mother the governess the servants who lived in this ten acre place with these people around them, the differences among them were not to them differences as they were to the three children who were of them, so one sees them and it is as the children know them, as they were really inside them as they were to the others of them among them. More and more it will come out in them the differences in all of them with the three young ones who are of them then, these as they find it to be true among them, in them whom they needed to be friends for them of the people around them, these who were different to them each one of them to them who were of them, and then there is the mother of the three of them and the governess and the servants and then the father of the three of them and some ways in which he was of all of them, of the people around them, and then in some ways he was not of them, but mostly there was everything in some way in him, mostly all the world was in him and it was all uneven in him as it is in all the world that made him, and more and more now it came to be in him that mostly he was filled up with impatient feeling, more and more then it came that his children were in opposition to him, more and more then his wife was not existant for him, then he needed things to fill him but this was all the later living for him, now he was just beginning with his impatient feeling, now he was as big as all the world around him, he was it and there was not any difference in him to the people around him. In his children there was already then a little of such a beginning, they were already then a little not all of him, a little outside from him, not to arouse fighting in him, not to arouse him to brush them away from him, just to be there and not be him and he would soon a little begin to know this in him. More and more the three of them Martha Alfred and David were really of them the poorer people they had in their daily living, the half country town being they had in them the half completely city feeling that there was in all of them. There were many kinds of people there living in little houses near them, some of them living well in a poor way there around them some living in a straggling kind of way near them, all of them were in some way part of the daily living of all of them the three children and the mother of them, all of them were more or less part of the real being of the children then, never really part of the real being of the mother of them ; always her real being which was not her important feeling, always her real being as she felt herself existing was the daily living with the three children as if they were still inside her and not apart from her and the well to do city living which was all there was of right being to her feeling. From her children she never came to have real important feeling of herself inside her, this could come to her from the Shilling family, a little from her husband as she felt toward him a little power, mostly from the servants and governesses who lived in the house with her, a little from the poorer people who lived near her.

There were many kinds of people then living around them. More and more the children came to know them, to be really a part of them to have the same being with them to have inside them the same half and half feeling, half country town feeling and half altogether a city feeling. Some of them were sometimes working for them, dress-making carpentering shoe-mending, odd jobs were done by some of them. These and the children of them were for the three Hersland children then nearly all there was of real being in them, Some of these came very close inside to them. For each one of the three of them Martha Alfred and David it was different ones among those who were around them who came close to them, with all of them there was changing and this will be a history of each one of them.

The household the mother father the three children of them, the governess and servants with them, they were all, all of them together then. More and more then it was then slowly coming to be true of them that the children were more entirely of them, the poorer people who lived around them, than they were of their mother then ; they were neither of the mother or of the feeling she had in herself then, nor of the way she felt herself then as being of the living that was all there was of right being to her. They were all three of them then more entirely of them the poorer people who lived around them then than they were of their mother then, than their mother was of them, though they were all there was of their mother's daily living then.

They were very many of them then the poorer people who were living around them, there were very many of them then and they were all of them in each one of them then different from all the others of them and this all three of the children knew very well inside them. They were a part of them, they were always together with them. The servants and the governess were to them as the mother was for them, the father gave a different feeling in them and this will be clearer for them as slowly the character in each one of them comes out from inside him.

There were many people living in small houses around them. Some of them were families of women, some of them were made up of some good ones and some who were not good to earn a living, there were families where it was a little hard to understand how they were living, nobody did any working, nobody had money that belonged to them. In some of the families around them there was a father who was really not very existing, no one was certain that he was a husband of the woman and the father of the children who all earned the living, such a one would just come

and eat and sleep in the house with them, with some there was no mother
and one was not very certain from anything the father showed in him or
that the children remembered about him that there had ever been one.
In one family there was a mother and she was a hard working woman,
there were children some at home, some away from them, some about
whom nothing was very certain, the father was not very certain, he was
not dead to them he was not very certain only not very certain in his
existence for them and in all of such families no one ever asked about
the things around them, and no one ever talked about the queer ways
anybody else had in him. All that was existing for any of them were
the things that happened to them.

In several of the families around them the father or a son had mysterious things he was doing every day in his earning of his living then.
Mostly there was nothing bad in any of them, one of them had an intelligence office where he was working, none of his family ever liked to talk
about him, it is often so with the work men do to earn a living, there is
nothing bad about them, there is nothing in the work that is wrong that
gives a reason why they should not do it then to earn their living, they do
it every day and earn a living then but somehow it is a feeling the family
have about him that they never talk as if he were of them. Sometimes
it is from the work he is doing, sometimes from the ways he has in him,
mostly there is nothing wrong in him, there is nothing bad in his earning
of a living, somehow it is not natural to his family to talk about him, to
act as if he were a part of their daily living, he eats with them, he sleeps
there with them, that is all that makes him then a part of them. Mostly
in the little houses in the part of the town where no rich people are living
the families many of them have such kind of mysteries in them. No one
ever talks about them. No one is ever certain with them how many
children there are of them, what some of them do to make a living, whether
there is a father to them, whether there is a mother to them, how they all
come to the money they have for their daily living.

The three Hersland children were of them, they were always of
the people with the people who lived in the small houses near them,
they were of them, they lived with them, they had the feeling of never
asking any questions of them, they had it in them to never ask any
questions about any of them, they had never any feeling to know anything about any of them that was not shown then in the daily living, no
one of such people as they knew there around them ever asked such
questions of any other one of them. Each one in a family then and every
family of them together then always lived on in their daily living, there
was a husband or a father to them or there was none, there was a mother
or a wife to them or there was none, there were more sons or less of them,
there were more daughters or less of them, no one ever asked any such
question of them, no one asked what they did for their daily living,

sometimes some of them would be gone a long time away from all of them, sometimes he would be rich then, sometimes he would come home then and be a hero to them, always there were uncertain things in any one of them to all of them and no one thought about them, no one knew them as uncertain things about any other one of them, no one ever asked any other one any question about them, mostly every one had it as right for him that each one of them should have a little house where his family was living, each family of them had a little house where any one of them and all of them did their eating and sleeping and washing, each one of them had his own way of earning a living, such uncertain things as each one of the families of them had in them are always there in all of them who are living then in the part of a city where no rich people are living, no one of them ever thinks about them, there is nothing for any of them except the things that happen every day to them, there is nothing for them except their daily living which is all there is then of them.

All of them who lived near the ten acre place where the Herslands were living in that part of Gossols where no rich people were living all of them then were good enough people and regular enough in their daily living and mostly all of the families of them had lived a long enough time where they were living then. Mostly all of them were honest enough men and women, mostly among them there were not any bad men and women. Mostly they were honest enough working men and women and their children went to school and went on to be decent enough men and women to go on living as their families always had been living. As I have just been saying there were not very many of them that were not good enough men and women. A few of them came to a bad end before they got through with their living but mostly all of them were honest enough men and women and they had good enough children and mostly they all made enough by working to keep on and be honest enough in their daily living.

As I was saying they were very different each one of them from the others of them, each family of them from all the other families of them. A great many of them had a little of an uncertain side to them, mostly in every family of them some of them had an uncertain something in them but perhaps the rest understood it about them, none of them ever spoke about them no one ever said it of them that they had uncertain things in them, perhaps it was all a natural way of being. Each one of them went on with his living and whatever came to any one of them was the natural way of living. It is queer in them in the families like them, the uncertain ways some of them seem to have always inside them. Perhaps it is all simple in them, mostly in all of these who lived around the Hersland family then, there was nothing that was wrong about them. Mostly they were all honest enough and good enough men and women with decent enough children.

There were many families of them. There was one family of them that was a family of women then, there was a father to them and he was not dead then or living away from them but mostly then it was as far as one could know them a family of women, a mother and there were three daughters then Anna and Cora and Bertha. There was a father of them, there was a husband to the mother of them, he was regularly with them in his eating and sleeping then, one saw him but somehow he was not really existing, he went every day to his working but that never made him any more of a real being. He went every day to his working, he came home to his eating and sleeping, he was regular in his living, he was regular in his working, he was not very real in existing. Many men and sometimes there is a woman and sometimes there are children of them, have such a way in them, they have such an uncertain feeling coming out from them, they are not real in existing.

The man then, the father of the three of them the husband of the woman then, was not existing for them, he used the little house with them for eating sleeping and washing, he went every day to his working. He was not existing for any of them, he was not existing for the Hersland family who were living in the ten acre place then near them neither for Mrs. Hersland and the three children then nor for the governesses and servants of them. With the father David Hersland, there was in him a little more of real existing, there was in him then that he was a man to feel it in him when another man spoke to him, when another man spoke as a master to him or as just a man to know him ; there was then in him a feeling of being a male thing then when Mr. Hersland met him. There would be a greeting between them when this one met with him, when Mr. Hersland came home from his day in the part of Gossols where the richer people were living, when he met him walking, when he met him coming home carrying something he had just been buying, there was in the man the being that made him speak to another man when he met him, there was in him a being that made the meeting with another man give to him almost a real existence in him, there was in him just such a little being so that he could give to another man a greeting, could so get into him a real being from the meeting he had then with a man in giving him a greeting ; there was in him, in such a kind of man and there are very many of them and they need men to give to them a feeling of existence in them, there was in this man just enough of a kind of being in him that always could make it certain that he was an object real in being, an object called man not woman the world around him then, and there are many of them and as far as any one can know such a one then that is all then that there is of him, perhaps there is more to him to the woman who is a wife to him or to his children who live in the house where he is living, perhaps there is a real existing to him but to all of those around him, to the Hersland family and the others who lived with them there was never in him any real existing, there was for all of them in the house where this man was living only a family of women, a mother and three daughters of them.

There was nothing wrong about him, anybody could see in him that he was a man and there are many of them made just like him, there is nothing wrong inside them, there is nothing very strong of existence in them, there is nothing wrong inside them, it is only that there is not very much of existence in them, there is a little in them, they are men when other men are with them, they are men when they are alone then, only then it is not very strong inside them, they are men then, they are alone then, existence is not very strong in them then, there is just enough of / such existence in them then that one can know them that they are men then when one thinks of them, one does not then when they are alone then ever think about them ever feel any existence in them.

With other men around them, existence in them gets to be a little stronger inside them, they come almost to feel themselves to be inside in them, there gets to be almost enough inside them of existence to make them then have other men feel that they really do exist then, but mostly in them there is not enough of existence to them to make women and children feel that they are really men inside them, men and having real existence in them, it is only when other men meet with them that the existence gets to be strong enough in them so that any one can know them and they can feel it in them that they are men and one with all the men around them, when they are alone with women or with children they have never in them anything of such a feeling, they have then nothing of real being, they go every day to their working, they come home to their eating and their sleeping, there is nothing wrong inside them, there is only nothing in them of real existence to them, it takes other men around them, it needs other men inside them, it takes other men to greet them, it takes other men around them to make of them a real being to be inside them and so it was with this one and there are many made just like him, and so this family then, it was to almost all who knew them a family of women then, the mother and three daughters of them Anna and Cora and Bertha then.

The mother's face was old now and a little wooden. She did dressmaking. She sometimes worked for the rich family near them, for Mrs. Hersland and her children. She was getting old now and a little wooden.

She was a foreign woman. No one knew it about him the husband who lived in the house with them whether he was or was not a foreign man. She was a foreign woman and she was a little old now and her face was a little wooden. She was a hard-working woman, she did dress-making, she earned a good enough living, they were doing very well with their living all of them then. The mother was a foreign woman, she had it in her to be really existing. She was existing for all five of them the Hersland family who knew her then, she was existing for her children, she was existing for all of them who lived in the houses near them, for all the people who ever came to know them, she was not important to them but she had in her a character for them.

The mother had existence in her in this she was different from the man who was a husband to her. She had existence in her, there was real existence to her, more than just enough to know she was a woman creature, she had existence in her, she had a character to her but she had nothing that was important in her, she was not important to any one around her she was not important to the three daughters who were then with her, in a way she was not important to the man who was a husband to her.

There was no past or present in her, there was existence in her, there was a character to her but there was nothing important inside her, there was nothing past or present or in the future that would be connected to her, but she had existence enough to make of her a really existent thing inside her, existence was strong in her in every moment in her, strong enough to make it to be real inside her, she did not need others around her to make existence inside her.

There was nothing connected in her with a past or present or future, there was existence in her, there was a character to her, she had no importance then to any one around her, she had the existence of the useful things around her, it was active in her this existence inside her, it was active in her and this gave a character to her, it was active in her and this was real existence inside her, this made every one who knew her know there was real existence to her, she had real existence in her but she had no importance inside her, there was nothing in her to connect her to a past a present or a future, there was real existence to her, she did not need others around her to make for her the existence she had inside her, they did not make it any stronger others who were around her the existence she had inside her, that was real in her, that was the character in her, that was all that there was of her, there was not in her anything to connect her with the past or present or future, there was real existence to her, that was the whole of her, she had no importance in her to any one of all who knew her.

As I was saying of her she was getting older now and her face and the body of her gave a wooden look to her.

There was nothing in her to connect her with the past the present or the future, there was not any history of her. They were three daughters to her and they then lived altogether, the mother the man who was a husband to her and the three girls Anna, Cora and Bertha. The only thing that could ever give to any one who knew her the mother of the three of them Anna, Cora and Bertha, the only thing that could ever give to any one who knew her a history of her was as they would see it in the history of each one of the three girls who had been once inside her, not of her then, though they were then inside her. The history of each one of them would never make a history for her, the three of them and each one of them made it that one could know about her the history of her. The history they each one of them went through before her as they went through their living and they were the daughters of her, was the history of her who had once had them inside her, once she must have gone through the changes that each one of them went through as they lived longer, there was no history in her, they never made any history for her, the history of them as they went on in their changing around her, each girl repeating in her in the changes that went on in each one inside in her was the repeating around her what once had been changes in her, they were not for her the history of her, they were not for her any past or present or future, there was not in her anything of history inside her, there was not in her any importance to her, there was not in her anything to hold her together with the three girls around her who went through their changes in front of her the three girls who once had been inside her, there was not in her any history of her, there was not in her any importance to her, there was in her real existence inside her, there was in her a character of her and that was all that was then her, that was all then that was ever in her, there was never any history in her, there was a history of her and that the three girls were living around her, they were having the changes she had had in her and now she was getting older and her face and body was getting to be wooden all through her and existence was always just the same in her, it was all there was of her.

The three girls Anna and Cora and Bertha went through the changes then and they were living then altogether, they went through their changes, the changes she had had in her, first they were in Anna then in Cora and then in Bertha and they were never to the mother a history of her, they were never to her a history inside her, there was never in her any connection inside her with a past or present or a future, these changes in the girls with her were like all the objects around her, like the making of dresses to her, like the changing of the eating from the green stuff they brought to her, through the cooking that was natural for her to the eating that came after, this was all to her like the changes in Anna and Cora and Bertha, they never made a history for her, they were not to her a history of her, they were the changes around her, and first it was in Anna then in Cora then in Bertha, each one of them had been once inside her, that was not a history to her, they were changing then around her, that was not history of her in her, she was getting older now and looking wooden, that did not change in her the existence inside her, that was a change like all the others in her, that was not any more of a history to her, existence was always just the same inside her and it would always be so in her until she died and that would be one more change of her, it would not be a change to her and so it was now with the girls around her, they went through their changes before her, they were not a history to her they were not for her a history of her, they were three daughters with her, they went through their changes one after another, they lived there in the small house all together she and the man who was a husband to her and the three girls who each one once had been inside her, and that was not a history to her, that was like all the other changes in her, that was like eating and dressmaking for her and so she had existence in her and she always worked hard and had a character in her and she never had importance for any one around her. She had existence in her like the useful things around her, she had character, she had had changes in her and now she was getting older and there was a little more wooden change inside her and so there would be changes in her until she would be all through with all the changes she had in her and always there would be real existence to her and always there would be character to her always there would never be a past or present or a future connected with her, always there would be existence in her, there would be changes, there would never be any history of her to her.

The eldest daughter of them Anna had come then to be a rather beautiful woman. No one thought it about them that all three of them would have that as a change in them. No one thought it about her the mother of them that she had had once a change in her like this change in them before she had borne any one of them. The eldest one had beauty then, now when she was grown to be a woman, all three of them one after the other came to have in them as one of the changes that went through them, beauty in them when they were not any longer children. Not one of the three of them had any signs in them of such a thing going to happen to them until it had happened in them. The one of them, to any one who began at any time to know them, the one of them who had come to be a woman then and to have this change into beauty which happened to each one of them, had it that this had already happened to her then, to any one who came then to know them it was a fact then that this one was a beautiful woman but this never made any connection for them to the other or other ones who had not had the change in them, the beauty in the one that had it then was like existence in the mother of them, it was in them one after the other of them as if it had always been in them, it had no connection in them with a past or future in them, it had no connection in them to any other changes that had been or could come to them, it had no connection with the others of them who were then with or without beauty in them, it had no connection with the mother of them, with the change she once had which was like the change in each one of them but nothing made any connection between any of them, to the mother of them, nor to the father of them for he had not any real existence in him to any one of them.

The change then came in each one of them and now it was Anna the eldest of them that was a beautiful woman to everybody around them then. The beauty in her then to any one who came to know all of them was, as beauty came to be in each one of them, a thing that when it was in any one of them then, was to any one who knew them then, something that was always in them always to be in them, always had been in them, in the others of them then there was not any sign of any such a change ever to be in them, in the mother of them there was nothing then that connected her with any such a change in them, there was nothing in her then to connect her with that one or with them, when there were more of them that had then this change in them, there was nothing in her that made it true for any one who knew her then that she had had in her any such change to connect her with that one or with them who had it then, that she had had it in her before she had borne them.   How any one knew it about them that the mother had had such a change in her before them, how any one knew it about them that the others of them would have such a change in them, that, no one who knew them could ever answer in them.   Perhaps it was the existence the mother had inside her for all of them, perhaps it was this that gave to every one who knew them no feeling of surprise in them that each one of them and the mother before them had, were having and were to have such changes in them, there was not anything to connect them together then except the existence in the mother of them, existence that was real in her for every one who came to know them, that never made her important to them but that made her a real thing to them, and this was what made it natural that all of them should go through, each one of them, the changes in them that every one of them had in them, this is what never made one think it about them that they would have such changes in them, that is what never made it a surprise to any one of them that they had such changes in them, it was the existence in the mother of them, this is what made real the changes in them to every one that knew them.   The existence in the mother of them is what made the change that was then in any one of them a final thing in each one of them, and the mother of them, to any one who knew them then.   The existence in the mother of them, at the time then when one knew them, made it, the change that was then them, to every one who knew them then, a thing that was forever in them, it was the existence that the mother of them had in her then that made whatever was in them to any one who knew them as if it were everlasting.   The mother had existence in her, she had no importance to her, there had been there would be changes in her but this never made any history for her, there was nothing in her to connect her with a past a present or a future, there was nothing in her to connect her with the changes in the daughters around her, to connect her with the man who was a husband to her, there was existence in her, there was no importance to her, there was no history in her for her, there was no history of her to her in the changes in the daughters there around her.

In the eldest daughter Anna there was more of importance inside her than there was in the mother of her, than there was in the sisters who went through·their changes later, than there was in her father who lived in the house with her.

In her there was not so much existence inside her as there was in the mother but there was more of importance to herself inside her, she was more important to every one who knew her, there was more of her in the things that happened to her, she was more important to the things that happened to her than her mother had ever been in all the living she had had all her life in her. Anna had inside her more importance in her, more than in her mother, more like that in her father, but with her there was real existence inside her, not so much existence as there was in the mother but existence enough to make alive the feeling of importance to herself inside her, enough to make others feel her, enough to make her important to every one that knew her. Anna had in her real existence to her, not so much as in her mother but enough to the making her living inside in her, she was important to herself inside from her own power in her, she was important to herself inside her as her father was when he was with other men around him to make him to be real inside him, when the father had men around him then there was in him a feeling of importance in him as a man among them and he was important to them then to his feeling, but really, in him there was no existing, it took other men around him to make him alive inside him, he had no existence in him. In the mother of them there was always strong existing but there was never anything of an important feeling, she was always existing, she was not important in her being, she was not any more existing with others who came near her in her living than she was when she was alone with her being, she was always existing, she was never important in her feeling, she was never important to any one who knew them, she was like any article around them, she had strong existence for them she was never in any way important for them, she had not in any way in her any changes for them, she was not important to any one of them.

There were three of them then Anna and Cora and Bertha. In Anna had come the change that made a beauty of her, she had less existence in her than the mother she had as much importance in her as the father, she had enough existence in her to make real inside her the important feeling she had in her.

It came to her to have things happen to her and in her, she had a career in her and later they will come out in her the things that happened to her.

The second daughter Cora had in her less existence than the mother and no important feeling in her, beauty came to her, things happened to her, there was nothing in her that made anything important to her.

Cora went through her changes a little slower than her sister Anna. They came in her slowly, they gave no importance to her, there was existence in her not enough to make her living, always, like the mother, there was not in her enough of existence like the mother to make a solid thing of her, there was in her a little uncertain feeling like that in the father but there was nothing in her that gave to her a sense of being important inside her from others being around her, others around her were as they were to her mother they were around her and that was all the meaning they had in her, they were around her, they did things to her, for her, they never gave to her as they did to her father and to her sister Anna a feeling of importance to herself inside her, they were as they were to her mother, things around in her ; in her, existence was not strong in her as it was always in the mother and so in her as in her father there was a little something uncertain and not solid to her, and all this will come out in her in the history of the Hersland family who came then more and more to know her.

There were three of them Anna and Cora and Bertha ; Bertha had in her less of existence in her than any of them except the father. Bertha had in her ehough of existence in her to make her alive when she was a little girl and there was not very much of her, she had not in her enough of existence to her to make her alive inside her when it came to her to be a young girl and later to have beauty in her and to be a woman then. There was not enough to her of existence in her to make her alive inside her when she had gone through in her with the change of being a little girl, not very much of her, even then she was not very living in her, she had not very much existence in her. She had a little more existence in her than her father, enough to make her living when there was so very little of her, then was the only time she had enough existence in her to make her alive inside her. No one who knew her could ever feel that there would be changes, there was not enough existence in her to any one who knew her to keep her alive through changes that went through her, the changes went on in her, they went on in her as they had done in her mother, in her sister Anna and then in her sister Cora, they went on slowly in her, she came later to have beauty in her, she never was very alive inside her, she never had existence like her mother who had existence like the useful things about her, she had not like her father importance from other people around her, when she was a little girl she had a little of such importance in her from the little existence that was then in her the little existence always in her that then kept her alive for there was then so little of her, more and more then as she grew bigger there was not any such importance there was not in her enough existence to make her alive inside her, and there was not any very real living to her, she had never in her any importance from other people around her, she was like her mother only she had very little of existence in her, so that is the history of her, she was alive inside her when there was very little of her when she was a little girl and then she was alive inside her and had in her a little of importance to herself inside her, she grew bigger and there was never then in her any strong existence to her, there was never in her enough importance to her to make it real in her, there was not later an uncertain feeling to her, there was in her the existence in her, the importance of it to her that had been in her when she was a little girl and was alive inside her for then there was so little of her. There was not in her later an uncertain feeling to her as there was in her father as there was in her sister Cora, there was in her always just the same being inside her, when she was a woman, when she had beauty in her, there was then inside her just the same existence in her just the same importance inside her that there had been when she was a little girl and there was not very much to her. She was like her mother, the little existence she had was really there in her, she was like her father, the little existence she had was important to her, she was not like her mother, the little existence was never very strong in her, she was not like her father, she could never get existence in her she could never get importance to her from other people around her, she had enough existence in her it was important enough inside her to make her alive in her when she was a little girl and there was not very much to her. There never came to be any more in her neither of existence nor of importance in her and later when she was bigger when she became a woman and had beauty, there was not in her enough of existence and of importance in her to fill her and so she was then later never very alive inside her, there was then of her, too much, for the existence and importance inside her. She was then, never, when she was bigger, when she was finished with the change of being a little girl and not very much to her, she was never after very alive inside her.

And now Anna had this change in her, she had beauty in her, Cora and Bertha were having the changes she had already had in her, there was yet nothing in Cora or in Bertha that could connect them with her, with the beauty change that had come to her.

The three girls Anna and Cora and Bertha went through their changes one after the other, now the beauty change had come in Anna, now when there was no longer in her a young girl's growing change in her beauty had come into her and to every one who knew her it was as if it had always been in her, it had no connection in her with her sisters Cora and Bertha nor with her mother. The mother had strong existence in her, she was getting older and her face and body was getting to be wooden all through her and existence was always just the same in her, it was always all there was of her. No one who knew them then the mother or Anna or Cora or Bertha, ever thought about the father, and so to every one around them then, this to every one that knew them was a family of women, there was the mother who was getting old now and a little wooden who was never important to any one who knew them who always had existence in her and that was always strong inside her, that never made any history in her, that never gave any importance to her she was existing then and existence always had been in her as it was in the useful things around her, there was no history in her, there was nothing in her to connect her with the past the present or the future, there was never any history in her there was a history of her and that the three girls were living around her, they were having the changes she had had in her, there was nothing then in her to connect her with the changes in the three girls who lived in the house with her, there was nothing in any of them that connected themselves with the others of them, there was nothing in them to connect them with the mother of them, there was nothing in the changes in them that made any one who knew them ever feel in them that she had had changes in her as the three girls had them then the three girls who were around her then, there was nothing in any of the three of them that made one feel in them that they would have in them the changes that any one of the three of them had had already in her, there was nothing to connect them with each other, they did go through their changes one after the other, there was never anything in any one of them to make any one who knew them feel that there would be changes in any one of them, a little more perhaps in Anna than in any of the others of them, in her, changes might come, in the other two of them Cora and Bertha and in the mother of them there was never any thing in them to make any one who knew them think a change would come in them, the mother was getting older now and her face and body was getting to be wooden all through her and existence was always just the same in her, it was always all that there was of her, Cora was a little wooden then, girlhood was almost finished in her, beauty had not come yet to be in her, Bertha was a little girl then, there was never in her as much existence inside her as there was in the mother or Anna or Cora, there was in her a little more existence than in the father, Anna had then beauty in her and was important then to every one who knew her, in her there was a feeling that there might come changes in her. Nobody ever thought about the father. This family to every one who knew them was a family of women.

There were many other families then living in the little houses near the ten acre place where the Hersland family were living in that part of Gossols where no other rich people were living, some of them were neat and made a good living like this family of women, some were not so well off in their living; some had a very straggling way of living, each one of the families of them in the small houses then had each its own way of living each its own uncertain ways of being, and this is a history of them.

There were many kinds of families of them living in the little houses near the Hersland family then. They were each one of them different from all the others of them, they were different each one of them from all the others of them in their way of living, in their ways of earning a living, in the things that had been in their lives in the earlier days of their living, in the things that would now happen to them, they were different each one of them from all the others of them then, they were different in all the ways that they had in them, they were different in all the things that made them important, in all the things that made them uncertain inside them, they were different inside each one of them from all the others of them in religion. Some of them then had religion in them, some of them had not anything of such a thing in them, all of them who had religion in them were different from all the others of them who had religion in them too in them. One of these families then was made up of a father and two children, a boy and a girl Eddy and Lilly and the father of them, there were many uncertain things about all three of them, about the living that they had had before in them, about there not being to them a woman to be a wife to him and a mother to the two children, about the way they had money to live on when not any one of the three of them did any working, about the kind of man the father was for it was very hard to know anything about him, about the character of the two children ; one thing was certain about them, they had religion in them, they were important in religion.

The father was a tall thin man, they said of him that he was a sick man, perhaps that was true of him, no one knew how anybody knew that about him, his children never said it of him, he was a tall thin blond man, he was always smoking and that was said by every one who knew him to be because it was good for him, he was important in religion.

There are many ways of being important in religion and this is a history of some of them, there are many men and many women and some children who have religion in them, there are many ways of having that in them. They are some who are important in religion, they are some who have religion and who are not important from the religion in them, they are many men and many women and some children who have religion in them and this is a history of some of them.

There are many of all these kinds of them, there were some of many kinds of them in the families that the Hersland family came to know then, more and more in their living then the Hersland children came to know them came to know the many ways many men and many women and some children have religion in them, the many ways some of them have to have religion make them important inside them, the way some of them who have religion never have any of such an important feeling in them, more and more then they came to know in the families that lived there around them the meaning the religion each one of them who had religion in them meant to the one that had it inside him, for there were many of them that had it in them many men and many women and some of their children.

This family the father and the two children Eddy and Lilly, all three of them had religion in them, there was no wife to him or mother to the children then. Slowly the Hersland children came to know them. They had it in them this man Mr. Richardson and his two children Eddy and Lilly Richardson, they had it in them all three of them to be important in religion, the father had always all his life had religion in him, he always had been important in religion, this is a history of the feeling in him, of the way his children too had it in them.

As I was saying Mr. Richardson was a tall thin blond man, he was sick then, so everybody said who knew him though his children never said it about him, he was sick then and he was always smoking and everybody said who knew him that that was because it was good for him, good for the sickness he had in him.

Any one who knew him would know that he had religion in him, that he always had had religion in him. Always one knew it in the two children that they had they always would have religion in them, religion with all three of them was a part of them, it was to all of them a part of their being, it was not a belief in them, it was of them like eating and sleeping and washing, for all these things and religion were part of their being, such was the nature of all three of them. Not that all three of them had the same nature in them, the three of them each one was very different from the other two of them, each one had their own nature in them, but all three had this in common that religion that eating sleeping and washing were natural to them, other things too were natural in them and all these things will come out more and more in the history of them.

There are many men and many women and some of their children who have at some time religion in them. There are some of all these, of the many men and many women and some children who have religion in them, there are many of these that have it in them as a natural part of them, who have religion always inside them, who need religion as they do eating and sleeping and loving and there are very many who have religion in them so from the beginning of them, in some of them this religion in them makes them important inside to them, with some of them this religion in them makes them important to every one who knows them, there are some who have religion in them as a natural thing in them and have always had such a thing in them and it does not give any importance to them.

There are some then who always have religion in them to whom it is as natural as breathing, there are some who have it in them who need it in them to complete them, there are some who have it like eating and sleeping, some who have it like loving, some who have it like washing, there are some who have it from a need in them to have it fill them when they have lost something that was once a piece in them ; some get from religion an important feeling, some have it and are important to every one who knows them, some never have in it any kind of an important feeling.

Mr. Richardson and his two children had always had religion in them, religion would always be in them like eating and sleeping and washing, not like breathing and loving. Religion was always in them, they had it always and it made all three of them important to every one that knew them.

To the father Mr. Richardson religion was like eating and sleeping and washing, all these and religion made him a continuous being, they were not outside him, they all were in him and they made him always continue in his existing. Religion had been in him always as a part of him, it was in him like sleeping, it was in him like eating, it was of him like washing, it had always been in him as a part of him, it had always made him important to every one who knew him, it did not make him important to himself inside him any more than eating and sleeping and washing made him important to himself inside him, it was a part of his continuous existing ; it did always make him important to every one who knew him.

To some who knew him, to some who had not any kind of religion in them, to some this religion in him was to them like lying but these did not understand him, there was in religion in him no more of lying, with him, than there was in washing any more than there was in eating or sleeping, this was very hard for some of them who knew him, some of them who never had any religion in them, to understand about him but always it was true of him, religion in him was like eating and sleeping and washing, it did not make him to himself important inside him, it made him important to everyone who knew him, it was there and they knew it in him, it was in him and whatever he should be ever found out in doing that would never make it different in him that religion was real inside him, that it was in him like his eating and sleeping and washing, that it never was, in him, lying any more than eating and sleeping and washing were lying. It was a part of him as they were a part of him, they were needed every day to remake him, to keep him going on in existing, so it was with religion and this in him made him important to every one who knew him.

The religion inside him, as I was saying, kept him existing, it was not that it filled a need in him, it was not that he used it in his living, it kept him continuous and existing as did his eating and sleeping. Religion was to him like eating and sleeping, religion was to him also like washing and it was this in him, the religion like washing that made him important to every one who knew him. Religion was to him as eating and sleeping was in him, religion was in him as washing was to him and this religion in him made him important to every one who knew him.

Washing is very common, almost every one does some washing, with some it is only for cleansing, with some it is a refreshing, with some a ceremonial thing that makes them important to every one who knows them. In those who have religion in them as washing is to some of them who make it a distinction in them, in some who have religion in them as washing is to some who do it as a necessary part of their daily living, such have from it a distinction ; washing is not a natural thing to happen like eating or sleeping, washing is not like eating or sleeping, it has in it a distinction and to them who do it every day as a natural thing to them, they have it in them to be important to every one who knows them, when religion is in any one as this washing is in some who have it in them, then such a one is important to every one who knows him.

Eating and sleeping are not like loving and breathing. Washing is not like eating and sleeping. Believing is like breathing and loving. Religion can be believing, it can be like breathing, it can be like loving, it can be like eating or sleeping, it can be like washing. It can be something to fill up a place when some one has lost out of them a piece that it was natural for them to have in them.

To be continuous in existing by an every day eating and sleeping is like what some have in religion, then it is not from a need in them, it is from the natural way they have in them to be continuous in their existing. Feeding and religion with such of them is every day natural to them. Washing is different from eating and sleeping. It is natural to some and it makes such ones important to every one that knows them. Some have religion in them as some have washing and they are always important to every one who knows them. To have washing as natural to them is some distinction to those who have it as natural in them, to have religion in them to be in them as washing is to some, those to whom it is natural from the beginning to have religion in them in such a way as some have washing is to make of them who have religion in any such a way natural to them important to every one who knows them.

Mr. Richardson had always had, from his beginning, religion in him. It was always natural in him as was his eating and sleeping and washing. He kept on this way in his existing, it was natural to him to keep on existing, it was natural to him to have in him religion and eating and sleeping and washing, he had had them all always from his beginning. It did not make him important to himself inside him, it made him important to everyone who knew him. There were many things in him and these will come out in the history of him. Always religion was in him, always he was important to every one who knew him. There were some who did not understand it in him, who thought it of him that religion was in him as a kind of lying but these did not understand religion in him, it was in him and had been in him from his beginning, it was in him as eating was in him, as sleeping was in him, as washing was to him. It did not make him important to himself inside him, it did make him important to every one that knew him.

This father Mr. Richardson and his two children Eddy and Lilly were different from any of the others who lived then in the small houses near the ten acre place where the Hersland family were living in that part of Gossols where no other rich people were living. Slowly the Hersland children came to know the three of them, they began to know then the character of the two children Eddy and Lilly Richardson, they never came to have in them, the Hersland family then, much more knowledge of the father of the two children Mr. Richardson. The character of Eddy and Lilly Richardson will come out then in the history of the Hersland children as they come to know it in them.

There were then many families living in the small houses near the ten acre place where the Hersland family were living then in that part of Gossols where no other rich people were living. There were many families of, for them, poor queer people living near them and each one of the families of them had in them their own way of living, their own way of going on existing, of having uncertain things in them, of earning their daily living. More and more the Hersland family came to know them, more and more the Hersland children came to be of them.

There were many families of them. Some of them had many children. Almost all of them had things in them to interest the Hersland children. Some of them were good companions to them in their out door living, some in the school life they lead together with them, some from the books and other things that they loaned to them, all these children in the little houses near them were in some way interesting to some one of the three of them either from what they were in themselves then or from their lives or what they had in their houses to lend to them, they were, all of these children of the, for them, poor queer people around them, they were all in some way interesting to some one of the three of them. They were, all of them, more and more interesting to the three Hersland children as these came always more and more to know them, as they came to be more and more a part of them. The Hersland children came to know them, they came to know others who knew these who lived near them, some who lived in other parts of Gossols and some of these others that the Hersland children came to know through the families near them, some of these others came later to be very important

to the three of them, some came to be important to the father of the
Hersland children, some also to the mother of them, all this will come
out in the later history of them.   This was the beginning of living for the
Hersland children, and more and more then they came to know the,
for them, poor queer people who lived in the little houses near them
in that part of Gossols where no other rich people were living.

So then it was then slowly coming to be true of them that the three
children were more entirely of them, the poorer people who lived around
them, than they were of their mother then, than their mother was of
them then, though they were all there was of their mother's daily living
then.

This was true of them then in the years when they were only beginning to know themselves inside them.   Later then in their living with
the same people around them, Alfred the elder son of the two boys then
was beginning to have inside him a feeling in him as there always had
been in the mother of them, he was beginning then not to be any longer
of them the poorer people who lived around them, more and more then
such a feeling went out of him and he was beginning to have it fill up
in him then inside him to replace the feeling that was not then any longer
in him, out of the feeling that gave his mother her important being.
In the daughter there was more in her then when she was older of the
kind of feeling that their father had in him.   In the younger son there
always remained in him all through his later living the feeling that made
him be one to him with the people that had been around him.   All
this will come out in the detailed history of each one of the three of them.
Now in the beginning they were all three of them of the people who lived
in the small houses around them.

To begin again then when it was slowly coming to be true of them
that the three children were more entirely of them, the poorer people
who lived around them, than they were of their mother then, than their
mother was of them then, though they were all there was of their
mother's daily living then.

They were all there was of their mother's daily living then but they
were nothing to her then of the important being that was beginning to
be strong inside her then.   They were to her in her then as they had
been when she was bearing them, they were part of her as her arms or
heart were part of her then, she felt them, she took care of them then
as she took care of her body out of which she had once made them
and so she always felt them.   Later she was lost among them, she would
be scared then and they were no longer of her then, they were not any
longer in her then to her, she was for them then a gentle scared little
thing.   She was lost among them then, sometimes they would be good
to her then, oftener she would not be existing for them then, mostly
she was scared then and the important feeling was dead in her then,

she had lost them, they were not of her any more then and she lost her body with them. Sometimes then they would be good to her, mostly they forgot about her, slowly she died away among them and then there was no more of living for her, she died away from all of them. She had never been really important to any of them, she was not important to her husband then for she was not enough to fill him now that he was shrinking away from the outside of him, she was not enough any more now to fill him, she was not in any way then important to her children for now they did not need to have in them the feeling that she had for them when they were for her as if she was still carrying them inside her still using herself up to make them from out of her, they were not in any way then any longer necessary to her, they had never been in her a part of her in the important being that was all that there was real to her of an important feeling inside in her. She was not then any more important to any of them when they were older, she was not important to her husband then for she was not enough then any more to fill him, not to her children, she never had been important to them after they had come to their individual feeling, they had never been in her a part of the important feeling to herself inside her, now she had a scared feeling in her, now she was lost among them and mostly they forgot about her, now she died away among them and they never thought about her, sometimes they would be good to her, mostly for them she had no existence in her and then she died away and the gentle scared little woman was all that they ever after remembered of her. Those who always after remembered about her were the servants, the governesses, the dependents who had been around her, they always were a real life to her, they were the important feeling in her, they always remembered about her, they had felt the real important being to herself inside her. This then is the history of how they came together with her to be in her and to give to her the important feeling inside her that was all there ever was of real being in her.

Her children were then a part of her, they were never any part of the important feeling of herself inside her that was beginning then to stir in her. It was slowly coming to be true of them then, the three Hersland children then, that they were more entirely of them, the poorer people who lived around them, than they were of their mother then, than their mother was of them then, though they were all that there was of their mother's daily living then.

Their mother then was just beginning to have in her the important feeling that had first become a little stirred up to be made inside her by her knowing the Shilling mother and the daughter Sophie Shilling and the other daughter Pauline Shilling. This important feeling that had then been a little begun inside her was now to be more stirred up in her, was to come to be almost a real thing in her by her living in that part of Gossols where no other rich people were living near her and in a kind of living that was not a natural way of being for her. Here she had around her, for her, poor queer kind of people in the little houses near her, in the house with her she had servants and governesses and seamstresses who made a life for her, her children who were then a part of her to her, and her husband and the certain little power with him she felt in herself to have in her, though mostly she had not in her for her husband or her children a sense of being important to herself inside her. This important feeling of herself inside her that had begun a little to exist in her from the Shilling family to her, was now stirred up to be more in her with the governesses and seamstresses and servants who lived in the house with her, and with the, for her, poor queer kind of people who lived in the small houses near her.

There are many kinds of men. Some kinds of them have it in them to feel themselves as big as all the world around them. Some have such a sense in them only when a new thing begins in them, soon they lose it out of them.

There are many ways of being a man, there are many millions of each kind of them, more and more in ones living they are there repeating themselves around one, every one of them in his own way being the kind of man he has in him, and there are always many millions made just like each one of them.

There are many ways of being a man and sometime one gets to know almost all of them, some sometime get to know all of them, there are many millions made of each kind of them, each one of them is different from all the other millions made just like him, this makes of him an individual, this in some of them makes in him an individual feeling to have inside in him, in some of some kinds of them there is almost nothing of such an individual being, perhaps always in every one in some way there is something of such an individual being, in all men, in women, and in the children of them.

There are many kinds of men, of every kind of them there are many millions of them many millions always made to be like the others of that kind of them, of some kinds of them there are more millions made like the others of such a kind of them than there are millions made alike of some other kinds of men. Perhaps this is not really true about any kind of them, perhaps there are not less millions of one kind of men than there are millions of other kinds of them, perhaps one thinks such a thing about some kinds of men only because in some kinds of men there is more in each one of such a kind, more in the many millions of such a kind of them, of an individual feeling in every one of such a kind of them. Perhaps in some kinds of men there are many more, in the many millions of their kind of them, there are many more of them that have in them a strongly existing individual being than in some other kinds of men other kinds of men of which there are not really any more millions made alike than there are of those kinds of men. Perhaps it is this strongly existing individual being in some of the kinds of men that makes it seem that there are less millions of them in the world of men than there are of other kinds of men other kinds of men who have in most of them less in them of such individual existing. Perhaps it is this in some of the kinds of men those kinds in which many of the millions of them have much in them of individual being, perhaps it is that which makes any one who knows any one of such kinds of men think him more different from the other millions of them made just like him the other millions of his kind of men, makes those who know any of such a kind of men, feel them to be more different one from the other of their kind of men than the ones of some other kind of men are different from the other millions of their kind of men to those who meet many of them. Always there are many kinds of men and always there are many millions made of each kind of them, there are many kinds of men and many millions of each kind of them, there are many kinds of women and there are many millions made of each kind of them, there are many children of these many men and many women and the kinds are often very much mixed up in them but more and more the kind that really is in each one of them more and more as one knows them it comes out to be clear in each one of them. Some kinds of men have, in most of the millions made of such a kind of them, have in them more of an individual being than most of the millions of some other kind of men. Some kinds of them have much more of an individual being as a nature in them than there is in other kinds of men. Each kind of them has in the many millions of that kind of them more, in some of them of individual feeling than there is in others of them. All this will come out slowly as it is written down about them, it comes out slowly in the living that every body is every day doing with all the many kinds of them, the many kinds of men the many kinds of women and the many kinds of children that have these many men and many women mixed up in them.

There are many kinds of men, there are many kinds of women there are many kinds of ways of mixing them in the children that come out of them. There are many kinds of men and many millions made of each kind of them. Some kinds of them have more in all of them of individual being than there is in some of the other kinds of men. In each kind of men, in the many millions of each kind of them there are always among them some with much, some with less, and some with little, and some with almost not any individual feeling in them some of such of them need other men around them to give the man an individual feeling in them, some men have in them so much individual feeling in them that they make their way through everything around them, some of them have it so much in them that they feel themselves as big as all the world around them.

There are some men who have always such bigness in them, there are some who have such a feeling in them when a new thing begins in them and then soon these lose it out of them. There are some who have such a feeling in them when they are first beginning their individual being, some of such ones never lose it out of them for they are always strong to be beginning and beginning is all of living to them. In some of such ones of them it comes in their later living to be only impatient feeling, they are then no longer beginning they are then full up with impatient feeling. Later in their living they have not enough in them any more of impatient feeling to fill them, they are old then and shrinking away from the outside of them so then it is in them the always beginning and being then in their feeling as big as all the world around them, then it comes to be in them only the being full up with impatient feeling and then it comes to be when they are old and weakening it comes to be a shrinking away of themselves from the outside of them, they are old men then and they have not any success in them, they are not any longer full up then not with big feeling or beginning or even any more with impatient feeling, they are old then and have not any success in them and it needs others then to make them full again inside them and mostly in their old age this does not happen in them, mostly in their old age such ones are never full inside them.

There are many kinds of men. Some kinds of them have it in them to feel themselves as big as all the world around them, some of this kind have it in them to keep this always in them all through their living. Some of this kind of men have such a sense in them only when a new thing begins in them, soon they lose it out of them. Some of this kind of men have such a sense in them only in their own beginning, later they lose it out of them. Some have it in them as their beginning and always they are beginning in their living and this feeling comes again and again to be in them with each beginning of their living and beginning in such of them is all there is of living. Some, and David Hersland who had come to Gossols to make his great fortune was one of them, some of such a kind of men have it in them to be as big as all the world in their beginning, they are strong in beginning and beginning things is all of living in them, then each beginning comes to be in them an impatient feeling. These never lose their big feeling they just begin a new thing and they are strong in beginning, they are as big then as all the world around them, they keep their big feeling for each time the beginning in them turns into impatient feeling they are then full up with impatient feeling, this makes them full inside them, they never have it in them to lose this feeling of being as big in them as all the world around them, they never can lose this feeling then until they are old men and weakening and then they shrink away from the outside of them and so they lose this certain sense of being as big as all the world around them for then they have this empty space in them where they have shrunk away from the outside of them and they have to be filled up again, they have not enough then of big feeling in them, they have not enough strength to have in them then a beginning, they have not enough of impatient feeling to fill them, they need other people to help them to fill them up inside them, they can never again have in them of themselves then a feeling of being as big as all the world around them.

As I have been saying there are many kinds of men and there are many millions made of each kind of them. David Hersland who had come to Gossols to make for himself a great fortune was of one kind of them. He was of the kind of them that feel themselves to be as big as all the world around them. Every one who knew him felt it in him. His children felt it less in him for they knew from their daily living with him that this was only in him when he was beginning, mostly he was filled up with impatient feeling. He had this big feeling in him, they knew it about him but, for them, it was his being full up with impatient feeling that was important to them in their daily life with him.

His children, in the way it almost always is with men, his children always were outside him, part of the world he was handling, sometimes using them sometimes brushing them away from before him, often fighting with them and always dropping or domineering them.

His children had it in them, in the way that almost all children have it in them, his children had it in them for a long time to be afraid of him. Almost all the time of their living together in the house with him they had such a fear in them, but really they had it less in them than many children for the fathers of them, they had it less from him as they learnt more and more to know it of him that he was mostly filled up inside him with impatient feeling, so they had always less and less of fear in them, they knew it more and more of him that he would not keep up anything against the wish in them, soon he would be changing, he never would carry out into action any anger he felt with them, it would soon be in him an impatient feeling and then there was not any more, for them, anything to fear from him. Always they more and more had this in them about him and so more and more they did not fear him. Always there remained a little fear in them for children never know all that a father can have in him. He may have it in him to be worse than they have ever known him, it is this uncertain danger to them that may be in him that makes a father always fearful to his children, it is in his voice, in his movements, in the sudden outbursts from him, children never can know really what is going on in the father of them as they know it in other children around them or in the mother of them. However the Hersland children learned more and more in their daily living that their father was mostly filled up with impatient feeling, they knew he had a big feeling in him, they felt this sometimes in him, sometimes it made them ashamed when they went about with him, sometimes they liked the big joyous feeling that it gave him but mostly for all three of them in their younger living with him the important thing about him was that he was filled up with impatient feeling.

Beginning was all of living with him, in a beginning he was always as big in his feeling as all the world around him. Beginning was almost all of living in him. Always he was beginning and always he was strong in his beginning, always then he was as big as all the world in his feeling.

There are many ways of beginning, there are some things in living that have in them always more of beginning than other things in living, education is such a part of living, eating and doctoring and making a great fortune in a place where everybody is beginning in their living.

Ways of educating children, ways of eating and doctoring, all have it in them to be always in a beginning.

In many people's living beginning is all there is of living, in many people's living it is dying ending that is to them all they have in them, some of these have always in them the fear in them of dying of ending, and then ending is in their feeling in every moment of their living. There are many ways for them of having such a feeling always in them the feeling of ending always inside them, some of them have it in a fear that is always in them, some have it in a sad feeling always somewhere inside them in them, some have it from a feeling that is not a sadness in them but a fullness of ending to them and these always are talking of how everything is always ending ; ending is all of living to many men and very many women, ending is all of living with them, and these have not a fear in them, they have not sadness in them, all that there is for them is ending and that gives to their living fullness and meaning. Such ones are very full of ending full of ending as some other men and some women have it in them to be very full with beginning, for such ones then there is, too, very much of meaning in ways of educating children, ways of eating and ways of doctoring. In all of these things then there is much beginning there is much of ending.

In ways of educating children in ways of eating and ways of doctoring there can be always to them who have in them beginning as all there is of living, much to content them ; for those who have in them ending as the important feeling in them they too can find it strongest in them for them in ways of educating children in ways of eating and ways of doctoring. These then who have for them as the whole of living either always beginning or always in an ending, these then can have it in them in many ways and with many kinds of feelings inside them, they can have it in a strong fear in them they can have it without any such a fear in them, they can have it with dying as always the strongest thing in them, they can have it with living as the most conscious thing in them, there are many ways that they can have it in them, with sadness or cheerful feeling in them, with energy or weakness in them, but always they have it together in all of them that ending or beginning is all of living to them, and for them ways of eating, ways of doctoring, ways of educating children are for them the strongest thing inside them.

In David Hersland the father of the three children whose lives we are now soon to be watching, to David Hersland beginning was all of living to him. For him there was in his living ways of eating, ways of doctoring, ways of educating his children, ways of making his great fortune here in Gossols where he was to make his important beginning.

There are many ways of eating, for some eating is living, for some eating is dying, for some thinking about ways of eating gives to them the feeling that they have it in them to be alive and to be going on living, to some to think about eating makes them know that death is always waiting that dying is in them, some of such of them have then a fear in them and these then never want to be thinking about ways of eating, they want their eating without any thinking, they never want to have the fear in them that comes to them with thinking about ways of eating, of ways of keeping health in them.

As I have been saying to some eating is a way of living, to some eating is dying. To many, now, thinking about eating is all of living to them, it is living, it is always beginning, it is like doctoring or educating children. David Hersland the father of the three children whose lives we will now soon be knowing was such a one, beginning was all of living to him, he had it in him in his beginning to be as big as all the world around him. He had it in him to be always beginning, beginning was living to him and this will come out in the history of him. He had it in him to be always beginning. There are some things in living that have it in them to have always more of beginning to them than other things in living, eating is such a part of living, eating and doctoring and educating children. Ways of eating, ways of doctoring, ways of educating children, all have it in them to be always in a beginning.

As I was saying David Hersland was a big man and he liked different ways of eating, he liked to think about what was good for him in eating, he liked to think about what was good for every one around him in their eating, and he was always changing, he was always beginning and often he was full up with impatient feeling ; this could be in him about the way of eating as it was in him about everything in his living. David Hersland was a big man, sometimes one felt about him that he filled up the whole world he looked so large then to every one who saw him, often he did not have such a bigness in him. Not that he was really such a large man to look at him but when he was full up with beginning he filled everything around him, he was as big then as all the world which was then in him to everybody who then saw him. As I was saying there are many kinds of men and there are many millions of each kind of them. As I was saying there are some kinds of them that have in them so much individual being in them that one can never think it about them that there are many millions made like them. Mr. David Hersland was of such a kind of them, he had it in him to be so full up with beginning that he was a big man filling up all the space around him, no one could come to think it about him then that there are many millions made just like him, but there are many millions made of each kind of men, there are many millions made who have such a bigness in them, some of them always have such a bigness in them every moment of their being, some have it only in their beginning soon they lose it out of them, some have it every time they are beginning and beginning is all of living to them, some of such ones are big in all their living, some have it in them only at moments in their living but all of them have it in them sometimes to be as big as all the world around them, all the world is in them and everybody can see it who then sees them.

David Hersland was such a one when he was in each one of his beginnings, soon then he would be filled up with impatient feeling and then there would be in him less of such a big feeling to every one who then looked at him, later in his life he was old and weakening and he then was shrunk away from the outside of him, he then did not have inside him enough to fill him, he was not then a big man to every one who saw him.

As I was saying there are many millions of every kind of men and there are many millions who have in them the kind of being David Hersland had in him. They have it in them some of them, as I have been saying, in all of their living, some have it in them in their eating, some have it in them in their drinking, some have it in them in business and their living, some have it in them in their loving, some have it so much in them that they have arabian nights inside them ; there are many millions of such a kind of them and this is a history of one of that kind of them, of David Hersland and the big ways he had in him.

As I was saying the father of the three of them whose lives we are soon now to be watching, Mr. David Hersland, had come to Gossols to make for himself his great fortune. There was for him, as I was saying, beginning as the whole of living, there was for him in living, eating and doctoring and educating his children and making for himself a great fortune. There were other things in him but they were not for him so important to him, they had not for him so much of beginning. As I was saying ways of eating were always to him living, they were to him always full of beginning and this is a history of the way he tried many of them. As I was saying there are many ways of eating, for some eating is living for some eating is dying, for some thinking about ways of eating gives to them the feeling that they have it in them to be alive and to be going on living, to some to think about eating makes them know that death is always waiting that dying is in them. Mr. Hersland always liked to think about what was good for him in eating, he liked to think about what was good for every one around him in their eating, he liked to buy all kinds of eating, he liked all kinds of thinking about eating, eating was living to him, eating was beginning to him, beginning was all of living in him, always he was interested in changing in having new ideas new ways of eating, eating was living for him, ways of eating were ways of beginning for him, eating was living to him and there are many millions always made just like him, many millions who have always new ways of eating in them, new ways of thinking about eating always inside them, for all of such then eating is living, to them.

There are many ways of thinking about eating, some who are always thinking about eating have not in them any love of eating, some who are always thinking about eating love to have eating going on inside them. Some of each of these kinds of men and women and children have it in them to think about what is good for them in eating, some do not have any such feeling in them eating is an end in itself for them, eating is what they need to content them. This is true of some of them who have not in them much love of the real eating going on in them, this is true of some of them who love the eating always going on inside them.

Mr. Hersland had many theories in him, eating was to him a pleasure when it was going on inside him, but to him that was not the important thing for him. The important thing to him in him were ways of knowing what kind of eating was good for him, ways of having in him new ways of beginning, this was important to himself inside him. Eating was not, to himself, eating, for him, it was living, it was theorising and believing, it was new ways of beginning. He loved to have eating going on inside him and then often, before finishing, he would be filled up, to complete him, with impatient feeling and then he would push eating away from him, then he would be changing, then he would find new things good for him, he would find in eating a new beginning.

Many men and many women and some children are always thinking of what is good for them in their eating. For some of these then eating is living for some of these then eating is dying, some find in ways of eating the continuing of living some find in ways of eating putting off a little longer their ending but dying is always inside them, some of these then, the many men and many women and some children who have it in them to be always thinking about eating about what is good in it for them, some of these then have not in them any love of eating, some of them have it in them to be loving the eating going on inside them,

Mr. Hersland was such a one but to himself it was never his loving the eating going on inside him that was important to him, it was his theories of eating, his changings, his beginning, new ways of finding ways of eating that were good for him, these were important to him.

In Mr. Hersland's ways of eating his children felt it in him that he was often filled up with impatient feeling. They more and more had it in them to know it of him that he loved to have eating going on inside him and more and more they came to know it of him that he, often then, before ending with the eating, would be filled up with impatient feeling and then he would push his eating away from him.

It was in Mr. David Hersland's ways of eating, his ways of doctoring, his ways of educating them, his ways of changing, that all three of his children, each one as they felt themselves inside them an individual being apart from others around them, began to feel it in them that the father of them was big in his beginning and soon then he would be full up with impatient feeling. This, the character in him, made a different impression on each one of the three of them and this will come out in them in the slow history of each one of them. The eldest Martha had it in her to be like him in never finishing but she was not then filled up with impatient feeling, she was not strong in a beginning she was not then as big as all the world as her father had it to be inside him. She had it in her in her later living to be often beginning, to be impatient but not to be full up with such feeling, she had it in her to be like him the father of them but she never had it in her to understand him, she had it in her to irritate in him his impatient feeling she had it in her always to be afraid of him but all this will come out later in the history of her as she grew older as she went away from all of them and then came back out of her trouble to him and always she was like him and always she could not understand him, always she could irritate the impatient feeling that he had always inside him then, always she was in a way afraid of the irritation in him that she always gave to him. The elder son Alfred had it in him not to be like his father in always beginning, beginning was not strong in him, there was more of his mother in him but he had it in him to be always in his later living full up with impatient feeling, he had no bigness in him as the father had in his beginnings, there was never any such bigness in him and always then he was full up with impatient feeling. He had it in him to see the bigness in his father in his beginnings and he had in him a great admiration for the big ways his father always had in him, he had never any such bigness inside him, always he felt it in his father and wanted to have it, too, inside him; more and more in his living he did not have any such bigness in him and later it was enough for him to be filled up with impatient feeling. This made a history for him. The younger one David had a bigness in him it was not like that in the father of them, it was not like the beginnings

that the father always had in him, it was always in young David that
he needed to have in him understanding of everything inside and around
him, that he needed to have in him understanding every minute inside
him why life was to him worth his living. His father never could
understand it in him : his father's being full up with impatient feeling
was always an irritation to him, his father's always beginning was always,
to him, failing, he knew his father had big things in him but it was his
being full up with impatient feeling that was irritating to David and
there was always a little in him of contempt that his father was always
beginning and then he would be full up with impatient feeling and then
he would be changing and then he would push everything away from
him.

The three of them came then more and more to know it about the
father of them that he had a great bigness in him, that he was strong
in beginning, that he would soon then be full up with impatient feeling,
that he would then push everything away from him or go away and leave
it there unfinished behind him, that he then would be changing and
soon then there would be in him a new beginning and he would then
be to every one who saw him as big as all the world around him.

This nature in him came out in him every minute in his living.
He had many things in him. He had in him his wife, she was never
very important to him, she was sometimes there as a tender feeling
inside him, she was a woman for him when he needed to have one, she
had in her an important feeling but this as far as he knew it was only a
joke to him, he never brushed her away from before him, he never
pushed her away from him, she was never existing for him except as
a woman when he had need of one, sometimes as a tender feeling in him,
sometimes as a joke to him, she never had any existence for him outside
of him. When she was not to him inside him she was never existing
for him and so he never brushed her away from before him. She would
do things for the children, sometimes he got angry with her then, mostly
he never knew she did them those things that he did not want that
they should have done for them, he never thought about it except when
he was angry with her for them, mostly she was not in any such way
important to him. Then there was for him in his living then the making
of his great fortune, for that he was always fighting and pushing men
away from around him and trying to brush them away from before him,
in this he had it in him, though here too he was always changing and
beginning, here he had it more in him than in any other thing in his
living, to keep on with his going, he was always changing and beginning
but mostly he kept on going much more than he ever had it in him to
keep on going to an ending in ways of eating in ways of doctoring in
ways of educating the children. In his home being he had around him
the many people who lived in the small houses near them, but they were

not important to him, they were like the governesses and seamstresses and servants and dependents there in the house with him, his being with all of these then was part of his wife's living with them and this will soon now come out in the living his wife did with them and with him. His children were for him, as it often is with men, his children were for him always outside him part of the world he was handling, sometimes playing with them, sometimes angry with them, sometimes loving with them, sometimes using, mostly fighting, and always dropping or domineering.

There were then living together Mr. David Hersland, his wife Fanny Hersland, their three children Martha and Alfred and David and in the house with them a governess a seamstress and the servants, in a part of Gossols where no other rich people were living. Near them were small houses with, for them, poor queer kind of people in them. Soon all of them living in the house came to know many of these, for them, poor queer people near them, some of these came to be a little dependent upon them, some of them came to be nearly all there was then of the three children's daily living that was important then to them.

They were all living, this family then, in a pleasant house in a ten acre place where living was very pleasant for them. They did there a little fancy farming, they had a little grain and fruit trees and vegetable gardening, they had many kinds of trees and sometimes they chopped down one of them, they had dogs and chickens and sometimes ducks and turkeys in the yard then, they had horses and two cows and sometimes they had young ones from the horses and the cows and that was very interesting to all of them, sometimes they had rabbits and always they had dogs, often they had a number of men working for them to get the hay in, sometimes they would catch rats and mice in the barn and that was very exciting to the children and sometimes to the father of them, and all around the ten acre place to shut all these joys in was a hedge of roses and in the summer many people came to pick them and then the family would let the dogs loose to bark at them and scare them, sometimes some one would come at night to steal fruit from them sometimes to steal a chicken and then there would be excitement for all of them and the dogs would be let loose to find the man but the dogs then were mostly not very anxious to get into danger with a strange man, they barked hard and that was all the danger there was for them or for the man who was stealing. And so they went on with the living all of them and mostly then their living was pleasant and interesting.

They were then regular in their living, the father was already then often full up with impatient feeling but in the beginning of their living in Gossols on the ten acre place in that part of Gossols where no other rich people were living, living was pleasant enough for all of them. Living was pleasant enough then for every one of them, living was often then more than pleasant enough for them, it was often full of joy to each one of them then, almost always it was pleasant enough there then to all of them.

Living was pleasant enough for all of them. The father had in him then much of changing much of beginning, he had ways of eating ways of doctoring ways of educating the children and he was always changing in them and this changing and then being full up with impatient feeling was already then a part of all of their daily living. The mother had her life with her husband and her children and her important feeling with the governess and servants and seamstress and the dependents near them, she had in her also her feeling of right rich living. The children, all three of them had it in them to be, in their feeling, more, of them, the poor people who lived around them, than they were of the family living then, at least this other life was, to all three of them, more inside to them then. They had their regular living, they had their school, their father and their mother and the three of them had the relation of each one of the others of them toward them, they had a governess and servants and men working, around them, they had all the joys of country living, and they had each one of them inside beginning then their own individual feeling.

Their father was always to all three of them, as it mostly is with men, their father was always to each one of them outside of them to them, part of the world to fear or fight, now and always for them. Sometimes they were very pleasant with him, sometimes loving to him, sometimes resisting to him, fighting or deceiving, always he was outside of them, always there was in him a danger to them, always they were never certain how far his anger might drive him, how far he would live his own life away from them. They never could have in them any such feeling about a woman or with children, it is only men who give to children this uncertain feeling, they never can know it about one of them how far the anger in him may drive him.

Life was pleasant there then for all of them. Always then in some ways trouble came to be inside in each one of them. As I was saying, in the early days of their living the father had it in him to be changing, to be full up with impatient feeling but this only made a reason to him for making a new beginning. This came out in him every day in his daily living.

As I was saying, they were regular enough in their daily living. The children had their schooling and that was mostly a regular thing with them, then they had various other ways of getting education and in these their father always had new ideas inside him.

All of the three children were beginning to have in them their own individual feeling. This began early in each one of them as it mostly is with children who have freedom in them and a father full up with beginning to commence them. Each one of them had already then their own kind of trouble inside in them, each one of them had soon a feeling about the ways of educating the way of getting new ways for the education of them, about ways of eating, that their father had then and always in him.

All three of them then began to have in them their own individual feeling, there was beginning soon in each one of them the being alone inside, each one of them in their own feeling. They were different each one of them from the others of them in the troubles they had then inside them, in the lonely feeling they had sometimes in them that they were alone each one in them, in the scared feeling they could have in them, in the hurt or angry feelings each one in their own way had inside them. They were different each one of them from the others of them in the troubles they had then inside them, in the lonely feeling they had sometimes in them that each one was alone inside and this was sometimes all they needed to content them. They were different each one of them in the troubles they had then inside them, in the feeling that they had each one of them toward the father of them, toward the mother of them, toward the governess and other people in the house with them, toward the people living in the small houses near them. Each one of them was very different inside from the others of them, in all their ways each one of them had different feelings from the others of them different ways of being alone inside in them, different ways of thinking feeling suffering and playing.

As I was saying, in a way life was regular enough for all of them then in the ten acre place in that part of Gossols where no other rich people were living cut off from all right rich being. As I was saying life was regular enough for all of them for the three children and the father and the mother of them. The children went to public school for their education. Their father had ideas about other things they should learn, other ways of doing besides the ways of the other children around them and it was in such things that he was always beginning.

Then there was their eating and their doctoring and the father always had new ideas inside him, new ways of beginning in ways they should have of eating and the doctoring that was good for children.

They were regular enough then in their daily living. The children were regular enough in their living, they were different each one of them from the other two of them, different in every thing in them for each one of them was of a different kind of being from the other two of them. The father and the mother mixed up in them made of each one of them a different kind of being from the others of them, this will come out more and more in them if they go on living as in old age they go on repeating what is inside them so that any one can know them. In their early living when they are no longer children this nature in them comes out less with repeating and so any one who knows them can know what is inside them. In children as it always is with young living there is much repeating but it is not then so surely themselves they are expressing, in their older living their repeating is then all that there is of them, when they are children their repeating does not tell what is really them, as young grown men and women it is much harder to know what is real in them but always they are telling, slowly they begin repeating, slowly we find it out about them what they have really inside them.

As I was saying they were regular enough in their daily living, regular as living comes to be in later living, regular in repeating but, as I was saying, in the regular repeating in mostly all children there is less that is really from them more that is just part of the regular living around them.

The three children had their regular school living.

There are many ways of taking teaching and each one of the Hersland children had a different way of learning from the other two of them, a different way of feeling about teachers and teaching, a different way of having pride in them and this came out very early in their living, in the regular public school training. There are many ways of having pride inside in one and always in receiving teaching the different kind of pride shows in each one. Martha, Alfred and David each one had a kind of pride in them but it was a very different pride in each one of them, it made a very different relation for each one of them to the teachers in the public school and to the governess at home and to the children around them, to the father of them and sometimes, not very often, to the mother of them.

The three of them Martha, Alfred and David had different ways of having pride in them in taking the teaching they had in school with the other children around them, in taking their father's ideas of things they should learn from the governess and other teachers he had to teach them.

All three of them had many kinds of education because of him. Sometimes they all three would be having just ordinary schooling. Sometimes all three would be having extra teaching, sometimes one or the other stopped going to school to try some other way of education that their father then thought would be good then for that one of them. Mostly though, in their younger living, they had all three of them fairly regular public school training and they had then each one their own feeling toward the life there with the teachers and the other children and this will come out in the history of each one. This will come out in the history of each one of them for I am thinking with each one of the three of them soon now there must be a beginning, I am thinking in each one of them soon there will be a beginning of a history of them from their beginning, and so slowly we can know it about them, each one of them, the real nature in them and the other kinds of nature mixed up in each one of them with the fundamental nature in them.

Mostly then in their young living they had **regular public school** training. Sometimes their father would be strong in **religion** and then this would make for the children complications in their **daily living.**

As I was saying in their younger living there was mostly a regular every day existence for them, in their younger living it was important to them that their father was as big as all the world around him, and it was then in him sometimes a little embarrassment to them, as I was telling, but mostly they liked it well enough the living with him and the things he was beginning and the ten acre place which was full of much joy then for all of them and the people in the small houses near them who were important then to all three of them in their daily living.

In their younger living, it was not very hard on them, their father's way of always beginning, they liked it too, the beginning, and the ending too, that was not so bad then for them, the impatient feeling in him was not then irritable inside him.

They had some troubles with him then in their early living, sometimes in ways of doctoring, sometimes when he thought it was good for all of them to have castor oil given to them, sometimes when he thought a chinese doctor would be good for them, sometimes when he had a queer blind man to examine some one of them ; but all this, and the ways of eating, ways of cooking, he thought good for them, will come out in the history of each one of the three of them, for in each one of them it had a different effect on them in their later living, these new beginnings in all their younger living, beginnings and new ways in doctoring and in ways of eating.

Sometimes in little things it would be annoying to them in their early living, his way of beginning and then never knowing that he was full up with impatient feeling and so had stopped and wanted others to keep on going. Sometimes this would be annoying of an evening. He would want to play cards and the three of them would begin with him, to please him. The children felt it to be hard on them when they would have begun playing cards just to oblige him and after a few minutes with them he would have arise in him his impatient feeling, and he would say, " here you just finish it up I haven't time to go on playing, " and he would call the governess to take his hand from him and all three of the children would have then to play together a game none of them would have thought of beginning, and they had to keep on going for often he would stop in his walking to find which one was winning, and it never came to him to know that he had made the beginning and that the children were playing just because they had to, for him. It was a small thing but it happened very often to them and it was annoying for them.

In their younger living life was pleasant enough for all of them in the ten acre place, though they had a governess and that was not always pleasant to them, their father was not always pleasant for them, their mother mostly was not very important to them. It was true of all three of them then that they were more entirely of them, the poorer people who lived around them, than they were of their mother then, than their mother was of them then, though they were all there was of their mother's daily living then.

Later in their living their father was angry when he saw it in them that they were not comfortable with the people who were always in a right rich living, when they came in contact with them. This feeling the mother never had about them. To her she was always of that right rich being, she never felt it in her that she was cut off from the way of being that was the natural way of being for her, she felt the sense of being important inside her, she never knew that that was different in her than it had been when she was of the old way of living that was natural to her. It never came to her to know it inside her that she had in her a feeling of herself in her that never had been in her and never would be in most of her own family who had gone on with the natural way of living for them. She did not know she had had an important feeling of herself inside her arise in her from being cut off from the natural way of living for her, from knowing the Shilling family and then from having later around her only, for her, poor queer kind of people, and governesses and servants and seamstresses and dependents there in the house with her.

She never really knew it in her that she was not really important to the man who was a husband to her. She never really knew it in her that she was not important to the children who had been once in her. In her later life when she was weak and breaking down inside her she felt it a little dimly in her, now she did not have any such feeling, she had a feeling of herself inside her, she had around her a governess and servants and a seamstress and dependents, she had her husband and her three children. She never knew it in her husband that she was always less and less important to him, she never knew it then that her children were then coming to be more entirely of them, the poorer people who lived in the small houses near them, than they were of their mother then, than their mother was of them then, though to her feeling then they were almost all there was then of her daily living. She never knew it that to the feeling in her of herself inside her her husband and her children were not important to her, they were of her as if they were in her a part of her, they were not important to her in the feeling of herself inside her that had come now to begin to be really in her.

Real country living feeling all three of the Hersland children in their younger living had inside them, a real country living feeling. This they had in them in the ten acre place with the hired men working and the chickens and ducks and fruit-trees and haymaking and seed-sewing and cows and some vegetable gardening. It was to them in their feeling real country living, it was to them earning a living in the hard country way and it was so that they then felt it inside them.

The three children had in many ways then in them the feeling of real country living. Their mother never had this feeling, with her it was always country house city living. In the children it was sometimes a real country living feeling that they had in them, and they were then very really a part of the life around them, of country ways of making a living, of cows and chickens and fruit-trees and hunting, and it was for them then in their younger living not country house city living, it was for them then real country living and country feeling and village life around them and hard-working country ways of earning a living.

The people in the small houses near them had all of them a half and half feeling, a half country and a half city feeling in them.

The three Hersland children had in them a country house city feeling only in their mother's feeling and with the governess and servants and dependents living there in the house with them. As it was true then of all three of them that they were more then of the poorer people around them than they were of their mother's living then, so it was true of the three of them that they had more in them the country feeling of the people around them than they had of the half city feeling that these people had in them. All of the Hersland children had a little too of the half city feeling that the people around them had in them. The country feeling and the city feeling the Hersland children had in them in their being part of the life around them was different than any feeling their mother and the servants and governesses and dependents living in the house with them ever had in any of them. Their father had a feeling more like that in them then, with him it was from his being as big as all the world around him, everything was in him, he had all of it somehow someway a little in him, city feeling, country feeling, and city country house feeling, inside him.

With the people living in the small houses near them Mr. Hersland mostly had in him city country house living, he was important to all of them, the only rich man in that part of Gossols where they were living. He was important to them then, the rich man, and they did not then know him any more than as his children then knew him. He was a pleasant enough useful enough man for them to have living in the big place near them. The queer ways in him never made them think much about him. They knew then more of the daily living of Mrs. Hersland and the children. The men in most of the little houses near the ten acre place mostly, like Mr. Hersland, only came to their houses for eating, for sleeping and for Sunday resting. He did the same, only he was a rich man, a pleasant man enough to them, a useful man enough when they would have any need of him. They never thought much about the queer ways he sometimes had in him, they never had then for him anything in the way of a personal feeling.

He was then for them a city country house person. He had it in him to feel other things inside him, sometimes to feel in him a real country living feeling, sometimes he brushed it all away from him, the country feeling, the city country house feeling living, he was then inside him a city man with city schemes and troubles and men around him, and then he walked up and down and his impatient feeling was irritable inside him and he would be muttering and talking to himself and jingling the money in his pockets then and more and more it came to be true of him that he walked up and down thinking, to himself inside him working, scheming, brushing men away from around him, domineering over them, going another way not knowing inside him that he was leaving them because they were then too many for him.

More and more then in their later living in the ten acre place in that part of Gossols where no other rich people were living there was for him no reality to country living, to city country house living. There was to him then in his later living more reality in the people living then around him, but this will come out in the history of him as each of his children get to know it then about him.

For the children it was in the beginning really country living, for the mother it was always rich city country house living. For the people around them in Mrs. Hersland then it was rich city country house living, in Mr. Hersland city being, in the three Hersland children each one a mixed thing in them of the three ways of feeling, rich city country house being country being and city being, and the mixtures of these three feelings in each one of the three of them to the people in the small houses near them is part of the history of each one of the three of them.

Each one of them had something in them then of real country feeling. In some one of them it was the fruit-trees, in some one the vegetable gardening, in some the cows, in some the chickens, in some the selling things from the place, in some the men working, in some ways in all three of them there was then something of real country living feeling, something of country life earning of a living.

They all three had it in them to have something of such country feeling. They got it in many ways, in hay-making, hay cutting, helping the men working, eating bread and vegetables, fruit as they were picking it, they got it from milking, and butter and cheese making, they got it from the seasons and the things they did to help things growing, they got it in every way around them, they got it in helping ploughing, in helping cut grass, and make the hay into bales for winter storing, they got it from playing Indians and having the darkness come around them, they got it from eating grass and leaves and having the taste in their mouths to bring back such things to them in their later living, they got it in every kind of a way then. They got it from the feeling of the wind around them, when they shouted with it around them, when they crouched down somewhere with it cut off from them, when they helped the men sowing seed with it blowing around them, and when the trees hit their own wood and made that queer sound that they got to have inside them. One can only get the real feeling of wind blowing in the country, in country living. Rain beating, and mud and snow and other ways of feeling the world outside them they can have in city country house living. Strong wind blowing needs real country living to give it a right feeling and this they all three of them each in their own way had then inside them. It was a very different way that each one of them had it in them, a different way too that their mother had it in her, that their father had it in him.

Real country living feeling all three of the Hersland children in their younger living had inside them, a real country living feeling. It was to them then in their feeling real country living, it was to them then earning a living in the country way. It was so that they then felt it inside them. In their later living it was different in each one of them. In Martha this being part of the country village living was not in her later living inside her to her feeling but it was inside her in her being. In Alfred there was in his later living nothing of this in him, not in his being not in his feeling ; he was of his mother then, the feeling she had had in her was what was in him then, the being important to himself inside her, the having in her the right rich being which was the natural being in her. In the younger brother David this early living was made by him into him as he made all his living in him, he made it a part of him, was something in him to be made over inside him to be a part of the whole of him.

As I was saying Mrs. Hersland never had inside her country living feeling nor city living feeling. She did not have such a feeling in her any more than the governesses and seamstresses and servants who lived in the house with her. She had a feeling of being part of the rich right being that was natural to her. She had always in her the feeling of rich city country house living with servants and dependents in the house with her, with near her, for her, poor queer kind of people who were employed by her, who were to her different from her, who were with her to her as they had need of her ; she felt herself inside her important to herself in her with such people always around her. Always more and more she felt herself important inside her. This came to be in her at its strongest inside her in her relation to a governess, Madeleine Wyman. Later it came to be less and less inside her. Later she was weakening inside her and her feeling of importance to herself inside her went out in her. She broke down a little, later, into weakness inside her. She more and more then had no strength in her, she more and more then was not important to her husband who was beginning then to have troubles in him that left him nothing of the tender feeling she had once been for him, she was less and less important to her children who were then so big inside them that she was then always lost among them. More and more then in her weakening she was not of them and superior to them the servants in the house with them and the people in the small houses near them. More and more she was weakening then, the feeling of herself inside her died out of her then. Her husband never thought about her then, she was lost then among her children who were then themselves inside in each one of them and fighting it out with all the world around them, she was not part of their world then, she was lost among them. She was not any longer then important to the servants in the house then. There was not any longer then a governess or a seamstress in the house with them. The people in the small houses near them were always less and less part of the daily living of Martha, Alfred and young David then. Mr. Hersland was the only one important to them then and so in every way the feeling of herself inside her was no longer kept up in her. Soon it all died out of the inside of her, she was weakening then and when all the troubles came to all of them in their later living she died away and left them and they all soon forgot that she had ever been important to them as a wife, a mother, a mistress living among them. One never forgot her in her later living and this was the governess Madeleine Wyman. With her had come to Mrs. Hersland to have it strongest inside her in all the living from the beginning to the ending of her, it had come to her to have in her relation to Madeleine Wyman and the family of Madeleine Wyman the strongest time in her of having a feeling of herself inside, of being important to herself in her.

Mrs. Hersland's living in the ten acre place with a husband, three children, always with a governess, a seamstress and servants in the house with her, and with, for her, poor people around her, was the important part of living to her, the part of living where she was nearest in her to being important to herself inside her as an individual power not only as part of the rich being which was natural to her.

She never knew it in her that it was different inside her than it would have been in her if she had lived in Bridgepoint with her family around her and the natural way of being for her always in her. Slowly the different kind of feeling of herself inside her grew to be more and more in her. It was at its strongest in her in her relation to the governess Madeleine Wyman and her struggles with the family of the Wymans who wanted to interfere with her. It was strong in her when she went a little later to visit at Bridgepoint and had her family around her. She was then herself inside her and that made a kind of a princess of her and they, her family, never knew it about her, she never knew it in her, that it was different inside her because of her having been cut off from the way of living that was the natural way of living for her. This was the end of the strongest time of being important to herself inside her. Then began the weakening of this in her, then began the weakening of the health in her, of herself inside her, of the whole of her. More and more then she broke down into weakness inside her and that was the beginning of her ending and she went on then slowly weakening to the end of her. She died away then and they all soon forgot her. The governess Madeleine Wyman was the only one to keep it in her that Mrs. Hersland once had been strong to feel herself inside her. Madeleine Wyman was married then and had a successful enough life then but always Mrs. Hersland was the most important thing, to her, that had ever been in her.

In their younger living all the three children Martha, Alfred and David, all of them had it in them to be more or less afraid of their father when he was angry or even playing with them. They never knew then how the anger in him might drive him, they never knew when they were playing with him when it might change in him to an outburst and then they never knew how far this burst would carry him and so like most women and all children, even when they would stand up against him, the man near them, they had in their younger living, all of them, more or less fear in them. This was not in all of them then a conscious feeling. They had each one then more or less of fear in them always when with him, when he would be connected to them in their feeling, in their actual doing. They had not then this about them in them as a conscious feeling then each one of them, they did not have then in them while they were connected to him a conscious feeling of more or less fear in them until after each time with him, then they would have more or less in them a conscious feeling in them of the fear that they had always more or less then in them with him. This was more or less true then of all three of them. Later in their living when it had come to be with him that he was all full up with impatient feeling, that then there was nothing in him that was not impatient feeling, then they had not any longer much fear of him, they knew it then about him that he was filled up with impatient feeling, they knew then that the anger in him never would drive him to any last act against them. More and more then as impatient feeling was all that there was of him, less and less then did they have in them any fear of him, more and more then they could stand up against him and he would always give way before them. Martha had always a little left in her even in his latest living of this fear of him, Alfred and David then had no fear of him, they could stand up to him and win out against him with not any fear inside them of where his anger might drive him. This was true of them in his later living, when his wife was no longer in him, when nothing was in him but impatient feeling. Later it went further with him, he was shrunk away then from the outside of him, he had impatient feeling in him but it was then weakness in him he had not enough of that then to fill him, he needed others then to fill him, he was then shrunk away from the outside of him. He needed then a woman to fill him and that was the last part of his living. Martha was then with him, she had come back out of her trouble to him, she was then there taking care of him, she had still a little fear in her of him, she had not then any power in him, she could not fill him, other women did it for him, and so he kept on to his ending.

There are many kinds of men and there are many millions made of each kind of them. The many millions of each kind of them have in them each one more or less of that which makes such a kind of them. Of the kind that Mr. David Hersland was he had a great deal of it in him, later it all turned into impatient feeling inside him, later then it became only a weakness in him, he was shrunk away from the outside of him, he needed others then inside him to fill him.

Mr. David Hersland had it in his strongest living to be as big as all the world around him, it was in him, he was all it in him, it was to him all inside him, he was it and it was to him all always in him. This was the big feeling in him and then he was strong in beginning. This was the biggest time of his living, when this was strong in him his big feeling his being strong in beginning his keeping going even with impatient feeling in him, before all of it in him turned into impatient feeling. This was the big time in his living, and this was when his wife was still in him as a tender feeling, when his children were first beginning to have in them individual feeling. This was the time of such a big feeling in him and then he was strong in beginning. The world around him, all, every moment, in beginning, it was then and it was all in him, and he was strong then and full up with beginning.

There are many millions of every kind of men, there are many millions of them and they have each one of them more or less in them of the kind of man they are and this makes a different being of each one of the many millions of that kind of them, that, the quantity in them of their kind of being, and the mixture in them of other kinds of being in them. There are many millions of each kind of men and other kinds of being are mixed up in each one of each kind of them but the strongest thing in each one of them is the bottom in them the kind of being in them that makes them. The bottom to every one then is the kind of being that makes him, it makes for him the kind of thinking, the way of eating, the way of drinking, the way of loving, the way of beginning, and the way of ending, in him. Other kinds of natures are in almost all men and almost all women mixed up in them with the bottom nature of them, and this mixture in them with the amount they have in them of their bottom kind of nature in them makes in each one a different being from the many millions always being made like him.

There are many kinds of men then and there are always many millions made of each kind of them. There is a kind of them that have it in them to be as big as all the world in their feeling, to be strong in beginning, and that is their kind of men. For such a kind of men the world around them is all in a beginning, for each of them beginning is the strongest thing in them. There are many millions of such a kind of men and they have it in all of them to be strong in beginning. In some of them, and they are mostly weaker in all their living, weaker than some of the other millions made of that kind of them, some of them keep on to their last minute with beginning, they are always a little weaker in their living, they are always to their last ending busy with beginning, some of such a kind of them have a great kind of bigness in them but they are weaker in their living than others of that kind of men, some of such ones of that kind of men have a great kind of feeling in them but it is in them only great in its beginning, it goes out into little things later in them, they must then have it in them to commence a new beginning to be big again inside them, they go on to their last ending in beginning, they are always a little weaker in living, they are always to their last ending busy with beginning. Some of this part of that kind of men have it in them to be big in their beginning, to have then a kind of greatness in them in the feeling they have inside them with beginning, and then it turns into an empty nothing in them, sometimes it turns into a blown up feeling in them, sometimes into a full emptiness that is then all there is of them then and keeps on so inside them to their ending. They are some then who keep on to their last minute with beginning, they are always a little weaker in their living, they are always to their last ending busy with beginning. There are some of the kind of men, the kind that have beginning as the strongest thing inside them, there are many of them many of the many millions of them, there are many of them who so sometime keep on going keep on going a little time with some one thing they have had in them as beginning ; there are some who sometime keep on going with something they sometime had as a beginning, keep on going with it then to their ending. These are some of the many millions of such a kind of men who have it in them to be as big in their feeling as all the world around them. There are some of such a kind of men who have it in them to push some one thing through to an ending something they have sometime had as a beginning, there are some of the many millions of this kind of men who have it in them to push several things through to an ending several things that they have had as a beginning in them. There are some who have something strong inside them that pushes through to an ending what they have in them as a beginning, some have such a success in them. Some have some time almost a success in them, some have something almost as a success inside them and then it breaks down in them, some of such of them try then with a new beginning, some of such of them break down inside them and there is then an end to them. Some have the beginning feeling in them turn into impatient feeling inside them as David Hersland had it in him. All of all the many millions of such a kind of men have it in them some time to be in them as big as all the world in their feeling, they have it in them all of them to be strong in all beginning.

David Hersland had a mixture in him and this will come out clearly in the history of him. As I was saying the biggest time in his living was when he was in Gossols near the end of that beginning when he was making his great fortune, when his wife was still in him as a tender feeling, when the important feeling she had in her then was a kind of joke to him, when she was not important to him but was not yet a trouble to him with letting the children be too strong for her to have them inside her to him, when his children were first beginning to have a little in them of an individual being. At the end of this beginning in him before he came to be full up with impatient feeling there was beginning in him impatient feeling, then his children were beginning not any longer to be part of their mother to him, they were beginning to be part of the world around him that he was domineering, fighting, brushing away from before him, sometimes breaking away from and leaving though he never knew this of himself in him, there was beginning then in him impatient feeling and in a joking way with a little irritation in him he brushed his wife away from before him, he was fighting then or domineering the men around him in his business living or brushing them away from around him or taking another way in a blustering fashion so as not to be beaten by them. This was at the beginning of the ending of his great beginning and this was when his wife had strongest in her her own important feeling. In the beginning of his great beginning he had a little of impatient feeling in him, always ever since he had had finished in him the adolescent being he had had a little impatient feeling in him but up to the beginning of the ending of his big beginning it had not had very much irritation in it for him or for others around him, he was hearty then and everything was in him then in his feeling, he was strong then in beginning, the world around him then to him was all every moment in beginning and he was it and it was all in him, and he was strong then and full up with beginning.

When a man is in the middle of his living it is very hard for any one who knows him, hard for himself or for others around him, for the men around him or his wife or other women or his children or the children who play with them, hard for any one of them to know him. Later

in his living when it comes to be inside him that it all settles down
inside him and he begins repeating in him the whole thing he is then
it is then easy to begin to know him, any one who stays with him then
can learn to know the kind of man he is then.   When a man is in the
middle of his living it is very hard to know him.   Mostly with women
in the middle of their living it is not so hard to know them, it is in them
when they are young women that they are like a man in the middle
of his living.   Anyhow it is very hard to know of most men and to know
it in many women in the middle of their living what there is in them,
what there is as a bottom to them, what there is mixed up inside them.
Slowly, more and more, one gets to know them as repeating comes out
in them.   In the middle of their living they are always repeating,
everybody always is repeating in all of their whole living but in the
middle of the living of most men and many women it is hard to be sure
about them just what it is they are repeating, they are in their living
saying many things then and it is hard to know it about them then
what it is in them they are repeating that later in their living will show
itself to be the whole of them to any one who wants to watch them.
Babies in repeating have not very many different kinds of ways of doing
it in them but growing old men and women in repeating show the kind
of men, the kind of women that is in them.   They show it in them then
which they are of the many kinds of men and women.   Perhaps babies
have it in them to be each one a little different from all the other babies
that are always being made but they have not it in them to have so
many different kinds of them as men and women have it in them.   Babies
have not it in them to show much to any one who sees them in their
repeating the kind they are then.   There are not so many kinds of
babies as there are kinds of men and women.   Growing old men and
women have in them the kind they are of men and women and that
comes out to any one that stays with them in the repeating that more
and more then repeats the whole of them.

Mr. David Hersland in his middle living was in Gossols making
his great fortune.   He had many things then in him, his living with
men around him in his business living, his living with his wife, his
knowing other men and women, his living on the ten acre place in that
part of Gossols where no other rich people were living his living on the
ten acre place with his wife and children and governess and servants
there in the house with him and with poor people in small houses near
them.   All these then came to know him, there was not then in him
yet the certain repeating that makes older men and older women clear
to every one that looks long at them, there was in him then all that
later would break down into repeating.   There was for him then his
business living, there was for him then his children beginning to have
in them individual being, there was for him then his wife and she was

having in her then her most important feeling. Every one who then saw him came a little then to know him but it was not easy then for them and this is a history of how each one of them then felt him.

There was a mixture in him of several ways in which his kind of men have it in them to work out in them the beginning which is the strongest thing in them and the feeling themselves as big as all the world around them. This mixture in him had many ways of coming out in him, in the middle of his living. It was not easy to know it certainly about him then which mixture was most him, always it came out a good deal in him to everybody who saw him or knew him then that he was a man who was in feeling himself inside him as big as all the world around him, that he was the kind of man who has it in him the being strong in beginning. In his middle living it was hard to tell which kind of a way this would work out in him, whether he had it in him to push on to succeeding in some one thing, whether something in him would push itself through to success through all the beginnings in him, whether it would each time break down in him, whether he would break down into weakness inside him, whether several things would come to a finish that he had as beginnings in him, whether all beginning in him would change off into another beginning, whether he would become bland inside him, whether the beginnings in him would break down into impatient feeling, whether there would be several of these things in him. In his middle living not any one could tell anything of this certainly about him.

As I have said once, to the people living in the small houses near them he was then in the big middle of his living, he was, in the beginning of their knowing him, to them, a queer man, with his big ways in buying and his way of owning everything around him to his feeling, they never then had trouble with him, he was then a good neighbor for them to have near them, a rich man to buy from them, they liked him but they had not then any personal feeling for him, he had queer ways in him but they laughed pleasantly for him for he was a rich man and they had a respect for him, he was a good neighbor to any of them who asked him to do anything for them, he was prompt in paying, he was large in buying, he was apart from them, they knew then nothing more about him, his children were a little of them then the people around him then, his wife lived among them the people around him then but above them in her country house feeling, Mr. Hersland was to them a city man and he had a home near them in that part of Gossols where no other rich people were living, to them then he was not living among them, he was a city man to them. They were as I have said about them, these people in the small houses near him, they were in their being half city and half country people. He was to them in the first beginning of their knowing him, a city man for their half country feeling. Slowly they came to know more about him in his country living, they first learned to know more about him as a man with a country house feeling in him, then it came to be for them that they knew him as a city man with a little country living in him, later in his later living they came to know in him city being with their half city feeling and this was for them the end of his living, the end of his being among them.

All men and all women, if they keep on in their living come to the repeating that makes it clear to anyone who listens to them then the real nature of them. In the middle living of most men and many women it is very hard to know them, with some of them it is much harder than with others of them. With women, mostly, it is easier to know them then, for there is with them in their middle living less complete mixing of the natures in them than in most men. They, many women, have not in their middle living so much in their way of being to make it all inside them mix into a whole as most men have it in them in their middle living, they have less in the conditions of their living to make the natures in them mix together with the bottom nature of them to make a whole of them than most men have it then in them. In their middle living there is stronger in them the simple repeating that makes them clear to any one who stays with them, with most of them any one who watches them then can come to know them. With most men, though many millions of the many kinds of them have this less in them, most kinds of men in their middle living are mixed up then to be a whole thing then and so it is harder then to be sure with them what is the bottom nature in them, how far this bottom nature of them will drive them ; and so children can not tell it of them then how far anger in a father will drive him, girls cannot tell it in a man then how far a feeling in him will bring him, business men and men working with him or under him, men he is directing, men who are fighting him, they are like his children, they are never certain in his middle living how far the power in him will carry him, then it begins a little more to break down into repeating in him, then more and more they see it in him just how far the nature in him will carry him, and so more and more then it breaks down into repeating in him and this goes on to the last end of him. His wife, a wife living with a man, knows it earlier about him in her feeling what is the bottom nature of him, knows it sooner about him than his children or the men who are with him in his business living. In the relation a wife has with a man, in loving, in eating, in drinking, in sleeping, in doctoring, there is more simple repeating, and so the wife living with him comes sooner to feel it in him in his middle living what will come to be later his repeating than any one else who can then know him. Mostly she knows it about him just at the beginning of his middle living, mostly no one else comes to be sure about it in him until toward the beginning of the ending of his middle living. This in a wife, most often, is mostly not a conscious feeling but she has it in her to know about him how far the feeling in him will drive him.

One never can know certainly in any one the nature of him when he is a boy or a young man for then there are many things to drive him that are not the nature of him, in the middle living it is only the nature in him that will drive him and this will come out then always more and more in him as he begins then at the beginning of the ending of his middle living to repeat more and more the whole of him.

With Mr. David Hersland then in his middle living, the men who were working with him, the men who were working under him, they all knew it about him that he was as big as all out doors in his feeling inside him, they knew it about him that he was strong in beginning, they never knew it about him then so that they could be certain then in them how far anything in him would go to an ending, how far the nature in him might drive him, how far there would be success in him, if there ever would come to him a breaking down inside him, what it would be that would fill him in his later living, what would be the repeating in his later living that would show the nature in him. His children had it in them to know it sooner about him than the men in his business living, they knew it sooner about him how strong it was beginning to be in him in his middle living that his beginning would break down into impatient feeling. They knew this about him sooner than the men with him in his business living, they knew it sooner about him how far his nature would take him, they learnt it about him from the anger in him but this to them too was in the beginning of the ending of his middle living. They soon knew then that his beginning would break down into impatient feeling, later they learned it about him that the anger in him would never carry him to any last act against them.

Some of the men who were in business living with Mr. Hersland were always afraid of him, afraid of the big ways in him, afraid of his way of strongly fighting, afraid of the big beginning in him, all through their being with him in business living they were afraid of him, they were afraid when with him when he would be beginning things with them. Later they would think, if it ever came that there was an ending in him in his success in making a great fortune, they would perhaps think then that they had always known this about him but in his middle living they could not know it of him, no one could then know it about him which way the beginning in him would work out through him. There was in him then for every one who knew him in his business living the being great in beginning, there was in him always then strong fighting, there was in him then brushing people away from before him, there was a little in him then a turning away from some of them in a blustering fashion as if he were brushing them away from around him though really then he was going away from them so that he could not know it in him that he could not brush them away from before him, there was in him a hearty way of laughing, a strong way of fighting, there was in him his business living, then in the middle of his living very little impatient feeling such as his children just about then were beginning then to know in him. In his middle living in his business working what was for his children impatient feeling in him in their troubles with him was for the men around him strong beginning, strong fighting, brushing people away from before him. All of them knew it about him that he was as big as all the world in his feeling, the men around him in his business living knew this in him because of his big way of seeing, his children felt it in him in the trouble they had in them when they were walking with him and they were ashamed because of the queer ways he had of doing.

There were many different kinds of men that knew Mr. Hersland in his business living and they had many different ways of feeling about the ways he had in him, about his strong beginnings, about his fighting everybody who was not to his feeling in him, about brushing people away from before him when he was going on with his beginning and full up with big feeling. Some as I was saying felt him to be a dangerous man for them, some of these went with him in beginning and then they liked it better to do their own finishing, for them even when he was carrying a beginning through perhaps to an ending the carrying it on by him had for them too much in it of beginning to ever be a comfort to them, some of these then did not fight him they began with him and then they went on in their own way to an ending. He would be then full up with beginning and with fighting, he might be going on too from the same beginning that he had begun together with them, he might be going on too to an ending but with him going on had always in it something of beginning and they left it to him to go on alone with his big feeling. They went on to their own ending. He was strong in fighting but as I was saying he had it in him to turn away in fighting into another direction in a blustering fashion and he never knew it in him that the nature in him would not carry him to the last fighting. He was strong in fighting and he liked it for he felt his strength then in him. He was strong in fighting he was not so strong in winning, more and more then at the ending of his middle living fighting in him turned into impatient feeling inside him, more and more then fighting in him in his late living broke down into weakness inside him. As I was saying he was strong in fighting, he was strong in brushing people away from before him. He would have in him then when he was fighting all the joy of being full up with beginning, he would have then when he was brushing people away from around him all the big feeling of being as big as all the world, inside him. When he was fighting, when he was brushing people away from before him, he was to himself then as if the whole world was in him, he was it, it was in him, there was not any difference then for him of him and all the world around him.

It was a very joyous thing in him this big feeling, everybody who saw him felt it in him, his children it made uncomfortable when they were out with him. The big feeling in him was not in him a big empty feeling, it was to him to be always strong in fighting, not so strong in winning, sometimes then in a blustering fashion he would go another way out of fighting, to himself then always it was that he was brushing others away from him, he never knew it in him that he went in this way out of fighting till his children told him when in his later living his impatient feeling made them angry with him.

It was a very joyous thing in him this big feeling in him, everybody who saw him felt it in him. Everybody who had anything to do with him had a very strong feeling in them about this big feeling in him. As I was saying every one of the many millions of this kind of men have it in them to have some time inside them a big feeling, a feeling of themselves inside them as big as all the world around them. In many of the millions of this kind of men such a big feeling is in them only as beginning inside them it never works out to a finish through them. Some of such a kind of men have it in them to work it through to a finish to a complete thing the big feeling that was in them. There have not been many millions of the many millions of the kind of men the kind that have such a kind of big feeling some time in them who work it out to an ending, in some of them it remains in them as beginning and they never lose it out of them and so it is a strong thing always in them, yes some have it in them through all their living to keep a thing in them in beginning it is always big inside them it is always as a beginning in them it never breaks down into weakness in them it never breaks down into new beginnings inside them it never breaks down into impatient feeling in them, it never comes to be swelled out and then empty in them it remains in them as big as the feeling in them of being as big as all the world inside them to their feeling, it remains in them always as a big beginning. Mr. David Hersland in his being had a mixture in him. There was in him all through his living a big beginning that was always in him to the last moment of his living, more and more in his later living it did not fill him, more and more toward the end of his middle living he was filled up with impatient feeling and the big beginning that was always in him to his ending was not important in him to those who then knew him, more and more to everyone then around him there was to him only impatient feeling but always in him to every one who knew him there was even when he was full up with impatient feeling there was always in him a big thing inside him there was in him a big beginning inside him. And this was in him, a big beginning, until the last of his living. Later in his living when he was shrunk away from the outside of him, when he needed women inside him to fill him, when his impatient feeling had broken down into weakness in him there was still spread out inside him a big feeling and that was the beginning always in him, the beginning that always was in him all through his living.

In his middle living then there were many ways of feeling this mixture in him by every one who then knew him. As I was saying there were many then who felt this big beginning in him and they also felt the danger in him of his strong fighting, fighting that did not carry the beginning in him to an ending, fighting that to his children was impatient feeling, that to some men who fought against him was a blustering turning away from them, that to some other men near him meant a brushing of them away from around him that to some men meant a living thing that they admired in him for it gave to such men a feeling of living inside them, that meant to some women a weakness in him so that they felt it in them that they could manage him by ingratiating diplomatic domineering—mostly in his middle living he brushed these away from around him but they did not lose then the feeling they had in them about him,—that meant to poor people near him a hearty nature in him, that meant to his children in their younger living a thing to make them ashamed when they were walking with him sometimes made them afraid of him and then in his later living made them angry .with him and in his latest living made them take care of him, made his wife feel her power with him and sometimes feel she had no importance for him, made him to the governesses and servants in the house with him a man who would not interfere with them for they could not feel a power in him for the feeling in him to them that in his business living made strong fighting in him they saw it in him in the daily living in the house with him they saw that it used itself up without touching the people he was fighting, there was to them no contact in him and so in the household living he did not count for them, it was Mrs. Hersland who was important for them.

In his business living, among the men who knew him, some were afraid of him, they were mostly not afraid to fight with him they felt it in them that he was strong in fighting and that most of the fighting would hit him, there were many then who were not afraid to fight against him for mostly people felt in him in his middle living that there was no danger in him for people he was fighting, dimly they knew it in them almost every one who then knew him that nothing in him would carry him to any last act against them there was no danger for them then they mostly all of them felt it so then inside them those with whom he was fighting, those whom he was brushing away from around him ; those who felt he was a dangerous man to have with them were men who were with him in his big beginnings and they felt in them even when he was going onward from a beginning they felt it in them that his going on had in it too much beginning to make them feel safe with him, so mostly they would then after a big beginning with him go their own way to ending, they would leave him with the big beginning always in him, they would leave him to his strong fighting to his brushing of people away from him to his going another way away from the man in front of him in his blustering fashion that was to himself a brushing away of the people around him.

He was strong then in beginning, he was strong in fighting, he was always changing, he was very strong in fighting. In his business living this came out in him, it came out in him in all his living, it came out in him in his ways of eating, in his ways of doctoring, in his ways of educating his children. In his business living no one went with him to an ending, always they would somewhere leave him and go on to their own finishing. To the end of his business living he had in him a big beginning, this never broke down into weakness inside him, this never broke down into impatient feeling, he was full then in his later living with impatient feeling and then later with weakness inside him but always in him too was a big beginning and this was in him to his ending. Mostly all the men in business with him went on to their own ending, some later when he was no longer living brought to a finish his big beginning but mostly all of them who were with him in his business living were with him in beginning and then they left him to his fighting, to his brushing people away from around him, to his going away from them in a blustering fashion which was to himself brushing them away from before him. In his younger living when he was working with older men above him he would be brought through them to finish out a beginning he had in him. He was always strong in fighting but then his being strong in beginning with others to bring it to an ending through him made him a big man to all then around him. Later in his living every one mostly left him to his fighting, to his brushing people away from around him to his going another way when as it mostly happened in him the nature in him did not carry him to the last end of fighting.

As I was saying men working with him in his business living mostly went their own way to an ending of the things they began with him. Mostly to all of them there was danger to them in his way of going on to an ending. There was for them too much of beginning in his way of ending. Those who followed with admiration in them were mostly men who had not enough in them of themselves inside them to begin a big thing with him, they were outside him they were outside his business living, they were full of admiration for him, they felt in them part of the big feeling of being as big as all the world around them when they were with him. These men were to him like the people in the small houses near him, in that part of Gossols where no other rich people were living, except that they came closer to him, they were not important to him they were not inside him for him but they were a comfort to him, they liked to know he had been fighting, they liked to know he had been brushing people away from around him, they were always there for him, they were not inside him to him, they were not important to him to his feeling, but they made a kind of support around him when he was resting up from fighting, they made a kind of cushion for him to keep him from knowing when he was through with fighting that he had not been winning. They were beginning to be important to him at the beginning of the ending of his middle living, earlier in his living they were all to him as the people in the small houses near him, in his country house living, he was hearty for them, he was a good neighbor to any one, he was good to do things for any one of them who asked him to do things for them. Some of them in the beginning of the ending of his middle living were more and more important to him as padding, not to fill him but to keep him from knowing it in himself that he was not strong in winning that the nature in him would not carry him to the last end of fighting which is winning, that when he turned away in a blustering fashion he was not brushing people away from him. He never knew it inside him that he was not brushing people away from around him when he went away from them in another direction in a blustering fashion until his children in his later living when they were angry with him for his impatient feeling said it to him. These men then in the beginning of the ending of his middle living were beginning to be important to him, they were then a padding, to him not inside him but around him. These men, some of them then, came to be in him a little like a tender feeling then when his wife was no longer in him as a tender feeling, they knew it always of him that he had a big beginning in him—that this was in him even when he was full up with impatient feeling—when later he was shrunk away from the outside of him, they always knew him to be strong in fighting and this in him made a strong living feeling always inside them to know him. In the beginning of the ending of his middle living some of such men were a little important to him.

As I was saying his children knew it sooner of him than the business men around him that he was full up with impatient feeling that the fighting in him would break down into impatient feeling, they knew it sooner about him than the business men around him that the anger in him would not carry him to any last act against them. His wife as I was saying knew it in her feeling sooner than the business men around him sooner than his children how far the nature in him would carry him, knew it sooner in her feeling how she could manage him, knew it in her feeling how in a way she was not important to him though this last never came to be a conscious feeling till at the ending of his middle living. The governess and servants in the house with him, as I was saying, liked him then in his middle living for his hearty laughing and the big ways he had of buying but they never felt in contact with him, his wife and his children were more real to all of them, this was true of all of them the servants and the governesses as they lived in the house with them, there was less of such a feeling in the governess Madeleine Wyman who was the governess they had with them in the beginning of the ending of Mr. Hersland's middle living, in the time when Mrs. Hersland had inside her the most important feeling of herself to herself in her feeling.

Mr. David Hersland then in his home living had always new ideas about ways of eating, ways of doctoring, ways of educating children, sometimes in a stubborn way he would go on a long time with some one way of them but this was mostly well at the end of his middle living, when his wife was not any longer strong in him, when she was no longer a tender feeling in him, when she was not any longer important to him. His wife had sooner in her than any one that knew him a feeling of how far the nature in him would carry him.   She knew this in her from living with him as a wife to him, from the simple repeating that a man has in him for the woman who is a wife to him.   He never felt it in him as a judgment of him this feeling that made her know about him how far the nature in him would carry him, she was to him never a thing outside him excepting when she was a kind of joke to him, she was always to him inside him, she never had for him any importance for him in her being outside of him, in such a part of her being she was either a joke to him or she was not important to him or he brushed her away from around him.   The men around him in his business living never made him feel in him how far the nature in him would carry him, to himself with them he was strong in fighting with them or against them or he was brushing them away from around him or they were not important to him.   The governesses and servants and the for him poor people near him were never important to him excepting perhaps in his later living when he was shrunk away from the outside of him and he needed a woman inside to fill him and this was beginning a little in him in the beginning of the ending of his middle-living, or else when there were some of them in him a little in his later living as a tender feeling as earlier his wife had been in him to him, or as they were in the beginning of the ending of his middle living important as a padding to him.   So he never knew it in him how far the nature in him could carry him, how he could not come to the last end of fighting, he never knew it inside him that he was not brushing people away from around him when he went away from them in another direction in a blustering fashion until his children in his later living when they were angry with him for his impatient feeling said it to him.   His children were for him not so completely outside him as business men around him, they were not in him as his wife was in him and as later some women and some men were in him, they were not of no importance to him inside him as some men and some women and the governesses and servants and people living near him were to him, they were outside him, they could get at him, in his later living when they were angry with him because of his being full up then with impatient feeling they told him what they thought of him, they made him feel it then inside him and this was all in the ending of his middle living.

A man in his living has many things inside him, he has in him his important feeling of himself to himself inside him, he has in him the kind of important feeling of himself to himself that makes his kind of man ; this comes sometimes from a mixture in him of all the kinds of natures in him, this comes sometimes from the bottom nature in him, this comes sometimes from the natures in him that are in him that are sometime in him mixed up with the bottom nature in him, sometimes in some men this other nature or natures in him are not mixed with the bottom nature in him at any time in his living many of such men have the important feeling of themselves inside them coming from the other nature or natures in them not from the bottom nature of them.

Many men have sometime in their living the important feeling of themselves to themselves inside them, some men have always this feeling inside them, most men have such a feeling more or less in them, perhaps all men and mostly all women have sometime in them a feeling of themselves to themselves inside them ; this comes sometimes from a mixture in them of the kind of natures in them, this comes sometimes from the bottom nature of them, this comes sometimes from the natures in them that are mixed up with the bottom natures of them, sometimes in some of them the other nature or natures in them are not mixed with the bottom nature in them, many of such of them have the important feeling of themselves inside them coming from the other natures not from the bottom nature of them.

Mostly all men in their living have many things inside them. As I have just been saying the feeling of themselves inside them can come in different ways from the inside of them, can come in different ways in some of the many millions of one kind of men from the other millions of that same kind of them.

A man in his living has many things inside him. He has in him his feeling himself important to himself inside him, he has in him his way of beginning ; this can come too from a mixture in him, from the bottom nature of him, from the nature or natures in him more or less mixed up with the bottom in him, in some, though mostly in all of them the bottom nature in them makes for them their way of beginning, in some of each kind of men the other nature or natures in them makes for them their way of beginning.

Men in their living have many things inside them, they have in them, each one of them has it in him, his own way of feeling himself important inside in him, they have in them all of them their own way of beginning, their own way of ending, their own way of working, their own way of having loving inside them and loving come out from them, their own way of having anger inside them and letting their anger come out from inside them, their own way of eating, their own way of drinking, their own way of sleeping, their own way of doctoring. They have each one of them their own way of fighting, they have in them all of them their own way of having fear in them. They have all of them in them their own way of believing, their own way of being important inside them, their own way of showing to others around them the important feeling inside in them.

In all of them in all the things that are in them in their daily living, in all of them in all the things that are in them from their beginning to their ending, some of the things always in them are stronger in them than the other things too always in them. In all of them then there are always all these things in them, ways of being are in all of them, in some of the many millions of each kind of them some of the things in them are stronger in them than others of them in them.

In all of them then in all the things that are in them in their daily living, in all of them in all the things that are in them from their beginning to their ending,—in all of them then there are always all these things in them,—in some of the many millions of each kind of them some of the things are stronger in them than others of them.

There are then many kinds of men and many millions of each kind of them. In many men there is a mixture in them, there is in them the bottom nature in them of their kind of men the nature that makes their kind of thinking, their kind of eating, of drinking and of loving, their kind of beginning and ending, there is then in many men this bottom nature in them of their kind of men and there is mixed up in them the nature of other kinds of men, natures that are a bottom nature in other men and makes of such men that kind of man.

In many men there is a mixture in them, there is in them the bottom nature in them the nature of their kind of men and there is mixed up in each one of them the nature or natures of other kind of men, natures that are each one of them a bottom nature in some of the many millions that there are of men and make of such men that kind of man.

In all the things that are in all men in all of their living from their beginning to their ending there can be as the impulse of them the bottom nature in them, the mixture in them of other nature or natures with the bottom nature, the nature or other natures in them which in some men of the many millions of each kind of men never really mix up with the bottom nature in them. Some of the things all men have in them in their daily living have it to come, in more men, only from the bottom nature in them than other things in them. Nothing of all the things all men have in them in their daily living comes in all men from the bottom nature of them. Eating, drinking, loving, anger in them, beginning and ending in them, come more from many men from the bottom nature of most of them than other things in them but always there are some men of all the millions of each kind of them who have it in them not to have even eating and drinking and doctoring and loving and anger in them and beginning and ending in them come from the bottom nature of them.

David Hersland had a mixture in him. He had as I was saying a big beginning in him a feeling of himself to himself of being as big as all the world around him. As I was saying he had a big beginning feeling in him all through his living to his ending. As I was saying his wife knew it about him in her feeling. She did not have it as a conscious thing in her in him but she felt it about him even before his children felt it in him, how far the nature in him would carry him.

As I was saying, in ways of eating, in ways of drinking, in ways of loving, in ways of letting anger come out from them about little things in their daily living, in ways of sleeping, in ways of doctoring, there is more, in strong middle living, of simple repeating than in other things in the middle living of vigorous active men and women. At the beginning of the ending of the middle living of vigorous active men and women, ways of thinking, ways of working, ways of beginning, ways of ending, ways of believing come to be in them as simple repeating.

In all men as I have been saying there are their own ways of bieng,

in them.   In some men some of their ways of being that more and more in
their later living settle down into simple repeating some of their ways of
being come from the bottom nature of them.   There are some men of all
the millions always being made of men there are some men who have only
in them a bottom nature to them.   From such men, and in all the
millions of every kind of men some of the millions of each kind of
them are such a kind of men they have in them only a bottom nature to
them, all their ways of being come in such men, some of the millions of
each kind of men, come all from the nature that makes their kind of men
that makes the kind of men that have all of them in them as bottom nature
in them their way of thinking, of eating, of drinking, of sleeping, of loving,
of having angry feeling in them, their way of beginning and of ending.
Every man has in him his own way of feeling about it inside him about
his ways of doing the things that make for him his daily living ; that is
the individual feeling in him, that is the feeling of being to himself inside
him, that is in many the feeling of being important to themselves inside
them, that is in some men a feeling of being important to every one around
them, that is in some men a feeling of being as big as all the world around
them.

David Hersland was of such a kind of men, men who have sometime
in them a feeling of being as big as all the world around them.   David
Hersland had a mixture in him.   He mostly came all together from the
bottom nature in him but there was in him too a mixture in him, and this
made him, in his later living, full up with impatient feeling.   There was
in him a mixture in him but with him it made a whole of him.

As I was saying some men have it in them to be made altogether of the
bottom nature that makes their kind of men.   Some have it in them to
have other nature or natures in them, natures that are the bottom nature
to make other kinds of men, and this nature or natures in them mixes up
well with the bottom nature of them to make a whole of them as when
things are cooked to make a whole dish that is together then.   Some have
other nature or natures only as a flavor to them, the bottom nature is
mostly the whole of them, some have other nature or natures in them that
never mix with the bottom nature in them and in such ones the impulse in
them comes from the bottom nature or from the other natures separate
from each other and from the bottom nature in them, in some of them
there is in them so little of the bottom nature in them that mostly everything that comes out from inside them comes out from the other nature
or natures in them not from the bottom nature in them.

There are many things in every man in his living from his beginning
to his ending.   Some of the things in men have it in them to come more
from the bottom nature of them than the other things in them but there
are some men of the millions of every kind of men that have it in them to
have almost nothing coming from the bottom nature of them.   Some of

the things in men have it to come from the bottom nature of men but there are some men of the many millions of every kind of men that have it in them to have nothing coming from the bottom nature of them. Some of the things in men have it in them to come more from the bottom nature of them, some of the things in men have it in them to come in more men not from the bottom nature of them. Some of the things in men have it in them to come more from the bottom nature of them but there are some men of the many millions of every kind of men that have it in them to have almost nothing coming from the bottom nature of them. There is from this on every kind of mixing in men. There is from that every kind of mixing and every kind of keeping separate of the natures in men; in some of the millions of every kind of men there is almost nothing in them in their living of the bottom nature of them, from that there is every kind of keeping separate and every kind of mixing of the natures in men to those millions of every kind of men who have in them only the bottom nature of their kind of men and have almost nothing in them of other kind of nature or natures in them. There is in men every kind of mixing and every kind of keeping separate of the natures in them. There are men who have nothing in them in their living of the bottom nature of them that makes their kind of men, there are men who have in them nothing of any nature in them excepting the bottom nature of them. There is from that every kind of mixing and every kind of keeping separate of the natures in men, from some men some of the millions of every kind of men with nothing in them in their living of the bottom nature of them to those millions of every kind of men who have in them only the bottom nature of their kind of men and have almost nothing in them of other kinds of nature or natures in them.

As I was saying men have in them their individual feeling in their way of feeling it in them about themselves to themselves inside them about the ways of being they have in them. Some have almost nothing of such a feeling in them, some have it a little in them, some have it in them always as a conscious feeling, some have it as a feeling of themselves inside them, some have it as a feeling of themselves inside them as important to them, some have it as a feeling of being important to themselves inside them as being always in them, some have it as being important to the others around them, some have it as being inside them that there is nothing existing except their kind of living, some have it that they feel themselves inside them as big as all the world around them, some have it that they are themselves the only important existing in the world then and in some of them for forever in them—these have in them the complete thing of being important to themselves inside them.

As I was saying in his middle living a man is more simple in his repeating of it in him of his ways of eating, ways of drinking, ways of doctoring, ways of loving, ways of sleeping, ways of walking, ways of having anger inside him than in his ways of having other things in him. A man in his middle living has in him already then simple repeating. It comes then that in his daily living often his wife has it earlier in her feeling how far the nature in him will carry him than anybody around him, not in her conscious feeling, not when she is talking about him, but in her feeling in her living with him.

David Hersland in his daily living had many things in him. He had his own way of loving. The way a man has of thinking, his way of beginning and his way of ending in most of the millions of every kind of men comes more from the bottom nature in him from the way of loving he has in him and that makes his kind of man, other natures are mixed up in him, but mostly his way of loving goes with his way of thinking goes with the kind of practical nature he has in him, goes with his way of working, comes from the bottom nature in him.

Some men have it in them in their loving to be attacking, some have it in them to let things sink into them, some let themselves wallow in their feeling and get strength in them from the wallowing they have in loving, some in loving are melting—strength passes out from them, some in their loving are worn out with the nervous desire in them, some have it as a dissipation in them, some have it as excitement in them, some have it as a clean attacking, some have it in them as a daily living—some as they have eating in them, some as they have drinking, some as they have sleeping in them, some have it in them as believing, some have it as a simple beginning feeling—some have it as the ending always of them such of them are always old men in their loving.

Men and women have in them many ways of living, —their ways of eating, their ways of drinking, their ways of thinking, their ways of working, their way of sleeping, in most men and many women go with the way of loving, come from the bottom nature in them.

Many as I was saying have not anything not their way of loving not their way of thinking coming from the bottom nature in them but coming from other nature or natures in them natures that are to other men and women bottom nature in them and make of them that kind of men and women. Many men and many women have their way of loving and their way of thinking and their way of working come from the mixture in them of other nature or natures with the bottom nature in them. There are many kinds of men and there are many kinds of women and some of the millions of each kind of them have it to be made only of the bottom nature of their kind of them, some have it in them to be made of more or less mixing inside them of another nature or of other kinds of nature with the bottom nature of them, some of them have it in them to have the loving feeling in them with their ways of thinking coming from the other kind of nature or other kind of natures in them not from the bottom nature in them.

Mr. David Hersland had a mixture in him. His wife was in him in his early middle living she was in him then as a tender feeling, when she was outside of him to him she was a little a joke to him, mostly she was not when outside him then important to him, later she was a little important to him because of the children and her resistance to him for them, then a little more and more then there changed in him a feeling of her being a joke to him to his brushing her away from around him, less and less then she was in him as a tender feeling, less and less then was she important to him.

In his earlier living when she first was a wife to him she was a little outside of him she could a little affect him she could a little resist herself to him, she was then in him a beginning as a tender feeling, she was then in him a little like a flower inside him, she was a little then outside him to him, she was then a little important to him as outside him, more and more then this came to be a joke to him, later then she came to be brushed away from around him.

David Hersland had a mixture in him. He was of the kind that have loving in them always in beginning and a little in getting strength from wallowing. In the beginning of his loving these two were mixed up in him and his wife was to him more than beginning more than a woman to him for his daily living she was a beautiful thing to him, she was an amusement to him, she was a pleasure to him to have resisting to him, she was a little in him as a tender feeling. More and more in his living loving was to him beginning until in his latest living he needed a woman to fill him, later when he was shrunk away from the outside of him he needed a woman with sympathetic diplomatic domineering to, entering into him, to fill him, he was then shrunk away from the outside of him he was not simple in attacking he was not really getting strength from wallowing, loving was more and more to him as a beginning feeling. Loving never came to be in him impatient feeling excepting when he felt his wife as outside of him, inside him in her early living she was a tender feeling in him, she was a gentle thing inside him, she was full up with children for him, outside him in his early living she was a pleasant resistance to him, she was a little a joke to him, she could a little manage him by resisting to him, then it came to be that a little more and more she was a tender feeling in him, a little, more and more, she was outside him, she was then more a joke to him when she was outside him for him, she was less and less important to him in her little resistance to him, more and more then she was no longer a tender feeling in him, more and more then she was in him as eating and sleeping when she was inside him, more and more then when she was outside him she was resisting for the children more and more then he brushed her away from around him for she was to him then only the children with no importance in her for him and his children more and more were stronger to do their own resisting were more and more important to be an irritation to him in his daily living could less and less be brushed away from before him by him. And so more and more it came to him that she was in him like his eating and sleeping, she was less and less in him as a tender feeling she was less and less important in him or to him as outside him, she was less and less a joke to him, she was less and less important to him as a resistance to him, she was less and less part of his children to him, and she more and more died away and left him and then she was not in any way important to him, he needed more beginning in his loving feeling to fill him than anything that she could give him, he mostly then forgot about her and that was the end of her living. Loving was always then in the ending of his middle living more and more in him a beginning feeling, he did not then get strength in him from wallowing in loving, he had not in him real attacking, he had in him in loving a beginning feeling, more and more he needed a woman inside him to fill him.

In his country house in his middle living he had in him in his daily living eating and sleeping and drinking and loving and impatient feeling and hearty laughing. He had his wife in the house with him and his children and servants and a governess and near him living in the small houses around the ten acre place where they were living in that part of Gossols where no other rich people were living he had, for him, poor people around him who all liked to have him as a neighbor to them. In his home living he had to him in him his feeling about ways of eating ways of doctoring ways of educating his children, he had in him his wife who was sometimes then in his middle living when his children were first beginning in them their individual feeling resisting to him, she was then still to him important for him, she was then still in him as a tender feeling, she was then still to him when she was outside him a pleasant joke to him, she could then still a little affect him by resisting to him. She was then in her strongest feeling of being important to herself inside her to her feeling, she was then in the strongest living with a man to be a husband to her in the rich way that was the natural way of being to her feeling, with her children still inside her to her feeling, with servants and a governess and a seamstress in the house with her in her daily living and she was of their daily living but above them in her right feeling of rich living, with around her the for her poor queer people near her, with the occasional visiting from rich people who did not live near her to disturb her from the life around her where she was cut off from the right rich living that was the natural way of being for her, and which made in her her feeling of being important to herself inside her and so then in her middle living she had in her the feeling stronger in her than any of her family who had gone on living the life that was the natural way of living for her the feeling of being important to herself inside her.

As I was saying men and women have many of them in them their individual feeling—their way of feeling it in them about themselves to themselves inside them about the ways of being they have in them.

Some have almost nothing of such a feeling in them, some have it a little in them, some have it in them always as a conscious feeling, some have it as a feeling of themselves inside them, some have it as a feeling of themselves inside them as important to them, some have it as a feeling of being important to themselves inside them as being always in them, some have it as being important to the others around them, some have it as being inside them that there is nothing existing except their kind of living, some have it that they feel themselves inside them as big as all the world around them, some have it that they are themselves the only important existing in the world then and in some of them for forever in them—these have in them the complete thing of being important to themselves inside them. Some have it as a feeling of being important in them from things they are doing, from religion in them, from the way of living they have in them, from the clothes they have on them, from the way they have of eating, from the way they have of drinking, from the way they have of sleeping, some from the way loving comes out from them, some from the way anger comes out of them, some have a feeling of importance in them from the kind of living they have in them and the others around them have in them, there are many ways of having a feeling of one's self inside one, there are many ways of having an important feeling in one, there are some who have in them a feeling of importance inside but not a feeling of importance of themselves to themselves inside them then, there are some who have inside them an important feeling in them but not an individual feeling in them, there are many ways for men and women to have themselves inside to them and this is a history of some of them.

Mr. David Hersland had in him a feeling of being as big as all the world around him, he had in him a strong feeling of beginning, of fighting of brushing people away from around him, of hearty laughing, in his middle living of pleasant every day living in his country house living. He had an individual feeling in him but it was the whole of him and the world around that was him to him, he never had in him a splitting of himself to himself until his children in his later living when they were angry with him for the impatient feeling he had in him told him what they thought of him told him how he never came to the right end of fighting which is winning, told him how he went away from those in front of him when to himself he was brushing people away from around him. David Hersland had an individual feeling in him, it was being as big as all the world around him, it was being big in beginning. In the ending of his middle living his wife was not important to him, she did not give to him anything in him of individual feeling. In the ending of his middle living he got it more and more from his children, a little from the governess and servants in the house with him, a little from the people living near him. At the ending of his middle living his wife was not any longer important to him she no longer gave him to himself inside him individual feeling.

Some men have it in them in their loving to be attacking, some have it in them to let things sink into them, some let themselves wallow in their feeling and get strength in them from the wallowing they have in loving, some in love are melting—strength passes out of them, some in their loving are worn out with the nervous desire in them, some have it as a dissipation in them, some have it as clean attacking, some have it as a beginning feeling—some have such a feeling always in them, some have it as the ending always of them, some always are children in their loving grimy little dirt then fills them, some are boys in their loving all their living—in their loving reckless attacking is strong in them, some are always young men in their loving, some have it in them like regular middle age living in them, some are old men in loving and this is in them all through their living. There are many kinds of loving in men, more and more this will be a history of them, there are many ways for women to have loving in them this will come out more and more in the history of women as it is here to be written, there are many ways for men to have loving in them, there are many ways that loving comes out from them, there are many ways for women and for men to have loving in them, this is a history of some of them, sometime there will be a history of all of them. There are many kinds of men and many millions of each kind of them, there are many ways of loving that men have in them and their way of loving makes their kind of man, there are many ways of loving in men and having loving come out from them and this comes in many of them from the nature of them their bottom nature in them that makes their kind of men, sometimes from the bottom nature in them mixed with the other nature or natures in them natures that are the bottom nature, the way of having loving in them, of other kind of men. There are many ways of having loving in them in men, there are many ways of having loving in them in women, more and more there will be a history of them, sometime there will then be a history of all of them.

David Hersland in his loving was of his kind of man having loving as beginning in him having loving as getting strength from wallowing, he was of his kind of man but loving was not very strong in him. He was in his loving, of his kind of man, not very strong in loving. Loving was in him always as a part of daily living but was not so very strong in him, not so strong in him as in many millions of his kind of men, there was more in him of being strong in beginning, of being to himself as big as all the world around him.

In his beginning family living his wife was in him as a tender feeling, she was a woman to him, she was a tender feeling inside him, she was a little a resistance to him and a little a joke to him, sometimes a leading for him for in her beginning with him she had a little a power to control him but always this was less and less in her for him.

David Hersland did not have it in him to be so strong in loving as many men of his kind of men have it in them. Many men of his kind of men have it in them to need the woman as a warm feeling inside them and she has always then a power in her over him; all men who have this nature in them the getting strength in wallowing as the bottom nature of them and with a beginning feeling too always then in them have it in them in their middle living to have a woman in them in their feeling as a warm thing in them, in some of them as a flower in them to their feeling ; some have loving then more and some less in their living. In his later living David Hersland had more need of a woman in him but that was not to be as his wife was in him a tender feeling a live thing in him it was to fill him up where he had shrunk from the outside of him, it was another kind of woman he needed then, not a beautiful thing inside him to be in him as a tender feeling but a thing to be alive, domineering, diplomatic, moving, entering under his skin by feeling herself him managing him and important to him in her filling him where he was shrunk away from the outside of him.

In the beginning of his living his wife was to him a certain power for him, inside him a tender beautiful feeling in him, outside him a joke to him and a resisting thing to him in little things for the ways he had in him, always having children in her for him.

There are many ways of family living, there are many ways of being a man to a wife, to his children, and to the servants living in the house with him, of being the wife to her husband in her living, being to her children and to the servants and dependents of her daily living, and then the children and then the servants to all of them. Mr. Hersland had his way of feeling about Mrs. Hersland and that is clear now in his feeling from the beginning to the ending of his middle living and then she died away and left him. In the beginning of his middle living she was a little a joke to him in her resisting and she had a little power in him then for the children, later she a little woman was with weakening inside in her living was lost then among the father and the resisting children, she was a little thing then to them and lost among them and more and more then she was not important to them and then she died away and left them. In her feeling for the servants and governesses and seamstresses in her daily living she had more feeling of herself to herself inside her in her feeling than in any other part of her living. She was with them outside him to her husband then, not very important to him, sometimes with her ways with them then a little a joke to him but mostly she had her own way then and then sometimes in a blustering fashion he let her do her own way while to himself brushing her away from before him. In her living with the servants and governess and seamstress in her daily living she had a feeling of herself to herself inside her, this was more of an individual being in her than ever had been in her when she was leading with her own kind of people around her the right rich living which was the natural way of being to her. She never to herself was cut off from the living that was the natural way of living to her but in her daily living that living did not touch her, she had her daily living with only dependents around her, she was of them and above them and that gave to her her feeling of herself to herself inside her, cut off from the equal living that was the natural way of living for her.

Her children in their younger living were to her still inside her, later they never gave to her any feeling of being important to herself inside her, more and more they were too large around her, she could suffer but they were not important in her in her feeling of herself inside her.

Being important to one's self inside one. Being lonesome inside one. Making the world small to one to lose from one the lonesome feeling a big world feeling can make inside any one who has not it in them to feel themselves as big as any world can be around them. Being important inside one in religion can help one loose from one the lonesome feeling a big world can give to one. There are many ways of losing the lonesome feeling a big world around can give to one. Many lose it before they know they have one, many all their lives keep their world small and so they never have in them such a lonesome feeling, some need religion in them to keep them from being lost inside them from having too much in them a lonesome feeling and a big world too big for them around them, some have in them a superior sense that makes the big world around them not strong enough to give then to them a lonesome feeling inside them, some have just a busy feeling in them and that keeps them from lonesome feeling in them, some never have it come to them that there is a big world around them, there are many who never have in them any such lonesome feeling inside them their living fills them they and their family and the people around them, but many in their living find it at some time in them that they have a lonesome feeling in them ; almost all men and almost all women, and mostly all of them when they were children, have such a kind of lonesome feeling at some moment in their living.

The important feeling of one's self to one inside one in one's living is to have in one then not anything of such a lonesome feeling. Sometimes in many women and some men it is not a lonesome feeling it is a weakening in them and somebody then takes care of them, in more women there is what might be a lonesome feeling as a weakening in them and then some one takes care of them or they die away then and so escape their lonesome feeling. Many women have it in them to float off into weakening, to lose themselves in religion and so escape from any lonesome feeling. Many women have it in them to feel that it never can happen to them the last end of trouble for them, they have in them the feeling that the world can never really be too much for them, this in many of them is religion in them, they are not important to themselves inside them, they are part of the important thing and in that they can never have the last end of evil coming to them, there are many women who have in them not an important feeling of themselves to themselves inside them but they have in them the sense that the last end of a bad thing cannot destroy them, some one will take care of them, something will save them, despair can never really fill them, they can never have in them the complete sense of a lonesome feeling in them ; it is like the feeling Mrs. Hersland had in her in her feeling that she was never really cut off from good rich right living which was the natural way of being to her, the for her natural way of living.

Mrs. Hersland had in her different ways of having herself inside her, of having important feeling in her. A feeling of herself inside her would never have come to be in her if she had gone on living in the way that was natural for her. Being important to herself inside her first came to be a little in her from the knowing Sophie Shilling and her sister Pauline Shilling and the mother Mrs. Shilling, later it came to be stronger in her from the living with the governesses and seamstresses and servants and dependents and being with them but above them all the time every moment of her living, not cut off to her feeling but really cut off in her living from the rich living that was for her the natural way of being.

Many women have in them the way of feeling that makes it for them that the last end of a bad thing cannot come to them, the last end of losing cannot come to them, the last end of trouble cannot destroy them ; many of such of them have not it in them to have an important feeling of themselves to themselves inside them, they have a feeling that they are a part of important being and the last end of a bad thing cannot destroy them, despair never can fill them, somehow something some one will then take care of them, the last end of a bad thing can never to the feeling of such ones ever come to really destroy them. Many of such ones have weakening in them and some one then takes care of them or else they die away and they never know it inside them that the last end of a bad thing has destroyed them, to themselves then in dying despair does not fill them, something to the last moment of their living something someone to such of them then in the last moments of their living will take care of them, but they are weakening and they are dead then but they have not had the lonesome feeling, despair has not ever been really inside them. Many have in them such a feeling, many have it in them as a religion. Many women who have never in them a really lonesome feeling have not it in them the thing that keeps it out of them as weakening they have it in them as resisting, they have it in them as superior feeling, they have it in them as going on always in living, as managing everything that can touch them, as being busy every moment with something, despair can never fill such of them, they never have in them a really lonesome feeling.

There are many ways then for many women not to have in them ever in their living anything of a really lonesome feeling inside them. There are then many ways of not having room in them for such a lonesome feeling, there are many ways of losing it out of them when it is a little in them, there are many ways of having such a lonesome feeling, there are some ways of having such a lonesome feeling always inside in one. Mrs. Hersland had in her then in her middle living a real feeling of being important to herself inside her in her feeling. If she had gone on in the living that was the natural way of being for her this never would have come to be real inside her, this would have been in her a real important feeling from the living that was natural to her but never a really important feeling of herself to herself inside her. She always would have had in her a feeling inside her that in her mother came out in the dreary trickling that was, almost all her later living, all that was of her. A little of such a feeling there would have always been in the daughter if she had gone on living the life that was the natural way of living for her but such a feeling would never come to be in her as it never came to be in her mother a feeling of herself to herself inside her, a feeling of herself to herself as important inside her. Some of her sisters and one brother had a little of the important feeling of the father, he had had a being that in any kind of living would have given a feeling of himself to himself as a religion. Mrs. Hersland had not in her any such a thing inside her, she had in her only the feeling that gave to her mother the dreary trickling that made all her, this in the daughter never had in it sadness and sorrow inside her it was in her a gentle pleasant timid sometimes an angry sometimes hurt feeling in her, in the living that was not the natural way of living for her it came to be inside her a feeling of herself to herself as important in her.

She had then in her, in her middle living it was strongest inside her, a feeling of herself to herself inside her. Once this came to be in her almost a lonesome feeling inside her but it really was not real enough in her, it did not come enough of itself from inside her, it never came to be altogether really a lonesome feeling in her.

There are very many ways for women to have loving in them, some have loving in them for any one or anything that needs them, some have loving in them from the need in them for some other one or for something they see around them, some have a mixture in them. There are some who have really not any loving in them. The kinds of loving women have in them and the way it comes out from them makes for them the bottom nature in them, makes them their kind of women and there are always many millions made of each kind of them.

Mrs. Hersland like almost all women had different things in her for loving. For her her children when they were little things around her it was not to her that they had need of her they were to her a part of her as if they were inside her, as they grew bigger and had their individual living in the house with her as they did not then need her to fight out their daily living with their father they did not feel any importance in her, they were for her then no longer a part of her, she had then weakening in her, she was a little thing then and they were so large around her, they were then struggling with themselves and with their living and with their father, she was weakening then and more and more they were not a part of her, she had not loved them because they had need of her, they were a part of her, then they were all struggling around her, she was a little thing then with weakening in her, more and more then they forgot about her, they were all struggling then around her, they were all of them having in them their individual living, they were all big then and she was a little gentle thing and lost among them and then she died away and left them. For her then with her children she was not of them who love those who have need of them nor of those who love any one near them because they have need of them. Some women have it in them to have children as part of them as if they were part of their own body all the time of their living. Such never have in them an important feeling of themselves inside them from the children that have come out of them, some of such of them can have it in them an important feeling from their children as it makes of them a larger thing being all one themselves and their children. Mrs. Hersland was of such of them of those who have in them not any important feeling of themselves inside them from their children. She was of such of them, the important feeling she had in her living came a little from her husband and more from the governesses and servants and dependents living in the house with them. She could not have in her a feeling of herself inside her from the children around her, they were to her like rich right living, they were a natural part of her, they could never give to her a feeling of herself to herself as important inside her. They were to her of her as her family living in Bridgepoint had been of her, important to her because they were her they were never cut off from her as she was never to her cut off from her the way of living that was the natural way of living for her.

Some women have it in them to love others because they need them, many of such ones subdue the ones they need for loving, they subdue them and they own them ; some women have it in them to love only those who need them ; some women have it in them only to have power when others love them, others loving them gives to them strength in domination as their needing those who love them keeps them from subduing others before those others love them. This will come clearer when this kind of women comes into this history of many kinds of men and women.

Mrs. Hersland was not of these two kinds then, she had a gentle little bounty in her, she had a sense in her of superior strength in her from the way of living that was the natural way of being to her, she had a larger being from the children who were always to her a part of her. She had in her a little power from the beauty feeling she had for her husband in his living with her ; she was for him then a tender feeling in him, she was for him then a pleasant little joke to him resisting to him, she was to him a woman for his using as she was to herself part of her children, that was the simple sense in her that never gave to her a sense of being important to herself inside her.

As I said once about her she had it a very little in her to have a very little sense of herself to herself inside her from a little power she felt in her with her husband when he first married her. She had then in her a little resistance of herself inside to him then, she was not yet then a joke to him when she had this little resistance in her, this little resistance of herself in herself in their early living together. More and more then it came to be to him a joke for him, more and more then her resistance to him was not of herself in herself to him, it was for the children and that was not a straight feeling of herself in herself inside her resisting, that was not to herself a resisting, that was getting something from him for the children, this never was in her an important feeling, always up to the last end of her weakening there was a little left over in her of her resisting to him the feeling of herself inside her, that never had anything to do with the children not when they were young and she was resisting so that they could have what she felt they should have in their living not when they were older and doing their own resisting and when they were all big, then, and she was lost among them. She never for her children had inside her any important feeling, she had when managing for a servant or a seamstress or a governess an important feeling, she had when a little resisting to her husband in their early living an important feeling. This little resisting in her in their early living together was the first faint beginning of herself to herself inside her the first beginning in her of herself inside her as an important feeling in her, this never went quite out of her even when she was weakening and had such a feeling very little in her, always it was there as a feeling left over, she always to her dying had it a little in her.

The kinds of feeling women have in them and the ways it comes out from them makes for them the bottom nature in them, gives to them their kind of thinking, makes the character they have all their living in them, makes them their kind of women and there are always many millions made of each kind of them.

Some women have it in them to love others because they need them, because these somehow are important to them because somehow these they have for loving belong to them, many of such of them subdue the ones they need for loving they subdue them and they own them ; some of them who have it to be of this kind of women have it in them to be almost of no importance to those they have around them in their living, to have the children belong to them as a part of them inside them, these are of the kind of them who always own their children who subdue those they need in living but these of this kind of women have it to have this that is them very lightly in them and Mrs. Hersland was of such a kind of them, these have it in them to be it so gently in them that it never comes out in them, with some it comes out a very little in them, with some it comes out sometime in their living, these then have it to be so timidly in them that their children are only a part of them it is with such of them only in such a way that they can ever own them, some of such a kind of them have it all so peaceably inside them that they have not in them the feeling of being themselves inside them, it takes some one around them to need them to be owned by them, to make such a kind of one own them, to make them feel it inside them that they are themselves inside them, to give to them anything of an important feeling. There are then this kind of women and many of them are very dependent all through their living but a little in them is an independent feeling and this comes out in them when there is any one around them who makes them own them, they have it in them then a feeling of themselves inside them, they need to have around them to have in them such a feeling of themselves inside them, they need some who make them own them and to such a one they are important any moment in their living. Mrs. Hersland had a very little such a feeling with her husband when she was first married to him, she had it in her when she was a little resisting to him; she never would have had much more in her if she had gone on living the life that was for her the natural way of being, she had it a little more in her feeling with the Shilling family in her hotel living, it came to be strongest in her living with a governess and a seamstress and servants in the house with her and to her, poor people around her, with always inside her country house feeling of right rich living, with nothing in her daily living being of such a living which was the natural way of living for her. She had it then in her to feel herself inside her and it was then strongest in her and came out in her with the governess Madeleine Wyman who was for her the one who in all her living was the one whom she had power over, not as part of her as her children were to her, but as outside of her. She fought with the family of Madeleine Wyman for her, she had a feeling then of herself inside her.

There are then two kinds of women, those who have dependent independence in them, those who have in them independent dependence inside them ; the ones of the first of them always somehow own the ones they need to love them, the second kind of them have it in them to love only those who need them, such of them have it in them to have power in them over others only when these others have begun already a little to love them, others loving them give to such of them stregnth in domination. There are then these two ways of loving there are these two ways of being when women have loving in them, as a bottom nature to them, there are then many kinds of mixing, there are many kinds of each kind of them, some women have it in them to have a bottom nature in them of one of these two kinds of loving and then this is mixed up in them with the other kind of loving as another nature in them but all this will come clear in the history of all kinds of women and some kinds of men as it will now be written of them.

Mrs. Hersland then was one of the one kind of them, of the first kind of them. In the Hersland family living during the middle part of the family living, when the children were beginning to have in them their individual living, when Mrs. Hersland was beginning to have strongest inside her her own important feeling, when Mr. Hersland was strongest in beginning and making his great fortune, during this middle portion of their family living they had three governesses in the years of living before the children were grown too big to have any need of such a person around them and each one of them was of another kind of woman and this will be a history of each one of them. There were many other women in their living, some of one some of another kind, some with mixtures in them, some were cooks and some were seamstresses around them, some were dependents in the house with them, some lived in little houses near them in that part of Gossols where no other rich people were living, and some were of the family or friends of some of such ones of them and this will be a history of all of them. There are many kinds of women then and many kinds of men and this then will be a history of some of the many kinds of them.

Many women have at some time resisting in them. Some have resisting in them as a feeling of themselves inside them. In some kinds of women resisting is not a feeling of themselves to themselves inside them. In some kinds of women resisting can only come from such a feeling. This makes two different kinds of women and mostly all women can be divided so between them. Patient women need to have in them such a feeling to be resisting, they need to have in them a feeling of themselves inside them to be really resisting to any one who owns them. Attacking women with weakness as the bottom of them have not it in them to need such a feeling for resisting, resisting is natural to them, it covers up in them the weakness of them. Concentrated women with not any weakness at the bottom in them do not need to have in them such a feeling, these are made up of resisting, concentration with them makes the whole of them makes for them the strength such a feeling as themselves inside them gives to patient ones to make resisting possible for them, attacking feeling gives it to others who really have weakness in them as the bottom of them. Such concentrated women have never in them any such resisting in them, yielding is the whole of such ones of them. This needs very much explaining, this makes a history of every kind of woman, this is a history of only a few kinds of them.

Many women then have resisting in them, many women have attacking in them, many women who have resisting and attacking in them have weakness as the bottom of them, some have not any such weakness at the bottom of them. These last mostly have much concentration of themselves inside them. Some women have not any attacking or resisting in them, some of such of them can have it in them when they have come into them a feeling of themselves inside them, some never have in them anything of such a feeling. Many women then have resisting at some time in them. Many women have religion in them, there are many kinds of women and each kind of them has it in those of them that have religion in them to have it of the character of them, mostly it is in them like the bottom nature that makes their kind of them that makes their kind of loving, their kind of resisting, if they have resisting in them, their kind of religion.

Mrs. Hersland never had her religion to be in her like his in her father, a thing to give to her a feeling of herself inside her, religion with her went with what would happen in her daily living for her, was in her not anything of resistance inside her, was simply a part of the gentle feeling in her like her children inside her, like the rich right living that was the natural way of living for her.

As I was saying many women have it in them to feel it inside them that the last end of a bad thing cannot come to them, that the last evil thing will not destroy them ; this is a common feeling with women who have in them resisting or attacking as the natural thing in them with a weakness at the bottom of them, these women have not in them a superior feeling, they have it in them that no last bad thing can overwhelm them that is to their resisting and at the same time the weakness of them gives to them the feeling that something some one will take care of them. This is in many of them a religion in them.

Mrs. Hersland was not such a one a last end of a bad thing could win and she would be hurt not angry when it had happened to them, she could be angry when she had a feeling of being herself inside her and so could then have resisting in her but this could never be in her in any real trouble or sorrow that came to her or to the children who were a part of her, then there was no important feeling of herself inside her, then there was no resisting in her, then she had a resignation to the pain that killed her, that was all the religion she had in her. Her mother had had always such a trickling sadness in her, this was all of her, this was all religion to her. Her father had had a feeling of himself inside him to make religion for him, he was all to himself always inside him he was the complete thing of such resisting, it was in him all religion, all religion was him he had it so all inside him. Mrs. Hersland had it then a little in her to have resisting in her, a feeling of herself inside her, she could then have anger in her but this could never be in her in any real trouble or sorrow that came to her or to the children who were a part of her, then there was no important feeling of herself inside her, then there was no resisting in her, then she had a resignation to the pain that killed her, that was all the religion she had in her.

As I was saying women who have resisting or attacking with weakness as the bottom of them never believe that the last end of a bad thing can come to them, that anything can really drown them, they have aggressive optimism in them, some of them then have aggressive optimism in them they have mostly all of them in some way religion in them, some have almost not any bottom weakness in them, some are all weakness inside them they have almost no attacking in them, sometimes with such of them their weakness makes them resisting, later this will be a history of several of all these kinds of them.

Some women have it in them to subdue those they need in loving. Madeleine Wyman the last governess was one of such of them and this will be a history of her living, with the Hersland family, with the mother, the father and the children.

The Herslands had a governess, a seamstress and servants living in the house with them. Mostly the Hersland children in their younger living were more entirely of them, the poorer people who lived around them, than they were of their home living. This was true of them, all through their younger living, all through the time they had governesses around them, their mother and their governesses never really knew it about them.

To begin then with beginning of the living of the Hersland family in the ten acre place in that part of Gossols where no other rich people were living.

There was then Mr. Hersland in the middle of his middle living, Mrs. Hersland in the beginning of the strongest time of being to herself inside her in her feeling, the three children in the first beginning in them of individual feeling. There were then the servants living in the house with them, a governess and near them in the small houses around them poor, for them, queer people to make for them their daily living.

They had foreign women as servants in the house with them when they could get them. Sometimes they could not get them. They had three governesses in their whole living in Gossols before the children grew too old to have one. One was a foreign born, two were american. The seamstresses were always foreign american, sometimes it was the family near them, sometimes it was one in the part of Gossols where rich people mostly were living, and then there was another one not near them but who would come sometimes and stay in the house with them. Mrs. Hersland with all of them had her important feeling, she had it in getting them, in keeping them, and whenever she had to get rid of one of them. She had always in her with them an important feeling, sometimes she had an angry feeling with them, sometimes a resisting feeling, she never let any interfering come between her and her acting toward them, she was always of them and above them, she had all of her feeling of herself to herself from them.

Many women have a feeling of themselves inside them from servants around them. There are many ways of having such a feeling in them. This is a long history of one of them.

Many servants get to have in them something that is almost a craziness in them, many have a very lonesome feeling in them not a lonesome feeling of themselves inside them just a lonesome feeling that makes queer, sometimes a little crazy women of them. This is in many of them. The irishwoman and one of the italian women had this a little in them. This makes them good fun for children living in the house with them. The children tease them, they are good to children around them, they always have to be sent away all of a sudden. The irishwoman and one of the italians was of this kind of women. The other servants were always steady women, each with their own way of being in them and this is now a history of all of them. This is a history of them and the seamstresses and the governesses and any troubles any one of them had with the others living in the house with them. This is a history of all of them and of the kind of important feeling Mrs. Hersland had in her from all of them and of the feelings the children each one had for each one of them and the relation each one had to Mr. Hersland.

Mrs. Hersland then was of the kind of women who have resisting in them only with a feeling of themselves inside them, Mrs. Hersland was of the kind of women who have dependent independence in them, Mrs. Hersland was of the kind of women, though she had this to be in her so timidly inside her so gently within her that mostly nobody ever knew it to themselves about her, she had it in her to be of the kind of women to own those they need for loving, to subdue any one who needs them to be important to them. She was then of them who have it in them not to have weakness as the last bottom of them, not to have it in them that the last end of a bad thing cannot come to them, she could have an ending, she could feel this in her dying, she could feel it in her weakening, she could feel it in her children when they were big and struggling and she a gentle little woman was lost among them, she never had in her an important feeling from her children, she had it in the living in Gossols in that part where no other rich people were living.

There are then two kinds of women, there are those who have in them resisting and attacking, and a bottom weakness in them, women with independent dependence in them, women who are strong in attacking, women who sometimes have not bottom weakness in them, some who have in them bottom weakness in them and this inside is a strength in them when they have children when they have strong loving in them when it is in them in such of them a fine sensitive weakness inside them, there are then such ones of them women who need others around to love them before they have any power in them from the weakness in them, in such of them attacking is a power in them but not when they meet with real resisting, the bottom weakness in them is only a power in them when those around them love them, so only can these have any power in them ; all these then all these women have not it in them mostly to believe that it never can come to them the last end of a bad thing to destroy them. All these then make one kind of the two kinds there are of women, the two kinds too there are then of men, and there are many kinds of such of them many strengths in them of this strength and weakness in them, many mixtures in them of the independence and dependence in them, many mixings and sometimes a mixing in the top of them with the other kind of nature of some men and women the dependent independent kind in men and women but more or less it is in them in all of this one kind of them it is in them to have independent dependence in them, it is in them to have attacking in them, to have aggressive optimism in them, to not believe the last end of a bad thing can come to them and destroy them, and then to have weakness as the bottom of them ; and in many of them this weakness is all there is to them, in some of them attacking is all there is of them.

The other kind of women and there are many kinds of such of them in the many millions always of women, this other kind of them need to own the people around them when this nature is strong in them ; they have many of them, a dependent patient way of living, but with the dependent nature in them they have never such of them, a feeling of themselves inside them, this comes out in them only with the bottom independence in them, when they feel themselves resisting, when it comes to them to own themselves inside them, when they own some one around them, some of such of them never have such a moment in their living, some of such of them never feel themselves inside them ; there are then always many women living, there are then these two kinds of them, this is now a history of some of each kind of them, sometime there will be a history of all of each kind of them and that will then be a history of all women who are living, of all the many millions who ever were or will be living and then there will begin a history of all the men and the two kinds of them for there are in men the same two kinds of them like with women and it works out differently a little in them for they are men and have themselves mostly more inside them in their living, there are then these two kinds in women and in men and always every one is of one kind or the other kind of them.

In their middle living in that part of Gossols where no other rich people were living the Hersland family had with them only women in the house with them. As I was saying servants often have it in them to be a little queer and children like to tease them, they have this queerness from cooking, from cleaning and from their lonesome living, from their sitting in the kitchen, from having a mistress to direct them, and children to tease them ; the Irishwoman and one of the Italian women that were cooking once for the Hersland family in their middle living had this queerness in them.

They had had then mostly in their living german women as servants in the house with them, sometimes they could not get them, once they had an Irishwoman, twice Italian women, once a Mexican. The Irish woman and one of the Italian women had a little queerness in them, the queerness that comes from being a servant and cooking and sitting alone in a kitchen and having a mistress to direct them and sometimes children to tease them, these had to be sent away all of a sudden.

Mostly the german women were very steady women, they did not have anything of such a queerness in them, sometimes the german girls they had with them were very young women and then Mrs. Hersland had to train them, some of such of them had natures in them that in their later living would come, from much kitchen sitting, from much directing of the mistress of the house to them, from much teasing from the children in the house with them, would come to make of them a queerness inside them that would make it come to them in their later living to be always sent away all of a sudden. In the early living of such ones they would not be sent away all of a sudden but the mistress of such ones would not then be sorry to lose them.

There were then as I was saying, when Mrs. Hersland could get them foreign servants in the house with them, there was always a governess in the house with them, there was often a seamstress staying in the house with them. There was always a man working in the garden but he never lived in the house with them.

As I was saying in most of their living they had german servants, but sometimes they could not get them, once they had an Irish woman cooking for them, twice Italian women and once a Mexican.

The german servants who lived with them mostly stayed a long time with them even those of them that were not altogether satisfying because until Mrs. Hersland had an angry feeling about some one she would never dismiss any one and angry feeling did not come to be in her very often. So mostly the servants stayed a long time with them, not those of them that had servant queerness in them, Mrs. Hersland never liked such a one, she wanted her servants so that she was of them and above them, she did not want them to have the kind of queerness in them that made strange beings of them, that always in a way made her afraid of them, servants were to Mrs. Hersland part of every day living, she never wanted them to have servant queerness in them, she was more then of them though always she was above them and she could come to have with such of them rightly an angry feeling.

Sometimes she would have young foreign girls or foreign american ones and she would train them, some of such of them would in their later living have servant queerness in them, mostly Mrs. Hersland did not keep such ones a long time, mostly she liked to have older women she felt herself more of them than with the young ones who needed to have her train them. She liked it better to have women who only needed directing and once in a while she would tell such a one how to cook something and with such of them she could feel of them and above them, she could with such ones have an injured feeling when they did something that was not right to her feeling, she could have with such a one rightly an angry feeling. She did not then like to have any one with servant queerness in them, she did not know it in herself that she did not like to have young girls to train but always these would soon be leaving, once one stayed on and on and Mrs. Hersland did not have with her rightly an angry feeling. She stayed on a long time until at last some one told about her that she was asking some one else to take her, that gave to Mrs. Hersland the injury that made it right for her to have an angry feeling in her and so at last she could dismiss her. This is the history of her. She was a blond little woman and with no feeling of cooking, or keeping anything clean in her, she always did what anybody told her, she had no sense of responsibility inside her, she had it in her to have lying in her that just came out of her whenever any one asked her, she had little curls in her blond hair, mostly every one thought her an ugly blond little servant, really she had a kind of little servant girl beauty in her. This is a history of her. She had not a servant nature in her but a servant girl nature in her that is the little dirty little girl character in her, the little dirty shrinking lying blond hair nature in her, not a woman nature in her. This was strong in her, in all the millions made just like her this is always stronger or weaker, this is the servant girl nature and there are always many millions made just like her.

Servant girl being is a kind of being that many millions of many kinds of women always have in them. Servant girl being in such of them is different from just servant being in other kinds of men and women. Servant girl being that is something of dirty or clean little girl being with the scared little lying always in such a one when there is much in their living and there always is in such ones of them for they need it to keep them going, to keep them cleaning, to keep them washing and working, to keep them from lying, much directing from the mistress living in the house with them, much teasing from children living in the house with them, much trouble with their loving so that nobody stops them when they go to their loving, much sitting in the kitchen with their hands so grimy nothing can clean them. Mostly such ones do not in their later living have servant queerness in them, they just get married most of them and just get old being that kind of them with many children always coming out of them and so they go on to their ending. Women who in all their living have this servant girl being in them are like in all women and always it is in all men and in all women that they have in them one of the two kinds of nature in them that is independent dependent or dependent independent nature in them. Servant girl nature in women then can be the independent dependent kind then with mostly only the dependent weakness in them with a scared dirty little girl crying and lying in them, mostly with nothing in them but the dependent scared weakness in them and no responsibility in them of being ever inside them and always a little in them and it mostly comes out in little tricks they have in them, little or much badness in them, a little of the attacking independent dependents always have in them. This is mostly in their living, in bad ones it can even come to stealing, mostly it is lying and finding ways to win to a ribbon, to moments in loving. Mostly when you catch hold of such a one by the arm to stop them there is not yielding, there is scared shrinking, there is lying, sometimes they do very good thinking, mostly in their later living a good many children come out from them, mostly they keep on working but always somebody is scolding them and this is a history of most of them.

As I was saying women with servant girl being inside them, not servant being that is a different kind of being that has not the grimy scared little girl lying as the bottom of them, such then have it in them to be of one kind or the other kind of them the independent dependent or the dependent independent kind of them. There is one kind of them who have a little attacking in them the independent dependent kind ; in them that comes out in little tricks and little dirty lying in them sometimes in stealing and other badness in them, in moments of leaving by themselves all of a sudden from where they were working when they are sure they can do better then and then there is a little grimy defiance in them, this is all the attacking there is in them, this makes of them independent dependent creatures for them and there will be written down here a history soon of one of such of them. There are then many millions always made of such of them, with always a servant girl nature in them and the independent dependent kind of being in them, there are then always many millions of such ones of them and always everywhere in every kind of living one can find such of them. Mrs. Hersland had the training of such a one of them, Mrs. Hersland had rightly an angry feeling when this one tried to get another place with out telling any one she was leaving. Mrs. Hersland had rightly an angry feeling then, she sent her away and soon there will be told the history of this one.

There are then in the women who have servant girl nature always in them, with every kind of way they can be living, with every kind of training that can come to them, there are always the two kinds of them the independent dependent kind of them and the dependent independent kind of them. Many of the independent dependent kind of them are pretty, scared young girls in their living, scaredness and lying, and shrinking, and a little attacking, and a little winning and prettiness and appealing are mixed up in many ways in them. Mostly in all of them these are always somehow somewhere in them, when they are working for their living, when they are young ladies in their living always there is some one always directing them, sometimes it is a mistress, a master, a mother or a father, a husband, some woman, or an aunt, a sister, or a man who is directing them. These things always are mixed up in them and more we will come to know all the history of all of them.

The dependent independent kind of women who have always in them the servant girl being in them have not in them anything of attacking, they have more weakness than shrinking in them, they have lying but it does not come out in little jerks out of them, it is never active in such a one, it is meekness and concealing in them ; and there will be later a history of all of such kinds of them.

Some women have it in them to be in all their living children, to have a childish nature in them all through their living. Some men have such a thing always in them, mostly men have it in them more than women to have in all their living a little childish nature in them. There are always then many millions of men and always some women who have always in them all through their living from their beginning to their ending child nature always in them. Some women have it in them all their living to have a grimy little girl nature in them, some have it in them to have a little girl sweet shrinking little lying nature always in them. All of such kind of them and there are always many millions made of them and they are in every place and in every kind of living, such have in them the nature that is in certain kinds of living servant girl nature and sometime there will be a history of every kind and every one of such of them. Some women have it in their living to have in them a being just before adolescent living, to have in them all through their living the fear of coming adolescence about beginning, in them, these always have it in them to be very lively so as to keep adolescence from giving sorrow to them, they are lively and they try all their living to keep up dancing so that adolescence will be scared away from them, these have not in them sentimental feeling, they have agressive liveliness in them. One can never be certain of this about them from their kind of living, they may be trying very exciting living, but in their walking they make a dance step not because they have it in them a lightsome feeling, they make it to keep in them a lively feeling, mostly they do not know it inside them that they do not want to have inside them the restlessness of adolescent living and so they keep up inside them always a lively feeling ; they make a dance step every now and then in their walking. There are always many women who have it all through their living to have such a just before beginning adolescent being in them. There are some men who have in them all through their living such a nature in them. There are then many millions always being made of such ones of women, there are some millions always being made of such ones of men. Some women have all their living their school feeling in them, they never get through, from their beginning to their ending, with such feeling, such being, such living, it is in them and nothing can change them, they are always school girls in their being, some of them always are as school girls in their feeling, some of them always are as school girls in their living, some women have some of this in them all through their living from their beginning to their ending, some have only this in them it

is always then all there is of them, there are many millions then who have
in all their living more or less in them of such being. Some women have
it in them and there are always many millions of them and they are to
themselves like men in their living there are many women who are always
vigorous young women energetic and getting information and busy every
moment in their living and sometime there will be a history of many of
such of them. Then there are many women, there are always many millions always everywhere of every kind of them, there are many women
who have some kind of woman nature in them and always in the millions
of all the kinds of them there is always in them one nature or the other nature in them, there is always some kind or every kind of mixture in them,
sometime there will be a history of every one of every kind of them, sometime there will be a history of everyone who ever was or is or will be living,
there must always sometime be a history of each one from their beginning
to their ending, of every one who ever was or is or will be living.   Sometime there will be a history of every woman, there will be sometime a history of every kind of them, there will be sometime a history of every part
of the living of every woman from her beginning to her ending.   This
is now a history of some of them.

There are many kinds of women and several of several kinds of them
were servants living in the house with the Hersland family and mostly
those were older women but sometimes Mrs. Hersland was training a
young one.

As I was saying Mrs. Hersland did not know she did not like to train
young ones and mostly they did not stay long but once there was a little
blond one who hung on.   She never did any better in her cleaning or
cooking than in the beginning, she always every minute needed directing,
Mrs. Hersland never knew she did not like to do this directing, she never
knew that she did not like it that with such a one she could not have rightly
an injured or an angry feeling.   At last she did have rightly an injured
and an angry feeling and that was for all of them then the end of that one.

Soon there will be a history of every kind of men and every kind of
women and every way any one can think about them.   Soon then there
will be a history of every man and every woman and every kind of being
they ever have or could have in them.   Sometime there will be a history
of all of them, and now to begin again with the servant girl being and the
servant being and the history of all of them who lived in the house with
the Hersland family then when Mrs. Hersland was beginning to have in
her strongest inside the feeling of being herself in her.

There were then many of them though mostly each one stayed a long
time with them but in these years of the Hersland family's middle living
with servants and seamstresses and governesses and dependents living in
the house with them, there were in all many women that gave to Mrs.
Hersland her important feeling.

There were then a few young girls who lived at some time in the house with them, some with servant girl nature in them, some with the one kind the independent dependent kind of nature in them, some with the other kind the dependent independent kind of nature in them. These as I was saying mostly did not stay long to get training, Mrs. Hersland never knew she did not want them, she never said she would not take them, after the one who stayed a long time and then gave to Mrs. Hersland a really angry feeling Mrs. Hersland never had one.

One of the foreign women, she was an older woman when she lived with them, she was such a one ; she had servant girl being, she had the dependent independent servant girl being, she stayed sometime with the Hersland family as the cook for them, she had in her the servant girl being of the dependent independent kind all through her living, there will be a history of this one.

Some young women who had servant girl nature in them came to know the Hersland family in their middle living, not as servants to them, some as dependents on them, some as living in the small houses near them, one was in a way of them in their living she was of the family of one of the governesses and they came later the Hersland children all three of them to know many of such of them.

Soon then there will be a history of every kind of men and women and of all the mixtures in them, sometime there will be a history of every man and every woman who ever were or are or will be living and of the kind of nature in them and the way it comes out from them from their beginning to their ending, sometime then there will be a history of each one of them and of the many millions always being made just like them, there will be sometime a history of all of them, there will be a history of them and now there is here a beginning.

There are then many millions always being made of women who have in all their living always from their beginning to their ending servant girl nature in them. Some of such of them are pretty little girls and happy in their living, some of such of them have much trouble in their living. There are then always many millions, in all the ways of living women have made for them, there are always many millions who have always in them all through their living from their beginning to their ending this servant girl nature in them, there will be now such a history of some of such of them, there will be now a history of some of the kinds of them, there will be now a description of the two kinds of them, the two kinds that divide all the kinds of men and women and sometime there will be a history of all of such of them, women who have such a servant girl nature in them, all of such of them who ever were or are or will be living.

Sometime then there will be a history of all women and all men, of all the men and all the women, of every one of them, of the mixtures in them of the bottom nature and other natures in them, of themselves inside them, there will be then a history of all of them of all their being and how it comes out from them from their beginning to their ending. Sometime there will be then such a history of every one who ever was or is or will be living, and this is not for anybody's reading, this is to give to everybody in their living the last end to being, it makes it so of them real being, it makes for each one who ever is or was or can be living a real continuing and always as one looks more and more at each one, as one sees them walking, eating, sitting, sewing, working, sleeping, being babies, children, young grown men and women, grown up men and women, growing old men and women, old men and old women, as one sees them every moment in their being there must be sometime a history of them, there must be sometime a history of each one of them and of the nature or natures in them, of themselves to themselves in their living, of the nature or natures mixed up in them and the coming out of this being in them from them from their beginning to their ending. Sometime there will be a history of all of the kinds of them and of each one of all the millions of each kind of them.

There are then always many millions being made of women who have in them servant girl nature always in them, there are always then there are always being made then many millions who have a little attacking and mostly scared dependent weakness in them, there are always being made then many millions of them who have a scared timid submission in them with a resisting somewhere sometime in them. There are always some then of the many millions of this first kind of them the independent dependent kind of them who never have it in them to have any such attacking in them, there are more of them of the many millions of this first kind of them, who have very little in them of the scared weekness in them, there are some of them who have in them such a weakness as meekness in them, some of them have this in them as gentle pretty young innocence inside them, there are all kinds of mixtures in them then in the many millions of this kind of them in the many kinds of living they have in them. In the second kind of them the dependent independent kind of them who have too all through their living servant girl nature in them, in this kind of them there are many of them who have a scared timid submission in them with a resisting sometime somewhere in them, there are many of them who have this submission as a patient meekness in them, they have not it in them many of such of them to ever choose their own way in living, to choose their own loving, to choose their own existing at any moment in their living, sometimes sometime some of such ones of them have resisting in them, sometimes this is in them a stubborn way they have in them, sometimes it is from too much directing of them and then they have resisting in them, sometimes from some one around them dependent on them, sometimes from feeling sometime in their living, feeling themselves inside them. There are many millions then of women who have always in them all their living this servant girl being inside them, always as it is in all men and women these are all of the one kind or the other kind of them of the independent dependent having attacking more or less sometime in them, of dependent independent who can have sometime resisting in them.

In all loving, in all the many millions always loving mostly there is one of them one of the two of them who is of the kind of them who have independent dependent nature in them, this one always in the two of them in loving does attacking in loving, sometimes it is in the man sometimes in the woman, and the other one then is of them who have dependent independent nature in them and these can have sometime more or less resisting in them, this makes the pair of them and this is always true in loving. This is not always clear in the beginning of a loving, sometimes it is the resisting that is in appearance like attacking, sometimes the attacking that has stubborness or weakness in it like resisting but more and more in loving more and more in their living this nature in them comes out of them in the repeating that is in all real being. It is true then that always every one is of one kind or the other kind of them the independent dependent or the dependent independent kind of them. It is hard to tell it about them, to describe it how each one is of the kind of them that is in that one. It is hard to tell it about them because the same words can describe all of them the one and the other kind of them, they are very different the one from the other kind of them, more and more perhaps it will come out clearly about them. It is hard to describe it in them the kind of being each one has in them, it is hard to describe it in them it is hard to know it in them, it is only slowly the two kinds of them come to be clear to every one who listens to the repeating that comes out of them, who sees the repeating that is in them the repeating of the bottom nature of them. Sometimes resisting comes like attacking, sometimes attacking seems like resisting, slowly it comes out from each one the kind of nature in them. So then this makes always a pair of them and this is always true in successful loving and this will soon then be a history of every kind of loving and how it comes from every one the nature of them.

Mrs. Hersland had dependent independent being, she could sometime in her have resisting. This is now a history of her and the servants and governesses and dependents who had to do with her. Mr. Hersland had attacking in him, mostly he was in his feeling as big as all the world in all of his beginning and all of his living was beginning, he never knew it inside him until his children told it to him when they were angry with him when impatient feeling filled him, he never knew that he did not go on to the last end of fighting that he had in him such a weakness in him ; this is now a history of him and of how the servants and the governesses and the dependents and his wife and children felt all these things in him.

All kinds of men and women have impatient feeling and sometime this will be a history of every kind of impatient feeling and of every kind of men and women who have impatient feeling. Now this is a history of servant living, of servants who have in them servant girl being, of servants who have in them servant being, of servants who have in them not any real servant being, of servants who have in them a mixing of some or all of these kinds of nature in them, of how it works out through them the two kinds of nature in all men and women the independent dependent and the dependent independent natures in all of them, this will be too a history of servant queerness and how it works in such of them as have this in them.

As I was saying Mrs. Hersland had mostly in her middle living in Gossols in that part where no other rich people were living older foreign or foreign american women as servants in the house with them. Sometimes she had a young one to train, Mrs. Hersland never knew it in her that she never really liked to do such training. They always then had german or german american older women as servants in the house with them, but sometimes Mrs. Hersland could not get any of them, once she had an Irish woman to to do the cooking, twice Italian women and once a Mexican, the Irish woman had servant queerness in her and she left all of a sudden, one Italian woman had servant queerness in her and she had to be sent away quickly without any warning, Mrs. Hersland never liked to have queer people near her she wanted her servants to be of the same kind of nature that was natural to her in the living at Bridgepoint the good living that was natural to her, she needed a servant around her that she Mrs. Hersland in her feeling could be of her and above her, she never wanted any servant to have servant queerness in her.

Some time then there will be every kind of a history of every one who ever can or is or was or will be living. Some time then there will be a history of every one from their beginning to their ending. Sometime then there will be a history of all of them, of every kind of them, of every one, of every bit of living they ever have in them, of them when there is never more than a beginning to them, of every kind of them, of every one when there is very little beginning and then there is an ending, there will then sometime be a history of every one there will be a history of everything that ever was or is or will be them, of everthing that was or is or will be all of any one or all of all of them. Sometime then there will be a history of every one, of everything or anything that is all them or any part of them and sometime then there will be a history of how anything or everything comes out from every one, comes out from every one or any one from the beginning to the ending of the being in them. Sometime then there must be a history of every one who ever was or is or will be living. As one sees every one in their living, in their loving, sitting, eating, drinking, sleeping, walking, working, thinking, laughing, as any one sees all of them from their beginning to their ending, sees them when they are little babies or children or young grown men and women or growing older men and women or old men and women then one knows it in them that sometime there will be a history of all of them, that sometime all of them will have the last touch of being, a history of them can give to them, sometime then there will be a history of each one, of all the kinds of them, of all the ways any one can know them, of all the ways each one is inside her or inside him, of all the ways anything of them comes out from them. Sometime then there will be a history of every one and so then every one will have in them the last touch of being a history of any one can give to them.

This is now a history of a number of men and women from their beginning to their ending ; these will have then the last touch of being that a history of any one can give to them, sometime it will be that any one who ever was or is or will be living, sometime then it will be even if they have had only a very little of any living, sometime then it will be that every one will have the last touch of being, a history of them can give to them, sometime then in my feeling there will be a history of every kind of men and women, there will be a history of every one from the beginning to their ending, every one will have sometime before the ending the last touch of being a history of them can give to any one.

So then we go on to our beginning of giving a history of every one from their beginning to their ending so that sometime there will be done a history of every one and every kind of one and all the nature in every one and all the ways it comes out of them. Every one then will be full then of the being a history of every one can give to them, every one of them will have that last touch of being a history of them can give to any one.

And so to commence again with the history of many of them and all the kinds there are of men and women.

Sometime then there will be a history of every one of every man and every woman from their beginning to their ending. Sometime there will be a history of every one and every kind of them and more and more then every one will understand it, how every one is connected with every one in the kind of being they have in them which makes of each one one of their kind of them. More and more then this will be a history of every kind and the way one kind is connected with the other kind of them and the many ways one can think of every kind of men and women as one more and more knows them as their nature is in them and comes out of them in the repeating that is more and more all of them.

There are then many kinds of them but all of them can be divided into the two kinds of them the independent dependent kind of them, the dependent independent kind of them, and more and more there will be a history of all of them so that more and more any one can see it in them. There are always then many kinds of men and women in these two kinds of them and sometime there will be a history of all of them.

To go on then now with the Hersland living in the ten acre place in that part of Gossols where no other rich people were living.

As I was saying Mrs. Hersland had mostly in her middle living in Gossols in that part where no other rich people were living, older foreign or foreign american women as servants in the house with them. Sometimes she had a young one to train, Mrs. Hersland never knew it in her that she never really liked to do such training, they always then had foreign or foreign american older women as servants in the house with them, but sometimes Mrs. Hersland could not get any of them, once she had an Irish woman to do the cooking, twice Italian women, and once a Mexican; the Irish woman had servant queerness in her and she left all of a sudden, one Italian woman had servant queerness in her and she had to be sent away quickly without any warning, Mrs. Hersland never liked to have queer people near her she wanted her servants to be of the same kind of being as that which was natural to her in the living at Bridgepoint the good rich living that was natural to her, she needed a servant to be around her so that Mrs. Hersland in her feeling could be of her and above her, she never wanted any servant to have servant queerness in her.

There were then not very many young women whom the Hersland family had as servants in the house with them. Mrs. Hersland never knew it in her that she did not like to do such training, no one of them excepting a little blond one ever stayed a long time with them. Mr. Hersland never knew that he had any feeling about such a kind of them but they were a little an annoyance to him. The Hersland family had many such young girls with servant girl nature in them around them from the houses near them, from the families of governesses or others living in the house with them, and so the Hersland children knew in their early living enough of such of them. As I was saying Mrs. Hersland never knew it that she did not like to do such training, after the one who gave to her after a long time a right reason for having in her rightly an injured and an angry feeling, she never had any such a one as a servant in the house with them.

As I was saying, more and more as one in passing looks at every one more and more then there comes to one the certain feeling that sometime there will be a history of every one, of all the kinds there are every one of men and women. Always as one looks at them as one lives on in the daily living that gives to one the feeling that in all real being there is always on and on repeating that comes out more and more and more in everybody's living, always then more and more one has in them the certain feeling that sometime there will be a history of every one, that sometime every one will have in them the last touch of being a history gives to every one. So then sometime there will be a history of every one and of every kind of men and women and of every kind of nature in any one of them and every kind of mixing there can ever be in any one and the way the nature in each one comes out from them, there will then sometime be a history of every one from their beginning to their ending, there will then be a history of every one even such of them that have only a little beginning and then an ending to them ; to every one then there will be a whole history of them, each one then sometime will have written a whole history of her, of him, and this will give to every one who ever was or is or will be living the last part of real being a history of them can give to any one.

There were then living on a ten acre place in a pleasant kind of living, Mr. Hersland and his wife and three children with servants and a governess and sometimes a seamstress in the house with them and near them poor people in small houses some of whom were more or less dependent on them. They had then pleasant living in this ten acre place, they had then their own kind of living and mostly it was pleasant enough for all of them, they had country living in them, they had city living in them, they had country house living in them, and always then living was very pleasant for all of them.

The three children were more then of the for them poor people around them than they were of their mother's or their governesses' or their father's living. They had a relation to everybody around them but mostly then inside them they were mostly of the living of the poorer people who lived in the small houses near them. Sometimes they were very much of the living of the servants in the house with them, sometimes of the family of the governess then living with them but mostly always then they were more of the living of the people living in the small houses around them than they were of the living of those in the house with them.

As I was saying some of the servants living in the house with them were sometimes important to the children, sometimes the children liked to tease them, sometimes to get what they wanted from them, mostly the servants and governesses and seamstresses were not as important to the children as the people living in the small houses near them.

There are then always many millions of women who are servants with servant nature in them, there are always many millions who have servant girl nature in them the kind of nature that makes of them a certain kind of being. These are then two kinds of them and there are many mixtures in them, in each one of them. Some of them the women who are living as servants to some one, there are many of them with servant natures in them, there are many of them with servant girl natures in them, there are many of them with servant mistress natures in them, many with mistress servant natures in them, there are then in the women living as servants to some one every kind of nature in them, there is every kind of mixture in them of one or more of all the kinds of being women have in them. Sometime there will be a history of all the kinds of being women ever have or had or can have or will have in them. Sometime and that will be a great thing there will be a history of each one, of the bottom nature of each one and the mixing of different being or kinds of being with the bottom nature and the way it comes out in her living, from the beginning, from her being a baby then and just beginning, from the way it comes out more and more in her living as she goes on repeating the way everybody always does in living, more and more then in each one in their living the history of each one comes out of them, more and more each one is repeating and each part of their living has its own repeating and makes of that part a history coming out from them, then in the whole living there comes out more and more and more a repeating that was in them always inside them, from the beginning to the ending ; this then is a history of them, this is a history of the bottom nature, how it works inside them, how it is mixed or not mixed up in them with the nature or other natures in them, sometime then there is a history of each one, sometime then there will be a history of every kind of women and of men, sometime there will be a history of each one.

There is then or will be then a history of each one who ever was or is or can be living. It comes out from them in the repeating which is sometime all of them. Many things come out of every one in their living and this is now a history of all that comes out of some of them.

Many things then come out in the repeating that make a history of each one for any one who always listens to them. Many things come out of each one and as one listens to them listens to all the repeating in them, always this comes to be clear about them, the history of them of the bottom nature in them, the nature or natures mixed up in them to make the whole of them in anyway it mixes up in them. Sometime then there will be a history of every one.

There are then many things every one has in them and this is a history of all of them in some of them.

As I said once almost every one has in them some kind of an impatient feeling, mostly every one has in them an anxious feeling and this is the way these work out in some.

When you come to feel the whole of anyone from the beginning to the ending, all the kind of repeating there is in them, the different ways at different times repeating comes out of them, all the kinds of things and mixtures in each one, anyone can see then by looking hard at any one living near them that a history of every one must be a long one. A history of any one must be a long one, slowly it comes out from them from their beginning to their ending, slowly you can see it in them the nature and the mixtures in them, slowly everything comes out from each one in the kind of repeating each one does in the different parts and kinds of living they have in them, slowly then the history of them comes out from them, slowly then any one who looks well at any one will have the history of the whole of that one. Slowly the history of each one comes out of each one. Sometime then there will be a history of every one. Mostly every history will be a long one. Slowly it comes out of each one, slowly any one who looks at them gets the history of each part of the living of any one in the history of the whole of each one that sometime there will be of every one

There will then sometime be a history of every one who ever is or was or will be living, mostly every history will be a long one, some will have a very little one, slowly it comes out of each one.

Mostly then the history of any one as it slowly comes out of them will be a long one, this is a long history now of many of them.

Every one then has in their living repeating, repeating of every kind of thing in them, repeating of the kind of impatient feeling they have in them, of the anxious feeling almost every one has more or less always in them.

There is then a whole to living, mostly everybody has for this an anxious feeling, some have not any such anxious feeling to the whole of them, many have the anxious feeling in every minute of their living, every minute is a whole to them with an anxious feeling which each minute ends them.

To many then in the history of all the kinds of them all the kinds of men and women who ever were or are or will be living, to some then and there are always many millions of them to some then the important thing is to have the history of all the kinds, the history of all the kinds that ever can be of men and women. To many and there are always many millions of such of them the important thing is to have written about every one around them the history of each one, the history of that one, of every man or woman who ever was or is or will be living for them, the history of each one as in their living from their beginning to their ending their history comes out from them. To some the important thing in them is their own history, the history of them and inside them, as in repeating it comes out of them. There are many men and women always livign and to them the important thing in living is in the different parts of living the being babies, children or young going to be men and women, or grown young men and women, and growing older men and women and men and women in their middle living, and growing old men and women, and then the end of all of them ; there are many millions then who always think and feel about all men and women in the parts of living and the kind of being every one has in them in those different parts of their living. There are then many millions who always feel this in them about others around them about themselves inside them, the important thing to all of such of them are the parts of living the being babies and children and young going to be men and women and growing older men and women, and middle aged men and women and growing old men and women and old men and old women and then that is the end of them in their worldly living. There are then many who feel this part living as the strongest thing in every one around them and in themselves inside them. There are then many millions, many many millions always living who want to know about what each one does all through his or her living, there are many who want to know about it in the history of every one what kind of feeling they had in them and how these feelings then came out from them in their living from their beginning to their ending. There are then many kinds of feelings in each one, there are many feelings in every one, there are many ways of hav ng feelings coming out of them, there are many who want to know it about every one around them what feelings they have in them, how such feelings come out of them, there are many millions then of women and of men who always think about this about every one around them, they want to know the feelings in each one of them and how it comes out from them, what the feelings in each one make of the life of such a one. There are many kinds of ways every one has in them of doing everything in their daily living, there are many who want a history of all such ways in each one. There are many who want their kind of history of only a few of all the people ever living, there are some who want a history coming out only from inside them, there are some who want a history to come out only from those just around them, there are some who want history coming out from some who were never and will never be anywhere near them, there is every kind of choosing, mostly every one wants a history of some one, mostly every one wants some kind of a history of some. Some few are always living who want about each one who ever was or is or will be living a history of every bit of them, of every moment in their daily living, of every kind of feeling they have in them, of every bit of them that comes out in them in repeating, of all the feeling in them and how it comes out from them in all of them in each one of them from their beginning to their ending, of every kind of men and women who ever were or are or will be living, of every part of their being and how in each part of their living their being shows itself in them, of the feeling in each kind of them and how it shows in each one their kind of them, how it comes out in each one in every part of their living from their beginning to their ending ; there are then some who want the whole history of every one, of the kind they are in them, of everything that makes them and ever can come out of them, of every bit of them in all their living ; there are then always some living who want of each one such a history of them, there are some of such of them now living and sometime there will be written by all of such of them a history of every one.

There are then many ways of having living inside one and having it come out from one, always then some one looks at each one, always the more one looks at every one the more one knows that sometime there will be a history of every one.

There are then many ways of having impatient feeling in one, there are then many ways of having an anxious feeling in one, this is now the history of some of them and the servant queerness that comes out of some servants who have in them impatient feeling and anxious being and later in their living from much sitting alone in a kitchen, from much eating without any one being then with them or around them, from much cooking, from much directing from the mistress in the house with them and from being with the children living in the houses where they are working have such servant queerness come to be in them ; there are then many women and many kinds of them who have sometimes servant queerness in them.

There are then every kind of women among the servants working in every kind of kitchen. There are some who have in them servant girl nature as the bottom of them.

The nature in every one is always coming out of them from their beginning to their ending by the repeating always in them, by the repeating always coming out from each one. Sometimes, often, one looking at some one forgets about that one many things one knows in that one, always soon then such a one brings it back to remember it about that one the things one is not then thinking by the repeating that is always in each one. Always then everybody is always repeating the whole nature of them and to any one who looks always at each one always the whole of that one one is then seeing keeps coming out of such a one. So any one can know about any one the nature of that one from the repeating that is the whole of each one. The whole of every one is always coming out in repeating. Always it is coming out of every one the whole nature of them in their daily living in the repeating each one has all the time in living. Every minute then in their living they are themselves inside them and they are repeating always and all the repeating together is the whole nature of every one coming out from them, coming out from them in their daily living, coming out from them in different ways in different moments of their living. Always then it is coming out of each one the whole nature of that one in the daily living of such a one in the repeating each one has all the time in living. Each minute then in the living of each one there is inside each one the being that makes that one and each one is repeating always this being that makes each one that one inside to that one and each one is repeating always and all the repeating together of each one is coming out always from each one, coming out from each one in the daily living each one is leading, coming out from each one in different ways in different moments of the living of each one.

Servant queerness in all of them who have servant queerness in them comes out of such of them as the kind of nature in them ; in each one having servant queerness in them it comes out of them by the nature of them, in the way they have always had in them impatient feeling and anxious feeling. Impatient feeling and anxious feeling has always been in each one of them in the way it was natural to their kind of them to such a one of their kind of them to have it in them and then it comes, the impatient feeling and anxious feeling, it comes to be that these get stronger and more mixed up in them then in such a one from their kind of living, from the kind of eating alone and drinking, from cooking and their kind of working, from sitting in a kitchen, it comes then that there is in such a one servant queerness in her being and the servant queerness is in her and comes out from her to make for her that kind of servant queerness that comes out of the nature in her.

The servants then living with the Hersland family, those who stayed a long time with them were older foreign or foreign american women. One of these had servant girl nature in her, she had submission in her, she could have sometime resisting in her. This never came to be in her in her living with the Hersland family, with them she never had any resistance inside her. Mrs. Hersland never had with her an angry feeling, she went away at last to take care of a sick brother.

There are then every kind of women among the women who are sometimes servants for some one. There are then every kind of women among foreign women among foreign american women who are servants sometime in their living to some one. Many of them have servant girl nature in them, many of them have servant nature in them, many of them have a mistress nature in them, many of them have a mixture in them ; there are then all kinds of women nature among them. About half of all of them have in them of their kind of them independent dependent nature in them, they are the independent dependents of their kind of them, the rest of them the other more or less half of them the women living as servants sometime in their living have dependent independent nature in them, they are the dependent independents of their kind of them. The nature in each one makes a long history of each of them and sometime there will be a history of every one and the nature in them and how in their servant living the nature in them comes out from them.

Mrs. Hersland got her important feeling of herself to herself from all of them from all the servants she ever had working for her or doing something for her in her living, Mrs. Hersland got her important feeling of herself to herself from all of them, from being of them and above them, from trying them, from directing them, from having in her sometimes from some of them an injured and an angry feeling, from having to arrange the relation of some of them to the governess living in the house at the same time. Some of them who had in them a certain mixture inside them never liked it that the governess was not of them and Mrs. Hersland had strongly then a feeling of herself to herself from making such a one understand the position a governess had and how a servant should behave toward such a one. Mrs. Hersland had then much important living with the servants, she never liked any one of them to have servant queerness in them, she never liked them to be so young that she needed to train them, she liked them to be older foreign or foreign american women, she liked to be of them and above them. Mostly she had very little trouble with them, sometimes she had troubles with the families of them, some of this will come out later in the daily living of the Hersland children in the history of each one.

Mrs. Hersland had then sometimes troubles with the families of them. Mrs. Hersland had her important feeling from servants who were with her in her middle living. Mrs. Hersland had from some of them an injured feeling, Mrs. Hersland had with some of them an angry feeling, sometimes it was with one of them sometimes with some one of the family of one of them. Mrs. Hersland had in her nothing of impatient feeling, she could have in her an injured and a bright angry feeling. Once one foreign girl had come to her from some one in Bridgepoint who had sent her because she wanted to go and this friend thought she would be a good servant for Mrs. Hersland to have with her. The girl did not want to stay, she wanted to go back to Bridgepoint, she said Mrs. Hersland should help send her, Mrs. Hersland had then an angry feeling in her, she said she did not have to help send her. The girl said she would have to help a little to send her, Mrs. Hersland said she would either not give her anything to help her or she would pay everything for her, she never would help to send her away from her, she would pay the whole thing for her, it was not right but she would pay the whole thing for her, she would do it all or nothing for her, she did not have to do anything for her, she would do the whole thing for her. Mrs. Hersland had in her a bright angry feeling inside her, it was wrong that a girl should behave so toward her. Mrs. Hersland had then rightly an angry feeling in her. She paid everything for her. This was Mrs. Hersland with an injured feeling inside her and an angry feeling then in her. There was nothing in her of impatient feeling in her, with servants she had never anxious feeling in her, she had in her sometimes an injured feeling and then an angry feeling and then she would send the one that had given it to her away from her, then she would pay for some one all expenses for her, when she had in her an angry feeling inside her there was no half measure in her, often she only had an injured feeling in her ; this time she had more angry than injured feeling in her. No one was then afraid of her, there was no terror in her anger for any one around her. Mostly she would then pay everything any one could in any kind of way ask of her to show them the right angry feeling in her.

There was never in Mrs. Hersland a bitter feeling in the injured or angry feeling in her with any servant in the house with her. She did not have in her impatient feeling, she did not have with any of them or the families of them an anxious feeling in her, she had inside her sometimes with them or with the families of them an injured sometimes an angry feeling in her, this never gave to her never made bitterness for her, Mrs. Hersland never had really any bitterness inside her, later she had a little dreary weakening sadness in her, later she had a scared feeling in her from her husband and her children grown big around her she never had in her impatient feeling in her she never had any bitterness in her, she had in her middle living for the servants and governesses and seamstresses and dependénts sometimes an injured feeling sometimes a bright anger.

To have an injured or an angry feeling in one is very common in ordinary living.   Injured or angry feeling may be in one with impatient feeling or with anxious feeling and it may be in one without any such being then in that one.   Mrs. Hersland had in her living, mostly in the beginning and in the middle of her middle living very much of such feeling, not much with her husband or her children but with the servants and seamstresses and governesses and dependents all those that gave to her the feeling of herself inside her.

The independent dependent kind of men and women have in them, most of them, mostly in their injured and their angry feeling a sense of impatient feeling or anxious feeling with a sense of their own virtue their own right inside them, they have not in them then mostly a consciousness of angry or injured feeling in them, to them then their angry feeling or their injured feeling flows from the outraged virtue or goodness in them, to themselves then they have not any angry or injured feeling as filling them but flowing from them because it is natural to have such a thing in them when their goodness or virtue is outraged by some one.   Mrs. Hersland was not such a one, she had in her dependent independent being in her, it was to her rightly an injured or an angry feeling she had then in her when some one around her did what it was not right for them to do toward her, she had then to herself rightly an injured and an angry feeling in her and to herself it was the injured or angry feeling that filled her, it was not right for the girl to ask Mrs. Hersland to help send her to Bridgepoint when the girl had no reason to leave her, it was right then for Mrs. Hersland to have in her an injured and then an angry feeling in her, it was then to Mrs. Hersland inside her that she had in her, rightly an angry and an injured feeling, then she would show it by doing nothing to help the girl who had no right to ask it of her or she would pay all her expenses for her.   Mrs. Hersland had rightly in her toward her an injured and an angry feeling, to herself then this was all that was then in her, it was not to her her own virtue or her own goodness that was then the important thing inside her it was the injured and the angry feeling in her, to satisfy that she paid all the expenses for her, she would do that or nothing for her, it was not to her her own virtue or her own goodness that was to herself urging her to do this for the girl who asked of her what she had no business to ask of her, it was to herself in her the injured and the angry feeling in her that needed to have this action to make it quiet inside her, it was to satisfy this in her that she would do anything or nothing for the girl who had asked her to help her when she had no right to ask her, it was not then to herself in her a sense of goodness and virtue in her ; this makes of her her kind of them the kind that has resisting and not attacking as the bottom nature in them ; she was of this kind of them then ,she had resisting not attacking in her as the bottom nature of her.

Mrs. Hersland was of this kind of them then, she had resisting as her way of being. This is not always clear in the beginning sometimes it is the resisting that is in appearance like attacking, sometimes the attacking that has stubborness or weakness in it like resisting but more in their living this nature in them comes out of them in the repeating that is in all being.

And so always whenever Mrs. Hersland had an injured or an angry feeling in her she did such a thing to satisfy herself inside her. This will come out more and more in her the kind of injured and angry feeling it was natural to have in her and the way it was natural for such feelings to come out of her. More this will be a history of these feelings in her, more and more this will be a history of the different ways the two kinds there are of men and women and all the kinds of the two kinds of them have every kind of feeling have every kind of way of having every feeling come out from them. Sometime then there will be more telling of the way Mrs. Hersland had injured and angry feeling. Sometime then there will be a history of every kind of feeling Mrs. Hersland had in her in her living and every way every feeling came out of her in her living. There will be then in the daily living of each one of the Hersland children there will be then in the history of the daily living of each one of the three of them a history of all the feeling and the way it came out of the mother of them the way it came out and so any one could see by looking that she was her kind of them the dependent independent kind of them the kind that have resisting as the bottom of them, the kind that have in them to themselves rightly in them an injured and an angry feeling and when they have this in them have not in them strongest inside them the sense of their own virtue or goodness then, they have then in them as the strongest thing then to themselves inside them this injured or angry feeling. Mrs. Hersland was of this kind of them then the dependent independent kind of women. Sometime there will be a long history of the two kinds of them and the feeling in them and the way feeling comes out of them.

There was then in the Hersland middle living pleasant enough living for all of them on the ten acre place with servants and seamstresses and governesses in the house with them.

As I was saying Mrs. Hersland had different seamstresses to do different kinds of sewing for herself and her children. This is now a history of all of them.

Sometime there is a history of each one, of every one who ever has living in them and repeating in them and has their being coming out from them in the repeating that is always in all being. Sometime there is a history of every one. Sometime there will be a history of every kind of men and women. Sometime there is a history of each one. There must be such a history of each one for the repeating in them makes a history of them. The repeating of the kinds of them makes a history of the kinds of them, the repeating of the different parts and ways of being makes a history in many ways of every one. This is now a history of some. This will be sometime a history of many kinds of them. Any one who looks at each one will see coming out from them the bottom nature of them and the mixing of other nature or natures with the bottom nature of them.

Every one then has a history in them by the repeating that comes out from them. There are some who will have sometime the whole repeating of each one they have around them, they will have the whole history of each one, there is repeating then always in every one, there is repeating always of the kinds of all women and men. There is repeating then always in every one ; that makes a history of each one always coming out of them. There is always repeating in every one but such repeating always has in it a little changing ; the whole repeating then that is always coming, the whole repeating that comes out from them every one who has living in them, the whole repeating then in them and coming out from each one is a whole history of each one.

Repeating then is always coming out of every one, always in the repeating of every one and coming out of them there is a little changing. There is always then repeating in all the millions of each kind of men and women, there is repeating then in all of them of each kind of them but in every one of each kind of them the repeating is a little changing. Each one has in him his own history inside him, it is in him in his own repeating, in his way of having repeating come out from him, every one then has the history in him, sometime then there will be a history of every one ; each one has in her her own history inside her, it is in her in her own repeating in her way of having repeating come out from her, every one then has the history in her, sometime then there will be a history of every one. Sometime then there will be a history of every kind of them every kind of men and women with every way there ever was or is or will be repeating of each kind of them.

The history of each one then is a history of that one and a piece of the history of their kind of men and women. Now there will be a history of one and then there will be histories of many more of them. Always then there will be long histories of each one.

There are then many things every one has in them that come out of them in the repeating everything living have always in them, repeating with a little changing just enough to make of each one an individual being, to make of each repeating an individual thing that gives to such a one a feeling of themselves inside them. I said each repeating in each one has each time in it a little changing, this sometimes comes nearly not to happening. Some keep on copying their repeating in their talking in the moving of their hands and shoulders and bodies in living, some keep on copying others around them, some have almost nothing in them of themselves inside them, every one has though always in them their own bottom nature their own kind of being, that is always in them repeating, that is always in them a real being.

Many go on all their life copying their own kind of repeating, many go on all their life copying some one else or some other kind of men or women's kind of repeating, some kind of being that they have not in them. Every one mostly has in them their own repeating sometime in their living, this is real being in them, many millions are always all through their living copying their own repeating, some have this in them because they are indolent in living, it is easier for such of them just to go on with an automatic copying of their own repeating rather than really live inside them their repeating. This is now a history of such a one.

There are then always the two kinds in all who are or were or ever will have in them human being, there are then always to my thinking in all of them the two kinds of them the dependent independent, the independent dependent; the first have resisting as the fighting power in them, the second have attacking as their natural way of fighting. As I was saying this is not always easy to know about them, it is not always easy to know which kind of these two kinds of being are in any one, it is hard to know it about them, it is hard to describe what I mean by the names I give to them. There are then these two kinds and always every one of all of them who have human being in them are of one kind or the other kind of them. Often, as I am saying, resisting is like attacking, the attacking like resisting. Often the meekness of the patient submission of the dependent side of the dependent independent kind of them seems like the sensitive scared yielding of the dependent side of the independent dependent kind of them. Each kind of them has in them their own way of loving, their own way of eating and drinking, their own way of sleeping, sitting resting and working, their own way of learning and thinking, their own way of having themselves come out from inside them ; always there are these two ways of being, mostly one who knows it well about them can tell which kind each one is of them, mostly one knows about them by always looking at them as the repeating in each one makes a history of that one. Sometime then there will be a history of all of them.

Sometime there will be a history of all of them. Sometime there will be written a long book, a history of all of them of the two kinds of them. Sometime it will be clear to some one the whole history of every kind of men and women, the two kinds of them, the kinds in each kind of them, the mixture of all of them. Sometime then will be written a long book, a history of every kind of men and women and all the kind of being in them.

Now this is a history of one of them. As I was saying Mrs. Hersland had three seamstresses working for her when she was living in Gossols in her middle living when she was strongest in her feeling of being herself inside her in her living. One of these was living in a part of Gossols between the part where the Herslands were living where no other rich people were living and the part where mostly all the rich people were living. She had this one to do most of the making her child Martha's better clothing and her own ordinary dresses for her ordinary daily living. Then she had one who lived in a part nearer where the rich people were living, she went to this one. Then there was the woman who lived in a small house near them, the woman who had the three daughters who all of them sometime had beauty in them.

The one who lived in between always worked twice a year in the fall and in the spring to make dresses for Mrs. Hersland and Martha and sometimes for the governess then living in the house with them. She always came to work in the house with them, she always ate there with them, and sometimes when she was in a hurry to finish her work she remained altogether in the house sleeping and eating. Her name was Lillian Rosenhagen. She was a large woman, she had black hair and she was tall and she had long heavy fingers that were tapering and heavy again just where the nails were commencing. Lillian Rosenhagen was a stupid woman and never said anything but the children could never forget having had her in the house with them. She was of the kind of them and there are always many always being made of them who have it in them to be stupid, to be heavy, to be drifting, and yet one never forgets them when one has known them, they do nothing but they have a physical something in them that makes them.

Every kind of history about any one is important then, every kind of way of thinking about any one is important to those who need a whole history of every one.

There is then a whole to living, mostly everybody has for this an anxious feeling, some have not any such anxious feeling to the whole of them, many have the anxious feeling in every minute of their living, every minute is a whole to them in an anxious feeling which each minute ends them.

As I was saying there are many ways of having anxious feeling in them in men and women. Anxious feeling in some is almost the whole living that they have in them, some have the anxious feeling every minute of their living every minute is a whole to them with an anxious feeling which each minute ends them. Some have very much anxious feeling in them but not every minute in their living, with some of such of them anxious feeling never makes an end to them, it goes on repeating in them but it does not ever to them make an end of them. Lillian Rosenhagen was such a one. Anxious feeling was in her always inside her coming to be strong in her whenever any little new thing was demanded of her, whenever she had to finish arranging anything whenever in a way there was any adjustment inside her to anything in her working or to any one around her.

There are then many ways for men and for women to have anxious feeling in them. Sometimes it is a wonder to any one who sees anxious feeling in almost every one, in every one's making a bargain, or selling, or buying, or hearing some one calling, or going to sleep, or wakening, in cooking, in ordering, many times in eating, in drinking, in coming and going. Mostly every one has in them more or less an anxious feeling, mostly every one has in them more or less impatient feeling, some have more anxious than impatient feeling in them, some have almost the same amount in them of anxious as impatient feeling in them, some have much more impatient than anxious feeling in them, many have every minute impatient feeling in them and every minute there is a beginning for them, many have impatient feeling in them and this has nothing in it of beginning for them, some have impatient feeling in them as always an ending to them inside them, many have it in them just as their own way of going on with their living. Anxious feeling can be in some as always an ending to them, it can be in some as always a beginning in them of living, there are some who have it in them as their own way of living.

In many, anxious being is impatient feeling and sometime there will be a history of many of such of them.

Lillian Rosenhagen had always repeating in her an anxious feeling, she had very little in her of impatient feeling. As I was saying Lillian Rosenhagen was very good at sewing, she was very steady at working, she had always in her repeating an anxious feeling when she had to do any ending or beginning.

Some have in them nervous feeling, this is different from an impatient feeling, this is different from anxious being, many have all of these mixed up in them. Lillian Rosenhagen had one kind of an anxious feeling, she had very little impatient feeling in most of her living, she had very little nervous being in her. This will now be a long history of the kind of anxious being in her and how it is different in her from in others who are made more or less like her.

There is a servant queerness in some, a queerness that comes out in them from the kind of anxious being, from the kind of impatient feeling sometime in them which comes to be from the kind of living servants have in them comes to be in such a one a servant queerness and every one in the house knows it in that one. There is then a servant queerness in many women and in some men who are working as servants and have a servant living in them. They have many of them a servant queerness in them and that comes out of them according to the nature of them, according to the kind there is in them of a bottom nature in them and the kind they have in them of mixtures inside them which gives to them the knid that is in them of the impatient being and anxious being in each one, the kind in them of such being inside them that with the servant living makes inside such a one servant queerness. There are many ways of having queerness in many men and women. There are many who have not any such queerness in them, many have things in them that others around them sometime think queer in them but there are many who have not such a kind of queerness in them that makes really a character in them. There are many men and women who have queerness in them, sometime there will be a history of all the kinds of them. Just now there will not be a history of such a one. Some dress-makers have a dress-making queerness in them, a queerness that comes from sitting sewing and always lying and there own kind of anxious feeling and their own kind of creating and own kind of nervous being, there are many of such of them. Lillian Rosenhagen was not of such of them, she had in her as I was saying anxious feeling, she had in her very little of impatient being, there never came to be in her a queerness inside her.

Lillian Rosenhagen never had any man who really wanted to marry her. They all liked her. Mostly every one who knew her liked her. She lived together with her mother and sometimes her sister. Sometimes the sister sewed with her. Often this one did not live with her mother and her sister. She had a very umpleasant nature.

Everybody is always in their living repeating, some all through their living have strong feeling in every moment of repeating in each time their repeating comes out from them. Some have feeling only in the beginning, repeating then goes on and on inside them ; some have feeling in them in the repeating coming out of them when they are changing in repeating ; many have very little feeling in them in most of the repeating coming out of them in their living ; many have not enough feeling in them to make it real repeating, in such of them it comes to be a copy of the repeating that once came out of them in feeling ; some copy others around them and make of this a repeating in them, some make of such a copying a repeating in feeling, some never have in such a copying a real repeating feeling.

There are then many as I was saying who all their lives are repeating and each repeating has in it as strong feeling as any part of their being, there are many millions always being made such of them, sometime there will be more understanding of the meaning in this saying. There are always many millions who only sometime in repeating have much feeling, in many of such of them repeating is just going on because they are living and in living one always goes on repeating, there are some who have not enough activity inside them to go in this way in their repeating, these have to copy themselves with a certain impulsion so as to go on repeating, they copy themselves in their way of talking, sometimes in their loving, often in their way of walking, of moving their hands and shoulders, in their ways of smiling, there have been some and always will be some who copy themselves so in all their living, in their eating and drinking, in every moment of their daily living.

I say some who have not much activity inside them have a kind of indolent and lethargic way of repeating, something in between just going on repeating and copying themselves to start them to keep going ; Lillian Rosenhagen was one of such of them.

I say that anxious feeling comes out of each one according to the nature of them, this has in almost every one every time it comes in them out of them more in it of real feeling in repeating than many things in many men and women. There are some men and women always living who can have in them anxious feeling repeating without much real being in such repeating. Lillian Rosenhagen was a little such a one.

Sometimes then the sister Cecilia Rosenhagen would be living with her mother and her older sister Lillian. Often she would leave them and live away from them. The Rosenhagen sisters were both born american. The father was not living. The mother was old then and did nothing but a little cleaning and cooking, the daughter Lillian did most of the supporting of the mother. Sometimes Cecilia would be helping but she never got as much money for working as Lillian and often she was not living with them.

As I was saying Lillian Rosenhagen did not have men want to marry her. She was good looking, she was tall and dark, she was a stupid woman. She had good dress-making instinct in her working. She was steady in her working. She had in her anxious feeling as I was saying, a little, every time she had to do something. Cecilia had in her anxious feeling as excitement always in her. She had a very disagreeable nature. She had always suspicion in her of every one around her, anxious feeling was always an exitement to her, she had a great deal of it in her.

Every one then has in their living repeating, repeating of every kind of thing in them, repeating of the kind of anxious feeling almost every one has more or less always in them, repeating of the way each one has of being stupid in their living.

Almost every one, always each one has a way of having a kind of stupidity inside them always repeating in their living. Every one then has in them some kind of stupidity inside them. In each one it is of the nature of that one, of the kind of stupid being that is natural to their kind of them. With some their stupid being is mixed up with anxious feeling, with some with their impatient feeling, in some with other things in them, in some it is just there in them it never mixes up inside them, it is just there, always in them, it is so steady and stilly in them it does not come out of them as repeating, it just lies there quiet, as the bottom of them.

Lillian Rosenhagen was such a one. She was a stupid woman. She had anxious feeling in her whenever any little new thing was demanded of her, whenever she had to finish arranging anything, whenever in any way there was any adjustment inside her to anything in her working or to any one around her. This was the anxious feeling in her, this had nothing to do in her with the stupid being in her that made her.

In many, anxious being is impatient feeling in them, and sometimes in many, it is a suspicious feeling always in them, in many it is an excited feeling that keeps them always changing and acting. In Cecilia Rosenhagen there was a little of all these three ways of having as feeling her anxious being. Mostly it was the last kind of them the excited way of being that was strongest in her in her anxious feeling, she had it in her to have a good deal of suspicious feeling, she had less in her her anxious being as impatient feeling. In some anxious being is in them a nervous condition.

As I was saying mostly every one has in them more or less anxious being, with some it is part of their stupid being, this was not so in the sister Lillian, it was true of the other one. Each one of them had in her her own stupid being and now this is a history of it in each of them.

Lillian Rosenhagen was four years older than her sister Cecilia. Cecilia had a very unpleasant nature, she had nervousness in her, she had suspicion in her, she had anxious being as excitement always working in her. She was not a good worker, she was not a bad worker, she could find people to employ her and they would always be ready to keep her longer than her suspicious temper would let her. As I was saying sometimes she would be living with her sister and mother and then anxious being would be such an excitement inside her that she would go away and live with any friend who would let her. She always had a new friend who would take her, then she would have her anxious being as a new excitement in her and she would come back to her mother and sister. Lillian never began again with her from any goodness inside her. She had no use for her sister, they had no use for each other, they both had stupid being in them and they put up with each other when they were together, they did not quarrel with each other, they did not enough touch one another to quarrel together.

They each one of them had in them their own kind of stupid being. In Lillian stupid being was the vague bottom to her that was always there when you looked at her. It made her, it had nothing to do in her with the anxious feeling sometimes in her, not with any trouble she had in her with her mother or her sister or a customer or the daily living and everything then that happened to her. She went on repeating because in living one goes on repeating, because that is the way one does in living. Lillian Rosenhagen went on living, sometimes she had a real feeling in her living, often she had in her a kind of anxious feeling, this she had in her whenever she had any adjusting of herself to her working, her work to a fitting of herself to any one who had then something to do with her. As I said she always then had a kind of anxious feeling in her, this never came to be sorrow in her, this never came to be a puzzled or a worried feeling in her, it was just such a kind of anxious feeling in her that made a little feeling inside her that was not just going on living in her, not a copying of herself in repeating in her, not just a drifting in her, it was pretty nearly a really anxious being in her. As I say she had a vague stupid being as a bottom to her. Mostly she went on repeating because repeating goes on always when any one is still living. She had a vague stupid bottom being, this was hardly repeating, this was just there lying in her as a bottom. She had a physical something that made an impression, that was some attraction. Mostly men did not want her for marrying, no man ever wanted her enough to have her marry him. She just went on living and dress-making.

Every one has in them their own history inside them, in each one the history comes out of them in the repeating that is always in them that sometime when all the repeating in them has been done by them and they are no longer living and so do no more repeating, that sometime will be a whole history of each one of them.

Sometime then each one will be dead and they each one will do no more repeating ; there will then have been, there will then be a whole history of each one. In some as I was saying repeating comes almost without any changing any differing from the other repeating in them, in some repeating always has some changing, in some repeating has each time real feeling, in some it has so little real feeling it is only copying their own repeating. There can be then every kind of repeating with every degree of changing to some which takes strong looking to be sure it is repeating. There can then be repeating with every degree of changing, with every degree of feeling. There can be strong feeling in each repeating and the repeating have almost no changing. There is every kind of mixing, there is excitement and nervous feeling in repeating that sometimes makes it seem to be changing, there is nervous or excited or anxious being around repeating that makes it sometimes seem like a fresh feeling. Even in anxious being there can be repeating without fresh feeling. There can be every kind of mixing, this is a history of some of them.

Repeating then is always coming out of every one, almost always in the repeating in every one and coming out of them there is a little changing. All the repeating in each one makes a history of each one always coming out of them. There is always repeating in every one but such repeating has almost always in it a little changing, the whole repeating then that is always coming the whole repeating that comes out of them every one who has living in them and coming out from each one is a whole history of each one.

Lillian and Cecilia Rosenhagen each in their own way of being had both of them very little changing in their repeating, very little fresh feeling in their repeating. Lillian Rosenhagen had as I was saying always when she had to do finishing or beginning or a little adjusting of anything or of herself to any one around her, had always then a little anxious being that had always in it a little feeling, that had always in it very little changing, it was very much the same repeating. Mostly, in her ways of doing there was very little in her of fresh feeling, mostly when she was with others there was in her very little of fresh feeling, she was just copying herself in her movements in repeating or else she had in her a little drifting ; she had in her as a bottom her indolent and stupid being that was in her but hardly came out of her as repeating. She had almost nothing in her ever of impatient feeling.

Cecilia Rosenhagen was very different from her sister Lillian. She had in her anxious feeling as the bottom and the whole of her being. No man wanted her to marry him. It was different with her from her sister Lillian, it was for a different reason. Cecilia Rosenhagen had in her anxious being as the bottom and the whole of her being. In her, anxious being was always in her excited feeling, any one who saw her knew this in her ; in her, injured feeling was always suspicious feeling, every one felt this strongly with her after a very little of her ; she always had a new woman friend to pity her and to commence with her, she never had any man who wanted to take care of her or marry her. It was different in her from her sister Lillian, neither of them ever came to marrying.

Cecilia Rosenhagen was a true spinster. Lillian Rosenhagen was not married because nobody had came to want her enough to take her. These two were very different in nature.

There is every kind of being in women who have it in common to have a spinster nature. Later there will be much discussing of this spinster nature. Now it is enough to know that Cecilia Rosenhagen had it in her.

So then they went on with their living to their ending Lillian and Cecilia Rosenhagen. No man ever married either one of them. They both went on in their own way living and dress-making to their ending. Mrs. Hersland liked to have Miss Lillian Rosenhagen in the house working. She was a good young woman for dress-making, she never gave to Mrs. Hersland anything of an injured or angry feeling.

It is very common to have in one injured or angry feeling inside one. Injured or angry feeling it is common to have inside in every one. Injured or angry feeling it is common to have sometime in almost every one. Anxious feeling and impatient feeling are more or less and sometime in almost every one. Every one has sometime something of such feelings in them. It is very common to have the injured or the angry feeling in one mixed in one with the impatient feeling and the anxious feeling sometime in almost every one. Anxious feeling, impatient feeling, injured feeling, angry feeling are all sometime in each one in almost every one who ever was or is or will be living. In many then impatient feeling and anxious being are mixed up in them in the injured feeling and the angry feeling almost every one has sometime in them. There are many then that have this mixture in them. The way it comes out of them, the way these feelings mix up in them, the way they mix up with other things in them make of each man or woman their kind of man or woman, make them one of the two kinds of men and women, make of them one of the many kinds in each of the two kinds of them.

There are then many who have mixed up in them anxious being, impatient feeling, injured and angry feeling. Almost every one has in them their kind of stupid being, mostly every one who knows any one knows this in them. There are some who have their stupid being mixed up in them with their kind of anxious being, their kind of impatient feeling, their kind of injured, their kind of angry feeling.

Lillian Rosenhagen had very little of any of this mixing. She did have a very little sometimes in her injured feeling in her, there was never very much of such feeling in her but when there was such feeling in her when there was a little an injured feeling inside her it was never in her impatient feeling or anxious feeling or even angry feeling ; but she could have sometimes in her a very little injured feeling inside her and this in her was connected inside her with the vague stupid being that was a bottom to her. That makes the being clear in her, there was almost nothing in her ever of impatient feeling and very little in her ever of angry feeling inside her. There was in her anxious being but that never had anything to do with the vague stupid being that was the bottom to her. There was in her not often but real in her sometimes an injured feeling that was not in her ever connected with the anxious feeling often in her with the anxious being of her, it was connected when it was in her, this injured feeling which was very real in her the times it came to be inside her it was connected in her it was part in her of the vague stupid being that was the bottom to her. This had very little in her ever to do with a love matter, almost never, almost never with her sister, a little more with her mother, almost never with a customer, it just sometimes came to be in her. As I said of her she had a physical something that went with the vague stupid bottom of her, that was pleasant in her, it was vague in her, she had never impatient feeling, or in living, anxious feeling, or in loving injured or angry feeling. No man came to ever want to marry her, she went on to her ending living and dress-making and now this is all the history of her.

With Cecilia Rosenhagen it was a different matter. Cecilia had a very different nature from her sister. No man ever wanted to marry her but it was a different matter from that in the case of her sister. In Lillian's case it was that no man had ever come to want her, no man ever wanted to have Cecilia ; that was quite a different matter. Everything in her came from her bottom nature, she always had excitement in her, she always had repeating in her and all the repeating in her was filled with the excitement always in her. She had not much impatient feeling in her, she had very much anxious feeling in her, she did not have very much real anger in her, she had always very much injured being in her. In her, injured being, anxious being, was a suspicious excited state inside her, these were always in her, these filled her when she was living with her sister, when she left her, when she came back to her sister and her mother, when she was living with any friend who would have her, when she was working for or leaving any one who employed her. Anxious being was always in her, it was always in her as injured feeling and an excited suspicious being, that made the whole of her. This did not come to be active in her very much from her sister, a little from her mother, more from any friend who let her live with her, a little from any one who employed her, but mostly she had it in her from everything around her, from every moment of being in her. Excited suspicious living of anxious being and injured feeling, that was the whole of her. She always had a new friend who let her stay with her and then she went to another and so on until she came back again to her mother and her sister and so on to begin again with another. This was a history of her, she was not a good workwoman but not a bad one either, she was good enough so that she would always find some one to employ her, she would always leave them while they were yet willing to keep her, she would have anxious feeling then in her as excitement, as a suspicious feeling, as an injured feeling in her and so then now there is a whole history of her. Sometime perhaps there will be another history of her.

There were then in Gossols in Mrs. Hersland's middle living three sets of women who did her dress-making. There were Lillian Rosenhagen and her sister Cecilia who worked for her in the house with her to make the ordinary dresses for her and her little girl Martha and sometimes for the governess then living with her, there was the woman who lived in a small house near the Herslands then in that part of Gossols where no other rich people were living, who did just working over and ordinary sewing, and there was then another dress-maker who lived in the richer quarter who made Mrs. Hersland's best dresses for her. There will be now a history of her.

There is a certain kind of women who have in them independent dependent nature in a certain kind of way in them. They have not servant girl nature in them. They have their own way of having independent dependent nature in them. This is now a history of one of them.

Such of them have more or less fear in them, they have very little in them of anxious being, they have some impatient feeling in them, they have courage in them and they have fear in them and they have a little impatient being and they have in them almost nothing of anxious being. As I was saying they have not in them servant girl nature in them.

They have not in them servant girl nature in them, they have in them very little of anxious being, they have in them only a little impatient being, they have not in them much injured being, they can have in them angry feeling. There are many ways then for women and for men to have anxious being in them.   These then have very little anxious being in them, they have independent dependent nature in them and so they have attacking in them as their natural way of fighting.   There are many women who seem from the kind of movement in them when they are doing anything in any way attacking anything in their living, there are many women who have then always in them something that seems anxious being in them. Such of them have attacking in them as their way of fighting but they have weakness in them or a sensitive being in them or a vague being in them or an empty being in them as the bottom of them.   These then have attacking as their natural way of fighting, many of them have attacking in them always only from some one else acting on them, some one else giving them ideas for figthing, some one else using them for living, some one else needing them for protecting or else because they are at the last need in them for some other thing.   There are many many millions always being made of such of them, they are wonderful instruments for other people's living, they never know it in them that it is other people's lives they are living.   As I was saying these have in them always in attacking something that is like anxious being in them, but this is mostly not true of them, it is mostly not true of them that they have anxious being in them for most of them and there are many men and many women of them most of them have not it in them to have consciously and most of them not to have any kind of fear in them.   One must have some kind of fear in one to have in one really anxious being, servant girl women have always such fear in them, dependent independent men and women have almost always fear in them, these have bottom earth feeling in them, they feel their pulses to see if they are living, any one with bottom earth feeling in them can have at some time fear in them, but this is not what is now being written.

Independent dependent men and women have attacking as a natural way of fighting in them, all independent dependent men and women have attacking as the natural way of fighting, the kind of independent dependent men and women, these of that kind of them who have very much in them of weakness or sensitive being or vague or vacant being as the bottom of them such of them have in them when it comes to them to have fighting in their living and most of them have a great deal in them of fighting, some of them have it in them then to conquer whatever it is in the bottom of them that does not help them in fighting, some of them harden themselves harden the weakness in them so that it does not stop them, some fill themselves with angry feeling to concentrate in them the vague being they have inside them as a bottom to them, some just go ahead with the vacant being lying there in them they go ahead and it gives to such of them a being like an anxious feeling but it is not fear in such of them it is only the vacant being in them, some get so strongly in them the fighting for some one around them that it takes away from them in attacking the sensitive feeling that might stop them. In all of such of them there is to one looking at them anxious being in them but this is not really in them, it is only the halting that comes to them in attacking from the kind of bottom in them, from the weakness or sensitive being or vague or empty being that makes the bottom of each one of such of them. These then have in them halting in attacking, they have not in them really anxious being, they have not in them really fear in them, they have not in them servant girl nature in them, they have not in them dependent independent nature in them, they have not really resisting in them, they may help their attacking by a kind of stubborness in them but this is never in such of them real resisting in them and sometime every one who lives near them learns to know it in them. The halting in them then in their beginning an attacking gives to such of them then an appearance to them not of timidity in them but of anxious being in them, sometimes anxious nervous being in them. They have not then really anxious being in them. Some time there will be here a history of many of them.

The other seamstress who did sewing for Mrs. Hersland in her middle living, the one who lived in that part of Gossols where richer people were living, the one that made for Mrs. Hersland then all her best dresses the ones she used for visiting, this woman then was of a kind of woman as I was saying who have in them very little of anxious being or impatient being, sometimes impatient being, a little of angry feeling, sometimes some injured feeling. She was not of them I have just been describing. She is near them but not altogether of them. She has not much attacking in her living, she has more gayety in being. She is of the kind very closely like the kind I have been just describing but she is of a different kind of women from them. She has not in her any servant girl being, she has in her independent dependent being, she has in her attacking as her way of fighting but she has not much fighting in her being, she has gayety in her being, she does good dress-making, this is now a history of her kind of women and there are men too who have this kind of being. This is a history of a kind then of men and women. This is a history of one woman of this kind of men and women.

Always then of each kind of being there are both men and women. Sometimes there are more women of that kind of them mostly made than men, sometimes there is a kind of being that comes oftener as men than women. Almost always in every kind of being there are millions always being made of men and women of that kind of them. Men have in them and women have in them some of them dependent independent nature in them, some of them independent dependent nature in them. There are many kinds of each of these two kinds of being men and women have in them. In all the kinds that are always in the world existing of each kind of them there are always some millions of men and some millions of women. This will come out clearer always as the history of every one of every kind who ever has or has had or will have human being in them comes to be written.

So then there was a woman Mary Maxworthing who did dress-making in Gossols and lived in that part of Gossols where richer people were living, there was this woman who had independent dependent being and had in her a certain kind of being and there are always being made many millions of women and there are always being made millions of men who have in them the same kind of being she had in her in her living.

She had attacking in her as her way of fighting but she did not have much fighting in her living, she had in her very little anxious being, she had in her a very little impatient being, she had gayety in living, she could have prudish feeling, she was a good work-woman.

Mary Maxworthing was clever not brilliant in dress-making, she had gayety in her living, she had very little in her of attacking, she had almost nothing in her of anxious being, she had very little fear in living, she had a little in her of impatient being, she had sometimes in her, injured feeling. She had not in her a stupid bottom to her, she had very little stupid being in her. She was as I said a very good dress-maker. She had as I was saying independent dependent being, when there was fighting in her there was attacking but there was very little fighting in her living, when there was weakness in her of the bottom giving way in her that is always in those who have the dependent side of independent dependence in them, when that weakness came to be yielding in her it was a sensitive yielding in her but there was very little of this in her, there was very little weakness or sensitive yielding at the bottom in her. She had almost no fear in her, very little bottom yielding in her, she had almost no anxious feeling ever in her, she had almost no stupid being at the bottom of her, she had a little impatient being in her, she had sometimes a little injured being in her ; any stupid being in her was connected with the little impatient being in her, with the injured feeling sometimes in her.

The difference between her and the other kind of women I have been just describing, the kind who have much bottom in them of sensitive being or weakness or vague being or empty being, with much in them of attacking, with very little in them of anxious being for they have not in them the kind of sense that gives fear inside them to men and women, the women then who have halting in attacking halting that looks like nervous anxious being in them not like timid being, the difference between such ones and such a one as the dress-maker Mary Maxworthing will come out later in the history of the Hersland daughter Martha, in the history of Julia Dehning. Now there is a history of Mary Maxworthing and her business of dress-making.

Mary Maxworthing then lived her own life, had her own way of dress-making, she was not of them who lived other people's lives in living. There are many of such of them many who have an instrument nature in them, many who have attacking in them as their natural way of fighting but have at the bottom of them sensitive being or weakness as the bottom of them or vacant being as the bottom of them or vague being as the bottom of them. Such of them have it in them often to live other people's lives in their living, some have it less some have it more in them, it depends in them on the proportion in them of fighting power in them, in the relation in them of the attacking instinct in them with the other bottom in them, it depends in them on the way stubborness is in them, in the way stupid being is in them ; the more there is in them of stupid being or stubborn being in them the more there is in such of them of resisting, of living their own lives in their living. There are some of them who have sensitive being or vacant being or weakness as a bottom to them or vague being in them to so completely fill them that it makes a personality in them and then they live their own lives in their living.

Sometime there will be some understanding of this nature in men and in women, soon it will show in Martha Hersland and in Julia Dehning, soon it will show a little in a sister of the first governess the Herslands had ever living with them. Mr. Hersland had a nature in him that has a connection with the kind of nature that I have been just describing, a connection in one direction, Mary Maxworthing had a connection in another direction. The relation who worked with Mary Maxworthing a young woman Mabel Linker had a far away connection with such of them. Lillian Rosenhagen was not at all of this kind of them, she had a vague bottom but she had dependent independent being. She was of a different nature.

Mary Maxworthing then in her later living was very successful in her business of dress-making, I don't mean to say she ever made a fortune, she never did make a fortune, she earned a very good living. She was very successful in dress-making, she never earned real distinction, she never in living did really very personal creating but she lived her own life in her living and she had a fairly successful life from her beginning to her ending. She had men who wanted her to marry them, when she was thirty-five she did marry and she married very well then, not well enough to give up dress-making but well enough to be very comfortable in living.

She had working with her Mabel Linker, she had other girls working for her but Mabel Linker was a kind of a partner. She was the daughter of a cousin of Mary's sister-in-law and was a very good almost brilliant dress-maker. Sometimes the two had a hard time keeping together, Mabel Linker was a little flighty sometimes and sometimes Mary Maxworthing had an impatient temper, always she had a little impatient being in her.

I like to tell it better in a woman the kind of nature a certain kind of men and women have in living, I like to tell about it better in a woman because it is clearer in her and I know it better, a little, not very much better. One can see it in her sooner, a little, not very much sooner, one

can see it as simpler, things show more nicely separated in her and it is
therefore easier to make it clear in a description of her. Such a nature as
Mary Maxworthing had in her is of the kind of nature that many men and
women have in them. It is clearer in her than in a man like her and
so I will describe it in her. Sometime it will be clearer just why and
how different her kind in a man is from her, this will all be clearer later.
Now this is a history of Mary Maxworthing, and her dress-making and
how Mabel Linker lived with her.

It is very interesting that every one has in them their kind of stupid
being. It is very important to know it in each one which part in them,
which kind of feeling in them is connected with stupid being in them.
Sometime there will be a history of every kind of stupid being in every kind
of human being in every part of the living of each one from their beginning to their ending.

Always it is important to know it in each one the stupid being in
them and the way it is connected in them with the important being in
them that makes each one that one, sometime then there will be a long
history of every kind of way any one can have stupidity inside
them. It is very important then to know it in each one and sometime
every one looking at any one can learn to know it in that one. Sometime
every one looking at any one will learn to know it in that one. Now there
will be a description of it in every one. Now there will be a description
of it in Mary Maxworthing.

There will be a description of the kind of stupid being Mary Maxworthing had in living, of the kind of stupid being the other kind of women
I was describing have in them, the stupid being Mabel Linker had in her
in her living.

Stupid being then is in every one, in some it is with the bottom in
them, in some with the other nature or natures in them, in some with the
feeling coming out of them. In some it is always repeating, in some it
is only rarely repeating, there is every kind of accent in repeating stupid
being, sometime there will be a history of all of them.

As I was saying every one has stupid being in them. It is very
important to know it in each one the kind of stupid being in them. Stupid being is not foolish being, it is not dull or senseless being, it is sometimes
foolish being, it is sometimes dull or senseless being, it is not always any
very certain kind of being, it is always in each one and sometime it comes in
some fashion out of every one.

Stupid being then will soon be certain in each one. This is now a
history of stupid being in some.

Stupid being then is somewhere in each one, in every one there is in
them the stupid being that is natural to them, that makes their kind of
them. There is then in every one their kind of stupid being and it comes
out in each one according to the nature of that one. In some, stupid

being is resisting. In many then who have independent dependent nature in them resisting is the stupid being in them. In those who have in them dependent independent nature, in them stubborness is a resisting that is natural in them with their kind of knowing, resisting in such of them is not the stupid part of them.

Each one as I was saying has in them their kind of stupid being, the kind of stupid being that is natural to their kind of them.

I say then in many who have independent dependent nature in them who have attacking as the natural way of fighting in them, who have weakness or vagueness or sensitiveness or emptiness as the natural bottom of them, in all of such of them stubborn resisting is almost always a part in them of the stupid nature in them, of the stupid nature every one has in them.

This was not so in Mary Maxworthing. She almost never had in her any stubborn resisting, the stupid being in her came with the impatient being in her, with angry feeling sometimes in her, with the injured feeling sometimes in her. She had really very little stupid being in her, she had not any stupid kind of bottom to her. She did not have really very much bottom in her, she had in her gayety and sensitive being in her enough to give her a sympathetic flavor, and a very little attacking in her but enough to make successful living in her, and impatient being in her enough to make it sometimes unpleasant to live with her, and impatient and angry feeling in her enough to give a stupid being to her, and injured feeling in her enough to keep her sense of responsibility to herself alive inside her. This is a history of her.

This is now another history of her, this is now a history of what happened to her. This is now a history of her and of Mabel Linker who lived with her.

Mary Maxworthing was one of the children of an american man and woman who had made a good enough living at farming.

Mary Maxworthing was one of the children of an american man and woman who had made a good enough living at farming. They still had a farm and some of their children lived with them. Their name was changed some in their american living. Mary came to Gossols to work for her living when she was about sixteen. She first earned her living by taking care of children. She did not find this very amusing. She liked children but she wanted freedom. She began to think when she was about twenty-one of some other way of earning a living. She thought over everything, a little dairy to sell butter and eggs and milk and cream but she did not like that kind of work and it takes a great deal of money to begin. She thought of millinering but she was not a very good hand at hat trimming, she was very good at sewing but she knew nothing about cutting and fitting. She was then about twenty-five when she came to this decision, when she decided to do dress-making. As I was saying she knew then nothing about cutting and fitting, she was very good at sewing, she had good ideas about dresses for women, she had a good sense of fashion.   So then she sent for her relation Mabel Linker who lived down in the country to come and join her.   She went on working at being nursery governess to earn a living for the two of them while Mabel was to learn cutting and fitting and dress-making from the beginning.   Mabel Linker was soon very clever at dress-making.   Soon they were ready to begin.   Then they started an establishment for dress-making in that part of Gossols where richer people were living.   They did not then have success with their undertaking.

Mary Maxworthing had a certain gayety in being.   She had not liked farming, she did not like taking care of children.   She did not like farming for that is a dreary way of living, not that she was a discontented person but she liked a certain gayety in living.   She had no wildness in her being, she was not really a thoughtless person, she was not a very conscientious person but she was conscientious enough for ordinary living, she was conscientious the way most people are in living, there was nothing reckless in her being.   She had a kind of responsibility to others and to herself in her living, she was not at all a wild or stupid being.

They were at first not successful in their business of dress-making, they had troubles with each other and with not having money enough to keep going until they had customers enough to pay them.

As I say Mary Maxworthing never liked the Maxworthing way of living, she never liked farming, it was to her a dreary way of living, she did not find it very pleasant taking care of children because it left her no freedom for living.   She preferred dress-making and it was very disappointing when she was at first not successful in this undertaking.

They had not enough customers to pay them to keep going, Mary Maxworthing soon used up all the money she had saved up to begin this undertaking, soon then the two of them began quarreling, soon then they had for a while to give up dress-making ; Mary had to go back to her place and once more begin to earn a living by taking care of children.

This was the way it came to an end for them the first effort for freedom, for Mary from nursery governessing, for Mabel Linker from sewing other people's cutting and fitting.

Mary Maxworthing had in her something of a despairing feeling when her undertaking came to such a helpless ending, when she had to go back to nursey governessing, when she had not any of the money left that she had been saving for five years for this undertaking.   Mary Maxworthing always had a certain stylish elegance in dressing, she had a good sense for fashion and a feeling for gayety without any wildness in her living.   There was nothing wild in her being, nothing reckless ever in her feeling, she had pride but not too much pride in her being, she had a reasonable amount of good sense and conscientiousness in living, she had started her undertaking with too much ambition for the money she had been saving and the talent she and Mabel Linker had between them. That is to say more money so that they could keep on longer waiting for people to know them or more distinction in their working might have kept them going ; but with the money they had for waiting and the talent there was in the two of them they were too ambitious in their beginning. What they had between them was not enough for such an ambitious beginning as they had made of their undertaking. Mary Maxworthing liked distinction, she had a certain ambition, she had not much attacking in her for winning but she had a certain kind of certainty of successful doing ; she had impatient being, she had a certain gayety in her being. Mabel Linker had not any sense in her to keep any one else with her from doing anything foolish, not that she would of herself have made such a beginning but she had not the energy in her for beginning, she had not the kind of sense in her for judging, she could never have any judgment of any way of beginning. Then they had trouble in their living. As I was saying Mary Maxworthing had gayety in being, she had very little almost not any anxious being ; she had independent dependent being and attacking was her natural way of fighting but there was very little fighting in her being, she had in her as a bottom a little but not very much sensitive being ; she had in her as a bottom almost not any stupid being. She had in her some impatient being, she could have in her a little injured being, she could have in her angry feeling, but mostly it was the impatient being that sometimes was nervous impatient being that made her interfering, that made her always sure of knowing, that was the stupid side to her being, that made the trouble between her and Mabel Linker when they were then working together. Mabel Linker had very little common sense, she had little twittering flighty ways in her but she was a good sewer, she was a good cutter and fitter, she was almost a brilliant dress-maker, but she had very little stability in her character. Mary Maxworthing began with almost an idolising of her and then there came trouble when they began living together. Then the money was all gone and they both had become a little bitter. Mary had then almost a despairing feeling in her. Mabel took it all as a thing that had happened to her and now there would be some other thing to happen to her. She took it not so much lightly as as a thing that was over and that was all there was about it to her.

This was only the beginning of trouble for her but she always took it as it came to her, not lightly but simply and flightily as it happened to her.

Mary Maxworthing had in her something of a despairing feeling at the failure of her undertaking, at her return to nursery governessing. At first she did not even get a position so she lived on with Mabel Linker who did enough work to support her. Mary Maxworthing had a miserable feeling then in her, she had not an anxious feeling in her because a living

for her was always around her, she could always find people to employ
her she had this always in her, but she had for the first time in her living
in her a discouraged sense of failure.

Mary Maxworthing then had, for her, a very helpless dreary feeling
at the failure of her undertaking. As I was saying it was not in her anxious
being for she knew very well she never would have any real trouble earning a living but there was then for her no freedom in living, no distinction
for her in the future. So she had in her, for her, really a despairing feeling. It was not a desperately despairing feeling but it was really, for her,
a despairing feeling. She and Mabel Linker still continued to live together. Mabel Linker went to work right away for another dress-maker,
it was hard work for her but this did not make really any very great
difference to her. For a little while then Mary depended on Mabel Linker to support her, after a little while some one employed her to help
out in a little store near her. She stayed there all of that summer. Later
she went to a friend of the last person who had employed her as a nursery
governess for her, and every one who knew her thought that the future
now was settled for her.

Every one who knew her had a certain feeling about her. Every
one who knew her had a secure feeling about her. There are many ways
every one knowing any one feel in them the character of that one. There
are very many ways then for people to feel other people around
them. There are some who make almost every one who knows them
have the same kind of feeling about them. In a way Mary Maxworthing was
such a one. Mabel Linker was not the least bit such a one, almost every one
who knew her had a different feeling. With Mary Maxworthing it was
a different matter, some liked her and some did not like her, but whether
one liked her or did not like her each one had about the same feeling about
her, about the same estimate of her. It is a queer thing though with
women and with men too like her, they can astonish every one and
Mary Maxworthing had this in her. There are always many millions
of women and of men being made like her. This is now a history of the
feeling about her, the estimate every one who knew her had of her, of
the thing in her that was a surprise to every one who knew her. The kind
she is will then always come to be clearer. Always one must remember
each one has their own way of feeling other people's nature.

There are then some kinds of men and women, some men and some
women of some kinds of nature who have it in them to have every one who
knows them have about the same idea of them. Some may like, some may
dislike them, some may be indifferent to such a one but all of them every
one who ever comes to know that one has about the same estimate of such
a one. This is now a history of such a one.

Mary Maxworthing was then such a one. She had a certain gayety
in living but no wildness no recklessness in her being and no one would think

such a thing from the certain pleasant gayety she had in living. She had attacking in fighting but really very little attacking fighting in her living and no one ever expected not to have it more strongly in her being than it really came to be seen as it came out of her. She had no reserve of fighting in her, every one who knew her knew just about how much strength she had in her. She had a little impatient being, a little unpleasant temper in her, a little insistence on interfering in her, a small amount of pride in her, enough of sensitive response to make a reasonable sweetness in her, a little tendency to angry and injured feeling in her but not very much of this in her not more of this in her than any one would expect from her. She had a reasonable sense of responsibility in her, a reasonable efficiency in her, she was in short what every one thought her. She could still then surprise every one who knew her. She was still then really what every one had thought her. It was what no one who knew her ever thought of her that the quality of being in her could ever lead her to have a certain thing happen, it did happen to her, this is a history of her then and how she really was what every one thought her. She really was what every one thought her, every one who knew her had about the same estimate of her, every one who knew her was surprised by something that happened to her. This is a history then of what happened to her and then how later a reasonable success came to her.

After she had to give up the dress-making, after she had used up all the money she had saved for that undertaking she had in her almost a despairing feeling, not anything of an anxious feeling, a little impatient feeling, nothing then of an angry or injured feeling. She had not then as I was saying anything of an anxious feeling, she was always certain of being able to earn a living, she had no fear in her in living, she had a despairing feeling for the loss of freedom and possible success and distinction, she had an impatient feeling, not altogether an irritable feeling, it was more in the nature of a purely impatient feeling because she had to go back to taking care of children.

This altogether made in her something very nearly a despairing feeling in her. She was then as I was saying still living with Mabel Linker. She had not yet found a position but this was not then worrying her, she knew she could always earn a living, she had in her then her kind of despairing feeling. Mabel Linker was earning then enough to support herself and her. This is now what happened to both of them.

Mary Maxworthing as I was saying was really whatever any one who knew her thought her and yet she now had something happen to her that surprised every one who knew her.

She had as I was saying in her then a kind of a despairing a little an impatient feeling, she had no really anxious or excited or fearful being then in her, she knew she could always get a good place for people always wanted her. She was then as I was saying not a very young woman. For the rest of the summer she finally began working in a store near her, then later she got a good position as nursery governess and everything was satisfactory to her. Mabel Linker was working then in the beginning of winter around in houses sewing but she expected soon to begin again working for herself, it was she now who had a chance in her of a future. Mary Maxworthing said nothing then of working with her. One day Mary Maxworthing took a day off to go to the hospital to see a doctor. She went alone not even Mabel Linker was with her.

As I was saying Mary Maxworthing was what every one thought her. Every one had about the same estimate of her. Something happened to her that surprised every one who knew her, surprised them that it should happen to her.

Mary Maxworthing had not any recklessness or wildness in her. She had very little weakness in her. She had a certain ambition a certain desire for freedom and distinction. She had no anxious being or fear in her, she had not very strong desires in her, she had a certain gayety in her, she had a reasonable sense of responsibility inside her, she had a certain delicacy and good sentiment in her, she was what every one who knew her thought her. She had a little impatient feeling in her.

She went in to the doctor, the doctor asked her a few questions and then examined her, "you know what's the matter with you", he said to her. She grew red, she had a little impatient feeling in her, she had no fear in her and no angry feeling in her. "I don't know what's the matter with me Doctor," was her answer.

She had I was saying never any anxious feeling in her, she never really had any fear in her. She did have a little impatient feeling always in her. She had had after the failure of her undertaking a little of a despairing feeling. Now she did not have this in her. When the doctor said that to her she had no fear or anxious being in her, she grew a little red, she had a little nervous impatience then in her. "You know what's the matter with you!" said the doctor. "I don't know what's the matter with me," was her answer. The doctor was a young man, he grew angry and he told her. She grew redder, she had more impatient feeling in her but she had very little shame or anxious feeling in her, she had a little more impatient feeling in her. "You'd better get him to marry you," said the doctor who was angry with her.

It is very interesting that every one has in them their kind of stupid being. It is very important to know it in each one which part in them ; which kind of feelings in them is connected with stupid being in them. Sometime there will be a history of every kind of stupid being in every kind of human being in every part of the history of each one from their beginning to their ending.

There is then stupid being in every one. As I was saying Mary Maxworthing had very little stupid being in the bottom in her being, her stupid being was mostly mixed up with her impatient being with her possible angry or injured feeling. The doctor was angry at her saying that she did not know what was wrong with her, he thought it was stupid bottom being in her or a way of deceiving in her, it was the stupid being in her that went with the impatient being in her. Sometime this will be clear in her. The doctor then was angry with her, "you know what is the matter with you !" he said to her.

She did not then say anything farther, she was not interested in what the doctor had further to say to her. It was of no importance to her. She had then finished the stupid being in her that went with the impatient being in her. She was through with being stupid in that kind of way of not knowing whether it had really happened to her. Later impatient feeling stupid being would be again in her, this will show in the later history of her but now she knew what was the matter with her ; she went home and it got told to Mabel Linker. It was told to Mabel Linker, Mary Maxworthing told it very directly to her, "I don't care I want a baby, so much the worse for me getting it in this way but I want it anyway." Mary said this always after she had told her.

Mary Maxworthing then had a baby in her, it had happened to her and it was a surprise to every one who knew her who learned it about her. It was the very last thing any one would have expected to happen to her. One would have thought surely Mary Maxworthing would make a man marry her before such a thing would happen to her. It was a surprise to every one who knew her. But she was always then the same that every one thought her only, as she said, alright there is nothing to say about it, it had happened to her. That was the end of the fact for her, that was not the end of the trouble for her, that was the end of the fact for her. As I was saying Mary had stupid being in her connected in her with the impatient feeling she had in her, with the injured feeling she could have sometime in her. She had no stupid being as a bottom to her, by and by this will be clearer. Mabel Linker had a hard time taking care of her. Gradually the people who employed her knew what had happened to her. They were surprised too that it could happen to her, she said nothing to explain how it had happened, she said, alright it has happened and she liked children and now she would have one. There was no hardness in her, there was then no really anxious being in her. It had happened and that was the end of that matter to her. Soon every one who knew her had the same feeling about what had happened to her. Every one continued to have the same opinion of her whether they liked her or whether they did not like her as they had had before this happened to her, then every one who knew her had still the same estimate of her.

She was then without real anxious feeling, the people who employed her were patient with the impatient being then in her. Mabel Linker took good care of her and stood all the impatient being then in her, the impatient being that was stupid being then in her, the impatient being that was irritating then in her to every one near her, the impatient being that made her very interfering and rather nagging.

This is now a history of what now happened to her and how Mabel took care of her, and of Mabel Linker and how they did and did not get along together, and what each one of them felt about the other.

Mary Maxworthing and Mabel Linker were from the same part of the country. They had always known each other. Mary was the elder. Mabel was about five years younger. Mabel Linker's cousin had married Mary Maxworthing's sister. Mary Maxworthing had always known Mabel Linker and had always been very fond of her. When Mabel came to Gossols to learn dress-making Mary almost idolised her. They were then always together, Mabel then always did what Mary told her. Mabel was then a stranger, Mary Maxworthing had already been in Gossols many years then and she took care of her. They got along very well together. As I was saying Mabel learned cutting and fitting and soon became very clever almost brilliant in dress-making, she had not the sense for fashion, she had not the sense for managing, she had very little sense about anything, she had to have some one to do directing and Mary Maxworthing did this for her in the beginning completely to Mabel's satisfaction. Satisfaction is not the right word for describing Mabel's feeling. In Mabel satisfaction was the not being aroused to escaping or resisting or in fact to any conscious feeling. Anyway they got on then very well in living and dress-making. Mary then had very little impatient being, her impatient being had then nothing nervous in it, not that she ever came to be a nervous person, her impatient being was not then too interfering and then too at that time she had for Mabel almost an idolising feeling. She liked to write down when she was sitting idling, "Mabel is an angel, angel Mabel," and this showed her feeling. She wrote this down with a pencil whenever she was sitting doing nothing, this was in the beginning when Mabel was learning dress-making, when they were first living together.

It was much harder to know it about Mabel Linker what feeling she had in her about any one around her. It was always very hard to know this about her. Perhaps she did not mostly have any very strong feeling in her. It was very hard to know it about her. When she had a lover it was then certain that she was crazy to have him marry her, she only lived in having him want her. Mostly with every one else around her one never could tell what was the feeling in her. They got along then very well as I was saying when they first began living together.

Mabel then had become a good dress-maker, Mary had put together money enough and they began then their working together. At first things went pretty well and then they had some trouble living together and they had not then enough money to go on waiting for a future. They kept on however for some time living together.

Mary Maxworthing did not have in her really an unpleasant nature, she did not really have in her a nagging temper. She had very little in her of anxious being or attacking feeling that makes unpleasant nature. She had in her very little nervous character, she had in her a little impatient feeling, she had a pleasant gayety in her. Her stupid being and her interfering never came from anxious being in her, they were not really unpleasant nature in her, they came from the little impatient being in her and the fact that she had not a very large bottom in her to her, she had a little sensitive bottom in her, a very little weakness as a bottom to her, almost no stupid being as a bottom to her, she had enough sensitiveness in her to make a pleasant sympathetic sweetness in her, she had very little fighting or attacking in her ; all the unpleasant and stupid being in her was with the little impatient feeling always in her, with the angry and injured feeling sometime in her. This is a history of how she and Mabel Linker did and did not get along together. Mabel had a very different nature.

There are many ways then that people have affection in them, there are many ways of having feeling about people near one. Each one then has their own way of having affectionate feeling in them. Every one has their own kind of affectionate being. Mary Maxworthing had her way of feeling about Mabel Linker, Mabel had her own way of having loving feeling. In every one there is their way of having in them affectionate feeling. In every one there is changing. Mostly every one has changing in them in their feeling about any one. Mostly every one never thinks about the changing the other one may be having in them. This is another matter though and now this is a history of the affectionate feeling and loving feeling Mary Maxworthing and Mabel Linker had in them and how each one affected the other one of them. As I was saying in the beginning Mary had for Mabel almost an idolising feeling, no one knew very much about Mabel Linker's feeling.

Mary had for Mabel then at first almost an idolising feeling. Mabel had a quality of brilliant dress-making, and sweetness in enduring, and no certain expression of her feeling, and a certain freedom in doing that looked like courage in her living but was only that she never saw anything except the thing that then filled her, she never had any reflection in her, she had a certain shrinking fear sometimes in her but that was only when somebody stopped her, she had a certain flighty freedom in her, she was almost a brilliant dress-maker. She never had any ideas in her, she had not much sense of fashion in her, she had not such sense in her but that was not necessary for her, Mary Maxworthing would run her, when she first lived with her Mary idolised her. As I was saying the failure of the undertaking was to Mary Maxworthing a loss of freedom, a loss of future distinction. Mabel had very little of this feeling, she had not much more freedom working with Mary Maxworthing than in any other kind of working, not that she did not like it better, she liked it better but the failure did not make all the difference to her. Later it went better because then she had a husband to urge her. But this is all history that will be written later. Always later although they stayed together it was not as it had been earlier, it was not then an idolising of her by Mary and a yielding by her because she had no way to resist her.

Freedom then in Mary Maxworthing was having her own choice in living, having some distinction. Freedom for Mabel Linker was loving one man and marrying him and working only under driving. She was brilliant then in working but she needed urging, she needed always some one else's starting. She had sensitive being in her to the point of creation, she was not of the kind of women that have instrument nature in them, she never did any one else's living, she always did her own living, when she loved her own loving, when she worked her own brilliant working, but always she needed other people to keep her going, to start her, to arrange for her, to hold her down when flightiness seized her ; she always lived her own life in living, she needed other people to start her, to give a beginning idea to her, she needed other people to arrange for her, to hold her when flightiness was in her. She had no fighting in her, she had very little sense of escaping in her, she had some stubborn being in her, when she seized a thing she needed in loving or living nothing could pull it away from her. She needed very few things so much that no one could take them from her, she had no sense in her, generosity had no meaning to her she would give anything to any one even when they did not ask her, she held on only to the thing in living that was life to her, she had not any strong feeling about anything except the man she needed for loving, the man she married and who was everything to her, everything else could slip away as it would from her. This made an ingrate of her, she had no sense of any one ever doing anything for her for she had no need in her, they did it she never felt anything about it in her, that made trouble for her later, that made it later hard for Mary Maxworthing to forgive her, this is a history of the trouble it made for her. She had independent dependent nature in her but the dependent side of it in her to the point of sometimes exquisite creation was the whole of her. She had none of the independent side of it in her, she had no attacking in her. Stupid being in her was a negative thing in her, she had no sense for ordinary living in her, she had no sense of anything that was happening to her, she had not enough of anything in her beside the sensitive creation that was her to make any sense in her, this was the stupid being in her ; that which was not in her was the stupid being of her, this made in her a lack of understanding and of living, it made an ingrate of her, it made very often a foolish person of her. Often it not being there made her flightiness control her, those who were not ever much interested really in her always said of her it was foolishness, silliness always in her, those who took a real interest in her said she had craziness in her.   She had independent dependent nature in her and the sensitive dependent side of it in her to the point of exquisite creation was the whole of her.   This is now a history of her, of her loving, of her marrying, of her dress-making, of her living with Mary Maxworthing.

When Mary came home from the doctor Mabel was told all that had happened to her.   Mabel did everything any one could have done for her in all the trouble that then came to her.

Mary Maxworthing had not a despairing feeling with the baby in her as she had had at the failure of her undertaking at dress-making.   She had a little more now of anxious being, she had none of despairing feeling, she had very little anxious feeling, she had none of despairing feeling, she had very little anxious feeling, mostly it was impatient feeling that filled her and injured feeling that so much bad luck should have come to her. A great deal of impatient feeling, considerable injured feeling and a little anxious feeling was what then mostly was in her.   She had none of the despairing sense she had had in her after her failure, this would not effect the future for her, so much the worse for her that it had happened to her, she liked children, so much the worse that it should have come so to her, she still loved the man, he loved her, sometime perhaps he would marry her.   As it happened he did marry her, he married her when she was thirty-five, when she was making her new beginning with Mabel Linker at dress-making and was succeeding.   He was a decent enough man and always wanted to marry her, his family wanted him to marry another girl who was richer, he had been away on business travelling all the time she had the baby and later, when he came back finally and could arrange it he married her.   It was a successful enough marriage for her.   Living was always successful enough for her.

But all this was much later now she is coming back from the doctor with some impatient feeling, a little anxious feeling and some injured feeling in her.   Mabel Linker then did anything any one could do for her, the people who employed her were much surprised at such a thing happening to her, no one who knew ever would have imagined such a thing would happen to her, but it did not change their feeling for her, it did not change anybody's estimate of her.   It had happened to her.   Everybody was good to her, everybody except the doctor who had got angry with her. He was young then, he thought she had deceipt in her, this was not true of her, she was as honest as most people are.

I don't mean that she had any great honesty in her.   She did not but she had medium honesty in her.   In her interview with the doctor there was no deceipt in her there was only the stupidity of impatient being in her.

She was as honest as most people are in living, she was as conscientious as most people are in beginning, to herself she was a little more conscientious than she really was in being, she could have in herself an injured being. She could feel that Mabel should have in her toward her a grateful feeling, she could have in herself an injured feeling, she was to herself more sacrificing, more conscientious, a little perhaps, not much more honest to her in her being than she really was in being or in living, she could have then injured feeling. Mostly, in her, she had more impatient being, more interfering, than she had angry or injured feeling. She could have angry and injured feeling.

Mostly one has injured feeling when one is to one inside in one's feeling more noble than one ever is in acting than one ever is really in being, one has then inside one injured feeling. There are many kinds of ways of having injured feeling in one. Sometime there will be a history of all of the kinds of them.

Sometimes there is much sweetness inside one to one's feeling and all the time nasty words are coming out from one, in many of such of them there is much sweetness in them in their feeling, many of such of them do not know that then mean or brutal things are being said by them, so then they have rightly in them injured feeling inside them when the others respond to the nasty things said by them to them. This is a very common way of having injured feeling in one, sometime there will be a history of all the kinds of them. Mary Maxworthing then had impatient being, she never knew that this really made her interfering, to herself it only made her want to have every one do what they were doing. She had in her a reasonably conscientious, honest being, to herself she had a little more of them and of self-sacrificing being than she really had in living. This could come to make in her injured and sometimes angry feeling. Just the kind she had in her of conscientious and honest being will come out more and more in the history of her as in her living it comes out of her.

She came back then from the doctor and then Mabel Linker and then her employer knew what had happened to her. Everybody then was very good to her. No one then who knew her changed then in their feeling about her, this had happened to her, she was always though what every one always had thought her. The doctor had been angry with her, but he was young and thought it deceipt in her, it was impatient being that was the stupid being in her.

Mabel Linker was working for her living, she had commenced again having work to do in her room and in a small way had commenced again a business of dress-making though often she had to go out sewing. Mary Maxworthing, when she would have a bad feeling in her, came to Mabel Linker to have her take care of her.

As I was saying too, no one knew it about her what kind of feeling Mabel Linker had in her for Mary Maxworthing. Perhaps it will come to be clearer later. Anyhow she then took care of her, and it was not an easy matter. Mary had not even then anxious being in her, she did have very much then impatient being in her, it was very hard sometimes for any one to put up with her.

Every one has in them their own history inside them. In each one the history comes out of them in the repeating that is always in them. Mary Maxworthing had always in her some impatient being, sometimes it had in her more and sometimes less importance in her being, sometimes it had in her almost a different meaning from other times in her living. Mostly it was in her her stupid being.

This came to be very strongly in her in the trouble she had in having her baby. She did not have then in her really any anxious being, she had then in her very much impatient being and feeling.

Finally she did not have a living baby, after six months it passed out of her, it was her impatient being in her that made trouble for her, this is a history of what happened to her.

Repeating then is always coming out of every one, from the kind of being always in them. Almost always in the repeating in every one and in its coming out of them there is a little changing. In Mary Maxworthing it was always the same kind of impatient being, sometimes it was in her, impatient feeling, sometimes it was, interfering with every one around her and nagging and complaining, mostly it was not complaining, sometimes it was impatient being and stupid acting. Impatient being was almost always in her, stupid acting, it was not always in her as impatient feeling

In her trouble with having the baby come out of her this was mixed up in her. Always there was then impatient being strongly in her, often there was stupid acting in her from the impatient being always in her, sometimes there was impatient feeling in her. This is now a history of these things in her. As I was saying she always had in her, impatient being. As I was saying impatient being was the stupid being in her. It was not always active in her, it was at this time often enough active in her. She did not have in her so very much impatient feeling inside her. At this time with this trouble in her, impatient being was more than usually active in her, it came out in stupid ways of doing and not doing, she had sometimes, for her, a good deal of impatient feeling inside her. Mostly in her, impatient being was not impatient feeling in her. This is now a history of what all this did in her.

As I was saying Mabel Linker took care of her. It was not an easy matter. Mary went to Mabel every time she felt badly inside her. She never would go to a doctor. This was the impatient being in her, this was the impatient being in her that was the stupid being in her, this will be clearer later.

Mabel Linker took care of her and it was not an easy matter. She would not go to see a doctor. Finally at six months the baby passed out of her. She almost died when this happened to her. Mabel Linker had sent then for a doctor. It came very nearly being too late then to save her. This did not scare her until it was all over. She did not really know what was happening to her. She did not like it when she heard it later, she had no desire for dying in her. All that happened to her was from the impatient being in her. Impatient being was the stupid being in her. Every one has in them their own kind of stupid being, every one has in them a stupid part in them, this is a history of stupid being in Mary Maxworthing and Mabel Linker. This is a history of what happened to each of them, of everything that was in them, of the kind of stupid being in each one of them.

As I was saying, at the beginning of their living together, at the beginning of their dress-making Mary had for Mabel almost an idolising feeling. No one ever thought about the feeling Mabel Linker had about Mary Maxworthing. That was not important to any one. Later every one who knew them came to think about it but this was in their later living ; in the beginning of their living together, in the beginning of their dress-making undertaking, the feeling Mabel Linker had about Mary Maxworthing was not important to any one, no one knew whether she had little or much feeling, this was not important then to any one, not even to Mary Maxworthing. This was because of the nature Mabel Linker had in her. Feeling in Mabel Linker for any one was something no one ever stopped to consider, it was enough that Mary Maxworthing liked living with her, it was enough for any one who knew her to know that when Mary needed her Mabel took good care of her. Later, feeling in Mabel became more important to those that knew her. Later there was a question in the mind of every one who knew her what kind of feeling she had in her. Later every one came to feel about her that mostly she had not any feeling in her. Mary Maxworthing later felt this in her. Later every one who knew her accepted this in her. Some were never very certain about her. She was different then from Mary Maxworthing, she was a very different nature. Every one had the same notion of Mary whether they liked or whether they did not like her, she could surprise them by something happening to her but every one had and always kept about the same estimate of her. This is now more history of her.

There are millions always being made of every kind of men and women. Some kinds of them have it in them to have a being that makes every one who knows one of such of them think that one a singular one but always there are many millions of such of them, as many millions of such of them as of them who have it in them to have every one who sees them think there are always many existing of their kind of them. More and more in living one finds this to be true of people around them. This is now a history of every kind of them of every kind of men and every kind of women who ever were or are or will be living, of every kind of beginning of them as they are babies and children, and now this is a history of these two of them, Mabel Linker and Mary Maxworthing.

There is always then repeating, always everything is repeating, this is a history of every kind of repeating there is in living, this is then a history of every kind of living. There is always then in every one, repeating, there are always being made then millions of every kind of being, there are always then living millions of every kind of men and women, there are and were and will be always existing millions of each kind of them, and the kinds of them from the beginning, and in every nation, are always the same and this is now a history of some of them. There are always then the same kinds of them and millions of them, millions of each kind there are of men and women always existing. Each one of all of them have in them their individual existing, their own history in them, their own living in them, and this is now a writing of the history as it comes out of some of them. There is then always repeating, there is then always individual existing. There is then always repeating, there is then always repeating in each one, in each kind of them, in pairs of them, in pairs of women, in pairs of men, in pairs of men and women. Always more and more in living it comes out how kinds of them in pairing are always repeating, this is true in loving, in friendly being between men and women. Sometimes in living one sees so many repeating, so many who seem when one knows them to be so individual there can never be any one anything like them, a pair of them with so individual a relation made up of two who are so singular in their being that it never seems that there can be others just like them. Always then one sees another pair of them and sometimes it is almost dizzying, it gives to each one of the pairs of them an unreal being, and then it comes again that one undertands then that repeating is the whole of living. Repeating is the whole of living and by repeating comes understanding, and understanding is to some the most important part of living. Repeating is the whole of living, and it makes of living a thing always more familiar to each one and so we have old men's and women's wisdom, and repeating, simple repeating is the whole of them.

As I was saying pairing of friends and pairing in loving is always a repeating of the coming together of the kinds of them and this is not just general repeating but very detailed repeating, wonderfully alike the pairs are then in character and looks and loving and living.

As I was saying Mary Maxworthing and Mabel Linker were not altogether successful friends in their living. Later they both were married and then things went a little better for them, also they were succeeding then in their business of dress-making. This was when Mrs. Hersland knew them, when they were again living and dress-making in that part of Gossols where rich people were living.

As I was saying Mary Maxworthing when she was having the baby taken, did not know how near she was to dying. All of it came from the impatient being which was her kind of stupid being. She did not know when the baby was passing how near she was to dying, afterwards she had about it almost an anxious feeling.

As I was saying it was hard on Mabel Linker then to take care of her. Not when the baby was passing out of her for then she had a doctor and was in a hospital with a nurse taking care of her, but before, when she would not see a doctor. She would not let a doctor see her, this was impatient being in her, she would not listen to Mabel Linker or to any one else who tried to advise her, she was full up with impatient feeling. Yes, of course sometimes she was bleeding, but she did not want to pay any attention ; she was full up then with impatient feeling. Later after it was over and she knew how near she had been to dying she had for a little while less impatient feeling, she had then in her, some anxious feeling. This was the end of that thing for her. She stayed then a year or two longer with the same employer. During this time Mary Maxworthing and Mabel Linker saw very little of each other. They had had serious troubles with each other.

As I was saying when Mary Maxworthing first had Mabel Linker live with her she had for her almost an idolising feeling. As I was saying men and women, women and women, men and men do so much repeating, it is almost startling as more and more one comes to know it of them. The repeating is not only of the general kind of combining as to their being men and women, as to their being big and little, alike or contrasting, independent dependent and dependent independent, it is likeness of the type of character combining with another and these two are very individual in their being and their relation and sometimes they have in them a kind of being that makes every one who knows them think there can never have been any one like one or the other of them, surely never any two like the pair of them and then one goes on in one's living and then there is repeating of the pair and then another repeating of them and then another repeating of them and always one has about each pair of them the strong feeling of their having each one of them strongly individual being and sometimes it makes of everything a strange world for living and sometimes it makes to one's feeling the world a pleasant and familiar place for living. Strangeness has no place then in living, to one's feeling, it is a familiar thing, living, and to some, such a feeling is the pleasantest kind of feeling they can have in their living.

Mary Maxworthing then is very clear now in her being. She is very clear now to every one. There are many millions always living with her kind of being. There are in every country in every kind of living, they exist with every kind of training. Sometime there will be a history of five of them, sometime there will be a history of all of them. Now this is a history of one of them.

Mary Maxworthing was what every one who knew her, whether they liked her or did not like her, thought her. She had not any recklessness.

or wildness in her. She had very little weakness in her. She had independent dependent nature in her but she had very little fighting in her, what seemed like fighting was mostly impatient being in her, she had very little attacking in her. She had a certain gayety in her, she had not good nature really in her, she had no heartlessness in her, she had enough sensitive being to make a pleasant sympathetic sweetness in her, that with the little gayety in her gave to her the charm she had in her. The very little attacking, the gayety in her, the impatient being in her, the certain practical feeling for fashion and for being a success, that was in her, gave to her her desire for freedom and a little distinction in the future. She had no sordidness in her, she had not much memory in her. More and more she will be clearer, in the history of her relation to Mabel Linker, in her relation to the man who later married her, in the way she came to the undertaking again of the business of dress-making.

As I was saying, during the trouble she had in her Mabel Linker took care of her. Later they had serious trouble with each other. Finally later when Mabel had a husband to urge her and Mary Maxworthing had a little money left to her they began again to be together, they more or less stuck together though they never really got along together. They had a reasonable success together. This is now a history of Mabel Linker and the nature in her.

Mabel Linker had a different nature. She had her own being in her. Every one has their own being in them. Every one has their own repeating in them. Every one is of a kind of men and women. Every kind of men and women is a kind of a kind of them. All the kinds of them are kinds of the two kinds of them. Sometime there will be a history of all of them.

There are then the two kinds of them, independent dependent and dependent independent. Mary Maxworthing was of the independent dependent, Mabel Linker was of the same kind of them but as one might say of extreme one end of that kind of them, while Mary Maxworthing was of toward the other end of them. This difference made an attraction between them, their being of the same kind of them made it that in the end they did not succeed in continuing friendly living. It is very interesting to know the range in one kind of men and women. This is now a little about one kind of them with Mary Maxworthing and Mabel Linker both of them of that one kind of them but at the two ends of that kind of them.

Men have in them and women have in them, some of them, independent dependent nature in them. Many millions of men and many millions of women are always being made of this kind, always about half of everybody living is of this kind of men and women. This is now a description of one part of them which makes one kind of this kind of men and women. This is a description of that part of them, that kind of them as women; later there will be a description of them as men. Always it is easier to know it in them, the details of a kind of them, in women, later this will be clearer in them. Now this is a history of the kind of them who have of them Mabel Linker and Mary Maxworthing.

As I was saying the two of them had difficulties, later in their living, had difficulty in remaining friends, in beginning again with dress-making. As I was saying they had both in them the same kind of being, that is to say one was one extreme kind of such being, the other was almost the other extreme kind of such being and now there is a description of them in the kind of being there is in them, later there is a history of their living as it came out of them, always there is a description of their character as in repeating it comes out of each one of them. So then.

There are as I was saying the two kinds of being in women and in men, independent dependent, dependent independent. The first of these have attacking as their natural way of fighting, resisting in such of them is sometimes impatient or dull or scared or stubborn or pig-headed stupid or vacant being, is sometimes a continuing of attacking ; resisting to the dependent independent is the natural way of fighting. Those then who have in them independent dependent being as the bottom of them have attacking in them as their natural way of fighting. Many of them have very little fighting in their living. This was true of both of these two who had independent dependent nature in them, Mabel Linker and Mary Maxworthing.

Those who have independent dependent nature in them may have practical and sordid nature in them but mostly they have not much earthy simple natural sense in them. This will be clearer as more of them come to be seen in the history there will be of such of them. As I was saying Mabel Linker and Mary Maxworthing had both of them independent dependent nature in them.

Mabel Linker had not an instrument nature in her, the sensitiveness in her made a kind of real creation in her, made her live her own living, do her own loving. To many there may be a confusion between the sensitive instrument nature that lives so strongly the lives of others that they seem to be their own creation and one like Mabel Linker. To any one that knows them well, sooner or later this comes to be clearer.

As I was saying then the instrument nature is one having sensitive being or power of idealising or power for seizing without knowing it other people's suggestion. If the seizing is their own volition that makes another being, that is not living other people's lives in living. So then there is a kind of men and women who have in them independent dependent nature in them and this is now to be a description of many variations in them and Mary Maxworthing and Mabel Linker, both of them, are of this part of the general independent dependent kind of men and women.

Sooner or later there will be histories of many men and women with independent dependent nature in them. As I was saying there is to be

Martha Hersland and Julia Dehning, there is to be a sister of one governess, and one governess with such a nature. Now there are Mary Maxworthing and Mabel Linker.

Perhaps, always it will become clearer, the independent dependent nature and later every one will see it in each one who have in them some form of such nature. Later dependent independent nature will be clearer and every one who sees any one will know it sooner or later in that one their kind of nature and the kind of the kind of nature they have in them and that in repeating comes out of them. Now then to begin again with independent dependent being, now to begin with Mabel Linker and Mary Maxworthing.

To begin again then with the instrument nature, with attacking being, with sensitive being, with weakness or vacant being, with little, with much bottom being, with little or much attacking in living, with unified or with separated natures inside each one, as in living it comes out of each one.

There are then many men and many women, more or less half of all that ever were or are or will be living, who have independent dependent nature in them. I will tell about it now in women because it comes easier to tell about it in them ; more and more, then, I will tell about it in men. It is the same in men as in women but it separates a little clearer in women and so it will make a kind of diagram for a beginning. As I was saying I like to tell in the beginning, I like better to tell it about women the nature in them because it is clearer and I know it better, a little not very much better. One can see it in her sooner, a little, not very much sooner, but on the whole it is clearer, things are more separate generally in her, perhaps it is a little clearer in her, perhaps I know it a little better in her.

As I was saying then, every one has in them their own way of being and this comes out of them in the repeating that is always in every one, in some it does not come to be very clear in them until their middle living, in some not until their later living, but sometime in every one the nature in them comes to be clear to any one who looks well at them, sometimes in their younger living, sometimes in their middle living, sometimes in their later living. As I was saying every one has in them their own way of eating, their own way of drinking, their own way of sleeping, their own way of resting, of loving, of talking, or keeping still, of waking, their own way of working, of having stupid being in them and coming out of them, their own way of having nasty feeling in them and coming out of them, in short then, every one has in them their own being and in repeating it is all through their living always coming out of them.

As I was saying more or less half of all who ever were or are or will be living have independent dependent nature in them, that is to say attacking is their natural way of fighting, resisting is stubborness and in many of them the stupid being in them, many of them have as a bottom to them sensitive or weak or stupid being, some have attacking that is fighting as almost the whole of them.   As I was saying this is all clearer in the women, as they have less in them a unification of these things in them, they have simpler reaction in them.   Everybody knows this now in women and now this is a history of all of them.

As I was saying then there are a kind of men and women who have in them independent dependent being and some of these have instrument nature, others are of the kind of Mary Maxworthing, others of the kind of Mabel Linker.   There are many kinds of them who have independent dependent nature in them and there are many kinds connected with these kinds of them and their history will come later ; Martha Hersland and Julia Dehning and Mr. Hersland and many others who came to know the Hersland children in some part of their living were connected then were of such a kind of nature.   It is clear then, independent dependent being is being when the natural way of fighting is attacking, dependent independent being is when the natural way of fighting is resisting.   There are some who have independent dependent nature in them and have no attacking, no fighting being in them, Mabel Linker was such a one .; there are some who have in them very little fighting in their living but all fighting in them is attacking and this is true of Mary Maxworthing. ·

There are then some who have in them sensitive being to the point of creating even to the point of fighting, there are some who have this in them ; there are some who have in them sensitive being and this makes them live other people's lives in living, these may have fighting from attacking being in them, these may have fighting in them from the sensitive being in them that makes them live other people's lives all through their living.   Later there will be written the history of such a one.   These have instrument nature in them, they need other people's lives for life enhancing.   Later there will be more history of such of them.   There are some who have instrument nature in them without the sensitive bottom to them, with stupid or vacant or weak or vague bottom to them and an idealising sense in them and a stupid stubborn way of resisting to everything except the one thing they have made their living and this is always in such of them some one else's thinking, feeling or being.   There are many millions always of such of them, sometime perhaps in Julia this will be interesting.   So then there are many ways of having instrument nature in one.   The dependent independents have it also in them, some of them, but with them, such of them as have it in them, it shows in different fashion from the independent dependent kind of them, such ones have earthy being, they have fear in them, that makes their way of being in them ; later in the living of Mrs. Hersland and Madeleine Wyman and Alfred Hersland and young David Hersland dependent independent being will come to be clearer.

Now then there is only independent dependent being we are

considering.   Later there will be more written of instrument being of this kind of them.   Neither·Mary Maxworthing nor Mabel Linker had this nature in them.   So then to go on with them.

As I was saying Mary Maxworthing had gayety in living.   She had very little fighting in her living but fighting in her was as attacking.   She had very little fear in her.   She had very little bottom to her, she had a little sensitive bottom to her enough to give a pleasant sweetness to her. She had a little weakness in her enough to make her a little yielding to attacking.   She had very little stupid bottom in her, most of the stupid being in her was of the impatient being always in her.   This was the disagreeable part in her, the little attacking in her was not enough in her to be an unpleasant being in her, injured and angry feeling in her was part of such attacking living as she had in her but these were not much in her. They were sometimes in her ; they were in her when she had the baby, that such bad luck should come to her.   They were in her about Mabel Linker, when to her thinking Mabel was ungrateful toward her.   This is now a history of Mabel Linker, and of her and Mary Maxworthing living together and their having trouble with one another and of Mabel's loving and then their beginning again dress-making together.

Mabel Linker had a very different nature from the other.   She had no impatient being in her, she had sensitive being in her to the point of creation.   She had in her independent dependent nature.   She had no attacking in her.   This is now a history of her.

Every one has in them always their own repeating, always more and more then repeating gives to every one who feels it in them a more certain feeling about them, a more secure feeling in living.   Repeating is more and more in every one the whole of that one the whole of every one, the wonder of each one is always more and more complete in each one as the repeating in them makes them a sure thing a thing certainly having being, makes for every one old men's and old women's wisdom, old men's loving and old women's feeling.   Always more and more then repeating is the certain thing in every one.   Always more and more then there is contentment in the secure feeling repeating in every one gives to every one.   Always then there is excitement for every one in the certainty of repeating in every one.   Always the wonder of each one as repeating in them makes a certain whole of them, comes to be a contentment to any one who sees them.   Always then repeating is in every one and every one is a whole then and there is a secure feeling in resting in this realisation sometime one can have of every one.   Repeating then is always in every one, sometime then there will be a description of all repeating and then there will be contentment in contemplation.   Anyhow repeating is always in every one. Anyhow repeating is always in the pairing of two of them.   This is now a history of two of them.

As I was saying Mary Maxworthing and Mabel Linker both of them were of the kind of them having in them independent dependent being. Mostly for successful living two living together, man and woman or two women or two men, there should be in them the two kinds of them, one independent dependent the other dependent independent, one with attacking as the natural way of fighting, the other resisting as the way of being ; but in loving and in friendly living this is mixed up in different ways to make a pair of friends for reasonably successful living. For loving to marrying to successful married living, there is always this combination, the independent dependent in one and in the other the dependent independent being. For loving then there is almost always this combination, in long successful friendly living there may be another mixing, a pairing of the same kinds of them. This will now be a description of some ways this is true in men and women, with every kind of nature in them.

Mary Maxworthing and Mabel Linker had then both of them independent dependent nature in them. Slowly it came out in them. Slowly they had trouble with each other. Later they began again together but that was then a business matter. Mabel had then her husband to urge her. Mabel's marrying made at first great trouble between her and Mary Maxworthing.

As I was saying, until Mabel Linker was full up with loving for the man who later married her no one ever had known what feeling she had in her about any one near her, about anything that happened to her. Perhaps nothing was important to her until loving filled her. Anyway no one ever knew what she had as feeling in her. She had as I was saying almost brilliant quality as a dress-maker. She had not much sense of fashion in her. She needed some one to urge her and start her. When a thing was suggested to her and she was pushed to begin she was almost a brilliant dress-maker. As I was saying no one knew very much what feeling she had in her. People who knew her had very different opinions of her. When Mary Maxworthing first knew her, first had her living with her, she almost idolised her. This feeling lasted in Mary through the beginning of their undertaking of dress-making. It died down in her when she had her trouble in her, her impatient feeling when they were not succeeding, her despairing feeling at the failure of her undertaking, her impatient troubled nervous feeling when she had her baby in her, her anxious feeling when she knew what had almost happened to her that her baby was dead and that she had almost died with her. And then Mabel Linker had her lover, Mary found ingratitude then in her, things got so that they could no longer live together. Then Mabel got married and much later when Mary had a little money left to her from some relative down in the country and Mabel had her husband to urge her, they began with their undertaking in that part of Gossols where richer people were living. Now they were more successful and things were different between them. Mary had now mostly the business managing and the excuses and the matching and the buying to do for the two of them and Mabel did the dress-making and she had in her with her husband's urging enough decision so Mary was stopped from doing too much interfering. They always did a fair amount of quarrelling but on the whole this time they succeeded fairly well with their undertaking. Then Mary married the man as I was saying, he had always wanted her to marry him and now his family would let him. His mother had not any longer any objection. Mary Maxworthing was succeeding well enough with dress-making, besides she saw that he would do it and it was not any longer any use objecting and resisting. This was about the time when Mrs. Hersland had them to make for her all her best dresses, all those she used for visiting.

As I was saying Mary Maxworthing when she had her baby in her had not then in her any despairing feeling but she had in her a troubled impatient nervous being. As I was saying, in their first living together she had for Mabel Linker almost an idolising feeling. She would write when she sat idling, "angel Mabel, Mabel is an angel", and this showed her feeling. She never thought anything about Mabel's feeling. Mabel was everything she wanted and that was enough for her feeling, besides it was almost impossible to know what Mabel had inside her. As I was saying Mary Maxworthing had gayety but never any wildness or recklessness in living. She had gayety in living, she had in her very little anxious being, she had in her always impatient being , she had some sensitive bottom enough to give with her gayety some attractive sweetness to her. Her gayety and her impatient being and what there was in her of attraction gave her some quality of domination, not so much as there was in her impatient being and interfering. She was then a pleasant enough person all through her living, she was a pleasant enough person with some quality of attraction. She was reasonably honest and conscientious in her living. In the beginning then she had for Mabel Linker an idolising feeling. When she was sitting idling she would often be writing, "Mabel is an angel, angel Mabel". She had for her this feeling, all through the beginning of their first undertaking. Then they had trouble living together, Mary was very interfering, she had a sense for fashion and she had given all the money they had for their beginning and Mabel never had in her any impatient being and she could endure a good deal of directing, but when they were not succeeding they began to have trouble between them. Not that Mabel said much or did much to show any changing in feeling but Mary felt that Mabel had not enough grateful feeling. Mabel never did have grateful feeling, after all she did the dress-making, after all she never thought much about Mary and her feeling, after all she was always willing, after all she never really heard very much of what Mary was always saying.

Mary Maxworthing had a certain gayety in living, she had ambition, she had impatient feeling. She had a certain power of domination, but not as much as she had impatient feeling which made her interfering and in a certain degree nagging. She had just enough domination to keep her from being too irritating.

Mary Maxworthing never had in her any grateful feeling to Mabel Linker for taking care of her, for doing all any one could do for her, while she was having her trouble with a baby. Mary was not like Mabel, she knew people should be grateful, she could have injured feeling in her. It was a little queer that she never felt that Mabel Linker had been good to her, that she should have any grateful feeling toward her ; perhaps it was because then she had so much impatient being in her and impatient being was the stupid being of her, perhaps it was because Mabel Linker had never any feeling in her of doing anything for her. Mary told her to do something and Mabel did it for her, there was no anxious feeling in Mabel Linker ever ; there was never any tenderness in her, Mary Maxworthing then had never any grateful feeling to her in her.

The idolising feeling in Mary Maxworthing for Mabel Linker did not change into something else in her. It just died out of her. Later when Mabel had gone away from her and was married Mary wanted to begin again with her but always again, when she got used to her, she had no strong feeling about her, she never had for her at any time, later, an idolising feeling, but she always wanted her more than Mabel wanted her. But Mabel really only needed the man who married her, Mabel never wanted anything else to come to her. Later with her husband to urge her she got to have more feeling for a future, she wanted then for him and for herself too then success in dress-making. She and Mary came together then. Mary had some money then and they began again in that part of Gossols where rich people were living.

Mary Maxworthing had then, when she had the baby in her, nervous impatient being, she had no feeling in her about Mabel Linker or any other person near her, the idolising feeling she had had for Mabel died out of her when freedom and distinction did not come to her, not that she had liked Mabel because Mabel could possibly help her to a future, not at all, but when Mabel was always with her, when Mary was not stirred up with planning for the future, when gayety was a little dead in her, when impatient feeling was in her, she had not any stimulation to have idolising feeling for Mabel Linker. Mary Maxworthing then had for Mabel, as for every one around her then, no feeling, she was full up with impatient being. Later then, when the baby was still-born and Mary knew she had been very near to dying, she had in her then anxious impatient, a little of nervous being, Mabel then had for her very little meaning, then later when Mary began to be herself again inside her Mabel had begun loving and Mary was disapproving. So there was never again a beginning in Mary of idolising feeling.

Mary Maxworthing and Mabel Linker were not altogether successful friends in their living. Later they both were married and then things went a little better between them. Mabel Linker had a husband then to make her important and to urge her inside her. Mary Maxworthing did not have a husband until some time after Mabel had one, until after she had begun again with Mabel the undertaking of dress-making.

Every one has then in them their own way of having injured feeling, Mabel Linker had never in her much of this inside her. Later with a husband to urge her to be inside her her important being, she could have such a feeling. Luckily then Mary Maxworthing had not yet her husband and so they got along together.

As I was saying when Mary Maxworthing was having her despairing feeling she lost all feeling about Mabel Linker. Mary Maxworthing had this in her, many women are like her, many men have this too in them, they have in them negative egotism in them. Later there will be histories of many of such of them.

Mary was not a complete one of such a kind of them. This is the kind they are then. Mabel Linker was not at all such a kind of one. This is now a description of them.

Many women then are always of them, many men have it in them, mostly it is a kind of them that are made more as women perhaps than as men. Every one then has their own way of having injured feeling in them. As I was saying many have it in them when they have more self-sacrificing, more noble being in them than ever comes out of them in living, when they have a noble sweetness in them to them and they are unpleasant or lazy even in living. Many of them who have negative egotism in them have lazy being as the bottom of them, lazy or vague or empty bottom to them. Some of them are dependent independent, some are independent dependent, all of them mostly have lazy or vague or empty or very little bottom to them. Some have much bottom in them and never get it into motion. Negative egotism then is when one has enough egotism never to follow any other leading, never to live anybody else's life in living, always to have the best reason why every condition in living is the wrong place for them and not to have enough egotism to live their own life, to do their own choosing, to really be resisting. These then never have any real choice in them, they have not resisting in them, they have very good reasons why there is no place for them, why conditions are always wrong to them. Often it takes years to know them, they are mostly nice women with tender hearts and pleasant natures in them, they are many of them so stirring in their living that it is hard to know it of them that they have lazy being as a bottom to them, they worry so much inside them that it is hard to believe it of them that they have not it in them to be active in taking trouble enough to be really living, they are very many then of all of such of them, they have such very good reasons for not finding any place for living, it takes a long time when one is living with any one of them not to be taken in by the good reasons they have for not choosing. Even when one knows them well their reasons are convincing, there is such good reason always in them and they are mostly pleasant people with tender hearts or active worrying in them and lazy being in them. Laziness is in many of them not easy to know of them. Many of them seem actively in motion many of such of them who have really lazy being in them. There are then many many millions always being made of women and of men who have negative egotism in them. Some then are always existing who come nearer real egotism, these have not enough egotism for choosing, for living, some by attacking some by resisting make for themselves a protection, they do not do their own living but they keep other people off oi them or clog them. There are many ways then of being in all these ways of egotism, sometime then there will be a history of all of them, a history of all of them, a history of every one, of every man and every woman who ever were or are or will be living, who have ever in them egotism, active, passive or negative.

Alright then, there is a negative egotism in many men and in women, in very many of them. Sometime then there will be a history of every kind of them.

As I was saying every one mostly has sometime in them some injured feeling. Mabel Linker almost never had any of it in her. Mary Maxworthing could have it sometimes in her. Mabel Linker had not in her any of the thing we have been just describing. She had in her individual being, she had in her sensitive being to the point of creating. She lived her own life in living. Mostly she was not doing much living, that is she needed urging to be working, she had flightiness in being, in loving she had her complete being, then she did real creating, she was alive then to her own feeling. Mary Maxworthing was more nearly of them who have in them negative egotism. She had a little gayety in living, she had a little sensitive bottom, but when she had impatient being as filling she had almost negative egotism. When she had impatient being then, she had not in her any sense of living, then all feeling for any one died out of her. Impatient being was not nervous being in her, it was not a bottom to her, it was sometimes the whole of her, it was stupid being in her. Mabel Linker had a very different nature.

As I was saying when Mary Maxworthing was looking to a future with freedom and a dress-making undertaking and a little distinction, she had in her a sense of herself to herself inside her, she had in her a sense of living in her, she had something of individual being in her. She had then for Mabel Linker almost an idolising feeling, this was important feeling in her. When she had despairing being in her she had only stupid being in her, she had not negative egotism then in her, she was just going on living because life was in her. All that then was in her was the impatient being that was in her stupid being and despairing feeling, not really despairing feeling, but dull being in her. Later when she had a very little anxious being in her and a good deal of impatient being in her, when Mabel Linker was taking care of her, she was nearer to negative egotism, she had excellent reasons for all injured feeling in her, she had excellent reason why everyone should take care of her, she had excellent reason for it to be right to her that Mabel Linker should take care of her, all she had done for her and all the trouble she herself now had in her, and so it was right that she should have Mabel Linker take care of her, and that was the end of that matter to her. Mabel Linker had no injured feeling in her, Mabel never had in her any sense of any one doing any thing for her, mostly Mabel did what came to her, she did well anything she started to do because it came to her, she did brilliant dress-making, it came natural to her, in loving she had her own living inside her. Later she had her husband to urge her, that gave to her a little more, always in her, a sense of herself to herself inside her.

Mary Maxworthing then had good reason not to have toward Mabel Linker any grateful feeling. Mabel took care of her. She had come near dying, now she was through with that trouble, slowly impatient being came to be more nearly a reasonably small part of her, and this was now to her an end of that matter.

This was then the end in her of anxious nervous being, she went back then to her old work and was not hoping and she had then negative egotism as the way of living, she had a kind of negative optimism as a way of thinking. It was then that Mabel Linker began loving, it was then that she and Mary Maxworthing almost came to the end of friendly relation. This is now the history of the two of them.

As I was saying Mary Maxworthing then had for a little time no hope for future freedom, she had just then no prospect for marrying, she was commencing to have again a little gayety in living, she had in her then still impatient being. Mabel Linker had commenced to have work enough at home to keep going. Mary just then had no hope of commencing dressmaking with her again. Mabel was flighty then and had no sense in managing. Mary was not taking much interest in what Mabel was doing, she had in her some impatient feeling, she had in her then very little important being of herself inside her to her feeling. She had in her then not much real living, she had in her then negative egotism.

It was alright for Mary Maxworthing to have the feeling she had in her about Mabel Linker. She had good reasons then for the feeling in her. It was the end of interest for her, it was the end of freedom for her, Mabel had no meaning for her when she had no connection with her, this came to her when she had her baby in her from the trouble in her that left her no feeling for any other because she had no live being in her ; later when Mabel was full up with love for the man who later married her there was nothing of her for Mary to feel in her, there had never been anything there really, for her, but when there was nothing else in Mabel Linker it had not made any difference to any one who knew her. Mary Maxworthing had then good reason for the feeling she had in her about Mabel Linker, Mary had had almost an idolising feeling about Mabel when they first lived together when they began their undertaking of dress-making together, when she would sit idling, waiting, dreaming, she would be writing, "Mabel is an angel, angel Mabel", this showed the feeling she had then in her about her. Then came the time when she was no longer hoping for the future, then there was some bitterness in her, then she felt Mabel should have more grateful feeling in her than she showed toward her, then came the despairing being in her and then the thing happened to her that surprised every one who knew her when her weakness and desire were more active in her because gayety and impatient being and ambition were then dead in her. Then she had not feeling about any one around her. Then there came to be in her, troubled impatient feeling, and Mabel took care of her. Mary was then full up with impatient being and Mabel took care of her like any other, neither the one nor the other then felt anything about the other. Then when that was over Mary knew how near she had come to be dying, then she had a little anxious impatient irritable being in her and then she and Mabel still lived together and then they quarrelled more and more with each other for Mabel was beginning then with her lover and so she had then the beginning of wanting to escape, a little, in her. Then Mary was beginning to have her former being, she had begun again taking care of children. Mabel then was beginning to succeed well enough with dress-making to work at home and keep going. She was flighty then and uncertain in her working and Mary was always scolding, not for her own sake for there was nothing in it for her, but for Mabel's sake so Mabel could get along and not have people leave her disgusted with her. Mabel was very flighty then with no one to hold her, she was getting then fuller and fuller of love for the man who later married her. Mary did not want this marriage for her, he was a young fellow, Mabel's lover, younger than she was and a poor money getter. Mary did not then have for Mabel any idolising feeling, she did not take much interest in her, she always scolded her, she had in her an injured feeling because Mabel had no gratitude in her, no feeling for any one around her. This was true enough about her, Mary always had good reasons for the feelings in her, it was true enough Mabel was flighty and had no gratitude in her and had no feeling for any one ever excepting the man who later married her. And so they did not get along at all together, Mabel always had more and more escaping in her, she had not come yet to have any feeling of herself inside her, this came to her later with a husband to urge her to make her herself inside her, but she had more and more of escaping being in her, she was always getting more and more full of loving and she never had had

in her any feeling for any one around her.   Before, it had not been important to any one the feeling in her for then there was not in her, loving or
escaping to make any one feel any lack in her.   Now it was different and
Mary Maxworthing had good reason for the feeling she had in her about
her.   Mabel was working then but flightiness was strongly in her and people who employed her often were disgusted with her.   They did not leave
her for as I was saying Mabel was almost brilliant in dress-making.   Mary
had no patience then with her, she had injured feeling in her for she was
then not of any importance to Mabel Linker.   She had injured and sometimes angry feeling in her then about her.   It was alright for her to have
then such a feeling about Mabel Linker, Mabel had flightiness then in her,
Mabel had escaping then in her, Mabel was full up with love for a man
who was younger and would never earn a living for her.   Mabel Linker
had then her own living in her.   She was full up with love for the man
who later married her.

Things then were always getting more and more unpleasant between
them.   Mary Maxworthing had injured feeling in her, she had impatient
being then in her, she was always scolding, she wanted Mabel not to have
such flightiness in her, she wanted to keep her from marrying.   Mabel
then had escaping being in her and she would then sometimes answer and
it was then a continued biting chatter whenever they were together and
they were always together, they could not keep away from one another.
Finally things got so bitter between them that Mary would have nothing
further to do with her.   Mabel could marry and then when sickness and
trouble would come to her she would know better.   Mary Maxworthing
would have nothing more to do with her or with her pauper lover.   Mary
had a hard feeling then in her about her, she had then impatient being and
injured being and angry feeling that together were in her as a hard sense
of knowing that bad things would come to Mabel Linker to punish her.
Mabel did not pay much attention then to her, she was having a little
trouble then with the mother of her lover.   The mother wanted her to take
another flat to live in and Mabel had no money to pay for anything and
she did not want to say it to her going to be husband's family.   Mary
Maxworthing had then always more and more of angry feeling in her about
Mabel Linker.   She told her then to get another machine to sew on, that
one was hers and she needed it now for herself and Mabel could go to her
lover's family and get them to give one to her, she thought they were such
nice people, let them show her.   Then Mabel's lover's mother made Mabel
promise not to invite Mary Maxworthing to their wedding and that was
for some time the end of any relation between them.   Mabel Linker then
was married and she and her husband had a happy enough existence.   The
husband's family had to help them and then his mother died and then when
Mabel met Mary they began to say "how do you do", again to one another.
Mabel with her husband, who was a nice bright man, to urge her, got on

a little better. More and more then she felt herself inside her. She was beginning to have work enough to occupy her. She had even a girl to help her. Later she and Mary got to be friendly again together. Mary had a little money left to her and with Mabel's husband to urge Mabel they began again a business of dress-making in that part of Gossols where rich people were living. Mary Maxworthing did the managing and the fashion and the excusing and the matching and the arranging for fittings and the arranging for paying and the changing, and Mabel the dress-making. They always had some trouble between them but this time they were successful enough with their undertaking. Later Mary Maxworthing married the man, as I was saying. They all four of them were successful enough in their living.

These then were the dress-makers Mrs. Hersland had in her middle living. The woman with the daughters, to do plain sewing and making over and putting on skirt braids and sometimes mending. Lillian Rosenhagen to make ordinary dresses for Mrs. Hersland and dresses for Martha and sometimes for the governess living in the house with her, and Mary Maxworthing and Mabel Linker to make her best dresses for her and once to make a dress for the last governess Miss Madeleine Wyman and there is now soon to be a history of this dress for her.

These then made Mrs. Hersland's clothes and clothes for her daughter Martha, sometimes for the governess living with her.

There were, as I was saying, in the middle living of the Hersland family, three governesses, a foreign woman, and a tall blond foreign american who later married a baker, and then Madeleine Wyman who was with them when Mrs. Hersland had in living, her most important feeling. This is now a history of the three of them and then there will be a little more history of Mrs. Hersland and Mr. Hersland and of them with them, and then there will begin a history of the three children, a long history of each one of them.

The first governess then was a foreign woman. She was a good musician.

It is very interesting that every one has in them their kind of stupid being. It is very important to know it in each one which part in them, which kind of feeling in them is connected with stupid being in them. There is then stupid being in every one. It was hard to know it in the foreign woman who was such a good musician and the first governess the Hersland family had living with them, it was hard to know the stupid being that was surely somewhere in her. It was hard to know her enough to know where to find it in her. She had a sister, in that way perhaps one could find it in her. This is now a history of her, and the sister and the Hersland family with her.

The sister was much younger. She was then in Gossols, then studying to be a teacher. She was always a little afraid of her sister. She always addressed her as sister Martha. It was very hard to find the stupid being in the governess even when she was with her sister. It was very hard to find stupid being in her then even when her sister was with her. She was then a woman nearly forty. She had been a governess ever since she was twenty. She had been, the last ten years, in America. She had brought her young sister with her, she wanted her to be educated to be a teacher, she wanted her to live in America where life would be easier. She herself did not like it in America, she wanted to go back to her old living where people spoke french and german and where it was natural for her to be a musician. It was not to her, natural to be musical in Gossols. She did not stay very long with the Herslands, her sister soon got a position as teacher and then the elder sister left her, she wanted then to leave America, this did not come to her, she got as far as Cincinatti and then somehow she never got farther. She stayed there and she gave music lessons and she never got any further and she stayed there always until she died there, and she never had left America. As I was saying it was not easy to know it in her the stupid being in her. As I was saying every one has in them their kind of stupid being. In almost every one sometime to every one it is clear in them which kind of feeling in them is connected with stupid being in them. There is stupid being in every one. It was not easy to know the stupid being in this first governess of the Herslands As I was saying she was a good musician. As I was saying she had been then almost twenty years in the occupation of governessing. She had been ten years in America, she had not much gayety in living, she had not in her anything of dreary being.

It is then very interesting always to know the stupid being in each one. It was hard to see it in this one. It was hard even to see it in her living with her sister and in this way it often comes out in women.

It was hard to know the stupid being in her for no one came close to her not even her sister. No one came close enough to her to know easily the stupid being in her. With some, you have to come close to them to know the stupid being in them. This first governess of the Hersland family was such a one. She had come to have some queerness in her. Was it queerness of herself inside her or was it governess queerness in her. It is hard to tell it in one when no one comes close to that one whether it is queerness in that one from the character, or from the life that one is leading, from conditions or to earn a living. There are many then who have queerness in them. This first governess of the Herslands was such a one, no one, not even her sister Olga even dimly inside her, ever was very certain what was stupid being in her. She had queerness in her but not enough to make a strange creature of her, just enough to keep herself together. No one was ever very certain whether keeping herself together was the queerness in her, whether it was governess queerness she had in her, no one was ever very certain of this in her not even her sister. To be sure her sister was a young girl when they were together. Later Olga the sister stayed in Gossols and her sister left her after having established her. There was almost twenty years between them, Olga was afraid of her sister, and then she was separated from her, and they never afterwards saw each other. And so Olga never came to be sure about her sister as to what was the stupid being in her. Perhaps it was the having to keep herself together. Perhaps it was the queerness in her. Perhaps it was the not having real queerness in her, just enough to keep herself together.

The first governess, then, did not stay a long time with the Herslands. It was not that any one of them wanted she should leave them. She did not make much of any impression on any of them. It made no difference to any of them her leaving or staying. She knew some funny foreign songs and the children liked to hear them and she was a good musician and that was all the meaning she had for them. As I was saying she had a little queerness in her but not enough to make her important to those near her. She had queerness enough to keep her together. As I was saying her sister was always a little afraid of her but she was twenty years younger and they did not live a long time together, her sister never came to know the meaning of queerness in her. She was to her, sister Martha, who gave the money to make her a teacher, who had given money so she had been kept at school after the father and mother had died and left her with no one to support her. Later when she had gotten a position and was earning her own living, she, sister Martha left Gossols and went to Cincinatti. They never again came together.

As I was saying the first governess of the Herslands had queerness in her, not enough to make any impression on any of the Hersland family in the time they had her, enough to keep herself together, enough to keep her sister from ever knowing any stupid being in her, enough as I say to keep her together, to make her. She had queerness in her. She had stupid being in her. Some have more and some have less character. This is the amount she had in her. Later there will be a history of her sister.

There are then many being made, many always existing of every kind of men and women. There are always, there always have been, there always will be everywhere in every kind of living millions of every kind of them. There are then always many millions of every kind of men and women. In all the millions of each kind of them there are all degrees of successful living. Some kind have more successful living in more of them than other kinds of them. But in all kinds of them there are all degrees of success in living in the many millions always existing of that kind of them.

The first governess the Herslands had with them was of a kind of men and women who most of them are successful enough in living and many of them come pretty close to complete failing but few of them completely fail in living, not many of them are really successful in living. Mostly they keep themselves from failing, this is mostly the successful being in them. Successful being in many of them is keeping themselves from failing. Some have more, some have less concentration in them, some have very much concentration in them, all of this kind of them have some concentration in them even if like in this one it is only as queerness, enough queerness to hold together the whole of them.

This first governess of the Herslands, who did not stay a long time with them, had in her, dependent independent being. The two, dependent and independent being were so balanced in her that resisting was almost attacking in her, that dependence was almost independence in her. It never really came to be a force in her, she had enough concentration of it all in her to make it in a sense seem like successful being in her, it was just enough in her, the concentration in her, to keep her from failure, it was as queerness in her and that gave her for some who saw her, more concentration than was in her. There was just enough queerness in her to hold her together. There was just enough concentration in her to keep her from failure. There was enough queerness in her to make character for her. There was not enough concentration in her to make success or failure, there was enough in her to keep her from failure, to keep people from coming close to her, to make her younger sister afraid of her, to give enough dignity to her to keep her always from giving way or failure. There was not enough in her to make any impression on any one around her, though when any one thought about her they remembered her as one having character, more character than they felt when they were with her.

She had dependent independent being in her. These were so balanced in her, that dependent being was like independent being, independent like dependent being in her. She was kept together. She had queerness enough in her to keep her together, to keep her from failure. This is a history of her. There are always many millions made like her, some have more some have less concentration in them, some have more some have less success in living. She always kept from failing to her dying. She never really had any success in living.

As I was saying she was a good musician. They liked her well enough, the Herslands, when she was governess to them but she made no impression on any of them. She did not give to Mrs. Hersland any important feeling of herself to herself inside her, to her feeling. Mr. Hersland had a theory of her in the beginning, he wanted to have a real foreign woman, a real governess with concentrated being, with german and french and who was really a musician. She was what he wanted then for his children and he employed her. When he remembered about her, when he saw her, or his wife or children mentioned her he knew she was what he felt they needed to have as governess in the house for the children. Theoretically, she was important to him, really she had no existence for him.

What she was was just what he wanted for his children, a foreign woman who knew german and french well and was a good musician. Then he forgot about her for she had never when with them any existence for him. Then when she left them after a little while with them because her sister had become a teacher and so she could leave her and she wanted to leave America, when she left them Mr. Hersland thought it was better that the children should have american training. They were american, they did not need french and german, they did not need to bother about music then, they could do that later, now they needed strength and gymnastics and out of door living, and swimming and shooting. And that was the end of the first governess for all of them.

They sometimes saw the sister Olga who was a teacher in Gossols but she never talked much about her sister Martha. The children liked Olga, they liked her, they liked to tease her. Mr. Hersland gave her good advice, when Mr. Hersland noticed her he was attracted by her. Olga was very different from her sister Martha.

She had as I was saying independent dependent being in her. She had very much vague being as a bottom to her. She had all sorts of attacking to make attraction in her. Later the children made fun of her. Later the vague bottom in her was stupid being and nervous being and sometimes silly being in her.

No one who knew her would think of her as a woman of a spinster nature. She was round and pleasant and men liked her and she had constant attacking ways in her to give to her more attraction and men could be in love with her and she wanted to have attention from them and she made them when they were anywhere near her give it to her, made them sure of her from her actions toward them and she had as a bottom a vague being and later this was in her as nervous being in her, never as impatient being in her.

No one would ever think of her as a woman with a spinster nature but this was true of her. She was as I was saying a pleasant person, more, even an attractive person. She was round and kind and pretty in a fashion. She had plenty of attraction and she was full up with attacking to give to herself more attraction.

As I was saying no one would ever naturally think of her as a spinster but this was true of her and more and more later it came to be clear in her. Always she had attacking in all kinds of ways to give to herself more attraction and always she had as a bottom a vague being so that she was a ways being baffling, always making for herself a stupid escaping, sometimes not an easy escaping, sometimes she had to escape by accusation.

She had in her independent dependent nature. Attacking was to her a natural way of fighting, she was full up with vague bottom and all the rest with constant pleasing attacking, she had never in her any real fighting. There was no connecting her attacking with her large vague bottom, with the large vague bottom in her that made her baffling, that later turned into nervous being in her. She had a spinster nature. No one who knew her ever thought about it in her. They never knew this in her. Every one just thought it was stupid being in her. Later the Hersland boys made fun of her.

Later there will be more history of her as Alfred Hersland comes to make fun of her, as Martha Hersland came to know her. Mrs. Hersland always kept track of her and was good to her. Mr. Hersland knew her in his later living when he had trouble. All this will be a history of her. All this will be written later. Everybody called her Olga. It was natural to be familiar to her.

There was then in the Hersland middle living this first governess who did not stay long with them. As I was saying when Mr. Hersland employed her, he was the one who interviewed her, she was the ideal for him. He wanted a real governess, a foreign woman with governess training, one who was a good musician, one who would talk french and german with the children. After she was with them whenever he noticed her he was certain that she was what he wanted to have for the children. When she left he had already in him a new beginning.

Now he wanted the children not to have their english spoiled by french and german. Now he was certain that music was a thing no one could learn when they were children. This was something every one should have in their later living, children should have freedom, should have an out of doors gymnasium, should have swimming and public school living, should have a governess who would live with them such a life and not teach them french or german, not teach them anything, just be a healthy person with them. And so this next governess was very different from the last one.

She was a tall blond woman. She had no queerness in her. Later she married a baker. She was a healthy person. There was no trouble for any one to know her stupid being. But it made no difference to any one that she had stupid being, that that was almost her whole being, there was nothing that any one wanted of her that made her stupid being a trouble in her. Stupid being was the whole of her. It was alright in her. It was not actively pleasant in her. It was just all of her.

She was not a music teacher, she had no french or german in her, she just knew the ordinary things and not very well either. The children knew the stupid being in her. Every one could see it in her, it was almost the whole of her. She had no evil in her, not much of anything in her, there was a great deal of her, she was tall and blond and stupid being filled her. She did not give it to Mrs. Hersland to have in her much sense of important being in her. They all, all the governesses and servants and seamstresses gave some of it some time to her but it was to come more strongly to her later through the third and last governess, Madeleine Wyman.

It is very interesting that every one has in them their kind of stupid being. It is very interesting to know it in each one which part in them, which kind of feelings in them is connected with stupid being in them. It is interesting to know it in each one the meaning of stupid being in them, it is interesting to know what each one finds as stupid being in every other one.

Each one then has in them stupid being, every one has in them their own way of eating, drinking, sleeping, resting, waking, wanting things and getting or not getting them. Each one has in them their own way of succeeding in living, or in failing. Each one has in them their own way of being, their own being in them, and sometime there will be a history of all of them.

Stupid being then is in every one. Stupid being then can be in every one mixed in them with their way of eating, or their way of drinking, or loving, or working, or waking, or resting, or doing nothing, or having pleasant or angry feeling in them, or succeeding or failing. Some can have stupid being mixed up with part of all of them, with some or a few or all the things in them that come out in them as repeating to make a history of them.

The second governess was a whole being, mostly to every one there was passive stupid being in her in every moment of her living. This is now a history of her.

There are some kinds of women and some kinds of men, there are then some women and some men of some kinds of nature who have it in them to have every one who knows them have about the same idea of them have about the same feeling about them. Some have more, some have less interest in such a one, some who know such a one may have a liking, some who know such a one may not have any such a feeling, some may have dislike in them toward such a one, some who know them never think about them, but every one who knows such a one has the same feeling about the being in such a one, the stupid being that makes such a one. There is a kind of being then that is very convincing. The second governess the Herslands had living with them was such a one. She was a big blond woman. She had just had an ordinary education.

There are many ways of being what every one who knows such a one thinks them.

There are many ways of being, there are many of many different kinds of men and women who give to every one who knows them the same feeling of them. There are many millions always being made of men and women who give to different ones who know them a different feeling of them. There are some, there are many of many kinds of men and women who give to every one the same feeling about them, Mary

Maxworthing in her way was such a one. The second governess the Herslands had was a very different kind of such a one. Every one who knew
her had the same estimate of her. The children laughed at her, they neither liked or disliked her, Mrs. Hersland had not any feeling about her.
Later this one married a baker. He was a big blond man, and they got
on very well together. She had children, she grew a little larger, her face
was thinner, she was a little dirtier then, not very much busier, she never
surprised any one who knew her. Her father and her mother had a dairy
farm and they managed to get along. She had a brother who was to
succeed the father. It did not make any difference to any one who was
her father or her mother or her brother. No one ever had much interest
about her, not even the baker, he liked her, they got along very well together, he gave the Hersland children cream-puffs while he talked to her.
She married and sometimes later the children or Mrs. Hersland or Mr.
Hersland would see her, she was a little grimier then, but nothing was
changed in her, she was a little larger, her face and neck were thinner, she
and the baker were satisfied with each other.

As I was saying men and women have many of them in them their
individual feeling in their way of feeling it in them about themselves to
themselves inside them about the ways of being they have in them.
Some have almost nothing of such a feeling in them, some have it a little
in them, some have it in them always as a conscious feeling, some have it
as a feeling of themselves inside them, some have it as a feeling of themselves inside them as important to them, some have it as a feeling of being
important to themselves inside them as being always in them, some have
it as being important to the others around them, some have it as being
inside them that there is nothing existing except their kind of living,
some have it that they feel themselves inside them as big as all the world
around them, some have it that they are themselves the only important
existing in the world then and in some of them for forever in them, these
have in them the complete thing of being important to themselves inside
them. Some have it as a feeling of being important in them from things
they are doing, from religion in them, from the ways of living they have
in them, from the clothes they have on them, from the way they have of
eating, from the way they have of drinking, from the way they have of
sleeping, some have a feeling of importance in them from the kind of living
they have in them and the others around them have in them, there are
many ways of having a feeling of one's self inside one, there are many ways
of having an important feeling in one, there are some who have in them a
feeling of importance inside but not a feeling of importance of themselves
to themselves inside them, there are some who have inside them an important feeling in them but not an individual feeling in them, there are many
ways for men and women to have themselves inside to them and this is a
history of some of them.

Mr. David Hersland had in him a feeling of being as big as all the world around him. He had his ideas of educating children. He was always full up with beginning. He was as big as all the world around him. He never thought about it in himself then, it was natural to him. Each beginning was in him such a feeling.

He had first seen the first governess they had and he had had a feeling in him that was the ideal governess for his children. She was a good musician, it was necessary then to him that they should have much music in their education. She was a good scholar in french and german, he talked to her about the way he would insist always that his children should talk french and german. She was an ideal to him, she was beginning to him, he would see to it that the children learned all this governess could teach them. He talked to her in the beginning often about them and his rules and wishes for them. Then she made no impression on him, she was not evident enough in the family living to attract his attention. She soon died out of him. Soon he forgot about the children and their education. Then she left them. Then he was angry with the children that they knew so little french and german.

Then there was in him a new beginning, he thought it better for their english that they should forget all the french and german the first governess had taught them. They should not spend time learning music when they needed physical training, he would have a good healthy woman, not a too well educated one, to help them with their lessons and to see that they did gymnastics and swimming. This time he wanted a big healthy woman. He did not want a small one that had no color in her face and was careful in every motion. He wanted a strong healthy woman, one who knew something about farming, one who did not spend her time in reading or piano practicing. He had in him then a new beginning. He wanted a big healthy woman who knew all about farming. The second governess then was such a one. Her father and mother had a dairy farm and she was a big blond woman and she had red cheeks and she was not a musician and she did not know any french and german and she had had only an ordinary education and she knew nothing about spending her time in reading. There was no question that she was the ideal Mr. Hersland had then in him for a governess for his children.

He never forgot about her altogether as he did about the first one. She was always some one to him, he liked big healthy women, she did not know much about farming but she listened while he talked to her about farming and about the children. Later he did not talk to her about the children, a little still about farming, but when he noticed her she made a certain impression on him. Later when she was married to the baker he would drop in to see her and eat a cake while he talked to her. He did not mind much that she was larger then and paler and a little dirtier in her dressing a little sordider, grimier. She was not important ever to the children but this will come out later in the history of the children as it will be written of each one of the three of them.

There are many ways for men to have loving in them and loving come out from them.

Some men have it in them in their loving to be attacking, some have it in them to let things sink into them, some let themselves wallow in their feeling and get strength in them from the wallowing they have in loving, some in loving are melting strength passes out from them, some in their loving are worn out with the nervous desire in them, some have it as a dissipation in them, some have it as they have eating and sleeping, some have it as they have resting, some have it as a dissipation of them, some have it as a clean attacking, some have it as a simple beginning feeling in them, some have it as the ending always of them, some of them are always old men in their loving.

Every one then every man and every woman have then their own feeling in loving, their own way of feeling in religion, their own way of laughing, of eating, of drinking, of going on living, of taking what comes to them, of looking for things to irritate them or content them, their own way of beginning and of ending.

Mr. Hersland then had his own way of being in him. The governesses had each one their own way of being in them. Each one had a certain effect on him.

It is very interesting that every one has in them their kind of stupid being. It is very important to know it in each one which part in them, which kind of feeling in them is connected with stupid being in them. There is then stupid being in every one. There is in every one their own way of living, of eating, of drinking, of beginning and ending, remembering and forgetting, of going on and stopping. There is then in every one their own way of responding to things, to any one that touches them, to everything in living. There is in every one repeating. There is in every one a different way of repeating in their beginning and in their middle living and in their ending. Sometime there will be a complete history of every one and of all the repeating in them.

Eating and sleeping then and drinking and being loving and working and waking and resting and doctoring and having religion and beginning and ending. Mr. Hersland was now in the beginning of his middle living. He was beginning then his habits of middle living. He was beginning then his regular country house living and governesses were then part of the regular living he had in him, with his eating and sleeping and talking and beginning. Habits were beginning in him. Repeating is always in every one, it settles in them in the beginning of their middle living to be a steady repetition with very little changing. There may be in them then much beginning and much ending, but it is steady repeating in them and the children with them have in them the pounding of the steady march of repeating the parents.of them have in them. Mr. Hersland then was beginning to have in him his repeating of beginning middle living. He had then in him eating and sleeping and hygiene and much beginning and hearty laughing and impatient being and a kind of interest in some people near him and some brushing away of his wife from around him and his regular derangements in his stomach and in his dieting. He had in him then the beginning of his middle living.

Every one, then, as I was saying, have in them, always, repeating. Every one who does not die before then has in them the steady pound of repeating in the beginning of their middle living. It becomes then more and more part of them, their way, their way of drinking, their way of beginning and of ending, their way of talking, of laughing, of having impatient being in them, their way of being attracted by women and by men.

There was then the beginning of middle living now in Mr. Hersland. It was in him then already in the beginning of their living in Gossols and having the first governess for the children. For Mrs. Hersland it was not yet in beginning. It came to her later with the governess Madeleine Wyman.

A part then of middle living in Mr. Hersland was his way of educating his children ; his daily habits then in his country living with his wife and his children and a governess to teach them. The ideas in him then about their education were his habits of beginning middle living. The attraction each governess had or had not for him, the impression she made or did not make on him was all part of his middle living. Later in the ending of his middle living it came to be a more sodden repeating. Now repeating was in him a varied vigorous pounding. This is now a description.

Mr. Hersland, as I said once when speaking of the kind of loving he had in him, Mr. Hersland had then in the beginning of his middle living, had his wife to content him. She was then a pleasant feeling in him, she was then a little of a joke to him, she had then still a little resisting for him, he then did not much brush her away from around him, he did not then forget about her existing, in his feeling, she was then still important to him. As I was saying, then in their younger living, still in the beginning of his middle living she gave him all the stimulation he needed to attract him, for his loving ; he was not then yet full up with impatient feeling, he had then yet a pleasant feeling in living and her resisting was important enough to him to hold him. Later he needed more to fill him, in his latest living when he was shrunk away from the outside of him, when he had not enough beginning enough impatient feeling to fill him, he needed then another kind of woman. This will come out later in the later history of him.

At this time then in this beginning of his middle living he had in him a cheerful sense of being, he had enough contentment from his wife, he did not then need much stimulation. He had in him then some impatient feeling but this was not yet very strongly in him. It came to be in him then when he was going to be very soon ready for a new beginning. It was in him then when there was an end then of something or it was continuing too long to suit him, whether it was his own or some one else's talking, whether it was his own or some one else's doing, that never made any difference to him, it was the sense in him of a new beginning that gave to him impatient feeling.

In the beginning of his middle living then some women were attractive to him. It was not then much of a need in him. Mostly then it was a joke to him. Later he had more need in him. This will come out in the later history of him.

There are many ways then of having some feeling about people near one. This is different in different parts of the living in one. Now this is a history of the middle living of Mr. Hersland, of the beginning and middle of his middle living. Later there will be a history of the ending of his middle living and then of his later living, in the written history of his children.

There are many ways then that one has feeling for people near them. This is now a history of feeling in Mr. Hersland in the beginning of his middle living.

As I was saying he selected the two first governesses for his children, the first was his ideal of a governess for them then, a woman with governess training, a good musician and having a thorough understanding of french and german. She was his ideal then. When he told her what his ideals were for his children, she made an impression on him. Mostly, later, he never noticed her, she made no impression on him, sometimes later when she listened while he told her what he knew about education she made some impression but it was always a reflection, it was only when she was listening that she made an impression and that was only by virtue of her training, the listening of somebody so well-trained in education made an impression on him, it was her training it was never herself that made an impression on him. When she left the Herslands he had not any longer much interest in talking to her training, he was already then full up then with a new beginning.

He had then a feeling that he wanted a big strong healthy woman to be with his children. They could get enough education from public schools and reading, he had had that kind of education, it would be the best thing for them. He told the governess what he wanted she should do for the children, what his ideas were about them. She listened to him but her listening was not stimulating, but she made an impression, he liked well enough to notice her then and later when she was married to the baker, when she was larger then and a little grimy he still liked to see her, he would stop by at her shop where she was sitting attending to the custom and he would eat a cake there and ask her how she was getting on and he liked that much contact with her.   Later there was a third governess Madeleine Wyman.

Mr. Hersland then in the beginning of his middle living wanted mildly a little attraction in women but mostly then it was not a need in him, his wife then was existent to him, he liked well enough a little looking at women who made on him then some impression.   So he liked a little to be with the second governess when she was with them and later when she was married to the baker.   She was a big blond woman.   She made a mild impression on him.   He liked to give her advice and talk about little things and later to eat a cake while she sat there sewing.   This was the beginning of his middle living.

There was then in Mr. Hersland in the beginning of his middle living beginning to be very completely in him as repeating his way of eating, of thinking, of laughing, of talking, of beginning, of having impatient feeling, of being attracted by women.   There was then in him beginning accented repeating that later would be louder and have less changing in repeating.   Later what was now an attraction to him would be then a need in him, later there will be a history of him.   Now there is enough history of him.   Now there will be a history of Mrs. Hersland and the important feeling she had in her with the third governess Madeleine Wyman.   Mr. Hersland had then in him now the beginning of his middle living repeating.   This is clear now in him.   Later there will be more description of this being in him as his children and his children's friends get to know it in him.

The kind of loving women and men have in them and the ways it comes out from them makes for them the bottom nature in them, gives to them their kind of thinking, makes the character they have all their living in them, makes them then their kind of women and men and there are always many millions made of each kind of them.

The kind of loving then women have in them and the ways it comes out from them makes for them the bottom nature in them, gives to them their kind of thinking, makes the character they have all their living in them, makes them their kind of women and there are always many millions made of each kind of them.

Some women have it in them to love others because they need them, because these somehow are important to them, because somehow these they have for loving belong to them, many of such of them subdue the ones they need for loving, they subdue them and they own them ; some of them who have it to be of this kind of women have it in them so lightly in them this being in them as to be almost of no importance to those they have around them in their living, to have their children belong to them only as a part of them inside them, these are of the kind of them who always own their children who subdue those they need in loving but these of this kind of women have it to have this that is them very gently in them and Mrs. Hersland was of such a kind of them, these have it in them to be it so gently in them that it never comes out in them with some it comes out a very little in them, these then have it to be so timidly in them some so dimly in them, some so gently in them, some so slightly in them that their children are only a part of them as having been once in them, it is with such of them only in such a way that they can ever own them ; some of such a kind of them have it all so peaceably inside them that they have not in them the feeling of being themselves inside them, it takes some one around them to need them to be owned by them to make such a kind of one own them, to make such of them feel it inside them that they are themselves inside them, to give to them anything of an important feeling. There are then this kind of women many of them are very dependent all through their living but a little in them is an independent feeling and this comes out in them when there is any one around them who makes them own them and with such a one they are important inside them any moment in their living. These are of the dependent independent kind of men and women. Mrs. Hersland had a very little such a feeling with her husband when she was first married to him, she had it in her when she was a little resisting to him ; she never would have had much more in her if she had gone on living the life that was for her the natural way of being, she had it a little more in her feeling with the Shilling family in her hotel living, it came to be strongest in her in her living with a governess and a seamstress and servants in the house with her and, for her, poor people, around her, with always inside her country house feeling of right rich living, with nothing in her daily being of such a living, which was the natural way of living for her. She had it then in her to feel herself inside her and it was then strongest in her and came out in her with the governess Madeleine Wyman who was for her the one who in all her living was the one whom she had power over, not as part of her, as her children were to her, but as outside of her. She fought with the family of Madeleine Wyman for her, she had a feeling then of herself inside her.

There are then two kinds of women, those who have dependent independence in them, those who have in them independent dependence inside them ; the first ones of them always somehow own the ones they need to love them, the second kind of them have it in them to love only those who need them, such of them have it in them to have power in them over others only when these others have begun already a little to love them, others loving them gives to such of them strength in domination. There are then these two ways of loving there are these two ways of being when women have loving in them as a bottom nature to them, there are then many kinds of mixing, there are many kinds of each kind of them, some women have it in them to have a bottom nature in them of one of these two kinds of loving and then this is mixed up in them with the other kind of loving as another nature in them but all this will come clear in the history of all kinds of women and some kinds of men as it will now be written of them.

In the Hersland family during the middle part of the family living when the children were beginning to have in them their individual living, when Mrs. Hersland was beginning to have strongest inside her her own important feeling, when Mr. Hersland was strongest in beginning and making his great fortune, during this middle living they had as governess with them Madeleine Wyman and this is now part of her history with them.

As I was saying some women have it in them to own those who love them, to subdue such then, these are of them who have dependent independent nature in them, they have resisting in them as their way of fighting. Some who have independent dependent nature in them and have attacking in them as their way of fighting, and have much strength in attacking have this way of subduing those they need for loving, this is another kind then of subduing from that in Madeleine Wyman or in Mrs. Hersland. Later there will be a history of all the kinds who have attacking subduing in them. Now there is a history of Mrs. Hersland and the moment she had in her with Madeleine Wyman as governess to her children and living with her, the time in her of the strongest being of herself inside her to her. This is now some of this history in her. This is now some of the history of Madeleine Wyman. This is now a history of the Wyman family and the struggle Mrs. Hersland made to keep Madeleine Wyman as governess in the house with her. This is the history of the nature in Mrs. Hersland and in Madeleine Wyman and in every member of the Wyman family. This then is to be now a long history of Madeleine Wyman. This is a history of the affection and the knowledge and the stupid being in her and the loving and the later living and the marrying of her and the death of her husband and her later living and her power of owning and subduing what she needed for loving and the nature in her and Mrs. Hersland's feeling for her and Mrs. Hersland's feeling inside her from the being with her and Mr. Hersland's feeling for her. Then later, in the history of the Hersland children, there will be more history of her. Now this is a fresh beginning. And now there will begin a long description of her.

Many women have sensitive being in them. Many have it as a bottom to them. Some of such of them have attacking as their way of fighting, some of such of them have resisting as their way of winning. Some of such of them have yielding of them as their way of subduing, some of such of them have resisting as their way of subduing. Some have weakening in them from the sensitive being as the bottom of them, some nervous being, some creating, some loving, some suffering, some yielding, some resisting. Mrs. Hersland had sensitive being as the bottom to her being, sometimes this was in her as suffering, sometimes as loving, sometimes as resisting.

Some then who have sensitive being as the bottom of them, some then of the many of them who have sensitive being as the bottom in them and have dependent independent nature in them, have resisting as their natural way of fighting, many then of this kind of them who have sensitive being as the bottom of them have not in much of their living much resisting. Many of such of them have not in their living very much fighting. Some have only for a little bit of their living real resisting in them, then they do not make any concession, then they have real resisting in them. Then the sensitive being in them turns into resisting being in them, this may lead to stupid acting by them, it is not stupid being in them, it is the way of fighting that should mean winning for them, when they have not enough in them for winning it often makes stupid acting, in them, it is not stupid being in them. Mrs. Hersland was such a one and it will come out in her living when she is herself inside her to her feeling. It came out a little in her in her loving, when she was young and a little resisting to her husband then to subdue him. It never showed in her with her children, not even when she was resisting her husband for them, resisting in her then was more nearly then attacking, it was defending them against him, sometimes it was real resisting against him, it never was in her ever in her relation to any of them, they were always inside her to her feeling or they were big around her, too big and she was lost among them. She never had any feeling of herself to herself inside her ever with any one of the three of them. In her relation to servants and governesses and the families of them when any of such ones tried to be interfering then she was to herself then complete in resisting, then to herself she had not any concession ever to make to any one of them. She could have sharp angry indignation then, she could have strongly then inside her resisting, she never then could have inside her any conceding. She then often did very stupid acting, it was not in her, this resisting, stupid being, it was that sensitive being was not in her to the point of really creating resisting. It was that made her resisting then stupid acting, it was not in her then stupid being. This is clear now.

Mrs. Hersland to herself was never cut off from rich right living. She was to herself cut off from Bridgepoint living, from eastern travelling, from southern feeling, she was not to herself cut off from rich living, she was to herself part of this being, in her Gossols living. She did not do much visiting but she was to herself always part of such living. She was to herself cut off from her family living, she was cut off from Bridgepoint living, she was in the west and eastern living was natural to her being. She had done travelling when she was younger, travelling with a cousin and a sister, she was now to her feeling cut off from such living. She was never to her dying, to herself, cut off from right rich being. She did not do much visiting, she was part of right rich being. This was herself in her feeling.

She was cut off from Bridgepoint living, from travelling, from eastern living, she had this to herself in her feeling, later she went to Bridgepoint and she was a princess to them, she was a rich woman, Mr. Hersland had then just made his great fortune. She was a princess to them, she was not of them, she never was to herself ever after the beginning of her Gossols living, ever again part of Bridgepoint living. She was always to herself cut off from eastern living, from her family being. As I was saying when she went much later on a visit to Bridgepoint she was a princess to them. Earlier her early eastern living was a romance to her feeling. Always it was a romance to her feeling. Always even after she had visited them and been like a princess to them, for them, with them, eastern living was a romance to her feeling. Always she was cut off from eastern living, she never was to herself cut off from ordinary right rich being.

Always then, eastern living, her early travelling, was a romance to her feeling, it was later a little a romance to her children. Later they had a sore feeling that their third governess shared it with them, that she owned the romance of the early living more than they owned it in them, more than it belonged to their mother in their feeling, it belonged then to Madeleine Wyman to their feeling, she owned the romance of their mother's early living, she owned then, later to their feeling, their mother's living, they had no freedom in their mother's living, later, in their feeling, Madeleine Wyman had the romance of their mother's early living as her possession. This was later a little a sore feeling in them, later when their mother's romance was no longer interesting to them, Madeleine Wyman had then come to own their mother and their father, to them. This was always a sore feeling in them.

Mrs. Hersland had then all through her living her feeling of being always a right part of right rich ordinary being. Her children then were more of them the poor people living near them than they were of their mother's living then, though they were all of their mother's being then, all of her daily living then. Her husband was beginning then to be more then of the daily living around him than she was of him, of the men and women near them, not so much as the children were then but more than she ever could be in her feeling. He was then in the beginning of the middle part of his middle living, soon then he would begin to be more full up with impatient being. The children then as I was saying were more then of the living of the, for her, poor queer people around them than they were of their mother's living then. Her husband Mr. Hersland was beginning to have in him more feeling of brushing people away from around him, of being of them whoever it was that was at the moment near him. It was then, Mrs. Hersland had in her, strongest inside her, her feeling of herself to herself in her, she had then her strongest feeling of important being in her of herself inside her and she had this with Madeleine Wyman living in the house with her.

There are many ways of being, there are many ways of loving. Some subdue the ones they need for their loving. There are many ways of subduing. There are many ways of owning other ones around one. This is a history of some of them. This is a history of two of them.

The Hersland family, then, had three governesses living with them. There was the first one, the good musician with a regular governess training, there was the second one without too much education, there was a third one and this is now a history of her.

This is now a history of her with her family, with Mr. Hersland, with Mrs. Hersland, with every one she ever knew in her living from its beginning to its ending.

This is now a beginning of the history of her, Mrs. Hersland talked a great deal to her. Madeleine always listened to her. This is now a history of their talking to each other. This is now a history of how they owned each other.

It is very interesting that every one has in them their kind of stupid being. It is very important to know it in each one which part in them which kind of feeling in them is connected with stupid being in them. There is then stupid being in every one.

There is then stupid being in every one, there is some subduing, some escaping in every one, there is some resisting and some attacking in every one. It is interesting to know it in each one what in them is stupid being for them, what kind of acting is stupid being in them, what kind of stupid acting is or is not stupid being in them. Sometime some one will know it of every one, what is and what is not stupid being in each one. This is now a history of two of them. This is now a history of more of them. This is now a history of Mrs. Hersland and Madeleine Wyman and the subduing power in each one of them and the escaping in each one of them and the resisting and attacking in each one of them and the stupid being in each one of them and the important being in each one of them. There is then now to be a history of the two of them, there is then now to be a history of the two of them and of all of the others near them, of the servants living in the house with them, of Mr. Hersland and later of the three Hersland children, of the Wyman family, the father and the mother and the two sisters and the brother of Madeleine Wyman. There is now then to be a history of all of these then, of Mrs. Hersland and Madeleine Wyman and of every one near them or connected with them. There was then as I was saying in Mrs. Hersland when Madeleine Wyman was living as governess with them, the time in her living when she had in her her completest feeling of being herself inside her in her feeling. This is now then a description of her being.

As I was saying Mrs. Hersland was never to her feeling, cut off from rich right living. She was to her feeling cut off from her family and from eastern living and eastern travelling. She was to herself cut off from it to her feeling even when later she went to Bridgepoint to visit her early living. She was always to herself then cut. off from her early being. Later Madeleine Wyman owned this early being. The three children later in their living had the feeling that Madeleine Wyman owned their mother's early Bridgepoint being, it gave to them a sore feeling. This is now a history of how the third governess Madeleine Wyman came to own Mrs. Hersland's early being and how Mrs. Hersland with Madeleine Wyman as governess in the house with them came to have in her her most important being of herself inside her and what feeling and being Mr. Hersland had in him.

Mrs. Hersland was never important to her children excepting to begin them. She never had a feeling of herself to herself from them. She was of them until they were so big that she was lost among them, she was lost then between them and the father of them.

Mrs. Hersland was never important to her children excepting to begin them. She was never, even to them, important to their being, they had later a sore feeling in them because Madeleine Wyman owned their mother and a little their father, entirely their mother later to them, they had a sore feeling in them, not because their mother was ever important to them, but she had made them, she so belonged to them, she was so part of the personal being of each one of them. Madeleine Wyman owning their mother, was to them, not an owning of them, but a cutting off a piece from each one of them. Their mother then was of them, they were not of her then excepting, as she was making them, Mrs. Hersland was never important to her children excepting to begin them.

Later there will be more history of the little sore feeling the children had in them because of Madeleine Wyman, who was married then, and their mother was no longer living, of Madeleine Wyman owning the mother of them. Later then in the history of each one of them there will be a description of the sore feeling they each one had in them at Madeleine Wyman's owning the mother of them and a little the father of them. Not that Madeleine Wyman had any influence over any of them, over the mother or the father or any one of the children. It was nothing of such a thing that happened to them. It was that she owned the mother of them by living in her feeling their mother's early living, by being the reason of their mother having in her then when Madeleine Wyman was with them the being herself to herself more inside her in her being than at any other time in all her living. So Madeleine Wyman owned Mrs. Hersland, to her children. She a little owned Mr. Hersland for them but that was mostly in so much as he belonged to the mother of them. Madeleine Wyman to them, to the children, never owned them, it was only the parents of them that she held in her possession. It was not a sore feeling ever in any one of the three of them that owning their mother and a little their father that she ever the least bit owned any one of the three of them. It was that in owning their mother's early living, in her feeling, owning their mother's moment of being most herself to herself in her feeling, owning their father's early living and their mother's feeling for their father then in her important being and their father's feeling for their mother then, it was by such owning that they felt something cut off from them. A part that should have been them Madeleine Wyman held in possession. It was not of them then, it was cut off from them. It should have been then as a piece of the whole of each one of the three of them. Madeleine Wyman held it in possession. In their very later living they each one had it again in them. They came again to own their mother and their father in them. In their early living they had about Madeleine Wyman a very sore feeling. They hated to hear her talking. Their mother and a little their father were really more important to Madeleine Wyman than they were to any of the three of them except as to having made them, to them, in their early living. They could not deny this to Madeleine Wyman. She had by her feeling of the importance of their mother in the world of beings, she had then by this a right to her owning, to her possession, they could not deny this any one of the three of them, it was not the importance of their mother as a being that counted for any of the three of them, it was that she was part of them, having made them. They were not any, any one of the three of them ever very much of her in their feeling. She was of them to their feeling. Not a lively feeling in them, it was important to them only when this possession was cut off from them by Madeleine Wyman's owning of her and her early living and her important being. She was then, Mrs. Hersland, important to her children, only to being them. She belonged to them then not by her important being in her feeling ; Madeleine Wyman then had a right to her possession. The children all three of them by her possession of the mother of them and a little of the father of them had cut off from them in their later younger living a part of them and they had then a right to their sore feeling at her possession of their mother and a little of the father of them. There will be now more history of Madeleine Wyman in this possession.

There is stupid being in every one. There is stupid being in every one in their living. Stupid being in one is often not stupid thinking or stupid acting. It very often is hard to know it in knowing any one. Sometimes one has to know of some one the whole history of them, the whole history of their living to know the stupid being of them. Every one then, mostly every one, has in them stupid being. It is hard to know stupid being in such a one as Mrs. Hersland or even in such a one as Madeleine Wyman. Stupid being in Mrs. Hersland was in her when she was acting. It was not in her when she was resisting but then she had very little resisting in her being. She had very little real fighting in her being, real fighting in her would be as resisting. She had very little of this in her in her living. She had a little of it in her with her husband in the beginning and always a little all through her living. She had a little of it in her with her children when they were first beginning, and then she was of them but soon they were not of her then and she had no winning fighting being for them or with them. Sometimes about a servant she had attacking being, later about Madeleine Wyman and that was in her stupid being. Madeleine Wyman had in her stupid being in wanting to be subduing. Not with Mr. or Mrs. Hersland, there she was yielding to be subduing and that was not in her stupid being, yielding was never in her stupid being, attacking was in her stupid being. With Mrs. Hersland and with Mr. Hersland too she had in her yielding and so she came to own them. She yielded herself to them and so she came to live in them and in their early living and then she came to own them. This was not in her stupid being. Stupid being with her was in her failing, in her attacking, in her sometimes when resisting. Mostly in her as attacking for subduing and this was in her stupid being. This was true of her with the Hersland children, this was true of her in her later living. This will sometime be clear in her as there comes to be completely a history of her, a history of all the living in her from her beginning to her ending.

There is then stupid being in every one. In many, one has to have a whole history of all their living from their beginning to their ending to know it in them. Mrs. Hersland was such a one.

Mrs. Hersland as I was saying was never important for her children excepting to begin them. She never had a feeling of herself to herself from them. She was of them until they were so big that she was lost among them, she was lost then between them and the father of them.

So then to begin again with the Hersland family's living with the third governess Madeleine Wyman with them and with a history of her and every one who came to know her and of the Hersland family with her. To begin again then with Mr. Hersland and his ideas about education.

To begin again with Mr. Hersland and his choosing of the governess for the education of his children. To begin again with Mr. Hersland and his theories of education.

As I said the first governess was a real governess and knew french and german and was a good musician. She was theoretically satisfying to him in the beginning but personally after she began living in the house with them she made no impression on him. Then his theories changed in him and he wanted a woman who was strong and used to farming and he got one and she was pleasanter for him for she had a physical meaning for him and then she married the baker and they all sometimes saw her after but that was the end of her governessing and for some time then they had no one. Then they heard of Madeleine Wyman who was everything. They needed a governess then so the father thought because the children had forgotten all their french and german and the daughter Martha that year had missed annual promotion. Besides in their half country living they needed some one to keep the family living apart from the living around them. Anyway in Madeleine Wyman they had everything, she knew french and german, she was an american, she had had good american schooling, she was a fair musician, she was intelligent and could talk as well as listen to Mr. Hersland about education, she wanted to listen always to Mrs. Hersland's Bridgepoint living, she felt always the gentle fine being in Mrs. Hersland's country house living, she was good looking, she liked walking and wanted to learn swimming. She had everything, every one was content then, her parents were glad to have her in such a good situation, every one was suited then and then there was a beginning. Madeleine Wyman was the third governess the Herslands had living with them.

Madeleine Wyman's father and mother were both living. There were in all, four children. Madeleine was the oldest of them, then Louise, then Frank, and then Helen. The Hersland children later knew all of them. Later there will be a history of them in the history of the three children. There will then also be a history of Mr. and Mrs. Wyman and the later living of Madeleine. Now there is a history of her, when she was a governess, and the feeling about her all through her living with them in Mr. and Mrs. Hersland. First then to begin again with Mr. Hersland and his feelings about education.

Some men then and some women have cowardly but not fearful being in them. This is true then of many of them who have cowardly being in them and are of independent dependent kind of men and women. The dependent independent way of having cowardly being in them, many of them, is to have always fearful being in them. These are given to supposing, they always see death and danger around them in their living. Mr. Hersland was not of them, he had independent dependent being, attacking was his natural way of fighting, resisting was weakness in him, he had not any fearful being in him, he could be a coward in his living, he could brush people away from around him, when he could not keep them brushed down from in front of him he went another way and he never knew in him that he was a coward then in living, he had no fearful being in him. Later his children told it to him when they were angry with him and the impatient feeling that then filled him. Mr. Hersland always had it in him to be strong in beginning, he always had it in him to feel himself inside him to be as big as all the world around him, later he was full up with impatient being. Always he had beginning in him, always he had theories of education, always he talked to every one around him, always he was advising every one, always he was talking about education, about eating, about drinking, about washing, about healthy living, about doctoring, about what men and women needed to make them successful in living. Always he was talking about eating and education and marrying, and drinking, and sleeping, and doctoring. Now there will be more description of the talking in him.

There are many ways then for women to like men, there are many ways for men to like women. Some like the other one for the health in them, for the life in them, some for other things in them, some need many kinds of things to content them in those they want to have near them, some need very little in them. For some health in another one, for some youth in another one is enough to content them. Some women want a man to be florid and have a reddish beard when he has one, some want him brown with a black one, some then want health, some want youth in those near them, for some one thing for some other things mean health in those near them. There are many men and many women who want to see people having lots of health, near them. For some men one kind for some men quite a different kind is to them a fine figure of a woman. Many men and many women want those near them to have strongly in them the feeling and appearance of healthy being, many men say it of women and of trees and other things near them, that's a healthy looking one, that is in such of them the highest kind of commendation. Mr. Hersland was such a one. Not in the woman he needed for a wife for him, she was pretty and dark, and healthy enough looking but that was not in her a striking thing. Mr. Hersland wanted his children to be healthy looking, in choosing the second governess he chose her for this being in her. In his middle living he needed this kind of fine healthiness in women to content him, later he needed a more active being in them, they had then to be energetic enough around him to fill him in where he had been shrunk away then from the outside of him. In his middle living then he wanted a woman to have a good figure and to be healthy looking. The second governess had been such a one and Mr. Hersland always had a certain pleasure in having her in the house with them. Later when she had married the baker he sometimes on his way home would stop to eat a cake and talk to her, tell her about what was the best way to give milk to the baby, to keep strong and not to need a doctor, what kind of a doctor she should have to take care of her, what was the right way for her to do to content her husband and save money and never have any trouble to come to her. He always gave advice to her; he ate a cake, he told her whether she was getting fatter or thinner, how to get thinner when she was getting fatter and later after she had had another baby and was always looking dragged and getting thinner, he would tell her what she should do to get fatter. He always gave advice to her, later always about her doctor and that she had a good man to be a husband to her a good baker and later when she was getting thinner what she should do to get fatter. He always gave advice to her. When she was beginning to be a governess to them he had talked to her about education and his children, later he mostly talked to her about eating and marrying, and gave advice to her about how to keep in condition.

With Madeleine Wyman it was a different matter. She was not a healthy woman to give pleasure simply by having health in her, and a fine figure. She was healthy but not the kind to make one feel it in her. She had a trim figure, she was not pretty, nor ugly either, she was pleasant and bright and had some energy. With her Mr. Hersland could always talk about education in a different way from that in which he talked with the second governess who had married the baker. Madeleine Wyman was young and had understanding in her, she was young and ready to try to carry out his theories in the way he wanted from her. She wanted to educate the three children in music, french and german, gymnastics, swimming, and with at the same time good american public school training. With the first governess it had been different. She always had listened to Mr. Hersland but she had a real governess being in her and she did what this governess being in her demanded from her. She was polite and intelligent but she had real governess being in her. After Mr. Hersland had gotten through telling her all the advantages of european education over american and she had politely agreed with him, there was nothing for him to say to her. He became indifferent later about telling this to her and so she had no existence for him although whenever he was conscious of her he had respect for the genuine governess being in her, for her being a thorough musician, for her really knowing french and german.

Madeleine Wyman then was a good person to listen to him. Better than the other two to him. Personally she was pleasant to him, she was not so large as an impression personally on him of agreeable healthy feeling as the second governess had been. She was more satisfying as a listener to him. Not so satisfying for advising, really she was more important to Mrs. Hersland than she was to him. She really had more advice from Mrs. Hersland than from him. He liked to talk to her but it was not a personal feeling. She had understanding in her, she was young and ready to carry out his feeling about education but really she was not very personal for him, she was very personal for Mrs. Hersland, she was to Mrs. Hersland a part of Mrs. Hersland's most important living. They had then for each other these two women very important being. This is now a history of them.

With Madeleine Wyman living in the same house with them, Mrs. Hersland had in her her feeling of being to herself inside her strongest in her whole living, stronger than later when she went to Bridgepoint to visit her family and was like a princess to them, a very rich woman from the far country and in her feeling for them a part of them but to them and really to herself then not a part of rich right living ; more important than earlier when she met Mr. Hersland and her marrying was then her important being. She had never then at any time in her living so completely to herself then a realization, a feeling of herself to herself, a being in herself to her own feeling important in her being, not from doing, not from feeling, not from being, not from having, not from anything in her living or her being but from being to herself in herself then an important person as she had then in her middle living with the third governess in the house with them.   Some one needed her, not for their living or their feeling, but needed her for their self-creation.   And so, it was in her middle living with Madeleine Wyman in the house with them that she had in her really individual being.

As I was saying the children later had a sore feeling that Madeleine Wyman owned their mother's early living.   They had a sore feeling because they were so, cut off from part of their own being.

Madeleine Wyman made Mrs. Hersland really an attacking being and this was the most stupid being she had in her in her living.   Mrs. Hersland then, was important to Madeleine Wyman to give to her individual being, with her feeling and living in her being to make for herself a being.   Mrs. Hersland then had from Madeleine Wyman individual being, from Madeleine Wyman's living her early being.   This is now again a history of them.

The Wyman family was foreign american.   The mother was always pretty foreign.   No one of their children excepting perhaps the second one Louise ever knew very much what their father had in him.   Their children did not really know much about what was in either of them, the father or the mother in the house with them.   The old people were too foreign to them for them ever to really know anything about them.   The second one Louise, Madeleine was the eldest of the children, the second one Louise was not foreign in her being but she was in some way nearer in understanding to the old folks who were very foreign perhaps not understanding to her feeling, but understanding to anyone to every one who saw her with them.   There seemed more connection between her and her father and her mother, there was not any connection to anybody's feeling between the foreign old woman and the old man, and anything in their living, there was not much connection to anybody's feeling between the old man and the old woman, perhaps they were not so very old then, they lived a long time after and so they could not have been so very old then, there was then to everybody who saw them not much connection between the foreign woman and the foreign man who was a little vague to every one, there was only the connection between that neither of them seemed to be connected with any other one.   Later when one knew the children better and still later when no one any longer saw any of them and only remembered them, one then could reconstruct the foreign father and mother out of the children and so could come to an understanding of them, a realisation that they had been alive then and human.   Later then there will be a reconstruction of them, not from any impression from them but from what their children had in them as nature in them and so the parents will come to be made soon to us out of the memory of the children as later one remembered them, the chil-

dren when one no longer saw them.   The mother and the father then were
to every one then disconnected from every one, a little less from the second
daughter Louise, she had some connection with them then to every one
who knew them.   Later there will be more description of this connection
of hers with them.   The Herslands had never then very much impression
of them, not indeed then or even later in their living, of any of the Wyman
family except Madeleine, although they later, especially the three children
and Mr. Hersland some too then, Mrs. Hersland was weakening then and
less then in everybody's living, came to know the others of them the two
sisters Louise and Helen and the brother Frank very well in their later
living.   They never however any one of them, the three Hersland children came to any realisation of them until later they remembered them
and reconstructed them and realised them and then reconstructed and
realised the foreign parents from a reconstruction from their reconstructed
children.   Every one had then when they knew them an impression
that the daughter Louise knew then what kind of woman her mother the
old foreign woman was and what a kind of a man she had as a husband
but no one ever knew how they came to have this feeling that this Louise
had such a knowledge of them, that she had such understanding.   This
is now a history of the Wyman family and the living and the being in all
of the six of them, the mother and the father and the four children, Madeleine, Louise, Frank, and Helen.   Now there will be a history of Mrs. Hersland to them.   Later there will be new history of them in the history of
each one of the three Hersland children.   Now then for the six of them,
the mother and the father and the four children Madeleine and Louise
and Frank and Helen, and Mrs. Hersland and a little Mr. Hersland to
them.   First there will be the impression every one had of them then and
the history of their living and then there will be a reconstruction of the
four of them from the memory of the impression of them and then a reconstruction of the father and the mother out of the reconstructed four children.   This is now then a history of them and of Mrs. Hersland and a
little of Mr. Hersland to them.   Later there will be a history of the three
Hersland children with them.

Madeleine Wyman stayed with the Herslands about three years and
then there was a struggle for her by her family who wanted her to marry
John Summer who wanted to marry her but was not very anxious to
have her, and she had not about it any very strong feeling but she liked
it with the Herslands as she was then living and she did not care very much
about marrying.   Later she married him and he was later then a more or
less sick man with his own ways in him of eating and doctoring.   He was
a rich man and her family wanted she should marry him.   She had no
objection then, only she liked it so very well being with the Herslands
then, she did not want any changing.   There was no way to really convince
her family that she was very well content to stay with the Herslands then,

Mrs. Hersland tried to convince them. Once to convince them she paid double wages to Madeleine Wyman and had Madeleine a dress made then by Mary Maxworthing and Mabel Linker who made Mrs. Hersland's dresses for visiting, to convince the Wyman family that Madeleine was best off with the Herslands then and should stay with them. There was then about three months of sharp struggle between the Wymans and Mrs. Hersland and Madeleine and a little Mr. Hersland with them. Then Madeleine had to leave them, the parents, that is the whole family of them, the Wyman family, would not listen to reason or to higher wages even or to a dress in the most fashionable way of dress-making. John Summer was content to have Madeleine stay where she was then. Sometime he wanted to marry her but there was no hurry about it for him. He had plenty of life before him to be married in. Later Madeleine went home and later then she married him and later then they adopted a little girl, they could not have any children, and later then they gave up this one, and later then he took to ways of eating and ways of doctoring and then he was no longer working and they were rich enough then to try every kind of way of eating and travelling and doctoring and she was faithful to him and he died then and this was many years after and Mrs. Hersland and Mr. Hersland had long been dead then, but Mrs. Wyman was still living, and now there is a history of all the Wyman family, of the six of them of the father and mother and Madeleine and Louise and Frank and Helen and of Mrs. Hersland to them and a little of Mr. Hersland to them. This is now the beginning of the knowing of the Herslands and the Wymans, this is now the beginning of Madeleine Wyman and her governessing.

This is now as remembering the Wyman family and reconstructing the children from remembered parts of them and reconstructing the parents from the reconstructed children, this is what the Wyman family was then. This is now a history of them. They were, none of them, people to make a strong impression. To every one then the second daughter was more of the father and mother who were very foreign than the other three children. No one knew quite why this was true of her and of them. Every one who knew them felt it in them. This is now a history of all six of them, of Mr. Wyman and Mrs. Wyman and Madeleine, Louise and Frank and Helen Wyman, of the nature in each one of them, of the living that came to each one of them.

The mother and the father, Mr. and Mrs. Wyman were not so old then as they seemed to be to every one who knew them then. They were very foreign, that made them then with grown up children a very old man and a very old woman. They were not so very old then for they lived a long time after, longer than Mr. and Mrs. Hersland who were young then to them. Mr. and Mrs. Wyman were old then to every one and mostly no one knew much about them. They were foreign now in one's later living by remembering their children one can reconstruct them and know what they were then. Mr. Wyman then had a nature in him a dependent independent earthy instrument nature in him and all being was vague in him, Mrs. Wyman had independent dependent being and it was concentrated being but not very efficient being, it was enough to make some attacking in her being, it was enough to make such attacking pretty persistent and sometimes insinuating, rarely winning but very often annoying. She was not efficient in her being but she was fairly insistent in attacking, sometimes insinuating almost hypocritical in her kind of attacking but on the whole not very efficient in her living, on the whole not very often winning. She could be persistent, insinuating, and annoying. She had some winning in persisting with Mrs. Hersland, her daughter for six months had double wages given to her and a new dress made by Mabel Linker and Mary Maxworthing and then after all she got her daughter to leave the Herslands so that later she would marry John Summer. But all this was not really winning, for Madeleine always intended to marry John Summer and Summer always intended to marry her, so really all that Mrs. Wyman had as winning in her was to be annoying to Mrs. Hersland and to give to her a sense of struggling, and to have had her daughter Madeleine get for six months more money then she was earning and a dress made by Mabel Linker and Mary Maxworthing. As I was saying Mr. Wyman had earthy dependent independent instrument nature. He was very vague in his nature. His son Frank was like him. Madeleine in efficiency was like her mother, in her kind of nature like her father. Louise was like her mother altogether excepting that there was less to her nature, less insinuating attacking in her being. Later there will be a history of her. She had some connection, to those who knew her, with her father and her mother. The son Frank was vague like his father and like him in his nature, only he was younger and had more beginning in him and more chance of later keeping going than his father had had who was foreign. Helen was even more spread and vague than her father ever had been, with her mother's nature in her. Later in her living queer things happened to her.

There is always then repeating, there is always then in every one beginning and ending, there is always then in every one stupid being, there is always then sometime some one to every one who ever was or is or will be living who knows the being in that one. There was then once a whole family of them the Wyman family, the six of them, Mrs. Wyman and Mr. Wyman and Madeleine and Louise and Frank and Helen Wyman. There is always then sometime some one who has it in them to envisage the whole life and being of every one. This is now then one who remembering can reconstruct the being in Madeleine and Louise and Frank and Helen and from them can reconstruct the being in Mrs. Wyman and

Mr. Wyman and so now there is a history of them. There is always then as I was saying some one to know the being in every one. Mostly every one knows the being in some one, some in many others around them, some not in any one. There are then many ways of knowing being in other people and this reconstruction is one of them. There will be now then a history of the Wyman family, of all six of them.

As I was saying Mrs. Hersland never had any real connection with them, any real feeling about any one of them excepting Madeleine. Mr. Hersland had less understanding, less connection with her being, the Hersland children had their connection with her mostly from remembering, from their sore feeling that their parent's early living had been cut away from them, not that any one of the three of them had a tender feeling for their parent's early living, it was only that it was part of their existing and not something for a stranger to be owning. Mrs. Hersland then of all the Hersland family had the most personal relation to Madeleine Wyman, Mr. Hersland as I was saying liked to talk to her liked her intelligence and her trim neat figure, liked the way she listened when he talked, and the way she was ready to carry out ideas he explained to her, to the three children then she was mostly then a governess to be in the house with them. Each of them had a different feeling about her then and that will be clearer in the history of each one of them. They were all three then as I was saying more of them then the poorer people living in small houses near them than they were of their mother's or their father's living then, than they were of rich country house living with a governess in the house with them. What each one of them felt in their being then about this governess living with them will come out later in the history of each one of them. In their later early living they came to know more of the three others Louise and Frank and Helen. Madeleine had been married then to John Summer, the three Hersland children never knew very certainly what then to call him or her. They then called Louise and Frank and Helen by their first names but they never were at ease then about what they should call John Summer or Madeleine. They never to the end felt very certain what was the right thing to call them. But this is all later history, the being in Louise and Frank and Helen is all later history, no one then in the Hersland family knew them, later the three Hersland children knew them, Mr. and Mrs. Hersland never knew much of the brother and sisters of Madeleine Wyman. They knew a little more of her father and mother. Not very much though, to Mrs. Hersland and Mr. Hersland Madeleine was apart from her family, to them her family had really no part in her, no right to interfere with them and with her, her marrying John Summer was to Mrs. Hersland and Mr. Hersland more their affair than the affair of Mrs. or Mr. Wyman. This is now a history of the trouble they all had together.

Mrs. Wyman and Mr. Wyman then to almost every one who saw

them then, hardly any one knew them then, to almost every one then they were very foreign, they were not part of any living, they were not part of their children's living, the children were another generation and american. To every one there was some connection between Louise and them, not that she was foreign but she was so clearly connected in kind with her mother's being that being young and of another generation and a part of american and not foreign being and a part of her sister's and her brother's living was not enough to cut her off from being part of the being her mother and her father too had in them. This was always true in her being and every one who knew them the Wyman family at any time felt this in them, though always to every one Louise was part of the younger american generation.

Madeleine Wyman was the last one of the three governesses the Herslands had had in the house with them in their middle living in that part of Gossols where no other rich people were living. When Madeleine Wyman was with them, then in the middle living of Mr. Hersland and Mrs. Hersland, Mrs. Hersland had in her her most important being, she had in her then her completest feeling of being herself inside her to her being. She had this in her from her relation to Madeleine Wyman. Madeleine was twenty-four then. She stayed with the Herslands two years, two years after, she married John Summer. Then she went away to another town with him and she came to Gossols sometimes and then she would see Mrs. Hersland. Later then she went travelling to live again the early being of Mr. and Mrs. Hersland which was her possession. Travelling, eastern living had for her this meaning, she was then again living the early life of Mrs. Hersland and Mr. Hersland then. Later Mrs. Hersland was weakening and later she died and then when Madeleine Summer met the young Hersland people she told them what their mother had been, she told them what travelling and eastern living had meant to her, Madeleine, it had meant the re-living of their mother's early living, of their mother's and their father's early being. Then later John Summer had queer notions of eating and much later he died and Madeleine went to live with her sisters and her brother, and mother who was not dead yet then. Sometime there will be a complete history of Madeleine Wyman's married living, it will be very interesting. Sometime there will be then a complete history of her being and her living and the living and being of all six of them, the Wyman family. This will be such a history in the long histories of each one of the three Hersland children. Now there is to be only a little suggesting of the being in each one. Now Madeleine has just come to be a governess to the Hersland family to live with them in that part of Gossols where no rich people were living.

Madeleine Wyman had had a pretty good education. She knew french and german, not as the first governess the Herslands had had knew them, but well enough to teach them. She was not a musician but she knew enough music to oversee the Hersland children's practising, she knew enough music to teach music when there were music lessons to be given. She had a good enough english education, she had a good enough american governess training. She and her younger sister Helen were the only ones of her family who had had much education. Helen was more modern than Madeleine in her feeling. She was more modern in using her education in her living and in her feeling, later when Helen Wyman came to know the Hersland young people she was more of them than any of her family had been for she was more modern, not more american perhaps but really more modern, anyway more of them, the Hersland children then at the ending of their first beginning living, than Madeleine or Louise or Frank even ever were of their generation. They had not many friends then the Wyman family. Frank and Helen Wyman were the first of their family to have friends of people around them. The others of the Wyman family had never been of any generation and so they had not friends of any of them who were of their generation.

There were then in the Wyman family, six of them ; the mother and father and Madeleine and Louise and Frank and Helen. The mother Mrs. Wyman had her nature in her. The second daughter Louise and the youngest daughter Helen were of her. The father Mr. Wyman had his nature, the son Frank and the eldest daughter Madeleine were of this nature.

The youngest daughter Helen was all spread and all vague in her nature. She had a good education for she was interested in studying, she was almost interested in writing. She was not so much interested in teaching but teaching was to be her occupation. As a matter of fact she never did much teaching. She did a little teaching but somehow the Wyman family always managed to have enough money to go on living, the father with his book-keeping, the daughter Madeleine first with governessing and then with marrying a rich man always could help them, later, much later, after trying many things Frank Wyman became a nurseryman and with Louise to help him and much later with Madeleine to help him he always kept going, he even took to marrying and having children and with plenty of help around him he always managed to keep going. So as I was saying Helen really never did much teaching although this was intended to be her occupation. There was no opening then for a girl like Helen except teaching, as I was saying she was almost interested in writing but this was never active enough inside her to start her going, just active enough inside her to make her more modern than her sister Madeleine who was the other one in the family who had had education. So then Helen was all spread and all vague in her independent dependent nature, but people who knew her had a friendly feeling for her. She was more of them the people who came to know them the Wyman family, than any other one of them. The son Frank was in that respect a little like her. The two youngest then Frank and Helen were more of their generation than Louise and Madeleine ever had been of the generation around them. So then Helen had vagueness in her like her father, she was spread out more inside her than any other of the Wyman family, she had independent dependent being in her, it was mostly as dependent being in her, it was all spread and all vague in her this being in her. As I was saying she never did much teaching though this was to be the end of her education. As I was saying she came almost to the point of being interested in writing but it remained as vague and spread out as her being, it never came to any thing. Later there was marrying in her living and that was a very strange proceeding. Later in the history of the Hersland children there will be a history of the marrying of Helen which as I was saying was a very strange proceeding.

Mrs. Wyman then had her nature in her. The second daughter Louise and the youngest daughter Helen were of her. The father Mr. Wyman had his nature, the son Frank and the eldest daughter Madeleine were of this nature.

The youngest daughter Helen was all spread and all vague in her nature.

The second daughter Louise was almost as concentrated as her mother but there was less to her nature. There was about as much efficient living in her but there was not any insinuating attacking, her attacking was more a steady pushing. It came to about the same thing as efficient being, it made her less interesting, less menacing, more agreeable to be knowing. It came to about the same amount of efficiency in her nature as her mother had in her and more than that in any of the rest of the Wyman family.

The important things in her living were the marrying, first of Madeleine, later the strange marrying of Helen and then the taking charge of her, later the helping her brother in his business of nurseryman ; the keeping everything going in the later Wyman living when old Mrs. Wyman's methods had no more efficiency for their living. And so she succeeded to her mother's living, she never was married, she never bore children, as I was saying she was of her mother's being but there was less to her nature, there was less variety in her when she was younger, when she was in her middle living, when she was older. There was less variety to her, there was no insinuating attacking to her, there was steady shoving in her that made up in her for any less active attacking there was in her than there was in her mother. She was a drier person than her mother. There was very little change in her, she always had much the same being in her. Her being part of the mother and father's being, that which every one who knew her felt in her was never important to her. To herself inside her she was not more part of her mother and father than were her sisters and her brother. To herself she was part of the livings of her sisters and her brother, that was important being in her, being part of the being of her mother and father was not important being to her. She did not know it in her that she was nearer them than were her sisters and her brother. If she had known it she would not have liked it inside her. Important being in her to herself inside her was being part of the living and the being of her sisters and her brother. It was the marrying of her sisters and the business of her brother that were important to her not the being and the living in her father and her mother. She was to herself then strongly of the being of her sisters and her brother. Her father and her mother were not to her very important inside her. Later then in the histories of her sisters and her brother, in the description of her mother and her father there will be more history of her.

The son Frank was almost as vague in his nature as his father.

He was tall then and had a long head and thick hair and at that time he had mild humor in him. He could make jokes at children, give him time he could make jokes at girls and at women. He was not slow but he was not very decided inside him. He was vague inside him as his father was inside him but he was younger then and pleasanter, he was blonder, and milder in manner than his father, but his father was much older and had dried down and he was not really quicker it was only that there was a tender youthful being in the son that threw over him a glamor of being slower and pleasanter than his father. The father was darker and drier and seemed to be quicker. Really they had about the same nature, the two of them, neither of them had an efficient nature. The son had an easier life because he had his sisters, and his wife, later. When he married her she was not stronger in her nature than he was in his nature, but he had the start of her by having his sisters around her. He always all through his living was tall and slow and pleasant and mildly joking and not lazy and not active either and there was always the appearance as if his women, Louise and Madeleine and his wife and Helen were holding him up so that he would keep on standing. His mother had never done this for him. While she was directing the family he had been drifting. He had tried one way of earning a living and then another way and then nothing. It was not till later that he became a nurseryman with women around him to support him. So Frank had a pleasant enough life all his living and successful enough life in his living. He and his father, as I was saying, were both of them alike in this nature. They both had resistance enough to keep going, the father in his book-keeping, with a wife and family around him that he felt only enough to awaken in him some resisting ; the son with enough resistance in him to have his women keep on holding him up while he pleasantly and vaguely kept on living. This then is a history of the two of them. Sometime perhaps there will be more understanding of the nature in the two of them.

The mother Mrs. Wyman had her nature in her. The second daughter Louise and the youngest daughter Helen were of her. The father Mr. Wyman had his nature. The son Frank and the eldest daughter Madeleine were of this nature. In the eldest daughter the nature of the father was more concentrated to make her. It did not make her really an efficient nature. She really had resistance in her.·

Madeleine Wyman had had a pretty good education. She knew french and german well enough to teach them. She knew enough music to teach music when there were music lessons to be given. She had had a good enough education. She had intelligence to listen with understanding to Mr. Hersland's talking. She had a kind of interest in his theories of education. She tried to put them into execution. This is now a little description of them.

She was then different from the first governess who was a real european governess and a musician, she was different from the second governess who had known nothing. She came to the Herslands in answer to an advertisement and Mr. Hersland had been pleased with her.

The three Hersland children then were having their regular public school living, they had then all the feeling of country children. They had too then every kind of fancy education anything that their father could think would be good for them.

The third governess was really then only to keep them up in music practising and a little in french and german, mostly then just to be in the house with them. Mr. Hersland was just then deciding that what the children needed was to be kept going and Madeleine Wyman had enough education in every direction to keep them going. Then too, they all of them had the feeling of needing a governess in the house with them. Mrs. Hersland liked her, Mr. Hersland took less interest in engaging her than he had with the first or second one. She came then to be a governess to them because they still had a feeling that the children ought to have some one and Mrs. Hersland liked her and Mr. Hersland had not much interest just then in education. Soon though he began to talk to her about what he wanted her to do for each one of the three of them and what he thought was the right kind of education for children and the difference between european and american education.

As I was saying Madeleine was like her father in her nature but this was much more concentrated in her than it was in her father or her brother, it was almost as concentrated as their kind of nature was in her mother and her sister Louise. It did not make her a really efficient nature but it gave real resistance inside her and it gave her a certain power with those whose ideas she tried to realise for them. This was the case with Mr. Hersland. It gave her power when she was part of some one's living as with Mrs. Hersland. It did not give her power in teaching because in educating she tried attacking and with this, for her, there was no succeeding so she had never any real power with any one of the three children.

Later she was married to John Summer. Later they had for a little while an adopted daughter. Madeleine had not wanted her, it was Summer who very much wanted children and did not seem to be able to have any of his own who insisted upon choosing and adopting one. They did not keep her long for soon they took to travelling and Madeleine had not wanted to have her and so they sent her back to the home from where they had gotten her. Madeleine as I was saying had not really an efficient nature, she had not much influence on any one near her. She had none on the adopted child although she nagged her as her mother had done when she had brought up her children, but it was as attacking in Madeleine for she had not wanted the child with her. And so what strength was in her was in living in other people's lives, not in attacking or even really in resisting. With her husband she had no influence, for she had not a feeling of living in him as she had with Mrs. Hersland and with Mr. David Hersland, and Mrs. Hersland's early living, with her husband she was a good enough woman, a wife to travel with him, to induce him to give up business and to take to travelling, but she had no influence with him in the things that were his living, his ideas of eating, of doctoring, of wearing warm clothing. He was a man who had these things in him as a sad religion. Later he died for them. Later there will be much history of him, and his doctoring, and later his dying, and always his strong feeling for ways of eating, for ways of doctoring, for ways of digesting. Madeleine then could keep him travelling, she could induce him to quit business living, she could make it that the adopted child no longer lived with them, she had really had no power in him, she had really no efficient being. She had it in her later to give a sore feeling to the Hersland children by to them owning the father and the mother. Earlier when she was a governess to them Martha sometimes had had a little feeling against her when Madeleine tried to carry out Mr. Hersland's theories of education. The Hersland children were not accustomed to having any one really try to be systematic in such realisation, they were accustomed to have only the pleasant new beginnings of new ways of learning and of out of door living. As I say Martha and sometimes a little David did not like her way of interfering with them, Alfred had not any such reason for a feeling for he was older than David, and a boy, not a girl like Martha, and so Madeleine had nothing really to do with him, Martha then, and a little David then, did not like her way of interfering with them, then they had no feeling about her being with their father and their mother , they really never cared very much then about anything going on in the house with them. They were then all three of them, the Hersland children, more of them, the poorer people who lived in the small houses near them than they were of their father's or their mother's living then. Mr. Hersland's tiving just then was the beginning of the middle living in his great fortune, lhe beginning of a struggling to resist a beginning of an ending to his fortune. The beginning of resisting was just then dimly beginning in him, he had not just then such a keen feeling about education. He talked to Madeleine Wyman then about his theories of education but they were not then so live in him as they had been. She tried to realise them for him, that to the children was interfering, that, to him, was not really interesting. He took less and less interest in the children just then excepting when they came up against him. That was then their only existing, for him. Madeleine was conscientious in trying to realise the ideas she knew he had in him. This as I was saying was to Martha and a little to young David, interfering. Later Madeleine had her own trouble in her and the children then went on with their living as was natural to them, having their regular public school living, having all the feeling of country children, having various kinds of fancy education and outdoor living, being of them the poor people near them.

Mrs. Hersland then had in her her time of being most herself to herself in her feeling. Her important being was then existing from Madeleine Wyman's living in her being, being in her early living, later needing protection against her parents' nagging, needing to be held against them by extra wages which Mrs. Hersland induced Mr. Hersland to give her and a dress made by Mary Maxworthing and Mabel Linker.

Later then there will be more description of Mr. Hersland and his ideas on education, later then in the history of each one of the Hersland children there will be a description of Madeleine Wyman's effort to realise Mr. Hersland's ideas of education. Now there is to be a description of Madeleine Wyman and Mrs. Hersland and the important feeling in her, and the trying of Mr. and Mrs. Wyman to make Madeleine leave her, and then the leaving of Madeleine and her later marrying John Summer.

The mother Mrs. Wyman had independent dependent nature in her. The second daughter Louise and the youngest daughter Helen were of her. The father Mr. Wyman had dependent independent earthy instrument nature, the son Frank and the eldest daughter Madeleine were of this nature.

The youngest daughter Helen was all spread and all vague in her independent dependent nature, more spread and vague in her nature, more spread and more vague in her nature than her father was in his nature. The second daughter Louise was almost as concentrated as he mother but there was less to her nature. The son Frank was almost a vague in his nature as his father. Dependent independent instrumen nature was concentrated to make the eldest daughter, Madeleine Wyman, but it did not make of her really an efficient nature. She had about the same concentration in her as her mother and her sister Louise had in their nature. There was real resisting in her, there was some power in her, there was not very much efficiency in her, there was about the same in her as there was in her sister Louise and in her mother. In her it was as dependent independent·instrument being, in them as independent dependent being.

Mrs. Hersland had as her being dependent independent gentle nature with some real resisting in her. Stupid being in her was attacking. Having the children as part of her, having a little resisting to her husband inside her, in her was her winning nature. Resisting winning was in her, in her relation to Mr. Hersland, to attract him, and so to come to be a little a real thing, inside him. Being part of them was her being with her children. She was of them as if they were still a physical part of her. Later they were big around her and she was lost among them and she had weakening inside her. Now they were really not of her, they were more of them the poor people around them than they were of their mother's living then, though they were to her all there ever was of being in her. Now her living was Madeleine Wyman's living in her and later, she and Madeleine resisting to the old Wyman's, Mr. and Mrs. Wyman's trying, by attacking. As I was saying attacking was in Mrs. Hersland stupid being. As I was saying this was in her in her resisting Mr. and Mrs. Wyman. This was in her sometimes with servant girls and their leaving, as I was saying earlier. It was in her most in her defending Madeleine Wyman against Mr. and Mrs. Wyman's trying to make Madeleine leave her.

Madeleine Wyman then as I was saying had come to be governess to the Herslands because a governess in the house with them had come to be a habit in the family living. They had had two of them, the first had left them to leave America, the second had married, and now it was natural to have a third one. This third one was the first one who was really important to Mrs. Hersland. Mr. Hersland found some important being in all three of them, they were like everything around him, part of him, part of the world around him, part of the beginning always in him. The second one had made more impression on him, she was a healthy woman, he liked to have a feeling of having her in the house with them. The first one had been mostly an ideal to him. The last one Madeleine, was pleasant to have listening to him, she had a neat figure, she was intelligent in listening, he had less active impression from her than he had from the one before her. None of them then, the first or second or third governess were really important then to the three Hersland children, they had existence for them, sometimes they interfered with them, sometimes they were pleasant to have in the house with them, but mostly they were not then any one of the three of them very important to the three children. Later this will come clearer, later in the long histories of each one of the three Hersland children which will now soon be commencing. First there will be a long history of Martha, then of Alfred, and then of young David, and of all of them together and of every one who ever came to know them. Before then there must be some more history of Mrs. Hersland and the important feeling in her that came to her from having Madeleine Wyman as governess in the house with her.

Mrs. Hersland as I was saying had in her then completely in her being the feeling of rich country house living, with servants and a governess and a seamstress in the house with them and not cut off from right rich living, although really doing very little visiting. To herself then, she and her husband and her children were part of right rich being, not doing much visiting, not needing to see much of richer people but always of them. To herself she was cut off from her family being and from accustomed living, to herself the other rich people in Gossols who were living there rich right living were too cut off from their family living, from their accustomed being. She was to herself leading rich country house living, it was a natural living to her being, it was all of her middle living, it was all her important living and her children's being, it was the natural living to her, to herself then she was leading rich right living, to herself then she was cut off from her family living, from eastern travelling. Madeleine Wyman then lived in Mrs. Hersland's feeling.

In Mr. Hersland, his early living was not, then in his middle living, in him, in his feeling. It was in him as part of him, it came out of him sometimes in talking, it was not in him then in his middle living nor in his later living, it was not in him then in his feeling. It was not important to him excepting as so much talking coming out of him. That was all the meaning his early living had in him to him and to every one who knew him. Even to Madeleine Wyman who lived in the early living of Mr. and Mrs. Hersland it was not as Mr. Hersland's early living that it was important to her being, it was as Mr. and Mrs. Hersland's early living that it made its impression. As I was saying it was a different matter to Mrs. Hersland who was to herself cut off from her family living. To Mr. Hersland eastern living was a past part of him, it was in him as being little as a baby or a child was in him, it was not something still existing cut off from him, it was part of him and not in his feeling. He had in him in his feeling, his beginning, his having it in him to be as big as all the world around him.

In Mrs. Hersland then it was a different thing, her early living was a continuous living that was going on then and she was cut off from it, to her feeling. When she later went to visit them her family who were still living in Bridgepoint in their natural way of living, she was still then cut off from them, she was of them but a princess to them, she was of them but a stranger to them with a husband and children who had not in any way any connection with them, she was of them but cut off from them by her Gossols living which was a different way of being though it was not a living that to herself was cut off from rich right being.

Madeleine Wyman then had in her the feeling of the early living of Mr. and Mrs. Hersland and this all her later life was an important part of her being and her feeling. She had this in her always as a possession, she had it in her more than Mr. or Mrs. Hersland had it in them, she had it in her as much as Mrs. Hersland had it in her talking, she had it in her more than Mrs. Hersland had it as a feeling, her having it in her gave to Mrs. Hersland her important feeling of herself inside her. Mrs. Hersland could never have had this in her from her own feeling, from her own talking of her early living, she would only have it in her from Madeleine Wyman having this as a possession.

It is clear then, Mr. Hersland had not in him any feeling of his early living, it was part of him because it had happened to him, it came out of him sometimes as bragging, sometimes as illustration, sometimes as moralising, but it was not really ever then in him in his middle or in his later living as feeling. It was in him only as having happened to him.

It is clear then that Mrs. Hersland had in her early living in her as something that was in her, in her middle living, as part of her feeling. Really, her being was her children and her husband and her country house living. To herself in her feeling she was never cut off from right rich living, really she was then not at all of such living, later when she met any of such of them she was cut off from them, to herself then it was not that she was cut off from right rich living, to herself then it was a little then that she was cut off from her family living and eastern travelling and visiting. This was stronger in her from Madeleine Wyman. It always had been all through her Gossols living, a little in her. It had not, before Madeleine Wyman was in the habit of listening to her, it had not been in her, a conscious feeling. Later then it was more consciously in her, it was really then not an important part of her being, it was really then an important part of her feeling herself inside her in her being. Her feeling herself inside her in her feeling was not an important part of her being, her feeling herself inside her to herself from her family being, from her children, a little from her husband, was the important being in her. Feeling herself to herself inside her was not really ever very important being in her. Feeling herself to herself inside her from her talking to Madeleine Wyman, from her defending her against her nagging father and mother was not really important being in her, feeling herself to herself inside her from having in her as part of her her family living, her husband and her children, her country house living, was important being in her.

As I was saying his early living sometimes came out of Mr. Hersland as talking. Mrs. Hersland's early living and her early living with her husband sometimes came out of her as talking, very often, to Madeleine Wyman in the house with her. It was very different in the two of them, in Mr. and in Mrs. Hersland.

As I was saying it came out of him, sometimes as bragging, sometimes as illustration, sometimes as moralising, sometimes as just talking, but it was not in him as feeling, it was not to him really then in his middle living an important part of his being. It was as I was saying early living to him, it had no more meaning than that in him.

In Mrs. Hersland it was in her as feeling, not really as very important feeling, but it had really meaning in her as feeling. It came out of her in talking, it had then to her real meaning, more even than it had to her feeling.

She had always talked some about her early living, when she was living at the hotel sometimes with Sophie Shilling, sometimes when she was visiting she would speak of eastern living to other ones in right rich living who had back of them too early eastern living, sometimes she told stories of it to her children, it was in her a little then as feeling, in the beginning in the hotel living it was in her fairly strongly as a feeling, not really a lonesome feeling, her children, her husband, Sophie Shilling, and Sophie's sister, Sophie's mother were then all the feeling really in her but she had then still a little in her a feeling of her early living and eastern travelling. As I was saying she would speak then of it but it did not then make her even a little important to herself inside her. This came to her later, this came to her when she told it over and over to Madeleine Wyman who was living then the complete being of Mr. and Mrs. Hersland in their early living. It came then to be in Mrs. Hersland her feeling of herself to herself in her feeling. This was not in her resisting or yielding, it was not like her being with her husband or her having anger in her or being a part of the children around her, it was in her like her being with the servants and seamstresses and poor people near her, being of them and above them, it was being herself inside her to her. It was the important being of herself to herself inside her it was not really the important being in her, important being in her really was herself as part of her family, as resisting to her husband or yielding in him, as being part of her children, as being part of rich right living.

As I was saying those having in them dependent independent being have in them resisting as their way of winning fighting. Resisting though is not their only way of fighting they can have yielding winning in them. Resisting and yielding then are not in them stupid being. Mrs. Hersland had in her dependent independent being. Madeleine Wyman had in her dependent independent being. Mrs. Hersland then had in her resisting and yielding to give her winning. Madeleine Wyman then had in her resisting and yielding to give her winning. Resisting and yielding then in both of them was not stupid being in them. Attacking then for both of them was stupid being. This is now a description of the different ways these things came out in them.

There is as I was saying two kinds of being, independent dependent, dependent independent. Resisting is to the dependent independent the natural way of fighting. Those then who have in them dependent independent being as the bottom of them have resisting in them as their natural way of fighting. Many of them have very little fighting in their living. This was true of both of them, Mrs. Hersland and Madeleine who both had dependent independent nature in them.

Resisting fighting is for these then who have dependent independent being in them not their only way of winning. They can have yielding and sensitive being and instrument being in them, sometimes for winning just to keep going, sometimes for winning to subdue some one near them.

Mrs. Hersland and Madeleine Wyman were then for a while then closely in each others living, Madeleine always then all the rest of her living was in her being in Mrs. Hersland's living. In Mrs. Hersland later there was weakening, she had never had Madeleine Wyman in her as real being. In Mrs. Hersland, real being was rich right living, her Bridgepoint family living and her marrying, and her country house living and her children. Later in her living she was weakening inside her, she was scared then, her children were big around her and outside her, trouble was coming then, the country house living was ending and often then Mr. Hersland forgot her as being and later then she died away from among them and they soon, all of them then, lost remembering her among them. So then this was real being in her this was really being herself inside her. This was a real history in her. Her early living, later when she talked so much about it to Madeleine Wyman it was real in her but it was important to her then more than it really was as being in her. It was sentimental feeling and romantic feeling in her, it was not real being in her. To Madeleine Wyman, this early living of Mrs. Hersland was being, it was real being inside her, inside in Madeleine Wyman, it was not sentimental and romantic in her, it was real being in her. It was a little too then real being in Mrs. Hersland but in talking it came to be to her feeling more important than it was then in her being. This was the difference then between them. Mrs. Hersland then had a real being from her early living but it was not, later then, so important to her being or her feeling as in her talking of it to Madeleine Wyman she made it come to be in her Mrs. Hersland's feeling. Later more and more when she was weakening, it was all fainter and fainter in her. In Madeleine Wyman, Mrs. Hersland and Mrs. Hersland's early living was real being. It came to be always stronger in Madeleine Wyman always more and more a part of her being, Mrs. Hersland and Mr. Hersland and their early living. Later the Hersland children had a sore feeling at her having such possession.

To begin again then with dependent independent nature, with resisting being, with sensitive being. To begin again then with dependent independent nature, with earthy instrument being, with little or much resisting, with little or much yielding, with little or much winning.

To begin again then with dependent independent nature, with resisting being, with sensitive being. To begin again then with dependent independent nature, with earthy instrument being, with little or much resisting, with little or much yielding, with little or much winning.

Neither Madeleine Wyman nor Mrs. Hersland had in them really efficient being. They both had in them some resisting fighting, some yielding winning. It showed in the two of them in very different fashion. Madeleine had in her really more instrument being than Mrs. Hersland had in her. Mrs. Hersland had in her more sensitive earthy being than Madeleine Wyman. Neither the one nor the other had really an efficient nature. They were very different from each other. Madeleine was drier and had more energy in her, not enough to carry her, to make for herself a living in her, but enough to make her want to listen and answer, and to carry into action Mr. Hersland's talking about education, enough to make her have later Mr. and Mrs. Hersland as a possession, enough to make her then have Mr. and Mrs. Hersland's early living a part then of her being. Mrs. Hersland had enough energy in her to be a mother, to be a little resisting to her husband in their beginning, to have the dignity in her of country house living and Bridgepoint Hissen family being, she had her own being in her, her children were a part of her, she had a sensitive and later a scared weakening being in her, she could have anger in her and a sharp indignant injured feeling, she had not instrument being in her. Later this will be clearer . More and more then it will be clearer the difference between the being in Madeleine Wyman and in her. They both had in them dependent independent being, it was in them in different fashion, Madeleine had in her instrument being, Mrs. Hersland had not in her such being, she had yielding in her but that was to loving in marrying, yielding in her to the being that was part of her as in her children and her sisters and her brothers and her mother and her father. She had not instrument nature, she had not any living in any being that was not in her a part of her. She was different then from Madeleine Wyman.

Neither the one nor the other of them had in them really efficient being. This came out more and more in them in their later living. This came out in them in their resisting to the trying of the Wyman family when these wanted Madeleine to marry John Summer.

As I was saying attacking in Mrs. Hersland was stupid being. It was in her when she had inside her her feeling of herself to herself in her, when she was resisting the Wyman family about Madeleine. In Madeleine, attacking was stupid being but she was then not showing such being, she had no attacking with which to resist her family's trying. Stupid being then was in her as attacking but it showed then only in her handling of children. Later she showed it with her husband, later when she had really no power over John Summer. She could sometimes stop him in business or in adopting a daughter, she could never really have any effect inside him. Now, then, stupid being as I was saying was in Mrs. Hersland's attacking to stop the Wyman trying, the giving Madeleine double wages and a dress made by Mabel Linker and Mary Maxworthing. Then Madeleine was not attacking, was not having stupid being excepting with the children in trying to carry out Mr. Hersland's ideas for them. Mostly then she had strongly in her instrument being. She was living in Mrs. Hersland's and in Mr. Hersland's being.

The Wyman family then the mother and the father with their children as a background to make a more solid seeming, won out then with trying, Madeleine went back to them and later married John Summer. She really had no objection to marrying John Summer, she did not want to leave the Hersland family, she was willing to marry John Summer later.

In all of them who have dependent independent nature in them, there is resisting and yielding and stupid being as attacking. Sometime there will have been written a history of many of them as by repeating it comes out of them. Sometime some one will know the amount of resisting, yielding and stupid acting there is in every one who ever has or has had or will have dependent independent being in them. Some have less, some have more of one or the other of these things in them, in some it changes in them in the different parts of their living, in the way they have in them excitement or nervous or quiet or melancholy or happy or contented or diseased or healthful or hungry or thirsty or tired or satisfied being in them. Mrs. Hersland then had stupid attacking being mostly in her when she was having important feeling of herself inside her with a servant or a governess or a seamstress or, for her, poor people to arouse it in her and to give to her indignant and injured feeling inside her. This then was strongest in her when Madeleine Wyman was with her, when she was making to herself a being by always telling of her early living, when she was resisting for Madeleine the Wyman family's trying, when she was making Mr. Hersland pay money for her attacking fighting. This then now is always getting clearer.

To begin again then with the dependent independent being in Mrs. Hersland.

It is interesting in each one, the success and failure, that one has in living. Every one has their own nature in them. This comes out of them as repeating. This comes out of them as making success or failure in their living. Mrs. Hersland and Madeleine Wyman had not in them either of them very efficient being, they had not success or failure in living, they went on well enough both of them from their beginning to their ending. This is now to be a history of each one of them.

Mrs. Hersland then had in her dependent independent being. She did not have in her much stupid being. That was in her only as attacking and that was in her sometimes when a servant or a seamstress or a governess or some one, living in a small house near them, did something that was to her not right for them to be doing, when such a one was ungrateful or unpleasant to her. Then she could have a sharp angry feeling in her, then she could have a hurt or injured, or hurt and injured feeling in her, then she would do something for such a one to show such a one that if they demanded something from her that it was not right that they should demand from her she would give them more than they had asked of her. This was angry and injured feeling in her. As I was saying this could be in her from a servant or governess or seamstress or people living in small houses near her. In her earlier living this could be in her from people she knew as friends to her or of her family, she could then in her early living sometimes have it in her from a sister or a brother, but in her later living in that part of Gossols where no other rich people were living this feeling in her came to her only from servants or governesses or seamstresses or store-keepers or dependents in the small houses near her.

She could have then a feeling of herself inside her. This was in her as a gentle dignity in her, as having as a part of her her early living, her country house being, her husband and her children. She could have then a feeling of herself inside her from angry or injured feeling in her, she could have a feeling of herself inside her from Madeleine Wyman's having her Mrs. Hersland's being as part of her. So then Mrs. Hersland had in her in living a sense of herself inside her. This was most active in her when Madeleine Wyman was living in the house with her.

Slowly there is building up a solid structure of the two different kinds of nature. Later any one who looks at any one will see the nature in them. Sometime then there will be a history of every one.

As I was saying Mrs. Hersland and Madeleine Wyman had neither of them a very efficient nature. They went on well enough both of them from their beginning to their ending. It must be clear soon the nature in the two of them and the difference between them. They had both of them dependent independent nature in them. Madeleine had an instrument nature and stupid being as attacking in her. This is now a history of her.

Mrs. Wyman the mother of Madeleine was a foreign american and always remained very foreign, not to herself but to every one who came to know them the Wyman family in their american living, Mrs. Wyman had independent dependent nature in her. She had in her not very efficient being, about as efficient being as Madeleine, enough to bring Madeleine away from Mrs. Hersland by her trying, enough to have Madeleine later married to John Summer, enough to keep her family going, but none of these were very hard things to be doing, she had not in her a very efficient nature. She had in her about the same efficiency as Madeleine had in her and that will later come to be clearer. She had in her about the same efficiency that her second daughter Louise had in her, Mrs. Wyman had more variety to her nature than her daughter Louise, she had about as much variety in her nature, Mrs. Wyman, as her daughter Madeleine had in her.

Mrs. Wyman then had in her independent dependent nature. The second daughter Louise and the youngest daughter Helen were of her as to nature, they had in them both, independent dependent nature. The daughter Louise had about as much efficiency in her as her mother, she had less variety to her nature, she had no liveliness of cringing in her as had her mother, independence and dependence in the daughter were solid substances inside her, in the mother were more lively and more cringing and more attacking and more lively in their changing. In the youngest daughter Helen there was independent dependent nature but this nature was in her as his nature was in her father, vague and uncertain and wide, and without ever any accentuation. Mrs. Wyman then had independent dependent nature in ner. The second daughter Louise and the youngest daughter Helen were of her in their nature.

Mr. Wyman was a foreign american like Mrs. Wyman but nobody felt it very much about him whether he was always foreign, he was foreign, it was not very important to any one excepting his wife and children. He had a dryness of being in him like that in the second Wyman daughter Louise, he had a vagueness in him like that in the youngest daughter Helen, Mr. Wyman then had in him dependent independent nature, the son Frank and the eldest daughter Madeleine were of this nature. The son Frank was like his father only he was always all his life fresher and younger. He had it in him always to have fresher and younger being in him than his father had had in living. He had it in him, the son Frank, with his fresher, younger being to have people like to take care of him, his sister Louise and his sister Madeleine and later his wife and later all three of them with the youngest sister Helen hanging on the outside of them, did this for him. There was in him all through his living fresher and younger being than his father had ever had in him. The eldest daughter Madeleine had in her nature like her father. It was not so earthy in her as it was in her father and her brother. It was not as vague in her as it was in her father, it was never in her so young and so fresh as it was in her brother, it was about as various and as efficient in her as her mother's nature was in her, it was not as solid in her as the nature in her was in her sister Louise, it had in her a little of the dryness that his nature had in her father, the variety and the efficiency that her nature had in her mother. This makes her clearer and now for a history of her.

All four of the Wyman children were born and brought up american. Madeleine had had a governess training. It was really a little more foreign than the training of the other three children. Louise in her training was between Madeleine, and Frank and Helen, these last two being entirely american, being entirely of their american generation in education and feeling. Madeleine was still a little foreign, Louise was between them but education was not really important in her being. She was to be all through her living important in running the family living, in helping and protecting Frank, and then Helen, then Madeleine in her marrying, then Frank in his business of being a nurseryman, then Helen after she came back out of her strange marriage experience back to them, and then Madeleine when she too came back to them with John Summer after their travelling when John Summer was dying of queer ways in eating. Always then she was of the living her brother and sisters had in them. She was not an instrument nature for she was un under-pinning always to them but all her living was her brother's and sisters' living and being.

Madeleine then had lingering in her a little, being foreign. She was american, her brother and sisters were american and her father and mother, in their feeling. They were all of them american, the mother and father were very foreign to every one that came to know them, Madeleine had lingering in her, a little, being foreign, Louise was very american in her feeling, Frank and Helen were simply american. Madeleine and Helen had most of the education, Helen was almost literary in her feeling, Madeleine had had a pretty good education for american governessing. She knew french and german, not as the first governess the Herslands had had knew them but well enough to teach them and talk french and german with the children when parents insisted that there should be talking of french or german. She knew then enough french to teach it to children, enough german to teach it and talk it and to listen with intelligence to Mr. Hersland's explanation of the fine qualities in foreign education. She was not a musician, she knew enough music to oversee the Hersland children's practising, for they had then, that was their father's theory for them, real musicians to teach them, she knew enough music to teach music when there were music lessons to be given, when parents had notions not so completed about education as the Herslands had then. She had a good enough english education, she was not like her sister Helen literary in her feeling, she had in short a good enough american governess training.

Madeleine Wyman came to be a governess to the Herslands, for the Herslands had not come yet to the understanding that for their then family living a governess was not any particular use to them. The children were having then their regular public school living, they had then all the feeling of country children, they had freedom in coming and going, they were then as I was saying more of them the people around them than they were of the family living then though they were then the large part of the family being. They had then their regular public school living, they had then too every kind of fancy education that their father could think would be good for them, they had out of door living and swimming and shooting and horse back riding and perfect freedom, they had not any need then in living for a governess in the house with them. More and more then this last governess became important in their mother's living, more and more then in the children's living she had no meaning, sometimes she would be interfering but mostly she had not even so much importance for them, this will be clearer in the long histories of each one of them.

More and more then this last governess was really then only in Mrs. Hersland's living. She was pleasant enough at moments in Mr. Hersland's living, but she was prominent only in Mrs. Hersland's living. Mrs. Hersland and Mr. Hersland never thought about her not being important in their children's living, she kept on being in the house with them and then came her people's nagging and then the arousing in Mrs. Hersland of attacking resisting and Mr. Hersland had not then about it any very strong feeling. He went, in her action, along with Mrs. Hersland but it was not then important to him. The children then had completely drifted away from governess training, they had then perfect freedom in living, the governess then was not existing for them. This was the last governess the Hersland children had living with them.

John Summer's father had come from the same part of the country as Mr. Wyman. They had known each other in Europe. The old Mr. Summer was dead then and his wife John Summer's mother did not like Mr. and Mrs. Wyman and never came to see them. She did not want to know that they were still living in Gossols in the same town with her. John Summer was not a young man now when he wanted to marry Madeleine Wyman, he was much older than she was, about fifteen years older. This match was not the work of Mrs. Wyman, it was only that Summer was used to Madeleine Wyman and he came to want to marry her. Madeleine was willing enough to marry John Summer, he was pretty rich and could go out of business after marrying and go travelling or any thing that would please her. Mr. Hersland thought it a good match for her, Mr. Hersland always wanted girls to use their sense in marrying and Madeleine Wyman certainly ought to marry John Summer. Mr. Hersland always believed girls should have common sense in them, he always gave them advice about saving money and marrying and cooking. He always gave advice to the second governess who was married to the baker, how she should act so that her husband would be contented with her. In his later living he was strong in sensible advice to women in their living. Now he said it would be the best thing Madeleine could be doing, marrying John Summer. Mr. Hersland always gave advice to the second governess who had married the baker, he would stop there and eat a cake and look at her and give her a lecture. He liked the feeling of women and he wanted them to have sense in them.

Mrs. Hersland always wanted Madeleine some time to marry Summer but she wanted it to be put off a little longer so that their feeling would be tenderer, so that there should not be any forcing from Mrs. Wyman.

Then too she wanted Madeleine to stay in the house with her for the important feeling in her through her, though she did not know this in her. Now her children were drifting away from being a part in her. Now Mr. Hersland was beginning to have more and more in him impatient feeling and brushing her away from around him. Mrs. Hersland did not know it inside her but she wanted Madeleine in the house with her, she wanted to have from her important being of herself to herself inside her. Now Mrs. Hersland had less and less in her the feeling of her children being in her as inside her, they were getting big then around her and were coming more and more then to be apart from her. She was beginning then more to have her husband forget her, country house living then was an old story to her, they never had visitors any more then and though to herself then she still always had inside her the feeling of rich right country house living, still then it was not lively to her feeling, there was nothing to make it strong then inside her, in her feeling. She had then her early living, her Bridgepoint family being, she had the talking of this to make for her of it to her then a stronger thing in her feeling than it really was in her being. This was then in those years in the middle of her middle living her important being in her talking, and her important feeling ; her early living, her marrying and her eastern travelling, Madeleine Wyman was then the important part of her important feeling. Her children were then not living by her being, her husband was then not living by her being, Madeleine Wyman was living by her being, from Madeleine Mrs. Hersland had then all her active important being and this is interesting.

Now it is clear, the kind of being Mrs. Hersland had in her and that which Madeleine Wyman had in her. More and more it is surer that this kind of describing leads to complete understanding of men and women. Sometime then there will be a complete history of every one who ever was or is or will be living.

To some beginning is always in their living, to some ending is always in them to their feeling, in them and in every one, to them. To some, it is different in their beginning, their middle living and their ending, the sense of beginning or of ending always being in them. In many there is always all through their living either beginning or ending always in their feeling, in themselves, in everything that happens to them, in everything that happens to every one.

Sometimes then to one all the world is full of beginning to them, to some then sometimes, all the world is filled up full with ending. To some then sometimes all the world is filled up full with beginning, to some then sometimes all the world is filled up full with ending, to some then sometimes all the world is filled up full with continuing. To some the world always is filled up full with beginning, to some everything and every one is always filled up full with continuing, to some always all their liv-

ing every one they ever see around them, everything, is ending. There
are then many kinds of ways of feeling. Every one has sometime some
kind of feeling in them of every one and everything, as always beginning,
always continuing or always ending, many have a mixture in them.

Repeating then is in every one, in every one their being and their
feeling and their way of realising everything and every one comes out of
them in repeating. More and more then every one comes to be clear
to some one.

Slowly every one in continuous repeating, to their minutest variation, comes to be clearer to some one. Every one who ever was or is or
will be living sometimes will be clearly realised by some one. Sometime
there will be an ordered history of every one. Slowly every kind of one
comes into ordered recognition. More and more then it is wonderful
in living the subtle variations coming clear into ordered recognition,
coming to make every one a part of some kind of them, some kind of men
and women. Repeating then is in every one, every one then comes sometime to be clearer to some one, sometime there will be then an orderly
history of every one who ever was or is or will be living.

Repeating then is in every one, repeating then makes a complete
history in every one for some one sometime to realise in that one. Repeating is in them of the most delicate shades in them of being and of feeling
and so it comes to be clear in each one the complete nature in each one,
it comes to be clear in each one the connection between that one and
others to make a kind of them, a kind of men and women. Repeating
is a wonderful thing in being, everything, every one is repeating then
always the whole of them and so sometime there surely will be an ordered
history of every one. More and more then this is a clear thing. Every
one has their own being in them, every one has repeating always in them
always of the whole of them, always the kinds of them come to be clearer
and the division again into kinds of them. Sometime then there will
be an orderly history of every kind of men and women and that will
be very interesting.

There is now then coming to be an ending of the beginning of the
history of the Hersland family. There are then now living in the ten
acre place in that part of Gossols where no other rich people were living,
Mr. and Mrs. Hersland and the three Hersland children. There will now
come to be a history of each one of the three children and in the history
of each one of them more history of Mr. and Mrs. Hersland and more
history of the governesses and the seamstresses and servants in the house
with them and more history of the families in the small houses near them,
and histories of every one they ever came to know in their living, all
three of the Hersland children. There is then to be a history of each
one of the children, there is then to be a history of the later living of Mr.
and Mrs. Hersland, there is then to be more and more a history of every

one who ever was or is or will be living. Sometime there will be written a long book that is a real history of every one who ever were or are or will be living, from their beginning to their ending, now there is a history of the Hersland and the Dehning families and every one who ever came to know them.

This is now a history of the Hersland family being and of the being of the people they came to know in their living. There has now been some description of the Hersland family and their living in the beginning and middle living of Mr. David Hersland and his wife Fanny Hersland. There has been already a little description of them. There will be later more description of them. There is now to be a beginning of the description of the being and the living in each of the three Hersland children. There is now to be a beginning of description of the being of the oldest of them, there is now to be a beginning of a description of the being of Martha Hersland and a beginning of a description of the being in every one she ever came to know in her living. Later there will be a description of the being in all three of the Hersland children and a description of every one they ever came to know in their living. Now there is a beginning of description of the being in the oldest of the three children, now there is a commencing a beginning of a description of the being and the living in Martha Hersland the oldest of the children and of every one she ever knew in her living. To begin then.

MARTHA HERSLAND

I am writing for myself and strangers. This is the only way that I can do it. Everybody is a real one to me, everybody is like some one else too to me. No one of them that I know can want to know it and so I write for myself and strangers.

Every one is always busy with it, no one of them then ever want to know it that every one looks like some one else and they see it. Mostly every one dislikes to hear it. It is very important to me to always know it, to always see it which one looks like others and to tell it. I write for myself and strangers. I do this for my own sake and for the sake of those who know I know it that they look like other ones, that they are separate and yet always repeated. There are some who like it that I know they are like many others and repeat it, there are many who never can really like it.

There are many that I know and they know it. They are all of them repeating and I hear it. I love it and I tell it, I love it and now I will write it. This is now the history of the way some of them are it.

I write for myself and strangers. No one who knows me can like it. At least they mostly do not like it that every one is of a kind of men and women and I see it. I love it and I write it.

I want readers so strangers must do it. Mostly no one knowing me can like it that I love it that every one is of a kind of men and women, that always I am looking and comparing and classifying of them, always I am seeing their repeating. Always more and more I love repeating, it may be irritating to hear from them but always more and more I love it of them. More and more I love it of them, the being in them, the mixing in them, the repeating in them, the deciding the kind of them every one is who has human being.

This is now a little of what I love and how I write it. Later there will be much more of it.

There are many ways of making kinds of men and women. Now there will be descriptions of every kind of way every one can be a kind of men and women.

This is now a history of Martha Hersland. This is now a history of Martha and of every one who came to be of her living.

There will then be soon much description of every way one can think of men and women, in their beginning, in their middle living, and their ending.

Every one then is an individual being. Every one then is like many others always living, there are many ways of thinking of every one, this is now a description of all of them. There must then be a whole history of each one of them. There must then now be a description of all repeating. Now I will tell all the meaning to me in repeating, the loving there is in me for repeating.

Every one is one inside them, every one reminds some one of some other one who is or was or will be living. Every one has it to say of each one he is like such a one I see it in him, every one has it to say of each one she is like some one else I can tell by remembering. So it goes on always in living, every one is always remembering some one who is resembling to the one at whom they are then looking. So they go on repeating, every one is themselves inside them and every one is resembling to others, and that is always interesting. There are many ways of making kinds of men and women. In each way of making kinds of them there is a different system of finding them resembling. Sometime there will be here every way there can be of seeing kinds of men and women. Sometime there will be then a complete history of each one. Every one always is repeating the whole of them and so sometime some one who sees them will have a complete history of every one. Sometime some one will know all the ways there are for people to be resembling, some one sometime then will have a completed history of every one.

Soon now there will be a history of the way repeating comes out of them comes out of men and women when they are young, when they are children, they have then their own system of being resembling ; this will soon be a description of the men and women in beginning, the being young in them, the being children.

There is then now and here the loving repetition, this is then, now and here, a description of the loving of repetition and then there will be a description of all the kinds of ways there can be seen to be kinds of men and women. Then there will be realised the complete history of every one, the fundamental character of every one, the bottom nature in them, the mixtures in them, the strength and weakness of everything they have inside them, the flavor of them, the meaning in them, the being in them, and then you have a whole history then of each one. Everything then they do in living is clear to the completed understanding, their living, loving, eating, pleasing, smoking, thinking, scolding, drinking, working, dancing, walking, talking, laughing, sleeping, everything in them. There are whole beings then, they are themselves inside them,

repeating coming out of them makes a history of each one of them.
Always from the beginning there was to me all living as repeating.
This is now a description of my feeling. As I was saying listening to
repeating is often irritating, always repeating is all of living, everything
in a being is always repeating, more and more listening to repeating gives
to me completed understanding. Each one slowly comes to be a whole
one to me. Each one slowly comes to be a whole one in me. Soon then
it commences to sound through my ears and eyes and feelings the repeating that is always coming out from each one, that is them, that makes
then slowly of each one of them a whole one. Repeating then comes
slowly then to be to one who has it to have loving repeating as natural
being comes to be a full sound telling all the being in each one such a one
is ever knowing. Sometimes it takes many years of knowing some one
before the repeating that is that one gets to be a steady sounding to the
hearing of one who has it as a natural being to love repeating that slowly
comes out from every one. Sometimes it takes many years of knowing
some one before the repeating in that one comes to be a clear history of
such a one. Natures sometimes are so mixed up in some one that steady
repeating in them is mixed up with changing. Soon then there will be
a completed history of each one. Sometimes it is difficult to know it
in some, for what these are saying is repeating in them is not the real
repeating of them, is not the complete repeating for them. Sometimes
many years of knowing some one pass before repeating of all being in them
comes out clearly from them. As I was saying it is often irritating to
listen to the repeating they are doing, always then that one that has it
as being to love repeating that is the whole history of each one, such a
one has it then that this irritation passes over into patient completed
understanding. Loving repeating is one way of being. This is now a
description of such feeling.

There are many that I know and they know it. They are all of them
repeating and I hear it. I love it and I tell it. I love it and now I will
write it. This is now a history of my love of it. I hear it and I love it
and I write it. They repeat it. They live it and I see it and I hear it.
They live it and I hear it and I see it and I love it and now and always I
will write it. There are many kinds of men and women and I know it.
They repeat it and I hear it and I love it. This is now a history of the
way they do it. This is now a history of the way I love it.

Now I will tell of the meaning to me in repeating, of the loving there
is in me for repeating.

Sometime every one becomes a whole one to me. Sometime every
one has a completed history for me. Slowly each one is a whole one to
me, with some, all their living is passing before they are a whole one to
me. There is a completed history of them to me then when there is of
them a completed understanding of the bottom nature in them of the

nature or natures mixed up in them with the bottom nature of them or separated in them. There is then a history of the things they say and do and feel, and happen to them. There is then a history of the living in them. Repeating is always in all of them. Repeating in them comes out of them, slowly making clear to any one that looks closely at them the nature and the natures mixed up in them. This sometime comes to be clear in every one.

Often as I was saying repeating is very irritating to listen to from them and then slowly it settles into a completed history of them. Repeating is a wonderful thing in living being. Sometime then the nature of every one comes to be clear to some one listening to the repeating coming out of each one.

This is then now to be a little description of the loving feeling for understanding of the completed history of each one that comes to one who listens always steadily to all repeating. This is the history then of the loving feeling in me of repeating, the loving feeling in me for completed understanding of the completed history of every one as it slowly comes out in every one as patiently and steadily I hear it and see it as repeating in them. This is now a little a description of this loving feeling. This is now a little a history of it from the beginning.

Always then I listen and come back again and again to listen to every one. Always then I am thinking and feeling the repeating in every one. Sometime then there will be for me a completed history of every one. Every one is separate then and a kind of men and women.

Sometime it takes many years of knowing some one before the repeating in that one comes to be a clear history of such a one. Sometimes many years of knowing some one pass before repeating of all being in such a one comes out clearly from them, makes a completed understanding of them by some one listening, watching, hearing all the repeating coming out from such a one.

As I was saying loving listening, hearing always all repeating, coming to completed understanding of each one is to some a natural way of being. This is now more description of the feeling such a one has in them, this is now more description of the way listening to repeating comes to make completed understanding. This is now more description of the way repeating slowly comes to make in each one a completed history of them.

There are many that I know and always more and more I know it. They are all of them repeating and I hear it. More and more I understand it. Always more and more I hear it, always more and more it has completed history in it.

Every one has their own being in them. Every one is of a kind of men and women. Many have mixed up in them some kind of many kinds of men and women. Slowly this comes clearly out from them in the repeating that is always in all living. Slowly it comes out from them to the most delicate gradation, to the gentlest flavor of them. Always it comes out as repeating from them. Always it comes out as repeating, out of them. Then to the complete understanding they keep on repeating this, the whole of them and any one seeing them then can understand them. This is a joy to any one loving repeating when in any one repeating steadily tells over and over again the history of the complete being in them. This is a solid happy satisfaction to any one who has it in them to love repeating and completed understanding.

As I was saying often for many years some one is baffling. The repeated hearing of them does not make the completed being they have in them to any one. Sometimes many years pass in listening to repeating in such a one and the being of them is not a completed history to any one then listening to them. Sometimes then it comes out of them a louder repeating that before was not clear to anybody's hearing and then it is a completed being to some one listening to the repeating coming out of such a one.

This is then now a description of loving repeating being in some. This is then now a description of loving repeating being in one.

There are many that I know and they know it. They are all of them repeating and I hear it. More and more I understand it. I love it and I tell it. I love it and always I will tell it. They live it and I see it and I hear it. They repeat it and I hear it and I see it, sometime then always I understand it, sometime then always there is a completed history of each one by it, sometime then I will tell the completed history of each one as by repeating I come to know it.

Every one always is repeating the whole of them. Every one is repeating the whole of them, such repeating is then always in them and so sometime some one who sees them will have a complete understanding of the whole of each one of them, will have a completed history of every man and every woman they ever come to know in their living, every man and every woman who were or are or will be living whom such a one can come to know in living.

This then is a history of many men and women, sometime there will be a history of every one.

As I was saying every one always is repeating the whole of them. As I was saying sometimes it takes many years of hearing the repeating in one before the whole being is clear to the understanding of one who has it as a being to love repeating, to know that always every one is repeating the whole of them.

This is then the way such a one, one who has it as a being to love repeating, to know that always every one is repeating the whole of them comes to a completed understanding of any one. This is now a description of such a way of hearing repeating.

Every one always is repeating the whole of them. Many always listen to all repeating that comes to them in their living. Some have it as being to love the repeating that is always in every one coming out from them as a whole of them. This is now a description of such a one and the completed understanding of each one who is repeating in such a one's living.

Every one always is repeating the whole of them. Always, one having loving repeating to getting completed understanding must have in them an open feeling, a sense for all the slightest variations in repeating, must never lose themselves so in the solid steadiness of all repeating that they do not hear the slightest variation. If they get deadened by the steady pounding of repeating they will not learn from each one even though each one always is repeating the whole of them they will not learn the completed history of them, they will not know the being really in them.

As I was saying every one always is repeating the whole of them. As I was saying sometimes it takes many years of listening, seeing, living, feeling, loving the repeating there is in some before one comes to a completed understanding. This is now a description, of such a way of hearing, seeing, feeling living, loving, repetition.

Mostly every one loves some one's repeating. Mostly every one then, comes to know then the being of some one by loving the repeating in them, the repeating coming out of them. There are some who love everybody's repeating, this is now a description of such loving in one.

Mostly every one loves some one's repeating. Every one always is repeating the whole of them. This is now a history of getting completed understanding by loving repeating in every one the repeating that always is coming out of them as a complete history of them. This is now a description of learning to listen to all repeating that every one always is making of the whole of them.

Now I will tell of the meaning to me in repeating, of the loving there is in me for repeating.

Always from the beginning there was to me all living as repeating. This is now a description of loving repeating as a being. This is now a history of learning to listen to repeating to come to a completed understanding.

To go on now giving all of the description of how repeating comes to have meaning, how it forms itself, how one must distinguish the different meanings in repeating. Sometimes it is very hard to understand the meaning of repeating. Sometime there will be a complete history of some one having loving repeating as being, to a completed understanding Now there will be a little description of such a one.

Sometime then there will be a complete history of all repeating to completed understanding. Sometime then there will be a complete history of every one who ever was or is or will be living.

Sometime there will be a complete history of some one having loving repeating to a completed understanding as being. Sometime then there will be a complete history of many women and many men.

Now there is to be some description of some one having loving repeating to a completed understanding as being. Then there will be a complete history of some.

More and more then there will be a history of many men and many women from their beginning to their ending, as being babies and children and growing young men and growing young women and young grown men and young grown women and men and women in their middle living and growing old men and growing old women and old men and old women.

More and more then there will be histories of all the kinds there are of men and women.

This is now a little description of having loving repeating as being. This is now a little description of one having loving repeating as being.

Loving repeating is one way of being. This is now a description of such being. Loving repeating is always in children. Loving repeating is in a way earth feeling. Some children have loving repeating for little things and story-telling, some have it as a more bottom being. Slowly this comes out in them in all their children being, in their eating, playing, crying, and laughing. Loving repeating is then in a way earth feeling. This is very strong in some. This is very strong in many, in children and in old age being. This is very strong in many in all ways of humorous being, this is very strong in some from their beginning to their ending. This is now some description of such being in one.

As I was saying loving repeating being is in a way earthy being. In some it is repeating that gives to them always a solid feeling of being. In some children there is more feeling in repeating eating and playing, in some in story-telling and their feeling. More and more in living as growing young men and women and grown young men and women and men and women in their middle living, more and more there comes to be in them differences in loving repeating in different kinds of men and women, there comes to be in some more and in some less loving repeating. Loving repeating in some is a going on always in them of earthy being, in some it is the way to completed understanding. Loving repeating then in some is their natural way of complete being. This is now some description of one.

There is then always repeating in all living. There is then in each one always repeating their whole being, the whole nature in them. Much loving repeating has to be in a being so that that one can listen to all the repeating in every one. Almost every one loves all repeating in some one. This is now some description of loving repeating, all repeating, in every one.

To begin again with the children. To begin again with the repeating being in them. To begin again with the loving repeating being in them. As I was saying some children have it in them to love repeating in them of eating, of angry feeling in them, many of them have loving repeating for story-telling in them, many of them have loving repeating being in them for any kind of being funny, in making jokes or teasing, many of them have loving repeating being in them in all kinds of playing. Mostly every one when they are children, mostly every one has then loving repeating being strongly in them, some have it more some have it less in them and this comes out more and more in them as they come to be young adolescents in their being and then grown young men and grown young women

To begin again then with children in their having loving repeating being. Mostly all children have loving repeating as being in them but some have it much more and some have it much less in them. Loving repeating being is more of that kind of being that has resisting as its natural way of fighting than of that kind of being that has attacking as its natural way of winning. But this is a very complicated question. I know very much about these ways of being in men and women. I know it and can say it, it is a very complex question and I do not know yet the whole of it, so I can not yet say all I know of it.

As I was saying all little children have in them mostly very much loving repeating being. As they grow into bigger children some have it more some have it less in them. Some have it in them more and more as a conscious feeling. Many of them do not have it in them more and more as a conscious feeling. Mostly when they are growing to be young men and women they have not it in them to have loving repeating being in them as a conscious feeling.

Mostly every one has not it in them as a conscious feeling as a young grown man or young grown woman. Some have it in them, loving repeating feeling as steadily developing, this is now a history of one.

Many men and many women never have it in them the conscious feeling of loving repeating. Many men and many women never have it in them until old age weakening is in them, a consciousness of repeating. Many have it in them all their living as a conscious feeling as a humorous way of being in them. Some have it in them, the consciousness of always repeating the whole of them as a serious obligation. There are many many ways then of having repeating as conscious feeling, of having loving repeating as a bottom being, of having loving repeating being as a conscious feeling.

As I was saying mostly all children have in them loving repeating being as important in them to them and to every one around them. Mostly growing young men and growing young women have to themselves very little loving repeating being, they do not have it to each other then most of them, they have it to older ones then as older ones have it to them loving repeating being, not loving repeating being but repeating as the way of being in them, repeating of the whole of them as coming every minute from them.

In the middle living of men and women there are very different ways of feeling to repeating, some have more and more in them loving repeating as a conscious feeling, some have less and less liking in them for the repeating in, to them, of mostly every one. Mostly every one has a loving feeling for repeating in some one. Some have not any such loving even in the repeating going on inside themselves then, not even for any one they are loving.

Some then have always growing in them more and more loving feeling for the repeating in every one. Many have not any loving for repeating in many of those around them.

There are then many ways of feeling in one about repeating. There are many ways of knowing repeating when one sees and hears and feels it in every one.

Loving repeating then is important being in some. This is now some description of the importance of loving repeating being in one.

Some find it interesting to find inside them repeating in them of some one they have known or some relation to them coming out in them, some never have any such feeling in them, some have not any liking for such being in them. Some like to see such being in others around them but not in themselves inside them. There are many ways of feeling in one about all these kinds of repeating. Sometime there will be written the history of all of them.

To begin again then with some description of the meaning of loving repeating being when it is strongly in a man or in a woman, when it is in them their way of understanding everything in living and there are very many always living of such being. This is now again a beginning of a little description of it in one.

Repeating of the whole of them is then always in every one. There are different stages in being, there is being babies and children and then growing young men or women and grown young men or women and men or women in middle living and in growing old and in ending. There are many kinds of men and women and soon now there will be a beginning of a history of all of them who ever were or are or will be living. There will be then here written a history of some of them. To begin again then with loving repeating being as a bottom nature in some. To begin again with the developing of it in one.

As I was saying children have it in them to have strongly loving repeating being as a conscious feeling in so far as they can be said to have such a thing in them. It gives to them a solid feeling of knowing they are safe in living. With growing it comes to be more in some, it comes to be less in others of them. Mostly there is very little conscious loving repeating feeling in growing young men and women.

In the beginning then, in remembering, repeating was strongly in the feeling of one, in the feeling of many, in the feeling of most of them who have it to have strongly in them their earthy feeling of being part of the solid dirt around them. This is one kind of being. This is mostly of one kind of being, of slow-minded resisting fighting being. This is now a little a description of one.

Slowly then some go on living, they may be fairly quick in learning, some of such of them seem very quick and impetuous in learning and in acting but such learning has for such of them very little meaning, it is the slow repeating resisting inside them that has meaning for them. Now there will be a little a description of loving repeating being in one of such of them.

The kinds and ways of repeating, of attacking and resisting in different kinds of men and women, the practical, the emotional, the sensitive, the every kind of being in every one who ever was or is or will be living, I know so much about all of them, many of them are very clear in kinds of men and women, in individual men and women, I know them so well inside them, repeating in them has so much meaning to knowing, more and more I know all there is of all being, more and more I know it in all the ways it is in them and comes out of them, sometime there will be a history of every one, sometime all history of all men and women will be inside some one.

Now there will be a little description of the coming to be history of all men and women, in some one. This is then to be a little history of such a one. This is then now to be a little description of loving repeating being in one.

Almost every one has it in them in their beginning to have loving repeating being strongly in them. Some of them have attacking being as the bottom nature in them, some of them have resisting being as the bottom nature in them. Some of both these kinds of them have more or less in all their living loving repeating being in them, it works differently in them to come out of them in these two kinds of them. Later there will be much description of the way it comes out from them and is in them in the different kinds of them. Now there is to be a little description of it in one having resisting as the way of winning fighting. This is now some description of such a one having loving repeating being developing into completed understanding. Now to slowly begin.

The relation of learning to being, of thinking to feeling, of realisation to emotion, all these and many others are very complicated questions. Sometimes there will be much description of them with the kinds of men and women with being in them, with mixtures in them, that complicates them. There will sometime be a history of every one. This is a sure thing.

Now again to begin. The relation of learning and thinking to being, of feeling to realising is a complicated question. There will now be very little talking of such way of being. As I was saying some have it in them to have slowly resisting as their natural way of being can have learning and thinking come quickly enough in them. This is then not bottom being in them. It is bottom being in some of such of them. This is very clear now in my knowing. Now to begin again with it as telling.

Some then who are of that kind of being who have slow resisting being as their way to wisdom have it in them to be quick in learning and in thinking and in acting. As I was saying in some this is not of the bottom nature in them, in some it is bottom nature in them for the slow resisting winning bottom to them was not put in in the making of them, in some it is in them but dull and not mixing in their living, in some it is not sensitive to action in their living, it is there in them going on inside them not connecting on with the rest of them. This is not just talking, this all has real meaning. These are all then of a kind of men and women who have resisting being as the real wisdom in them. In some of such of them they seem to be winning by acting by attacking they live so very successfully in living but nevertheless they are of the kind of them that have resisting winning as their real way of fighting although never in their living does this act in them. Careful listening to the whole of them always repeating shows this in them, what kind they are of men and women.

To begin again. This is now some description of one having loving repeating as a way to wisdom, having slowly resisting winning as the bottom being. As I was saying learning in such a one and thinking about everything can be quick enough in the beginning.

The important thing then in knowing the bottom nature in any one is the way their real being slowly comes to be them, the whole of them comes to be repeating in them.

As I was saying some can have quick learning and nervous attacking or one or the other in them with slow resisting being in them as their natural way of winning. There is every kind of mixing. There is every degree of intensification. There is every degree of hastening the resisting into more rapid realisation. There is every degree of hurrying. In short there are all degrees of intensification and rapidity in motion and mixing and disguising and yet the kind he is each one, the kind she is each one, comes to be clear in the repeating that more and more steadily makes them clear to any one looking hard at them. These kinds then are existing, the independent dependent, the dependent independent, the one with attacking as the way of winning, the other with resisting as the way of wisdom for them. I know then this is true of every one that each one is of one or the other kind of these two kinds of them. I know it is in them, I know many more thing about these two kinds of them.

Slowly they come to be clearer in every one, sometime perhaps it will be clear to every one. Sometime perhaps some one will have completely in them the history of every one of everything in every one and the degree and kind and way of being of everything in each one in them from their beginning to their ending and coming out of them.

This is then a beginning of the way of knowing everything in every one, of knowing the complete history of each one who ever is or was or will be living. This is then a little description of the winning of so much wisdom.

As I was saying the important thing is having loving repeating being, that is the beginning of learning the complete history of every one. That being must always be in such a one, one who has it in them sometime to have in them the completed history of every one they ever can hear of as having being.

There are so many ways of beginning this description, and now once more to make a beginning.

Always repeating is all of living, everything that is being is always repeating, more and more listening to repeating gives to me completed understanding. Each one then slowly comes to be a whole one to me, each one slowly comes to be a whole one in me, slowly it sounds louder and louder and louder inside me through my ears and eyes and feelings and the talking there is always in me the repeating that is the whole of each one I come to know around, and each one of them then comes to be a whole one to me, comes to be a whole one in me. Loving repeating is one way of being. This is now a description of such being.

Always from the beginning there was to me all living as repeating. This was not in me then a conscious being. Always more and more this is in me developing to a completed being. This is now again a beginning of a little description of such being.

In their beginning as children every one has in them loving repeating being. This is for them then their natural being. Later in conscious being some have much in them of loving repeating being, some have in them almost nothing of such feeling. There are then these two kinds of them. This is then one way of thinking of them.

There are two kinds of men and women, those who have in them resisting as their way of winning those who have in them attacking as their way of winning fighting, there are many kinds, many very many kinds of each of these two kinds of men and women, sometime there will be written a description of all the kinds of them. Now this division is accepted by me and I will now give a little more description of loving repeating being and then go on to describing how it comes to slowly give to me completed understanding, loving repeating being always in me acting, of this one and that one, and then there will be some description of resembling coming to be clear by looking at the repeating in men and women and then there will be more history of Martha Hersland and the being coming out of her all her living and the being in every one she came to know in living.

Always then from the beginning there was in me always increasing as a conscious feeling loving repeating being, learning to know repeating in every one, hearing the whole being of any one always repeating in that one every minute of their living. There was then always in me as a bottom nature to me an earthy, resisting slow understanding, loving repeating being. As I was saying this has nothing to do with ordinary learning, in a way with ordinary living. This will be clearer later in this description.

Many have loving repeating being in them, many never come to know it of them, many never have it as a conscious feeling, many have in it a restful satisfaction. Some have in it always more and more understanding, many have in it very little enlarging understanding. There is every kind of way of having loving repeating being as a bottom. It is very clear to me and to my feeling, it is very slow in developing, it is very important to make it clear now in writing, it must be done now with a slow description. To begin again then with it in my feeling, to begin again then to tell of the meaning to me in all repeating, of the loving there is in me for repeating.

Sometime every one becomes a whole one to me. For many years this was just forming in me. Now sometimes it takes many years for some one to be a whole one to me. For many years loving repeating was a bottom to me, I was never thinking then of the meaning of it in me, it had nothing then much to do with the learning, the talking, the thinking, nor the living then in me. There was for many years a learning and talking and questioning in me and not listening to repeating in every one around me. Then slowly loving repeating being came to be a conscious feeling in me. Slowly then every one sometime became a whole one to me.

Now I will tell of the meaning in me of repeating, of the loving repeating being there is now always in me.

In loving repeating being then to completed understanding there must always be a feeling for all changing, a feeling for living being that is always in repeating. This is now again a beginning of a description of my feeling.

Always then I am thinking and feeling the repeating in each one as I know them. Always then slowly each one comes to be a whole one to me. As I was saying loving repeating in every one, hearing always all repeating, coming to completed understanding of each one is to me a natural way of being.

There are many that I know and always more and more I know it. They are all of them repeating and I hear it. They are all of them living and I know it. More and more I understand it, always more and more it has completed history in it.

Every one has their own being in them. Every one is of a kind of men and women. Always more and more I know the whole history of each one. This is now a little a description of such knowing in me. This is now a little a description of beginning of hearing repeating all around me.

As I was saying learning, thinking, living in the beginning of being men and women often has in it very little of real being. Real being, the bottom nature, often does not then in the beginning do very loud repeating. Learning, thinking, talking, living, often then is not of the real bottom being. Some are this way all their living. Some slowly come to be repeating louder and more clearly the bottom being that makes them. Listening to repeating, knowing being in every one who ever was or is or will be living slowly came to be in me a louder and louder pounding. Now I have it to my feeling to feel all living, to be always listening to the slightest changing, to have each one come to be a whole one to me from the repeating in each one that sometime I come to be understanding. Listening to repeating is often irritating, listening to repeating can be dulling, always repeating is all of living, everything in a being is always repeating, always more and more listening to repeating gives to me completed understanding. Each one slowly comes to be a whole one to me. Each one slowly comes to be a whole one in me.

In the beginning then learning and thinking and talking and feeling and loving and working in me mostly was not bottom being in me. Slowly it came out in me the feeling for living in repeating that now by listening and watching and feeling everything coming out of each one and always repeating the whole one gives to me completed understanding.

There was a time when I was questioning, always asking, when I was talking, wondering, there was a time when I was feeling, thinking and all the time then I did not know repeating, I did not see or hear or feel repeating. There was a long time then when there was nothing in me using the bottom loving repeating being that now leads me to knowing. Then I was attacking, questioning, wondering, thinking, always at the bottom was loving repeating being, that was not then there to my conscious being. Sometime there will be written a long history of such a beginning.

Always then there was there a recognition of the thing always repeating, the being in each one, and always then thinking, feeling, talking, living, was not of this real being. Slowly I came to hear repeating. More and more then I came to listen, now always and always I listen and always now each one comes to be a whole one to me.

This will be clearer now in a description of how several men and several women came to be a whole one to me. Later then there will be more description of the knowing of the kinds there are of men and women, of the resembling that makes kinds of them around one. Now there will be a little description of the slow way repeating makes a whole one to me. Later there will be again a continuing of the description of the living of the Hersland family, the father and the mother and the three children.

Now this is the way I hear repeating. This is the way slowly some men and some women, each one, comes to be a whole one to me.

There are many that I know and always more and more I know it. They are all of them repeating and I hear it. More and more I understand it. Always more and more I know it, always more and more it has completed history in it.

Every one then has their own being in them. Every one is of a kind of men and women. Always then I listen and come back again and again to listen to every one. Always then I am thinking and feeling the repeating in every one. Sometime then there will be for me a completed history of every one. Every one is separate then. Every one is always repeating the whole of them.

Sometimes it takes many years of knowing some one before the repeating in that one comes to be a clear history of such a one. Sometimes many years of knowing some one pass before repeating of all being in such a one comes out clearly from them, makes a completed understanding of them by some one listening, watching, hearing all the repeating coming out from such a one.

As I was saying always then I listen and feel and say and come back again and again to the repeating in every one. Sometime then each one comes to be to me a completed being. This is now the slowly completed history of some.

There are many that I know and I know it. They are many that I know and they know it. They are all of them themselves and they repeat it and I hear it. Always I listen to it. Slowly I come to understand it. Many years I listened and did not know it. I heard it, I understood it some, I did not know I heard it. They repeat themselves now and I listen to it. Every way that they do it now I hear it. Now each time very slowly I come to understand it. Always it comes very slowly the completed understanding ot it, the repeating each one does to tell it the whole history of the being in each one, always now I hear it. Always now slowly I understand it.

There are many that I know and always more and more I know it. They are always all of them always repeating themselves and I hear it. Always I stop myself from being too quickly sure that I have heard all of it. Always I begin again to listen to it. Always I remember all the times I thought I had heard all of it all the repeating in some one and then there was much more to it. Always I remember every way one can hear only a part of it, the repeating that is the whole history of any one and so always I begin again as if I had never heard it.

Always I love it, sometimes I get a little tired of it, mostly I am always ready to do it, always I love it. Listening up to completed understanding of the repeating that sometime is a completed history of each one is all my life and always I live it. I love it and I live it. Sometimes I am tired in it, mostly I am always ready for it.

Mostly in the beginning as I was saying I heard repeating, I was learning, thinking, talking, living not really anything I was really knowing. Slowly I came to be living, loving thinking, feeling, hearing every one repeating, beginning again and again so as to feel all changing, remembering all the ways one always can come to be mistaken. Sometime there will be more history of it the way some young people live it the beginning and then slowly the bottom in them comes to be all them. Sometime there will be a history of all young living, feeling, talking, thinking, being. Some have their real being in young living, some do not have it then in them. Later there will be a history of all of them, of every one.

To begin then again with a little description of my coming to completed understanding of some now that I am always hearing, seeing, feeling all being in each one repeating. Later there will be a description of earlier learning. Now there will be some description of realising some, now when hearing repeating is my natural way of learning. To begin then.

There are many that I know and always slowly I understand more and more of it, the way I know it, the way I come to know it. There are many that I know. Always slowly I understand more and more of it. Slowly each one that I know comes to be a real one to me.

Every one has their own being in them. Slowly in listening, seeing, feeling all the repeating in each one of them slowly each one of them comes to be a whole one to any one that so hears and feels and sees them. This is now a little description of some, this is now a little description of how hearing, feeling, seeing repeating in some makes of such of them to such a one completed beings. This is now a little such a description to lead up to kinds of men and women. To begin then.

Every one I am ever knowing slowly comes to be a whole one to me. Each one slowly comes to be a whole one in me. Sometimes for many years some one is baffling. I hear them and I see them and I feel them in all the repeating I can see and hear and feel from them and seeing, hearing, feeling does not give to me completed understanding of the completed being in them.

Sometimes some one for many years is baffling. The repeated hearing, seeing, feeling of repeating in them does not give to me then a history of the complete being in them. Slowly then sometime it comes to be clearer of them, I begin again with listening, I feel new shades in repeating, parts of repeating that I was neglecting hearing, seeing, feeling come to have a louder beating. Slowly it comes to a fuller sounding, sometimes many years pass in such a baffling listening, feeling, seeing all the repeating in some one. Then slowly such a one comes to have real meaning. Many times I begin and then begin again. Always I must not begin a deadened following, always their repeating must be a fresh feeling in my hearing, seeing, feeling. Always I must admit all changing. Always I must have a sensitive and open being, always I must have a loving repeating being. Often listening to them is irritating, often it is dulling, always then there must be in me new beginning, always there must be in me steadily alive inside me my loving repeating being. Then sometime every one is a completed being to me, sometime every one has a completed history to me. Always then it comes out of them their whole repeating, sometime then I can feel and hear and see it all and it has meaning. Sometime then each one I am ever knowing comes to be to me a completed being, and then always they are always repeating always the whole of them.

There are many that I know then. They are all of them repeating and I hear it, see it, feel it. More and more I understand it. I love it, I tell it. I love it, I live it and I tell it. Always I will tell it. They live it and I see it and I hear it and I feel it. They live it and I see it and I hear it and I feel it and I love it, sometime then I understand it, sometime then there is a completed history of each one by it, sometime then I will tell the completed history of every one as by hearing, feeling, seeing all repeating I come to know it. Now I will just tell a few short histories to explain it, to explain hearing, feeling, seeing repeating and understanding being by it. Now I will tell a few short histories in it to show loving repeating being in me and how I use it.

As I was saying every one I am ever knowing slowly comes to be a whole one to me. Each one slowly comes to be a whole one to me. Some come to have for me complete meaning quicker then others of them. Mostly all of them come pretty slowly to be a whole one to me. This is now a little description of some who have come to be inside me as a whole one to me, some very slowly, some quicker to me. Always I am hearing, feeling, seeing all repeating in them, always I have as a bottom loving repeating being.

Everybody is a real one to me, everybody is like some one else too to me. This is always there in me this and loving repeating being, always, in me.

Everybody is a real one to me, everybody is like some one else too to me. Every one always is repeating the whole of them. Each one slowly comes to be a whole one to me. Each one slowly comes to be a whole one in me.

Some one coming to be a whole one in me is now what I am describing. Every one is like some one else too to me, that will have more meaning later when I am talking of the kinds there are of men and women. Always every one is repeating the whole of them, that is always there to bring to me completed understanding. That is always there in every one to some one. That is always there in every one to be a complete history always coming out of them.

To begin then again with a few of them who slowly come to be each one of them a whole one to me.

Each one slowly comes to be a whole one to me. Each one slowly comes to be a whole one in me. Every one always is repeating. As I was saying sometimes it is very irritating hearing, feeling, seeing repeating in some one, in every one. More and more then when such a one is a whole one to me, more and more then as loving repeating is all my being, more and more then I am happy in my loving repeating being. Now then.

Each one slowly comes to be a whole one to me. Each one slowly comes to be a whole one in me. This is now a description of learning one.

There are then many ways of learning, there are then many ways of having men and women come to be a whole one to me, come to be a whole one in me. To begin now with one.

This one very slowly came to be a whole one to me. This one very slowly came to be a whole one in me. Always now this one is a complete one to me. Always now all the repeating I am hearing coming from this one has real meaning. This is now a description of this learning.

Each one slowly comes to be a whole one to me. Each one slowly comes to be a whole one in me. This one very slowly came to be a whole one in me. This then is now a description of one way of learning to listen, feel and see all the repeating in some. Then there will be descriptions of other ways of learning. Now to begin again with this one.

Each one slowly comes to be a whole one to me. Each one slowly comes to be a whole one in me. With some, right understanding of the repeating always coming out from them takes many years of loving repeating being in me to bring me to such understanding.

Each one slowly comes to be a whole one to me. Sometimes listening, feeling, seeing, repeating in such a one is very irritating. Slowly it comes clear and the one comes to be a whole one to me.

There are many ways then of learning the complete being in any one, this is now a description of one. There are many that I know and I know it. Sometimes it takes many years to learn it. Sometime each one is a whole one to me. Sometime each one is a whole one in me. Sometimes after I have them so I lose them and then I must begin again to learn them. Mostly when I know them they keep on being a whole one in me. Some are easier to keep as a whole one to one than others around one. Some are easier to hold as a whole one when one is thinking of them, some are easier to keep as a whole one when one is hearing them coming out from them. There are all kinds of ways then of knowing, there are all kinds of ways then of remembering, there are all kinds of ways then of losing a thing after it is knowledge in one. Each one then sometime is a whole one to me. Each one then sometime is a whole one in me. This is now a description of one. This is now a description of one who very slowly came to be a whole one in me. This is now a very short description of learning this one.

Sometimes it takes many years of listening, seeing, living, feeling, loving the repeating there is in some one before one comes to a completed understanding of such a one. Sometimes it is very irritating to do such hearing, seeing, feeling living. Always there is loving repetition being in one doing such listening, seeing, feeling, often it is then very irritating, always then loving feeling for repetition can make one go on living, hearing, seeing, feeling all the repetitions coming out of such a one. As I was saying almost every one has some one who sometimes has listened to all the repeating in that one. This is from the loving feeling some one sometime has had for that one. Every one mostly, sometimes has listened to all repeating in some one, has heard and felt and seen all the repeating in some one. Mostly every one has sometime had some one hear and see and feel all the repeating coming out of them. Some have it to love every one. Some have it to love many men and many women or many men or many women, some have it to love the repeating in them, some have it to love every one and the repeating in every one, some have it to love some and to love repeating in every one. This is now some description of learning of complete understanding in such a one.

Every one then sometime comes to be a whole one to me. Each one sometime comes to be a whole one in me. Always loving repeating is my way of being. This is now some description of my studying.

There are many that I know and always more and more I know it. They are all of them repeating and I hear it. More and more I understand it. Always more and more I see it, hear it, feel it, always more and more it has to me completed history in it.

Every one has their own being in them. Everybody is a real one to me. Each one sometimes is a whole one to me. Each one is sometimes a whole one in me. Some come very slowly to be a complete being to me.

This is now a description of learning to listen to all repeating that every one always is making of the whole of them. This is now some description of learning to hear, see and feel all repeating that each one always is making of the whole of them. Each one as I was saying sometime comes to be a whole one in me, each one sometime comes to be a complete being to me. Sometimes after they are this to me I keep on knowing it inside me, sometimes I lose it, sometimes I doubt it, it is too clear or too vague or too confused inside me. Sometime then I have it all to do again. Always I keep on hearing, feeling, seeing all repeating in each one for always it has more and more being to my feeling.

This is now then some description of my learning. Then there will be a beginning again of Martha Hersland and her being and her living. This is now then first a little studying and then later Martha Hersland will begin living. Now then to do this little studying.

As I was saying each one sometime is a whole one to me. Sometimes some one very very slowly comes to be a whole one to me. Every one is a real one to me. Every one always is repeating the whole of them.

Every one is sometime a puzzle to me. Every one is sometime a whole being to me. Some one sometimes is many years a puzzle to me. Sometime every one, each one is a whole being to me.

Some one sometimes for many years is a puzzle to me. Some slowly come to be a whole one in me. Some all of a sudden come to be a whole one to me. Mostly every one is sometime a puzzle to me. Mostly every one is for some years a puzzle to me. This is now a little a description of how one was a puzzle to me and then came to be clear inside me, came to be a whole one to me. More and more then as they are a whole one to me they are friendly to me there inside me. Always they come to be more and more in me. Always they come to have more and more meaning to me in the repeating which then they are doing clearly to me, of the whole of them.

Many of them then are many years a puzzle to me.

Slowly then each one comes to be to me a whole one, always they are repeating the whole of them then.

Every one is puzzling to me, some for some reason others for other reasons, always every one is puzzling, sometime every one becomes a whole one to me, mostly then they go on repeating clearly to me the whole of them, sometimes they commence again to be a puzzle to me, sometimes I lose the way of hearing clearly the repeating of the whole of them that always every one is always doing.

This one then was puzzling for many years to me and then slowly this one came to be a whole one to me, many others then came to be clear to me. Always then this one has been a whole one to me, always then the whole of this one always is repeating to me. Often, as I was saying, it is very irritating to be listening, irritating when it is puzzling, irritating just to be hearing repeating. More and more as each one is a whole one to me repeating from them is not irritating to me, it is friendly there inside me, they are then each one a whole one in me.

This one then for many years was puzzling to me. Slowly then this one came to repeat clearly to me the whole being and then this one came to be a whole one to me.

Slowly then this one came to be a whole one to me.

Always then I was listening, feeling, looking, always then I was hearing, feeling, seeing the repeating always coming out of this one and always it was puzzling, and mostly it was irritating listening, and always this one was not then a whole one to me.

There is a certain feeling one has in one when some one is not a whole one to one even though one seems to know all the nature of that one. Such a one then is very puzzling and when sometime such a one is a whole one to one all the repeating coming out of them has meaning as part of a whole one. When some one is not a clear one to one, repeating coming out of them has not this clear relation. Then such a one is puzzling until they come to be a whole one. Then repeating coming out of them has clear meaning.

Always then I am hearing, feeling, seeing the repeating always coming out of every one. Loving repeating being is in me always every moment in my living. Sometimes as I was saying hearing repeating is very irritating. Always sometime it comes to be to me a completed history of each one I am ever knowing.

As I was saying, then always I was seeing, feeling, hearing all repeating coming out of this one. As I was saying often it was irritating. As I was saying it was not for many years a clear repeating of a whole being. Slowly then this one came to be a whole one to me. This is now some description.

Sometime each one comes to be a whole one to me. Sometime the bottom nature in each one, the other nature or natures in each one, the mixing or not mixing in them of the natures in them comes to be clear in each one, each one then is a complete one, each one then keeps repeating the whole history of them.

Some then are puzzling a long time, almost every one is puzzling, mostly every one is puzzling to me, sometime mostly every one comes to be a whole one to me.

As I was saying there is a bottom nature in every one, the other nature or natures in them may be of their kind of men and women, if they are at bottom resisting the other nature or natures in them may be of a kind of resisting, they may be of a kind of attacking being. All this is very confusing. All this is very puzzling. Always more and more I know it of each one the being in them the mixtures in them, always more I come to have a completed understanding of each one.

As I was saying every one sometime is a whole one to me. Every one sometime is a complete being in me. Sometimes for many years some one is puzzling, slowly then they come to be clearly a whole one, then all the repeating coming out of them always tells and keeps on telling to me the whole of them. Always then this repeating of the whole of them has more and more completeness to me, more and more of beauty for me, more and more a friendly feeling in me.

In learning one I have been describing there was very long listening, often listening was very irritating, there were many years of puzzled being, there were many years then of believing in the heard, seen, felt repeating which was every one's hearing, feeling, seeing, without puzzling, slowly then there came to be in me a puzzled feeling, slowly then I knew I was not hearing all the repeating this one was doing, I was not feeling, hearing, seeing the repeating that was a complete history of this one, always then I was puzzling, slowly then the repeating coming out of this one was a complete history of this one. Always I am listening to, feeling, seeing what every one thinks about any one. Always I am ready to feel some one will hear some repeating coming out of one that I have not begun yet to see or hear or feel in that one. Always then I am seeing, feeling, hearing what every one else sees or feels or hears as repeating in each one. So then always sometime there will come to be in me a complete seeing, hearing, feeling of the repeating coming out of each one making a complete history of each one.

One then I have been describing was to me a very slow long learning. Always in the beginning the repeating I was hearing, feeling, seeing coming always out of this one was to me a complete history of the being of this one, the being I was first describing that every one who knew this one felt was the being of this one. More and more then hearing this repeating was irritating, more and more then there was in me always a beginning again of listening to, of seeing, feeling the repeating coming out of this one. Slowly then there came to be in me puzzled feeling. Slowly there came to be in me a feeling that it was not a complete repeating I was hearing, not a complete history of her being. Then always I had in me a puzzled feeling, slowly then there came to me to see in this one other repeating that always was repeating but that slowly came to have meaning. Always I was hearing, feeling, seeing every one else feeling, listening to, seeing this one. Slowly then this one came to be a complete one to me. Slowly then all the repeating came to be a complete history of the being of this one always coming out of this one always repeating the whole of the being this one had all of her living. Slowly then every one, everything always helping , slowly then, I always listening, looking, feeling, always then I slowly, always hearing, seeing, feeling came to have this one to be a whole one to me, came to have this one to be a whole one inside me. Always then more and more I heard and saw and felt all the repeating always telling the whole being in her, more and more then I had in me a completed friendly feeling of the whole being that was this one.

Each one comes to be a whole one to me. Each comes to be a whole one in me. Some come very slowly to be a whole one to me. Some come fairly quickly to be a whole one in me. Some come fairly quickly to be a whole one in me, and then this whole one which was just outlines comes to be more and more filled up for me. Some come to be very slowly a whole one to me. There are every kind of way to have men and women, in their beginning, in their middle being, in their ending be a whole one inside any one to that one. Sometime there will be a description of every kind of way any one can know anything, any one can know any one.

Some one sometime comes to be a whole one to me, there are many ways of learning in me, there are many ways of loving learning in me, there are many ways of keeping everything that learning has given to me, inside me. There are many ways then of having some time to have it come that some one is a whole one in me. This is now some description of another one coming to be a whole one to me.

Sometimes I know and hear and feel and see all the repeating in some one, all the repeating that is the whole of some one but it always comes as pieces to me, it is never there to make a whole one to me. Some people have it in them to be in pieces in repeating the whole of them, such of them almost come never to be a whole one to me, some come almost all their living in repeating to be succession not a whole one inside me. Sometimes sometime such a one has a way of loving which makes a whole one of such a one long enough to hear the whole repeating in such a one as a complete one by some one. Such a one comes then sometime to be a whole one and then one loses the whole one repeating of them and they are pieces then of repeating and always it is changing back to pieces of repeating from the little time of loving that a little time makes of them a whole one. There are very many of them and this is now a little a description of the nature in this kind of them, this is now a little a description of learning to know them to make of them a complete one.

Every one then sometime is a whole one to me, every one then sometimes is a whole one in me, some of these do not for long times make a whole one to me inside me. Some of them are a whole one in me and then they go to pieces again inside me, repeating comes out of them as pieces to me, pieces of a whole one that only sometimes is a whole one in me.

There are then a kind of them, a kind of men and women, there are very many of them always living who have it in them to be inside them to be mostly to every one, to be always to mostly every one pieces coming out of them, pieces that never make of them a whole one, not because of complication in them, not because of difficulty of envisaging them but because really such of them are in pieces inside them, always in their living. This kind then of men and women have it to have it to be true of them that nothing in them dominates them, not mind, nor bottom nature in them, nor other nature or natures in them, nor emotion, nor sensitiveness, nor suggestibility, nor practicalness, nor weakness, nor selfishness, nor nervousness, nor egotism, nor desire, nor whimsicalness, nor cleverness, nor ideals, nor stimulation, nor vices, nor indifference, nor beauty, nor eating, nor drinking, nor laziness, nor energy, nor emulation, nor envy, nor malice, nor pleasure, nor skepticism. It is not as it is in some that there is contradictory being in them, there is not in such of these of them domination of anything in them to make contradiction, to make changing of one thing to another in them. Always they are in pieces then but pieces are not disconcerting to them or any one, hardly not puzzling. Some of such of them sometimes then make melodrama of themselves to themselves to hold themselves together to them. Some of such of them make of themselves to themselves and sometimes to other ones that know them a melodrama of themselves to make to themselves each one of themselves a whole one to themselves and sometimes to make of themselves a whole one to others around them. This is a very interesting thing, this is sometimes the explanation of melodrama in some one.

Some then some men and some women are not whole ones inside me for long times together. Sometime one of such a one was a whole one in me and then it was clear to me why such a kind of one was not for long times continually a whole one in me.

In first beginning to know such a one if they make of themselves melodrama to make to themselves a whole one of themselves to themselves then such melodrama is very confusing, it is not natural melodrama to them, melodrama in such of them is mostly not a natural way of being, mostly such of them have pride to hide themselves to themselves from knowing that there is not a whole to them, pride to hide this from themselves and from every one. So then melodrama in such a one is confusing. When melodrama is taken from such a one then they remain confusing, there is nothing then to guide any one to know them as a whole then such a one.

Such a one, now with no melodrama, just there as many pieces to some one, remains confusing, not because they are not acting, not because they are not repeating, they may be acting, every one always is repeating, it is that nothing in them is dominating, they are in pieces to themselves then and to everyone. They have not weakness, nor laziness, nor dullness to make them confusing. They are in pieces, there is not in them anything dominating, not the bottom nature in them, not other nature or natures in them, not confusion in them, not struggle or contradiction, or weakness or indifference in them. So then such a one is puzzling.

Sometime then as I was saying each one comes to be a whole one to me, sometime then each one comes to be clear inside me, sometimes as I was saying it is slow growing this coming to completed understanding inside me, sometimes it is a quick illumination, sometimes it is a mixture of these two ways of learning knowing, sometimes it is other ways of learning knowing in me.

As I was saying every one is surely sometime puzzling to me. As I was saying such a one, one being in pieces was a long time puzzling to me. Always this one was in pieces though always loving being was a louder piece than other pieces in that one.

So then such a one by not going on being a whole one after being illuminated by seeming a whole one by that one's way of loving was not any longer puzzling. This gave to me then an understanding of the being in such ones, such a one then was not together for long times as a whole one to me but to my understanding then from that time on always was a whole one to me.

Every one then sometime is a whole one to me, every one then always sometime comes to be clear to me, comes to be really a whole one inside me.

This is clear then that there are many ways of hearing, feeling, seeing repeating come out of every one. Always then I am seeing, hearing, feeling all repeating coming out of every one. Always then sometime every one I am ever knowing comes to be a whole one to me. This is now a little a description of another way of learning one.

Sometime then every one I know comes to be a whole one to me. Mostly every one comes very slowly to be a whole one inside me. Mostly every one is sometime and sometimes for a very long time a puzzle to me, sometime some one only very slowly comes to be a puzzle to me. Sometimes some one is never really a puzzle to me, sometimes some one suddenly comes to be a whole one to me. Often now when I know as much as I know now of kinds of men and women, some men some women come to be quickly a whole one to me, mostly still yet they come very slowly to be whole ones to me, mostly yet each one is a long time a puzzle to me, earlier every one mostly came very slowly to be a whole one to me, sometimes then some one came suddenly and soon to be a whole one in me, sometimes then some one was never really a puzzle to me. This then is another way of learning in me. This is now then a little a descript-ion of such a learning of one, one who was not really more than for the time of intensely looking for one time of seeing a puzzle to me.

This is now a little description of learning quickly, one.

There was one, I knew some things about this one, I knew a number of things about this one, I had heard descriptions of this one, I was interested but not more than I am in every one. I was not then very much interested in this one. As I was saying I had heard descriptions of this one, they were ordinary descriptions, they were not very interesting, they had not very much meaning. Then I saw this one, then I looked intensely at this one, then this one was a whole one to me. Then the whole being of this one was inside me, it was then as possession of me. I could not get it out from inside me, it gave new meanings to many things, it made a meaning to me of damnation. I had then to tell it to this one, that was the only way to loosen myself from this one who was a whole one in me. I had then to tell this one of the meaning in damnation that this one being a whole one inside me had made clear to me. Always then later this one was a whole one to me, it was then a gentler possession of me inside me than when this one first was a whole one inside me, a damned one to me. It was still true to me later inside me the whole of this one but it did not then possess me. This is then one way of learning a whole one, by seeing them completely by one long looking at them. This is now a little more description of this one and being possessed by this one as a whole one inside me. To begin again then.

There are many that I know and they know it. Very often I tell it, mostly I must tell it, sometimes I tell it because I like to hear it, sometimes I have to tell it to loose myself from it. This one was one that I knew then and I made this one know it. I told it then to loose myself from it. Mostly very slowly each one I know comes to be a whole one to me, mostly I tell it then because I like to hear it, sometimes I write it, sometimes I tell some one else, not then, about it. Mostly I tell it and I write it, mostly I tell it or I write it, there are many that I know and they know it. Mostly in some way I tell it.

This one then very soon knew it, very soon then I had had to tell it. This is now some more description of it.

There are many that I know and they know it, they are all of them repeating and I hear it, sometimes I tell it, mostly I tell it, there are many that I know, they are all of them repeating and I hear it, sometimes I see a whole being in it, sometime, always, I see the whole being in it. There are many that I know and they know it, sometimes they soon know it, sometimes I soon tell it, sometimes I wait a long time to tell it, sometimes I slowly tell it. There are many that I know and mostly always sometime they know it.

There are many that I know, they are all of them repeating and I see it, feel it, hear it. Always I listen to it and look at it and feel it, sometime always I understand it. There are many that I know and they know it, sometime each one is a whole one to me, mostly then I tell it, sometimes it is a long time before I tell it, sometimes I tell it as soon as I know it, sometimes I begin to tell it before I really know it, sometimes I tell it puzzling at it, sometimes I slowly tell it. There are many ways then of learning the whole one each one is from the repeating always coming out of each one. There are many ways of telling it to each one what is the whole of them, there are many ways of telling it about them what is the whole being in each one. Sometime, then, each one is a whole one to me, I was just now beginning telling about one. As I was saying this one was not one I ever thought about or felt before I knew this one as a whole one. This is interesting then as one way of learning. This was interesting then as a way of telling for then this one possessed me by my feeling the whole being that made all this one's repeating and I had to tell this one the whole being that was the whole of this one, the whole meaning of the repeating that was the being of this one so as to free myself from the possession this one's whole being being inside me then had of me. This now is to be a little more description of the being in this one and the feeling in me in learning the whole being of this one and the meaning of the repeating of this one and the telling of my knowing it and what I knew, to this one.

There are many that I know and they know it. This time I knew it and suffered in it and was possessed by it, the knowledge of it, and I told it to this one to free myself from it. This is a little more description of my knowing it and of my telling it, and some description of what I knew and what I told of the whole being in this one always coming out as repeating from this one.

There are many that I know and they know it. This one I knew quickly and then I told it and then this one knew it and this is now a little history of all of it.

There are many kinds of men and women and I know it, each one is a real one to me, each one sometimes is a whole one to me, they repeat it and I hear it and I see it and I feel it, each one sometime is a whole one to me, sometime, always, I tell it.

There are many kinds of men and women and I know it, always I know some of it, always more and more I know more of it. There are many that I know and they know it. There are many that I know and sometime I tell it, somehow, somewhere, all of it.

There are many then now that I know, there are many then now that know I know it. Every one always is repeating the whole of them. Every one sometimes is a whole one to me.

Always then I have known some, more and more I know more of them, more of men and women, more and more then always I know of the kinds there are of them.

Every one has their own being in them, every one always is repeating the whole of them, they repeat it and I hear it and sometimes I get a whole one inside me from listening, looking feeling it. Sometimes I quickly understand it, sometimes I quickly tell it. This is now a history of the way some one did it, this is now a history of the way I understood it, this is now a history of the way I told this one the whole of it, the whole repeating always coming out of this one and the meaning of it, the being in it.

Sometimes then I know many things of some one, always I am knowing more and more of such a one, this one is not ever then puzzling to me, everything is interesting, all is some history of some one but sometimes there is no interest in me to see a whole to some one, I go on knowing things of them, I talk and hear and remember all about such a one, there is no puzzling in me about such a one then for I am not then interested in understanding, there is a whole to such a one yes, there is sometime to me a whole to every one, I am seeing, hearing, feeling things and remembering things of such a one, there is no problem, no puzzled feeling about such a one then to me. This one then that I am now beginning a little to describe farther was such a one to me. I knew many things about this one, I remembered, I heard many things that were interesting, that were amusing, I remembered them, there was in me then no puzzling, there was nothing of a whole being in all of them to me, but I was not thinking of the whole being in them, they were interesting things to know about some one, everything is interesting to know about any one, everything is important to know about every one, but I was never puzzling about this one. All the things I knew were interesting I was not feeling any need of a whole being in this one, and then once I looked hard at this one and then there was a whole being always afterwards repeating to every one from this one after my telling all the being in this one, the whole being in this one, and this is very interesting.

Always then I listen and come back again and again to listen to every one. Always then I am thinking and feeling the repeating in every one. Sometimes it happens that I have a complete history of some one, of the meaning of all the repeating in them the first time I look hard at them, mostly this is in me a slow thing, learning understanding, mostly I come back again and again to listen to the repeating in every one before they are a whole one, before there is to me a whole history of the being in them. Always I come back again and again, it has happened that sometimes I have had the whole history of some one the first time I looked long at them, mostly this is a slow thing, always even when understanding happens like with this one the first time of hard looking, always, then I go back again and again to listen, to fill in, to be certain. This then was what happened to this one in my learning, this is now a little a description.

The nature in this one was not like any of those I have been just describing. Everybody who knew this one knew everything, there was no deceiving of any one by this one, everything in this one always was repeating to every one who ever listened to this one, and this one was not made up of pieces and none of the pieces dominating, this one had a very real bottom, a very real domination inside that one of that one's own being, the thing with this one was to understand the meaning of the repeating all the repeating this one was always doing. What was important was to have applied to this one completed understanding. This one was not puzzling really to any one, this one had nothing of the nature of the being that was always coming out as repeating hidden, it was all there, all always repeating, all always being dominated by the bottom being and all that then was needed was to understand the meaning, that was very interesting, that was what I did by one hard looking. This is now a little more description of this one.

This one then as I was saying had it to have as being really the nature as dominating and every one that looked at or listened to or felt this one knew all of the repeating always telling over and over again all of the history of this one. This time then it was a question of understanding the meaning of the being in one.

This now is very interesting in relation to the being in this one, whose learning, in me, I am soon now to be describing.

There was then in the first one I was describing, all of the being always repeating but all the repeating any one knowing this one ever was hearing, feeling, seeing could be understood as meaning that this one was always giving all her loving to every one and always there was no place for her in living, always there was no place for her in living. Always every one felt this in her and always every one was explaining there being no place for such a one in living by specific good reasoning, always dimly every one had a little a puzzled feeling, always every one, really every one who ever knew this one was really sympathising, really believing because all of it was really there always repeating.

Slowly then this one came to be a whole one in me. As I have said in writing, often, for many years some one is baffling, the repeated hearing of them does not make the completed being they have in them to any one. Sometimes many years pass in listening to repeating in such a one and the being of them is not a completed history to any one then listening to them, sometime then it comes out of them a louder repeating of that which before was not clear to anybody's hearing and then such a one is a completed being to some one listening to the repeating coming out of such a one, there is then to some one a complete history of such a one, this mostly comes slowly to the one who is learning the being of such a one, this was the history of learning the first one that I have been describing.

The third one then of whose learning I am beginning now a description, this third one then I have been a little describing was very different from this first one, every one who ever knew or saw or heard of this one always knew all the repeating always coming out of this one, all the complete history of this one. No one ever knowing this one did not know all the repeating in this one but always there was in no one a complete understanding of the meaning of the being in this one, and this is now to be some description, description of the being in this one, description of the learning of the meaning of the being in this one, description of the telling of the knowing of the meaning in this one.

As I was saying the first one I was describing always had then to every one the very best reason for there being no place for this one ever for living, no place ever for this one in living. This last one, the one I am now describing has with this first one some connection, always then this last one always had the best reasons for not realising the living being in living and every one always was always helping and no one ever was understanding for every one always was convinced of the good reasons this one had for not being able to realise real being in living and always this one was trying and always every one who saw this one was helping and this now is very interesting.

As I was saying always every one knew the whole repeating of this last one, every one who ever knew this one really knew all the repeating coming out of this one, always then it was a question of meaning to make of this one a whole one inside one.

Every one always is repeating the whole of them, some to every one who knows any one of such of them, some one repeating the whole of them so that every one who knows them hears the whole repeating in them. The important thing then with such a one for every one as I was saying knows with such a one that they are hearing all the repeating coming out of such a one, the important thing then with such a one so as to get such a one to be a whole one to any one seeing, feeeling, hearing such a one, the important thing then is hearing, feeling, seeing all the repeating coming out from such a one is to realise the meaning of the being, it is not enough to realise all the repeating in such a one.

This one that I have commenced describing had in being going at the same time asking and refusing, infinite tenacity in holding on to anything that was there to this one's seizing, always not really wanting what was being held so grimly by this one. Always then there was denying in this one, mostly one thinks of fundamental denying as scepticism, as evil acting, this was not so of this one, denying and trying holding with tenacious gripping was always there in this one. Always then every one who ever knew this one knew this as always repeating, tenacity in holding, desiring believing in religion, always every one who ever knew this one saw these always coming out as repeating, no one seeing it come out of this one as repeating had any realisation that always it led to denying, always to negation, that grasping and asking, opening and closing could not be the same movement in action without ending in denying everything, and both being completed expression of this being and always together there repeating and so neither coming to be really existing there was not in this one consciousness of struggling, always it was in this one then as denying always then there was in this one no reality of experiencing, never any stopping gripping to be asking, never stopping asking to be steadily gripping, always asking and gripping in the same repeating, always so ending in denying. The spirit of denying that comes to be the whole of such a one, there can be in such a one no real experiencing, a hand cannot be closed and open, it ends in such a one denying that a hand is really existing.

As I was saying every one always is repeating the whole of them. Every one is repeating the whole of them, such repeating is then always in them and so sometime some one who sees them will have a complete understanding of the whole of each one of them, will have a completed history of every man and every woman they ever came to know in their living, every man and every woman who were or are or will be living, every man and every woman in each one's beginning, middle and ending, every man and every woman then who were or are or will be living whom such a one can come to know in living.

Every one always is repeating the whole of them. This one that I am now describing always was repeating the whole being as every one always is doing. This one was not like the first one I was describing then, every one who knew this one heard, felt and saw all the being in this one always repeating, nothing of important being in this one was not loudly repeating.

As I was saying I knew all the repeating in this one mostly from other people's telling, no one ever was understanding the meaning in the repeat ing, no one then was understanding the reason of this one never really realising being, never winning anything this one ever was really want- ing. Every one, as I was saying was hearing, feeling and seeing clearly all the repeating there ever was to be ever coming out of this one to any one. There was never then in this one any repeating that every one who was ever hearing, feeling, seeing this one did not feel and see and hear in this one always all through their knowing this one. This one then mostly did not give to any one a puzzling feeling, everything was clear in this one to every one, everything in this one was clearly repeating to every one who ever was really listening, to every one who was hearing, seeing, feeling the repeating coming out of this one, the important thing then was understanding the meaning in the being of this one, always every one was hearing, feeling, seeing all the repeating there ever was in this one, it was seeing the meaning of all the being in this one that was interesting and this came to me then in one very hard looking at this one.

Always then sometime each one comes to be a whole one in me, al- ways then sometimes every one is a whole one to me. Everybody al- ways then sometime is a real one to me. Every one then has always sometime their own being in them to me. Sometime then every one is a whole one to me, sometime then every one has a complete history for me. Always then sometime each one is a whole one to me.

As I was saying every one who ever came to know this one really knew all the repeating in this one, no repeating in this one was not sounding loudly to every one who ever came to know this one. As I was saying I knew then all the repeating in this one a little from every one's telling, mostly it was not puzzling, every one evidently had been hearing all the repeating there ever was coming out of this one. As I was saying it was interesting but not overwhelmingly interesting for it was not puzzling, every one knew all the repeating in this one, the wanting in this one of believing, the desire of having believing, the tenacity in gripping everything this one ever was having, the feeling in this one for wanting everything with goodness in it, the not realising anything, every one then who ever knew this one knew the eagerness of desiring, the lack of succeeding, the tenacity in holding on to all possessing, every one then knew all these always repeating in this one, always it was in every one describing this one a describing of all these things in this one, there was then never any realising of how these things came to be this one, every one always was helping this one for always to every one there were such good reasons why this one should have much helping, some always were trying to loose the hold on possession, others always were trying to strengthen to desiring faith and goodness, always every one was helping, always no one was understanding that a little even very much strengthening of wanting believing or a little even very much weakening of holding possession of gripping could never in such a one have any real meaning, for always at the bottom this one was gripping and asking, always this one was opening and shutting the hands at the same instant of being and that always would make denying the only real thing in such a one's being, nothing else could ever really happen, never could there come the miracle of simultaneous opening and gripping.

It is clear then now to every one. It is clear then now to every one that every one who ever was knowing this one always was hearing, seeing, feeling all the repeating in this one, always then the important thing was understanding the being always repeating, realising denying as the real being in this one.

As I was saying then I knew all the repeating in this one, a little from my own listening to this one, mostly from other people's descriptions of this one. I knew then all the repeating in this one, it was interesting to know the repeating in this one, all repeating of any one is interesting to any one having loving repeating being, having loving repeating being to completed understanding as being. Always then as I was saying repeating is interesting to me, always then I was interested in all the repeating of this one, it was interesting but it was not then a problem to me, this one then was interesting, not so very interesting to me, and then as I was saying I met this one and then I began and then all the repeating in this one had meaning. This one then was to me at the end of looking the complete thing to me that every one sometime is to me. This one was then a complete one to me, this one was then a solemn load inside me. This is now then a little more description of my knowing this one as a complete one and then of my telling of my knowing to this one.

As I was saying every one always is repeating the whole of them. As I was saying sometimes it takes many years of hearing the repeating in one before the whole being is clear to the understanding of one who has it as being to love repeating, to know that always every one is repeating the whole of them, to have it that sometime each one is a whole one to that one. These then the ways I have been describing are some of the ways then that such a one, one who has it as being to love repeating, to know that always every one is repeating the whole of them, comes to a completed understanding of every one.

Sometimes then as I was saying it takes many years of hearing and seeing and feeling the repeating in some one before the whole being of that one is clear to my understanding. This then was not the way of my learning this last one as a whole being. As I was saying I knew all the repeating in this one, every one who knew this one knew all the repeating in this one. I had never felt it a puzzle in this one, I had not had that kind of interest in this one and then it happened that I saw this one and then it happened that I looked hard at this one and then this one was a whole one to me, this one was a depressing solemn load inside me, then I had this one inside me and this one was to me inside me a being having damnation as the way of being and this then was a new thing in me, damnation had not had before any meaning for me, this one was not an evil one, a wicked one, but a damned one to me, this one was then a whole one inside me. This is now to be a little more description of this one in me and of my telling it to this one.

This one was then a whole one to me, this one was then a solemn saddening load inside me, not from evil or conviction or from willing or from reasoning but from asking and gripping in the same breath of being and both being complete expression of a being and so neither really having meaning to such a being not making really inside such a one any struggling.

This one then after this one hard looking was a whole one to me, was a whole solemn load inside me. This one then always was repeating to me the whole being in that one, the resulting to such a one of suffering damning. This one was then a whole one to me. This one was then a whole one inside me, was as a solemn load inside me.

Each one is then sometime a whole one to me, this one was then a whole one in me was a solemn saddening load inside me, gave to me the first meaning there ever was to me of the meaning of damning in all human religion, was a very serious solemn load inside me, and a ways it was there inside me this one as a whole one in me and always this one was repeating to me the whole being, the whole history of this one and a ways it had meaning and always then it was to me the compelling of me to understand the reason there is in damning, this denying and never having any realisation of anything really existing was to me a state of really suffering damning. This one then was as I was saying a whole one then inside me, a whole one to me after the ending of that looking, a serious solemn saddening whole one in me, and always more and more I was seeing, hearing, feeling this one repeating the whole being there was in this one and always then it was to my completed understanding the completed spirit of suffering damning, that was then the whole of this one.

Always then this one was a whole one to me. As I was saying each one sometimes is a whole one to me, sometime one always is a whole one to me, I am never losing the feeling of such a one being a whole one inside me. This one always was a whole one to me, always then I was seeing, feeling, hearing all the repeating coming out of this one, always then this one was a solemn load inside me.

As I was saying there are many that I know and I know it, there are many that I know and they know it, they are many that I know and I tell it. There are many that I know and I know it, there are many that I know and they know it, there are many that I know and I tell it, I know it and I tell it, they repeat it and I see it, and I hear it and I feel it and I tell it. Always then there are many that I know and to some of them I tell it. This one was then a whole one to me, this one then was a whole one inside me, I know it and I tell it, I knew it and I told it and this is now some description of my then telling of it.

This one was then a whole one inside me. Always sometime each one is a whole one to me, always sometime I tell it to some one the whole one each one sometime is to me. Always then sometime each one is a whole one to me, each one then sometime is a complete one to me, a complete one there inside me, always sometime then I have each one as a whole one always sometime then I tell it to some one, very often I tell it to that one the one that is a whole one then in me.

There are many that I know and always more and more I know it. They are all of them sometime a whole one to me. More and more I understand it. They are all of them repeating and I hear it, they are all of them always repeating the whole of them and always more and more I know them. There are many that I know and they know it. They are all of them always repeating the whole of them and I understand it. They are, each one of them sometime a whole one to me, they are all of them, always then, repeating the whole of them and I know it and I understand it. I know it and I tell it. Always sometime I tell it. Mostly always when it is complete in me I tell it.

There are many that I know and I know it. They are repeating always the whole of them and I understand it. They are, each one then, sometime a whole one to me. I know it and I tell it. Mostly, when it is complete in me, I tell it.

Mostly, then when it is entirely, completely in me, the whole of them, and I know it, then I tell it. Mostly always I tell it, mostly I tell it to that one who is a whole one then inside me, sometimes I just tell it to any one who will listen to it. Mostly then when any one is entirely completely in me, mostly always then I tell it.

This is now then a little a description of my telling of it. As I was saying mostly always when some one is entirely and completely a whole one to me, I know it and I tell it, sometimes I tell it to that one that is then entirely and completely a whole one inside me to me, sometimes I tell it to any one who will listen to it.

Always then I tell it, always then when any one is completely a whole one to me, mostly always then I tell it. This is now some description of one time of telling it, telling it to that one who just was then a whole one to me.

As I was saying each one is sometime a whole one to me, is a whole one inside me, each one then sometimes gives to me a sense of being filled up inside me with that one, then a whole one inside me. Each one then is sometime a whole one in me, I know it and I tell it, I am filled up then with that whole one inside me and I tell it and then it settles down inside me to always hearing it repeating in such a one, filling 'n and changing and being a completer and completer history of that one and always then it is quietly there in me and I like it. Sometimes it is disturbed in me and again completely fills me and then again it settles down in me. Then again it is quietly there in me and I always like it. Always I am then learning more and more the history of that one, always more and more there is then meaning in all the repeating coming out of that one but there is then not so much need in me to tell it, it is then steady pleasant, sometimes exciting, learning in me and always I enjoy it but then it is quieter inside me and I am then not all filled up with it and so then though always often I tell it, all of it, pieces of it to any one who will listen to it, I am not then all filled up with it and I can then really be without really needing to tell it, I can then get along without really then ever telling it.

As I was saying each one sometime is a whole one to me. As I was saying mostly when it is complete to me and I first really know it, really and completely and filled up with it then I tell it. Mostly then I have to tell it. Mostly then I am filled up with it and it comes out of me then as telling it, sometimes to the one that is then a whole one to me, sometimes then to any one who will then listen to me.

There are many then that I know and sometime each one comes to be a whole one in me, sometime then each one then a whole one inside me fills me, sometime then I know that one and sometime then I tell it the whole one that I then know that I know as a whole one as a whole being then. Always then more and more I know that one, always then more and more I hear and feel and see all the repeating coming out of them, always I am telling everything, more and more I tell everything, always I tell it when I come completely to know it the being in one, when I come completely to understand, when they are a whole one inside me and I am filled up with it.

Mostly always when it is once complete in me I tell it, always often, more and more I know it, always often, I very often tell it, always when it is once complete in me I have to tell it, I am filled up then with it, telling it is then always in me, always then I tell it. This is then a little a description of one telling of it.

There are many that I know and always sometime I tell it. Sometimes I slowly tell it, sometimes I tell it and then more and more I tell it, sometimes I tell it and then slowly I keep on with telling of it. There are many ways of telling it. Sometimes I tell it when I am still puzzling with it. Mostly always when it is complete in me I tell it. Mostly then I learn more and more the meaning in it, often then slowly I tell more and more of it. Mostly when it is complete in me once and I am all filled up with that one then I have to tell it. Sometimes then I tell it to any one who will listen to it. Sometimes then I tell it to the one who is then a whole one inside me, I am filled with that one then as a whole one and to that one then I tell it.

As I was saying this one that I have been just describing was a whole one to me, a serious solemn filling inside me. This one was then complete in me, this one was then a serious solemn filling in me, always then this one was in me suffering damning trom the being in this one and this was a new realisation in me and so then this was complete then inside me, this one then being a whole one inside me, this one then completely filling me inside me, I knew it then and I told it then, I told it then to this one.

As I was saying then each one sometime is a whole one to me, each one sometime is a whole one inside me. Mostly then I tell it to some one. This one then came after one hard looking to be a whole one inside me. I was then all filled up with this one. I told it then to this one the whole meaning of all the being in this one.

As I was saying I know many women and many men. I know many of them as babies, as children as growing men and growing women as grown men and grown women as growing old men and growing old women, as grown old men and grown old women, and every kind of being they ever have in them. I know many then of them very many of them and sometime each one is a whole one to me, each one is a whole one inside me, each one then has real meaning for me. Sometime then each one is a whole one to me, sometime then each one of them has a whole history of each one for me. Everything then they do in living is clear then to me, their living, loving, eating, pleasing, smoking, scolding, drinking, dancing, thinking, working, walking, talking, laughing, sleeping, suffering, joking, everything in them. There are whole beings then, they are themselves inside them to me. They are then, each one, a whole one inside me. Repeating of the whole of them always coming out of each one of them makes a history always of each one of them always to me.

There are many then that I know, and I know it, I know it and mostly always sometime I tell it. Each one sometimes is a whole one to me, always sometime I know it, mostly always sometime I tell it. Mostly when I am full up with it I tell it, I know it, I am full up with it and I tell it.

This one then the one I have been just describing was a whole one inside me when the meaning of the being in this one was a clear meaning to me, I was full up then with this one inside me, I was full up then with this one, I would tell it then to almost any one who would listen, I would tell it then to this one the one that was a whole one then inside me, the one then filling me all up inside me. I knew then the meaning in this one, the meaning in this one was a complete thing and then I told it to this one.

There are many that I know and I know it, there are many that I know and there are some of them to whom I tell it that I know it. This then was one of them then. I knew it and I told. This one was then a whole one to me and I told it then to this one.

Mostly always then each one I am ever knowing sometime, sometimes is a whole one to me, mostly always then when I know it, the whole being of some one, I tell it and sometimes I tell it to that one. Mostly then when I am filled up with it, the whole meaning of the whole being of some one, I tell it. I know it and I tell it. I am filled full then with it and I tell it. Mostly always then I tell it when I am filled up full with the whole meaning of the whole being of some one, I know it and I have to tell it, often I tell it to any one who will listen to it, sometimes I have to tell it to that one whose whole being then having meaning as a whole one to me is then filling me full up with it.

I know then sometime the whole being of every one I am ever knowing and always sometime, often sometimes I tell it. Mostly always when I am filled up full with it I tell it, sometimes I have to tell it, sometimes I like to tell it, sometimes I keep on with telling it.

I know it and I tell it, this is now some description of the ways of telling it, of the need of telling it, of telling it to any one who will listen to it, of telling it to the one whose being I am then understanding.

Always sometime every one I am ever knowing is a whole one inside me. Always then sometime I know the meaning of the whole being of every one I am ever knowing. Sometime, then I know it, sometime then I tell it. There are many ways of knowing, as I have been telling, there are many ways of telling. Always then when I come to know the whole meaning of any one, that one is then there inside me. I am more or less filled up then with that one, sometimes I am filled up so full with that one that I must tell it then to every one, sometimes I am filled up so full with that one that I must then certainly tell it to that one. There are many different ways then of feeling knowing inside one. Mostly always sometime I must tell it of each one to some one, sometimes I must tell it of some one to every one, sometimes to many and not then to that one filling me then, sometimes I must tell it to many and to that one, sometimes I must tell it mostly to that one. It is all a very complicated condition having knowing any one inside in one. Mostly always I sometime tell it to some one. Mostly when I am filled up with some one I tell it then to that one and to others then, sometimes I never tell it to that one, mostly sometime I do tell it to that one. Mostly then sometime each one I am ever knowing is a whole one in me, mostly sometime I tell it to that one, sometimes I tell it very little, sometimes very slowly to that one, sometimes very gently, sometimes very completely, sometimes very quickly, sometimes very greatly, sometimes just in little pieces to some, sometimes all but a little of it to some one. Always then sometime each one is a whole one in me, mostly always I tell it sometime to that one. Sometimes then I have to tell it when I am all filled up with it, sometimes then I tell it to rid myself a little of it, sometimes because I am so full of it it keeps pouring out of me all the time when I am first having it. This was then the way I was filled full of it after looking at and so understanding the last one I have been describing. I was filled full up with it, I knew it and I told it, I told it to this one, the one whose being as meaning made me then all full of that one then inside me, I was knowing it then, I was then all full up with it, I was then full up to the telling of it. This is now the history of that.

Being filled up with some one who then is a whole one inside one is to some a natural way of being. Knowing and telling is to some their natural way of complete being. This is now some description of one of such of them.

Knowing and telling then is to some their natural way of complete being. This has been some description of one of such of them.

Always then sometime each one is a whole one to me, always then I am listening to, looking at, feeling the whole being always then repeating in each one, always then I am knowing the meaning of the nature or natures in each one, always then I am telling the meaning of the being in each one.

Hearing, feeling, seeing all repeating coming out of any one I am ever knowing, knowing sometime the meaning of the being in every one I am ever knowing that is having sometime each one I am ever knowing a whole one to me, hearing, seeing, feeling then always all the repeating coming out of every one I am ever knowing, understanding sometime the meaning of the being in every one, being sometime filled up full with the whole being in each one I am ever knowing, being sometime then full up with the complete being of each one I am ever knowing, being full up with it with the completed knowing of it, being fuller and fuller with it, being sometime all filled up with it, filled up completely with it, filled up full with it sometimes to the quick telling of it, sometimes to the slow telling of it, sometimes slowly filling up with it, sometimes more sometimes less quickly being filled full up with it is all always sometimes in me. Always then sometime each one is a whole one to me, always then sometime each one I am ever knowing is a whole one inside me, always then sometime I am filled full with each one then a complete one every one I am ever knowing, always then sometime I am filled full with each one I am ever knowing as a whole one then inside me, always then I am filled full with some one filled full of the meaning of one then filling me full up with that one then, full up to the point of telling the meaning of that one sometimes to every one sometimes only to some, sometimes to that one the one that is then the complete filling of me, and always then sometime then there is a complete understanding of each one I am ever knowing, and always sometime there is coming out of me some telling of all the knowing being in me, sometimes it comes out of me I am filled full of knowing and it bursts out from me, sometimes it comes very slowly from me, sometimes it comes sharply from me, sometimes it comes out of me to amuse me, sometimes it comes out of me as a way of doing a duty for me, sometimes it comes brilliantly out of me, sometimes it comes as a way of playing by me, sometimes it comes very slowly, sometimes it comes very repeatingly, sometimes very willingly out of me, sometimes not very willingly, always then it comes out of me. I know many men and women, know them in many stages of their being. Always more and more I know them, I know them and mostly I tell them, always then more and more I know them, I know them and mostly I tell them. There are many then that I know and they know it. I know them, I know the repeating of themselves always coming out of them, I know them and mostly I tell them, always more and more I know I know them, always more and more they know I know it, I know it and I tell it, this is now some history of it. To begin again then with knowing it the being in some one and telling it, telling it to that one. To begin again with the knowing of that one, the last one I was describing and the telling it to that one.

Always then I am telling to some one all the being in some. There are many that I know and I know it, always then I am telling some one it. Always then I am telling some one all the being in some, sometime then I am telling to all of them all the being in every one. Always then I am telling to some one all the being in some one. Always then sometime I am telling all the being in every one to every one. All the time then I am telling all the being in each one I am ever knowing to some one, all the time then I am knowing some one, all the time then I am telling that to some one, sometimes to that one, mostly always sometime to some one.

Mostly always then I am learning to know some one, mostly always then I am telling some one the being in some one. Mostly then I am learning some one, mostly then I am knowing some one, mostly then

I am telling some one. So then this is in me living being, learning, knowing and telling and mostly then all three of them are always in me mostly always. This then is living being in some, learning, knowing, telling, this then as I was saying is living being in many of them always living, this is now a little a description of it in one.

So then to begin again with learning, knowing and telling. Mostly then there is mostly always keeping going learning, knowing, telling in my being. Always then as I was saying loving repeating is always there in me as being, always then as I was saying sometime each one I am ever knowing is a whole one to me, always then, as I was saying, knowing all the being in some one is always coming to be in me keeping going there inside me, always then as I was saying knowing some one is filling me all up inside me, always then I am telling some one all the knowing there is then in me.

This then a way of being, learning, knowing, telling, this is then the being in me. There has been much writing of listening to repeating, of hearing, feeling, seeing, knowing all repeating, of feeling knowing each one sometime as a whole one, now then there is a little writing of the telling of the knowing always in me.

So then always every one is repeating the whole of them, always then sometime each one I am ever knowing is a whole one to me, mostly always then I am telling my complete knowing of each one to some one, often I am telling it to that one, the one whose complete being is then completely filling me then there inside me. This is now a little description of such telling to one.

As I was saying every one who ever knew this last one knew all the repeating ever in this one, ever coming out of this one, always then this one was really not giving to any one any really puzzling feeling, always then I knew all the repeating every one knew in this one and always coming out of this one, always then I never had any puzzling feeling about this one. Every one really then knew all the repeating ever coming out of this one, every one then who ever was knowing this one knew all the being in this one, mostly then no one could have about this one any puzzling feeling, no one felt any puzzling feeling then about this one, every one who ever knew this one knew all the being that ever came out of this one as repeating, no one then had about this one a puzzling feeling, every one only knew that this one found no meaning in the living of this one's being. There are always many such men and women. Mostly then no one found this one puzzling, this one was greedily seizing and humbly asking, this one was tenaciously gripping and never getting holding, this one was always close-fisting and always opening the hand in imploring begging. Many then are of such a kind of them but mostly asking and seizing in most of them are really in being in them, in this one they made up a complete denying, nothing then in this one was really being.

As I was saying every one who was ever knowing this one knew always all the repeating always coming out of this one, all the frenzied seizing all the pitiful asking, mostly then every one who ever was knowing this one thought about it in this one as these being in this one in contradiction, in many these ways of being are making a contradiction, in many all these ways of being are really vital being in them, in this one it was a different thing from the others having contradictory being in them, in this one it was a negation of real being, it was the real spirit of denying in this one. Every one then as I was saying every one who ever came to know this one always knew all the repeating that ever was coming out of this one, every one then knew the being in this one, no one then had any puzzling feeling about this one, no one then knew the meaning of the being in this one. This one then at the end of looking came to be a whole one to me, there was not really ever any puzzling feeling in me about this one, I came then sometime to look at this one, this one became then completely to me a whole one, this one then was a whole one to me, this one then was a whole one inside me, I knew it and the knowing of it filled me, I knew it then the meaning in this one, I was filled full then more and more with the being in this one, more and more then I knew it inside me, more and more then it filled me, I knew it then and more and more then it filled me and then it came to possess me, it was then a complete filling of me there inside me the being in this one, I knew it then and soon I told it to this one, I knew it then and I told it to myself and then more and more I knew it and more and more I told it and then more and more I knew it and then I told it to that one, more and more then I told it to that one, always more and more then I told it to that one.

Always then sometime each one is a whole one to me, always then sometime each one is more or less filling me up inside me, always then sometime I tell it all more or less to some one, very often I tell it all more or less to that one. This one then was a whole one to me, this one was then completely a filling up inside me, more and more then the knowing of the meaning in this being was in me there completely as a filling to me there inside me, more and more then I knew the meaning in all the repeating always coming out of this one, soon then I told it to this one, always then more and more I told it to this one.

Kinds and ways of being, kinds and ways of having being coming out in repeating, many of them are very clear in kinds of men and women, in individual men and women. Realising kinds and ways in being, learning in being, thinking to feeling, realising meaning in being, realising way and kinds of sensitiveness and emotion, meaning of stupidness in being, ways of knowing, ways of telling, ways of being resembling, all these always are in me filling me with seeing, feeling, learning understanding, filling me sometime to telling.

It came then that I heard the meaning of the being in that one, that was to me then a real thing, the meaning of the being that was all the being in this one. I heard it then, more and more I knew it in all the ways it was in this one in all the ways it did and had and would come out of this one, the being in this one. Sometime then all history of this one will be complete to some one. Always then the repeating in this one was forming in me as a complete history of this one.

There was then this one, there will then be sometime a complete history of this one, perhaps there will be a complete history of this one in some one, perhaps never really inside any one. Each one sometime is a whole one to me, then I am hearing or feeling or seeing some repeating coming out of that one that makes a completer one of that one, always then there may be sometimes more history of that one, there may then be never a whole history of any one inside any one. Mostly then that is a melancholy feeling in some that there is not a complete history of every one in some one. Slowly then that feeling is discouraging to one loving having a whole history of every one inside in one. Perhaps slowly then there is really in such a one more and more knowing of the meaning in each one that one is ever knowing. Always then for such a one there must be many new beginnings. Always then for such a one there must be a feeling that that one such a one is then knowing is a whole one, always each one is a whole one, always each one has a whole history of them always coming out of them, sometime some one will have in them a whole history of each one. Always then more and more each one sometime is a whole one and then sometime it is hard to hold this one as a whole one inside one and then the one having knowing each one that one is ever knowing as a whole one as the way of having living being in that one, such a one having the whole one that that one is having inside then of some one come to pieces in them, have new repeating in them, have new meaning in them, always then sometime the one having knowing each one they are ever knowing as a whole one as the living being in that one, such a one then sometimes is having all a wrong meaning to the being of some one then seeming to be a real right whole one then inside that one and always then there is sorrowing feeling in such a one and always then there is new beginning in such a one and always then there is struggling in such a one to make that one then inside them as a whole one give up in them the wrong whole meaning and to keep in them all the repeating that really was in that one this one then was thinking knowing as a whole one. Sometime then each one is a whole one to me, sometimes then there is a real complete one there inside me, sometime then I know something, mostly then I begin again, always then I am feeling, seeing, hearing all the repeating coming out of any one I am ever knowing, sometimes I am telling the whole feeling I have in the whole being of some one I am then knowing and having then as completely filling all my being, and then I am beginning again with more knowing and more and more then that one I am then knowing has for me then **meaning.**

This one then that I was last describing and then describing the meaning in the being in that one and then describing the telling of the meaning of the being in that one to that one, that one then knew then the meaning of the being in that one ; that one always like every one that ever knew that one always knew, had always known all the repeating always coming out of the being in the living of that one, now that one knew the meaning of the being that made that one and it was a very serious feeling knowing that that was the meaning of the being, that denying was the meaning of the being in that one, that always there was in that one no way of ever realising real feeling, real being, that always it made up into denying. This one then knew the meaning of that being, I had told it to this one as I was saying, this was then in this one the first moment in the being of this one that was not denying. This is clear then, it was clear then to that one, it was to that one giving up asking, it was to that one then loosening gripping. This one had then a revelation, this one then had a new beginning.

This then happened to this one, this one then had a real realisation of the being in this one and that was the beginning in this one of realising living, that was the beginning in this one of a being that was not in its meaning denying. This then came as a religion, this then came as a revelation, this one was then not asking and had the feeling of having been given living, this one was not asking and was receiving, this one had loosened gripping and so a little the hand was open to receiving, this was then the first being in this one that was not denying. By and by there was more changing. There will be now then more description.

Slowly then there was in this one increasing realisation of real being. As I was saying this one not asking had the moment of receiving, loosening gripping had a little the power of accepting, slowly then this came to be the new meaning of the being always there in this one.

This one had then a new beginning, always then from then on this one was changing, always then this one was repeating, always then knowing this one seeing, feeling, hearing the repeating coming out of this one, always then I was knowing more and more all the meaning there ever was or could or would be in this one in the being that was all the being in this one, always then this one was a whole one there inside me, always then I was knowing the complete meaning in the being in this one, always then this one was repeating all the being in this one, always then there was changing in this one and always there was in this one the being that every one who ever knew this one always knew as coming out of this one and always repeating.

As I was saying this one then knew the meaning of the being in this one making a denying in this one of everything, I knew it from looking at this one, I knew it then and I was filled up then with this one, I knew it and then I was telling it to this one and always more and more I was telling it to this one and then this one was knowing the meaning of the being always repeating in this one and then there was in this one a beginning, there was then in this one real despairing, there was then in this one a stopping asking, a little loosening of gripping, there was then in this one some receiving, a being able to take what is given in the hand a little loosened in gripping, this then was in this one religion, this then was in this one a new meaning in being, a real realising of living, a beginning believing something. Then it went on and on in this one.

As I was saying this one was a little loosening gripping and a little this one received in this loosening, seizing believing and then this one was gripping this believing, this was then the new meaning in the being in this one, this and receiving, really receiving something. Not denying, receiving something, tenaciously gripping that this one had and always sometimes again would be a little receiving in moments when remembering, this one would a little moment be stopping asking, always then a little loosening gripping would give to this one a little at such moments power of receiving, then this one would be tenaciously holding this this one had then been receiving, always then this was the new meaning in the being of this one.

Sometime perhaps it will be clear to every one the whole being of some one. Sometime perhaps it will be clear to some one the being in any one. This is then a beginning.

This is then a beginning, always then there is some winning knowing. Sometime perhaps it will be clear in some one the being in any one, always then there is some winning knowing, always then there is some one keeping going learning, sometime perhaps it will be clear to some one the whole being of some one. This is then again a beginning.

Mostly every one is resembling some how to some one, every one is one inside them, every one reminds some one of some other one. Each one has it to say of each one he is like such a one I see it in him, every one has it to say of each one she is like some one else I can tell by remembering. Every one is always remembering some one who is resembling to some one. Every one is themselves inside them and every one is resembling to others.

This is then a beginning, always then there is some winning of knowing. Sometime perhaps it will be clear in some one the being in any one. Always then there is some winning knowing, always then there are some keeping going in learning. Sometime perhaps it will be clear to some one the whole being of some one. This is then again a beginning. This now is learning understanding of resembling to realising kinds in men and women. Every one has their own being in them. Every one is of a kind in men and women. Every one is resembling somehow to some one.

Everybody is a real one to me, everybody is like some one else too to me.

Everybody has their own being in them. Every one is a kind of men and women.

Everybody is a real one to me, everybody is like some one else too to me. Every one is one inside them, every one reminds some one of some other one, every one, mostly every one, has it to say of mostly each one that one ever is knowing, that one ever is seeing, that one is like such a one I see it in that one. So it goes on, every one mostly sees in each one something that is like something in some other one. Everybody is a real one to me, everybody is like some one else too to me, everybody has their own being in them to me, every one is of a kind of men and women to me. There are many ways of making kinds of men and women. In each way of making kinds of them there is a different way of feeling them as resembling. These are now some of the ways I know it in them which ones are like which other ones of them. Everybody then has to me their own being, that is them, every one then is like some others in some ways and that makes each one of them of a certain kind of men, of a certain kind of women, of a certain kind of men and women. Everybody is a real one to me, everybody is like some one else too to me. Resembling, in each one to other men, to other women, to other men and women, makes sometime a way of complete understanding of each one, everything then they do in living is clear to one who knows resemblances and differences and kinds in men and women, their way then of living, loving, eating, pleasing, smoking, scolding, drinking, dancing, walking, talking, beginning, ending, sleeping, laughing, working, everything in them is clear then. Everybody has their own being in them, every one is of a kind of men and women.

Every one has their own being in them. Every one is of a kind of men and women. There are many very many kinds of men and women, there are many very many kinds of men, there are many very many kinds of women. There are many ways of making kinds of them, this is now a description of all the kinds of ways there are of making kinds of them, all the kinds of ways there are of making kinds of women, all the kinds of ways there are of making kinds of men, all the kinds of ways there are of making kinds in men and women, all the kinds of ways there are of making kinds of them in all the stages of each of them in them all from their beginning to their complete ending, all the kinds of ways there is in them of being and having being coming out from them, all their kinds of ways of being themselves inside them all of them and all the kinds of ways the being in them comes out from them, all the kinds of ways they ever effect any others any other one ever in any kind of way ever connected with them. To know all the kinds of ways then to make kinds of men and women one must know all the ways some are like others of them, are different from others of them, so then there come to be kinds of them. So then to sôme one each one must be a real one and each one must be like other ones in some ways and like other ones in other ways and some must know all the ways some one is resembling to or different from some other one and other ones and so sometime there will be a completed system of kinds of men and women, of kinds of men and kinds of women.

To begin now a little such a grouping ; each one must be a whole one, each one must be to some one like some one else, like some other one.

Everybody is a real one to me, everybody is like some one else too to me. Almost every one in looking at any one mostly feels that that one they are then seeing, is like some one else they have known in their living, sometimes they know it in remembering, sometimes it is puzzling to them, sometimes they tell it and no other one then sees it with them, always there are different ways of feeling resemblances between people any one is knowing, always then there is remembering and disagreeing about resemblances between every one, always then mostly every one sees some one resembling the one they are then remembering, mostly every one feels resemblances in men and women. It is important then to make kinds of them, kinds of men and women, it is important then to know all the ways there are of being resembling, always then every one is a real one always then every one is resembling in different kinds of ways to different ones, always then all through the living of any one they are being resembling to different ones, always then there are many kinds of being, always then there are many ways of feeling, knowing kinds in being, always then each one is a kind of man, a kind of woman, a kind in their beginning, a kind in their going on, a kind in their ending, every one is of a kind of men, a kind of women, a kind of men and women, a kind in beginning, a kind in going on and in ending. Always then for understanding, each one must see the meaning in all the ways of being kinds of men and women, some have a feeling for some things in being others for other things in being, each one has their own way of feeling kinds in men and in women, in babies, in children, in growing young men in growing young women, in men and women. There are then all these many ways of knowing, feeling kinds in men and women, always then there are many ways of knowing, feeling, thinking, talking, using kinds in men and women. Always then each one is a whole one and in many ways of a kind of men or of a kind of women.

Mostly this is all always confusing every one in talking, feeling, thinking, using, seeing any one, always each one has their own way of feeling kinds in them, always each kind of them has their kind of way of knowing men and women. Making each one a kind of men and women in enough kinds of ways to have everything included in the kinds of them, everything that is in the being of that one, that is understanding that one. That one is then a completed whole one then to that one, the one having that understanding of that one. That is very exciting, that is very interesting, that completed understanding is to some all the meaning in their living.

Always then each one one is ever hearing talking, knowing feeling, thinking, seeing, each one has their way of seeing each one they are ever knowing, each one has their way of feeling kinds in men and women. Always then that one that has it to want to have understanding of any one, that one always must have a feeling always of the ways all the ways, the many ways of knowing, feeling kinds in men and women. This then as I was saying is very exciting. This then is now some description of one way of learning to know kinds in men and women. Always I am telling of learning kinds in men and in women. Always then everybody is a real one to me, everybody is like some one else too to me. Always then sometime each one comes to be a whole one in me.

Always I am learning, more and more then I am knowing many kinds in men and women, many ways of making kinds in men and women, always I am learning, always it is interesting, often it is exciting, always I am learning, sometimes I am really learning all the being in some one, always more and more each one is to me a kind of one, always then I am learning more and more of bottom ways of being resembling, always I am learning more and more of the kinds of mixing that are confusing to any one looking, always then more and more there are steadily grouping kinds of men and women to me, more and more I know where each one I am ever seeing belongs in the grouping, more and more then it all grows confusing, I am always knowing more and more and then it gets all mixed up to me all mixed up in each one all mixed up in each one I am learning, each time there is in me a clear understanding of any one and I go on to another one or back to one I was earlier understanding that one is all a confusion from the last learning, each time then when there is a clear understanding of any one it is confusing with the next one, knowing more makes more grouping necessary in men and women and then all of a sudden this new grouping is a clear thing to my understanding and then sometimes all of a sudden I lose the meaning out of all of them I lose all of them and then each one I am then seeing looks like every one I have ever known in all my looking and there is no meaning in any of my grouping and then there is in me again a beginning and always sometime there will be clearly existing kinds of men and women, grouping of them by the bottom nature in them, by the mixing of other nature or natures with the bottom nature of them and so then sometime there will be a complete history of each one who ever is or was or will be living. It is very interesting, often very exciting, mostly very confusing, always steadily increasing in meaning.

There is now a little a description of my learning. There will be now then a little indication of what I have been learning, what I am now knowing, then there will be again a beginning of Martha Hersland in her beginning.

Everybody then is a real one to me. Sometime every one is a real one to me, everybody too is like somebody else always then to me. Slowly then there comes to be to me kinds in men and women. Slowly then they are grouping inside me into kinds of them, kinds of men and women. Every one then has their own being in them, every one is then to me of a kind of men and women. This will be clearer now in a description of how several men and several women came to be each one of them the beginning of a group for me. That made them for me each one of them a kind of them, a kind of women and men. Later then there will be more description of the learning of the kinds there are of men and women, of the resembling between them that makes kinds of them around one.

Now then there will be a little description of the learning of men and women as kinds of them, of the resemblances that are there in the nature in them, in the bottom nature in them that makes one kind of a way of making kinds of them.

Now this is the way resemblances among men and women have meaning to me to make kinds of them. Now this is the way I am learning men and women, knowing kinds in them.

Every one has some feeling of knowing kinds in men and in women, some have some feeling of knowing kinds in men and women. This is now then to be some description of my knowing kinds in men and women. This will soon be clearer in little descriptions of some of them as kinds in women and men.

This is now a little a description of my learning kinds in men and women. Mostly every one as I was saying has some feeling of knowing kinds in men, mostly every one as I was saying has some feeling of knowing kinds in women as I was saying some have some feeling of knowing kinds in men and women. Mostly every one sees resemblances between some men, between some women, some between some men and women, and men and men, and women and women. There are then as I was saying many ways of making kinds in men and women.

There will be now more description of the learning of knowing of the kinds there are of men and women, of the resembling that makes kinds of them around one. As I was saying always each one is sometime a whole one to me, each one always is like some one or many other ones to me.

This is then the way I do my learning, slowly knowing each one, more and more seeing each one as a whole one and at the same time as a kind of men and women, slowly more and more having everybody in me as a real one, slowly more and more knowing resemblances all the resemblances existing, slowly more and more having confusion and then slowly again and again beginning and getting clearer the kinds of them and then losing them in more complicated differences and resemblings and so always more and more I am understanding and always more and more I am changing and always more and more I am beginning and always more and more I am having uncertainty in my feeling and always more and more I am certain and always more and more there are distinct kinds of them kinds of men and women, and then sometimes there are so many ways of seeing each one that I must stop looking.

This will be always then a longer and longer description always longer with my living and my knowing.

Always then I am seeing the resemblances that make kinds of them kinds of men and women and always I come back again and again to see it in them. Always then I am thinking and feeling and learning resemblances in men and women, always then I am making kinds in them.

Every one then has their own being in them. Every one is of a kind of men and women. Always then I see resemblances in each one to another one to other ones and always I come back again and again to looking at that one and always I am seeing something, and always I am having a confusion inside me about that one and always I am beginning again and again and again and then sometime that one is a whole one to me, that one is of a kind of men and women from the bottom nature in that one and always then sometime it is clear about that one to me the nature or natures in that one with the bottom nature in that one and then sometime I know of that one all the kinds of being in that one, all the kinds of ways that one is of kinds of men and women.

Always then I am thinking and feeling and seeing all the ways the one I am then knowing has of being resembling to any one. Every one as I was saying mostly every one feels and tells about resemblances in men and women, mostly every one has a feeling of kinds in men, of kinds in women, of kinds in men and women. There are then as I was saying many ways of feeling kinds in men and women.

Mostly then as I was saying every one has some feeling of people resembling each other, some have it more some have it less in them the feeling that people are resembling, some are always looking for resemblances, some are then with that very annoying, some are always saying this one is like some one I can tell it by remembering, some are always thinking that every one is resembling a few they have known in living and these then often are annoying, always then mostly each one feels something of interest in seeing resemblances between some one and some other one or ones sometime, some feel this very often, some feel this all the time, mostly then there is a good deal of discussing mostly then there is a good deal of irritation, mostly then there is a good deal of difference of opinion about the ways people are resembling, about resemblances between some one and some other one some one then is seeing and some one else is then not feeling. Always then there is in living much finding of resemblances between men, between women, between men and women, between children, and mostly always then when any one tells it to any one there is much discussing often very much irritation. This is then very interesting. There are then often some who find every one they are ever knowing resembling a few men and women whom these sometime have had come to be in them a certain kind of men and women, these then make many of those they are seeing of these few kinds of them. Mostly then every one has some feeling for resemblances and for kinds in men and in women and in men and women.

Now then to begin again understanding, to begin again learning men and women, to begin again seeing them as whole ones each one and each one as kinds in men and women. As I was saying each one I am ever knowing some time is a real one to me, as I was saying each one I am ever knowing sometime is like some one else too to me. Always then I am learning always then I am remembering, I am puzzling, I am in a confusion, always then I am coming back again and again and seeing, feeling, thinking all the ways any one can see that one, all the ways that one is resembling to any one, slowly then each one I am ever knowing is a whole one to me, slowly then I can learn other ones from having that one a whole one inside me, more and more then I am understanding kinds in men and women, more and more then I am learning different values in resemblances existing always between each one and others of them, sometime then each one comes to be to me a completed being. This is then now a slow description of my way of learning, this is then now a little description of some whom I am knowing.

Every one is themselves inside them, mostly every one reminds some one of some other one of some other ones, every one has it to say of some one some of many, he is like such a one I see it in him, she is like some one else I can tell it by remembering. Mostly every one is sometimes thinking that some one is resembling the one at whom they are then looking. So, many always go on thinking that every one is resembling to others, and often some one is disagreeing some one to whom such a one is pointing out resemblances does not agree with that one. This is very common. There are many ways of feeling kinds in men and women. People disagreeing about ways of being resembling, people seeing different ways of making kinds in them often makes such irritation, sometimes exciting, sometimes confusing, sometimes to some one puzzling.

There are many ways of making kinds in men and women. Each way of making kinds of them comes from a different way of feeling knowing them as resembling. There are many ways then of feeling knowing kinds in men and women. Sometime some one will know all the ways there are for people to be resembling, some one some time then will have a completed history of every one, every one who ever is or was or will be living. There are many ways then of knowing kinds in men and women, there are many ways then, there is a way of feeling them as kinds of them by ways of doing that come from education and tradition, kinds of them that come from the ways that make a nation, there are ways of seeing kinds of them by the kind of learning in them, tastes, beliefs, fondness for walking, working, doing nothing, there are ways of feeling kinds in them in color resemblances and gentlenesses in them, and courage, and ways of showing angry feeling, there are ways of knowing resemblances in them from occupation giving certain habits to them, there are ways of seeing kinds in them from their being always young, always old in them, bright all of some of them, dull all of some of them, moral all of some of them, immoral all of some of them, lazy all of some of them, very energetic always some of them, then there are samenesses in the looks of many of them that makes kinds of them to some and sometime some one will know all the ways there are for people to be resembling, some one sometime then will have a completed history of all of them.

There are all these ways then and many more of them of feeling knowing people to be resembling and then there is the way that I am always seeing, the resembling that makes the two kinds of them, independent dependent kind of them who have attacking as their natural way of winning fighting and the dependent independent kind of them who have resisting in them as their natural way of winning and then there are so many complicated kinds of these two kinds of them so many ways of mixing, disguising, complicated using of their natures in many of them, so complicated that mostly it is confusing to me who know it of them that there are these kinds of them and always more and more I know it of them and always it is confusing for sometimes a resisting one spends most of living in attacking, an attacking one spends most of the living in resisting, sometimes some one is mostly all attacking and just at the bottom there is a contradiction of the whole nature of them, there are so many complications then in all this that I am knowing, it is all a very difficult thing to be really understanding. I know very much about these ways of being in men and women, I know it and I can say it, I know it and I can write it, it is a very complex mixing the being in all men and in all women, I do not know yet the whole of it, I do know now very much of it, I cannot yet say all I know of it.

Mostly everybody now is like some one else to me, like many others to me, in some ways like some in other ways like others and now more and more there are to me some of each kind of them that are mostly only of that kind of them, and so more and more there come to be to me clearly a certain number of kinds of men and women.

Kinds in men and women then are to many always in men and

women and in many different ways of feeling and thinking. Mostly to every one there are kinds in men, kinds in women, kinds in men and women.

There are then as I was saying many ways of feeling kinds in men and women, every way of feeling kinds in men and women must be in such a one that sometime has in that one all the history of all men, of all women.

Kinds in men and women then are existing to mostly every one. To many feeling kinds in men and women is a part of learning men and women, to some kinds in men and women are parts of learning men and women, to some feeling kinds in men and women is to have sometime each one such a one is ever knowing a completed whole one to that one. To such a one always there is continually more variation and more resembling and sometimes it is so confusing that such a one must stop looking. Then when some one is a whole one and a complete one of a kind of one or the kinds in one are complete to one knowing that one, then it is very satisfying.

Everybody then is mostly a real one to me, everybody is now like some one and like some other one and then again like some other one and each one sometimes is a whole one to me.

This being resembling, this seeing resemblances between those one is knowing is interesting, defining, confusing, uncertain and certain. You see one, the way of looking at any one in that one that is like some one, the way of listening, a sudden expression, a way of walking, a sound in laughing, a number of expressions that are passing over the face of that one, it is confusing, too many people have pieces in them like pieces in this one, it began as a clear resemblance to some one, it goes on to be a confusing number of resemblances to many then, some resemblance that is very clear one is not remembering then it is baffling, more and more resemblances come out in that one, perhaps that one is not independent dependent and yet that was so clear in the beginning, more and more then with knowing resemblances are multiplying and being baffling and confusing and always each one of all these resemblances one who sometime wants to have this one as a whole one, wants to really know kinds in men and women must completely feel, admit, remember and consider and realise as having meaning. This is then a beginning of learning to make kinds of men and women. Slowly then all the resemblances between one and all the others that have something, different things in common with that one, all these fall into an ordered system sometime then that one is a whole one, sometimes that one is very different to what was in the beginning the important resemblance in that one but always everything, all resemblances in that one must be counted in, nothing must ever be thrown out, everything in each one must be included to know that one and then sometime that one is to some one a whole one and that is then very satisfying.

Sometimes as I was just saying everything in any one, all the resemblances in that one point to that one being one kind of men and women and then, say an independent dependent kind of one, and then when one looks more and more closely at that one the bottom nature in that one is a contradiction to all the rest in that one, is so to say dependent independent being and everything one ever was knowing of that one has to be always still remembered but now it all has a new direction. Knowing completely then any one gives a solid basis for seeing the meaning of any being that has in it resemblances to that one. Always then it is important with each one that sometime that one is to the one learning kinds in men and women a whole one, a complete one so that there can then be a solid basis of comparison of understanding the meaning of the being in some one who is resembling in any way to that one who is to the one learning, then a whole one. Sometime as I was saying there are so many ways of seeing, feeling resemblances in some one, some one resembles so many men and women that it is confusing, baffling, then the one learning kinds in men and women is despairing, nothing then to that one has any meaning, it is then to that one all of it only an arbitrary choosing and then that one must stop looking, that one then must begin again then and always never forgetting anything that one ever has seen as a resemblance in the one that one is then learning. Sometime really each one will then be a complete one to that one. Sometime really each one will be a completed, understood person, understood in kinds of men and women. This is a real way of learning, sometime then there will be a complete history of every one, everything then they do in living, each one, will be clear then to the one that has really learned all the kinds there are of men and women, all will be understood then in them, their living, loving, eating, working, resting, pleasing, smoking, scolding, drinking, dancing, walking, talking, sleeping, beginning, ending, attacking, resisting, winning, losing, everything. There are whole beings always, they are themselves inside them, they will be whole ones then to the others who have learned to know them, they will be each understood by being known as their kind of them.

I do know very much of the being in men and women. I do know very many of them. I do know the resemblances in them and the kinds of them, the divisions into kinds of them that is important for the understanding of them. I do know many of them, I know them, I understand, I explain them, they are themselves then to me, they are whole ones to me, I know it and I tell it, I know it more and more and more and more I tell it. Always I am thinking about it, always I feel the being the whole being sometime in each one, I know it sometime and I tell it sometime. I learn it as I see it and feel it and hear it as they repeat it, I understand it and then I understand in another one that is like the one that has then become a whole one to me, I learn new variations in it then from this now one and then sometime this one is a whole one to me and I begin again then with this one to know kinds in men and women and so on and always there is more to learn about it, there is more to know about it, there is more to tell about it.

This will be clearer now in a description of how several men and women each one came to be a whole one to me, a kind of men and women to me and then by resemblances between them and others of them there came to be more understanding of each kind in men and women in me and then other kinds in them to me. Later there will be more description of the knowing of all the kinds there are of men and women, of the resembling that makes kinds of them around one. Now there will be a little description of some, of the kinds they are, of learning by resemblances between men and women the being in them.

The way I think of every one is like this. This is the way they come to be in groups to me, in groups that have in them to be that those in them are resembling each one to the other one. The way I know them as resembling, that I have been just explaining, in every way that any one can see any one of them. The way I think of each one is like this that I will now begin describing.

In recognizing them as being of one group or of another group of them, that is one kind or another kind of men and women, everything in them, anything in them, their looks, their feelings, their expressions, their way of doing anything, their way of doing everything, everything, anything in them is to be noticed in its resemblance to something in another one. So then there come to be groups of kinds of men and women. So then as I was saying I come to know them, sometime all of them I am ever knowing, as kinds in men and women. Sometimes it is very confusing, sometimes very simple, sometimes very certain, sometimes very uncertain, sometimes for a long time baffling. There are then kinds in men and women. Sometime there will be a description of all the kinds of them.

The way I think of each one is like this. I think of them as having a bottom nature in them, as having sometimes mixed up in them other nature or natures with the bottom nature in them. This is now to be a little description of the way I always think of each one of them to lead later to a description of some of the kinds of men and women.

I think of each one I am ever knowing. Each one sometime is a whole one to me. Each one has a bottom nature in them of one kind of men and women. Each one may have in them other nature or natures in them mixed with each other or separate together in them. This is the way I think of men and women.

This is now a description of the way I feel and think the natures in them.

As I was saying each one has a bottom nature in them. Each one is one of a kind of men and women.

Each one has a bottom nature in them, each one has or has not another nature or other natures in them besides the bottom nature in them. These may be of the same kind as the bottom nature, they may not. This is now then a description of the way I feel and think the nature and natures in men and women.

This is then the way I feel the nature, the bottom nature, the other nature or natures, in men and women, this is then the way I feel each nature in each one of them. Each nature then is of a kind in men and women.

This is then the way I feel each nature in men and women, this is the way I feel the nature and make groupings of them, groupings of kinds of them.

The way I feel natures in men and women is this way then. To begin then with one general kind of them, this is a resisting earthy slow kind of them, anything entering into them as a sensation must emerge again from through the slow resisting bottom of them to be an emotion in them. This is a kind of them. This bottom in them then in some can be solid, in some frozen, in some dried and cracked, in some muddy and engulfing, in some thicker, in some thinner, slimier, drier, very dry and not so dry and in some a stimulation entering into the surface of the mass that is them to make an emotion does not get into it, the mass then that is them, to be swallowed up in it to be emerging, in some it is swallowed up and never then is emerging. Now all these kinds of ways of being are existing and sometime there will be examples of all these ways of being, now all these ways of being have it in common that there is not in them a quick and poignant reaction, it must be an entering and then an emerging mostly taking some time in the doing, the quickest of these then are such of them where the mud is dry and almost wooden, where the mud has become dry and almost wooden, or metallic in them and it is a surface denting a stimulation gives to them or else there is a surface that is not dry and the rest is dry and it is only the surface of the whole mass that is that one of which there has been any penetrating, and in some in whom the whole mass of the being is taking part in the reaction in some of such of them habit, mind strongly acting can make it go quicker and quicker the deep sinking and emerging. This is then a kind of them, the resisting kind of them, and there are many kinds of that kind of them. This is a very sure way of grouping kinds in men and women. I know it and I see men and women by it. Mostly to any one now it means nothing. I will begin again then this explaining. This group I have been describing are those that have resisting winning as their natural way of being. I will begin again explaining. There are a kind of men and women who have resisting as their way of winning fighting. There are another kind of men and women that have attacking as their way of winning fighting, these have poignant and quick reaction, emotion in such of them has the quickness and intensity of a sensation, that is one kind of men and women. Later I will tell more of them. Now I must begin again with the resisting, the dependent independent the kind I have been beginning describing in a way that may mean nothing to any other one, in the way I feel bottom being in men and women, in the way I make kinds in them, in the way each one comes to be a whole one to me seeing that one.

Resisting being is one way of being. This is now a description. As I was saying there are kinds of them kinds in men and women and there are kinds of kinds of them kinds in kinds in men and women. First then there are large groupings of them, the grouping into two kinds of them those having resisting, those having attacking as their natural way of winning fighting, dependent independent, independent dependent, these two kinds of them. Each group then has in a way the same way of hand-writing, the same way of succeeding, the same way of beginning, the same way of loving. Many of them are very baffling, many in each group of them, for there are in many of them other nature or natures in them, sometimes then they are very baffling, sometime to some one the bottom nature in them is certain, the kind the bottom nature in them is, and then, though it may take a long time to know the complete being in them, they are not any longer baffling. Soon a few short histories will be given of learning the bottom being in some and so clearing up the problem of them which for a long time was confusing, which always is confusing to any one not knowing the bottom being in that one.

This is clear then, bottom being is the natural way of winning, loving, fighting, working, thinking, writing in each one. This is not anything about good or bad in them, in each one, about more or less brains in them but the kind of brains, the kind of good, the kind of bad, the kind of loving, the kind of fighting, the way of working, being in them at the bottom of them.

This is a very certain way of knowing, grouping men and women, understanding, seeing the kind of natures in them, making certain of the resemblances between them. This is then a universal grouping, always everywhere with every education there are these same kinds of them, some are a complete thing of one kind of them, some are very little just at the bottom one kind of them and all the rest of them are other kinds of them, there are in them every degree of mixing, every degree of emphasising, some are the whole of their kind of them, some are only part of their kind of them ; to commence again then with my way of seeing them and then the way of knowing the resemblances between them and so the making groups of them. To begin again then with my feeling of bottom nature in each one.

There are then the two general kinds of them, the attacking kind the independent dependent kind of them, the resisting kind the dependent independent kind of them. There are all extremes of these two kinds of them, resisting kind that is almost always feverishly attacking, attacking kind that is almost always stubbornly resisting, the independent dependents that are almost all independent, almost all dependent, the dependent independent that are almost all dependent, that are almost all independent, it is often very confusing but the distinction has meaning, mostly to every one reading there is not any understanding, that is very certain, sometime to some one it can have meaning, always then there is going on explaining of the meaning of this dividing of men and women into these kinds of them.

There must now then be more description of the way each one is made of a substance common to their kind of them, thicker, thinner, harder, softer, all of one consistency, all of one lump, or little lumps stuck together to make a whole one cemented together sometimes by the same kind of being sometimes by other kind of being in them, some with a lump hard at the centre liquid at the surface, some with the lump vegetablish or wooden or metallic in them. Always then the kind of substance, the kind of way when it is a mediumly fluid solid fructifying reacting substance, the way it acts then makes one kind of them the resisting kind of them, the way another substance acts makes another kind of them the attacking kind of them. It and the state it is in each kind of them, the mixing of it with the other way of being that makes many kinds of these two kinds of them, sometime all this will have meaning. Now there will be a little more description given of these two kinds of substances and their way of acting and the kinds in each kind of them and then there will be given short histories showing learning kinds, learning individual ones by knowing this way of seeing, feeling bottom nature in men and women.

I know it and I want to tell it. I see it the bottom nature in each one I am ever knowing, sometimes, in each one. I see it, I see it and know it, its likeness and unlikeness to bottom nature in another one, I know and I want to tell it. I know it and I want to tell it and sometime some one else too will know it. I know it and I want to tell it and sometimes some one, some will know it. This is then the way I see it.

As I was saying there are two general kinds of them, the resisting, the attacking kind of them. There are two general kinds of them, there are many very many kinds of these two kinds of them, there are many very very many mixings in every one of some of all the kinds of them, in some of some of both the general kinds of them I know this now and now I will describe more of it. I will now describe natures in all men and women. In each one, some nature is the bottom nature of them. All natures are kinds, they are like natures in other men and women. This is now a little a beginning of the grouping of them.

First then to consider the general resisting group of men and women, considering them now only the bottom nature, which is resisting, in this group of them, leaving out now any considering of mixing in them of other nature or natures in them, of other forms of resisting nature in them besides the kind of-resisting being that is bottom nature in each one, of any attacking nature or natures in them that are mixed up in them. It is clear then that it is now the general group of resisting beings that are to have now a describing, there will be a little explaining of the attacking being in resisting being. There is now to be here a short description.

As I was saying this is one way of seeing being, bottom nature as a substance that has a way of acting that makes one general kind of being, that makes all of that kind of them have it in common to have a certain way of fighting, thinking, loving, succeeding, beginning and ending, this is of course in each one affected by the quantity of bottom being in each one of their kind of being and of the other nature or natures in each one and so often it is all very confusing. Often in very much of any one's living it is very hard to know which nature in them is bottom nature in them, sometime this comes to be clear in each one, it is always there and repeating in each one, sometimes it is loudly sounding and after any one has heard it clearly in some one it is always there to that one, always repeating. The bottom nature then is clear in that one. In some it is clearer when they are very young, in some when they are young, in some when they are not so young, in some when they are old ones. Always in each one it is there repeating, sometime some one knows it in each one, sometime some one will know it in every one that one is ever knowing.

To begin then. The resisting kind of them. Many are of this kind of them and I know it in them. They are it, they live it and I know it. Sometime then I understand it, they are it, they live it and they repeat it, sometime then I know it when I see it, hear it, feel it in them, sometime then when they are of this kind of them I know it of them, sometimes for a long time it is baffling in some one for it is not clear in them, sometime it is clear in each one the bottom nature in them, when it is resisting being in them it makes certain kinds of ways of being, loving, thinking, fighting in such of them. They are it, they live it and sometime I know it. They are it, they live it, sometime they show it, sometime I understand it and now I will tell it the way I see it. I will tell the way I see and feel and hear and know resisting being in those that have it, then I will tell the way I see and feel and hear and know attacking being in those that have it, I will tell of the kinds there are in it and how by resemblances between those of that kind of it I know it, I will give then more examples of knowing it.

The resisting kind in men and women and how I feel it. They are it, they live it, sometimes I know it. Always sometime in each one sometime. I know it. I understand and I can tell it. I will wait a little longer before I tell very much about it. Now there will be only a little description of it. Slowly there will be a complete description of it, coming out of me, and sometime there will be written all any one knows of it. I know it and now I will tell a little of it.

The resisting kind of being in men and women and how I feel it, how I know it in them. They are it, they live it, they repeat it, sometime I know it in them, this is now some description of the way I realise it.

The bottom nature in many then is of the dependent independent kind of being there can be in men and women, these have resisting fighting as their natural way of winning. In such of them reaction is not quick and poignant in them, in such of them emotion has not the poignancy of a sensation. I know it in them, always sometime I know it in them, often it is hard to know it in them from the mixing of the other kinds of nature in them. Perhaps now I will give just a little description of it, later I will give more description of it. I understand it and I can tell it. I will wait a little longer before I tell very much about it. Now there will be only a little description of it. Slowly there will be a complete description of it coming out of me and sometime there will be written all any one knows of it. I know it and now I will tell a little of it.

Resisting being in men and women. This is now then a little a description of my realising resisting being in men and women. This is then now a little description of my realising resisting being in some.

There are many that have resisting being in them as a bottom nature to them, sometimes I know it in them. There are many then that have it, I know it and sometime I tell it, they are all of them showing it in the repeating they are all of them doing all their living, sometime I know it in each one of them, sometime I know it and sometime I tell it. There are many that have it, that makes all of them one kind of men and women. I know it in them in each one of them of men and women I am ever knowing who have it and sometimes I understand it, I know it and understand the action of it in each one of them that have it, in each one of them that I come to know of that kind of men and women. There are many then that have it, about half of all men and women are of the kind of men and women having resisting being as a bottom nature in them, the rest of them mostly have attacking being in them. This is a general division. I understand a good deal of it, I can tell more and less than I understand of it. I am now going to tell less and more than I understand of resisting being as a bottom nature in many men and women who have it.

Resisting being then as I was saying is to me a kind of being, one kind of men and women have it as being that emotion is not as poignant in them as sensation. This is my meaning, this is resisting being. Generally speaking then resisting being is a kind of being where, taking bottom nature to be a substance like earth to some one's feeling, this needs time for penetrating to get reaction. Those having attacking being their substance is more vibrant in them, these can have reaction as emotion as quick and poignant and complete as a sensation. Generally speaking, those having resisting being in them have a slow way of responding, they may be nervous and quick and all that but it is in them, nervousness is in them as the effect of slow-moving going too fast and so having nervous being, nervous being in them is not the natural means of expression to such of them, some have quick response in them by the steadily training of themselves to quicker and quicker reaction and some of them in the end come to seem to have quick reaction as their natural way of being, mostly in such of them this is a late development in them and that is natural from the kind of being in them. Attacking being often has nervousness as energy as a natural way of active being in them, often these then lose the power of attacking with the loss of nervousness in them. There are so very many ways of knowing these two kinds in men and women. I know so very many of them, I will not now tell of very many of them. Mostly the resisting being when they have conservative being in them have it from not having the activity of changing, the attacking kind of being have conservative sense in them from convictions, traditions, they are attackingly defending. Mostly those having in them resisting being have more feeling of objects as real things to them, objects have to them more earthy meaning than to those who have attacking as their natural way of being. Mostly then objects to those having attacking being as their natural way of being have for them meaning as emotion, as practically to be using, as beauty, as symbolism, that is to many of them their natural way of seeing anything they are knowing, to those who have resisting being as their natural way of being an object is it itself to them, the meaning, the use, the emotion about it, the beauty, the symbolising of it is to such of them a secondary reaction, not altogether at once as in those having in them attacking as their natural way of being. So then those having resisting being have also in them passive adaptibility strongly in them when they are not really resisting while those who have attacking being are generally more active in adapting, they may have yielding in them or stubborness or sensitive responsiveness in them when not attacking they have not generally speaking passive adaptibility in them. They are very different then the attacking and the resisting kind in men and women. This division has real meaning. Sometime when I am all through all my writing, when all my meaning, all my understanding, all my knowing, all my learning has been written, sometime then some will understand the being in all men and women.

I am all unhappy in this writing. I know very much of the meaning of the being in men and women. I know it and feel it and I am always learning more of it and now I am telling it and I am nervous and driving and unhappy in it. Sometimes I will be all happy in it.

I know it and now I begin again with telling it, the way I feel resisting being in men and women. It is like a substance and in some it is as I was saying solid and sensitive all through it to stimulation, in some almost wooden, in some muddy and engulfing, in some thin almost like gruel, in some solid in some parts and in other parts all liquid, in some with holes like air-holes in it, in some a thin layer of it, in some hardened and crack- ed all through it, in some double layers of it with no connections between the layers of it. This and many many other ways there are of feeling it as the bottom being in different ones of them ; different men and women have resisting being as their natural way of being, always I am looking hard at each one, feeling, seeing, hearing the repeating com- ing out of each one and so slowly I know of each one the way the bot- tom in them is existing and so then that is the foundation of tne history of each one of them and always it is coming out of each one of them.

This then this bottom nature in them, the way it is made in them makes the bottom history of them, makes their way of being stupid, wise, active, lazy, continuous, disjointed, is always there in them, in some their kind of them is more, is less, is the same all through their living, is more or less affected by the other nature or natures in them if they have other nature or natures in them, can be stimulated or hurried or slowed but never really changed in them, can come very nearly to be changed in them, can never really be changed in them, really not ever to my knowing, really not ever really changed in them. This then is very certain and now to speak again of attacking being. Attacking being as I was saying has it to be that emotion can be as quick, as poignant, as profound in meaning as a sensation. This is my meaning. I am thinking of attacking being not as an earthy kind of substance but as a pulpy not dust not dirt but a more mixed up substance, it can be slimy, gelatinous, gluey, white opaquy kind of thing and it can be white and vibrant, and clear and heat- ed and this is all not very clear to me and I will now tell more about it.

This is the way I am thinking of it. In the one in which I first learned to know it it was like this to me. It was like this to me in the first one I came to know it, the substance attacking being is, in its var- ious shaping. In this one it was so dull, so thick, so gluey that it was so slow in action one almost could think of it as resisting but it was not resisting earthy dependent independent being, it was attacking, stupid, slow-moving, it was independent dependent being, it was a different sub- stance in its way of acting, reacting, of being penetrated, of feeling, of thinking than any slow resisting dependent independent being and now there is to be here a very little explaining of how I know this as a kind of being.

In this one then, as I was saying it was attacking being but very slowly getting into motion but not because it the stimulation was lost into it and had to be remade out of it but because it being shaken it was a slow mass getting into action. I know this distinction, it has real meaning, I am saying it again and again and now I begin again with a description.

This then the attacking being was first clear to me in one having it as a slow, stupid, gelatinous being that when it got moving went on repeating action, never could get going any faster, had a nervous anaemic feeling that was part of its getting moving and keeping going. The resisting medium has a different kind of action as I was explaining. Now this attacking being when it is vibrant can be nervous and poignant and quicker than chain-lightning, there can be to it a profound complete reaction having the intensity of a sensation. Its sensitiveness is different in kind from that of the resisting kind of being, its sensitiveness is quivering into action not a sensitiveness just existing, but this is all too much to be now explaining, wait and I can tell it, clearer, always it has to be told as it has been learned by me very slowly, each one only slowly can know it, each one must wait for little pieces of it, always there will be coming more and more of it, always there will be a telling of every way the two kinds of being are different in everything and always it is hard to say it the differences between them, always more and more I know it, always more and more I know it, always more I come back to begin again the knowing of it, always I will tell it as I learned it, sometime I will have told all of it, always I am telling pieces of it, more and more I will know it, more and more I will tell it, sometime it will be clear to some one and I will be then glad of it.

This then is attacking being to me, this then was the way it came first to be clear in me, in one in whom it was slow moving, and in others then I knew it when it was quick and poignant and complete and I saw it, and I knew it as the same substance as this slow moving mass and in all its forms of acting more and more then I knew it. In some as I was saying it is as emotion, in some it is as passion, in some it is as sensitive responding ; it has a way of thinking, loving, acting, different in kind from that of resisting being and some time, and it is a very long time too I know it now I am beginning telling all I know all I am always learning, sometime there will have been a complete description of these two kinds of being.

In some then this quick and poignant and profound reaction has to break through a resisting being lying on it and then it is very interesting in the changing in the action it takes to get through the covering, sometimes it is in some more quivering vibrant at the bottom than through the rest of it and then it is lighted and set in motion the rest that of itself never has more activity than quivering by the more vibrant part at the bottom, sometimes all of it is not more active ever than quivering, this is true in some, in some it is all vibrant and completely poignantly passionately acting, in some its nervousness its most vigorous action, in some it is a big mass always slowly moving but would like to stop acting and a resolute will, a mind, a conviction, education in such a one keeps it moving, sometimes it stops moving, there are so many ways, there are such a various kind of mixing that can be in any one, sometime there will be a history of each one, sometime there will be a description of all the ways resisting being can be in any one, all the ways attacking being can be in any one.

This then is then one way I have been seeing kinds in men and women, the way I see the bottom natures and other natures in them. Always I see them as kinds, always as kinds of substance and ways of that substance being in them as bottom nature. Sometime all this will be clearer. This is then the way I see kinds in men and women. This then makes every one sometime a clear one, a whole one to me, this is now soon to be more description of such learning by me, of such understanding of the being in men and women.

As I was saying often for many years some one is baffling ; the repeated seeing, hearing, feeling of the being in them does not make clear the nature of the bottom being in them. Sometimes for many years some one is baffling and then it is clear in that one and then by resemblances between that one and other ones many are clear then. This is now some description of such learning. This will be now little short descriptions of learning six of them and how knowing others before helped with these and how knowing these helped with others later. This is now then a little more of preliminary studying.

There are many that I know and always more and more I know it, they are all of them repeating, they are all of them in some way resembling one to others of them, more and more I understand it, sometimes in each one I know the bottom nature in them, sometimes in each one I know all the natures in them, sometimes each one is a whole one to me, sometime of each one there is a complete history to me.

There was one then, this one was not baffling for such a long time, this one was of the resisting kind of them.

Sometime each one comes to be a whole one to me. Sometime the bottom nature in each one, the other nature or natures in each one, the mixing or not mixing in them of the natures in them comes to be clear in each one, each one then is a complete one, each one then keeps repeating the whole history of them.

Some are puzzling a long time, every one is more or less puzzling sometime, mostly every one is puzzling to me sometime, sometime mostly every one comes to be a whole one to me.

As I have been saying there is a bottom nature in every one, the other nature or natures in them may be of their kind of them the same kind as the bottom nature in them, if they are resisting, the other nature or natures in them may be of a kind of resisting, they may be of a kind of attacking being. All this makes some one sometimes for a long time very baffling. All this makes each one always sometime puzzling. Always more and more I know it of each one the being in them the mixtures in them, always more and more I will come to have a complete understanding of every one I am ever knowing. This is now a description of my understanding of one.

This one then was not baffling for such a very long time, this one had times of being puzzling to me, mostly after a real beginning of understanding it comes to me very steadily, not quickly not slowly, this one was of a resisting kind of them with the attacking kind of resisting being almost to the point of succeeding as part of the being in this one. This is now to be some description of this one.

The first one of those that further back I was describing as showing my way of learning to have each one come to be a whole one in me, that first one was to every one as the natural way of being was one having every one always wanting to have her be with them every one who knew her then, and always every one was flattering her to make it up to her that there was not ever any place for her in living, for always to herself and to every one there was always a good reason why not any condition was the right condition for her living, for always to herself and to every one there was always a good reason why not any condition was the right condition for her living. But always a little somewhere there was a feeling that this was not all the meaning in the being in this one, slowly then some felt in this one the muggy resisting bottom that kept her from ever giving herself to any one unless some one needing her engulfed her by a need of her, they engulfed her then some when they had to have some one. Slowly then some came to know in this one the resisting bottom in this one, slowly then some came to see it in this one that she was of them needing to be owning those they need for loving, this is part of this kind of resisting being as I was saying about Mrs. Hersland but in this one it never came to any realisation for this one never really owned any one, resisting to keep from yielding to the need of having other people's having loving feeling, resisting accepting just an ordinary quantity of loving feeling from any one, this kept this one from yielding herself enough to any one so as to own any one, wanting giving loving and having resisting being kept this one from being engulfed by other ones excepting when some one drowned this one, kept this one mostly from ever yielding enough to own any one. As I was saying sometimes some one engulfed this one, always this wore out this one, it was never freely yielding herself to engulfing then, it was wanting to keep ahead of being engulfed by giving and this was very wearing to this one.

Some then knew this being in this one, slowly then hearing, feeling, seeing all the repeating in this one, slowly then hearing, feeling, seeing every one who knew this one's feeling about this one made it clear to me the whole being in this one, I came then to hear repeating the muggy resisting bottom that kept her ever from giving herself to any one unless one engulfed her by completely using her, by a need of her to comfort them in some sorrow when they had to have some one, by using her and giving nothing to her. This one then had this resisting being that with all the need in her of having loving given to her kept her from ever giving herself to any one even for a little loving of such a one, kept her from ever having a place for really living.

But this is not all the meaning in this one, she had in her to be muggily resisting except when some one was engulfing her, but also if she could have given herself to some one it would be to own them. She was of the kind of women that have to own the ones they need for loving. This one then never owned any one, and this was that she could not give herself enough to any one to own them, sometimes some one owned this one but this one then was so drowned by this one's owning that she could not loose herself enough to own them, she could only cling to wanting to give to them just enough to keep herself from being completely drowned by that one's owning of her. If she could once be drowned by some one completely to not wanting to give to such a one she might have owned some one for loving but this never could come to be in her, she was too busy being drowned when she was drowning, she had not then any strength for owning. So then this one never owned any one, sometimes she was almost drowned by engulfing by some one needing her then. This is interesting and now this one I am now to be describing is of the same family as this one but it is in this one a very different thing this one can engulf those this one needs for living. This will be very interesting.

This is a little of the way I feel the resisting being in this one and this is the way it acts in this one. Later then, and I have already been beginning, I will then compare it with the resisting being in one. These two then are of the same kind of them but this being in them is very different in its action. To begin then.

The first one the one when it is lightish brown and gritty a little and sometimes very fluid and thin and sometimes almost dried hard and not really smooth then, in this one then it has a very different action this bottom nature from that in the one where it is dark and smooth and murkier and always about the same state of being a thickish fluid state there in her. These then are two kinds of a kind of men and women. This is now some description of the differences in being and acting, resisting and attacking, loving, owning, yielding, having vanity and stupid being in them, practical and ideal being in them.

The first one then as I was saying has as bottom nature in her being, resisting, this was then the action of this bottom nature in her that she never really gave herself to any one to own them, though always she wanted to be giving herself to some one, always she wanted to be owning every one, sometimes some one would be engulfing this one, but she was resisting then, and once when she was not resisting some one engulfed her so completely that what she is, the bottom being in her, was watered so thin that it was not of strength enough to cling to any one as dirt to hold them, to stick on them as it would if it were thick enough to own to inclose them by encasing them. This is true then that this one had it to be that the resisting substance was sometimes very thin and never thick but sometimes almost dried up into a grey brown, it looked browner thin, a little more grey when it was not wet, very thin, stuff in her. This being in her then made it that this one never gave herself to any one and never owned any one, sometimes was drowned by some one, always was a little gritty to the feeling of every one. Another one then one I am now beginning to describe as knowing, this one then was darker, smoother, thicker always a thick fluid in the being in her, in the bottom nature of her. There are many men and many women of both these two kinds of the one kind of them, the resisting engulfing kind of them, of men and women.

This second one then had as I was saying a thicker darker smoother, always as a thick fluid, the bottom nature in her. This one then had a power of engulfing some she needed for living, this one then could own some but mostly this one did not need any one, this being in her was enough to give to her a sense of superiority inside her, she had in her the sense of completely engulfing anything she needed for living and so she had in her a complete vanity a complete sense of superiority to every one. The other one had a sense of being aggrieved at never really owning any one. This one in her thicker, dark, murkier smoother bottom .being had not any such feeling, mostly this one was not engulfing any one but the sensation of the feeling of potential engulfing gave to this one a complete sense of superior being to every one, there was no need then in this one for action. The other one, the first one, from her never owning any one and having the feeling of not engulfing any one needed that every one should be flattering to keep this one from feeling too much the fact that there was no place for living for this one, the other one did not need such consolation, there was not any place for living for the other one but this was not a need to her, the vanity in her from the bottom substance of her made her completely then impervious to the need of any place for living, this one then when she was not engulfing any one and mostly this one was not engulfing any one this one was then engulfing her own self in the bottom nature in her and this gave to her a complete vanity of being in her, always there was there in her herself to be completely engulfed in the bottom nature of her and this gave to herself a sense of power and this was complete vanity in her and there was then no need in her of a place for living for her.

Sometimes the being in her led to reckless outbreaks from her. As I was saying resisting being as its way of attacking, attacking mostly in such men and women has not in it the strength for winning fighting, mostly it is weaker than the personal quality of resisting in such of them.

In some who have resisting being, attacking is their way of living and mostly such of them are not very strong in winning in living or in fighting although they are, some of such a kind of them, fairly successful in practical living. Winning in loving or in fighting is the test in such of them. Some time this will be clear in them, the men and women having resisting being, sometime there will be very much description of the way of attacking in these men and women having resisting being as their natural way of being, as their way of loving, as their way of winning fighting.

The first one, the one I was before describing, this one had attacking in living but mostly it was in her as the finding of their being no place to her for living, this was mostly all there was of attacking being in her, always knowing, always finding the good reason why not any place was a place for living to her. The other one had it as making her sometimes have reckless being in her, attacking being at moments was in her, she was then not to herself engulfing any one but the sense of superiority always in her the vanity that was completely inside her there could let her be reckless in attacking and mostly she was then not succeeding, but this did not then lead to any thing for always there was in her complete the vanity and superiority inside her that the power of completely engulfing herself always made in her. These two are different then, the differences are interesting. They are then two kinds of one kind of a general kind of being in men and women, they have each of them then as a bottom nature in them one kind of one kind of a general resisting kind of being.

There is another thing in the two of them, efficiency in doing anything. Always in the first one there is a desire to run things and this one does not do these things very well nor very badly either but to herself efficiency is strong in her and this is part of the wanting to own other ones for her living and mostly they do not really have her own them and this always is part to her of there not being any place for living for her. Owning others is a right to her, doing it is not ever very successful in her, always then this one has this desire and always then this one does not ever give herself to do it for any one for really this one must own another one to really contentedly to herself to do the thing for that other one. Sometimes as I was saying some one engulfs this one and then this one can do things for the other one, it is the nearest to owning any one this one ever comes to do in living. Always then not owning any one is the tragedy in this one, always every one flatters this one to make this one feel a little moment that this one owns them or some other one. The second one, engulfing herself giving power to this one, superiority in herself to every one, and complete vanity then being in her, this one does not need doing anything for any one to give to her a sense of owning them. This one is efficient enough in acting. Mostly to this one this is not interesting. These then have in them two kinds of engulfing resisting being as bottom natures in them.

Every one has their own being in them. Every one is of a kind in men and women. Each one has a bottom nature in them, this nature is of a kind of nature that makes a kind in men and women.

Everybody is a real one to me, everybody is like some one else too to me. There will be now more descriptions of kinds in men and women, of the likenesses and unlikenesses between them, of seeing kinds in men and women in the bottom natures of them. Every one has some feeling of knowing kinds in men and women. This will now be more description of some ways of feeling kinds in men and women.

More and more then there will be histories of all the kinds there are of men and women.

Each one is of a kind of men and women from the bottom nature in them. This is then one way of making kinds in men and women.

Sometime each one comes to be clear to me, the kind they are then from the bottom nature of them comes to be clear to me, makes of them then to me this kind of men and women. This then sometime comes to be clear to me in each one the bottom natures in them making kinds for me in men and women.

Sometime then the bottom nature in each one is a certain thing to some one knowing that one. Sometime then the bottom nature in each one is a clear thing to some one. There is then a kind of understanding of that one. Sometime each one comes to be a whole one to some one, the bottom nature in that one, the other nature or natures in that one, the whole being, living, way of doing everything, the whole history of that one comes sometime to be clear to some one.

Sometime each one so comes to be a whole one to some one. Mostly sometime mostly every one I am ever knowing comes so to be a whole one to me and now I am telling of the learning of this in some, the learning having them as a whole one to me.

Sometime then mostly each one comes to be a whole one to me. Sometime the bottom nature in each one, the other nature or natures in each one, the mixing or not mixing of the natures in them comes to be clear to me in mostly every one I am ever knowing, each one then is a complete one to me, each one then keeps repeating the whole history of them, this is now some description of my learning to hear, see and feel the whole repeating coming out of some.

As I was saying there is a bottom nature in every one, the other nature or natures in them may be of this kind of men and women that is of the same kind as the bottom nature of them, they may not be of the same kind of them. If the bottom nature of them is resisting the other nature or natures in them may be all resisting, some kinds of resisting and some attacking, all of the other natures in them may be of kinds of attacking, if the bottom nature in them is a kind of attacking being the other nature or natures in them may be of kinds of resisting, of kinds of attacking, some of kinds of resisting, some of kinds of attacking, some may have only a bottom nature to them, some may have almost nothing of bottom nature to them, there is every kind of mixing, mostly in each one it is very confusing, often each one one is ever knowing is for a long time baffling.

Some are puzzling a long time, almost every one is more or less puzzling to every one, mostly every one is puzzling to me, sometime mostly every one comes to be a whole one to me.

Always then I am learning some one. Mostly every one comes very slowly to be a whole one to me. Mostly every one is sometimes and mostly for a very long time a puzzle to me, sometimes some one only after a long time of learning that one comes to be a conscious puzzle to me.

Some can have a bottom with other nature or natures in them not mixed up with the bottom nature in them. Such of them are very puzzling and when sometimes such a one is a whole to one such ones always are in parts to one but all the parts are there in that one to one and all always repeating in that one and all repeating coming out of such a one has meaning as parts in one. When some one is not a whole one to one repeating coming out of them has not this clear relation. Such a one as I am now describing is not in pieces, is a whole one. All of such a one is almost completely one and then the bottom of that one is of a different kind from the rest of the whole one and that makes this one not confusing but baffling and sometimes a clear whole one, and then at last a completer whole one. When some one is not a whole one to one repeating coming out of them has not clear relation but sometimes repeating coming out of one has the clear relation of a whole one and it is not the whole of that one that the one feeling the clear relation in all the repeating is really knowing, there is a bottom nature that is different from all the rest of that one. Sooner or later some one knowing this will know it of this one, in the beginning of not being certain that the whole one one is knowing is the whole of that one is a strange feeling, not doubting, not puzzling, not baffling, just incompletion. Then such a one is a little puzzling until that one comes to be a whole whole one. Then the repeating coming out of such a one has clear meaning.

This was one, that I am now describing, was to this one and to every one, of the resisting kind of them, slow, earthy, dependent independent kind of them and as such a one was to this one and to every one that knew this one a whole one. The bottom being in this one was not resisting being , it was attacking being, reaction in this one was poignant and quick in this one but it was to this one and to every one who knew this one slow in this one because it passed through the whole rest of this one that was resisting, slow, earthy kind of being and so this one was not slow-minded but long-winded, this one had complete quick poignant decision and reaction and then passing through the rest of being in this one it made it to be to this one that it was slow-deciding, germinating in this one and it was no such thing. This was interesting to know for this one had been a whole one to the other way of feeling this one, but it was not the whole of this one, and this understanding of this one gave a completely new meaning to the being, to the history of this one.

To explain again. This one was mostly smooth, resisting self-sustaining, dependent independent being, this was the being in this one to this one and mostly to every one, only the history of the living of this one was not completely what the history of such being is in those having such being as the whole of them. Mostly this was not puzzling as it might be some other thing in this one, some incompletion of condition in this one, and this one was as this being so completely a whole one. Then it came to be clear in this one that this was not the whole of this one. The bottom nature, and the bottom nature in this one always was acting but never to this one in the talking this one did of the being in this one to any one was it existing, nor to any one not paying much attention to the history of the living in this one but just to the ways of doing things in this one was it existing, the bottom being in this one as I was saying always was there acting and sometime it was clear to some one that this one was not at the bottom slow, resisting, self-sustained, dependent independent being, at the bottom this one was quick feeling, attacking, sensitive, independent dependent being and that gave to the history of this one a new meaning.

There is one thing very interesting. Those who have this kind of mixing, all of them one thing except just the bottom and that not mixing with the rest of them but always acting, are always romantic in their notion of themselves in living. This is a natural thing, everything in them is one thing, resisting or attacking being as it may happen, everything they or any one can see in them is this thing then a complete one and yet the bottom of them always acting is another thing. This is bound to make them, such of them, have a complete creation of their own being a completed conception of their own being and always it is not the whole being in them, indeed it is never the true meaning of their being and so they have many of them a very romantic feeling in being. This is very interesting. There are many ways of having romantic feeling of one's own being, this is one of them, sometime there will be descriptions of many of them. It is very interesting to know all the ways of having romantic feeling of one's self in living. These then that I have been just describing are not romantic in living, the bottom being in them is too actually acting in them and that determines the history of them, they are romantic in the contemplation of their personality, not knowing the determining thing in them the bottom being and so they romantically conceive themselves as a whole of what is all them but the bottom being in them that really determines the being, way of doing, the history of them.

Now there will be a description of another kind of contradiction between bottom nature and the other natures in men and women. To begin again then.

This one then too is of the kind of them that have it to be a romantic temperament, a feeling of themselves as being guided by a destiny always from the beginning and unchanging. All of these then, this last one and this one, have it to be to themselves that they are as they are and nothing can change them, not from firmness of will in them, not from intention or resolution in them, but from the destiny of them always in them from the beginning. These are then this kind of men and women, all of this kind of romantic temperaments with to them a fixed destiny in them, all of these then are an almost complete one thing with another bottom, this keeps them such of them from being a complete unification of being, the bottom of them that is the opposite kind of being, if they are all resisting then the bottom always active in them is attacking being with all the quality of that kind of attacking being, if all the rest of them is attacking being the bottom being in such of them and always active in them is resisting being with all the quality of that kind of resisting being, this makes in such of them romantic feeling of themselves as being unchanging. They, this kind of men and women only know in themselves all except the bottom being in them and that makes them to themselves unchanging, having a destiny from the beginning, these then do not know in themselves the bottom being that interferes and acts and sometimes to them spoils their history for them, these then only know in themselves all the rest of themselves except the bottom being in them. This is very interesting. Perhaps Napoleon was one of this kind of men and women.

This one that I am now describing had it to be all of the being excepting the bottom being overwhelmingly powerful attacking being, and as a bottom being there was in this one the earthy type that is of the kind of resisting being that is earthy, indolent, slowly engulfing. This one then had it to have as a bottom being indolent earthy being, practical and easy and slowly engulfing in its natural way of winning, with not much energy in acting, with almost not anything of attacking being of the resisting being and this was just there as a bottom, all the rest of the being in this one which was destiny and living to this one was keen and synthetic and poignant and complete attacking being.

All through the early living of this one the bottom being was just there alive in this one and always acting but so to speak not interfering to domination, to being the real being in this one as controlling being. More and more as this one grew older and the fire of youth and the energy in this one did not hold the whole of this one together, the nature in this one separated into the top and bottom both active but not acting together. This made this one then stupidly obstinate with the attacking top in this one, lethargic with the resisting indolent bottom in this one, vain-glorious with the sense of destiny and success of the top being in this one and nervously irritable with the disturbed bottom being in this one. This is then one kind of being in men and women, these then have been two examples of this kind of being, sometime every one will understand all being in men and women.

These then are one kind of way of being one with the bottom attacking, one with the bottom the resisting kind of them, these two I have been just describing. Then these are one kind of way of being these two that I have been just describing where there is the contradiction I have been just explaining. Now this is to be a description of a kind of being where all the nature is of one kind of being and yet where there is a contradiction in the being. To begin then.

Mostly every one is sometime and sometimes for a very long time puzzling. This one I am now going to be describing was for a long time a puzzle to me. This one as I was saying was, the whole of this one, of one kind of being, of attacking being, but this one was contradictory and confusing and for a long time a very long time puzzling. This is the history of my learning this one, this is a description of the being in this one.

Thinking one's self good is very important to understand in each one. Goodness and stupid being in each one it is very important to understand in each one. Each kind of them then, each kind of men and women have their own kind of stupid being, their own kind of goodness or badness in them, each kind in men and women have their own way of feeling themselves as good inside them. Some have very much of this in them, some have very little of this in them. Some have very much stupid being of their kind of them in them, some have very little of their kind of stupid being in them. Some have very much of the goodness of their kind of being in them, some have very little of it in them. Some have very much of the badness of their kind of being in them, some have very little of it in them.

Each kind of them each kind of men and women have the kind of stupid being, the kind of goodness, the kind of badness of their kind of being in them, each one of them have the feeling of their goodness inside them in the kind of way their kind of being always has such feeling.

This is now some description of the way each kind of men and women have their own kind of way of having stupid being in them, their own kind of stupid being in them, their own kind of way of having goodness in them, their own kind of goodness in them, their own kind of way of having badness in them, of having their own kind of badness in them.

Each kind of men and women has a certain kind of stupid being, a certain kind of goodness and a certain kind of badness that is their kind of them, that is in common to all men and women of their kind of them, part of them like their kind of way of loving, fighting, working, thinking, eating, drinking, enjoying, disliking, having impatient and angry feeling.

Now there will be some description of the way each kind in men and women has their own way of having stupid being, goodness, badness, knowing their own goodness, knowing their own badness in them. I tell all this now, now when I am still a little puzzling at it. Sometime I will understand it, then I will tell more of it. Now I tell it when now I am still puzzling at it.

Each one then is of a kind of men and women. Each one then has a bottom nature of a kind of men and women in them, many have other nature or natures in them.

Two that I am now going to describe a little are each one of them of one kind of being completely. Each one of them was puzzling, one, the first one was a very long time to me baffling, this was a very curious thing and I will now begin to tell about it, to explain it, the being in this one, the learning in me of the being in this one. I tell it now when now it is still a little puzzling. I know it a little and I begin now to tell all I know yet of it.

Every one has their own being in them. Every one is of a kind of men and women. Each one is a separate one and yet always repeated.

There are then many kinds in men and women. There are two kinds of them, there are many kinds of these kinds of them, there are many kinds in each one of the many kinds of each kind of them.

Supposing there is one kind of them, that some one knows say ten of that kind of them among those that one has come to know in living. Now in these ten of that kind of them some have this kind of being that makes this kind of them as bottom being, some have other kinds of being mixed up in them with this bottom being in them. Some of these ten of them have not this kind of being as bottom being in them, they have some other kind of being in them and have this kind of being, that of the ten of them, mixed with the bottom being in them. There are some of these ten of them that have in them only this being in them, the being that makes alike these ten of them in their way of being, doing everything, feeling, loving.

As I was saying each kind of them has its own way of being stupid, being loving, being good, being bad, winning fighting, believing in themselves as being good, believing in themselves as being bad.

Each one has in him, has in her their own kind of being, each one has in him, has in her that kind of being stronger in some parts than in other parts of them, some have it in them drier, wetter, stronger, weaker, the kind of being that is their kind of being in them.

More and more I would like to make it clear to some one how I see men and women, how I see kinds in men and women. I know a good deal of it now though always I am puzzling, beginning again and again and again, feeling it all is fabrication and always I am knowing that really I see a very certain thing in my way of seeing kinds in men and women, that I am really understanding the meaning of the being in them. I know a great deal then and I tell it now when I am still puzzling.

This is a hard thing I am now beginning explaining, it is a fairly clear thing now to me, it is not all clear yet to me, I tell it now when now I am still having a good deal of puzzling thinking in my learning understanding.

There was one then and he was very puzzling. This one was to me a very long time very baffling. This one seemed all of one kind of being, this one seemed a whole being to me always and always I was not understanding. This one had been and was really something in living, this one had done important working, this one was a whole one and yet this one was not a whole one and yet surely there was in this one only one kind of being, it was very puzzling.

Say these ten then, they each one have in them some way, somehow, in some part of them a being common to all of them. Each one of them has his or her own being, each one of them is separate and resembling. Each one of them have a kind of being in them, some of them have several kinds of being mixed up in them, all of them have one certain kind of being in them, some of them have only that one kind of being in them. The one I am now thinking of describing was one of such of them, this one then had one kind of being and this was clear and yet this one was a contradiction inside him, this one was for a long time very baffling. This one is now fairly clear to my understanding, I am describing this one now when I am still a little puzzling over this one.

I know for fairly certain now something of the meaning of the being in this one and I am now beginning the telling of the meaning of the being in this one though now still I am a little puzzling over understanding this one.

As I was saying, take one kind of being, say ten men and women have this kind of being, some of these ten have other kinds of being mixed up in them but that is not what I am now discussing.

As I was saying, take ten men and women having in them a kind of being in them, not a general kind of resemblance between them but a pretty close resemblance between them, this is now a pretty small subdivision of men and women, of course there are many millions always living of this kind of them but say I have in all my living known ten of them, that is now a subdivision, a particular kind of them that have each one of them a kind of being in them that is very definite in its character in each one of them giving to each one of them a very definite way of learning, loving, fighting, escaping, having stupid being in them, having moral or unmoral or immoral meanings in them.

This then now is clear, this is a definite kind of being, this being in some way in all of these ten men and women. This kind of them is one subdivision of attacking being. This kind of them have it in them to mostly succeed fairly well in living, some of course are failing, some of every kind of being are succeeding and some are failing but some of kinds of men and women have it to have more of them succeeding than failing, some kinds of them have more of them failing than succeeding, some kinds of them have it to be divided about even in succeeding and failing in living.

This kind of being then that all these ten have in them is a kind of attacking being. In these attacking is mostly not very active in them, loving in them is attacking being and most of them have it to have loving strongly in them but in most of them loving being in them is overflowing into nervous being in them, this nervous being in them is not energy in them as it is in some where loving is nervous being, in these of them nervous being is an excess in them, they have much passion in them, it is active in them, it is nervous being in them, nervous being in them is not active loving or attacking being in them. This is very clear in them to any one knowing them, every one mostly who knows a fair number of men and women knows certainly some of them, sometime some one perhaps will know the kind of men and women I am now trying describing. It is very discouraging, I begin again.

This kind of them then has not attacking as very active in them, mostly they have in them much loving but there is in it so much nervous being draining them, not entering into the active being in them that many of them are not really active in loving. This kind of them, the kind of being these ten have in common is very clear to me from knowing these ten of them, I will now begin again to try to describe them.

These then as I was saying, those having this being in them are of the attacking kind in men and women, they most of them succeed very well in living, most of them have very considerable loving being in them, most of them have much nervous being in them. The nervous being not being energy in them gives to many of them the appearance of there being much repression in them, this is not as true of them as it seems from the nervous being always showing. The repression is an interpretation others have of them for this kind of nervous being that these have in them that is not energy in them is something like the nervous being that is generated in some men and women whose nervous being is energy in them, from repression.

All of them have this same kind of nervous being in them then, all of them of whom I have been speaking, these ten of them. Some have it more, some have it less in them, all of them have it in them and it is not energy in them, it is not from repression in them, it is part of their kind of being, those who have attacking being but not much attacking action in them, a considerable capacity for succeeding, a considerable capacity for loving. It is very important to know then that in this kind of them nervous being is not energy of action, not a result of suppresing themselves in their loving or their living.

Mostly this kind of men and women have it in them to have more loving, nervous being, intelligence, success in living, than activity in attacking, emotion and feeling and enthusiasm. These then have mostly much common sense but these have not much practical sense in living. All this is very interesting and so now I must begin again.

These ten of them have in them the same kind of being. There will be now some more description of the being in them. This last that I have been saying about the practical sense in them is not very well expressed yet and so now I will try again.

This kind of being is as I was saying an attacking being with not very much attacking fighting in them, these have in them mostly the quality of succeeding well enough in living, they are opportunists in living and they have moral conviction. Let me begin again then, I will begin again to explain the being in them.

As I was saying earlier those having attacking being have it in them to have in them a strong sense of the meaning, the emotion, the use of the facts every one knows in living. Those having in them resisting being have stronger in them a realisation of the thing itself that makes the fact rather than the sense of the meaning of the thing, the use of it. The resisting kind can love money and living not for the use, emotion, meaning, but for the thing itself as a thing existing. Sometime I will make this clearer but this must do now as a beginning.

This kind then that I am now describing have as I was saying attacking being but not much activity in attacking, they have sense for facts as attacking being have them but they have not much instinctive emotion about them or sense of the use of them, they have in short no dramatic sense for facts in living but being of the attacking kind of being these have a sense for the meaning of facts in being and so it comes that this kind of them are opportunistic, highly rationalising, unimaginative, having no instinct for meaning in anything but regarding only the meaning and the use in things, having no instinct for quality in people but wanting completely to understand and use them.

I will take for more understanding of them the moral sense in them. Say one of such of them being as is true of most of them strongly wanting success in living, such a one knows then that honesty is the best policy for him. This one then will completely realise the meaning in this saying, to him it is wisdom, as the way necessary for him to be acting to be succeeding. So far it is opportunism in him, the embracing of this conviction that honesty is the best policy for him. This then is the meaning to him in honest living, and then such a one embraces this as a moral principle, such a one then holds to this if it means ruin to him, such a one has rationally and opportunistically embraced this way of being, this one then makes of this an absolute conviction, a complete moral principle for living, this one then has no sense for opportunistically adapting himself in detail in living, such a one has no practical dramatic sense for living, such a one has attacking being but no activity in attacking, such a one has embraced a creed from the sense of succeeding, of rational opportunism, it is then a moral conviction in this one, this one then has no imagination for facts or people but this one can build a complete system for living and if such a one has a good head on him, such a one is mostly successful enough in living. Herbert Spencer was such a kind of one.

These then, these ten of them have it to have in common a kind of being that is of the attacking kind of being but these have not much activity of attacking in them, many of these are successful enough in living, mostly these have pretty strongly loving being in them, these have mostly strongly nervousness in them and this nervousness is not part of energy in them, it is not energy in them and that is the reason there is very little attacking being in them, it is something like that kind of nervousness that comes from repression in some men and women but mostly repression is not in this kind of them, mostly these are opportunists at the bottom of them though they all of them mostly at some time make of some principle a rationally constucted system and then make of that system a moral conviction, and so these of them are a curious spectacle of opportunism, rationalising passion, moral conviction, nervousness, much love, emotion.

Mind then in all of this kind in men and women is highly rationalising, mostly these have not much instinct for being in things and in men and women. What these realise as being in things and in men and women is mostly true and alright for a beginning for living but these then do not react to it in living, these rationalise it and from that they come to a principle in living that from then on all their life guides them. These have not then a capacity for growing from experiencing for they have made their conviction from their early realising and then it is in them a principle of living, mostly in all of them this original realisation in them is a fairly intelligent rationalised opportunism.

Perhaps this is clear now to some one. It is certainly a clear thing for some one to be understanding, this is certainly a clear thing in this kind of men and women.

These have then mostly quick clear minds but the results of their thinking are not quick in coming as they are all of them complicatedly rationalising, some of them think they have slow minds but this is not true of them, they have the quick minds and quick impressions of the attacking kind of being, but their minds being so rationalising it takes them some time to complete the whole thing, their mind begins with each thing and they think they are slow in taking impressions because mostly they are closed to impressions from anything as their mind when it is formulating is occupying the whole of them and until their mind opens them again they are closed to impressions and so as I was saying these mostly have little power of experiencing.

Now all this leads to very complicated things in each one having in them such a being, those having good minds, better minds than capacity for experiencing, such can have some principle of growth in them, for their minds can keep them open to all impressions they are capable of receiving and can make the most use of those impressions that they have received inside them. Those having mind only about as strong as the power of receiving impressions in them, such of them just keep going, they are fairly successful in living some of them, there is not much growth in them. There are some of them who have finer power of receiving impressions than quality of mind to direct them and these then more and more are stultified in their living by running themselves by their minds as all of those having this kind of being always do run themselves. This is now a description of learning the last kind of one as a whole one. This then is now a description of one of them, one of these ten of them.

This one for many years was baffling to me. It was evident that all the being in this one always was repeating to every one's hearing, it was evident that in this one there was not a mixture of many kinds of being and yet this one was baffling, this one had strange contradictions in him. This one said of himself that he had a slow-working mind, this one had to himself and to every one a moral passion for goodness in him, this one was to every one generous and disinterested in thinking and in being, this one was an opportunist in living, this one had very fine sensibilities to beauty and to luxury in living, this one very often was not open to any such impression, this one had a passion for being loving, this one had not any really passionate loving in him, this one had a fixed scheme of living for grace and beauty and had no grace in him and no power of creating beauty in the conditions of living around him, this one had much ambition and was very successful in living, this one then was baffling and for a long long time I was puzzling and puzzling and now this one is a clear one to me.

Each one, as I was saying, having a kind of being in them has that being in them in different intensities, proportions, they have in them too most of them different kinds of beings mixed up in them but that is not what I am now considering. Each one then of these ten of them of this kind of them that I have been describing, all of these ten of them then that I have known in living has it in them to have this nature in them the kind of nature that is common to all these ten, in different proportions, different intensities, different relation of one part to the other part of the nature and so each one of them had their own being in them, each one was separate, each one was resembling to the others of them. Some of them have other natures too in them that make the things I have been describing, acting differently in them, some of them had this being that I have been describing as a bottom nature to them, others have it as a nature mixed up with another kind of nature in them, one of them had it as the whole being in him, and this one I am now beginning to describe my learning as a whole one.

Each one sometime is a whole one to me, each one sometime is a whole one in me, this one for a long time was baffling, this one now is a whole one to me, this one now I am again beginning describing learning.

Each one having the kind of being in them that I have been just describing has in her or in him more or less of all the things, all the things in him or in her, I have been describing. Each one of these then has more or less opportunism in their feeling about living, each one of them has loving being that is of the attacking kind but not active in attacking, often very desiring, sometimes appearing engulfing, sometimes never coming into the relation of loving. Each one of this kind of them have a mind that is slow only because it takes much time in going through many logical processes to a conclusion, not slow in actual action, not slow in developing, mostly all of this kind of men and women are quite the same in ways of thinking, learning, understanding, quite from their beginning, there is then in the minds of this kind of men not much developing. Each one of them of this kind in men and women has more or less in them the way of making of whatever was the beginning of their living and the conclusions from this beginning a principle that in some is like a firm moral resolution. In all of this kind of them this acting of the mind in them cuts them off from experiencing, they are of the attacking kind in men and women, things are important to them as use, emotion, passion gives them meaning but these have not any of them activity in attacking being and so they have not imagination or dramatic sense of meaning in them, they have not a spontaneous relation to things in living, in some way in each one of them it, the experience, must go through their more or less rationalising mind before reaction acting to the fact is in them and so then they are not often getting into trouble but most of their living they are not experiencing. This is strange in them when they have strongly in them a love of beauty and luxury in them and this will be soon the history of one of such of them. In all of them then all these ten who have it to have this being in common in them, in all of them there is more or less actively in them all these things I have been describing, mostly in each one there is enough more of one part than another part of this being in them to make the meaning of their being a fairly clear thing in them, to make their living and their being have a fairly clear meaning, in some of these ten there are other natures in them, in some other nature as bottom being in them but that we are not just now considering. As I was saying many having a being in them have the balance of that being in them so kept that one kind of living, one kind of existing is natural to them and has meaning, this was true then of most of these ten of whom I have been talking, it was not true of all of them.

In one the one I am now beginning describing, the one who was a long time baffling to me, all these things I have been describing as the being of this one kind of being were equally strongly in him, all these things then, all of them were equally strongly repeating in him all through his living and so this one was baffling, for mostly in every one all the qualities in a kind of being are not equally active in them. This made this one baffling. This made this one puzzling for this one had profound impression by beauty and this was complete and poignant and quick in him and he had the rationalising mind acting on each piece of impression and shutting him off from getting deep and poignant and complete impressions from things before him and so he was puzzling, he had opportunism so strongly in him that each time he was open to a new relation with anything in life or a man or a woman he acted in this way toward them and also he had created for himself a whole rationalised scheme of living of beauty and goodness and fairness to every one because that was the way to make the living that would be successful and beautiful, to him. Always to himself he was always open to feeling beauty and goodness and nobility in living, always to himself he had made a scheme of complete living in luxury and success and winning admiration, always to himself he could completely understand everything with his mind which was to himself a great thing in him, never was he ever knowing that his running himself by his mind which was making always for him his theory of beauty and goodness and luxury was closing him to impressions of beauty and luxury and learning. This he never knew in him. He did not know his kind of a mind had never any relation to experience excepting as a beginning, when his mind was working he was shut off from experiencing, such being the way a mind works in this kind of being, and so this one was baffling, no one would ever expect one person, one man or one woman, would have in the completest form all the parts of a kind of being and so this one was baffling, there was complete contradiction in him and yet he was all of one kind of being, this one then was baffling and for a long time this one was not a whole one to me and then I understood the meaning in him, he had it in him all the qualities of this kind of being that was in any of these ten that I have said all had in them this kind of being.

This is very clear to me now. Now I am not any longer puzzling about this one. This is not very clear yet in my telling. This will be clearer when I have told of the loving being in this one.

There are many ways of having loving feeling, this one that I am now describing had loving feeling in every kind of way any one having the kind of being common to these ten could have it in her or in him.

Each kind of being has then its own way of loving, of having loving

feeling, of having it and having it to themselves as themselves acting in
it. This one, the one I am now describing had it in every way this one's
kind of being can have it.

Those having this kind of being have as I was saying much nervous
being that is not energy in them as attacking being, as loving, though it
is very much like repressed active being or repressed loving being, but
it is not that in them. This so far is clear to me. I am telling all this
now, now when it is still a little a puzzle to me.

So then this one had all the ways of having loving being this kind
of them can have it in them. Mostly this kind in men and women have
a good deal of loving being in them, though in many of them it does not
in them come to loving any man or any woman for as I was saying attacking being is not active in them, and in many of them loving being is just
there in them, being there in them as nervous being is in them which is
not attacking energy in them. Generally then in this kind of them although there is much loving being in them it does not express itself in
loving any particular one until some particular one having very strongly
being in them enormously stimulating these makes the loving being
in them active to loving that one. It is not, and this is very important
to know in them and to remember of them to understand this kind of
them, it is not that loving being is not awakened in them, it is very lively
in most of this kind of them in every moment of the living of this kind
of them, there is not restraint in this kind of them, it is that this kind of
them are of the attacking kind in men and women and attacking activity
is not active in them. This is now clear in them in the loving in them, in
the thinking in them, in the practical living in them. It is clear to me
now of them. I am not now any longer in a puzzle about them. Perhaps
sometime it will be clear to some other one from the description I have
been giving of them.

So then that is loving women in them, loving men in them, but this
is not the only loving feeling in them. These have in them another kind
of loving feeling in them, affection for goodness and beauty and nobility
in everything and in men and in women and an affection for the feeling
of being able to feel inside them loving for luxury and extravagance and
sinning. I am now describing this in them now when it is still a little a
puzzle to me. Perhaps it will be clearer to me. Now I will tell it as clearly
as I know it. I will tell it, a little confusing it as I tell it , for it is so that
I now know it. Sometime I will know more of it. Then I will certainly
tell more of it.

They have then this kind of them, they have much affectionate being
in them, not emotional affection in them but affection like the kind of
thinking being there is in them, to making of something they were experiencing as important to them a principle in them to be always in them.
Sometimes this is affection for some one, some kind of thing, for goodness,

nobility and virtue and beauty and luxury and sinning and succeeding in living by doing anything. In such a one then one of this kind of them affection that is like a moral principle in them can be for any or some or all of these things that I have been naming, and then it is with these then as in their living as I have described it in them, affection for any of these things is a constant thing in them as constant as the ruling principle they embrace with their minds for living after having rationalised it from some experiencing.

So then these ten of this kind of them all have in them the kind of loving being this kind of them have as their natural way of being. They have, most of them, very much loving being, but they have not attacking as active in them though they are of the attacking kind of being and so all of them to get it as attacking in them the loving being in them have to have strongly stimulation. Mostly all of them have much loving being always in them and mostly always every one who ever knows any one of them knows this in them but mostly always as I was saying they need very strong stimulation in the being in the other one to make it an attacking thing in them. It is not repressed in them, it is not dormant in them, it is there as evident in them to every one who knows any one of them as is the nervous being in them that is not attacking energy in them. They have then all of them, some more some less in them, but mostly all of this kind of them a good deal of such kind of loving being in them. They have in them much affection in them mostly all of them and this is in them like the thinking being in them like the rationalising some experience they have chosen and then made into a conviction like a moral principle. These then do this with a feeling for any one, with a feeling for anything, any feeling that has convinced them, they make this then, this kind of them into a conviction and they are not often getting for this new experiencing, just as they are not in working and thinking in relation to experience, as a continuous thing in living. This is clear then to some one, it is clear now to me and now I tell it, knowing it now to clearly understand it.

The one of the ten of them that I have been describing had all these kinds of ways of having loving feeling strongly in him in his living and so this one was perplexing.

Now I will finish up this one. Now I will tell of my learning this one. of this one coming to be a whole one to me.

This one was for a long time baffling to me. I was telling every one of this one when this one was still a very baffling one to me. Now this one is mostly all clear to me inside me. This one is now a whole one to me. This is the way I learned this one so that this one was a whole one to me.

As I was saying every one always is repeating the whole of them. As I was saying sometimes it takes many years of hearing the repeating in one before the whole being is clear to the understanding of one who has it as being to love repeating, to know that always every one is repeating the whole of them, to have it that sometime each one is a whole one to that one. This then the way I am now describing learning this one, this then is one of the ways then that such a one, one who has it as being to love repeating, to know that always every one is repeating the whole of them, comes to a completed understanding of every one.

This then is now a little a description of the way I learned this one so that this one is a whole one to me.

Now I will finish up this one. Now I will tell of my learning this one, of this one coming to be a whole one inside me.

This one was a long time perplexing to me because this one was very evidently made up of only one kind of being and yet always there were absolute contradictions in his being. There is a kind of being say in ten men, each one of these ten have the kind of being that is common to all the ten of them in him as being more emphasised in one direction than in the other direction. For instance in this kind of being that I have been just describing one of these ten will have the being in him so that there is in him much more strongly affection for succeeding in living than for other things in him, another will have the being in him so that the loving women is most strongly in him, some one will have the being in him so that rationalising, logical thinking will be the strongest thing in him, some of them will have the being in them so that in each one of them the having the thing they have made a moral conviction as moral conviction to perhaps almost fanaticism as the strongest thing in her or in him, this may be in one of these as a conviction of denying, of skepticism, of opportunism, of socialism, of monarchism, of irreligion, of anything. There are some then of this kind of them that have the power of experiencing strong affection for beauty or luxury or truth as strongest in them. In each one of these all the other things in this kind of being are in them but mostly in all of them there is one part of this kind of being that is strongest in them. This one that I have been just describing was different in this from these others that I have been just mentioning. This one had mostly everything of this kind of being as equal in strength in him.

This one said of himself that he had a slow mind, this one had a good mind and ran himself with this mind. This one had a capacity for profound, poignant, affectionate, intuitive experiencing of beauty, in him. This one was running himself by his mind and so, often, was shutting himself off from experiencing, his mind not letting him feel beauty in anything that his mind was not already rationally admitting as a thing to be so experiencing. This one then had the affection for truth and nobility and loyalty and made of them a moral conviction, this one had the affection for luxury and succeeding in living and being a superior being and this one made of these things a moral conviction. This one had wanting loving women in him and this one had protecting them as a moral conviction, this with loving luxury and succeeding in living and truth and loyalty and courage, and having in him the quality of not having attacking being as active in him, not having loving as attacking in him, all this made this one very confusing.

This one then was perplexing, slowly it came to me to know it to be true of him that he had not, as this one thought he had, a slow developing mind in him, the mind in him was slow only because it went on logically working when all the actual learning had been done by this one as experiencing and it seemed slow because this one believing that his mind was developing things for him let this mind run him and keep him from poignant experiencing and so this one was to himself a person slowly developing himself and everything in him and this was not true of him, he was slow-minded to himself then not because he had any slow-minded resisting being in him but because his mind was just doing with rationalising what this one had already done with experiencing. This then led to bad things in this one in developing for this one more and more believing in his mind as slowly developing in himself and slowly developing learning, let himself be run by it himself and his mind was not as fine an instrument as his experiencing and so running himself by his mind was not for this one a true way of developing. For some of this kind of them it is the true way of developing, for this one of them it was not the true way of developing.

It is now a little clear perhaps to some one how this one was perplexing to me to make of this one a whole one, always this one was then a puzzle to me, two things then made this one clear to me, the knowing that his mind was not a slow steadily developing thing, the recognition that although there was only one kind of being in this one it was not a unified thing in him. It was not unified in him as I found out by more thinking about this one because this one had all the parts of the kind of being that was his kind of being equally strongly in him and that then could not be a unified one for there was nothing making a bottom and so then this one was clear to me, this one was then a whole one to me, this one then was such a one as I have been describing.

Now to give a little description of one who was of the resisting kind of being and had a different kind of complication from that in this one I have just been describing but one who also had only one kind of being in him.

This one was one of one of the kinds in men and women that have resisting being in them. As I was saying when I was describing resisting being, these, those having resisting being in them, can have this being in them in various ways depending on the conditions so to be speaking of the substance in them, the substance that is them.

This one that I am now beginning a little to tell about to make the fifth one of the six that I am now describing in this explaining of the way natures are and are mixed up in men and women, this one had in him resisting being and one kind of resisting being only in him and not any other kind of nature in him. This one was perplexing too to every one but this one was perplexing mostly to every one for a different reason from that in the case of any of the others that I have been describing. This one was perplexing to every one by reason of his failing to succeed in living and this in this one was perplexing to every one that ever came to know this one. This is now a little a history a little an explanation of this one, a little a description of learning to understand the being in this one.

This one was then of the resisting kind in men and women but as I was saying, sometimes it is not easy to know it in one whether the being in that one is of the resisting kind in them or of the attacking kind in them. This is now perhaps to some one a little clearer in the way I know it in men and women from the description I have just been giving of a kind of them that have attacking being more or less as static in them.

It is not then always easy even after much knowing of some one to know whether the being in that one is attacking or resisting, in them.

As I was saying, resisting being in some is in such a thin layer in them that reaction in them is as quick in them as in those having attacking being in them. In some, as I was saying, those have resisting being in them have this in them as a mass dry in the centre and only actively penetrable for reaction by them of the surface of the being in them. In these then resisting being may be very quick being, in some of such of them it may be almost brilliantly quick being in them but mostly in those of them that are brilliantly quick the central portion of them is not dead dry in them it is living enough in them to give meaning to the clever quick surface reaction in them. This is very clear to my feeling, this is very clear in my knowing of this kind in men and women, this must then sometimes be clearly made into a description. I am now beginning again to make a description of this kind of being in men and women.

There are then many millions always living having resisting being in whom the resisting solid mass of being in each one of them is not acting and so such of them never in their living are slow in their thinking or their working. In such of them the part in them that is active in them is the surface of this being and this gives to such of them clever thinking and being. There are all varieties in this kind of them as there are in all the kinds of them in all the resisting kinds of them in all the attacking kinds of them. I am always feeling each kind of them as a substance darker, lighter, thinner, thicker, muddier, clearer, smoother, lumpier, granularer, mixeder, simpler like every kind there is of earth or of anything and always I am feeling in each one of them their kind of stuff as much in them, as little in them, as all of a piece in them, as lumps in them held together sometimes by parts of the same sometimes by other kinds of stuff in them and always sooner or later for each one I am feeling the stuff in them acting in them and so sometime each one I am ever knowing comes to be made of something really existing that is them and each one of them sometime then is to me a kind of stuff that all of a certain kind of men and a certain kind of women have in them as the material in them that is bottom nature in them, that is other nature or natures in them. Each one then sometime comes to be to me made out of a real something that always is there acting and that is that one and sometime then I really know that one, I really understand the meaning of the being in that one.

The one I am now beginning to describe a little for there will not be here now much description of this one, this one was of the resisting kind of them and there was in this one clever being for this one was of the kind of them I have been just describing, the central mass in this one the slower fairly clear brown not completely dry mass in him was not so active in him as the surface of the mass in him that was quickly cleverly reacting. But in this one this caused trouble in him that the central mass was not quite dry in him, in some places the central mass was profoundly active and this made a complication in this one that made it that this one was not successful in living and this is very very interesting and this is now a little a description of this one in which description there will be a mingling of the history of this one, of the description of the being in this one, of the learning by some to understand the meaning of the being in this one.

This one as I was saying never really succeeded in living and that was surprising to every one for this one was very clever and quick and energetic, this one had really a quality of bottom thinking, this one was strong in keeping going at working and always this one was not succeeding in living, was not really succeeding in anything. Always this one, though always this one was working steadily and sometimes very cleverly, this one never really finished anything. Always this one was capable of real thinking and always this one was never understanding anything in himself or in any one. And always this one knew it in him that he was failing. Always this one had an exalted nature in him and always this one was not in any way petty in his being and always this one was always failing in being decently good to any one. Always then this one was failing in living and this was perplexing him and perplexing to every one that ever came to know this one, that ever came to think about this problem. This was the history of him.

The being in him was as I was saying resisting being and this one had in him only the one kind of being, that was the bottom nature in him, there was not in him any other nature or natures of any other kind of being in him and in this this one was like the last one I was describing. This one was very different though from the last one I was describing for this one had not all the being in him possible to the kind of being that was his kind of being. This one had however certain parts of the kind of being in him that were natural parts of his kind of being, that without other parts of that being being in him made a fundamental contradiction in his being and this was the meaning of the being in this one.

To begin again then with thinking of a mass of being of the resisting substance very active at the surface and active inside toward the center only here and there, this was the being in this one and this caused the trouble in this one.

Always then this one had in him active in him isolated spots in the central resisting mass in him, these were in him as the conceptions that were the starting in him of various schemes of working, mostly the actual working in him was done by the quick clever surface of him, always then these central live spots in the whole mass of him would be reacting to all the mass of work the surface of him had been doing and there was not enough self-consciousness in him to know that it was a poorer kind of work than he had wanted that he had been doing and it was to him only that that time he had not succeeded in doing the work he had been planning, and he must just begin again. So it went on with him and so he never was finishing anything and the two kinds of activity of the being in him being that they were of the same kind of being in him never came to struggle together in him they just went on in him and so he never was succeeding in his living, he never was succeeding in anything, he never could finish anything with all his steady energetic patient working.

So then when some one has in her or in him separate pieces active of the one kind of being in them and not adjusted so that one is dominating or when as in the last one I was describing some one has all the pieces possible of one kind of being equally active in him such a one can never really come to a completely self-conscious being, such a one may be successful in living but such a one never has in him a unified being, mostly such a one has not in him any struggling of the pieces with each other in him. Of this last I am not yet absolutely certain.

The meaning of the being in this last one came to some who had often at moments thought about this one. Mostly no one puzzled about this one, failing in living in this one, though succeeding in living could have come to this one to every one, had something about it curiously inevitably to any one who ever came to know this one, and so as I was saying mostly no one really puzzled about this one. One day some were thinking about the queer history of this one and they began to think about a specific case in which this one had not finished something and then it came to be clear to them for they realised then that this one always was planning and criticising his complete work with the chunks of slow solid central intelligence and feeling in this one and always this one was working with the surface of this one and this one was not self-conscious ever to criticise his way of working, only to criticise the specific result he had been achieving and so this one always had to be beginning again and this was then the history of this one. Sometime prehaps there will be written a complete history of this one, sometime perhaps there will be written a complete history of every one.

Now to give one little additional example. There will be very little telling about this one. This one was different from the two last ones I have been describing, this one had a mixing of natures in him and very little in him of each of the kind of natures in him. There was as a bottom being in him a kind of resisting being. This one had as bottom being rather turgid resisting being. This one had not much bottom being in him, not much of this rather turgid resisting being in him. This one had such a kind of bottom being in him, enough of it in him to be always evident in him to any one really looking at him. This one had other natures mixed up in him with this bottom nature of him in him. There was then not so very much bottom nature in him, all that there was of it was of this quite turgid between sodden resisting and engulfing resisting being. There was enough of this in him as a bottom nature to him so that every one really looking hard at him knew this in him. It was in this way, by looking at him and so understanding, that one knowing this one knew the bottom nature there in this one.

There were then other natures in this one. There was in this one mixed up with the bottom nature in this one two other kinds of natures in this one, one a kind of resisting being, one a kind of attacking being. The kind of resisting being that was in him was of the kind that I was describing in the first of these six that I am now finishing. It was a kind of smooth dark very thick engulfing being that has with it as a way of being, much complete vanity and separation from contact with any one and much needing of indolence and elegance and luxury to make life a pleasant thing for such a one, elegance in luxury is a need for such a one. The kind of attacking being there was in this one was of the kind that I have been just describing in the one before the last one I have been describing. This being gave to this one I am now describing an affection for all beauty in living and in being, it gave to this one that in the beginning of his conscious living this one had embraced as a conviction the need of steady, unexalted, slightly ambitious working.

This one having the rationalising mind of the kind of attacking being that was one of the natures in him this one then knew very early in his living that loving a beautiful life and needing elegant luxury for pleasant living and yielding to these things in him would soon lead him to be dominated by the bottom being of him, the sodden resisting mixed with engulfing resisting bottom being in him and this would lead him so that sooner or later the beautiful life would be turned by him into an ugly one. This one dimly then knew this in him, this one as I was saying had mixed up in him the kind of attacking being that has it to be rationally minded and amibitous of succeeding in living and having a power of it making itself into a life-long resolution and a carrying of it out completely during a whole living as if it were the natural way of being in him, an instinctive being in him, the kind of living best suited to the purposes rationally embraced by such a one. This one then that I am describing knew that steady unexalted working which was not to this one the whole natural way of being was the only way of living for this one to keep this one from making ugly, beautiful elegant luxurious being that was in him and that in this working this one must not wait for the stimulation of experiencing, working must go on in him always and experiencing and needing elegant luxury and the bottom being in him must just be there acting while always this one was working, always this one was succeeding fairly well in living. Perhaps later this one would not succeed so well in living, perhaps this one would be more and more worn out with his working. Perhaps this is what would happen to such a one. This is a description of one, one who had it in him to not be able to have a beautiful elegant luxurious life in living because then later the bottom being in this one would make the beautiful life an ugly one. This one then lived by energised conviction in the attacking kind of being there was in him mixed with the other being in him. This one then was one that one could know the bottom being of him by looking at him, mostly in his living he was working by energised conviction, sometimes he would be worn out and then he would be not succeeding very well in living but the balance of natures in him would be in him as it had been always in his living. There was not then in this one any active struggle of the natures in him, but keeping them so balanced in him although it was not an effort in him for energised vocation of working was as naturally active as all the other kinds of being that were in him, that being the peculiarity of the type of attacking being that this one had in him, the keeping them so balanced in him was wearing, not to him, for it was not an effort in him, but was wearing to his whole being, his whole being would wear itself out by excessive spontaneous equilibration and so this one more ard more then would be not successful in living but always up to the ending of the acting living in this one the equilibration of natures in him would be what I have been describing. Here ends then the describing of the learning of the natures in the being of six kinds in men and women.

Now then to begin again the history of Martha Hersland and of every one she ever knew in living. Always there will be here writing a description of all the kinds of ways there can be seen to be kinds of men and women. There will be here then written the complete history of every one Martha Hersland ever came to know in her living, the fundamental character of every one, the bottom natures in them, the other natures in them, the mixtures in them, the strength and weakness of everything they have inside them.

Now then to begin again with a few men and women and now to begin those of them as beginning. Now to begin again the history of Martha Hersland, to give a history of her as beginning. Then to go on with the history of Martha Hersland and of every one she ever came to know in her living. Now to begin with the beginning of the living of Martha Hersland. Now to begin the description of the being in Martha Hersland in her beginning.

Sometime there will be a complete telling of all young living, feeling, talking, thinking, being. Some have their real being to themselves in young living, some do not have it then to themselves in them. Later there will be a description of all the kinds of ways there are of feeling themselves in young being.

This is now some description of being, of men and women in their beginning, when they are children, they have then ways of being resembling to each other that some of them lose in their later living, there will be now some description of Martha Hersland in her beginning.

Soon now there will be much description of the being in men and women when they are young, when they are children, when they are babies, when they are growing into young men and young women, there will be then soon much description of the being coming out of them then as repeating, then when they are beginning, when they are babies and children and then growing into men and women.

This will soon be a description of many men and women in beginning, the being young in them, the being children.

This is now a beginning of a description of the being in Martha Hersland as beginning.

In some the nature in them is clearer when they are very young, in some when they are young, in some when they are not so young, in some when they are old ones. Always in each one it is there repeating, sometime some one knows it in each one, sometime some one will know it in every one that one is ever knowing.

Sometime there will be a history of all young living, feeling, talking, thinking, being. Some have their real being in young living, some do not have it then in them. Later there will be a history of all of them.

One little boy does something to another little boy who does not like it, he shows no sign of reacting to it the little boy who does not like it. He seems not to know and then not to remember to be angry with it, his reaction is so slow to it. Then he hits out and often the first little boy is surprised at it. This often happens when one little boy does something to another little boy who does not like it.

This is the way many little boys do it and they are of many kinds the little boys who do this when some other little boy, some little girl, some one does something and they do not like it.

This is then the way many little boys do it, this is the way that some little girls do it.

One little girl, one little boy, some one, many do something to a little girl who does not like it, she shows just then no sign of reacting to it, the little girl who does not like it. She is not angry, she seems not to remember then to be angry, her reaction is not there then to it. Then she does something violent to show it and often then the one that did something to that little girl is surprised at it, that one then has forgotten all about it. This very often happens when a little girl, when a little boy, when some one does something to a little girl who does not like it.

This is then the way many little boys and little girls do something when some one does something and they do not like it. They are of many kinds the little boys and little girls who do something in this way when some one has done something and they have not liked it. Some women and some men do this way in their later living, many little boys and many little girls do this way when they are very little ones and then later they change, it changes in them the way to do it, the way to act to any one who does something and they do not like it. Some have their real being in young living, some do not have it then in them. Now there will be a description of some who have and some who have not their real being in young living.

There are many then little boys and little girls who have the way of acting I have been just describing when some one does something to them and these then do not like this thing that one has been doing, has done to them.

As I was saying some one does something to some little one who does not like it, the little one then shows no sign of reacting to this thing, the little one that does not like it. The little one shows then no feeling, the little one then is not remembering, the little one then does some violent thing to the one that has done the thing the little one was not liking. The other one then has forgotten and is surprised at the violent action of the little one. This often happens when one little one, when some one, does something to a little one and that little one does not like that thing.

As I was saying this is often happening. As I was saying there are many little ones who have this way of acting when any one has done something they have not been liking.

As I was saying there are many kinds of little ones who have this kind of way of acting when some one had done something they were not then liking. This is then a very common way of acting. There are then many little ones who have this way of acting when some one has done something they were not liking.

So then there are many kinds who can have this way of acting when they are little ones, many kinds of men and women.

As I was saying some have their real being in young living, some do not have it then in them. As I was saying in some the nature in them is clearer when they are very young, in some when they are young, in some when they are not so young, in some when they are older or ending. Always in each one it is there and repeating.

As I was saying this way of acting that I have been just describing can be in various kinds of men and women when they are little ones, when they are in beginning. There are very many little ones that have such a way of acting when some one has been doing something they have not been liking. In some it is from the being in them, in some it is from being being in beginning then in them.

Some have their real being showing in young living, some do not have it showing very clearly in them then. Always in each one it is then there repeating. Always in every one sometime it is clear to some one.

There are then many kinds of men and women who have the kind of way of acting I have been just describing, when they are little ones. Some of such of them have attacking being in them as bottom being in them, some of such of them have resisting being in them as their natural way of fighting. This is not very clear then from the action in them when some one has done something they have not been liking. There must be always a description of every way some one can think of men and women, in their beginning, in their middle living, in their ending. There must be always an expression of every way some one can feel kinds in men and women in their beginning, in their middle living, in their ending. Every one has their own way of seeing every one they come to know in their living. Always then all this makes a completed history of every one.

Every one then has their own way of seeing every one, every one has some that are more complicated to them than other ones. To some every one is or is not a man or woman, in their beginning, in their middle living, in their ending, like every other one. Some say of some one they are seeing, he is like every other one, some have a very different feeling seeing this one, every one has some way of making kinds in men and women, every one finds some one some time confusing, not easy to be certain of the kind that one is then, mostly every one sometime comes to a decision about each one, some come very nearly to never deciding about some one, some find it harder to decide about children what kind of being they have in them, some about men, some about women, some about many, some about almost every one, some about almost no one.

There are then many ways of feeling, of thinking men and women in their beginning, in their middle living, in their ending. Some are very confusing to some, others very confusing to others, some because of their being, some because of their training, some because of their ambition, some because of the activity some because of the quietness in them, some because of the nature in them being in beginning, some because of the nature in them being complete in them, some because of the nature in them being coming to an ending.

Each one sometime is a whole one, in them. Each one sometime is a whole one, to some one, to themselves inside them, to some one knowing them, sometime in their living. This coming together of them to be one inside them, in some comes to be in them in the beginning of their living, in some in the middle of their living, in some at the ending of their living, they come together inside them to be a whole one in them, sometime, mostly every one. Some come together to be one in them in different kinds of ways in different times in living, some seem to come together and are not really together then, some really come together as one and come together really sometime as another whole one inside them, mostly when some one has come together to some one it makes that one more or less interesting than that one was before to the one knowing that one. To some then the one that has come together to be a whole by reason of having come together is then no longer interesting, the mystery of that one is then ended to the one knowing that one as a whole one, this is not very uncommon.

Some are so uncertain in their kind of them, the kind that have the being that is them not very strongly in them, or else very thinly spread out in them, or rather vacant in them, or very mixed up in them, there are many that almost never really are a whole one inside them or are a whole one that is almost without form and substance in them and these then when one knows this of them, these who then never come really to be a whole one to any one, to themselves inside them, these then have not any interest to any one as not being a whole one in them. Mostly those having it as possible to be really a whole one are interesting until they come together inside them to themselves or to some one, mostly after that they are to many that know them less interesting ; many after that coming together are more interesting to those that knew them, mostly all of them those becoming then more, those becoming then less interesting, in short mostly all men and women coming to be a whole one inside them and to those that know them are more simply repeating themselves to every one.

Some as I was saying are more whole ones in them when they are little ones some when they are young ones, when they are beginning their living, than they are any other time in their living. Some and many men and women are of this kind of them are more entirely whole ones in them and to every one in their middle living. Some in the ending of their being are really whole ones to themselves and to others for the first time in their living.

This coming together in them to be a whole one is a strange thing in men and women. Sometimes some one is very interesting to some one, very, very interesting to some one and then that one comes together to be a whole one and then that one is not any more, at all, interesting to the one knowing that one, that one then is shrunken by being a whole one, some have not that happen to them by being a whole one, some are richer then, all are solider then to those knowing them when they come together inside them. It is very strange this coming together to be a whole one. As I was saying some come together as different whole ones in different times in their living, some seem to come together inside them but this is not real in them, some by their thinking, by their living come to come together as a richer whole one than could have been expected from them, often there is some little thing in some one those knowing that one are hardly noticing and that keeps that one from coming together until that one in his being has come to be richer than any one knowing that one, than that one ever expected to be in his being, sometimes some one has something in them that seems not important being in them and that keeps them open to growing and that one comes together then later as a richer whole one than any one knowing that one thought ever to find that one, and then there are very many of them that lose rich being with losing their younger living, there are many that lose it with losing a certain kind of stimulation, there are many that have a covering of passion, of emotion, of quick or slow reaction to everything, that covers them, and sometime to some one they come together to be a whole one without that covering, sometimes sometime to every one, inside them they come together to be a whole one without any one then feeling the covering on them which is not lively then in its active being and such a one may then be very dissapointing, such a one is a dry whole one when every one knowing that one felt that one a rich whole until that one came together as a dry whole one. And so on and so on, the ways of coming together are many and interesting, more and more to every one, every one sometimes is a whole mostly every one sometime comes together in them as a whole one. Some as I was saying almost never come together in them as a whole one, some of such a kind of them are then not any longer interesting when it is almost certain of them that they will not come together in them ever to be a whole one inside them, some of such of them keep on being tantalising because they come so nearly again and again to be whole ones inside them.

This then of coming to be whole ones sometimes in them which is sometime in mostly all men and women, this is very interesting. Some as I was saying never come really to be a whole one inside them not at any time in their living not in their beginning, not in their middle living, not in their ending. These are of many kinds, some have it that they never come to be a whole one in them because they are made of little lumps of one kind of being held together or separated from each other, as one comes to feel it in them, the lumps in them from each other by other kind of being in them, sometimes by other kind of being in them that is almost the complete opposite of the lumps in them, some because, the lumps are melting always into the surrounding being that keeps the lumps from touching, in some because the kind of being in them is spread out so thin in them, that everything they have learned, that they like to be in living, all reaction to everything interesting, in them, has really nothing to do in them with the thin spread being in them. There are other ones who have many kinds of being in them and none ever really dominating, and there are many kinds of ways of being so that at no time really such a one is a whole one in them but really mostly every one sometime comes together in them to be a whole one, in some part of their living, sometimes earlier in their living in loving or in working and then later in their living in natural development of themselves settling in them. There are many ways of disguising the whole being in each one, some have a stronger disguise in their beginning than in their middle living or in their ending. Soon now there will be some discussing of the disguising of whole being in young living.

Some as I was saying never come to be whole ones inside them. Some are always whole ones though the being in them is all a mushy mass with a skin to hold them in and so make one. Such a one is a whole one and of such a one I am now beginning a description.

These others I have been describing that have it in them to be made some of lumps of one kind of being held together by other kind of being in them, some where all the kinds of being are mingling in them, some where there are little lumps of being and none of them connected with the other lumps that are part of them, and all the other kinds of them that never have it in them to be a whole one inside them not at any time in their living, though they may be active enough in living, these then all of them are very different from the one I am now beginning describing.

This one, the one I am now beginning describing was of the independent dependent kind of them, this one was of that kind of them, the independent dependent kind of them, the mass that in the different kinds of them was worked into different concentrations to make them. This one then that I am now describing, and always there are many existing like this one, this one then was a whole one ; and all those having independent dependent being have the kind of material being that is the whole of this one.

Sometime there will be a description of a complete undifferentiated one that is of the dependent independent kind of them. Now there will be a little description of this one a completely undifferentiated independent dependent one, and then there will be a description of how Martha Hersland was made like this one only more concentrated in her being and then there will be the history of the beginning of being in Martha Hersland.

This one then, this one that is a whole one, a mushy mass of independent dependent being with a skin holding it together from flowing away from this one, holding it together to make of this a whole one, this one then is a real one, and always there are many living just like this one in their being, though each one of them is a whole one, separate and yet very resembling the one to the other one, and each one is an individual one to themselves and each one is a whole one.

This one then is a whole one, is all of one kind of one and all of it in this one, the being in this one is of the same consistency and concentration. This one is of the independent dependent kind of being.

This one always is and was and will be a whole one, always in this one's beginning, in this one's middle living, in this one's ending, always this one was a whole one, the same kind of whole one from the being a baby to the being a dying and dead one. Always this one is a whole one and this is now some description of this one.

It is interesting to see the substance that is independent dependent beings in so many ways in so many kinds of men and women, it is interesting to see this substance that has so many kinds of ways of being in many kinds in men and women, it is interesting to see it completely fluid in this one, to see all its activities in this one, sometimes it is an uncomfortable feeling to know it so well from this one when one is knowing some kinds of men and women having in them independent dependent being, sometimes it makes one turn away from seeing the being in some so that one will not know it too clearly in them that they have in them independent dependent being and that is the being in the one I am now beginning to be describing. Independent dependent being is the being in the one I am now beginning describing. There will not be here now much description of this one, there will be here now a little description of this one and how this one was a whole always in all the living of this one, in the beginning, in the middle living, in the ending of this one. There will be a very little description now of this one and then a real beginning of Martha Hersland who is of the independent dependent kind of them.

This one then was as I was saying always a whole one. This one was a whole one always, a whole one because there was only one kind of being in this one always in the same lax condition and with a skin to separate it from the world around this one. This made of this one a whole one.

This one is very existing to my feeling. This one is of the independent dependent kind of them. This one was always a whole one, this one all her living was repeating the whole being there was in this one and it was all always completely there to every one, the whole being in this one, to every one who ever knew this one, always there to every one when this one was a baby or a little one, or a young girl or a young woman, or a woman in her middle living, or in her ending. There are always very very many women, very many men like this one, always existing. This one was and is and will be always a real one to every one that ever knew or knows or will come to know this one. This one is a real one in herself and to every one. This one is of the independent dependent kind of them. This one all her living was always a complete one and every one always knew the whole being of this one. This is now some description of this one.

This one is then of the independent dependent kind of them, this one is all independent dependent being in solution. Of this one now I will give a very little description.

This one is all independent dependent being in solution, this is now a little description of this one, one of the independent dependent kind of them, one always all her living always a whole one, one being independent dependent being in solution, one being all her living always of the same concentration of being, the same whole one, when this one was a baby, a young one, an older one and then an old one and then dying and then no longer one and always then there are others like this one. Always there are many many millions of every kind of men and women and this makes many stories very much realler, there being so many always of the same kind of them. It makes it realler then when in a story there are twelve women, all alike, and one hundred men, all alike, and a man and a woman completely resembling the one to the other one of them and always then it makes circuses more interesting for always then each one doing something in a circus is a kind of men or women and each one is completed, concentrated at the moment each one has the music stopped and does the hard thing one has been preparing all his life and that makes a living for that one, makes the living of that one ; this is then very interesting and always circuses more and more are interesting to any one interested in kinds in men and women and now to begin again with this one the one that was of the independent dependent kind of them, that was all independent dependent being in a flabby state of being, that was always a whole one for this one had a skin that held this one from flowing over everything and that made this one a whole one, that made this one an individual one as every one is who ever is a man or woman and so then this one is a real one and now there will be of this one here now a very little description.

This one was then once a very little one, a baby and then a little one and then a young girl and then a woman and then older and then later there was an ending to her and that was the history of this one.

This one always was the same one to herself and to every one when she was a very little one, a baby, and then a little one and then a bigger one and then a very considerably bigger one and then a sick one and then no longer one.

This one was always the same whole one to herself and to every one when she was a very little one, then when she was a little one, when she was then a bigger, when she was a very considerably bigger one and then when she was just continuing and then when she was ending and dying.

This one always then was the same one, sometimes she was bigger than at other times, sometimes she was fatter, sometimes she was sicker, sometimes she had children around her, always she was held together to be one, to be a whole one by the skin of her, always she was of the independent dependent kind of them, always this was all the history of her.

In some the nature in them is clearer when they are very young, in some when they are young, in some when they are not so young, in some when they are getting older, in some when they are old ones. This one was always to every one the same one. This one always was the same one. When this one was a little one, a very little one, an older one, a very old one, always this one was the same one, always this one was all independent dependent being in solution. Knowing this one completely is then a very important thing, knowing this one completely will make it easier to know all of the men and women having in them independent dependent being, all the kinds there are of independent dependent kinds in men and women.

This one then was in the beginning a little baby and then a little girl and then a woman and always every one knew all the being in this one, the being that was never changing in concentration or in action. This one was a flabby mass of independent dependent being held together by the skin surrounding for so this one had individual being. This one then was one that had this meaning, the being all independent dependent being in possibility of formation. This one then was a very important one, there are always many millions of them living and each one of them is held together as a whole one by the skin of each one. This one then is independent being in solution.

As I was saying those having independent dependent being have attacking as their way of fighting, loving, winning. Resisting in such of them as I was saying is mostly in them stupid being. This is the natural being in them. This one was so slow always in her attacking that it mostly was resisting in her as it mostly, the attacking being in this one, just was barely in motion.

This one was of the independent dependent kind of them, attacking being was so slow in action that it made of this one a mass that was resisting, that was mostly all stupid being. This one was as I was saying of the independent dependent kind of them. This one started somewhere into action, it all would be slowly wobbling and so make what was attacking being but any one coming against this one would only be feeling it as a mass to stick in and so think it as a mass resisting, really this one was of the independent dependent kind of them, really this one had attacking as a way of fighting, as a way of loving. This one was a whole one because this one was held together by a skin, as I was saying. This one always was a whole one, when this one was a young one, a very young one, an older one, a very old one. This one was like many other men and women, this one was like many many other men and women as having independent dependent being. This one then was like very many other babies when this one was a baby too, this one was like many other children when this one was a child, this one was like many other young men and young women when this one was a young woman, this one was like many other men and women when this one was a woman, this one was like many other old men and old women when this one was an old woman, this one was different from all the others of them for this one had her own skin and so was separated from all the others of them that have or had or will have the same kind of being to make them, they each one of them are different from all the others of them like them for each one, every one, has their own skin that cuts them off from all the other ones and so each one, even of this kind of them, are individual ones, whole ones to themselves and to everyone ; this one was like many very many men and women, this one was like all of them that have in them independent dependent being, that have in them anything of independent dependent being. This one then is interesting, knowing this one is then an important thing. I know this one very completely in the whole being of this one. This one is then the simplest form of independent dependent being. Every one having in them anything of independent dependent being is connected with this one then by the being in that one and by the being in this one. This is then now the beginning of really knowing independent dependent being in every one ever having in them any of such being. More and more there will be much description of independent dependent being. More and more I will know more of independent dependent being. More and more there will be more understanding in every one of independent dependent being.

Some have their real being in them in young living, some do not have it then in them. Now there will be some description of young living in some.

Some have their real being in them in very young living, some do not have it then in them. Now there will be a little description of very young living in one.

This one, and the one I am now beginning describing is Martha Hersland and this is a little story of the acting in her of her being in her very young living, this one was a very little one then and she was running and she was in the street and it was a muddy one and she had an umbrella that she was dragging and she was crying. "I will throw the umbrella in the mud," she was saying, she was very little then, she was just beginning her schooling, "I will throw the umbrella in the mud" she said and no one was near her and she was dragging the umbrella and bitterness possessed her, "I will throw the umbrella in the mud" she was saying and nobody heard her, the others had run ahead to get home and they had left her, "I will throw the umbrella in the mud," and there was desperate anger in her; "I have throwed the umbrella in the mud" burst from her, she had thrown the umbrella in the mud and that was the end of it all in her. She had thrown the umbrella in the mud and no one heard her as it burst from her, "I have throwed the umbrella in the mud," it was the end of all that to her.

It is very hard telling from any incident in any one's living what kind of being they have in them. Kinds in being is a subject that is very puzzling. Martha Hersland had independent dependent being but this that I have just been telling might have been in the living of a little one having independent dependent being, might have been in the living of a little one having dependent independent being, might have been in the living of a little one having a mixture in its being. This then was in the living of Martha Hersland when she was a little one but as I was saying it is very hard to know from anything in any one's living the kind of being in them. Slowly some one comes to know the being in some one. Slowly then now every one reading will know all the being in Martha Hersland. This is then a beginning.

Some have the real being in their living in their young living, some do not have it then in them. Now there will be some description of young living in some.

Sometime there will be a history of all young living, feeling, talking, thinking, being. Some have their real being mostly in their young living, some do not have it then at all in them. Later there will be a history of all these, of every one.

There are many ways of making kinds in men and women when they are in their beginning when they are children. They are then each one of them like some others, like some other children, they are each one of them something of themselves then, always somehow a little, some much very much, themselves inside them, each one, and each one are like many other ones, many other children. There are many ways of making kinds in men and women in their beginning, there are many ways of making kinds in children. In each way of making kinds of them there is a different system, a different way of feeling, a different way of thinking them as being resembling one to others of them. Martha Hersland as I was saying was of the independent dependent kind of them. Martha knew in her early living a certain number of children, some I have already been describing, now there will be more history of some, more history of others of them. As I was saying Martha was throwing the umbrella in the mud with angry feeling as she was telling and nobody was hearing. As I was saying no one knowing this as having been Martha's way of acting then when she a little one was filled full of angry feeling, with despairing feeling, with responsible feeling, with frightened feeling, no one then could be very certain of the kind of being Martha had in her. Not any one could know then whether Martha was of the kind of them having attacking as their natural being, the kind of them having resisting as their natural being. Some have their real being in young living, some do not have it then in them. In those having it then strongly in them sometime some one watching them can know it in them. Mostly it is harder to know it in them then in their beginning than in their later young living. Always it is a difficult thing, in some it is almost impossible in their beginning living to know the being in them, in some it is easy then. Now there will be a little description of young living in some.

Knowing a map and then seeing the place and knowing then that the roads actually existing are like the map, to some is always astonishing and always then very gratifying. To some there is the same thing in living and to such a one seeing each one they are knowing as young ones and older ones and very old ones, and seeing them then as having in them the kind of being that hearing others talking, and reading what others have written, makes every one know is the nature of human being knowing this then in every one at each period in them is to some as I was saying astonishing and then gratifying, is to some as I was saying knowing a place after knowing a map of such a place is to some to their feeling an astonishment and then a gratification. This is then always there all their living in some, that is to say these ones come to know in those of them that are of their own generation, not children being, though in some even that is known to them by hearing and reading, in other children around them, they being then children, in some of such of them then there is a self-consciousness then enough to make them know then even when they are children children being, it comes to be more strongly in them then when they are young men and women, it comes to be to them then almost overwhelming as astonishment and gratification in their middle living to find themselves and those of their own age around them looking like men and women in their middle living, acting, living like men and women in their middle living, this is then to them very astonishing, to some it is gratifying, to some of such of them it is terrifying, they are then, they themselves and others around them as they remember their fathers and their mothers when they themselves were children, this is then as I say to many of such of them who have this in them very astonishing, to some very gratifying, to some even terrifying, and there are then all kinds of feeling in between about this thing.

This then, this realising is strongest in men and women of those around them of their own age in living when they themselves are having in them then that living that is to them the thing they have known like a map of living and then they know it in those around them of their own time of living and in themselves then and to many very many it is then astonishing, to some then gratifiying, to some then almost terrifiying, to some it is overwhelming then to know it really then inside really completely then inside them, that all living is always repeating, that they are like every one else who has or ever has had or ever will have in them middle living, like them in the way they are then in their looks, in their troubles with their health or happiness or working or children. It is to many then overwhelming that they know then that everything they have been hearing or reading about living is true of them, that they are in their middle living, that all those they are knowing of about the same age as they are themselves then are then also in that middle living that they have known always from reading, from seeing, from hearing and that is to many very astonishing, to some who have it in them to love repeating in living very gratifying, to some who are beginning to be a little weary then very satisfying, to many then almost or completely terrifying. This is then there, the understanding of being in middle living in such a one, and then there is in such a one an understanding of men and women they are remembering who were when they knew them in middle living, there is then in such of them a new realisation of every one, for every one must have sometime in them middle living.

There are then many who have sometime in them the feeling I have been describing with a map and seeing the place and knowing then the roads are really existing like the maps of them. This is to very many always each time astonishing.

They are some who have then a feeling of knowing other children, knowing themselves, they themselves being then children, as being like the children they know from reading from hearing people talking about being in children. Mostly every one does not know it in this way, the being in children, many know it only from remembering themselves and others who were around them then, from knowing children, from knowing sometime every one, from having children of their own or from other ones around them having them, from knowing some in their later living whom they remembered as children but did not realise then the being in them. Mostly every one a little sometime in their living realise themselves and others as being like children, like men, like women they have come to know in reading or from hearing about them.

There is then the knowing kinds in men and women from the character in them, the nature in them, the mind, the passion, the way of winning, working, loving, dying, having religion in them, the way of giving and the way of receiving, and the way of taking, and the way of accepting, and the way of escaping in them ; there are many ways of knowing kinds in men and women from habits of training, of grammar, of playing and washing and working in them, and doing nothing ; there are then many very many ways of knowing kinds in men and women, from prettyness and ugliness in them, from ways of dressing, from all the ways they have of being and then there are ways of knowing men and women as being in their beginning, as babies and children, and then being young grown men and women, and then men and women in their middle living, and then men and women in their ending.

Some find it harder to decide about children what kind of being they have in them, than about men and women as young men and women, than men and women as men and women in their middle living, as men and women in their ending. Some find it harder to know what kind of being they have in them, the women than the men, some find it harder to know what kind of being they have in them the men than the women. Some find it harder to know the being men and women have in them when they are young men and women than at any other time in their living, some find it harder with men and women in their middle living then when the disposition in them is changing to middle living disposition, in many to impatient irritation, some find it harder to know real being in men and women in their ending then when loving, feeling, religion, have queer ways of showing in them, always then some are very confusing sometime to some, mostly every one has some way of making kinds in men and women, mostly every one finds some one sometimes confusing, mostly every one sometime finds some one very confusing not easy then to be certain of the kind of being one has in her or in him, mostly every one comes to a decision sometime about the kind of being in each one, some come very nearly to never deciding about some one, some as I was saying find it harder about children what being they have in them, about men and women when they are beginning than at any other time in their living.

Some have their real being in them in young living, some do not have it then in them. Now there will be some description of young living in some.

Now there will be some description of young living, feeling, talking, thinking being. Some have their real being in young living, some do not have it then in them. All have their real being in their young living to some, not any one has their real being in young living to some. To begin then with a little description of many ways of feeling being in young living, of feeling, thinking, the being, understanding the being of men and women when they are in their beginning, when they are babies, when they are children, when they are growing into being young men and young women.

To begin then again with a little description of feeling, thinking kinds in babies and in children, in understanding the being and kinds in being in men and women when they are in their beginning, when they are babies, when they are children.

Some then are understanding kinds in children always. Some then have more feeling for kinds in children for being in children than for being in men and women in grown up men and women. Some find being in children more confusing for to them the being in children is the being in men and women in beginning and so to them children are confusing as being natures in beginning. Children are confusing and deceiving to many. These then are to some very difficult to knowing, the being in children is to some a very difficult thing to be understanding. The being in children is very confusing to any one wanting to understand being in men and women. The being in children is then often very confusing, this is because being in beginning the nature in them is then almost hidden, or disguised, or uncertain, or changing, or too loudly in them. Children are then often very confusing for they are often all of them doing the same thing and the nature in them does not affect them, they have many of them then not their own way of eating, drinking, playing, laughing, crying, having angry feeling, kicking, screaming, loving, deceiving, some have then their own individual way of doing but mostly in children it is a general kind of action a general kind of way of acting when any one does anything to them and they are not liking this thing some one has been doing to them. Always it is hard to know the real being in any one from knowing things any one has been doing, with children it is even more confusing, the same kind of acting is done by children that have every different kind of nature in them when they are happy, when they are playing, when they are cheating, when they have angry or injured feeling. Mostly then the being in children, the individual being in each one is very difficult for any one even living with them to be knowing, it is often almost hidden, or disguised, or uncertain, or changing, or too loudly in them, and so they have not then really in them individual being. Slowly then they come to have in them more and more their individual being. Slowly more and more individual being comes out of them as more and more they are themselves inside them.

It is very hard to know of any one the being in them from one or two things they have been doing that some one is telling about them, from many things even that they have been doing and that one knows of them. Knowing real being in men and women is a very slow proceeding and always more and more this is very certain.

As I was saying it is almost harder to know it in children and young men and women the being in them than in older men and women. Not every one thinks that this is certain. As I was saying many many kinds of little boys that in their later living have very different ways of reacting when some one has done something and they do not like the thing some one has been doing, many many men who have very different ways of acting when some one has done something they are not liking, very different natures in them, when they were little boys and some little boy, some one did something they were not liking, they showed no signs of reacting to it then and then later they hit out and often the little boy the some one who had done the thing to them they were not liking had forgotten, so long was the little boy who was not liking the thing the other one did to him in responding. This is true also of women, many kinds of women with very different kinds of natures in them, when they were little girls and some one did something to them they were not liking showed at first no reaction and then they showed angry feeling when every one had forgotten the thing the little girl had not been liking.

In some men, in some women, this shows real nature in them, in some it is just that nature is in them in beginning, and so children are very confusing to the understanding.

In some the nature in them is clearer when they are very young, in some when they are young, in some when they are not so young, in some when they are old ones. Always in each one it is there and repeating, sometime some one knows it in each one.

As I was saying some have more feeling for kinds in men and women when men and women are in beginning, some have more feeling for kinds in men and women when men and women are babies than in any other time in their living, some have more feeling for kinds in men and women when men and women are children than at any other time in their existing. As I was saying, to some, being in children is very confusing because the nature in them is in its beginning.

As I was saying it is very hard telling from knowing something some one did sometime, the nature in them. As I was saying it is very difficult to know the nature in a man or in a woman from knowing even quite a number of things they are doing ; it is even harder to know the nature in children from the action in them as I have been just saying, that is true of many children, not of all of them by any means and that must never be forgotten.

As I was saying Martha Hersland when she was a little one a very little one and the others were running ahead and she had the umbrella for one of them and she was struggling to catch up with the rest of them and they were disappearing and she was being filled fuller always with angry feeling and resentment and desperation and she was crying out, "I will throw the umbrella in the mud," and nobody was hearing and she was repeating again and again and then in a moment of triumphing she did throw the umbrella in the mud and then she went on crying and saying, "I did throw the umbrella in the mud," this is a description of an action that many very different kinds of children could have been doing when they were left behind struggling, Martha Hersland did this and she was a little girl then and slowly now there will come to be a complete description of the nature in her that this I have been just describing does not now help very much to be understanding.

Now there will be some description of Martha Hersland in her young living and the children she knew when she was beginning living.

I was telling of the living of the Hersland family in Gossols on a ten acre place and of people living in small houses near them and it was then that Martha Hersland was a child and was knowing children. She knew some children at the public school near them where she and her brothers had their american education, some children that were living then in the small houses near the ten acre place where the Hersland family were living then as I was telling and some other children who knew these children. She knew some children at the public school. Some children were living near them in the small houses as I was telling and she knew them and knew some other children who knew these children. And then she knew some children who sometimes came to see them, the Hersland children, who were the kind of children she naturally should have been knowing, from the kind of people Mr. and Mrs. Hersland should naturally be knowing, but these children were never important in her living. Mostly then she was knowing children living near her, and children knowing these children.

Mostly then, Martha, and as I was saying this was mostly true of all three of them of all three of the Hersland children, Martha when she was in the beginning of her living was more of them, the children, the people living in the small houses near them and the friends of these people, of these children, than she was of her family living, of her mother's and father's country house living. She was then not at all of the living that would naturally have been her kind of living, of well-to-do living.

She was then, as a child, as a young girl, almost until she was a young woman of the being of those living in small houses near them.

Much description of the being in the children living in the small houses near the ten acre place where the Herslands were living and of children living in other parts of Gossols and knowing these children will be in the description of the beginning being of the youngest of the three Hersland children, in the history of David Hersland. Now in the history of the beginning of the being of Martha the oldest of the three Hersland children there will be more a description of how other children felt the being in her, how every one felt the being in her and so there will be a description of her as every one who knew her felt her, now, in her beginning, and then, later in her living.

There will then be much description of the being in the children living in the small houses near them and of many other children in the history of the beginning of the youngest of the Hersland children who was really more of them, these children, than his brother or his sister ever had been. Now this is a description of the beginning of the being in the eldest of the Hersland children, in Martha Hersland and there will be now much description of how every one ever knowing Martha felt the being in her, other children knowing her, her governesses and the servants and her brothers and her teachers and her mother and her father and later other girls and boys and later her lover and later her husband and then very many who then knew her and then again her brothers and her father, and again then everybody who then and on from then to her ending knew her.

All three of the Hersland children as I was saying were when they were children very much of the living of the people living in small houses near them. The youngest of the three Hersland children David Hersland was so entirely of them when he was in his beginning, of them, of the children at school with him, of children knowing these children and the children living in the small houses near the Hersland family then, was so entirely of the being of all these children that in the description of the being in him there will be very much description of the being in many of them. In the child being of the second Hersland child the elder son, Alfred Hersland there was also a little of this that he was very much of the living of the people around him but it was not in him so completely inside him as it was in the being of the younger son David Hersland, the youngest of the three Hersland children. Then Alfred Hersland was very much sooner through with having it in him the living of the people around him as part of the being in him than either his younger brother or his older sister. He was then really less of them the poor people around him than either of the other two Hersland children but nevertheless in his young living in his playing and in his being interested then, he too was very much of them the poor people near them, though it was never really very deep in him and it was very soon all ended for him. He was then, Alfred Hersland in a sense in his being less really of the being of the people living in small houses near him, more of the people it was natural for him to know in his living though he was not of them at all in his beginning than his brother or his sister and this will come out very clearly in the history of him that will be written after the history of Martha has reached its completion. It will be interesting then to know it in each one of the Hersland children just how they were of the living of the, for them, poor people near them.

As I was saying David, the youngest of them was of the living of the people living in the small houses near them, of their living, of their children's living, David had really inside him the living and the being of the people living in the small houses and of the people that knew these people and the children that knew these children and so they, all of them the being in them the natures of many of them will come to have much description of them being given in the very long history of David Hersland that will be written after there has been written some descriptions of Martha Hersland and then of Alfred Hersland. So then sometime there will be much description of the nature of many of the men, women and children, of the families the Herslands knew in their living in the ten acre place in a part of Gossols where no rich people were living, where there were not living any who would naturally have been friends then of the Hersland children if the Hersland family had been living the well to do living that was really natural for them. There will then in the history of young David Hersland which will be a very long one there will be much description of many people who lived near them the Hersland family then. As I was saying Alfred Hersland was very much less of them the people then living around him than his younger brother David than in a sense the daughter of the Hersland family, the eldest of them of the children, Martha. Alfred was of them in playing in quarrelling, in taking excursions for hunting and other things and in bycicling and in many ways, then, and when he was beginning to be somewhere near being a young man. This will all be told in the history of him which will be begun after there has been written a little description of the whole being and all the living of his elder sister Martha which is now what is here in beginning. So then in the history of David Hersland there will be much description of the being and the nature of the people near the Hersland family when Martha, Alfred and David were children and until they were young men and women, in the history of Alfred Hersland there will be descriptions of his being with them of Alfred's being with the people around the Hersland family then and what he did with them in the way of playing, quarrelling and living. Martha Hersland was more of the living and the being of the people around them then than Alfred ever was really inside him but not so much of them as David was of them and now in the history of Martha Hersland there will be a description of them only in the sense of what way they, the people knowing the Hersland family then, knew her and felt her.

This is now clear then, by and by there will be much description of the being and the character in many of these people, families, men, women and children that the Hersland children knew when they were children and on from them until they were almost young men and women, in the long history of David Hersland that will be written after there has been written some of the history of Martha Hersland and of Alfred Hersland the two elder Hersland children. There will then be written also the meaning of these men and women to Mr. and Mrs. David Hersland the father and the mother of the three Hersland children. So then all that will happen, all that will be written after there is written some description of living and the being of the two elder Hersland children. First then now there will be written some description of Martha Hersland in her beginning. After there has been written something of the history of her living some description of her being, there will be written a history of her brother Alfred up to the time of his marrying Julia Dehning. After that will be written the whole long history of the youngest of the three children David Hersland and all through there will be written some history of the father and mother and of all the governesses and servants living in the house with the Hersland family. So then to begin again. In the history of young David Hersland there will be written much description of the character and living of every one the Hersland family ever came to know in all the time they were living in the ten acre place in that part of Gossols where no other rich people were living. In the history of Alfred Hersland there will be much description of the things Alfred did with and to them, all of them whom the Hersland family came to know then. Now in the history of Martha Hersland there will be much description of how every one knowing the Hersland family then came to feel and know her and them, what every one knowing them felt in her and in the Hersland living, what every one knowing them and knowing her felt about her, knew about her, felt about them, knew about them.

There are many ways of disguising the whole being that is each one, some have a stronger disguising of them in their beginning living, stronger then than in their middle living, or in their ending. In many this is now true of them. Soon now there will be some discussing of the disguising of whole being in young living. Now there will be some description of how every one who knew Martha Hersland knew and felt the being and the living she had in her, how her father felt her, how her mother felt her, how the servants felt her, each one of them, how each one of the governesses knew and felt her, in short how every one who knew her then, men women and children who knew her then, knew her then, felt her then. To begin then.

As I was saying it is very hard to know the being in some one from some few things they have been doing, it is hard knowing any one but sometime each one knowing any one has some feeling of that one.

There are many ways of disguising the whole being, in each one. Some have a stronger disguise in their beginning than in their middle living or in their ending. Some have a stronger disguise in their middle living than in their beginning living or when they are ending living. Some have a stronger disguise when they are ending living than at any other time in their living. Some do not have at any time in their living more disguising of the real being in them than at any other time in their living. Martha Hersland was one of such of them. This is now the way every one knowing Martha Hersland felt the being in her.

Martha Hersland was of the independent dependent kind in men and women. The one I was describing as being independent dependent being as in fluid condition and held together to be one by the skin surrounding that one was of the same kind of being then as that in Martha Hersland, in Martha the being was in a little more concentrated condition but the proportion of attacking and obstinate resisting and quickness and hesitation and ways of being always in every part of living a whole one was the same in Martha Hersland as in the one I was describing as being independent dependent being in completely fluid condition and being a whole one only, and always being one, by having a skin to hold it in and to separate it so from every one and make it so an individual one. Martha then was of the independent dependent kind in men and women, Martha had this being then in more concentration in a more solid condition than the one I was earlier describing. It is a little true now to me of Martha and a little true to me of many men and women having independent dependent being in them that the being in them being like the one I was describing, the one having all independent dependent being in solution in a fluid condition, and my knowing independent dependent being so well in that one and that one being such a fluid whole one, gives to me seeing them an uncomfortable feeling to know it so well from this one I was describing, the being in them, the activities in them, in some having independent dependent being; sometimes it makes me a little turn away from seeing the being in some having in them independent dependent being so that I will not know it too clearly in them the being that they have in them, all the meaning of the being in them and that is a little now the way I am feeling in looking at the being in Martha Hersland and now all the same I am beginning completely to realise all the meaning there is in the being there is in her and always now I will look straight on at her. I will know all the being in her. Martha was of the independent dependent kind of them as I was saying, she was as I was saying like the one I was describing that was independent dependent being in completely fluid condition and always was a whole one in the beginning of the being there was in that one in the middle of the living of that one, in the ending of the living of that one. Martha then was like that one in the relation of things in her being, she was more concentrated more solid than that one, it was not only the skin that kept her apart from other ones, there was actual individual being always in Martha but Martha was a whole one, in her beginning, in her middle living, in her ending, she was all through her of the same concentration, of the same nature, always it was the same being in her, that in her in her beginning, in her being a baby, a little one, a little bigger one, and so on. Always Martha like the other one I was describing was a whole one.   This is now some description of what each one who knew her felt in her, this is now some descriptions of the nature in her, of the living that was in her.

When she was a very little one sometimes she wanted not to be existing.   This is a very common thing in every one in the beginning of their living.   This is a very common thing in mostly every one in the beginning of their living.   Many want then not any longer to be existing, mostly then when they are very little ones they are never thinking I wish I had never come into existing, they have not then any such a feeling, they often say then I wish I had died when I was a little baby and had not any feeling, I would not then have to be always suffering, I would not then now have to think of being frightened by dying, I wish I had been dead when I was a very little one and was not knowing anything.   It is very interesting the way anybody feels about dying, about not existing, about everything, about every one.   Always more and more this is very interesting.

There are ways then that those having in them independent dependent being feel about living, feel about dying, feel about never having been, if they have any of such a kind of feeling in them, that is common to all of them as being different from the way those having in them dependent independent being have of feeling.

More and more there will be understanding of these different ways of feeling their own being, feeling anybody else's being, feeling the ending of themselves and the ending of any one, feel their not existing, that makes one kind in men and women, makes that kind different from other kinds of them.   There will then be a very little always being made that slowly will make a great deal of description of the feelings in each kind in men and women about everything.

As I was saying Martha was of the independent dependent kind of them.   As I was saying it is hard to know the kind of being in any one from just a description of some thoughts, some feelings, some actions in them for it is in their feeling of themselves inside them that the kind of being in them shows in them and that comes out of them slowly in their living, that comes out of them always as repeating, this is very very difficult to make any one understand from a description of them.   This is now what I am always trying.   I know much of all this and sometime sometimes I can make some one else know it by my explaining, I am never very certain but always there is again and again for me a beginning of this trying.

As I was saying many little ones have a feeling about not wanting any more to be living, some want to have been dead when they were little babies and not knowing anything, some want to be dead then so that every one will miss them, some want to prove themselves all noble by dying, some are just tired of struggling when they are little ones, there are such ones, and some of such of them have independent dependent being that does not succeed then in winning fighting by attacking. Martha was a little such a one, and more and more this will show in all her living. Always there was in her much attacking, mostly there was in her nervous feeling, mostly there was in her not much winning, early then she had at moments tired feeling. Never did she know that really she was failing in attacking, always she had in her nervous feeling showing that she had been failing to every one, it was not excitement or weakness or yielding or escaping or blustering as it is in some, some who have independent dependent being and are failing in attacking, in some who have dependent independent being and yet always are attacking though attacking is not for them the way of winning fighting, but in Martha Hersland all ot her being was independent dependent being, attacking was her way of winning fighting, mostly she was never winning mostly she did not really know this in her, she had nervous feeling in her that showed the failure in the fighting she was doing, all this will be clearer when there will have been completely given the feeling every one who ever came to know her at any time in her living had about her.

Always Martha was a whole one, she had only this one kind of being. She always was a whole one, all her living she was repeating the whole being, the kind of being that was the whole being of her, mostly all her living she was a whole one, to herself, to every one. There was in her always one kind of independent dependent being as I was saying and it was mostly all always completely there to every one, the whole being in her to every one who ever knew her, always there then to every one, when she was a baby or a little one, or a young girl or a young woman, or a woman in her middle living, or in her ending. Mostly then always she really was a whole one. Mostly then always every one who knew her had about her such a feeling. This will come clearer in the history of her.

She was as I was saying of one kind of independent dependent being and all her living there was about the same concentration to her, the same relation of attacking and succeeding and failing and nervous feeling and stupid being and understanding and tired feeling in her. Martha was then once a very little one, a baby, and then a little one and then a young girl and then a woman and then she was older and then later there was an ending to her and always all through this living in her she was the same whole one inside her and to every one who knew her.

In some the nature in them is clearer when they are very young, in some when they are young, in some when they are not so young, in some when they are getting older, in some when they are old ones. Martha was mostly always to every one who knew her the same whole one, when she was a little one, a very little one, an older one, a very old one, mostly always then she was to every one about the same kind of a whole one. She was of one kind of that kind of them and mostly all her living there was the same concentration of the being that was her, the same proportion of one thing to the other things active in her.

As I was saying those having in them independent dependent being have in them attacking as their natural way of winning fighting, as their natural way of winning in loving. As I was saying those having in them dependent independent being have in them resisting as their natural way of winning fighting, have resisting as their natural way of winning in loving. This then is the being in those having in them independent dependent being, this then is the being in those having in them dependent independent being. These then are the two different ways of being in men and women and always this, one way or the other way of being, always then one way or the other way of being, independent dependent being or dependent independent being is in each one, every one who ever was or is or will be living.

Often it is very confusing for as I was saying sometimes, very often, one having in her or in him independent dependent being, that is having attacking as their real way of winning fighting, winning in loving, such a one seems really to be always resisting. This then the kind of being in some one is sometimes, is one might say truly very often, very confusing, for one, having in them really as being attacking as the way of winning fighting, as the way of winning loving, always sometimes every minute in their living to themselves and to every one knowing them seems to be resisting, seems to be so fighting and winning, so loving and winning. This is then very confusing to every one knowing that one. Slowly then the real fighting being, the real loving being in that one comes to be understood by some one, sometimes not really by any one, mostly in every one, sometime by some one. This is true then of very many having in them independent dependent being, that is those having in them attacking as their real way of winning fighting, attacking as their real way of winning loving, it is true in many of them that to themselves mostly, and mostly to every one ever knowing them, they have in them resisting as their way of winning fighting, resisting as their way of winning in loving. In those having in them dependent independent being that is those having in them resisting as their real way of winning fighting, resisting as their real way of winning in loving, there are very many of them who seem to themselves sometimes and mostly always to every one ever knowing them seem to be always and incessantly attacking, seem to be always winning by attacking in fighting and in loving. Sometime it comes out of them that they are not really winning, more and more perhaps it comes out of them that always attacking they are never really winning, sometimes sometime some one will know it of them that attacking is not in such of them the way of winning fighting, winning loving, in some sometime every one who knows them knows it sometime of them, that attacking is not in them the way of winning fighting, the way of winning loving. It is very confusing for every one realising this description must be really understanding that failing does not prove it to be true of some one that attacking is not the real way of winning fighting for one doing their fighting by attacking. Many having in them attacking as their natural way of winning fighting fail to succeed to winning by attacking, fail to succeed in loving by attacking. They may fail then those having in them such being, they may even succeed by resisting those having in them attacking as their way of winning and yet these then are of the kind of them having attacking as their natural way of winning fighting, as their natural way of winning loving, are in short of the independent dependent kind of them. Of those having in them resisting as their natural way of winning fighting they are often for a long time to every one, to themselves then and they are bragging of it and they have it in them to themselves and to every one that they are always succeeding by attacking, and sometimes they are really never failing, to themselves and to others who know them and yet always to some one knowing the whole sum of them the whole completeness of their living some one can know it in them that attacking is not in them their real way of winning fighting, of succeeding in being loved and in loving. So then as I was saying it is very confusing and sometimes one only knows really the kind of being in some by the kind of yielding in them, the kind of sensitiveness in them for there is in each kind of being, in independent dependent being, in dependent independent being a kind of way of yielding, a kind of way of being dependent, a kind of way of having sensitiveness in them that makes that kind of them. There is then in independent dependent being a kind of way of yielding, of having sensitive being that is different from the kind of way of yielding of having sensitive being in dependent independent kinds in men and women. There is a kind of way of yielding, of being dependent, of having sensitive being in those having in them dependent independent being that is different from the kind of way of yielding, of having dependent being, of having sensitive being in those having in them any of the kinds of independent dependent being. In short there is one way of having dependent being, of yielding, of sensitiveness, of having stupid being, of having feeling about objects, about practical living that goes with having attacking as the natural way of winning fighting of winning loving, of winning anything and there is another whole system of being that is very different from this, a way of yielding, a way of having sensitiveness in being, a way of seeing and feeling everything in living, a way of choosing a way of reacting to everything that goes with having it as being, the winning fighting by resisting as the real way of being, the winning anything in living, loving and everything by resisting. So then sometimes there will be much very much description of the way of yielding in each one having in them one or the other of these two kinds of being, independent dependent, dependent independent, that is of every one, of all men, of all women.

As I was saying the one I was describing that had all independent dependent being in solution, this one had as all of those having independent dependent being in them have it as being, this one had attacking as the natural way of winning anything. This one as I was saying had all the being in a flabby kind of state that made this one when this one was attacking made all the being in this one then when the being in this one was in motion made it that the being in this one, all the being of this one, was then when attacking just in a state of motion and so to any one feeling this one this one would seem to have resisting being as the natural way of acting for the movement of the whole being in this one, this one being then in a state of attacking really was then to every one knowing this one in this state of action, for it was so slow the moving of the whole being that made this one, that any one coming in contact with this one then or any such a one, sticking so to speak in the mass of this when meeting this one would think of this one as resisting but this was not true of this one then or of any of such of them that have independent dependent being in solution in them, it is stupid being in them that wobbling in them that is their moving that is so slow and uncertain that to any one knowing them, feeling them, seeing them it is not in them as attacking moving activity in them but attacking that is the being in this one and in the others like this one having in them each one independent dependent being. And so then often this kind of a one is from the spreading of the being in that one always then slower and slower in moving in the attacking activity of such a one, and very very often with such a one the attacking never coming to real action as a using of the energy generated in the attacking feeling in independent dependent being of such a kind of one, makes such a kind of one a nervous kind of being and this is then the way independent dependent being can in some be very confusing for attacking does not seem to be the way of active being of them and so it takes much knowing of the being in men and women to realise the action in them. This one then the one I was describing had then independent dependent being but attacking never came to really be ever an action and so this one was to many very resisting, stubborn in resisting and this was only because attacking being in this one never came to be anything more than the whole mass of being that was this one being just moving. As I was saying before, this one that I was describing was the least possible concentration, the most diffuse possible kind of existing of independent dependent being. As I was saying this one a little more concentrated was what made the being of Martha Hersland, Martha who is now soon to be a complete one to every one reading this description. As I was saying the one I have been just describing had with this attacking always much nervous being. As I was saying this one I was describing being made a little into something having a little more concentration would be the being I am now beginning describing. As I was saying the one I was describing was of the independent dependent kind of them, this was the being too that Martha Hersland had in her. The one I was describing had independent dependent being in its weakest concentration, Martha Hersland had independent dependent being in a state of a little more concentration. As I was saying all her living the first one I was describing was a whole one, always a complete one to herself and to every one, this then as I was saying, being always a whole one to herself and every one all through her living was a thing every one will know soon in Martha Hersland. The first one then I was describing was of the independent dependent kind of them that is one having attacking as the natural way of winning fighting, this is the being, the independent dependent being, is the being that is in Martha Hersland, the one I am now again beginning describing, the oldest of the three of them, the three Hersland children.

As I was saying there is a kind of way of yielding, a kind of way of having sensitive being that every one having independent dependent being have in them as their way of being. There will be just now very little description of this in any one. Later there will be very much description of this in every one having in them independent dependent being. Now there will be mostly a beginning of understanding of attacking and resisting and stupid being, and nervous being, and a little of the yielding and the sensitive being in some having in them independent dependent being and now there will be a beginning of all these in one and this one is Martha Hersland the oldest of the three Hersland children.

As I was saying when Martha was a very little one, the Herslands were living in a ten acre place and they were poor people in small houses living near them and the Herslands had a governess and servants then living in the house with them.

Later when Martha was a little bigger, she went to a school near them where the children living in the small houses near them went too to get their instruction and Martha was of them then of all of them the poor people near them ; the Hersland children always had then a governess in the house with them. This made two different kinds of living for them, this was more troublesome to Martha than to the two other children who were boys and so not really in actual relation to the family living and the governess in the house with them. To begin now a description of what every one knowing Martha Hersland when she was a little one felt or knew or thought of the being that now every one reading is commencing feeling, knowing.

As I was saying, when Martha was a very little one and just beginning to go out with other children the governess was never then with the Hersland children, any of them, when they were very little ones and went out with other children. The children were of the living of the people about them, they had that kind of living feeling in them, the kind of living feeling natural in the people living in the small houses near them. The Hersland family then, the Hersland children all three of them had the living feeling in them of the people about them. Mr. Hersland had not the living feeling of the people about them completely in him for he went every day into a very different kind of living but he had a good deal of it in him for his past living was not strongly ever in him. Mrs. Hersland had no other daily living than her household and her children and the living feeling of the people in the small houses near them but in Mrs. Hersland there was always in her as her real living feeling for her, the past living, the right rich american living that was the natural way of living in her. The three children as I was saying had each one of them more in them then of the living feeling natural to the people then around them than they had the living feeling belonging to the kind of living natural to the children of the father and the mother of them. Each one of the three of them Martha, Alfred and David Hersland had in them the living feeling natural to the poorer people around them differently in them. This will come out in the long histories of each one of them. This is now a long history of the oldest of them, Martha Hersland and this is now a beginning of description of the way she had in her to be of them the people living near the Herslands in small houses near the ten acre place where the Herslands were living then in that part of Gossols where no other rich people were living.

As I was saying when Martha was a little one, when she first went to school and this was very soon after the Herslands began living in the ten acre place in that part of Gossols where no other rich people were living for Martha had been born when the Herslands had just come to Gossols and were living in the hotel as I was saying, in the hotel where Mrs. Hersland knew Sophie Shilling and Pauline Shilling and Mrs. Shilling; and so as I was saying when they came, the Hersland family, to live on the ten acre place where they went on living to after the time when Martha a. grown woman came back out of her trouble to live again with them, Martha the oldest of the three Hersland children was old enough to begin her schooling, was old enough to begin having living feeling forming in her, to be of them the people living near them.

As I was saying Mr. Hersland believed in independence for his children, in democratic schooling for them, in having a governess in the house with them for their education, in healthy out of door living.

Martha Hersland then when she was a very little one, when she was a little one, when she was a bigger one, when she was running her own living, when she was a lost one, when she was shrunken when she was older, and always all of her living every minute in her living was the same one, the same whole one, to herself and to every one ever knowing her being. She was as I was saying a little more concentrated version of the one I was just describing. Like that one she was always all her living a whole one, like that one always all her living being a whole one had not really much meaning. This is now again a beginning of the being Martha had in her all her living.

Some have their real being in young living, some do not have it then in them, all have their real being in young living to some, not any one has their real being in young living to some.

Martha Hersland had in her independent dependent being as I was saying. Martha in her young living was a whole one, always all her living Martha was a whole one. Sometime she was older, sometimes she was happier, sometimes she was nervouser, sometimes she was farther from and sometimes nearer failure, always she had the same being in her, always she was of the independent dependent kind of them, always she was like the other one I was describing excepting that Martha had independent dependent being in a little more concentrated form in her and so she would keep together even without the skin of her to hold her, one part would stick to the other part of her, she would not be flowing everywhere if there was not a skin to hold her, so then she was a little in more ways a whole one than the one I was describing that had independent dependent being in solution.

Always then, as I was saying, Martha was a whole one. When Martha was a little one, as I was saying she was of them the poorer children living near the Hersland family then and she went to school with them. When she was a little one as I was saying the Hersland family always had a governess living in the house with them to educate the Hersland children in music, french and german and any other kind of education Mr. Hersland at any other time thought it would be good for them to be having. The Hersland family then had a governess living in the house with them when Martha was a little one and then on to when Martha was quite old enough not to like them ever to be interfering with anything she wanted to be doing, with any kind of reading or knowing any one or any way she was learning anything. Then later than that they the Herslands still had one and then more and more the governess living in the house with them had really nothing to do with the Hersland children, but always as long as a governess was in the house with them the governess would be a little sometime troublesome to Martha Hersland and her living then.

To those knowing Martha Hersland then when she was a young one when she was beginning her individual being, she was then a whole one, to no one quite entirely pleasing, but most of those knowing her then liked her well enough whenever they thought about her and sometimes then they did not like her.

As I was saying she went to school with the children near them, the for the Hersland children, poorer children near them. As I was saying when the

Hersland family moved to the ten acre place Martha was already old enough to begin her schooling.   As I was saying then when she was a very little one and she was coming home with them, they went faster than she could then, they left her then and she was running with the umbrella one of them had left with her after saying she would carry it for her and she was saying I will throw the umbrella in the mud and then she was crying, I have thrown the umbrella in the mud, and then later she got home and the umbrella was not with her but one of the other ones one of those who had left her went back that day later and got it for her.   Then she was a very little one and just beginning knowing the children near her. When she was a little bigger she was in her living almost entirely of them the people near her.   As I was saying they mostly all liked her well enough when they thought about her, they did not think very much about her, sometimes when they thought about her they did not like her.   She was for them mostly then as if she had been one of them in her natural way of living, there was nothing in her to make her a different kind of child from the others of them, she was of them and yet a little sometimes it was troublesome to her and for them in her that she was not of them in the living that would have been natural for her.   It was more important in her for them when a little they were beginning all of them to have loving in them, for she not being of them a little must not get into a kind of trouble that would be alright for them in the kind of living that was the natural way of living for them.   Neither they nor she really knew this inside them ever in their living but it was a little troublesome there to her and for them, troublesome as the governess was in her living, not really ever interfering, sometimes a little attempting to be interfering, always there as being a thing that had no meaning really in her living but could not ever have been there ever if the living that was then for her real living had been for her her natural way of living.   Slowly this came to be in her as something stronger, something slowly making a difference in her as she grew older. Slowly then things happened to these children she knew then as they grew older that would not happen to her as she grew older.   She was living very much their life when she was not at all any more of them ; this is now a little more description of the being in her and how they felt her every one who then knew her.

Mr. Hersland as I was saying, in his middle living had in him much impatient being.   Mr. Hersland as I was saying had in him independent dependent being as a bottom nature to him, as most of him.   Martha Hersland as I was saying had independent dependent being as all the being in her.   Always more and more I am understanding independent dependent being and all the kinds of ways it has of being, making different kinds in men and women.   Always more and more I am understanding dependent independent being and all the ways it has of being in the kinds of men and women having such being in them.   Always more and more then I am understanding being in all the kinds there are ever existing of men and women. To commence again now with Martha Hersland and how her father Mr. David Hersland felt her.

As I was saying Mr. Hersland had a strong feeling about educating his children. Mostly always it was strongly in him the feeling of the need of educating them, always it was changing in him, the feelings he had in him about what kind of education was the right kind of education for them but always that is mostly always there was one thing constant in him the wanting them to be individual and independent. Sometimes when they were too much of one kind of living he had a new theory of independence for them that took the form of restrictions on the liberty they were enjoying and sometimes he wanted that they should be as they would have been if they had had the living that would have been natural for them and this came to him a few times in the living of his daughter Martha and he tried to make her over but mostly he wanted them to have an education making them to be strong and independent. About their living the life of the poor people near them, he never really thought about this in them. Mostly as I was saying when he was in the country it was to him as if he were of their living, he had then no sense of social distinction, they were poor men and he was a rich one, he never wanted then his children to have any position. His feeling about his daughter Martha then in the beginning was that she was of them, later that she could learn from them what they all knew in living, later when she sometimes met people it would have been natural she should be knowing he was impatient at the way she was looking and he was full up then with impatient feeling. Mostly she was never important to him, very much later in her living she filled him very full of impatient feeling. As I was saying they were both of them of the independent dependent kind of them. There was a great difference in the way they had in them each one of them independent dependent being.

Mr. Hersland to his children when they were old enough to realise him was very full of impatient feeling. They were then afraid of him though they knew it of him that he never would go as far as his anger could drive him. They knew this of him more and more until almost they were not afraid of him.

Mr. Hersland had in him independent dependent being, his daughter Martha had in her independent dependent being. This being was very different in Mr. Hersland than in Martha Hersland as I was saying. This is now some description of the differences between them. This is now some description of the feeling in Mr. Hersland in different parts of her living about his daughter Martha and what he thought and said about her. To begin then now with a little description of the different way their being was in the two of them.

When Martha was a little one she was a whole one, always she was a whole one. When Martha was a young one she was a whole one. She was not very interesting to her father or to any one who knew her, then in her young living. She was not very interesting ever to her father or ever very interesting really to any one who ever knew her.

Sometimes she was a little interesting to some one. She was never very interesting to her father or to any one knowing her in her young living. She was never really interesting to her father in her living. Later in his living she was always with him. In her young living as I was saying she was really not very interesting to any one. Always as I was saying she was the same whole one. When she was first a young woman she was a little interesting to some. She was never really very interesting to any one. Always, as I was saying, all her living, she was the same whole one.

She was as I was saying of the independent dependent kind of them. More and more it is interesting, more and more I am understanding the being in men and in women. More and more I am realising that each kind of men and women each kind of the two kinds of them have completely in them in whatever kind or condition of being any one will find them, with more or less intelligence, with more or less strength, with more or less weakness in them, with more or less originality or energy or interest or success or failure in them, each kind of them, all the men and women of each of the two kinds of them of each kind of the two kinds of them have the same way of eating, drinking, loving, hating, succeeding, failing, fighting, escaping, have the same kind of being in them as all the others of the same kind of them and that makes grouping of men and women always to me more interesting. Sometime in my explaining it will be interesting to every one, it will be interesting in explaining men and women for every one interested in understanding men and women.

Mr. Hersland as I was saying had in him independent dependent being. As I was saying more and more in his living he was full up with impatient being. As I was saying he had it in him to always be strong in beginning, to be very strong in attacking and then he would go another way to another beginning never knowing that he had not finished to really winning, never knowing this in him, not really even when in his later living his children when they were angry at the impatient being then in him and not then being any longer afraid of him knowing then that he never would be carried through to the end of the anger in him told it to him. He never really knew it in him but this was the being in him as I was saying. He never knew the being in his daughter Martha until she in his old age living managed for him, until she came back out of her troubles to them and then he was beginning already to be shrunk from the outside of him and she was then not interesting to him. She never really was interesting to him. He never knew it in her that she had independent dependent being in her, because for him she was not thorough in anything, she was always beginning and never really beginning anything. This was in her for him when she was a little one and then when she was beginning her education it was annoying to him for always he was really beginning and always she was almost beginning and then when he was changing she was then really beginning and then it was to him in her stupid being, that she was nervous then and not finishing anything, not thorough in anything. His feeling was very different with his two sons who each in their way were annoying to him but Martha was annoying to him being as she was of the same kind of being as the being that was in him.

Martha as I was saying always was a whole one, as I was saying when she was a young one she was of the living of the people living in small houses near the Hersland family then. She was completely of their living then, the governess the Hersland family had living with them was sometimes troublesome to Martha in her living but only one of them the last one Madeleine Wyman was ever really troublesome and that was when she was trying as I was saying to carry out in the children and mostly on Martha who was a girl and older the ideas of education Mr. Hersland had then in him. It was then that Mr. Hersland came to a realisation that Martha was not really thorough in anything. Martha was hard-working and did well enough in her schooling but when he wanted her to have disciplining, to make strong beginnings in french and german and music and swimming and exercising and dancing, as I was saying she was always a little mixed up in beginning and then had a nervous confusion from the changing and Madeleine Wyman was thorough and annoying to her and then Martha was completely of them the poorer people near them. As I was saying Martha was interesting enough then to every one but not really very interesting to any one knowing her then. As I was saying she was more completely of them the poorer people near them when the governess Madeleine Wyman was living with the Hersland family in the house with them and for some years longer than she was of any other living, was more of them in her feeling, in her living, in her understanding of all living but always then all of them the poorer people living in small houses near them were having things happen to them, the young boys the young girls whom she knew then which was not of her future living to have happen to her then and always neither she nor they knew this in them but always it was there between them and Martha was then there in living neither bird or beast or good red herring and she did not know it nor did any one else know it of her then.

So then Martha's young living was very confusing to her then but she did not know it in her then. She had in her as I was saying independent dependent being, she had attacking as her natural way of fighting but as I was saying she was only a little more concentrated in her being than that other one I was describing and so when she was in motion except in jerks there was not really very much action, there was very much nervous being and confusion and this was in her stupid being and always all her living she was the same one the same whole one I have been just describing.

This then was the young living in her. It was well enough but rather confused inside her. Confusion always was strong in her. All of her when it was in motion just was sort of knocking together, and that was mostly all the active being in her and that was to many who knew her obstinacy and resisting in her and to her father it was that she was never thorough. Sometimes there was stronger reaction for a moment in her, anger, or a deep commotion for something that was a disgrace to some one or to her and then she was a little more than the whole one that she mostly just was and was mostly to every one.

This was then the being in her. Always then she was not very interesting to any one knowing her. Her mother had never a very lively realisation of her. Her mother more and more was external to her when she Martha was to her mother no longer inside her. Not that Mrs. Hersland ever knew this in her, always she had a feeling of having had and having her as a child as part of her and always she had her dresses and her hats and all as important to her but as I was saying Martha was then when she was growing completely as completely as there was really living being in her of them the poor people living in the small houses near the Hersland family then. As I was saying later there was a difference, that they were having living that could not be in one going to be having a different future from that that any of them would have as natural to them. Earlier when she was a young one, yes there was a little difference between them for she had a father and a mother to them and these other children could be conscious of the father and the mother of her and she had a governess living in the house with her and servants and all that that made her in ways of living, but mostly to them then the poorer people living in the small houses those that knew her then they did not feel the difference to be a difference that in any way cut her off from the living natural to them only they could sometimes be conscious of the mother or the father or the governess or the servants when they were with her, when they were not with her, not from anything in her but from their being really existing the father and the mother and the governess and the servants of the Hersland family. So then in her younger living she was not cut off from them by her future for the children she was then knowing were young then and not having any such feeling. Almost not at all then was she in any way cut off from them. Sometimes they as I was saying, from hearing other people or their parents talking, from seeing them or from something that Martha said in talking could be conscious of Martha's mother or father or governess or servants living in the house with her and so they might be just by a shade cut off from her but mostly then she was completely of them the children and the poor people living near them. As I was saying she was really then, Martha, not very interesting to any one knowing her then. She was completely of them then the people living in small houses near the Hersland family then. She had no feeling in her of a different kind of living in her. All the active living there was in her was of the living of the poorer people near her.

As I was saying when she was quite a young one there was not any feeling in any of them, not in the parents of these children then any feeling that she was in her feeling cut off from them by not being able to have some things happen to her that could not happen to any one having the kind of future that was the natural kind of future living for her. As I was saying a little such a feeling came when she was somewhat older, when she was older with them, but in her younger living there was not in herself not in any one of them, a little perhaps in her mother and the governesses and servants then living in the house with her, not any in her father then not anything of such a feeling. And so she was completely of them then to them to all of them the children and the other people living in the small houses near the Hersland family ten acre living place then, she was completely then of their living then always even when the children or the others were conscious of the existing of Mr. or Mrs. Hersland or the governess or the servants living with them.

At this time Martha was completely of the living of these people near her, of the children and the parents of them, then in her younger living. Later as I was saying there was the developing of feeling the natural future for her in her in them and in her father and a very little in her and always a little more and more in all of them. And then it came that she went away to another kind of living. This is now a little history of how they felt her when she was young, when she was a little older, every one who then came to know her. There will be then a little description of the transition to another kind of living that then came to her.

When she was quite a young one, as I was saying, she was then quite completely of the living of the children and the people living near the Hersland family then when the Hersland family were living in that part of Gossols where no other rich people were living then.

She was completely of their living then. She could have happen to her then what could happen to any of them in their living, in their schooling, in their playing, in their quarrelling, in their liking, in their disliking, in their being interesting one to the other of them.

As I was saying Martha Hersland was not then very interesting to any of them, she was good enough at doing anything, they were friendly enough with her most of them, they did not most of them think very well of the way she did quarrelling whenever she did any of that with any of them. One little boy wanted her to do loving the little boy who with his sister lived with the father who smoked to help his asthma but this was not very much of a success for Martha then had a nervous feeling and was not very daring and was not very understanding and had a confusion that was a little like wanting, a little like obstinate hesitation, a little like being afraid of everything, a little like a very stupid way of being, and the little boy then forgot about her being existing for really Martha was not then to any one very interesting. Martha was alright then but she was not interesting enough to be successful in quarrelling or in loving then, they all of them forgot her a little when she wanted to be quarrelling or they were quarrelling or they wanted to be loving or she wanted to be loving. Perhaps a very little it was that she was not quite entirely completely, altogether of them, perhaps it was that she was not then really interesting to any one. She was of them then so that she was living their living entirely then with them and they did begin with her then in loving or in quarrelling as they did with each other in their living then but as I was saying she was not interesting then, the being in her as I was saying when it was active was just knocking together in her and that made in her a little confusion and she was not stupid in ordinary living and she was not interesting and that was her younger living.

When she was a little older she was still always with them the people near the Hersland family then in that part of Gossols where no rich people were living then. She was with them then living their kind of being, hearing them talking and knowing everything happening to them but not any of them then included her with them in quarrelling or loving, not even as making a beginning. The natural future for her was then separating them. She was still very much with them, with the girls she would help the mothers cooking or setting the table, she knew their daily living, she helped them in wiping the dishes when they were washing them, and was with them and always then she was not of them even as she had been to them when she was a younger one and she never knew it then and they never knew it then. She was not any more interesting then. Something happened to her then that made her now for a little time more than the whole one she was all her living to herself and perhaps a little to some who then and later knew her, it was really just a little accentuation of being put in motion and of that I will now give a very little description.

No one knew very much what Martha was feeling about anything when she was in her young living. She was not ever telling very much of her feeling then to any one, and never to any one in the family living. Not any of the Hersland family ever were telling each other very much about what feeling they had in them. Martha was really not telling any one very much in her young living the feeling she had in her about anything and then in a way too it was not in her ready for telling. It had not form in her yet, feeling in her, there was really then no way for her to tell any one anything about her feeling.

Now there will be a little more telling of the kind of a whole one she

was, of the kind of nature there was in her.   There will then be a little
more telling of the moment in her when the movement of the being in her
was a little faster, came to be almost violent emotion in her.   There will
then be a little telling of her living, what she was knowing, what she was
feeling in her young living.   There will be a little telling of how much she
had heard about living and how much she had seen, how little and how
much she knew then and what then happened in her when she saw something that really made all her being move together and faster than it had
ever had motion before in her.   There will be then a little telling of how
much she had heard about anything in living, how much she had heard,
and how little she knew and what she saw then and what she felt then
when she saw something that I will now soon be telling.   This is now a
little description of how much she had heard and how little she knew and
what she saw in her young living.   There will then be a description of her
seeing a man hitting a woman with an umbrella in another part of town
from that in which the Herslands were living and of her consequent deciding to go to college and get that kind of education.   To begin then.

Martha as I was saying was of the independent dependent kind in
men and women.   Martha as I was saying had it in her to be of the kind
of them that have attacking as their natural way of winning fighting.
Martha as I was saying was of this kind of them.   Martha as I was saying
was mostly never really attacking.   Martha as I was saying when her
being was all of it in motion, and mostly when any of it was in motion it
was all of it in motion and then it was mostly as pieces knocking together
in confusion and in nervous being and not then into really attacking, sometimes it could happen but this was not very often, yes in a sense a very
little of it was in her very often, but enough of it to really make an action
was not in her very often, sometimes it could happen that there was a
strong impulse and then there was a strong movement of her being of all
the being that was Martha Hersland and always then it never really even
then came to be really attacking, it just went off into very strong knocking
together of pieces of the being in her, a livelier confuson inside her than just
the ordinary confusion in her and that was all there was of attacking in
her in the most active being ever in her.

This was the being in her it was independent dependent being the
being that has attacking as the natural way of winning in fighting or in
loving but as I was saying the being in her never got into motion to carry
on to anything as object in attacking, it just remained inside her as knocking together in her to be a confusion and a nervous being in her.   She had
in her as I was saying, independent dependent being, that was all the being
there was in her.   As I was saying attacking being was the natural way
of winning fighting in her but attacking never came to be really an action
carrying on to anything outside her.

She was as I was saying in her young living not very interesting to any one who then knew her. She did not then, as I was saying tell very much to any one any feeling she had in her, really then nothing came to be in her clear inside her to tell any one if any one was there to listen to her. This was true of her mostly all her young living as I was saying.

She was then as I was saying all her young living completely of them the people living near the Hersland family then, she was then not of the living of her father and her mother. As I was saying later in her young living she was very annoying to her father, she was not ready enough to be beginning and then there was confusion in her when he was changing to a new beginning and this was often like stubborn resistance and often then her father would begin to have in him very much impatient feeling and some anger. And always then Martha a little was beginning to be beginning and a little so then she had in her her own feeling and a good deal then she was afraid to hear him when he was beginning with her though always she felt it a little in her that it was really all impatient being in him and that he never would carry it through against her as anger the annoyed impatient angry feeling he had then toward her. As I was saying all this was mostly a trouble to her when the governess Madeleine Wyman was beginning to take charge of her. This was too annoying to be only confusing in her, what right had Miss Wyman to be forcing her, Martha, and resistance was then in Martha a thing having in her a clearer meaning than any time before in her living. Really Martha was afraid of Madeleine Wyman more in a way than she was of her father, Madeleine Wyman was a compacted power that kept going and always was there and there was not really any way of getting away from her when one was in the house with her. This was then the beginning of more concentrated consciousness of feeling in Martha this experience with Madeleine Wyman. This did not last a long time as I was saying earlier. Madeleine Wyman came soon to be only of the living of Mr. and Mrs. Hersland, not at all of the three Hersland children. Always she was sometimes troublesome to them but more and more as I was saying she was only of the living of Mr. and Mrs. Hersland and not at all of the three Hersland children. Always as I was saying she was troublesome to them then and later in their living and there will be later more history written of the feeling about her in each one of the three of them. Now there is to be a little description of Martha Hersland and what she knew and saw and heard in her younger living.

As I was saying in her younger living she was not really ever very interesting to any one knowing her then. As I was saying all the living there was really in her then was of the living of the children and the sisters and the brothers and the fathers and the mothers of the children that she was knowing then. The Hersland family living was not really important then as living for her being then. As I was saying all the active living really in her, in her younger living, was the living of the people living in small houses, the people who were as I was saying half poor city people half poor country people in their living and their feeling.

These were then the ones that gave to her living in her younger living all the meaning living had in her then.

As I was saying these children, these people, had in them all of them the feeling of city living and the feeling of country living. Martha Hersland in her younger living was completely of them as I was saying. Martha Hersland had then in her young living the kind of feeling about living that they had in them. There was as I was saying always the difference of her having a different kind of father and mother and way of living from any of them but that was not there in her feeling and was not there in their thinking, it did however make a difference in her understanding of things that happened among them. As I was saying in her very young living and then a little later in her young living she was completely of them the people living in the small houses there then there where there were no rich people living excepting the Hersland family as I was saying. She was completely of them, of their living, of their way of feeling living in her later younger living and yet already as I was saying there could be in her a little less really being of them even than there had been because already then future living was important in the present living of all of them and her future living was a different thing from their future living. As I was saying she had not been so very interesting to any one in her younger living, to any one of them. As I was saying there would be in them a little beginning with her too in quarrelling one little boy as I was saying tried a little in loving, in things they should not be doing and really she was not resisting but it could not come to anything for there was not in her anything really active inside her then, she was really not even so important to them then any of them than when she had been a very little one but really as I have been saying she never really was interesting to any one in her younger living.

As I was saying in her later younger living she was completely with them and yet then she was the most cut off from them for then future living was beginning to count in the being and feeling and doing of all of them and always her future living more and more certainly was a different thing from that of those she was knowing then. She was then not really then very interesting really to any of them then.

She was completely with them then in her daily living then, then in her later younger living. She was always with them then, then in her later younger living, she would be with them whatever they were doing when she was not at home studying in some one of the ways her father then was thinking was important for her to be doing.

She was with them then, in the day-time, in the evening, all the time she was with them, the people living in small houses near them. Some of the girls and some of the boys had already commenced to be working.

I was saying that there was one family living in a small house near the Hersland family then of a mother a foreign woman who was rather wooden, and a father who was not important to any one, and three daughters who each one sometime came to have real beauty in them. It was the second one of them whom Martha knew very well in the later part of her young living. She had not come yet to have beauty in her this one, she was just beginning to work out to learn dress-making. The older one who was working in the city somewhere had come to have her beauty and there were queer things one heard then about her of her marrying a rich man, a man whose family made much money making chocolate and every one had heard of them from eating the chocolate they were making and the name sounded very italian and somehow every one knew though no one of them had ever seen him that he was a handsome fierce looking black-moustached man and a very rich one. None of the family of this girl ever said anything, Martha Hersland did not know really where she heard all about the oldest girl for when she thought it over she knew no one had told her. It came to be in her then like something she had dreamed about some one and so it had all of it no real meaning for her. She knew dimly that all of them the three Banks boys one of whom was learning tele-graphing, one of whom was learning shoemaking, the other learning nothing and perhaps sometimes stealing something, she knew they knew the three girls and said things to them that Martha was never really hearing but as I was saying Martha was not really interesting then to any one and inside, her feeling was not active to be to herself or to any one a thing possibly having then any expression. The young Rodman boy was to her a little more an active awakening because he said things to make her be understanding. There were two of them, the eldest a big lumbering fellow and this young one who made fun of her whenever he saw her and he just annoyed her and that was not really very active then in her. She was, as I was saying, of them, she was always with them, all of them, she heard them talking, she knew what they were doing, she would listen to the mothers and the fathers of them talking, she had no other notion of living than that she saw and heard and felt and had when she was with them and always her future would be a different one and so she was not then understanding what all of them were living for to her her future living was unknown and so she had no present living, with all of them then it was a different thing, their present living was their future living and so she was not really ever then of them.

As I was saying Martha was not then really interesting to any one. As I was saying feeling was then in her not very clear to herself or to any one. As I was saying she was annoying then to her father by her not making very good beginnings and not being as he put it really thorough in anything. No one of his children ever were to him in their younger living really thorough in anything. The other two were interested in resisting beginning or in beginning, he had not any such a satisfaction, as I was saying, with his daughter and she was then in her later younger living annoying to him. He wanted her to learn housekeeping then and to him it was a good thing for her to be with them the poorer people living near them so she could do what all those other girls she knew could do as to cooking and dress-making and of course Martha could not really do them and sometimes then he asked her to do some such thing and then of course she could not do it for him and then he would be full up with impatient feeling that she could not do that thing, that always she was not as he put it ever thorough in anything. And always all this time she was studying in one way or another, with tutors or a teacher from the school near her and sometimes by herself and then there came to be a change in her and for her. Always her mother was not very close to her. The mother was there always for all of her children but this was for Martha only when she was a little sick or for dressing or for an occasional visiting. This was the time when Mrs. Hersland was having in her her most important feeling of herself inside her as I was saying. So Martha was not then really very interesting to any one. Martha always was a whole one as I was saying. Martha was not then really very interesting to any one.

There will be much description of the feeling her brothers had about their sister in the long histories that will be written later of the two of them. There will be very much written of the feeling the father Mr. Hersland had about her in the history to be written later of the ending of the being in him. There will never be very much written of the feeling that the mother had about her. Always then, as I was saying, to each one she was a whole one. There has been now a little written of how those who knew her when she was a young one, felt her. As I was saying mostly she was not really very interesting to any one. As I was saying she was then not very interesting to any one who then knew her. The servants and the governesses excepting perhaps a little Madeleine Wyman when she was trying to carry out on her the theories of education Mr. Hersland always was explaining then to her had not very individual feeling about her. She was one of the Hersland family to them. Some of her teachers at the school where Martha got her american education had a little more feeling about her. Some of them almost were nearly interested in her. She could have a kind of earnestness in her, it never came really to be there in her in her young living and to some of her teachers then it was that she had a stupid way of being resisting, of being obstinate in her, but as I was saying sometimes a little one of them almost would be interested in her particularly after a governess or her father had been there to talk about her, to explain about her, to arrange about her. So then as I was saying Martha Hersland in her younger living was not really very interesting to any one who then knew her.

Martha Hersland as I was saying was always a whole one. Martha as I was saying was of the independent dependent kind of them. The being in Martha as I was saying was mostly always just in a state of being in confusion. There was as I was saying in Martha very much nervous being accompanying the confusion in her being whenever the being in her was in motion. Mostly always the being in her was in this kind of a confusion. As I was saying Martha was of the independent dependent kind of them. This is now again a little a description of the being in her.

Martha was as I was saying of the independent dependent kind of men and women. Martha was one of this kind of them and had it as being to have this kind of being all of it that was in her of the same degree of concentration, that is to say that there was no part of the being in her more accented, more effective in her than another part of the being in her. That is to say it was like this in her. The one that I was describing and that was a whole one only ever by the skin of her holding her together there might be one who might be like her and so then this one though still of the independent dependent kind of them would have this being with different accents different meanings in different parts of the being that was this one. Some have all kinds of combinations of kinds in them and some as I was saying have even another kind of substance mixed up with them, the dependent independent kind of being as we were saying. Now Martha Hersland as I said in the beginning of this description of the being in her was like the one that I was describing that was all independent dependent being in solution and in so fluid a condition that this being is only made an individual one by the skin separating it from flowing over everything near it to lose itself in everything and not have individual existing, Martha Hersland then as I was saying was like this one only Martha was a little more solid and there was a little more solidity to her but as I was saying there was not much more really effective movement to her. The other one the first one I was describing when substance that was all of her was set in motion mostly it just sort of bobbled up and down in her it was not active enough to give any onward attacking motion to the whole of her that was made by the skin of her holding her together and so there never came to be real attacking in her indeed as I was saying it was to most every one seeing her, this one, as if she had resisting being in her for the substance of her was a heavy slightly sticky one as I was saying and though attacking being was the way of active being in her it came to it that she was really resisting because she never got to anything more than a little bobbing motion and this one was so an obstruction; always of course there was a slight attacking action to her for that was the nature of the being in her but to every one feeling her it was resisting, stupid being, obstinacy of a dull kind in her, and that was the being in her. Now Martha Hersland as I was saying was like this one only a little more solid and so when there was a strong emotion to give motion to her there could be more real attacking being in her than there ever could be in the one I was just describing. As I was saying Martha had as being a substance solid enough so that Martha's skin so to speak was part of the substance of her, she was a whole one then more than just by being held together by a skin as was the case in the other. Martha then had a little more real attacking movement in her than the other one I was describing who in mixture of being was just like her. Martha had not really very much forward attacking motion in her. Mostly in her too it was a confused interaction and made a confused being in her that was to many knowing her stupid being in her. This was in her to many knowing her like resisting being in her but as I was saying she had not really in her resisting being as a way of winning, as a way of fighting, as a way of loving, as I was saying confused being that was resisting being in her to many knowing her was stupid being in her, was failure in her.

As I was saying Martha when she was a young one was not really very interesting to any one who knew her then. She was until she was nearly, almost, a young woman of the feeling and the living of poorer people as I was saying, more than she was then of any other living. She was in her daily living of their living and their feeling as I was saying. This is now a little description of the feeling and the living she then had in her. She was always then as I was saying of the living and the feeling of the people, and the other people that knew them, of people in very small houses living near the Hersland family then. She was of their daily living then as I was saying. This is now a little description of what she knew with them and what she did not know with them then.

As I was saying Martha Hersland was all through her younger living of the feeling and the living of, for her natural family living, poor people. She was of the daily feeling and the daily living of them more than she was of the daily feeling and the daily living of her family living and feeling. She was then as I was saying of the daily living and the daily feeling of the people near her who had in them as I said of them half city feeling and half country feeling. She was as I was saying as much as there was in her then of feeling and living of their feeling and their living. She was with them often in the evening, she was with them more or less in the day time, she was of their daily living and their daily feeling more than she was then of any other feeling or living. As I was just saying she was with them often in the evening when she was not any longer a very young one, she was with them then very much of the day-time, she was as I was saying of their daily living and their daily feeling almost all the daily living and the daily feeling there was in her then.

She was with them as I was just saying often in the evening now that she was no longer a very little one and very much of the day-time. Some of them, the younger ones whom she knew then were beginning now to go out working and she saw them when they came back from their working and she was with them then and she was with them then again in the evening. As I have said almost all there was of daily living and daily feeling then in her was of the daily living and the daily feeling of these young people and their friends and relations and this was not very important to any one then that this was the daily living and the daily feeling of Martha Hersland then. Sometimes Mr. Hersland suddenly remembered that Martha should not go out in the evening, mostly he did not pay much attention to the daily feeling and the daily living in her then. Sometimes as I was saying he would suddenly remember she should not go out in the evening alone with these young people near them and then he would forbid her going and he would tell her that she should stay in the house and be with her mother and then he would lecture her brother that he did not take better care of his sister. "You have to take care of her sometime and you might as well begin, the sooner the better. You will have to do it sooner or later, I tell you." "I'll take mine later" said the brother but he was careful that his father did not hear and he went out that evening as he did many evenings as I will be telling later in the long history of the living of him, but on that evening Martha Hersland could not go out to be with the others. Mr. Hersland's remembering that she should not go out in the evening did not happen very often. Mostly she went out in the evening and the day-time. Sometimes her father coming home from the city and seeing Martha standing in the yard of some of the small houses talking would get very angry that she was not at home studying. He could often get very angry and be full up with impatient feeling as I was saying whenever he remembered that Martha was his daughter and was not just what he would have her. At this time they had not any governess living in the house with them. Madeleine Wyman had left them and they had no governess after this one. Mrs. Hersland then did not have much meaning in the family living. She was weakening a little inside her then as I said when I was describing the living in her, she was lost then between her big children and the father of them as I was then saying then when I was describing the being in Mrs. Hersland. So then as I was just saying Martha was in her daily living and her daily feeling more of them the people in small houses near the Hersland family then than she was of any other daily living or daily feeling then. As I was saying she was with them often in the evening, as I was saying she was not then very interesting to any of them then. As I was saying the future which would be different for her in kind than the future of them made a separation between them in the things she was knowing with them and the things they were knowing among them, in the things she was feeling with them and the things they were feeling among them, in the things she was doing with them and the things they were doing among them, in the way she was interesting to them and the way they were interesting to each other among themselves then. As I was saying all there was of daily living and daily feeling in her then was of the daily feeling and daily living they had among them. As I was saying in a way she was separated from them, though all the living and feeling she had in her then was the living and feeling she had from them, by the future living that would be different in her living from the future living any of them would naturally be having.

As I was saying she was then not really very interesting to any one. She might have been a little interesting a couple of evenings to Harry Brenner but she never really was interesting to him.

As I was saying she was then of their daily living and their daily feeling, the poorer people near them, and she was with them a good deal in the day-time and she was with them very often in the evening. As I was saying sometimes her father remembered that she should not be out with them in the evening and he would forbid her going out that evening and he would lecture her brother Alfred because he did not take care of his sister who should not go out in the evenings in the way she was doing and the father was full up then as I was saying with impatient feeling and then that would be the end of his interfering with Martha's daily living and daily feeling and Martha's going out in the evening. The mother Mrs. Hersland was then as I was saying in the history of her living lost then among her children and the father of them. Always then in her young living Martha was of them the people near them and this was of her until she was almost a young woman.

As I was saying she was of them the poorer people in her daily living and in her daily feeling, as I was saying she was not so interesting to any of them as they were to each other then and this was mostly because of the future living there was for her in her and a little perhaps from the way being was in her but mostly it was from the future living of her that was naturally to be different from that of those she was then knowing. As I was saying she was not so interesting to any of them as they were to each other then and she was not feeling and living and understanding anything really in the way they were doing then. As I was saying she almost might have been interesting to them from her almost being interesting a couple of evenings to Harry Brenner who was one of them but she did not come to be really interesting to him. Perhaps it was the future living in her that made her not come to be really interesting to Harry Brenner then although there was almost a beginning of being interested in him. That was the end of it though then, she never as I was saying was really interesting to any of them then.

So then this was the being, the living, the feeling, the understanding in Martha Hersland up to her almost being a young woman this that I have been describing. Her father as I was saying had many ideas about her education and then he had impatient feeling in him that she was not the kind of daughter he had wanted to have as a daughter to him. The mother as I was saying then had only a dim feeling then of the being, and the living, and the feeling there was then in her children. Things were a little dim in her then but to herself then she and they and the father of them were still then of the living that was the natural living for them. To herself inside her they were never at any time neither she nor her husband nor her children nor their family ever really cut off from the living that was the natural living to them. Really she was then lost among them, that was the real being in her then, really the being in herself and in her husband and her children was really then a very dim thing to her then but always there was in her the feeling as I was saying of being in herself and in her husband and her children part of the well to do living which was the natural being for her, the only being she ever had had, to her feeling, in her.

So then as I was saying Martha Hersland in her daily feeling, in her daily living was of the daily living and the daily feeling of the people living in small houses near the Hersland family then living in the part of Gossols where no other rich people were living. Her father as I was saying was of their daily living and their daily feeling too somewhat then and on Sundays when he walked and stopped to talk to them and sat down in the houses with the women when they were cooking and ate something there in the kitchen with them and felt inside him a feeling that they were women there in a room with him. Then it was to him a good thing, then when he had this kind of feeling of them the women in him, then he thought and said it was a good thing Martha should learn how to do things, cooking and sewing and living and feeling like the women he was seeing then having as women in him to him, then when he was sitting with them in the kitchen or sometimes in their little gardens. Then he said Martha should learn the living they had in them, and he said it to them and then he said it to Martha when he saw her. This was one way he had of feeling about her being of the daily living and the daily feeling of these people living near them. Then sometimes of an evening as I was saying he would see Martha leaving the house and he would suddenly remember then she should not go out of an evening, that was no way a daughter of his in his position should be acting and then he would tell her he would see to it that she should stay home and he would employ some one to look after her and make of her the kind of educated person that it was right he should have for a daughter. And so as I was saying Martha Hersland until she was almost a young woman was in her daily living and in her daily feeling of them the people living in the small houses near the ten acre place where the Hersland family were living then and she was with them and in the houses of them a good deal in the daytime and she was a good deal with all of them in the evenings in the later part of her young living and as I was saying she was not really then interesting to any of them and as I was saying she was not then really feeling and really living and really understanding the living and the feeling that they had together then amongst them. This was the daily living and the daily feeling in Martha Hersland and the being in Martha Hersland this that I have been just describing when it came that she had an awakening into realler feeling and then she came to have a real attacking moment and it lasted to her beginning her university education. This is now a little description of this in her.

As I was saying she had a being in her that was mostly in a condition always all her living of being in a state of confusion inside her. This gave to her always very much nervous being in her, this made her to every one often very stupid in resisting and very slow in beginning and very foolish in not remembering anything that she should have been learning in her living. This will come out very clearly in the description of her living with her husband and then later with her father after she had come back to live with him after all the trouble she had in her living. It will come out very clearly then the being in her, the confusion always in her that made her to every one knowing her mostly always very stupid in resisting and really very slow and yet very jerky and unexpected in beginning and very foolish in not remembering what having been experiencing something any one would have supposed she would have been really learning.

Now there will be a little more description of her daily living, of the living and the feeling of the living and the feeling of the people in the little houses near the Hersland family then in her young living and the ending in her of this living and this feeling.

The kind of being she had in her I have already a little been describing, the kind of a whole one that she was and the nature and the kind of way her being was active in her. There has been too a little description of how much she had heard and how little she knew in living. As I was saying she was not then really very interesting to any one. No one knew anything very much then of what she was feeling about anything then and she did not know what she felt then about anything in living and nobody knew what she felt then about living and really she did not clearly then feel anything.

This was the way she was then when one day when she was alone in another part of the town where she had gone to take a lesson in singing she saw a man hit a woman with an umbrella, and the woman had a red face partly in anger and partly in asking and the man wanted the woman to know then that he wanted her to leave him alone then in a public street where people were passing and Martha saw this and this man was for her the ending of the living I have been describing that she had been living. She would go to college, she knew it then and understand everything and know the meaning of the living and the feeling in men and in women. She would go to college and she told it then to her father and her mother and they had no objection, no one was paying very much attention and she began her preparation and she came to know some other young girls and young boys, not rich ones like those it was natural she should then be knowing but more of her natural kind than any she had known before in her living. One of them John Davidson she knew very well then and he and she played music and sang together and then she was ready and then she went to college for more education. This is to be now more history of, in her, the ending of her older young living and her subsequent going to college and of the man she met there and who there married her.

As I was saying Martha then was once a very little one a baby, and then a little one and then a young girl and then a woman and then she was older and then later there was an ending to her and always all through this living in her she was the same whole one inside her and to every one who knew her.

In the description of her that I have been writing so far Martha has been a very little one, a baby, and then a little one and then a young girl and then about to become a young woman and always then in a way to herself inside her and to every one knowing her she had been the same whole one.

This was then as I was saying in a way always true she was always the same whole one inside her and to every one ever knowing her.

In some the nature in them is clearer when they are very young, in some when they are young, in some when they are not so young, in some when they are getting older, in some when they are old ones. Martha was mostly always to every one who knew her the same whole one, when she was a very little one, a little one, an older one, a very old one, mostly always she was to every one about the same kind of a whole one.

And this in a way always was true of her, all her living she was the same whole one, there was very little change in her, mostly all her living the whole of her was repeating completely, when she was learning, when she was loving, when in her later living she was still struggling. She was then all her living the same whole one, there was the same concentration of being in her, the same the proportion of one thing to the other things active in her.

As I was saying this was in the main true of her, she was of the kind of men and women and there are always many many millions of them and they are of every kind in a way of men and women, that is of independent dependent or dependent independent kind of them who are all their living the same whole one who always are repeating the complete whole thing they always are in themselves and to every one, who have the same concentration of the being in them always all their living when they are babies, when they are young ones, when they are older ones, when they are old ones, who have the same proportion of one thing to the other things active in them every minute in their living.

As I was saying Martha Hersland was of this kind of them though there were moments in her living when it seemed a little different in her for sometimes she really got into motion and mostly as I was saying motion was just confusion in her, it never came to movement in her it just was mixing up of being inside her.

As I was saying she was of the independent dependent kind of being those having in them attacking as their natural way of winning fighting, as their natural way of winning in loving, and as I was saying mostly in her, commotion in her did not make an actual attack by her for her and this was not there really to herself inside her, to herself there was real movement in her, but to every one then there was only stupid resisting and nervous being in her and this was mostly the whole history of her

As I was saying this was not quite the whole history of her, it did come to happen in her, sometimes in the living, in the history of her, that the shock of commotion in her was so strong as to give a forward movement to her. As I was saying that happened once to her when she was a very little one when she threw down the umbrella, it happened every now and then in her, it happened, as I was saying, when she saw the man hitting the woman in the street with his umbrella to rid himself then of her and of the asking in her. When she saw this it was not a horror she had in her, really she had not any very certain feeling in her, mostly in her living, as I was saying, she had not any very certain feeling, mostly as I was saying it was confusion, excitement and nervousness she had in her when there was movement inside her, then as I was saying, when she saw the man hit the woman with an umbrella and she was just then passing, she had not then as I was saying any distinct feeling then in her about what she had been seeing, not then and not then later, but it gave a motion to her, it gave her direction to getting for herself a university education.

This then that I have been describing is the being in Martha and now there will be more history of her.

As I was just saying that which I have been describing is the being in Martha Hersland. I have been describing the living and the feeling she had in her until now she was almost a young woman and a new life was to begin for her.

As I was saying she started then her preparation to get for herself a college education. As I was saying no one was objecting. Her father Mr. Hersland was not very much interested just then in his children. She had teachers and she could be taught enough by them to pass her entrance examination. She began a little then to know other kinds of young girls and boys than those that she had until then been knowing. She played duets in the evening and sang with John Davidson who was preparing to go away to get an eastern education. She was less and less and then almost not at all with them the people living near the Hersland family then, and then as I was saying she went to get her college education. This is now to be more history of her and how she came to have a lover and how he came to marry her and how he came then to leave her and what happened then to him and what happened then to her. In short this is now to be a history of all the living there ever was in her, all the being in her.

As I was saying there was not then very much change in the being in her, she was always then the same whole one, at first there was a little more movement in her, she learned a little at first how to have definite feeling in her, she learned that in the college life around her but it was not really the being in her and all this will come out in the history of her. This is now then more history of her. Now then there will begin to be a little history of another, of one of those who came to know her, who came to the same college where she was learning to do the things I have just been describing. This is now the beginning of the history of him as I am saying. This is now a little description of the living there had been in Phillip Redfern.

There was then in the living of Martha Hersland the being born in the hotel where the Hersland family was living when Mr. David Hersland came to Gossols to make for himself a great fortune and brought with him his wife little Fanny Hissen who was to know there the Shilling family who where to make in her the beginning of the feeling of herself inside her. There was then in the living of Martha Hersland that her father Mr. David Hersland and her mother Fanny Hersland came together to make her and she was born in the hotel where Mr. and Mrs. Hersland were living when they first came to Gossols where Mr. Hersland was to make for himself a great fortune and where Mrs. Hersland was to have mostly a living that was not the way of living that it would have been natural for her to be having. Martha was born then in the hotel and Mr. Hersland was just beginning then to succeed in winning fighting and Mrs. Hersland was beginning then through knowing the Shilling family, Sophie Shilling, Pauline Shilling and the mother of them to have a little in her to herself inside the feeling of herself to herself in her that it was not really natural for her to have ever really in her. Then in the living of Martha Hersland she was a little one in the ten acre place where the Hersland family lived a little later and there it was that Mr. Hersland was winning fighting and then having impatient feeling in him and then being full up with impatient feeling and then having in him beginning failing in winning and then having in him only beginning and there Mrs. Hersland had always more and more in her from the for her queer poor people near her and the servants and governesses in the house with her the feeling of importance of herself to herself inside her and then she had there in her the beginning of the weakening in her the being lost among her children and her husband living in the house with her. In the living of Martha Hersland she was a little one in the ten acre place and she was then living there the half-city half-country living of the people around her and she went to school then and she was healthy enough then and happy enough then and she was always then getting older and getting bigger and she had some troubles then and always she was of them the people in the small houses near the ten acre place where she was living then and she had always the living in her and the being in her I was describing and sometimes she got a little fatter and sometimes a little thinner and sometimes she was happy enough and often she was not so happy and mostly always she was healthy and sometimes she had uneasy feelings in her and often her father was a trouble to her and often the governess was troublesome to her and mostly her mother was not very important for her and she went on and the family living of the Hersland family was changing some as I was saying and a little Martha was changing in her as the family living was changing around her and when it came to her to want her own education no one was paying much attention to her, each one of the Hersland family had then themselves inside them to themselves each one, the father as I was saying and the mother as I was saying and Alfred Hersland and his brother David as I will be saying in the history of the two of them. Always a little then Martha had trouble with each one of them, the family living in the house together, her father and her mother and her brother Alfred and David the younger brother but mostly then they none of them were really important to her, she was all taken up then with the being in her, mostly each one of them then the family living together were taken up then by themselves then each one by the being in them and that was the history of the Hersland family, then when Martha went to college for more education. This was then the living of the Hersland family when Martha was having it in her that she was a young woman, this was the history of all of them then, that they were each one of them taken up with the being inside of them then, the father Mr. Hersland with much impatient feeling then in him, the mother with important being in her from the governess Madeleine Wyman who came often to see her and from having weakening commencing then in her, Martha from the having seen the man hit the woman with the umbrella and so then having in her the need of a college education for her, the brother Alfred who was then beginning to do things that were full of interesting feeling for him, the younger brother David who was beginning then and always from then it went on in him to find the meaning for him of something in each day of living that would make living have meaning for him, each one of them then the Hersland family then were each one of them all taken up with themselves inside them and this was the history of them as I was saying when Martha went away from them to get a college education. Each one of the Hersland family was then each one of them too much taken up with the being inside themselves then to pay much attention to another one. Martha went away to college then, as I was saying, and there she was learning to be like them the young men and women of her generation and there as I was saying she came to know Phillip Redfern.

Phillip Redfern was born in a small city and in the south western part of this country. He was the son of a consciously ill-assorted pair of parents and his earliest intellectual concept so in his later living he was always saying as I will soon be telling, was the realisation of the quality of these two decisive and unharmonised elements in his child life. He remembered too very well his first definite realisation of the quality of women when the inherent contradictions in the claims made for that sex awoke in him much confused thought. He often said that he had often puzzled over the fact that he must give up his chair to and be careful of little girls while at the same time he was taught that the little girl was quite as strong as he and quite as able to use liberty and to perfect action. In his later living he said that when he was a very little one this had been so much a puzzle to him, little girls then, to him, had everything, he wished then when he was a little one and this was a puzzle to him, he wished he had been a little girl so and so have everything.

His mother was his dear dear friend then and from her he receiv- ed then all the thoughts and convictions that were definite and con- scious then and for a long time after in him. She was an eager, impetuous, sensitive creature, full of ideal enthusiasms in her being, with moments of clear purpose and vigorous thinking but for the most part was excitably prejudiced and inconsequent in sensitive enthusiasm and given to accept- ing and giving and living sensations and impressions under the con- viction that she had them as carefully thought out theories and prin- ciples that were complete from reasoning. Her constant rebellion against the pressure of her husband's steady domination found effective expression in the inspiring training of her son to be the champion of women. It would be a sublime proof of the justice of all the poetry of living so she was al- ways thinking for the son of James Redfern to devote the strength of the father that was soon to be in the son of him to the winning of liberty, equality, opportunity, beauty, feeling, for all women.

James Redfern was a man determined to be master always in his house. He was a man courteous and deferential to all women, he never came into any vivid relation with any human being. He was cold and reserved and had a strong calm attacking will in him, and he was always perfectly right in doing everything. This was always true of him. He never knew it in him that his wife had a set purpose in her to make their son any particular thing in living. Such a thing could never be a real thing to him, such a thing no woman he could have living in the house with him could have in her, to him. It could have no meaning such a fantastic notion and then too she never said it to him. It would not have any meaning excepting as words if she had ever said it to him.

The things that have no meaning as existing are to every one very many, and that is always more and more important in understanding the being in men and women.   Often it is very astonishing, it is like seeing something and some one who always has been walking with you and you always have been feeling that one was seeing everything with you and you feel then that they are seeing that thing the way you are seeing it then and you go sometime with that one to a doctor to have that one have their eyes examined and then you find that things you are seeing they cannot see and never have been seeing and it is very astonishing and everything is different and you know then that you are seeing, you are writing completely only for one and that is yourself then and to every other one it is a different thing and then you remember every one has said that sometime and you know it then and it is astonishing.   You know it then yes but you do not really know it as a continuous knowing in you for then in living always you are feeling that some one else is understanding, feeling seeing something the way you are feeling, seeing, understanding that thing, and always it is a shock to you sometime with every one you are ever knowing and many never really know it of any one that they are feeling, seeing, understanding a different way from them and this is very very common.   As I was saying it never would come to Mr. James Redfern to be realising that Mrs. Redfern had a destiny for their son such as being a champion of women.   Such a thing would be a fantastic dream that could come from sickness in some one and nothing more to him and as I was saying she never said it to him.   Mr. Redfern was very willing that Mrs. Redfern should be the tender dear friend of their son, he was too simply certain of the being in himself and in his son to pay much attention to the emotional influences that Mrs. Redfern brought to bear on him then when he was a young one.   He was simply certain, that was the being in him, that his son would be a rational man.   Emotional women and romantic children had pleasant fantastic dreams that were alright for them.   He demanded from his son then obedience and in his presence self-restraint and for the rest when Phillip was a man being his father's son would make him the man all the Redferns had been.

Phillip Redfern when he was a man was to most every one who ever came to know him a person having in him a strange and incalculable nature.   The strong enthusiasm of emotion of his mother's nature early awoke in him with the stimulation she was always then giving to him very much interest to him for the emotional life he could have in him. The interest for knowledge and domination were in him equally strong and from the beginning he devoted himself to meditation and analysis of the emotions he had in him.   The constant spectacle of an armed neutrality between his parents early filled him with an interest in the nature of marriage and the meaning of women.

Many children who are always in the society of older men and women have their elder's feelings in them and these older men and women in their talking and their feeling if they have very decided quality in them to give to them the children always with them a knowledge of life quite out of relation to the reality of the children's experiencing and sometimes such a one one of such children while knowing and accepting many facts that his elders would have listened to in astonished horror from him often will be really ignorant of the meaning of the simplest things that happen to every one living which other children have in them as natural things for them to be knowing then. Phillip Redfern then had in him then when he was a young one and was living with his mother and his father as the only people then for him in him, his own living where there was much knowledge from reading and thinking, wonderful dreams, keen analysis, much real emotion of sympathising and very little experiencing of beginning living.

From his father then and from his mother too then, then when he was a little one Phillip Redfern learned careful and scrupulous courtesy to women and to himself and to every one he was ever seeing or feeling or meeting in books or in living or in his hearing talking or in his dreaming, and from his father then power of reserve and these were in him without the determined standards that governed the elder Redfern. Phillip learned his principles from his mother and these were in her longings and aspirations rather than reasoned settled purposes and experiencing and they were real in him though really then he did not believe in them though then and longer he lived by them.

When Phillip was beginning to be a young man he went to college as I was saying in my describing the living of Martha Hersland. He had never been to a school, his learning had been gathered from his father and largely by himself in reading. Now for the first time in his living he with his brilliant personality for he had that then to himself and to every one, keen intellect, ardent desires, moral aspirations and principles that he knew he could know by analysing them were not well reasoned principles for him to have in him but were to him as his mother's being was in him as a dear dear friend inside him, was to be thrown into familiar relations with young men and women.

The college of which Redfern became a member was the typical co-educational college of the west, a completely democratic institution. Mostly no one there was conscious of a grand-father unless as remembering one as an old man living in the house with them or as living in another place and being written to sometimes by them and then having died and that was the end of grand-fathers to them. No one among them was held responsible for the father they had unless by some particular notoriety that had come to the father of some one. It was then a democratic western institution, this college where Redfern went to have his college education. This democracy was too simple and genuine to be discussed by any one then. No one was really interested how any man or woman of them came by the money that was educating them, whether it came through several generations of gentlemen to them, whether it came through two generations or one, whether one of them earned it for herself or for himself by working, or teaching, or working on a farm or at book-selling or at anything else that would bring money to them in the summer or whether they earned a little by being a janitor to a school building in the winter or had it given them by some one interested in them. This democracy was then almost complete among them and was the same between the men and women as between the men, as between the women. This democracy was really almost complete among all of them and included very simple comradship among them all, all of the men and women there together then. The men mostly were simple, direct and earnest in their relations with the women there being educated with them, the men, most of them treating them with generosity and kindliness enough and never really doubting even for a moment their right to any learning or occupation the women, any of them were able to acquire then. The students were many of them earnest experienced men and women who had already struggled solidly with poverty and education. Many of them were interested in the sciences and the practical application of them but also there was among them a kind of feeling and yearning for beauty and this then often showed itself in them in much out of door wandering, and was beginning a little with some of them to realise itself in attempting making pictures and sculpture.

It was of such a sober minded, earnest, moral, democratic community that Redfern was now become a part. His moral aspirations found full satisfaction in the serious life of the place and his interest in emotional enthusiasm found a new and delightful exercise in the problem of woman that presented itself so strangely here. At this time the return to honest nature to him, was complete delight in him for elaboration was then not so necessary in his conviction but that vigor and force unadorned then made him forgetful of subtilty and refinement. The free simple comradship of the men and women at first filled him with astonishment and then with delight. He could not feel himself a part of it, he could not love the sense of danger in the presence and companionship of women, his instincts bade him be on guard but his ideal he felt to be here realised.

Among the many vigorous young women in the place there was Martha Hersland. She was a blond good-looking young woman full of moral purpose and educational desires. She had an eager earnest intelligence, fixed convictions and principles by then, and restless energy. She and Redfern were students in the same studies in the same class and soon singled themselves out from the crowd, it was all new, strange and dangerous for the south-western man and all perfectly simple and matter of course for the western girl. They had long talks on the meanings of things, he discoursing of his life and aims, she listening, understanding and sympathising. This intercourse steadily grew more constant and familiar. Redfern's instincts were dangerous was always there as a conviction in him, his ideals simple and pure was almost always real inside him, slowly he realised in this constant companion the existence of instincts as simple and pure as his ideals.

They were going through the country one wintry day, plunging vigorously through the snow and liking the cold air and rapid walking and excited with their own health and their youth and the freedom. "You are a comrade and a woman," he cried out in his pleasure, "It is the new world," "Surely, there is no difference our being together only it is pleasanter and we go faster," was her eager answer. "I know it," said Redfern, "I know it, it is the new world." This comradship continued through the three years. They spent much time in explaining to each other what neither quite understood. He never quite felt the reality of her simple convictions, she never quite realised what it was he did not understand.

One spring day a boy friend came to see her a younger brother of John Davidson who used to play duets with her and all three went out in the country. It was a soft warm day, the ground was warm and wet and they were healthy and they did not mind that. They found a fairly dry hill-side and sat down all three too indolent to wander further. The young fellow, a boy of eighteen, threw himself on the ground and rested his head on Martha Hersland's lap. Redfern did not stop a start of surprise and Martha Hersland smiled. The next day Redfern frankly came to her with his perplexity. "I don't understand," he said. "Was it alright for Davidson to do so yesterday. I almost believed it was my duty to knock him off." "Yes I saw you were surprised," she said and she looked uneasy and then she resolutely tried to make him see. "Do you know that to me a western woman it seems very strange that any one should see any wrong in his action. Yes I will say it, I have never understood before why you always seemed on guard". She ended pretty steadily, he flushed and looked uneasy. He looked at her earnestly, whatever was there, he certainly could not doubt her honesty. It could not be a new form of deliberate enticement even though it made a new danger.

After two years of marriage Redfern's realisation of her was almost complete. Martha was all that she had promised him to be, all that he had thought her, but that all proved sufficiently inadequate to his needs. She was moral, strenuous and pure and sought earnestly after higher things in life and art but her mind was narrow and in its way insistent, her intelligence quick but without grace and harsh and Redfern loved a gentle intelligence. Redfern was a hard man to hold, he had no tender fibre to make him gentle to discordant suffering and when once he was certain that this woman had no message for him there was no way in which she could make to him an appeal. Her narrow eager mind was helpless.

It was part of him elaborate chivalry and she though harsh and crude should never cease to receive from him this respect. He knew she must suffer but what could he do. They were man and wife, their minds and natures were separated by great gulfs, it must be again an armed neutrality but this time it was not as with his parents an armed neutrality between equals but with an inferior who could not learn the rules of the game. It was just so much the more unhappy.

Mrs. Redfern never understood what had happened to her. In a dazed blind way she tried all ways of breaking through the walls that confined her. She threw herself against them with impatient energy and again she tried to destroy them piece by piece. She was always thrown back bruised and dazed and never quite certain whence came the blow, how it was dealt or why. It was a long agony, she never became wiser or more indifferent, she struggled on always in the same dazed eager way.

Such was the relation between Redfern and his wife when Redfern having made some reputation for himself in philosophy was called to Farnham college to fill the chair of philosophy there.

There was then a dean presiding over the college of Farnham who in common with many of her generation believed wholly in the essential sameness of sex and who had devoted her life to the development of this doctrine. The Dean of Farhman had had great influence in the lives of many women. She was possessed of a strong purpose and vast energy. She had an extraordinary instinct for the qualities of men and rarely failed to choose the best of the young teachers as they came from the universities. She rarely kept them many years for either they attained such distinction that the great universities claimed them or they were dismissed as not being able enough to be called away.

Phillip Redfern had taken his doctor's degree in philosophy, had married and presently then he came to hold the chair of philosophy at Farnham college. Two very interesting personalities in the place were the dean Miss Charles and her friend Miss Dounor.

Redfern had previously had no experience of women's colleges, he knew some thing of the character of the dean but had heard nothing of any other member of the institution and went to make his bow to his fellow instructors in some wonder of anticipation and excitement of mind.

The new professor of philosophy was invited by the dean to meet the assembled faculty at a tea at her house two days after his arrival in the place. He entered alone and was met by the dean who was then just about beginning the ending of her middle living. She was a dignified figure with a noble head and a preoccupied abrupt manner. She was a member of a family which was proud of having had in three successive generations three remarkable women.

The first of these three was not known beyond her own community among whom she had great influence by reason of her strength of will, her powerful intellect, her strong common sense and her deep religious feeling. She carried to its utmost the then woman's life with its keen wordly sense, its power of emotion and prayer and its devout practical morality.

The daughter of this vigorous woman was known to a wider circle and sought for truth in all varieties of ecstatic experience. She mingled with her genuine mystic exaltation a basal common sense and though spending the greater part of her life in examining and actively taking part in all the exaggerated religious enthusiasms of her time she never lost her sense of criticism and judgement and though convinced again and again of the folly and hypocrisy of successive saints never doubted the validity of mystic religious experience.

In the third generation the niece of this woman, the dean Hannah Charles, found her expression in still wider experience. She did not expect her regeneration from religious experience and found her exaltation in resisting.

Through her influence she was enabled to keep the college in a flourishing state and to keep the control of all things entirely in her own hands but she was anxious that in the teaching staff there should be some one who would be permanent, who would have great parts and a scholarly mind and would have no influence to trouble hers and before many years she found Miss Dounor who ideally fulfilled these conditions.

Miss Dounor was a graduate of an eastern college and had made some reputation. She was utterly unattached, being an only child whose parents died just before she entered college and was equally detached by her nature from all affairs of the world and was always quite content to remain where she was so long as some took from her all management of practical affairs and left her in peace with her work and her dreams. She was possessed of a sort of transfigured innocence which made a deep impression on the vigorous practical mind of Miss Charles who while keeping her completely under her control was nevertheless in awe of her blindness of worldly things and of the intellectual power of her clear sensitive mind.

Though Miss Dounor was detached by the quality of her nature from worldly affairs it was not because she loved best dreams and abstract thought, for her deepest interest was in the varieties of human experience and her constant desire was to partake of all human relations but by some quality of her nature she never succeeded in really touching any human creature she knew. Her transfigured innocence, too, was not an ignorance of the facts of life nor a puritan's instinct indeed her desire was to experience the extreme forms of sensuous life and to make even immoral experiences her own. Her detachment was due to an abstracted spirit that could not do what it would and which was evident in her reserved body, her shy eyes and gentle face.

As I was saying Phillip Redfern had been invited by the dean to meet the assembled faculty at a tea at her house. He entered in some wonder of anticipation and excitement of mind and was met by the dean Miss Charles, "You must meet Miss Dounor" she said to him breaking abruptly through the politeness of the new instructor who was as I said south-western. Redfern looked with interest at this new presentment of gentleness and intelligence who greeted him with awkward shyness. Her talk was serious pleasant and intense, her point of view clear, her arguments just, and her opinions sensitive. Her self-consciousness disappeared during this eager discussion but her manner did not lose its awkward restraint, her voice its gentleness or her eyes their shyness.

While the two were still in the height of the discussion there came up to them a blond, eager, good-looking young woman whom Redfern observing presented as his wife to his new acquantance. Miss Dounor checked in her talk was thrown into even more than her original shy awkwardness and looking with distress at this new arrival after several efforts to bring her mind to understand said ; "Mrs. Redfern yes yes, of course, your wife I had forgotten." She made another attempt to begin to speak and then suddenly giving it up gazed at them quite helpless.

"Pray go on as I am very anxious to hear what you think," said Mrs. Redfern nervously and Redfern bowing to his wife turned again to Miss Dounor and went on with the talk.

An observer would have found it difficult to tell from the mere appearance of these three what their relation toward each other was. Miss Dounor was absorbed in her talk and thought and oblivious of everything except the discussion, her shy eyes fixed on Redfern's face and her tall constrained body filled with eagerness, Redfern was listening and answering showing the same degree of courteous deference to both his companions, turned first toward one and then toward the other one with impartial attention and Mrs. Redfern her blond good-looking face filled with eager anxiety to understand listened to one and then the other with the same anxious care.

Later Redfern wandered to a window where Miss Hannah Charles, Miss Dounor and Mrs. Redfern were standing looking out at a fine prospect of sunset and a long line of elms defining a road that led back through the town of Farnham to the wooded hills behind. Redfern stood with them looking out at the scene. Mrs. Redfern was listening intently to each one's thinking. "Ah of course you know Greek," she said with eager admiration to Miss Dounor who made no reply.

It happens often about the twenty-ninth year of a life that all the forces that have been engaged through the years of childhood, adolescence and youth in confused and sometimes angry combat range themselves in ordered ranks, one is uncertain of one's aims, meaning and power during these years of tumultuous growth when aspiration has no relation to fulfillment and one plunges here and there with energy and misdirection during the strain and stress of the making of a personality until at last we reach the twenty-ninth year, the straight and narrow gateway of maturity and life which was all uproar and confusion narrows down to form and purpose and we exchange a dim possibility for a big or small reality.

Also in our american life where there is no coercion in custom and it is our right to change our vocation as often as we have desire and opportunity, it is a common experience that our youth extends through the whole first twenty-nine years of our life and it is not till we reach thirty that we find at last that vocation for which we feel ourselves fit and to which we willingly devote continued labor. It must be owned that while much labor is lost to the world in these efforts to secure one's true vocation, nevertheless it makes more completeness in individual life and perhaps in the end will prove as useful to the world, and if we believe that there is more meaning in the choice of love than plain propinquity so we may well believe that there is more meaning in vocations than that it is the thing we can first learn about and win an income with.

Redfern had now come to this fateful twenty-ninth year. He had been a public preacher for women's rights, he had been a mathematician, a psychologist and a philosopher, he had married and earned a living and yet the world was to him without worth or meaning and he longed for a more vital human life than to be an instructor of youth, his theme was humanity, his desire was to be in the great world and of it, he wished for active life among his equals not to pass his days as a guide to the immature and he preferred the criticism of life in fiction to the analysis of the mind in philosophy and now the time was come in this his twenty-ninth year for the decisive influence in his career.

Cora Dounor had on her side too her ideals which in this world she had not found complete. She too longed for the real world while wrapped away from it by the perverse reserve of her mind and the awkward shyness of her body. Such friendship as she had yet realised she felt for the dean Miss Hannah Charles but it was not a nearness of affection, it was a recognition of the power of doing and working, and a deference to the representative of effective action and the habitual dependence of years of protection. What ever Miss Charles advised or undertook seemed always to Miss Dounor the best that could be done or affected. She sustained her end of the relation in being a learned mind, a brilliant teacher and a docile subject. She pursued her way expounding philosophy, imbibing beauty, desiring life, never questioning the things nearest her, interested only in abstract ideas and concrete desire and all her life was arranged to leave her untouched and unattached but in this shy abstracted, learned creature there was a desire for sordid life and the common lot.

It was interesting to see the slow growth of interest to admiration and then to love in this awkward reserved woman, unconscious of her meanings and the world's attention and who made no attempt to disguise or conceal the strength of her feeling.

Redfern's life experience had been to learn that where there was woman there was for him danger not through his own affections but by the demand that this sex made upon him. By this extreme chivalry he was always bound to more than fulfill the expectations he gave rise to in the mind of his companion. Indeed this man loved the problem of woman so much that he willingly endured all pain to seek and find the ideal that filled him with such deep unrest and he never tired of meeting and knowing and devoting himself to any woman who promised to fulfill for him his desire and here in Cora Dounor he had found a spirit so delicate so free so gentle and intelligent that no severity of suffering could deter him from seeking the exquisite knowledge that this companionship could give him. And he knew that she too would willingly pay high for the fresh vision that he brought her.

It is the french habit in thinking to consider that in the grouping of two and an extra it is the two that get something from it all who are of importance and whose claim should be considered ; the american mind accustomed to waste happiness and be reckless of joy finds morality more important than ecstacy and the lonely extra of more value than the happy two. To our new world feeling the sadness of pain has more dignity than the beauty of joy. It takes time to learn the value of happiness. Truly a single moment snatched out of a distracted existence is hardly worth the trouble it takes to seize it and to obtain such it is wasteful to inflict pain, it is only the cultivators of leisure who have time to feel the gentle approach the slow rise, the deep ecstacy and the full flow of joy and for these pain is of little value, a thing not to be remembered, and it is only the lack of joy that counts.

Martha Redfern eager, anxious and moral had little understanding of the sanctity of joy and hardly a realisation of the misery of pain. She understood little now what it was that had come upon her and she tried to arrange and explain it by her western morality and her new world humanity. She could not escape the knowledge that something stronger than community of interest bound her husband and Miss Dounor together. She tried resolutely to interpret it all in terms of comradship and great equality of intellectual interests never admitting to herself for a moment the conception of a possible marital disloyalty. But in spite of these standards and convictions she was filled with a vague uneasiness that had a different meaning than the habitual struggle against the hard wall of courtesy that Redfern had erected before her.

This struggle in her mind showed itself clearly when she was in the company of her husband and Miss Dounor. She would sit conscientiously bending her mind to her self-imposed task of understanding and development, when in the immediate circle of talkers that included her husband and Miss Dounor she gave anxious and impartial attention to the words of one and the other occasionally joining in the talk by an earnest inquiry and receiving always from Redfern the courteous deference that he extended to every one, to everything, to all women. She listened with admiring attention particularly to Miss Dounor who genuinely unconscious of all this nervous misery paid her in return scant attention. When she was not in the immediate group of talkers with these two she kept her attention on the person with whom she was talking and showed the burden of her feeling only in the anxious care with which she listened and talked.

She was not to be left much longer to work out her own conclusions. One afternoon in the late fall in the second year of their life at Farnham, Miss Charles came to the room where she was sitting alone and in her abrupt way spoke directly of the object of her visit. "Mrs. Redfern," she began "you probably know something of the gossip that is at present going on, I want you to keep Mr. Redfern in order, I cannot allow him to make Miss Dounor the subject of scandalous talk." She stopped and looked steadily at the uneasy woman who was dazed by this sudden statement of her own suspicion, "I, I don't understand," she stammered. "I think you understand quite well. I depend upon you to speak to him about it," and with this the dean departed.

This action on Miss Charles part showed her wisdom. She knew very well the small power that Mrs. Redfern had over her husband and she took this method of attack only because it was the only one open to her. Mrs. Redfern could not accomplish anything by any action but she was a woman and jealous and there was little doubt, so the dean thought, that before long she would effect some change.

Martha Redfern's mind was now in a confusion. Miss Charles had added nothing to her facts nevertheless her statement had made a certainty of what Mrs. Redfern had resolutely regarded as an impossibility. She sat there long and long thinking over again and again the same weary round of thoughts and terrors. She knew she was powerless to change him, she could only try to get the evidence to condemn him. Did she want it, if she had it she must act on it, she dreaded to obtain it and could not longer exist without it. She must watch him and find it all out without questioning, must learn it by seeing and hearing and she felt dimly a terror of the things she might be caught doing to obtain it, she dreaded the condemnation of Redfern's chivalrous honor. She did not doubt his disloyalty she was convinced of that and she still feared to lose his respect for her sense of honor. "He is dishonorable, all his action is deceit," she said to herself again and again but she found no comfort in this thought, she knew there was a difference and that she respected his standard more than her own justification.

In the long weary days that followed she was torn by these desires, she must watch him always and secretly, she must gain the knowledge she dreaded to possess and she must be deeply ashamed of the ways she must pursue. She was no longer able to listen to others when her husband and Miss Dounor were in her presence, she dared not keep an open watch but her observation was unceasing.

Redfern was not wholly unconscious of this change in his wife's manner perhaps more in the relief that she ceased her eager efforts to please him than in the annoyance of her suspicious watching. Redfern was a man too much on guard to fear surprise and with all his experience too ignorant of women's ways to see danger where danger really lay.

It was the end of May and one late afternoon Mrs. Redfern filled with her sad past and sadder future, sat in her room watching the young leaves shining brilliantly in the warm sunshine on the long row of elms that stretched away through the village toward the green hills that rose beyond. Mrs. Redfern knew very well the feel of that earth warm with young life and wet with spring rains, knew it as part of her dreary life that seemed to have lasted always. As she sat there in sadness, the restless eagerness of her blond goodlooking face was gone and her hands lay clasped quietly without straining, time and sadness had become stronger in her than desire.

Redfern came into the house and passed into his own study. He remained there a short while and then was called away. As soon as he was out of sight Mrs. Redfern arose and went into his room. She walked up to his desk and opening his portfolio saw a letter in his writing. She scarcely hesitated so eager was she to read it. She read it to the end, she had her evidence.

Categories that once to some one had real meaning can later to that same one be all empty. It is queer that words that meant something in our thinking and our feeling can later come to have in them in us not at all any meaning. This is happening always to every one really feeling meaning in words they are saying. This is happening very often to almost every one having any realisation in them in their feeling, in their thinking, in their imagining of the words they are always using. This is common then to many having in them any real realisation of the meaning of the words they are using. As I was saying categories that once to some one had real meaning come later to that same one not to have any meaning at all then for that one. Sometimes one reads a letter that they have been keeping with other letters, and one is not very old then and so it is not that they are old then and forgetting, they are not very old then and they come in cleaning something to reading this letter and it is all full of hot feeling and the one, reading the letter then, has not in them any memory of the person who once wrote that letter to them. This is different, very different from the changing of the feeling and the thinking in many who have in them real realisation of the meaning of words when they are using them but there is in each case so complete a changing of experiencing in feeling and thinking, or in time or in something, that something, some one once alive to some one is then completely a stranger to that one, the meaning in a word to that one the meaning in a way of feeling and thinking that is a category to some one, some one whom some one was knowing, these then come to be all lost to that one sometime later in the living of that one.

This is very true then, this is very true then of the feeling and the thinking that makes the meaning in the words one is using, this is very true then that to many of them having in them strongly a sense of realising the meaning of the words they are using that some words they once were using, later have not any meaning and some then have a little shame in them when they are copying an old piece of writing where they were using words that sometime had real meaning for them and now have not any real meaning in them to the feeling and the thinking and the imagining of such a one. Often this is in me in my feeling, often then I have to lose words I have once been using, now I commence again with words that have meaning, a little perhaps I had forgotten when it came to copying the meaning in some of the words I have just been writing. Now to begin again with what I know of the being in Phillip Redfern, now to begin again a description of Phillip Redfern and always now I will be using words having in my feeling, thinking, imagining very real meaning. As I was saying Phillip Redfern was to very many who knew him a queer one, he was to very many who knew him a bad one, he was to some who knew him so good a one that he was almost a real saint for them. This was true of him then and now I will begin a little more description of the kind of being in him, of the kind of being he had in living, of the many millions men and women always being like him.

He was of the kind of men and women who, in the end, to every one, have been as if they had been a failure. They are many of them, many of this kind of them, many of the kind of which Redfern was one, that have had very much reputation, have been well known for their living, for the being in them, in their living very many of this kind of them. These see themselves, always have, do and will see themselves all their living as virtuous, as heroic, as noble, as successful, as beautiful, as whatever is the best way of being to them, see themselves so through the weakness as well as through the strong things in them. Many men and many women see themselves as virtuous always in their living, this is a little now very interesting.

Many then have it in them that their weakness is a virtue in them. There are very many of this kind of them then. Johnson when he forgets his emotion, the emotion he had when he was friendly or loving or fighting, Johnson when he forgets his emotion and declares it to have been all the other one's doing attributes his having yielded to this indulging in loving, fighting, friendly action, to the weakness in him of always yielding. This weakness of his is uppermost in him and to himself, having forgotten that he had been himself wanting the thing he had once, later in describing, feeling of thinking the action over he says it was because he has the weakness of never being able to resist any one who wants anything. Perhaps Johnson began but later he forgets his having been wanting the thing, he remembers only that always he does anything anybody wants him to be doing, that is the weakness in him that is to him the whole principle of the being in him. Frank Hackart attributes his doing anything to the philanthropy in him, she was lonesome and threw herself on him, took possession and what did he do but take care of her. This later in telling, in remembering, in feeling is always the history of any woman and him. Mary Helbing always puts it down to, that they wanted it and she gave it but she had no responsibility, it was because she was so game that she did it, that is always the reason she does it, she is so game she never refuses anything that is a challenge, there is never anything that she is ever wanting in her living that she is ever getting. Sarah Sands puts her yielding down to unsuspiciousness, that is the reason she yields, she is so easy, that is the secret of it. Phillip Redfern was of this kind of them, he was to himself completely chivalrous, completely a gentleman, women, every one should always have complete courtesy always from him. And they are right all of them, all these things, each thing in each one, are characteristics in each one but they all think that one characteristic is the whole of them, they all of them forget the other things in them that are active in them, they all have it in common that in remembering anything they forget all the emotion they had then in them and so it must have been the other person's fault it happened, anything. All of them in remembering have not had any emotion except the one and so they had none then and so it must have been the other person. This is a little now very interesting.

As I was saying Phillip Redfern was of this kind in men and women.

There will be now more description of virtuous being, virtuous feeling in men and women. There will be now some description of religious feeling in some men and women, of virtuous and religious feeling in them, of the being in them, of the sensitiveness in them, of the worldly feeling in them, of succeeding and failing in them. First then there will be more description of the kind of being in some men, men like Phillip Redfern, of religious, virtuous feeling in some men.

As I was saying some of the things all men have in them in their daily living have it to come in more men, only from the bottom nature in them than other things in them. Nothing of all the things all men have in them in their daily living comes in all men from the bottom nature of them. Eating, drinking, loving, anger in them, beginning and ending in them come more from many men from the bottom nature of most of them than other things in them but always there are many men of all the millions of each kind of them who have it in them not to have even eating and drinking and doctoring and living and anger in them and beginning and ending in them come from the bottom nature of them.

Men in their living have many things inside them, they have in them, each one of them has it in him, his own way of feeling himself important inside in him, they have in them all of them their own way of beginning, their own way of ending, their own way of working, their own way of having loving inside them and loving coming out from them, their own way of having anger inside them and letting their anger come out from inside them, their own way of eating their own way of drinking, their own way of sleeping, their own way of doctoring. They have each one of them their own way of fighting they have in them all of them their own way of having fear in them. They have all of them in them their own way of believing, their own way of being important inside them their own way of showing to others around them the important feeling inside in them.

Mostly every one has some kind of way of conceiving of themselves as a strong one, as a weak one, as a good one, as a bad one, as a virtuous, as an honorable one, as a religious, as an irreligious, as an unreligious one.

Mostly every one has some kind of way of conceiving of themselves, as a strong one, as a weak one, as a good one, as a bad one, as a virtuous one, as an honorable one, as a religious one, as an irreligious one, as an unreligious one.

Some as I am saying have honor in them and religion from the nature of them when this is strong enough in them to make it their own inside them. Some can make their own honor, some their own living, some their own religion, some are weak and can do one thing, make one thing their own, some are strong enough and all of it, loving, honor, and religion in them, all of it is some one else's, of some one else's making, some can just resist and not make their own anything, there are many of them. Some out of their own virtue make a god who sometimes later is a terror to them. Out of their own virtue they make a god who sometimes later is a terror to them. Some make some things like laws out of the nature of them, out of the nature of some other one. Some are controlled by other people's virtue, and then it scares them. Listen to each one telling about their own virtue and that grows to make a god for them, grows to be a law for them and often afterwards scares them, some afterwards like it, some forget it, some are it. Some honor what is right to them for them to be doing. Some separate honor from the doing of the thing, have it as a feeling.

Some love themselves enough to not want to lose themselves, immortality can to them mean nothing but this thing. Some love themselves negatively, then impersonal future life is for them alright, a good enough thing. Some love themselves and others so hard that they are sure that they will exist even when they won't, they do to themselves exist even when they don't, these have a future life feeling, an individual thing, some love themselves and they are it and that is all there is of it in them and they do not have future life in them to be an important thing. Men and women have being in them all of them when they are living. Many men and women have in them a feeling of future life in them, very many of them, some for this life, some for another life, some for both lives, this and another one, some have a stronger, some have a weaker feeling of themselves inside them, some have more, some have less loving in them for themselves than other ones have in them, some have more some have less loving in them for other ones than others have in them, some have more some have less feeling for some thing than other ones have in them and all these things in each one are part in them of the virtuous feeling, of the religious feeling they have in them each one, each man and woman, each one having man or woman being in them, each man or woman has some being in her or in him.

There are some who have not any feeling of virtue in them. There are not very many of them. There are perhaps some millions of them. Mostly every one as I am saying has in her or in him some kind of feeling of being of virtue in living. Some from the things they feel as weakness in them, some from the things they feel as strength in them. Phillip Redfern had it in him to make a virtue for him of a thing he felt as a weakness in him. There are very many of this kind of them, many, very many men, many women.

Mostly all of this kind of men and women have some kind of religion in them. This is now a little a discussion of the being in some of them.

As I was saying Phillip Redfern was of the kind of men and women, and there are always many men of this kind of them and some women of this kind of them, who have in their living a good deal of reputation from the living and the being in them and then they are not successful in living successful in the whole of their living and to many knowing them they are romantic in their living, or beautiful, or dramatic in their living and to some, saints in living, and Redfern was such a one and to most every one he was a man always failing in his living, and to Miss Dounor he was a saint among men and to Mrs. Redfern he was wonderful in the honorable courtesy in him and mostly every one sometime thought he was a bad man and mostly to every one he was a man given to lying. He said once of some one, "Lathrop tells a lie as if it were the truth and I tell the truth as if it were a lie." He was to himself a man simple, sensuous and passionate and that was to himself the whole of him. As I was saying his weakness was to himself the strength in him and so always all his living to every one who ever came to know, excepting to some to whom he was a saint in suffering, to every one mostly he was failing from the weaknesses there were in him. To himself as I was saying he was a simple, sensuous, passionate being from whom chivalry demanded he should be always yielding when he himself was not active in feeling. He was a man always on guard, with every one always able to pierce him. That was the living he had in him.

For the rest of his days he was a literary man and sometimes a politician. He plunged deeply into the political life of his time and failed everywhere, in this life as in all of his human relations his instincts gave the lie to his ideals and his ideals to his instincts. It was interesting to many to witness the life of this man, to see him go up again and again, against the yielding spirit in him, go up with unwearied courage only to meet with certain defeat. He was himself the only one of all the lookers on who dreamed of victory. The others whether watching with indifference, with deep sympathy or stern condemnation, with malicious or righteous triumph knew that he would fail, but he always struggled on filled to the very end with hope and courage, always defeated and always ready to make the fresh assault.

As I was saying there was a Johnson who had made some reputation in his living, by the living that was romantic to every one knowing, by the being in him and always he was certain in telling, feeling, and thinking that everything that had happened to him when as was the way in him, he was finished with that thing, that it was because he was weak and open to any suggesting and that made it happen that he was in a relation and he had the right to get out in any way he wanted for that was the right he had to defend himself when every one had him where they wanted to have him because he was so weak to every one's suggesting. He would brag of things he had done when he was filled up with them and always he was filled up with them and he would know he had a right to run away or do anything to defend himself for every one could hold him by suggesting to him by the sensitive suggestibility in him and this was his great weakness in him and he made of it the principle of his living to himself in his talking, thinking, feeling, and he was of the kind of them and perhaps Lord Byron and Oscar Wilde were of this kind of them, he was of them who become romantic, heroic, beautiful, saintly by the weakness in them that is there always acting, that is true of them, but always these are doing things and boasting of them in their active living. There are very many of such of them. Redfern was such a one. A Johnson I was describing was such a one. Some have only this a little in them enough to make them very sentimental in their living, some have it a little more in them than those having it just as sentimental being in them and some of

such of them are men's men and some of such of them are women's men.
And Hackart that I was just describing was one of such of them. Some
have it just a little more in them than the sentimental ones and they are
dramatic in their living and there are very many women and there are
very many men who have this being in them and a Sarah Sands was such
a one as I was just saying. There are some who have this way of being
only in spots in them. There are many such of them, many women and
many men of such of them.

As I was saying such a one as the Johnson I have been just describing, when he forgets his emotion that made him do a thing, always declares
it to have been all the other one's doing, attributes his having yielded to
his own weakness of being very susceptible to suggesting that being the
thing in him uppermost in him to make a principle continuous in him of
living. This is all different from self-righteousness which is a way of being
that everything in one is right and should be so considered by every one,
self-righteousness is believing that the one acting is so right that if every
one acted like them everything would be right in living and every one
would be a good one. This is a very different thing from the feeling that
I am describing. These that I am describing make a principle to free
them, from the weakness in them. It is a weakness, they are always
saying it of them, one that he is too susceptible to suggesting, another
that when a woman needs protecting of course he must give her that because she is a weak thing and he is always weak in yielding protection to
a weak woman, another because she is so unobserving that she has no
realisation of what anybody is doing though maybe it is her vanity that
keeps her from really seeing. All these things are true as characteristics
in each one of them that make a principle of them, these things are in
each one of them, that is quite true of them but they all think that characteristic is the whole of them and so they have not to themselves the
responsibility of the condition. Some are noble in it, some are not, but
all of them are sure of it, for that is the principle of their being, to each
one of them. In short, they all, each one of this kind of them forget their
emotion they had in the thing they were doing, and so to themselves
after, it must have been the other person's fault that it happened, this
thing, and these then after have no emotion of this thing, unless they are
living it again in imagining and then they are the same as when they had
it really in them, always else they have not the emotion, it is the other
person's fault the thing happened between them, these have no emotion
that they are remembering except the kind of weakness they know always
to be in them each one and so they had no emotion then, they knew that
well in them, and so it must have been their weakness and the other
person's willing them that made them have this thing in them.

As I was saying Phillip Redfern was such a one. As I was saying all
this is very interesting in the meaning of virtue and religion that such a

one has in them. This kind of being can be in them having independent dependent or dependent independent being in them, having any kind of being in them.

Johnson when he forgets his emotion and declares it to have been all the other one's doing, attributes his having yielded to his own weakness, that being the thing in him to him uppermost in him. Frank Hackart attributes his to philanthropy, she was lonesome and threw herself on him, took possession, and what did he do but take care of her. Melanctha put it down to that they wanted it and she gave it but she had no responsibility, it was because she was so game that she did it. Sarah Sands puts her yielding down to unsuspiciousness, that is the reason she yields, she is so easy and that's it. All these things are true as characteristics in each one but they all think that characteristic is the whole of them. It isn't. They all forget their emotion and so it must have been the other person's fault it happened and they have now no emotion and so they had none and so it must have been the other person's.

Phillip Redfern as I was saying was of this kind in men and women. He was always on his guard and always a woman could reach him inside his guard and he must do then what it was right for a man always on guard to do when he was touched inside the guard. He must give them their revenge and always again they would touch him. He must always be elaborately on guard and always he must give them what they asked of him when they touched him in spite of his guarding himself from them. This was the way his being worked in him.

As I was saying many men and some women, many women and some men of this kind of them make a good deal of reputation in their living from the living and the being in them. Mostly all of them, at least very many of them, any way it is not uncommon among them that they make a failure of the whole of their living, mostly they want to succeed in winning recognition, mostly they get some from their living, very many of them are failing in the whole of their living, often some one thinks one of such of them a saint, a hero, a very noble person, often very many think such a one to be a very bad one. Phillip Redfern as I was saying was such a one. There were very many different ways of feeling the being in him as I am saying. This has been now a very little description of the being in him. As I was saying, to the ending of his living he had the same living in him and as a whole living, his living was failing.

Phillip Redfern then had to himself a feeling of the being in him that was to him in a way a simple thing. Phillip Redfern was to Miss Dounor a man of saintly strength and courage and chivalrous feeling and self-sacrificing. Phillip Redfern was to Mrs. Redfern a man before whom she wanted to be intelligent, and honorable in acting and in feeling and delicate, and to be pleasing by knowing Greek and naive realism. Phillip

Redfern was to very many a man who was always lying.   Phillip Redfern was to very many a very brilliant man gone altogether wrong.   Phillip Redfern was to very many a man always wronging every one.   Phillip Redfern was to many a very brilliant man and a very weak one.   Phillip Redfern was to some the kind of man I have been just describing.   This has been now a little history of him.

Virtue and virtuous feeling in men and women is a very peculiar thing. More and more there will be a description in this writing of all the kinds of ways any one can have virtue in them.   Now there will be a very little description of virtue in men and women and then there will be a little more description of their sensitive being.

Every one has then their own way of being important inside them from the things in them each one that are virtues in them to them, or vices in them to them, or strong things in them, to them, or weaknesses in them to them.   Mostly every one has some kind of way of having some distinction inside them to themselves to their feeling and their thinking and their talking.   Mostly every one has some kind of way of feeling some distinction in them, some from the tastes in them, some from the not having tastes or any way of doing anything in them, some as I was saying from the strong things in them, some as I was saying from the weak things in them.   Mostly every one has some way of finding themselves inside them more or less distinguished, they have this feeling mostly every one, more or less inside them always in their living. Mostly every one is in some way a distinguished man or a distinguished woman inside themselves to themselves from something, from doing, being something, from not doing or being something, from doing things like some one, from doing things like every one, from doing things better or worse than some one, from doing things not so well or better than almost any one, from doing something and not doing some other thing, from doing some things and never doing some other things, there is every kind of thing that can give distinction and mostly every one has some kind of distinguished feeling in themselves to themselves inside them.

Being virtuous, being sentimental, being dramatic, being religious, being anything is interesting in each one having in them that thing that they have in them.   Being distinguished each one inside them by something, to themselves in their feeling, is very interesting.

Sometime I want to understand every kind of way any one can have the feeling of being distinguished by the virtue they have in them.   Someime I want to understand every kind of way any one can have the feeling of being distinguished in them and every kind of thing that can give any one a feeling of such distinction in themselves inside them.   Sometime I want to understand the complete being in each one and all the details of their coming to have in them their kind of feeling, imagination, thinking, knowing, certainty inside them, virtuous feeling in them, anything in them that gives to them inside them the feeling of being distinguished to themselves inside them.

I want to know sometime all about sentimental feeling. I want to know sometime all the different kinds of ways people have it in them to be certain of anything. These and virtuous feelings in each one, of themselves to themselves having virtue inside them, is to me very interesting. Always more and more I want to know it of each one what certainty means to them, how they came to be certain of anything, what certainty means to them and how contradiction does not worry them and how it does worry them and how much they have in them of remembering and how much they have in them of forgetting, and how different any one is from any other one and what any one and every one means by anything they are saying. All these things are to me very interesting.

As I was saying virtuous feeling and being certain of anything is to me very interesting. Having virtuous feeling and any certain feeling, that is being certain of anything is to me very interesting in every one. Having certainty in them is in each one, of the kind of way that their kind of men and women have it of having it in them. Having certainty in them is a thing very interesting in each one having a certainty of anything in her or in him. Certainty and virtuous feeling and religion, these are to me all three just now very interesting. Shortly I will try to tell a little of the way some come to have their certainty in them. Some build certainty up with little and little sure things and make a pile of them, some are summary and all embracing in the certain feeling they have always in them, some are certain of almost anything, some are hardly certain of anything, some have to have a complete system for each certain feeling in them, some have a sense of dramatic arrangement to complete the scene of the certain conviction, the certain emotion they have in them and the complete scene changes for them with each new certainty they have in them. Certainty worries some and some never have certainty to be a worry to them. Some have certainty by comparison, by comparing the thing they have then with what any other one they are knowing is having, some never compare anything with any one, certainty is a real thing in them, in some of such of them as a little pile they are gradually increasing, in some in something that they keep there inside them always of the same dimension. Some need company to keep their certainty from freezing or melting or evaporating or in some way disappearing. Some need company to keep any certainty in them, some like company around them while they have their own certainty inside them, some need to have the certainty in the presence of the company that they need to have with them. Certainty is certainly very interesting. I wish I knew all the kinds of certainty all the kinds of men and women ever existing have in them. Certainty and virtuous feeling and important feeling in men and in women is to me just now very very interesting.

As I was saying the kind of certainty, the kind of virtuous feeling, the kind of important feeling any one has in them comes from the nature of them, from the kind they are of men and women. Some men and some women are strong enough to make their own kind of certain feeling in them, some are weak and can do one thing their own in the way of a certainty in them, some are strong enough in living and all of it all the certain feeling in them is some one else's, some can just resist and not get any one else's certain feeling and never make any of their own certain feeling to be inside them, some have everybody's certain feeling in them, some have a sentimental sense of the beauty and the loveliness and the truth of certain feeling and it is so lovely and so noble and everybody is so good and so beautiful and everybody has some certain feeling and in some such a feeling of certain feeling is a real thing. There are many ways of being sentimental, sometime there will be some description of some kinds of ways of being sentimental. Out of their own certain feeling some make a god who sometimes later is a terror to them. That is a kind of feeling that some have about laws of nature as they call them. Many make of their certain feeling a god which later terrifies them. Some are controlled by other's certain feeling. To some it is a comfort such a certain feeling. Some have it that some one else's certain feeling scares them. Listen to each one telling of the certain feeling in them. It is very interesting. Some like their own certain feeling, some later forget it, some later are scared by it, some later are it. Some love their certain feeling enough never to want to lose it, some have it when they are not any longer believing in it, some can completely lose it, some get mixed up with theirs and other ones and they have very much trouble with all of it, all the certain feeling they ever come to know in living. Some love their certain feeling and they never lose it, some love it and they sometime lose it, some always are looking for it, some are immortal in themselves by it, some neither have it nor haven't it, some are to themselves only a part of it. Some love it so hard that other people have it. Some have it, some never really have it, some never really own it. Many need company for it, this is very common. Some need drama to support it, some need lying to help it, some love it, some hate it, some never are very certain they really have it. Certain feeling in men and women is very interesting.

What was Phillip Redfern's way with certainty and virtue and distinction in himself to himself inside him. He was to himself as I was saying simple, sensuous and passionate. This was not really a description of him to any other one. This was all he ever said to any one of the being in him. This was the feeling he had in him of the being he had in him. He never said it any differently of himself to any one. He was to himself of the good kind in men and women, he was on guard because women and other things were dangerous things, he always felt he would be winning and always he was failing and this was always happening to him. Always to mostly every one he was lying. Always he was telling all that it was right for him to tell to any one. That was the way any man would act, of that he was very certain. No man would tell more than he should tell if he was the kind of a man Redfern would speak of as a good one. This was very certain knowledge in him, in Phillip Redfern. He was certain always that he was telling all that it was right for him, for any man to tell to any one. To mostly every one he was a man who was mostly always lying about himself and about every other one who had any relation to him. This was true in his living, he was telling all that it was right he should be telling to any one, every one was always feeling, always saying that he was mostly always always lying. To himself it was not a virtue in him that he was never telling anything more about anything about himself about any one than it was right that he should be telling, it was to himself then, this in him, not a virtuous feeling in him, it was a thing it was natural for him to be doing, never to tell anything, it was not right that he should say really to any one. He had not then from this any feeling of virtue in him. He had a feeling of virtue although it was as he felt it in him a weakness in him that he always kept himself on guard so that temptation should never come close to him. This was to him in a way a virtue in him, that he always was on guard so that no woman, nothing he did not want should touch him, should come close to him. This was to him a virtue in him, though it was from the weakness of him that he needed to be always guarding but it was a weakness of what can any man do when a demand is made upon him, kind of weakness in him, that was a weakness that any man who was a man must have in living, and so he Redfern always being on guard had from that to himself a virtuous feeling in him, and this then as I am saying is very common. One man Johnson as I was saying had it that he always ran away and left the other one to manage any trouble they had made together and this was a weakness in him, yes, but it was a consistent thing in him and he needed it for living, and it really was wisdom in him, this thing and so in a way it was a virtuous thing in him. Some have this kind of virtuous feeling in resisting always all experiencing. There are many ways as I was saying of having this kind of virtuous feeling.

As I was saying people having in them any of the kinds of being I have been describing very often have very much reputation in their living sometime from the living and the being they have in them. Very many of them in their living are to some one believing in them, saints or heroes or beautiful creatures or wonderfully romantic creatures in their living and are to very many people knowing them, liars and cowards and bad men and bad women and to themselves they are men and women having in them a weakness yes and a virtuous feeling yes and a certain feeling of the real distinction of the consistent action their weakness entails on them.

Johnson as I was saying always attributes his having yielded to be in any situation to his own weakness that being the uppermost thing in him to him and always then that being the true reason he is in the situation he is in, to himself then, he has it as the only right thing for him always to be doing then is escaping and he always then does run away and leave the other one with the trouble or the blame of the situation they both were in. Hackart attributes his troubles, when he has any, and he often has them to the philanthropy in him, she was lonesome and took possession of him and what did he do but take care of her and so after all when some one else needs him, he must leave her for of course he must help the one that needs him most, that's easy for any one to see and that is what Hackart is always doing, being a man's man and a woman's man and philanthropic in his feeling. Another one puts her yielding to her grit and she has given everything, herself and everything and then the other one wants more and that is a ridiculous thing and of course she will not pay any attention to the clamoring of that other one who has been given everything and by one who never wants anything from any one. Another put her yielding down to guilessness and always believing anything anybody wants to make her believe and then she gets sick and must defend herself by attacking and she ought really to learn to attack the other one before she has suffered by them but this can never come to her because of the nature in her to be always believing in every one. Redfern always was on guard, that was his contribution to defending himself and then some one came close to him and then he gave that one always all her living everything she ever wanted from him. He always gave to every one who ever was in any relation with him completely everything they could ask of him every minute in his living and to the ending of their or his living. This was a certain thing in his feeling, he gave every one unceasingly everything they could possibly demand of him. That was his being and his living to himself all his living. That was his being and his living to one or two and these made a great person or a saint of him to them and to very many he was one who was in a complete sense a man never trustworthy in anything, never realising his obligation to any one. This then has been some description of the being in Phillip Redfern. To the last hour of his living he was faithful to the certainty of having been faithful to every one who ever had come to have any claim upon him. To the last hour of his living he was to himself completely giving himself to any one that had come to touch him. Always he was guarding himself, always to the last moment of his living to himself, always to himself to the last moment of his living he was faithful to everything he owed to every one and any one.

This is now then a little more description of the being in three women who had each one their own feeling about him, Miss Dounor, Miss Charles and his wife Mrs. Redfern. This is now a little more description of the being each one of the three of them had in them the being and the completed living of each one of them.

To begin then with Miss Dounor, her feeling and her living and her feeling Phillip Redfern in her living.

To very many, to, sometimes any one would think, mostly every one some one's way of loving, some other one's way of loving, some other one's way of living, some other one's way of keeping somethings and not other things, of throwing away some things and not other things, some one's way of buying some things and not buying other things is a foolish one. Mostly every one finds that things other ones are wanting are very foolish things for any one to be wanting, for that one to be wanting, to be buying, to be keeping. Each one has in him a very certain feeling of things any one having any sense in them should be wanting to have in living. It is very hard for mostly every one to understand why another one has that way of loving, that way of being angry in them that they have in them. Some try to understand the other one's way of doing these things but mostly every one finds it very puzzling. What can any one want with buying, keeping, wanting any such thing each one says of something some one has been wanting, buying, keeping. This is very common. Very many could forgive some one anything excepting the way that one has angry feeling or injured feeling in them. Some could let anything pass excepting the kind of way some one has of loving. That gives them an angry feeling, that is all there is about it to them. It is very very common that some one could forgive anybody anything excepting the way they have of having angry or injured feeling in them. This is very very common. Some can never understand the queer ways in another one. Mr. Hersland always was saying to his three children that the ways they had in them were only habits, there was no need they should have these ways in them. He had ways in him, they were him to him, the ways his children had in them were habits and it was not at all necessary that they should have any such habits in them. Many think that some one, some others could do the work they are doing in some other way from the way these are doing their working. As I am saying it is very, very common that some one could forgive some one anything excepting the way they have angry feeling, or injured feeling or loving feeling in them. Now then to begin a little description of the being in some women and the feeling they each had about the other one and the feeling they each one had about Redfern.

Perhaps no one ever will know the complete history of every one. This is a sad thing. Perhaps no one will ever have as a complete thing the history of any one. This is a very sad thing. Sometime each one will have made a complete history of them in the repeating always coming out of them. Sometime perhaps some one will really know it of some one, that will be a very contenting thing to some. Some seeing a mistake in their copying, say then, oh how can I ever be certain, perhaps I have made many mistakes I have not been noticing. This is a sad thing. Some every time they see a mistake they have been making say, if I almost did not see this one in reading it again, very likely there are very many I did not see for I would not have seen this one if I had not been noticing very carefully when I was seeing this one, and this is a very sad thing. Some say then, I noticed this one and so always I am noticing all the mistakes I am ever making and that is very pleasant if any one can believe what they are hearing from some one, and then some one says with a mistake they have been noticing, this is certainly the first mistake I have ever made in copying and that is comforting too only one can hardly at all believe that one and then some one says of a copying, I never make any mistake in copying and that is almost irritating to be hearing for always every one is making mistakes and that is a very sad thing.

Perhaps no one ever will know the complete history of every one. This is a sad thing. Perhaps no one will ever have as a complete thing the history of any one. This is a very sad thing. Surely some one sometime will have a complete history of some one. All this gives to some a very despairing feeling. Some one is hearing something, and they think then, it is only by an accident that I have heard that thing, I have known that thing, always there are many things that I am not knowing, that is very certain, every one always is repeating, that there is not any denying, certainly sometime some one always paying all attention must know sometime the history of some one. Perhaps no one ever gets a complete history of any one. This is very discouraging thinking. I am very sad now in this feeling. Always, hearing something, gives to some a sad feeling of realising everything they have not been hearing and that they are not knowing and perhaps they can never have really in them the complete history of any one, no one ever can have in them the complete history of any one and that is then a very melancholy feeling in them. There is a little comfort to some of such of them that always every one is repeating the whole of them, that always every one always is repeating all the being in them and then that is a little a comfort to such a one and then such a one knows always how important each repeating in each one is to make a completer realisation of that one and how each repeating is more and more a completion of the history of the being of each one and then such a one knowing how many repeatings out of each one that one is not hearing has in that one a very dreary feeling. Sadness is then in that one, sadness and gentle melancholy despairing. Repeating is in each one, yes, always coming out of them, yes that is a little a comforting, each repeating is important to be knowing and that is interesting and that is a sad thing to one wanting to have in them complete histories of men and women.

Sometimes in listening to a conversation which is very important to two men, to two women, to two men and women, sometime then it is a wonderful thing to see how each one always is repeating everything they are saying and each time in repeating, what each one is saying has more meaning to each one of them and so they go on and on and on and on repeating and always to some one listening, repeating is a very wonderful thing. There are many of them who do not live in each repeating each repeating coming out of them but always repeating is interesting. Repeating is what I am loving. Sometimes there is in me a sad feeling for all the repeating no one loving repeating is hearing, it is like any beauty that no one is seeing, it is a lovely thing, always some one should be knowing the meaning in the repeating always coming out of women and of men, the repeating of the being in them. So then.

Every one is a brute in her way or his way to some one, every one has some kind of sensitiveness in them.

Some feel some kinds of things others feel other kinds of things. Mostly every one feels some kinds of things. The way some things touch some and do not touch other ones and kinds in men and women then I will now begin to think a little bit about describing. To begin then.

I am thinking it is very interesting the relation of the kind of things that touch men and women with the kind of bottom nature in them, the kind of being they have in them in every way in them, the way they react to things which may be different from the way they feel them.

I am thinking very much of feeling things in men and women. As I was saying every one is a brute in her way or his way to some one, every one has some kind of sensitiveness in them. Mostly every one has some inner way of feeling in them, almost every one has some way of reacting to stimulus in them. This is not always the same thing. These things have many complications in them.

I am beginning now a little a description of three women, Miss Dounor, Miss Charles and Mrs. Redfern. I am beginning now a little a realisation of the way each one of them is in her way a brute to some one, each one has in her way a kind of sensitiveness in being. This is now some description of each one of the three of them Miss Dounor, Miss Charles and Mrs. Redfern.

In listening to a conversation, as I was saying, repeating of each one and the gradual rising and falling and rising again of realisation is very interesting. This is now some description of the three women and as I was saying of the sensitiveness in each one of them to some things and the insensitiveness to other things and the bottom nature in them and the kinds of repeating in them and the bottom nature and the other natures mixed with the bottom nature in each one of them.

Sensitiveness to something, understanding anything, feeling anything, that is very interesting to understand in each one. How much, when and where and how and when not and where not and how not they are feeling, thinking, understanding. To begin again then with feeling anything.

Mostly every one is a brute in her way or his way to some one, mostly every one has some kind of sensitiveness in them.

Mostly every one can have some kind of feeling in them, very many men and very many women can have some understanding in them of some kind of thing by the kind of being sensitive to some kind of impression that they have in them.

Some kinds of men and women have a way of having sensation from some things and other men and women have it in them to be able to be impressionable to other kinds of things. Some men and some women have very much of sensitive being in them for the kind of thing they can be feeling, they can then be very loving, or very trembly from the abundant delicate fear in them, or very attacking from the intensity of the feeling in them, or very mystic in their absorption of feeling which is then all of them. There are some men and women having in them very much weakness as the bottom in them and watery anxious feeling, and sometimes nervous anxious feeling then in them and sometimes stubborn feeling then in them. There are some who have vague or vacant being as the bottom in them and it is very hard to know with such ones of them what feeling they have ever in them and there are some with almost intermittent being in them and it is very hard to tell with such of them what kind of thing gives to them a feeling, what kind of feeling they ever have really in them. As I was saying mostly every one sometimes feels something, some one, is understanding something, some one, has some kind of sensitiveness in them to something, to some one, mostly every one.

As I was saying some men and some women have very much of sensitive being in them for something that can give to them real feeling. They can then, some of these of them, when they are filled full then of such feeling, they can then be completely loving, completely believing, they can then have a trembling awed being in them, they can have then abundant trembly feeling in them, they can then be so full up then with the feeling in them that they are a full thing and action has no place then in them, they are completely then a feeling, there are then men and women, there are then women and men who have then this finely sensitive completed feeling that is sometime all them and perhaps Cora Dounor was one of such of them. Perhaps she was one of them and was such a one in loving Phillip Redfern. Perhaps that was the whole being she had in her then.

Each one as I am saying has it in them to feel more or less, sometime, something, almost certainly each one sometime has some capacity for more or less feeling something. Some have in them always and very little feeling, some have some feeling and much nervous being always in them, some have as a bottom to them very much weakness and eagerness together then and they have then such of them some sensitiveness in them to things coming to them but often after they are then full up with nervous vibrations and then nothing can really touch them and then they can have in them nervous vibratory movement in them, anxious feeling in them and sometimes stubborn feeling then in them and then nothing can touch them and they are all this being then this nervous vibratory quivering and perhaps Mrs. Redfern was such a one Mrs. Redfern who had been Martha Hersland and was married now to Phillip Redfern and had come to Farnham and had there seen Phillip Redfern come to know Miss Dounor and had been then warned to take care of him by the dean of Farnham Miss Charles. She never knew then, Mrs. Redfern never knew then that she would not ever again have him, have Redfern again. This never could come to be real knowledge in her. She was always then and later always working at something to have him again and that was there always in her to the end of him and of her. There will be a little more description of her written in the history of the ending of the living in her father, in the history of the later living of her brother Alfred Hersland who now just when her trouble was commencing was just then marrying Julia Dehning, in the history of her brother David Hersland her younger brother. More description of her will be part of the history of the ending of the existing of the Hersland family. There will be very much history of this ending of all of them of the Hersland family written later.

The dean Miss Charles was very different from either Miss Dounor or Mrs. Redfern. She had it in her to have her own way of feeling things touching her, mostly there was in her less reactive than self-directive action in her than there was in the two women who were just then concerning her, Miss Dounor and Mrs. Redfern.

It is hard to know it of any one whether they are enjoying anything, whether they are knowing they are giving pain to some one, whether they were planning that thing. It is hard to know such things in any one when they are telling when they are not telling to any one what they know inside them. It is hard telling it of any one whether they are enjoying a thing, whether they know that they are hurting some one, whether they have been planning the acting they have been doing. It is hard telling it of any one whether they are enjoying anything, whether they know that they are hurting any one, whether they have been planning the acting they are doing. It is very hard then to know anything of the being in any one, it is hard then to know the being in many men and in many women, it is hard then to know the being and the feeling in any man or in any woman. It is hard to know it if they tell you all they know of it.   It is hârd to know it if they do not tell you what they know of it in it.   Miss Cora Dounor then could do some planning, could do some hurting with it, that is certain.   This is perhaps surprising to some, reading.   To begin then with her feeling and her being and her acting.

As I am saying she had it in her to be compounded of beautiful sensitive being, of being able to be in a state of being completely possessed by a wonderful feeling of loving and that was then the whole of the being that was being then in her and then it came to be in her that she could be hurting first Miss Charles and then Mrs. Redfern, then Miss Charles and Mrs. Redfern by planning.   This is then the being in her this that I am now with very much complication slowly realising, not yet completely realising, not yet completely ready to be completely describing, beginning now to be describing.   The dean Miss Charles was a very different person, she was of the dependent independent kind of them.   To understand the being in her there must be now a little realisation of the way beginning is in very many persons having in them a nature that is self growing and a nature that is reacting to stimulation and that have it in them to have these two natures acting in not very great harmony inside them.   Mrs. Redfern as I was saying in a long description that has been already written was a very different kind of person from Miss Dounor and Miss Charles. These are then the three of them that were struggling and each of them had in them their own ways of being brutal, hurting some one, had each of them their own way of being sensitive to things and people near them.

Sometimes I am almost despairing.   Yes it is very hard, almost impossible I am feeling now in my despairing feeling to have completely a realising of the being in any one, when they are telling it when they are not telling it, it is so very very hard to know it completely in one the being in one.   I know the being in Miss Dounor that I am beginning describing, I know the being in Miss Charles that I am soon going to be beginning describing, I know the being in Mrs. Redfern, I have been describing the being in that one.   I know the being in each one of these three of them and I am almost despairing for I am doubting if I am knowing it poignantly enough to be really knowing it, to be really knowing the being in any one of the three of them.   Always now I am despairing.   It is a very melancholy feeling I have in me now I am despairing about really knowing the complete being of any one of each one of these three of them Miss Dounor and Miss Charles and Mrs. Redfern.

Miss Dounor as I was saying was to Redfern the most complete thing of gentleness and intelligence he could think of ever seeing in anybody who was living, Miss Dounor had it to have in her the complete thing of gentleness, of beauty in sensitiveness, in completeness of intelligent sensitiveness in completely loving.   She was the complete thing then of gentleness and sensitiveness and intelligence and she had it as a complete thing gentleness and sensitiveness and intelligence in completely loving. It was in her complete in loving, complete in creative loving, it was then completed being, it was then completely in her completely loving Phillip Redfern. And always to the ending of his living in all the other loving and other troubling and the other enjoying of men and women in him he was faithful to the thing she had been, was and would be to him the completed incarnation of gentleness and sensitiveness and intelligence, gentle intelligence and intelligent sensitiveness and all to the point of completely creative loving that was to him the supreme thing in all living. Miss Dounor was then completely what Redfern found her to him, she was of them of the independent dependent kind or them who have sensitive being to the point of creative being, of attacking, of creative loving, creative feeling, of sometimes creative thinking and writing. She was then such a one and completely then this one and she had in her completely sensitive being to the point of attacking. She could have in her a planning of attacking and this came to be in her from the completeness of sensitive creative loving that she had then in her then when she was knowing Phillip Redfern.

Perhaps she was not of this kind of them. Perhaps she was at the bottom, of the resisting kind of them. I think she was of the resisting kind of them and so she needed to own the one she needed for loving, so she could do resisting to planning making an attacking. I am almost despairing, yes a little I am realising the being in Miss Dounor and in Miss Charles and Mrs. Redfern, but I am really almost despairing, I have really in me a very very melancholy feeling, a very melancholy being, I am really then despairing.

Miss Charles was of the kind of men and women that I speak of and have spoken of as the dependent independent kind of them. I will now tell a little about what I mean by self growing activity in such of them and reactive activity in such of them. As I was saying a long time back when I was describing the dependent independent kind of them, reaction is not poignant in them unless it enters into them the stimulation is lost in them and so sets it, the mass, in motion, it is not as in the other kind of them who have it to have a reactive emotion to be as poignant as a sensation as is the case in the independent dependent kind of them. Miss Charles then as I was saying was of the kind of them where reaction to have meaning must be a slow thing, but she had quick reactions as mostly all of them of this kind of them have them and those were in her mostly attacking being as is very common in those having in them dependent independent being.

It is so very confusing that I am beginning to have in me despairing melancholy feeling. Mrs. Redfern as I was saying was of the independent dependent kind of them and being in her was never really attacking, it was mostly never active into forward movement it was incessantly in action as being in a state of most continual nervous agitation. They were then very different in their being the three of them Miss Dounor and Miss Charles and Mrs. Redfern and they had each one of them their own way of hurting the other ones in their then living, of having in them sensitiveness to something.

It is hard to know it of any one whether they are enjoying anything, whether they are feeling something, whether they are knowing they are giving pain to some one, whether they were planning that thing. It is a very difficult thing to know such things in any one any one is knowing, very difficult even when they are telling that one all the feeling they have in them, a very difficult thing when they are not telling anything. It is a very difficult thing to tell it of any one whether they are enjoying a thing, whether they know that they are hurting some one, whether they have been planning the acting they have been doing. It is a very difficult thing to know anything of the being in any one, it is a very difficult thing to know the being in any one if they tell you all that they themselves know of it as they live it, if they themselves tell you nothing at all about it. It is a very difficult thing to know the being in any one. It is a very difficult thing to know whether any one is feeling a thing, enjoying a thing, knowing that they are hurting some one, planning that thing, planning anything they are doing in their living. It is a difficult thing to know the being in any one if that one tells to any one completely all that that one has in them of telling, it is a very difficult thing to know the being in any one if they are not telling any one anything that they can have as telling in them. It is a very difficult thing to know it of any one the being in them, it is a very difficult thing to tell it of any one what they are feeling, whether they are enjoying, whether they are knowing that they are hurting some one, whether they had been planning doing that thing. It is a very difficult thing to know these things in anyone, it is a difficult thing if that one is telling everything they can be telling, if that one is telling nothing. It is certainly a difficult thing to know it of any one whether they have in them a kind of feeling, whether they have in them at some time any realisation that they are hurting some one, whether they had planned doing that thing.

Miss Dounor had come to live with Miss Charles, they had come to know each other in the way that it was natural for each one of them to know the other one of them. The two of them then had come to know Mrs. Redfern. They both had come then each in their way to know her and to feel her and to have an opinion of her.

Miss Dounor had this being in her. She could have some planning in her, this came from the completeness of pride in her. This now comes to be clearer, that she had as completely pride in her as sensitiveness and intelligent gentleness inside her. She had in her pride as sensitive, as intelligent, as complete as the loving being in her when she was loving Redfern. She had in her pride as sensitive, as intelligent, as complete as the being ever in her. She had always had in her a pride as complete, as intelligent, as sensitive as the complete being of her. She had in her a pride as intelligent, as sensitive as complete as the being in her. This made it that she had planning in her, this made attacking sometimes in her. This never made any action in her toward a lover, this gave to her a power of planning and this was in her and she could be wonderfully punishing some around her. This could be turned into melodrama if the intelligence in her had not been so gentle and so fine in her, this in many who are like her is a melodrama. In her it made her able to do some planning against some to punish them not for interfering but for existing and so claiming something that entirely belonged to her. What was in Redfern to him himself a weakness in him was to her a heroic thing to be defending. Pride was in her then as delicate, as gentle, as intelligent as sensitive as complete as the being in her. This is now more description of her. This is now some description of the way she could be hurting another, how she could be feeling another, how she could have planning in her, how she did have planning in her. This is now more description of her and the being in her. I am now a little understanding the whole of her, I have in me still now a little melancholy feeling.

Miss Charles was of the dependent independent kind of them as I was saying.

Everybody is perfectly right. Everybody has their own being in them. Some say it of themselves in their living, I am as I am and I know I will never be changing. Mostly every one is perfectly right in living. That is a very pleasant feeling to be having about every one in the living of every one. Mostly not very many have that pleasant feeling that everybody is as they are and they will not be very much changing in them and everybody is right in their living. It is a very pleasant feeling, knowing every one is as they are and everybody is right in their living. Miss Dounor was as she was and she was not ever changing, Miss Charles was as she was and was not ever changing. Mrs. Redfern was as she was and always she wanted to be changing and always she was trying.

Miss Dounor as I was saying was as she was all her living and was not really ever changing and she was very right in her living and she was very complete in her being and her pride was as complete in her as her being and so she could be planning her conviction of how far Mrs. Redfern should not go in presumption, how far Miss Charles should not go in her interfering, how completely Phillip Redfern was a saint in living and in her devotion and she could carry out all this in its completion. Mrs. Redfern had no understanding in desiring. Phillip Redfern always should give her always would give her always would give to every one anything she, anything they were ever asking. This was the being in him. Asking was not presumption in Mrs. Redfern, desiring was presumption and Miss Dounor could then have in her a planning of perfect attacking. Always Mrs. Redfern should have anything she could ever ask of anyone, that was a very certain thing. Always Mrs. Redfern should have, would have from Mr. Redfern anything she was ever asking of him. Always then to them to Mr. Redfern and to Miss Dounor then, always then Mrs. Redfern had everything from Redfern that she ever could ask of him. This was then a very certain thing. Always then Mrs. Redfern had the right to ask anything and always she would have anything she should ever be asking of Phillip Redfern. She had in her, Mrs. Redfern, no intelligence, no understanding, in desiring, Miss Dounor had in her then a perfect power of planning the attacking that should keep Mrs. Redfern in her place of condemnation for Mrs. Redfern had not in her any intelligence in desiring, she had a right to anything she ever could be asking and she would have it given to her then whenever she asked for anything. Mrs. Redfern was never changing in her being, always she was trying, always she was without understanding in her desiring, always Miss Dounor could completely plan an attacking when the time came for such action to restrain Mrs. Redfern in her unintelligent desiring.

Miss Dounor was then perfectly right in her being. She was never changing, she was completely loving, she was completely understanding desiring, she was complete in the pride of attacking in her complete sensitive, completely intelligent, completely gentle being, completely understood desiring. Mrs. Redfern had no understanding in desiring. Mrs. Redfern always was trying to change the being she had in her to find some way of having intelligent desiring in her, always she would have from Redfern anything she could anything she should anything she would ever ask him to be giving to her. That was the being in her.

There were three of them then, Miss Charles, Miss Dounor and Mrs. Redfern.

Miss Charles was then not permitted by Miss Dounor to interfere with the being inside her, ever at any time in their living. Miss Charles was never asking anything of any one. Miss Charles was then one of the dependent independent kind of them. Miss Charles was then one having general moral and special moral aspirations and general unmoral desires and ambitious and special unmoral ways of carrying them into realisation and there was never inside her any contradiction and this is very common in very many kinds of them of men and women and later in the living of Alfred Hersland there will be so very much discussion of this matter and now there will be a little explanation of the way it acts in the kind of men and women of which Miss Charles was one.

Some have it in them some having in them a being like Miss Charles some of such of them have it in them to have it in the beginning very strongly in them that they have generalised moral aspirations, strongly detailed moral struggles in them, and then slowly in them comes out in them that they are vigorous egotistic sensual natures, loving being, living, writing, reading, eating, drinking, loving, bullying, teasing, finding out everything, and slowly they get courage in them to feel the being in them they have in them, slowly they get courage in them to live the being they have in them. Some like Miss Charles keep on having tranquilly inside them equally strongly in them moral aspiration general and detailed in them, egotistic expedient domineering as a general aspiration and as detailed living in them. Some are always struggling, some of this kind of them, some get to have in them that the moral fervor in them in the general and specific expression of them get to be the whole of them, some get to have it all fairly mixed up in them. This is now a little description of how one of them when she was a young one one of the first kind of them who slowly came to have the courage of feeling and then living the real being came to have the struggle as a beginning. Later then came the courage to be more certain of the real being. This is now a little piece of such a description of such beginning experiencing.

As I was saying in many of such ones there is the slow reacting, slow expressing being that comes more and more in their living to determine them. There are in many of such ones aspirations and convictions due to quick reactions to others around them, to books they are reading, to the family tradition, to the lack of articulation of the meaning of the being in them that makes them need then to be filled full with other reactions in them so that they will then have something. Some then spend all their living struggling to adjust the being that slowly comes to active stirring in them to the aspirations they had in them, some want to create their aspirations from the being in them and they have not the courage in them. It is a wonderful thing how much courage it takes even to buy a clock you are very much liking when it is a kind of one every one thinks only a servant should be owning. It is very wonderful how much courage it takes to buy bright colored handkerchiefs when every one having good taste uses white ones or pale colored ones, when a bright colored one gives you so much pleasure you suffer always at not having them. It is very hard to have the courage of your being in you, in clocks, in handkerchiefs, in aspirations, in liking things that are low, in anything. It is a very difficult thing to get the courage to buy the kind of clock or handkerchiefs you are loving when every one thinks it is a silly thing. It takes very much courage to do anything connected with your being unless it is a very serious thing. In some, expressing their being needs courage, for, foolish ways to every one else, in them. It is a very difficult thing to have courage to buy clocks and handkerchiefs you are liking, you are

seriously liking and everybody thinks then you are joking. It is a very difficult thing to have courage for something no one is thinking is a serious
thing.

As I was saying Miss Charles had in her what I am calling dependent independent being, that is being that is not in its quicker reacting poignant in its feeling, not having emotion then have the keenness
of sensation as those having independent dependent being have it in them.
Miss Charles was then such a one.

This is then a very common thing as I am saying. Miss Charles
had in her this being. As I am saying there are two ways then of acting
in a being like those I have been just describing. The acting from the
personality slowly developing, the acting from the organised reaction
to contemporary ideals, tradition, education and need of having, before
the developing of their own being, completed aspiration. Often these
keep on as they did in Miss Charles and no one is knowing which is the
stronger way of being in such a one. Sometimes there is as I was saying
in the beginning very much struggling and then slowly the personality
comes to action and that one drops away the early filling, sometimes the
early filling comes to be the later filling and in such a one then there is
not any changing. This is quite interesting and will be always more and
more dwelt upon. This then was the being in Miss Charles and this
was the meaning of her action with Miss Dounor and Mrs. Redfern and Mr.
Redfern that I have been describing.

There will be now a very little more description of the being in them,
of the virtuous feeling in them, of the religious feeling in them, of the sensitiveness in them, of the worldly feeling in them, of the succeeding and
failing in them, in each one of the three of them, Miss Dounor, Miss Charles
and Mrs. Redfern.

Every one has their own being in them. Every one is right in their
own living. This is a pleasant feeling to have in one about every one.
This makes every one very interesting to one having such a feeling in
them. Every one is right in their living. Each one has her or his own
being in her or in him. Each one is right in the living in her or in him.
Each one of these three of them were right in their living. This is now a
little more description of the being in each one of them.

It is a very difficult thing to know it of any one whether they are
enjoying anything, whether they are knowing they are giving pain to
some one, whether they were planning that thing. It is a very difficult
thing to know it of any one what is the kind of thing they are sensitive to
in living, what is the bottom nature in them, whether they will in living be
mostly succeeding or mostly failing. It is hard to know such things in
any one when they are telling everything they have in them, when they
are not telling to any one anything of what they know inside them. It
is a very difficult thing the telling it of any one whether they are enjoying

a thing, whether they know that they are hurting some one, whether they have been planning the acting they are doing. It is a very difficult thing then to know anything of the being in any one, it is hard then to know the being in many men and in many women, it is a very difficult thing then to know the being and the feeling in any man or in any woman. It is hard to know it if they tell you all they know of it. It is hard to know it if they do not tell you what they know of it in it. Nevertheless now almost I am understanding the being in the three of them Miss Charles, Miss Dounor and Mrs. Redfern. There will be now a very little more description of the being in them, of the virtuous feeling in them of the religious feeling in them, of the sensitiveness in them, of the worldly feeling in them, of the succeeding and failure in them, in each one of the three of them Miss Charles, Miss Dounor and Mrs. Redfern.

Miss Cora Dounor could do some planning, could do some attacking with it, that is certain. This is perhaps surprising to some reading. To begin then with her feeling and her being and her doing, and her succeeding and her failing.

She was then complete in her loving, she had complete understanding in desiring in all her relation with Phillip Redfern, she had completely then the realisation later in her that Phillip Redfern was saintly and she had then in her the complete possession of her adoration, the complete understanding and possession of her adoration of the saintly being in him, and this was then in her a complete succeeding in being and in living. This was not exactly virtuous or religious being in her this was complete understanding desiring and complete intelligent being in her and this was in her succeeding in her being and in her living. This is very certain. This was in her succeeding in her being and in her living. She had then in her complete understanding in desiring, she had then completely in her completed intelligence in adoration and this was complete being in her and it was a complete possession of her and by her and this was then completely succeeding in living. This is now very certain.

She had then complete succeeding in her living as I was saying, she had in her complete pride in her and this could be in her strong sensitive attacking but this was not completely a succeeding in her living. As I was saying Mrs. Redfern had in her no intelligence whatever in desiring, this was in her then presumption in her to Miss Dounor, not the things for which Mrs. Redfern was asking, Mrs. Redfern had the right to ask for anything or everything, it was desiring in her that was a thing Miss Dounor could rightly condemn in her and later she made it very certain to every one that Mrs. Redfern had no intelligence no understanding in desiring and then at last Mrs. Redfern reproached her and so then in a sense Miss Dounor was then failing in her being completely proud inside her. Mrs. Redfern attempting to attack her, attacking her even though failing in attacking was a failing of the complete intelligent pride in the understanding sensitive planning attacking pride in Miss Dounor and so Miss Dounor in her living was not then completely succeeding. This is certain. There was then complete succeeding in Miss Dounor in her loving in her completely understanding desiring, in her complete intelligence of adoration, in the completion of the being then in her, there was in her then some failing that Mrs. Redfern could attack her with going on attempting desiring. This is all very certain.

Miss Dounor held Miss Charles from really touching her real being, she did not hold her from really touching Redfern's being. She never recognised this failing in herself inside her but it was a failing of the completeness of pride in her and later much later when Redfern was no longer existing in living it made them separate from one another, later it in spots made Miss Dounor bitter. Miss Charles then was not succeeding in keeping Miss Dounor with her, she was winning by not then having any remembrance in her of the trouble she had had with her. Miss Dounor then was succeeding and failing in some ways as I have been saying. There was real succeeding in her as I have been saying, there was real failing in her as I have been saying. This is all very certain. This has been some description of the being in Miss Dounor and of her failing and of her succeeding.

Miss Charles was of the kind of them the kind of men and women I know very well in living. I know very well all the varieties of this kind of them. In each kind of them they are nice ones they are those that are not such nice ones, they are pleasant ones and they are unpleasant ones, they are those having that kind of being in them so lightly it hardly then makes them that kind of them, there are then some of them having that being in them that kind of being in them so concentratedly it is a wonderful thing to see them, to see a kind of being so complete in one man or in one woman. Miss Charles was of a kind of being I know very well in living, very well indeed in living, I know very well all the varieties of the kind of being that Miss Charles was in living in all the very many millions ever living having had or having that kind of being in them. Some then of a kind of being are nice ones, some of that kind of them are not very nice ones, some of that kind of them are not at all nice ones. Some of a kind of them are nice ones of that kind of them and then they have a mixture in them of other kinds of being in them and then that one is not a nice one though that one has a nice kind of one kind of being in that one. That often makes one a very puzzling one to every one. There are then all kinds of ways of being one kind of them in men and women. Some are a nice kind of a kind of them, and some are not a nice kind of that same kind of them. Sometimes being in one who is a nice one of a kind of them and then has other things mixed up in them is very perplexing and sometimes no one in such a one ever comes to an understanding of that one. Well then that is true then that of each kind of them there are nice ones and nice enough ones and not very nice ones, and not at all nice ones and very horrid ones. This can be in them with any strength or weakness of their kind of being in them, it is from the mixing and the accenting and the relation of parts of their kind of nature in them. There is one thing very certain of each kind of them of each kind there is of men and women there are nice ones and then there are not at all nice ones of them. And about some mostly every one is agreeing and about some there is very much disagreeing and there are very many ways of feeling every one and every one has their own being in them. Yes every one has their own being in them and yes every one is right in living their own being in them and this is a very difficult thing to be realising and it is a very pleasant thing to have inside one when it comes to be really in one.

Miss Charles was of a kind of men and women I know very well in all the kind of ways of being they have in them. Miss Charles was one of the independent dependent kind of them. Miss Charles was one who was herself a very strong one in her being and it slowly came to be more and more filling inside her. Miss Charles was one who had it in her to have reaction in her to influences around her when she was younger, to desires in her, to tradition and mob action and to very many things then and they made moral aspiration in her they made a reformer of her, they made an aggressive attacking person of her and when she was a young one all this then almost completely filled her. She was as I was saying of the dependent independent kind in men and women and resisting, slow realisation was the bottom way of feeling and of fighting and of understanding in her. This came then slowly to be stronger in her, this made then of her one that could be feeling and understanding brilliant men and brilliant women, brilliant and sensitive men and brilliant and sensitive women, made her feel them then and choose them then, then when her resisting sensitive understanding had come to be more completely the whole filling in her, then when slow steady detailed domination came to be then really filling then inside her, then when reforming attacking was changed in her to the personal being that then was mostly all the filling in her. It was never all the filling in her always she had in her a little of the special reforming attacking which was reaction in her, quick reaction to things and conditions around her and always she had very much in her of the generalised moral attacking conviction that came from the generalisation of her attacking and that made a righteous moral person of her and this is a very common thing and later there will be endless discussing of the meaning of this kind of moral being in all kinds of men and women, the generalised conviction and the relation of it to the concrete living, feeling, being in them, but this will come later in the beginning of the understanding of Alfred Hersland that will pretty soon now commence to be written.

Miss Charles was of the dependent independent kind of them. These have it in them then to have when they have quick reaction in them that is not a stirring from the depths of them these have it very often that this in them is a violent attacking, often continuous bragging, often moral reforming conviction, often nervous action in them, often incessant talking, incessant action, incessant attacking in them and this is in those of them that are the pure thing of dependent independent being and attacking is not their way at all of winning fighting. There are some who have in them resisting being and they have in them attacking being as another nature in them but that is a different thing from this thing that I am now describing, from the being in Miss Charles. Miss Charles was completely dependent independent being, attacking was not her way of winning fighting, it was resisting as I was saying in telling what she did to win her fighting for Miss Dounor with Redfern. That was then when she was a young one when she was no longer a young one, when her own being was almost completely then her filling, when there was in her the generalised moral emotion that came from the reaction that filled her a good deal in her young living, reaction that made attacking being then in her, in her who had in her to have resisting as her way of winning fighting, that was then what gave to her then attempting dominating every one by attacking and this is a very common thing in those having in them dependent independent being, this is a very common thing in them in their young living when their real way of winning fighting has not come yet to be in them. I am not saying that those having in them dependent independent being cannot have in them religion and moral or reforming passion as the expression of the being in them, there are very many of them who have it in them as I was saying, the old man Hissen had it in him and there are very many of them of this kind of them and there are very many of many various kinds of them of the dependent independent kind of them that have religious or virtuous or moral or reforming passion in them as the whole expression of the being in them but these express this then by resisting fighting which is their way of winning fighting. As I was saying there are many having in them dependent independent being, and there are some of them who have it in them only when they are younger ones and some have it in them very strongly in them up to their ending, there are very many of them who have much attacking of quick reacting, much attacking in bragging, in being quickly certain of everything, of being very quick in judging everything and these then some of them are mostly all filled up with this kind of reacting attacking in them which is not in them their real way of winning fighting. This is a very important thing to know in men and women, a very important thing to know in them in knowing them, in judging of the power in them of succeeding or of failing in their living. The independent dependent kind in men and women can have quick reaction that is completely poignant, that is attacking, in them, that is their real way of winning fighting. Those having in them dependent independent nature in them have not real power in quick resisting, in attacking fighting, many of them have this filling them all their living, many of them have this filling them in their young living when their own way of winning fighting is not yet developed in them enough to fill them, some have almost nothing of this kind of acting in them some of the dependent independent kind of them. All this is very important, very very important, sometime there will be very very much description of every kind of being in every kind of men and women.

Miss Charles was of the kind of them the kind of men and women I know very well in living. I know very well all the varieties of this kind of them. Some of each kind there is of men and women are very nice ones of their kind of them, some of each kind there is of men and women are not nice ones at all of their kind of them. Miss Charles was not a very nice one, she was not a not nice one at all of her kind of them. Being nice or not a nice kind of one, a pleasant or unpleasant kind of one was not in her an important thing. This is a very certain thing. She was as I was saying in her younger living aggressive in her detailed and generalised conviction of morality and reformation and equalisation. Later in her living she went on in the direction she had been going but her methods then were from the being in her and that then mostly entirely filled her. That made her control everything, every one near her by steady resisting pressure and that was then the way of winning in her. Everything near her, every one near her, every detail of everything was then more or less completely owned by her. She was of the kind of them who own the thing they need for loving. Later as I was saying Miss Dounor left her, Miss Charles had a little owned Redfern almost and Miss Dounor many years later left her and Miss Charles went on always to her ending completely owning the college of Farnham.

There has been now enough description of Miss Charles. There has been enough description of Miss Dounor. There has been enough description of Miss Dounor and of Miss Charles. There will be now a very little more description of Mrs. Redfern.

At the time of the ending of the living of the Redfern's at Farnham, Alfred Hersland was just coming to his marrying of Julia Dehning. The Redferns after the ending of their living at the college of Farnham never lived anywhere together again. Mrs. Redfern never understood this thing. Always she was expecting it to begin again their living together until after the complete ending of being in Redfern. That made her certain then that they would never live together again.

After the ending of their Farnham living the Redferns never lived anywhere together again. Mrs. Redfern never understood this thing. She never knew that she would not ever again have him. This never could come to be real knowledge in her and she was always working at something to have him again and that was there always in her to the end of him and of her. First she was travelling and studying and then she was working to make· some women understand something and many laughed at her and always she was full of desiring and always she was never understanding in desiring. When there was the end of her living with Redfern her brother Alfred was just coming to his marrying Julia Dehning. Martha was then travelling and studying and then she came back to be with her father and her mother was weakening then and later she was dead and Mr. Hersland lost his great fortune and Martha then took care of him. There will be now a little more description of her and then of her with him. There will be a little more description of her written in the history of the ending of the living in her father, in the history of the later living of her brother Alfred Herslard, in the history of her brother David Hersland. More description of her will be part of the history of the ending of the existing of the Hersland family. There will be very much history of this ending of all of them of the Hersland family written later.

There will be now a little more description written of her and of her living with her father when she came back to the family living back out of her trouble after the ending of the living in Phillip Redfern.

After the ending of the Redfern's living at Farnham the two of them, Mr. and Mrs. Redfern never lived anywhere together again. Mrs. Redfern never understood this thing. Always she was expecting it to begin again, their living together and always she was studying and preparing herself to be a companion to him in intellectual living. Always then she was studying and striving and travelling and working. And then he was dead and then she knew they would not live together again. Then she was certain of this thing.

That was her living then until he was dead and she went back to the ten acre place where then her father and mother were living and her mother was weakening then and a little while later then she died there and Martha finished her living staying with her father who had then lost his great fortune.

No one knowing Mr. Hersland in his middle living could have really been completely certain that he would never bring through to a completed beginning anything in his living. I was saying that he had in his middle living, the need in him, of having people around him, who were not in him in his feeling, who were there around him getting from his beginning the realisation of their being, he was to them life enhancing. This would have been in him, this need in him in the middle of his middle living what ever would have been the power of completion in him, for it is a need in all of them who have in them the being big in a beginning. As I was saying no one knowing him could really be completely certain then in him before the complete ending of his middle living about the completeness of beginning in him, the carrying power in him of a beginning and going on in action.

No one knowing Mr. Hersland before the complete ending of his middle living could have been completely certain that he would never bring through to a completed beginning anything in his living. No one knowing Mr. Hersland in his middle living could have really been completely certain that he would never bring through to a completed beginning anything in his living. Later in the ending of his middle living he was beginning to lose his great fortune. His wife was dying and dead then and Martha was living with him and his sons Alfred and David were in Bridgepoint then. Martha was living with him at the ending of his middle living and from then on. As I was saying no one knowing Mr. Hersland in his middle living could have really been completely certain that he would never bring through to a completed beginning anything in his living. Later in his middle living he was beginning to lose his great fortune, at the ending of his middle living he had pretty completely no great beginning in him and Martha his daughter was then living with him.

Martha had never in her, as I have been saying understanding in desiring. After the ending of her living with Redfern she went about travelling, studying, working, and some laughed at her then and she went on and always she could never understand this thing.

Martha had not in her any understanding in desiring. She went on as I was saying not hoping but intending to get ready to live again with Phillip Redfern and be intellectually a companion to him. She went about travelling and studying and working and intending to be completely the thing Redfern wished a wife who lived with him to be and she went on intending to be completely this thing, and very many laughed about her then and she never saw Redfern again. She never understood this thing. She had no understanding in desiring. Redfern died young. When he was dead Martha came home to Gossols and it was then the beginning of the ending of her father's middle living. He was beginning then to lose his great fortune. He was full up then pretty nearly with impatient feeling. Martha had no understanding in desiring, she would always after a meal offer him sugar to put in his coffee and he never took sugar in black coffee and she never learned this thing and he was then completely filled up with impatient feeling. He never liked to be helped in putting on anything and always Martha helped him on with his coat and always he would be completely then filled up with impatient feeling. Martha Redfern then lived at home all the time her father was losing his great fortune and then he was needing attacking women to fill him where he was shrunk away from the outside of him but he did not want to be filled so with Martha then, not then or later in his living, she was never inside him to him, she offered him sugar and he never took sugar in black coffee, never and she tried to help him on with his over coat when he was leaving and he never had wanted such a kind of attention and Martha always commenced again and again for Martha was always full up with desiring beginning, and he then he was full up then with impatient feeling only he was not really completely full up then with anything, he was then shrunk away from the outside of him, at least this was then beginning in him.

As I was saying no one knowing Mr. Hersland in his middle living could have really been completely certain that he would never bring through to a completed beginning anything in his living. In the ending of his middle living he was beginning to lose his great fortune. He had then still beginning in him, mostly then he was full up with impatient feeling, later he was shrunk away from the outside of him.

No one knowing Mr. Hersland in his middle living could have really been completely certain that he would never bring through to a completed beginning anything in his living. I was saying that he had in his middle living the need in him, of having people around him, who were not in him in his feeling, who were there around him getting from his being strong in beginning, big as all the world in his feeling, getting so a realisation of their own being, getting from him the enhancing of being in them. This would have been in him, this need of having men around him who received then from him the enhancing of the being in them, this would have been in him then in his middle living, whatever would have been the power of completion of him, whatever strength he could have in him much or little in him of carrying a beginning through to a complete winning, for it is a need in very many men and very many women in their middle living, it is a need in all of them who have in them the being big in a beginning. As I was saying no one knowing him could really be completely certain then about the power in him to be completely succeeding to be completely failing, to be succeeding or failing in his living no one who knew him before the ending of the middle living in him, not those men who were around him and got in them from hearing, feeling, seeing, hearing about the big beginning always in him got in them the enhancing of the being in them, not these then in his middle living could know it in them of him whether he would have succeeding as the complete being in him, failing as the complete being in him. These could not know it then of him. Those men who began beginning with him and then left him to do their own ending, being afraid of the way of going on with a beginning in him, wanting to be doing their own ending, these could not be certain in his middle living whether he would be ending his beginning in success or in failing. These then up to the ending of his middle living could not be certain of it about him. Those men who were fighting against him, those whom he was brushing away from around him, those whom when he was not succeeding in brushing them away from before him, he went another way then and he was full up with beginning action and he did not then really know it in him, these could not know it certainly in them of him, later they might think they had been certain about him, they were not then certain about him not any of them completely certain then, this is a certain thing, none of them of any of them he was brushing away from before him, he was not succeeding in brushing away from before him, those he was fighting against or those who were fighting around him, none of them had in them to be certain then in them whether he would be succeeding or failing in his completed living. It is a most difficult thing to tell about very many men whether they will be succeeding or failing, it is a most difficult thing to know it about them. No one can be certain of them, of very many of them before the complete ending of their middle living whether they will be succeeding or failing in their living. In many men and in many women, the character in them comes completely to be repeating and one can know it completely in them as in repeating it comes out of them, one can come to know of them the complete limits of the variation of all repeating in them and yet one, no one can yet be completely certain of them whether they will be succeeding or failing in the whole living of them. And this is always and always a certain thing and always and always it is more exciting the knowing in one completely the character of them, the whole repeating in them, the whole range of being in them and yet not then being completely certain of them whether they will be succeeding or failing in living.

There are many kinds of men and women as I have often been saying and some of one kind of them have more succeeding in them than others of that kind of them, some of that kind of them have more failing in them than others of that kind of them and some are very uncertain about whether there is succeeding or failing in them, it is an uncertain thing always about them to their ending.

No one knowing Mr. Hersland up to the ending of his middle living, not any men knowing him then, not any of them could be certain whether he would be succeeding or failing in his completed living. Not any women knowing him then whether they were feeling power with him or in him or not feeling anything much about him, not his wife, not any governess or servant living in the house with him, not any woman managing him or not succeeding in managing him not any woman could be really certain about him before the ending of his middle living whether the beginning in him whether the being in him would be a completion of winning in him, or succeeding or failing in him. Not his children when they were angry with him for the impatient feeling that filled him and they knew then that he went away from men and from them and from women when he could not brush them away from around him, not his children when they were angry with him and told him how they knew the being in him, not his children then were completely certain in them, could be really certain whether he would be completing his living in succeeding or in failing. It is a very difficult thing, an exceedingly difficult thing to know it of very many men even when one is certain of all the being all the possible variations of repeating ever coming out of them, to be certain whether they will be succeeding or failing in living. It is an exceedingly difficult thing in very many men and very many women to know it of very many men and very many women, it is an exceedingly difficult thing to know it of them whether they will be succeeding or failing in their living. One can know the complete being in them, all the repeating coming out from them and it is then still very often not before the ending of their middle living that one can be really certain whether they will be succeeding or failing in living. No one knowing Mr. Hersland in his middle living could have really been completely certain that he would never bring through to a completed beginning anything in his living. No one then not any one from any way of knowing not any man not any woman not any children could be really certain about him, not from any way of knowing him, not from knowing all the being in him, all the repeating ever coming out of him could have been really certain before the ending of his middle living that he would not be succeeding in living. At the ending of his middle living he was beginning not succeeding in living, he was beginning losing his great fortune.

It is so very exceedingly a difficult thing to know about the going to be succeeding, the going to be failing in living in a very great many men and women, it is an exceedingly difficult thing although one can know of them all the being they have in them, all the variations of repeating of the being in them ever coming out of them. No one knowing Mr. Hersland up to the ending of his middle living, not any of the men knowing him, feeling him, seeing him, hearing him, hearing about him, working with him, working against, working with him some and against him some, not any man or any woman or any one of his children could really be certain about him before the ending of his middle living, from any way of knowing, from knowing anything about him or in him could really be certain that he would not be succeeding in living. At the ending of his middle living he was beginning not succeeding in living, he was beginning losing his great fortune.

More it is certain that each one has his or her own being in her or in him and always in repeating in all their living it comes out of them and more and more of each one one comes to know of them all the possible variations in each one of the repeatings always coming out of them and each one then steadies down to be a whole one to some one watching and understanding. This is very certain, always each one has their own being in them and always each one is repeating the whole being in them and always then more and more some one can be certain about them the being in them the complete gamut of variation in the repeating of them. And always about very many of them even then it is an exceedingly difficult thing to know it of such a one, one is so then knowing, whether they will be failing or succeeding in living. I have been repeating again and again that no one knowing Mr. Hersland in his middle living, knowing Mr. Hersland before the ending of his middle living could really have been completely certain that he would, that he would not bring through to a completed beginning anything in his living, that he would be succeeding or failing in living. No one could be really certain about him about succeeding or failing in living until the end of his middle living. He was then beginning definitely not succeeding in living, he was beginning then really losing his great fortune. There will be more description of Mr. David Hersland, always more description of him, always in this history of many men and many women. There will be a little more and a little more description of him always in this history of many men and many women.

It is an exceedingly difficult thing in very many women and in very many men to know it of them whether they will be succeeding or failing in living. I have been saying it very often about Mr. David Hersland, it is true about very many women and very many men of all the kinds there are of men and women. It was as I have been repeating what no one could tell for certain about Mr. David Hersland. No one could tell it about him before the ending of his middle living for certain, not any one, whether he would be succeeding or failing in living. At the ending of his middle living he was beginning not succeeding in living, he was beginning losing his great fortune.

It is an exceedingly difficult thing to know it of any one whether they will be succeeding or failing in living. It is an exceedingly difficult thing to know it of any one. It is a very difficult thing to know the complete being in any one but always more and more it comes to be certain in each one one is knowing the complete being in them, sometime too it almost comes to be certain about them whether they will be succeeding or failing in living. In some it comes to be certain to some, to some one the complete being in them and still it is not a certain thing whether they will be succeeding or failing in living, Mr. Hersland as I have been saying again and again was one of such of them. There are always many of such of them in all the kinds there are of men and women. Mr. Hersland then was very completely such a one, Martha, his daughter, Mrs. Redfern was less completely such a one, it came very nearly being certain that she would not be succeeding in living but she might have been succeeding in living. It was not a certain thing, not completely a certain thing and it was not a certain thing that she was not succeeding in living not succeeding in living before the ending of her living.

There will then be more description of Mr. David Hersland and always more description of him always in this history of many men and many women, there will be a little more and a little more description of him always being written, always in this history of a good many men and a good many women.

There will be more description of Martha Hersland, Mrs. Redfern, written in the history of the ending of the living of Mr. David Hersland, her father, in the history of the living and the later living of her brother Alfred Hersland, in the history of her brother David Hersland and in the history of the ending of his living. There will be always more history of her and it will later come to be part of the history of the ending of the existing of the Hersland family. There will be very much history written of the ending of all of them of the Hersland family written later.

ALFRED HERSLAND AND JULIA DEHNING

I have been giving the history of a very great many men and women. Sometime I will give a history of every kind of men and women, every kind there is of men and women. Already I have given a history of many men and women. Sometime I will be giving a history of all the rest of them. This is now pretty nearly certain. I have been already giving the history of a very great many men and women, I will be now giving the history of a number of more of them and then of a number more still of them and then still of some more of them and then this will be the end of this history of very many men and women. Sometime then I will give a history of all of them and that will be a long book and when I am finished with this one then I will begin that one. I have already begun that one but now I am still writing on this one and now I am beginning this portion of this one which is the complete history of Alfred Hersland and of every one he ever came to know in living and of many other ones I will be describing now in this beginning.

Sometime I want to understand every kind of way any one can have the feeling of being distinguished by the virtue they have in them. Sometime I want to understand every kind of way any one can have the feeling of being distinguished in them and every kind of thing that can give any one a feeling of such distinction of such virtue in themselves inside them.

Being distinguished each one inside them by something, to themselves in their feeling, is very interesting. Being virtuous each one inside them by something, to themselves in their feeling is very interesting. Being right each one inside them by something to themselves in their feeling is very interesting.

Many have a very certain feeling a sure feeling, about something inside them. Many have a certain feeling about something inside them. Many need company for it, this is very very common. Many need a measure for it, this will need explaining. Some need drama to support it, some need lying to help it, some love it, some hate it, some never are very certain they really have it. Certain feeling in men and women is very common.

Some as I am saying have sure feeling in them, have honor in them and religion from the nature of them when this is strong enough in them to make it their own inside them. Some can make their own honor, some their own loving, some their own religion, some are weak and can do one thing, make one thing their own, some are strong enough and all of it, loving, honor, certainty and religion in them, all of it is some one else's, of some one else's making, some can just resist and not make their own anything, there are many of them. Some out of their own virtue make a god who sometimes later is a terror to them. Out of their own virtue they make a god who sometimes later is a terror to them. Some make some things like laws out of the nature of them, out of the nature of some other one. Some are controlled by other people's virtue, and then it scares them. Listen to each one telling about their own virtue and that grows to make a god for them, grows to be a law for them and often afterwards scares them, some afterwards like it, some forget it, some are it. Some honor what is right to them for them to be doing. Some separate honor from the doing of the thing, have it as a feeling.

Some love themselves enough to not want to lose themselves, immortality can to them mean nothing but this thing. Some love themselves negatively, then impersonal future life is for them alright, a good enough thing. Some love themselves and others so hard that they are sure that they will exist even when they won't, they do to themselves exist even when they don't, these have a future life feeling an individual thing, some love themselves and they are it and that is all there is of it in them and they do not have future life in them to be an important thing. Men and women have being in them all of them when they are living. Many men and women have in them a feeling of future life in them, very many of them, some for this life, some for another life, some for both lives, this and another one, some have a stronger, some have a weaker feeling of themselves inside them, some have more, some have less loving in them for themselves than other ones have in them, some have more some have less loving in them for other ones than others have in them, some have more some have less feeling for some thing than other ones have in them and all these things in each one are part in them of the virtuous feeling, of the religious feeling they have in them each one, each man and woman, each one having man or woman being in them, each man or woman has some being in her or in him.

I want to know sometime all about sentimental feeling. I want to know sometime all the different kinds of ways people have it in them to be certain of anything. These and virtuous feelings in each one, of themselves to themselves having virtue inside them, is to me very interesting. Always more and more I want to know it of each one what certainty means to them, how they come to be certain of anything, what certainty means to them and how contradiction does not worry them and how it does worry them and how much they have in them of remembering and how much they have in them of forgetting, and how different any one is from any other one and what any one and every one means by anything they are saying. All these things are to me very interesting.

As I was saying virtuous feeling and being certain of anything is to me very interesting. Having virtuous feeling and any certain feeling, that is being certain of anything is to me very interesting in every one. Having certainty in them is in each one of the kind of way that their kind of men and women have it of having it in them. Having certainty in them is a thing very interesting in each one having a certainty of anything in her or in him. Certainty and virtuous feeling and religion these are to me all three just now very interesting. Shortly I will try to tell a little of the way some come to have their certainty in them. Some build certainty up with little and little sure things and make a pile of them, some are summary and all embracing in the certain feeling they have always in them, some are certain of almost anything, some are hardly certain of anything, some have to have a complete system for each certain feeling in them, some have certainty in them and they do not know it then in them, some have to have it come out of them as action and then they are not certain, some are certain only after there is not any more action in them from that certain thing in them, some have some action in them and then slowly they know they have certainty in them, some have to understand a thing to accept it and then afterwards they have certainty in them, some have hardly any certainty at all ever really in them, very many have very many certainties always in them, some have a sense of dramatic arrangement to complete the scene of the certain conviction the certain emotion they have in them and the complete scene changes for them with each new certainty they have in them. Certainty worries some and some never have certainty as a worry to them. Some have certainty by comparison, by comparing the thing they have then with what any other one they are knowing, hearing, seeing is having, some never compare anything with anything in any one, certainty is a real thing in some, in some of such of them as a little pile they are gradually increasing, in some as something that they keep there inside them always of the same dimension, in some as something they have because they are defending that thing, in some as something they have because they are attacking some one for that thing, in some as something that gives to them for that thing a stubborn feeling in them. Some need company to keep their certainty from freezing or melting or evaporating or in some way disappearing. Some do not know they have certainty in them, do not ever concern themselves with such a thing. Some have it, some do not have it in them. Some have it sometimes, some have it sometime in them. Some have it and do not know it. Some have it and do not know it until it is acting. Some are not certain then when it is acting that they have it in them. Some have it and lose it while they are speaking. Quite a number have it and lose it while they are speaking or acting. Some almost always almost have it and they do not have it just at the last moment before they are certain. Some are very energetic to express it but always they do not have it in them. Some are energetic to express it and they always almost have it in them. In some it passes very easily out of them. Very many lose it every second in their living. Some are always thinking they are losing this thing. Some need company to keep any certainty in them, some like company around them while they have their own certainty inside them, some need to have the certainty in the presence of the company that they need to have with them always in their living. Certainty and virtuous feeling and important feeling in men and women is very interesting. I wish I could know everything of any such thing I would then be a very wise one to every one.

Some feel some kinds of things others feel other kinds of things. Mostly every one feels some kinds of things. The way some things touch some and do not touch other ones, and kinds in men and women then, I will now begin to think some about describing.

It makes me a little unhappy that everything is a little funny. It makes me a little unhappy that many things are funny and peculiar and strange to me. It makes me a little unhappy that everything and every one is sometime a little queer to me. It makes me a little unhappy that every one seems sometime almost a little crazy. It does make me a little unhappy that every one sometime is a queer one to me. It does make me sometime a little uncertain, it does sometimes make me very uncertain about everything and always then it is perplexing what is certain what is not certain, who is a queer one, what is a funny thing for some one to be wanting or not wanting or doing or not doing or thinking or not thinking or believing or not believing.

It does certainly make me a little unhappy that every one sometime is a queer one to me. It does certainly make me a little unhappy quite often that every one is really inside them or in thinking, in doing or in feeling or in believing a queer one. It certainly does make me an uncomfortable one and sometimes a little an unhappy, a gently almost melancholy sulky one that every one sometime is a queer one.

More and more in living each one is certain that other ones have believing something in them that is almost an impossible thing for each one to believe that any other one can really be believing, any other one who is not a crazy one. Always more and more in living each one, every one is learning that other ones are believing something thinking something, that one thinks another one is doing something that one only would be doing if he is a crazy one and the other one is not a crazy one and the other one is believing a thing that to some one is not possible that any one not a crazy one could really be believing. This is a very common thing. This is a very common thing and very many more and more in their living come to a realising that other ones are believing things and it is more and more interesting and sometimes very depressing to any one of such of them that wants to be understanding the being in men and women. This then is as I am saying a very common thing that others are believing things that it seems absolutely impossible those ones should be believing and often it is altogether puzzling and more and more in living if any one is listening to other one's thinking and believing, more and more this is borne in on that one. Always it is very interesting, sometimes it is surprising, sometimes puzzling, sometimes depressing, sometimes a very funny thing and in every kind of a way always to one listening to other's repeating always more and more it is borne in on such a one.

As I have been saying each one has their own being in them, each one has their own sensitiveness to things in them, each one is of a kind of them. Of each kind of them some are more completely themselves than others of their kind of them and this is now a very long discussion of the way being is in some and in others of one kind of them and then of being in some and in others of all the kinds of them all the kinds there are of men and women.

Disillusionment in living is finding that no one can really ever be agreeing with you completely in anything. Disillusionment then in living that gives to very many then melancholy feeling, some despairing feeling, some resignation, some fairly cheerful beginning and some a forgetting and continuing and some a dreary trickling weeping some violent attacking and some a letting themselves do anything, disillusion then is really finding, really realising, really being certain that no one really can completely agree with you in anything, that, as is very certain, not, those fighting beside you or living completely with you or anybody, really, can really be believing anything completely that you are believing. Really realising this thing, completely realising this thing is the disillusionment in living is the beginning of being an old man or an old woman is being no longer a young one no longer a young man or a young woman no longer a growing older young man or growing older young woman. This is then what every one always has been meaning by living bringing disillusion. This is the real thing of disillusion that no one, not any one really is believing, seeing, understanding, thinking anything as you are thinking, believing, seeing, understanding such a thing. This is then what disillusion is from living and slowly then after failing again and again in changing some one, after finding that some one that has been fighting for something, that every one that has been fighting something beside you for a long time that each one of them splits off from you somewhere and you must join on with new ones or go on all alone then or be a disillusioned one who is not any longer then a young one. This is then disillusionment in living and sometime in the history of David

Hersland the younger son in the Hersland family living then in a part of Gossols where they alone of rich people were living there will be completely a history of the disillusionment of such a realising and the dying then of that one, of young David Hersland then.

This is then complete disillusionment in living, the complete realisation that no one can believe as you do about anything, so not really any single one and to some as I am saying this is a sad thing, to mostly every one it is sometime a shocking thing, sometimes a shocking thing, sometime a real shock to them, to mostly every one a thing that only very slowly with constant repetition is really a complete certain thing inside to give to them the being that is no longer in them really young being. This is then the real meaning of not being any longer a young one in living, the complete realising that not any one really can believe what any other one is believing and some there are, enough of them, who never have completely such a realisation, they are always hoping to find her or him, they are always changing her or him to fit them, they are always looking, they are always forgetting failing or explaining it by something, they are always going on and on in trying. There are a very great many of them who are this way to their ending. There are a very great many who are this way almost to their very ending, there are a great many men and women who have sometime in them in their living complete disillusion.

There is then as I am saying complete disillusion in living, the realising, completely realising that not any one, not one fighting for the same thinking and believing as the other, not any one has the same believing in her or in him that any other one has in them and it comes then sometime to most every one to be realising with feeling this thing and then they often stop having friendly feeling and then often they begin again but it is then a different thing between them, they are old then and not young then in their feeling.

Young ones sometimes think they have it in them, this thing, some young ones kill themselves then, stop living then, this is often happening, young ones sometimes, very often even, think they have in them this thing but they do not have it in them, mostly not any young one, as a complete realisation, this thing, they have it in them and it is sometimes, very often then an agony to them, some of them kill themselves or are killed then, but really mostly not any of them have really realised the thing, they may be dead from this thing, they have not realised the thing, it has been an awful agony in them, they have not really grasped the thing as having general human meaning, it has been a shock to them, it may perhaps even have killed completely very completely some of them, mostly then a young one has not really such a thing in them, this is pretty nearly certain, later there will be much description of disillusionment in the being of David Hersland who was always in his living as I was saying trying to be certain from day to day in his living what there was in living that could make it for him a completely necessary thing.

This is then a very little description of feeling disillusionment in living. There is this thing then there is the moment and a very complete moment to those that have had it when something they have bought or made or loved or are is a thing that they are afraid, almost certain, very fearful that no one will think it a nice thing and then some one likes that thing and this then is a very wonderful feeling to know that some one really appreciates the thing. This is a very wonderful thing, this is a thing which I will now be illustrating.

Disillusionment in living is the finding out nobody agrees with you not those that are and were fighting with you. Disillusionment in living is the finding out nobody agrees with you not those that are fighting for you. Complete disillusionment is when you realise that no one can for they can't change. The amount they agree is important to you until the amount they do not agree with you is completely realised by you. Then you say you will write for yourself and strangers, you will be for yourself and strangers and this then makes an old man or an old woman of you.

This is then one thing, another thing is the perfect joy of finding some one, any one really liking something you are liking, making, doing, being. This is another thing and a very pleasant thing, sometimes not a pleasant thing at all. That depends on many things, on some thing.

It is a very strange feeling when one is loving a clock that is to every one of your class of living an ugly and a foolish one and one really likes such a thing and likes it very much and liking it is a serious thing, or one likes a colored handkerchief that is very gay and every one of your kind of living thinks it a very ugly or a foolish thing and thinks you like it because it is a funny thing to like it and you like it with a serious feeling, or you like eating something and liking it is a childish thing to every one or you like something that is a dirty thing and no one can really like that thing or you write a book and while you write it you are ashamed for every one must think you are a silly or a crazy one and yet you write it and you are ashamed, you know you will be laughed at or pitied by every one and you have a queer feeling and you are not very certain and you go on writing. Then some one says yes to it, to something you are liking, or doing or making and then never again can you have completely such a feeling of being afraid and ashamed that you had then when you were writing or liking the thing and not any one had said yes about the thing. In a way it is a very difficult thing to like anything, to do anything. You can never have again either about something you have done or about something any one else has done the same complete feeling if some one else besides the first one sees it, some other one if you have made it, yourself if you have understood something, you can never again have the complete feeling of recognition that you have then. You can have very many kinds of feelings you can only alone and with the first one have the perfect feeling of not being almost completely filled with being ashamed and afraid to show something to like something with a really serious feeling.

I have not been very clear in this telling, it will be clearer in the description of master and schools in living and in working, and in painting and in writing and in everything.

It is a very queer thing this not agreeing with any one. It would seem that where we are each of us always telling and repeating and explaining and doing it again and again that some one would really understand what the other one is always repeating. But in loving, in working, in everything it is always the same thing. In loving some one is jealous, really jealous and it would seem an impossible thing to the one not understanding that the other one could have about such a thing a jealous feeling and they have it and they suffer and they weep and sorrow in it and the other one cannot believe it, they cannot believe the other one can really mean it and sometime the other one perhaps comes to realise it that the other one can really suffer in it and then later that one tries to reassure the other one the one that is then suffering about that thing and the other one the one that is receiving such reassuring says then, did you think I ever could believe this thing, no I have no fear of such a thing, and it is all puzzling, to have one kind of feeling, a jealous feeling, and not have a fear in them that the other one does not want them, it is a very mixing thing and over and over again when you are certain it is a whole one some one, one must begin again and again and the only thing that is a help to one is that there is really so little fundamental changing in any one and always every one is repeating big pieces of them and so sometime perhaps some one will know something and I certainly would like very much to be that one and so now to begin.

All this leads again to kinds in men and women. This then will be soon now a description of difference in men and women morally and intellectually in them between concrete acting, thinking and feeling in them and generalised acting, thinking and feeling in them.

Many women and men have a completely sure feeling in them. Many men and women have certain feeling with something inside them.

Many have a very certain feeling about something inside them. Many need company for it, this is very common, many need a measure for it, this will need explaining, some need drama to support it, some need lying to help it, some are not letting their right hand know what their left hand is doing with it, some love it, some hate it, some never are very certain they really have it, some only think they love it, some like the feeling of loving it they would have if they could have it. Some have a feeling they would have it if they had their life to live over again and they sigh about it. Certain feeling in men and women is very interesting.

As I was saying in many there is the slow reacting, slow expressing being that comes more and more in their living to determine them. There are in many of such ones aspirations and convictions due to quick reactions to others around them, to books they are reading, to the family tradition, to the spirit of the age in educating, in believing, to the lack of power of articulating the being in them that makes them need then to be filled full with other reactions in them so that they will then have something. Some of such of them spend all their living in adjusting the being that comes to active condition inside them in their living to the being they have come to be in living from all being that has been affecting them in all their living, some of such of them want a little in them to create their living from the being inside them and they have not the power in them for this thing, they go on then living the being of every one that has been making them. It is a wonderful thing how very much it has to be in one, how it needs to be so strongly in one anything, how much it needs to be in one anything so that thing is a thing that comes then to be done, it is a wonderful thing how very much it needs to be in one anything, any little any big thing so that that thing will be done by that one. It is a wonderful thing as I was saying and I am now repeating, it is a wonderful thing how much a thing needs to be in one as a desire in them how much courage any one must have in them to be doing anying if they are a first one, if it is something no one is thinking is a serious thing, if it is the buying of a clock one is very much liking and everybody is thinking it an ugly or a foolish one and the one wanting it has for it a serious feeling and no one can think that one is buying it for anything but as doing a funny thing. It is a hard thing to be loving something with a serious feeling and every one is thinking that only a servant girl could be loving such a thing, it is a hard thing then to buy that thing. It is a very wonderful thing how much courage it takes to buy and use them and like them bright colored handkerchiefs when every one having good taste is using white ones or pale colored ones when a bright colored one gives to the one buying them so much pleasure that that one suffers always at not having them when that one has not bought one of such of them. It is a very difficult thing to have your being in you so that you will be doing something, anything you are wanting, having something anything you are wanting when you have plenty of money for the buying, in clocks in handkerchiefs, so that you will be thinking, feeling anything that you are needing feeling, thinking, so that you will be having aspirations that are really of a thing filling you with meaning, so that you will be having really in you in liking a real feeling of satisfaction. It is very hard to know what you are liking, whether you are not really liking something that is a low thing to yourself then, it is a very difficult thing to get the courage to buy the kind of clock or handkerchiefs you are loving when every one thinks it is a silly thing, when every one thinks you are doing it for the joke of the thing. It is hard then to know whether you are really loving that thing. It takes very much courage to do anything connected with your being that is not a serious thing. It takes courage to be doing a serious thing that is connected with one's being that is certain. In some, expressing their being needs courage, in foolish ways, ways that are foolish ones to every one else, in them. It is a very difficult thing to have courage to buy clocks and handkerchiefs you are loving, you are seriously appreciating, with which you have very seriously pleasure with enjoying and everybody is thinking then that you are joking. It is a very difficult thing to have courage for that which no one is thinking is a serious thing.

Some have a measure in living and some do not have any measure to determine them. Many in their living are determined by the measure of some one, they are to themselves to be like some one or very near to what that one is for them, they are like some one or are something like some one, they have then a measure by which they can determine what they are to be, to do in living. Such then are always followers in living, many of such of them have their own being in them, all of such of them have some being in them, all of such of them have a measure that determines them, they are themselves inside them, they need only come very near doing, being some certain thing which is established already as a standard for them by some one who did not have any standard to make her or him some one and that one is a master and the others having themselves inside them and such a one as a measure for them are schoolmen, and now there will be very little description of these things in men and women for it is something that is important in the being in David Hersland the second son. The important thing now to be discussing is concrete and abstract aspiration, concrete and generalised action in many men and women of very many kinds of them and now there will be a beginning of discussing the feeling in each one of being a bad one, of being a good one, the relation of aspiration and action, of generalised and concrete aspiration and action.

It happens very often that a man has it in him, that a man does something, that he does it very often, that he does many things, when he is a young one and an older one and an old one. It happens very often that a man does something, that a man has something in him and he does a thing again and again in his living. There was a man who was always writing to his daughter that she should not do things that were wrong that would disgrace him, she should not do such things and in every letter that he wrote to her he told her she should not do such things, that he was her father and was giving good moral advice to her and always he wrote to her in every letter that she should not do things that she should not do anything that would disgrace him. He wrote this in every letter he wrote to her, he wrote very nicely to her, he wrote often enough to her and in every letter he wrote to her that she should not do anything that was a disgraceful thing for her to be doing and then once she wrote back to him that he had not any right to write moral things in letters to her, that he had taught her that he had shown her that he had commenced in her the doing the things things that would disgrace her and he had said then when he had begun with her he had said he did it so that when she was older she could take care of herself with those who wished to make her do things that were wicked things and he would teach her and she would be stronger than such girls who had not any way of knowing better, and she wrote this letter and her father got the letter and he was a paralytic always after, it was a shock to him getting such a letter, he kept saying over and over again that his daughter was trying to kill him and now she had done it and at the time he got the letter he was sitting by the fire and he threw the letter in the fire and his wife asked him what was the matter and he said it is Edith she is killing me, what, is she disgracing us said the mother, no said the father, she is killing me and that was all he said then of the matter and he never wrote another letter.

It happens very often that a man has it in him, that a man does something, that he does it very often that he does many things, when he is a young man when he is an old man, when he is an older man. Some kind of young men do things because they are so good then they want every one to be wise enough to take care of themselves and so they do some things to them. This is very common and these then are very often good enough kind of young men who are very good men in their living. There will soon be a little description of one of them. There are then very many men and there is then from the generalised virtue and concrete action that is from the nature of them that might make one think they were hypocrites in living but they are not although certainly there are in living some men wanting to deceive other men but this is not true of this kind of them. One of such of these kind of them had a little boy and this one, the little son wanted to make a collection of butterflies and beetles and it was all exciting to him and it was all arranged then and then the father said to the son you are certain this is not a cruel thing that you are wanting to be doing, killing things to make collections of them, and the son was very disturbed then and they talked about it together the two of them and more and more they talked about it then and then at last the boy was convinced it was a cruel thing and he said he would not do it and his father said the little boy was a noble boy to give up pleasure when it was a cruel one. The boy went to bed then and then the father when he got up in the early morning saw a wonderfully beautiful moth in the room and he caught him and he killed him and he pinned him and he woke up his son then and showed it to him and he said to him "see what a good father I am to have caught and killed this one," the boy was all mixed up inside him and then he said he would go on with his collecting and that was all there was then of discussing and this is a little description of something that happened once and it is very interesting.

It happens very often that a man has it in him, that he does things, that he does something, that he does many things when he is a young man and an older man and an old man, that he feels always in a way about everything, that he is a good enough man in living, that he is a very good man.

Some kinds of young men do things with a feeling that they are teaching people to be strong and good ones and to take care of themselves and they are doing something and almost every one would say it was a very wicked thing this thing they are doing and in some it makes of them a very unpleasant person and some of such of them are not the least bit unpleasant ones because they have no mixing between the generalised conception and the concrete action. Many old men do things to keep themselves warm then, when they are old ones and they are needing to be warm then. Some of them are cold then and they need to be warm then and need to be warmed up then, and some are shrunk away from the outside of them then when they are old men and need some one to fill them and they do concrete actions then and their generalised sensation is keeping warm then, their generalised intention is of keeping warm then and this is all very interesting and always if Alfred Hersland and Mr. Herman Dehning and George Dehning come to be clear ones in this describing always then sometime many will be completely understanding this being I am now understanding, now completely understanding.

There are very many kinds of men. In each kind of them there are some of them who have it in them to have the being in them so that the concrete things they are doing are very different from the generalised feeling in them of what it is right and decent and good and bad to be doing. There are very many kinds of men, quite a number of kinds of them and of each kind of them there are always very great many millions of them always living and very many millions of them always have the being in them, very many millions of each kind of them that the being in them is so in them that the concrete actions, feelings in them are very different in them from the generalised feelings strongly in them and this is true of many of all the kinds there are of men and these then may be sentimental from this thing, and it may be very simply in them, they may be very unpleasant then from this thing and they may not be unpleasant unpleasant to hardly any one from this thing and this is something that in all the living of every one of them is interesting in them, in all the living of a great many men is interesting to them.

There are so many of them, each kind of them does it differently from the other kinds of them, each one of a kind of them does it differently from the others of that kind of them and in some it is more in the thinking than the feeling, in some more in acting than in thinking and in feeling, it is a very complete thing to be understanding, each one has in him his own being, each one of them has in him his own way of repeating this thing in him, each one has in him the way of having this in him that his kind of men have it in them. Women have it in them, that will come later in writing.

It happens then very often that a man has it in him that he does something and that thing is a concrete acting and no one would ever think that man had done that thing and that man is a good man, and he does it very often.

It happens very often that a man does something and he does it very often and it is an awful shock to him if sometime some one tells it to him and as I was saying one of such of them was a paralytic from being told it by one of his children in his later living and always such a man does a thing and it is a concrete thing and as a man he has many concrete actions in him and these he does very often and in his living, in his feeling a complete generalised sincere feeling always completely him, not a sentimental thing, a real thing in him by which he very often is completely living and he does a concrete thing and does it very often does many of them that have no place in his generalised sincere feeling and sometimes it is told to him and he can be killed then and almost by hearing this thing said of him so strongly is it in him that he is not doing that concrete thing, that he has never done that thing. These then this kind of them are not self-righteous men who think the way they do things should be the way of all men, they are not men like those I was describing who make an ideal out of the weakness in them, they are the men they very ordinary men who have it in them to believe that that they have inside them in their living in their feeling in their thinking what all good decent men have in them in their thinking, in their living, in their feeling and this is a generalised conviction of themselves to themselves always in them, all their living, and they see themselves in their living, and their being and their thinking, in their feeling as good enough men, good enough fathers, good enough husbands, good enough citizens, and always they are seeing themselves as each of them and so they see all of their concrete actions and sometimes and very often they are doing something, that thing they do very often and that thing is a thing not any man who is a good enough man would be doing and mostly a very great many of them of these who are to themselves completely good enough men are very very often doing such a thing and it is to them when they are young ones and a little older ones that they are doing it to be instructing to others so that other ones will know something and when they are older ones they do it then because in their realler feeling they know things are not so important as they once were thinking they were to them and every one, and then when they are old ones they need any way there is that can warm them and always to themselves they are the generalised good enough men and always then they are doing very often a thing somethings that are not included in such a generalisation and then sometimes it is told to them, it comes to them, very many never have it brought in to them a very great many of them, some of them have it brought in to them and some of such of them have their lives broken are made sick men then and all this is very common, this is the being in very many millions of every kind of men and this is interesting and this is soon to be a history of Alfred Hersland and his connection with the family of Mr. Henry Dehning.

It is very perplexing the generalised conception which is of virtue in many men and many women and the concrete feeling that is not of virtue in them. This is perplexing, one comes then to understand this thing as a complete thing and then always it is a shock to that one as in living cases of this always are being thrust upon that one. Some one builds up convictions from some other one, some know then that they do not believe that thing and some do it then because it is a pleasant thing, some do it to please some one, some begin to believe it and then they lose it and they don't say anything, some begin not to believe and then they come when they are older ones to believe what they began with as not believing but saying it to please some one, very many then in very many ways have other ones convictions come to be the determining frame for them, some believing it then, some who are not believing it then, very many who do not know then whether they do or do not believe that thing. This is a common thing, very many men do it, very many men do it because they are in it, very many men do it for very many women, for some women, very many men do it for men and for women, and for other women, and for children, very many do it for very many, very many do it for some, very many do it for some one, very many do it for themselves in their living. There are very many women there are very many men who are always saying if they had their life to live again they would live a different one, they would learn very many things, they would do serious reading. There are very many who always are going to be doing more serious reading, more staying at home of an evening.

It is certain that many men and many women, very many of them have a generalised conception of being which is them and concrete feeling and acting in them that is very often, sometimes always in them that is a very different thing to others from them in them to them.

Sensitiveness, measure, kinds in men and women, cowardice and courage, kinds of sensitiveness in them, originality and personality in them, generalised and concrete feelings and thinkings and activities in them this is all really very enormously interesting.

Every one, every kind of one, they are there living, each one having in him, each one having in her, each one having their own being, every one, every kind of one. I am realising the whole of human being. They are all each one of them themselves inside them, each one is of a kind in men and women. Each one is a whole one, each one has all there is of their own being sometime in them, each one always is repeating the being of them, always, and all of them are each one of them themselves each one, their own selves in them and always each one is of a kind of them and always more and more in every kind of living, in every kind of country, climate, civilization, always always there are the kinds of them the same kinds of them and some of each kind of them are very strong ones, and some are very weak ones, and some of each kind of them are in some kinds of ways leaders and some of each kind of them are mostly always following, and always each one of them have their own being in them and some of each kind of them are very good ones, some good enough ones, some pretty good ones, some pretty bad ones, some of each kind of them are very bad ones and always each kind of them have their own way of thinking, feeling, loving, talking, laughing, eating, drinking, fighting, pleasing, disliking, beginning and ending. Often there are very much mixings of kinds of them in very many of them but always there are very many of each kind of them pretty completely only their kind of them and some kinds of them I know very well in living, some I don't know so quite completely in them the being in them, some I am only beginning knowing, very many kinds of them are to me now then very puzzling, and always always always, there are the same kinds of them having in them their way of eating, drinking, sleeping, loving, hating, wakening, understanding, sensitiveness in realising anything, realising something, dullness, stupid being in them, quickness and slowness in them, suffering, enduring, quarrelling, agreeing, everything, in them everything, there are then these certain kinds in men in women and always then they are existing and there are very very very many men and very very very very many women always existing, each one having their own being in them and there are then a number of kinds of them but not such a great many kinds of them and sometime there will surely then be written a complete description of all the kinds there are of men and women.

There are then kinds in men and women. Some of each of the kinds of being there are existing have it in them that they have very greatly sensitiveness in realising, of their kind of being. Some of each kind of them have almost nothing in them of the kind of sensitiveness in realising of their kind of them and some of such of them, not having in them any sensitive realising of their kind of them can have it in them very excellent thinking, very solid fighting of their kind of them and many of such of them of such a kind of them are to very many greater men than those having sensitive realising of their kind of them, they are then many of such of them to very many of them that know them geniuses without weakness in them, these then are the very strongest thing that there can be of schoolmen, of followers who to very many are real leaders in living, in thinking, in feeling. George Dehning was such a kind of one and in the history of David Hersland there will be so very much description of every kind of a way men can have their kind of being in them.

The thing that is the important thing now in this part of the long history of a family's being is the kind of being in Alfred Hersland and in Mr. Henry Dehning. The thing that is the important thing to be understanding is being good in being and in living. To begin then now about being a good one, about all the kinds of ways of being a good one men and women have in them, all the kinds of ways I can think about them now in writing and the funny ways it can come out of many of them.

Being good in living is something, it is in some way mostly in every one, it is a very peculiar thing sometimes, and sometimes not a very peculiar thing. Being good in living is certainly a very important thing, it is in some way mostly in every one, in some way in very many women and in very many men it makes them what they are in living, it makes very many what they are to every one and to themselves in all their living. Being in some ways a good one is very common, it is a very common thing, it is in some way in very many men and in very many women.

Being good then is a thing about which there will now be very much writing. I have been already describing quite a number of ways men and women have it in them to be good ones in their feeling and their thinking and their being, in themselves to themselves, in themselves to other ones, to many other ones, to a few other ones, to every one that knows them, to hardly any one, to almost not any one, to one, to more than one. Being good then is a thing that is very interesting. Being good is a thing that is very often puzzling to very many having it in them, to very many men and women, being good is very often to very many not at all puzzling, there has been some description of some kinds of ways of having goodness in them in some men and women already given. Now there will be a new beginning of understanding this very interesting thing.

Kinds of being in women and in men is a peculiar thing. Kinds of being in men and women is peculiar, that there are always the same kinds of them existing is a peculiar thing. It is extraordinary the kind of things people are thinking, believing and feeling, always very often each one is thinking feeling believing something, sometimes they can afterwards be changing in that thinking, feeling, believing, knowing, but always very often no one, not anyone, not anything can change that thinking feeling believing knowing in them and the thing they are thinking believing, feeling or knowing is a thing that very many men and women like them are certain no one could possibly be ever thinking feeling believing knowing, and this is the peculiar thing that makes living the thing we are all doing, this understanding this realisation that other ones really have such kinds of thinking believing feeling knowing as completely them this makes very many men and very many women when they cannot change any one makes them then disillusioned in their living some of them, some when they are young ones and that is one kind of thing, some when they are older ones that is another kind of thing. Kinds then in women and in men in men and women is a peculiar thing. Yes certainly it is a peculiar thing, that and some other things that are now beginning being written.

There are many ways of thinking, feeling, knowing, believing in many men and women in all there ever are or were or will be of men and women. There are very many of them, each one has her or his own being in them, each one is of a kind or of several kinds in men and women each one has their own nature in them, mostly every one, always each one has many things in them are sometime are mostly always believing knowing feeling many things in them that if the others knowing really could really believe that these had in them would make them think those others were really crazy ones. Mostly very many all their living think other ones are not really feeling thinking believing knowing doing the things those are really are feeling believing thinking knowing doing, if they believed it of them that they really are believing thinking feeling doing knowing believing the things they really are believing knowing feeling doing thinking they would think them to be really crazy ones and they would be afraid of them.

There are many then believing thinking knowing feeling doing things, mostly every one is feeling knowing thinking doing something, doing feeling believing knowing thinking a very great many things that if any one really knew it about them any one knowing them would be thinking that one a crazy one, would be afraid of such a one, and no one knowing that one is thinking such a one really a seriously crazy one and that is because mostly every one does not really believe any other one really believes thinks knows feels does the thing, the many things that one really does do, think, feel, believe, know in living. Sometimes it is a funny thing to know it about some one the things they really can know and feel and believe and do and think in them, sometimes it is a very puzzling sometimes it is a very frightening thing, sometimes it is an impossible thing and mostly every one is contenting themselves with feeling that that other one is not really feeling thinking doing knowing believing the thing the things they are doing knowing believing or thinking that they never did have such things in them that they are just talking that it is really all different in them. One once who was a very intelligent active bright well-read fairly well experienced woman thought that what happens every month to all women, she thought it only happened to Plymouth Brethren, women having that religion. She was a child of Plymouth Brethren and had only known very intimately Plymouth Brethren women. She had known other women but it had not happened to her to have known about this thing. She was a child of Plymouth Brethren and she thought that what happens to all women every month only happened to Plymouth Brethren women, women having that religion, she was twenty eight years old when she learned that it happened to every kind of women. This is not an astonishing thing that she should have believed this thing. Every one mostly always is thinking feeling believing knowing something that is to every one else. when they know it about them a thing no one that was not a crazy one would be thinking feeling believing or knowing. Mostly every one can be content with being certain that the other one never did believe that thing.

There are a very great many men and women and they are very well educated intelligent ones who are very certain that a river can not flow north because water can never be going up hill in a natural way of flowing. They are very certain of this thing and when one understands it about them, some of them, it is astonishing that they can really be thinking such a thing and sometimes it takes almost a quarrelling to make them realise that a river can flow north and that north is not going up hill. They are knowing then that north is not going up hill when they think of it as travelling, they think of north as up hill when they think of it as water flowing and this is very common. Such things then are very common, every kind of way there ever can be of thinking feeling believing knowing doing is common and the way mostly every one has it in them the way one has it in them of knowing feeling, believing thinking doing is a thing that every one knowing that one if they really thought that one was really believing feeling thinking knowing doing as that one really is, was and will be thinking feeling doing believing knowing would be thinking that one a crazy one, that one a fool, that one a liar and a bad one, would be afraid or hating or despising or pitying that one or completely puzzled by that one. Mostly then no one really is ever believing any other one really can be believing feeling thinking doing knowing, the things the other one really is feeling believing thinking doing knowing.

Kinds of being in women and in men is a peculiar thing, that there are always the same kinds of them existing is a peculiar thing. That there are so very many always existing of each kind of them is a peculiar thing. That there are so very many always existing of every kind of them is a peculiar thing. When one sees a very great many of any thing, if it is jewels, or exotic fruits or old furniture or any precious thing in any place then always one is thinking they must be cheap there, they have so many of them it must be that they are selling them cheap they have so many of them and one mostly always has this feeling and this is the kind of feeling very many men and women have about men and women, there are so many they must be cheap things and one can use them any way one can be wanting them without any thinking about them and this is a very natural thing and then when it is a store and one wants to buy the rare thing or something where they have so many of them and then one finds out one has to pay them the same as in the stores where there are only a few of these things that they have for selling and that is always astonishing, that is to some always a certain shock to them and this is now beginning to be very true of men and women everywhere where men and women are living, they come just as high where there are a great many of them as where there are a few of them. But this is another thing, always to my feeling there are a very great many men and women always existing, always to my feeling there are a very great many of each kind of them always existing, always to my feeling each one of them is an expensive thing to be learning to be understanding and now I begin again.

I will now begin a little the writing about goodness and religion and sensitiveness and feeling and loving, and realising and understanding and thinking and doing and knowing in every one, in every kind there is in men and women.

One builds up other people's convictions, other people's intuitions other people's loving and virtue and religion, this is a very common thing. Some build up other ones convictions, other one's intuitions, other ones loving and virtue and religion, this is a very common thing. Very many men do it for very many women, very many women do it for men, and for other women, and for children, very many men do it for very many children, very many men do it for very many men, very many do it for themselves in their living, very many women, very many men do it for themselves in their living do the creating of their intuitions, their convictions, their loving, their virtue, their religion.

It is very interesting the way it happens sometimes. Some one one is loving tells one to do something to do it very often and then the one loving that one knows it then will know where the one told to do it does that thing, the other one who is to be doing that thing is not in the beginning certain that the one loving that one knows it when that one does that thing, the thing the other one loving that one tells that one to do very often for the one loving and that one then not with that one doing that thing will know that that one is doing that thing. It happens then very often that in the beginning the one doing the thing the one loving them is asking of them so that the other one not being with her or him then will know that he or she is then doing that thing it happens very often that the other one that is asked to be doing a thing is not then certain that the other one the one that has the believing that the other one doing that thing that one will be knowing then when that one is not with that other one who is doing a thing, it happens very often that in the beginning the one of whom the doing has been asked by the other one the one certain that he or she will be knowing it when he or she is not with that one it happens very often that in the beginning the one not certain that the other will know it does it with a different feeling, does it with a very careful feeling then and later then when that one is certain that the other one is not certain when that one has been doing that thing because of tests such a one has been making it happens sometimes such a one goes on carefully doing that thing religiously doing that thing would be a way of stating it then for it would then be a ritualistic thing and there are others who would not let themselves ever test such a thing but go on always doubting but always more or less doing the thing, not from the loving in them but from the belief in them built up so in them that the other one really has intuition and that is the way it goes very often with having intuition, always then some one gives to some one conviction of intuition, some give it to themselves in living, very often others give it to them, there are then very many men and women and some of them have more some less sensitiveness in them and always it is hard to tell it of them of men and women what is sensitiveness in them what is made inside them by themselves by every one they are knowing in their living.

Dead is dead.   To be dead is to be really dead said one man and there are very many men who really feel this in them, to be dead is to be really dead and that is the end of them.   To be dead is to be really dead and yet perhaps that is not really the end of them, some men feel this in them.   Dead is dead yes dead is really dead yes to be dead is to be really dead yes, to be dead is to be really dead and that is the real ending of them yes, but still, yes to be dead is to be dead, to be really dead yes, and yet always there is religion always existing and it is better to have everything, to be dead is to be dead some men are feeling knowing thinking believing in them, very many men are feeling thinking knowing believing it in them and some of them some of such of them have it in them that they know that religion is always existing, dead is dead, that they know pretty entirely completely really in them yes dead is dead they really know that in them, religion always is existing, dead is dead yes that is true then, and then they go on in living always doing their religion.   Dead is dead yes that is certain and they go on having their religion and they are not believing and their religion is believing that dead is not dead, to be dead is to be not really dead, dead is dead of that they are really certain some of these then and they go on then having their religion doing everything in their religion and to their religion to be dead is not to be really dead of that their religion is almost certain and they are almost certain in them always that to be dead is to be really dead, yes dead is dead they know that in them, they know that in them, they do everything any one can do in their religion and their religion is very certain that to be dead is not to be really dead and these men are very certain that to be dead is to be dead, that dead is dead.   This then is very common.   There are these then and there are then those that have it in them in living that dead is dead only partly in them and in them is the very constant realisation that every one, they themselves, are believing that religion is a right thing to be having and religion is always saying though you are dead you are living and these then could know it as an active living in them that dead is dead, that is in instinctive living in them but always in their talking, very many of them always in their feeling, some of them always in their doing, some of them in their thinking, some of them always in their believing have it in them that every one has religion in living, they have religion in them, dead is not dead then everybody is of this then very certain and always dead is dead is the simply instinctive living in these men then and very many of these then have it in them that they are those having concrete action that is very often very different from what these are certain all decent men and they themselves are always doing, these then can as I was saying kill the butterfly in the morning because they are so good to their son when in the evening just before they completely persuaded him the son that killing butterflies is a cruel action no good man should be doing, and some of such of them as I was saying can have it in them that they have done something very often and later in their living a daughter can write to them that what that daughter is doing that is a disgrace to the family then came to be a way of doing from the things the father was often showing to her when she was a young one and such a one then can have a paralytic stroke from the shock of realisation, of dead is dead and that by religion to his saying that dead is not dead and of the difference in him of general and concrete conviction.

There are a very great many then that have as a concrete realisation always in them that dead is dead, that things are as they see them, that they are doing things when they are doing them and these then can have it in them that they realise as a generalisation that to be dead is not to be so very really dead, that things are not perhaps what they are to them, that they are living with other men around them who have it in them to have religion in them which is certain that to be dead is not to be a really dead one and these then have it in them to equilibrate themselves to this opinion, the opinion the conviction of being not dead when they are dead of having virtue in them when they are not doing any good thing of never doing anything any good man cannot be doing when really they are doing that thing very often and this is a generalised sense in them all through their living and always then they are really living the dead is dead living as a concrete living. To some having this equilibrating, this generalised conception is only sentimental in them, in some it is a way of being important to themselves inside them to make it strongly in them this generalised equilibration in them, to very many it is a very simple thing of being like every one for every one to mostly any one is like this in their living is being of a conviction that dead is not really dead, that good is progressing, that every one is a good one in some way of endeavoring. This is a very common thing then and always and always it will in its simple in its complicated forms will be interesting, will be illuminating in the being and the living of Alfred Hersland and Mr. Herman Dehning and his son George Dehning.

Explaining ones vices by ones virtues is one way of feeling, thinking, believing, knowing, thinking believing, feeling, knowing oneself inside one in living. This is a very different thing from that which I have been just describing as sometimes perplexing, as very common, the generalised conception which is of virtue in many men and many women and the concrete feeling and acting that is not of virtue in them. Explaining ones vices by ones virtues then is one way of feeling thinking knowing believing the being inside in one different from that I have been just describing, different from the being in Redfern which I was once describing which was as I was then saying was an explaining ones virtues by the vices in them. There is then explaining ones virtues by ones vices and others then explain their vices by the virtues in them. There are certainly a very great many ways of having virtuous feeling in them in men and women and yet after all there are not such a very great many ways of them, there are a good many ways though and this is now some more description of virtuous feeling, being, thinking, knowing believing, in men and in women. Later then there will be very much discussion of different kinds of sensibility and way of having it in them in men and women.

A man having it in him to have the generalised conviction of good being as completely him and the concrete acting of being a mean spirited and tyrannical man in living and always taking everything he can that it is not dangerous for him to be taking and never giving anything that is not taken from him, one of such a kind of them can have it in him to be always speaking and very often in his talking it comes out again and again that he is a good man, and a noble man, and a very angry one whenever any one ever is doing anything that he knows of them that is not a fine action a good generous way of doing, thinking, believing, feeling. and sometime perhaps some one might say to him a sister-in-law or a brother-in-law of him, of such a one, why did you do that mean thing to that man, and he would then say to such a one, because he was such a mean man he deserved all I could give him to get the best of him, and then the brother-in-law or the sister-in-law might say then to him, but you say you are such an awfully good man how could such a good man as you are do such a mean thing to any one, and then such a one would be answering, a good man could do such a thing to another mean man, didn't I do that thing to that mean kind of a man and don't you know don't every one always know it in him that I am a good man, you know that, and then there would be no answer that could touch him. Such men are very common, they are very often not full up with religion these are good men that is the conviction that is the feeling of themselves inside them to themselves in them, that is the complete being in them to themselves completely in all the believing, feeling, doing, thinking ever in them. These then are not being good in the name of god or in the conviction of religion, they never do a bad thing in secret as some do who are good men in the name of religion or virtue or of god can do it and then not be letting their right hand know what their left hand is doing, no, such a one as I have been describing has it as a completed generalised conviction his own virtue as him and is himself completely constantly himself to himself in his being, has the complete thing of being important in all living from the completed realisation that he is completely a good noble generous human being and such a one never has any need of any secret action, such a one tells every one everything he does in living, any mean thing, any bad thing, anything, for always it is there completely in him that he did this thing and a good man could, would, does do that thing, he did that thing, he a good man who never does anything he should not be doing did this thing does something and so it is right for him to do that thing and he can tell it as a thing he was proud to do in living, everything he ever does in living is a thing he is proud to be telling to every one, he is completely a good man, he has no need of secret living, everything he is ever doing is a thing he can be boasting he was doing for he is completely a good man, he is not a good man in the name of religion of god or of his country or of his profession, he is a good man completely a good one to himself inside him, that is important being in him, that is his being to himself inside him, that is all being in him, he is the complete thing of a generalised conviction of virtuous being.

All these kinds of ways then of having virtuous being, feeling, thinking, believing, doing, knowing inside in one are very interesting to be describing, studying, realising, understanding. It makes then one way of realising kinds in men and women the realising of the different ways different ones have virtuous feeling in them. I have already been describing some of them, I will now be describing others of them.

Many have virtuous feeling from something inside them. Many need company to have it, this is very common. Many need a leader for it, this is in very many women and very many men. Some need drama to support it, some need lying to help it, some always need to leave out something in their telling anything to have it, some need always to leave out something in their feeling, in their doing, in their knowing, in their realising, in their believing, and they have it mostly in them, some need always to leave out pieces of everything they have in them to make for themselves the complete creation of virtuous being of themselves to themselves inside them. Many have virtuous feeling about something inside them. Some need drama to support it, some need lying to help it, some need company to feel it, some love it when they have it, some do not then love it, some hate it, some are it, some are burdened with it, some enjoy it, some never are very certain they really ever have it. Virtuous feeling in men and women is what I am now a little describing.

Some then and these are now another kind of them from any I have been describing, some then have an ideal in them and always they poetically, romantically, dramatically, idealistically, sentimentally conceive themselves as doing that thing and they are not good at inventing and they are always doing everything and they leave out mostly everything in telling anything and they are always then very fond of telling this thing and so they have it in them to be idealistically, romantically, sentimentally, dramatically one thing and that is always in them an ideal thing. These then are such ones as would have it in them to be to themselves supposing it is a chaste one or a forgiving one that kind of one completely in them. Being with them, knowing them, some of them, it is climbing mountains for always when you are thinking you have heard the whole thing about the ideal they are to themselves in themselves to every one a new peak comes up behind and you begin again climbing, they are not really chaste then such a one yes that is certain they will sometime tell that thing but the claim then comes from a new kind of relation in them that is a real one of a completely chaste thing, they violate that one and then a new one is to them the complete thing of idealistic romantic chastity for them and always in their telling they leave out everything that can destroy the truth of the latest idealistic chastity in them, and then every one knows of that new violation and they are then creating a new idealism and again they are telling everything with leaving out in their telling, feeling, thinking, believing anything that shows another violation they have been making of their idealistic conception, and these then go on and they go on and everybody laughs about them that such a one should have idealistic romantic conceptions of chaste being and always this one has a new one and always this one then in telling is leaving out everything that tells the last violation of the latest idealistic romantic dramatic conception of chaste being and these then are lying but not by invention but by idealistic romantic dramatic sentimental omission and that is then very amusing and I know just now several of such a kind of them and everybody can laugh at them sometime.

This happens very often with very many in loving, they are explaining that with that last one they were not real in loving, this they are now doing is really loving, always before they have not been really loving that is certain, this is very common in loving, it is very common very often in women, it is very common it is very often in men in their real feeling, in their real thinking, it is very common in men and women it is very common in loving in women and in men it is very common in loving often in men and women.

Another form of having virtuous feeling is thinking what any one is doing is only a habit in them, and this is pretty common in men, quite common in men and in women.

This way of feeling then is that not any one is really a bad one that is hardly any one, mostly every one does a thing because it is a habit and all that they need then is to change their habit to some other thing, some other way of doing that thing doing something and that one will be a good one. This is fairly common in men and women this way of having a feeling about virtue in other ones and in themselves then, in some it is stronger in beginning, when they are young, but in very many having this kind of conception it is in them all through their living. They are not actually ever changing the habits they have in them neither is any other one they are knowing but that does not affect their conviction that doing bad things is only a habit in themselves and in every one, and this is indeed quite common in men and in women.

Another very common way of having virtuous feeling about oneself inside one is from having always the sense of being oneself inside one and so one oneself doing something does it, a wrong thing, with a different feeling from any other one and so it is not really then a wrong thing. This is very common even with many women many men who have not much personality in them, who do such very bad things as a regular way of living that no one not knowing would ever think it of them that they know it in them that they themselves inside them with the feeling of themselves inside them made it that the wrong things they were doing were not so bad as when other ones did that wrong thing. They are themselves inside them, they feel themselves inside them, each one of them and so then the things they are doing are personal things, not mercenary, vulgar things like those the other ones doing the same things are doing. This is very common in women, this is very common in men, each man mostly each woman mostly has a feeling of their own being, of being themselves inside them in them and that in itself makes each one doing something less bad in doing that thing than any other one doing that thing. A man painting, a painter exhibiting has such feeling. A painter was saying that exhibitions are so disgusting because just looking one sees that all the pictures are bad and that is disgusting, one's own pictures are hanging there and one looking at them and realising that they are bad things knows by remembering how each one of them happened to come to be not a good one and that then makes it alright for there are reasons that one's own pictures are not good ones while with all the others they are bad ones and that's all there is to them, there are not reasons to explain them to the feeling of any one looking at them and this is a very common way of having a conviction of virtue in them in a wonderfully large number of men and women.

There are others who build it up in pieces the virtuous being the virtuous feeling in them, slowly they build it up in living, slowly carefully and always they are adding, piece after piece is being added by them to make sometime pretty completely a whole thing and some of these are very good ones indeed in living and some are not such very good ones, but very many of them are very good ones in living. Some of such of them may have many other things in them that are not such good things in them but these do not affect the good thing of them, the good part of them, the virtuous being in them that these are steadily building up in them by steady adding, sometimes quickly sometimes slowly but always, mostly always, very often safely, completely safely in them. There are so many of them then men and women that have virtuous feeling in them, important being in them from virtuous feeling in them that it is a large undertaking to understand it and realise it and describe it and I am now not any longer beginning the doing this thing.

There are some who have very much virtuous feeling virtuous being in them, some who have not so much virtuous being virtuous feeling in them, some who have very little, some who have hardly any and some who have not any interest in any such a thing.

Some have virtuous feeling in them from having in them concrete and generalised virtue always really in them. Some have virtuous feeling in them from having in them concrete and generalised virtue almost always really in them. Some have virtuous feeling in them from having in them concrete and generalised virtue very often really in them. Some have virtuous feeling in them from having in them concrete and generalised virtue sometimes really in them. Some have virtuous feeling in them from having in them concrete and generalised virtue sometime really in them.

There are lots more ways of having virtuous feeling in one than these that I have been describing. I am keeping them back now from crowding on me, slowly they will come to me and out from me, this has been a description of a few of them and there are lots of them but I have been already describing a good many of them and always I am understanding women and men more and more by listening to them as in repeating it comes out of them the telling by them of how goodness is in them even in those who never are really talking about any such a thing. Always sometime it comes out of every one the way they have virtuous feeling in them and always more and more to me it is interesting.

It is very perplexing the generalised conception which is of virtue in many men and many women and the concrete feeling and acting that is not of virtue in them. This is perplexing, this is sometimes not at all perplexing, mostly it is perplexing always to the families of them, those knowing always the kind of them, this kind in men and women. Alfred Hersland will soon then be interesting. There will soon be a description of him begun.

There are many ways of being and of loving and of winning and of losing, and having honor in them, and horror of something, and religion in them and virtuous feeling being believing and thinking in them from the nature of them when this is strong enough in them to make their own in men and women. Sometimes some one to every one is strong enough to make his own or her own living thinking feeling being loving, horror, working and religion and virtuous feeling and this is not then true of that one, this one is one having anticipating suggestion and then being like a resounding board to the suggestion they were anticipating and so giving it forth then so that to themselves then and mostly to every one they are strong to do their own living, to make their own opinion and virtue and working and thinking and loving and religion and this will soon now be some description of such a one. Some then can make their own honor, and virtue and work and thinking and loving and religion. Some can make their own horror, some their own loving, some their own religion, some are weak and can do one thing their own, some are strong enough and all of it is some one else's thinking, feeling, doing, religion, virtue in them, they are strong enough men and women. There are some can just resist and not make their own anything. Some out of their own virtue make a god who sometimes later is a nuisance to them, a terror perhaps to them, a difficult thing to be forgetting. Some are controlled by other's virtue and religion and that scares them, it is a superstition to them and always after it is a scared part of them. Some like religion, some forget it, some are it, some have a prejudice against it. There are many who love themselves enough to not want to lose themselves from living, to not want other people, existence to lose them, to very many women, to very many men this comes to be as a religion in them, this makes religion a real thing to them. Some love themselves so much immortality can have no meaning for them, the younger David Hersland was such a one, there will be a long history of him sometime written. Some love themselves negatively and they like thinking about immortal living. Some love themselves or other ones so forcibly in them that death can have no meaning as an ending, these are then certain of existing, these then are made to have religion, that is certain, some do not have it then in them, really they are certain that every one is continuing, they may not know it as religion, they mostly all of them sometime know it in them. Some love themselves so completely or some other one that they think they exist when they don't, will exist when they won't, are in communication with them when they certainly are not, some of these do not make it as a religion, they have it as a conviction as a certainty in them, these have a future life feeling in their present living. This is pretty common. Some have fervent loving in them for themselves or some one with very much fear in them and some of such of them have religion in them and very many of such of them have none.

This is now to be a little a very little description of some having in her or in him the feeling of original creation from anticipated suggestion and the way virtue then is in them, in such of them. Then there will be a beginning of the being in Alfred Hersland after this little description which has not much to do with anything but is to me interesting has been made, as I was just saying.

Some have very much sensitive being in them, very many have sensitive being as creative activity in them, very many have it as an instrument nature in them, some of them have it so that they can be almost creative by resonating, resoundingly anticipating another one's suggestion before that suggestion comes as a completion and such then are often for the very longest kind of time really puzzling as having in them sensitiveness to the creation of real personality in them as original activity in them and these very often have it in them that they are intelligent and so can reflect and then reflect about the thing they are creating from anticipation of the suggesting of other one's to them, they are quicker, these then, quicker really than chain lightning and sometimes for a very long time these are confusing. Sometimes these then can be understood by one when one realises of them that they are as greatly one thing as any other thing if the proper influence has come into the circle of their living and that never to themselves when they are beginning a new thing did the other thing the last thing they were creating, the last kind of thing they were doing completely express the personality of them to their thinking, such of them are never failing in anything, they are always succeeding, later they are always certain they have not completely expressed the personality in them in the last thing they were doing, they are now completely expressing the personality in them and then later in remembering they know they have not completely expressed the personality in them and always in each kind of thing they are doing they are succeeding, they are never stopping doing the last thing because they are tired of doing that thing, they are beginning a new thing without really leaving the last thing ; in their generalised living, slowly every one can come to know it of them they are not really original in inspiration, it comes then that it is change but not an evolution of them everything, there is no generalised conception that forms itself from them in them, they may be fairly successful in living they may not be successful in living, always then they are quicker than chain lightning really in their sensitive being.

The weakness of the being in them may come to be clear from the virtue feeling in them, from religion in them, from the way they need for that always to have company around them, this is generalised being in them and they need close company around them to support them, they cannot for this do concrete working that gives to every one the illusion that inspiration is inside them. This is pretty clear to my thinking, not completely clear yet and I am now telling it here to a little rid myself of it and to begin again to think and feel about it. Sometime I will have to do much more realising, understanding the sensitive being in men and women, it is a completely necessary thing and I am always working and thinking and feeling and I will not now say any more about this thing, this is enough now and I have been relieving myself enough now of my wisdom.

Perhaps this description that I have been just making has a little after all to do with something in this writing. This then and other things that have been written have something to do with preparing the understanding of myself then and some others perhaps then for the being in Julia Dehning.

There must be much alternating all through in this writing of preparing to be describing Alfred Hersland and the living in him and Julia Dehning who came later to be marrying him. These two then will be mostly all of them in this part of this writing and always I am alternating between them and always a little preparing understanding one and a little preparing understanding the other one and so sometime perhaps everything will come to be showing something and that will be then a happy ending of all this beginning.

Sensitive being is completely interesting. It will sometime be a long book that one when everything is written about sensitive being and kinds of it and the meaning of it in every man and every woman. Sometime it must be done for so only can there be written a history of every one.

All this describing then of virtuous being, feeling, knowing, thinking, in men and in women makes it right now to begin the complete understanding and description of the living and the being in Alfred Hersland and every one important in his living.

Alfred Hersland, the kind he is of human beings is to me very clear just now very clear inside me as grown up men and women, I have very many of the kind that are his kind of them now in me, I am mostly now completely filled up with that kind of them, that kind in men and women, with many individual ones of them, with many women of that kind of them with many men of that kind of them, I am just now very completely full up with the kind Alfred Hersland is in being, with men and women very many of them of that kind of them, with many of them, one just like him, that is all of him in my imagining, with some a little more one kind a little more another kind, with many who are of the same kind as he is among men and women but very different from him, I am full up very full up now with a whole large group who are all more or less connected in kind with him, with Alfred Hersland as he is completely now inside him, a complete one, I have then so many men and women in me now who are of his kind in men and women and they are in me now, I am completely full up with them now, completely filled up with them filled up with them as men and women, all full up with that kind of men and women and I must now begin again and slowly live it in them the beginning of them, I am filled up quite entirely filled up quite full up with the kind of them with all the varieties of them of this kind of them as men and women as women and men, I am all completely quite completely full up with this kind of them in men and women and all the kinds of them connected with this kind of them, I am completely now pretty nearly entirely now full up with many men and many women and all of this kind of them the kind of which Alfred Hersland is one, completely filled up with them but only as completely men and women, I must a little now be filled up full with them with these then as beginning as children, I must be completely full with them and I must be full up with them too as children and I am now beginning a little to fill up with them as children, I am filled up full with them as young men, young women, as very young men and very young women, as older men and older women, as growing old men and growing old women, as old men and old women as dying and dead ones, I am then pretty completely entirely filled up full with this kind of them with very many men and women with complete men and complete women with this kind in men and women the kind of which Alfred Hersland is one and of kinds closely connected in character with his kind of them, I am very full then of his kind in men and women, I am very fairly full of a kind of them he will have one of as marrying him, the kind there is in Julia Dehning which is a very different kind from his kind of them, I am fairly full of the Julia Dehning kind of them as children, as completely men and women, I am very completely full then, I am quite completely full of the kind there is of men and women of which Alfred Hersland is one and now I am waiting to be a fuller one, I am waiting to be a completely full one, I am waiting to be full up with that kind of them all there are of that kind of them as children and I am now as I am saying waiting.

To begin again with Mr. Hissen the grandfather of Alfred Hersland. This one was as I was saying a man having it in him that he was really all that there was of religion, he was a man as I was saying a man completely being that thing to himself inside him, a man living that thing completely every moment in his living, a man holding them as part of him his wife and children to be a part of him when they were in the house with him, and he was all there was of religion, when they had left him for their own living they were then not any longer in him part of him, he was then again all there was of religion, he was a man then having a connection with such as those I was describing who have it to be completely to themselves that they are completely a good one only those that I have been describing have it in them to have concrete living in them and generalised conviction of themselves besides in them and seeing themselves in the light of the generalisation and the generalisation comes from the conviction of being that is not in concrete existing really in them, in Mr. Hissen then it was a different thing, his generalisation was a complete generalisation from the complete feeling acting being thinking in him, he was completely then all that there was of religion, he was living knowing being thinking feeling believing that he was himself all that there was of religion and he was concretely living every minute in this being and concrete and generalised being was the same being in him and he did not think that when he would be dead he would be living, dead was dead to him and religion was living to him but not living when he was no longer a live one, he was in himself all that there was of religion, dead is dead, he was very certain, religion was not in him a contradiction of this thing, religion was him, he was all that there was of religion, religion was all that there was of religion, he was it so completely in him that he was not ever judging any one, not himself, not any one, he was himself to himself inside him, he was all there was of religion, he was alive when he was living and was then all there was of religion, he held his children there when they were living in the house with him, when they had left him they were no longer in him of him, he was not then ever judging any of them, when he was alive he was to himself completely living completely religion, when he would be dead he would be a dead one he could not have any fear in him, he was a completely whole one then, there was not in him any contradiction between being a dead one a really dead one and religion, he was in himself all that there was of religion, he lived completely the living of being completely himself all there was of religion, he was so, not ever judging any one not himself not any one not his children, they were him when they were part of him, they were not him when they were not a part of him and that made him a complete thing always in living, generalised and concrete living, feeling, being, knowing, thinking, believing, had in him no complication, he was then the complete thing of being all there was of religion, of being certain that to be a dead one was to be really then a dead one, to have this in him as religion, to be himself completely all there was of religion, to be living concretely every moment every day his religion living concretely and as a generalisation. This then is the being in Mr. Hissen who was the grandfather of Alfred Hersland and this then is one of the kind of them that one must be understanding to understand the being in Alfred Hersland which I am hoping very soon now to be beginning describing. This is one then, I will now describe others of this family of kinds in men and women, for soon now I will describe Alfred Hersland for I am completely always nearer understanding that one and yet there are some difficulties that I am still feeling and I am very full up now with this kind of them the Alfred Hersland kind of them and still I am feeling some difficulties in the completion, they are not yet to me all of them entirely completely yet whole ones inside me, I am waiting and I am not yet certain, I am not yet impatient yet in waiting, I am waiting, I am not now again beginning, I do not feel that I need to be again beginning, I am in the right direction, I am only now just needing to be going, I am now only just waiting, I am going I think very soon to be keeping on going, I have been describing Mr. Hissen again the grandfather of Alfred Hersland, I will now tell a little more of religious desiring in some of this kind of them, some who have fear and idealisation in them, Mr. Hissen had not this in him, dead was dead to him, religion was completely all him in him, he was not judging any one, he had not any fear in him, he died of old age when he came to be a dead one, to be dead was to be dead of that he was very certain, he had not then any fear in him, he had not in him ecstacy or idealisation, he had completion in him, he had all that there was of religion for him in him, when he would be a dead one he would be dead of that he was completely certain, he was then a complete one, concrete and generalised conviction was the same in him, he was the grandfather of Alfred Hersland, he was one of one kind in men and women, I am now pretty settled in my direction, I am still now waiting, I am still now not going on, I am still now waiting and that is what I am now doing.

This then the being in Mr. Hissen the grandfather of the three Hersland children is one way of having religion, feeling of virtue, in one, it is an important thing to have it completely inside me the feeling of religion in Mr. Hissen. It is pretty completely inside me now and still a little I am waiting, I will now soon be describing one who had another way of having religion, the complete other extreme and still of the same kind of them as Mr. Hissen and then I will be describing the in between kinds of them and so then I will come again to Alfred Hersland. And all of these then are of the resisting kind of them the dependent independent kind of them and now then again a little I am beginning to be waiting. I will be waiting quite a little now before I begin again.

There are some who naturally are knowing dead is dead but these are not then certain that to be dead is to be a dead one. There are many who are saying to be dead is to be a dead one but these then are not very certain that to be dead is to be really a dead one. There are some who are practically speaking completely certain that to be dead is to be a really dead one but always these then are afraid in living and always these then are a little afraid of being a dead one, some then are very completely afraid of becoming a really dead one some of these then are thinking feeling when they are being completely afraid of being a completely dead one when they will be dead ones that perhaps then to be dead is not to be really a dead one, they knew it in them that to be dead is to be completely entirely a dead one, these are certain then of this thing and they are afraid then every moment in their living that it will come to be in them that they will come to be a really dead one and then many of these then have it in them as a fear in them that to be a dead one is to be really a dead one and they know that is really in them that to be dead is to be really a dead one and so then they have it in them that they think they have it in them that they are believing then that to be a dead one is not to be really a dead one and then they do not know it in them whether that is really a comforting thing to them, they do not know it in them whether they are ever really thinking that to be a dead one is not to be really dead then and these are not certain whether it is a comfort to them any such a feeling and there they are then these then full up then with fear inside them every kind of fear they can possibly have then for they have it in them that to be dead is to be a dead one and they have it in them to never to be wanting to be such a kind of a really dead one and then they have it in them from this fear in them coming out of this fear in them that they will soon come to be a really dead one, that perhaps a dead one is not really a dead one and then they have the fear in them of a dead one not being then a really dead one and fear then is complicated in them and there are a very considerable number of such of them always existing and fear then makes of them that they have a generalised conception that they have religion in them and virtuous being in them and this is of the feeling in them that comes from the reaction in them from the fear in them of being a really dead one that perhaps being a dead one is not really being a really dead one and always then these have in them as a continuous concrete realisation and this is always being in them that to be dead is to be completely really a dead one.

Some have it as a complete feeling in them that to be dead is to be dead and this then a world without ending is in them for to be dead is to be a dead one and so then not any thing to them has ever any ending. Everything then to such of them is going on forever and forever to them and always then to be a dead one is to be a dead one and always then there is a continuing for ever and ever to such of them of everything and so then to these of them there is no ending of anything and living and being a dead one is to these then the very same thing and to be a dead one is to be a dead one and to be a living one a living one and to very many of these dead and living are all one and these then have in them religion as being of everything that is never ending and some of these then come to have it in them this I am describing to be certain that to be dead is to be a dead one and to be living is to be a living one and that always everything is never ending, come then to have it in them as loving being in them and these then can come to have it in them that they are of them that have it to be of the kind of them that own the thing they need for loving and so then these then having it as loving in them that nothing is ever ending and to be dead is to be a dead one and to be living is to be a living one and that nothing is ever ending and have this in them as loving being and own the thing they need for loving are very interesting in religion.

All these then that I have been describing all these then all these kinds of them that I have been describing I am thinking as of the resisting kind in men and women, the dependent independent kind of them.

These then some men and women always there are a good many of these living who have it in them to have resisting being and some way of feeling that to be a dead one is to be a dead one and have in them religion from this thing mixed up with this thing in them, these then that I have been describing are of the resisting kind in men and women, they are of that kind of them that have loving in them as resisting and owning those they need in loving not from stubborn feeling not for attacking but from the dependent independent right way of winning fighting. There are very many kinds of this kind in men and women, some of each kind of all these kinds of them have religion in them. Later after very much waiting and very much history of Alfred Hersland has been written there will be very much description of the way sensitiveness and religion is in the attacking kind in men and women and this will be written in the description of Julia Dehning who came to be marrying Alfred Hersland as I have already very long ago been telling. There will then be very much description of virtuous feeling and religion in the description of Julia Dehning, of virtuous feeling and religion in the attacking in the independent dependent kind in men and women. There will be very much description of virtuous feeling acting thinking being in the description of Mr. Henry Dehning and of old men having it in them virtuous feeling being thinking There will be a description of a kind of way of having virtuous feeling in the description of Mr. Dehning. There will be a description of George Dehning and the little one Hortense Dehning in the history of the younger Hersland brother David Hersland. Now I am still waiting to be beginning really beginning the history of Alfred Hersland from the beginning of his living.

There have been then now, been in this description, the three generations of men and women. There was then Mr. and Mrs. Hissen and the old Mr. and Mrs. Hersland, there was then Mr. and Mrs. David Hersland and these then had three children Martha and Alfred and David and the history of Martha has been now already mostly written, not completely altogether written but a good deal written and now there will be beginning to be written the history of Alfred Hersland and every one he ever came to know in his early living, in his marrying and in his later living.

There was then Mr. Hissen and Mrs. Hissen and Alfred Hersland had it in him to have a good deal in him Mr. Hissen being but it was a very different thing in him this being in him than it was in Mr. Hissen. Alfred never had in him at any time in him religion, he was a mixture then of old Mr. Hissen and old Mr. Hersland who was a butcher when he was a young man working and who was a man who had important feeling in him from having been a little important then in religion. Alfred Hersland then, to be certain of the being in him, was of the resisting kind of them in men and women and now then I will wait again and soon then I will be full up with him, I am now then not completely full up with him. Now I am again beginning waiting to be full up completely full up with him. I am very considerably full up now with the kind of being in him, I will be waiting and then I will be full up with all the being in him, that is certain, and so then now a little again once more then I am waiting waiting to be filled up full completely with him with all the being ever in him.

There are then some living who are saying that to be a dead one is to be really a dead one and these then are not very certain that to be a dead one is to be really a dead one. They are then some who have it in them that dead is dead and these then are not very certain that to be dead is to be a dead one. There are then very many who in living have it in them that dead is dead and these then are not certain that to be a dead one is to be a really entirely completely certainly altogether dead one. There are very many then of these always living, perhaps Alfred Hersland was one of this kind of them. Perhaps he is of this kind of men. Perhaps he is not this kind of a one, not one of this kind of them of women and men. Anyway this much is certain, he was of the resisting kind of them, he is of the resisting kind of men, of the dependent independent kind of them. He is certainly of the engulfing resisting kind in men and women.

Of these Alfred Hersland was not really one, Julia Dehning was of this kind of them. They can be either attacking or resisting kind of them. There are some, indeed there are a very great many of them, I know some of them always in living, there are many of them some very successful in living some very brilliant in living, some not successful in living, some of every kind of them as to succeeding and failing, there are a very great number of them always living women and men who have it that the being the root of being in them is intensity of emotion and these then are doing, feeling believing many things in living, some many things very different from those other ones of that kind of them are feeling, thinking and believing, many of them very different things from what they have been and will be believing feeling thinking doing knowing and always each thing any of these are feeling thinking believing knowing doing is for them completely bathed and floated by the intensity of emotion that is all being in them and these have it that to themselves inside them they are deeply profoundly moved by the thing and really then they are really profoundly moved by the emotional intensity in them, not any thing in them, in those of them that are completely this kind of them not anything they ever are feeling thinking knowing believing doing in living has any other value than any other thing they are ever feeling knowing doing thinking believing for always all of the being in them is intensity in emotion and very many of such of them have sometime very strongly religion in them and mostly always virtuous feeling in them, that is natural for them to be having in them as any one understanding anything of human being certainly will be more or less realising. These then and there are a very considerable number always existing of them as I am saying are often succeeding very well in living and are brilliant ones in living and some of them are weak and stupid ones in living and there are all degrees in between but always it is certain that these have in them emotional intensity as being in them and often for a very long time they are puzzling, they are often for long years puzzling to some one for it is a very difficult thing to know it of them that not anything they are ever feeling knowing thinking believing understanding is profoundly in them when they are so completely moved and enveloped by and enveloping that thing, it is a very puzzling thing very often with these for they come so nearly to be original in living feeling thinking being knowing believing and they are really not then original ones and it is disconcerting for often one is a very long time convinced by them by such of them who are so completely themselves living by that thing in them then which is not them but is sustained by the intensity of emotion which is the really truly them. It is very certain that these then are very strong ones for following in religion for being certain of virtue in them, these must be that for otherwise they would know that they had not originality in them, this will be all so very interesting when I am going to be describing Julia Dehning, this is a completely interesting thing but now there must be a beginning to the real realisation in me of Alfred Hersland and his living, I have been doing a very great deal of waiting, waiting is to me very interesting for always something is coming or else nothing is coming and there is eating, sleeping, laughing, living, talking and a little tickling in the body and the mind then that is very pleasant to any one liking waiting and then there is always the drowsiness of going to be lively waking and all this is in me in waiting and I like very well doing waiting and now perhaps a little more I will be waiting but always I am a little near to beginning and now once more again I am waiting and now I am contenting myself again with waiting and that is a very pleasant feeling a pleasant thing for any one content inside them with it in them.

I am always now feeling the temper stirring in Alfred Hersland the kind of temper he had in him when he was a boy and when he was a man and he had a temper in him that is a common thing with those having in them resisting being tending to the engulfing kind of that kind of them and Alfred Hersland had this kind of angry action in him although he was not an angry or a sullen person mostly in him.

I am very nearly full up with him with Alfred Hersland and his kind in men and women. It is all filling in me now to over flowing. Alfred Hersland was a very little one and then a child and then a boy then. He learned to understand talking and answering and it was surprising when he began this thing as it is with every one. Once one sees a little one and he is not understanding anything any one says to him and he is not trying to do anything and then in a very little while a couple of months of living and he is understanding and answering and is trying to have things, that he can have a liking for then and that is a very certain thing and Alfred Hersland had this in him and later then he was a boy in his living and then he was coming to be a very young man and he had it then in him to be wanting to be helping his sister to have freedom so then he was very certain and he wanted to be helping and to be instructing and to be a good deal an example to his brother who was a younger one and he was then beginning resisting for every one to his father then, and his mother then had about him a strong feeling of worrying when he was a little late for dinner in the evening and later to be missing him when he had left them to go to Bridgepoint for his college education and he was then certain he was a man devoted to everything and every one and he always wrote to every one then to be good ones and he was a man then and then very much later he was marrying Julia Dehning and all this then was in him as much later living and in the beginning he was a little baby and then beginning understanding and talking and then a boy then and then a boy coming to be going to be a very young man and then he was full up with public feeling for every one living in the house with him, his sister, his brother, his father, his mother, every one, in the beginning then he was a very little one, this is now then the beginning of the complete history of the being and the living of him.

It is a nice thing, it is mostly pleasant for every one when the eldest son is the eldest of the children, in family living. This was not the case with Alfred Hersland, he was the eldest son, he was not the oldest of the three Hersland children, Martha was the oldest of them, it is very certain that mostly in family living it is a pleasanter thing when the oldest one of the children is the oldest son, this most generally is pleasanter for every one, for that one who is the oldest one, it is not such a pleasant thing for that one when a woman a girl a sister is the older one when he is the oldest son, this mostly then makes it a little a difficult thing when he is a son and not the oldest one of the children, in family living. Very often in family living when one is not the oldest of the three children but is the oldest son, very often then he is such a one as I am soon going to be describing as Alfred Hersland. Very often in family living when one is not the oldest of the children but is the oldest son, very often then that one is such a one as Alfred Hersland was in his living. I know now three of such of them who have it in them to be of the kind of them that Alfred Hersland is and who have it in their living that they were the oldest son and that they had a sister who was a few years older and that put them in a position that I will now soon be describing in the early living, in the beginning of being a young man in the living of Alfred Hersland.

Alfred Hersland then is now to every one a young one, this is now a history of him. He was a good enough looking one, many said he was a very good looking one.

Sometimes in reading, sometimes in thinking, sometimes in realising, sometimes in a kind of a way in feeling, knowing repeating knowing always everything is repeating, knowing that there will be going on living is saddening. Sometime then in reading, in realising anything, a little sometimes in feeling something it is saddening to be thinking, feeling, realising that always everything, is repeating, that sometime some one is a young one and that now some one is in their middle living and that now some one is an old one and sometimes it is a queer feeling in one this and then not anything, not writing, reading, dying, being a dead one, living, being a young one, being one is a real thing inside in one then and always then it is certain that always every one is living and every one has their being in them and every one is feeling thinking knowing something and always then it is certain that every one is like some other one and everything is existing and it is saddening then and existing is not a real thing then to some one feeling then every one as existing and being themselves inside them and some one being like some one and each one being either a young one or a middle aged one or an old one and sometimes then this is a little a dreary thing and sometimes then it is a very queer thing and mostly then it is all then something and mostly then it is certain that everything is existing and mostly then it is inside in some one that not anything is a real thing, that it is dreary to be writing.

I am feeling always that I am not certain that I am ever really full up with any one in being as a young one, it is such a difficult thing to be a young one inside one, an older one inside one, to be any age inside in one, I am feeling that it is a very queer thing to be knowing some one who is a young one, to be knowing any one, I am not then having any one inside me now in my realising, not myself inside me in my feeling, I am living that is certain, I am now beginning a little again feeling that I am not yet full up with the being in Alfred Hersland. I am now again beginning waiting.

I have not any more any one in me to my feeling. Always then there is Alfred Hersland and I know very well what kind of being there is in him. I have not any one in me to my feeling. Not Alfred Hersland then and and so again now I am beginning waiting.

How can any one know it in them that they are a young one, that they are a middle aged one, that they are an old one. Mostly there is not any way to know it inside in one that one is a young one that one is an older one that one is an old one, there is not any way of knowing such a thing inside in one, mostly then each one must be told it by some one and mostly then that one does not then really know it in them. Mostly then there is not any way any one by themselves can know it in them that they are a young one a very young one, a young one not such a very young one, an older one, a good deal older one, an old one, a very old one. There is not then any way any one can know it inside them the difference in them of being a young one or an older one when some one is not somehow telling it to them, some other one, this can be a telling by that other one this can be a telling by the other one because the other one is existing at another stage in living. I have been seeing a young man and have been talking very much with him and he is quite a young man and he is very much like one I was seeing very much when I was quite a young one. Now this one that I am now seeing is quite a young one that is to me very certain and there is in me a feeling that to any one to himself now there is not very much meaning in many things he is now always saying and yet I know it by remembering that that one that I was knowing very well when I was quite a young one and who is so very like this one, I know that that one was not then to himself or to me then a young one, I must date it to myself to be really certain that that other one who is in being just like this one was then such a young one, young as this one is now in his being, it is certain that that other one was such a young one, he is not now to my remembering of that time a young one, he was at that time to my feeling as now I am remembering he was at that time to my feeling then not at all a very young one, he really was then as old as I am now in my feeling, for it is certain not any one is any age inside them to their feeling, every one is inside them living, that is about all there can ever be in them really of feeling of themselves inside them, that they are living inside in them, they cannot be inside in them any age inside them not any one and that makes it a very hard thing to be really realising a young one or an old one or any one, or one's own self inside one, and now I am not going to be doing this thing with Alfred Hersland I am now only going to be telling the being in him and the living in him and what he did in living with any other one. Not any one in them is to themselves any age inside them. They know in them by looks and looking at other ones and talking and knowing things they are thinking, have been thinking, by things they were and will be doing, by realising by an effort in them or simply in them things happening in them by remembering but really then not any one is to themselves anything but only just living inside them, that is all feeling of themselves inside them that they can have in them with not anything to help them by telling them or by their seeing others then to help them.

Always then Alfred Hersland had a being in him that now I am beginning describing. Always Alfred Hersland was living to his ending. This is the being then that is in every one, they are existing until there is an end of them. Each one has their own being in them, each one is of a kind in men and women. Alfred Hersland was of a kind of men and women as I was saying, he was the eldest son but not the eldest child as I was saying and that had some effect on him as I was saying it does have on those that are eldest sons but not the eldest child in family living, and Alfred Hersland was all through his early living living with poor people near him and in a way he was of them, he did things with them as I will now be telling and then he left home to go to Bridgepoint for his college training and before that he was at the stage of being very instructive and very desirous to be the head of his family and a good citizen and after he left he was a tender feeling in his mother's living and then he had some kinds of loving in him and then as I was saying he came to be married to Julia Dehning and later then his father was losing his great fortune and then too Martha was beginning having trouble in living and later then his brother David was influencing him and later then Alfred Hersland was having very much trouble in his married living and many people came then to be important to him and then there was more and more living in him and this is now to be a complete history of him. I am now almost all through with waiting. I am now beginning to be free with the being of him inside me in my feeling. I am now completely certain that not any one is to himself inside him in his or her feeling any age inside them.

Alfred Hersland was the eldest son and the second child of the Hersland family and the Hersland family then were living on a ten acre place in a part of Gossols where no other rich people were living and the Herslands were then rich people, Mr. Hersland was then a very rich one, Mrs. Hersland had it then and always that she was naturally a natural part of rich living, but being rich ones was then not inside them as a feeling important in the Hersland children living, they were then all three of the living of the poor people in small houses and a half country half-city living feeling. Alfred Hersland was then such a one in his living, and living was then the important thing in him and slowly then family living came to be important to him, but now in the beginning when he was a very young one, family living was not important in him. This is now to be a complete history of the living in him all his living. When he was quite a very young one family living his family position was not of any importance in him, then it came to be more important, then very important in him, then after his marrying Julia Dehning very much less important in him. Always all the time he was living in Gossols even when family living was important to him he was living with the poor people near him. Later after he married Julia Dehning he in a way came back to such a living although they were then different ones he was then knowing.

Mostly it is very hard realising about another one that that one is not thinking, is not thinking when it would seem that thing is a thing they would naturally be doing. It is very hard for any one who is ever doing writing to be really realising that very many are not doing thinking, remembering, it is a very hard thing to be realising about other ones and then it is a very hard thing to be realising that some who would naturally be thinking the kind of way one writing is thinking are not ever thinking that kind of a way about anything, about something. It is a very hard thing then knowing what any one ever is seeing, feeling, thinking, I am all alone now and I have then an unreal lonesome feeling, it is like a little boy who was howling and they all rushed out to help him, I am all alone, he said, and all of a sudden it had scared him. It is not frightening to some but it is hard work for them then for such a one may then perhaps be almost in need of beginning again.

Every one was a whole one in me and now a little every one is in fragments inside me. There are a very great many not now in me, mostly every one now in me is in pieces inside me. Mostly not any one now is a whole one inside me. Alfred Hersland is in fragments inside me, I will now begin again and it will be a describing of pieces then, pieces of perhaps a whole one. Perhaps not any one really is a whole one inside them to themselves or to any one. Perhaps every one is in pieces inside them and perhaps every one has not completely in them their own being inside in them. Perhaps each one is in pieces and repeating is coming out of them that is certain but as repeating of pieces in them. Repeating is always coming out of each one that is certain, in all moments of despairing that is certain, that every one always is repeating. That every one always is repeating is a certain thing.

I am very certain of that thing that every one always is repeating the being in them, sometimes it is to me as pieces that do not make any meaning as a whole one. Mostly always sometime each one is a whole one to me, very often each one is in pieces to me. Always every one is repeating, repeating and repeating the being in them and always repeating is coming out of each one, always all through all the living they are doing, always all their living and sometimes it is exciting to know it in them, sometimes a very dreary thing, sometimes a very discouraging feeling for living, sometimes a friendly one and sometimes then it makes of some one not such an important one as one had thought them, sometimes then it makes of some one a more important one than one had thought them, sometimes it is a habit in one to expect it of them the repeating from some one.

Now then, mostly every one is a good deal in pieces to my feeling, Alfred Hersland then now is such a one to my feeling, a good deal in pieces to my feeling. Always all his being is always repeating in all his living. He is a good deal in pieces to my feeling.

He was not then the oldest of the Hersland children, he was younger than Martha and that always makes a difference in a boy's living, not that Martha was very important to him in his early living but there came to be for him when it came to be in him when he was a going to be young man and was coming to feel like a good citizen and having strong family feeling, it came to him then to be directing and he was not then the eldest of the Hersland children. He did help Martha some then, he did help her a little to be able to go to college as she was wanting to do then but they were not very interesting ever to each other Martha and Alfred Hersland, a little then when she was to go to college Martha was a little interesting to Alfred then and very much later in her living when Alfred was having trouble long after he had been married to Julia Dehning he was a little then a little interesting to Martha who was then taking care of her father in Gossols after he had lost their great fortune. Alfred then was a little really interested in Martha when she was leaving home for a college education, later he and his brother David were a little interesting one to the other one when they were living in Bridgepoint together after Alfred was married and then later, and the mother Mrs. Hersland had a tender feeling in her for the clothes Alfred had left with her and the room he had slept in, when he left the family living to go to Bridgepoint to do his studying, and Mr. Hersland he never had in him a very certain important feeling about Alfred excepting a little when he might have been needing him or when a little Alfred might be opposing him but really then the three Hersland children not any of them were really important ever to Mr. David Hersland to his feeling. He had sometimes a kind of feeling about one or the other of them because of something, some specific thing, but mostly Mr. Hersland was as big as all the world in his feeling.

Every one to me just now is in pieces to me. That is to say every one is to me just now as pieces to me. That is to say that each complete one is only as a piece to me, that all there is of each one at anytime in them gives to me a feeling of pieces not of a whole thing, that is to say I am having just now with each one I am knowing or remembering a feeling an emotion from them as if they were each one not a whole thing. I have this perhaps not altogether with every one but I have it just now with a good many of them a good many that I am knowing, knowing now or remembering now and most of the time now I have such a feeling. A little it comes to me I am certain from my realisation that many of them are not completely thinking or feeling the way a complete one of their kind of them would be thinking or feeling. They are thinking and feeling in pieces then now to me to my feeling just now in my emotion and that makes of them to me pieces of being, makes all there is of them of each one, not whole ones, this is very strongly in me just now in my feeling, very very strongly in me, men and women very many of them those I am knowing those I am remembering, not all of them, I do not say that it is true of all of them even just now in my feeling but very many a great many of them are to me just now in pieces to me. There are pieces then and that is whole being, there is a piece then and that is the whole being of some one, they may be, such a one may be completely of one kind of being, but it is only a piece of such a kind of being as that one is in being. It is not such a very joyous feeling, having the emotion of having every one as a piece to one, it does make of everything a thing without ending and all the time then there is not any use of anything keeping on going. Why should anything any one keep on going if not ever at any time anything any one will be a whole one, what is the use of anything or everything keeping on going if not at any time I will not be having a sensation that any one anything will be a whole one, once every one sometime was a whole one, now mostly every one is a piece of a one, not all the being as a complete one and yet every one has their own being in them and putting all of each kind of them together to make a whole one can not be to me a satisfaction, cannot give to me any real satisfaction can not be a satisfactory way in my feeling of having completion of having anything or any one a whole one cannot give to me any reason why the world should keep on being, there is not any reason if in repeating nothing is giving to me a sensation of a completed one, I have then this in me now and mostly every one I am knowing or remembering is to me just now a piece of a kind of being and every one is themselves inside them, that is always to my feeling certain and so then feeling each one is a piece of a kind of being and always then feeling each one is entirely existing so that each one is not a part of any whole thing I cannot to myself have any very real satisfaction from getting together all the ones there are of a kind of them, to make a whole one, that is, not to my feeling, that cannot give to me an emotion of satisfaction, that is not to my feeling satisfying and so then I am not feeling each one is sometime to me a whole one, no then no, I am now feeling that mostly all of them every one I am knowing every one I am remembering is to me a piece of being and so then there is not any use in the world going on existing so that every one can keep on with repeating a piece of being, not any use at all then to me to my feeling, not any use then really to any one and this is now then the real state of feeling I am now having.

Alfred Hersland is to me a piece of being, he is not in me a whole one, this is certain, mostly every one is to me a piece of being, every one has their own being in them, Alfred Hersland has his own being in him, alright, I know it of every one, I know it that every one has their own being in them, I know it and always I feel it, I always feel it and I always know it, every one has their own being in them yes every one, every kind of a one, every one that ever was or is or will be living, yes, alright, I know it of every one that every one has their own being in them, Alfred Hersland had his own being in him, yes every one has their own being in them, yes that is alright, I know that of them, I know that very well of them, I know every one has their own being in them, I feel it of them, I know that always in every one, always in each one, always of every one, yes i know that each one has their own being in them and I am saying that mostly every one is a piece of being, not a whole one in them and so then there is not any use of the world going on for any one, and there is not any way of making a complete one of any being by putting together all of some kinds of them all of any kind of them for each one has their own being in them and so after all there is not any way of making a whole one. Every one to me just now is as a piece to me, that is to say each one mostly is not a complete one of anything to my feeling, each one just now to my feeling is a piece of something and that is to me very certain by my very strongly realising in every one the way they are not thinking, feeling a complete thing of their kind in feeling and thinking. Now then Alfred Hersland is a piece of being to me and now I will tell of it the way I feel it in me, the way I feel him and every one just now in me.

Alfred Hersland had a kind of being in him that in some who have it in them makes of them very good ones, some not such very good ones. This is in a way true of every kind there is of being. Of the kind of one that Alfred Hersland was in his being they range from very good ones through to pretty bad ones but this is true of every kind there is of men and women. Alfred had it in him to have his being in him so that it was a little passionate in him, not very affectionate in him, not so as to be very good in him, not really ever very bad in him, sometimes as aspiration in him, more or less as ambitious in him, sometimes as virtuous and didactic in him. The kind of being he had in him was of a kind of being that in some having it in them makes of them devout in religion, makes of them mystic in religion, so as to let themselves be absorbed, all existing, some of them having this kind of being in them have religion in them but then it is like that in the grandfather of Alfred Hersland, Mr. Hissen. Some having this kind of being in them are meek enough in living and yet a little dominating in family living and are just enough in thinking and impersonal in feeling, and some of such of them need to have as a wife to them some one very vibratingly existing to give to them enough stimulation to make them keep really alive inside them. All these then are of the resisting, the dependent independent kind of them. Some of them have the being in them very murkily passionate inside and some of these then are trying to engulf every one near them to be lost inside them, to be swallowed by them and some of them are not interested in very many persons near them but some of them they need to have engulfed by them and so then Alfred Hersland was of the kind of them the resisting dependent independent kind of them, the kind that own those they need for loving. Many of such of them do not really in their living need any one for loving, in a way Mr. Hissen the old man important in religion, being inside him all there was of religion was such a one of this kind of them. Alfred Hersland then to my feeling has being in him as pieces only of being, he is himself inside him, he has being in him, he has really living in him, every one has real being to me in them but as I am saying very many to me now are pieces of being and yet they are themselves inside them, I know that of them, I know that in them, I know that in myself with them, and so then to me then just now then in my feeling, very much mostly every one is as pieces of living, pieces of being, to me then now to my feeling, pieces everywhere of something are existing and repeating, repeating of pieces of something and yet whole ones are inside them are repeating all around me as living, feeling, being, thinking, existing and in a way then not whole ones and not a part of anything because they are one each one all there is of them and so then just now to my feeling it is a little fragmentary all there is of living and keeping going is only in everything because it is not ended yet and that is then my feeling just now inside me and Alfred Hersland is to me a real being but not having completion in the sense of a whole meaning, everything then every one, that is mostly every one mostly everything is just now to my feeling as pieces of being, pieces alive completely inside them and so always repeating as a whole one but having not meaning as a whole one. Alfred Hersland then was a kind of them he had a kind of being in him that was in him as more or less engulfing, somewhat passionate, not very bad, certainly not very good, engulfing resisting dependent independent being, needing to own those he would need for loving, very often needing some one poignantly alive to influence him.

Of the kind of one that Alfred Hersland was in his being they range from very good ones through to pretty bad ones, from very tyrannical ones to very just ones, from very good ones through to pretty bad ones, from very religious ones to completely skeptical ones, from very dominant ones to very meek ones, from very passionate ones to completely indifferent ones and all of these in their living are of the resisting kind of them the dependent independent kind of them, those of them should have then needing to own those they need for loving. Alfred Hersland then had in him to be a little passionate and engulfing, a little meek and a little tyrannical in living, a little didactic and superior in aspiring, and certainly not really a very good one and in religion mostly not believing and yet not being really completely certain that to be dead was to be really completely a dead one, he had it a little in him to be a little going to be saving himself by a little religion in himself or in somebody very near to him whom in a way then he was owning.

Of the kind of one that Alfred Hersland was in his being, the kind of them men and women having in them such kind of being range from very good ones through to pretty bad ones, have all kinds of mixtures in them, have every kind of way of living are many of them pretty successful in living, some very successful and some pretty miserably failing, some pretty steady with the being in them, some pretty intermittent and some meek and some very weak in being and all this is true of every kind there is of men and women.

I am thinking now of six of them that have such a kind of nature in them like that in Alfred Hersland and these have it very differently in them than he had it in him and then there was his grandfather Mr. Hissen of whom I have written. There was one and he was not very successful not very not successful in living, he was successful enough in living and he had it in him to be impersonal and just and kindly enough with mostly every one, and he had not any engulfing passionate nature in him, not at all any such a kind of this kind of being in him, and he was almost altogether certain that to be dead was to be really a dead one and he did not altogether completely like it such a feeling and he could be a little not certain of it inside him though mostly altogether he was certain that to be dead is to be really truly a dead one and he liked it very well that his wife who could be making lively living feeling was very certain that to be dead was not at all to be a dead one and he liked it then that she was such a kind of one and mostly then this one was successful enough in living, and kindly and not meek and not given to aggression and master in his own house by patient overseeing and successful enough in living by patient persisting and this then is all there is now to be written of the living this one had in him. This one then was of the resisting kind of them that have it in them not to be engulfing, not to be aggressive nor meek in their resisting winning, to be needing to be owning those they need for loving but to be only loving one human being, to be kindly but impersonal really with every other one. That is all then of the being of one of the six of them.

Another of the six of them was one having it in him to have a good deal in him of the engulfing passionate being of his kind of them but the being in him was not really ever in action, it never amounted to any more in him than to be a little wiggling in him and that was all then, he wanted it to be in action, he wanted to be passionate, and succeeding, and aspiring, and despairing, he tried it always all his living, he was always a little scaring and filling with hope his family for the despair and the possible activity in succeeding in living in him and mostly then nothing ever happened and he came as near in his living as a man can come to failing who is not completely failing in living. He loved a very pale anaemic woman but he never came to marrying, he was always a man considered as perhaps promising successful living and so it went on and on and he was an older one and still he himself and a little some other ones had still a hopeful feeling that this one would sometime be really succeeding, would really be doing something. This then has been a very little description of another one of the six of them.

Another one of them had the passionate murky engulfing being in him in a completely concentrated form that made him active, sensitive, amusing and successful, quite successful in living. He was always loving but it never was a trouble to him, he was so active he never was knowing that he was engulfing the other one, that he owned those he needed for loving. He was a very active, sensitive, amusing, successful enough person and the murky engulfing passionate resisting being that made him was so concentrated in him that he was a compactly existing being and in a way not interested in anything or any one he was not just then really needing. He was a very nice, a nice, amusing, sensitive, successful enough one of this kind of them, the passionate engulfing resisting kind of them, in this one this being was quite a concentrated pleasant thing. This is then all there will now be written of this one.

Another one had it in him to be completely certain in all his acting and his feeling and his living that to be dead is to be a dead one and so this one must keep on being a live one and must have everything he can be seizing to keep by him and always this one in his talking and his thinking and his feeling was very certain that he was very certain that to be dead was not to be a dead one and if it were, what then, a really noble man would not let it effect him and he was most certainly such a one. This one then had this being, the resisting being I have been describing as not really in him as engulfing as not really in him not engulfing, as not really in him as passion and yet as just enough in him as passion to give him a little something that made it that mostly one would not trust him and yet that for very many he had some real attraction. This one had some aggression of resisting being in him, this one was quite successful enough in living.

This one that I am now beginning describing had murky passionate resisting being but its action in him was very intermittent and it was at different times in very different conditions in him. Sometimes it was in him in a fairly concentrated condition and it made of him some one very quick and sensitive and charming and a musician, sometimes it was very quiet in him and then sometimes it burst out as uncontrollable temper in him. Twice in his life it lead to loving and both times then it made trouble for him for he was not strong enough in persisting to be able to keep on owning the ones he needed for loving. This one was not very successful in living.

This one was very successful in living, this one that I am now beginning describing. This one had this being not at all as murky not at all as engulfing, he had it in him as efficient emotion, as active practical reasonably aggressive resistant action, as steadily and not too sensitively in him, as warmly affectionate and rationally self-understanding. He was a little sentimental and this was all the weakness there was in him. The being in him was perfectly adjusted to steadily succeeding in living. Sometime perhaps there will be a very long history written of him and four others very like him, perhaps in the history of David Hersland and George Dehning.

This then has been, a little, descriptions of six kinds of being that are kinds of the kinds of them that Alfred Hersland was in living. As I was saying of the kind of being there is in Alfred Hersland there is every kind of variation. There has been now made very short descriptions of six of them. This is now time then for the really beginning describing the living in Alfred Hersland from his beginning.

As I was saying he was not the oldest of the three Hersland children. Every one knows this now of him. He was the oldest son but not the oldest one of the children in the family living. Being the oldest son and not the oldest of the children has always a certain effect on one having such a position in a family living. That is pretty nearly certain. Alfred Hersland then as I was saying was the oldest son but not the oldest of the children. Martha Hersland was the oldest of the three children. There has been already written a complete history of her living and her being, a pretty nearly completed history of her. She was the oldest of the three Hersland children, Alfred Hersland was three years younger. This is now the beginning of a complete history of his living, the beginning of the regular description of the being he had in him. To begin again then, to begin now with him, to begin now again trying to describe him as a quite young one, as beginning in his living. To begin then.

Alfred Hersland, Alfy as every one then called him was as a young one of the living of poor people living in small houses in a part of Gossols where the Herslands were the only rich people living. Alfy was of the living of poor people in his daily living then as was his older sister Martha then and his brother who was then quite a little one. All three of the Hersland children were of this living for a good many years in their beginning. It was different in Alfred than it was in Martha, than it was in David Hersland, that I have already been saying. In Alfred it was his daily living then, it was nearly all the living then in him. It was half country half city living. Alfy knew very many poor people then in his young living. In a way then he was then completely of them, completely of their living then. He was different in his living with them in a way than Martha and David were. He was completely then as a young one of the living of poor people, a half city half country poor people living. He was always then with these kind of men and women and children.

All three of the Hersland children Martha and Alfred and David were in their young living more of the living of the poor people living near them than they were of their own family living then. Each one of them was in his or her way almost completely in their young living of the living of poor people in a part of Gossols where the Herslands were the only people who were rich of all those living there. All three of them Martha, Alfred and David were then in their young living of the half country half city living of poor people living in that part of Gossols where the Herslands then were living. Each one of the three Hersland children had each one her or his own being in her or in him. Each one was very different from the other two of them, Martha had one kind of being, and

Alfred had one kind of being and David had a kind of being and the being in each one was different from that in each of the other two of them.

Each one of the three of them the Hersland children were then in their young living each in their own way with their own being in them of the living of people living in small houses and being in feeling half city half country men and women and children. All three of them of the Hersland children had this living inside them and around them then when they were beginning living, for a number of years each one of them, and in each one it was a living that was in them in each one different in feeling from each of the other two of them. Each one then of the three of them were freely living when they were each one of them young ones with people living near them. Martha was of the people near her as I was saying and in her as I was saying then she was in a way completely of them and completely not of them, she was of them completely in her daily living and in her feeling, she was completely not of them because of the future living that would be a different one from anything that any of them would naturally be having. Martha was in a way completely in her daily living completely in her feeling all through her young living of the being of the people living in small houses near them, of the women and the men and the children and then later she was more and more completely not of them because of the living that would be her natural future living. She was of them in her feeling, she was completely cut off from them from the future living that would be natural to her in their feeling. She had not then in her feeling in her younger living any feeling of living that was different from their living in them only she had in her her future living and so then she was to them completely cut off from them. She had not in her in her younger living very much almost not any feeling of the living, the rich right american living that would have been a natural living for her to be having. She was to her feeling like those with whom she was mostly then entirely in her young living living. She was pretty nearly altogether like them then in her feeling, she had more money and she did not have to work to earn any and that was a natural thing in her living and then in her feeling she was completely of them and this was in her all of her young living. In Alfred Hersland it was a little different, he really did more things with them than Martha ever did with them. He did everything with them all through his young living but always somehow he had it in him that his mother never was cut off in her feeling from being part of rich right american living. This was not in him as thinking, his mother was not then important to his feeling, she was not then really in any way very important to him, his father was a rich man, every one who knew him knew this about him, Alfred Hersland was completely living the living half city half country of people around him, somehow always he had it in him that his mother was part of rich right american living, this was in him as a kind of realisation of rich surfaces in aesthetic feeling, this was in him and his father was a rich man and always he was completely doing everything with those boys and girls and men and women who were living in that part of Gossols where he was living. He did everything with them, he was completely living with them, he did everything they were doing, he did everything with them and they with him, he was completely then living with them.

He was doing all his daily living with the children and the women and the men living in small houses in that part of Gossols where the Herslands were the only rich people living. The Herslands were rich people of rich american living as the natural way of living. In a way Alfred had never had any real experiencing of this kind of way of living, he really did not know very much of any one who was living this kind of living, sometimes some with their children came to see the Herslands and then the Hersland children had to play and talk with these then these children living the rich american living, and the Hersland children mostly were not interested in them, Alfred had not any liking for them, he liked to have all the fruit picked even before it was quite ripe before it was really ready for picking so that those children who were coming to visit them should not be using their trees to pick fruit and enjoy it. Alfred never liked it that these children should be at home in his orchard, picking fruit and eating it and taking it home with them, he liked very well picking fruit and climbing trees, his own trees with those children that were in his daily living, he never did like it that children coming with their parents on a Sunday visit well to do american families should come and pick fruit in his orchard and enjoy such things then when they came occasionally to visit the Herslands in a part of Gossols where not any other rich people excepting the Herslands were living. Once when some of them were coming, Alfred with David and Martha to help picked all the fruit although most of it was green then, it was mostly cherries just then, picked it all every bit of it and put it in the barn to ripen and he did this so that the children coming to visit them should not be climbing the trees and helping themselves as if it were in an orchard of their own. He made David and Martha have such a feeling too in them, it was a mixed feeling in Alfy then, he was then just beginning to feel in him responsibility for family living, he was just beginning then to feel in him that he was an american citizen, he was just beginning to feel in him then his daily living and liking that realisation that he was then beginning to have in him. He was beginning then a little dimly to have a realisation of the fact that his mother never in her feeling had been really cut off from rich right american living. He was just then completely living with the people living near him, he was doing all his living with them, living was interesting to him then, he was more and more then beginning to be really living his living with their living. He had in him not any disliking for the rich american living but he did not want the children of that living to make themselves too much at home in his garden in his orchard with the flowers and the fruit that was part of his daily living then.

Each one of the three Hersland children had each their own way of living and feeling their early living. This is now to be a description of the way Alfred lived and felt his early living.

As a boy Alfred Hersland, Alfy as they called him was doing everything he was doing with these boys, those children living near him. He did everything he did with them, mostly he did everything they did in living, he did everything he did then in his daily living with them. He was then completely of them in doing everything he did in his daily living with them. As I was saying he did mostly everything they did in their living. He certainly did everything he did in his daily living with them. He was of them then. He was of them, Martha Hersland, David Hersland, all three of the Hersland children were of them the people in small houses near them in their early living. Each one of them, of the three Hersland children was of them in the way it was natural for that one to be of people around her around him. Each one of the three of them certainly was of the children and women and men who were their neighbors then in all the young living each one of them had then. Each one of them certainly then was of the daily living of these then, the people near them more than any one of the three of them were then of their own proper family living. Martha Hersland was pretty completely of the living of the people living near her when she was a young one, more than she was then of her mother's or her father's or her brother's living then. Alfred Hersland, Alfy as these then all called him did everything he did in his younger living with them with these people near him. David Hersland also was of them the people near him but then he was of every one in a way and mostly always of himself inside him and soon now there will be a beginning to him. Each one then of them certainly did have their young living in company with the people living near them then and certainly each one of them had their living inside in them in the way it was natural for such a kind of them as each one of them was inside them to have it in them. Martha then had it in her in her kind of way, of having it in her. She was of them these people in her younger living. Alfred, Alfy as they called him, had it in him then when he was a boy and also then when he was a little older as it was natural for him to have it in him. He certainly then when he was a boy lived all his daily living with them, mostly then he did what they did in living, certainly he did everything he did with them, this was true of him when he was a boy, it was pretty nearly true of him when he was a little older, it was more or less true of him all the time he lived there near them.

The grandfather of the Hersland children Mr. Hissen had it in him to be completely certain that when he would be a dead one he would be dead completely dead, of that he was completely certain, he was so a complete one, concrete and generalised conviction was the same in him, he was in himself then to himself always in him always all there was of religion, he was the grandfather of the Hersland children, he was the grandfather of Alfred and David Hersland, he was the grandfather of Martha Hersland but she was not related to him in being, he was the grandfather of Alfred and David Hersland, they were related to him by their being, he was the grandfather of Alfred Hersland, that is certain, this is now beginning to be a description of Alfred Hersland and the being in him and the living that came out of and to him.

Alfred Hersland was a boy and living then with for him poor people, children, men and women. He did everything that he was then doing in his living with them, he was then completely of them, he was then completely with them when he was a boy and among them. Later when he was still doing everything he was doing with them, when he was still doing mostly everything they were doing with them, it was then a little different in him, he was pretty completely then doing with them everything that they were doing, he was doing it pretty completely entirely then his life with them, he was pretty completely then almost entirely then doing with them everything that they, older girls and boys, and men and women in the small houses near the Hersland ten acre place were then doing, he was then completely doing and doing pretty nearly entirely everything they were doing and doing it with them and it was a little a different thing in him than when he was a younger one, already he had then a feeling like a feeling for quality of richness and finish in anything, he had already a little beginning of feeling in him that his family was not really then never had been cut off from the rich american living, the natural living for them. He did not know it then and the little he knew then was not pleasant to him, he did then mostly entirely everything those living in small houses near him were doing and he did it with them, he did not know then really anything of this rich right american living that was the natural Hersland way of living, he knew nothing of this then, he did not really think of such a thing, a little he had in him then a little family feeling about managing his sister and being a good citizen, his mother was not then important to him, his father was a rich man he knew it then but he did not then really feel this in him, he had not any realisation of this then in him, and always then he was doing everything and with them, very completely indeed then what these people were doing who lived near him and always then he did not know then and the little he knew of them who had it in them, right rich american living was not pleasant to him and yet in him beginning was a little feeling that some way somehow he was inside him a being never really cut off from rich right american living. When he was a younger one this was entirely completely not in him, a little later when he was completely doing everything the ones near him were doing and very much with them and with the feeling of them and himself as of them in him still somewhere in him there was in him what his mother had in her as always there inside her that he was of a being that had it as a natural thing that nothing in him was cut off from rich right american living, and always then he was completely living with them the people near him living their living having their feeling being completely then of their living in his acting, in his living, in his thinking, in his feeling.   Each one of the Hersland cnildren had their own being in them each one of them had a different way from the two other ones of having the living with the people near them in them. Martha had her being, had her feeling in their living, had her way of being completely of them the people near her, in her younger living.   Alfred had his being in him, he had his way of feeling the living he was doing in his young living.   He certainly was doing everything these near him were doing and doing it with them and feeling it as they were feeling in it then and this is now then some history of his living then, of his daily living then.

Alfred Hersland was with them in his daily living with the people living near him, with the boys around him in his daily living and he did then everything he did with them and he did then everything they did in their daily living and he had not in him then anything at all of family living.   When.he was a boy, when he was beginning his living he lived his daily life then doing everything he did then with the boys the women and men living near him.   He did his roller skating, a little shooting, some camping, a good deal of fishing, some going about the country selling fruit he had been picking with them in the orchard in the ten acre place where the Herslands were living and any other fruit belonging to any of them that they could use for selling, he did everything in his daily living with them, he was with them when they were with girls then and he did with the girls everything a boy does when he is with them.   He had then public school living.   He did his daily living completely with them, he did everything they were doing then, this was the history of the living he had in him when he was a young one : he did everything then with these then living near him, he had then his being in him and his daily living and this is now then to be a description of the living then in him with the being in him.

There were then the Banks boys who lived near him, there were three of them, it was the oldest one who was mostly with him, the second one George who had lost two fingers from a sickness he had that no one ever mentioned to him was the one with whom David Hersland later did his living.   The oldest Banks brother Albert, who later in his living did shoemaking, George later was a clerk and pretty successful in living, the third brother then a very red faced freckled one who could crow very well and always was on fences doing this thing and his later living came when the Herslands did not any longer any of them any more know what happened to any one in that part of Gossols and so there is not to be any telling of his future living, Albert was a good deal in these days with Alfred Hersland and then he began shoemaking and he was not very good at learning at school and once he had a furious anger in him there and he scared every one in the school by drawing a pistol although it was an empty one and he was told not to come any more and he then began learning shoemaking but he was a good fellow to be with for any one and pleasant enough and he and Alfred did everything together then until the shoemaking began and then he went with men and Alfred was not so completely with him then. These Banks boys had in them all three of them half city half country living, Alfred had in him completely half city half country living, when he began shoemaking city living came to be more strongly in him, Albert then went on with his half city half country living, he went on then living with those then near him who kept on in them being half city half country in their feeling. There were some of them who kept on having half city half country feeling some of those living near the Herslands then and after Albert Banks began learning shoemaking Alfred Hersland was mostly with them. The one who might have been interested in Martha if she had been more interesting to him was one of such of them. Alfred when he was not any longer a boy in his living was for a little while a good deal with this one. He did then, Alfred did then pretty nearly entirely everything that this one, that this crowd of them were doing then in their daily living. Alfred was beginning to have a little in him beginning then the feeling of family being but it was not in him then yet as in any way determining and he was then completely entirely doing in his daily living what these having in them half country half city living were doing.

There were a number of little houses in this part of Gossols and Alfred knew a good many of the people living in them. In a good many of them the same people kept on living all the time the Herslands were living in a ten acre place there, in some of the houses there was much moving, people would be very often coming and going. Once there was a family that stayed one year there and there were two children an older boy and a very young one, the older one Louis Champion was very much with Alfred then, the little brother was a nuisance to them, Alfred did a good deal of roller skating, some camping out and more or less fishing with Louis Champion. Louis was a pleasant fellow and good-looking.

Alfy was often out in the evening, in the summer he was out a long time almost always every evening. Sometimes he went out with some of them living in small houses near him, sometimes some of them would be playing hide and go seek around the Hersland house with him. Albert Banks was often playing, going about with him of an evening. They were together very often in the evening. Alfy was very often out in the evening with some of them living near him. In the summer he was out a long time almost always every evening. Very often he would be going off somewhere to do something or he would be standing around with them or they would be all of them hanging around together in a vacant lot that was near to where all of them were living. Sometimes they would be chasing all around all of them, sometimes some of them would be hiding and running on the Hersland place as I was just saying. Albert Banks was often then with Alfy in the evening, less at first after he began learning shoemaking, earlier when he was still going to school he was almost always together with Alfy on a summer evening. All the year Alfy was very often out in the evening when he was a little older boy and in the summer he was out a long time almost always every evening. Sometimes he was out with some of them he was doing everything with in his daily living, sometimes they would be together playing hide and seek in his orchard and in his garden. Albert Banks as I was saying would be then almost always with him in the evening, he would often be playing hide and seek in the Hersland orchard and garden with them, this was before he was thinking of beginning learning shoemaking. Frank and Will Roddy often were with them all in the evening. Frank and Will Roddy often were there in the evening at the Hersland place playing with Albert Banks and Alfred Hersland and David. They were often playing hide and go seek in the summer in the evening. Sometimes some girls would be with them, sometimes Martha Hersland would be with them. Every now and then there would be some girls playing along with them. Albert Banks and Frank and Will Roddy for some time were almost always together with Alfy in the evening. Albert Banks as I was saying later began learning shoe-making, he was then not so very much with Alfy and the Roddy boys who were still then a good deal together in the evening. Frank Roddy later in his living went into the country to earn his living. Will Roddy later went into a cigar stand, clerking, and then his father died and he had a little money and he came to be a partner and then he and the other one failed and they were not fair then they very much favored one creditor, they had some trouble, later very many years later some of the Herslands happened to hear from some one that Will Roddy was in jail because of something he had been doing. He was supposed not to have been very honest and afterwards he was in jail. He was a little fellow and very quick.

So then Alfy and Albert Banks and the Roddy boys were often playing hide and go seek in the summer in the evening. They were a good deal together mostly every evening as I was saying. They were very often together in a vacant lot playing or hanging around together somewhere and often enough they would be chasing around in the Hersland orchard and garden. Sometimes there some girls would be with them. Sometimes then Martha Hersland would be with them. Alfred and

David very often were playing hide and go seek with Albert Banks and the Roddy boys and sometimes some others, in the Hersland orchard and garden. Sometimes some girls would be with them, sometimes then Martha Hersland would be with them. Sometimes then they stayed a long time in the orchard, later then Alfred said to Martha he would tell her father, she had no business to be playing. Sometimes he would be angry and later he would threaten her if she would not do something he wanted her to be doing he would tell her father she was playing hide and go seek in the evening. Sometimes later there would be quarrelling and Alfy would be saying Martha should not be playing that evening. Sometimes Alfy would make Martha go in. He would say if she did not go in he would tell her father she was playing hide and go seek in the evening. Don't you know any better than to come along, he would say to her. He was then a little beginning to have in him the feeling that he was a good citizen, that he was the oldest son, he did not know then yet very specifically why she should go in, she did not know then very specifically why she should go in, they neither of them knew very specifically why she should not be playing hide and go seek in the evening but Alfy was beginning then to have such a feeling about himself in him that he should send her in and later then if she did not do something he wanted she should be doing he always said he would then tell his father she had been playing hide and go seek in the evening and then she always had a sullen fear inside her. Neither of them then as I was saying knew very specifically what they were meaning. Martha, Alfred and David Hersland all three were out a good deal in the evening. Alfred was often out in the evening, in the summer he was out a long time almost always every evening. He was then doing everything with the children and women and men living near him, he was then doing everything mostly that they were doing, he was doing everything he did with them. He was then mostly always out with them in the evening. He was then and when he was older he was then with them, some of them sometimes with a good many of them in the evening. He was always then doing everything he was doing then with them. Alfred all his younger living was out very often in the evening, then and later in his Gossols living he was often out in the evening, in the summer he was out a long time almost always in the evening. Mostly he stayed entirely in that part of Gossols where he was living. Mostly he never went away from the crowd living near him. Mostly he in the evening when he was a young one when he was an older one stayed in that part of Gossols where the Herslands were living, was with them the people living in small houses near him.

There were some whom he knew who were living in another part of Gossols and he sometimes saw them, sometimes he saw them very often. This is now to be a description of them, of all of them. There were two families of them that the Hersland children came to know and each of them lived in a different part of Gossols. They had no connection with each other. The Fishers one of these families then were friends of the woman who lived near the Herslands and did dress-making sometimes for Mrs. Hersland. Sometimes Mary Fisher came to see the second daughter Cora who was not yet come to be a really pretty one. Sometimes Mary Fisher's brother Henry came with her and so the Herslands all of them came to know them and they each one in their way all excepting Mrs. Hersland came to know the Fishers very well. Mr. Hersland came to know them very well later, Martha and Alfred and David Hersland came to know them earlier. They were six of them of the Fisher family, four children and a father and mother. Mr. Fisher had something to do with horses, that was the way he made a living. The Hersland children never came to know him. They sometimes saw him and spoke to him. Henry the second son they came to know very well all of them. Henry went bycicling very often with David Hersland. Mary was the only daughter and all the Hersland family came to know her. Later Mrs. Hersland came to know her a good deal and Martha Hersland always liked her. Mrs. Hersland liked her well enough but never came really to know her. Alfred used·to stay in her kitchen talking to her. Jim was the oldest son and brother. The Herslands did not, any of them, ever come to know him. The Fishers were all proud of him, he was a commercial traveler and was apart from them. Slowly it came out about him that he was going to ruin from a taste for liquor. Later he took a cure and was better, none of the Herslands ever saw him, not any of them ever came to know him. Mrs. Fisher was a tall kindly faced kind of woman. She was always good and mostly always in the kitchen. All the Herslands came to know her, Mrs. Hersland never really came to know her. Henry Fisher was a very reliable person, he was very pleasant always to Martha Hersland, he and David Hersland did a great deal of bycicling together. Alfred Hersland was at the Fishers sometimes for an evening. They were not really ever very important in his living.

Another family with whom the Herslands Martha and Alfred and David, never Mr. and Mrs. Hersland, spent an evening were the Henrys and these were not really important to them. They came to know them quite by accident having sat next to them at a theatre one afternoon and then they went to see them. They went there quite often in the evening one or two or all three of the Herslands then. Mr. and Mrs. Hersland never came to know any of them of the Henry family. There were four children, James Henry a tall thin one who played the violin while the other ones danced in the evening. Henry a pleasant enough sensible enough fellow to be knowing, Rose Henry a little dark one and Carrie Henry who was just one of them. The Herslands would go there and eat dinner with them, Mrs. Henry browned potatoes, pealed, when she roasted her meat the way french people do them, the Herslands always ate very many of them, the forks and knives the Henrys used for eating were worn down very thin, later then James Henry played and all of them danced pretty solemnly in a quadrille. This happened quite often in the evening. The Henrys were really not important in the living of any of the Hersland children. Later then they did not see any of them, Mr. Henry later killed himself and every one wondered if he had been crazy when he did this thing. They were not any of them ever important in the living of Martha, Alfred or David Hersland.

Alfred as I was saying was in Gossols when he was a very young one and when he was a little an older one. Sometimes then later he saw a little sometimes of Olga the sister of the first governess the Herslands had had in their Gossols living staying with them. Sometimes the Wyman family made up to him. This is the way he had all these in him this that I am now beginning describing. This is now beginning to be a history of him, a history of Alfred Hersland of all the being and all the living in him.

Alfred played the violin some, he played it very well. He had some musical feeling, he had quite a bit of musical understanding, later in his very early Bridgepoint living he was very much interested in playing and in understanding. He made for himself some reputation as an intelligent amateur musician. He came to know then in Bridgepoint in his early living in Bridgepoint a young man who was making music a profession and did some rather nice composing. Later this one gave it up and went into a clothing manufacturing business in which his brother and father needed him, but this is all later history of Alfred Hersland, this all was in his Bridgepoint living, this is now a history of him and a description of the being in him in his Gossols living. He had then in him in his younger living a good deal of musical feeling. All the three of them Martha, Alfred and David in their younger living took lessons to learn to play on something. Alfred was the only one of the three of them who had any really musical feeling. Martha took a little interest once in playing and she did a good deal of practicing just before she left Gossols for her college education. David was interested in understanding but he never did any practicing, he was interested again later and always everything was interesting to him sometime and later there will be a very long history of everything and of him written.

Alfred had really some musical feeling in him. Once in his later Gossols living he had a really interesting teacher. This was a man named Arragon. He was a very interesting man, he interested Alfred very much then when he was teaching him. Alfred never wanted to be a musician as a way of living never really at any time in him but music and understanding musical feeling was for a little while all the feeling in him, while Arragon was near him. Later there will be some little history written of this man, not very much but a little and that will come in the later Gossols living in Alfred Hersland.

This has been now a little description of the living in Alfred Hersland and now there will be more description of him, of the being in him and the living in him.

Alfred Hersland was neither popular nor very unpopular with those that knew him. He was not pleasant nor unpleasant to any one, he did everything he did with those he was knowing then, he really did with them mostly everything they were doing. He was not at any time left out by them. He always all his Gossols living did everything he was doing with those he was near then in living, and he always then did with them everything that they were doing. He was never then left out by them. To them his future living was not important in him to cut him off at all from them. He did everything he was doing then with them, he did mostly everything they were doing with them. He was himself inside him, later as I was saying he had some feeling in him that he never had been cut off from rich american living, later then this came to be in him, he still then did everything he did with those he was knowing in Gossols where he was living, not altogether though then, he was beginning knowing some other women and some men, he saw something then of Ida Heard the school teacher and so did his music teacher Arragon this is all to be written later.

Alfred Hersland then was himself inside him, he was perhaps not a very complete one, as I was saying some, a good many just now are pieces to me, they are themselves inside them. Alfred Hersland is one of such of them. He was certainly himself inside him, perhaps he was not such a very complete one, this is a little my feeling of him just now and I have mentioned it again. He was himself inside him, he was of the engulfing resisting kind of them in men and women, he was perhaps not a very complete one, he was to mostly every one not very pleasant not very unpleasant, he was not popular or unpopular with men or with women. This is now to be some description of the being in him.

He was some one to himself inside him that is certain, this is now to be a long description of the being in him. There will then be more description of his Gossols living.

Now there will be description of the being in him and then more history of his Gossols living.

Some know more or less of men and women what the being in them are going to be making them do from minute to minute in their living, some have not at all any such knowledge in them of men and women. Some have a little such knowledge in them about some one when they have known that one completely entirely from the top to the bottom all through them for a good deal of the living in them. Some even then are very apt to be believing that any minute that one will go much farther in doing

something than that one really ever will be doing, much less far in doing
something than that one is really ever going. This is quite common.
There are a very great many who are very certain that some one will
be doing something and these then have it in them to be easily quickly
very completely forgetting all the times they are mistaken. But then
it certainly is certain that some have more feeling for what others are
going to be doing from minute to minute in their living than others have
it in them. Some have an exaggerated notion of the way they do not have
it in them. But some and I mention it for I am one of such of them have
practiced very often in thinking to be planning the action of some one
they are knowing very well in living and always then though often they
know the general direction mostly always they think something is going
to be happening much sooner than it does really happen or much later
than it does really happen or much more strongly than that one is going
to do that thing or much more weakly than that one is going to be doing
that thing and very often then too such a one is wrong about the kind
of action that some one they are knowing very well is going to be doing.
I am very busy mentioning this thing because I have always been very
interested in seeing how very wrong I can be when I am telling about
any one how they are going to be living from day to day in their living.
And yet more and more in my living I come to be more understanding
of the complete meaning of the being in each one I am knowing, I get
to be more able more and more to know of them what will be the quality
of living of working in them what on the whole will be the quality of succeeding and failing in them and always then I want to be mistaken I
want to make mistakes so that I can see something in them which makes
of that one a more complete one, always then I want to be more certain
of all the variations that makes some one so very much like some one
really different from that one. Always then more and more I want to
be feeling completely feeling the complete being, all the being in each
one I am ever knowing and feeling in them the kind and quality and quantity of work and living and loving in them. I can never have really much
feeling of what specifically they will be doing from moment to moment
in their living I have not any dramatic imagination for action in them,
I only can know about action in them from knowing action they have
been doing any of them, I mention this so that every one can be certain
I do not know this about any one any men or women, I tell about the
living in them from the living they have had in them I cannot ever construct action for them to be doing, I have certainly constructive imagination for being in them, sometimes with very little watching I have pretty
complete realisation of pretty nearly all the being in them. I just felt like
mentioning this thing and so I have just mentioned it here so that every
one can be certain that I have not any dramatic constructive imagination. I am always more and more and that is certain realising under-

standing constructing with complete imagination the complete being each one of men and women. The actual things each one are doing I only know from knowing the actual detail in the actual living of each actual one I am ever knowing. I certainly more and more am always more and more realising the being in each one I am seeing. I am always more and more realising kinds in men and women, the being in each one of each kind of them. I have mentioned this because I have been feeling for some time like mentioning this thing, sometime I will make more of this and will illustrate it then. This will come to be done very much later in my living. Of that I am almost certain.

Now there will be some description of the being in Alfred Hersland and then after that has been a little written there will be written more history of his Gossols living and more description of those with whom he was then in his daily living. There will then be written a description of him in his Bridgepoint living and of his later marrying Julia Dehning and of every one whom he knew just then and then there will be more history written and there will be more and on and on then until somewhere nearly to the end of him. And then sometime later there will be written the ending of him and of his generation in the Hersland living.

This then is now to be a little description of the being that was him, as I was saying being is interesting to me and I have some understanding of being in men and women. As I was saying the being in Alfred Hersland is more or less like a piece of a whole one but always he had his own being in him, in a way he was himself inside him and this is now a little description of my feeling about being in him, about being in a good many men and women. Almost every one sometime is a piece of one not a whole one, almost every one sometime is a whole one. This is true of many men and women to me of mostly every one. I will now try to understand my meaning in this feeling.

To be using a new word in my writing is to me a very difficult thing. Every word I am ever using in writing has for me very existing being. Using a word I have not yet been using in my writing is to me very difficult and a peculiar feeling. Sometimes I am using a new one, sometimes I feel new meanings in an old one, sometimes I like one I am very fond of that one one that has many meanings many ways of being used to make different meanings to every one. Sometimes I like it, almost always I like it when I am feeling many ways of using one word in writing. Sometimes I like it that different ways of emphasising can make very different meanings in a phrase or sentence I have made and am rereading. Always in writing it, it is in me only one thing, a little I like it sometimes that there can be very different ways of reading the thing I have been writing with only one feeling of a meaning. This is a pleasant thing, sometimes I am very well pleased with this thing, very often then I am liking a word that can have many ways of feeling in it, it is really a very difficult thing to me to be using a word I have not yet been using in writing. I may know very well the meaning of a word and yet it has not for me completely weight and form and really existing being. There are only a few words and with these mostly always I am writing that have for me completely entirely existing being, in talking I use many more of them of words I am not living but talking is another thing, in talking one can be saying mostly anything, often then I am using many words I never could be using in writing. In writing a word must be for me really an existing thing, it has a place for me as living, this is the way I feel about me writing. I have been mentioning this thing for I am just now feeling a learning in me for some words I have just been beginning using in my writing. Now I am going on with a description of being, ot being in pieces and as whole ones to my feeling, of being in Alfred Hersland as I was saying.

I will not go on about pieces and whole ones in everybody's being. Each one mostly sometimes is a whole one to me. Very often later then they are pieces to me some that have been sometimes completely whole ones to me. That happens then to me quite often, that happens to me again and again. Sometimes some one I have been feeling as a completely whole one from the loving being in that one comes then to me all of a sudden to be loving loving more than loving some one something and that one then is a piece of one to me, not any longer the whole one I was feeling. Then I begin again very often and make of this one a new whole one beginning again with this piece and remembering everything I ever knew of this one. One then has been to me a whole one having complete loving being, such a one then comes to have to me loving loving more than loving anything and that realisation of that one makes that one to me then not a whole one. This may come to me of some one, of any one, of all who are whole ones to me. I may have in me then some realisation of them and that realisation makes them not a whole one. Every one is not a whole one, now I am waiting a little for an inspiration about this thing to explain completely my feeling. I will now soon be telling my feeling about men and women, about whole being in them, about them as a piece of living each one about them always all each one having their own being in them, always then each one of them each one who ever was or is or will be living. Then there will be a complete description of being in Alfred Hersland for my realisation.

Alfred Hersland was of a kind in men and women as I was saying. He was the eldest son but not the eldest child as I was saying, and that had some effect on him as I was saying. I am writing everything as I am learning anything. I am writing everything as I am learning anything, as I am feeling anything in any one as being, as I am having a realisation of any one, I am saying everything then as I am full up then with a thing, with anything of any one. I am certain that some are sometime whole ones to me, that some are sometimes a piece of their kind of them in me, always I am certain each one is existing, they are themselves inside them, sometime mostly every one is a whole one to my feeling, very often before then very often after then that one is not a whole one in my feeling, that one is a piece of the kind of being that is the being they are of in being. This comes then very often to be in my feeling and just now I am quite a little far from certain that each one is a whole one and always I am certain somehow always each one is existing inside them and that in a way sometimes gives to me a very unsatisfactory way of feeling being for not any one then is completely a whole one to my feeling mostly not any one and yet they are not each one parts of a being to my feeling each one then is existing inside in them and I am then not very well satisfied with my feeling all being. I am having that kind of feeling a good deal when several of them that have been completely whole ones to my feeling are not any longer such completely whole ones, as I was saying this can happen in them from realising that they are not original but anticipatorily suggestible some one that was to me as one completely self-suggested in living, or it can come from some one having been a completely loving being and then this one is not really loving the one they were completely loving and loving is not the complete being in them. Some come to be pieces of themselves as a whole one from there being anger in them, failure, stupid being that makes a dead piece in them, uncertain being, weakness in them sometimes makes of them a piece sometimes of their whole one and some and a little in a way Alfred Hersland was such a one never come to be a whole one to me, he always has been a piece of himself as a whole being and now I begin again.

I have not been very interesting in explaining being in men and women in my feeling as I am just now having it a good deal in me. That is quite certain, sometime later I will do it again. Now I will begin with the being in Alfred Hersland. I am not yet quite full up with the being in him. Again I am beginning waiting. Again I am beginning a little to feel him. I am still hoping to be more certain in my feeling. I am waiting and waiting, I have not in me now any impatient feeling. Pieces in being, whole ones in being, words saying what I am wanting, words having existence in them to my feeling, Alfred Hersland and the being in him and the kind he was of men and women all these things will come soon to be more completely in me, that is certain.

Alfred Hersland was of a kind of men and women. This is now some description of that kind of them.

Some one seems to be talking in such a very different kind of way to mostly every one than I am ever hearing from that one and sometimes then I do not think of any one really telling me what that other one has been saying, at least it is a very difficult thing to realise that one can have such a free talking in him when always I have not heard it coming out of him. For many years I was slowly learning that very often some one is not talking in my hearing the way he is talking when some one else is listening. For very many it is a very difficult thing to be realising the effect they have on men and women. I have often been listening again and again to some one, have been very much with them and always then they have, that one a certain kind of way of talking that seems then to be the completely natural way of talking in them, I have seen such of them talking from suffering, from excited feeling, from happy feeling in them, from gayety and from being very serious inside them and then some one tells me about them about such a one that that one says such and such a thing in talking is always saying such and such a kind of thing always in talking and that is then to me astonishing, very astonishing, and then sometime I realise it of them slowly that such a one, that one, can be saying that thing, always having such a kind of talking coming out of them that it is a natural thing in them and slowly then always then I am always learning how each one is talking to every one and more and more then slowly then I am listening.

A little again now to me each one is a whole one sometime. A good deal to me now yet each one is a piece of living and always inside them is their own being. Always to me there are kinds in men and women that is certain and now then to begin again describing the kind of one Alfred Hersland is in living, all the kinds there are of that kind of them, all the kinds of ways there are in me of learning them of feeling them.

There is a kind of a kind of them and Alfred Hersland was one of this kind of a one, one of the kind of them that are one kind of the engulfing resisting kind of them that have it mostly all of them to have it that mostly every one knowing them feels it of them knows it in them that they are a piece of being and always they have it in them very many of them to be very alive inside them, to be to themselves a being very much living and aspiring, very much really existing. There is a kind of every kind there is of being that have it in them to be a piece of being very much to every one and those then those of that kind of them are active inside them in being, are active and aspiring, are very completely live ones in their existing and these then are a good deal to a good many knowing them completely a piece of being and as I am saying there are some kinds of every general kind there is in men and women of all the kinds of them there are some kinds of each kind of them that have this in them the being to mostly every one knowing them as pieces of a being and as I am saying some of these kinds of them are very active and aspiring in their being and their living and Alfred Hersland was one of such of them and now I am beginning inquiring into the being of such of them into the being of all of such of them who have it in them to be to very many knowing them pieces of being and having active and completely aspiring being in them completely and continuously aspiring being in them. Alfred

Hersland then was such a one. As I was saying he was of the engulfing resisting being, as I was saying he had active and aspiring being in him, as I was saying he was mostly to every one ever knowing him a piece of being and this is now to be a history of the living in him, a description of the being in him, an inquiring into the connection in being between him and all those other ones that like him are pieces of being to mostly every one knowing them. There are a very great many men and women that are such of them. Alfred Hersland was of these then was such a one this is now then again the continuing of realising the kind of them that have it in them to be a piece of being to mostly every one knowing them. Alfred Hersland as I am saying all his living was such a one, was one of this kind of them.

Some one has milk brought to the house by the milkman and it is wasted and yet always that one is continuing having that amount of milk brought in because that one is thinking that sometime that one will be a sick one and then if the milkman has not the habit of bringing milk every day to that one then when that one is a sick one that one will not have milk brought every day by a milkman. It will be too late then to be beginning then when that one is so sick that one cannot go out to order anything. One having in that one a feeling that nothing should be wasted by any one living can have such a way of doing with a milkman bringing milk for that one. Such a one can have it that that one never throws away anything, never wastes anything in living and always there is more milk there than that one can be using in the daily living, in a kind of a way this is very common, not about milk left, but about a way of feeling in living and a way of acting. This is in a way common. Mostly then I have just now a feeling mostly such a one is part of a being. Mostly just now I have a good deal of such feeling that every one is not a whole one that each one is not ever a complete one. One quite young one was loving another one and that one was saying to the one that one was loving, I only love them like you with dark hair and brown eyes for I am a blond one and I could only be loving a dark one. Then this one saw a picture of another one, I could love that one said this one. But that one is a blond one, the one this one was thinking of loving told this one and you just said you could only love a dark one, yes that is true but I think I could love that one, and this is very common, and always there are very many having it always in them that they are a piece of being and always each one is a whole one in the sense that each one is being really in them is existing and sometimes then very often there is to me not any kind of a whole one really in any one and anything and now I am not really caring any more anyway about this thing, about being being a whole one in any one in any way.

Always there are very many of every kind there is in men and women who are to mostly every one knowing them pieces of living, they are themselves too inside them. Perhaps Alfred Hersland was one of these, I am now beginning a description of the kind of being the kind he is of men and women have in them.

These then all of them have it in them that they are resisting and some of them are engulfing in resisting and some of them are slowly resisting and many of them are superficially attacking and all of them have it in them to some way own those they need for loving.

Mostly then these the resisting kind in men and women have it in them to feel very strongly the completely existing of everything, they have it in them to be certain that everything in a way is made out of real earth the way it was done to make Adam that is to say the resisting kind of them in their feeling have it to be certain that a thing is existing more than that a thing has a use and can give to them an emotion. These have it in them then mostly that emotion is not as poignant in them as sensation, that is then their way of being although as I have been saying some of such of them can be engulfing, some vacant in them, some certain that to be them is to be attacking to be quick and poignant in emotion and to be that to mostly every one seeing them doing their living. In a way though always it is true of all of them all of those having in them this being I am now describing, that they have a slow sure feeling that everything is made out of earth and has that kind of very certain existing. Sometime I am hoping to make it completely clear inside me and in my expressing the two kinds there are in men and women and all the kinds there are of these two kinds of them. To begin again with the kind Alfred Hersland was in living, the kind he was and some of the kinds more or less connected in kind with his kind of them. I am going on now with a history of him, a complete history of him.

Some always are lying when any one is asking anything and then they come to be saying I don't know that thing and then they come to telling the true story about that thing. That is the way they do about everything about anything and this is quite common.

It is very hard to know it of any one whether they are lying that is to say it is very hard to know it in any one whether they are knowing the relation between what they are saying and what had happened what is happening to them. It is a very difficult thing to know it of any one whether they, to themselves, are saying what is not what they are thinking. Lying, stupid being in men and women, religion, aspiration, sensitiveness to any one to anything in men and women, appreciation and enthusiasm, emotion and being afraid in them of something of anything of everything of any one, of almost every one, all these then are very interesting in men and women and very often, very very often it is a necessary thing to know all the being every bit of the being in any one to know it of them what they have in them of these things inside them of lying and aspiration and stupid being and virtuous feeling and important feeling and religion and fear and realisation of material existing. It is necessary then to know of some all the being in them to be certain of them whether they are lying, whether they are feeling, whether they are believing, whether they are understanding, whether they are afraid, whether they are good, whether they are bad, whether they are important inside in them to themselves inside them. It is a very difficult thing then to know the being really in mostly every one. Very often when some one is knowing the complete being of some one that one is still only a piece of a being, there is not in the being of that one a quality of completion, there is no reason why that one from the being in that one should keep on existing, should have kept on existing and when that one is a dead one it is an accidental kind of thing that that one should be an ended one, it is not a completed or a cut off thing the ended one, and that is a very common thing to be feeling about many men and many women. This is a kind of feeling almost every one knowing him had about Alfred Hersland as I have been saying again and again.

I will now give some description of a considerable number of men and women of kinds connected in kind with the kind of men and women of which Alfred Hersland was one. There will be now some description of each one of a considerable number of men and women each of a kind of men and women of one kind of the kinds of them that are connected in kind with the kind of them of which Alfred Hersland was one. In the description of these there will be an explanation with the description of each one of them of the way each one is a complete one sometimes to some one or not a complete one.

There will then now be a description of a considerable number of men and women, there will be then now some further expression of the feeling some one every one has about some one about every one. There will be now perhaps more understanding of the way each one is or is not sometime a complete one. There will now perhaps be some understanding of lying, aspiration, religion, feeling, being, thinking, in a considerable number of men and women, in a number of kinds of the resisting kind of being in men and women. To really again begin then. Later there will be a complete history of Alfred Hersland, later there will be a complete history of Julia Dehning.

To begin now then just now with little descriptions of a considerable number of men and women who all of them are some kind of the resisting kind in men and women. To begin this then.

Some as I have said already somewhere earlier in my writing, some of the resisting kind of them have it in them to have generalised feeling that is of ideal aspiration and concrete feeling that is in continual action and of very material seizing and holding. Some as I have been saying already in my description have it in them to be completely certain that to be dead is to be really truly a dead one and always then perhaps to be a dead one is not to be really truly a dead one and it is a good thing then to be married to one who is certain that to be dead is not to be really a truly dead one. This is true of some this is true of the first one that I am now describing. This one was not meek not aggressive not arrogant not egotistical in living, this one could have resisting in him, this one like very many having such a kind of being was fairly slow in action and in feeling, if he was not slow in feeling and in acting and in listening such a one would not be certain that he himself was doing that acting, listening, feeling, such a one would be thinking that something was happening, it would be over and that one would not be realising that he himself was listening, feeling, acting, and this is very common with many having in them dependent independent resisting being. This first one then that I am now beginning describing had resisting being as fairly sensitive being as slowly reacting being as not at all engulfing being, as a complete being only this one was not quite entirely certain that to be dead was to be a really dead one and he liked it that the wife that he had always with him was certain that to be dead was not to be at all a dead one. This one that I am describing, this first one had resisting being as completely sensitive, fairly slowly reacting, this one was not meek not aggressive in living, this one was persistently and patiently and in detail dominating in family living, this one was very just in thinking and in judging, this one had not very much imagination and was impersonal in feeling, this one had pleasant affection, this one had completely honest action, this one had a good deal of fear a good deal of affection in him, this one was quite a good man in living, this one was pretty certain that everything is existing, this one had loving and such things reasonably in him, this one could have it in him to have it that he found himself even a better one than he really was in living but really he was a very good one in living and though a little he had the abstract conception of himself as a more ideal one than he was in concrete feeling, mostly he was realising pretty completely all that he was really experiencing, only a little he was not realising that having a little fear in him that to be dead was not to be really a dead one did not make in him an experiencing that he was a better one than actual living in him made him. He was as I was saying glad to be having a wife who was completely certain that knowing that to be dead was not to be at all a really dead one made every one a very much better one than each one really was in living. This is then a complete history of the being in this one. This one then was a sensitive, slowly reacting, fairly affectionate, quite good, reasonably just and a little fearful and quite impersonal and somewhat loving quite very good resisting independent dependent one. This one was pretty completely a whole one to himself and to mostly every one, this one then is different from the one I am next going to be describing in being a completely slowly reacting completely sensitive one.

This one that I am now describing was of a kind of one that are very many of them quite successful in living. This is now a description of several of them. This is a kind of resisting dependent independent men and women.

These have it in them mostly to make every one feel it about them that they are very strong ones in living, they have solidity in them, they are like wood or iron and have a solid being in them and every one knowing them is certain that they are good ones and they are independent and intelligent and loyal and not timeserving and yet always they are succeeding in living succeeding in loving, a little arrogant but not unpleasant to mostly every one knowing them, very successfully knowing successful people in their living though not seeking to know such ones, it just comes to them. Some of such ones are not completely successful in living, some of such ones have a pride that is a little more sensitive than the being really in them, some have a romantic imagination that is too active for the being in them but mostly this kind of them are very successful in living and this is to be now a little more description of this kind of them.

Resisting being in them is as it were solid and firm and hard but never aggressive being in them. It is not profoundly sensitive in them, it is as it is with wood when in a tree it is living and then when it is completely useful as a piece of wood to be used for working into a shape for using and it is a solid thing then, an honest thing then, a thing to be adapted for good using, a solid reliable thing then, a completely existing thing then, a thing sensitive in the sense that it repays good handling but not a thing sensitive in the sense that a tree living having living growing being is a sensitive thing. These then this kind of resisting men and women who I am now describing have this in them and they have it in them some of them so completely this being in them that they are to many knowing them completely strong men, completely geniuses in living without any of the weaknesses in them that geniuses most generally have in them, that men successful in living most generally have in them. These men are very interesting, I know now five of such of them and only one of these five of them is not really a successful one and that one has a pride in him and a romantic imagination in him that is too sensitive for the solid dead wood being in him. This kind of them of men are very interesting to me in the being in them, they are very pleasant companions mostly always all of them loyal, reliable, delicate in their feeling, honest, earnest, never toadying, decently prudent and decently courageous in living, always giving to every one a conviction that they are a very strong one and they are mostly always succeeding very well in anything that is a life work to them and though they are laborious in their working they are really pretty quick and graceful in their working generally although strength is the quality in them that seems strongest in them but really strength in them is the solidity of block wood, bar iron in them really then these in their living can be completely adapted to their living, these then can be completely succeeding in living, these then can have sentimental feeling, and pride in them and romantic imagination but really this cannot at the bottom of them disturb them they are completely solid they can be completely adapted to living. I will come back again and again to describe this kind in men and women. I will come back again and again to every kind there is of men and women. These then that I have been describing have a lack in them, they are complete enough in living, they are each one completely different from every other one, they are themselves inside them but in a true sense they have not in them individual being, they are the very cream of schoolmen the very best thing there can be of any one following a master and working with him. They are individual to him, they are themselves completely inside them to themselves in them. These then are very good men mostly, loyal and earnest and efficient and successful in living. They are solidly learning and solidly resisting to be winning. Their working in its resulting is very often a quick and graceful and a little a dull thing. They are sensitive and strong and active to mostly every one having to do with them. They interest me very much, mostly unless I am a very sad one every one is to me very interesting. Sometime certainly I will tell more and then again some other time I will know more and then sometime I will tell more and so on and so on of this kind in men and women.

I am altogether a discouraged one. I am just now altogether a discouraged one. I am going on describing men and women.

I know one, he is of the resisting kind in men and women and he is completely an instrument being he is so completely that in a sense he has no volition though to very many knowing him he is almost a crazy one in living out ideas he has in him. I know this one, he has it in him to have vibratingly sensitive resisting being, that is all him and always when he wishes to do any working he must put himself quiescently ready so that something will play on him, some influence something and then it vibrates through him and he makes something does some work and not even really making himself a quiescent being is volition in him, it is simply a shutting off from himself by an almost senseless feeling of resisting any other thing, it is not choice in him of something and volition certainly is the act of choosing. This one as I am saying and I know very many who know him this one as I am saying is to very many an obstinate exaggerated self directing completely self-directing one and this one is completely an instrument nature, this one is like a violin a completely vibrating thing to anything that really can effect him. This one, I know this one very well in his living, this one in his loving is not loving as mostly men and women are doing who love the attacking kind of them if they are resisting kind in them, the resisting if they are of the attacking kind of them this one as I am saying in his loving is completely loving a resisting one, one like himself and this is very interesting. Mostly when one needs heightening of the being in them they get it from those very like them, for loving they need those different from them, for courage and emulation and influencing those like them and sometimes some love those like them and these are mostly then instrument natures or natures needing pretty complete influencing throughout their being but this is a very complicated question an excessively complicated question and sometime I am going to write a book and it will be a very long one and it will be all full up, completely filled up with pairs of them twos of them, sometimes threes and fours and fives but mostly with twos of them, twos of men, of women, of women and men, of men and women. Now to say just a little more of this one this instrument one that I am knowing pretty well now in the living in him. This one was not really succeeding very well in living, this one would not be succeeding very well when he was not any longer a young man, when he was an older one and had not any longer youthful beauty feeling and vibration in him and then too he would come to have fixed ideas in him, that would be a natural thing for him, and then perhaps later he would come to be a crazy one or just one that was failing in living. Some like him not so completely vibrating having some volition in them might be successful in living, some like him having a dulled vibration in them and fairly stupid feeling in them and much desire for good eating and drinking and sleeping can be successful enough in living. I know some of such of them, sometime oh sometime, really truly sometime there will be a description a complete description of every one.

Now I will be describing four men, I know them all pretty well, two of them the first and the last are fairly whole ones inside them to mostly every one, the two others are mostly pieces of living to mostly every one knowing them.

I know these four pretty well then, they are all in a way of the engulfing kind of the resisting kind in men and women, the four of them have that in common in every other way they are very different each one of them from the three others of them.

The first one has engulfing being so brightly, so gayly, so concentratedly in him that it is a very fresh and gay and juicy thing in him the being in him. He is quite successful in living this one, quite successful in loving and always all his living he has had very much loving in him. He has not much real independence of action this one, he needs some one to start him to do everything excepting dancing and loving, this comes to him from the mere existing of women in the world around him. In mostly everything else some one starts him and he is very gay then in keeping going. When he is a sad one he does not want to see any one, that happens sometimes to him, he cannot start himself then, no one is starting him then, he is a sad one then and not succeeding in living. Really he is a very lively one in living and on the whole not unsuccessful in living. He is completely sensitive and not at all a bad one not a bit a bad one but not really a very actively good one he has no initiative for taking any responsibility on himself for himself or for any one. Always though he is responsible for himself, living gives him that initiative and he goes on living, sometimes he is a little fussy and then he remembers his father was so before him, he would like to be a different person not be like his father in any way and there he is he finds himself being just like his father after all the different kind of living that he has been having. This one has a genuinely sensitive being, this one is not a selfish one, self-seeking, this one is not apparently engulfing and yet really this one is completely of the engulfing resisting kind of them, this one has this being in him that is certain. It is gay and sparkling in him it is well concentrated in him, it is an engulfing resisting being that is certain.

The second one, I know this one from the history of him from letters he has written, this one has engulfing murky being as hopeful and yet as a weak thing in him. He needs so much stimulating that after he was not any longer a very young one he could not get enough of it to keep going, he never engulfed anything really in his living not himself, not any one not any woman not any man, but he was always hopeful that sometime he would do this thing, hope was always there in him, when he was a very young one he was vigorous in aspiring, later he was not vigorous in anything but always hopeful and always of the engulfing resisting kind of them though never really engulfing or resisting anything. This was the being in him, he was not an unattractive one, sometime there will be more history of him written of his loving and of his not supporting himself by working and of his despairing and of his always hoping. This is enough of him just now, alright then.

This one the third of these four of them I know very well indeed now and it took me a very long time to know him but that is not what I am now telling. This one was of the engulfing murkily resisting kind of them but he mostly was too ambitious and had too much vanity in him and was too self-sacrificing for any one to know it of him. He was really truly such a one, that is certain. He had very much vanity and self-sacrificing and affection and ambition in him and only slowly it came out of him that he was a rather dry engulfing murky resisting being. There will be here very little description of him, he is a very important one to be well known because he has the being in him so confused in him that it teaches one a great deal to completely learn him. I like him and I know him I will now tell a little more about him.

Every one is sometime a little a lovely one to me. Some are sometimes quite very lovely ones to me, some are more some are less lovely to me. Sometime for a little almost every one is a lovely one to me.

Every one I have been describing I will be describing I am describing, every one I am I can ever be knowing is sometime a little, more, a very lovely one to me. This is a very nice feeling in me inside me when some one is really a lovely one to me. Mostly every one pretty nearly every one certainly every one is sometime a little a lovely one to me. Some one is very much a lovely one to me. Each one certainly is sometime sometimes a lovely one to me. All these I am describing have it in them to have been sometime to be sometimes a lovely one to me. Every one, each one is certainly sometime a little a lovely one to me. This one I am now describing was for sometime really a quite lovely one to me. This one as I was saying was of the dependent independent resisting murkily engulfing kind of them but as I have been saying this was rather gently and a little drily in him and mostly not any one knew it of him that he was of the engulfing murky kind of them. This one was a very gentle one, a very affectionate one, a really very self-devoted one, a really very ambitious one, a really very vain one, a really very appealing one and always also a fairly aspiring one, and always there was murky engulfing in this one but it was a little dry a little very pretty in this one. This one was to very many quite a lovely one. This one's living and being is quite interesting, sometime there will be written a very complete history of this one. This one mostly to every one who really came to know this one very well was a piece of being not a very completely whole one. Sometime there will be a complete history of this one.

The fourth one of these four of them that all have it in them to have murky engulfing resisting being was very little to me a lovely one. He was very really a lovely one to his wife and she was older than he was and he really was not a bad one not a good one not a bad one, he was not a very lovely one to most of those he came to know in living. Every one is to me sometime a little a lovely one, that is pretty nearly certain.

This one was of the engulfing murky resisting kind of them but engulfing was in him the swallowing of very little things, he never had it in him to do any large swallowing, he never was really engulfing a woman he was engulfing, she needed to thrust herself inside him and so he a little was doing swallowing and often he had it in him to be wanting to do to be be doing engulfing but he never really knew it in him, he was of the murky resisting engulfing kind of them but he had it in him only really as nibbling. To himself he was a very noble one, to himself he was almost a heroic one, to himself he was completely a good man, completely entirely a good one with not any mean ways in him and this really was a very natural thing seeing that murky resisting engulfing being was a nibbling swallowing thing in him, this could not be himself to himself inside him, that is certain, and so to himself inside him he was a completely good one almost a heroic one. If any one if his sister-in-law said to him but you nibbled and swallowed that thing that was not a noble thing to be doing, he would be saying, I am a good one my wife knows that every one knows that and if I did that thing it was the right thing for me to be doing. He was not a bad man this one, he was to himself completely almost heroically a good one, to his wife who was never quite completely engulfed by him she wanting to be completely engulfed by him felt him to be completely entirely a very lovely one, to his wife he was completely entirely a good one as he was to himself completely inside him. This is enough now of this one, he was to mostly every one a complete enough one, this will be now some descriptions of some other men and women.

One having in him very thickly in him murky resisting engulfing being often threatened he would kill himself and he sometimes made a poem before he was ready to kill himself because he could not have in living what he needed to completely content him. This is now a very little description of this one. This one is quite an interesting one, this one is rather strong in his living in his being this one is fairly successful in living. This one as a very young one was not a very adroit one, was rather reckless and given to having things happen to him, had courage in him, was a pretty hard one to manage, was quite a funny one. He was when he was a young one a reckless one, quite in almost a foolish way a daring one and in a way very many liked him very well then and not any one then could in any kind of a way manage him. When he was a little older then he was quite affectionate with his brother and his father, his mother was less interesting to him, his brother was very fond of him, his brother was older, his father liked to hear him say funny things then, and then when he was a little older again this one not yet any more than quite a young man he was quite a stingy one, a very prudent one, a very openly suspicious one, quite popular with men, not very interesting to women, quite devoted to his brother, quite cold in his relations to any one having any need of him, completely without enthusiasm, quite openly suspicious as I was saying, very prudent in his business living and quite a good business man, and as I was saying completely certain that he should take care of himself completely that not any one would do this thing for him. This was the being in him and as I am saying it was interesting. When he was quite a young man he decided on marrying and then when his mother tried to interfere with him he told the people that his mother was a bad one and he told her that he had written a poem and now he would kill himself and she believed him. This one as I am saying was openly a suspicious one, openly a man thinking only of his own well being, he was quite a funny one, he was very popular with men, he was not very interesting to women but they mostly did not at all dislike him, he had been when he was a young one quite reckless and quite daring, he always had all his living very affectionate ways in him, he always was certain that he would be master in any house

which was his own house completely master of it and always he was a
pleasant and quite a funny fellow and he could be openly flattering and
openly suspicious and he was both all of his living and always he was
very funny to every one, very amusing, as I was saying he was always
pretty popular with men and not at all unpopular with women. He
had his passionate resisting engulfing being in him quite alive and completely in between aggression and resisting, he was not attacking with
it, he was not resisting with it, it never was doing one thing or the other
thing neither aggressive in it or resisting in it, he had all the qualities of
it of his kind of being, they were all complete alive and living in him, they
were so to speak not in motion, this as I am understanding is the being
in him, he had almost not any really stupid being in him, he was completely his own being and this was completely alive, completely not moving
in him. This is the way I am now understanding this one, it is very
certain that I must sometime completely be understanding this one for
I am constantly now feeling thinking about knowing certain ones in a
way connected with this one and it is important to me that I sometime
understand them, it is important to me very important indeed to me that
I sometime understand every one, I am always keeping on wanting to do
this thing mostly all the time, certainly pretty nearly all the time, yes
always somewhere in me that is certain, always somewhere in me, mostly all through me I am hoping that sometime I will be understanding
every one every kind there are of men and women knowing, feeling, completely realising them, each one, every one, and sometime I certainly
am hoping to be completely understanding several I am knowing that
are a kind of them connected in kind with the kind of which I have just
been a little describing one. I am then certainly going on with my hoping. I will now go on with my description of a considerable number of
men and women, some men, some women, all of the resisting kind in men
and women.

This one of whom I am now going to be giving a very little description is not completely of the engulfing kind of the resisting kind of them,
he is a murky passionate resisting one but not a really engulfing one, he
is as near to being an engulfing one as one can be without being one. He
is as near an engulfing kind as one can be who is not it at all but is completely disturbed in loving so that it is really in him that in a way he is not
an engulfing kind of a one. This one then in a way is connected with
Mr. Hissen the grandfather of the Hersland children in his kind of being,
this one has in him religion, very completely in him but he is not a complete one, he is not complete inside him completely all that there is of
religion in him, he is lost in loving, lost in religion, not completely a lost
one but sometimes quite completely a lost one, has to be afraid inside
him to be rescued by some one from the quite completely lost condition
of him. This one is not then a very complete one inside him, that is

natural from the being in him. This one like some others like him loses himself from inside him by loving feeling by religion in him, this one then does not do this completely in him, he is a little all himself inside him and so then this one all his living is a very incomplete one, always then he is not succeeding very well in living, mostly then some one masters him enough so that he does not completely fail in living completely lose himself out from him and he too a little helps with this being with the being in him that is in him that makes him a little the complete thing in religion in himself inside him. This one then in a way in loving, in religion, loses the feeling after the emotion, must then begin again and this is a natural thing from the nature of him, he is not at all engulfing, he is as near to it as any one can be who completely entirely is not it. I am finding this description very interesting. I am understanding more and more now the being in him. This is all that I will now be writing of him. He was quite an elegant one quite a graceful one in his expression, in his daily living, when he was a young one he was quite completely an idealist then, always he had religion and loving in him. This is all I am now going to be saying about him.

I have known several of a kind of them of the resisting engulfing kind of them men and women of this kind, I have known completely some of them this kind of them, I have known absolutely entirely completely one of such of them, I have known pretty entirely completely another of this kind of them, I have known men I have known women of this kind of them of one kind of the engulfing resisting kind in men and women, and these have it that vanity is complete in them, pride is not in them, vanity is complete in them, seizing anything they are thinking they are needing in living is complete in them, elegance is very completely in them, desiring completely successful feeling is completely in them in such of them, feeling what they are needing to give to themselves or any one distinction is very completely in them, feeling about anything itself is not very much in then, realising the complete meaning, feeling the complete elegance of distinction feeling it completely in them, seizing everything anything they are needing for such complete realising of distinction in themselves and in every one is completely in them, vanity as I am saying is completely in them, simplicity in realising that they are completely elegant and completely needing distinction is very important in realising any one of such a kind of them. It is a very important thing to know it of these then that they have complete vanity in them, that they have complete feeling for the thing for anything any one is needing to really give to them real distinction. These then are as I was saying one kind of the engulfing resisting kind of them, they are completely then engulfing resisting some of such of them and the thing they are completely engulfingly resistingly winning is anything everything that can give to them distinction. They have vanity completely in them so completely in them that they have in them perfectly simplicity in seizing anything they are needing. They have vanity and elegance so completely in them that they have not any pride in them they do not need to have pride in them to protect them to themselves inside them from anything. They have vanity completely in them, some of them have some engulfing passion in them some have very little engulfing passion in them, such of them have not any affection really in them, such of them mostly are not thinking about feeling in them anything of itself in them, they have elegance of being, they have complete vanity inside them, they have completely in them the realisation of every one who is a distinguished one, of themselves as having distinction in them. Some of such of them are judging every one by the intelligence in them, all of such of them, are always judging every one, they must always be judging every one such a one, all the being in them is the learning by them the distinction they must by the being in them be seizing. They have not in them such of them the feeling for a thing itself, they have not loving for anything itself, they have in them the needing of seizing distinction, they have in them a complete need of judging for they must always be judging every one as to whether that one has distinction in her or in him, by judging they can decide then about this thing about every one, they cannot have the feeling for the thing that any one by loving that thing has come to have distinction in her or in him, they have in them only the need in them of judging whether some one has come to have distinction and always such a one has complete vanity in being, they have not any need of any pride inside them to protect themselves inside them and so then, such a one, as I am saying such a one is complete seizing judging every one for distinction. They have then such ones the instinct for realising distinction, for judging people and things that merit distinction, they have not these then most completely not the emotion of the things that gives to people distinction. Consequently for them, learning is to teach themselves or have some one teach them to recognise and realise the things that those people realise who have achieved distinction and that can only be done by such of them by their learning to realise detail in thinking and feeling, so that these judging some one as a distinguished one can enter into that one's distinction by realising what that one judged to be distinguished by them is thinking and feeling. These have then to learn carefully what it is they have seized and are seizing, these can then go on successfully living, always these are judging, mostly these are completely seizing what they are needing. I am hoping always hoping to be making a complete history of all men and women completely, completely and more completely of them, these then that I have been just describing are connected quite closely connected all of them with the kind that Alfred Hersland is of men and women. These I have been describing are very clearly in me, pretty nearly completely clearly in me and I am pretty nearly completely understanding them and some of them certainly are of such a kind of them I will be describing again and again.

I still am going to be describing a considerable number of kinds of men and women and some now are not very engulfing of the resisting kind in men and women. Of some of these that I am now going to be describing I am going to be describing inquisitiveness in them. Inquisitiveness in men and women is very interesting. Some have very much of this in them, some of these I am going to be describing have it almost as complete being in them the amount of inquisitiveness in them, and the meaning of inquisitiveness in them. I am now going to be describing a considerable number of men and inquisitiveness and loving and affection in them and slowness and succeeding and failing in their living is very important in them in the understanding ot them. There will be then now a very considerable number more of men and women with resisting being in them that I will be liking to be describing. To begin again now with diminishing this considerable number. I am beginning now again.

Curiosity and suspicion these two things are often very interesting, this one that I am now beginning describing had these very completely in him, and always then this one had these more simply in him than any one knowing him was realising, he had inquisitiveness in him for the mere satisfaction of asking and knowing, he had suspicion in him because suspicious feeling was a pleasant feeling in him, he used inquisitiveness and suspicion in living, that is certain, no one knowing him could deny that of him, but often he was not using such things, he was just inquiring, he was just asking because his attention was caught and he liked to know everything and he liked asking and often suspicion was in him because suspicion was an easy way to be feeling for him about everything and a very pleasant feeling to have inside him. This one was of the resisting slightly engulfing kind in men and women, resisting and engulfing was equally in him. In many I have been describing engulfing is stronger than resisting, in this one resisting and engulfing was pretty nearly equally divided in him, he was thick but not too thick not too dry in his being, he could take complete impression from everything he was learning, he was always asking, he was continually suspecting, he was quite successful in living. This is now to be a little a description of the questions he was always asking, of the suspicion always in him.

Some men and women are inquisitive about everything, they are always asking, if they see any one with anything they ask what is that thing, what is it you are carrying, what are you going to be doing with that thing, why have you that thing, where did you get that thing, how long will you have that thing, there are very many men and women who want to know about anything about everything, I am such a one, I certainly am such a one. A very great many like to know a good many things, a great many are always asking questions of every one, a great many are to very many doing this with intention, a great many have intention in their asking, a great many just have their attention caught by anything and then they ask the question. Some when they are hearing any one talking are immediately listening, many would like to know what is in letters others are writing and receiving, a great many quite honest ones are always wanting to know everything, a great many men and women have a good deal suspicion in them about others and this has in them not any very precise meaning. A great many are liking to know things but do not do much asking, a great many have not any such a feeling. A great many have a very great deal of suspiciousness in them, a great many have almost not any of this being in them. This one that I am now describing was one who was always asking and mostly always every one was wondering what was this one meaning by the questions he was asking and often later this one would perhaps be using information he had had from asking questions but asking questions in him was not a thing in him that came from wanting to be using some time information he was gathering, very often asking questions in him was simply from a catching of his attention by something. Once this one asked some one he was visiting, just suddenly,—and this door here does that lead into the hall or directly out into the garden,—and that was all he said then about this thing and afterwards every one was thinking he would be using this against them but really then this one was wondering did the door lead to the hall or directly to a garden. If such a one, one having this kind of a way is of the resisting engulfing type and fairly successful in living and slow and sudden and quite suspicious of every one, almost certainly then every one will think it to be true of such a one that this one always is asking questions for purposes of winning, perhaps of cheating, certainly ror some distant manoeuvering. This is very common. There are very many having in them rather engulfing rather resisting being who are slow and sudden, who are a little absent when any one is asking them anything, who are suspicious and quite trusting, who are often asking questions for in their being being in slow action and always more or less moving they have it that their attention is always a little wandering waiting for something inside them to do something and so then these of them are very busy having their attention caught by anything and asking questions about everything and very often every one knowing such of them are very suspicious of them and mostly these then too have constant suspicion in them as constant as the questioning in them. This is very common then with this kind of being. I am not yet through wih my description of this kind of resisting engulfing men and women.

A great many men and women have very much suspicion in them

of everything of every one. A great many men a great many women have steadily suspicion in them of everything of every one. A great many have this in them from the beginning of living in them. A great many very many of the resisting, dependent independent very earthy men and women have complete suspicion, little steady suspicion of everything of every one always in them. They do not have it from experiencing in them they have it in them as a natural thing, they have it in them like a child walking and certain that every step they are going to be tumbling. This is very common, very many men very many women very many having resisting being in them have it in them to be suspicious always of every one of everything. This is in them very often when they are quite kindly quite trusting, very many then having resisting being have it to have very naturally in them always in them always steadily in them from their beginning that they are suspicious of every one of everything, always suspicious always steadily suspicious inside them, this one then that I am describing has suspicion always in him, there will be now a description of several of this kind in men and women. I am now going on with my description of one, who was naturally a completely suspicious one.

Many having resisting being have it in them all their living when they are beginning and then on to their ending have it to have suspicion always naturally in them and this is a natural thing for them to have in them because they having resisting being have it in them to be knowing that always some one is doing attacking. Resisting being in them is in meaning that always some one some where is attacking, resisting being is in them in some of them, in very many men in very many women as having in them completely naturally always very much suspicion. Very many men and women have in them completely all their living very complete suspicious feeling very many men and women with resisting being. Very many men and women with attacking being have suspicion in them completely in them, sometime I will be telling very much of them. Very many men and women have hardly any kind of suspicious feeling ever in them. There are very many ways of having suspicious feeling many kinds of ways many degrees of such feeling, now I am giving a not very long description of one having in him very complete suspicious feeling, very much suspicious feeling about men, very much very complete suspicious feeling about women and this one was quite a successful one in living and this one had very much inquisitive feeling in him and this one was pretty completely resisting in his being pretty completely engulfing in his being and always very many felt it about him that every bit of asking in him and every bit of suspicion in him was really deep wisdom in him and always then he had completely resisting being in him completely engulfing being in him, complete suspicion in him, complete inquisitiveness inside him, and always then he had enthusiasm and very much

feeling about something and always he was asking about everything
and always he was having suspicious feeling in him and altogether he was
sufficiently a wise one, and very often he was just asking because he saw
something and very often he was just suspecting because he had resisting being in him. This is one then that is to me a completely interesting one. Every one is to me a completely interesting one, this one is to
me very completely an interesting one. I like feeling the being in this
one, sometime yes certainly sometime I will be telling all the feeling I
have in the complete being in this one. As I am saying suspicious feeling is very interesting, very very interesting. Sometime later I will
tell very much about one kind of them of the resisting kind of them that
have it in them to have suspicious feeling as a completely interesting
thing in them. I hope I will not be beginning now to tell about this kind
of them. Perhaps I will tell a little about such of them in among this
considerable number of men and women of the resisting kind of them I
am just now describing. I really do not want to begin now about them.
I will not begin now about them that is certain. I will completely understand them later and will be telling then about them. I certainly will
not write anything now about them. That is now certain. I have been
writing now about a considerable number of the considerable number
I am now describing of the resisting kind of them. I will now begin a
pretty short description of another one of them. That is to be a little
description of one having rich resisting being and being a little too quick
perhaps quite a little too quick in ripening. This one had in him quite
some inquisitiveness in him, not any suspicion in him. This is to be now
quite a short description of him.

This one then as I am saying was of the resisting kind of them, that
is to say resisting was the way of winning in him, that is to say this one
was in a way slow in reacting, that is to say this one in a way was needing
to own those this one needed for loving, this was all true and this was
all not true of this one and this one was completely of resisting being,
this one was all made completely all of only resisting being. This one
then really was very early a completely highly developed one, this one
was very flowing in the completely creating power this one had inside
him, this one was a quite inquisitive one, this one had hardly any suspiciousness in natural ordinary daily living in him, this one was really
not owning the one this one needed for his loving. This one as I was
saying was of the resisting kind of them, not of the engulfing kind of them,
of completely sensitively resisting being and the resisting being and sensitive being was pretty nearly equal in this one, it was pretty nearly as
sensitive as resisting but not quite completely so in this one it was a little
more sensitive than resisting and so this one was quick in developing,
early in flowering and this one was always trying to be a slower one and
this one really never was in living a really slow one. This one was as I

was saying not a suspicious one, resisting being was not strongly enough in him as protecting to give to him a suspicious feeling toward everything and every one. This one was not really owning the one this one needed for his loving. This one could only own one this one needed for loving by getting rid of the one this one needed for loving and then this one would not be having the one this one needed for loving and then where was this one, he was where he needed the one he needed for loving and taking her back again made him then lose the power of owning this one, the only way he could own this one was by getting rid of this one or by secretly letting some other one love him, in this way then this one to himself inside him could own the one he needed for loving. He really could own the one he needed for loving by sending her away from him, he then did not have near him the one he needed for loving, to himself inside him then he could own that one by letting, by making some other one love him and mostly then he dreamed of this thing, he did this thing. This is now a clear complete description of one having resisting being.

This is now to be a description of another one having resisting being, not engulfing resisting being, just resisting being, this one was a very nice one, a very pleasant gentle, sensitive, fairly resisting, sometimes angrily resisting one, this one had some suspicion in her in living, this one could have very often an injured feeling, this one had quite a good deal of inquisitive feeling in her, this one needed to own to a considerable degree those this one needed for loving, this one had children and children were to this one a piece of her cut off from her that were as it were equal to her and she was as they were, the same in living, thinking, feeling and being. This one as I was saying was a gentle, often injured, fairly angrily resisting one, quite inquisitive, with enough suspicious feeling to be defending other ones when it was not at all her business to be interfering and so this one a very nice a completely in a way honest one could do something that was not a pretty thing for this one to be doing. This is what this one did once in her living.

This one that I have been describing had not real suspicious feeling, this one was of the resisting kind of them but this one had very much more sensitiveness than resisting being and resisting being was in this one not a kind of thing to make of this one really a suspicious one. This being in this one resisting being in this one was in this one a sense of really being gently minute by minute in living and so this one when this one was adding up anything would always be adding it by one and one and one. This one had it to be very careful in living and always this one would be counting everything by one and one and one. Counting everything this one was spending by one and one and one and one and one and one was in this one resisting being was in this one recognition of real existing of everything. This one could have very much injured feeling, this one could have injured feeling very often could have it for herself for other ones for any one and this one sometimes was very mixed up in doing anything by injured feeling for one and not for another one and for that other one then and for this one herself this one inside this one then and this one then was sufficiently complicated by injured feeling inside this one and injured feeling was the only complicated thing in the being and in the living of this one. This one was as I was saying a very gentle a very sensitive one, this one was a resisting one, this one was not at all an engulfing one, this one from the mixing of a little softly resisting being and very much gentle and sensitive being had in this one suspicion only as injured feeling. Some having this kind of being and having sensitiveness not delicately and sensitively in them and resisting slightly engulfing in them are completely suspicious and completely injured always in their living and these very often have it in them to having being persecuted as a mania in them. There are very many having such being in them, later I will be telling a few little things that sometimes are happening in living in the living of this kind of men this kind of women. As I was saying this one I am now just a little describing was not at all not even a little bit an engulfing one, this one was a softly resisting one a really earthy one really feeling always in living that existing anything existing is really there in being and always this one was doing all the counting this one ever was doing by counting one and then one and then one and then one. This one as I was saying had not really suspicious being, this one as I was saying had much and quite often very warmly really injured feeling, for herself in herself, for some other one, for any other one and this injured feeling was in the being of this one the only complication. Once some one, a young cousin, this one I am describing was then coming to the beginning of the middle living in this one, once a young cousin told this one, the cousin was very fond of this one, that the cousin never wanted to be eating dinner at the house of another one another cousin of this one, that he liked very much indeed being with his cousin but he did not like it at all for a place to be dining, this was then all that was said just then. Later then the first cousin the one that said this to the one I have been describing, asked this cousin who had just come to be engaged to be married then to come and take dinner with him. This one then the cousin asked to dine by the other cousin of the one I am describing happened to mention to the one I am describing that he was going to be dining next week with this cousin. This one I am now describing had then completely inside this one an injured feeling for this one that was going to be dining with the other one that this one should be going to be dining with the other one when the other one would not dine with that one because it was not a pleasant thing and so this one I am describing told the one going to be dining with the other one what that one had said about dining with him. Then of course this one would not dine with the other one. And all this came from there being in this

one I am describing a soft resisting, a gentle sensitive being with not any
suspiciousness in being and not any engulfing and not any egotism so
that this one had to have in this one that everything that could be aggression or suspicion or worldliness in living or individual feeling was in this
one injured feeling, a very little angry and a very much hurt feeling and
so this one had injured feeling quite often and very much for this one,
for some other one, for any other one.

I will describe now very little a very different kind of one from that
one I have been just describing.   There will not be then very many more
of them of the considerable number left then.   There will perhaps then
still be left about six of them, six kinds of them and perhaps there will
be added a few more to make another generalisation but really there have
been already done a considerable part of the considerable number of the
resisting kind of them that I am now describing.

This one then is quite a different kind of a one from the last one I
was describing.   This one as a whole one is like a cannon-ball lying on
a bag of cotton, the cannon-ball lying on a cotton bag as a complete thing
was the whole of this one.   This is in a way a description of this one,
there will be now a very little more description of this one.

Children are always thinking are very often thinking that their
mothers are very lovely looking and that is very often because mostly the
child is always close up to the mother close to her when the child is looking and mostly being close like that as a habitual thing is to find that one
a lovely thing a lovely looking one.

This one that I was saying was a whole one which was like a cannon-
ball resting on a bag of cotton was the cotton part finding the cannon-
ball lovely looking being always so close to that thing and the cannon-
ball was finding the cotton lovely looking that being so closely always
to that thing.   To explain then.   This one then was one having solid
enough dull not very lively, not lively at all fairly dry resisting bottom,
a bottom that might have been engulfing if it had been a lively dark wet
thing, but this was not true of it then at all that it was engulfing, it was
entirely not engulfing.   As I was saying many having engulfing being
and not having resisting being enough in them are very aspiring and this
one then had aspiration like what might have been engulfing in the bottom being the bottom being which was not at all engulfing.   Some of
this kind of them have it as a bottom being something that is more nearly
engulfing and these then have more active aspiration as ambition, these
have then more nearly some power of very nearly engulfing something
but this one was as little engulfing as such a kind of them can be in living,
just as amiable and ideal in aspiration and aspiration in this one as I was
saying was like the cannon-ball resting on the bag of cotton, it was completely beautiful always to all that cotton and this one was always living
near light and beauty near to the aspiration, the cannon-ball and this

one was then as I was saying amiable in intention and clear and large worded and hesitating in expression. This one is an interesting enough one. I am knowing quite well three of these of them, one is more nearly engulfing, one has of him the very largest size in bags of cotton, one and this is the one I am realising in now describing was a little skimped in the cotton foundation. This is not a funny description, I was not certain I should say anything of the cannon-ball and the cotton, I was almost certain I would not say anything in this description about the cannon-ball and the cotton, it was not in me a natural way of conceiving any one, some one conceived this one as a cannon-ball resting on a bag of cotton, I used that in my description, this is not to me a natural way of talking, I have been using it here as I am saying. Now I will begin describing another one and that will be leaving only a few more to be describing of the considerable number of them that I have been describing of the resisting kind of them. This one that I am now beginning describing is of the resisting and sensitive and suspicious kind of them and now I will be telling a few stories about such of them.

It is very hard with some to be realising what kind they are this kind of them when they are quite old ones. It is a very difficult thing to be realising of some kinds of them one has been knowing before the beginning of their middle living what they are as old ones, these in living. When one is oneself a fairly old one, one will be knowing a little more perhaps of this thing, one is knowing a little of something of this thing from old relations one is knowing and one knowing all the family of these then is perhaps a little knowing what these are as younger ones in living. These that I am now describing are a kind of them that when they are old ones no one is paying much attention to them. They have then as old ones the same being in them I am now describing, they are mostly not any too successfully living all their living, they have when they are old ones the same being in them, mostly then not very many then are paying much attention to them then, these when they are old ones in living, these that I am now describing.

These then that I am now describing are a kind of them that have sensitiveness that is complete suspicion in them, these are of the kind of them·that are themselves completely important to themselves inside them, they have resistance in them much less than sensitiveness as suspicion in them. Suspicion in these of them comes out of the sensitiveness of them before the sensitiveness in them gives to them inside them really an emotion and so in these in living suspicion is as it were the whole of them, the complete emotion always in them. This sensitiveness in them that is in them a suspicion before it is an emotion in them from anything is always every moment in such of them. That these have it in them that sensitiveness makes for them suspicion before they have from anything a complete emotion is the reason that these mostly are not very successful in living, they are a little successful many of them and when they are older ones or old ones, no one, not any one is paying much attention to them. These then in a way are not really earthy, not really resisting, not at all engulfing, these then in a way are not certain that dead is dead, that things really are existing, these can have superstition and religion and prudence and fear and almost a crazy kind of thinking in them. This is now some stories about some of them.

I feel it and I brood over it and it comes then very simply from me, do you see how simply it comes out of me, you see, I feel it and I think about it and then I know it and I know then it is a simple thing, why are you always saying then it is a complicated one when really it is a very simple one this thing, do you see now it is a very simple thing this thing, do you see that this is a simple thing like everything why then should you make of it a complicated thing when it is a simple thing, do you see now that it is a simple thing this thing, why do you make everything a complicated thing, do you see, this is a simple thing, everything is a simple thing, you make everything a complicated thing when everything is a simple thing, do you see, it is a simple thing, you say it is a complicated thing, do you see, everything is a simple thing that is certain, do you see, that is certain. Very many are always saying this thing, it is very common, to be certain, to be really certain that some one is really feeling thinking seeing that that one is really feeling thinking seeing what that one really is seeing feeling thinking is certainly a quite rare thing. Mostly then it is a difficult thing, a patient solemn thing to be really certain that any one is really feeling seeing thinking believing what that one in the way that one really is feeling thinking seeing believing is feeling thinking seeing believing anything. These then I am now describing who are completely for themselves suspicious ones, who have it in them to have emotion in them become suspicion before it is a real emotion of anything for anything about anything in them, these have it completely to be certain that every one is doing feeling seeing the thing that one is feeling doing seeing believing when such a one is not agreeing with them, when such a one is feeling thinking believing doing anything that such a one is doing that thing for a mean or wicked or jealous or stupid or obstinate or cursed or religious reason, it is not a real feeling believing seeing realising, that this one having suspicion in him is certain. One of such a kind of one once liked very well some one and then that one forgot to give this one five cents that this one had paid for that one and then this one hated that one, had no trust in that one for this one was certain that that one knowing that this one was too sensitive to be asking did not think it necessary to pay that one, he never could believe that any one forgot such a thing. This is an extreme thing of a way of feeling that is common to all of these of them. Another one once was always certain that some one who one time told him that he would sometime later be successful in teaching meant it that he would not be successful in painting and that this was because that one was jealous of this one although that one had just met this one. This one was certain that every one sometime would do a mean thing to him and always each one to him sometime did this thing. Once one said to him I hope you will be successful in the city where you are going to earn your living. That means that you think my way of working rotten, you know very well no one making a living there is doing good work to your thinking, it would be a better thing to say what you are thinking straight out, said this one. One of such a kind of them was always asking and always getting and always he was certain that every one was doing the thing they were doing because they wanted to make of him a poor thing and some of such of them are always having difficulty with partners and others and any one and then as I am saying when they are older ones not any one pays very much attention to them. These are some and more or less like them are very many a very great many always living who have it in them that anything to them makes an emotion that is suspicion before it is real emotion in them.

In some connected with them, sensitiveness that in these I have been just describing turns into suspicion before it is sensation or emotion about a person, a thing done, or anything, in these turns into cleverness in them or self-protection in the sense of doing nothing and breaking all engagements and giving up all obligation. In some it turns before it is really a sensation into a sensual passion. This is all very interesting surely to any one really believing really being certain completely certain that different ones are different in kind from other kinds of them are really different in experiencing. This is in a way a very difficult thing to really truly believe in one, that some one really has a completely different kind of a way of feeling a thing from another one. Mostly every one in practical living needs only to be completely realising their own experiencing and then need only to be realising other ones experiencing enough to be using them, the ones experiencing. It is a very difficult thing to really believe it of another one what the other one is really feeling, it is such a very long learning anybody must be having to be really to be actually believing this thing. I do this thing. I am a rare one, I know this always more in living, I know always more in living that other ones are really believing what they are believing, feeling, what they are feeling, thinking, what they are thinking, always more and more in living I know I am a rare one. There are not very many having this very completely really in them.

To go on now then describing a little more some of these I have been last mentioning. Some of these are having their sensitiveness making of them clever, or self-protecting, or sexually wanting anything, without having really emotion from the thing from the sensitiveness in them.

These are of the resisting kind of them and might to some seem to be engulfing but they are not really resisting or engulfing. Sensitiveness turns
into suspicion, cleverness, self-protection, sexual action before it comes
as an emotion and these mostly then never have sensitiveness in them
leading to emotion by reaction to a person or thing or action. These
then are interesting. To be telling then now a little more of some of
them.

These then all of them have it in them that everything turns inside
them to suspicion, to cleverness, to self-protection, to sexual emotion,
to sensibility of a kind that is a thing that is called sentimental, before
it comes to produce emotion from the thing about the thing in relation
to the thing itself inside them. There is one, I knew this one quite very
well once and last week again I was seeing this one and now I am quite
a good deal understanding this one, this is one and in this one everything
was in this one sensibility of a sentimental kind, this was in this one not
very much as suspicion as I was saying it is in some, and in this one everything, nothing had any meaning excepting as arousing a feeling of sentimental sensibility that was the same thing whatever was the thing that
came to this one as touching this one. This one was pretty completely
to every one completely socially one and this is quite a common
thing. Sometime a history of her and her two mothers and her
sister will be written and I have been telling that it will be written
to several of them. She was as I was saying completely such a
one and as a younger one was sharp and interesting and then she
was a married one and then she was large and dull. This was after
she succeeded fairly at the beginning of her middle living in coming
to be a married one. She had not then any reaction at all in living for she was then in her married living living with bottom being reacting and there was no bottom being in her, living, at all in her then and
every one said it was such a surprising thing that she should be then so
completely a submissive and indifferent and inefficient and a little a timid
one then when she had been before her being a married one so altogether
an emotional and dark, expressive and clever one but it was just this
thing that I am saying that I am now pretty well understanding that
makes it a completely a natural thing, she had not ever had anything
that did not turn to sensibility before it reached her in her and when she
was a tired one and married and fatter then there was not this then. She
is an interesting one, really she is a very interesting one, she is quite a
pretty ugly one now but not in any way now an active one as now I am
completely realising. It is an interesting history the history of all of
this kind of them. It is a very interesting thing the history of this one.
The complete family living of this one is a thing I could make a remark-
ably interesting thing to any one, that is certain. I have been telling that
to this one. This one did not like very much to hear me say that thing,

it is a certain thing that it is an interesting thing to me and I could tell it so to every one, I have been telling it to this one that I can make it a completely interesting thing. This one was not liking it very well then. Sometime I will be feeling completely the telling of it and then I will be telling it, I have told this one that I will tell it then. This one will not know then it is this one. That is the very nice thing in this writing. Sometime I will tell everything, everything. Mostly I do tell anything.

One of this kind of them I have been describing has it that everything is in her as cleverness, or self-protection from any stimulation, never an emotion about a thing. This one would, if she could, have real emotion but it never is even a little bit in her of herself, inside her. Sometimes it is, a moment, a real feeling in her, something from something, when it is made to be in her by some one by force holding her from having it turn into cleverness, suspicion, sentimental believing, self-protection and so giving it a chance to sink into her so that she has a reaction to it really in her. This has a few times happened to her. This one is always feeling that some one should do this for her. Holding her from being her way in her so that emotion can be in her has been done for her. She never can do this for herself, ever. She is in her feeling certain that every one in this way should be doing for her. She is all her living needing that some one do this thing. She has it in her as a feeling that the world owes it to her to do this for her. She has not ever any really grateful feeling, she has only the emotion that some one wins in her for her. It is an interesting game to play in her and very many do it for her. Then they lose the power and she has to have another. She does not know that she is certain that the world owes this to her.

This one then would have it in her to be certain that to be dead was not to be at all really a dead one, this was what this one wanted to have in her as realisation, as emotion, this conviction is what this one was very certain the world owed her. This is what this one wanted that she should have in her, have as emotion inside her, this emotion in her is what every one knowing should do for her inside her. Very many coming to know her tried to give it to her, always she was wanting to have this inside her, the conviction, the emotion that to be dead was not to be really a dead one. This was the history of the living in her. She had in her as I was saying to have it that nothing gave to her really an emotion about that thing. Every thing touching her aroused in her suspicion, cleverness and self-protection. She wanted to have conviction and emotion that to be dead is not to be really truly a dead one. She wanted this in her, this realisation and emotion, in her, and then too she would be certain, she knew then she would then be really certain completely certain that every one was a very much better one than each one really was in living. She was certain, pretty nearly certain that if she were really completely certain that she was really knowing that to be dead was not to be at all a really dead one she would then be knowing that every one living was really a very much better one than each one really is living and this would be a very pleasant feeling for her to be having. Always then she was needing to be completely certain that she was really knowing that to be dead was not to be really at all a dead one and always she was unconsciously feeling that the world owed her owed it to her to give her this realisation. This was a history of her. Perhaps she never came really to have it in her, perhaps she came to have it a little in her, always some one was working in her for her, this is a history of her. This is an amusing thing, this history of this one. Sometime a very detailed history of this one will be an amusing thing to be writing, to be reading. Now I will not tell any more detail of this one.

Some as I was saying have it in them to have this kind of reaction I have been describing as sexual emotion and one such a one that I am knowing is quite an interesting one, quite an extraordinary one and sometime I will tell some of the exciting things in her living but not now, now I am going on describing three more kinds of resisting being. These I have been describing are resisting being in the sense that they would be resisting if they had any real emotion in them about anything but really they have not that in them and resisting being in them is a thing in them one is knowing in them from resemblances between them and those really resisting in living. Enough of this kind of them then now as I am saying, I will begin again some time with them, that is almost certain.

I am now going to give very little description of three other kinds in resisting being and then perhaps a few more will be adding themselves in but I am hoping that not very many will be adding themselves then because I will be wanting to be going on writing the history of Alfred Hersland which will certainly be more interesting now that every one knows so very much more of resisting, of resisting engulfing being in men and women.

This one I am beginning describing is a little connected on with these I have been just describing and is a little connected on with the next one I will be describing which is to be the kind of resisting being who are continually attacking. This one then is not an easy one to be describing, I will begin a little slowly now to be thinking and then I will do a little a very little writing. To commence now with my thinking. I am thinking now of this one.

This one is of the resisting kind in men and women, might have been of the engulfing kind of them, was not at all of the engulfing kind of them was only a resisting one, had a feeling of being an engulfing kind of them which made this one have very much emotion of dominating with stern action.

This one was of the resisting kind in men and women, this one had a little, had quite a good deal, had very often, had in a way always the emotion of dominating by engulfing, this made this one in her inside her in her feeling and often in her talking melodramatic in description, really this one was resisting, quite nicely, quite successfully a resisting one, not at all really an engulfing one, quite a good deal an engulfing one to herself inside her in her feeling. Feeling herself to be being an engulfing one gave to this one melodramatic sensation of being an important one,. this one was quite a bit an important one in living by the resisting being that was really winning being in her. A little with an animal or with her children she was a little to herself then and a little to them an engulfing one, really she was not at all an engulfing one, she was certainly completely a resisting one. As I am saying being to herself inside her an engulfing one gave to her melodrama of herself to herself inside her, melodrama in herself to herself inside her in her living with other ones, really there was not melodrama in her living mostly in her, a little with a little child or an animal around her, really not at all in living in her. She had from this melodrama, in her later, a history inside her of the past living in her and this was of her as a completely dominatingly engulfing being in her living. This one then certainly was in living simply a resisting sensitive fairly of the resisting sensitive being, dependent as dependent independent ones have it to be dependent in them, not at all in bottom being an engulfing one. This one then is connected with the group I have been describing by this conception she had of her own being but she was different from these I have been describing for she had not the being in her of being something from sensitiveness in her as these have it really in them. In her it was melodrama. She was really steadily winning resisting sensitive bottom dependent independent being. This one is connected with the one I will now be describing because this one made out of this being she had in her a little to herself and to very little ones near her a kind of attacking being, of dominating by stern attacking and this was from the, to herself, engulfing being in her. Really this one was not really at all an engulfing one. Really this one I have been just describing is not so completely clearly in my feeling as I would have them I am describing. It is there, but not so absolutely there as a realisation, that I can be content with owning what I am knowing. I will not then say now any more about this one. I will now say a little about another one, one who was of the resisting kind of them, not at all of the engulfing kind of them, one who was to herself and to every one always an attacking one. This one was attacking the way a boy is when he is thrown into water and is scared then and every kind of way is hitting the water so as to keep the water from drowning him. Such a boy makes very much splashing. This is the kind of attacking this one had in her living, this one was so scared she was always hitting out in every direction, this one had little moments of knowing she was a timid one, mostly she was certain she was a very attacking successfully attacking one.

This resisting one was very often, and mostly always, bragging, was very often certain that to be the one that one was in living was to be one quick and poignant in emotion and quick in vigorous attacking. This one was this to a considerable number seeing this one doing living, knowing this one all her living. This one was this, was an attacking one to mostly every one seeing this one doing all the living in this one. In a way as I was saying it was true of this one. A boy thinking he is drowning is hitting the water every kind of way to keep it from drowning him and as I am saying he is making very much splashing. Resisting then was the being in this one, hitting in every direction was the living in this one, bragging always that this one was doing more hitting than any other one was always in this one, engulfing was not at all in this one. This one knew sometimes that she was really a timid one. This one was not winning by resisting, not by sensitive dependent being, because this one was always hitting away making a whirlwind around this one so that not anything could come near this one to attack this one. This one was not really a successful one in inner living, not in loving, not in winning permanently any one, not in winning permanently with working, resisting was the way of winning for this one and this one was not ever in living really resisting to anything, this one was always hitting in every direction, this one was really a slow one, this one was to herself a very quick one, this one was hitting in a quick enough fashion but she was not hitting anything she was attacking, hitting in every direction one must sometimes hit something, this one sometimes hit something, to this one she was always hitting something, to a good many knowing this one she was always hitting something.

This one was very certain in a foolish way of being timid and always hitting out at anything that she had really intuition, that she was really certain that to be dead was not to be at all, why not a bit, a dead one. This one was telling this very often. This one was telling this in a way once to several listening. This one is a very common type of resisting being and I know very many of this kind of them and all of them are certain of themselves to be certainly knowing whether to be dead is to be or not to be a really dead one. That is complete attacking, by them. This one was telling of the way this one was certain. This one was telling that she was certain some one was a bad one. She knew it she was certain, she knew it by intuition, she knew it by her feeling, she knew it because she knew that to be dead is not to be at all, not the least bit a really dead one. This one as I am saying was completely a resisting one but this one never was really resisting, this one was, even she herself knew that a little, a timid one, she knew she was afraid always with a man. This one was a very typical one of the resisting kind who are always attacking and attacking is not at all the way to winning for them. These then are incessant in attacking, they are never at all resting from attacking, mostly they know that they are not winning in loving, mostly they think they can be certain that to be dead is to be or is not to be a dead one, they are mostly always not really winning in loving. This one that I am describing was not ever winning in loving, this one was certain that this one had a feeling that was certain about being a dead one was to be not a dead one. This one was certain of the intuition this one had of every one. This was really in this one from the dependent being in this one and the stupid attacking in this one. This is the way this one told of one complete intuition.

There is a whole series of this kind of them that I know in living. I saw yesterday afternoon two of them together and one of these two of them did not do very much attacking and she was successful in loving and she was very dependent and very independent in the way dependent independent kind of them have it in them to be winning. I knew once very well another one of this kind of them who was always doing considerable attacking and always doing very much bragging and always wanting to be thinking inside in this one and telling it to every one when this one heard mentioned anything done that this one was doing everything quicker and stronger and farther and shorter and slower and happier and sadder and weaker and completer and every other kind of more or lesser that any one can conceive of anything, than any one. But always this one was really solidly winningly resistingly dependently independently living. This one had it as a simple conviction that this one could do everything, this one did mostly everything, this one was certain that to be dead was to be a dead one, attacking was almost in this one not a stupid thing but it was in this one stupid being because after all this one was completely a resisting one and dependent independent was the being in this one. This one had dependent and independent being so well balanced in her living that almost attacking and bragging was not stupid being in this one but really it was stupid being in this one in the final meaning of the being in this one because this one really was winning in loving and living and working by resisting being and all the attacking being in this one was hitting to keep away attacking from coming and was not really the natural way of winning fighting as an attacking and so then this one was of this kind of them I am describing but this one was completely and entirely an efficient one. The other one that I have begun describing the one that was the first one of this kind of them that I mentioned in my writing, was always splashing always hitting in every direction, was in a way quite a competent one but really was a timid one, was one not successful in loving, was one that as a poor one would not have been successful as a whole in living, was not successful as this one thought this one inside this one to be a successful one but was to very many knowing this one a very, a strikingly successful one. Really this one was not a successful one in loving and that is interesting.

This one had two kinds of ways of having stupid being, one was as timid being, one was as attacking being. Of the attacking being I have been giving a description. Of the timid being I have given only a very little description. As I was saying this one had it to think that this one was certain that to be dead was not to be at all a dead one. This was a comfort to all the stupid being in this one to all the dependent being in this one. This was a comfort to the stupid being in this one, to the timidity and to the attacking feeling and acting always in this one. Intuition, feeling this one had intuition was stupid being in this one. This one was not at all in many ways a stupid one. This one was a stupid one when between timidity and universal attacking this one had intuition. "Yes I can always tell what any one is, what a man is, what a woman is, what a child is, what a very little child is," said this one. "I am very certain in my feeling, just listen. Once I met a man, I knew this man was just the kind of a man I knew he was, I was certain when I saw him, every time I saw him I was certain, once he came into this house and I shook hands with him, I was more than ever certain that this man was the kind of a man I had thought him. I don't see him very often, I would never meet him if I could avoid him, I never make a mistake about a person about a man or a woman or about children when I have an intuition."

This one as I am saying had stupid being from a timid feeling, completely a timid feeling, from being quite the dependent kind of the dependent independent kind of them and from the attacking acting, attacking living that was always to this one and to every one all the living in this one. This one liked the feeling of being certain that to be dead was not to be at all a dead one, this was very satisfying to the timid feeling and the attacking being in this one, this was stupid being in this one, this one was not wise in loving or in religion, this one was quite efficient in every day living, this one to very many was quite a successful one, to very many a brilliantly successful one. This is all I will be writing now about this one, this is not enough really about this one, I ought to be writing very much more about this kind of them, all I think about this kind of them is inside me quite sure, quite certain, I do not yet think all that can be thought or felt about this kind of them, I do think and feel more about this kind of them than I have just written. I have not just now a very patient feeling about writing about this kind of them. I want to be having soon a completely patient feeling in writing the description of all resisting being, of all resisting engulfing being, in writing the history of Alfred Hersland. I will now write one more description and will so be ending just now the considerable number of resisting ones I have been describing. I will then go on to a little generalising and then to patiently feeling in me the history of Alfred Hersland and all resisting engulfing being.

When I have not been right there must be something wrong. Every one says to me I am always certain I am right about everything and I must be certain of that thing because otherwise there is something wrong and that is a wearying, wearing thing and then I must be beginning learning everything.

I have been very glad to have been wrong. It is sometimes a very hard thing to win myself to having been wrong about something. I do a great deal of suffering.

I have been glad to have been wrong and I have felt certain that this was making me a really joyous wise one. I have been very sad to have to bring myself to be certain that I have been wrong about something. This is now a little more history of me and the kind of suffering I can have in me. This is a little a description of the suffering I do have in me.

When I have not been right there must be something wrong. That is what I say to myself inside me. That is what some one sometimes says to me. This has been said to me. This I do say to myself inside me. When I have not been right there must be something wrong

This is in a way the meaning of all living in me. This is the way I have suffering in me. When I have not been right there must be something wrong. I have been very glad to have been wrong. It is sometimes a very wearing thing to have been wrong about something.

I have it in me in being that I am resisting in being, I am fairly slow in action and in feeling, if I am not slow in acting and in feeling and in listening I am not certain that I myself am doing that acting listening feeling, I would be thinking something was happening, it would be over and I would not be realising that I myself was listening, feeling, acting. When I am very slow in listening feeling thinking realising then I can still need to have it that I am still to be slower in doing anything. When I have not been right there must be something wrong. I may then perhaps be quicker in listening feeling realising, I must then be slower in concluding. I have very much wisdom. I want sometime to be completely understanding every one so that sometime I will be right about every one. And now I am not knowing anything at all really of the feeling any one has in them when they are between fourteen and eighteen. I certainly will be needing to know this thing. I know now I do not know at all the feeling in such of them, those being at that time of living, I cannot then really be right about every one yet, that is certain. When I have not been right there must be something wrong. I know that very well in me. Some one says I feel that in me. I certainly do feel that in me. I am hoping sometime to be right about every one, about everything. I do. I certainly do hope this thing. That is to say I want to realise every one, I want to write a history of every one. Sometime I want to be right about every one. Perhaps I am right now about some. Perhaps I am right now about a good many men and women who are and were and will be living. Perhaps I am right about almost all of them. Certainly when I am not right something is wrong and I must know it in me, in them then. I want to write a history of every one. Sometime I want to be right about every one. Perhaps I am right now about some. Certainly I am right now about a very great many men and women about the being in them. Certainly I am right now in my realising of a very considerable number of them, of men and women who were and are and will be living, of a very considerable number of kinds in men and women. Sometime I want to be right about every one, I want to realise every one. Sometime I want to write the history of every one. Always when I am not right something is wrong. Certainly I am right about a very great many, that is certain. Sometime I want to be right about every one. I want to be completely realising every one sometime. This is what I am wanting. Sometimes I am very glad to have been wrong. Sometimes it is a very wearing thing bringing my feeling to the realisation that I have been wrong about something. Sometimes it is such a tempting thing to let it go that I have been right about something. I want sometime to be right about every one. I want sometime to write a history of every one, of every kind there is in men and women. It would be such a satisfaction always to be right about every one, such a certain, active feeling in me. I want sometime to be sure when I know something that I am completely right in my certain feeling. Sometime I want to be completely certain. I am one that in this way am wanting to be completely certain, am wanting to be right in being completely certain and in this way only in me can it come to be in me that to be dead is not to be a dead one. Really to be just dead is to be to me a really dead one. To be completely right, completely certain is to be in me universal in my feeling, to be like the earth complete and fructifying. This is doing talking. I will now begin again. I really am wanting to be sometime right about every one. I am wanting sometime to tell about secrecy in those having in them resisting being, Sometime later in the history of Alfred Hersland I will be discussing this thing.

I have now described the considerable number of kinds of the resisting kind of them that I was going to be describing and I have now finished doing this thing. I will now be adding a very few not only of the resisting kind of them but of both resisting and attacking ones to make another generalisation but really there have been already done the considerable number of the resisting kinds of them in men and women that I was going to be describing. These few little additions are now just for finishing and to be a little commencing explaining relation between kinds that are resisting and kinds that are attacking and kinds that are kinds in men and women.

Lena, Maria and Hetty and others that I am not now naming adapt their loving to any one who is interesting. They then want, not to own them, not to influence them, but to feel power in themselves through them, to know inside them that they are knowing by knowing them the things the one who is interesting is knowing. These end up very often by marrying a man very popular with men who only like them out of all women, who can only be owned by them, of all women. Some are possessed by a passionate desire for the thing the interesting person is realising and such ones are a little different from these others. Some want distinction for themselves and so they are different. Some, Hortense and Martha are such of them, care enough about the man they are loving being interesting to need to love one having genius, these two have more real personal passion, more founded courage in them than Lena or Maria or Hetty. Some want to do the thing itself as if they themselves could do the thing that makes the distinguished one a distinguished one even if they know they cannot do this thing to make of themselves in it a distinguished one. Some of such of them do not know that they began to do that thing from loving a distinguished one and some of such of them are so stubborn in doing that thing that they cannot learn about that thing from the one they are adapting themselves to, the distinguished one.

I am thinking. I am not yet certain. Every kind I have been describing of the resisting kind of men and women can be found with a different action in the attacking kind in men and women. I am thinking. I have now described a kind of them and I know some of them and some of them I have known in loving, known very well in loving and some are of the attacking and some of the resisting kind of them and I have been describing them together so that any one can see why I am thinking that there are attacking kinds correlative to the resisting kinds I have been describing.

Lena and Maria are of the resisting and Hetty and Hortense and Martha are of the attacking kind of them and all of these have a way of loving that in a way is common to all of them, a way of adapting their loving to any one who is interesting to feel power in themselves through them.

But all of this is one thing and now being in Alfred Hersland is something. I have been describing a considerable number of men and women having resisting being in them. Alfred Hersland had resisting engulfing being in him. Having been understanding so many having resisting being in them makes it more certain that I am understanding the being in Alfred Hersland.

Alfred Hersland had resisting being somewhat engulfing resisting being in him. He had not anything at all of the attacking kind of being in him. He was all of engulfing resisting being.

Alfred had it in him to have his being in him so that it was a little passionate in him, not very affectionate in him, not so as to be very good in him, not really ever very bad in him, sometimes as aspiration in him, more or less as ambition in him, sometimes as virtuous and didactic in him. The kind of being he had in him was of a kind of being that in some having it in them makes of them being devout in religion, quite aspiring in their living, quite ambitious for succeeding, makes of them mystic in religion so as to let themselves be absorbed all existing, some of them having this kind of being in them have religion in them. Some having this kind of being in them are meek enough in living and yet a little dominating in family living and some of such of them need to have as a wife to them some one very vibratingly existing to give to them enough stimulation to make them keep really alive inside them. All these then are of the resisting the dependent independent kind of them. Some of them have the being in them inside and some of these then are trying to engulf every one near them to be lost inside them, to be swallowed by them and some of them are not interested in very many persons near them but some of them they need to have engulfed by them and so then Alfred Hersland was of the kind of them the resisting dependent independent kind of them, the kind that own those they need for loving. Many of such of them do not really in their living need any one for loving.

Alfred Hersland to my feeling has being in him as pieces only of being. This is now to be more history of him. He was of the resisting engulfing kind of them, his being was a little passionate, not very affectionate, not so very good, not really so very bad in him, somewhat as aspiration in him, a good deal as ambition in him, possibly as religion in him, certainly as weakness in him, not altogether as successful in him. He had his being in him and to very many being was not complete in him. He was not a very strong one, he was not altogether a weak one. This is now to be completely a history of him and the living he had all together in him.

Very many never learn anything from the experience with themselves they have in living. Very many are never at all learning anything with the experience they are having of themselves in their living. Very many are always expecting out of themselves what they could have certainly been learning that they would not ever be succeeding in doing. Very many are not all their living learning anything from the experience they have with themselves in their living. This is very common. Alfred Hersland in a way was such a one. All the Hersland men in a way were such ones in their being, Mr. David Hersland in his living, Alfred and David Hersland in their living. Alfred Hersland was in a way such a one. This is now to be a complete history of him.

There is always, perhaps there is always something in what every one says about any one. In some way anything, everything any one, every one says about any one is a true thing. Each one says something about some one and that one says something says a number of things sometime about herself or himself and everything any one, anything any one says about that one anything that one says about that one everything that one says about that one is in a way a true thing. Always then sometime there is a complete history of some one, sometime there will be a complete history of Julia Dehning. Sometime there will be very many descriptions of some one, there will sometime be very many descriptions of Julia Dehning. Now there is to be more description of the being Alfred Hersland had in him always in all his living. Very soon now there is to be very much description of the living in Alfred Hersland and of the people Alfred Hersland came to know in living, and now I am feeling a complete realisation of the difference between affection and passion and soon there will be a description of Alfred Hersland knowing the man who was a musician and of Alfred Hersland knowing the woman who was the sister of the first governess the Herslands had had living with them in the ten acre place in Gossols. These two were a little important to him in his early living as I have already been saying. I am very interested just now in the difference between passion and affection and I will now tell about a man and then I will describe the musician Alfred Hersland came to know in his early living a Mr. Arragon who was really foreign.

I am always more and more realising that some are pieces of being always in living and some are not such pieces of being in their whole living. Later then I will be describing being in Alfred Hersland and all the living he had in him. Just now as I am saying I find it that I am writing about a man who had inspired affection in him for beautiful things in living and this one was a puzzle to me and then I knew it of him that it was inspired affection not passion he had in him. Arragon had passion that was not poignant in him but it was passion, this one that is now strongly in my feeling is one having inspired affection and not at all any passion in him. This one in his young living to the beginning of his middle living was to very many knowing him, to himself always inside him one having really passion about beauty in living. This one had then inspired affection not passion in him but inspired affection was so freshly poignantly in him and his intellect could use it so well for him that to himself then and to every one then he had real creation of passionately understanding beautiful things in living. More and more then this one in his middle living was not any longer creating his realisation of beauty in living, this one was then living on the approximation others made for him of everything this one wished to have beautiful around him and for living. This one then never could make for himself the beautiful luxury he was needing. Inspired affection for beauty in him awoke in others the need of creating as nearly as these could do what this one needed as beauty in living. This one could not create his own taste in luxury in living, he could not create his own taste for a woman. A woman, everything in his living created itself to approximate to the taste this one would have created if this one could have created the thing this one wanted to have to arouse in him inspired affection. This one then after beginning his middle living never created anything, never in his living did this one create loving not for beautiful things not for a woman, this one had inspired affection in him and to himself and to every one it was passion, it never was passion in him and more it came out in him as more and more in living this one needed that other ones by their creating approximated to what his taste would have been if he had had passion instead of affection for luxury and beauty in living and so this one more and more was declining because this one came more and more to have affection for things others created to be what this one would have wanted to have in living if this one could have created what this one was needing to have to arouse him to inspired affection and this is a history of this one. Now this one as I am saying had not passion in him, not for beauty not for a woman not for anything, but this one had inspired affection and it is an interesting thing that this one had as a woman who chose herself for him one who was as this one was of the attacking type in men and women, this is an interesting thing. I am very happy in realising this thing. I am hoping that this is really the complete history of this one.

Arragon who was a little important in the living of Alfred Hersland was different from this one I have been just describing. Arragon had passion in him but it was not poignant in him but brilliant and emotional and sentimental. I will now begin a description of his being and of what Alfred Hersland lived through with him. Later then I will be describing Ida the school-teacher and the kind she was in men and women. Now to begin again with the musician.

I find it very interesting to know the difference between affection and passion, I will now just a little describe a kind of them having passion of which Arragon the musician who came to know Alfred Hersland when Alfred was just beginning being a man inside him was one. I know three very well of this kind of them and very many more or less connected with this kind of them. All these I am now describing, the one I have just been describing are of the attacking kind in men, the independent dependent kind of them. These then that I am now describing all have really passion in them passion that makes them creating or feeling in themselves creating feeling of something of very much in living. To begin then. Alfred Hersland was of the resisting engulfing kind of them, these I am now describing are of the passionate creating seizing attacking kind in men and women.

There are many kinds of ways of being of the attacking kind in men

and women that is certain. I am already realising a considerable number of them. I am .realising pretty completely realising a very considerable number of ways of having resisting being in them and I have been
already describing, very well describing some of those I am always now
realising. I am realising now some of the attacking kinds of them. There
are many kinds of them and I am realising some of the kinds of them.
I have been realising Mr. Henry Dehning and Martha Hersland and Redfern and I was saying that Cora Dounor was of this kind of them but I am
thinking in that I was mistaken I am thinking Cora Dounor was certainly
of the resisting kind of them. There are almost border cases that is certain I am realising some of that kind of them and I will be describing that
in describing the sister of the first governess the Herslands had had living with them. Now I am describing a musician Arragon who was a
man having in him as I was saying passion but this was not poignant
in him although to himself and to mostly every one it was poignant in
him because he had so much weakness and sensitiveness and romance in
him. This one then was of the attacking kind of them as I was saying.
I am remembering that I mean by attacking being those having it in
them that emotion is poignant like sensation, that use and purpose and
organisation and synthesising and imagining and everything in relation
is as true in them in beginning as the thing being existing. The resisting kind of them have it in them that a thing being existing is more real
to them than use or purpose or meaning in anything, the attacking kind
of them have it in them that emotion is as poignant as sensation and use
and purpose and meaning and relation as primary as existing. Mr. Hersland was of the attacking kind in men and women, so was Redfern as I
was saying so was Martha Redfern, so is the one I have been just describing as affectionate and never passionate in living and now I am describing this being in another one in Mr. Arragon a musician and I will tell
quite a little now about him and Alfred Hersland liked him very much
when Alfred was coming to be a young man as I have several times been
saying. Arragon had attacking passion in him but as I was saying it
was not very poignant in him. In Redfern it was poignant but not rich
enough to sustain him, in Mr. Hersland it was poignant and rich but not
steady in him, in the one I have been just describing it was as affection
and not passion and in Arragon and it made him a pretty good musician,
it was rich but not poignant in him and he made up for it in him by weakness and sensibility and feeling himself to be a really great one and by
having moments of really inspired feeling when almost he made it in himself by loving by weakness by talking to be poignant inside him.

This kind then of which Arragon was one is quite common. Every
kind of being is quite common. That is certain. There are very many
always existing of each one of all the kinds there are in being. That is
certain. Anyway it would be certain but it is certain to me because I

am more and more realising I know a considerable number of each kind I am ever knowing. More and more in living I come to know enough of each kind of them to make groups of them. Sometime I will be able to make a diagram. I have already made several diagrams. I will sometime make a complete diagram and that will be a very long book that will tell all about each kind there is of men and women. But just now I am thinking of this one kind of them, the kind of which Arragon was one.

This kind of them as I have been saying are those having in them attacking passion. As I was saying I know just now pretty well three of them. I know too this one that I am now describing, that makes then four of them. In a way as I am saying Redfern was one of such of them. There are some connected with this kind of them that have this being in them passionate attacking as highly suggestible emotion in them. That is one kind of them, sometime there will be much description of such of them. Some are connected with this kind of them that have it in them to be so stupidly in them that it really makes of them that all their life they are obstinately resisting everything, these are connected with Mrs. Redfern, these are connected with Julia Dehning, these can sometimes sometime in their living get an impression but mostly all of their living they are obstinately resisting losing their attacking passion. There will sometime necessarily be very much description of them. Then there are some who have attacking passion so sensitively so delicately in them that mostly they are delicately vibrating and only sometime is the thing going fast enough in them to make such of them really attacking. Some of such of them are very lovely ones in all their feeling living, sometime there will be a long description of a lovely one. These then will be leading to a whole group having in them flavor realising as complete existing and sometime I will tell so very much about such a kind of them. And then there is the group that do not have it at all as passion but as affection as I was saying. And then there are some that are steadily pressing in attacking, some who perhaps in their living are always really winning. Then there are some in whom passion is emotion before it can be acting as passion and all these groups are of course extremely interesting. Now I am describing one group of this group of them who have it in them to have attacking passion in them and some have it in them poignantly and they are weak in living, and some have it poignantly and their natures are not abundant in them and some have it in them poignantly and they are rich in beginning and they are always all their living in beginning and some have it poignantly in them and are rich in being and are rich in developing in being and in living and some have it poignantly in them and nothing is good enough to hold them and some have it poignantly in them and they are not strong enough to keep anything and some are practical with it and some are not at all practical not even sensible with it and some do not have it poignantly in them and this musician Alfred Hersland knew in his younger living was one of such of them.

I like thinking about kinds of them in men and women. I like feeling men and women each one as of one kind of them and that I can that sometime I will know others like them. It makes it to me a very pleasant world for living. It makes it simple to be certain that each one every one has their own being in them that each one every one is of a kind in men and women and that always there are existing very many of each of these kinds of them. This is a pleasant thing for me to have as certain in me. I know then there can be a history of each one and of all kinds all the kinds in men and women. This is a pleasant feeling, this is comforting to me just now when I am thinking of every one always growing older and then dying, now when I am thinking about each one being sometime a sick one each one being sometime a dead one. This gives to me then a pleasant feeling knowing kinds in men and women now when I am thinking that sometime each one will be an old one and then each one will be a dead one. I can understand that knowing there are kinds in men and women would not be a comfort to every one. I can understand this thing. I have it in me as a very pleasant feeling that always there are kinds in men and women and always there are very many existing of each kind of them. I have it in me then as I am saying this thing as a very pleasant feeling as a pleasant complete feeling, as a completely contenting feeling and I am knowing sometime each one will be a dead one and I am knowing each one has their own being in them and I am knowing each one is one of a kind in men and women and as I am saying I am having a pleasant completely completed feeling and always then it is a comfortable and calming thing this being certain that each one is one of a kind of them in men and women and that there are always very many of each kind existing, that each one has their own being in them is then completely interesting, that each one sometime is to be a dead one is then not discouraging, and so then I am having a completely pleasant and completed feeling, I who am completely certain that each one is of a kind in men and women, I who am always almost always knowing several of each kind of them I come to know in living, I who am expecting sometime perhaps to be knowing all there ever can be, were or are or will be of kinds in men and women. I have then even with sombre certain feeling that each one is always an older one and sometime a dead one I have then knowing each one is of one kind in men and women I have then a pleasant feeling, a contented a completed feeling as I have been saying. I have a quiet sombre feeling I have not so much an afraid feeling in being living now when I am certain, and I am knowing them, that there are a number of kinds in men and women, not such a great number of them, quite a number of them. Each one is themselves inside them, each one every one is of a kind in men and women. This is to me a completely satisfying thing. I am beginning again now to describe one kind of them, one of one kind in men and women.

This musician, whom as I was saying Alfred Hersland knew in his younger living was of the sensitive passionate attacking kind in men and women but passion was not really poignant in him, sensitiveness was very spread out in him, to himself and to mostly every one passion was poignant in him and he could be ruining himself by loving but passion was not poignant in him and in a way this made him a very good musician, sensitiveness was in him and not concentration and this is a kind of them that to very many knowing them are those who are not successful because of passion and of weakness in them. Mostly those of this kind of them who have passion as poignant in them they have a different way of not succeeding, they do not come so nearly to succeeding, they do not appear again when they have gone down with the sensitive passionate weakness in them, they have less power of recuperation. Some of these succeed very well in living, there certainly are some of every kind there is in men and women who succeed very well in living, very many of this kind of them come very nearly to completely succeeding, very many of them have very much weakness, I am getting a little diffused about them, I have several in me all at once and they are crowding and they are coming out as a facile mixing and I am beginning again now with each one of them.

Very many of this kind as I have been saying have not passion poignantly in them, very many of this kind of them have passion very poignantly in them, all of this kind of them are very sensitive in being, they are all of the sensitive passionate attacking kind in men and women. Two of those who were and are crowded in me just now are of the kind of them not having the passion poignantly in them. Three of those that were crowding each other in me of this kind of them are of the poignant kind in passion of this kind of them. I will go on a little with these poignant kind of them and then I will go on with Arragon the musician who had not passion as poignant in him.

To begin then again. To begin with those having passion poignantly in them of the sensitive passionate attacking kind in men and women, the sensitive passionate attacking independent dependent kind in men and women.

This one that I am now thinking about describing had passion poignantly in him that is certain. He had the conviction of being always completely creating everything in his living. He had passion poignantly in him that is certain, he was creating some part of his living, he certainly was not in any way completely creating all the living he had in him. Very often he was certain that he would be creating everything in his living if there were not so many things to make him nervous to disturb him. Mostly to himself he certainly could be creating everything in his living. He certainly did create something of his living, he certainly had passion poignantly in him. As I was saying to himself he was comletely creating all his living, not that to himself he really was creating all his living for always and that he was always feeling he had very much to make a nervous restless person of him, but certainly he was to himself a being that could be creating everything in all his living. Passion was poignantly in him that is certain, he did create something in his living that is certain, more and more in his living he was having nervousness in him and not creating everything in his living in the way that to himself it was certain he could be creating everything in all his living. Always more and more then it was right for him to be seizing creating everything he could be seizing creating in his living. More and more then he had this in him, always all his living he certainly was creating something of his living, always he was certain he could be creating everything in all of his living, always he had nervousness in him and this was to him that things were interfering to keep him back from creating everything in his living and so more and more he would be seizing creating anything and so more and more to every one he was such a one and more and more to himself, always to himself he was one who should be creating everything in all his living. This is then a complete history of him. Passion was ceitainly poignantly in him, he certainly was not ever creating everything in his living, he was to himself one who certainly could be creating everything in all his living, he was then one who always more and more in his living would be seizing creating anything. This then is a complete history of one, a very complete history of one and I am understanding this complete history of this one.

Every one has their own being in them, every one is of a kind in men and women. Only a very little sometimes this is not an important thing inside me to me. Sometimes it is not an important thing inside me, sometimes it is a little a dreary thing, making of everything that there is not anything inspiriting to be a live one. Sometimes it is a little this way in me but mostly always it is an important thing inside me that every one is their own self inside them, that every one is of a kind of men and women. Always to me, to be a dead one is a sombre thing, to be certain that it is existing, always there has been in me the being very much afraid of this thing, always it is to me a sombre thing in living, sometime later in the history of David Hersland there will be very much description of this sombre feeling in some. Mostly as I am repeating it is an important thing inside me that each one is themselves inside them that each one is of a kind in men and women. Mostly and I am saying it again and again it is an important thing, always an important thing, mostly always an important thing. Each one is themselves inside them, each one is one of a kind in men and women, this is an important thing always in my living, it is sometimes a very pleasant feeling, it is very often a very pleasant feeling in me, mostly always it is completely an important thing inside me. I am living, I am certain, I am important in me in my realising that each is themselves inside them that each one is of a kind in men and women, I have very often a very pleasant feeling, I have sometimes a very sombre feeling. I have just now a good deal a quite sombre feeling. I am beginning now again telling, feeling, being certain of the kind of being there is in one kind in men and women. Always each one is to me completely their own selves inside them, I have never a sombre feeling that that is not a certain thing. Always each one is themselves inside them, always each one is of a kind in men and women. Always kinds are connected with other kinds in men and women. Sometimes I want to be describing lots and lots of kinds in men and women, I want to be going on and on and describe one and then another one and then connections between them and then perhaps I am mistaken and I am hurrying and crowding and then I am not certain and then I am wondering perhaps it is not completely an important thing, perhaps not anything is inspiriting in living, but always in me really I am certain that it is an important thing in me and I am telling that each one has always their own being in them that every one is one of a kind in men and women, mostly then this in me is important feeling, mostly this is in me pleasant and exciting, sometimes there is in me very sombre feeling, always there is in me that it is interesting that each one is themself inside them that each one is of a kind in men and women. Mostly always I am important with this thing.

I am important with this thing. There is a kind of them then of the attacking kind of them that I have been describing. These have sen- sitive passion in them. In some it is a very poignant thing in them, in some it is not such a poignant thing. I have described one in whom it was a poignant thing. In some in whom it is a poignant thing it is religion in them, in some it is denying in them, in some it is aspiration and these are disappointed idealists in living but this is not what I am telling, I am describing now a musician, one having a very good con- centrating intelligence in him, a spread out vibrating sensitiveness in him, an aspiration to be religious and exalted in all feeling, a wanting to be always loving, a succeeding in being very often very complicated in much loving, a success in living and then a good deal of failing and then a very great deal of failing and then not altogether failing. As I was saying passionate being was not poignant in him, he had a very great deal of it in him, he was a good musician, he was a foreign one, he was in Gossols and then he was not altogether failing not altogether succeeding, there he was living, he was to very many knowing him an adventurer in living, really he was one not having passion as very poignant in him but having in him a good deal of it in him of this non-poignant passion, a very great deal of sensitiveness and aspiration in doing much loving and perhaps having religion, not so very much aspiration for succeeding or failing.

Alfred Hersland as I said in beginning about his knowing this man came to know him when Alfred was coming to the beginning of the ending of his young living. This one was then a little important to him, not very important to him, not any one was very important to him then, he was slowly growing up then and he had his being in him and he had it as being that at that time in his living not any one was very important to him, this friend and teacher was as important as any one was then to Alfred, he was a little important to him. I am remembering very well now the being in Alfred Hersland.

Alfred Hersland had it in him that he was then living the living of people near him, he was doing then everything those near him were doing in living, he was then living the living of Mr. Arragon and doing everything he did that he could do with him. Alfred was as I was saying of the resisting engulfing kind of them having in him very much aspiring in living, having in him a fair amount of passion in living, having in him a very considerable feeling for distinction and elegance and beauty and richness in living having in him very considerably at times violent feeling in him of wanting to be doing with every one he was knowing what they were doing that he wanted to be doing with them. He had then very much pleasing feeling in doing with him what Arragon was doing in living, as I was saying Alfred Hersland really had musical feeling and musical understanding in him, he never had it at all in him that he wanted to be a musician. As I was saying Mr. Arragon was a little but was not very important to Alfred Hersland inside him, not any one could be then really important to Alfred Hersland inside him then, Alfred had his being inside him then, Alfred was of a kind in men and women, that was all the history of Alfred Hersland then and he was living the living of those near him and he was doing everything he was doing in his living with those he was then knowing and he was then doing everything they were then doing in their living. He was as I said before in a way then of the feeling of his natural rich american living but really always he was living the living and doing everything that they were doing of those near him. He was as I was saying of the engulfing resisting kind in men and women and he had in him a fair amount of passion in living and always then he was living, he was doing everything those near him were doing in living. Mr. Arragon was at one time very much with him. He was a little important as important as any one to Alfred Hersland then. Not any one was or could be really important to Alfred Hersland then. Alfred was of the engulfing resisting kind in men and women, not very strongly really resisting, not very strongly really engulfing, quite very strongly aspiring, quite strongly feeling distinction and elegance and beauty in living and richness as I was saying, quite often angry in resolving and very angry in beginning doing what every one near him was doing in living. He had his own being then, he was of a kind in men and women.

He was very pleasant to himself in being with Arragon and he liked it very well and it was a rich feeling in him that Mr. Arragon was having him with him in doing his living. Not anything was completely important to Alfred Hersland then.

I am not content, I have not had it come out without pressing the description of Mr. Arragon the musician. It should come out of me without pressing without any straining in me to be pressing, I can be doing thinking to be helping, I should not be doing any pressing and any straining, I have been doing a little it has not come to be a complete thing simply coming, it is to be then to rebegin to come out from me. Always each thing must come out completely from me leaving me inside me just then gently empty, so pleasantly and weakly gently empty, that is a happy way to have it come out of me each one that is making itself in me, that is the only way it can come to be content for me in me, it can come out fairly quickly very slowly with a burst or gently, any way it feels a need of coming out of me, but being out of me I must be very pleasantly most gently, often weakly empty, this one then Mr. Arragon is not so happily then out of me, he is then still there inside me, I will let him come again when he is more completely ready, of the kind he is in living that has come out very pleasantly from inside me, his own being in me has not come out to be out of me so satisfactorily. Sometime then he may be better done, to begin again then the being and the living Alfred Hersland had in him.

Some are a very long time puzzles to me, this one the musician Mr. Arragon is not a puzzle to me, he is quite completely in me, and all of it is understood inside me, pretty well understood by me inside me, it is the coming out of me that has not been satisfactory. It has come out of me as little pieces never making a complete one, I will be a little slow and then it will come better done, I hope I am certain of this thing. I am not waiting, I am forgetting so that this one can come when this one can come as a satisfactory one without my disturbing this one by any impatience about this one. I have been describing very many men and very many women many of the resisting, some of the attacking kind of them, as I have often been saying there are many kinds of mixing a bottom attacking breaking through resisting nature in the same one, pressing through resisting nature in the same one, acting separately with resisting being in the same one and resisting being in the bottom doing all kinds of twisted complications with attacking being in the same one. There are very many kinds of mixing, I have described some of them, and then there are some and these are certainly very difficult ones in whom the character of the being is completely oppositely acting and there are border line cases where the one is almost the other kind of a one. And sometimes then I think it is all foolishness this I am writing and thinking and feeling and having as important being and then I give in to not thinking or feeling or being an important one and then I see it again and I am simply certain and I am naturally thinking, feeling each one as a kind of a one in the way I have been telling and I am then again a completely important one. Alfred Hersland in his living knew a number of kinds in men and women. I am beginning now very regularly again the history of the living and the being in him.

Alfred Hersland as I have certainly been realising is of the resisting more or less engulfing kind in men and women. As I was saying those having in them resisting being are those having in them realisation of things as existing as more in them than as things having relation. Those having in them resisting being have not emotion in them having really poignancy in them like sensation. This is then a thing to be now completely believing. Those having in them resisting as their complete way of being in living are those having in them as I was saying earthy being in the way of really being certain that everything that each thing is really an existing thing, these have it in them that completely in them existing is the thing they know inside them that everything each thing really is really existing. As I have said often there are many variations in this thing and there are those having this being who come from the way of having this being in them to be certain that not anything is really existing and all that is complication and I have been telling I will never be ending my telling of all these kinds of ways of being but again and again I am certain that the resisting kind in men and women have it in them to be certain as a bottom being that really each thing is existing. Now some as I am saying of the resisting kind of them are of an engulfing kind and these too are certain that each thing they are engulfing is really a thing really existing. These then too have it that sensation is in them more poignant than emotion, that a thing existing is nearer knowledge in them than things being in relation. The attacking kind in men and women are just the other way as I have said and I will be saying. The resisting kind in men and women are such then, they have complete realisation naturally in them that things that each thing is really existing. Now see what is true in them. They have this in them, they have curiosity and imagination based in them on the real realisation in them that each thing is existing. Yes. In a kind of them of which Alfred Hersland is one this is not solid in them although the being in them is this kind of being in them. This realisation of things being existing is in such of them but these being comparatively intermittently resisting and engulfing their curiosity and imagination is sometimes quite often disconnected with the realisation that things that each thing is really existing. These can have it in them to be aspiring without being then founded in them on a realisation that each thing is existing, these then can have engulfing passion in them that does not really seize the thing they could be realising as really existing. These then come to be quite considerably in their living that they are a part of a being. Curiosity can in such of them turn into cleverness in living for it is not then based in them on the realisation that each thing is really existing.

This is being in Alfred Hersland. He liked being with Arragon, he had really musical realisation in him then and always he could have it in him. He liked being with Arragon, liked realising music with him, he had also very much then in him a pleased feeling of being doing everything in living with Arragon that Arragon was doing then in his living. Mostly Alfred Hersland did what he did in his living, did with them what others did in their living as being something he was then doing but there was in him with Arragon a little more important and pleasant feeling of himself to himself inside him by doing with him with Arragon what Arragon was doing then in living. Alfred was beginning then a little too to pass this on to his brother and his sister, this was the beginning of being a little aspiring and also a little being a head of family living in his being. He had really then some realisation of musical meaning, he did then everything he was then doing with Arragon and he was doing then pretty nearly everything Arragon was then doing in living. This then is the beginning the little beginning of middle living in Alfred Hersland. As I was saying Arragon was not then very important in Alfred Hersland, he himself inside him not really yet in being was really the only important thing inside him in Alfred Hersland could be the only important thing really inside him. In a way Alfred was not one really to be deeply influenced by anything and that is a natural thing in him. In his middle middle living he was really more effected by some, all his early middle living, all his young living he certainly had none to be really important to him in him or for him, he was different inside him at different times in this living, sometimes more sometimes less to himself inside him in him, but always then he had his being in him and always then in a way the whole of him was part of being, and always then he was doing everything he was doing with those living near him and mostly he was doing everything they were doing in living, and sometimes he was quite sometimes not so much important to himself inside him, and always in a way he was never in being in living cut off really from rich american living. He knew at this time as I was saying Olga who was Ida the sister of the first governess the Herlsands had had living with them, Ida was then a school-teacher, Alfred laughed at her, he liked her, Arragon liked her, there was not much history of this liking for her. Sometimes Alfred saw a good deal of her, once he wrote her a real love letter. She was in a way angry then and told him he was not a good man and should not come to see her. Arragon thought there would be some history of a feeling in himself for her, he found out for himself and from what Alfred told him about himself and her that there was not being really a history in either one of them knowing her. She was in a way a queer one to mostly every one knowing her that there was not a history in any one's knowing her. I will try now to describe her.

I am having a glimmering of understanding two, one a man and one a woman and they are very different from each other and with them are very many and a considerable number of them have been silly ones almost without any meaning in being almost not being themselves inside them to my feeling, being such very silly ones as to me almost not to be existing, being like funny things in dreaming and now they are to me connected with some who I am really understanding then having flavor of something as being a complete thing to them. How can there be existing a flavor when there is nothing to have the flavor, that is foolishness in talking, there are many who are often all their living thinking they are being this thing. These are a kind of them, I will tell about them. Now I am thinking of some who are not to themselves existing in a flavor they are not to themselves existing in a way as something they are realising, they have been to me very often so disconcerting, they were silly ones to my feeling, they are not silly ones to most every one knowing them, I am seeing a little now perhaps that they are existing.

These then I am describing, I will keep only those just now in my feeling those having in them one kind of being not a mixture in them. I was describing the being in Alfred Hersland that made of him to me to very many knowing him a part of a being. He has in him only one kind of being but as I was telling pieces of it get separated off from other pieces of it by not being completely acting, flavors, reactions, by-products get disconnected and keeping on going in him and things get all disarranged in him so that this one is a part of a one in living, the bottom in him resisting and engulfing is not rich or thick or solid or ample or active enough in acting to make a complete being in my feeling in him, and always then that is there as being in him. These that to me in their living were silly ones not having any existing not from doing silly things but from there not being any connection between what they were seeing and doing and feeling and saying and always it all went on at once and kept on being all the being in them ; these then are like this to me now, they are in a way of the flavor group which group as I was saying have it in them to be believing that flavor is existing without anything to be making a flavor without anything being a flavored thing. These then that I am now describing who were vague and silly ones often to my feeling pleasant ones often to my feeling, astonishing often to my feeling, disconcerting often to my feeling, these then live but they do not make themselves important to themselves in it. Those ones I have been understanding were to themselves important in the flavor living they were feeling in them and these then I came to understand by realising the bottom being in each one of them and sometime I will be giving a very interesting description of many kinds of these kinds of them who are to themselves living a flavor life in living, are to themselves only a flavor in their being, I have an interesting collection of these kinds of them and the being in them and passion and affection in them and the kind of flavor they are to themselves in themselves and the kind of flavor they are to every one to some one knowing them but all that very interesting collection I know in my living I will not be just now describing, very likely I will not describe them for some time yet as I am liking to think of describing them. These then these others I have commenced now describing are in a way connected with these these I have commenced now describing who are so vague and disconnected and puzzling and are saying and feeling and doing and seeing all at once and there is not any connection any one can be seeing and it is not in them as it is in some that bottom being in them is so slow in acting that other things in them are making confusion and bottom being never arrives in them to be doing anything, no these are different from these, everything in these is going at the same rate in them only the action is so vaguely in them that things in them do not keep in connection and these then are not to themselves inside them in the way of making themselves to themselves inside them to be themselves in them. These then live in a life but they do not make themselves important to themselves in it. One is at bottom a fairly dull not too stupid, fairly solemn, unthinking, believing, lethargic, not completely non-poignant resisting person, and this one is actively living doing all little things stubbornly because it is pleasant tasting and lively doing pleasant living in a vigorous interesting fairly delicately sensitive constant state of appreciation. The other one the woman is a practical, anarchistic, attacking, servant girl person not feeling any difference between being a dirty one or a clean one having ugly things or nice ones in anything near this one, having a need for seizing everything to use in a servant girl fashion and always this one is living a life of independently loving beauty in living having justness in appreciation and needing a delicate flavor in loving and not keep anything that does not want to be kept by this one. These two then to themselves are not really important inside them from either being in them, they are really actively living what I am calling the flavor living and passively living the other living. Olga who was Ida whom Alfred Hersland and Arragon knew once as I was saying is in a way like these only living in her is a very much more exciting occupation to herself and to a good many a little knowing her in her living. She was a stupid resisting, stagnant, dull fairly sensible one in bottom being and this being was so stagnant in her it is very hard ever to be really certain whether she was of the resisting or attacking kind of them but really she was of the resisting kind of them. This being as I am saying was stagnant being in her and as vapor there was in her a nervous almost crazy kind of asking every one to be a lover to her and this was in her and she was a substantially pretty good-hearted honest round one and so not any one can understand that there is never any history in any man ever knowing her when she is always so constantly asking every one to them to be a lover and to keep on making love to her and she was always then going on with them. This was living in her, this was being in her. To herself she was not living really in either way of her living, she was really living both of them and to herself inside her she was never certain that she was living in either one of them, in the two of them. The one she is actively living the nervous sexual asking to be object of all loving, the other one she is passively living. This then is the being and the living in Ida and so then there was not any history in the knowing of her in Mr. Arragon, in Alfred Hersland. A good many who were young laughed a good deal about her, many did not believe that any one could ever think they could want to have her and really there was never any history in any one's knowing her really, and she was a little confusing to herself sometimes then and very much a puzzle to very many others then. This is all I know now about her.

This then is certain that not any one really was very important in the living of Alfred Hersland in his young living. As I was saying he knew a good many then, he was doing with them what he was doing then in his living, he knew a good many then and he was doing in his living with them what they were doing in their living then. I have described some of them. As I was saying the family of Madeleine Wyman were sometimes trying to be pleasant with him. The mother Mrs. Wyman could flatter him but she did not really flatter him and that was not an unpleasant thing to his feeling but he did not for that want to see her again. Sometimes he was quite a little with Madeleine Wyman's brother and her younger sister but not enough to be different really in him from knowing any other one in his living. The older Wyman daughter could be pleasant to him by taking an interest in him but that was only in him as making a little less flattering what her mother had left on him. Really there is not any use now remembering more about them for him. This was all young living in Alfred Hersland this I have been describing. There was more young living, of course there was a good deal more young living in him. There was young living in him, there was his being inside him, he lived the living of those he was then knowing and soon then he went to Bridgepoint to begin his middle living. He went there and then he came to making a living and to marrying Julia Dehning and to knowing a fair number of men and women.

The Hissen relatives were glad to see him, it was very pleasant for them to see one of their sister's children, and to know really that the Gossols living was existing, really existing. They were pleasant cheerful quickly curious and always a little doubting and it was pleasant for them to see Alfred and to feel him and to ask him how his mother was and to hear him and to see that though he was a fairly tall one he looked a little like them and was very pleasant in liking them. The Hersland relatives too saw him and for a while he lived with his aunt and she was interested in him but it was not such a pleasant thing in her and at first he was very much with the Hissen men and women and he was a little tender with them. He liked being in Bridgepoint and he began studying and he played the violin a good deal then and he was with his relatives a good deal then and he began to know then some who knew them and others then and he was very nice then and he had a pleasant feeling of living in him then.

It was very pleasant being in this Bridgepoint living, it was very pleasant to him to be seeing, as it is to Gossols' children, many relatives who knew him and had seen him when he was a baby and were thinking then in seeing him of his father and his mother and he was in them the only one, and it was very pleasant for him as it is for Gossols' children to hear the thunder cracking and the lightning shooting and the leaves piling up and then snow coming looking white and then dirty when he was looking up to see it falling and then it was pleasant for him to see skating and then to see a green spring beginning, it was a pleasant thing like it is to some to hear a cuckoo sounding and to be slowly convinced by some one that it is not a clock but a live bird calling. It is a pleasant thing to come somewhere and be having such a thing happen a very pleasant thing. Alfred had a pleasant feeling and with the Hissen men and women quite a pleasant tender feeling in him in his living and to them all then he was a pleasant one quite a very pleasant one and to himself inside him then he was pleasantly being with every one. He had in him then the feeling Hissen people naturally have in them and he was to them too then a tall one and coming from Gossols and being of them and it was pleasant and they were curious and they stayed around him and were touching him then to really feel him and he was of them and he was pleasant inside him and he was a little tall for them and he and they liked him and he was living with a Hersland aunt then and this was the beginning of Bridgepoint living in him.

This was pleasant feeling in living that Alfred had then. This can come to those living in Gossols and knowing some and being happy enough in living and enjoying doing things and then such a one coming to many with a pleasant feeling of every one knowing every one and every one knowing that one and every one a little curious and remembering and touching that one to be interested in remembering and at the same time feeling that that one is a tall one, this is very pleasant to some who have been all their living living in Gossols, not at all pleasant to some who have not been living in Gossols, not at all pleasant to some who have been living all their living in Gossols, it was very pleasant feeling in Alfred as I have been saying.

This is a comforting thing in being a great author inside one that always even with much lonely feeling and much sighing in one and even with not pleasantness inside any one just then when it is a very sombre burden then that one is beginning having coming saying that pleasant living is a pleasant thing and to be explaining how some are liking pleasant living. Not every one is liking pleasant living. Alfred as I was saying when he first came to Bridgepoint living was liking it very much that he was then in pleasant living and then he was a little being in love and that was then almost still pleasant living even though the Hersland aunt with whom he was living was trying to be interfering and was just a little breaking into for him the pleasantness of pleasant living he was having then. The Hissens were a little interfering then, were sometimes having hurt or angry feeling, but that was for him then not a part of not pleasant living. Certainly for quite some time Bridgepoint living was for him pleasant living. He had some loving in him then, he had some tender feeling in him then, he was liking music very well then, he had pleasant living in him then, he had aspiring in him then but it was not yet then come to be in him as something that was to be an active thing in him to make living for him in him. It was quite sometime later then that he met Julia Dehning.

Alfred of course in his feeling loving was feeling it differently in him at Bridgepoint than he had felt loving when he was in Gossols. Mostly until he met Julia Dehning he was not very seriously feeling loving, that was really true though of him, in Bridgepoint before he met Julia Dehning, the second year that he was living in Bridgepoint and studying he was really feeling loving in him, he wanted then to quit studying and earn a living in a business so that he could then soon be marrying and this was very troublesome then to his Hersland aunt with whom he was then staying who was not willing that he should be loving then to marrying and then Alfred's mother came to see him and she was supposed to stop him from marrying but really she was ready to let him and was ready to give presents to all of them and then it was over in him because the girl then was gone to another city and was writing then to him. One of the Hissens aunts, one who was married to a gentle Hissen man made fun of the girl then to Alfred and did it very often and did it very well then and did it with letters he showed her that the girl wrote to him and then his mother who had been a princess to the rest of the Hissen men and women, so she must be to them being herself to herself inside her then and having been living in Gossols to them, went home then and all the Hissens then helped Alfred to not want then to be marrying although then he was not being so much with them, he was not any longer then feeling full up in him with the pleasant living they had in them, he had not then any longer in him tender feeling pleasantly in him. He always liked them well enough all his living but they were not then at all filling him full up with pleasant feeling. He went on studying then, he came then to know more and more men and more and more women and three years later and then already perhaps his father was beginning the losing his great fortune and his mother was beginning completely weakening and Martha was beginning to have her trouble seriously in living and David his brother was coming to Bridgepoint too to do more studying, these things in the living in Gossols were not then really important in Alfred Hersland when he was coming then to know Julia Dehning, Gossols living was inside him then pretty completely not any more in him, Hissen living was not then any more in him, he always had his own being in him he had now pretty completely his own living in him, in a way now a little he was not quite doing in his living what every one near him was doing, he was not doing then in his living, whatever he was doing with them. This then is really completely then beginning of middle living in Alfred Hersland and this is to be now more regular history of him. There will soon be ever so much description of being in Julia Dehning and in every Dehning and now a little I will be telling a little more of beginning middle living in Alfred Hersland in his first beginning Bridgepoint living.

He knew a number then in these days of his early Bridgepoint living but mostly not any of them were later in his living, those who were later in his living were some that I will be later describing. In the beginning living he was interesting to some as realising musical meaning, and mostly then he was pleasantly young and quite tall and always giving romantically scientifically restrained superior information and playing the violin not very well but always able then to be directing the one playing with him. There were then women and men who liked him, not enough to make it very different in him from those he had been loving in his early living, but he was a little older now and soon he was quite a good deal older and he had been really loving then and he had been assisted in not loving by his aunt Hilda Hissen who did this very nicely for him to herself then and to him and he was ready then soon to be one who was one to be impressive to Julia Dehning as I was very long ago saying. This then was the beginning of middle living in Alfred Hersland. David Hersland his brother came to Bridgepoint then, he found some letters that Alfred had forgotten that the girl had written to him and David made fun of Alfred then and soon then Alfred was loving Julia Dehning and this was to David as to Alfred too a serious thing this living and then this marrying by Alfred of Julia Dehning. This was then the complete beginning of middle living in Alfred Hersland.

I wish every one knew every one and liked having me telling them about the being that each one has in them about the kind of one each one is of men and women. It would be a very complete thing in my feeling to be having complete lists of every body ever living and to be realising each one and to be making diagrams of them and lists of them and explaining the being in each one and the relation of that being to other beings in other men and other women and to go on then explaining and realising and knowing the complete being in each one and all the kinds there are in men and women. Not many find it interesting this way I am realising every one, not any I am just now hearing, and it is so completely an important thing, it is a complete thing in understanding, I am going on writing, I am going on now with a description of all whom Alfred Hersland came to know in his living. Mostly no one will be wanting to listen. I am certain. I am important inside me and not any one really is listening to me. I am wishing every one knew every one and wanted to have me make diagrams of all the kinds there are of men and women and the place in this diagram of each one. It would be very contenting to me and I am now not beginning again but going on with my explaining and describing and realising and knowing and being certain.

I see so many who I am very certain will not be at all interested in my being certain that each one is himself inside him, that each one is of a kind in men and women, that I can make a diagram now including a very considerable number of kinds in men and women and that sometime I will be able to explain the being in each one and make a scheme of relations in kinds of being with each one having in them the way of eating, thinking, feeling, working, drinking, loving, beginning and ending, feeling things as being existing of their kind of being, with sensitivenesses and suddenesses and impatient and patient and dependent and independent being of their kind of them and succeeding and failing of their kind of them and I will be able to make groups of them and it will be such an interesting and such an important thing in my feeling, in my being, and I will be making groups of them of each kind of them with some of each kind of them succeeding some failing some in between succeeding and failing, some having more of something of their kind of them in them than other things of their kind of them and each one then I am ever knowing comes sometime then to be such a clear one to my feeling and I could want to have every one know every one so that each one could see the meaning of my explanation and always I am certain that so very many I am always knowing are not wanting to completely listen to me in my explaining and many are not understanding that they must be hearing me completely and they are not doing this thing and here I am and I am certain, at least I am mostly always certain and yet always I am of the dependent independent kind of them and always in me there is quite a good deal always of dependent despairing and always I am knowing and always I will be knowing always now I am certain that mostly those I am knowing do not want, cannot be completely listening and it is such a complete being in me and I am important that is certain and here I am full up now with knowing that mostly those to whom I am explaining are not completely hearing.

Alfred Hersland was in Bridgepoint doing in the beginning very pleasant living. He was not remembering then very much of his Gossols living, and then he was not remembering very much his pleasant tender feeling in the pleasant living he had in him with the Hissen men and women and young men and women and the young men and women that knew the young Hissen men and women. He always had a little remembering in him of wanting to be marrying the one he did not marry then and always he remembered his aunt the aunt who had married a Hissen man, who had slowly shown him that this one whom he wanted then to be marrying was not one to have him. He remembered this very well, he did not remember much about the Hersland aunt who interfered with him. Alfred Hersland was a little not very good at remembering but he remembered more or less about wanting to have married one then although he never later wanted that. he had married this one. He did want for quite some time very completely certainly to marry this one and this one certainly then wanted to be married to him but he did not marry this one.

When Alfred Hersland came first to know Julia Dehning he was not remembering any longer very much in him any of the early Bridgepoint living that he had had in him. He was remembering as I was saying sometimes then that he had really wanted to marry one and he remembered then that he had been living in Gossols when he had been a very young one. This was mostly all his remembering then. He was then not really knowing any he had been knowing when he was beginning Bridgepoint living. His Hersland aunt was then connected with him. She knew Mrs. Dehning. The Hissens were not then connected in him with him, not that he had ever had any quarrel with them but always in living in mostly every one there is a keeping going that keeps making different ones come to be connected in them with them and now then as I was saying Alfred Hersland was coming to know Julia Dehning. As I was saying there was not then in him really any family Gossols living, really not any Hissen Bridgepoint living. The loving that I said he had in him when he wanted to be marrying and earning a living in some business so he could be married without waiting that lasted about two years before it was completely ended in him and then there was about a year and a half in him and then he came to know Julia Dehning.

There are then resisting and attacking kinds in men and women. Alfred Hersland is of the resisting kind of them, Julia Dehning of the attacking kind of them. The resisting kind as I have been saying and having not been yet complete in telling, the resisting kind of them are naturally and ultimately completely certain that things have really ordinarily materially existing being, they are existing, they are in relation, they have quality as beauty and smells and use and perhaps purpose and perhaps many other kinds of meaning but always then for the resisting kind of them they are really existing, having existing like any dirt in any field or in any road or any place or any garden. These then are of the resisting kind of them and these then have the ways of thinking and feeling eating, drinking and loving and curiosity and obstinacy and beginning and ending and being dead and being living and working and resting and hoping and not hoping for anything in a way characteristic of this resisting kind of them. Now this is certainly true of them and at the same time what with engulfing being in them and misplaced parts in them and attenuation in them and delicacy in them in being so that they are reversing and dependent timid being in them and aspiring being in them, the being in them gets so complicated in them sometimes too when they have dramatic being in them and aggressive self-defensive being in them, all this can so confuse kind of being in them that even when they have not any attacking being in them as a good many have it in them it is very perplexing even to me when I have been looking such a very long time at one of them. For instance there are a kind of them that are really completely certain that to be dead is not to be really a dead one, that nothing is really existing, these are certain that nothing is existing except everything, they are completely certain that everything is existing, they are of the resisting kind of them they must be certain that things are existing, and they make everything existing and so lose out of existing anything. They lose themselves and everything in being certain that everything is really existing completely simply existing, that is resisting being having mysticism, this is quite common. This is a very complete religious kind of being and these are of the resisting kind of them. I am just mentioning this thing to show that resisting being can be very confusing to be understanding.

Those having in them attacking being the attacking kind of them can have mysticism in them that is very certain. Sometime I will tell all I ever can know about these things. Those having attacking being as mysticism lose themselves in attacking complete emotion, anybody can see how different this is from the way resisting kind of them have mysticism in them. The attacking kind in men and women feel and need and see and use relations between things as coming to them as ultimately realisation more completely even than things being existing. These then can have as I am fond of saying but am now a little tired of repeating emotion having poignancy like a sensation. This is the characteristic then of attacking being, that being in relation is more completely to them of things than things being existing. This makes them attacking as anybody can see by understanding. This is attacking being then. Julia Dehning was of the attacking kind in men and women. This is now to be a history of Julia Dehning and those Julia knew in living and of her marrying Alfred Hersland and of every thing.

Some have very pleasant living when they are very young men and women, some have anything but pleasant living in them then. Very many have quite pleasant living in them then and when they are writing it then in diaries and letters to themselves and others there is not very much pleasant living in them then. It is a pretty difficult thing to be remembering, in a way ever to be certain about whether one is having, has been having pleasant living. It is quite a difficult thing to know it in them to know it of them quite young men and quite young women whether they are whether they were having pleasant living A very considerable number of very young men and women are not having very pleasant living in them. It is very difficult to know it inside in one in remembering or in living whether one is having then pleasant living. Pleasant living is a very difficult thing about which to be certain. A great many are thinking that mostly every one is having pleasant enough living, a great many are thinking that not any one is really having pleasant living, a great many are thinking that some are having pleasant living. A good many are thinking every one should have pleasant living in them. A certain number are thinking every one could have pleasant living in them, I find it quite puzzling to be certain about any one whether they are having pleasant living in them. As I was saying Alfred Hersland in his early Bridgepoint living had quite completely pleasant living. I am almost certain. Later then living was exciting and interesting and gay and varied and absorbing and perplexing and sometimes disconcerting and sometimes uneasy in him but it was never again I am thinking quite so pleasant in him. Perhaps it was pleasant in him in his later living, it is very hard to be certain about any one about pleasant living in them, a very difficult thing indeed to be certain about this in any one at any time in the living any one has in them. Certainly his early Bridgepoint living was pleasant in him. This is quite reasonably certain. Later he was not remembering this early pleasant Bridgepoint living. It was not important in him. Really nothing was important in him until his first loving. He had always had his own being in him, that in a way was important inside him, not anything was really important to him until he wanted to stop studying to be marrying. It was his wanting to stop studying to be marrying and his then slowly not wanting that this one should have him that was important to him. He soon was forgetting his loving this one, he never was really forgetting having been wanting stopping studying and beginning working at anything so that he could be married then. He never really forgot stopping wanting to be married to this one. Not that that was really very exciting but it was important to him, more important than anything that he ever had had in his living. Later then he was older and was beginning to know Julia Dehning.

He always had his own being in him, he was always himself inside him. This always was in him. Sometimes he was himself to himself inside him, sometimes he was not so much himself to himself inside him. Mostly everything any one says about any one, that one says about that one in a way is a true thing.

He always was himself inside him. He was not ever really knowing what could and what could not come out of him. Very many are not ever really knowing what will and what will not come out of them. Each one is himself inside him, is herself inside her that is certain. Very many are not knowing what is in them to really come out of them. Very many are not ever coming to know of them what is in them to come out of them, many who in a way do know something of the being that is them. This is a pecular thing. Watching carefully repeating in each one, one can come then to know of each one what is in them each one to come out of them, many men can be certain of themselves that something else will not then come out of them, some one else can be certain about them that not any really different thing, different way of doing anything will come out of them, these can not ever come to be really realising of themselves inside them that something more completely so that it is different will not be coming out of them. This is very common.

He was himself inside him, of course he was, all his living. Always he was not realising that not any really different thing could come out from him. You see one has to be very careful about being certain what is being in any one. A great many are certain about what is being in some one and although they may not be altogether wrong about that one they mostly always are not realising all the being coming out of each one. You have certainly to be very fond of waiting, very fond of realising each repeating, very fond of understanding each one is always really repeating, very fond of waiting to be hearing, seeing, feeling a great deal of repeating out of each one to be at all ready to be realising the complete being in each one, to be realising what will not be coming out of some one. Mostly each one is repeating but mostly each one is not realising their own thing as repeating in them. It is a queer thing to me who am really entirely loving repeating that mostly not any one is seeing feeling hearing themselves as doing repeating. Perhaps it would not be pleasant to most of them, indeed very many of them are quite certain they do not at all love repeating. So then a very great many never can come to be realising what can and what really cannot come out of them. As I am saying one must be very fond indeed of waiting, of hearing, seeing, feeling repeating to be really certain about any one what can and what can really not come out of them. Sometimes one can be fairly quickly certain about some one and sometimes it takes quite a considerable time to be really certain but always it is quite well to be waiting a considerable time to be really certain from realising the repeating coming out of some one, what can and what cannot come out of that one. As I am saying very many a very great many are always beginning having a completely new thing coming out of them to themselves inside them or waiting to have something coming so completely out of them that it is really in that quality of being a complete thing to be a new thing to be coming out of them, and this is very common. It is really extraordinary that all the repeating coming out of them all their living is not discouraging but then mostly not any one is really loving being repeating and so each one can never be really certain about what can and what really cannot come out of them. Each one has their own being in them, each one is of a kind in men and women. Alfred Hersland as I am saying had his own being in him, he was not to himself all his living repeating, that is not quite true of him, he was to himself a good deal repeating all his living, mostly every one are to themselves a good deal repeating all their living but not really completely repeating, not repeating so that they can sometime quite soon even be considerably certain what can and what cannot really come out of them. Some are quite certain, quite a number are quite certain, a very great number are never really inside them certain. And mostly not any of them are to themselves all their living always repeating, some are of course to themselves all their living repeating, but mostly not very many are to themselves loving repeating of themselves all their living. So then very many are living, very many are aspiring, very many are arranging, very many are telling the being to be coming out of them in their living that can never be coming out of them and I am not now telling about young ones or about those who are failing in living, I am telling now about a great many who are living. Being always repeating the whole being all of one's living is such a lovely thing to my feeling. Mostly every one is saying they do not love repeating. I am realising the being in very many men and women, I am realising what can and what cannot come out of them each one and always I am loving all repeating, repeating all the being in each one over and over again is such a lovely thing for me to be realising. And yet mostly every one is telling that they do not love repeating, they do not think it at all a lovely thing, they are not repeating their whole being always all the time in living, something will soon be coming out of them to show every one what more being there is in them. And here I am almost all alone in really completely loving repeating, loving it that each one all his living is repeating all his being. I am now completely realising all the being Alfred had in him, I will now tell how in repeating it all came out of him. And always too now I will be beginning describing Julia Dehning.

Every one is always knowing the reason why they themselves are failing in succeeding. Each one is knowing certainly each time why he is not succeeding in living. Each one is always knowing why she is succeeding in failing. Mostly not any one has much of such a feeling about other ones why they are failing to be succeeding. Always each one is repeating in telling each time the reason for not then succeeding. Mostly as one gets used to hearing it from any one they get a little tired of that one. Each one then has their own steady complete reason for each time of not succeeding. Very many as I was saying are not learning about themselves in living. They are not learning about themselves from themselves in their living. The reason for not succeeding comes out each time freshly from them ; to very many then that one is always going on repeating ; that one then is always making a bright finding a discovering of the reason that one is not that time succeeding, that one is always fresh in discovering what is to every other one then an inevitable repeating not having really any meaning. It is a thing a great many are not doing, learning about themselves from themselves in their living. It is very satisfying to very many who are living who were living who will be living that there are reasons always then explaining each failing in succeeding. As I was saying Mr. Hersland's children told it to him later when they were a little tired of the impatient being always in him and when they were then not any longer at all afraid of his doing anything to scare them. He did not then really hear them, he was always fresh then as he always had been in discovering a reason for each failing of succeeding. Mostly of every one each one finds it of them that they are repeating discovering a reason for each failing. To themselves each one it is a specific thing each reason each time of failing to be succeeding, to mostly every other one sometime the reason each one is giving for each time of failing is repeating a completely feeble one. As I was saying there are quite a number always living, quite a majority in men and women who are not learning themselves in failing, from themselves in their living. I am now realising Alfred Hersland to himself inside him. Alfred Hersland in a way was not failing in his living in a way was not succeeding in his living. Alfred Hersland was not really learning anything from his being in his living but then really that was not an important matter in him, Alfred Hersland was not really a learning kind in living. He learned something that is certain, mostly he was aspiring in living, mostly he was not succeeding, mostly he was not failing in living. Repeating and repeating and repeating and beginning and ending and being a young one and then an older one and then an old one and then not any longer one one ; I am sometimes inside and sometimes including this realising. The relation of content and reflection, the relation of being and living, the relation of learning and stupid being, this is in me in my feeling, certainly in me now and I will be now doing expecting.

Alfred Hersland married Julia Dehning. They were not successful together in their married living, this is to be now a complete history of them and of every one connected with either of them.

Very many have it in them that they are throwing always off from them the little too much they are always having of everything. Some are not having really too much of anything, of everything, some are forgetting whether they have been having too much or not enough of everything in getting another thing, some are responding with complete excitement to each thing, some have enough excitement in them to be responding to that thing and being in a state of having excitement in another thing, some have it that they are always aspiring to be completely full up with a thing. Alfred Hersland had one way of being in him, Julia Dehning had her way of being. Alfred Hersland had aspiring in him to be completely full up with something. Julia Dehning had very much excitement in being interested in each thing and continuing and being interested in some more thing. Julia Dehning had very much excitement in being an interested one. They both of them were not failing in a way in the whole of their living each one, they not either of them were really succeeding in their being either of them. This is now to be a history of each of them and of every one.

Loving is a thing a great many are doing. Marrying is a thing a great many are doing. There are very many degrees of having loving in men and women. Loving is a thing each one is sometime doing in a way natural to them to be doing. Just at first I am thinking about six or seven who are doing loving. Alfred Hersland and Julia Dehning were doing loving and were marrying. I could give descriptions of lists of men and women who are sometime doing loving. I have just been explaining to one how one I am knowing just now is doing loving. I am feeling very much just now how two I am knowing are feeling in being loving. I am letting myself go into Alfred Hersland and Julia Dehning and the loving being they had in them when they came to be thinking of marrying. I will tell now a little about loving.

It is a simple thing for very many men and women for some of their living, for very many men and women for a good part of their living, for a good many men and women for all their living to be believing, to be certain that each one is really a quite nice one, every one is a nice one. This is really very very common. In a way it is a natural way of feeling

for after all for very many women and for very many men it is not a
reasonable thing that any one they can come to be knowing could be not
a nice one. It is such a very simple thing really to be certain that each
one in a way is a nice one, perhaps one can be certain of a way of loving
that one has that is not a nice way of having loving and yet really one can
not be really believing it in the way of knowing that that one is not a nice
one. Yes it is true the way of loving in that one is not a nice one but
then that one is a nice one and any one having that way of loving is not
a nice one and very many are then completely content in them that all
this is a true thing, that that way of loving is one making that one not a nice
one, that that one is a nice one, that that one has the way of loving that
not any nice one can have in them and very many find it inside them
completely satisfying to be completely certain of these three things being
all true of some one they are knowing. This is quite simply common.
I have been hearing some one saying this again and again and I have been
explaining the kind of loving being the one had in her that made that one
not a nice one and it all is completely satisfying. And it is quite an easy
natural way of feeling in very many women in very many men this way
of feeling about men and women. Some men and some women have very
much suspicion in them about mostly every one and these can have in
them do have in them these simple ways of being certain of niceness and
not niceness and not possibly niceness and quite niceness all in one. There
are some who are really completely certain that each one is a nice one,
sometimes such a one is really certain that some are really not at all nice
ones and some then have confusion in them for they can never come to
be really understanding how any one can come to be really not a nice
one. Thinking every one really quite a nice one is really quite common.
This is a very important thing in a way in having loving feeling and now
I will be describing a little some loving feeling some I have been just
knowing have in them. I will be describing just now some loving so as
to be realising the relation of feeling each one, some one, a nice one to
feeling loving for each one, for some one. This will bring me on then to
describing Alfred Hersland Julia Dehning loving and marrying.

There is one that is certainly a nice one. This one is certainly a
very nice one. I am knowing this one. I have been explaining this one
to some one who was and is and will be certain that this one is a nice one
and is certain that this one has a way of loving that is not a way a nice
one could have loving in them. This one then is really seriously a nice
one. This one is certainly a nice one. This one has a way of loving
that not any nice one could have in them. This one is certainly a very
completely nice one.

Mostly those who are complete ones in living have it in them that
content is at least as full as thinking, realising, questioning, loving, dreaming, talking, aspiration, beginning, ending, quite completely as full in

them and very many have it that this is not true of them and those these
then are sentimental or virtuous or finicky or enthusiastic or aspiring and
reflective or temperamental or eager or sudden or intelligent or a number of these things in living. This is very common as every one knows
of very many women and men. Alfred Hersland was aspiring in living.

The thing in one that may come and may not come to be loving
feeling in that one is sometimes concentrated, sometimes very diffused
in them, sometimes in lumps in them and sometimes in different ways
in them. Sometime I will be describing pretty completely ways of loving,
ways of liking oneself and other ones, ways of eating, ways of drinking,
the liking some kinds of eating and not other kinds of eating, liking or not
liking drinking, being wearied or not wearied with liking anything in all
the kinds I can come to know of men and women. Always ways of
eating, and things to eat different ones are liking are to me quite concentratedly exciting. Now then I am describing a little and pretty feebly
in a good deal of confusion a little about ways of having loving feeling.
As I was saying the one I am now describing had not had loving to come out
of this one as really feeling wanting to be loving. This one as I was saying
was a nice one. I know now a fair amount about feeling loving, quite a
good deal now, of that some are now quite certain. I will tell now a little
more about one. This one as I was saying was quite well known for being
a very nice one, a very nice one in dressing, in getting ready every day
for living, in being an engaged one who was not yet a married one.
This one then was quite known by being a very nice one, a quite delicately
nice one. This one as I was saying was seeing everything not nice ones
were doing when she was walking or travelling. She was a little vacant
in a way, this one. She had as I was saying being that was made up by
adding little pellets together which were never mingling. Each little
pellet had part of seeing everything not nice ones were doing. Being
made up of little pellets made this one a delicately nice one, an engaged
one who was not a married one. When this one made jokes about loving, about not being a nice one and this one did this quite often, it was
done with that part of each pellet that was always seeing whenever this
one was travelling or walking what not nice ones were doing. This one
as I was saying was really quite certainly a recognised delicately nice one.
This one was certainly convincingly a quite completely delicately nice
one.

Loving being, I am filled just now quite full of loving being in myself
and in a number of men and women. Loving is to me just now an interesting, a delightful a quite completely realised thing. I have loving being
in me more than I knew I could have in me. It was a surprising thing to
find it so completely in me. I am realising loving being in quite a number
now of men and women, completely realising for them, completely real-

ising in them loving being. I am loving just now beautiful loving, I am loving nice loving, I am loving just now every kind of loving. I am realising just now very much and quite some kinds of loving. I am thinking now that it is a difficult thing to be knowing without very careful waiting and then a little more waiting besides the waiting that was pretty nearly enough waiting how much any one is, what kind there is in any one of loving. A very great many have very many prejudices concerning loving, more perhaps even than about drinking and eating. This is very common. Not very many are very well pleased with other people's ways in having loving in them. Some are very much pleased with some ways of having loving and not with other ways of having loving. Some are wanting people to be very nice in having loving being in them. Some are pretty well ready to let most people do the kind of loving they have naturally in them but are not ready to let all people do the loving the way loving naturally comes to be in them. A very considerable number of men and women have different ways of having loving in them. I have different ways of having loving feeling in me I am certain; I am loving just now very much all loving. I am realising just now with lightness and delight and conviction and acquiescing and curious feeling all the ways anybody can be having loving feeling. I have always all along been telling a little about ways of loving in different kinds in men and women. I will tell now a little more about specific loving in some specific men and women.

Some are never really knowing how much or how little they can be loving. Some are never really knowing how much they are loving. They are looking at some one they are loving and they are thinking they are not really completely loving they could very easily be forgetting the one they are loving, and then they are completely full up then with loving, and they never at any time can be realising that really they are loving more or may be less than they are thinking they are loving. I can understand this thing, I cannot really ever be really realising that I can really be having really loving feeling. This is perhaps more common in the resisting than in the attacking kind in men, at least it would be a very natural thing if it were a common thing with those having resisting being as their way of having loving feeling. There are then kinds in men and women and each kind has a way of loving that in a way is common to each one of that kind of them. As I was saying, now as I am saying some know very well the complete feeling of being a loving one inside them. It is a very wonderful thing when one is not certain with loving to be seeing some one completely certain in having completely quivering, complete loving feeling, to be all loving and certain that they are really all loving. There are then attacking and resisting kind in men and women. There are sensitive attacking, and trembling attacking, and quivering attacking, and obstinate attacking, and rushing attacking, and piercing attacking, and cowardly attacking, and withdrawing attacking, and steady attacking, and enthusiastic attacking, and mystic attacking that is attacking to lose itself in complete emotion, and narrow attacking that is destroying everything that is not to be there as an object to be attacked to exaltation, and ambitious attacking, and sullen attacking, and quick attacking, and planned attacking, and necessary attacking, and sudden and intermittent attacking, and confused attacking, and dutiful attacking, and troubled attacking, and slow attacking, and stupid attacking, and wobbling attacking and then there are engulfing resisting and simple resisting and vacant resisting and surface resisting and yielding resisting and stubborn resisting and solemn resisting and earnest resisting and seductive resisting and fiery resisting and intermittent resisting and attacking resisting, and confused resisting and dulled resisting, and emphatic resisting and sympathetic resisting, and fearful resisting, and very timid resisting and trickly resisting and suspicious resisting, and embracing resisting and in short there are very many kinds of ways of having loving feeling in men and in women.

As I was saying some are not ever really certain they are really loving and they are looking at one they are loving and they are thinking they could easily be forgetting that one any one they are loving, that not any one is really loved by them, that they are really not having loving feeling that is real ever in them and such then are wondering, and adoring one really having certain loving feeling. It is a very wonderful thing to such a one, one not being certain that some one can have complete energy complete certainty in loving, that some one can have emotion to have poignancy like a sensation. Such a one, one never really believing that the feeling in them is really loving feeling can perhaps come to believe it of themselves by experiencing that always they are spontaneously acting as if they were completely loving, and repeating in them of such action sometimes does convince such a one. They know they are loving because they are doing what some one who is loving would naturally be doing and this gradually brings conviction to them. Some turn it then into a sentimental feeling so as not to lose it out of them, a few keep it as really needing to be constantly repeating to keep them in their conviction. This then has been a description of some loving.

As I was saying a great many have prejudices about people being loving. Some say alright all but one way of loving, another says alright all but another way of loving, some say not very many kinds of loving are right loving, some say all ways of loving are really ways of having loving feeling. I like loving. I like mostly all the ways any one can have ot having loving feeling in them. Slowly it has come to be in me that any way of being a loving one is interesting and not unpleasant to me. That came very slowly to be in me. I like loving then as I am saying. I will tell now then a little more about loving in women and in men.

Sometimes it is very puzzling that so many are certain that they are really loving some one. Sometimes I am wondering about how they can be so very certain. And then they have so many ways of thinking out the loving in them. And then they have ways of beginning loving and ways of ending loving very many men and very many women and ways of marrying and not marrying that certainly are puzzling and believing that they can and cannot bear to be loving and not living, they can and cannot be learning loving, and ways of being brave and being cowardly with loving and with those that they are loving that are very complicating. Sometimes some one who is always ready to be fighting and ready to kill and be killed by any one when he thinks it right for him to be an angry one sometimes then such a one being really wanting to be completely dominating in loving, being an attacking one gets frightened and has a feeling of loathing when one who is not any longer loving him though he is still loving that one threatens to really injure him. How should that one knowing that the other one is not any longer loving be so afraid when the other one threatens to really injure him. Is it that until then he could never, he being an attacking one, could never really realise that the other one was not loving him. Why should a courageous one be afraid when one who has once loved him threatens to hurt him when he would not be afraid earlier or later of that one. Is it vanity or the bitter feeling of being really an abandoned one lonely and suffering because some one is really positively not loving that one. I think it is in mostly every one, in certainly a good many women and men a kind of the last one left on earth all alone feeling when they are realising even when they are not any longer loving that one that some one really truly completely actually does not any longer love them. But all this is just something that is happening. Now I am telling a little more about loving.

Alfred Hersland and Julia Dehning came to have some loving feeling and then they came to marrying. I am beginning again a history of them.

I was seeing one to-day who reminded me very much of another one I have seen doing very much loving and both of these certainly are in a way in living that is a natural way to feel about the being, the acting and the living in them. These were in a way quite different ones these two in their complete living I am certain but they both being of the resisting kind in men and women were and are and will be so completely on fire always every minute in existing that they are not really ever resisting anything and being of the resisting not of the attacking kind of men and women the fire of it is burning any one besides being just burning is burning that one by accident of conflagration, are burning themselves by accident of being themselves in a fire that is burning. I know just now two of such of them, one of such of them I know quite well in all loving, the other one I am just seeing sitting, standing, running, looking, a little in talking, breathing and I will not be seeing any more in living, I have not been seeing any more in living. The loving in such of them is naturally from the being of them what any one understanding now the being in such can be realising. All the ones in between these and engulfing ones, between these and completely resisting ones are existing. I have seen quite a number of them. I am seeing these days very many kinds of men and women. Sometimes now I am tired out and irritated and not at all amiable about them because they are not some of them like any other one I have been knowing. Sometimes then now I have a very irritable feeling in looking and sometimes some one these days and I am looking steadily at them are very completely illuminating a kind in men and women. I am these days seeing men and women. I am these days looking and looking and looking at them and then I am all worn out and irritated by being wearied with seeing and not seeing being in them. I see a very considerable number just now of men and women. I am wearied and not weary with my learning always more and more and then not being really ever certain. I am a happy one, that is quite reasonably certain. I am quite a very happy person. I am quite completely a very happy person seeing very many men and women.

I am listening just now to many women loving one, a resisting one who is not burning. This one certainly is not burning, not burning himself or any one by conflagration. This is one of the resisting kind of them I have been describing not having any weakness in him and all the romantic strength of intelligent and active genius to very many knowing him. This gives in him some appearance of burning to some. One having as I was saying being like wood cut and excellent and hard and sometimes made into shapes very fanciful and delicate and perhaps symbolic but always being solid wood cut and not sensitive to being a weak thing by being a thing having sap flowing. This one then as I am saying is always being one having many loving him, insisting upon loving him, clinging adoring, following, needing him. He is having very many kinds of women always loving him. He is a very nice man really in his loving. He is sentimental a little and solid and firm and gentle and complete in loving and not any longer loving.

Sometime I will describe very many who are loving in their living. I have now described some, and I am feeling very many loving everywhere in living. I am feeling a very great many men and women, I am feeling a very great many men and women doing loving. More and more I will be satisfied with every kind there is in men and women of being, doing loving. Now I am really beginning again about being in Alfred Hersland and in Julia Dehning.

Alfred Hersland as almost any one can tell now by remembering was of the resisting engulfing kind in men and women, not a very complete one in being, fairly aspiring in being and in living, not really failing not really succeeding in the whole of the living in him, not completely certain

that to be dead was to be really a dead one, not quite completely entirely
utterly certain that to be dead was not to be really a dead one. Julia
Dehning I am just beginning describing. Julia Dehning was of the attacking kind in men and women. Julia Dehning was of the kind of attacking
kind who mostly are spending their living resisting being at bottom changing in their way of doing any attacking. They are attacking with some
excitement everything to mostly every one seeing them, really they are resisting all their living any changing in their feeling of attacking. In a way
then at bottom they are mostly all their living not having any
stimulation. Mostly to every one they are excitedly every minute being
stimulated by something. I am going to tell a good deal now about attacking being. I am beginning preparing myself now to be courageous to do
this thing. I am feeling a little weak now in courageous feeling as is quite
common in my living. I am remembering and remembering attacking
being. I am a little realising this thing. I am beginning again now remembering realising attacking being in men and women, in Julia
Dehning.

Hopefulness is to me very interesting. Any one expecting anything
to be coming out of them, being fairly certain in being a hopeful one is
to me fairly interesting. There have been in me feeling very nearly to
being a completely miserable one in having another one fairly certain of
having something coming from them, of being fairly completely a hopeful one.
There are very hopeful ones having resisting being or engulfing resisting
being in them, there are hopeful ones having attacking being. I will
now soon be describing hopeful being in men and women having attacking being in them. I have been pretty miserable sometimes seeing them,
hearing them, feeling them. I have been quite very miserable hearing,
feeling and seeing some, some are having complete hopefulness of enthusiastic or excited or passionate attacking being. I have not had a miserable
feeling from seeing or hearing or feeling attacking hopeful ones who are
completely fighting ones or pushing ones or winning ones in living. I
have not been miserable about them, not at all, I have not been miserable
for them the excited or enthusiastic or passionate ones, not at all, I have
been a miserable one because I have been always a little pretty nearly
certain that I would be ending failing and every one enthusiastic or passionate or sensitive or excited in attacking would then make me a jealous
one, a miserable one having a sad and sombre feeling, being certain that
to be dead was to be really a dead one and that I pretty nearly certainly
would be always being nearer and more nearly a completely dead one.
I had very much such being in me and I was a sad resisting depressed
jealous one then and now I am telling this thing.

Attacking being and resisting being have each their way of having
hopeful feeling. Some have very much hopeful feeling, some have less,
some have none, some have pretty nearly none, some not any at all really

hopeful feeling. Each one has their own way of having in them certain feeling, hopeful feeling. I am loving to know every one having or not having hopeful feeling in them, certain feeling in them. I am wanting to know every one who ever was or is or will be living, all the being in each one of them, all the kinds there are of men and women, all the ways each one has anything ever in them everything they ever have in them in them.

It is certainly a very queer thing to be certain sometime about some one that they have been all their living that kind of one in their being. It is certainly a most queer feeling of dreaming that one has in one when one is certain about some one of the being in them and then is remembering the being in that one that was in that one when one was not really knowing that one very well but still quite well. It is a very queer feeling of dreaming that one has then. It comes then sharply to one then to be deciding whether one is really then ever certain about anything, any one. And yet I certainly am certain that sometime I am really completely knowing some one and very often I have in me a queer feeling like dreaming. It is then a curious thing in feeling to be coming to learn to know very completely any one. I have come to know very completely now, pretty nearly completely now Julia Dehning and I am now beginning to tell all the being in Julia Dehning as I have been learning to be realising the being in Julia Dehning. Julia Dehning was of the attacking kind in men and women. I have mentioned this thing. Julia Dehning was of one kind of the attacking kind in men and women. I have told a little about this kind of the attacking kind in men and women. I will slowly quite slowly I am hoping be telling the complete history of Julia Dehning, I will slowly certainly fairly slowly be describing all the being of Julia Dehning, I will be always telling a very good deal about attacking being in men and women. I will be telling a good deal about hoping and loving and liking to be a cold or a hot one in the attacking kind in men and women. I will be always somehow managing to be remembering learning being in Julia Dehning. I am writing the history of Alfred Hersland and Julia Dehning and of every one pretty nearly every one they came to know in their living, of pretty nearly every one who came to know them or to know about them. I am remembering always that each one is repeating always all their being, I am remembering that very often I am very much not knowing what they are saying to other ones, what they are feeling, how they are not feeling and doing what I am thinking and hearing they are saying and doing, I am remembering that very often they are having being in them and I am supplying in them in my feeling what they certainly have not been having in them. In short I am remembering and I am a little melancholy with it in me now I am quite certain. I would so be content with knowing everything. I am giving now a history of Alfred Hersland and Julia Dehning. It is puzzling that each one has had being in them and have been repeating the whole being of them and I have not been hearing seeing feeling all the being in them. Yes it is certainly true of them of very many men and very many women I have not been hearing more than a part of the repeating coming out of them. They are each one always repeating all the being in them. I am certain. I am hearing always very much repeating coming out of each one I am ever knowing. I am not hearing anywhere nearly all the repeating coming out of them each one I am ever knowing. I am always hearing, seeing, feeling repeating coming out of each one I am ever knowing. I am knowing kinds in men and women. I am not hearing a wonderful amount of repeating always coming, I am now quite certain. I could be so happy knowing everything. I could be enjoying so much having curious feeling about every one if always more and more I could certainly be hearing, feeling seeing all every bit of repeating coming in any way out of every one. I am enjoying having curious feeling about every one, I like every bit of repeating I am hearing, I get an awful sinking feeling when I find out by an accidental hearing, feeling, seeing repeating from some one what I have not been hearing, feeling, seeing as repeating in this one and then I am saying if it had not been for this little accidental thing I would not have known this repeating in this one and it is so easy not to have such an accidental happening. Alas, I say then, alas, I will perhaps not really ever be knowing all the repeating coming out of each one. I know some of the repeating coming out of Alfred Hersland and Julia Dehning and some others whom they knew and some others who knew them and I will now be describing what I am desolately feeling is all being in them. I am desolate because I am not certainly hearing all repeating, I am almost sulking. I am beginning now to go on with my history of the Dehning family and of Julia Dehning and of her marrying and of the Hersland family and of Alfred Hersland and of every one they any of them came to know in their living. To begin again then from pretty nearly the beginning. I am remembering everything I have been telling. I am always loving all repeating. I am realising kinds in men and women. I am realising Alfred Hersland and Julia Dehning. That is I am certainly somewhere near to a fairly complete realisation of them and of some whom they knew each one and who came to know them either of them. I am a little tired now with all this beginning again. I am hoping that I am going on again.

The Hersland family living was different from the Dehning family living. The Dehning family living was that of right very rich american being. It was the living of the Dehning family being and the living of the Dehning family living, very rich american living. The Dehning family was different from the Hersland family. There was Mr. Henry Dehning and Mrs. Dehning and Julia Dehning and George Dehning and Hortense Dehning. They were each one themselves inside them, they made together then a family living, they were living then right very rich american living. Mr. Henry Dehning had his being in him, Mrs. Dehning had her being in her, Julia Dehning had her being in her, George Dehning had his being in him, Hortense Dehning had her being in her, this is to be now the history of all the living in each one of them, of the family living they had in living, of the living they had each one with each one of the others of them and with themselves inside them, this is to be the history of every one almost every one they ever came to know, any one of them in living, the history of every one who came to know of them to know of any one of them, of any one ever connected in any way with them, in any way with any one of them. There are a great many men and women always living. This is to be now some history of some of them.

Mr. Henry Dehning was a foreign american, he was living then the living of a very rich american, he was a very different kind of a person from Mr. David Hersland. They never met in their living. This will have been and will be a history of both of them. Mr. David Hersland as I have said was full up with beginning and later full up with impatient feeling. Mr. Henry Dehning was not at all the same kind in living as Mr. David Hersland. Mr. Henry Dehning was married to one who was of the attacking kind in men and women, Mr. Henry Dehning was a resisting kind of them that was so diffused in smoothly and compactly resisting that he seemed to be always steadily to be attacking. He would very often not be hearing what any one was saying to him. He was a very nice man, he was quite entirely almost a good man. He was pretty nearly completely a quite successful man. He was loving to his wife and to his children, he was ready to listen and to understand any one's wanting to be doing something. He and his wife lived together like very many good men and women, his wife was not too good a woman but she was a good woman, not a bad one. She was pretty harsh in any attacking, he was not gentle but he was smoother in resisting. They were really very nice and good and pleasant and successful and happy and content in married living. They both came to be a little worried with being old ones and having to take care of their own and each other's older troubles as older people come to have them with the body wearing they have then in them. She made him do what she wanted him to do, he made her do what he wanted her to do, they made each other do what they wanted each other to do, very much less were they doing this thing with their children. They were very rich american man and woman living very well the right very rich american living.

I have been telling very much of Hersland family living. I will now be telling something of Dehning family living. I will be giving some history of each one of them. Mr. and Mrs. Dehning were really very nice very rich good kind quite completely successful a little troubled american man and woman. I am now beginning repeating with fuller repeating the living in them, the living they had in their living.

The Dehning family each one and as family living was different enough from the Hersland family each one and Hersland family living. The Dehnings as I am saying were really always all their family living living the living as right very rich americans. Mr. Dehning as I was saying in the beginning of writing after he was born came to America quite a poor person with brothers and sisters and a mother and a father all quite poor like him and he was quite a nice one then and he came to be quite a very rich one. Mr. Hersland came to the making of a large fortune out in Gossols as I was saying but as I was saying he was not in his family living living right rich american living. The Dehnings were all their family living living the right very rich american living. They were really very nice ones in this living, they were very different from the Herslands when the young Dehnings came to be knowing the young Herslands. The Dehnings were living completely nicely as family living very rich right american living. Each one of them of the Dehning family had their own being in them, all together they had a family living in them.

Mr. Dehning was quite a good man, a good business man, a good enough citizen, a good husband to his wife and a good enough father to his children. He was quite a careful and generous and kindly man and always could be fairly made by his wife to do what she would have him, he was also fairly ready to listen to his children when they wanted anything in their living. He was as I am saying quite a good man, a quite good man in business living, a quite good man quite entirely a good man in his family, in his daily living. He came to be an old man and was then a little shrunk then from outside him. His wife was sick then, a good deal in taking care of him, keeping him from eating what was not good for him, keeping him then from smoking which was then bad for him, keeping him then from any excitement of business living which was then a thing the doctor had quite forbidden to him. Later then she was a sick one and while he was shrinking some away from the outside of him, she died from too much coming to be inside her for her living. She left him then wishing he had been the one to be the dead one for the sake of the children. She knew he certainly would be needing something to fill him, something to warm him now he would be shrunk away a little from the outside of him. Not any man certainly not the man she had known all her living could not be managed to be married by a woman and then there would be trouble with money and her children and it would have been better that he had been the first one to be the dead one and then she would have been handing the money over very entirely to the children. She was the first one to be a dead one as I am saying and he did not as a matter of fact marry any one but it was it is surely certain a little struggle for his children with a sister-in-law and some one else to help him to keep him from marrying. All this will be told later in the history of George Dehning and Hortense Dehning and Julia Dehning.

As I was saying the Dehning family living was very different from the Hersland family living. Mr. and Mrs. Dehning and Julia and George and Hortense Dehning all were living all their family living completely and pretty nicely and quite pleasantly and fairly freely right very rich american living. They lived it very well then. It was quite a pleasant thing in them. It was not quite entirely a pleasant thing in them but it was quite a good deal a pleasant thing in them. There were five of them Mrs. Dehning and Mr. Dehning and Julia and George and Hortense Dehning, this is to be now some description of them again and some description again of family living in them and some description of some people knowing them. Then there will be more description of the marrying and married living of Julia Dehning and Alfred Hersland.

One is telling and I am hearing that there is not a need in every one to be a courageous one to do ordinary living. Some are doing ordinary living without any need in them to have courage in them to do that thing. Very many are needing very much courage in them to do that thing, to be every day completely living ordinary living. For some it takes courage to be killing anything, like a buzzing thing or a fly, to buy anything, to sell anything, to eat anything, to drink anything, to remember anything, to want anything, to forget anything, to decide anything, to like anything. Some and some one is telling this to me and I am listening do not need courage for any such thing. The attacking and resisting kind in men and women, those having attacking naturally do not need much courage for just daily living. Mrs. Dehning did not need much courage for daily living, Julia Dehning had so little that she needed as courage for daily living that it went over to her being too energetic not to be nervous in her daily living. The nervousness of attacking and resisting being is interesting. I am now beginning to be ready to completely feel being in Mrs. Dehning. I am a little not ready yet to feel being in Mr. Dehning. I am almost ready to feel all being there is or was or will be in Julia Dehning.

It is a very difficult thing to believe that any one has seen everything in anything and that one has just glanced at that thing and you have had to be looking very long at that thing. Some one has just glanced at a book and you have read that book and the other one knows everything in that book, in short the other one is a quick one and you are a slow one, it is a very difficult thing to really find it convincing that that one has really been reading that book in such a quick glancing. That one is telling all the things in the book that is certain, to mostly every one any one being a slower one or a quicker one in detail of daily living is an astonishing thing, a thing very difficult to be realising a thing to be believing because of its being a thing every little minute is proving, a thing that always is a little not a real thing like seeing any slight of hand performing. It is a very difficult thing being really certain of anything any one is doing in any kind of a way any one is naturally acting. I am beginning now to be describing Mrs. Dehning. Mr. Dehning is not completely in me yet, I am certain. Mrs. Dehning is quite in me, I am certain. Mrs. Dehning is an attacking, a harsh continuous, not too quickly, fairly good, attacking one. She was to herself and to every one a good enough one in all her living. This is to be now a description of her being and a little description of all her living. She was an attacking one, she could be a very gay and cheery one, she was a pretty stupid one, she was fairly quick and not a very quick one. She was an important one. She was important to herself to every one. She was a little a lonesome one in dying, she was knowing that her husband who was a very good man and a very devoted one would be needing a woman to fill him, she knew his children should not want for their sake that he should marry some one. She was a little a lonesome one in dying.

When he was sick, Mr. Dehning, she could make him do what she wanted him to be doing by doing quite excited attacking. He could make her do what he wanted her to be doing. They were to mostly every one not very sweet in their living together then, really then they were quite sweet in their living together then. They could each one make the other one do what they wanted the other one to be doing. Mrs. Dehning could be a cherry and quite gay one, she was quite an ambitious one, she was a crudely attacking one, she was not a very quick one, she was quite completely in her being feeling a stupid one, she was to herself important to every one, she was quite really an important one, she had a good deal of sense for living, she was mostly then a quite good enough one.

Mr. Dehning was quite entirely a mostly good enough one. He had quite a great deal of sense for living. He was not in feeling a very stupid one, he was quite in feeling not a stupid one, he was not a gentle one but he was quite a complete one, he was then for very many a gentle one, he was not really a gentle one, he was quite a complete one, he was quite a good one to be listening to any one who wanted to be doing anything, he was quite a completely successful one in living, when he was an older one he was a little a worried one from being an old one, from not being really a complete one in his children who were not in him complete ones, who were struggling ; his wife always had been in him to be him a complete one although she was a crudely harsh one because she really had some sense for living because really she could and always did make him do what she wanted him to be doing because he always could and did make her do what he wanted her to be doing. They were pretty even then altogether in their living, in their being, in their being quicker and slower, attacking and resisting, having courage and patience and sense in living, having ambition and success, and failing a little in coming to be old ones and dying.

This is to be now more history of both of them, not so very much more description of the two of them.

There was then the Dehning family living, the right very rich american family living. There was then the Dehning very rich good enough family living. Mr. and Mrs. Dehning were very completely living very rich american right family living. They had country house living and city living. They had both of them sense for living, this is now to be a considerable amount more of description of them.

There are many who like it in their living to have more ready than they can be using. Mr. Dehning was in a way such a one. Mrs. Dehning was not in a way not such a one. Mr. Dehning was such a one, was believing in being such a one. Mr. Dehning was quite certainly such a one. Mr. Dehning was a very successful one quite entirely a successful one, Mr. Dehning had always in living more ready than he needed to be using, than he could be using, than he was using. Mrs. Dehning was not such a one. Mrs. Dehning was not such a one by her own being in her but she was one having it in her to be realising always completely inside her that they had it in them as family living, all their family living to have more ready than they were using. They were quite reasonably pleasant in this thing. Mr. Dehning was entirely justly pleasant in this thing. He had this being in him he had always certainly more ready than he was using. This made him what he was to every one this with the rest of being in him. This is to be now a little more description of him. Certainly he had it in him, certainly all his living to his dying, that he had more ready than he was needing to be using.

Mrs. Dehning was not an old woman when she came to be a dead one and she looked a younger one than she was then. He was not an old man a very old man when he came to be a dead one. They were both of them living and dying and dead ones of the right very rich american living. This will be now more history of the Dehning family living. This is to be now more description of Mrs. Dehning and Mr. Dehning. Mr. Dehning was always believing in having a good deal more ready than he was using. Mr. Dehning was always ready to be listening to any one wanting to be doing anything. Mr. Dehning was quite a pleasant one to have as a father to any one. He was to himself an important one to be giving advice and to be listening to any one who really wanted to be doing anything. He was a little an important one inside him from believing that every one should have more ready than they were needing. He was to himself an important one from always certainly having more than he was needing. This was important being in him. Being ready to listen to any one who was wanting to do anything was important being in him. Being an attacking one was important being in Mrs. Dehning. Being a very rich one was important being in Mrs. Dehning. Being the mother of children with whom she was showing was important being in

Mrs. Dehning. Making Mr. Dehning do what she would have was gay and satisfactory important being in Mrs. Dehning. Mr. Dehning and Mrs. Dehning each of them had important being of themselves to themselves inside them, each one of them was an important one in living. This is to be now more description of them.

Mrs. Dehning had nervous being, that is to say she had attacking being and very often that was exciting to her being and made her have in her nervous being, later in her living when Julia was leading Dehning family living Mrs. Dehning had nervous being from being one a little following feeling being one leading in attacking. Later she had nervous being with lonesomeness and walking in a restless fashion and wanting to be having something like a dog she had once only she was afraid then that when she would lose him she would be afraid that another one would not be a nice one. She had nervous feeling then of being very certain that she had been all her living a good woman, a good enough woman and an important one, an important enough one and now she was telling this thing again and again and Julia was not happy then nor succeeding then in married living. She was then, Mrs. Dehning, taking very good care of Mr. Dehning, she was sometimes then very attacking in making him do something that was good for him. They were living then being important in each other making each other do something then good for each other one to be then doing. Mrs. Dehning was not such an old one when she came to dying. As I was saying she was certain if Mr. Dehning had not been left by her being a dead one he would not make it harder for every one by wanting to be marrying again as any man being left certainly would want to be doing. Mrs. Dehning certainly was very worried about this thing as she was certain that he would be living when she was not any longer living with him. Mrs. Dehning as I was saying was one having attacking being. This is to be now some more description of her.

Mrs. Dehning was not an unpleasant one. No certainly not, Mrs. Dehning was not an unpleasant one. She was not a pleasant one. This is to be now some more description. Mrs. Dehning was an important one. She was an important enough one. Mrs. Dehning lived very well the Dehning very rich american living. She was in a way a gay one, she was very often quite a gay one, she certainly was very often very unpleasant to very many having a pleasant time when she was among them. She was very often not a pleasant one. She was in a way a stupid one, she was by way of stupid being that was being in her crude in attacking, in being an important one, she could be as I was saying and certainly was a nervous one. She had sense for living, that is certain. Now I will tell more of Dehning family living.

Mrs. Dehning was a whole being. It is very difficult remembering the whole being in any one. It is very difficult remembering the whole of them of any one. Realising the being in them as attacking or resisting is very good for remembering the whole being in any one. Mrs. Dehning was an attacking one. She had sense for living, she was not then a really stupid one. She was not as strong as her attacking, she was then not such an important one as she was in living, she was a stupid one in being unmeaning in being a harsh one, she was a nervous one in being one following because her daughter Julia was leading, she was a gay one in being one having life in her being, she was a good one in making her husband do everything that was good for him when he was a sick one, she was not a bad one in living in not having any need to oppress any one to her being. She was one then who was living the very right rich american living all her living. She was one not having this living as an unpleasant thing, she was one having stupid being in harsh attacking for not any winning, she was in this thing quite completely a stupid one. She was not an old woman when she was a dead one, she was a completely stupid one in attacking for not any winning. She was attacking for not any winning very much in every day of living. She was in such attacking a stupid coarse and not a gay one. She was a gay one in having her being alive in her all her living. She had sense for living in having been making her husband do what she needed for her living he should be doing, in having been doing all her living what he needed she should be doing. This was being then in Mrs. Dehning. This is remembering all the being in Mrs. Dehning. All this I have been telling is remembering all the being in Mrs. Dehning.

Mr. Dehning was a whole one in living. He lived after Mrs. Dehning was a dead one. He had then luke-warm being needing to be warmer to be really living. He was a dead one without coming to be again a really warm one. This is very common. This is very common when a man is an old man needing to be careful of eating, drinking, smoking and everything and his wife is a dead one and he has grown children and he is a rich one and he likes to be again a quite warm one. Mr. Dehning was really a quite good enough man for all living, for any kind of living he ever could have in him from his beginning to his ending.

Mr. Dehning could listen to any one wanting to do anything. Mr. Dehning could listen to his children to any one of them wanting to do anything. Mr. Dehning was not really listening to Mrs. Dehning when she wanted that he should be doing something. As I said of them he did what she needed he should be doing for her living in her being, she did what he needed she should be doing for his living in his being. He was of the resisting kind in men and women but really he was not to any one resisting, he was always listening to any one who wanted to be doing anything. He had really sense for living. He lived very well very rich right american living. He had lived all of his living. He liked very well all of his living. He would have been liking it better if his children had been more actively succeeding. He was very well doing all of his living.

He liked it very well that he liked hearing what any one could tell him that they wanted to be doing. He liked it very well with every one, with any of his brothers or his sisters or their children. He liked this completely well in him in his living. Mr. Dehning lived very well, quite completely well very rich right american living. There will be now some more description of him.

When he was a young one he was most likely quite a good one, not a very exciting one, quite a pleasant one, entirely an efficient one, quite a pleasant one. He was then very likely a reasonably social one, a little a quiet firm good one, a little a one wanting a woman to own him by attacking loving. He was one then probably a little then sometime telling a little to some one what a good one should be doing in being one doing living.

I am thinking, I am knowing, when I am reading, when I am hearing, when I am seeing, when I am writing, when I am talking, that very many are not feeling thinking believing what some one thinks every one is naturally believing feeling thinking. Mr. Dehning as I am saying often was a man more and more in living always listening to any one wanting to be doing anything. Really then he was listening to any one wanting to be doing anything, really he always had sense for living, really sense for living, really though he was believing that each one in a way was believing feeling being something that some certainly are really never believing feeling thinking.

Mr. Dehning very likely when he was a young man and then when he was beginning middle living was one who sometimes was telling what a man living the life a reasonably good man should be living should be doing. He was a man who all his living really was not ever really failing. He was a very rich american. He was married to Mrs. Dehning. He had three children Julia, George and Hortense Dehning. He had playfulness in him in living, he needed his wife to be owning him by attacking, he needed to be a wise man in pleasant advising, he needed to be an important man by being always ready to be listening to any one wanting to be doing anything. There will be written now some history of him.

He was a man who came to be by living living very completely the living of a very rich american. He was a man in his later living quite reasonably often telling the history of the living he had been all his living doing. He was a man many were likingly admiring without ever thinking much about what he was in all his living. Certainly when he was a young man and a man beginning middle living he was one having very much sense indeed for living. When he was quite a young man certainly he sometimes then was telling some one what a man living a reasonably good kind of living should be doing all his living. Surely all his living he was quite reasonably a fair man to be living with men, with women, with children. He always more and more was ready to be listening to any one who really wanted to be doing anything. This was all being in him, all that I have been describing. He came to be an old man a little luke-warm inside him and wanting then to be a warmer one. This is certain. I think I have been telling for just now enough history of him.

This then has been now a little description of Mrs. Dehning and Mr. Dehning, there will be now written a little more description of the Dehning family living, there will be then be written a description of Julia Dehning. The history of George Dehning and Hortense Dehning will be written in the long history to be written of David Hersland and that will be written after the complete writing of the loving and the marrying and the being and the living in Alfred Hersland and Julia Dehning and ever one they knew and who came to know them or to know about them. I am going on then now telling about Dehning family living, about Alfred Hersland and Julia Dehning loving and marrying and living.

I like very well to know it of each one what kind of living they have been, they are doing, they will be doing in living. I like knowing the living in each one. I like to listen to any one, I like to hear the living they have in them, I like to know the kind of feeling, thinking, doing each one has in her, has in him. I like to hear everything. I like to know all living. I like to know the living in any one. I like very much to be realising every kind of living. I like very much to be realising in each one the living they had, they have, they can have in them. I like so very much to be really feeling every kind of way there is of having living feeling. I am always more and more realising that not any living any one ever is or was describing is not existing. There are so very many kinrs of ways of living, of feeling living always existing. I like always to be listening to stories of feeling living. More and more and more there are to me many kinds of ways of feeling living. I am remembering my beginning feeling kinds in feeling living. I am certain I cannot ever be realising any more kinds of living, of feeling living than I will have been hearing from some describing. I certainly never will be knowing all the kinds of ways there are of feeling living. Of that I am really certain, I am always feeling I can perhaps not certainly but still possibly come to be realising pretty nearly all the kinds there are in men and women. Perhaps I cannot but I certainly have a very good deal such a feeling. I certainly am knowing I certainly will not be realising very many kinds of ways of feeling living. I have just been a little beginning this thing, realising kinds of ways of feeling ways in living. I am realising fairly well the Dehning family way of living. I have a pretty helpless feeling with feeling all the kinds of ways there are of living, of feeling ways of living, of having ways in living. I feel like one a little beginning and certainly not going to be making very much of progressing. I am remembering

I always was very halting in realising ways of living, ways of feeling ways of living. I am learning but not really grasping these things in me, that is certain. I am loving to be knowing all the kinds there are in men and women, all the being each one has in him all his living. I am being then a very happy one in knowing kinds in men and women, in being certain that sometime there will be written a complete history a complete description of all the kinds there are in men and women. I am completely then living in being certain of kinds in men and women, in each one having their own being in them, in being certain that sometime some one will be knowing certainly all the being each one has in living, all the kinds there are in men and women. This is then complete being in me, complete living in me, the kinds there are in men and women, the kind of way each one has in that one to be naturally loving, working, feeling, anything, everything. I have in me completely halting learning in realising ways of living in men and women. I have learnt some. I am learning now some more, a fair number more from some one. I am haltingly learning, beginning learning this thing, I am remembering how each kind of way of living was a thing not real and having been needing that I should be convincing myself that it really was really an existing way of really living. I have not with ways of living that slow openness of steady realisation, that joy in always being certain that it is repeating, I know ways of living are repeating, I am not realising them as repeating, I know it of them, I do not really truly feel it in them. I do not know whether I am clearly expressing now a feeling. I will sometime begin again telling how I am not really realising ways of living.

I am realising each one always sometime. And just now I am seeing each one having something, some kind of thing in them that is interesting that I was not naturally seeing they were having. That is making for me a new way of feeling living. I do not know whether I am liking this thing. I am of the resisting kind in men and women. I am not very certain I am liking it that I am beginning a realising a quite new way to me of feeling living. As I was saying it is not a natural thing to me to be realising ways of feeling living. It is a natural thing to me to be realising in each one some being, a good deal of being, sometimes all the being they have or can have or did have in them. To me ways of feeling living is different in some having in them almost quite completely the same way of being. As I was saying the Dehnings had in them very rich right american living. That is then one way of feeling living. As I am saying I have all my life not naturally been learning realising ways of feeling living. I am now being taught by some one that some have a way of feeling living that I have not ever been realising. I like it although it is to me upsetting learning anything I am not naturally learning. I have been learning all my living very much that to me was upsetting as being not to me a natural thing to be learning. If it is to me completely a not natural thing to be learning I certainly am ending with not having been learning that thing, I will be knôwing sometime whether it is not a completely not natural thing for me to be learning to be realising, ways of feeling living with different kinds of living.

The Dehnings then were then living, very pleasantly, quite entirely decently, not very aggressively, pretty freely, quite contentedly, fairly advancedly, thoroughly generously, quite gayly, pretty entirely cheerfully, right very rich american living.

As I am saying I am learning just now to be seeing in each one things that are interesting in them that it is not certainly easily natural for me to be observing, realising of them. This is leading to being more open to realising ways of feeling living that are different to different kinds of ways of living. I like seeing things in each one that are interesting, I even in a way like learning seeing a new way of seeing new, to me, things in them. I like it in a way I say, I find it hard to let myself not resist at all to this thing. I am resisting, I am too doing this thing. Sometime I will know what I am now doing. That is just now to me a little a comforting thing. I am beginning again going on telling the history of the Dehning family living, of Julia Dehning, of her marrying and loving and living and learning or not learning.

The Dehnings liked living. They all did that thing very well, quite well as people go, in doing this thing. They all of them all of the Dehnings liked very well being in living. They all had in a way some sense for living. This is to be now some history of all of them and of the living in them.

They all quite entirely liked living, all five of them. They all went on living up to the end of their living. This is to be now the history of each one of the five of them, of all of them. This is to be now a history of Dehning family living, of Mrs. Dehning and Mr. Dehning and Julia and George and Hortense Dehning. I am beginning now this history of all of them. I am beginning now with Julia Dehning, in her family living, in her married living, in all of her living. There will be all the time then now a description of the living of all of them of the Dehning family living then. I am beginning now again.

Some have all their living nervous being, nervous feeling. Julia Dehning had quite a great deal of nervous being the bigger part of her living. Some have nervousness from sensitive being in them, some do not have nervousness from sensitive being in them. Some have nervousness from ambition in them. Some have nervousness in them pretty nearly all of their living. Some do not have nervousness in them in their living and then it comes to be in them and then they come to be dead ones or perhaps really crazy ones and it is a very difficult thing to know it of some one whether nervousness is just nervousness or will be something stronger in them. Very many have very much nervousness in them all of their living. Some have nervousness from sensitiveness in them, some from ambition in them, some do not have nervousness in them most of their living. Julia Dehning was not such a one. Julia Dehning had nervousness a good deal in her in her living, it was not in her from sensitiveness, it was not in her from ambition, it did not come to be more strongly in her, it was always all her living a good deal in her, it was not excitement in her, it was attacking being in her being resisting to any changing of her way of having attacking being. This was in her all her living. This is now to be some history of her.

Living having meaning to any one doing living, being living, this is a thing very many are feeling, being certain in, denying. As I was saying Mr. Dehning and Mrs. Dehning had each one of them in their own way sense for living, in some way living had in them for them really meaning. Mrs. Dehning was saying when trouble came to them she could not really understand it that any one having been so reasonably charitable to every one should have it that things should happen to their children but always then she would go on being a good woman because she was always certain to do this thing, so she was saying. And later then when her children were not thinking about her being in her in living she did not then see any reason why she should go on thinking about what it was, all that she could do for them and with their father for them but certainly she would be going on doing everything for certainly she always was a little certain she would go on doing everything. She had then as I was saying sense for living. She was of the attacking kind in men and women, she was nervous with being one attacking without needing, without feeling winning, she was nervous with being not following not leading in her children's later living, she was not nervous with winning attacking in living her living with Mr. Dehning, with many men and many women, she was nervous with very much attacking and this she had always in being with harsh attacking for not any winning, she was not nervous in being a gay one in living, she was nervous with not following and not leading in her children's later living. Mr. Dehning was not a very nervous one, he was a nervous one in dying, in being a sick one for dying, he was a nervous one in sudden action in being one not warm enough for living in his later living. Mostly in his living, in his broad careful even resisting, in his listening to any one who wanted to do anything, in his feeling that sometime each one should do a right thing, he was not nervous in living. Julia Dehning was a good deal of her living a nervous one. This is to be now some history of such a one, of some of such of them.

The Dehning family living was then a fairly free very rich very decent right american living. As I was saying in the beginning of telling Dehning family living, the Dehnings liked country house living, they liked very well fairly free, perfectly decent, quite generous very rich right american living. They certainly did live this thing.

Julia was then the oldest of the Dehning children, George was con-

siderably younger and- Hortense was a good deal younger than George
Dehning, Julia was then the beginning of Dehning completely american
living.   This is a description of her being and of her living, of her loving
and of her marrying, and of all of her living.   Julia then was an american.
Julia had her own being in her, she was of a kind in men and women.
This is to be now a desription of being in her and of living in her.

Each one is inside them being that one.   Mostly every one has some
way of feeling living in them.   Each one has ways in them that are in
other ones living with them.

Mostly every one has living having some kind of meaning to them.
Very many like it that they are doing something, living, working, loving,
dressing, dreaming, waking, cleaning something, being a kind of a one,
looking like some one, going to be doing something, being a nice one,
being a not nice one, helping something, helping some one, winning,
conquering, losing, forgetting, being an influence in being a living one
being a dead one, having courage to be going on living, having a troubled
living, being a worried one, cleaning themselves all their living, learning
something, beginning something, forgetting something, ending something,
liking old things, leaving something, liking everything, liking pretty nearly
nothing, being disgusted with everything, liking new things, leaving
pretty nearly nothing, liking changing, liking being a quiet one, liking
fighting, being one making a peace between all men and all women, and
all women, and all men, fighting things out to finishing, being honest
in living, being failing for a reason, being just failing, being just succeeding, being lucky, being an unlucky one, being a really completely successful one, being one submitting to everything, being loved by every one,
being one submitting to almost nothing, being one certain that one should
be one submitting to being a good one, being hated by a good many who
come to know them, being certain of spending money, of being saving,
being one loving god, being one loving living, being one loved by god always
in being living, being one loving god and living, being one needing religion,
being one not needing anything for living, being one not needing any
one, being one not needing any religion to support them, being one afraid
in living, being one always shivering with living, being one not having
any realisation of shivering in living, being one liking eating, being one liking thinking, being one liking waking, being one certainly not afraid
to be dying, being one liking starving, being one liking to do anything,
being one liking to be resting, being one liking working, being one certainly
not afraid of doing anything, being one liking to be in pain for themselves
or some one, being one liking cold days in out door living, being one liking rainy days around them, being one liking hot sunshine on them, being
one certainly not afraid of anything, being one getting sick with cold
or hot or raining weather on them, being one not liking any fresh air
on them, being one not able to be breathing without much fresh air on

them, being a funny one, being one not liking funny ones, one not liking queer ones in living, being one liking swimming, being one tired of ocean bathing before they have really been in more than twice in a season, being one excited with learning anything, being one needing everything because anything was food to living for that one, being one being excited at leaving anything, being one learning always a little something, being one not thinking very much about anything, of any one. There are all these ways then of having living having meaning and there are innumerable other ones, do not crowd so on me all the other ones, I know very well there are very many other ones, I know very well I am not knowing all the ways men and women are feeling living, I know very well I am not knowing all the ways any one can have living have meaning. I know very well I do not know all these things. I know very well I could be very happy knowing everything. I know I am quite a happy one knowing something of being. Now I am always hearing of ways some have of feeling living and they come crowding and I am resisting so that I can be slowly realising and always I am knowing I can never really be knowing all the ways there are of feeling living, all the ways there are of having living having meaning. I am knowing something of kinds of being in men and women, I could know sometime, if I could know completely all I could be knowing, all the kinds there are of men and women. I am comforting now my feeling by saying this thing in my complete feeling again and again. I am beginning now a history of living, of feeling living, of living having meaning in Julia Dehning and Alfred Hersland. I have been telling something of the kind of being each one of them had in them. I will tell very much more about the being each one of them had in them.

Julia Dehning was all her life resisting any changing in attacking. She was always resisting not attacking and so she was an obstinate one not hearing what any one was saying. She was always listening to every one who had a way of doing anything, and had nervousness in doing it then, she was always all the time then resisting being any kind of an attacking one that she had not always been in all her living, she was harshly doing everything that she knew about from hearing any one who was doing anything and she was all her life resisting any changing in her attacking. She was then the daughter of Mrs. Dehning and Mr. Dehning as I am saying.

I know so well the kinds there are in men and women. I know so well the kinds that are connected and the way they are connected with other kinds in men and women. Julia Dehning was one having attacking being and she was completely a stubborn one to not hearing anything that was something to be a changing in any way anything in her attacking. As I was saying Mrs. Dehning had sense for living. As I was saying Mr. Dehning had sense for living. Julia Dehning was not one really failing in living, Julia Dehning was one not having really sense for living.

Julia was one having really to every one courage for living, Julia Dehning was of the independent dependent kind in men and women, she was of that kind of them and having power over those who were already loving with her, who were already overwhelmed by attacking being in her, she was one who was in a way certain that always some one would be there to hold her when the last end of failing came so that it would not touch her, to herself and to every one she was one not having any such dependence in her, she was one always fighting whether to winning or to losing, always courageous to be fighting, and in a way this was true of her and always there was there in her that some one would be there holding her when the last end of fighting was in her, though to herself and to every other one this was not in her as a thing she was needing for living, really though she could be not knowing she was not fighting by the strength of herself in her when the last end of fighting was in her and to herself then she was keeping going on fighting by courage in her in every one near her; really as I am saying of her she had not sense really for living in her, really she had not really feeling in her whether she was fighting for winning or for losing, really she had not faith in her that she was fighting for winning, really she did not have any feeling that was independent dependent one in living, really she had not really sense in her for living, really it was a very difficult thing to know this in her, to know she was not having any one do what she needed of them, that she was not ever doing anything any one needed that she should be doing, for really she was not failing in living, really she had much support and loving in living, really she was some a loving one in living, really she was all her living fighting and winning a good deal in fighting, always she was learning everything, always she was really living to herself and to every one. And yet she was completely not hearing, feeling, seeing anything that was in any way changing any attacking being she had all her living in her. She married Alfred Hersland whom I have been already a good deal describing, this is to be a history of the living and the being in her and of the slow learning her that was in very many knowing her. I will be telling now of how a good many different ones felt about her.

She was to mostly every one a completely honest one. She was to mostly every one an earnest, an excited and an ambitious one, she was to mostly every one one fighting to be successfully a winning one by steady fighting all her living, by courage in resisting being worn out by any one else's attacking, she was to every one one being one leading in all fighting she was doing all her living, she was one having complete conviction that thinking and working and being an interested one in everything was something giving meaning to her being in all of her living. This is to be now some description of the way some were realising being in Julia Dehning.

Many women like their children, some like children being as babies, some like children being young ones, some like children being older ones, some like their children being young men and young women, some like their children being young men, some like their children being young women. Julia Dehning liked her children as little babies which was surprising to very many who knew Julia Dehning quite well in her living, knew quite well her being. She liked children all their living, she used all energy to learn everything, she liked them completely as being little babies and this in a way was surprising, not really surprising perhaps but all the same somewhat surprising. Some women then are of the attacking kind in living, some are of the resisting kind in living. Julia Dehning was of the attacking kind in living. I have said sometime that it is the resisting kind that need to own those they need for loving. Now many of the attacking kind of them need to own those they need for loving but they need to own them by attacking them to hold them, attacking them to seize them and they can be doing this completely with a little baby being with them. Some resisting ones are completely loving children when they are little babies because then they are completely owning them by possession, by the baby being of them to them some of them. Some of the attacking kind of them being of the dependent kind of them like the little babies as then they are together dependent ones being together completely a dependent being. Julia Dehning was of the independent dependent kind in men and women. Sometime much later I will tell something of women and children with them. Now I will only tell about Julia Dehning loving and marrying and what some knowing her thought of her as she was then being.

It is a very difficult thing to really let one's self be certain that they are not sorry when every one is thinking they should be sorry, that they are not glad when every one is thinking that they are going to be a glad one, that they are not liking to be doing something for some one they are loving when that one is thinking they are glad to do that thing, that they are not pleased to see some one when it is a natural thing for them in their living to be glad to see such a one, that they are not moved by some one being suffering when they being reasonably tender-hearted should be moved then, that they are not remembering their own little needs when it is not a decent time for them to be mentioning them. It is a very difficult thing, some from superstition, fearing something bad will happen if they let themselves know that they are what not any one not having bad things going to be happening to them would be in feeling, some from natural conviction that they are feeling always what is right for them to be feeling, some from the sentimental feeling that it is such a nice feeling feeling the right way in living, some from not being really certain that to be a dead one is to be really entirely a dead one, some from being quite certain that to be a dead one is to be not at all a dead one, some from having a fear in them that then something will happen badly to some one, some from generous loving, some from enthusiasm, some from being really that kind of a one one having some such feeling, it is a very difficult thing to very many in living to let themselves be saying feeling thinking what they are thinking feeling saying when something happens to them happens to some one. I am saying this long thing because I am feeling that this is a necessary thing to be realising in learning knowing any one and yet it does very much happen that one is having very really much more feeling the way any one naturally is supposing they are having about anything about everything than they themselves are thinking they are having. I have been learning in my living all the being in many men and many women, in Julia Dehning. I am always wanting to be realising the whole being in each one of them, by feeling, by thinking, by knowing by talking, by remembering. I am going to be telling very soon now what very many felt in knowing Julia Dehning, what Julia Dehning felt in living, what being what kind of being Julia Dehning was inside her.

As I was saying she was of the attacking, the independent dependent kind in men and women. As I was saying she was all through her living resisting having any changing in her being one doing one way of attacking. As I am saying she had in a way not really a lack of successful living, really though she had not really sense for living. That is what any one now certainly can be realising.

Each one is certainly like some one, having something in them of the father and the mother of them. Mrs. Dehning was a stupid one in being one attacking harshly and not for any winning, and not tor any winning of anything, not for winning excitement or sensation or feeling or power or religion or good or bad anything or anything. Julia had stupid being in being completely one completely resisting any changing in her attacking. Mrs. Dehning was a nervous one as I have been explaining. Julia was a nervous one as I have been saying. Mrs. Dehning had really sense tor living. Julia had not really sense for living. Julia then was a young woman. This is now to be a description of Julia Dehning, of what others were feeling in Julia Dehning.

Some are knowing in living by their feeling that they are liking something. Some are not knowing by their feeling what thing they are liking. Some have so very much feeling that the feeling covers anything to liking, some have so much excitement in living that that thing covers everything. Some can need everything for anything can be food to them. Very many, quite a number are living and not telling by their feeling what they are liking. A good many are living and are telling by their feeling what they are liking. As I was saying Julia Dehning came to the marrying of Alfred Hersland. This is the way they came to be loving, the way I have told once, the way I am now telling.

Some liked very much the being and the living in Julia Dehning, some did not like at all the being and the living in Julia Dehning ; to some it was, the living and the being in Julia Dehning, not a pleasant not an unpleasant thing. Julia Dehning was not a harsh one in attacking without winning as her mother was in her feeling. Julia was a stupid one in resisting any changing in her being as attacking. Julia was a crude one then and in such a way a stupid one but not really a harsh one. She was one to herself and to every one having complete courage for living. Really as I was saying she had not really sense for living and so really then she had not really courage for living, she had completely courage for resisting any changing in her being in her way attacking, not really complete courage for this thing, she was of the independent dependent kind of them.

I am feeling attacking kinds a little harshly just now in me, I am now beginning again to have in me complete feeling of attacking being in men and women.

Attacking kind are often very sweet ones to very many, poignantly sweet ones and generous ones in living. Attacking kind often have it in them to be as bad, as harsh, as crude as they feel in them to any one because they know in living they are generous ones needing to be attacking some one to have them love them. I know this as certain. This gives to them the right to be harsh or crude or eager as they have it in them that they have it in them for living that they are generous in emotion, as they certainly are, in poignant feeling, the need of attacking to win what they are needing for living. Those having resisting being have it in them very often to be afraid if they are too completely resisting not any one will attack them enough to win them and they are uneasy then in them. This is certainly not true of all attacking and all resisting, these things I have been saying of attacking kind in men and women of resisting kind in men and women, it is true of quite a number of them. So then many of the attacking kind in men and women feel it in them as a completely natural thing to be as harsh as crude as active as eager in attacking as they feel it to have it in them. Many of the resisting kind in men and women have it to be very dubious about the doing all the resisting they have in them to be doing. Many have attacking being have sweetness and courage in attacking, and harshness and crudeness and eagerness in attacking. I am now thinking about men and women having it in them to be certain they are right in living.

As I am saying some knowing Julia Dehning like completely the being and the living she had all her living, some did not like it at all, some liked it well enough as I was saying. Some liked it and then liked it well enough and then did not like it. Some liked it very much and then liked it well enough. Some as I was saying did not like it.

To mostly every one Julia had complete courage for living. Slowly some came to understanding that really she had not sense for living, that she had almost complete courage for not changing any kind of attacking being she had in living. She had real courage in her, that is certain. She had sweetness in her that is certain. She had stupid being in her that is certain.

I will tell now more about attacking being, about enthusiasm, about being certain in living, about what other ones are feeling, thinking, saying. I know Julia Dehning. Certainly I know Julia Dehning. Yes of course I know Julia Dehning. Have I not certainly come to know Julia Dehning. I certainly have come to know Julia Dehning, I know Julia Dehning, I have known Julia Dehning, I am thinking I will know Julia Dehning. How do I know Julia Dehning, I know Julia Dehning as one at the end of her beginning living, at the beginning of her middle living, at the middle of her middle living. I know Julia Dehning as one having in her living marrying Alfred Hersland. I know Julia Dehning in the Dehning family living, I know Julia Dehning some as Mrs. Dehning, some as Mr. Dehning, some as George Dehning, some as Hortense Dehning, as each one of them, as each one of them then knew her in their living, in her living. I certainly do know Julia Dehning. How do I know Julia Dehning ? I know Julia Dehning as a kind of a one, as one of a kind in men and women. I know Julia Dehning having her being in her in her living. I know Julia Dehning being certain that she was a really living one. I know Julia Dehning being certain in being living. Yes I do know Julia Dehning. I certainly can say I do know Julia Dehning. Julia Dehning was one having being in her all her living and being quite an important one in living. Julia Dehning came to marry Alfred Hersland, that is certain. Julia Dehning was one always being one having completely courage for living in being one having completely living being in resisting being one having changing from sensitiveness in ways of attacking, in having changing from hearing, seeing, feeling anything in the attacking being in her.

I am remembering, really I never do forget one having being in her, attacking being in her and always to every one this one was one not having attacking in her but resisting being in her because this one had this being in her as being so like soft not set jelly in her that this one was one by her skin cutting her off from any other one and this one had attacking being that never did more than just wobble in her and any one moving at her was sticking in this being in her and so she was to every one a resisting one but really this one was of the attacking kind in men and women. Now I was telling how Martha Hersland had attacking being that was in her indeterminate nervous excitement inside her. Now I am telling of Julia Dehning that she was one having complete resisting to any changing in her attacking, as stubborness then to mostly every one realising this in her in her living, and was one not having really sense for living, one having really courage always in living, being one that needed everything for anything can feed her and now I certainly understand the relation in being between her and these two I have been just rehearsing as being and I am certainly certain I am certainly knowing being in Julia Dehning.

I wish every one was feeling being the way I am telling it now in my writing and that not any one could understand it without hearing me tell it as I am now doing. I could like that very well I think now when I am not remembering listening, when I am not remembering loving everything, loving being and repeating in every one. I think it would be so very nice if every one knew how completely it is a necessary thing to realise being the way I am realising being, and then I am explaining this thing, and then I am being one really explaining everything. I really do like being in every one and so I am very happy even with not every one really realising the important thing that I can explain being in every one, with hardly any one realising this thing. I am telling now the history of the living in Julia Dehning, a description of the being in Julia Dehning, and what I know of her being, what many know of being in her in her living.

I am thinking about how any one feels anything, learns anything. I am thinking about Julia Dehning. I am thinking about dependent and independent being, dependent independent, independent dependent being.

I am thinking about attacking being. I am thinking about how the attacking kind in men and women react to anything, I am thinking about the way they have sensitiveness in them. I am thinking about how I am going to be telling about the being in them, the attacking kind in men and women.

I have been describing some of the attacking kind in men and women. I must now I am thinking tell about being in some more of them.

I am knowing very well, I am knowing very many men and women having attacking being in them, independent dependent being. I am feeling some of them. I am realising many of them. Now I have it as something I am doing, describing being in the independent dependent kind, the attacking kind in men and women.

Sensitiveness to anything, to something in any kind of the attacking kind in men and women, the independent dependent kind in men and women is something I am now beginning describing. I know certainly in daily living sensitiveness in the attacking kind in men and women in independent dependent kind in men and women. I can certainly know what I am meaning by sensitiveness in them, I am now beginning giving what is in me as realising sensitiveness in being and independent dependent kind in men and women.

Sensitiveness is in men and women of the independent dependent kind in men and women, in those having it that they can have it in them that reaction is complete and poignant and quick in them so that they can have emotion as poignant in them as a sensation. This is in a way the foundation of my explanation. I am beginning again telling everything.

How has any one sensitiveness in living ?˙ They have it in them as their way of being. Now let me see, I who am realising now sensitive being in the attacking kind of them, let me see if I can say this thing now in the time I am living. Each one I have been knowing having attacking being, having their kind of sensitiveness in them is remaining in my feeling, they are crowding now in my feeling, they all have it in them to have sensitive being of the attacking kind of being of the independent dependent kind of being in them. They have then sensitive being some of them of independent kind of independent dependent being, they have sensitive being in them some of them of dependent kind of the independent dependent kind of being. Some have sensitiveness in them that makes of them that they are to themselves and to every one possessed by each one ever coming near to them. Some have with this kind of sensitiveness in them emotion, some passion, some practical desiring, some fear, some depression, some exaltation, these then are such having it in them that they are completely and always responding to any one coming near to them in the way of sensitiveness of complete reaction of realisation of the being of some one being near them. Some as I am saying have this with passion, some with emotion, some with intention, some with desperation, some with much lying, some with conviction, some with religion, many with feeling of knowing everything coming to be happening, some have it thickly in them, some thinly in them, some with much independent attacking, some with almost not any attacking, some with gladness in them, some with the desire of being an important one in living. These then have it in them that sensitiveness is complete and always in them to everything coming near them, it may be thick or thin, or stupid or dull or timid or aggressive in them, or fairly intelligent in them. These are then many of them very full of wanting always having new things in religion. These are very often having it in them to be very interesting to quite a number knowing them. Some are very sweet with this thing, some are very gentle with this thing, some are wanting to make money, or position or win something for some one with this thing. Mostly these then are not really succeeding in living. Some have with this thing sense for living in them, mostly they have not in them most of such of them very much sense for living in them. These then are not those having sensitiveness in them to mystic religion as being really in them. Those wanting to have mystic religion in them those of the attacking kind of them are those having it in them to be attacking complete emotion to be in that thing. Such have it in them to have complete sensitiveness in them to something they are realising as a complete thing to be attacking by a complete effort of being in that thing by the attacking by them of that thing. Such as these have it in them mostly not to have poignant passion in them but complete attacking in them and very many of them have not attacking in them only for religion, they have it for pure reason, for pure affection, for much succeeding in living, and mostly these then too very many of them though being very successful indeed in living have not really in them much sense for living. I know a whole lot of these in living. I hope I will be seeing that I am rightly realising the being in them and that it is as I have been describing and as I will be going on sometime describing.

Now there are some having attacking being in them having sensitiveness in them as passion in them and these can have it in them to be successful, to be failing in living, to be wise or foolish in living, to have sense for living, to have not too much sense for living, to have much, to have little sensitiveness in them, to have it thinly, thickly, intermittently in them, to be using it in every way in living, to have it very delicately in them, to have it fairly coarsely in them, but mostly these having it in them although they may be succeeding although they may be failing, are not really without some sense for living in them. They can be anything, some practical, some religious, some earnest, some careless, some ambitious, some critical, some very weak in living, some very intermittent in doing anything, all having passion in them as sensitive being.

Then there are some having attacking being as sensitive being as emotion in them, these can be quite melancholy often in living, these can be quite aggressive in living and to every one can be content and energetic in living, and self-satisfying and these can have it in them that they have trouble in having it as being that sensitiveness is in them as emotion, they can have it that they have not in them any power of resisting when they have it not in them to be practical in living. I know now some of such of them. I will certainly sometime tell more of such of them. Two of such of them are just now in my feeling every minute in my living.

Then there are some having attacking being that have sensitiveness in them as being really excitement inside but mostly these then do not have it in them to have sensitiveness really in them. Perhaps they have spots of sensitiveness in them, times for sensitiveness in them.

Now I will begin telling a little about how some come to learn or not learn in living. Always I am telling of the attacking kind in men and women. Always now I will be keeping on telling of the attacking kind in men and women until I have given a good description a really good description of Julia Dehning and what every one who knew Julia in living thought about the being she had in her all her living.

Surely every one has a way of learning something. This is now to be very little description of how some connected in being with Julia Dehning learn what they do learn in living, this then is connected with sensitiveness in them as is of course a natural thing as any one ever thinking about learning can certainly be understanding.

I am now understanding all the ways the attacking kind in men and women have sensitiveness in them. I am feeling some having attacking being in them having sensitiveness in them and I am not understanding what way sensitiveness is in them.

I have been seeing some, I have been knowing some some, I have been hearing about some having attacking being in them and I am not realising of them the way sensitiveness is in them. I have not been loving any of this kind in men and women, I would like to be loving some one some, of this kind in men and women. I would like to be knowing certainly the way sensitiveness is in them in this kind of the attacking kind in women and men. I am feeling some one of this kind in men and women. I know some thing of the character in them, something of the way they do some things in living, but they are a kind of them that are really different from these kinds I have been describing. I will not now be telling my troubles to every one. It is enough that I have been saying that I am not understanding all the ways sensitiveness is in the attacking kind in men and women.

I am realising some sensitiveness in some who have attacking being in them. Soon I will tell complete histories of each one having sensitive being in them. That will certainly be helping to make a long book interesting. I could tell it very completely now of some. I will not just now be beginning this thing. I am certainly now writing a history of being in Julia Dehning being living.

As I was saying some having attacking being in them, having independent dependent being in them have it in them to have sensitivenes in them as passion in them. I was telling about one having attacking being and having it as wobbling, having it as being in this one as a soft jelly mass making of this one an individual one by the skin of this one separating this one from any other one. I have been telling about attacking being in Martha Hersland, in Mr. David Hersland in Redfern. I have been telling something of attacking being in some others because I was telling then about such other ones. I am remembering pretty completely everything I have been telling. I am always thinking I am not remembering what I am going to be telling what I have been telling but really I am remembering pretty well what I have been telling, what I am telling, what I am going to be telling. Now I am telling about some ways of having sensitiveness and learning in some having attacking being, independent dependent being in them.

Julia Dehning as I have been saying was always resisting changing the attacking way she had had, was having, would be having all her living. As I was saying she had not really then sense for living. As I was saying she was not really an unsuccessful one in living. As I was saying

Mrs. Dehning was stupid in attacking when she was attacking and not for any winning. This was in her always in her daily living. As I was saying Mrs. Dehning had some sense for living. As I was saying she was an important enough one in daily living.

There are very many who are wanting to be learning in their living. Some as I have been saying of Julia Dehning are wanting anything because they are feeling that anything can feed them. Some something like Julia Dehning can feel having teaching, some something like Julia Dehning can feel a little the thing some one has been teaching them, some something like Julia Dehning can be feeling giving teaching, some something like Julia Dehning are every minute feeling teaching to them feeling teaching from them, either feeling teaching being given to them or being given by them, always then feeling teaching, always then feeling teaching being given, this is very common with many having in them not really any sensitiveness to the teaching itself that has been given, that they are giving. To begin again. There are many having sensitiveness in them to some one teaching, to there being one teaching some one, to their teaching some one and have in them the very least possible sensitiveness to the teaching that is being taught then. This is very common. Some have not any in them sensitiveness to the thing taught by any one and these have it in them to have really sensitiveness to there being teaching done to them, by them, to some one, by some one. Now this is certainly quite common and this is bringing this writing always nearer to Julia Dehning. As I was saying Julia needed anything because in her feeling in her being everything could be feeding her in living. Now as I was saying Julia had being that was one resisting, being stupid in resisting anything that could be touching her in relation to her always being in her way persisting in attacking. Really then Julia had not in her any way of learning anything. Really she had it in her that she was being an excited one in seizing everything, seizing anything to learn that thing and always then she had it in her being that she was a stupid one in not being able to not be a resisting one in a stubborn way to anything teaching her in any way to be an attacking one. This then is being in her and as any one can see it would make of her one not having really sense for living, one having not necessarily failing in living, one being one interesting to some, one being one certainly in a way having courage in living. As I was saying she was of the attacking, of the independent dependent kind in women and men. She had dependent being in her of the independent dependent kind of being but this really was in her only when rarely it did happen to her some one did tell her she had not really any way of learning in her. Then she had it in her as the dependent independent dependent attacking kind in women and men have it in them, she had it in her to be certain that not the last end of a bad thing could happen to her and then surely some one did have it to be certain that she certainly could learn something and so then she had it in her this not as a religion but she had in her then the certain feeling of right conviction. And see then every one reading this thing that this one Julia Dehning had conviction in her that she was one to be an attacking one resisting any one changing any attacking in her being and she was one seizing being one learning and always then really she could not be learning anything. It is a clear thing then that she had not in her anything of religion. It is certainly a clear thing this thing that she did not have in her with dependent independent dependent being in her anything in her of religion, she could and did and would have and mostly must have conviction, she must be having the sensation of certain feeling to be going on attacking, having courage really in all of her living. She was completely then a stupid one in being a resisting one resisting any changing in her being in a way an attacking one having courage in living. She had then certainly not sense for living. She was then certainly in living not one failing in living. She was one seizing being one learning anything, learning everything, she was one feeling being one needing anything, needing everything because not anything was teaching anything in her being. She was one seizing anything that was teaching because she was one having it in her feeling that everything was feeding her in living. She had courage in living, she had not sense for living, she had dependent being in her being of the independent dependent kind as I have been saying, she was not really failing not really succeeding in living. She was one quite interesting to some, quite unpleasant to some, quite irritating to some, quite stimulating to some, quite stupid to some, quite unusually bright to some, quite loving and pathetic to some, quite cold and self-seeking to some, entirely generous and courageous to some, quite failing in really attacking to some, quite entirely honest to some, quite failing in being honest in knowing that sometimes she was lying to some, quite earnest and sensitive to teaching to some, quite impenetrable to anything to some, quite really nice to quite a number knowing her in living, quite open-minded to some, quite completely obstinate to some, quite nervous and fairly excited to every one. This is to be now a history of living in her, of being in her, of what each one knowing her felt in her, what those living with her felt about her, how one can know her, how one can come to know any one, of being in every one.

This then is certain, feeling that there is and was and will be teaching being given always every day to some one by some, to every one by every one is very much in very many moral feeling, completely moral feeling, completely moral conviction. This is very often in very many not having any feeling in them for anything any one is learning any one is or can be teaching. There being teaching always being given makes of living a moral operation to very many living. Julia Dehning as I was saying was completely needing feeling that always in all daily living teaching was being given by some one by a good many of mostly every-thing. She was needing learning learning everything for anything could be a food to her that she could have as learning. She had then certainly from this thing completely a moral conviction. She did this needing learning from being one needing to be going on living. This is in very many women in very many men, in pretty nearly ever so many women and men. Teach-ing then being existing is being existing as being in moral being in very many pretty nearly a very great many men and women.

Some are feeling each thing they are liking and are not learning anything in living. Some of these have religion in them, some of these have themselves inside them to them as all being in them, some of such of them are completely loving some one. Many are feeling everything in living are not learning anything in living, I know very well one of these in my living and this one has complete feeling of each thing and this one is delicately vibrating and completely loving something and not having any religion, not any moral feeling, not any interest in any opinion. I know by reading and by hearing of two having it in them that they are completely feeling everything, each thing and are not learning anything in living. These have religion in them, these are certain that the having so much feeling in them with each thing is meaning that they are real-ising that a god is loving them. I know one and that one is in a way like Julia Dehning and this one is feeling each thing in living and not learn-ing anything and always having a conviction that it is a necessary thing that this one is learning everything so that this one can be having mean-ing in living and this one has moral conviction. This one needs it that every one is learning everything. I know one who is in living living in her being and completely living with her being and this one is feeling everything and not learning anything in living and this one is needing feeling everything in living and not learning anything in living to make it for herself a complete thing that she is living with her being. Some who are feeling everything feeling anything in living have a little a very little power of realising each thing they are feeling, these could learn something in living if each thing was not succeeding another thing. Some of these can come to learn something in living. Some can learn something in their liv-ing, Julia Dehning in a way was not such a one. These I have just been describing are some with attacking being in them who are not learning, not succeeding, not necessarily failing in living, some of such of them are quite important to a number knowing them in living. They are not really important in living. They have not really sense for living. I am going now again to commence my regular description of being in Julia Dehning, of Dehning family living, of Julia's meeting and marrying and loving and not learning, and not enduring Alfred Hersland, and of her complete living. I am beginning again, not from the beginning this time that is certain.

The Dehning family as I was saying were living quite completely pleasantly very rich right american living. They were living this in a free way, in a quite generous way, in a completely pleasant way in a fairly energetic way, in a quite successful way, in a fairly gay way, in a quite spirited way, in a fairly peaceful way, in not an ambitious way, in a quite fairly simple way, in a quite thoroughly completely easily pleasant fairly happy reasonably contenting and contented way.

Family living is a thing a family in a way is realising. Sometimes a family is not at all realising that thing. Mostly a family is in a way knowing the kind of family living they have in them. Sometimes it is a queer thing to have them telling family living. Sometimes it is a very funny thing when some are explaining a family living, sometimes it is a foolish thing, sometimes an irritating thing, very often a quite tedious thing. Family living is a peculiar thing because not any one, mostly, is deciding family living and always each one is himself or herself inside her or him and family living is in a way a combination that in a way is not coming from any one. Sometimes it is coming from some one, sometimes it is a combination thing, sometimes it just happens to be existing. As I am saying the Dehnings had family living in them that was not really expressing Mr. Dehning or Mrs. Dehning or in a way the two together nor in a way the three children. Really one knowing each one of them would be thinking family living would have been a different thing in them from what it really was in them. Really I suppose certainly it was a combination of being in Mr. Dehning and Mrs. Dehning and the three children.

Family living is a pleasant thing when each one likes to be hearing some telling about what each one likes to be doing in living. Family living when not any one is liking to be listening to what another one is liking in living is not at all a pleasant thing. It is a very difficult thing, for very many, to keep on being one liking to be hearing about what another one in the family is liking in living. So then family living comes to be not any longer existing and sometimes then it is a very troublesome thing. In the Dehning family living they kept on all of them for a really very long time of living being ready to be listening to what each one liked in living, needed in living, had in living. Dehning family living as I was saying was quite completely a long time a quite pleasant thing. Julia was not really perhaps listening enough to Mrs. Dehning having living to make it later a completely pleasant living but Julia was listening to all the other ones and all the other ones could listen to all the other ones telling about living in them and so really Dehning family living was really pretty nearly a completely pleasant thing.

It certainly is quite entirely a difficult thing to keep on a long time with several living in a house together, a family to go on really listening to what each one is telling, to what each one is needing, having for living.

Each one can find it a more or a less difficult thing. Mostly each one sometime commences to be doing less of this thing in family living as they come to be in middle living. As I was saying Mr. Dehning liked it in him to be listening to any one wanting to be doing anything. He was a completely good man in family living, in doing all living he had in him. Each one of the Dehning family was quite good for Dehning family living.

As I was saying Mr. Dehning liked it inside him that he was ready to be listening to any one wanting to do something. This was in a way pleasant being of important feeling in him. Mrs. Dehning was not listening when Julia was marrying Alfred Hersland. In a way though she was listening. Later George and Hortense Dehning were feeling very much listening inside them. Julia Dehning was not then making Dehning family living, she was a little then leading to her mother's feeling who was one having it in her feeling that she was one leading in attacking. Not that really in a way either Mrs. Dehning or Julia Dehning were making family living, or really leading Dehning family living, they really each one, Mrs. Dehning earlier, Julia Dehning later, were giving their own feeling of being one needing succeeding in having something in living as a stamp on Dehning family living. They were neither of them ones having a needing of attacking for winning, they neither of them had really much ambition in them, they really had it in them to be needing to be succeeding in having something that would be for them a stamping by them of Dehning family living. Each one of them had in them their own being of which I have been already giving some description. Mrs. Dehning had some sense for living, Julia Dehning had not really sense for living. Each one of them was quite important as living. Mrs. Dehning was one quite succeeding in living. Julia was one succeeding in living, failing too in living. Mrs. Dehning was one not really failing in living. The Dehning family living is then something I am describing. Julia Dehning and Alfred Hersland came to be married ones, I am describing this thing.

Mr. Dehning was one learning in living. Really he was not one coming to have more and more sense for living. He had certainly in his early and middle living very much sense for living, he always all his living had sense for living.

He was in Dehning family living. Mr. Dehning, Mrs. Dehning, Julia, George and Hortense Dehning were in Dehning family living. Julia came to marrying in the beginning of the ending of middle living in Mr. and Mrs. Dehning. Mrs. Dehning had sense for living, neither more nor less all of her living, Mrs. Dehning could be learning in living. Mr. Dehning was a little coming to be in him an important one from being one listening to any one wanting to be doing anything.

Julia began her living by attacking to be marrying Alfred Hersland attacking in family living. As I was saying Julia was one not really winning, she was really doing what she was feeling she was needing to be going on being one living. She was really then keeping on being in family living although she was attacking to be living in marrying Alfred Hersland. That is history of living in her, that will be always what I am telling of being in her being living.

Julia had not the emotion of ambition, she had not ambition in her as emotion, she had it in her, ambition, as attacking and not for winning, she had some intention of ambition, not very much but some, she had ambition in being one resisting any changing in attacking being in her. Alfred Hersland had ambition in emotion, he had ambition in intention, he had not so much ambition in being one having resisting engulfing being. It is a thing that is very interesting that those having in them that ambition is not as emotion in them have it that to very many knowing them they are very sweet in living, very careless in living, very unworldly in living, very unselfish in living. Some of such of them have ambition in them as Julia Dehning had as I am saying. It is in a way a nice thing to be one not having ambition as emotion for these then knowing this thing of them can be doing what they are neding in living and always they do not need to be holding back or ashamed in them because they are not really self-seeking to any one, knowing it in them that ambition is not an emotion in them. Alfred Hersland had amibtion as emotion in him, he had ambition as intention in him, he had not ambition as acting as resisting engulfing being in him and so then he was in a way failing in living. He was not completely failing in living. Julia Dehning and Alfred Hersland came to know each other and came to be married and to living together and this is to be now a history of the living in them.

Julia was all her living in a way of Dehning family living. As I was saying Mrs. Dehning, Julia Dehning was of Dehning family living. They were not really making Dehning family living any more than any one in the Dehning family living. They were in a way always putting on themselves a stamp that was in a way from their own being in being a part of Dehning family living. In a way they were a little more exciting in being stamping in themselves for themselves a way of being part of Dehning family living, a little more exciting than Mr. Dehning or George or Hortense Dehning. Really as I was saying of them they were not actually very exciting, really then, as Mrs. Dehning was not really exciting in harsh attacking as she had not then feeling of being winning she was not then winning anything, she was one in any feeling and Julia Dehning who as I was saying had not really sense for living was not winning in being one resisting any changing in her being in one way in attacking living, in not learning anything in living. So then really not any one of the Dehning family were really exciting, they were each one of them reasonably important in living, they were really not at all exciting. The Dehning family each one were certain as being much more exciting. The

Dehning family were living very well very rich american living. This is to be now more history of each one of them.

The Dehning family living was successful living for all of them, all five of them, the Dehning family living was a successful, generous, pleasant, reasonably important very rich american living. Quite generous, quite pleasant, quite reasonably a successful very rich right american living, almost a completely american living, always fairly excited, sometimes fairly profoundly agitated, mostly always fairly pleasant fairly generous, very completely each one having anything they could be needing, quite simple in emotion, country house and city living.

It was a reasonably important living, the Dehning family living, each one of them were reasonably important each one of them in their living. As I am saying they werey mostly all of them fairly excited with living, all of them certainly living in living, as I was just saying not really so very exciting in being. There is to be more description of them.

It is very hard for any one to tell in any other one how much that one is loving another one. It is very difficult to tell it about any one how much loving they can have they do have in them. It is difficult to know of any one what kind of loving they have in them, certainly it is difficult to know that in any one, it certainly is very difficult to tell it of any one at any time how much of their loving they have in them, they can have in them, how much loving there is in them of their kind of loving for any one.

Alfred Hersland and Julia Dehning came together, they certainly came to marrying. It was very difficult to tell in either of them how much of their kind of loving they had then in them for the other of the two of them.

Julia Dehning as I have been saying was of the attacking kind in men and women. Alfred Hersland as I have been saying again and again was of the engulfing resisting kind in men and women. Julia Dehning certainly could have some loving in her for some one, Julia was in Dehning family living, she was certainly one to have some loving in her for some in living, she certainly was having loving in her then for Alfred Hersland. Alfred Hersland as I was saying had not really any living that was important to him until he came to loving one and wanting to stop studying so that he could immediately marry that one and then a little later he did not want to be loving. That was the first thing important to him in living as I was saying. He had aspiring being in him as I was saying of him. He came to loving and marrying Julia Dehning. He had loving in him for her then, in a way he always had some loving in him for some one. They both then Julia Dehning and Alfred Hersland had it in them to have some loving for some one, for the other one, for some, in them.

Mrs. Dehning as I was saying had some sense for living. Julia was important enough in living, was not really failing in living, was really quite important as living, was really one very courageously completely living her living, was fairly attacking, was one not having really sense for living. Did Alfred Hersland have sense for living, any sense for living, I am not quite certain, I think he had a little sense for living, not so much as he was one being stupid in aspiration, in ambition, as he was an engulfing resisting one not really resisting, not really engulfing, but perhaps he had a very little bit of sense for living, else he probably would have been completely failing in living, a little sense for living came to be in a way in him and then he was again a loving one and then he was failing but not really completely failing in living. He was then even almost succeeding in living.

Julia Dehning and Alfred Hersland then when they were marrying each other did certainly have loving in them each one of them for the other one. I have already told about their coming to be needing to have each other for living and loving. They did certainly come to marrying. They did certainly succeed in not succeeding in their married living. This is to be now some description of loving being in each one of the two of them and of their marrying and of their married living.

The description of the loving being in Julia Dehning and then in Alfred Hersland and the relation in Julia of her being loving to family living, the loving being in Julia and the stupid being in her and the family living to her, and then more loving being in her.

It is very difficult in quarrelling to be certain in either one what the other one is remembering. It is very often astonishing to each one quarrelling to find out what the other one was remembering for quarrelling. Mostly in quarreling not any one is finding out what the other one is remembering for quarrelling, what the other one is remembering from quarrelling.

I have been telling something about living in men and women having resisting being in them, having engulfing resisting being in them. Some of such of them have quite a good deal of loving in them, some of such of them have more loving in them than they can feel in them some have less loving in them than they are believing they have in them, not having it in them to have emotion poignant like a sensation as those having attacking being have it in them. Some having resisting being having attacking in them to keep themselves from having to be resisting being very dependent of the dependent independent kind of them say they are having very much loving, they may have very much loving in them, say they have very little loving in them, they may have very little loving in them. Those having engulfing being may have very much, a little or quite some loving in them. These sometimes have very much more loving feeling in them than at other times in their living, some of them.

These may tell that they have very much loving feeling in them with conviction, they may tell that they have little loving feeling in them with conviction.

Those having attacking have it as I am saying to have emotion having in them the poignancy of a sensation. Some having attacking being can certainly have this very dully in them. Many can have it in them that they are telling about having it very much in them, some of such of them have it very much in them and some of such of them just have it some in them. Some of the attacking kind of them can be very excited about telling it about themselves, sometimes very often, and some of such of them certainly have it very lively in them, some have it quite deadened in them. Some can have very much emotion in telling about it to themselves and every one and they have quite a great deal of it really in them, some have it very much in them in telling of it and it is in them that they have it really in them, yes they certainly have it really in them only it does not make them do what they think it will, it does, it did make them do in living. Some have a great deal of it in them but it is not active in them but I will not tell all the ways I can think of that those having attacking being have emotion in them. Some as I am saying of the attacking kind in men and women are very much excited always in being, in living in any living, in being one being living. Some of such of them have very much emotion in them, some not so much, some quite a bit, some really very little in them. Some of such of them have it in them that they are not having emotion with the excitement of being in living in them, they have emotion in them. Some are all their living, some of such as these I am describing, some are all their living having been having really one fairly large emotion and are resisting any changing in them of this emotion in them and are very excited in living from being excited ones and stubborn ones in living. Some of such of them have sense for living, some of such of them have not sense for living. Some of such are very stupid ones in being, some of such of them are quite sensitive in being. Julia Dehning was of the kind having one emotion all her living and not being ever changing, and being stubborn in resisting and excited in being living, and not sensitive in being and not having sense for living.

This is to be now more description of loving and marrying and quarrelling and family living.

When some one having been feeling all their living one way of feeling living comes to be feeling in them another way of feeling living, that is disturbing to them. Sometimes then one is from that time on a more or less sick one. Sometimes some one likes this in them. Sometimes they do not like it in them. Sometimes some one has all their living been doing something and having for doing that thing excited feeling in them and then some one does that thing for them with not any excitement in that one and then the other one is left with not any excited feeling and that is sometimes a pleasant thing and sometimes a completely distressing thing. Some never can lose excitement out of them not with any one's showing them. Julia·Dehning always had an excited way of being needing anything and as I was saying she had really loving being all her living and as I was saying that was not exciting in her really, not very exciting and always she was stubbornly resisting being any different in attacking by her being.

Julia and Alfred and Dehning family living and loving and learning and quarrelling.

Some know of themselves in their dressing, in their daily living in everything what they are and what they are wanting from every one, from any one. Some know what they are wanting but they do not have it in them in their daily living, in their dressing to show it to any one. Some can show it while they are with some who have the same being in them and then later when they are left alone cannot really be remembering what it is they wanted to be to show to any one, to every one. Some know what they want to be and can build it up by little pieces and do again and again. Some know what they are and see it as a complete thing and make that thing in daily living. Some know what they are and are always cutting and fitting and fitting and cutting and painting and sometime they come to be that thing in dressing and daily living and then they can lose that thing. Some cannot see the thing they are in daily living and in dressing nor what they want to be in daily living and in dressing. Some see what they want to be in daily living and in dressing and then they are a little less than that thing so that they will not be queer to any one. Some have really the feeling of inventing themselves in daily living and in dressing, some are really doing this thing, some are feeling themselves doing this thing. I will tell more about this thing. Julia Dehning as I was saying was all her living after she was herself to herself in living wanting to be creating living in learning everything in daily living, furnishing, dress-making, decoration, cleaning herself and everything, resting, reading, being a good one, being a useful one. She was doing this then and she came to loving Alfred Hersland. She was doing this thing, she was as I was saying one not having really any way of feeling in learning. She came to loving and marrying Alfred Hersland. She had loving being in her, she had Dehning family living in her feeling.

One knows what effect that one wants to produce to that one, to any one, in that one existing, in the daily living that one has for living. That one does not feel that one as a finished thing, that one works from something that one is knowing pretty quickly to something that one has been not really knowing and then that comes to be to that one a known thing and then that one sticks there in that thing. That one does not want to be conspucious in living but does want to be intelligent and elegant. This then is a personal ideal, that that that one has for daily living and so this one has feeling of being always creating all the daily living, the being in that one, really that one is going from something that one has been knowing to something that one has not quite been certainly knowing and sticks there in that thing.

Another one needs to be for living what that one is certain any one like that one is in being and in living. That one can be that in living when there are others realising what that one being that kind of a one is in living, when others being that kind in living are with that one in daily living. This one needs these then for being what this one is certain any one being like this one is in daily living. This one when this one is not being kept in living being by others being what this one is certain this one is being in living, by others being certain that this one is in living what this one is certain any one like this one is in living, loses the grasp really on what is what this one is certain any one like this one is in daily living. Another one never loses realising what it is that this one is certain is being in this one and always this one is building it up by little pieces. This one never comes to be a completer one. Very often this one is a vague and stupid one and not really being in living and so then always this one keeps a little pile by always adding to make this one what this one is certain from what this one and every one expects of this one this one is in daily living. Some see themselves as a whole one and they cut and add boldly to make themselves the whole one. Some slowly possess it, some never know what it is and never possess it, some only know what is not it when they see themselves not it in daily living. Julia Dehning was one having certainly a needing of being learning everything. Julia was in a way not feeling in learning anything. Julia had loving being in her that is certain. She was certain of having honesty for living as every one having Dehning family living have in them. She was certain of having courage for living. This thing she had in her in daily living, this she could not ever have in her as developing. It was in her that was certain, she had attacking being in her that was this thing in her, she had attacking being in her that was being needing learning anything. She had it in her to be completely stubbornly actively passively resisting any changing of the attacking being in her, she had then not really sense for living, as any one can know now by a little feeling being in her. She was not really failing in living, she was not really succeeding in living, she was fighting very well always for her being one living, being honestly a courageous one, being one needing to be learning everything. She had very much active nervous being in her. She had excitement in being one doing her daily living in living. She had really passion in her but not enough to make it right that she should have so much stubborness in her of not changing her attacking, not enough to make it right that she should be such a nervous one in daily living, should be one so excited in learning anything.

I will begin again now with a description of Julia Dehning.

Julia Dehning came to be married to Alfred. They were not very successful one with the other in married living. It is certain that each one in quarrelling is remembering a different thing for quarrelling. This is to be now more description of daily living in Julia Dehning.

Julia and Alfred each one in daily living, aspiration, ambition, taste, feeling, moral being, quarrelling, family living.

I am describing what is to me a beautiful thing, learning being in women and in men. Every little bit, every single bit of learning being in women and men is to me a beautiful thing. I am telling always about what is to me a beautiful thing, that is learning being in women and in men. A very little bit I am ever learning is to me a beautiful thing. Learning being in women and in men is to me really a completely beautiful thing. Every bit of repeating I am doing while I am learning being in women and in men is to me a completely really beautiful thing. Being one learning being in women and in men ought then to be always making me a very happy one. I am always learning being in women and in men. I am sometimes quite a melancholy one.

I have learnt pretty completely being in Julia Dehning. I am remembering now being in Julia Dehning. I am realising now being in Julia Dehning. I am feeling now more realisation of being in Julia Dehning by always more realising the connection between being in her and being in women and in men who have the same kind of being more or less in them. Julia Dehning was quite an important person in being a person being living.

Really she was not failing in living, really she was not succeeding in living, really she had much support and loving in living, really she was quite an important one in being living, really she had courage in being one being living, really she had loving being in her, really she had a need in her that there would be some there certain to be supporting, really she always had support and loving in her living, really she was quite an important one in living. Really she had much support and loving for living, really she had courage in being one always being one living, really she was one having courage to be going on being in living, really she was one resisting and being one not feeling hearing seeing anything that could be changing anything of attacking being she had in living, she was one needing learning everything, needing learning anything so that she would be using all her being living, as she was not learning anything, for living attacking being which was the being in her. So then she was not really defeated in being living, she was not succeeding, not failing in living, she was quite an important one in living, she had loving and support in her living, she had not sense for living.

Julia Dehning was quite a sweet one to some, poignantly sweet one and generous in living and having careless domination in living and having thoughtlessness in being one needing everything and having complete courage always in being one always being living, in being one winning learning to be living. This was the feeling some had all her living in Julia Dehning. Some had different feeling in her living in her. Mostly every one had a feeling of courage for being one needing living in her all of her living. Mostly every one was feeling in her that she was needing to be feeling learning everything because anything could feed her. Some had a certain feeling that she was not ever learning anything in living. Some were certain that she had really sense for living, some were certain that she did not have in her at all sense for living, some were never really certain about this thing about her.

She was one certainly having generous emotion in the sense that she was knowing she was attacking in living to be winning what was not for herself as a thing to be enjoying but what was needed so that she could be one having honest living, having earnest learning living, having Dehning family living. She was one that to herself and mostly every one was completely living for honest living, for learning living, for Dehning family living. Really she was not learning anything in living, really she could never have the last courage of knowing that sometime she was not honest in living, really she was needing loving and support in Dehning family living. Really then it could only come to any one as a slow thing to be realising that she had not complete courage in being one living, that she had not sense for living. So then she could have it really in her that it was sweet and generous and aspiring for her to be as harsh as crude as active as eager in attacking as she could have strength for it in her being. And this was right for her to herself and to mostly any one feeling loving being in her. This is true of very many having attacking being in them and poignant and generous loving being in them as complete being for them. This then was not stupid being in her, stupid being in her was resisting having any changing in the attacking being of her, having not any sensitiveness of being in her from more living in her. This made of her one not learning anything in living, having real then not sense for living. I will tell more gradually about this thing.

Alfred Hersland had ambition in him, Julia Dehning had ambition. Not either one or the other of them as I was saying was really failing in living, was really succeeding, had really sense for living, was really defeated by living.

Alfred Hersland had aspiration in living, had an aspiration to be succeeding. Julia Dehning had aspiration in living, had aspiration in being one learning and to be then completely living. Alfred Hersland had failing in him had failing to be one succeeding in something, Julia Dehning was then one not succeeding in being, was one not really learning anything for living. It was then right that they should have come to be two loving one another and then coming to marrying and then coming to be not succeeding in married living. Some have it right for them to be loving and marrying and succeeding in married living, some have it right from the being in them to be loving each other and marrying and not succeeding then in having married living in them for those two of them together then. Some have it to be right for them from the being in them to be loving one another then and not then to be marrying. Some who are loving one another do not have it really that it is right from the being in them that they are loving for each other then. And then it is right from being in some one that that one should love some one, should not love some one, should be loved by some one, should not be loved by some one. Anyway it certainly was alright from the being in them that Alfred Hersland and Julia Dehning should come to be loving one another and marrying and not succeeding in their married living.

They were married then and they did not succeed in their married living together then. They were each one of them not really succeeding not really failing in their living.

Really it is a very difficult thing in living for some to be certain that they are believing in loving, that they are believing in being honest in living, that they are believing in any one being a good one. It is so terribly mixed up and how does one know living, loving, thinking, honest being, feeling, goodness in living, and yet one is doing thinking, living, loving, honest action, goodness in living, and some one else is being a good one, an honest one, a loving one, a thinking one, a feeling one and always then one is knowing everything in one and one is not believing what one is knowing inside them and one is knowing what is going on in them and one is not believing that thing and how then is one really certain that loving and feeling and thinking and goodness and honesty is in them and how is one not certain and what is then the satisfaction of having been of being of going to be being a living one and that one is not certain that loving that thinking that honesty that goodness is something in them and that one is not then certain. One is saying, of course he would do that thing, he is a middle aged man and he needs to do that thing, he needs to do that thing, yes I have a passion, I have a passion for my children, yes he has a passion, he has a passion for his reputation, he is a middle aged man and he has a chance to do that thing, of course he will do that thing, why should he not do that thing, it is honest for him a middle aged man to do that thing, they need that thing or else they would not pay him to do that thing, of course he is a loving man, of course he loves his reputation, of course he is a middle aged man, of course he has three years to make him a very rich man, of course he is an honest man, of course he is a good man, I respect him, everybody respects him, he loves his reputation, he has a very good reputation, certainly some are loving, some are honest, some are good ones, some are thinking in living, certainly some are certain of this thing, certainly I am certain to be certain of this thing.

I am certain to be certain of the thing that some have loving in them, that some have thinking in them, that some have honest action in them, that some have goodness in them, that every one has being in being living. I am certain to be certain of this thing with some kind of meaning and I am not then going to be terribly in a twitter in me about this thing. I am going to be certain of this thing, and why not be certain of this thing why not be certain of this thing as certain as of being being in every one having living as being in them. I am going to be certain of this thing. I am going now to be describing honesty and goodness and loving and thinking and living in Julia Dehning and Alfred Hersland.

To some it is an encouraging thing a very encouraging thing that mostly every one has plenty of courage in them for daily living. To some it is a wonderful thing that not everything scares every one. It is so easy for some to be scared by mostly everything, by every little bit of daily living, it is a very fine thing, a fine fine thing for such of them to be really certain that not everybody is scared by everything. Very often some are living a long time in living believing that every one is really scared by everything. Some are not ever really believing that any one is scared by everything. As I was saying it is certainly an encouraging thing to some that some are certainly loving, some are certainly thinking, some are certainly feeling, some are certainly honest ones, some are certainly good ones. I have said that this is to be a description of being in Julia Dehning and Alfred Hersland, I am remembering this thing, that is certain.

Mr. Dehning soon came to thinking that Alfred Hersland was not an honest man. Julia Hersland soon came to be certain that Alfred Hersland was not an honest one. Mr. Dehning was an honest enough man in living. That is certain.

Julia Dehning and Alfred Hersland were married and commenced being together for all of their daily living. Mr. Dehning came to think that Alfred Hersland was not an honest enough man to have in the Dehning family daily living. Julia Hersland was quite certain that Alfred Hersland was not an honest enough one for any Dehning family living. The Dehning family were certainly quite honest ones for daily living. Alfred Hersland certainly was not quite such an honest one in some of his daily living.

It is to some a quite difficult thing to be certain that they have loving, that they have thinking, that they have feeling, that they have honest daily living, that they have goodness in them. It is not at all a difficult thing for some to be certain of themselves in living, to be certain about other ones in living whether they are loving, whether they are feeling, whether they are honest ones, whether they are good ones, whether they are thinking in all of their living. As I was saying Mr. Dehning came to be thinking that Alfred Hersland was not an honest man enough for Dehning family living. As I was saying Julia Hersland came to be quite soon quite entirely certain that Alfred Hersland was not an honest enough one to be having as one having with her all his daily living. As I was saying Alfred Hersland was one really not failing really not succeeding in living, he was one having some aspiration for succeeding in living, he was one having engulfing resisting being in him, he was one having some loving being in him, he was one having some thinking in him, he was one certainly not going to be honest enough in the Dehning family way of living.

They all of them had some loving feeling in them. Mr. Dehning, Mrs. Dehning, Julia Hersland and Alfred Hersland. They each one of them certainly could have some loving feeling in them. They each one of them could have very little loving feeling in them. In living Dehning family living each one had in them some loving feeling. Alfred Hersland had some loving feeling in him. The Dehning family living as I said before was very right very rich american living quite pleasantly, quite generously, reasonably honestly, reasonably lovingly, somewhat urgently existing. Julia Hersland in married living was expecting different living from Dehning family living, so she was thinking, she wanted a very much more earnest and exciting american living than the Dehning family living and always then it was certain that in her she was certain that she had it in her to be really having Dehning family living as every one reasonably good ones had it to have in them, Alfred Hersland was not really then of Dehning family living, Julia was really then always of Dehning family living. Mr. Dehning was then fairly slowly quite certain that Alfred Hersland was not such a reasonably honest one as Mr. Dehning needed for business living. Julia Hersland had come fairly quickly to be certain that Alfred Hersland was not the kind of a one she needed for fairly honest daily living, Alfred Hersland was really not failing then, really not succeeding then in living, Alfred Hersland had then important feeling for being one aspiring to succeeding in living. Alfred Hersland had then some loving feeling in him, that was not then to him in him important feeling. Julia had then in living loving feeling, that was then important feeling in her to her then. Mr. Dehning had some loving feeling in him then, he always had some loving feeling in him, this was always important to him in him. Mrs. Dehning had some loving feeling in her, this was not important then to her in her or really then to any one.

Alfred Hersland was then not really succeeding not really failing in living. Mr. Dehning as I said of him had it in him some then, he had it in him all his living, he had it in him more and more in his living to be listening to any one wanting to do anything. He was quite entirely one listening to any one wanting to do anything. Mostly in living he was a man quite certainly judging that some men would do and some men would not do something and always he had it in him to be listening to any one telling about doing anything. Alfred Hersland as I was saying was married to Julia Dehning. Alfred Hersland as I was saying was not really then failing was not really then succeeding in living.

Mr. Dehning was an honest man. He surely was an honest enough man. The Dehning family each one of them was certain sometime in her in him that they were honest ones for living. The Dehning family surely each one sometime were certain that they were honest enough for living. They were each one sometime certain that they were really honest ones in living each one sometime in her or in him. The time came sometime to Julia Dehning when she was surely certain that she was one honest in living.

It was easy for Julia Dehning to be certain sometime that she was completely an honest one for living. It was never possible then that she should not be certain that she was completely an honest one for living. It was quite easy surely for Julia Dehning to be certain that she was completely an honest one, that Dehning family living was completely an honest enough one for any living. It was quite certainly easy for Julia Hersland to be certain sometime that she was one completely honest for daily living. It was certainly then certain that she would be then all her living certain that she was certainly a completely honest one for all daily living. She could certainly be certain that Alfred Hersland was not a completely honest one for daily living. Julia Hersland was then one resisting all her living having in her any changing in being one being one way of being an attacking one. In a way Julia Hersland was succeeding, in a way Julia Hersland was not succeeding in living.

Julia Hersland had some loving feeling in her, Alfred Hersland had some loving feeling in him. Mr. Dehning had some loving feeling in him, Mrs. Dehning had some loving feeling in her, George Dehning had some loving feeling in him, Hortense Dehning had some loving feeling in her. This is to be now histories of each one of them.

Mr. Dehning was whatever any one thought him. Some are really what mostly every one thinks such a one is in living. Mr. Dehning was such a one. Mr. Dehning then in a way made Dehning family living. Julia Hersland came to be certain that she was one having Dehning family living as beginning of all being in her. As I said she was one wanting to be learning anything, needing everything as anything could feed her for her being one doing living. As I said once in telling of her loving and marrying Alfred Hersland he was one to her really doing learning in living. Always as I was saying she was not doing any learning for living. As I was saying sometime she came to be certain that she was a completely honest one for living. This was in her all her living then as really every bit of learning living in her living. She was one certain that she was an honest one for all daily living. She was certain that Dehning family living was honest enough for all daily living. She came to be quite certain that Alfred Hersland was not honest enough for any daily living. This was in her then sometime and always then she was certain of this thing all the rest then of her living and as I was saying she was one completely resisting any changing in the attacking being that was really living in her. All her living then too she was going on learning everything and always then really she was one succeeding some, not succeeding some, more, sometime quite failing in living. Really then as I was saying perhaps she had not really at all sense for living. She married Alfred Hersland, she came quite soon to be certain he was not honest really for any daily living. She came to be quite certain then that she was a completely honest one for daily living, that Dehning family living was a completely honest one for family living. As I was saying she had some loving being in her, Alfred Hersland had some loving being in him, Mr. Dehning had certainly some loving being in him, Mrs. Dehning had some loving being, George Dehning had loving being in him, Hortense Dehning had some loving being as being in her living. This is to be now then again and again histories of all of each one of them.

Why should they not each one of them know it in them that they each one of them had some loving feeling in them. They did each one of them know it in them sometime that they had some loving feeling in them, some of them were quite often certain that they had some loving feeling in them, some of them were certain that they had some loving feeling in them, each one of them certainly sometime was certain that that one had some loving feeling.

Julia Dehning, Julia Hersland certainly then had some loving feeling in her and sometimes she was quite certain of this thing. Alfred Hersland certainly had some loving feeling in him and very often he was certain of it being there in him. Mr. Dehning had certainly some loving feeling in him and certainly it was a simple thing for him to be mostly always certain of this thing. Mrs. Dehning had certainly some loving feeling and she certainly sometimes was quite entirely certain of this thing. George Dehning had certainly some loving feeling in him and he certainly was really quite often certain of this thing. Hortense Dehning had some loving feeling in her in all her living and she was fairly certain of this thing. This then is a true thing that each one of them Julia Hersland and Alfred Hersland and Mr. Dehning and Mrs. Dehning and George Dehning and Hortense Dehning had some loving being in her or in him.

There was then Dehning family living. Julia Hersland had been of Dehning family living. She had been needing learning anything, all her living she was needing learning everything as anything could feed her for being one wanting to be living. She came to loving and marrying Alfred Hersland. This is an interesting thing to some. This has been quite an interesting thing to some. The being in Julia Hersland, the loving being, the living being in her is an interesting thing to some. She was then as I was saying one having independent dependent being in living. This is a history of her and of every one.

I am beginning more and more to feel being in young girls, in young women. I am beginning more and more to know the being they have in them. I do not yet know the being in all of them, I do not yet know all the being in all of them. I see one kind of them that I do not know at all as being and I see that kind of them again and again, I see again and again one and another of that kind of them. I do not know at all the being in them, in any of that kind of them. I know then now always very much always more and more the being in women, the being in them when they are young girls coming to be going to be young women. I know always more and more what men are coming to be doing in their living, I do not know very much more now of the being of men when they are young boys coming to be going to be men. I certainly do now know very much more of the way being is in young girls in their living. I certainly do know quite a good deal of this thing and it is a very pleasant thing in me to be more and more knowing this thing. Why is it a pleasant thing in me to me to be more and more knowing this thing. It is a pleasant thing in me to me to be knowing this thing because it is to me a completely pleasant thing to be knowing everything and it is to me a completely pleasant thing in me to be feeling in me delicately inside me the being that I am coming to be knowing through knowing some one, through knowing any one. I am feeling always in me knowing every one through some one feeling any one, every one in them, I am feeling that one and that one is feeling any one, is feeling every one, and sometimes it is a completely delicate thing so feeling any one feeling every one. Sometimes it not at all a delicate thing so feeling some one feeling any one, everyone, sometimes it is a completely delicate thing, feeling some one feeling every one, feeling any one. Always all my living I am feeling some feeling other ones and this I am liking in living. Sometimes as I am saying it is a very completely delicate thing feeling some one feeling any one, feeling every one. I am having now a completely delicate feeling in feeling some one feeling any one, feeling some one. I am now completely beginning to be feeling being in young girls, in young women, and this is to me a very pleasant thing, really a delicate completely pleasant thing.

As I was saying Julia Hersland had in her some loving feeling. It is certainly pretty certain that she had some loving feeling in her. She was loving and then marrying Alfred Hersland and then certainly coming to not loving Alfred Hersland. She was of Dehning family living. She was certainly in a way always loving and perhaps coming always to have more and more loving feeling for her father Mr. Dehning. Mr. Dehning in a way certainly really did make Dehning family living. In a way Dehning family living was not really what Julia Hersland was at all living in her living, in a way that was all she was ever living. As I was saying she was not putting any of her being into making Dehning family living. She came sometime to be quite certain that she was an honest one in daily living, that Dehning family living was honest enough living for any daily living and then as I was saying she was always all her living needing to be learning anything and as I was saying she was really not learning in living and she had her own being as I was saying attacking independent dependent being, that is courage for living, that is having some one supporting when the last end of a bad thing was on her in her living and not then feeling that she was having to be having such support although having in her really loving feeling for the supporting being then in her living. She was certainly then one not using her being for living because she certainly was not learning anything in living, she certainly had some loving feeling in her in her living, she certainly was sometime completely certain that she was an honest one for daily living, she certainly was not learning anything ever in living for living, she certainly was not learning anything ever in living her living, she certainly was not ever learning anything, she certainly was completely feeling needing learning everything, she certainly was completely feeling needing learning anything, she certainly was not failing completely, not succeeding completely in living, she certainly was one being alive in living. She certainly was one having some loving feeling in her in her living. Alfred Hersland certainly had some loving feeling in him in his living. He came to loving Julia Dehning and then marrying her and then somewhat loving her and somewhat keeping on loving her and then not loving her and then later he was really loving another and he was never really of Hersland family living in the way of having anything very loving in him or any way of being certain that Hersland family living was important enough for daily living and always he had a very little loving feeling for Mr. Hersland and Mrs. Hersland and Martha Hersland and David Hersland and always then he had some loving feeling in living, certainly Julia Hersland and Alfred Hersland each one of them had some loving feeling in them in each one of them. They had then each one of them come to be loving and marrying, each one of them then had certainly some loving feeling then for some one, some aspiration for something important to them from being one living. Julia Dehning had been a young girl and then an older one and then one needing for her feeling to be all her living learning everything, learning anything, needing to be marrying Alfred Hersland. Alfred Hersland had been a young man having it in him that not anything had been in living really important to make for him aspiration to be one succeeding. This had come to be in him after he had been going to stop studying to earn a living for one he was then loving and had then come not to be any longer loving that one. He had come then to have really aspiration in him for succeeding in being important in succeeding. He had as I was saying all his living some loving feeling in him. Julia as I was saying was a young girl and then was really alive in her to her in her being and needing to be learning anything to be learning everything and having courage to be living in being alive in her to her in her being and being then not learning anything and being then of Dehning family living and being then certain but not then with it as conviction that she was an honest one in living, that Dehning family being was honest enough in any daily living, and always then she was not one not having completely courage for living and always then she was one succeeding in being in her living, and always then she was completely anything completely everything she ever was in living because as I am saying she had not ever really sense for living because as I am saying she had always in her some loving feeling, because as I was saying she always was alive in being in her living. She was then all her living as I was saying not so very interesting. She was as I am saying of those having attacking being, independent dependent being, those having it to have in them emotion to be poignant like sensation. This is to be now certainly a complete history of her and of any one coming to be knowing her in any living.

Mostly every one is certain that when they were young they did anything and then they were not tired or not feeling well from doing this thing. I am certain this is not what is really ever happening. I am certain many have not feeling well and very tired feeling when they are young ones and have been doing something. It is a very curious thing this being a very tired one, a very disturbed one, one not feeling well when one was a young one and then being this when one is an older one, really mostly every one is all their living when they are quite completely young when they are young when they are older when they are old ones repeating not feeling well, being a disturbed one, being a very tired one. Very many are not really knowing this thing in living. I am knowing this thing in living. Each one is repeating all their living being a tired one, being a disturbed one, being one not feeling well again and again.

This is to be now a description of Julia Dehning and Julia Dehning coming to be Julia Hersland and Julia Hersland then. She was then all her living repeating being in her way a tired one a disturbed one a one not feeling well again and again. Mostly not any one is really certain of their way of being a tired one, being one not feeling well being a disturbed one until they are an older one. Each one, every one is always repeating their being in being again and again a disturbed one, a tired one, a one not feeling well in daily living.

How wise it is to be knowing every one is repeating all their living being tired ones, being disturbed ones, being ones not feeling well quite often. As I am saying mostly every one is not knowing that they have been again and again repeating being not well, being a disturbed one, being a tired

one in their young living. When young ones are very tired ones, are
disturbed ones are not well ones they very often are not at all remembering that thing, when they are older ones they are sometimes remembering when they are tired ones from doing something, disturbed ones from
living, not well sometimes in daily living. Some are remembering in
their young living being tired ones and disturbed ones and not well ones,
some are very well remembering this thing. Julia Hersland who was
Julia Dehning was one who was not remembering having been a tired
one, a disturbed one a not well one in young living. She hardly could
be remembering being not a well one, a tired one, a disturbed one, in her
middle living. This is to be now some history of being in her.

Some have liked very much the being and the living in Julia Dehning.
Some have not liked all the living in Julia Dehning. Some have liked
the being in Julia Dehning. Some have liked and have not liked the being
in Julia Dehning. As I was saying she had all her living the same way
of having tired feeling, of having disturbed feeling, disturbed living, the
same way of being sometimes not well in daily living. I remember the
way I had tired feeling and disturbed feeling in my living when I
was a young one now when I have it when I am not any longer such a
young one. Julia was not really ever remembering that she had all
her living the same being a tired one, the same being a disturbed one,
the same being sometimes not well, as daily living. This was being in
her to know this in her, to not really remember this inside her. I remember tired being and disturbed being and being not well in daily living,
sometimes from eating, sometimes from drinking, sometimes from excited feeling. As I was saying Julia Hersland all her living was completely
resisting changing anything in her being a living one having a kind of
attacking, she was one resisting really learning anything from having
been living, she was one really wanting to be learning anything, to be
learning everything for anything could really be a food to this one. So
then all her living she had had disturbed living, disturbed feeling, tired
feeling, not feeling well in daily living and really she knew this thing, she
could really be quite reasonably knowing this thing really she was not
ever really remembering this thing. She was then one being alive in
living, she was one having some loving feeling, she was one learning sometime to know for certain that she was for herself and every one honest
for daily living, she was one having learned to know as certain that
Alfred Hersland was not an honest one for daily living, she was one coming
to have it known as certain that Hersland family living was honest
enough living for any daily living. She was one then not learning anything
in living. She was one then needing to be learning anything, she was
one then completely resisting being in any way changing in being one
living in some attacking being, she was one having courage to be one
being going on living, very much courage for being one going on living,

she was one having all her living a way of having tired feeling, disturbed feeling, disturbed living, not feeling well in daily living and being one quite reasonably knowing this thing and being one not really ever at all really remembering this thing. This then is a description of being in Julia Hersland born Julia Dehning. As I was saying she and Alfred Hersland were not really at all successful for their married living, anybody now can realise this thing, certainly, surely any one now with any sense for understanding when I am explaining now can be realising this thing.

Loving being in each one of them, what the mother and the father and each one felt toward every other one just after the marrying. Some loving feeling then in each one of them.

Loving being in each one of them, what Mr. Dehning and Mrs. Dehning and Julia Hersland and Alfred Hersland and Hortense Dehning and George Dehning each one felt toward every other one of them just after the marrying of Julia Dehning with Alfred Hersland is what I am now beginning to be a little describing. Some loving feeling then in each one of them I have said again and again was in them each one of them. I said Julia had really not sense for living, she was completely resisting any changing by learning of being in her being in her as attacking, she was then really not learning anything in living, she was then not doing anything any one was needing, she was really then not having any one really doing anything she was needing, she was then always she was really living in her being and really she was not failing in living and really some liked very much the being in her in her living, and really some liked and did not like being in her, and some really did not like being in her, and to herself and every one and really then she had courage in being one going on being one living. So then she had really not sense for living, she had really loving feeling in her in all of her living. Some can have resisting to any changing in any attacking being in them and can have from that being in them sense for living, really courage for winning in attacking being. Julia as I was saying had it to have quite completely active all her living needing to be learning anything, to be learning everything, she had it in her needing to have as somewhere in her that some one would keep it from coming to her the last end of any bad thing. And so then she not learning anything in living from not having any not resisting any changing in attacking being in her had not any sense at all really for living in her in her living. Now I will tell something about loving being.

Some are sweet ones to some, some are sweet ones to hardly any one, some are quite sweet ones to mostly every one, some are somewhat sweet ones in living, some are not sweet ones in any living they are doing. Some having resisting being are very sweet ones, some having attacking being are very sweet ones. Some are, some are not sweet ones, each one of these I am now beginning to be describing as having some loving feeling Mrs. Dehning and Mr. Dehning and Julia Hersland and Alfred Hersland and

George Dehning and Hortense Dehning had some sweetness in them.
Many having attacking being have sweetness in them, many having resisting being have sweetness in them.

I would like to be sometime some in love with every one. I will
not be sometime some in love with every one. I would like certainly to
be sometime in love some with every one, to have every one sometime in
love with me and then I would be certain what way each one had loving
being being in them. I really would like then some to have each one,
every one, any one having loving being to my feeling and then I could
have it in me to be certain what way any one, in which way each one
having loving in them have loving feeling in them and coming out from
them. Not every one will ever be loving this one, that is certain and so
this one and I am this one will not be completely certain of loving being
in each one. I will be quite certain about loving being in some, I will
be completely certain about loving being in some, I will be somewhat
certain about loving being in mostly every one. There are some who
are not telling, showing, meaning anything about loving being in them to
me as I look long at them, some kinds in men and women. I do very
much regret this thing. I would like very well to have loving being from
some one of each kind of them to me, to some one I am completely knowing. I regret that I do not know completely loving being in every kind
there is in men and women. I see some kinds of men and women, I look
long at some of these kinds in men and women and I see nothing of the
way they do their loving. And then I am very much regretting I do not
yet know everything.

Julia Hersland was of the attacking kind in men and women having emotion when having emotion poignantly like a sensation. She had
very considerable excitement in being one going on with living, she had
very much nervous being in being one needing to be learning everything,
she had some dependent being in being one having right Dehning family
living in her as being, she had stupidity in being one resisting really learning in living, she was one having some passion in needing having some
loving relation, she was one having some worn out feeling in not having
completed passional loving, she was one having much courage in being
one being honest for winning all living, she was one being sweet to some by
being needing that some one had been keeping her from having the last
end of a bad thing happening, she was courageous to many in having it
as being that she was really going to be going on living, she was a harsh
thing to the feeling of some in being one not remembering having tired,
disturbed, not well feeling, she was a hard thing to some from having it
as being that she was not attacking for winning, that she was attacking
to be going on with being one living in the being that had been all her living from the beginning. This is then quite a full description of being
in her.

I know all loving being in her, I will now describe this thing. I know all loving being in all the Dehning family each one and in Alfred Hersland who was married to Julia Dehning and I will now begin a description of all the loving being in each one of them, ever in any one of them. Alfred Hersland and Julia Dehning were married. Each one of the two of them had some loving feeling in them then, each one of the Dehning family had some loving feeling in them then. This will be now some description of loving feeling in each one of them then.

They were married then. Married living was then beginning to be in them in each one of them Julia Hersland and Alfred Hersland and for them in Mr. Dehning and Mrs. Dehning and George and Hortense Dehning. Every one of them had then for them, every one of Dehning family living, feeling of married living in them. Julia was having then married living, married loving. Julia knew she certainly was learning then anything. Alfred Hersland came then to be of Dehning family living. Mr. Dehning could commence then to have some pride in him in the married living of Alfred and Julia Hersland, he could then have in him beginning to be listening when Alfred Hersland could begin to be talking about doing anything in his living. Mrs. Dehning had then come to have feeling for married living in Mr. and Mrs. Alfred Hersland. She could then fondle him some, Alfred Hersland, and make of him a son-in-law in Dehning family living. She could be then in Dehning family living as she always had been and Julia having married living was a part of her but apart from her. Mrs. Dehning then was completely then feeling their married living nicely and with a good deal of active contented feeling which was just then just beginning to be a little commencing in Mr. Dehning. She was not at all then helping Mr. Dehning to this thing, each one then of the two of them had in them their own individual feeling in feeling married living in Julia and Alfred Hersland. Hortense Dehning then was always needing loving Julia in all of her living, she Hortense was then a really young girl in her feeling and this in her then could not be at all a thing to be ever then noticed in her by any one. George Dehning was then in Dehning family living, that was all that was in him then in feeling married living in Julia and Alfred Hersland then.

There are some who have not in them enough to last out not being a moral one, not feeling moral conviction throughout their living. There are some who have not in them enough power to learn anything in living, although needing to be learning anything for being living, so that they can go on without having it in them a moral conviction that some one is teaching some one something in all living. There are some not having in them enough needing to be learning anything, although they are completely always needing to be learning anything, to be not bothered with being certain that they have honest being for daily living. Not any one having really in them moral feeling is really believing any other one is really liking frivolous living, is really believing that they are not really needing learning anything. This then is a description of Julia Hersland having been just then a married one. As I was saying she was in her feeling needing learning anything for everything to her feeling could be food to her for her to be one really living in going on being living. This was then not enough in her as I was saying so that she did not come then to be completely certain that she was honest for daily living, that Dehning family living was honest enough for any daily living, that Alfred Hersland was not honest for daily living. So then she was one having moral conviction that she was honest for daily living, that there was teaching existing in living. This then is moral conviction, this is not religion this is moral conviction. Religion in such a one is being certain that the last end of a bad thing will not come to such a one. Moral conviction in such a one is being certain of honest being for daily living, of teaching being always going on being existing. Julia Hersland then was a married one, she had completely feeling in her needing to be learning anything, this was in her but was not really filling her to keep her from being certain about honest being for daily living, about teaching being really always everywhere somewhere existing. This then was Julia Hersland having become a married one.

Mr. Dehning as I was saying was a little coming to be having it in him that he was to begin inside him listening to what Alfred Hersland could be telling him about what Alfred Hersland really was needing to be one completely being in living. This was then just a little then beginning to be in Mr. Dehning when Alfred and Julia Hersland had become quite entirely then married and living so then. Mrs. Dehning was then completely in her in their married living being beginning. She was completely in herself then inside her then, Mrs. Dehning, she was then of married living in them, she was then completely then again all of herself inside her to make her herself again then. This was then married living beginning in them in her then. She had completely in her then inside her the beginning married living in them, she had completely in her then inside her the being of her. This was beginning married living then of Alfred Hersland and Julia Hersland in her.

Hortense Dehning as I was saying was in her for herself then really quite nicely living any living in Julia then, and so then Hortense then was living inside her beginning married living of Julia and Alfred Hersland and this was not then an important thing to any one and only to Hortense for remembering. As I was saying George Dehning was living in Dehning family living, certainly he was living in that living then and so he was living in Dehning family living in the beginning married living in Alfred and Julia Hersland and that is enough then about him. To go on then.

As I was saying once, Alfred Hersland was needing something to

make him completely be then one being really living. This is then to
be some description of his coming not to be having, to be having this
thing.

Mr. Dehning had all he could be needing to be successful in living.
As I was saying more and more it was important being in him really to
be listening to any one wanting to be doing anything.

Each one has their own way of telling some other one what they are
needing for being succeeding in living. Some are stammering some
when they are telling this thing of their needing something to be then a
successful one, to some one. Some tell this quite quickly to any one,
some tell it quite quickly but not to any one, some almost do not tell
this thing to any one, some seem to be one not telling this thing to any
one some of such of them then tell this thing quite completely to some.
Each one is himself is herself inside her inside him in telling this thing, in
telling of needing something to be making that one a successful one in
living. Some are very convincing in telling this thing, some are not at
all convincing in telling this thing, some are more some are less convincing in telling this thing, some are convincing to some in telling this
thing, some are not really convincing to any one in telling this thing, some
are convincing to mostly every one in telling this thing. As I was saying it
was coming to be always more important being in Mr. Dehning to be listening to any one wanting to be doing anything. Mr. Dehning was everything he was needing for his successful living. This is certain. Mr.
Dehning was one being quite successful in all of his living. Alfred
Hersland came to be a little convincing to him, not really to the completeness of being convincing to him in telling what he would be needing to be
one quite successful in living but then Alfred Hersland was then being of
Dehning family living. Mr. Dehning was certainly living then being
in Dehning family living, he was one having it always more in him as
important being listening to any one wanting to be doing anything, he
was one having quite altogether everything he was using for quite completely successful living, he was certainly one certain that not any one
should be not having something in living they were not then using, certainly he had feeling that Alfred Hersland to be succeeding would have to
be using everything he had for living and so he Alfred Hersland was a
little never really convincing in being one going to be succeeding to Mr.
Dehning but then Mr. Dehning was in Dehning family living, Alfred
Hersland was in Dehning family living, listening to any one wanting to
be doing anything was always more and more important being in Mr.
Dehning, Mr. Dehning came then to enough then for completely listening
came then to be convinced by Alfred Hersland's telling what Alfred
Hersland was needing for succeeding in living.

Mr. Dehning liked very well then hearing any one telling again and
again what any one was needing for succeeding in living. As I am saying

always more and more it was important being in Mr. Dehning being one listening to any one telling about what they were needing to be doing to be really living in their living. As I am saying Mr. Dehning liked very well then some repeating, Alfred Hersland then was really then repeating with pretty steady aspiration that he was needing something to be succeeding in being one living.

I am beginning to like conversation, I am beginning to like reading some thing about some that I never before found at all interesting. I am beginning to like conversation, I used not to like conversing at all, and social living, and so going on and on I am needing always I am needing something to give to me completely successful diversion to give me enough stimulation to keep me completely going on being one going on living. That is a description of some being in me, this is then some history of me. So then I am beginning now to like conversation.

As I was saying Alfred Hersland was telling then after he was a married one with a reasonable steadiness in aspiration, with quite a really complete enthusiasm, with eagerness but not with insistence in telling, with quite sufficient pleasure in repeating, with quite a great deal of honesty in hoping, he was telling then what he was needing to be one really succeeding quite well in living. He was then in Dehning family living. He was then just married to Julia Dehning.

I was saying that I was coming to now be interested in conversing and this is to me now completeness in diversion which is what I am having to make of me one going to be going on living. I have been having all my living completeness in diversion and so I have been one all my living been one going to be going on being living. Each one then who is not stopping being going on living is one having it in them in some way to be one going on going on being living.

Mr. Dehning as I was saying was one quite completely succeeding in living, he was one going to be going on in being one being living and always it was more and more important in him in his being that he was listening when some one was telling what that one was going to be doing in living, was going to be needing to be doing what that one was going to be doing in living. So then it was always in Mr. Dehning that he was listening to some one telling what they were going to be doing in living, what they were going to be needing to be going to be doing something. As I am saying Mr. Dehning had in him to be really listening to some one telling such a thing to him. As I was saying he was not really listening to Alfred Hersland until Alfred Hersland was really in Dehning family living, then sooner than it was right to him by listening he was doing more than listening and this is to be now some history of this thing.

Anybody can understand that Mr. Dehning was one really listening to any one wanting to be doing anything, really listening to any one. Anybody can understand that this always was in Mr. Dehning and al-

ways was more and more important being in him. Any one can understand that really with Alfred Hersland he came not to be so really listening as it was in him to be doing really in his living. Alfred was in Dehning
family living and Mr. Dehning always was listening to any one in Dehning
family living wanting to be doing anything and Alfred was in Dehning
family daily living, he was in Dehning family living and not born to be
this thing and he was one really earnest in aspiring, really honest in hoping, really enthusiastic in believing, really thorough in repeating.
Alfred Hersland came then to be beginning.

Alfred Hersland came then to be beginning succeeding in living.
This is to be now some history of this thing.

Julia was one not really attacking for winning, she was one not needing to be really living, she was really doing what she was feeling she
was needing to be doing if she were to be one really being living in
going on living. She was really then all her living keeping on being
in family living although she was attacking to be going on being living
by learning anything. That is a history of her. She was certain then
after she was a married one that she was an honest one in daily living,
that Dehning family living was honest enough for living, she was
then always then and always in Dehning family living. She was
always then attacking to be learning as if she could be one going to be
really living in being one going to be going on as living. Really then she
was all her living in Dehning family living. Really then as I have been
saying quite often she was not attacking to be winning, any one can now
understand this thing. To very many she was one attacking to be winning, really then she was in a way like Mrs. Dehning who too was stupid
in being one attacking and not for any real winning of anything.

Any one can then now be understanding being in Julia Hersland
and can be understanding then Dehning family living, and can begin
again now to be getting ready to be understanding being in Mr. Dehning
and in Alfred Hersland and how they came to be doing with themselves
and each other what they came to be doing. This is a way of saying I
could be such a very happy one if every one really was certain that I
was really a very wise one. I like it that I am feeling that I could be a
very happy one if every one were certain I was a completely wise one.
Really I like it very well that I am not really certain, that mostly not any
one is really certain. It is a nicely disturbing feeling, this thing. I am
now completely realising being in Mr. Dehning and Alfred Hersland.

That thing that I was saying that some have not ambition as emotion in them and these then are to mostly every one not ambitious ones in
living and some of these have very much ambition as really being in them
and some have it as intention and not emotion in them and some really
do not have it as emotion, as intention, as being in the being in them is
really very interesting. I can understand this thing from having been

knowing some who are ones older ones are very much liking, really these
have it in them sometimes to be very much needing to be succeeding
in living for the being in them and yet not having ambition as emotion,
as intention in them really not having at all ambition as emotion, as
intention in them, makes of them then those being very sweet in living,
being full of sweetness then and light and life to very many knowing
them. Some not having any ambition as intention, as emotion in them
have not any ambition in them but these are just being in living, they
are really not actually succeeding in living. Some of such of them are
being very completely well in being living, this is another thing. Now
I am thinking of Julia Hersland and Alfred Hersland, now I am thinking of one having really not ambition as emotion, almost not ambition
as intention, quite completely ambition as being, now I am thinking
of one having completely ambition as aspiration, considerably and hope-
fully and even enthusiastically and eagerly, ambition as intention, not
really ambition as being. This is to be a history of Alfred and Julia
Hersland.

Mr. Dehning had come then as I was saying to be doing differently
than listening to Alfred Hersland. He gave him a good deal of money as
a loan for Alfred to be really then beginning to be succeeding in living.

Alfred certainly did have a very little real sense for living, else with
being one aspiring in emotion, and ambitious in emotion and intention
and not ambitious in being and not really succeeding in being one resisting
and not really succeeding in being one engulfing he would not have been
one ending living with not being then one having been really completely
failing. He was not ever really succeeding in living. He was one not
really learning anything very much by having been in living. He was not
well in the beginning of his middle living believing he was beginning
to be one going to be really going on succeeding in living. Now I am
going on. Now go on.

Succeeding is to me just now very interesting. Some are certainly
succeeding in living, some are certainly not succeeding in living, some are
in between. I have been coming just lately to be understanding more
and more the being in each one and the way being in each one makes of
each one one succeeding, one not succeeding, one in between succeeding
and not succeeding in living, one succeeding some, one succeeding sometime, one succeeding sometimes, one not succeeding at all in living, one
not succeeding quite often in living, one beginning with succeeding, one
succeeding and then not with any more succeeding just keeping on going.
I have come more and more to understanding the being in men and women
in relation to their succeeding and failing in living. I have been making
groups of them groups of men and women and grouping the being in them
in relation to ambition, to succeeding, to failing in them. I have been
explaining some men to some and it is certainly an interesting thing to

be doing this thing. I am hoping sometime to write a complete history of men and women, I am beginning to be hoping this thing again, I am filled up now so much with learning so much about men and women and feel so much wisdom in me now inside me completely organising that I am coming again to be almost certain that I can sometime be writing the complete history of every one who ever was or is or will be living. I will sometime be writing complete histories of pairs of people who are connected in living. I am now telling about some succeeding, some failing in living.

It is very difficult in quarrelling for either one to be certain what the other one has then in him that is making him then do quarrelling. This is often quite astonishing. This is sometimes quite entirely astonishing that not one quarrelling is certain of what the other one has in her, in him for quarrelling. This can be really astonishing when any one later is learning at all what was then in another one. And then it is such a very difficult thing ever to believe the other one when the other one is telling what was in him for quarrelling.

It is certainly a difficult thing to believe another one about quarrelling in that other one with one. Very often then it is not a thing any one can be doing believing then the other one. Sometimes it is a thing some one can be doing believing the other one. Mostly then every one comes sometime more or less in them to quarrel with some other one, with mostly every other one sometime. A little quite a little, quite a good deal, quite some, quite almost not at all, quite often, quite seldom, quite certainly, quite slowly, quite suddenly, quite gradually, certainly there is quite a good deal in every one or some quarrelling with some one, with quite a number of them that sometime for that one are being living with that one in the living that one can have in that one. This then is to be now much description of Dehning and Hersland quarrelling. They certainly did quarrel some.

They certainly did quarrel some all of them. They certainly did quarrel completely, some of them. This is to be now some history of all of them.

Now I am writing of being successful in living, of quarrelling in being living. Now I am writing of having loving feeling in them some men and some women of being ones succeeding in living some men and some women, of being doing some quarrelling some of these men and some of these women. This is to be now more history of each one of them.

Quarrelling is to me very interesting. Beginning and ending is to me very interesting.

Mostly every one does some quarrelling. Quarrelling is to me very interesting. Beginning is to me very interesting. Ending is to me very interesting. Every one is beginning and ending in their living.

Mostly every one is sometimes quarrelling with some one. Quarrelling as I am saying is to me very interesting. Beginning is interesting, ending is interesting.to me as I have been again saying. Mostly every one is sometimes quarrelling with some one, mostly every one is beginning sometime ending with some one. This that I am now writing is a history of Dehning and Hersland living and quarrelling.

Quarrelling is not letting those having attacking be winning by attacking, those having resisting being be winning by resisting, those having dependent being be winning by dependent being, those having engulfing being be winning by engulfing being. This is quarreling in living, not letting each one by some one be winning by the being in them. This is certainly quarrelling in living. There is a great deal of quarrelling in living, that is reasonably certain and that is a very natural thing as certainly very many are not winning with the being in them.

Quarrelling is then this thing. Sometimes it is like not writing only for one's self and those not knowing one. Quarrelling is then certainly mostly that each one is not winning, to some one, with the being in them, quarrelling is then certainly then mostly that some one is not winning then, for some one, with the being in them. That certainly is quarrelling. That certainly is continually happening in living in any living by every one, by any one.

Quarrelling then is some one not winning by the being in them for some one, to some one. This is now to be some history of some quarrelling.

Now any one can be understanding how Julia and Alfred Hersland, how Mr. Dehning and Alfred Hersland how Mrs. Dehning, how each one came to be quarrelling, how Mr. Dehning and Julia Hersland and Mrs. Dehning then came to be quarrelling with Alfred Hersland. Surely any one can now understand this thing. Surely now every one can now understand this thing.

Mr. Dehning was helping Alfred Hersland as Alfred Hersland had wanted Mr. Dehning to help him. I was saying that Mr. Dehning came to help Alfred Hersland in the way Alfred Hersland had been wanting Mr. Dehning to help him. I told something about this thing.

Julia and Alfred Hersland were still living a married living when Mr. Dehning was not going into any house where Alfred Hersland was staying and Mrs. Dehning was still going to see Julia where she was living. Alfred Hersland was then not beginning to be succeeding. He was really not altogether failing.

Mr. Dehning had come to be certain that he could be explaining to any one that Alfred Hersland was not honest enough for daily living, that he could really convince any one of this thing.

He certainly had good reason for convincing every one, he certainly could have convinced mostly every one. He could convince almost any one of this thing. He was quite certain and he had good reason for being quite certain that any one could convince any one of this thing.

As I was saying Julia Hersland very soon after commencing having married living was certain that Alfred Hersland was not an honest one for living, she was certain of this thing, she came at that time then to be to herself completely knowing it as certain that she was an honest one in living an honest one for living, she had always been knowing that Dehning family living was honest enough for any daily living, in daily living.

Beginning anything, going on with anything, ending come to anything to any one ever living is to me an interesting thing. This is being now more description of everything ever existing in Mr. Dehning, Mrs. Dehning, Alfred Hersland, Julia Hersland, George Dehning and Hortense Dehning and any one coming to know any of them very well in their living.

It was a natural thing for Mr. Dehning to be certain that he could convince any one that Alfred Hersland was what he knew him then to be in daily living. It was a perfectly natural thing for Mr. Dehning to be certain of this thing, Mr. Dehning did not talk so very much about this thing. Really he told it again and again to Julia and Mrs. Dehning and George Dehning some in Dehning family living but this was a natural thing for Mr. Dehning to be doing then. Really he was naturally completely certain that he could certainly convince every one that he had been completely right in not any longer having Alfred Hersland in any family living where he Mr. Dehning was having family living. He was certain that this thing was a right thing. He never thought or said then that Julia should have come to be certain not to want to be married to Alfred. He certainly never did say this thing then, that is he never really certainly said this thing. He said quite often that Alfred Hersland was not honest enough for any daily living. He was quite certain of this thing. Any one certainly could be convinced of this thing if there could come any reason for convincing any one of this thing. Mr. Dehning said this thing when it was right for him to be saying this thing. Mr. Dehning had completely natural feeling in him about this whole thing. This then has been a description of Mr. Dehning and Alfred Hersland having been in Dehning family living. This is to be now more description of being in each one and in some together in living of these I have mentioned again and again.

Alfred Hersland had ambition in him. Julia Hersland had ambition for living. Not either one or the other of them had really sense for living, not either one or the other was really in the whole of living succeeding or failing. They had each of them ambition in them. They had ambition differently in them each one of them. Mr. Dehning had ambition in living. Mrs. Dehning had ambition. This is to be now some description of ambition, and honest living, and loving being and daily living and succeeding and failing in each one of them.

Alfred Hersland then was for Dehning family living, not honest in daily living. He was much later when he was working with some men then fairly successful in living. He could be then when working with certain men quite a successful enough one in living. He had not really sense for living, he had not really not any sense for living. He had as I was saying not any ambition in him from the resisting, from the engulfing being in him. He had a feeling from the resisting and engulfing being in him some feeling of succeeding in living, of feeling something elegant in him in living for him. He had then too, from the resisting and engulfing being in him with this feeling of feeling something being quite elegant in him and in living and some feeling of succeeding being an elegant thing in being living, quite a good deal of vanity for living. As I was saying really aspiration and amibition was really stupid being in him because really he was one not winning by being resisting, really not winning by being engulfing. He had aspiration in him, he had ambition in him, as I was saying he had not really feeling of anything being important in him until he was loving and wanting to stop studying to marry that one and then not wanting to marry that one. He had not ambition and aspiration in him by the being of him. He had aspiration and ambition in him, beginning when something was important to him, as something of emotion, as certainly a good deal of intention. So then aspiration and ambition as emotion was almost sentimental being in him it was not in him from being one able to be succeeding able to be winning by the being in him, aspiration and ambition as intention was really stupid being in him, they were not from being in him but from needing to be having what he needed to be having to have anything be important to him which was not from the being in him important to him. He was then certainly for Dehning family living not honest for daily living and to himself then he was a man having it in him to have that he was not quite certain that to be a dead one was to be really not a dead one. He had some loving feeling in him, he could with not winning resisting and engulfing being have violent temper sometimes in him. He was one then to Dehning family living not honest in daily living. He was one very much later, and working with some men, not really not successful in living.

Certainly some are loving, some are honest, some are good ones, some are thinking in living, certainly there are some in living having some of thinking, loving, good being, honesty in them. Some have certainly some of something really in them. Certainly they have.

Some have pretty honest living in them always in their daily living and are liking it very well that they have some reputation for this thing. Mr. Dehning really was such a one. Some come to be sometime completely certain that they are completely honest ones in living and then all their living they are completely freely attacking with this thing. Julia Dehning was such a one. She was really not feeling it as being that there was for her a reputation of being an honest one in living, she liked it that the Dehning family living, Mr. Dehning, had a complete reputation of honest living in daily living, her being an honest one in daily living was a thing when she came to be living with it inside her completely in her she could be using all her living for all the attacking she was ever doing to be winning. Alfred Hersland was not believing that not every one was thinking that he was an honest enough one for daily living. He never really was certain that any one excepting Mr. Dehning was really believing that he was not an honest man for any kind of daily living. He never was really certain that Julia could have really been believing this thing if she had not been then and all of her living in Dehning family living. Julia was certain of this thing that Alfred Hersland was not honest enough for daily living when she came to living in married living. She came very quickly to be very certain that to her then she was one living in her being which was one being complete in honest living and she was soon then coming to be attacking in all her living with this thing. Mr. Dehning as I was saying was one having completely in him for him the reputation of being one really completely honest enough for any daily living. Mrs. Dehning was one honest enough for any daily living, and she had feeling of Dehning family living having a reputation for this thing but the kind of reputation she was always feeling they were having was the kind one comes to be having when one is a dead one, when one is not any longer in living, she was really in living quite completely an honest one. Each one then of the four of them Mr. Dehning, Alfred Hersland, Julia Hersland and Mrs. Dehning had a different feeling in their having reputation of being an honest enough one for living.

This is then what was happening. Mr. Dehning had come quite slowly to be certain that Alfred Hersland was completely not an honest enough man for any honest enough daily living. Mr. Dehning had come quite slowly enough to be certain of this thing. He had as I was saying never been really certain that Alfred Hersland was really for him in Dehning family living and then he was certain enough of this thing to be pretty nearly completely listening to Alfred Hersland telling about anything he needed to be doing to be really living in daily living and then he was still not quite entirely completely listening and he was already then giving Alfred Hersland what Alfred Hersland was needing to be beginning to be living in daily living to be beginning to be living to be one succeeding in living, Mr. Dehning then certainly came to be certain that Alfred Hersland was not honest enough for any daily living and Alfred Hersland was quite certain then that Mr. Dehning was completely in him certain of this thing. Mr. Dehning did not see Alfred Hersland any more at all then to speak at all to him in any daily living. Mr. Dehning was certainly certain that he could convince any one that certainly Alfred Hersland was not honest for any daily living. Mr. Dehning could certainly convince almost any one of this thing. Mr. Dehning did certainly not just then begin anything to convince any one of this thing.

Julia Hersland came very quickly to be really certain that Alfred Hersland was not an honest one for any daily living and as I was saying she was one having then certainly complete courage for being one going on being living. She knew then as being in her that she was one being honest always in being one being living, having courage always for being one going to be going on being living. She was always then needing to be one going to be learning everything. This has been then a complete description. She was quickly certain that Alfred Hersland was not honest for any daily living. This then was then for Alfred Hersland not a serious thing, this was then not in him then as important in him, as being living then in him as being really something really exciting. As I was saying in a way Julia Hersland was not an interesting one in being living. She was an interesting one in being living to some, that will be again more history of her.

Mrs. Dehning was certainly not certain from any being in her that Alfred Hersland was not honest enough for any daily living. She could and did come to be quite certain of this thing. As I said of her she was completely an honest one in being one being living. As I was saying she was feeling reputation as being as if some one were already a dead one. As I was saying she was one mostly attacking harshly in living but not for any winning. As I was saying she had sense for living. As I was saying she was always being in her stupid being in being one feeling anything. So then she was not certain from any being in her being there to her in her that Alfred Hersland was not honest enough for any daily living. She certainly came to be certain of this thing. So then she was going on talking to Alfred Hersland for quite a long time in daily living and then it came that to hear him or to see him or to know of him made her completely then a nervous one.

I will be telling about feeling being in George Dehning and Hortense Dehning in the history of David Hersland that will certainly sometime be written.

I have given a description of Alfred Hersland and Julia Hersland not succeeding in married living, of Alfred Hersland not succeeding in being one beginning to be succeeding in living from being in Dehning family living. As I was saying later he was not failing in living, he was fairly succeeding, later when he was working with some other men.

This is to be now more history of married living of Mr. and Mrs. Hersland and of Mr. Dehning living and Mrs. Dehning being living.

The Herslands Alfred and Julia were living married living. They had a baby and it was quite a strong well one but it did not live to be a very old one. It got sick and died of something. As I was saying Julia loved babies being little babies and her children. This first one was a little boy and Mrs. Dehning thought that he was one looking very much like the father of him. Mr. Dehning had seen him and saw him very often and he was glad that his daughter Julia had a baby and loved him.

They had later Julia and Alfred another child and this one was a girl and Mrs. Dehning was certain that this one would be in Dehning family living, this one was already looking like the mother of her. Mr. Dehning often saw her when the nurse was with her, the baby, and he liked it very much that Julia was happy in having a little girl who was like her. Then there was a little boy who was quite a weak little one and about this one it was not quite certain although Mrs. Dehning was pretty nearly certain that he was quite a good deal like the father of him. This one was quite a weak little one in commencing but he came to be quite a strong enough little one a little later in his living. He was certainly a good deal like the father of him, Mrs. Dehning often said this about him but he had it a little in him to be like his young uncle George Dehning. Mrs. Dehning did not say this very often Mr. and Mrs. Hersland then were living then married living as I am saying.

The Herslands Alfred and Julia Hersland did not go on being in married living. It was a natural thing as I was saying that they should not be succeeding in married living, the two of them.

As I was saying Alfred Hersland came later to loving another. Julia Hersland too came later to loving another. Each one of them as I was saying was not succeeding was not failing really in living.

I can feel myself in myself going to be being an old one. I can feel being in some going to be old ones in the living of these and I can not feel being in some when these are going to be beginning to be old ones. I can certainly more and more feel old being going to be in men and in women in each one. I am beginning a little to feel young being having been, very young being having been in each one in all women and all men. I certainly can feel being old ones in a good many now when I am feeling being in them. I like to be feeling them being old ones in every little thing in every piece of being in them. I cannot so well feel being in them having been very young in them. I am a little beginning to feel this thing, I am just commencing then in really feeling this thing. I am feeling again and again in myself going to be an old one. I do not like this thing, I certainly do like this thing. I certainly do like ending being in all men and in all women. I certainly do not at all like this thing. I certainly have completely a queer disturbed mixed with sombre feeling in this thing. I certainly do really completely need feeling certainly this thing in every one that each one is sometime ending in being living.

Alfred Hersland and Julia Hersland went on then for sometime being living. Sometime then they went on being living in married living with each other and then they were not and then they had more living in them and then one and then the other one was ended in being living. This is then to be all history of them. I will be going on to the ending in all description of every one, of any one.

How can anything be different from what it is. I do not know any such a thing. Very many are knowing this. I am not knowing this thing.

I am not knowing anything being different from what it is. Very many are knowing everything being different from what it is. Once this was to me an astonishing thing. Now it is not to me at all an astonishing thing.

I am thinking now about everything being what it is, everything not being what it is, something being what it is, nothing being what it is, something not being what it is to some, I am thinking of this thing and I am thinking about sense for living in men and women.

I would like to be thinking about some being practical in their being and some not being that thing in their being but I am not just now feeling any understanding of this thing and so I am not thinking about this thing. I have been expecting some time to be soon thinking about this thing. I am not as I have just been saying thinking now about this thing. I am thinking now as I have been saying about something being what it is, not being what it is to some men and some women. I am thinking about every one having it or not having it that something that everything is what it is, not what it is to them each one of them, that nothing is what it is, to some one. I am too thinking and going soon now to be telling very much about sense for living in men and women.

Those in Dehning daily living, those in Hersland daily living each one of them came to know some men and women, in being one being living. Each one any one having living being has some sense for living or has not any sense for living pretty nearly not any sense for living. This is to be now some description of sense for living in men and women.

Some have sense for living from having realisation in them that each thing they are knowing is such a thing as it is to them and really knowing this in them. Each thing has then to some of such of them the value that thing has really for any one needing that thing for being one going on living. Some are knowing in them that each thing they are knowing in living is the thing that thing really is being but they are not feeling that thing as really value to any one for any one to be going on living. I will sometime be telling some more about this thing.

Kinds in men and women. I am seeing kinds in men and in women so many kinds in them. Sometimes I am seeing a number of one kind of them, some other days I am seeing a number of other kinds of them. I wish I knew everything about them, I wish I knew everything about each one, I wish I had a complete record of each one, what each one did, what each one had as being in her in him, what each one could be doing, thinking, feeling, knowing. I certainly do wish that I knew everything about being and doing and feeling and knowing being in each one. I do not yet that is certain, I am almost not hoping that I will sometime know everything about every one, I only know that I wish that I did sometime know everything about every one all through the living being ever in each one.

Nobody knows, nobody can know, and I am telling it very often, nobody knows nobody can know how I am wanting to know everything about every one. I am seeing so many just now having living being in them succeeding or failing much or some in living, nobody knows, nobody can know how I want to know all the being ever in them. Nobody can know how tired I get looking so hard at them, nobody knows how much I want to know all the being there is or was or will be in any man or woman ever living. Nobody knows and I tell it very often, nobody knows this thing. Nobody can know this thing being in me that I am telling very often, nobody knows what I am wanting, that I am wanting to know completely all the being there ever was or is or will be in any one.

I can certainly not really tell this thing to any one so that any one can completely believe this thing that I am really wanting to be knowing all the being ever having been, going to be, being in any one. No one can really believe my needing really needing to be having this thing, really needing this thing for living.

I tell you every one that I am seeing very many kinds in men and women, a very great many men and women, and all the kinds there are of them. I tell it again and again that I am seeing a very great many men and women, such a number of them and I am seeing kinds in them and I tell every one that I am doing this thing, that I am knowing this thing. Nobody knows, nobody knows that I am really needing to be knowing everything ever in any man in any woman, any being, all being ever in any woman in any man. Nobody knows that I am completely needing to be completely knowing this thing. I am seeing a very great many men and women. I am seeing kinds in them. I do not know all the being in each one of them.

I see very many men and women. I look at them, some have been succeeding in being one being living, some are succeeding, some will be succeeding. Some have not been succeeding in being in their living, some will not be succeeding, some are not succeeding. Some have sense for living and are not succeeding, have not been succeeding, will not be succeeding in living. I will tell something now about sense for living in women and in men.

I see very many just now who are living and I look at them. I see very many just now. I am asking some of them to do something, some of these do what I ask them to do and some do not do what I ask them. Some do in a way something when I ask them to do something. I am as I am saying seeing now very many men and very many women. I am seeing each one of them doing several things for living, some are asking, some are talking, some are standing, some are waiting, some are working, some are eating, some are sitting, some are drinking, some are writing, some are loving, some are forgetting that they had begun doing something, some are thinking every one should understand what they are saying, some are feeling that every one near them are ugly ones for living, some are laughing, very many are rushing some are washing themselves or other things, some are dressing, some are having their feet swollen and hurting them as they are standing, as they are walking, as they are sitting, as they are working. Anybody then can see then that I am seeing just now very many men and very many women.

As I am saying sense for living is something that is to me quite interesting. I can tell something now about this thing in men and women.

I can tell something more about this thing about having sense in living, by living, for living, I can tell some more about sense in men and in women. I sometimes can tell very much about sense for living in men and women. I have been telling to some quite a good deal about this thing.

I am thinking now about one kind and I am knowing now not really knowing all of them but really knowing being in them in some of this kind in men and women. I am knowing three of them of this group of them as men. I am knowing one of a group of them as a woman. I am knowing another of another group in men and women as a woman, some of another group of them some as men and some as women. I am knowing another very large group of them and I am knowing these as everything they ever are in living some of them. I am trying to begin now telling what I am knowing about sense in men and in women.

I am now not doing anything but telling about sense in living, sense from living, sense of living, sense for living, sense about living in men and in women. I am telling everything to be away where I am not just now learning so that I am going to be completely telling all I am knowing about sense for living in men and women and I am not yet doing this thing and I am not yet really certain that I am now going to be having everything away so that I will be telling this thing. I certainly do not now certainly know this thing. I am putting everything away from me in me so that I shall be soon telling all this thing. I will now go on putting everything a little more away from me in me so that I certainly will not be telling anything that is not this thing. I like this thing putting everything away from me in me so that I will be telling this thing. I will tell this thing. Certainly I will tell this thing. Pretty nearly everything is away now and I am very nearly telling this thing. I am certainly not leaving anything not put away from me inside me so that now I certainly can be telling something. I certainly can be telling this thing.

I am liking to be thinking about sense for living being in some of each kind there is in men and in women. I am liking to be thinking about making kinds of them in men and women in relation to sense for living being in them. I am liking then as I am saying just now to certainly be putting everything away so that now I am thinking kinds this way in men and in women.

Do I know everything of having sense in being living, well, I do not think I do, I do not know knowing everything about having sense for living. I have said something about having sense for living. I am going to be saying something about having sense for living. I have just been being seeing one certainly having had and having and perhaps going to be having sense for living. It was interesting to me to be seeing this one. I saw one having sense for living but this one was one having sense for each little piece of living and this never made in this one sense for all the living in this one. This one had so much sense for each little piece of living this one was doing that it was astonishing. This one had not really sense for living for big pieces of living in him. I saw another one and this one had not had much sense for living but this one had not then at all really needed this thing, this one then had sense for living and then it was sense like a good many have it in them a dull thing in this one as being like a really married one and then this one had more sense for living and was a very careful one and then this one came very early in her living to being a really dead one and not any one was then remembering loving this one as much as one would have throught from all the being in this one many would be remembering loving this one.

I am thinking now again of three having really succeeding in living, really sense for living in them and these have it for a whole living in them and these do not have it that they are really learning in being one going on living, these have it in them that at one time they are realising completely succeeding in living and they are then really completely succeeding in living, and then they are realising completely succeeding in living and there are more seeing them and they have more of a building in which they are then living and they are then completely succeeding in living, and then they are realising again succeeding in living and then they have more again to see them and they have again a bigger building in which they are then and they are then again completely succeeding in living and not any at all are they learning anything from having been at all in any living and so on and so on and these then are the most wonderfully succeeding ones in living and always they have not it at all in them to be learning at all anything in being being living. These then are men and women succeeding in living, having sense for living, certainly sense for winning, not any sense for learning from having been one being living, not really sense for feeling being living, certainly some sense for feeling being winning, certainly sense for having working under them not any one going to be winning, not having any sense for trusting any one working for them, really sense for winning in living, really sense for always winning a bigger living, always changing to winning a bigger living, always not learning anything from being one being living, always then succeeding for living. I am seeing three of them. One of them is being one making a big business of something, one of these is making a to be always larger to be for him to be in, one of these is one everybody is knowing in every country now that that one is one being living.

Some as I was saying have really sense for living, there are as many ways of having this thing as there are kinds in men and women and I have certainly been saying that there are quite a very great many kinds in men and women.

Some are saying that they have it that they can by remembering be certain that each one they are knowing were sometime younger ones. Some are certain that each one they are knowing are getting to be very old ones. Some are certain that each one they are knowing are not changing, they were not very much younger ones, they are not coming now to be very much older ones. There are different ways of feeling oneself and other ones as to any one coming to be older, having been younger ones. This and having sense for living is to me just now very interesting.

Every one being a young one, having been a young one, being an older one, having been an older one, being an old one and having been and going on being an old one, having been and going on being a young one, having been one not an old one not a young one and going on being not a young one not an old one is to me very interesting. I cannot really get away from this thing as being everything there is in any one being one being living. I really cannot get myself away from this thing. This is any one being living.

I really am thinking that every one is living in being in some way one having sense for living, in being in some way one being one going on being living. Some have come to be not any longer living ones. Perhaps each one ever living will be coming sometime to be not any longer one being going on living. Perhaps each one sometime is not any longer one being in living. I am certainly repeating this thing which is to me something I am certainly thinking is perhaps being in every one.

Some are changing the size in being in them in the living in them. I am seeing some doing this thing in being ones going on being in living. I like seeing every one and then I very much do not like at all seeing every one. Some have changing in size in them inside them in being in them, some are not changing in the size in them in the being of them inside them. There is one she has been changing the size in being inside her in living and this one is not a young one is not an old one. There is one and this one is almost an old one is changing the size in her in being and this one was really a fat one and is now quite entirely a thing one, this one then is one changing being in this one and this one is really not a fat thin one but really then a really thin one and then this one is quite dull then to any one listening to being in that one. And some one is a thin one, that one was not a young one not an old one and this one was a funny one in being one being in being in him a fat one.

I certainly pretty nearly like being in each one. I do not like listening too many days one after the other to some. I am now doing this thing. I will then know something. Each one always is repeating. This is certain that each one always is repeating all the being in that one. This sometimes is quite a dull thing for me when I am listening, not that each one is repeating all the being in them that is never to me a dull thing but the thing they are repeating can be to me quite a dull thing.

I am still not telling all I know about sense for living. Perhaps I am not yet quite ready to be telling everything about this thing. This then is going to commence again being the history of every one and among them of the Herslands and the Dehnings.

Sense for succeeding in living, sense for feeling being in living, sense for being one going to be going on being living, these three are different things, quite entirely different things and some having one have the others, some have almost none of any of them, some have some of one of them, I am thinking just now of one having some sense for succeeding in living, some sense for feeling being one being living, not any sense for being one going to be going on being living. This is one and I am feeling this one. Some will be remembering this one, some will not be remembering this one. I am feeling this one. This one is one certainly having some sense for suceeding in living, is one having certainly really sense for being one feeling being living, is one having certainly having certainly never been having any not any sense for being one going to be going on being living. Mrs. Hersland, Mrs. Alfred Hersland was one having as I was saying sense for being one going to be going on being living. Mrs. Hersland, Mrs. Alfred Hersland, Julia Hersland was one then quite different from this one I am just now describing.

This one I am just now describing, this one I am just now really feeling is one then really having sense for really succeeding in living, is one having sense for really feeling that that one is really being in living, is one being really in living, is one not ever having been being one going on being living. As I am saying any one will not then when this one is not any longer being in living, will not be remembering really this one having been being in living. This description then is a description of this one. This one then is one really feeling being in living, really this one is really being this, this thing, being one really feeling being in living, really feeling all the being this one was being in being living, this one then really was quite entirely in the living this one had in being one being living, feeling of all being this one was in being living. Am I really then saying this thing that I am now feeling in the being being in this one, that this one was and in a way it was sometimes quite a completely bubbling thing that this one had sense for some succeeding in being one being living, it was sometimes quite very often entirely a thing that any one really could be remembering that this one was really perhaps having quite sense enough for succeeding in living and this one certainly was then feeling all the being this one was in being one being living. This one was then as I was saying not really at all like, quite different then from the being in Julia Hersland. I will tell now more about both of them.

This one is then one I am now knowing completely in being one, I am being that one, completely realising the being in this one. I really did not think I would be so soon doing this thing, realising being in this one, and then I was, I am realising the being in this one and I like realising the being in this one, and I will be remembering this one although I am not sure that I can be certain to be really realising remembering this one. I will though certainly be remembering this one, yes I will be remembering this one, really I am certain of this thing, I certainly will be remembering this one, I am certain of this thing.

I am feeling now in every one the sense for being one being in living that each one has in them and the way each one has that sense in them and the way each one is beginning being one being one succeeding being one not succeeding in everything, being one beginning and going on and ending in being one being living.

I am feeling very much sense for living in men and in women, in every one I am seeing doing being in living, being one going on being living, I am feeling very much this thing when I am seeing one being a young one, when I am seeing some one being not a very young one, when I am seeing somebody who is quite certainly not a young one, when I am seeing any one.

Very many have been here living and talking and some of them have been very much loving some one, and all of them have it in them to have some sense in being one being living. Some of them are not very interesting to very many knowing them in being in the way that one is one having some sense in being one being living. Very many have then been here and are living and are having each one some sense for living and some of them are quite successful ones in being living and very many of them are quite enough successful in being living to be going on being those being living in being living. Very many then are here and have it in them very many of them to have some sense in being one being living and very many of them are succeeding in living so that until their ending they are those being those going on being living. There are then very many here and mostly each one of them of these that are here have it in them to have in them some sense in being one being living and very many of them are succeeding in being living, are succeeding in living so that each one of them of these are those going on being living until there is naturally a complete end to being in them. There were a number here, some of them have been loving some one quite a good deal in being one having some sense in being living, in being one being living, in being one succeeding well enough in being living to be going on being one being living. There are then often very many here and each one of them, that is certainly quite a number of them, some perhaps not and I am not just now telling about them, mostly then very many of them have it in them to have some sense in them in being one being living, some of them as I was saying quite a good deal sometimes are loving some one, quite a number of them as I am saying are succeeding well enough in being living to be of them and there are very many of them always living a very great many of them always being living who have it to be succeeding enough in being living to be of them those who are going to go on being in living until they are not any longer being living. This is then sense in being living in very many who are here very often, this is the way they have sense in being living in them. As I was saying Julia Hersland and Alfred Hersland were not such a man and such a woman. No they were not really of such of them, they were really of such of them they did go on being living, they were not of such of them, in a way they did not go on being living, they were as I was saying a little differently in them each one of them from the other one of them as to sense for living. As I was saying Julia Hersland had not really sense for being one being living, as I was saying she had strength for being one going on being living, as I was saying Alfred Hersland was one having some little sense for being one being living, as I was saying he was not ever really very much living in this thing in the sense for being one being living that there was a little in him. As I was saying they were both of them nearly succeeding, nearly altogether failing in being those being in living. I am not yet certain that I am finished with general telling about sense for being in living in men and women. I am almost certain that I am now really interested in this thing. There are then very many here, who have it in them to have some sense in them in being one being living, some of such of them quite often are really loving some one, very many of them are succeeding in being one being living well enough to be one going on in being one being living.

There were to-night eight of them and each one of them had in them some ways of not having any sense for living at all in them. There were eight of them and each of them have very much of not any of some kind of sense for living in them. I was telling one of them this thing in telling this one how he had sense for living so that he would be completely succeeding in being one being living. This one had sense for living in being one being quite certain from experiencing that in being living he could be one succeeding in living, be one having some feeling for being one being living. He is then one having certainly in him from experience in being one being living a realisation that in being one being living one can be one succeeding in living. This one has not been in living very penetratingly making any other one feel this thing, this one has certainly quite entirely learnt to be realising that he could be succeeding in being one being in living. This one is then one having really sense for being living. This one is one having it in him to certainly be succeeding quite some in living. This is one then having it in him to be realising that he can be, that he will very likely be succeeding some in living. He is one as I am saying having other people knowing this thing with him but then it is not an exciting thing, really not to him, really not to any one, he has been learning this thing, he has always been quite certain that he is working, he is certainly one always having been quite liking to be where he would be when he could be learning to be really realising that he was certainly to be one succeeding some in being living. I was telling this one then that this one really had sense for living in him. It was not at all an exciting thing telling this to him. I told it to him and always then I was certain that that he had some sense for living was not at all a thing to give to him to give to any one enough excitement so that any one could go on telling him this thing, telling him that he had sense really for living.

As I was saying there were eight of them and each one of them had it in them to have in them in a way not any sense for living, and I have told about one of these eight of them that she had not any sense for being one going to be going on being one being living. This one then was a dead one and then this one was moving a little then but then that was not really a disturbing thing, no not to me even, now when I am not any longer a quite young one.

There were then eight of them and one of them had really not really at all any sense for being one being living, not any sense at all really for being one ever having, ever being, ever going to be living. This one then certainly never had been having, never would have been having, never should have been having any sense at all in being one being living. This one was one really in a way not failing in living, this one was one to whom in a way one would be listening and then this one was a completely one not having ever been having any sense in being one being living and then not any one was listening to this one. It would have been an astonishing thing that any one could be having not any sense for living as this one was having this thing, it would have been an astonishing thing if so many had not been coming so nearly to listening to this one so that they did not really realise that not any one could listen to this one. This one really is an astonishing one, this one really has not any sense in being one being living. I will tell very much about such a one. This one was not certain that this one was one really being living and really this one was not such a one and this one was a beautifully astonishing one in being one really being one to whom very many were almost listening and being one being so completely one not having anything of having any sense in being one being living. This one really was one being beautifully astonishing. I know this one.

There were then eight of them. One was one having sense for living in being one not knowing what kind of sense for living very many very like this one are having in being living. This one had really then sense for living in being one not knowing the sense for living some like this one have in them and then too not knowing this thing made of this one quite a foolish one, made of this one a stupid one that was a quite funny thing when one was knowing this one.

There were as I was saying eight of them having in them each one of them some ways of not having any sense in being living in them. One of them was one having sense for being living in him enough so that he never came to have responsibility which would crush him. He could have been quite certainly a worried one but really in his living he was one who was almost not at all a worried one. He had then sense for living in having been in all living certain to be one who would have been a worried one if he had not been one not becoming a worried one. He was one then having sense for living, in being one feeling being living enough to have sense for living so that he did not in living by trying for all living become a worried one. He was quite entirely a really nice one this one and he had sense for living to the really living everything any one could need from him. He was certainly quite entirely a complete one, a very nice one, a one not having come to be a married one, and he had sense for being one being living not having come to be a married one, he was one not having sense for living in being one not needing to have been coming to be a married one. I cannot help mentioning it again that he was really a very nice one to have been going on and not be a worried one and be a living one, a very nice one with sense for living, with not sense for living.

There is another one then the sixth one having so much sense for living and so little sense for living that it is a sweet delight in this one this thing to every one, no really not to every one, I cannot really say it is a sweet delight this in this one to every one, it is such a thing certainly to some.

There is another one having certainly sense in living and certainly this one would be having a good deal of sense for any living if this one in telling about sense for living was not then forgetting to be living in having sense for living. This is enough about this one. There is another one and that one then makes complete the eight of them and this one has sense for living and this one is as big as all the world will be when it is a completed one, in beginning feeling and this one is then completing the world then being all in him and this one then is then really inside him is then having really completely sense in being living and this one then does not then complete the world to make of it a complete one and this one then has still sense for being living, this one then has not sense in being one being living.

I am now going to be telling that Julia Dehning and Alfred Hersland were living in their house and having some kind of married living in them then.

I am interested in having sense for being in living in men and women, I am interested in men and women succeeding in living, I am interested in men and women being married ones and being ones having or not having sense of being in married living, in being ones succeeding in being married ones, succeeding in married living.

I am very much interested in men and women having sense for being ones being in being living, for men and women having sense for being ones succeeding in being living, succeeding feeling being living, succeeding in winning anything in being one being living, succeeding in living to themselves to any one, in men and women being married ones. I am very much interested now in this thing, in these things in men and women, I am interested just now in every one. I am interested in every one in having in them sense for being one being in living. I like very much just now looking at any one, at every one, I like very much just now to be reading about any one having been doing anything, I like very much just now hearing about any one being in living, about any one having been doing, being doing anything, I like seeing pictures of any one and I like very well knowing everything I can be knowing about every one. I like this thing just now, I am liking just now knowing about every one that each one is having or not having in some ways sense in being one being living and that each one is in some way being one succeeding, not succeeding, not going to be succeeding, pretty nearly succeeding, not at all succeeding, perhaps going to be succeeding, pretty nearly succeeding, almost succeeding, succeeding or not at all succeeding or not succeeding or very well succeeding in living. I like it as I am saying just now knowing about each one in any kind of married living they have in them. It would be such a pleasant thing to very many thinking, feeling, telling about men and about women to have it in them to be just now, to be often liking to be thinking about men and about women having in them some sense, not any sense for being in living, some sense and very little sense and very much sense for being ones succeeding in living. It would be then a little to them that it would be a pleasant thing for them to be certain that very many men and very many women are always being just now being living.

This then is in me just now in my feeling and I am telling this thing and I am feeling that just now there are very many men and very many women married ones, that there are just now very many men and very many women having in them sense for being feeling themselves and sometimes some one and sometimes some and sometimes themselves to them as being in being living and there are men and women living just now and having in them hardly any sense for being one being in living, and that men and women are having or are not having sense for being ones succeeding in being living, succeeding in living. I am then telling now of being in men and in women. I am telling now about some being married men, some men, and some being married women, some women. I am telling now about some having in some ways sense for being ones being living, some having in some ways sense for succeeding while they are being in living, I am telling something now about every one. I am telling very much now about being married in some who are just now living in being married ones. I know some of such of them just now and I am now going to be telling something about each one of them. This then will be more description of Mr. and Mrs. Hersland being married ones, of other ones being married ones.

I am thinking about some who are living. Some of these are married ones in living. Some of these are not married ones in living. I am thinking about some who are living. Some of these certainly have not been ever married ones in living, some of these have certainly sometime been married ones in their living, some of these certainly have been sometimes married ones in living. I am thinking about some who are living. I am thinking about a good many who are living. Some who are living are going on being living, some who are living are not going to be going on being living. I am thinking about a very great many who are living, some of these are liking very well being in living, some are not really liking it that they are being in living. I am then thinking very much about a great many who are living. Some of these as I have been saying have in a way sense in being in living, some of these as I have been saying have in a way not sense really for being in being living. Some of these as I have been saying are living just now and I am knowing them just now when they are doing this living, some of them are certainly living just now and I am not knowing them just now doing their living. I am then certainly just now thinking about very many men and very many women being living.

Some as I am saying, some men and women are married ones in living and some are not married ones in living. Some as I am saying are married ones again and again in their living, some as I am saying are not at all ever married ones in their living. Some then certainly are sometimes married ones in their living. Being a married one is an interesting thing to me I am certain. Being married ones is an interesting thing to some, is not a very interesting thing to some. Being a married one is an interesting thing sometime to some one and is not an interesting thing sometime to that one. Being a married one is more is less an interesting thing to some one in the living being in that one. Some then are certainly sometime in their living a married one. Some being sometime in their living a married one are sometime finding that thing an interesting thing in them to them. In a way being a married one was an interesting thing to Alfred Hersland in a way it was not an interesting thing to him. Being a married one was in a way a very interesting thing to Julia Hersland, in a way it was not a very interesting thing to Julia Hersland.

I am thinking just now certainly thinking just now about some men, about some women. I certainly am just now thinking about men and about women. I certainly am just now thinking about some men, I certainly am just now thinking about some women. I am not certain that I cannot very soon have finished writing a complete history of all men and all women. This is a new feeling for me to have in me. This is a new thing to be inside me, this that I am not certain that I will not have very soon now have brought to a completion all the history of all men and all women so completely that not any more ever can be as a new thing written. This is a new feeling to have in me. I am not really certain I am going to be liking to have this as a thing to be completely in me. Perhaps I will be certain I am knowing completely everything of being in men and in women. It would be an exciting thing to be certain really of this thing having had the complete history of every one already finished in writing. I will not be having it as certain this thing, I will go on being one every day telling about being being in men and in women. Certainly I will be going on being one telling about being in men and women. I am going on being such a one.

I am wondering whether each one is an interesting thing in being one being living. I am wondering about this thing.

I am knowing some one wanting that each one is certain that everything is in the world to any one being living. I know another one who is certain that not very many things are in the world to any one being really living. I know some one who asks questions always about these things and I am remembering the words that one is using in asking about everything in asking about anything. That one is wondering whether any one is having anything in being one being really living. I am wondering whether this one is one really being almost now a quite old one. I am wondering just now whether I am not already really understanding all the being there ever can be in any man and any woman. I am almost being certain that I am understanding all being ever having been, ever being, ever going to be in any man, in any woman. I am almost certain I am understanding just now everything about being in men and women.

I am certain I do not know completely yet all the detail of all the kinds there are of men and women. I am almost certain I am understanding just now all there is of being in men and in women when they are beginning, when they are in middle living, when they are ending.

It is quite certain that I am realising just now being being in all men and in all women and the way this is in them in each one of them. I am understanding just now very much and I am not just now telling very much. I will soon now certainly be telling very much. Thinking about sense in being in living in men and women, thinking about some being and some not being married ones in being living has been to me a thing I have been very completely enjoying. I am now one knowing being being in men and in women.

I am thinking about some being and some being not married ones in being living, I am thinking about some being completely not married ones in being living, I am thinking now about every one. I will be telling just now about being being in every one.

It is a funny thing to me, a peculiar thing that each one is not knowing that living is what is certainly in them and each other one is one being one having it in them that they are ones being living. I know that each one very often is really forgetting this thing that one is one having it that that one is one having being living as being and that every other one each one is one having being in them of being one being living. Mostly every one is sometime forgetting this thing about that one, about every one.

And so then I am knowing everything because really I am not ever forgetting this thing that I am one being one having living in being and that every one is having it in that one that that one is having living being in being that one.

I am then one in a way certainly one knowing everything. Some are ones in a way knowing everything. Some are ones not in a way knowing everything. Some are knowing that some are in a way ones knowing everything. Some are never feeling anything about any one knowing everything. Mostly every one is sometime, is sometimes feeling about some one in a way knowing everything.

Alfred Hersland was the one then Julia Dehning was marrying. She married him as one she was marrying. He was one being one she was marrying, she was one being one he was marrying and each one of them was the one the other one was marrying and loving then. Each one of them was marrying the other one needing that one then and loving that one then. Each one of them then married the other one needing that one then for loving and living and being then being the one they were needing to be being in living.

Julia Dehning married Alfred Hersland. They were married and living then not very successfully to each of them married living. It is certain that each one of them was needing the other one then for being in living what each one of them was needing for being in living in them. Each one of them was then being in living and was then certain to be needing being in living. Each one of them was succeeding was failing in living. Not either of them had in a way really sense for living in being living. Each one of them in a way would be certain to be going on being in living. Each one of them was going on being in living.

Julia was one as I was saying one needing to be one being going on being living. Julia was such a one all her living. All her living she was one needing to be going on being one being living. All her living she was one as I have been saying one needing to be one going to be going on being living.

So then Julia was married to Alfred Hersland. She married him and was loving him and was certain then and not by thinking about this thing that she was one going to be going on being living. This was being in her then. This was always being in her all her living.

Julia Dehning then married one she was needing then for the being in her that was being one who was needing to be certainly always going on going to be living. This was being in her and she was then not thinking about this thing. Alfred Hersland then as I was saying was thinking about being one being aspiring in being succeeding in living. They were married ones Julia and Alfred Hersland. This is to be now more history of some coming to know them.

It is not such a very difficult thing going on being living as it seems to be to some thinking about this thing about going on being living. It is quite an easy thing for a great many having living being in them. This is a thing to surprise some that really this thing is not a difficult thing. To some it is quite a difficult thing being one going on being living. To very many, for very many it is not at all a very difficult, to quite some it is not the very least bit a really difficult thing, to be one going on being one being living, being in being living.

To some it is quite a surprising thing that it is not a very difficult thing to very many, being ones going on in being ones being in living. Julia Hersland certainly all her living was one being one going on being living, as I am saying she was not having it really in her to be from being in her one having really sense in being to herself being in living, in having really sense for living from being in her, from having been in living all her living. She was one certainly though going to be all her living going on being living. She was one really not from being in her being one succeeding in living, succeeding in being living to her inside her, she was one certainly going to be from being in her one going to be going on being one going to be living all of her living, that is certain. When she was ending she would come of course to be one not any longer being in living but that would be simply that she had come then sometime to be a dead one, not that she had ever come to be one not going to be going on being one going on being living. Really then she was one as I was saying needing learning anything because anything could be feeding her to be one going to be going on being living and indeed then she was one needing to be resisting really learning anything to be at all changing attacking being in her which was in her to make of her being one going to be all her living going on being living. This is in a way a full description of her, there can be more description of her. This will be some more description of her.

Certainly some are in their living married ones. Certainly there are some having it in being that they are ones going to be going on being living and these can have it in them to be in living attacking to be winning, these can have it in living to be learning something. Some of such of them can have it to be learning something more and more in living, some can have it in them to be really learning the same thing again and again. Julia as I was saying really was not learning anything and this is a nice thing to be certain of in thinking out being being in Julia all her living. Julia was then as I was saying one needing being one having it that she was learning anything. She was completely then when she was doing this thing marrying Alfred Hersland. She liked it a little then and then it went on to come to be quite soon a beginning of a long ending, a long dividing of themselves from living with each other any more in being in living.

Pride and egotism and vanity and ambition and succeeding and failing I like to think about now in each one. I like thinking about pride and egoism and vanity and ambition and failing and succeeding in each one I am knowing because it is very interesting to know these things being in those having these things in them.

I was just telling some one interesting things about each one of them in that family having it in them that egotism in them did not in them make them doing very well the thing they had some talent to be doing. One of these had it in that one to be one having some talent to be working to be interesting in something to every one and this one had it in him to have it that for him in him he was one living in being one needing to have it that he was one being one having pride in having been possibly beginning something and this one was an unhappy one inside him when he was a young one and quite a thin one and then he was one coming to be a rather heavy set one and some thought that then he was coming to be a quite happy one but happiness was not then in him. He knew this then, his brother and his sister all of them were certain of this thing then. One of these had it that she had vanity completely in her as egotism in her and she had then a pride in feeling this to be there concealed inside her and egotism filled this one to keep vanity in her with pride to keep it from being a trouble to her as knowledge to any one of her and this one was one having been going to be and being to herself and some a distinguished woman in being one leading some one only nobody was ever really following that one and this one was one really to herself and to every one one not having it as being to be one going on being living, and this one was dying in having slowly less and less leading in her of some one with not any one following and this one then would have been listening while I was telling her this thing only just then her mind certainly was wandering and not any one then was following this mind in her being then wandering. This is one I will perhaps not be ever seeing again and yet as she might say perhaps I will, who knows certainly then that I will not ever see this one again.

There was another one of these that had it in her to be one quite ordinarily wallowing and engulfing in loving and ordinary enough in being not a very stupid one and like a good many in being one giving and taking and this one had it that egotism in her was not having any reinforcing for any of this being that was being in her but was in her as being to her that she was one needing to be one doing everything any one was needing and this one was then an unhappy one and a rich one and every one was flattering this one and every one was quite certain that this one would always be living and they would always be flattering this one to keep this one as one going on being living and sometime there will be histories and histories written of these women and these men. One of this family was really succeeding in living having it in him that egotism in him went to make him into complete carrying out power in him to be a busy man coming to be a very rich one and so this one had effective ambition in him and this one was a dead one when he was not a very old one and some were not really very sorry that this one was a dead one although not any one was really very glad that this one was a dead one.

Julia Hersland and Alfred Hersland neither one of them were at all like the family of women and men I have been just describing. Julia Hersland was one going on being in being living, Alfred Hersland was one not failing not succeeding in living, not having altogether not any sense for living, not having really sense for living, was one who was twice a married one and was one who was sometimes a very loving one. Julia was one who might have been twice a married one but really she was only once a married one and she was in a way a loving one. This is to be now a more detailed account of what happened in their living in each one of them, to each one of them.

Alfred Hersland married Julia Dehning and was then living in married living in a way in Dehning family living. He had then later help from Mr. Dehning so that he could be having what he knew then he was needing to be one succeeding in living. He was not then succeeding in living and Mr. Dehning came then to be certain that Alfred Hersland was one not honest enough for any, for him, daily living. Julia Hersland had been, before Mr. Dehning was, certain of this thing certain of this thing about Alfred in her married living with him. Mrs. Dehning was certain then that Julia never should have been allowed to be married to him and this was in her then a very certain thing.

Julia Hersland was the wife of Alfred Hersland and was not coming to having successful married living with him. She had children, two children, she came to know very well David Hersland brother of Alfred Hersland. She did not ever marry again as Alfred Hersland did. She might have done this thing. Now I go on with him, then I go on with her. I am going on with him, then I am going on with her.

Hersland had not then when Mr. Dehning was helping him, had not succeeded in beginning really successful living, he was then one not to every one failing in living, he was then certainly one having been one, Mr. Dehning was certain any one could be understaning, as not being one honest for daily living in any living any one Mr. Dehning was having with him could be living in, any one Mr. Dehning was knowing in daily living could be having as being in daily living with such a one. Hersland then and Julia Hersland were living then in married living, Mr. Dehning was then certainly not ever seeing Hersland then, he was not ever then entering in any house where Hersland was living then. Did Hersland ever know certainly that Julia would be certain that Hersland was not what Julia was needing for honest daily living if Julia had not been certain by reason of having a father still living in Dehning family living, did Hersland really ever believe this thing that Julia was certain of this and not by having because of her father being one making Dehning living Dehning living feeling of honest being not being in Hersland in some living of daily living in him, was Hersland really not ever in him certain of this thing, of this being certain in Julia that she would not be needing the being in him for any daily living even if she had not then had a father living making Dehning family living, Julia was certain that Hersland might have been certain of this thing, Julia was certain that he would be certain of this thing and that then he would not be saying he was certain of this thing, Mr. Dehning was certain enough that Hersland was certain of this thing, Mrs. Dehning was certain to be talking on and on to herself and to Julia and to every one in Dehning family living who was then not listening and that was every one then about being certain about this thing and David Hersland who was later then talking about this thing to Julia and George and a little sometime to Hortense Dehning was certain that Alfred was one who was not certain that to be dead was to be really a dead one and David Hersland was a young man then and was completely then hoping to be discovering this thing as certain in Alfred Hersland that Alfred Hersland was not certain that to be dead was to be really and truly a really dead one. So then there was then married living and having been having children and a father-in-law and a mother-in-law and a brother-in-law and a sister-in-law both quite young ones and a brother then in Alfred Hersland's living and Julia Hersland and not really failing to every one knowing him then and not really beginning being succeeding to himself then and beginning to know some then who came to see him then and not ever seeing Mr. Dehning then but some seeing of Mrs. Dehning then and some seeing of George Dehning then and some living then in the house with him of his brother David Hersland who was studying in Bridgepoint just then. He came later in his living to know other ones and as I was saying he was not in his living succeeding or failing. To some he was quite a good deal succeeding, to some he was quite a good deal failing, to himself he was a good deal succeeding, sometimes he was telling about being a good deal succeeding in living, sometimes he was to himself a good deal failing in being in living. He knew very well in all of his living Patrick Moore, and later Minnie Mason. Later he married Minnie Mason. As I was saying he was not failing, certainly not altogether succeeding in being in living. Later he had about almost completely an angry feeling in not liking Mr. Dehning and Mrs. Dehning and Julia Dehning, and George Dehning and Hortense Dehning and mostly then he was certain that he had loving feeling in him, that he had and had had and could have and would have some loving feeling for Julia Hersland and her children and he was then needing completely to be one being living loving Minnie Mason who had been a married one and later was one married to him. He was one almost one to himself, to some, to his brother David Hersland, to several, sometimes almost not to any one having that he had had, did have, would have loving feeling for Julia Hersland and her children. He was one as I am saying who was not ever one having it being needing having ambition in being one being living from the resisting, from the engulfing being that was being in him. He was one having ambition in intention and aspiration from being one having vanity in him from engulfing being that was in him not winning being in living. He was then a man having people liking him in living, having people despising him in living, having some people loving him in living, having some people liking him pretty well, having some people certainly not liking to have him being liked by them. He was one who had married living with Julia Hersland, with Minnie Hersland. He was one knowing very well some men and working with some men. He was one not having enough sense for living for anything really more than being married to Minnie Mason, than for working pretty well sometime with some men, than for being almost persuading his brother David that he Alfred had really some loving being always in him. He had not sense for living enough for having aspiration and ambition and being marrying Julia Dehning and being persuading Mr. Dehning to be almost believing that he Alfred Hersland needed something that Mr. Dehning could give him to be beginning to be succeeding in living and being one making Mrs. Dehning willing to have him be petted by her in Dehning family living and make her later then a very nervous one. So then Alfred lived and went on living and ended one having in him not enough sense for living to be one failing, to be one succeeding in living. He was one ending being in living having loving feeling in him, being a married one, having been really working quite well with some men, being pretty nearly a completely hated one in Dehning family living, being certainly a completely hated one in Dehning family living and being then a tradition as a hated one not honest in daily living in Dehning family living ; and then Julia Hersland was dead and I am not finding it very interesting knowing what was happening later to the children of Alfred and Julia Hersland. He did not have any children in his married living with Minnie Mason.

Julia had complete courage as being one certainly going to be going on being living. Julia had sweetness in her that was very certain to some coming to know her. Julia had honesty in being one having in her Dehning family living and being then stamping that thing with her being one certainly very certain to be one going on being living. She was one needing to be learning anything, everybody came to know this thing, every one comes to know this thing in knowing this one in living, Julia had certainly courage in living sweetness in living to some knowing being being in her in all of her living as she was going on being one going on certainly being living. Alfred never came to be loving her as being one certainly having sweetness in her to some knowing being being in her, in a way Alfred was not loving her as being one certainly going to be going on being living, in a way he was loving her as being one going to be going on being living. He was loving her some then as being one certainly going to be going on being one being living, he was certainly loving her some as one being one certainly needing to be learning anything, he was certainly loving her some as one attacking but not really for winning, he was one loving her some for being one not really winning by being attacking, he was really not loving her for being one resisting learning really anything so that she could not have any changing in being one attacking, he was one not really coming to be hating Dehning family living and always then he could have a very angry temper about this thing. He was one really then not having really hating really ever in him, she could have hating him come to be in her, the Dehning family could have a tradition of hating him be in them as a thing they might have been inheriting, the Hersland family could mostly not be feeling hating them the Dehning family very personally in them.

Julia came then later to be really completely separated from him, she came then to be going on being living, she might have then come to be marrying some one, she did not then come to be marrying any one, that was in a way an accidental thing, she might have come then to be marrying one, she did not then marry that one, she went on certainly being one going on being living, she was succeeding well enough then in going on being in living, she had children as I have been saying and as I said of them I am not finding it to me at all an interesting thing to be telling just now about living coming to be more and more in them.

So then there has been written some history of Julia and Alfred Hersland, there will be written now a little more detailed description of living being in each one of them with the people knowing each one of them.

Some are quite certain that they have some friend, some friends who are stronger than they are to do some thing but then these are ones doing the thing in a way that is not for that thing a completely perfect way of doing that thing and that one who is not such a strong one as a friend of his is in doing that thing is one doing that thing to make that thing a completer thing. In his beginning in living important living Alfred Hersland had not at all in him to him such a feeling about any other one. Later in his living after he was married to Minnie Hersland and she helped him with Pat Moore to tell him this to be inside him he could then know a little in him that he had friends stronger than he was in doing something. He never had this really completely in him but at moments in his later living he had it almost completely inside him. Only at moments in his later living as I was saying and then not really completely inside him but somewhat certainly in his later living at moments then when Pat Moore was not so intimate but still pretty intimate with him and Minnie Mason was married to him he had this pretty nearly completely at moments inside him that he had friends, that he certainly had a friend stronger than he at doing some thing for living but that he himself had it in him to do that thing and to do it very perfectly very perfectly indeed, very completely indeed, very completely certainly completely and perfectly and he knew this at moments in him and he told it to his children who were the children of Julia Hersland sometimes when he sometimes for a little time saw one of them. He was then one certainly not failing, pretty nearly really succeeding then in his later living.

Patrick Moore in a way admired him and Alfred Hersland in a way was always all his living knowing him.

Patrick Moore was one in a way succeeding very well in living. There was another one who was knowing Alfred Hersland some then. Mackinly Young was knowing him then but that was because Young was knowing Moore a little and was going to be a musician. Then there was James Flint who knew Alfred Hersland quite well and then knew Julia Hersland and then knew David Hersland very well and he knew Minnie Mason very well and Alfred Hersland met her then. James Flint always more or less all his living knew Moore and he knew David Hersland as long as David was living, not seeing him very often but always knowing him. I will begin now continuing the history of Alfred Hersland and Julia Hersland and of some who came to know them. I am beginning coming to the beginning of the ending of my description of Alfred and Julia Hersland. To begin then.

Mackinly Young knew Moore a little. Young was a musician, he was certainly serious in that profession, he certainly was serious in going to be one going to be making something important in musical composition. There are very many who are very serious ones in going to be doing something in the way of artistic creation. There are very many who are working many hours every day with serious intention. Young was one who had it in him to be one always steadily working, having certainly real feeling in being one certainly seriously going to be going to do something that would be certain to be a good thing. He was one having as I was saying power for steady working. He was one having certainly a sense for being one certainly being living. He was one not continuing in being living being one having certainly sense for being one being living with being one having certainly the power to be day after day steadily working. He certainly had sense in being one being in living, he certainly had sense for being one feeling being in living. This was rising up slowly from the depths of him and mostly then he was every day steadily working and this which was really sense for being in living which was really in him was so slowly rising in him that he being one steadily seriously earnestly continuously working made for him a cover to him and sense in being one being really living rather did not make any more than a touching of this thing the cover of him which was being one completely seriously steadily working. Let me explain again. This one then was as I was saying a man and his name was Mackinly Young. He was a musician. He was completely seriously working every day in his living. He was certain that he needed to be one to be really living to be one creating something in writing music that certainly would be a thoroughly good thing. This one Mackinly Young was one having certainly a feeling of being one really being living, he was one being really in being living, he was one having certainly sense in being living. He was one seeing with his thinking, feeling in his working that everything he was learning was really something and each day in his living he was really learning something. He was one certain that everything he was learning was something he could be using to be doing the thing he seriously was certain he needed to be doing to be one really being in living. He was one steadily learning more and more and always then when he was composing the only thing that was anything were things that really were not anything, were just suggestions of there being somewhere inside that one a sense really in being living. Not anything this one was learning was coming into connection with the sense of being one being living that was in this one. It was this way with this one. This one in seriously steadily daily working was really a practical man that is to say each thing he was learning was for the doing of something. He was one always working and really then he could do that thing he certainly had been learning but then that was not creation. No certainly not, that was not creation. And yet sense for living was in him but it was a thing to rise slowly in him so slowly that

it almost stopped and .went so slowly like molasses very thick that not
anything he could be learning could be helping him with this thing. Not
at all and really then it was some sense for living he certainly had in him
but not enough to be one so seriously so earnestly certain to be winning
doing a really completely good thing, not continuous enough in oozing
to be making sense for him in all the arguments he was always indulging
in, just enough to make him again and again say completely funny penetrating things, not too penetrating even but thoroughly interesting as
funny things but that again not any too often. He was one then who if
he was not one melancholy by the nature in him or too worrisome would
certainly end up by teaching something and being certain that the ones he
was knowing would never work hard enough or be serious enough to really
do the thing. However he knew Pat Moore very well and continued to know
him. In a way he really liked Alfred Hersland, he never thought Alfred
would really succeed in doing anything, he thought Pat Moore might
succeed very well in living, he thought James Flint would succeed in living but that was not of any interest to Young, he continued to know
Alfred Hersland for some years, he came to know Minnie Hersland and he
liked her very well and he always came to see the two of them and always
he liked very much to see Pat Moore quite often. Pat Moore was a very
different kind of a man, this is a description of what he was in being and
in living.

Patrick Moore was not a musician but he liked it that his friends
were good at that thing. He was in business and in a way was a man
completely succeeding, excepting when he was very worried because he
was a poor man, was a man quite completely for the being and the living
in him succeeding in living.

Patrick Moore was of the resisting kind of them and his being was
alive and very lively inside of him. His being was completely alive and
quite lively inside him and he was one succeeding in living excepting when
he was worrying about being a poor man a very poor man sometime in
his living and this was a strange thing to be in him to many that knew him.
This is something that is important in any one coming to know him that
he was a man succeeding in living, being alive inside him and lively inside
in him and worrying sometime that he was a really poor man and not
worrying any one else with this thing. He was never a very poor man
but he was very often as is common not a quite rich one. He was never
a very rich one, he was when he was at the ending of his middle living and
to the end of his living then quite a rich one. He was married then and
his wife was quite a rich one. He was one doing real estate business and
was one almost every one was liking. As I said of him he had always
some admiration for Alfred Hersland and he was quite certain that
Hersland would never be really failing in living. He had some understanding of Hersland not continuing to be living with Julia Hersland and

loving his children.   He had feeling for Alfred Hersland marrying Minnie Mason.

He liked Flint very well and always was ready to have Flint come to see him.   He liked Young very well and often he did not for a very long time see him.   He admired Young for being one so thoroughly working and working and arguing.   He liked every one very well and very often as I was saying he was worrying about being a poor man but really he was not ever troubling any one with this thing.   He was as I was saying of the resisting kind in men and women and as I was saying being was alive in him always all his living, it was very lively really inside him.   He was one liking some, liking a good many, admiring some, admiring a good many, he was one very many were liking and he was one really succeeding in living, he was one having really all his living livelily in him sense for feeling being one being living, he was one as I was saying worrying sometimes and for quite long times about being a poor man, not about being one failing in living, that was not being in him, but about being a poor man, but, as I was saying, he was one not really ever worrying any one with this thing.   I will tell more now about him and the other ones in his being living.

I would certainly like to be knowing it of each one just how succeeding, just how failing in living comes to be in them in living from the being in them.   I would certainly like to know this of each one who ever was, who is now living.   I certainly would like to know it about each one just how the being in them connects itself with any one, with anything, with every one so that that one is succeeding is failing in living.   I certainly cannot tell any one how very much I would like to know this in each one. I am completely filled up with wanting to be completely certain about every one about the being in them and the failing and the succeeding and the succeeding and the failing they have in them in their living.   I look at every one, I read about each one, I think about each one, I listen to each one, I listen to about each one, I listen to any one, I listen to every one, I look at any one, I look again and again, I listen again and again and again, I am thinking very often about each one, I certainly would like to know it about every one about the being in them and the way being in them makes failing and succeeding in them. I am much less interested in their being good ones or bad ones, clean ones or dirty ones, rich ones or poor ones, well-mannered or badly-mannered ones, sick ones or well ones, I want to know about each one the being in them being in them to make of them ones succeeding, ones failing.

That is what I want to know about each one, being in them making of them ones succeeding, ones failing, ones succeeding and failing, ones failing and succeeding in being in living.   This is what I want to know about each one and I never can know everything and perhaps I never can know everything about this thing.   Very likely I can never know everything about this thing. That is to me a thing made of me, one certain to be one some day certainly ending. I like living but I am certain that I cannot know everything and so I know certainly that I will be one some day not being any longer living. This is not to me now a sorrowful thing, this is to me now quite a certain thing. I like being living, I like too being certain of something, I am certainly certain of something.

This is to be now a description of successful living of not successful living being in Pat Moore and Alfred Hersland and Mackinly Young and James Flint and Minnie Mason and David Hersland. I tell about successful living about failing in these now because I want to be telling about it in every one and I cannot just now do that thing because I do not just now completely know that thing.

I know a good deal now about being in men and women, about being in some one, in some, in many making in them each one their succeeding, their failing in being living, in being in living, in being going on being living. I know this now so that I could have it in me to know very much about succeeding and failing in men and women and yet I am not certain I will very soon be knowing really very much more about this thing. I really have not very much hope in me that soon I will be knowing very much more about succeeding and failing being in men and women. I seem just now in me to be a little, a good deal stopping in being learning about this thing in men and women. If I tell about being in some men some women making for them succeeding making for them failing in being living, in being in living, in being going on being in living, in being going on living, perhaps then a little I will be beginning again learning something of being being in men and women making succeeding and failing in them.

I am getting to find it more and more interesting being one feeling it in every one the being in them making them to be succeeding, to be failing in living.

James Flint liked Patrick Moore very well. He admired him. James Flint began his beginning living as a musician, he ended his beginning middle living as a manufacturer of clothing. He was a man certainly succeeding in living and yet not one succeeding well enough to be at all startling. He was one succeeding in living. He was one certainly being living in being in living, certainly very solidly this thing and always then he had a quick way of doing things in music and manufacturing that were a little quicker than solid succeeding in him and this then kept him from being one really quite startlingly being one succeeding in living. He was one as I was saying completely succeeding in living, being certainly one solidly attacking in successful winning and always then as I was saying he was lightly attacking and successfully lightly attacking quicker then he was solidly attacking and this was in him in being a musician and this was in him in being one manufacturing clothing and this was in him and he was one not being at all in his living an astonishingly successful one. As

I was saying he admired Pat Moore and liked him very well indeed and Moore was one certainly successful quite well in living and being entirely alive inside him and very lively inside him with this live being in him. Not any one was close to Pat Moore in Moore's being alive in being living and Moore was succeeding well enough in living and not any one was wanting him to be succeeding any more than he was succeeding and he was sometimes worrying a good deal about going to be a very poor man but he never worried any one with this thing and yet Flint was not quite entirely satisfied with Moore being in his own living. James Flint certainly was satisfied with being being alive in Moore and very lively in him and Moore being one succeeding in living. Flint did not need to have Moore succeed any more than Moore would be succeeding in living but somehow to Flint it was as if Moore should have been a little more poignantly succeeding, that is to say he should not be more poignant in being, in living, in succeeding but somehow being succeeding as he Moore was succeeding should have been a more poignant thing to some one, to any one, not to Moore, not to Flint, not to any woman, not to any other man, but somehow some way to some one. Flint then in a way was not completely satisfied with Pat Moore. As I was saying Flint and Moore knew each other and Flint had come to know Minnie Mason, Flint was a man a good many came to know in living and Minnie Mason came to know Moore and Young, and Hersland came to know her and some years later a number of years later Alfred Hersland was married to her. They all came to know David Hersland as was a natural thing. Now I will give a very short description of Minnie Mason and Minnie with each one of them and Minnie Mason marrying and married to Alfred Hersland.

Some have sense for living from having realisation in them that each thing they are knowing is such a thing as it is to them and really knowing this in them. Some are knowing in them that each thing they are knowing in living is the thing that thing really is living.

Some have in them completely the emotion of knowing something is something without feeling in them that any thing is anything. This certainly can be in men and women. There are many ways of having sense for living, sense of being living in them in men and in women. Some have completely the emotion of something being what they are needing for being one going on being living and some of such of them have not at all in them any feeling of any one thing having it as being the thing they are needing to be having it be to have them be ones going on being in living, being in living, being living. Some have some of such feeling and not any such thing, not any such feeling has any value for them.

I am knowing one who knew Young some and Flint a little and heard of Moore and came once to dine with Alfred and Minnie Hersland and this one was one being certain that he was one loving with intensity a powerful thing and this-one was one loving with intensity the emotion of feeling a thing being a powerful thing and so this one was always hoping but really never being one doing anything that gave to him satisfaction. And this is very common. I am not just now liking every one, not at all, each one is too completely herself, himself inside her, inside him and repeating sometimes with some changing, sometimes with more emphasing, sometimes with a weakening feeling, sometimes more loudly, sometimes more faintly the being in that one, and I certainly do just now not want to be certain of this thing and I am completely certain of this thing and I know now certainly there are very many, most every one not wanting to be certain inside them that each one is repeating always all the being in them being themselves inside them. I can see just now in me that for very many living this is not at all a romantic thing this knowing that each one always is repeating. I know that mostly every one will not ever be really certain of this thing. I, I am always certain of this thing, I mostly am all solid in this thing, that is full up, that is satisfied, that is comfortable, that is interested, that is noticing, that is stirred by this thing, I will not just now be mentioning again this thing.

Minnie Mason married Alfred Hersland when he was loving again in his living and they were succeeding well enough in being in married living. They went on being in married living. It interested them enough, it interested some others in the beginning, mostly it was not so very interrsting their being in married living, their succeeding well enough in married living, Alfred Hersland succeeding well enough in living, mostly every one they were knowing succeeding well enough in living. I am interested in this thing.

Minnie Mason certainly did love very much and very often. She certainly did very much of this thing. She came to loving one and being loved by that one and to marrying that one and marrying then was almost then a successful thing for the two of them. It was not then a successful thing. She had had come then to almost marrying another one instead of the one she married then and that would have been almost a successful thing in having married living. She came later as I was saying to marrying Alfred Hersland, that was quite a successful thing in having married living. As I was saying she was one certainly loving very often, she was one as I was saying certainly loving very much and as I was saying she certainly did this thing very often. In a way she went on knowing the one she had been married to, in a way she went on knowing every one. She knew James Flint and he knew Patrick Moore and Patrick Moore knew Alfred Hersland and Minnie Mason married Alfred Hersland. She was as I was saying in a way knowing every one, she, as I was saying, in a way went on knowing each one she ever had been knowing. In a way she went on knowing the one she had been married to, the one she almost had been marrying, she was then successfully marrying and being in married living with Alfred Hersland. She was then going on knowing James Flint and Moore and even Young then as I was saying.

Pat Moore thought it certainly a very good thing that Alfred Hersland married Minnie Mason. He said to every one he thought it a very good thing. He did think it to be a very good thing that Minnie Mason married Alfred Hersland. He knew Minnie and he knew Alfred and he always went on knowing them and he very often took dinner with them. Flint did not see any of them very often, he sometimes saw them. He saw Moore, and he saw Hersland and Minnie Hersland when he came to see them, Young did not see any of them often. He did sometimes see them, he did sometimes see Mr. and Mrs. Hersland and he did once in a while see Moore and once in a while he saw James Flint. They all thought it was a very good thing that Hersland and Minnie were married and living contentedly in married living and were then succeeding quite well in living. Moore was quite certain that it was a good thing that Hersland and Minnie were marrying.

Some are very happy loving some one, some are very happy then loving another one. Some one is very happy in loving one, some one is very happy in loving and then is very happy in loving another one. Minnie Mason was such a one. It is quite common to be quite happy sometime in being loving. It is quite common to be happy in loving one and to be happy in loving another one. This is quite common. Minnie was quite happy in loving one and she married that one and she was quite happy in loving another one and she did not marry that one and she was quite happy in marrying another one and she did marry that one. Certainly it was quite right, Moore was certain of this thing, that any one with the name of Minnie Mason should be happy in loving some one. Minnie was happy in loving one and she was happy in loving that one. She married that one, she was almost then succeeding in married living with that one. She did not keep on being married to that one, she in a way always was knowing that one, she in a way always knew it as quite a happy thing in her living that this one certainly would be doing something when she asked him to be doing something. She was very happy just then when she was marrying this one in loving another one and she was never going to be marrying and she never married that one and she certainly would have been certainly almost succeeding in married living with that one. She was in a way all her living knowing this one, she was in a way certain that this one would be doing anything she would ask him if she ever would come to asking him to do something. She was then later as I was saying happy in loving Hersland. She married him, she was succeeding then in married living, he was succeeding then in living. She was of the resisting kind of them but resisting was in her constantly trickling out of her as steadily trickling attacking, very often she was doing very much lying as I was saying. She had really sense for living as I was saying. Resisting being came trickling out of her, there was a great deal always trickling out of her, it was as attacking being to mostly every one knowing her, as I was saying she had sense for living, as I am saying she and Alfred Hersland successfully went on living in married living until they came one and then the other of them to be old ones and then dead ones.

Minnie Hersland had had and in a way had not at all had sense for being in living. She was not in a way continuing in being living but in a way she was by not stopping being living. She was then in a way all her living continuing being living, in a way she was not ever to herself inside her in being being, continuing being living. Going on being living in men and women in all of them is an interesting thing. Each one has that in them the way their kind in men and women can have it to have it in them.

Minnie then all her living was in a way continuing being living, in a way she was not ever in her being continuing being living. As I was saying she was loving very much and very often, as I was saying in a way she had sense really for living, as I was saying she was in a way always going on knowing any one she ever had been knowing.

These are all now living these I have been, these I am now describing. They were then, Alfred Hersland and Julia Hersland and each one of them knew some who were then doing living.

Some have sense for living by the emotion in them, some have sense for living by being certain that each thing is existing. Some have not any sense for living by emotion, by being certain that each thing that everything is existing, some of such have it in them that they are certainly going to be going on living. As I was saying Julia Dehning was one almost not having any sense for living, she was one certainly going to be going on being living, what there was in her of sense for living was sense of living by emotion being in her.

She did certainly in a way have a little a very little sense of living from emotion in her, she did certainly have it in her to be one going to be going on living, this was courage in her to her and to every one ever knowing her. She did as I was saying have sweetness of a little having sense for being living by having really emotion in a way in her, not emotion as loving, emotion as being in living. She had in a way this really in her.

As I could be saying there are some living to be ones being good for living, there are some living to be ones making themselves and others good for living, there are some living because they are certain that there is some good to some one in their being living, there are some living certain that each one has some good in living, there are some living needing to be certain that sometime some one will be a good one, there are some living hoping sometime to be certain that some will be good ones in living, there are some living who are certain that not any one not being a good one is really being in living, there are some living that are not certain by their thinking that any way is a good one but they have it in them to be only able to be living by considering living in the way of something to be done to be a good one to make some one be a good one to have it that in living there are there will be good ones, there are some in living that are certain that they must be one being a good one, there are all these and then there are as one might say schools of each one of these ways of being of many being these things with not much feeling in them of such a thing to make them be doing much living.   I will now tell about Julia Dehning and a whole lot more of men and women.

Some men are certainly sometime loving a woman. Some women are certainly sometime loving some man. Some men are sometime certainly loving some woman. Very many men are thinking the woman they are loving a very wonderful thing. Very many men are sometime loving, each one of them, some one. Some of these are not really thinking the one they are loving to be such a wonderful one. Many women are sometimes in their living loved by some man, some are needing this for being one to themselves being living, some are liking such a thing very well for keeping on being living, some are excited in this thing, some are certain that they are going on living having this thing, some are always thinking they are not going on in living having this thing, and then they are very many the women who are as it were schools following in the feeling of some one having a feeling in them of having, having had, going to be having some man loving them. There are some women, quite some of them who have it as being that they are completely feeling one thing when they are feeling that thing, these then are wonderful ones to any one loving them, they are eternal things having it in them to be completely one thing, these may be ones having any kind of thing in feeling but each time feeling is in them they are feeling that thing with the whole of them and these can then give to any one loving them the feeling that being one is a thing not having any beginning or any ending and so then many being in the state of having loving for them, by some one of such of them many have it in them then that infinite and eternal has really meaning. A thing not beginning and not ending is certainly continuing, one completely feeling something is one not having begun to feel anything because to have a beginning means that there will be accumulation and then gradually dying away as ending and this cannot be where a thing is a complete thing. So then many women give to the men loving them the awe-inspired feeling of realising an eternal thing. And that is very satisfying and so very many men are very much liking having this kind of loving given to them. Now I am saying this is in some women, not only in loving but in living, they are completely feeling something. There are a very great many woman living not at all completely feeling anything and they are sometimes loving some one and they are sometimes being loved by some one. Loving is a very nice thing to very many doing that thing, it is not at all a nice thing to very many doing that thing. Now as I am saying Julia Hersland, who had been Julia Dehning came to know a good many men and women in her living. In her younger living she had not known any one not in Dehning family living or visiting. Now she was coming now when she was no longer succeeding in married living she was coming to know some men and women. She came to know David Hersland brother of her husband Alfred Hersland. She came to know James Cranach and his wife Miriam. She came to know Theodore Summers and to know very well then William Beckling, and she came to know pretty well not so very well because Helen really did not like Julia Hersland in her daily living, she came to know Helen Cooke. Julia came to know Rachel Sherman although Rachel was certain that Helen was right about her feeling about living being in Julia Dehning as some called her then, and then later Rachel married Adolph Herman and then with not any changing in her feeling she was a very dear friend in her feeling and in Julia Hersland's feeling. And Julia had known and then was not any longer knowing Charles Kohler, and then there was Arthur Keller whom in a way every one was quite certain would come to be sometime a brother-in-law to her and then there was one she was certainly needing to be one certainly to be existing as being one certainly teaching some one something, Linder Herne, and then there was the whole family that were relations to her, and then there was Florentine Cranach who was a cousin of James Cranach and then there was Hilda Breslau who might come later to be a sister-in-law to her but who really later married another, Ernest Brakes who was a painter, and then there was Selma Dehning who had married into the Dehning family and then had not any love for any one who was not a Dehning and then there was Ella and Fred and their little baby, Robert Housman who came very often to stay with them the Dehnings and with Mrs. Hersland, and then there was Mrs. Conkling the aunt of Selma Dehning and then there was a cousin of Mrs. Conkling and she had five children and they were all girls and all in a way earning their living and very nice girls in home living and Julia liked going out with them. And then there was a doctor who did not do any practicing Dr. Florence Arden who was quite an entirely magnificent woman and Julia liked meeting her when she met her at any concert or at any meeting and then there was a very rich man Mr. James Curson and his wife Mrs. Bertha Curson who were extremely delighted to know Mrs. Hersland and Julia Hersland was completely happy in spending some time in the country with them. That's all just now.

There are some women, there are some men who are all their living certain that they are not liking it that every one is living the way each one is living, that they are not liking it that they are living the way they are living, that they are not living another way in living. Some are certain that they are needing that every one should be in a way trying to be a good one, some are all their living certain of this thing, some are all their living in the living of being certain of this thing, some could be certain of this thing, some can and are, some are certain of this thing that each one should be one trying to be a good one they are completely certain of this thing and they are then of the school of this thing and they are that all their living certainly one certain of this thing that each one should be one in a way trying to be a good one.

Julia knew Mr. and Mrs. James Miriam Cranach and she knew Theodore Summers and she knew William Beckling and she knew very many other men and women, this is certain. All of these were in some way certain that each one in living should in a way be doing something so that everything would be a good thing for some one. So then to give a little description of Theodore Summers and Miriam Cranach and James Cranach and William Beckling. And then to give some description of Julia Hersland knowing each one of them. Theodore Summers was one certainly quarrelling so as to make some kinds of men do something so that some should be certain that they were having for living what they were needing. Theodore Summers certainly was hotly quarrelling sometimes for this thing.

In a way Julia liked very much understanding Summers being one quarrelling to win somthing, in a way she wanted to follow after him, in a way she certainly did not follow after him. Later she did not at all follow him.

Summers was certainly in a way to Julia for a time complete in important living of being one certainly giving it to her to have for living certainly learning something, but he did not give it to her that Dehning living was certainly completely honest living because he was not ever feeling anything about anything like any such thing and so then he was not really important to her. He had completely energy in living, he was not one certainly going on being living as Julia Hersland certainly was going to be going on doing and so in a way Summers was not to Julia really completely in her living, I will tell a little more a little later about him.

Miriam Cranach was really a friend to Julia Hersland and that was an important thing and that was in a way not at all an important thing. Miriam was a resisting one really being living in a religion, a religion that in a way was completely certain to be leading any one to be certain that not any one would be a good enough one to help themselves or any one and it did not lead Miriam to this thing and it did lead Miriam to be certain of this thing. Julia Hersland was certain that Miriam was completely an honest one for daily living but she was not needing Miriam for this thing, she was not needing Miriam for the religion in Miriam, she was not really needing Miriam, she and Miriam were completely faithful friends in living and this was not important to any one as being inside in any one and both of them were certainly in a way living inside in them, and this is certain, and in a way it is a little a strange thing and I will tell sometime some more about this thing.

Julia Hersland might later have come to marry William Beckling but William came then to be quite a sick man and he had then certainly to take care of himself in living and he would not then marry any woman. I will tell more about him. He was in a way one in a way acting as if he were almost certain that some one should be a good one for living. This is all now for just beginning a description of living in him.

Mostly all of these whom Julia knew then met the others she knew then but very many did not like some of the others they met then. Some did like very much some of those they met then. Some did not come to know any of the others they met then . Some did come to know some of the others they met then. As I was saying Julia had in a way not come to have any friends in her personal living in her younger living. This is quite common. This is quite astonishing to those who have had friends personal to them to their living but it is certainly very common, quite extraordinarily common that young women and younger ones and young men and younger ones have not had any one who was personally a companion to them. As I am saying this is really extraordinarily common. It is also very uncommon as I am saying and very many are knowing.

Julia Dehning then had in a way in her younger living not had really any one personally a companion to her then, she was herself inside her and giving a stamp then decidedly to herself to every one of herself on Dehning living as being in her being living. She was then being in Dehning family living, that is now certain.

Now then to begin again the long list of those she came to know as Mrs. Alfred Herland, some of them she knew earlier, certainly William Beckling, a very little Miriam Cranach, quite well in Dehning family living Charles Kohler, she had heard of Adolph Herman and as for the rest perhaps she had met them, knew of some one knowing them, perhaps not, that really is not an important thing to any one excepting to me who am interested in knowing everything every little thing. I will then begin remembering these things. Julia Hersland too knew David Hersland, she in a way knew some that knew him, he in a way knew every one she knew then, she in a way knew about some of those Alfred Hersland was knowing then. She did not later know anything of those Alfred Hersland was knowing.

Really almost all her living she knew William Beckling, she did not come to marry him, that was because he became a sick man and was certain then that it was not right for him to marry any woman. She knew Theodore Summers a few years, she always sometime heard something about him, later when she did not any longer often see him. It was a little then an important thing in her living as part of really learning anything, as part of being one certainly and she was certainly such a one as part of being in courageous being one going on certainly going on being living.

She came to know the Cranachs after she was a married one. They had a little known William Beckling, they did not care about him, they had known David Hersland, they liked knowing him. Julia afterwards to the end of her living knew them really for her daily living. There will be a history written a short one of her and each one of them. Helen Cooke knew Julia after she was Mrs. Hersland. Helen knew Mrs. Cranach, she knew William Beckling, she knew David Hersland, she really did not interest herself really to know any of them then. She later came to know David Hersland as a thing interesting to her for the living being in her, she always all her living knew Julia Hersland, she did not find that at all interesting. Rachel Sherman married Adolph Herman, Adolph Herman knew William Beckling, Rachel Sherman knew Helen Cooke very well then and she met William Beckling and Mrs. Alfred Hersland and then Adolph Herman and then she married him. I will tell about that thing. The Hermans in a way always went on knowing and later learning anything with Mrs. Hersland. That was interesting. I will tell about this thing. Charles Kohler was one in a way in Dehning family living, later they were not certain that in a way he had been in Dehning family living, for some time then not anybody in Dehning family living saw him, Julia sometimes saw him then, she never was certain whether he had been in his feeling ever in Dehning family living. He was not in any way to any one in Dehning family living or to any one knowing Julia Hersland an important one. Linder Herne was a man certainly teaching something. Julia had heard of him, she liked it that all the rest of his living she could know him.

Arthur Keller as I said she came to know as he came to be perhaps going to be a brother-in-law. I will tell about him later in the history of David Hersland. Then there was Hilda who married Ernest Brakes and she might have married George Dehning. I will tell a little about her now and more about her later, she never completely wanted to know Julia Hersland and yet she liked it very well that she did know Julia Hersland. She married Ernest Brakes and she sometimes met the Dehnings later when she went out somewhere. Then there were other ones as I said in telling about those Julia was knowing, I will begin again telling about every one Julia Hersland was knowing.

There certainly are kinds in men and women. There certainly are things hurting each one living. The things hurting each one hurt them in the way their kind of them, their kind in men and women are hurt by anything. Sometimes it is astonishing to some one that they are effected by something in a way and that is the way their kind of them in men and women are certain to be affected by that thing and they did not know of which kind they were and that they would be effected the way their kind in men and women is always being effected by something and so they found it completely astonishing to know it of themselves that they were effected that way by that thing. Some know quite certainly by the middle of their middle living how they are going to be effected by each thing. Very many are never really certain about this thing. Quite a number come to be quite certain about this thing. Some can be certain about other ones about this thing. Some are quite certain but are not really knowing this thing, some are not certain and are not really knowing this thing.

Each kind then in men and women have it to have that all of them are hurt in the same way by something that can hurt them. This is just now in me by my feeling. Some of each kind of them have it to be much less hurt than others of their kind of them by anything. Some of each kind of them can be almost quite completely hurt by something hurting them. Each kind of them in men and women have it in them to have their own way of having frightened feeling in them from something really scaring them. Some of each kind in men and women are not very much frightened by anything scaring them. Some are very much scared by something frightening them. Some easily have their way of being frightened in them, some need very much frightening to have their way of being frightened, the way of being frightened of their kind of them come out of them.

I am beginning now telling more of Miriam Cranach who was of a kind of them of whom many have it to have religion in them so that they are in living really ones having really inside them and outside of them distinction from this thing. Some of such of them are fairly happy ones in living but very many of such of them are happy really only by religion. These are of the resisting kind in men and women, that is to say they are of the dependent independent kind. They have it in them not to be really dependent, not to be really independent. They have completely the sensitiveness of resisting being but they are not sensitive to anything that is not to their feeling connected with the relation of themselves of some one to the universal feeling. They have not at all engulfing being although some of them almost suggest such a thing, they have not at all resisting although some of them very much suggest such a thing, they seem to be resisting because they are not responding to anything that is to them whatever meaning that word many have for them not god-given. They seem some of them to be engulfing because they are completely sensitive to that thing. These have it very often that they have not any power of expressing themselves about anything that does not completely touch them. Many of these if it were not for the looks of them would seem from their talking or their writing generally to be quite stupid ones.

Miriam was such a one. I will not tell very much just now about her because sometime later when I tell more about men and women I will tell about Miss Ortenried who married Olaf Lawson. I will then tell all I know then about this kind in men and women, how they have religion in them, how they can be hurt by something, how they can be frightened when something has scared them.

I told something about Miriam Cranach knowing Julia Dehning Hersland. I have already told something about this thing.

Always something is happening and one is then feeling something and sometimes one is then one knowing how some other one felt when something was happening. Some one can understand then always sometime how some other one was feeling sometime about something.

William Beckling was one who was almost for him completely, brilliantly succeeding in living, and then he came to be a sick one and he was certain then that it would not be right for him to marry a woman.

Beckling then was almost completely brilliantly succeeding in living as I was saying. He did not begin early in his living to be so brilliantly succeeding, but about the middle of his middle living he was certainly almost quite brilliantly succeeding.

Almost all these I have been saying who were knowing Julia Hersland were succeeding pretty well in living. Ernest Brakes who married Hilda Breslau who might have come to marry George Dehning was never succeeding any too well in living. They were happy ones enough in being living Brakes and his wife Hilda. Henry Sherman and his wife Rachel were in a way successful in living quite successful in living, in a way quite happy in living, happy enough in living, they were to very many knowing them and to themselves all their living very happy quite successful ones in being living. They were loving each other that is certain and were pleasant to each other completely in being husband and wife living together and going about together. They both had much intention, much aspiration, much conviction, much sensitiveness in living, they did not have very much that hurt them but some things did hurt them, perhaps some things frightened them that is not certain. They did not have religion but they each had complete devotion to being certain that each one was to be one really and truly working, was one really and truly working. These came to know Julia Hersland always more in their living and in her living. They came to be almost always more or less in each others daily living. I can not describe them more because I do not know what to be certain about in thinking about them. Sometime I will be more certain and then I will begin again about them.

I will tell more now about Julia Hersland and each one she came to know in living and how she came to know them and I will tell more and more about all the living ever being in her.

I could go on and on, I am so certain that it would be a very important thing if some other going on being living, some other ones going on being in living could be knowing really how to be distinguishing the resisting from the attacking kind in men and women, could be understanding the way having it in them to have religion in them is in them of the resisting kind of them, is in them of the attacking kind of them. I am so certain that I am knowing a very great deal about being being in men and in women that it certainly does seem as if something would be missing if not any one could be coming to know from me all of that everything. And now I am sad with this thing for certainly I will be going on with all this thing and certainly then not any one will be rightly certain about some one which kind of being that one has in them resisting or attacking and how religion is in that one. But then I am remembering that every one being ever in living is pretty well used to this thing that some one has it to have knowing realising something and not any one else even later has that thing and so then I will go on writing, and not for myself and not for any other one but because it is a thing I certainly can be earnestly doing with sometimes excited feeling and sometimes happy feeling and sometimes longing feeling and sometimes almost indifferent feeling and always with a little dubious feeling. I could though be so wise and I am so wise and it would be so nice for me to be certain that from me some other one could be a wise one a little less wise than I am who am the original wise one. I could then be so pleased with this thing with being certain that with me there would be an increasing of wise realisation, and then I am remembering it is like when I was a younger one I was for years so sorry about things important in something being lost and some one being a dead one by an accident when he was a young one and then later I was certain I would not be using that thing that was lost and would not be reading something if it had been written and if I did not need that thing, very likely not any one would be really needing that thing, and whatever any one is having is plenty good enough unless they want some other thing and perhaps they will find that other thing, and anyhow nobody can be a wise one in the way I am just now a wise one, so I will go on and go on and if anybody comes to be like me a wise one why then there will have come to be another wise one. I am almost certain I am completely a wise one. I will not tell any more now about this thing. I will tell now some more about religion and about attacking and about resisting being and I will tell some more now about everything and perhaps sometime I will be sad again about not any one ever having the understanding of being in men and women that I am having.

Julia Dehning came to know each of them, some men and some women, and so for now to finish them and her up. Sometime and it will be in the history of David Hersland that it will be done I will be telling more about each one coming to be sometime a completely dead one. I like it very much that each one all their living have it that they are in some way being living ones. Very often to very many they are very faintly repeating to themselves to any one that they are being living ones then when they are living. Some are not when they are dead ones letting any one having known them be really certain that they are then dead ones. Always then I am certain that sometime I will be telling very much more about every one being in their living living ones and being sometime then really a dead one, dead ones. Being living and then being a dead one, I am certain that I will always be telling more and more about these things to every one. Being a very happy one makes it that I can tell each one sometime about this thing about being a living one and about being sometime then a dead one. I like very much being a happy one, a really widely certainly happy one. I like very much being a very happy one. I can tell to myself too and to every one that each one in the way it is in him is being in his living and each one is sometime then a dead one. I say that I will certainly tell more and more about this to every one. I will certainly always be telling about every one being in being living and every one being sometime a dead one.

Julia Hersland was being in living and certainly sometime she came to be a dead one. Julia Hersland certainly was being in living and she certainly sometime came to be a dead one. Julia was as I was saying one not failing, in a way not succeeding in living. Julia in a way certainly was quite an excited one in being one being in living. Julia certainly was one keeping on being in living all her living and then she was a dead one. Julia was in a way in living not a happy one, not an unhappy one, in a way quite a happy one. Julia was certainly one in a way not having been one feeling in living. She was one in a way succeeding in living. She came to know quite a number of men and women and quite a number of men and women came to know her and she was one having certainly it in her to be one being going on being in living.

She came to know a good many men and women in living and a good many men and women came to know her and they, mostly all of them, were succeeding in living and in a way she was one having been succeeding in being in living. She was of Dehning family living as I was saying. She was not of Dehning family living. She went on living being in living as I was saying. She came sometime to be a dead one. Many others had come by then to be dead ones. Some had not yet then come to be dead ones. There are very many always living that is certain. There are very many always living. There were then once very many living. Julia Hersland was one being going on in living. She came sometime to be a dead one. Julia knew some then when she was being living and they were then being living, and they knew her then some.

Julia came to know some. She came to know each one of them some sometime in her living. Julia came to know them those I have been mentioning each one of them some sometime in her living. Julia came to know them each one of them sometime in her living. I was just telling some one yesterday evening that some one has it not to have in them the poignancy of experience that that one thought that other one had in living. That one had concentration in expressing experiencing, that one had not concentration in experiencing. Having concentration in experiencing is common but then again it is not so very common. There was one that I was seeing yesterday evening and this one was of the slow resisting and engulfing kind in men and women and this one was quite solemn and this one was not such a solid one in being a slow resisting engulfing one as this one was in expression and so this one was solemn. This one could really be thinking about some one, this one had imagination, this one had sensitiveness for coming to be realising ways of doing something, this one had not sensitiveness for realising the feeling of something having being really existing, this one had the feeling of having feeling of being really existing, this one then had slow solemn expression. I was telling some one yesterday evening, no I do not think I was telling any one this thing yesterday evening. I would have been telling some one yesterday evening if I had not in a way not been wanting to tell that one this thing, that each one could be finding another one interesting if each one felt another one being in act of feeling the way that one really is feeling being living. I cannot come to be more certain ever of anything than I am of how very interesting it is to me in my being one being living to be certain of the feeling there is being in each one and how that feeling comes out of each one as expression. The one I was going to be telling this thing to last evening is one having it that he is sympathetically realising this about each one who has been expressing himself in something written or painted or winning in fighting or governing, or thinking or discovering, this one cannot be rightly certain although this one is very often telling about this thing and this one is very often quite certain what the being is in any one as experiencing when the expression is not a formulated one. Now I can learn it by loving repeating, loving repeating is in me and so to me every one is having as it were coming out of them formulated expression. Loving repeating in me makes of me then one understanding being in men and women, and the relation of expression coming out of each one to the being making them of them. So then any one can know that being one loving hearing seeing feeling repeating has made of me a very wise one.

I am commencing now again a description of Julia coming to know some men and some women sometime in her living. I am beginning again describing being and expression of the being of them coming out of them of some men and some women Julia came to know in living.

It is a queer thing that some one wanting to be giving and giving some one something is not giving that one what that one is wanting. It is a queer thing that some are wanting to be giving some something and are giving some something and are not giving them what they are wanting, what they are needing for their living. It is a queer thing that some are realising sometime that some other one is seeing, is remembering something that one cannot be seeing by looking, cannot be remembering by any kind of trying to remember that thing. It is a queer feeling to be really certain that one is not remembering the way another one is remembering, is not seeing the way another one is seeing, it is a queer feeling to be completely realising the way another one is seeing something another one is realising something and to be quite certain by realising that one can not be seeing, cannot be remembering that thing. It is a completely queer feeling, this that I am describing. It is a completely queer feeling to be realising that some one is seeing something, is feeling something is remembering something, to be completely realising that one being feeling, being remembering, being seeing something and to be completely realising that one realising another one's feeling seeing remembering that thing cannot one's self feel see and remember that thing. I can say that having such a feeling is completely having a queer feeling in being one being living. I can say that I am having completely a queer feeling when I am realising that I am not being feeling, seeing, remembering something when I am completely realising some one else being feeling, seeing, remembering that thing. I have then a completely queer feeling, I have been having a completely queer feeling, I have been realising some one being able to be feeling, remembering, seeing something and I have been realising that I am not able to be feeling, remembering, seeing that thing. It is not a completely queer feeling if one is not completely realising some one's experiencing something and completely realising not being going to be, not being experiencing that thing. This thing then is the complete thing in having complete queer feeling in living. I well tell about this again and again. It is in me now, it will be in me again and again. It is in me now, it will be in me very often. I am now beginning the ending of my telling about the living in Julia Hersland and Alfred Hersland and other women and other men knowing them.

Some one was saying of some one that he was an interesting one, he wanted himself to be such an earnest one, his father was not an earnest one that was a thing he was used to in his living, his mother was an indolent one, he was pretty well used to that thing that she was an indolent one, his brother was certainly not an earnest one he had not any hope that he could be in living, a fellow who was such a one as his brother was, an earnest one, he himself was not ever keeping going in being an earnest one, this one then was as another one said of him one asking very much of himself in living and he was not succeeding, very likely would not be succeeding in going on being an.earnest one and he was not a disappointed one one disappointed with living, he was one not really filled with any earnest feeling in being one being living, he had earnest feeling of knowing that not any one in his family had been being in living an earnest one and this made of him in a way one who could be in living if he would be, a disappointed one. So then as some one said of this one this one was one feeling it in him that he might have been expecting having earnest feeling coming to be being inside him but he did not come to be expecting this thing as he was almost certain that his father did not have ever inside him earnest feeling, that his mother certainly was one going to be going on being indolent in being living, that his brother certainly never would have anything in him of earnest feeling, and then he to himself as one to be realised by him would not come to have inside in him certainly earnest feeling, that was very likely to be not in him this earnest feeling that he was expecting from some one inside him. So then this one as this other one said of him was a very moral man. He certainly asked a great deal of himself, that is what this other one said about this one, this one that the other one said was one who was certainly a very moral one in his being one going on being living. This one then as I was saying was a very moral man in being one expecting very much from himself inside him in his being one being living. He certainly was not having it in him very expectantly feeling this expectation of having earnest feeling going on being in him but he certainly was a moral one in having this very certain realisation that not his father not his mother not his brother not himself in learning living was an earnest one in feeling anything.

   It is a very amusing thing hearing some realising other ones being moral ones in living. She should do it, she wants so much from herself to herself in living, let her pay herself for being one going to be going to be a good one. That is what some one is saying about some one. It is very interesting to be helping some one going to be a good one. It is certain that some are going to be good ones in living. It is certain that to some this is in some other one very unbecoming. It is certain that to some this in some other one is very becoming. I have been helping some with this thing with coming to be going to be a good one. I have been helping some very much in this thing. Each one is herself, is himself inside her inside him and it is certainly a very interesting thing helping each one, helping some of each kind of them to be going to be a good one. I have sometimes been helping some, with very much feeling and serious consideration and steady struggling and earnest attention, I have sometimes been helping some to going to be a good one in their living for them. I have quite often been doing this thing. I am now going on telling a little more about the middle living in Julia Hersland

and in some coming to know her then. She was then to herself inside her one honest in all daily living, one certainly having courage in being one certainly going to be going on living, one certainly going to be learning anything, one certainly to herself inside her in a way certainly a good one.

One cousin is dead, another is quite a sick one. That is not so strange as they are then in the middle of their middle living, it is not strange and yet it is certainly something one is not wishing to have happening just then. It is natural that when there are very many of a family living and very many cousins and some aunts and uncles living that sometimes some of them should be sick ones, even that once in a while one of them should come to be a dead one. In a way it is a strange thing because very often for many years not any one in the family connection is a seriously sick one, not any one is ever thinking of any one they are then knowing as any where near to any dying. Sometimes it happens that one cousin is quite a sick one, sometimes it happens that all the uncles are dead by then and only two aunts are still living. Sometimes it happens in a family living that all the aunts and some of the uncles are still living. Sometimes it happens that the aunts and uncles that are sisters and brothers of the mother of some one are all living and the mother the sister of these uncles and aunts is the only one of that family who is not then any longer living. Sometimes it happens that pretty nearly every one of the brothers of a father of some one are not any longer living and the father then after some more years of being living is not any longer living. There is then sometimes in family living when there is not any one who is then a seriously sick one, that there has not been any one during many years coming to be not any longer a living one. Some have some feeling in them that sometime some one who is a cousin will be a seriously sick one and some one who is a cousin will come to be not any longer living. Some are feeling that sometime quite a number who are cousins to them will not be any longer living. Julia Hersland was in the ending of her middle living. Mrs. Dehning had been for sometime not any longer living. Mr. Dehning was not any longer living. Julia Hersland went on being one being living until well to the end of her older living. She had a brother George and a sister Hortense. These were both a good deal younger. She had children who were living. She was not really ever married again although of course it would have been quite a natural thing for her to marry again and to marry William Beckling. He came as I said to be a sick one but he really did not come to be a dead one until the beginning of his old living. You never can tell anything certainly about such a thing.

I am certainly going to be telling more about feeling being in living. I will tell some more about feeling being in living, feeling certain that one is being in living in some and then in some other men and women.

I will not worry any one just now with this thing. This is in me for me and I am certainly not scaring myself with this thing. I certainly would not be frightening any one in living. I certainly would be wanting every one to be certain that they are feeling themselves being living.

Some like the being they have in them. Some are frightened and then they do the thing that frightens them. Some are glad that when they have been sick ones it was of a kind of sickness that was not a very expensive one. Some when they have a sickness need expensive medicine to cure them. Some are certain that some other one is always certain to be needing to have money spent, and that they are of the kind in men and women who even when they come to be sick ones have a kind of sickness come to them that does not need expensive medicine for curing. Some are certain that they would be strong to be struggling if they were anywhere where they needed to be winning by fighting, one was saying that she was the kind of one who would be holding out until she would be a dead one because it was what she needed for her satisfaction, but she said she would not really be holding out as she might have been doing because she would not want that her husband should be losing a chance to be earning a living by working. Some are quite right in saying that they are one being one strong to be winning, some are quite right then in saying such a thing and these then some of them are winning in living and some of them are not winning in living. Some are quite right in saying that they are one to certainly injure some one and then it is some one not that one who is injuring that one. Some are quite right in saying they are one to injure some one, some do then injure some one, some do then not injure some one. Some are quite right to be asking a question after they have been silently listening while other people have been talking, some are quite right in not then letting themselves be asking a question. Some are certainly quite right to be listening very quietly very often, some are quite right to be almost never doing this thing.

I will tell now a very little more how Julia Hersland and some others did something, did everything.

Each one is coming gradually to be knowing in their living what way being is inside in men in women when they are quite young ones, completely little ones, older ones, middle aged ones, old ones, then each one comes gradually to be knowing how being is in men, in women when men when women are about sixty, about fifty, about fifty-five, about forty, about forty-five, about thirty, about twenty-eight, about twenty-six, about twenty-two, about eighteen and fourteen and eleven, and seven and five and three and two and under one to being only just beginning being in iving. Each one gradually in living is realising how being is in men, how being is in women at different ages in them, each one comes in living to know more differences than just very young living, young living, middle living and old living. Again and again it is a startling thing to some one to be learning pieces of this thing of the way being is at different ages in men and in women. I am just now a little realising how old men and how old women mostly are when they are sixty-one. I have learnt a good deal about how being is in men between twenty three and forty-two. I know a good deal about twenty-seven, twenty-five, twenty-nine, thirty, thirty-two, thirty-four, thirty-seven, forty and forty-two and then I know a little about fifty-seven and now I am learning something about being in women and in men when they are sixty and sixty-one. I know a good deal about them when they are very little ones, two and three years old in living, something about them when they are eleven, a very little when they are seventeen almost nothing when they are eighteen and fifteen. I know a very little about them when they are twenty-one. I know that being is very differently in them at different ages in different kinds in men and women. I know that some when they are sixty are healthy ones and some then when they are sixty are not at all then healthy ones. I know some when they are sixty are pretty well worn then and some are dead before they come to be that age in living and some are quite young men and quite young women in eating, sleeping, moving, talking and enjoying, and always then each one is learning in living how being is in each one ever living at different ages in their being living and I, I am just now being quite an astonished one, finding it quite astonishing to be really realising being sixty years old and being in living in men and in women.

Alfred Hersland came to be older than sixty in living, Julia came to be a little older in living, Minnie who married Alfred later did not come in living to be sixty before she came to an ending, Mr. Dehning came to be sixty and he was pretty well beginning then to be quite an old man, Mr. Hersland came to be older a good deal older than sixty before he was not any longer one being living, he was when he was sixty in a way then a completely old one, he was then in a way then not at all a completely old one. I will tell about being old ones later in the description of Dehning and Hersland family living being completely then for that generation ended and ending.

Minnie Mason as I said was married to Alfred Hersland. She would never have it that she would not be married to him when they were beginning to be needing being one in living. She certainly saw to it that they could then be married and quite reasonaply happily married then. She knew David Hersland then. She told him she liked him and she would be a nice sister-in-law to him. She was quite a nice sister-in-law to him. She had not really much interest in Alfred having been married to Julia Dehning excepting only that it would be certain that Julia should be freed from him so that she herself should marry Alfred Hersland when they came to need to be together for living. So then Alfred Hersland went on living as I am saying. Julia Hersland went on living as I have been saying. I will tell now a little more about these things, about being in living.

Certainly some are loving each other more in living than mostly any one is loving any other one. This was not a thing ever coming to be in Julia Dehning, this was not a thing that ever came to be really in Alfred Hersland. They had loving being sometimes in them each one of them. I have said this of them again and again. Almost every one ever knowing either one of them thought of each one of them that they had each one of them sometime loving feeling in them. I have told about loving feeling being in Alfred Hersland. I have told about loving feeling being in Julia Dehning. In a way loving feeling could be quite poignantly in Julia Dehning and she could have sweetness in her then as being in her then. In a way though as I was saying she had always in her stupid being as having it in her to be always resisting having any way in her of really learning anything and in a way she did not have any sweetness in her with this being in her. This stupid being was certainly always being in her and active enough inside her. In a way then she certainly had not really sweetness as actively in her as there was not any sweetness in her with the stupid being of her active in her and stupid being in her was always active inside her. She certainly was one not learning anything in being one being in living, she was one certainly having a dominant courage in her from being one certainly going on being living, she was one having certainly earnest intention as being in her from being one always wanting to have teaching being in the world as always existing, she was one being fairly interesting from being one being really excited in being one always being living, she was one certainly being harsh and being troublesome and being without realising anything without feeling anything in being one needing anything as anything could be to her as something on which to be feeding, she certainly was one having affection and being in Dehning family living, she was one having certainly sometimes loving feeling and having this poignantly with sweetness in being and sweetness in kissing and she was one certainly having stupid being as being in her all her living so that she was everlasting, actively resisting changing at all in attacking. She was one as I was saying not succeeding not failing in living. I am not certain I will just now tell any more about the being in Julia Dehning. Later I will tell more about her in the history of David Hersland that I will now very soon be writing. Certainly I will then tell more of her and of some who knew her and whom David knew by knowing her and some who knew him and then knew her because he knew her just then.

I certainly will not tell any more now about being in her, about living in her, I certainly will tell some about being in her, about living in her, later. I certainly will later be telling something that I have not yet been telling. I do not yet know about her what I will be telling about

her later. I certainly will be telling more about her later. I am quite
certain of this thing.

When I was a young one I was needing some one to teach me something I was needing just then. I was then at the ending of my beginning being in living. Some one then began teaching me that thing I was
needing just then, that one was then teaching me that thing I was needing
just then. I was paying that one for teaching me that thing, the thing
I was needing just then. Once I was saying to this one I will not be paying you to-day, I will pay you in three weeks, you will wait till then, I
said to this one. This one said yes I will wait until then, but I am now
asking you to tell me what you are meaning when you are saying to me
and to yourself then that you have not money to pay me to-day for this
thing. Do you mean that you cannot get the money to pay me to-day,
is that what you are meaning, that you cannot get it to-day if you need
it to day is that your meaning. I said no that is not my meaning, I mean
that I have not the money to-day and that I will have it in three weeks
that is what I am meaning by what I am saying. You mean you will
not get it to-day because you are feeling you are not really needing to
have it to-day that is your meaning, said that one. No I said that is not
the way to understand this thing, I have not got the money to-day and
I will have it in three weeks from to-day, my brother sends me my money
every month that is what I mean by what I am saying. That is what I
am meaning said that one, you are needing the money to-day to your feeling, I am needing the money to-day we will say to my feeling but you do
not need the money to-day to your feeling, that is what you are meaning,
money is a thing like working you are giving it when you are feeling that
you are needing the money to be giving it, I am giving work because I
am needing money to be receiving it, said this one. I had a confused
feeling then. Money was something I was owning yes, but not owning
because it was like being in myself that I needed to be living, having
money was as natural to me then as being in living and I could not be
spending it irregularly, I must spend it as an income. I had it yes but
not to give except when regularly I had some. It was confusing that I
was so certain I had not the money then and yet certainly I could get the
money then but it was not possible to get the money then for I could
not feel I could be needing really to be spending the money I could get
then when it was not the time to get this money as money to be spending.
Some have such a feeling in living, some have not such a feeling in living.
Some cannot really believe it that any one is spending money when they
are not certain that the family have money that gives that money to
them. Some really can never believe this thing of any one. Some are
certain that every one who is not living by daily pay for working can ever
be without having enough for some kind of living. I am feeling always
more and more in living how certainly some are certain of something.

In a way it is a personal thing for them, in a way it is a family affair in them, in a way it is a way of living in a national way for them, in a way it is a way of living of the local way in them, in a way it is a way of living their kind in men and women have in being in living. It is certainly quite completely a difficult thing for any one to be remembering how any one else is doing their daily living, in a way it is quite a difficult thing for some, for quite a number of men for quite a number of women to be remembering how they were getting along from time to time to be in living. It is very often astonishing to be realising complete being in living in men and in women. It is certainly astonishing to know it of each one what that one has done in being in living in himself inside him, to himself inside him, with other ones, with some other one, to any other one, to some one. I am saying this thing because I am in living and because very many men and very many women are living. I am saying this thing because I certainly am going on being in living because very many men and very many women are certainly going on being in living.

Alfred Hersland and Minnie Mason and Patrick Moore and James Flint and Mackinly Young and David Hersland and George Dehning and Hortense Dehing and Julia Hersland and Theodore Summers and William Beckling and Helen Cooke and James Cranach and Miriam Cranach and Rachel Sherman and Adolph Herman and Charles Kohler and Linder Herne and Arthur Keller and Florentine Cranach and Hilda Breslau and Ernest Brakes and Selma Dehning and Ella Housman and Robert Housman and Fred Housman and Florence Arden and James Curson and Bertha Curson and Hilda Gnadenfeld and Algar Audenried and every one who knew any one of them were sometime being in living, were all their living going on being in living.

All men and all women ever having been, being in living are certainly feeling something in them about going on being in living. Each one of them certainly sometimes is going on being in living doing something and then is going on being in living doing some other thing. Each one ever having been in living has certainly been in living feeling certain in some way of doing something. It is as I say certainly to some an astonishing thing to be knowing in some other one the way that one has it to be in living certain about being one doing some thing in some way in the living of that one. Certainly some one is very often certain that not any one really is certain in doing something in some way, that that one is certainly not certain enough in doing that thing that way to be ever in the living of that one really doing that thing in any such a way in the living of that one. As I am saying each one ever having been, being in living is doing something in some way, is certain in some way in being in some way being living, is going on in some way being in living, certainly mostly every one.

As I am saying there has been being there is being in some of these

I have been mentioning, in Alfred Hersland and Martha Hersland and Julia Dehning and David Hersland and George Dehning and Hortense Dehning and William Beckling, and Minnie Mason, and Charles Kohler and Pat Moore and Florence Arden and James Flint and Robert Housman and Adolph Herman and Mackinly Young and Selma Dehning and Hilda Breslau and Arthur Keller and James Flint and every other one they were any of them ever knowing and every other one living when any of them were going on being living and every other one being living when they were not any longer going on being living any of them or any other one, before any one of them were being in living being then being living, every one then of all these certainly sometime in a way was going on being in living, was certainly being some way in being living. This is enough to say just now about each one of them. This is what I am saying just now about each one of them. I will certainly say this about each one of them again and again. This is the ending of just this way of going on telling about being being in some men and in some women. This is the ending of this way of telling about being having been and being in Alfred Hersland and Julia Dehning.

DAVID HERSLAND

I do ask some, I would ask every one, I do not ask some because I am quite certain that they would not like me to ask it, I do ask some if they would mind it if they found out that they did have the name they had then and had been having been born not in the family living they are then living in, if they had been born illegitimate. I ask some and I would ask every one only I am quite certain very many would not like to have me ask it if they would like it, if they would very much dislike it, if they would make a tragedy of it, if they would make a joke of it, if they found they had in them blood of some kind of a being that was a low kind to them. I would like to know how every one can be feeling about such a thing, if they have any feeling about any such thing. David Hersland was the younger son of Mr. David Hersland and Mrs. Hersland. In his younger living he never thought about any such thing as that about which I have just been telling. In his later living he liked thinking about feeling such things, thinking such things being in men and women. Some when they are quite young ones are thinking then about such things. He was never at all when he was a young one thinking about any such thing. This is to be now a history of him.

What am I believing about living. I am believing that I am not certain when I am saying something from being one being then being loving that I am meaning anything by what I am then saying, I am not certain that I am not then having being in being one being loving that is being that is having the meaning as being of what I am then saying. I am believing that I am not certain about being being in one meaning what one being in being loving is saying. I am believing that I am not certain being being loving in one is in one then meaning what that one is then saying. I am believing that I am not certain that being is not in one meaning what that one being then being loving is saying. What is it I am knowing about living, I certainly am not knowing that I am not knowing everything about being in living. I am not certain that I am knowing everything about being living. I am not certain that I am not knowing everything about being living. I am not certain that I am knowing everything about being living.

I know that I am not certain about what I would do for some one what I would not do for some one. Not any one is certain so that acting by them shows it to any one what they would do for some one, what they would not do for some one. Each one then would do something for some one, would not do something for some one, would do something for any one would not do something for any one. Some are quite certain about themselves in this thing. Some are quite not certain about themselves in this thing. Not any one is rightly certain about themselves about this thing. Perhaps not any one is really certain about themselves about this thing. Perhaps one is certain about that one about this thing. I know I am not certain about what I would do for some one, what I would not do for some one.

Some one having some one who was with them become a dead one could be saying, when some one was saying something, that one does not know he is a dead one, he will never know that thing. He does not know he is a dead one, some one said of some one who was a dead one. Some one could be certain that some one who is a dead one would not know he was a dead one, some one could not know that some other one who was a dead one would not know that that one was a dead one. Some one then has been quite certain that some one who was with them when that one was a dead one did not know then that that one was a dead one. Some have been certain that every one who is a dead one does not then know that that one is a dead one.

It is a surprising thing sometimes to be learning which ones of some one has been knowing are quite certain and say the thing then as a very simple thing that anybody can be knowing that some one who has been with them being a dead one is not knowing that that one is a dead one.

It is certainly something that some are saying when some one who was with them is a dead one that that one is not knowing then that that one is a dead one. Some like very well to be hearing some one say this thing that some one is a dead one and is certainly then not knowing this thing. Some like very well hearing this thing. Some are not wanting ever to be hearing any thing about any one ever being a dead one. This will soon now be the beginning of a description of living that David Hersland did before he came to be a dead one.

Some are satisfied with having been living when they are come to be a dead one with not having had in them any very sick feeling, any very bad thing to be doing, any very hard work for them in them, not any queer feeling of not having had their head quite right inside them. Some are satisfied then with having been living ones when they have come to be a dead one, some are not satisfied then with having come to be then a dead one. Some are satisfied, some are not satisfied with having been one being living. Some are quite satisfied with having been one having living in them, some are not satisfied at all with this thing. Some are very well satisfied with having come to be a dead one, some are not at all satisfied with this thing.

Some one gives to another one a stubborn feeling when that one could be convincing that other one if that other one would then continue listening. Some are certain that sometimes they can be convinced by some one. Some are certain they are sometimes convinced by some one. Some are certain that they could be conceived sometimes by some one but that they will not be letting themselves ever have any such a thing happen to them. Some like being convinced of some things by some, by some one.

Some one and I certainly never did think that one ever could do such a thing has it to be so strongly repeating the facts that one is remembering that almost always I am always convinced that I have been wrong in my feeling. I certainly am not certain whether I ever can be certain whether I ever am when I am feeling something justified from my way of feeling anything in having such a feeling when this one is repeating the way that one is remembering everything. Some one said about some one who was saying something that seemed a very foolish thing to some one about how some one did something, but that one was not saying foolish things, she was judging from the feeling of being convenienced and inconvenienced that she would be having and that was all that concerned her in her judging. It was not a foolish thing then that that one had been saying. No, there are many ways of not being a foolish one in being living. There are certainly lots and lots of them of ways of not being a foolish one in being in living. So then some certainly could be convincing me of many things if I go on listening. I am quite certain that this is certain.

David Hersland was a dead one before he was a middle aged one. He was then never in his living an old one. He was dead before he came to the middle of his middle living.

I am coming to know some whom I have known as middle aged ones, as young ones. This is a pleasing thing.

David Hersland was a dead one before he was a middle aged one. He was then never in his living a middle aged one. He was dead before he came to the middle of his middle living.

I have come to know some as being young whom I have been knowing as middle aged ones as coming to be old ones, I know now what ones being young ones will come to be middle aged ones like some I have been knowing as middle aged ones. This seems an easy thing. It is a very difficult thing.

It is hard to be certain to one's feeling that some one one has been knowing is a dead one, will not be a growing older one. Some one was saying that his grandfather had been a dead one before his grandfather was finished being a young one.   That is a queer thing that a grandfather was never in his own middle living.

I am coming to know now more and more of a group of them in men and women what kind they are when they are young ones, when they are middle aged ones, when they are old ones.   To-night I came to be certain about one group of them what kind they are when they are young men when they are young women.   I am not yet certain about some groups of them what they are when they are old ones, I am not certain about some groups of them what they are when they are middle aged ones, I am not certain about some groups of them what they are when they are young men when they are young women, I am not certain about some groups of them what they are when they are young ones ycunger than young women and young men.   I am certain I am not yet knowing all the kinds there are in men and women.

David Hersland was come to being one not being living before he could come to be a middle aged one.   He was not ever then an older one, an old one, a middle aged one.   He came to be a dead one after a considerable beginning of his middle living.

I know now how quite a number of groups that there are of men and women are ones existing when they are young ones, that is young women and young men, that is just ending their beginning living, just beginning their middle living.   I am beginning to know of some groups in men and women, what they have as hands and faces and ears and bodies to them and being in them, and ways of acting in them when they are young men and young women, older young men and young women, middle aged men and women, old men and women.   I do not know yet very much about what any group of them are when they are young children. I am slowly spreading very slowly spreading to them, I have not yet spread to them, not at all reached to them yet in spreading out in knowing being in groups of men and women.

As I was saying David Hersland was a dead one before he was a middle aged one.   He was dead before he came to the middle of his middle living.   He was then never a middle aged one, he was then never an old one. He was one of a kind in men and women.   Certainly each one is one of a kind in men and women.   I am knowing more about being in each group of them when every one of a group of them is a young one, and an older one, an old one.   I am knowing then being in some groups of men and women as it is in them when they are young men or women, older men or women, old men or women.

No one will listen while I am talking.   Some have very much such a trouble in being one being living.   Some have not at all any of such trouble in them.   Some will listen when I am talking.   Some will not listen when I am talking.   Some will listen while they are fat ones, they do not listen when after dieting they have become thin ones. These then listen to other ones and some of these other ones could not get any listening from them before the dieting that made these come to be thin ones from having been fat ones. Some are listening to me now and before they were always listening every evening to another one. They are listening to me now, I like them to be listening. Some who are young men and young women are listening to me now very often. Some who are now young men are listening to me now very often, they listen to me and I am talking very much now quite often to them. Some are very faithful in being ones listening and these are not listening very often. I know very well one such a one. Some quite older ones are listening but then really I am not talking very much when they are listening. Some have it to be certain that not any one ever is listening when they are talking. Some of these are mistaken, some of these are not mistaken. Some of these come to know it in them that they are not listening being so certain in them that there can not ever be conversation in any living for them. This will be soon a description of being in David Hesland and how men and how women listened to him, how some listened to him, how others listened to him, how some heard him doing talking but never listened to him, how some did not ever hear him doing any talking, how some forgot about him, how some remembered him, how some talked to him, how some said they would prefer not having ever to talk to him, how some had to talk to him, how some stopped talking with him, how some being with him liked what they were then doing, how some being with him sometimes did not at all like that thing, how some told him everything that they could think of telling and how some were sorry they had told him and how some were not sorry they had told him and how some wanted to go on telling him more and how some forgot they had told him anything. This is then to be a description of David Hersland of being and listening and talking and being liked and disliked and remembered and forgotten and going on being living and dying and being a dead one.

Some are listening to me and I tell them then the being they have in them. I tell them what they have what they have not in them, how it comes together, how it does not come together in them, how the being they have in them is important to them, how it is not important to them, how it can be active in them, how it can be not active in them, why they like having their being in them, why they do not like having their being in them. Mostly every one has listened some when I have been telling them about being in them. Some have listened and I have thought that they were believing what I was telling them and then many years after they have been telling that they were certain then that I was telling them then what I had not any reason to believe was true of them. And sometimes then later when they tell me such a thing they find it that I am not certain that I was not then doing this thing. Some make of themselves a new one by my telling them about the being in them and to very many then they are quite a new one and to some then they are not at all a new one, they are quite an old one. Some like listening and later then they have a frightened feeling that I will influence them to be another one, they do not like very well some of them what they are in living, they do like some of them what they are in living, they are quite certain they do not want me to be influencing them. Some are listening and I am talking and I am talking and then they ask a question and then I say to myself that words can have a meaning to some one and a meaning to some other one and that I was talking and that that one was intelligently listening and that that one has then asked this question. I have told so many so much about the being in them. I will tell I am quite certain some more about the being in them. This will be now much history of talking and listening. I talk one way and listen one way and talk other ways and listen other ways and so probably does every one. This is to be now very much description of talking and listening, of a number of young men and young women talking and of a number of older men and older women talking and of each one of them the young men and young women and the older men and the older women listening.

Some are certain that sometime some could be different ones in being in being living, some are certain that sometime every one will be a different one in being in being living, some are hoping that sometime some one will be a different one, some are certain that they are believing that something can be different in living sometime for some, some are certain that they are believing that something can be different in each one, some are believing this thing about men some are believing this thing about women, some are believing this thing about men and women, some are thinking they are believing this thing, some are not believing that they are believing this thing, some are always believing this thing, some are not always believing this thing, I am not believing this thing, another one is not believing this thing, another one is not believing this thing, another one is believing this thing, another one is believing this thing, another one is believing this thing, another one is believing this thing, another one is not believing this thing, another one is not believing this thing, another one is not believing this thing, another one is believing this thing, another one is believing this thing.

This is to be a history of David Hersland and of his coming in his living to be thinking again and again and very often of coming to be a dead one. This is to be a history of him and of his coming to be thinking of coming to be a dead one and of his thinking about coming to be a dead one and about being a dead one and about his coming to be a dead one.

This then is to be now a history of David Hersland and of talking and of listening and of thinking about being dead ones in men and women

men being in being living. This then is to be now a history of David
Hersland and of his talking and of his hearing talking and of his listening
and of other ones doing listening and of very much talking and of
thinking and feeling and of everything that ever was or is or will be being
in some men and some women doing living. This then is to be now commencing being a history of David Hersland being in living and being talking and being listening and being talking and listening and being talking
and being talking and being talking and being listening and being listening. This is then to be now a history of him.

Every one has experiencing in being one being living. I am saddening with not feeling each one being experiencing as each one is having that thing. I am saddening with this thing. There are so many
being in living and there are so many that I am knowing by seeing and hearing being in living and each one of these is experiencing in being living and
I cannot be feeling what way each one is experiencing, I who am suffering and suffering because of this thing. I am in desolation and my eyes are
large with needing weeping and I have a flush from feverish feeling and
I am not knowing what way each one is experiencing in being living and
about some I am knowing in a general way and I could be knowing in a
more complete way if I could be living more with that one and I never
will live more with every one, I certainly cannot ever live with each one in
their being one being living, in my being one being living. I tell you
I cannot bear it this thing that I cannot be realising experiencing in each
one being living, I say it again and again I cannot let myself be really
resting in believing this thing, it is in me now as when I am realising being
a dead one, a one being dying and I can do this thing and I do this thing
and I am filled then with complete desolation and I am doing this thing
again and again and I am now again and again certain that I will not
ever be realising experiencing in each one of very many men and very
many women, I can realise something of experiencing in some of them, in
them as kinds of them but I am needing to have it in me as a complete thing
of each one ever living and I I know I will not, and I am one knowing being
a dead one and not being a living one, I who am not believing that I will be
realising each one's experiencing. I do not want to realise each thing they
are experiencing, I do not care anything about such a thing, all that I
am needing to be one being living is to be realising completely how each
one is experiencing, with what feeling, thinking, believing, creating and
I I am very certain that I will not ever be completely with each one doing
such a thing, I will be doing something in such a thing with kinds in men
and women, with some of some kinds of them but not with each one not
with every one, no certainly not with every one. No certainly not with
every one, completely, certainly not, and more and more knowing some
one experiencing and completely knowing that one makes it certain that
if I could live with each one I could realise the experiencing in each one

and I cannot ever live with each one, I certainly never will be living a good deal with each one ever having been living.

David in beginning living was hearing some, was feeling some about somethings being things that one should be doing so as to be one going on being living. Such a thing as not changing a thing when one was beginning putting it on one way and such a thing as counting some things and not other things and such a thing as arranging clothing so that not in any way could he be putting one thing on the way he had been putting that thing on the other morning and stepping on something and not stepping on something and thinking something and then certainly thinking then another thing, and doing something and certainly then be doing another thing, and hoping something and saying then another thing, and walking around something and walking around that same thing and never walking again around that same thing, as I was saying when he was one beginning being living he was hearing then when he was one beginning living some things, he was feeling then some things about needing somethings being happening so that he could become one going on being living and he was then as I was saying hearing some things, he was then feeling some things that needed being so that he could be one going on being in being living.

He was one then as I was saying commencing being in living and he was then a little an older one and this is to be now a complete history of him and of listening and of talking and of some doing listening and doing talking.

One and then another and then another one and then another one said something and then some other one said something and some one can listen to every one who says something. There are not so many kinds in men and women, I have just been seeing pictures of about fifteen kinds of them, kinds of men and women, there are more than that of course of kinds in men and women as I feel being being in them but there are not so very many kinds in men and women. Each one talks a good deal in being in living even those who do not do very much talking. Every one who ever was living talks a good deal that is certain. Every one ever living talks a good deal, some are talking and others are listening and those then talking are thinking that those then listening are ones not ever doing very much talking and some of them do very much talking and some of them do not do so very much talking. Some one talks a good deal in being living, every one listens a good deal in being living, this is to be now a description of talking and listening, this is to be now a description of being and living in David Hersland, of David Hersland.

There are not then so many kinds in men and women. Each one of every kind in men and women is as I am saying doing very much talking doing very much listening in being living, some of each kind in men and women do more talking in being living than others of that kind of them, some of each kind in men and women do more listening than others of that kind of them, some of each kind in men and women do more talking and more listening than others of that kind of them, that kind in men and women. I am saying that there are not so very many kinds in men and women as I am feeling being in men and women, but as I was saying each one of a kind in men and women has being in that one being differently in him from being in any other one of that kind of them. I am now beginning describing being in David Hersland, I will be telling very much now about talking and listening, I will be describing in many various ways quite a number of men and quite a number of women.

Each one is mostly all his living all her living, a young one, an older one, one in middle living, an old one to themselves, to any one, to some one. That is to say not any one is all his living all her living to any one, that is to say not any one hardly is feeling another one being a young one and then an older one and then an old one. It is a very strange thing this thing and an interesting thing that almost not any one is to any one is to themselves inside them one having been in all parts of being living. That is to say it is very striking one man is writing about some one and that one about whom that one is writing is to that one say an old man. That one writing tells about that man being a young one, tells about that man being a middle aged one and always it is a description of the old man who was once a young man, a child, a middle aged man, it is not a description of a young man a middle aged man or a child. It is the same thing if some one is a child to some one feeling that one, telling about that one, that one may be described as an older one, a middle aged one an old one but it is always then a description of a child having become a middle aged one, an older one, an old one. So then this is certain that each one is to some one for all of the living ever in that one a child, to some one, a baby, to some one, an older one, to some one, a middle aged one, to some one, an old one, to some one. I am not saying that not any one can be feeling more than one stage of being in themselves, in any other one, but I am really almost saying this thing. It is an interesting thing that each one in a way is feeling the world being existing in this kind of way too in them. Those feeling the world an old thing are only feeling this thing, those feeling the world a new thing are only feeling this thing, those feeling the world to be having had a past living are only feeling it as a thing having description and so on and so on and it is extraordinary how not any one can be convincing in telling about one being a young man if they are feeling the living being in that one being that of an old one. Mostly every one is in some place in being living to every one knowing that one and that is the complete realisation that each one is having of that one. Always then this comes to be to me more an extraordinary thing that not any one can really be telling the whole history, can really be realising the whole going on of being in them, that not any one can be telling the whole history of any one, that not any one can be realising the whole time of being going on being of being in any one. I do certainly think this to be an extraordinary thing. Mostly then as I am saying not any one is feeling any other one really having been in living a young one an older one a middle aged one, an old one. Really then mostly every one all the living of some one is feeling that one to have been a young one or an older one, or a middle aged one or an old one.

Listening does not help one with this thing because as I am saying each one is feeling themselves as having been an old one, a middle aged one, a younger one, a young one all their living and when they an old one talk about themselves as a young one, it is a description of an old one having been a young one, not a realising of being a young one, and so on and so on and so each one is in themselves in feeling one having been in all living a young one, or an older one, or a middle aged one, or an old one.

I did use to find this very perplexing this difficulty each one has of realising whole being having been going on being in any one, in themselves inside them. It is a very useful thing that always in living there are some being young ones some being older ones, some being middle aged ones, some being older ones so that one can always be certain that not any one has been living without all the being in them having been going on being as being a young one an older one a middle aged one, an old one. As I was saying listening is not helping any one very much with this thing, knowing ones self inside one is not helping one very much with this thing, talking about being having been in one is not helping one very much with this thing. Knowing family living is helping some with this thing, having little ways in moments inside one in feeling, in doing something perhaps is helping something with this thing, mostly not anything is really helping one doing this thing, realising the whole being having been, going on, going to be going on in any one. So then I am not thinking about doing this thing. I am thinking about telling about being being in men and in women, I am thinking about telling about talking and listening that some men and some women are doing, that mostly every one is or was or will be doing. I am thinking then about telling about knowing being being in men and in women. I am thinking then about listening and talking being, going to be being, having been being in some men in some women.

David Hersland was interested in dying, in loving, in talking, in listening, in ways of eating, in ways of being going on being in living. He came to be a dead one when he was coming to the beginning of the middle of his middle living ; this will be now a complete description of the being being in him and the living he was having in being one being living.

He was one interested in ways of eating, in loving, in ways of being going on being living, in dying, in listening, in talking. He was one living in needing to be certain always and that always every day in his living that he was understanding that living was a thing that he wanted then to be doing, that he was then realising as being, as beginning or as going to be beginning or as going to be ending.

He was one certainly interested all his living in listening, in talking, in loving, in dying, in going on going on living, in ways of going on being living. He was one certainly all his living interested in talking, he was one certainly all his living interested in listening. He was one certainly all his living very much interested in talking, he was one certainly all his living very much interested in listening, this will then be soon a description of talking, of ways of being one interested very much in talking, of ways of listening, of being one very much interested in listening. I can certainly say that David Hersland was certainly very much interested in listening, in ways of being one being listening, I can certainly say that David Hersland was one very much interested in talking, in kinds of talking that kinds in men and women are doing, in kinds of talking men and women doing any talking are doing. He was one then certainly interested in talking, certainly interested in listening. He was one in his living certainly doing listening, he was one in his living certainly doing talking. This then will be then soon now some description of talking being done by men and women, of listening being done by men and women, and then there will be some description of David Hersland and certainly he was in his living doing some talking, doing some listening, he certainly was all his living interested in talking interested in listening, interested in his being one talking, interested in his being one listening, interested in ways of talking in men and in women, interested in ways of listening in men and in women, interested in his own way of talking, interested in his own way of listening. He was one then certainly all his living very much interested in men and women being ones doing talking, being ones doing listening. As I was saying he was one interested in living interested in dying, in loving, in talking, in listening, in ways of going on being in living. He was one certainly interested in ways of going on being living, of going on being in living he was one certainly interested in being one going on being living, in going on being in being living, he certainly was interested in every one's being one going on being living. He was then certainly one interested in any one's going on being living, he was certainly interested in ways of going on being living, ways of going on being in being living. He was one as I was saying interested in talking, in listening, in dying, in going on being living, in going on being in being living, in loving. He was one certainly interested in dying, in listening, in talking, in going on being in being living, in loving. He was one then certainly interested in being one wanting to be certain each moment in being living that he was wanting to be one then being living. As I was saying he was very much an interested one in realising ways of being one going on being living, in listening, in talking, in ways of eating, in loving, some in going to be beginning, some in ending, in dying, some in going to be ending. He was then in living mostly an interested one. He was in living then almost mostly an interested one. He was then in living one being an interested one in ways of being one going on being living, in his being one going on being living, in dying, in loving in ways of being one eating to be going on being living, in his way of eating something, in his way of eating for being one going on being in living, he was as I was saying in being living one interested in ways of being one being talking, in ways of being one being listening. He was as I was saying one being one pretty nearly completely interested in being one being living, in any one's being one being living. As I was saying he was one pretty nearly completely interested in living being existing. He was one as I am saying pretty nearly completely interested in this thing. He was one as I am saying all his living pretty nearly completely interested in this thing. He was then as I am saying pretty nearly all his living interested in his being one being living. As I am saying he was all his living pretty nearly completely interested in his being one being going on being living. He was one then as I am saying one almost completely interested in being one being living. He was then as I am saying mostly all his living one being almost completely interested in his being one being living. He was all his living interested in loving, in dying, in ways of going on being living, in talking, in listening, in ways of eating. He was one almost completely interested in being one being living. He was one all his living interested in ways of eating, ways of being one going on being in living, in listening, in talking, in dying, in loving. He was one mostly all his living almost completely interested in his being one going on being living.

I am now beginning a description of being having been in David Hersland, the being, the living in him, the talking and listening he was doing in living, the ways he was eating, loving in him, dying in him, going on being living in him when he was one going on being living in living. I am now beginning a description of David Hersland and I will give one description after another description of the being in him and the living in him and the talking he did in living, and the listening he did in living, and the loving he did in living, and the going on being living he did in living and the dying he did when he was being living and I will give one description and then another description and then another description and then another description and then I will give another description and another description of the being in him and the talking he did in living, and the listening he did in living, and the things that were interesting to him in listening and in talking that any one was then doing, and the dying he was doing in being in living, and the going on being in living that he was doing in being in living, and the loving he was doing in being in living, and the ways of eating that were interesting to him while he was being in living. As I was saying he was mostly all his living almost completely interested in being one being living. He was mostly all his living almost completely interested in any one being living. He was mostly all his living completely interested in some one being one being living, in some being living. He was as I was saying interested all his living in any one being one going on being in being living. He was then one certainly interested in talking, in listening, in dying, in loving, in ways of going on going on living, in ways of eating, he was certainly then one mostly all his living almost completely interested in his being one being living, he was certainly one interested in some being ones going on being living.

I will now be telling about David Hersland being one of Hersland family living, having Hersland family living as living for him, having Gossols half country half city living as a way of having living in him. I will now be telling about living being in David Hersland when he was quite a little one when he was a bigger one, when he was as big one as he ever was in being one being living. I will now be telling about being being in him and I will tell of course a good deal about the being being in him. Naturally I will tell a great deal about living and being being in David Hersland. He was living in Gossols in a part of Gossols where not any rich people were living. He was living the Hersland's half-country, half-city living. He was living the half country half city living of the men and women and children living in that part of Gossols where the Herslands were living. He was living the living he was naturally living from the being he had as being in him. This is to be now some description of him. This is to be now of course very much history of him. This will be naturally a description, some description, many descriptions of very many men and very many women. This will be then very much description of David Hersland, of being, of living, of dying, of listening, of talking, of going on being living, of going on being in living, of ways of eating.

David Hersland was all his younger and young living living in Gossols and he was knowing then the Hersland family and any one knowing the Hersland family then and he was knowing every one living in the part of Gossols he was living in, mostly every one, and he was knowing some others too then. He was talking some then and listening some then, certainly he was listening some then and talking some then. I have already told something about his having been one listening some then about his having been one talking some then.

David Hersland would have liked it very well all his living to like every kind there is of women. He would have liked very well to have had this in him all his living. He would have liked all of his living to feel beauty in any kind there is of women. He would have liked it very well to feel in him beauty being in each one in all women. He would have liked very well in every bit of being living to be feeling each woman a beautiful thing to be being in living. He certainly would have liked very well all his living to be finding every woman every kind of woman a beautiful one in being loving. This is to be then a history of living being in David Hersland, of loving, listening, talking, going on being living, dying, ways of feeling going on being living in him. He is then one I am going to be now beginning describing.

He would have liked it very well to be having all his living each woman ever living to be a beautiful one to him. He wanted it then that all his living every woman he could come to be knowing should be to him, would be for him a beautiful one. He wanted this thing all his living. He wanted always that any woman, that every woman was a beautiful woman to him, was a beautiful woman being a woman being living. He was then one certainly being interested all his living in dying, loving, ways of eating, ways of going on being in living, talking and listening. He was one then all his living one certainly almost being one completely interested in being one being living. This is to be now a history of living being and having been in some men and some women.

David was one being then being one almost completely interested in being living from the beginning of his being one being living. As I have been saying this is to be now a description of his being one being living. I am beginning now this description of him, a description of all living being in him of all the being in him.

I am realising being in some men, men succeeding completely in living, I will tell sometime about some of them. Some men are very active in being living, some men are not so very active in being living, some men and some women are very active in being living, some men and some women are not very active in being living. Some men are very active in being living and are succeeding very well in being living, some men are very active in being living and are not succeeding very well in being living, some men and some women are succeeding very well in being living, some men and some women are not succeeding very well in being living.

Some men and some women have being very actively in them and are succeeding very well in being living and are not very convincing to some knowing them all their living, some men and some women have being very actively in them and are succeeding very well in being living and are convincing to very many knowing them all their living. I certainly will try to tell all I am realising of being in men and women. I will try sometime to tell all I am realising of being in some having being very actively in them and succeeding completely well in being in living and being convincing to many knowing them all their living, of being in some having being actively in them and being ones succeeding completely in living and being convincing as being really interesting to some knowing them all their living, of being in some having being actively in them and being ones succeeding astonishingly succeeding and being convincingly interesting to some and being certainly not convincingly interesting to some and being some convincingly interesting to some and being some not convincingly interesting to some, I can try to tell all I am realising about being being in men and in women. I can try to realise completely all being in each one. I am trying to be realising all being in each one. I am quarrelling with some, I am hurting some, I am winning with some, I am beginning with some, I am being hurt by some, I am neglecting some, I am wanting some, I am forgetting some, I am happy with some, I am kissing some, I have been telling some I did not know that that one was feeling that thing and that one was telling me then that that one did not know I was feeling that thing, I certainly did have resentment against some one, I certainly did not like what some one did when I was doing something, I am trying to be realising being, I can try to do this thing. This is to be now a complete description of all the being I ever have been realising as being in David Hersland and very many he knew and ones who knew him. This then is to be a description. This then is to be a history of him and of some whom he knew, of some who knew him, this then is to be a history of all of him and of some whom he knew, of all of him and of some who knew him.

He began living and this is to be now a little description of that beginning. He went on being living and this is to be then a description of that thing. He still went on living and this is then to be a description of that thing. He came to be a dead one and this will be then a description of that thing. He began being living and this is to be now some description of this thing.

I am troubled with men and with women, I am troubled by men and by women. I am troubled that each one is experiencing each thing they are experiencing the way each one is experiencing each thing. I do not want that any one should experience anything any way but the way each one is experiencing that thing. I certainly do not want it that any one should experience anything in any way that that one is not experiencing a thing. No I do not want anything to be at all a different thing in the way each one is experiencing each thing, no I do not want anything to be different in experiencing than it is in each one, I certainly do not, I may but I doubt it, I certainly do not, I am certain of this thing. I certainly do not want any one to be experiencing anything in a different way than the way they have it in them to experience that thing. I am troubled as I was saying with each one being one experiencing the way each one is experiencing, I am troubled by each one experiencing the way each one is experiencing each thing. I am troubled, I say I am very much troubled by each one being that one experiencing each thing as that one is experiencing that thing. I certainly am very much troubled with this thing. Each one is experiencing each thing in the way that one is experiencing each thing. I certainly do not at all want that each one should not be experiencing each thing the way that one is experiencing that thing. Some say I do want each one to be experiencing differently from the way each one is experiencing each thing, I may but I doubt this thing, I certainly am certain that I do not want that each one is experiencing each thing differently from the way each one is experiencing each thing. So then I want it that each one is experiencing each thing the way each one is experiencing each thing. I certainly do not want it that each one is experiencing each thing in a way each one is not experiencing each thing. I am as I am saying troubled with each one experiencing each thing the way each one is experiencing each thing. I certainly am troubled by each one being experiencing each thing the way each one is experiencing each thing.

Some are not succeeding in living, some are succeeding in living. Some are feeling some one to be one succeeding in living, some are not feeling that one to be one succeeding in living. Some are ones being certain that sometime something will be working in a different way from the way that thing is now working. Some are certain that everything will be working differently from the way everything is now working. Some as I am saying are understanding something one way, some as I am saying are understanding something another way. Some are beginning with understanding, some are ending with understanding. Some are realising experiencing in some one when that other one has done something. Some are realising experiencing in some one when that some one has commenced doing something. Some are realising experiencing in some one when some one has completely done something. Some are realising experiencing in each one while each one is doing being experiencing. I certainly am very troubled by each one being one experiencing each thing they are experiencing.

I said there are very many men and very many women always being living. I said there are very many men and very many women experiencing each thing they are each one experiencing. I said there are very many men and very many women always, there certainly are very many men and very many women always living.

David Hersland knew very many being living while he was one being living. He knew some when he was a little one, an older one, one beginning being in middle living. He certainly did know quite a number who were being living while he was being living.

He knew some of them longer than he did other ones, he talked more to some than he did to other ones, he forgot some more than he did other ones, he listened to some more than he did to other ones, he liked some better than he did other ones, he loved some more than he did other ones, he was liked more by some than he was by other ones, he was remembered more by some than he was by other ones. He knew then a good many who were living when he was living. There were a very great many who were living when he was living. He knew some who were living when he was living. There were some whom he knew all his living, there were some whom he knew a very short time in his living. I certainly will be trying to tell about each one ever having been, going to be, being living, I certainly will now tell about each one David Hersland was knowing and about each one who knew him.

I certainly am now trying to be beginning telling about each one David Hersland knew in his living about each one who in his living knew him. I certainly am now trying to be beginning to tell about David Hersland being living, I certainly am going to be trying to tell about David Hersland being living, about each one he knew when he was being living, about each one who while he was being living knew him. Many women have it in them to be sometimes loving some one. Many of such of them have it in them then to be laying their hand on that one, to be feeling inside in them then and out from them the way any one being one having feeling of being some one directing any living is feeling, being some one giving something is feeling, being some one receiving something is feeling, being some one many might be finding it necessary to be respectfully addressing is feeling, being some one who is some one who is an important one by reason of being one being born to be in living is feeling. This feeling in the one having that feeling is mostly a very nice thing to that one having that feeling, it is sometimes a very nice thing to the one loving that one, it is sometimes not at all a nice thing to some one loving that one, it is sometimes a nice thing to some seeing that one having that feeling, it is to some seeing one having that way of feeling a very funny thing, to some a very unpleasant thing, to some a serious thing, to some a curious thing. However it is certain that very many women having feeling in them of loving some one have then a feeling of being some one having it in them to be important to every one as being one having been born to be living. They are then acting that way in being one being one loving some one. As I am saying some have one feeling about such a thing, some have another feeling about such a thing. Some have a feeling of being impressed by any woman having such a feeling of being one being important by being one having been born to be living in being in living, being important as being one being born and being living. Very many women as I am saying are sometime, are sometimes loving some man and as I am saying some of such of them have it then in them to have of their kind of them the feeling and the manner then of being one having it in them to be one directing living. Very many women are sometime, are sometimes loving some man and as I am saying some of such of them have it then in them to have of their kind of them the feeling and the manner then of being one having it in them to be one being important by reason of having been one being born to being in living. As I am saying very many women are sometime, are sometimes loving some man and as I am saying some of such of them have it then in them to have of their kind of them the feeling and the manner then of being one having it in them to be important to every one because of being existing and that is enough as it is to any one in any position where they are and not anybody ·in any way can move them. Anyway very many women having loving in them are having then the feeling and the acting of being ones being born important ones to any one. As I am saying each one having this feeling is acting then the way their kind of them is naturally acting having such a feeling. As I am saying some feel one way some feel another way in feeling, seeing some woman having such a feeling. David Hersland as I was saying was one having it that each woman having loving in them had on him some effect to make of him in some way one submitting to that one. He was then one in a way doing very much submitting. Some liked this in him, some did not like this in him, some found him one very unpleasant in being one being living, some found him very attracting in being one being living. Any how this is to be now a complete history of him and this time I am certain to be beginning with his beginning being one being in living.

Some come to be a dead one before they come to be a middle aged one, some come to be a dead one before they come to be an old one. Some come to be a dead one before they come to be the ending of the beginning of their middle living. David Hersland came to be a dead one before he came to be at the ending of the beginning of his middle living.

Quite a number come to be dead ones before they come to be old ones. Quite a number come to be dead ones before they come to be middle aged ones. Quite a number come to be dead ones before they come to the beginning of coming to be a middle aged one. Some then really come to be dead ones before they come to the ending of the beginning of their middle living. Some of these might have been succeeding in living if they had gone on being living, some of these might have been not succeeding in living if they had gone on then being living. Some then come to be quite really dead ones before the ending of the beginning of their middle living. Some do not come to be dead ones before the ending of their beginning middle living. Quite a number do not come to being dead ones before the ending of the beginning of their middle living. David Hersland as I was saying came to be a dead one before he came to be at the ending of his beginning being in his middle living. David Hersland might have been one succeeding if he had gone on being living, David Hersland might have been one not succeeding if he had gone on being living. So then certainly some men, some women come to be really dead ones before the ending of the beginning of their middle living. Certainly quite a number of men and quite a number of women come to be dead before they come to be at the ending of the beginning of their middle living. Some as I was saying of these if they had gone on being living would have been succeeding well enough in living, some of these as I was saying would certainly not have been succeeding very well in being living.   David Hersland as I said of him was one who came to be one being dead before he came to be one beginning being in the middle of his middle living, he was one as I have said of him who might have been one succeeding in living if he had been one going on being living, he might have been one failing in living if he had been one going on being living.   Some who have come to be dead ones before they have come to the beginning of the middle of their middle living would certainly have been succeeding if they had been ones going on being living.   Some who come to be dead ones before the beginning of the middle of the middle of their living would have been really failing if they had gone on being living.   I am going now to be telling about being and living being in David Hersland from his beginning being in living to his coming to be one not being any longer being living.   I cannot tell to any one how completely very many come to be dying and quite dead ones before they come to the beginning of the middle of their middle living.   I am telling to myself that I am certain of this thing.   I am telling that some of these would have been succeeding in living if they had been ones not coming to be dead ones before the beginning of the middle of their middle living.   I am also telling that some of these would have been failing in living if they had been ones going on being living to the ending of their middle living, if they had been ones going on to being old ones in being living.   As I am certainly saying David Hersland was one coming to be a dead one before the ending of the beginning of his middle living.   This is now to be a complete history of being and living in him.

Not any one could be certain all their living that any other one is completely living their living.   Almost not any one can be certain that any other one is completely living the living of that one.   Mostly not any one is believing all their living that any other one is completely living the living of that one.   Mostly every one is believing that some one could be completely living all the living of that one.   Some to themselves inside them are believing they are completely living the living of them.   Some to themselves inside them are not believing that they are completely living the living of them.   Mostly not any one is believing of any other one that that one is completely living the living of them. Some are believing that some one is completely living the living of that one. Some could be believing that some one is completely living the being in him, some could be believing that some one is completely living the being in her, some could not be believing that any one could be completely living the living in that one.   Mostly not any one is really believing that any other one is completely living their living, some are believing that some are living completely the living in them, very many are not believing anything about this thing, mostly every one is believing something about this thing.   So then very many are always being living.   There are some certainly believing that some one can be completely living the living in them, some are certainly believing that every one can be completely living the living in them. Certainly some are certain that some are realising meaning in being one completely living their living, certainly some are certain that every one can be realising the meaning in being one completely living their living, some are certain that perhaps some one can be realising the meaning of being one being completely living in their living, certainly some are certain that certainly not any one can be realising any meaning in one living completely all their living.

Certainly then each one is himself each one is herself, certainly.

Certainly then each one is himself each one is herself certainly then each one is that one in being one being living. Some are certain that each one could be one being certain of something. Some are certain that some could be ones being certain of something, some are not at all certain about any one being certain of anything, some are quite certain about every one being certain about one thing, some are quite certain that every one is certain about the same thing, some are not at all certain about every one being certain about the same thing, some are thinking that some time they might come they might come to have come to be certain that every one is certain about the same thing, there are very many quite certain that every one can be certain about the same thing, there are very many quite certain that every one is certain about the same thing, there are some there are many quite certain that not every one is certain about the same thing, there are some certainly certain that each one is certain of something, there are certainly some quite certain that very many are not certain of even one thing, there are certainly some quite certain that some are not ever certain of any one thing, there are some who are not certain about any one being certain of anything, there are certainly very many certain that every one is certain of the same thing, there are certainly very many certain that every one can be certain of the same thing, there are certainly some that are certain that not every one can be certain about the same thing, there are certainly some who are certain that each one is certain of something, there are certainly some that are certain that not each one is certain of something, there are some that are coming to be certain of something about every one being or not being certain, there are some not coming to be certain about each one being or not being certain about something. There are some saying something and saying it again and again, there are some saying something and not saying it again and again, there are some saying one thing and then saying another thing, there are some saying one thing and then saying another and then saying another thing, there are some saying one thing and saying it again and then saying another thing and saying it again and again and again. Mostly every one is more or less always saying something. Mostly every one is sometimes saying something. Mostly every one is quite often saying something. Sometimes one is saying something and another one is saying the same thing, sometimes one is saying something and another one is not then saying that thing, sometimes one is saying something and another one is saying that thing and then is saying another thing. This is very often happening. Very many then are always being living. Mostly every one is more or less saying something quite often and mostly every one is more or less hearing that some one is saying something. This is to be now a complete description of David Hersland before his beginning being in living and sometime there will be some description about some thinking about his being about his not being one living completely his living. I said of him that he came to be one not any longer being living before he came to be at the end of the beginning of his middle living. This will be now a beginning of description of being and living in him.

In beginning his living David Hersland was of course a very little one and he was then quite interesting to some. In beginning his living he was of course not remembering anything and there were some who later remembered about him then. In beginning his living he was of course completely a very small one, he was beginning living and he was then going on in being living and he then went on being in living and he was then not such a very little one. He was then in being one beginning being in living a very little one. Then he was going on being in living and always more and more then he was coming to be not such a very little one. He was in beginning being living a completely small one. As I was saying he was a younger one, he came to be living after Martha and after Alfred Hersland had each of them been sometime living. Mr. Hersland had always intended to have three children and as I was saying there had been two and these two had not gone on being living and so David Hersland came to be living and sometime later in some way he heard this thing when he was still quite a young one and he had it in him then to be certain that being living is a very queer thing, he being one being living and yet it was only because two others had not been ones going on being living. It was to him then that he was certain then that being living was a queer thing. As I said of him in a way he was needing it that every moment he was one being one being living by realising then that he was one needing then being one being living. He was in a way then as I was saying needing to be certain that he realised in him every minute in being living needing being being living. He certainly was one for sometime going on being living. He went on for sometime being one going on being living. As I was saying he could have it in him to be feeling that it was a very queer thing to be one being living. He was one that could be realising very much and very often that he was needing being one being living. He was one needing to be understanding every minute in being living what meaning there was to him in his needing to be to him one being being living. He certainly then could have it in him to be going on being living. He certainly could have it in him to feel it to be a queer thing to be one being living. He was one then as I was saying who was a very little one in beginning living as mostly every one must be in being one beginning being living, he was then one beginning being living, he was then a very small one, he was the youngest of the three Hersland children, he was quite pleasant to the Hersland family then, all his living he was not unpleasant to any one of them the Hersland family, this is to be now quite a complete history of him.

One man has one kind of way of feeling something, something that is existing. Something is an object being existing, it can be anything any kind of a thing. One man sees it as a thing having solidly being existing. This man has it that he realises a thing having solidly being existing, he does not realise that a thing has character making it a particular thing, he does not realise that it has expression its way of telling any one that it is that kind of thing, he does realise it as having existence in relation to other things being existing that is to say he does realise that other things are at the same time solidly existing and each thing has to have its room for being existing and so for each one to have this solid existing makes a relation being between things being existing. This is one man having realisation of anything.

Another one has it that he has it to be realising completely the character of each thing, anything, has it to be realising completely the way each thing would be telling the character it has in being living by repeating if each thing could be expressing the character of that thing to any one. This one has that thing so that each thing is existing, not by description, by really being in having completely character in being existing. This one has then a realising a complete realising of each thing being in relation to any other thing. This one has completely the realisation of this thing. This one has some sense of a thing of each thing being solidly existing but not so much as this one is needing to make this one be a slow one in growing realisation.

There is another one and this is the one that is different from these two. This one has realisation of a thing having solid existing, this one has realisation of character in each thing, this one has realisation of relation existing between everything so that each thing is existing at the same time as every other thing is existing and this one has emotion in him about each one of three things he is realising about each thing. This is another kind of a one.

There are some who realise it of each thing that it is a pretty thing, there are some that realise it of each thing that it is an ugly thing, there are some who realise it of each thing that it is a funny thing, there are some who realise it of each thing that it is a tender thing, there are some who realise it of each thing that it has a pretty color, there are some who realise it of each thing that it has a pretty shape, there are some who realise it of each thing that it has a meaning, there are some who realise it of each thing that it is a queer thing, there are some that realise it of each thing that it is an unpleasant thing, there are some who realise it of each thing that it would be pretty if it were in a garden, there are some who realise it of each thing that it would be a nice thing if it were in a room with simple furnishing, there are some who realise it of each thing that it is a thing a nice thing when it is in a room which is not a very light one, there are some realising that each thing is part of a story any one can be telling about anything, there are some that are realising each thing is a nice thing if it is exciting to love that thing, in a way then every one has it in them to feel something about things being in being existing.

Now I am telling about another one. One this one has a gift of expression of expressing something and that is a beautiful thing that is to say the means of expressing something in this one is a beautiful thing and this one is one wanting to be expressing the existence the character of anything. Now this one has complete emotions about the means this one has for expressing anything, this one certainly has not any emotion about anything that is being existing. This one has not a realisation of something being solidly existing, this one has not a realisation of the character of anything, of the way anything could be experiencing being existing, this one has not any realisation of anything being in relation to any other thing and this is a natural thing when one is realising the being in this one. This one is needing being one realising anything as existing so that this one can be having something to be using his beautiful means of expression on. So then this one has a practical realisation of everything being existing.

These then are some ways of being ones realising anything. I will not now tell about other ones. I will not tell now about other ones.

David Hersland as I was saying was one wanting it that he should be one realising every minute what there was in life to be a thing going on being doing. He was one doing this thing in all of his living from the beginning of being one being living to the end of his being one being living, that is to say from his being in the middle of his beginning being living to the ending of the beginning of the middle of being living.

As I was saying the last one I have been just describing was one needing to be certain that things are existing so that he could be using his beautiful means of expression. There are some having not such beautiful means of expression who are needing for their means of expression that they have as being, are needing realising that things are existing, are practically needing this thing. There are some, and these are a different kind, in whom the means of expression is the thing really existing, and these are to themselves not needing it that they have a practical need of realising things being existing. I cannot tell enough about every one, certainly not. Then there are very many realising objects not as being existing but as being acting one in relation to another one, this is very common, for very many of such of them things are really being existing, for very many of such of them things being existing is only a practical thing so that they can be being in relation, they are not really being existing they are acting for themselves, for some other one, toward themselves, toward some other thing but now I am getting empty of realising and so I will not now be saying any more about any one, not completely empty of realising but emptier than I have been.

David Hersland was then certainly for himself almost completely, for some other ones completely, for some quite some interesting. He was then one being completely interesting to some, almost completely interesting to himself as being one being existing, quite interesting to very many, he was in short one quite interesting in being one being living to very many and a little some to almost every one knowing him. This is certainly now to be a history of him, of his being one being living and being to quite some quite interesting.

So then each one has a kind of way of feeling everything being existing and this is to be now a complete history of David Hersland knowing everything he knew in being one being living and of everything any one he came to know knowing anything came to know in being living. Certainly now I will begin again.

Very many are talking, very many are listening, David Hersland certainly in being one being living was one being one talking was being one listening. Certainly he was one beginning being one being talking being one being listening quite from the beginning of the middle of his beginning being one being existing in being living. He was one then certainly all his living being one being listening being one being talking. He was interesting to quite a number in being one being listening, he was interesting to quite a number in being one being talking. Quite a number were interesting to him as being ones being listening, quite a number were interesting to him as being ones being talking. He was one as I was saying who was wanting to be needing it that every woman was to him a beautiful one in being living. This was in him from the ending of the middle of his beginning living to the ending of the beginning of his middle living and then he was one not any longer being living. Certainly wanting to be needing that every woman was a beautiful thing in being one being living was in him in the beginning of his being in his middle living. This is to be now a description of being in him and of living in him in the beginning of his being one being living.

Two knowing each other all their living might tell each other sometime what each one of them thought the other one had been, thought the other one would be doing in being living. Two having known each other very well in their living might tell each other what each one thought really about the other. Two knowing each other very well in living might be doing this thing. Two knowing each other very well in living might know each one what that one thought of the other one. Two knowing each other very well in living might be thinking that they were knowing what the other one knew about each other one. Two knowing each other very well in living might be knowing what each one thought about each other one. Two knowing each other very well in living might be thinking they are knowing what each one is thinking about being and about living in the other one. Two knowing each other very well in being living might be thinking they are not knowing what the other one is thinking about the other one. Two knowing each other very well in living might be telling each one of them to some one what they are thinking of the other one. Two knowing each other very well in living might not be telling any one what they are each one of them thinking about the other one. Two knowing each other very well in living one of them might be telling the other one sometime what that one was thinking of the other one. Two knowing each other in living one might be telling some one sometimes what that one thought of the other one. Two knowing each other very well in living one of them might be sometime telling some one what that one had often been thinking about being, about living in the other one. Two knowing each other very well in living one of them might sometime tell some one what that one had come to think about the being and the living in the other one. So then very often there are two living knowing each other very well in living. Some of such of them then are certain that they are knowing what the other one thinks of that one. Some are not certain that they are knowing what the other one thinks of that one. Some are knowing what the other one thinks of that one. Some are not knowing what the other one thinks of being and living in that one. Some are often wondering what the other one is thinking of being and living in that one. Some are never at all wondering about what the other one is thinking about that one. To some it would be a pleasant thing to know certainly what the other one is thinking about that one. To some it would not be at all a pleasant thing to know certainly what the other one is thinking about being and about living in that one. Some sometime talk to some one about what the other one is thinking about being and living being in that one. Some sometimes talk to the other one about what the other one is thinking about being and living being in either of them, in one of them. Some are talking to every one they are knowing about what the other one is thinking about being and living being in that one. Some are for a very long time having a feeling of being one knowing about thinking about being and living in both of them in both of them. Two of two of them sometimes for a very long time have a quite certain feeling about knowing about thinking about being and living in both of them in the two of them. Certainly there are very often in living being two of them knowing each other certainly very well in being living. Certainly very often one of them has a feeling of knowing or not knowing what the other one is thinking about the being and living in that one.

David Hersland as I was saying was one being interested in his being one being living. He was one being interested in quite a number of other ones being ones being living. Some are not interested in ones being living. David Hersland was interested in ones being living. He was one as I was saying almost completely interested in being one being living. He was one, as I was saying, to himself almost one being completely, almost being completely living. He was one interested in some being ones being living. He was one in a way interested in every one he came to be knowing, in any one who came to know him. He was one as I was saying interested in his being one being living, almost completely interested in being living, he was one almost completely living. This is to be now some description of his being a quite young one in living.

They talked in different ways about different things, some talked in some way about something then talked in another way about something, some talked in some way about something then talked in another way about another thing, some talked in the same way about a good many things, mostly every one talked a good deal about something, mostly every one talked a good deal about a number of things. Mostly, all his living, David Hersland talked a good deal about something, mostly all his living he talked a good deal about a good many things. He liked it certainly so mostly every one was saying sometime about him to do a good deal of talking, in a way to himself and to very many knowing he did not like doing a good deal of talking. Any way he certainly did considerable talking while he was one being one being in living. As I was saying he came to be a dead one at the end of the beginning of his middle living. To some this was a very sad thing, to some this was a sad enough thing, in a way to some it was not at all an interesting thing, to some it was for quite a very long time a very interesting thing. Some found it then a very interesting thing to be wondering whether he would have been one having been succeeding in living if he had been one being living a reasonably long time. Some certainly thought this to be an exceedingly interesting question.

As I was saying the Herslands lived where a good many other people were living when David Hersland was a young one, was beginning being in living. As I was saying each one he was then knowing talked some about something, talked some about a good many things. David Hersland then talked some about something, talked then some about a good many things. He was then one talking and listening and so was everybody else doing that thing, those he was seeing then. He was living in Hersland family living then, he was living in that part of Gossols living then where the Hersland family were living then. This is to be now some description of living he was doing then and the living some other ones were doing then in their daily living.

Some one and that one is quite reasonably an observing one is seeing some one sitting and that one is to very many looking an interesting enough one and then that one the one that is reasonably observing says of this one the one sitting and being interesting to quite a number who were looking that way just then that this one is certainly quite entirely a stupid one, that one can tell that by observing that one and knowing so that that one is not at all really an interesting thing. This one then tells about that one the one sitting and it is certainly true what the one telling is telling about that one, it is quite a good description and it is pleasantly then an astonishing thing to be certain that the one describing the other one from observation is extraordinarily of the same quality and having been having the same history in being living as the one that one has been describing and quite correctly describing as one not interesting in being living and one at whom very many are quite a good deal looking. This kind of thing happening was the interesting thing in some being in being living to David Hersland in almost any part of his being in living. As I was saying of him he certainly was one wanting to be needing that every woman ever living should be a beautiful thing to him in his feeling.

David Hersland was one certainly enjoying some kind of things that were happening. He certainly very often was enjoying things having been happening. This is to be now a quite complete history of him from his beginning to his ending.

He was playing some when he was a young one, he was believing somethings then pretty nearly believing some things then, reading some then, talking some then, listening some then, eating a good deal sometimes then, deciding some things then when not anybody had asked him to decide a thing, being listened to some then when he was deciding some thing then, liking it pretty nearly entirely then that some were listening while he was deciding something then, pretty nearly entirely liking it that he was one being going on being living then. He knew a good many then, a good many in a way knew him then, he was living in Hersland family living then, he was living inside him to himself some then, he was living half country half city living then, he was almost living the living of many he was knowing then in his daily living, he certainly was almost then completely liking being one going on being living. He talked a good deal all his living as I was saying, he certainly a good deal did not talk in all of his living, he listened some that is certain, he talked some that is quite certain. He was one going on being in living until he was at the end of the beginning of his middle living and then he came to dying and then he was a dead one. In his beginning living he was doing different things in his daily living, this is to be now a description of living and of being in him.

One who knew David Hersland a long time in living was one certainly living so that that one later in the living of that one should certainly be one certainly not marrying a certain one. This one might be loving that one, this one certainly was one living in being living so that certainly that one to that one was one certainly one never going to be marrying a certain one. Very many knowing of this one, knowing this one a little would be saying that this one was certainly sometimes going to be marrying a certain one, not any one really knowing this one ever did any thinking about this one going to be marrying that certain one, it was not a thing to any one really knowing this one needing any thinking, it was a thing that everybody knowing this one took as being of course certain that this one would never be marrying that certain one. Certainly everybody knowing very well the two of them were certain that each of them were certain that that one never would be marrying the other one. This one then married that certain one. Now did this one have it that this one had not been knowing that every one knowing this one very well was very simply certain that that one would not be marrying a certain one or did this one have it that this one was knowing this thing. Did this one have it that once this one was knowing that thing and when this one came to be one going to be marrying the certain one was not knowing this thing. It certainly was to every one a simply inevitable thing that this one would never be marrying a certain one. This one certainly married that certain one. Every one really knowing this one never came to knowing whether it had perhaps not ever been an inevitable thing to that one that that one was not ever to be marrying that certain one, not any one knowing this one ever came to know that for this one it had been an inevitable thing that this one was not ever to marry that certain one. To some knowing this thing it was a puzzling thing and then it was to them that that one had married that certain one and they knew them very well in their married living. To some it was not a puzzling thing, they were not ever thinking then when this one had been once married to that certain one, they were not ever thinking about that one ever having been going to be married to any one, to that certain one. To some it was not a puzzling thing, it was a thing like something having been a lost thing that never had been a thing any one had found before it was lost. To some it was a thing that was not puzzling at all and yet was different from what every one knowing anything was certain could be happening, to some of such of them it was not at all a puzzling thing. To some it was a thing that was like being a dead one and certainly perhaps one being a dead one is not knowing it then that that one is then being a dead one. To mostly not any one was it at all exasperating, to mostly not any one was it really exciting that that one had married a certain one and it had been to every one knowing them a simply inevitable thing that that one would not ever marry that certain one. So then that one had married that certain one. Certainly every one knowing either one of them very well had been simply certain like being certain of being one being living that that one would not ever be marrying that certain one. In a way, as I say, when that one then married that certain one, it was not to very many of those having been simply certain exciting, it was to very many of those having been simply certain that this one would not marry that certain one not puzzling, it was not to any one knowing them and having been simply certain at all exasperating, it was not to all of them who had been completely certain that that one would not ever marry that certain one when that one married that certain one really exciting. And this was a strange thing to be in David Hersland in being one being living. This one as I am saying was one knowing David Hersland very well in living. This one was one David Hersland knew very well almost all his living. David Hersland was one having it as I was saying that he was one wanting to be having it that he was completely needing to be certain every minute in being living of having it that he was realising that there was being a reason in being living so that he could be one going on being living. He was one as I was saying certainly needing every moment in his living to be one needing to be reasoning to be realising that he was one to be one going on being living. As I was saying he knew very well the one that came to marry a certain one when he had been completely quite certain that that one would not be marrying a certain one and it was not to him completely exciting, it was not to him completely interesting that this one had then married that certain one and that not he, not any one that he knew then knew then whether that one had or had not ever been completely certain that one could certainly not ever marry that certain one. As I was saying David Hersland knew this one very well, this one knew David Hersland very well, as I was saying this thing was not then when it had suddenly happened, and it happened certainly quite suddenly, it was not then to David Hersland completely interesting, it was not then to David Hersland completely exciting, this that it was not then or ever later than then a completely interesting thing a completely exciting thing to David Hersland is certainly a curious thing. David Hersland is one I am now beginning describing. I certainly will tell a good deal of everything I know about living and about being in him.

It is a nice thing to some that some one is certain that every one would be thankful perhaps to him certainly at any rate thankful, just thankful if they could be having it completely shown to them what way they could be living so that living could have a meaning to every one when every one had come to be thankful for understanding living having such a meaning. There are very many certainly being certain that everybody could be thankful if everybody could be thankful. Some are quite certain that anybody could be thankful if everybody could be thankful. Some are quite certain that some one is really certain that every one could be thankful if every one were really coming to be ones being thankful ones. Very many then are quite certain that each one could be wanting what every one could be wanting. Very many then are quite certain that certainly every one could be wanting what each one could be wanting. Mostly a good many are saying that some one who is certain that every one could be wanting what every one could be wanting is a very nice one. Each one is certainly being living, each is one certainly being sometime a dead one. Does each one being one being living need it to be perhaps liking that thing. Does each one being living need it to be sometime wanting something. Does each one coming to be a dead one, need it to have it that he could be wanting what every one else perhaps could be, could have been wanting. Does each one who has come to be a dead one know then that he is a dead one. Does any one having come to be a dead one know then that he is a really truly dead one. Certainly a very great many are very certain that they are thinking that each one is or could be wanting a certain kind of meaning in being one being living, and then some one is not then being such a one and is it then really completely puzzling, completely exciting, completely interesting to any one that some one could not be wanting what every one certainly is realising everybody could be wanting. I will certainly now commence telling a good deal, that is, as much of a good deal as I will be telling of being being in very many being living. Many men and many women are being living, have been, will be being living. I will now tell a good deal that is I will tell all I will be telling about being being in men and women, in some men and in some women. I shall now just be repeating that I certainly am knowing there is being being in men and in women being living, I will just repeat this now again and again and again and then I can be certain enough of this thing to be leaving it without being then looking at it and so then I can leave it and it will be then keeping going and I can go ahead and be fooling and mixing up everything in telling about being being in David Hersland and this I hope sometime to be doing but not this evening, no certainly not this evening, no certainly not now when I am looking to be just repeating that being is in men and in women who are being living.

Some are not very much interested in their being living in living and they are a little interested in this thing. They are going on being in living and they are not very much interested in their being living in living and they are a little interested in this thing in being one being living in living. Some of these are then going on and going on being living in living and they are not then very much interested in this thing and they are a little interested in this thing. Some of such of them are going on being in living and they keep on going on being in living and they are not much interested in this and they are a little interested in this thing. Quite a number of such of them are keeping on being ones being living and they are not some of such of them ever very much interested in this thing and they are a little interested in this thing. Some of them are going on being living and they are certainly not ever very much interested in this thing and they certainly are a little interested in this thing.

David Hersland was one being living in living and certainly he was one almost completely interested in being one being in living, this is to be now certainly some description of this in him, this is certainly to be now some description of being of not being very much, of being a little, of being almost completely interested in being one being in living. David Hersland was one being living to the ending of his beginning being in middle living I am realising that being is in men and in women being living, I can now be not repeating this thing, I can now go on and go on and go on a little more then and a good deal more then about David Hersland and about his knowing some and about some knowing him.

David was a young one and knowing a good many then and some were knowing him then. He was doing things then every day with himself, with some one else, with other ones, and he was then being one being a young one in being living. He was knowing then quite a number of ones being living and some were knowing him then. He liked it then being living, he always almost completely liked it being living. He was then a young one being living and he knew some then who were being living then and some knew him then. He was then a quite young one.

Some are wondering about other ones about how they have enough money to support them. It is a very mysterious thing sometimes to some one about living coming to be paid for by some one. Some find it quite a strange thing that some one was not doing anything and that one is doing something and that one is knowing then how to do that thing and some one is paying that one for doing that thing. To some it is an astonishing thing that any one can be doing anything so that some one can be paying them something for that thing. To some it is not at all an astonishing thing that some one is knowing how to be doing something so that some one is paying that one something for doing that thing. To some as I say being one being earning a living is a thing that is astonishing, to some being one earning a living is a thing that is not at all in any kind of a way astonishing. Those living in Gossols as I was saying in the part of Gossols where the Herslands were living were ones living in small houses as I was saying and some knew about how some made money to be ones going on being living and some did not know this about some of them how they were earning money so as to be ones able to be going on being living. Some as I was saying were doing something and anybody looking could be seeing them doing that thing and could be seeing some one, some paying them to be doing that thing. Some were not doing things that every one could be seeing them be doing. Some were not doing anything that any one could see would be a thing any one would be paying them anything to be doing. In a way certainly some of them were not making money so as to be ones going on being going on being living. Certainly some of them were not to themselves to any one making money enough for any such a thing, for any going on being living. Sometimes it was a puzzling thing about some family living in some house then in that part of Gossols where the Herslands were living about who it was that was in that house living. Sometimes not any one that said anything really knew anything about that thing. It was confusing and then mostly not any one was really confused by that thing.

David Hersland all his living knew quite a number who were being living then and quite a number who were being living knew him then. He knew quite a number who were being living, he knew quite a number when he was a young one, some knew him then, as I was saying all his living he knew quite a number who were living while he was one being living. Certainly some he was knowing were doing something and some one was paying them something for that thing, certainly some he was knowing were doing something and not any one really was paying them anything for the thing they were doing, certainly there were some he was knowing who were really not doing very much any one thing and some of these had money then and some of these did not have money then. Mostly all his living David Hersland would have liked it very well to be knowing it about each one what they were doing, what they had been doing, what they would be doing to be earning money to be ones going on being living. This was all his living a thing that was quite interesting to David Hersland knowing this thing about each one he was ever knowing. Sometimes about some one such a thing was very confusing sometimes about some one he was knowing in living, sometimes he was confused about this thing about some one, sometimes he was not confused about this thing about that one, sometimes he was not listening enough to some one to be really understanding this thing about some one how that one was having money enough to be one going on being living, sometimes he was listening very much to some one and he listened to every one knowing that one and it was not confusing about that one but he never could find out about that one about the money that one had to be one going on being living. Always all his living this was to him an interesting enough thing about each one he was knowing what money they had and how they had that money for daily living. As I was saying all his living he knew a good many who were then living, as I was saying all his living a good many knew him. As I was saying when he was in his beginning living he knew a good many who were living then, as I was saying when he was in his beginning living a good number knew him then. He was then as I was saying living in the part of Gossols where the Hersland family were living then and the Hersland family were living on a ten acre place then and there were very many living in that part of Gossols where the Herslands were living then and these were living in small houses and as I was saying David Hersland knew them, he knew a number of people then, some knew him then, I will be telling something now about being in him and knowing other ones being in him and other ones knowing him being in him. I will tell now about his being one beginning being living.

Mostly every one at different parts in their living when they are very little ones when they are a little bigger ones when they are not any longer very young ones when they are quite not very young ones when they are ones beginning being in their middle living when they are ones being in their middle living when they are ones ending being in their middle living when they are ones coming to be growing old ones when they are ones come to be old ones have a feeling about some one having angry feeling in them have some feeling about any one that has for them angry feeling in them. Mostly every one has some feeling about angry feeling being in some one, about angry feeling being inside them, about angry feeling in any one. Some have all their living about the same feeling about some one having angry feeling about having angry feeling themselves inside them about any one having angry feeling in them. Some have a very different feeling about angry feeling being in some one about angry feeling being in any one about angry feeling being inside in them in different parts of their being in living. Some are certainly changing in their feeling about angry feeling being in any one about angry feeling being in some one about angry feeling being inside in them as they are going on being living. I am telling now about angry feeling being in some one about angry feeling being in any one about angry feeling in one inside that one to that one and I am saying that some are changing while they are being living about their feeling about each one of these ways of being and some are not changing in their way of feeling about angry feeling being in any one in some one in some in themselves inside them, and some are changing very much in their living about angry feeling and some are not changing very much in their feeling about angry feeling and some are changing one way and some are changing another way. Each one of the Hersland family could have angry feeling in them. Some of them were changing in being living about angry feeling being inside them, about angry feeling being in some other one, about angry feeling being in some one, about angry feeling being in some, and some of these were not changing much in their living in their being living in feeling about angry feeling being inside them, being in some one, being in any one, being in some. They were all of them changing somewhat in their living in their feeling about angry feeling, some of them were changing very much while they went on being living about angry feeling being in them being in some other one being in any one. Certainly some of them were changing very much in their feeling about angry feeling being in them, being in some, being in any one, some of them were certainly hardly at all changing, not very much changing in their feeling about angry feeling all the time that they were living.

There were very many living there in that part of Gossols where the Herslands were living and some knew them and some knew some of them and some knew of some one of them how that one had angry feeling in that one and some of the Hersland family knew of some of those who lived near them how they had angry feeling in them. Some of these who knew the Hersland family then, knew some of the Hersland family then did not know how those of the Hersland family they knew then had angry feeling in them. Each one of the Hersland family knew some of those living near them without knowing of them how they had angry feeling in them.

Each one of the Hersland family could have some angry feeling sometimes in them. Each one of the Hersland family did have sometimes some angry feeling in them. David Hersland knew something about angry feeling in him and in each one of the Hersland family who could have angry feeling, that is to say he knew something about angry feeling being in each one of the family of the then Hersland family. Mostly each one of the Hersland family knew something about the way each one, each other one, all of them could have angry feeling in them. As I was saying some of them changed in their living about angry feeling being inside them, inside any other one, inside all of them and some as I was saying some of them did not change very much in their feeling about angry feeling being in any one of them, in all of them, in them.

Mostly every one then is having some feeling about angry feeling all their living. This can be then certainly some description of angry feeling being in men and in women in all parts of their being living and in all kinds in men and in women. Mostly every one then certainly has some feeling of being sometime an angry one, has some feeling of some other one being sometime an angry one. Mostly a good many have some feeling about angry feeling being existing in themselves and in other ones. Some are liking angry feeling being in them, some are certainly not liking angry feeling being in them or having been in them, some are certainly liking angry feeling having been in them. But this is not now to me an important thing, the liking angry feeling inside in one, the not liking angry feeling inside in one. It is now an important thing to me that certainly mostly every one has angry feeling in him sometime and mostly every one has some feeling about angry feeling being in him, being in some other one, being in any one and that some are changing very much in their feeling about angry feeling in themselves, in some other one in any other one while they are being in living and some are hardly at all changing in their feeling about angry feeling in themselves in any one while they are being living. Some knowing some in that part of Gossols where the Herslands were living knew about the way angry feeling was in them when it was in them and some did not know this thing about some they were knowing then. Each one certainly in the Hersland family then could have angry feeling sometimes in them. Each one of them did have sometimes angry feeling in them, some knowing some of them knew of them how they had angry feeling, some knowing some of them did not know how they had angry feeling in them. Some knowing some of them knew how one of them had angry feeling but not how the others of them had angry feeling. Some of the Hersland family were certainly changing very much in their feeling about angry feeling being in any one from the beginning to the ending of their being living, some of them certainly changed some in their feeling about angry feeling being in any one from the beginning of their being living to their ending, each one of them certainly changed some about this, that is a natural enough thing when any one is passing from being a very little young one through to a bigger older one, to a middle living one to an older one, to an old one to a very old one. David Hersland in his being living certainly was changing very much in his feeling about angry feeling in any one. That is certainly a very natural thing. Each one of the Hersland family could have angry feeling in them. Some knew how each one of them had angry feeling in them, some did not know how each one of them had angry feeling in them, some did not know and then they did know about angry feeling in them in each one of them. Each one of the Hersland family certainly had their own way of having angry feeling in them. Certainly each one knew something about how each one of them had angry feeling in them when they had it in them. The Hersland family had not very much angry feeling in them for any one to be noticing, they had some angry feeling in them sometimes each one of them for some one to be noticing. Some had angry feeling more often in them than others of them. David Hersland had angry feeling in him once in a while not very often, Alfred Hersland had angry feeling in him once in a while not so very often, this is to be now a history of David Hersland.

Some are wanting to be needing in their living to have some one have some angry feeling. Some are needing it in their living to have some one have some angry feeling. Some are needing angry feeling being existing, some are wanting to be needing angry feeling being existing. David Hersland was one sometime in his living wanting to be needing having angry feeling being existing he was sometime in his living needing angry feeling to be existing, he was sometime in his living not wanting any angry feeling to be existing, he was sometime in his living completely wanting not angry feeling being existing, he was sometime in his living having an angry feeling about angry feeling being existing, he was sometime in his living completely needing having angry feeling really being existing, he was one wanting sometime in his living that not any angry feeling should be existing.

Some are needing angry feeling being in some one existing, some are needing angry feeling being inside them being existing, some are wanting to be needing angry feeling being in some existing, some are wanting to be needing angry feeling being sometimes existing inside them, some are wanting to be needing that angry feeling be not existing in any one, not in themselves inside them, some are having angry feeling and they are never certain whether they are needing whether they are not needing that thing, some are having some one having angry feeling and they are not certain whether they are liking whether they are not liking that thing, some are having angry feeling inside them and they are not certain whether they are liking whether they are not liking that thing, some are having some having angry feeling some one having angry feeling and they are not certain whether they are needing or whether they are not needing that thing. Certainly very many are sometimes having angry feeling in them, certainly very many are having others having angry feeling for them, certainly very many are having some one having angry feeling for them, certainly very many are having some often having angry feeling against them, certainly very many have some to have angry feeling about them, certainly a very great many have some one having angry feeling about them, have some one having angry feeling against them, have some one having angry feeling with them.

To some it is extraordinary that any one having angry feeling can then come to be convincing. Some having angry feeling come then to be convincing about something to some one. Some came to be very convincing to David Hersland when they had angry feeling in them sometime in his living. Some did not come to be convincing to him about anything when they had angry feeling in them, sometimes in his living not any one having angry feeling was convincing to him about anything, sometimes in his living almost any one having angry feeling in them were convincing to him then about something they were saying then, certainly for sometime while he was being living some certainly some one was mostly always convincing about something when those, when that one, were angry ones, was an angry one. Certainly very many living are changing in their feeling about any one being an angry one about some one being an angry one, about they themselves that one being an angry one. Some certainly are very different in different times in their living in their feeling about angry feeling being existing. Some are not changing very much in the time of their being living in their feeling about angry feeling being existing. Each one certainly has in them their own way of feeling, of changing in feeling about angry feeling being existing. Very many come to know in being living quite a number who are then existing. Some come to know of some they are then knowing how they have angry feeling in them, some do not come to know of very many they are knowing how they have angry feeling in them, some come to know of quite a number they are knowing how they have angry feeling in them. Alfred Hersland came to know of some he was knowing how they come to have angry feeling in them. David Hersland came in some way to know of quite a number he came to know in being living how they came to have angry feeling, what they do when they have angry feeling. As I was saying sometimes when he was living he was one wanting to be needing that not any one was having angry feeling, as I was saying sometimes in his living he was needing, to be one going on being living with any meaning in that thing, that not any one having angry feeling in being in living that not any angry feeling was being existing, sometimes in his being living he was wanting to be needing that there was angry feeling quite a good deal of angry feeling existing, sometimes while he was living as I was saying of him he was quite needing that angry feeling was really existing, as I was saying he was in his living one changing about ones having angry feeling being ones being convincing about something. This is to be in a way a history of him and of every one that he ever knew and of every one who ever came to know him or of him.

Some have different feeling about each one having angry feeling. Some when they are young ones have different feeling about each one having angry feeling. Some have a feeling about one having angry feeling and that one has angry feeling and that one can do anything, having angry feeling, and mostly that one does not do anything when that one is having that angry feeling and some one being then a young one has it in that one then to be completely certain that that one is wanting to be needing that not angry feeling be existing, that one then the one being then a young one has it in that one that any one having angry feeling is one not convincing any one of anything certainly not convincing any one of anything certainly quite completely not convincing any one of anything, angry feeling then is to that one when one that one is knowing who could be doing anything in having angry feeling and mostly is not doing anything in having angry feeling is having angry feeling, angry feeling is to that one when one that one is knowing is having angry feeling angry feeling then is to that one something that that one is certainly wanting to be needing to have not ever existing, certainly to that one then not any one having angry feeling could be convincing about anything, that is one way of having feeling in some one, in some, in some one when that one is a young one, in some when they are young ones, in some when they are older ones, in some only when they are young ones, in some only when a certain one is having angry feeling, in some when any one is having angry feeling, in some when every one is having angry feeling, about angry feeling being existing. So then certainly some when they are young ones are feeling about some one, one who could be doing anything when having angry feeling and who sometimes is doing something when having angry feeling and sometimes is not doing anything when having angry feeling, are feeling about angry feeling when angry feeling is in that some one that they are certainly wanting to be needing that not any angry feeling ever is existing, that certainly not any one could be convincing to any one, who was óne ever having, ever going to be having angry feeling. As I am saying some have such feeling about angry feeling when they are young ones when angry feeling is in a certain one. Some as I was saying are having such feeling when they are older ones when angry feeling is in a certain one. Some have such feeling as I am saying about angry feeling when they are young ones when angry feeling is in some, some as I am saying have such feeling about angry feeling when they are older ones when angry feeling is in some, some as I am saying when they are young have such feeling when angry feeling is in any one, some when they are older as I am now saying have such feeling about angry feeling when angry feeling is in any one, some as I am now saying when they are older ones have such feeling about angry feeling being existing, some are ones having such feeling about angry feeling being existing when they are young ones in being living. Alfred Hersland had such feeling about some one having angry feeling when he Alfred was not a young one not yet an older one, he had not such a feeling about any one having angry feeling when he was a young one, when he was an older one. David Hersland had such feeling about some one having angry feeling when he was a young one, he had it then not so much in him when he was beginning being an older one he had it again in him when he was going on a little being an older one he had it in him then some about every one, about any one having angry feeling, he did not have it in him not really in him not at all wanting having it in him at all when he was going on still more being an older one, he had it a little in him then, he was not wanting it at all then to be in him for him to be one going on being living, he certainly did not want it then to be in him he did not have it then in him for his living, for his being one being living. Some he knew when he was living were ones having such feeling when he was knowing them, some he knew in his living had been sometime having such feeling about angry feeling, some whom he knew in his living would certainly be having such feeling about angry feeling. Some who knew him when he was being living when he was not having it to be needing such feeling thought that he was having such feeling about angry feeling, some thought then he was wanting to be needing such feeling about angry feeling when he was not wanting to be needing such feeling. He knew very many while he was one being living. I am saying again, quite a number knew him while he was being living. I am saying again, some felt one way of feeling about angry feeling in him, other ones felt other ways of feeling about angry feeling in him. I will slowly be describing every one feeling about angry feeling in him, about his feeling about angry feeling in him, I will be describing his feeling about angry feeling being in him, about angry feeling being in any one, about angry feeling being in some. He certainly did very often a good deal of talking a good deal of listening about angry feeling being existing. Angry feeling was very often quite interesting to him.

In some one, in some to some, in some to some one sometime, sometimes, to some sometimes, all the time of their being living, to some one sometimes all the time of that one being living there is not anything to convince of anything. Sometimes such a one who not in any way has power of doing anything when that one is being an angry one, who certainly is not convincing about anything in being one being living, that is to some one, has it to have it to give that one that some one angry feeling of being one not then able to be doing anything to be expressing any angry feeling to be completely then filled up with furious angry feeling to be then only completely doing smiling. Some then being in family living with some other one, some then are existing in living and then some one has it to have because of that one being something, doing something, completely furious angry feeling, completely not doing anything to be to them telling anything to any one that that one is having completely furious angry feeling, completely smiling and the one that is making the one have this in that one this completely furious feeling, this completely not doing anything to be showing any one that that one is having completely furious angry feeling, this completely smiling is one not having it to be able to be doing anything in any way to that one that is then having completely furious feeling not convincing that one, not pleasing that one, not injuring that one, not in any way to that one or in any way for that one meaning anything to any one in being one being living. Certainly this can be in some being living, this way of being one having angry feeling, this certainly when some are coming to the ending of the middle of their young living comes to be in them very often. Some have it in them some all of their living, some have it in them some in the beginning of the middle of their young living, some of them have it in them some at the ending of their young living, some have it in them some to the beginning of the middle of their middle living, some but mostly not so very many have it in them some all their living, quite a number certainly do have it some all their living this then this way of having angry feeling come to be in them, this way of having angry feeling in them, quite a number certainly of women, quite a number certainly of men. Certainly David Hersland could have it in him to have this in him when he was in the beginning of the middle of his being in his young living, he could have it in him until almost the ending of his young living, it is certainly not completely certain that he could not have it in him any time in his being one being living which was to the ending of the beginning of his middle living. He was not knowing much about this being in any one when he was one being in young living any such a way of having angry feeling, he could come to be certain in him that such a way of having angry feeling is not at all uncommon. He certainly sometime came to be certain of this thing that very many have it, had it, could have it in them to have this way of having angry feeling come to be in them, be in them. Very many do not come to have angry feeling come to be in them, be in them, very many do have have it sometime to have angry feeling coming to be in this way in them, be in this way in them, very many do not, very many certainly very many sometime do come to have angry feeling come in this way to be in them, do have angry feeling in some such way in them then.

Certainly each one has their own way of having angry feeling in them, certainly some having angry feeling come to be in them from some one not having it to have it from being one being in living having any way of being one acting to affect them, to convince them have it then to have angry feeling in the way their kind of them, in the way that one has angry feeling. Each one certainly has angry feeling the way it is natural for that one to have angry feeling in that one, that is mostly every one. Some do not have it completely to have angry feeling in them the way it is natural to have angry feeling in them but this is another thing, certainly mostly every one has more or less completely in them when they have angry feeling in them their way of having angry feeling in them. I have just now been telling about David Hersland, I have been just telling about David Hersland and about Alfred Hersland and I will tell more about angry feeling being in women being in men being sometime in every one having ever angry feeling in them, about any one having angry feeling, about some having angry feeling.

Angry feeling again and again is in each one being in any family living, being in any living, this is pretty nearly certain. Angry feeling again and again is in one being one being in a family, being in any living. Angry feeling again and again is in one in different ways in one in one being in any living, being in any family living. Mostly each one being in any family living, mostly each one being in any living is having to have in that one again and again angry feeling from each one that one is knowing in the family living, from each one that one is knowing in any living. Perhaps it is certain that not every one is having angry feeling in that one from each one they are knowing in any living. Perhaps it is certain that each one in any family living is having again and again the same kind of angry feeling from each one being with that one in that family living. Perhaps this is really certain. Perhaps it is certain that each one has from each one being, from each one being doing something the same kind of angry feeling again and again. Perhaps it is really certain that almost every one has a different way of having angry feeling with each one that one is knowing and perhaps it is quite certain that mostly every one has that way of feeling angry feeling from some one being in living, from some one doing something, again and again. It is perhaps almost completely certain that each one being in some family living is having some angry feeling about each one in that family living and about each one in a certain kind of way of having angry feeling and in each way of having some angry feeling having it again and again. Perhaps not every one is having a different way of having angry feeling with different ones in their living, perhaps some are not having angry feeling in some way again and again.

Some are having pretty nearly completely angry feeling again and again, some are not having completely angry feeling again and again, some are not having anywhere nearly completely angry feeling again and again, some are having quite completely angry feeling again and again.

Some are having angry feeling, mostly every one is having some angry feeling. Some are knowing something about this thing, some are not knowing anything about this thing, some are knowing very much about this thing, some are remembering what they have been knowing about this thing, some are needing to be forgetting everything they were ever knowing about this thing, some are wanting to be needing to be remembering what they could be knowing about this thing.

Each one certainly has their own way of feeling about angry feeling being in them, having been in them, going to be in them. Each one has their own way of knowing has their own way of not knowing about angry feeling having been, going to be, being in them. Each one has it to be remembering about angry feeling, each one has it to be not remembering about angry feeling, in their own way each one of them. Certainly each one has their own way of remembering and forgetting angry feeling being, having been, going to be in them, each one certainly has their own way of remembering and forgetting knowing about angry feeling having been, being, going to be in them.

Each one certainly has their own way of feeling, of thinking, of remembering, of forgetting about angry feeling having been, being in them, going to be being in them. Mostly each is one in some way liking in some way not liking having angry feeling having been, being, going to be being in them. Some are almost not at all liking having, having had, going to be having angry feeling, some are almost completely liking having angry feeling, some are almost completely liking having had angry feeling, some are almost completely liking going to be having angry feeling. Some are certainly liking some ways of having angry feeling in them some are certainly not liking other ways of having angry feeling in them, some other way of having angry feeling. Some are liking that some are knowing they are having angry feeling. Some are sometimes liking that some are knowing they are having angry feeling. Each one has angry feeling in different parts in that one being one being living, each one has angry feeling from some one from some that one is knowing in being living. Some are almost quite certain that not any one is knowing they are having angry feeling when they themselves are knowing they are having angry feeling.

Some are quite certain that very many are quite certain that they are having angry feeling and they themselves are quite certain that they are not having not at all having angry feeling, sometimes then these have been having angry feeling, sometimes then these have not been having having angry feeling, sometime others have not been thinking these were having angry feeling when these were thinking those others were thinking that thing, sometimes others have been thinking these were having angry feeling when these were thinking those others were thinking that thing.

Some then have angry feeling about each one they are knowing and are having it again and again. Some are certainly having it again and again from each one being with them in them in family living and for each one are having a certain kind of angry feeling and are certainly having it again and again.

Each one has then the angry feeling in them of their kind of them, of their being one being living. There are different ways of having angry feeling in different ones who are having it that one being with them in family living, being with them in some living is one not having it to have it that that one can be doing anything to the one then having angry feeling but is one doing something, being something that is certainly the reason why the one having angry feeling just then is just then having angry feeling in that one. Certainly there are in this way of having it happen that angry feeling is in some, different ways of having angry feeling in the one having then angry feeling. As I am saying some certainly are then needing to be wanting not to have it that they themselves that any one is certain that they are having then angry feeling. Certainly some are needing when such angry feeling is in them are needing it that not any other one is knowing that they are having angry feeling inside them. Some are certainly then when they are having such angry feeling in them are certainly then needing to be certain themselves then inside them that they are then having angry feeling in them. Some are needing certainly needing when they are having such angry feeling in them are certainly needing that some one some other one is knowing it then that they are having then such angry feeling in them. Some are ones when they are having such angry feeling in them are ones wanting to be needing that some other one is knowing it of them that they are then having such angry feeling in them. Some are ones wanting to be needing it that not any one ever can be knowing that they are ones having such angry feeling in them. Some having such angry feeling are ones wanting to be needing it that they are ones not then knowing it that they have inside them any such angry feeling. Some having such angry feeling in them are ones needing to be wanting then and always in them about such angry feeling in them that they are not knowing it inside them that they are having in them such a way of having in them angry feeling. Then there are ones certainly not ever being ones ever remembering having been having in any such a way angry feeling. Then there are some certainly needing that they are wanting that not any one should ever be remembering anything about any one ever having any such a way of having angry feeling. Then there are some certainly very well remembering that they are ones having been having such an angry feeling and some of these then are ones really needing that not any one, that they not themselves inside them are ever mentioning that they have been having any such a way of having angry feeling in them and there are some of this kind of them that can never be listening when any one is mentioning such a way of having angry feeling, and there are some of such of them who are certainly not hearing when any one in any way is mentioning such a way of having angry feeling, of such angry feeling having been sometime in that one. Certainly to very many having such angry feeling in them it is a thing they are mostly not at all liking, certainly some, quite some having it in them to have such angry feeling in them are in some ways needing it to be wanting it to be in them, some are in some way coming to be liking it to be inside in them such a way of having angry feeling in them, some are in some way coming to be liking it inside in them such a way of having angry feeling in them, some are almost completely liking it having such a way of having angry feeling in them some of those having angry feeling in them from some one not being one in any way doing anything to that one in any way able to be doing anything to that one but being one being in the family living, being one being in some living of that one and being one being then in being living, being one doing something in being living. Certainly Alfred Hersland was one being in the family living of David Hersland. Certainly there were very many in the living of David Hersland sometimes in David Hersland being one being living. Certainly some of these were sometimes ones making it that David Hersland had in him angry feeling and these then were then ones not being ones able in any way to be doing anything in the living of David Hersland he being one being then being living. Alfred Hersland was one certainly one when David Hersland was in the beginning of the middle of his young living, one not doing anything in the living, in the living David Hersland was then living, certainly David Hersland had then angry feeling from Alfred Hersland being one then being living being one then doing something. Certainly David Hersland had sometimes angry feeling in him and this was in him and it was in him in the middle of his young living and this was in him because Alfred Hersland was being then one doing some particular thing. Certainly then sometimes Alfred Hersland was knowing that David Hersland was having angry feeling in him. Certainly sometimes when David Hersland was having angry feeling in him in this way in him Alfred Hersland was not at all then knowing this thing. Sometimes Martha Hersland would be knowing this thing that David Hersland was having angry feeling in him in this way in him, mostly she was not knowing this thing, David Hersland certainly always knew it in him when he was having angry feeling in him in such a way inside him, sometimes later he could be explaining such angry feeling when he was explaining something and Martha was listening, sometimes he could come to be almost thinking it a funny thing to have been having any such angry feeling he could be thinking it to be a funny thing to himself inside him he could be sometime almost mentioning this thing to some one that it was a funny thing to have been having angry feeling in any such way inside him, certainly he sometime sometimes could be mentioning this thing that he was thinking it to be a funny thing that he had angry feeling in any way inside him, he certainly sometime could come to be completely thinking that it was a very peculiar thing to have been having such a way of having angry feeling, to have been having sometimes inside him such a way of having angry feeling, he could be completely explaining to himself and sometime to some one and sometime to some that it was a peculiar thing to have been having such angry feeling inside him. He certainly could be sometime completely explaining such angry feeling, he certainly could be explaining completely explaining that this was a peculiar thing that this was quite a funny thing having been having such angry feeling in him, he could certainly sometime be completely certain about the explanation of this thing, about this being a funny thing, to himself and to some. He was one as I was saying having had quite reasonably often such a way of having angry feeling in him when he was in the middle of his young living. He was one in a way having such a way of having angry feeling in him when he was one being in the beginning of his middle living. He was quite certainly not one having any such angry feeling in him in any such a way when he was in the ending of his young living. This is quite clear then, he had certainly a good deal of such angry feeling in him and quite often in the middle of his young living, not any in the ending of his young living, certainly some and fairly often in the beginning of his middle living, more or less then to the ending of his living which was in the ending of the beginning of his middle living. He had angry feeling in such a way in him pretty much the same way in him when he had it in him and yet there were differences and sometime these differences will be coming to be showing themselves in his coming to be having it that every one is knowing other things in him that every one knowing him could be certainly knowing.

There are different ways of having angry feeling when some one is teaching some one something. There are different ways of having angry feeling when some one is trying to teach some one something. There are different ways of having angry feeling inside each one who is having angry feeling with some one teaching that one.

One is being one some one is teaching and that one can be certain that that is not at all a good way for that one to be teaching that one that thing. One is being one some one is teaching and the one some one is teaching can be quite completely certain inside that one that the one that is teaching that one is one not knowing anything about that thing. That one the one some one is teaching something can be certain of this thing that the one teaching that one is not teaching that one in the right way of teaching that thing, can be certain of this thing when that one is quite in the beginning of the middle of young living.

Some one is one to whom some one is regularly teaching something. Some one is one whom some one is teaching. Some one is one whom some one is regularly teaching something and that is in the middle of the young living of that one, is quite in the beginning of the middle of the young living in that one and that one is then one in the middle of the middle of the young living of that one and is then in the ending of the middle of the young living in that one and is always quite certain that the one regularly teaching that one something is one not knowing anything about the thing that one is teaching. Certainly David Hersland was one not admiring any teacher any one teacher teaching him in any fashion until David Hersland was one at the ending of young living at the beginning of the beginning of his being in middle living and then he certainly was admiring some who were teaching, regularly then teaching him then something.

Some can be quite certain when they are in the beginning of the middle of their young living can be quite certain that not any one teaching them something is one knowing anything about that thing. Some of such of them are not in any way pleasant ones for those then teaching them to be teaching. Some of such of them are not at all unpleasant ones for those then teaching them to be teaching. David Hersland as I was saying was of such of them that I have been describing and certainly he was not then to every one teaching him an unpleasant one, he was certainly then not to every one then teaching him something a pleasant one.

Certainly mostly every one in being one being in young living is one being one some one is regularly teaching something. Certainly some are then quite certain to themselves inside them that not any one teaching them then something is knowing anything really about the thing they are then teaching. Certainly some are certain of this thing to mostly every one knowing them then. Certainly some are certain of this thing to some one knowing them then. Certainly some are needing to be wanting to be certain of this thing. Certainly some are wanting to be needing to be certain of this thing. Certainly very many are pretty nearly completely certain of this thing. Some are certainly mostly always completely certain of this thing then when they are in any part of the middle of their being in young living. David Hersland was, certainly, was one of such of them. He was one feeling in such fashion. He was not then admiring any one of those who was then teaching him something, who was then being a teacher for him in a regular fashion.

Certainly some do not at all think about this thing whether the one teaching them anything is knowing anything about that thing. Certainly not, they certainly are not at all thinking about this thing in any one regularly teaching them anything, very many who are being taught something, very many who have been taught something. When I asked something they did not answer that question, certainly they can teach some something, did they or did they not answer the question I asked, certainly not, certainly they did not answer that question, certainly they answered about a good many things, let me know if they answered my question, certainly they did not answer my question, the question I asked, and I will ask a question again, they will not answer the question I will ask them to answer. When I asked something they did not answer that question, certainly not, certainly they did not answer that question, certainly they said something about that thing, certainly they did not answer my question, they answered some questions, they certainly did not answer that question the question I asked them, I will ask them again, they certainly will say something, they will not explain that thing, I will ask about some other thing, they will not be able to explain that thing, I am certain that they cannot explain anything anything I ask them. Some can when they are in the middle of their young living, in any part of the middle of their young living can be saying such a thing to themselves inside them. Some can say such a thing to themselves inside them, in only one part of the middle of their young living. Very many do then say such a thing to themselves inside them. Very many do say such a thing to some other one. Some do say such a thing, almost, to the teacher teaching them. Some do say such a thing to the teacher teaching them. Some are hearing some one say such a thing. Some are listening when some one is saying such a thing. As I was saying David Hersland was one certainly saying such a thing sometimes to himself inside him, sometimes to some one, sometime to the teacher teaching him, sometimes to the teacher teaching him, he was one saying such a thing in all of the middle of his young living. In some, saying such a thing is an important thing, being one saying such a thing is an important thing. Certainly some who have been ones saying such things are not important ones, excepting while they are saying such things, to any one. Some saying such things are needing being ones thinking about the things, such things, being said by them. Some saying such things are needing to themselves inside them being ones having been saying such things. Some are certainly for a good deal of the time they are ones being living are ones needing in some way being ones saying such a thing. Different kinds of them in men and women are saying such things in the way their kind of them can say such things. Each one has their own being inside them and each one saying such things is using the being in them for the saying of such things, is feeling with the being in them about having been, about being one saying such things. Certainly this has close connection in very many, such things with angry feeling being in them. Certainly some are not needing that some one should be one to interfere with them by being one being one teaching something, they are quite certain. Certainly they can then have angry feeling some of them, some of them do then have angry feeling. Some of them do not then always have angry feeling, some have then almost not at all angry feeling, they have different kinds of feeling, some do then always have angry feeling, some do then sometime have angry feeling. Certainly David Hersland was one not by any means always having then angry feeling, when he was thinking, when he was feeling, when he was saying such things. He very often did not then have angry feeling, he could have then the need in him to be explaining to the one teaching him what he was thinking about them, he could have it in him sometimes to be completely disregarding their being existing, he could sometimes be thinking about them and not hearing them and they were then ones teaching him, he could be one almost completely listening and then certainly he would be needing to be teaching them, he could be wanting them not to be a bother to him while they were ones being ones teaching him something, he could be one almost having them being ones being not existing and they certainly were existing then to themselves and to every one as ones being ones teaching him something. As I was saying he was one certainly not pleasant to those teaching him something, he was one certainly not unpleasant to those teaching him something, he was unpleasant to some, almost completely unpleasant to some, he was not quite completely pleasant to any of them, he was very nearly completely pleasant to some of them. He was one sometimes needing to be doing some other thing when some one was being one teaching him then something. This certainly could happen to him, it certainly did happen to him again and again.

One was one not completely certain that each one teaching that one something was one not knowing anything about the thing that one was teaching. This one was completely certain that some teaching that one something were ones not knowing anything about that thing. This one was one almost completely certain about some teaching that one something that they were ones not knowing anything about the things they were then teaching to that one. This one in being one being an older one was quite certain that not any one having been teaching that one in any regular way anything was one knowing how the teaching of that thing should have been done. This one then was one who in later living being in that one was certain that not any one who had been teaching that one anything knew anything about teaching, about teaching that one, about teaching any one. This one was one quite certain in his later living that teaching was something that some one should be understanding. This one in being one being later in the living in that one was certain then that that one was one having it then that that one was teaching something, was having it then that that one was not one learning anything then by talking and listening, was one then certain that that one knowing how thinking can be done, and certainly that one did then know that thing, was one then certainly one to be teaching any one and then that one really would not then be doing teaching, to that one inside in that one, as not any one not knowing about the way of doing thinking, not realising the way of doing thinking would be one profiting by such teaching and such a one would not be needing that thing, that teaching that this one could be doing. There was then such a one and this one was then in the beginning of the ending of the middle living in that one. This one was then one certainly having angry feeling that was irritation, that was impatient feeling while this one had been a young one and any one had been teaching that one something. This one was one certainly not at all pleasant to very many having been teaching this one. This one was interesting to some teaching this one. This one was quite pleasant to some teaching this one. David Hersland was not like this one. David Hersland was a different kind of a one. This one was one having it to be realising very well the way each one doing thinking is doing thinking, this one was one not realising very well which way any one was experiencing anything and the relation of doing thinking in each one doing thinking with the way each one is experiencing. This one was then one certainly having angry feeling when this one was a young one in having any one teaching that one anything in the way any one was then teaching that one. This one was then completely the same one in being one coming to be an older one. This one was one certainly doing thinking, this one was one certainly knowing about thinking being done by men and by women doing thinking. This one then was different from David Hersland. David Hersland was not like this one I have just been describing. David Hersland was one certainly often certain that the one that was then teaching him was one not understanding that thing. David Hersland certainly sometimes carefully explained, to some one teaching him, that thing. As I am saying David Hersland was one not like the one I have been just describing. David Hersland was one certainly doing thinking, David Hersland was certainly one talking and listening, the one I have been just describing was one doing talking and listening, David Hersland was one wanting to be needing to be one teaching each one something, he was one certainly coming to be early in his middle living a dead one. He was one certainly finding it often a troublesome thing to have a governess living in the house with him as he was one to himself needing to be reading almost anything, certainly a certain thing, and sometimes a governess said something about such a thing. He could find it a pleasant thing to have a governess living in the house with him and he did find it to be a pleasant thing and then again and again it was not at all a pleasant thing but mostly it was not to him at all a serious thing, they were not any of them really regularly teaching anything to him.

There are some who are certain, in being ones being in later living, who are certain that they could have been ones having it that they had teachers really knowing something and then if they had had them they would have been ones living a different way in being ones learning in being living in being one being in being living. There are in each kind in men and women some having such feeling in them. David Hersland was not at all one of such of them. It is a curious thing that the one I was describing as being one certainly knowing about thinking being in any one is in a way such a one. Surely this one is not such a one and yet in a way that one is such a one. That one is such a one although certainly not any one to that one was when that one was a young one was one really knowing how to be teaching something to that one and that one when that one was in the later living in that one was understanding thinking being in each one thinking and was one certainly thinking and one then certain that he would be one not teaching as it was not a thing that one was then feeling any one could be understanding excepting one not needing that thing and this one was surely then one certain that some one when that one was a young one could have been teaching that one something if the one teaching that one had been understanding teaching. As I was saying in a way David Hersland was one like this one, in a way David Hersland was one not like this one, certainly David Hersland was one certain about almost every one teaching him when he was a young one that they were not understanding what they were teaching and if they were understanding what they were teaching were not understanding how to be teaching. He was not certain about every one, he was to some teaching him a quite completely pleasant one.

There are some not thinking, not feeling about their knowing anything, not having angry feeling in them with those teaching them regularly but have very much such feeling about some teaching them in some irregular fashion. Some being ones some one is teaching it is just the other way in them. David Hersland was certainly not of either of these kinds of them, being one some one is teaching.

There are many kinds of ways of having angry feeling, each one certainly was having sometimes angry feeling when that one was being one some one was teaching, each one certainly is having sometimes angry feeling when that one is being one some one is teaching.

Some are thinking, some are feeling, some are thinking and feeling, some are thinking some one is feeling, some are thinking some one is thinking, some are thinking some one is feeling and thinking, some are feeling some one is thinking, some are feeling some one is thinking and feeling, some are feeling some one is feeling. These are so very many ways of thinking and feeling connecting, not connecting, of being existing, of not being existing, there are so many ways of realising and not realising thinking and feeling being, thinking being, feeling being, feeling not being, thinking not being, thinking and feeling not being, some kind of thinking, some kind of feeling not being in some one.

Certainly it is a trouble to me to be doing this thing. I certainly cannot in any way know it is a trouble to you to do this thing when you asked me whether you should or should not do this thing and then did what I said you should do about doing this thing. I certainly can be realising it is a trouble to me to do this thing, I certainly cannot be realising it is a trouble to you to do this thing. You asked me and I told you and you did what I told you and now you are thinking I should have been feeling that you were doing that thing from the feeling you were having about that thing. You certainly asked me what you should do about doing that thing, I certainly told you what you should do about doing that thing, you certainly did what I told you to do about doing that thing.

Some are younger ones than other ones, some are asking ones by being ones not feeling it to be ones to be deciding ones, some are ones being ones quite certain that other ones can be ones working to do deciding, some are ones liking other ones to be ones to be ones being quicker ones, some are ones not being ones realising anything inside them at any time before it is a completely finished thing, and certainly very many in their being ones being living are ones are being ones to whom some one can be saying, is saying, will be saying what I have just been telling some one said or could have said or might have said or will be saying or is saying to some one. This is to be some description of angry feeling being in men and in women about such a thing, in all of them. This will be then some description of one kind of angry feeling, of some explaining and then some more angry feeling and some more angry feeling and then sometimes not any more angry feeling and then sometimes more angry feeling being in men being in men and in women.

It would be easy to have angry feeling, for some, if they were not coming to be certain that some other one was one coming to be one not thinking anything that was an important thing to be doing as thinking. Very many are having sometimes and quite often angry feeling about some one and then that one comes to be for them one certainly not being one doing important thinking or feeling or acting and this one then is going on being asked advice by the one having had and now not having any angry feeling about that one. So then asking advice and taking advice is one thing and asking advice and taking advice is another thing and that in the same one in relation to the same other one. Giving advice and talking to some one is one thing and giving advice and talking to some one is another thing in the same one giving advice and talking to the same other one.

Some would like to be certain about some one who has been one talking to them giving advice to them whether that one is one really one not important in feeling and in thinking. Some are thinking very often about wanting to be certain about this thing. If they were certain about this thing they certainly would not be having in them in any way that is certainly not in most ways angry feeling against that one. Some are never really certain inside them about this thing, some are certain and then they are not certain about this thing in some one who has been one talking to them giving advice to them when they asked advice of that one. Some are completely certain and they have angry feeling in them when that one is talking to them, giving advice to them that they are asking of that one. Some are certain of that thing that the one having been one talking to them often and giving advice to them when they were wanting to have advice given to them is one not important in thinking and in feeling and are not at all in any way angry inside in them when that one is talking then when that one is giving advice to them.

Asking advice is in some kinds in men and in women, in some men and women of many kinds in men and women. Asking advice means a different thing in one than it does in another one in the being in them. Giving advice is in the same way in some kinds in men and women, is in some men and women of very many kinds in men and women. It means different things in the being in different kinds in men and women.

David Hersland was one certainly giving advice some from well in the beginning of the ending of young living. It meant something in the being in him. He was one who certainly could have angry feeling in him in being one giving advice to some one, mostly he was one not having angry feeling in giving advice to any one. He was one who certainly did come to be certain about some one about some who had been one talking to him who had been ones talking to him, giving advice to him when he was asking for advice to be given, he was one certainly coming to think of some one, of some of such of them that they were ones that that one was one not important in thinking not important in feeling and mostly then Hersland did not have then any angry feeling in him about that one, about them, he could have sometime in coming to be certain angry feeling about some one of such of them. Mostly he did not have angry feeling inside him in being certain about any one.

As I was saying he was one giving advice certainly a good deal of advice in being one being living.

Some certainly are liking to be working with sharp knives or sharp scissors, some are not liking to be working with sharp knives or sharp scissors, some have angry feeling when some one has been sharpening the knives or scissors they have been using, some have angry feeling in them when some one has sharpened a knife or a scissor for them, some have very angry feeling when some one will not let the knife or scissors they are using be sharpened so that they will be sharp ones, some are very angry when some one is wanting to be using knives and scissors which are not sharp ones and is preferring them to be not sharp ones. Some are asking always that some one sharpen the knives or the scissors they are using, some are angry when they find that some one will not sharpen a knife or a pair of scissors for them.

As I was saying Martha Hersland was the oldest of the three Hersland children. Certainly she could have angry feeling, certainly she could ask advice sometimes from some one, she did ask advice sometimes that is certain, she certainly did ask advice sometimes from David Hersland. David Hersland did quite often enough give advice to Martha and she quite often enough took the advice he gave her. Certainly she very often listened very much to him. He certainly listened some. As I was saying he was one who certainly gave advice quite often while he was one being one being living. He certainly listened some to advice that might have been given to him. Some are thinking that he was one not at all ever listening, he certainly did listen some.

Some are certainly not listening to some and some of such of them are certainly listening some then. Some are feeling about some other one that that one is repeating very much and that that one is very certain that that one is not liking any one to be repeating in talking and certainly that one is repeating and repeating and repeating. Some are certain about such a one that that one is one mostly having an angry feeling when that one is listening and sometimes that one is not having then an angry feeling and certainly sometimes then that one is having angry feeling. Certainly very many are sometimes quite certain about some other one that that one is not listening to everything that one is hearing and that that one is one judging in that one as one being one having been listening completely to everything that one has been hearing and certainly that one has not been listening to everything that one has been hearing. Mostly every one sometime is certain of this thing in every one and very many when they are certain of this thing have then very much angry feeling in them. Each one has their own way of having angry feeling in them and coming out of them.

Angry feeling is coming, coming, not coming, certainly not coming to be in them in some. Angry feeling is certainly coming to be in them in some. It is really a surprising thing to some that they have been having really angry feeling in them. Some are certainly not feeling in them before, during, after they have been having angry feeling any of the feeling that would be for them in their thinking, in their feeling, in their realisation angry feeling. It is a curious thing that certainly certainly very many are not feeling any feeling in them giving to them angry feeling and yet certainly they are just then having angry feeling in them. This is happening quite often to some. Some are ones of such a kind of them and of some of such of them not many are knowing that they are having angry feeling in them when they are having angry feeling in them. In a way David Hersland quite often was of such of them. Some of such of them have it that they would be to themselves having angry feeling if they had more realisation in being one feeling some of them, some of such of them are ones who would not have been having angry feeling if they had all the feeling they were having just then being active in them to them, some would be having angry feeling to themselves then if they could be certain to be going on having angry feeling. In a way as I was saying David Hersland was such a one. In a way he had never in him really a complete angry feeling, in a way he had sometimes almost complete angry feeling, in a way really inside him he had sometimes very angry feeling in him, in a way he had inside him not ever any really angry feeling in him. He could be telling his sister Martha sometimes about angry feeling being existing in some. Certainly she would ask him quite often about angry feeling being existing in some.

Some are not understanding that every one is not always knowing that every one can come to be a dead one. Some are always being ones being quite certain that each one sometime will be coming to be a dead one. Some are certain every minute in their living that each one ever living will come sometime to be a dead one. Some are certain that each one will come to be a dead one, are always certain of this thing. Some of such of them have quite an angry feeling when they are realising that some other one is not always certain of this thing that each one sometime is being one coming to be a dead one, that sometime each one ever living is a dead one. Some who are certain of this thing are always in their living having angry feeling when some one is not certain of this thing in being one being living, that each one is sometime a dead one. Some who are all their living completely certain that each one is sometime certain to be a dead one have in part of their living very angry feeling when some one is not certain of this thing. Some who are living are in a way having angry feeling and having irritated feeling, some who are certain all their living that each one sometime is coming to be a dead one, when they are hearing some talking who are not ever feeling about each one coming to be a dead one sometime. Some who are certain that each one will sometime be a dead one have some angry feeling in them all their living when some are not listening to any one who is telling that sometime every one will be a dead one. Some are pretty nearly certain all their living that each one sometime will be a dead one. Some are completely certain all their living that each one ever living will come to be a dead one sometime. Some have sometimes in their living angry feeling about what other ones are feeling or are not feeling about each one being sometime a dead one.

Certainly some are very every minute certain that sometime each one ever living will be a dead one. Some of such of them are having angry feeling inside them in being one being certain of this thing. Some are not always being completely certain that sometime each one will be a dead one. Some are having angry feeling inside them about this thing.

Some are having angry feeling about some such thing about being certain about every one being a dead one sometime, about always being cerain about this thing, about not often being certain about this thing, about never coming to themselves inside them being completely certain, completely not certain every minute about this thing, about not remembering this thing, about not listening about this thing, about other ones not saying they are certain about this thing, that they are not certain about this thing, about others listening, about others refusing to listen to this thing that each one sometime is a dead one, some are having angry feeling in them about such a thing sometime in their living and then in parts of their living they are having very little angry feeling about such things and part of their living they are having remembering having angry feeling about such a thing and part of their living they are not having at all angry feeling about such things. David Hersland was one of such of them. He certainly all his living was talking some and listening some he was talking a good deal and listening a good deal in his living, he certainly was sometimes talking, he certainly was listening very often to talking about each one coming to be sometime a dead one.

Some are certain that they are understanding why every one is being living. Some are certain that they are understanding why any one is being living. Some are certain that they are understanding that every one who is living is living. Some are certain that they are understanding that any one who is living is living. Some are so certain that they are understanding that every one who is living is being living that they are boasting about this thing and sometimes some one hearing them telling about this thing has angry feeling in that one. One can have been in living, to that one and to mostly every one, one certain that every one is living in being living but that that one is not understanding this thing living being in any one. Such a one can have it come then, to that one, that that one is understanding this thing, living being in every one being living, and then that one is finding that one to be a very different one from what that one has ever been in being living and that one is telling that thing and telling it so much and in such a way of telling it again and again that some are then certain that that one is a different one and some are not certain and some are certain that that one is not a different one from what that one has been and some of each of these kinds of them have in them then angry feeling, some of them have some angry feeling, some have very little angry feeling, some have very much angry feeling about that one.

It is certainly interesting what each one feels, thinks, says, knows, would like to know, does not care about knowing about living feeling being in anything, in any one, in every one. It is certainly a very exciting thing to some to feel something in them about living being in men and in women. It is not at all, not the least bit an exciting thing to some to feel anything about living being in men and in women, in anything, in everything.

Some one has been one to that one, to every one knowing that one, one certainly not going ever to be certain that living being in any one, in every one, in everything, is a thing that one is ever going to be understanding and then all of a sudden, sometime when that one has been changing in some way in doing something, that one is one to keep on telling that that one certainly does understand everything that is to say living being in men and in women. Certainly such a one can have then angry feeling but, very often, almost mostly, such a one is not just then having angry feeling and certainly some are having about such a one then angry feeling and some are not having then about such a one any angry feeling.

David Hersland was one who almost came to be one certain sometime to be completely understanding being being in men and in women being living. He was one certainly almost and not so very often still quite often coming to be certain of being one completely understanding everything. As I was saying he had sometimes then angry feeling, certainly some had about him then some angry feeling. Sometimes then he had not any angry feeling. Certainly there were some then interested about him then who had not then angry feeling. Some who were not very much interested had about him then angry feeling, some who were not very much interested in him then had not then about him any angry feeling. As I was saying he was almost one having it to be in him to be completely certain that he was understanding everything again and again and sometimes all of a sudden. As I was saying he was almost such a one, he was quite often almost such a one. There are certainly some coming to be quite certain, some all of a sudden, that they are understanding everything. Some have about some such a one very angry feeling, David Hersland did have in being living about some of such of them angry feeling, about some others of such of them he had a very gentle feeling, about some others of such of them he had a very sympathetic feeling, about some others of such of them he had a very interested feeling, about some others of such of them he had a scared feeling, about some others of such of them he had really a completely surprised feeling, about some others of such of them he had a very silly feeling, about some others of such of them he had an annoyed feeling, about some others of such of them he had quite an indifferent feeling, about some others of such of them he had sometimes a very earnest feeling, about some others of such of them he had intensely an inquiring feeling, about some others of such of them he had a disgusted feeling, about some others of such of them he had a very sorrowful feeling, about some others of such of them he had a disappointed feeling, about some others of such of them he had a feeling that made him be one going on scolding them every time he thought about them, about some others of some of them he was not certain but perhaps they really did understand everything and then sometimes he was quite certain that they did not understand everything and then sometimes he had a humble feeling perhaps they were understanding everything and then sometimes he had a certain feeling that they were not understanding everything. As I am saying David Hersland was one having it to be almost one to be sometimes completely certain that he was understanding everything.

Certainly some in one way of being ones being living, some in other ways of being ones being living come to be certain, some gradually, some all of a sudden, some sometime, some sometimes, some quite often, some very often, come to be certain that they are understanding every one being one being living. Some as I am saying are having when they are having this thing angry feeling, some when they are having this thing are not having it to be having any angry feeling. Some about such of them have angry feeling, some have not any angry feeling about any one of such of them. As I am saying there are very many ways of coming to be certain of being one understanding living being in men and in women. As I am saying there are very many ways of being impressed of not being impressed by any one of such of them, by some of such of them, by many of such of them, by every one of such of them.

There are certainly many ways of feeling, of thinking, of liking of not liking living being in men and in women, living being existing. Very many are convinced that living is a real thing, something they are certain is existing, some are not so certain of this thing. Some are content with living being existing, some are not at all content with this thing. Some are certainly certain that if every one were understanding everything that not any one will only be wanting to be certain only that living is being existing. Some are so certain that understanding anything is amusing to every one, and certainly it is not it is not at all amusing to some it is not at all interesting to some. Some are so certain that understanding anything is interesting to every one that they are certain that sometime every one will be understanding something. Some are so certain that understanding everything is a necessary thing that they are certain that sometime they will be understanding everything. Some of such of them come to be certain that they are understanding everything, to some of such of them it comes all of a sudden.

As I was saying some of such of them have angry feeling in them then, as I was saying some of such of them have not at all angry feeling in them then. As I was saying David Hersland in a way was almost such a one.

If he feels it and he knows it and he tells it and he thinks it and he says it, clearly tells it why then perhaps it is something and perhaps it is not anything. Some are certain that clear thinking and clear telling and certain feeling and complete emotion are something some one can be doing. Some are certain that sometime they will be having complete emotion and certain feeling and clear thinking and eloquent expression. Some are certain that they are having clear thinking and complete emotion and adequate expression and absolute conviction. Some are certain that they have been having clear thinking and complete emotion and complete conviction and adequate expression. Some are certainly very clearly thinking, some certainly have then complete conviction. Some are certainly having complete emotion and are clearly thinking and are having adequate expression and perhaps are really having then absolute conviction. Some are certainly having sometime complete emotion and adequate expression. Some are perhaps having sometime complete emotion and clear thinking and adequate expression. Some are perhaps having clear thinking and adequate expression and some emotion, very much emotion and pretty nearly absolute conviction. Some are certainly having clear thinking and adequate expression and considerable emotion. Some are certainly not having completely clear thinking and complete emotion and adequate expression and absolute conviction.

Some one is certain that some other one is doing clear thinking, is having adequate expression, is having almost complete conviction, is certainly not having complete emotion. That one is certain that the other one is one having pretty nearly complete emotion, not at all any clear thinking, not at all absolute conviction, might easily be having adequate expression.

Which is then the important one, certainly one of the two of them. One of the two of them is certainly in a way the important one. One of the two of them is certainly in a way not the important one.

David Hersland was certain that really one of them was the more important one. David Hersland was one certainly in a way not having complete emotion, certainly in a way doing clear thinking, certainly in a way having adequate expression, certainly having very nearly absolute conviction. He had absolute conviction. He had clear thinking, he had adequate expression, he felt inside him complete emotion.

Some are working hard to be ones telling some one something. Some are working and are telling some one something. Some are not working hard to tell some one something. Some are not working hard and they are then telling some one something.

To some spirituality and idealism have no meaning excepting as meaning completest intensification of any experiencing, any conception of transcending experience has to some not any meaning. To some anything to have meaning must be existing, to some anything to have meaning must be being, having been going to be experienced as something existing by some one. Many who are carefully and completely thinking have it to leave out something they have been, they will be, they are, they can be experiencing and this is a very natural thinking as very many who have it to be ones clearly and completely reasonably thinking have it to have it that they are thinking to be solving a problem and naturally then they are not thinking into them everything they can be experiencing. Some are quite certain that any one very clearly thinking are not ever completely experiencing, some are quite certain that any one clearly thinking is leaving out very much that should be being remembered by that one. Some certainly have a conception that everything should be intelligible to some one, certainly some of such of them are to some others, listening to them, not convincing. Some have it to be experiencing that they are experiencing more than experiencing and this is to very many completely convincing and it is to some completely convincing in some, and it is altogether convincing to some and to some it is convincing when these having it in them to have such experiencing of something that is not experiencing explain their experience, to some it is not then convincing. To some, some having experiencing of something which is more than any experiencing are convincing when they are explaining this thing. To some it would be a very pleasant thing if not any one having such experiencing ever got mixed up between what was, what is, what will be to that one and how it comes to be, how it came to be, how it will come to be, in short the explanation, the description, the condition what as experience to them was without any condition.

As I am saying some are working in being ones being thinking, some are not working in being ones being thinking. Some are certainly thinking and working in being one being thinking and certainly coming to an ending in their thinking and doing it the thinking as a complete thing and certainly carefully doing that thing and certainly clearly telling the thinking they have been doing. Some certainly then have not been putting in everything that any one could be experiencing that is connected with the thing about which they have been thinking, some will not put in some experiencing, some cannot put in some experiencing, some are certain that they have put in all that experiencing, some put in almost all experiencing that has anything to do with that thing when they are thinking about that thing.

Certainly to be completely experiencing, to be clearly thinking, to have real conviction, to have enthusiasm, to keep on going in doing thinking and having experiencing is a very enjoyable thing. Certainly very many are very clearly thinking that is quite a number are certainly quite thinking quite clearly. David Hersland was such a one. He certainly had enthusiasm, he certainly could have some experiencing, he certainly was needing for his own satisfaction to put in everything any one could be experiencing in thinking about anything. He certainly was one completely wanting to do this thing. He was one in a way doing this thing. He was one in a way never coming to be completely doing this thing, he was one having almost absolute conviction, he was one having real enthusiasm. He was one not being certain that experiencing being intensified was spirituality and idealism. He was not certain that one could not be experiencing something that was a different thing. He almost came to be certain that one could not be experiencing something more complete than any experiencing, he came to be almost certain that one can be experiencing something that is more than experiencing. He came to be certainly quite certain that not any one could explain such a thing, he came to be almost certain that perhaps he could sometime explain such a thing.

Some certainly and certainly they were not expecting to be doing that thing come sometime to be explaining what they were certain certainly was not existing. This is quite common. Some certainly come to be quite certain that something is existing that they were completely certain was not ever existing. David Hersland was in a way not at all such a one.

Many are very logical in being ones being thinking. Some demonstrate something in being ones being thinking. Many are very logical in being ones being thinking. Some keep on demonstrating something. Many are very logical in being ones being thinking, some of these are demonstrating something, some of these are beginning demonstrating something, some of these are not really demonstrating anything, some of these are occasionally demonstrating something. It is like this, many who are logical ones are while they are being logical are always experiencing being one being living, some while they are being logical ones are being ones experiencing a great deal of being ones being living, some while they are being logical are experiencing very little of being ones being living, some while they are being logical have at times the conviction of being ones experiencing being living, some are certain that being logical ones makes of them ones being ones experiencing being living and this is perhaps true of them. The way each one is experiencing the amount each one is experiencing living is then a thing that some one is knowing, that some one is not knowing, that some are not knowing of themselves inside them, that some are knowing of themselves inside them, about which some have conviction, about which some do not have conviction, about which some have conviction and they certainly are not knowing what they are certain they are knowing, about which some have conviction and they certainly are knowing what they are knowing, about which some are not knowing that they are having a conviction, about which some are having a conviction and are not certain of that thing, about which some are quite certain they have not any conviction, about which some are certainly not knowing everything, about which some are knowing more than others are knowing, about which some are knowing very much, about which some are knowing hardly anything.

So then experiencing being one being living is a thing about which some are knowing very much in themselves, in other ones. Experiencing being one being living is something some have very much in them. Experiencing being one being living is something many are certainly having some. Experiencing being one being living is certainly something every one is having some. Certainly some are having more than others are having of being one experiencing being one being living.

Surely some one is meaning something by what that one is saying. It would be a nuisance for some not to be certain of this thing. Some one is meaning something when that one is saying something. Certainly in each one there is a connection between what that one is saying and that one is meaning, certainly in some way there must be some connection. Each one has their own way inside them of meaning something, each one has their own way of having connection between what that one is meaning and what that one is thinking, between what that one is meaning and what that one is saying, about what that one is meaning and what that one is feeling, about what that one is meaning and what that one is certain is conviction in that one.

It would be a nuisance for some not to be certain of this thing that each one has some connection in them between what they are meaning what they are saying what they are feeling, what they are thinking, what they are certain about in being one being living.

Certainly some are pretty certain that there is not enough connection to make it interesting, in very many, between what they are meaning, they are thinking, they are feeling, they are saying, they are certain in something existing.

I mean, I mean and that is not what I mean, I mean that not any one is saying what they are meaning, I mean that I am feeling something, I mean that I mean something and I mean that not any one is thinking, is feeling, is saying, is certain of that thing, I mean that not any one can be saying, thinking, feeling, not any one can be certain of that thing, I mean I am not certain of that thing, I am not ever saying, thinking, feeling, being certain of this thing, I mean, I mean, I know what I mean.

And certainly some one is right in saying such a thing, such a one some of such of them certainly are right in saying such a thing. Some of such of them have it that the moment of sensibility, emotion and expression and origin is all in a state of completion and then it is a finished thing and certainly then that one was meaning something and he was saying I mean, I mean, and it was all finished and then there was another something and this one certainly very often said I mean. That one said that very often in being one being living.

Surely in some way there is some connection between what each one is meaning and saying and feeling and thinking and being certain of in living. Surely it would be a very great nuisance to ones being ones being living if there were not some connection in each one between meaning and feeling and saying and thinking and being certain in each one.

Some are quite certain that there is very little connection certainly not enough to make it interesting between what every one is meaning and what every one is thinking and what every one is saying and what every one is feeling and of what every one is certain. David Hersland, yes he might be one of such of them.

Some are quite certain that there is enough connection to make it completely interesting between what every one is meaning and what every one is thinking and what every one is feeling and of what every one is certain. David Hersland was certainly one of such of them.

Some are certainly knowing what they are meaning, some are certainly not knowing what they are meaning. Certainly every one in a way is meaning something, certainly every one in a way is saying, is thinking, is feeling, is quite certain of something.

Which way some one is meaning anything, which way some one is meaning everything, how some one is meaning what that one is saying, meaning, feeling, thinking and being certain, what that one is doing, feeling, thinking and of what that one is certain, how that one is going on meaning something, meaning anything, meaning everything, which way that one is going on meaning what that one is saying, feeling, thinking, doing, what connection there is in that one between living in that one and being in that one, how that one is liking is not liking what that one means to any one knowing that one, how that one is liking is not liking what that one is not meaning to some one, to any one, how anything coming into that one comes out of that one, how some things coming into that one hardly are coming out of that one, how much the things coming out of that one are different from the things going into that one, how quickly and how slowly, how completely, how gradually, how intermittently, how noisily, how silently, how happily, how drearily, how difficultly, how gaily, how complicatedly, how simply, how joyously, how boisterously, how despondingly, how fragmentarily, how delicately, how roughly, how excitedly, how energetically, how persistently, how repeatedly, how repeatingly, how drily, how startlingly, how funnily, how certainly, how hesitatingly, anything is coming out of that one, what is being in each one and how anything comes into that one and comes out of that one makes of each one one meaning something and feeling, telling, thinking, being certain and being living.

Certainly the way of experiencing anything and expressing that thing is the being being in each one. Certainly there are groups of men and women as to ways of experiencing things in being ones being living, certainly there are groups of them who in a way have the same ways of experiencing in them and these have each of them ways of experiencing something. Each one of them are meaning something to themselves inside them, to any other one, in being ones being living and having their own way of being ones experiencing anything, of being ones expressing anything.

Some are not knowing what kind they are of ones experiencing, of ones expressing, very many are not knowing what kind they are of ones experiencing, of ones expressing. In a way David Hersland did know very well what kind he was of ones experiencing, of ones expressing, in a way he never came to be completely certain that he was not perhaps another kind of a one experiencing, another kind of a one expressing.

Some have almost a way of saying what they are meaning. Some have a way of thinking, a way of feeling in them and a way of needing to be meaning something in them and they have for very much of their living almost a way of saying what they are meaning and for part of their living they have a way of saying what they are meaning. Some have a way of feeling something and almost a way of thinking something and they have all their living a way of saying what they are meaning. Some have all their living a way of saying what they are meaning. Some have a way of saying what they are meaning dimly. Some have a way of saying what they are meaning dreamily. Some have a way of saying what they are meaning doubtingly. Some have in their living a way of saying what they are meaning and then they have not a way of saying what they are meaning, they have not then any way for them of saying what they are meaning. Some certainly are slowly coming to a way of saying what they are meaning. Some certainly any time in their being one being living are ones having a way, having ways of saying what they are meaning.

Some certainly are ones feeling completely feeling something, are ones thinking very well about everything, are ones certainly to themselves sometime going to be needing to be ones saying what they are meaning and some of such of them are saying what they are not meaning while they are not saying what they are meaning and some then are not saying anything when they are not saying what they are meaning. Some of such of them are certain that sometime they will be ones saying something saying what they are meaning. Some of such of them are almost certain that they will not ever be saying anything, saying what they are meaning. Some of such of them are sometime saying something, saying what they are meaning, some of such of them are not sometime saying something, saying what they are meaning. David Hersland was not at all one of any such a kind of them.

Some are quite certain that they are knowing what each one saying anything is meaning by what they are saying. David Hersland was in a way one of such of them. Some are quite certain that each one is meaning something when they are saying anything. In a way David Hersland was almost such a one. Some are certain that each one is one wanting to be meaning something by what that one is saying. David Hersland was not such a one, he was somewhat such a one sometimes in his living. Some are certain that each one is one not wanting to be meaning something by what that one is saying. David Hersland was hardly ever at all really such a one. Some are certain that each one is one liking it to be one meaning something by what they are saying when they are saying anything, David Hersland was pretty nearly one of such of them.

Some are believing that mostly every one is meaning the same thing in being one being living. David Hersland could have been one being such a one, David Hersland was not one being such a one. Just the way each one is experiencing what they are experiencing, how much they are experiencing in the way they are experiencing, how much of the time in being one being living they are experiencing much, they are experiencing little, how strongly they are experiencing what they are experiencing in the way they are experiencing and what way and how much they are thinking, what connection there is in them each one between experiencing and thinking, what result it has all in them as meaning and how and when and what way they are telling what they are meaning, that is a thing certainly in each one interesting to some, that is a thing in every one interesting to some, that was a thing certainly completely interesting to Hersland, a thing he needed to have completely interesting to him, a thing about which he was completely thinking and in a way he was one wanting to be needing to be one completely certain that there was not complete interest in him in any such complete realisation, in a way he was one needing to be completely certain that he was complete in needing the realisation of experiencing and thinking and meaning and telling in all men and women, in a way he was one wanting to be needing to be certain to be interested in not being certain that any such realisation would be complete living for him. He was one sometimes in being one being living feeling one way of wanting to be needing to be a complete one and sometimes in being living feeling another way of wanting to be needing completeness in being living, he was one sometimes wanting to be needing not completeness in being one being living. He was one certainly very much an interested one in experiencing, in thinking, in meaning, in telling being in men and in women.

Some one is feeling very strongly about something, that one is thinking about the thing about which that one is having then strong feeling, that one then is telling about the thing about which that one is having then strong feeling. This one is telling about the thing about which that one is having then strong feeling, certainly not any one is having then strong feeling about that thing excepting the one telling about that thing. Not any one perhaps could have strong feeling about that thing excepting the one telling about that thing. There are some who have it in them to have strong feeling about something and perhaps not any one ever being living could be having that kind of a strong feeling about that thing. David Hersland was not such a one. Some one is feeling very strongly about something, that one is thinking about the thing about which that one is having then strong feeling, that one then is telling about the thing about which that one is having then strong feeling. This one is telling about the thing about which that one is having then strong feeling, certainly one other one is having then strong feeling about that thing, the one telling about that thing is having then about that thing strong feeling and another one. David Hersland was not such a one one having strong feeling about something and thinking about that thing and telling about that thing and having one other one having then a strong feeling about that thing. There are some having a strong feeling about something, they are thinking about that thing, they are telling about that thing, there are other ones then having strong feeling about that thing about which these ones, such a one, is feeling a strong feeling, is thinking about, is telling about. David Hersland was one of such of them ones having strong feeling about some thing and thinking about that thing and telling about that thing and these being then some who are having then strong feeling about the thing, about which the one had been having strong feeling, about which that one had been thinking, about which that one had been telling.

Some are remembering how something was happening when they are feeling about that thing, when they are thinking about that thing, when they are telling about that thing. David Hersland was pretty completely one of such of them. Some are remembering what was happening when they are telling about something not when they are feeling about that thing not when they are thinking about that thing. Some are remembering what was happening not when they are telling about that thing, not when they are feeling about that thing, they are remembering what was happening when they are thinking about that thing. Some are remembering what was happening when they are feeling about that thing and not when they are thinking about that thing but when they are telling about that thing. Some are remembering what was happening when they are feeling about a thing and when they are thinking about that thing but not when they are telling about that thing. Some are remembering what was happening when they are feeling about a thing, not when they are telling about the thing, not when they are thinking about the thing.

Some are certainly clearly thinking completely clearly thinking, some have all their living been pretty clearly thinking, some have it to be needing to be to themselves what they are that is one certainly thinking clearly completely clearly about anything about which they are thinking. Some of these certainly are thinking very clearly about anything about which they are clearly thinking, some of these are boasting, not to themselves, some yes to themselves, some to some others, some to very many others, some to one, of this thing. Some are certain that they are not boasting about this thing, some are quite certain they are not boasting about this thing, some who are telling it very much and very often that they certainly are clearly thinking about anything they are thinking and they certainly are thinking clearly about anything about which they are thinking are completely certain that telling about this thing by them to a good many, to every one is not boasting. Some who are clearly thinking, who are thinking clearly about everything about which they are thinking are needing to be certain that they have come to the right conclusion, sometime about everything. David Hersland in a way was not such a one. Some who are thinking clearly about everything about which they are thinking are not certain that they will sometime come to a right conclusion about anything about which they are thinking clearly. Some are certain that if they can keep on clearly thinking they will certainly sometime come to a completely right conclusion about everything about which they are thinking clearly that is about anything about which they are really thinking. David Hersland was in a way not such a one. Some certainly are thinking very clearly about anything about which they are thinking, some certainly can keep on pretty well thinking clearly about everything about which they are thinking.

Each one has his has her own way of being one experiencing in being one being living. Each one is of a kind in men and women, of a kind of way of being one experiencing, of being one experiencing anything, of being one experiencing being one being living.

Each one in some way can know, each one in some way cannot know, each one in some ways does know, each one in some ways does not know of each one some one in some ways can know, some one in some ways cannot know, of each one some can in some way know, some can in some way not know what they are meaning by being one being living, each one, how they are thinking, how much and what way they are boasting, how they can and how they cannot be experiencing, what some other one could be meaning who might be having almost such a being in them as that other one has in them. Certainly some are not thinking about anything and these are ones very clearly certain about many things and are clearly certainly expressing what they are knowing and they are not changing when others are changing. Certainly some are not thinking about anything and they are clearly feeling something and they are clearly telling that thing, and they certainly are not changing when they have not been feeling a new feeling about the thing they have been clearly telling, their feeling. David Hersland might have been one of such of them, he was not one of such of them, he certainly was one thinking about mostly everything about which he was having feeling. He might have been one not thinking about anything but having clearly a feeling about that thing and clearly expressing the feeling he was having and not doing any thinking and not doing any changing and having then more clear feeling and clearly expressing that clear feeling. He might have been such a one. He certainly might have been such a one. He certainly was one having clear feeling about some thing, he was one certainly thinking about things, he certainly was one clearly expressing what he was feeling when he was clearly feeling something, he was one certainly thinking about almost everything, he was one in a way needing to be having complete thinking, he was one not really wanting to be needing complete thinking, he was one certainly thinking about almost everything.

He was certainly to some one in a way boasting about being one being living in being one being the one he was then. To very many he was certainly one not boasting about this thing He was one certainly to himself one sometimes boasting of this thing, he certainly was one liking to be to some, one boasting of this thing.

Mostly every one is needing some one to be one listening to that one being one being one boasting. David Hersland in a way was not one needing one to be one listening to him being one being one boasting. There certainly were some who were listening then to him. He was one in a way not really needing this thing and that was because he was one so clearly telling what he was so clearly feeling. He needed some to be listening while he was thinking, he did have very many to listen while he was thinking, he almost was not needing this thing. Some who are thinking are very much needing some one to be one boastingly listening, some who are thinking are needing some one to be listening to them and saying something and not really saying that thing. Some are needing to be having some one saying something and they are not seriously considering the serious thing they are needing that some one is saying while they are thinking. David Hersland could in a way be one of such of them. Very many are completely ones of such of them.

Thinking, boasting, listening, remembering, forgetting, feeling, and meaning, and telling are in some being living.

Some are certainly completely interested in going on being living, some are not completely interested in this thing, some are almost completely interested in this thing. In a way David Hersland was not completely interested in this thing, in a way he was almost completely interested in this thing.

Some are thinking about being interested in this thing, about being interested in going on being living. Some are telling every one how interesting it is to be interested in this thing. Some are boasting about being completely interested in this thing, some are boasting about not being at all interested in this thing. Sometimes it is astonishing that some one has been forgetting that that one is completely interested in this thing. Some are pretty nearly always remembering that they are completely interested in this thing. Being ones completely interested in being ones going on being living is what very many are certain is not all of living to them. Being ones completely interested in being ones going on being living is what very many are having as very nearly all of living for them. Each one ever living is certainly sometimes completely interested in being one going on being living. David Hersland as I was saying was in a way not completely interested in this thing, was in a way almost completely interested in this thing. He was one certainly talking about this thing, he was one certainly listening to some talking about this thing, he was one certainly sometimes boasting about being one perhaps sometime going to be completely interested in this thing, he was one certainly mostly remembering about being interested in this thing, he was one certainly sometimes quite forgetting about any one being interested in this thing, he could certainly be feeling something about the meaning of this thing, he certainly could do very much thinking about the meaning of this thing.

He could certainly be feeling something about being one going on being living, about any one going on being living, he certainly could think very much and very often about any one being one going on being living. He could certainly feel something about this thing, he could certainly think very much indeed about this thing, he could certainly feel a little something about this thing, he could certainly feel a little something about any one not going on being living, he could certainly think very much about this thing.

Some are thinking very much in being ones being living, some are not thinking very much in being ones being living. Some are thinking very much about being ones going on being living, in being ones being living, some are not thinking very much about being ones going on being living, in being ones being living. Some are feeling very much about being ones going on being living, some are not feeling so much about being ones going on being living. Some are certainly boasting very much about feeling about being ones being going on being living, some are boasting very much about being ones not feeling very much about being ones going on being living. David Hersland went on being living until he was at the ending of the beginning of his middle living and then he was not any longer going on being living.

Some are changing while they are living in their feeling about being one going on being living, about any one being one going on being living. Some are changing very much in their feeling about this thing. Very many are changing very much in their feeling about this thing during the time they are being one being living. Some do not change so very much in their feeling about this thing while they are ones being living. David Hersland certainly changed some in his feeling about this thing while he was one being living, he certainly did not change so very much in his feeling about this thing in being one being living. He was one thinking very much and very often about any one going on being living, he certainly thought very different things about this thing at different times in his being one being living. Each one in a way is feeling something about ones going on being living, about that one being one being living. Certainly each one feels in some way something about such a thing.

Feeling and thinking about ones, about that one being going on living, thinking, boasting, listening, remembering, forgetting, feeling, and meaning, and telling about being one, about being ones going on being living is in some going on being living.

Some are having a very delicate feeling and they are ones that can be thinking and they are ones sometimes delightfully telling something, beautifully telling something, touchingly telling something, quaintly telling something, freshly telling something and they are ones dully telling something and flatly telling scmething and harshly telling something and telling and telling and not telling anything, and telling something so that some one can be saying certainly that one was thinking that other one was not knowing anything and certainly the one was knowing that that one was certain that the one was not knowing anything. Some are having quite a delicate feeling and they are often thinking and they are telling what they are meaning and certainly it is sometimes quite a beautiful telling they are doing and certainly sometimes not a beautiful telling that they are doing. Some are feeling very delicately and they are thinking and they are completely telling very beautifully something. Some are feeling delicately and they are not doing very much thinking and they are sometimes quite beautifully telling something. David Hersland was not of any of these kinds of them. Some are not feeling delicately about anything and they are thinking very much and very often and they are sometimes almost beautifully telling about something. Some are not feeling at all delicately about something and they are thinking very much and very often and they are persisting and they are sometimes almost really completely beautifully telling something, almost beautifully telling something, almost completely telling something, almost beautifully completely telling something. David Hersland was not of any such a kind in men and women. Some are certainly quite not having any delicate feeling about anything and they are persisting and they have complete realisation of being one loving everything and they are thinking very much and very often and they are quite completely delicately thinking and such of them can be ones succeeding very well in being ones being living, they can be ones not feeling beautifully or delicately about anything, they can be ones succeeding very well in being ones going on being living, they can be ones living very completely to be ones teaching being good ones in being ones going on being living. David Hersland was not one of such of them. Some are feeling delicately about something and are not feeling delicately about any other thing, some are feeling delicately and sensitively and completely about some things and not about other things, some of these are thinking very much and very often, some of these are almost completely telling beautifully about something, David Hersland was in a way one of such of them.

Some are thinking to make a thing a complete thing more when they are younger ones than when they are older ones. Some are thinking to make anything a complete thing more when they are older ones than when they are younger ones. Some are wanting to be needing to think some thing to be a complete thing more when they are younger ones than when they are older ones, some more when they are older ones than when they are younger ones. Some are needing to be thinking a thing a complete thing when they are younger ones and when they are older ones. Some certainly are all their living needing to be thinking something to be a complete thing, some are certainly needing all their living to be thinking everything to be a complete thing. Some are certainly all their living wanting to be needing to be thinking everything to be to them a complete thing, some are certainly all their living wanting to be needing to think some thing out to be a complete thing. David Hersland was certainly sometimes in his being one being living almost needing to be thinking something out to be a complete thing, he certainly was in his younger living, he certainly was sometimes in his older living needing to be sometimes thinking everything out to be a complete thing. He was not in his living ever completely wanting to be needing to be thinking everything out to be a complete thing, he was certainly in his living, in his younger living certainly and perhaps in his later living almost completely wanting to be needing to be thinking something out as a complete thing.

David Hersland was of a kind in men and women having it in them to have feeling clearly in them, to be telling clearly the feeling they have in them, to have very much feeling in them and to have it in them, some of them, very often. David Hersland was one who was thinking very much and very often and he was certainly thinking very clearly when he was thinking and he certainly was thinking very much in being one being living. He was one in a way needing to be thinking out a thing to be a complete thing. He was one feeling clearly, telling clearly what he was clearly feeling, he was one feeling very much and very often. He was one wanting to be needing to be feeling having every woman being in some ways a beautiful one. He was one feeling very much and very often, he was one feeling clearly and completely what he was feeling. He was one telling clearly what he was feeling. He was one thinking clearly very much and very often. He was one in a way needing to be one thinking things to be completed things, he was one then making anything a transparent thing and then it was a little a confused thing for certainly he was wanting to be needing to be feeling that any woman was in some ways a really beautiful one. He was one clearly thinking clearly feeling and doing both very much and very often and that together made it that he was one needing in a way to be thinking everything to be a completed thing and in a way then he was not succeeding in being in living for then he came to be one making everything a pretty transparent thing, a thing so clear that it was a sparkling thing, a thing so clear that it did not have beginning or middle or ending and as I was saying it was not a completely clear thing as certainly he was pretty completely wanting to be needing to be feeling that any woman that could ever be existing was in some way a really beautiful thing.

David Hersland was not any longer living and some one had a trunk that he had had and always liked to use it when that one was travelling. Some one was very indignant that he had come to be a dead one and almost went out to where he was not any longer living to complain to some one about this thing. Some one knew only some time later after David Hersland was not any longer living that he was not any longer living and that one felt it to be a completely strange thing that David Hersland was not any longer living and after that it was not a strange thing and after that it was not a real thing as certainly he could not have been one being living, and after that there was another one very much like David Hersland and that one was already not any longer living the one like David Hersland before the one who had known David Hersland knew about this one. There was another one who had certainly been one going to be very sorry if anything happened to David Hersland and that one was sorry when David Hersland came to be a dead one. There was one who was excited about David Hersland having come to be a dead one because David Hersland certainly might have been going on being living if he had not come to be a dead one. This one was excited again and again about this thing. There was one who was tenderly completely a sad one and then always was about this thing about David Hersland being a dead one a tenderly complete sad one. David Hersland then in a way was one having been living in being living. David Hersland was of a kind in men and women. There are many kinds in men and women. Each kind has a way of thinking, of feeling, of experiencing anything.

Some have babies in being one being living, some do not have any of them, David Hersland never had any of them. Some would like to have them, some would not like to have them. David Hersland was never really wanting to be needing to have much feeling about having babies in being one being living. He did not have any of them. He did not ever come to have very much feeling about he himself having them. He could come to have feeling about some needing to be wanting to be having some of them, about some needing to be wanting not to be having some of them.

Some do have many of them. Some do not have many of them. Certainly some completely do not want to have any of them, some almost completely do not want to have any of them, some certainly completely want to have some of them, some certainly completely want to have one of them, some certainly completely want to have many of them, some almost completely want to have many of them, some almost completely want to have some of them. Certainly very many are interested in some wanting, in some not wanting to have any of them, some are not at all interested in anybody wanting in anybody not wanting to have any of them. David Hersland was certainly not completely, not almost completely interested in anybody wanting in anybody not wanting any of them. Being a baby was not to him completely interesting. It was not to him completely uninteresting, certainly not completely uninteresting, really certainly not completely uninteresting.

David Hersland was certainly one needing to be saying something about babies and men and babies and women. Babies and men and babies and women were not to him completely interesting. He certainly sometimes was talking and certainly sometimes was listening to talking about babies and women, about babies and men. Babies and men, and babies and women were not to him almost completely interesting. He certainly sometimes and sometimes quite often talked very much about babies and men, and babies and women. Certainly many are talking sometimes and sometimes very often about something and that thing is not to them completely interesting and that thing is not to them almost completely interesting and they are liking very well the talking they are doing about this thing and they are liking very well the listening they are doing to any one talking about this thing. Certainly then babies, having them, not having them was not completely an interesting thing to David Hersland was not almost completely an interesting thing to him.

Some things were completely interesting things to David Hersland, some things were almost completely interesting things to him, some things he was wanting to be having as completely interesting things to him, some things were almost completely not interesting things to him.

Certainly some remembered that David Hersland had said something sometimes about any one having, about any one not having, not going to be having, going to be having, having had, not having had, liking, not liking having babies. Certainly some remembered what David Hersland had been saying about such a thing and some were talking quite often about what he had been saying about such a thing and some were certainly talking quite often about such a thing and not then any more remembering very much about what he had said about such a thing and some were not then, some of such of them, remembering that he had talked sometimes about such a thing and some were, some of such of them, were remembering very well that he had some times been talking about such a thing. He certainly had been talking some sometimes about such a thing, he certainly sometimes was convincing some one of something when he was talking about such a thing.

Certainly every one can have been one, can be one imagining something, some are imagining everything to be anything, some are very carefully imagining something to be anything, some are dreamily imagining something to be anything, some are daintily imagining anything to be something, some are very carefully imagining again and again the same thing to be something, some have earnest feeling in imagining everything to be anything, some have a tired feeling in imagining something to be anything. Some are telling very much and very often the way they were, the way they are, the way they will be imagining anything to be something, some are very much interested in their being one having been, being, going to be being one imagining everything to be something some are very much interested in their own imagining everything being something and in every one else's imagining everything being something, some find it very interesting that every one else is imagining everything being something. Some were imagining some things being some things when they were young ones and then were imagining everything being something when they were older ones. Some are talking very much and very often about being one being imagining in being one being living. Some are very convincing in being one telling about being one being imagining in being living.

Sometime each one has been telling very much and very often what that one is thinking about that one being one being imagining in living, being one talking in living, being one listening in living, being one succeeding in living, being one failing in living. Sometime each one has been telling very much and very often about living having been, about living being in that one.

Some have been doing something very often, they have been doing that thing very much and very often and yet they are not then knowing being in being one doing that thing, that is to say some one may be one living all the living of that one doing some one thing again and again with many men and many women and this one then has not been learning anything about how to be one doing that thing. Some one might be one ruining many men and many women certainly was one ruining one and certainly then that one might be one not knowing anything about ruining about not ruining any one, might be one certainly not knowing anything about ruining men and women, might certainly be one not knowing anything of being being in men and women who are who are not ruined by that one, in short it is sometimes surprising how some are not being ones having had experience in being ones doing something when they have been ones doing something. Some have been ones doing something and really then they have not very often done that thing. It is surprising very often how some who have been ones doing something have been ones very rarely doing that thing, and some who have been ones doing something have been doing that thing very often.

Every one certainly is telling very much and very often everything in being one being living and some are listening to some and some are listening to many and some are not doing very much listening and some are listening more and then are listening less and some are talking more and some are talking less and each one is one being living and then each one is one going on being living all the time that one is one being living, and each one is sometime a young one and each one is sometime quite a young one.

Some are jumping when they are young ones, jumping from a place and are landing way below from where they were jumping and it is a pretty thing to see them doing, and many of them when they are doing this thing are not hurting themselves in landing. Certainly very many when they are young ones are jumping a long distance and are landing somewhere and to some of such of them it is not an important thing at all to be knowing where they are going to be landing when they are beginning jumping. Some are certain that not any one is such a one when they are a young one, some are certain that every one when they are jumping even when they are quite young ones have it that it is to them an important thing to be certain that they can be landing safely somewhere below the place from which they have been jumping. Some are certain that mostly every one when they are young ones are ones jumping and not being ones being interested in knowing that they will be landing somewhere and not be ones having been hurt by jumping. Some are quite certain that being young ones is being in some way in being living, some are quite certain that being young ones is in some one way of being in being living and in others another way of being in being living. Some are quite certain that there are some ways in being living that every one being a young one has then in that one. Some are certain that this is not a true thing. Some are certain that not any one being a young one, having been a young one has been then one saying a certain thing, some are quite certain that mostly every one having been a young one is one then not saying a certain thing. Each one being in being living having been a young one is remembering, is not remembering having been being then. Some are certain that not any one is remembering very much in having been a young one, some are certain that every one is remembering very much in having been a young one. Some are certain that they are remembering completely having been a young one and then some one who was a young one too then is remembering and that then makes it to the first one that that one really is not at all remembering being living in being a young one. Sometimes this is a pleasant thing, sometimes it is a thing indifferent to that one, sometimes it is a thing making that one feel a feeling of being one having been existing without having been one going on in being one being living. Some are not listening to other ones remembering being a young one, some are listening very often to other ones remembering being a young one. Each one being living is certainly one having been one going on being living.

Many when they are being young ones are talking very much and very often, many when they are being young ones are ones going on being livng, many when they are being young ones are sometimes ones not going on being living. Many when they are young ones are being ones going on being living and they are then remembering this thing and they are then forgetting this thing and they are sometimes ones telling something about being ones not going on being living.

Some are certainly not remembering being ones being young ones, some are certainly remembering and very clearly remembering and remembering completely being young ones in being living. Many are quite certain they are remembering being young ones in being living. Many are completely certain they are not remembering being young ones in being living. Some are remembering some one being a young one in being living, some are not remembering any one being a young one in being living.

David Hersland in the beginning of his being living was being a young one. There were others then being young ones. Some had then one way of being in being young ones and others had then other ways of being in being young ones and David Hersland was a young one then and later some of them remembered their being in being young ones then and some did not remember much of their being in being young ones then. David Hersland remembered some of them being in being young ones then, something of some of them, a little something of being a young one then, certainly something of being being in him when he was being a young one and sometimes he was one quite certainly remembering being in being a young one and sometimes he was one quite certainly not remembering being in him as being in him in being a young one. Certainly some are remembering better than others being young ones in being living.

There are such very different ways of feeling any one being a dead one and any one being a living one at different times in being one being living. Certainly to very many being living when they are being young ones being a dead one is a thing that is a thing a little terrifying, not very exciting, quite interesting, not happening, certainly not happening. To some it is a thing completely terrifying when they are young ones, certainly not happening, certainly not interesting, certainly very often being a thing that one is a good deal remembering. To some when they are young ones it is a thing happening, it is a thing terrifying them, it is a thing mostly forgotten, it is a thing quite interesting. To some it is a thing completely forgotten, quite interesting, not happening, might be quite terrifying. To some it is a thing, when they are young ones, needing to be then completely forgotten, sometimes then completely desolating, sometimes then making in that one that that one is wanting to be certain that it is something not happening, is something not happening, is something that that one is finding interesting, is something that that one is then a good deal forgetting.   In a way David Hersland was such a kind of one.

Some when they are being young ones are certainly not certain that anything is not existing and then they certainly are certain that not anything is existing and then they are wanting to be needing that anything being that anything not being existing is a thing completely interesting to them and then it is not really at all then completely interesting to them and these are ones being ones going on being living some of them and David Hersland was one of such of them.

Certainly there are very many who being young ones are not certain about anything being existing, anything being not existing and are sometimes feeling completely in them about such a thing.   There are some who when they are young ones are not certain about anything being existing, about anything being not existing and are not feeling anything at all in them about any such thing.   Certainly some when they are young ones are quite certain that everything is existing, certainly some when they are young ones are wanting to be needing to be quite certain that not anything is existing.

There are certainly very many going on being living when they are young ones, a very great many being young ones are being then ones going on being living.   Some are certainly then and later remembering having been ones then going on being living, certainly some then and later are not remembering having been then ones going on being living.   Some are remembering then when they are young ones going on being living are remembering it then that they are young ones going on being living and then later are forgetting that they were remembering this thing when they were young ones.   David Hersland might have been one of such of them.

There are a very great many being young ones and there are a great many having been being young ones.   David Hersland knew some who were being young ones and he was a young one then, David Hersland knew some being young ones and he was not really being a young one then.   There certainly have been and are being very many being young ones.   Each one has their own way of having it in them being a young one when that one is being a young one.

Certainly some are ones having been young ones and ones then having been talking very much and jumping very much and being then being ones almost completely ones certain then that they were ones completely feeling being ones talking and being ones jumping.   Very many certainly are not when they are young ones feeling themselves to be completely ones then jumping then talking.   Some are ones certainly not altogether completely then, when they are young ones, feeling themselves then in being being ones jumping then, being ones talking then, being ones then completely jumping and talking.   Very many later are remembering themselves having been ones feeling themselves being completely one jumping completely one talking when they were young ones. Some are certainly being ones when they are young ones doing very much jumping doing very much talking then when they are young ones, some of such of them are certainly then feeling themselves to be ones pretty nearly completely ones being ones talking being ones jumping, some of such of them are certainly then not completely then feeling themselves ones being completely ones being jumping, completely ones being talking. Certainly very many when they are being young ones are ones then talking then and jumping then and certainly some of such of them are ones certainly feeling themselves being completely then ones talking, ones jumping. Some and certainly some of them are ones that are not ones anybody would be thinking were feeling themselves being such ones are ones not feeling themselves at all being ones completely jumping completely talking when they were being young ones. In a way Hersland was such a kind of a one. In a way he was one certainly not one completely feeling being one jumping being one talking when he was being a young one. In a way he was very nearly completely feeling himself being one being talking being one being jumping when he was being a young one. Certainly he was quite a good deal one being one feeling being completely one jumping completely one talking then when he was a young one. Each one certainly is one being a young one when that one is one beginning being living. Some are remembering being one beginning being living, some are not remembering being one beginning being living. Some are ones who might be remembering and were and some are ones who might be remembering and were not. In a way David Hersland was one of such of them. In a way he was one who might have been remembering he was a young one and very much he was one not remembering. He certainly was one knowing very many when he was a young one many who were then being ones being young ones.

Some are saying some one looks like some one and then some other one says yes and then they are both laughing and then they are telling another one about this thing and they are all then laughing and laughing and they keep on then for a very long time laughing and beginning telling one another about this thing and sometimes then they are not telling one another about this thing and sometimes they are not then telling some other one about this thing but certainly then they can be, they are laughing then. Some are telling that some one is like some one and that one telling that thing has angry feeling and is getting having more and more angry feeling in telling this thing while the one that one is telling this thing is certainly not saying that this one is finding a resemblance that is convincing to this one. Sometimes some are beginning telling about something and then certainly a number are saying something and certainly very many of them are having then angry feeling and they are then talking and talking and talking and telling that thing and every minute each one of them is having angry feeling. Certainly some are talking each one about a thing and each one is having angry feeling and they are ones going to be playing something then and certainly mostly each one of them is talking then and certainly mostly each one of them is having angry feeling in them and perhaps it is quite exciting to all of them then and perhaps it is not really exciting to most of them then. Certainly some are talking very long times and quite often and another one is with them and is talking very long times and quite often and another one and another one is with them and each one of them is certainly talking very long times and quite often. Certainly each one being living is beginning being living and certainly some of such of them are doing these things in being ones being then being living.

David Hersland was one being one beginning being living and there were others then being ones beginning being living and they sometimes were with each other then and sometimes some were with some then and others were with others then. Certainly each one every one being living is being one sometime beginning being living and this is in different ways in them in each one ever living.

To some certainly not any one is ever a young one. To some not anyone is certainly to themselves inside them a young one. Some are certain that not any one is ever to themselves inside them a young one. Some are doubting whether any one is to themselves inside them to themselves then a young one. Some are certain that no one is ever to themselves inside them a young one. Certainly not any one is being to themselves a young one inside them to some. Certainly any one is being to themselves a young one inside them to some. To some, certainly not any one is ever a young one. To some certainly every one is sometime a young one. To some every one is sometimes a young one.

Certainly each one has a way of feeling about young being, about beginning being living in that one, in every one. There are certainly very different ways of feeling about being young ones, about anybody being a young one, about that one being a young one, about anybody having been a young one, about that one having been a young one.

Certainly each one is beginning being living when they are beginning being ones being living. Certainly some are not to themselves in being living being young ones. Certainly some are to themselves in a way in being living young ones. Some perhaps are to themselves in being living in the beginning of being living really being young ones. Each one ever living is certainly sometime beginning being in living. There are certainly many ways of being to oneself in being one beginning being living. To some certainly not any one is ever a young one. Certainly not any one is one being to themselves a young one inside them to some. To some certainly not any one is ever a young one. Certainly each one is one beginning being living. Certainly not every one is to themselves inside them then one beginning being living. Not every one is one to themselves inside them having been beginning being living. Certainly in a way David Hersland was such a one, he certainly in a way was such a one one certain in a way that not any one is ever a young one. He was one in a way not ever to himself inside him one being a young one. Certainly there are very many being ones and always there are very many of them and very many of them are such of them are ones being certain then that not any one is ever a young one, being certain then that one is not then a young one, being certain then that one is not one having been a young one. David Hersland was one being once beginning being in living. There were very many then being ones beginning being in living, some of them were in a way young ones then inside them to them, some of them were not in a way young ones then inside them to them.

Being one needing to be listening to some one is being in some when they are young ones, when they are older ones, when they are middle aged ones, when they are old ones. Being one needing to be listening to some one is what very many being in living are being in being one being living. Certainly very many are ones needing to be listening to some one to be ones certain to themselves to be ones going on being living, going to be going on being living. Some are needing being one listening to some one while they are young ones, while they are older ones, while they are begining being in middle living and then they are ones listening to some one and some of such of them are then ones not needing to be listening to some one. Some are needing some one to be very convincing in being one to whom they are listening. Some are certainly needing this thing very much in being one being living. Some are needing this thing sometimes in being one being living. Some are needing this thing and are needing it again and again. Some are not needing this thing but it is certainly a comforting thing to them to be having this thing. Some are having this thing and it is a comforting thing to them and they are wanting to be needing this thing. Some are wanting to be needing this thing and they are almost needing this thing. Some are wanting not to be needing this thing. Some are having some one being a convincing one to whom they are listening and it is then almost a comforting thing to them and they are then ones wanting to be needing this thing and then it is coming to be in them that they are not having this thing. In a way David Hersland was one of such of them, in a way it was something he was having and it was then in a way a comforting thing to him and then in a way he was wanting to be needing this thing and then in a way he was certain not to be having any more of this thing and of their being some one being convincing to whom he was listening. When he was a young one he was almost knowing that he was wanting to be needing this thing, when he was an older one he was knowing that he was having this thing and having it again and again, when he was older he was knowing that he was wanting to be needing this thing and that certainly he was not going to be having anything of this thing and perhaps he was then going to be completely needing this thing and perhaps he was going to be then not at all needing this thing, and then he did not go on being one being living.

Certainly he was one being living when he was being a young one, he was often then quite certainly one being almost completely interested in being one being living, he was then quite often wanting to be one being completely interested in being one being living, he was then one quite often almost completely interested in being one being living. He certainly then went on being living, he did this thing certainly all of his being living in being in young living. He certainly when he was a young one was needing then sometimes to be sure that he was one being living, this is certainly what some being living are needing when they are ones being young ones in being living. David Hersland certainly was one almost completely one being living when he was being a young one. Some he was knowing then were certainly being completely living then and being then being young ones in being living. Some he was knowing then were not quite completely being ones being living then, some were quite a good deal not being ones being completely living then when they were being young ones in being living. David Hersland did a good deal of living in being living then when he was a young one. He was knowing very many then and very many knew him then. He remembered some of them in his later living and he did not remember some of them. He certainly was one almost completely then interested in being one being living then.

Certainly every one being living is being one going on being living and some are then knowing that thing and some are then not knowing that thing and some are remembering doing that thing and some are not remembering having been doing that thing having been going on being living. Certainly every one being living is one going on being living, certainly very many are not remembering having been doing that thing, certainly very many are remembering having been being doing that thing. Certainly every one living is one going on being living, certainly every one having been living is one having been going on being living. Certainly every one being living is one going on being living. Some are doing some things then, some are not doing some things then, some are enjoying some things then, some are not enjoying some things then. Some are certainly needing to be ones knowing they are being ones going on being living, are needing to be doing some things that are things that are making them be feeling that they are being ones going on being living by being, things that any one is needing to be one going on being living, that is breathing and breathing and breathing. There are very many such of them always being existing, there are very many certainly knowing then that they are ones going on being living then when they are doing more breathing than just breathing in being living. Very many are doing very much breathing to be ones knowing they are going on being living, very many are certain to be ones going on being living when they have been regularly doing more breathing than breathing to be being living. Some certainly are liking very much being living doing this thing. Quite a number are liking very much being living doing this thing being ones knowing then being one going on being living.

To some certainly every one is always a young one. To some certainly some one is almost always a young one. Certainly any one being living is then one going on being living. Certainly some are breathing more than they are always breathing and certainly some of such of them are ones knowing then that they are ones going on being living. Some are knowing they are ones going on being living when they are young ones, some are not knowing they are ones going on being living when they are young ones, some are ones not knowing it then when they are ones going on being living in being young ones, some are ones knowing it then when they are young ones knowing that they are ones going on being living then.

Some when they are being young ones are liking being ones going on being living, some when they are being young ones are not liking it being ones going on being living. Certainly some are then wanting to be liking being one going on being living, some are certainly then not wanting to be liking being one going on being living, certainly going on being living. David Hersland was sometimes not liking being one going on being living, he certainly was one sometimes, almost always, liking being one going on being living then. He certainly was one going on being living then, he certainly was sometimes knowing this thing then, he certainly was sometimes almost knowing this thing then. He was doing some things then and some others were doing some things then and he was doing some things and some others were doing the things he was wanting to be needing to be doing then, and he was doing some things then, and he was doing some things he was needing to be doing then and some others did things then when he was doing things, and some were doing things then and he was going to be doing things then, and he was doing things then and some others were doing things then and some others were going to be doing things then, and some were doing things and he was doing things and some others were doing things and he was going to be doing things and he was needing to be doing things and he was doing things and he was wanting to be doing things and he was doing things and some others were doing things and some others were going to be doing things and some others were wanting to be doing things and some others were doing things and some others were needing to be doing things and some others were doing things and some others were doing things.

Certainly some when they are ones being dreaming and they are young ones then and ones being dreaming then are ones then not dreaming then about anything. There are certainly some being young ones and ones being dreaming then and they are then not being ones dreaming then about anything. There are some being ones being dreaming and they are young ones then and some of them are ones dreaming then about something, certainly some of them who are ones being one being dreaming and being ones being then young ones are ones dreaming then about something. Some certainly are ones being dreaming when they are ones being young ones and some of such of them are ones being ones not dreaming then of anything and some are ones certainly some of them are ones dreaming of something. Some when they are being ones being young ones are ones sometimes then being ones being dreaming and some of such of them are ones dreaming then of something, sometimes when they are then ones dreaming then and sometimes are ones not dreaming of anything when they are ones being young ones and being sometimes then ones being dreaming.

One is doing something and then doing that thing again and then doing another thing and then doing that thing again and then doing the one thing and then the other thing and that one certainly would be doing some other thing and doing that thing again and would be then doing another thing and would be doing that thing again and would then be doing the one thing and then would be doing the other if that one were not doing the things that one is doing in being one being living. Certainly some are doing something and doing that thing and doing another thing and certainly some are completely ones needing to be ones doing that thing and that thing again and then some other thing and then that other thing again and then one thing and then another and then another thing to be ones being being ones living. Certainly some are doing something and are doing it again and are doing another thing and are doing it again and are doing the one thing and are doing the other thing and are completely wanting to be needing to be doing the one thing and the other thing to be one being living. There are some that certainly are almost completely wanting that they should be ones needing to be one doing one thing, to be one doing that thing again, to be one doing another thing, to be one doing that again, to be one doing the one thing and the other thing, to be one needing doing the one thing and the other thing to be one being living. There are some who are almost completely wanting that they should be one who is one that is needing being one doing the one thing and doing it again and doing another thing and doing it again and doing the one thing and the other thing to be one being living. Certainly each one being living is doing something and doing another thing and the one thing again and the other thing again and the one thing and the other thing and something and that thing again and something. Each one being living is one being one doing something and doing it again and another thing and something and another thing and doing something and doing another thing again. Each one being living is one doing something and doing that thing and another thing and that thing and another thing and another thing and that thing and another thing and another thing again. Certainly each one living is one in some way doing something, doing another thing, in some way needing doing something, doing another thing, in some way wanting to be needing doing something, doing another thing, doing another thing and doing something again and another thing again and another thing again. Some are certainly needing to be ones doing something and they are doing one thing and doing it again and again and again and again and they are doing another thing and they are doing it again and again and again and they are doing another thing and they are doing it again and again and again and such a one might have been one doing a very different thing then and doing another very different thing then and doing another very different thing then and doing that then each or any one of them and doing it again and again and again. Certainly some are ones being living and are ones being ones doing something and doing it very well in doing it again and again and again. Certainly some are ones being living and are ones doing something and doing it well and not doing it well in doing it again and again and again and again. Certainly some are ones being and are ones doing something and are ones doing it quite well and are ones doing it quite well in doing it again and are ones doing it again and again. Some are ones being living and doing something and are doing that thing and are doing some other thing and are doing some other thing and certainly they are then doing some other thing and certainly they are doing each thing and hardly any one is doing anything better than such a one is doing anything. There are some being living and they are doing something and they are doing that thing and they are going on doing that thing and then they are not any longer doing that thing. Some are quite doing something in being living. Some are being living and are quite steadily and completely doing something. Some are being living and they are then doing something and they are then doing that thing again. Some are being living and certainly they are ones doing something and are then ones being living. Certainly each one being living is one in some way doing something in some way being living to some in being one doing something, is in some way being living inside that one in being one doing something, is in some way needing being being living, is in some way needing being doing something, is in some way wanting to be needing being doing something. Each one being living is one doing something and doing it again and doing some other thing and doing it again and doing the one thing and doing the other thing and doing another thing and doing one thing and the other thing and doing another thing and doing it again.

Certainly some are ones completely being living to themselves inside them. Some of such of them are ones being ones doing some thing and another thing and doing the one thing and the other thing and doing them again and doing them again and doing them again and again. Certainly some are ones completely being living and they are this thing to themselves then, they are this thing to some other one, they are ones being completely living in being ones being living and doing something and another thing and another thing and doing some of them again and again and again and again. Certainly some are ones being ones completely being living and when they are ones being living and are ones being completely living in doing something and doing that thing again and doing some other thing and doing that thing again and again and again and being one doing such a thing again and doing some other such thing and doing it again and again and again and again and being one being one completely living and being such a one to every one, certainly to any one knowing that one, knowing anything of that one.

There are some when they are being living and when they are beginning being living are ones completely being living and are ones completely being living to themselves then and to mostly every one and are ones being completely being living doing many things and doing them, most of them, very often. There certainly are some being living who are ones certainly being ones completely being living and are such ones and any one can be completely certain of this thing being one knowing such a one, being one knowing any one knowing such a one. Certainly there are very many being completely living in being living and are such to any one and are ones doing some thing and another and another thing and doing one again and again and again and doing the other thing again and again and doing the other thing again and again and again. Certainly there are some being ones completely being living in being living and doing something and doing it again and again and doing another thing of the same kind of thing and doing it again and being one being completely living in being one being living. Certainly some are ones completely being living in being living and are such ones to any one, to every one and certainly there are ones being living not being ones completely living that is not to some knowing them knowing of them and some of such of them are ones certainly doing something and certainly doing another thing of the same kind and another one of the same kind and doing each one of them very much and very often and again and again and again and again. Certainly some are ones being ones completely being living to themselves in being living and some knowing them are certain that this is not being in them in some of such of them that they are ones being completely living in being living. There certainly are ones who are ones not being completely living in being living to themselves then and some are certainly certain that some of such of them are ones being completely being living in being living and some are certainly certain that some of such of them are not ones being completely living in being living. Certainly each one being living is beginning being living and some are then knowing this thing and some are not then knowing this thing, those being in being beginning being living. Some who are beginning being living are then knowing that thing. Some who are beginning being living are then not knowing that thing. Some beginning being living are almost then knowing that thing. Certainly some beginning being living are quite certainly not knowing anything at all of any such thing being in being living. Certainly there are many ways of being ones being completely living in being living, being ones not completely living in being living. There are certainly many ways of being ones completely being living in being young ones, there are certainly many ways of being ones not completely being living in being young ones.

When one is a young one one is a young one. Certainly when one is a young one one is then a young one. In a way one is knowing then that one is not then a young one, in a way one is knowing it then that one is then a young one. When one is a middle aged one one is then a middle aged one. In a way one is knowing then that one is then a middle aged one, in a way one is knowing then that one is not then a middle aged one. When one is an old one one is then an old one. In a way one is knowing then that one is then an old one, in a way one is knowing then that one is not then an old one.

When one is a young one one is a young one. Certainly when one is a young one one is then a young one. In a way one is knowing then that one is then a young one, in a way one is knowing then that one is not then a young one. When one is an older one one is then an older one. One is then in a way knowing then that one is then an older one, one is then in a way knowing then that one is not then an older one.

When one is a young one one is a young one. When one is a young one one is certainly then in a way a young one. When one is a young one one is certainly in a way then not a young one.

When one is a young one one is a young one. One is a young one and is then in some ways then not a young one. One is a young one and is in some ways then a young one.

One is a young one and one is knowing in some way that one is a young one. One is a young one and one is knowing in some way that one is not a young one.

One is a young one and is knowing that one is not a young one and is knowing that one is a young one. One is an older one and is knowing that one is an older one and is knowing that one is not an older one. One is a middle aged one and is knowing that one is a middle aged one and is knowing that one is not a middle aged one. One is an older one and is knowing that one is a middle aged one and is knowing that one is not a middle aged one. One is an older one and is knowing that one is not an older one and is knowing that one is an old one. One is an old one and is knowing one is an old one and is knowing that one is not an old one. One is an older one and is not knowing one is an older one and is knowing one is an older one. One is a very old one and one is knowing one is a very old one and is not knowing one is a very old one. One is an older one and is knowing one is an older one and is not knowing one is an older one. One is a young one and one is and one is not knowing one is a young one. One is a young one and one is knowing one is not a young one and one is knowing that one is a young one. One is a young one and is then knowing that one is a young one and is then knowing that one is not a young one.

One is a young one and is knowing and is not knowing then that that one is then a young one. One is a young one and is knowing then that that one is not a young one, is knowing then that that one is then a young one.

David Hersland was a young one, he was knowing he was then a young one, he was knowing that he was then not a young one. He knew some who were young ones then. Some of them were knowing then that they were young ones then and knowing then that they were not young ones then.

Every one is doing something in being a young one in being living. Some are jumping and some are then not jumping very much and some are not jumping well enough then so that they are interested in doing that thing, and some are jumping then and it is an extraordinary thing that they can do that thing so wonderfully, the thing they are doing then, the jumping they are doing then. Some are jumping then and mostly not any one is jumping a longer distance than they are jumping. Some are jumping and they go on jumping and it is certainly very satisfying to be one then jumping. Some are jumping and certainly it is a very wonderful thing the jumping they are doing. Some are jumping and anybody would be satisfied with jumping in such a way unless they were ones jumping in quite a different way. Some are ones jumping very well and it is quite interesting being jumping then and certainly not any one would not be an interested one in being one jumping in the way these are jumping, David Hersland was one of such of them. Certainly he was jumping and jumping very well and jumping quite often. Some when they are jumping are wonderfully jumping. David Hersland knew some of such of them. Every one is doing something in being a young one in being living. Very many are jumping then and David Hersland was jumping then and he jumped very well and was quite interested in jumping then. Some jump quite wonderfully when they are jumping. Some are interested in such jumping, some are wanting to be doing such jumping. David Hersland was interested in such jumping, he was almost wanting to be doing such jumping. He jumped very well when he was one doing jumping, he was not feeling very much about wanting to be doing wonderful jumping. He did extremely good jumping when he was one doing jumping.

Every one is doing something in being a young one in being living. Mostly every one is doing something when they are being one being young ones. Certainly jumping is doing something. Some are doing a good deal of jumping when they are young ones. Some are doing then very wonderful jumping. Some are jumping very well then. David Hersland jumped very well then.

Each one when that one is a young one is knowing then that that one is a young one, is knowing then that that one is not a young one, each one when that one is a young one is not knowing then that that one is then a young one, is not knowing then that that one is then a young one.

Some when they are young ones are knowing then very well that every one is certain to be sometime a young one. Some when they are young ones are feeling that they are then completely knowing this thing. In a way they are completely then knowing this thing, in a way they are not completely then knowing this thing. Some are certainly when they are young ones not in any way completely knowing the thing that every one is sometime a dead one. Very many are in some way knowing this thing that every one is sometime being a dead one, very many are knowing something of this thing when they are being young in being living. Very many are not knowing very much about every one being a young one, very many when they are young ones are not then knowing very much about this thing. Very many are not knowing very much about every one being a dead one, very many when they are young ones are not then knowing very much about this thing. Certainly David Hersland in a way knew almost completely then when he was a young one that every one would sometime be a dead one, in a way he did not at all completely know about this thing about every one coming to be sometime a dead one, then when he was being a young one in being living. There were very many being young ones in being living then when David Hersland was being a young one in being living. David Hersland knew some who were being young ones when he was being a young one, he knew some of them and he was with some of them some of the time then and he did some things with some of them and he did not do some things with some of them and he certainly talked enough then with some of them and he did not talk very much to some of them and he was going to talk some with some of them and he certainly would have liked sometimes not to have talked much with some of them, but mostly he talked a good deal with a good many of them and he mostly always could have talked more with most of them and certainly he did not talk to some and he would have liked to have talked to them but mostly he talked a good deal with a good many of them and he did things with some of them and he was being young in his living when others were being young in their living and he knew a good many of such of them and he did some things with them and he talked some with them and he certainly did know some of them being young ones in their living when he was being a young one in his living.

Some do not do things very much with others who are being young ones in living when they are being young ones in being. Some do very much do things with others who are being young ones in living when they are being young ones in being living. David Hersland did things a good deal with some who were being young ones in being living when he was a young one in being living, he did not do some things with any one who were being young ones in being living when he was a young one in being living.

Certainly every one who is being is being living. Certainly some are certain that in being living they are ones feeling that being living is some thing. Certainly some being living are feeling that being living is something. Certainly very many in being living are feeling that being living is something. Very many are feeling that being living is a thing making of them ones being existing. Some are feeling that being living is a thing not making of them ones being existing. Certainly being existing is something very many are feeling in being ones being living. Certainly very many are very often doing something, certainly very many are going on living for quite a long time. Certainly very many are always feeling themselves then being existing. Certainly very many are certain that being existing is something. Certainly some are sometimes feeling that being existing is almost not something. Certainly some are sometimes feeling that being existing is not something. Certainly quite a number being living are feeling that being existing is not anything. Certainly a very great number are feeling that being existing is something. Certainly David Hersland was sometimes feeling that being existing is something. Certainly David Hersland was sometimes feeling that being living is not something. Some are quite certain that being existing is not anything. David Hersland was almost certain of this thing that being existing is not anything. Some are certain that being existing is something. Certainly David Hersland could be almost being certain of this thing that being existing is something. David Hersland when he was a young one could be feeling that he was completely certain that being existing is not anything. David Hersland when he was a young one was feeling that he was as nearly certain, as any one could be who was not completely certain, that being existing is not anything. David Hersland was feeling when he was a young one that he might come to be certain that being existing is not anything. David Hersland was certain then when he was a young one that being existing is not anything, and he was completely certain of this thing, and he was as completely certain of this thing as any one can be who is not completely certain of this thing, David Hersland was almost completely certain of this thing then when he was a young one certainly almost completely certain that being existing is not anything. He was completely certain of this thing that he was feeling this thing that being existing is not anything. He was almost completely certain of this thing that being living is not anything. He was completely certain of this thing that being existing is not anything. He was almost completely certain of this thing that being existing is not anything. He was completely certain of this thing that being existing is not anything. He was almost completely certain that being existing is something, he was almost completely certain of this thing then when he was a young one, he was almost completely certain that being existing is something, he was completely certain that he was feeling completely feeling that being existing is something, he was completely certain that being living is something, he was almost completely certain that being living is something, he was almost certain, when he was a young one, that being existing is something, he was completely certain then of this thing that being existing is something, then when he was a young one. He was feeling certain, then when he was a young one, that he was almost certain of this thing that being existing is something, he was feeling certain then when he was a young one that he was almost certain of this thing that being existing is not anything. He was one being living and he was one feeling something about being existing. Very many are ones being living and very many of them are ones feeling something about being existing. Very many are ones feeling something about existing, when they are young ones. Very many are being living and all of them are being young ones in being living and some of them are ones feeling something about being existing. Feeling something about being one being existing is in very many being living. Feeling something about being existing was in David Hersland in being one being living.

Some are wanting to know about some one whether that one is a young one or is an older one. It is an important thing to know that of some one. That one being a young one is in a way one being one kind of a one and that one being an older one is then in a way not that kind of a one. Some one is being one being living and that one is then a young one. That one is a kind of a one. That one being that kind of a one is being one living in a certain way, thinking and doing in a certain way and that one is one certainly doing that in a way one way being a young one and in a way in a different way being an older one. It is an important thing to be knowing of that one, of any one whether that one is then a young one or an older one. Some are knowing about some one that that one is an older one and that one is not then an older one, that one is then in the very beginning of the middle living of that one and not in the middle of the middle living of that one. Perhaps that then is the reason that one is doing something in the way that one is doing it then. Perhaps that is not the reason that that one is doing that thing the way that one is doing that thing then. Perhaps that one will be doing that thing that way in the ending of the middle of the living in that one. Perhaps that one will not be doing that thing in that way at the ending of the middle of the middle living in that one. Certainly I am asking each one how old that one is just then. Certainly I am doing this thing. David Hersland was a young one in the ending of the beginning of the ending of young living and he certainly was then one that some were needing to be asking how old he was then and certainly some were thinking then that he was as old as he was then and certainly some were thinking then that he was older than he was then. Certainly he was at the beginning of the ending of young being in him then and he certainly was knowing quite a number who were being living then and some were young ones who were younger than he was then and some were ones who were as old as he was then and some some were ones who were older ones than he was then. He had been knowing very many all his living and some were older ones than he was then and some were younger ones than he was then and some were just as old as he was then. Certainly all his living he knew quite a number who were being living and quite a number knew him. Sometimes in his being living he was not knowing so many who were being living and not very many knew him. Sometimes in his living he knew quite a number who were living. Sometimes in his living he did not know very many who were living. Sometimes in his living very many knew him. Sometimes in his living there were not very many who knew him.

Sometimes, to some one, knowing anybody in being living is to that one something really existing. Sometimes, to some one, knowing somebody is to that one a thing that in a way is not really existing. Sometimes some one is wondering about this thing. Sometimes that one is not wondering about that thing. Certainly some are not ever wondering about such a thing. Certainly some are knowing somebody and that thing is existing. Certainly there are some who are doing this thing. Certainly some are knowing somebody and that thing is not existing. Certainly there are some who are doing this thing.

David Hersland was certainly one having all of such ways of being being in him. He certainly was one knowing some one and that thing being existing to him, he certainly was one knowing some one and that thing being not existing to him. He certainly was one knowing some one and that thing being sometimes being sometimes not existing to him. He certainly was one wondering about such a thing. He was certainly one not wondering about such a thing. He certainly was one being existing inside him to him, he was certainly one being not existing inside him to him. He was certainly one wondering about such a thing. He was certainly one not wondering about such a thing.

Certainly sometimes he knew a number of people being living and he knew some of them in some way and he did not know some of them in that way and he was then knowing some in that way some of those he had been knowing in that way and he was not knowing some then in that way some of those he had been knowing in that way and he was knowing then some of those in that way some of those he had not been knowing in that way. He certainly sometimes in being living knew quite a number of ones being living. He certainly sometimes in being living did not know very many being living. He certainly was one having ways of knowing ones in him, and certainly he was sometimes having very many ways of knowing ones being in him. He certainly had very many ways of knowing ones being in him and certainly sometimes in being living he was knowing very many being living and certainly sometimes in being living he was not knowing very many being living. He was one wondering about knowing ones in being living, he certainly was one wondering quite often about being one knowing ones being living.

The way some other one is not frightened by something, the way some other one is frightened by something makes some one, make some almost certain that not any one is existing. The way some other one is frightened by something, the way some other one is not frightened by something makes some wonder whether they are realising being being in any one. Some other one being frightened by some one, some other one not being frightened by some one makes some feel uncertain whether they are themselves being living. Some other one being frightened, some other one not being frightened by something, by some one make some certain that that other one is not understanding anything. Some certainly are not believing another one who is then a frightened one, who is then not a frightened one. Some are explaining to some one who is not a frightened one by some thing that that one is not understanding what a thing it is the thing that is not frightening that one. Some are certainly then completely being astonished ones in realising that that one who is not frightened by one thing is frightened by another thing which is certainly not a dangerous thing and the other thing is a dangerous thing and why should any one be frightened by anything that is not a dangerous thing and why should any one not be frightened by anything that is a dangerous thing. Some certainly are frightened by some things that are not pleasant things, some certainly are frightened by some things that are dreary things, some certainly are frightened by things that are dangerous things, some certainly are frightened by things that are dirty things, some certainly are frightened by things that are lively things, some certainly are frightened by things that are quick things, some certainly are ones being frightened by things because those things are slow things.

David Hersland was one all his living learning to be believing that what frightened some one did frighten that one, that what did not frighten some one did not frighten that one. David Hersland certainly was one all his living trying to be learning to be one believing this thing believing that what frightened some one did frighten that one, that what did not frighten some one did not frighten that one. He was sometimes being one, in trying to be learning this thing, one who was certain that not any one is being existing. He was sometimes one certain that what was frightening that one was not frightening that one, that what was not frightening that one was frightening that one. He was explaining very often that he was not believing that what was frightening some one was frightening that one, that what was not frightening that one was not frightening that one. Certainly he was one trying to be one learning to be believing that what was frightening any one was frightening that one, that what was not frightening some one was not frightening that one.

He was in his living sometimes knowing very many who were living. Sometimes in his living very many who were being living knew him. He knew quite a number who were being living when he was a young one then when he was a young one.

Some one was not having angry feeling when he was asking why any one is doing anything. This one did not have angry feeling when some one was explaining that each one did the thing that each one was doing so as to be satisfying the wanting to do that thing that each one had then inside in them. Some are wanting to be asking why each one is doing the thing each one is doing and have not any angry feeling in asking this thing. Some one was explaining that each one doing anything, certainly some of them, were doing that thing to satisfy the feeling of wanting to be doing that thing. Some one was asking what was the use in doing anything and the one asking this thing did not have any angry feeling when that one asked that thing. Some one was explaining that the use of doing a thing was to be satisfying the need any one had to be doing that thing and this explanation did not give to the one receiving this explanation any angry feeling, it did not give to that one any satisfied feeling, it did not give to that one any sad feeling, it did not give to that one any angry feeling. Some are not having any angry feeling when they are asking why any one is doing anything. Some are not having any angry feeling when they are asking why each one is doing the thing each one is doing. Some are not having any angry feeling when some one is giving an explanation of why each one is doing what each one is doing. Some are not having any angry feeling when some one is explaining why any one is doing anything. Some are not having any angry feeling when some one is explaining that each one is doing what each one is doing and is in some way completely explaining that thing, some are not then having any angry feeling, some are not then having any satisfaction, some of such of them are not then having any sad feeling, some of such of them had been then perhaps expecting to be having some satisfaction, some of such of them are not having any weary feeling, some of such of them are not having then disappointed feeling, some of such of them are not then having any excited feeling, some of such of them are not then not asking why each one is doing what each one is doing, some of such of them are not then having any angry feeling.

Some are explaining that each one is doing the thing each one is doing because they are needing to be doing that thing, because they are needing to be wanting to be doing that thing, because doing that thing is a thing that is feeding them, because doing that thing is a thing that they are needing to be doing so that they can be ones doing something that they are ones needing to be wanting to be doing, because doing that thing is a thing that is something any one will be doing who is one needing to be one doing some things that this one is needing to be doing, because doing that thing is a thing in some way satisfying that one as being the one being that one. Some having some one explaining each one being one doing what each one is doing are not having then any angry feeling . Some of such of them are explaining that exchanging anything is a completely pleasant thing and they are not exchanging anything just then, some of such of them are explaining that exchanging anything is a completely pleasant thing and they are exchanging a good deal just then, some of such of them are not having in them any angry feeling, some of such of them are asking then why each one is doing what each one is doing, some of such of them are hearing some then explaining that thing, some of such of them have not in them then any angry feeling.

In a way David Hersland was one not completely asking why each one is doing what each one is doing. In a way David Hersland was not ever completely explaining why each one is doing what each one is doing. In a way he did have angry feeling in him in asking, in listening, in explaining, this thing, certainly he did very nearly did not have angry feeling in him about any of this thing. Certainly he might have been one completely asking about this thing about why each one is doing what each one is doing. He might have been one certainly he might have been one completely explaining this thing why each one is doing what each one is doing. He was not ever completely asking this thing, he was not ever completely explaining this thing. He might have been one having completely angry feeling in asking, in explaining, in having explanations of this thing, he certainly was not ever completely angry in asking about this thing, in explaining, in hearing some one explaining this thing. He was one who certainly might have been one completely asking about each one doing the thing each one is doing, he was one who certainly might have been one completely explaining each one doing what each one is doing.

David Hersland was not completely asking himself, asking any one why each one is doing what each one is doing. Sometimes he was almost completely asking this thing. He might have been one sometime completely asking this thing. He might not have been sometime completely asking this thing. He was not ever really completely asking this thing. He certainly might easily be thinking, any one might easily be certain about it about him when he was living that he was one completely asking this thing. He certainly was not completely asking this thing. He certainly was not ever completely explaining why every one is doing what each one is doing in being living. He might have been one explaining this thing, he might have been one not explaining this thing. Certainly many were certain that he was one having been being, going to be being explaining this thing. He could be one needing wanting to be explaining this thing. He was not ever completely needing wanting to be explaining this thing. He was not then ever really in living completely explaining why each one is doing what each one is doing in being living.

He certainly might have been one completely listening to any one explaining this thing why each one is doing what each one is doing. He was pretty nearly completely listening to any one who was one explaining this thing. He was then one sometimes explaining something. He was then sometimes wanting to be needing being one completely explaining everything. He was then sometimes almost completely needing wanting to be one explaining everything. He certainly listened very much and very often and certainly he very nearly completely listened when he listened to very many who were explaining everything. Certainly he was one who was listening, who was explaining, who was asking, who was answering in being one being living. He was one certainly completely clearly feeling a good deal in being one being living. He certainly was one clearly thinking. He certainly was one pretty nearly completely explaining everything. He certainly was one pretty nearly completely asking about each one being one doing the things each one is doing. He was a young one and he was an older one and he was a little older then and then he was not any longer living. He certainly sometimes then was knowing very many who were living then. He certainly sometimes then was known by some who were living then. He certainly was one who was in a way completely clearly feeling some things. He certainly was one who was in a way very completely clearly thinking. He was in a way one pretty nearly completely needing to be wanting to be completely asking about each one being the one that one is in being living. He was one certainly wanting to be needing to be certain that somethings being existing are beautiful things being existing. He was one certainly not in a way completely feeling such a thing. He was in a way completely clearly feeling what he was feeling. He was one certainly not completely explaining everything. He was one certainly not completely asking about each one being the one that one is in being living. He was one feeling some things clearly feeling some things. He was one knowing some very well in being one being living. He was one who was doing some things. He was one clearly thinking in being living. He was one listening and talking and asking and answering. He was one, and certainly

some were certain of this thing, he was one clearly feeling, clearly thinking, completely clearly feeling, completely clearly thinking some things,
and he was then feeling and listening and talking and asking and answering and almost completely then needing to be sometime explaining everything. He was not ever really completely needing to be explaining everything. He was not ever completely explaining everything. He might
have been one completely explaining everything. He might not have
been one completely explaining everything.

He was one and certainly there were some who were certain of this
thing, he was one almost completely listening to any one who was explaining everything. He was one and he certainly was that to some he
was one not in a way completely listening to any one explaining everything. He was one who certainly to some was very nearly explaining
everything. He was not one explaining everything. He was not completely needing to be such a one.

To be young, to be older, to be middle aged, to be older, to be old,
each one is a way of being and each one means something to each one being
living. In a way being young means something to every one and it is
not the same thing. One is a young one that is to say that one is in the
beginning of being living, that is to say that one is not yet a middle aged,
is not yet beginning to be a middle aged one. That one is thinking, is
feeling about being being in that one, that one is telling about that
thing. That one is doing something and is thinking about that thing.
That one is not then to that one one being a young one that is to say that
one is not then to that one, one beginning being living, that one is then to
that one one being living one being one doing something and thinking
about that thing, one being one thinking, one being one feeling, one helping some one to be one doing something, one realising the way some other
one should begin doing something, one telling some one how that one
should go on doing something. This one then is in a way not a young
one that is to say this one is in a way not one being one being beginning
in being living. This one in a way is a young one, that is to say this one is
one not feeling something, not thinking something, not being in being
living one being what that one will be being when that one is an older one.
That one is then in a way a young one and is in a way beginning being
living and this is then in this one, and this one is one not then having
that thing in that one that is being a young one, is not then having that
thing in that one as something that one is needing to be one deciding
anything, to be one directing some other one, to be one working and feeling and thinking, and that one is then a young one and this is in that one
as being and that is then making that one be the one that one is then in
being living.

David Hersland was such a one in being a young one, he certainly
was then one being one not needing it to be a young one to be one being

then living, to be one being then working and thinking and feeling and directing some and deciding anything. He was then a young one and being then a young one made it that he was one being existing as being one doing anything, feeling anything, thinking anything, deciding anything, directing anything in the way that he was then doing such a thing, then when he was a young one.

Some are needing themselves being a young one, an older one, a middle aged one, and older one, an old one to be ones realising what any one telling about different ways of feeling anything, of thinking about anything, of doing anything is meaning by what that one is telling. Some are needing themselves being a young one, an older one, a middle aged one, an older one, an old one to be one being certain that it is a different thing inside in one being a young one, from being an older one, from being a middle aged one, from being an older one, from being an old one. Some are needing themselves being different ages in being living to be realising that each one is different in being one being feeling, in being one being thinking, in being one doing anything, in being one deciding anything, in being one directing anything in being a young one, in being an older one, in being a middle aged one, in being an older one, in being an old one.

David Hersland was such a one. David Hersland was needing being at different ages in being living to be realising the different ways any one can be thinking, feeling, doing at different times in being living, in being a young one, an older one, a middle aged one, an older one, an old one, a very old one.

Some are needing being at different ages in being living to be to themselves one doing something, thinking something, feeling something, directing some, deciding something. David Hersland was such a one. Some are needing being at different ages in being living so that they can be realising that each one is feeling differently, is thinking differently, is doing anything differently, is deciding differently, is directing anything or any one differently at different ages in their being living. David Hersland was such a one.

David Hersland was a young one and he was then thinking and feeling and doing some things and deciding some things and directing some things and directing some whom he knew then, directing some of them in doing things, directing some of them in thinking things, directing some of them in feeling things. He was directing some then in thinking about some things, he was directing some then in their feeling about some things. He was deciding some things then and deciding some things then for some who were knowing him just then. He was one then being living all his living. He was one being one being living to himself inside him almost all of his being living.

He was one being a young one, David Hersland was in a way being a young one when he was a young one when he was in the beginning of his being living. He was one being a young one in a way being a young one when he was a young one. He was experiencing then, in a way he was experiencing then being a young one, in a way he was not experiencing then being a young one. He was a young one when he was in the beginning of his being living and in a way he was then experiencing that thing. He was a young one when he was beginning being living and in a way he was not then experiencing that thing. In a way he was not then a young one then when he was in the beginning of his being living and he was then experiencing that thing experiencing being not then a young one. He was in a way not a young one then when he was in the beginning of his being one being living and he was in a way then not experiencing that thing experiencing being then not a young one.

He was one experiencing being one being living all of his being living. He was experiencing being at some age in being living in all of his being living.

He was one experiencing being living then when he was a young one. He was one experiencing being a young one then when he was a young one, he was one experiencing not being a young one then when he was a young one.

He was one experiencing living being in him, he was one experiencing living being in some when he was knowing them who were knowing him then when he was a young one. He was experiencing in them their being a young one some who were then being young ones, he was experiencing in them their not being young ones some who were then young ones. He was experiencing being not young ones in some who were not then young ones. He was experiencing then some being young ones in some who were not then young ones. He was experiencing living then when he was a young one, he was experiencing being living then. He was experiencing being living all his living, he was experiencing living all his living.

David Hersland was sometimes certain that he was living in being one having very much feeling in being one being living. He was sometimes certain of this thing. He was sometimes certain that he was not living in being one having very much feeling in being living. He was sometimes certain of this thing. When he was in living in the beginning of his being living he was sometimes really certain that he was living in being one having very much feeling in being one being living. He was sometimes then when he was in the beginning of being living, he was sometimes then certain of this thing. When he was in living in the beginning of his being living he was sometimes then really certain that he was living in being one not having very much feeling in being one being living. He was sometimes then when he was in the beginning of being living, he was sometimes certain of this thing.

Some are almost really certain sometimes that they are ones being living in being one having very much feeling. Some are almost really certain sometimes that they are ones being living in being one not having very much feeling in being living. David Hersland was sometimes really certain that he was one having very much feeling in being one being living. He was sometimes really certain that he was one not having very much feeling in being one being living.

He knew some who were living when he was living. He was certain about some of them that they were ones having very much feeling in being ones being living. He was sometimes not completely certain about this thing, about some he was knowing having very much feeling in being ones being living. He was sometimes certain that he was one being living having very much feeling in being one being living. He was sometimes certain that he was one not having very much feeling in being one being living. He was one having very much feeling in being one being living and then he was clearly thinking about such a thing. He was one not having very much feeling in being one being living and he was very clearly thinking about this thing. Certainly he was always thinking quite clearly about something. He certainly was quite clearly thinking about very many things, he was one clearly thinking in being one being living.

He was one knowing it about some that in a way they were ones clearly thinking, that in a way they were ones not clearly thinking. He was not knowing it about some that they were ones clearly thinking, that they were not ones clearly thinking.

He was one knowing some who were living while he was living and certainly some of them were completely certain that he was one clearly thinking about everything. He was one knowing some who were living while he was living and some of them were certain that he was one living in feeling very much in being living.

He was knowing some who were living while he was being living. He was sometimes telling some of them about his being one clearly thinking, he was sometimes telling some of them about his being certain of being one living in feeling very much in being living, he was sometimes telling some of them about his being certain of being one living in not feeling very much in being living, he was telling some of them about his thinking clearly about being being one feeling very much in being living, he was telling some of them about his thinking very clearly about his being one living in not feeling very much in being living. He was one living in being one feeling very much in being living. He was one living in not feeling very much in being living. He was one clearly thinking about something, he was one very clearly thinking in being one being living.

He was one certainly knowing that he was one being living. He was one certainly thinking, certainly clearly thinking about that thing. He was one knowing some who were living while he was being living. He was one certainly clearly thinking about that thing. He was one certainly feeling very much in being living. He certainly was clearly thinking about that thing. He was one certainly not feeling very much in being living. He certainly was clearly thinking about that thing. He knew some who were living while he was living, he was feeling something about some of them, he was clearly thinking about that thing. He was one needing to be one clearly thinking about something, about almost everything. He was one wanting to be needing to be one clearly thinking about something, about almost anything, about everything. He was sometimes wanting to be needing some other thing, he was sometimes not wanting to be needing some other thing. He certainly was sometimes wanting to be needing some other thing. He was sometimes almost needing some other thing. He certainly was always needing to be quite clearly thinking. He was sometimes almost needing some other thing. He was sometimes wanting to be needing some other thing. He was sometimes not wanting to be needing some other thing. He knew some who were living while he was being living. He sometimes knew quite a number of them. He sometimes did not know very many of them. He was feeling something about some of them. He was sometimes feeling something about quite a number of them. He was sometimes thinking clearly about some of them. He was sometimes feeling very much about some of them. He was sometimes not feeling very much about some of them. He was sometimes feeling something about some of them.

Perhaps very many would be pleased to be with him. Perhaps very many would be pleased to be with some one, to be with him quite often. Perhaps very many would be pleased to be with him and that was a thing that any one would expect would be what very many were feeling. Any one might expect that very many would be with him very often if he wanted very many to be with him. Certainly some would be quite certain that very many would not want to be with him, some would be quite certain that not very many would want to be with him very often. Some could be quite certain that hardly any one would be pleased to be with him very often. Certainly very many were quite certain that very many would be pleased to be with him very often. Certainly some were pleased to be with him quite often. Very many might have been pleased to be with him quite often, some were pleased to be with him quite often.

David Hersland knew some who were living while he was being living. He was with some of them very often. Some were pleased to be with him very often. Some were pleased to be with him but they were not with him very often. Some were certain that any one might be pleased to be with him quite often. Some were certain that not any one would be pleased to be with him very often. Some certainly were with him very often. Some were certainly very pleased to be with him very often. Some were with him very often, some were not pleased to be with him very often. Some were with him quite often, some of such of them were very pleased to be with him. Some were with him quite often, some of such of them were not pleased to be with him. Some were very certain that some one would be very pleased to be with him very often. Sometimes some one was very pleased to be with him very often.

David Hersland certainly knew quite a number who were living while he was being living. Some of them were very pleased to be with him very often. Some of them were very pleased to be with him quite often. Some were very pleased to be with him and not very often. Some were pleased not to be with him very often. Some were not pleased when they were with him. Some were not at all pleased when they were with him. Some were certain that any one could be pleased to be with him. Some were certain that some would be very pleased to be with him and to be with him very often. Some were certain that not any one would be pleased to be with him very often. Some were certain that not any one could be pleased to be with him. Some certainly were very pleased to be with him very often. Some certainly were very pleased to be with him quite often. Some certainly were very pleased to be with him. Some certainly were not very pleased to be with him. Some were with him very often. Some were with him quite often. Some were not very often with him.

Some did not believe that anybody did not like to be with him sometimes. Some did not believe that anybody ever really liked to be with him. He sometimes knew that some one did not like to be with him, some sometimes were certain that he knew that thing, some sometimes were not certain that he knew that thing. He knew that some one sometimes did like to be with him. Some were certain that he did sometimes know that thing, some were not certain that he did sometimes know that thing.

When he was living he was knowing some and some knew him. He was knowing ones in different ways in different times in his being living. Some knew him and some of such of them were certain that they did not like this thing did not like knowing him. Some knew him and they were quite certain that every one who knew him would sometime like him. Some knew him and were quite certain that any one knowing him might come to like him, and they were quite certain that some knowing him did not like knowing him, and they were certain that some knowing him were completely liking this thing liking knowing him, and they were certain that he might come to be knowing that some who were knowing him were not liking that thing liking knowing him, and they were certain that he might not come to be knowing that some were not liking to be knowing him some who were knowing him.

He was one living in being living and sometimes he was knowing very many who were living then and sometimes he was not knowing very many who were living then. Some he was knowing were very often with him and some of such of them were completely then liking this thing, some of such of them were almost completely liking that thing, some of such of them were quite liking that thing, some of such of them were not liking that thing, some of such of them were wanting to be not liking that thing, some of such of them were needing to be not liking that thing not liking being with him very often. Some who were knowing him, sometime were wondering whether they should ever be telling him anything about any one's liking about any one's not liking to be with him. Certainly some who were knowing him were quite often wondering about this thing about whether they would ever be talking with him about any one's liking about any one's not liking to be with him. Certainly he was one completely listening, completely talking in being one being living. He certainly was one sometimes knowing very many who were living while he was being living. He was one certainly very many were quite pleasantly liking. He was one some were not so pleasantly liking. He certainly was one some were almost liking. He was one certainly clearly thinking in being living. He was one clearly telling anything he was telling. He was one almost completely clearly feeling something. He was one almost completely clearly thinking, certainly very often quite completely clearly thinking. He was one certainly not completely needing being one clearly thinking. He was one not needing being one clearly feeling. He was one certainly almost completely needing being one being in being one completely clearly thinking. He was not needing being one being in being completely clearly feeling. He certainly was very nearly completely needing being one completely clearly thinking.

He knew very many who were being while he was being living. He was one living in being one almost completely clearly thinking. He was one pretty nearly feeling very clearly what he was feeling. He was not needing this thing, he was not living in needing this thing. He was living in needing almost needing being one completely clearly thinking. He was one certainly needing to be feeling something and not to be clearly feeling this thing. He was one almost completely clearly feeling what he was feeling in being living. He certainly was almost completely needing feeling something and he was not at all clearly feeling that thing, he was not needing to be clearly feeling that thing to be one being living. He was clearly feeling what he was feeling, he was not living in clearly feeling what he was feeling. He was living almost living in being one completely clearly thinking. He was one who was almost completely clearly thinking. He was sometimes knowing very many who were living while he was being living, he was sometimes not knowing very many who were being living while he was being living. Some he was knowing were almost completely liking his knowing them then. Some were not liking his knowing them then, some were almost completely not liking that thing his knowing them then. Some were completely liking this thing his knowing them then. Some were liking it very well his knowing them then. Certainly some were sometimes very much liking knowing him. Some were not liking knowing him. Some were certainly quite needing knowing him. Some were wanting to be needing knowing him. Some were wanting not to be needing knowing him. Some were very nearly completely pleasantly knowing him. Some were wanting to be completely pleasantly knowing him. Some were mentioning this thing. Some were certainly not mentioning this thing. Some were certainly sometimes wondering about talking to him about knowing about not knowing some he was sometimes knowing. Some did sometimes talk to him about this thing. Some certainly did not talk to him about this thing.

Understanding being in some one makes the one understanding the being in some one come very nearly to telling that one the one whose being is being understood by the one understanding the being of some one makes that one come sometimes very near to telling the one whose being that one is understanding that that one will certainly never be doing the thing that that one is needing to be one going on being living. Some one is understanding the being in some one. That one might be telling that one the one whose being that one is understanding that that one will never be doing the thing that one is needing to be doing to be one really going on being living. Some one is understanding the being in that one. Certainly that one whose being is being understood then is one not going to be doing the thing that one is needing to be doing to be one going on being really living. The one understanding the being in the other one might be telling that one this thing. The one understanding the being in the other one is very nearly telling that one this thing. The one understanding the being in the other one is certainly not telling the other one this thing. The one understanding the being in the other one is knowing that that one will never be telling the other one anything about this thing.

The one understanding the being in another one and understanding then that that one will not ever be doing the thing that one is needing to be doing to be one being to that one inside that one one going on being living, is telling the one that one is understanding is telling that one this thing that that one will not ever be doing the thing that one is needing to be doing to be one going on, to that one inside that one, one going on being living. Certainly some one to whom some one understanding the being in that one has been telling that thing is not ever completely forgetting that thing, is not ever completely forgetting that that one will be one not going on being living, not really going on being living.

Some one understanding some one and being certain that that one will not be doing the thing that one is needing to be really one going on being living, is certainly hoping that some other one understanding that one will not ever tell that thing to the one certainly not going to be doing the thing that one is needing to be one going on living. That one is not telling that thing. Certainly that one did not ever tell that one that thing, did not ever tell that one that that one would never be doing the thing that one was needing to be doing to be one really going on being living.

Some one is understanding some one sometime and that one is then certain that the one that one is then understanding is one certainly not going to be doing the thing that one is needing to be doing to be one really going on being living. Perhaps that one the one not going to be doing the thing that one is needing to be doing to be one going on being living would be wanting to have the one understanding that one tell about understanding that one. The one understanding the other one is telling that one about being one not going to be doing the thing that one is needing to be doing to be one really going on being living. The one being pretty nearly certain then that the other one understanding the being in him is really telling what will be happening that is that that one will not ever be doing the thing that one is needing to be doing to be one really going on being living, is sometimes almost forgetting this thing that this one will not be doing what this one is needing to be doing to be one really going on being living.

Some one understanding being in some one is certain not ever to be telling that one that that one will not ever be doing the thing that one is needing to be doing to be one going on living. Some one understanding some one is telling that one and explaining that thing completely explaining that thing that that one that that one is understanding is one certainly not going to be one doing the thing that one is needing to be doing to be one going on being really living. That one the one not going to be doing the thing that one is needing to be one going on being living is completely understanding the explanation of that thing that the one understanding that one has been giving.

Some one is certain that the one that one is understanding then is one that will certainly not be doing the thing that one is needing to be doing to be one going on really being living. That one the one the other one is understanding is one certainly not going to be doing the thing that one is needing to be doing to be one really going on being living. The one understanding the one not going to be one doing the thing that one is needing to be one going on being living is not mentioning this thing to that one. The one the other one is understanding, the one who is not going to be doing the thing that one is needing to be doing to be one going on being living is sometimes quite certain that that one will be surprising the one who is understanding the being in that one.

David Hersland was understanding the being in some one and was telling that one then about this thing about understanding the being in that one. Some one was understanding the being in David Hersland and was not telling him about this thing was not telling about understanding the being in him. David Hersland was understanding the being in some one and was certainly never telling that one very much about that thing about understanding the being in that one. Some one was understanding the being in David Hersland and was telling him something about this thing something about understanding the being in him.

Some one was not understanding the being in David Hersland and was telling some other one about this thing about not understanding the being in Hersland. Some one was understanding something of the being in David Hersland and was telling some other one about that understanding of his being.

Some one was not understanding the being in David Hersland and was asking David Hersland about this thing about not understanding the being in him and David Hersland was explaining about this thing about that one not understanding the being in him. Some one was understanding something of the being in David Hersland and was asking some one who was not understanding the being in Hersland to explain that thing, the not understanding in the one not understanding, the understanding in the one understanding something.

One not understanding the being in David Hersland was asking every one knowing that one to explain that one not being one understanding the being in Hersland. Some one understanding the being in David Hersland was explaining that some one was understanding some of the being in David Hersland and that that one was one who was not needing any more explaining for certainly that one needed that David Hersland was not needing any more explaining. Some one was understanding the being in David Hersland and this was one needing that some other one was not understanding the being in David Hersland. One was understanding something of the being in David Hersland and was sometime telling about this thing that that one had been understanding something of the being in David Hersland and that one was then forgetting this thing forgetting the understanding of the being in David Hersland. Some one was not understanding the being in David Hersland and was not ever forgetting this thing not ever forgetting not understanding the being in David Hersland. Some one understood the being in David Hersland and was explaining this thing explaining understanding the being in David Hersland to every one understanding the being in David Hersland. Some one was understanding the being in David Hersland and was sometimes explaining this thing, sometimes explaining the being in David Hersland. David Hersland was the son born of his mother Fanny Hersland after Martha Hersland, Alfred Hersland and two who did not come to be ones going on being living were born out of her. He was the son of Fanny Hersland and her husband David Hersland. David the son was something like his mother and something like his father. He was something like his sister Martha, he was something like his brother. He was different, quite different from his mother and his father and his sister and his brother. He was remembering in his being living that the one who was his mother and the one who was his father and the one who was his brother and the one who was his sister was his mother, was his father, was his brother, was his sister. He was not remembering in his being living sometimes he was not remembering anything about any one being his mother, any one being his father, any one being his sister, any one being his brother.

He was living the living each one in the Hersland family was living when the Hersland family was living their family living. He was living a living not any other one in the Hersland family living was living when the Hersland family was living the Hersland family living.

He was one needing to be one being living to himself inside him and to be one sometimes having some be certain of this thing he certain that he was one being living to himself inside him. He was one needing to be one being living to himself inside him and to be one sometimes having every one not knowing anything of any such a thing being in him of his being one being living to himself inside him.

He was one being living to himself inside him and some were knowing this thing, they were not mentioning this thing, they were not remembering this thing, they were knowing this thing and he was one to them living in being living and not then knowing them in being one being living with them.

He was one being living in being one being living to himself inside him and he was not remembering this thing and he was knowing this thing and sometimes he was certain that some were knowing him in knowing this thing and sometimes he was certain that some were not knowing him in knowing this thing. He was sometimes certain that he was knowing some he was knowing he being one knowing himself being one being living to himself inside him. He was sometimes certain that he would be one knowing some he was knowing if he could be one not knowing it inside him that he was one being living to himself inside him. He was sometimes certain that he was knowing some knowing him he being one being quite certain that he was not knowing that he was being one being living inside him. He was one being quite certain that he was not knowing any one knowing him he being one knowing inside him that he was one being living to himself inside him.

Surely he said some things and did some things that some said he said and did. David did some things alone when he was a young one, some things he did not do alone when he was a young one.

Some are knowing some one, are hearing that one say some things, are knowing that that one is doing some things and it is then when that one is telling some other one what that one has been hearing what that one has been knowing that some other one is a surprised one. Surely some one is saying the things that some other one is hearing that one saying, certainly that one is saying those things, only it happens that some other one never happens to be one hearing any one saying such things.

Surely David Hersland was saying some things, was doing some things that some said he said and did. Surely he was saying some things and some said he said such things and some were certain that he had not said any such thing and some were wondering about his saying such a thing, and some were wondering if some are saying the things some are saying they are saying, and some are certain that some are saying some things and some are ones not being ones hearing such things.

Surely David Hersland said some things and did some things that some said he said and some said he did. Certainly some knowing him were wondering if he had been saying some things he had been saying, certainly some knowing him were wondering if he had been doing some things he had been doing.

When he was a young one he did some things alone and when he was a young one he did not do some things alone. Certainly he did some things that he was certainly wondering, when some one was telling that he had been doing, that he was wondering if he had been ever doing any such a thing. Certainly he was saying some things and certainly when some said such things to him as things he had been saying he did not recognise them as a thing he could ever have been saying. Certainly some are doing the things and are saying the things some are saying they did, some are saying they said. Certainly David Hersland did some things some said he did, and said some things some said he said.

Sometimes some one knowing some one is saying that that one said something and it is something that would astonish some to believe that one was saying and surely that one had been saying that thing because the one telling about the thing was one certainly not one having it to be one thinking any such thing, hearing any such thing from any other one. Sometimes it is very astonishing to some knowing some one to be knowing everything that that one they are knowing is saying, everything that one they are knowing is doing. Certainly it is very often astonishing to some one when that one comes to be knowing what some one that one is knowing has been saying. Certainly each one is saying very much in being one being living. Certainly something some one has been saying is astonishing to some one when that one comes to be hearing that that one has been saying that thing.

Surely each one certainly did some things and said some things that some said he did and said. Certainly it is astonishing to some one hearing that some one has said something that that one has said. Certainly it is astonishing to some one knowing that some one did some thing that that one did. Each one is doing some things in being one being living. Some are knowing such a one, any one. Some are knowing what this one is saying in being living, what some one is saying is believing is some times hearing some other thing that this one has been saying that some one has been saying, and then the one knowing this one is wondering whether the one did say such a thing and then sometimes is one finding it to be very astonishing that the one is one saying such things and then some time is one hearing the one saying such things and then is one not then astonished at knowing the one as being one saying such things in being one being living.

Certainly each one in being one being living is saying some things, is doing some things. Certainly each one knowing any one is hearing some of the things that one is saying. Certainly each one knowing some one is hearing some things that that one has been saying to some other one knowing that one. This is sometimes something that astonishes the other one the one then hearing what the one that one is knowing has been saying to the other one.

David Hersland said some things in being one being living and some heard him saying some things and some repeated what he had been saying. Sometimes he was not certain that he had, that he had not been saying some things he was hearing then, sometimes he was certain that he had not been saying any such thing and sometimes he had been and sometimes he had not been saying the things he was certain he had not been saying. He said some things and sometimes he was certain that they were not things he could have been saying but he was not certain that they were not things he had been saying. He was one saying some things in being one being living. Some certainly were certain that they had been hearing every kind of thing he was saying in being one being living. Some of such of them had been hearing every kind of thing he could be saying. Some of such of them had not been hearing every kind of thing he had been saying. Some of such of them were sometimes wondering about such a thing about not having heard every kind of thing he was saying.

David Hersland said some things when he was a young one, said a good many things when he was a young one and some heard very many things he said then and some heard very few of the things he said then. Some were certain that they heard very many of the things he said then when he was a young one and some were certain that they heard every kind of thing he said then when he was a young one.

Certainly David Hersland said some things then when he was a young one that some said he said then. He knew that he had said some of them. He did not know whether he had said some of them. He knew he did not say some of them. He did say some he knew he did not say, some he knew he did say, some he did not know whether he did or whether he did not say, he did say some he knew he could not say, he could not have said as they were not the kind of things he did say. He did not say some of the things he knew he did not say the kind of things he could not say because they were the kind of things he did not say.

Each one in being living is saying things, is doing things. David Hersland in being living was doing things, was saying things. When he was a young one he did some things alone, when he was a young one he did not do some things alone. When he was a young one he said some things and some heard the things he said, and he said some things and some did not hear the things he said. Some told some other ones some things he said and astonished them. Some told some other ones that he did not say some things and that astonished them. Certainly he said some things in being one being living then when he was a young one, certainly he said some things that some said he said, certainly he said some things that some said he had not said. Certainly some are saying some things to some one listening and it is quite astonishing that they should say that thing and it is not at all astonishing that they should say that thing. Certainly sometimes they are astonished at having been saying that thing and certainly sometimes they are not astonished at having been saying that thing. Certainly sometimes some are astonished at that one having been saying such a thing. Certainly sometimes some are wondering about that one having been saying such a thing. Certainly some are not ever believing that that one has ben saying such a thing. Certainly some are certain that that one is one often saying such a thing. Certainly some are saying that it is a very simple thing that that one is saying such a thing. Certainly some are wondering if he will ever say such a thing again the thing the one said to some one who was listening.

Certainly when one is a young one some one is hearing that one saying something that not any one else is hearing that one saying and very often that one is telling some other one that the one said that thing and is telling that thing and pleasantly and simply telling that thing and the one hearing that thing hearing that the one was saying such a thing is wondering if the one was saying that thing or whether the one telling that the one was saying that thing is simply and pleasantly imagining that the one was saying that thing.

It certainly is astonishing that each one is saying all the things each one really has been saying. It certainly is astonishing that any one can be saying so many kinds of things so many things as every one is saying in being living. This is astonishing to some, interesting to some, exciting to some, simple to some, doubtful to some.

David Hersland was a young one when he was one being a young one, he knew some then, some knew him then, some heard him saying some things he was saying then, some heard him saying these things and saying other things, some did not hear him saying any of these things then, some heard him saying many things, some heard him saying a few things. He was one saying things. Each one is one saying many things in being one being living.

Some were with him very often when he was a young one. He was with some one very often when he was a young one. Some one was with him very often when he was a young one. He was with some very often when he was a young one. He did some things alone when he was a young one, he did some things with some other one when he was a young one, he did some things with some other ones when he was a young one.

One thing is certain, some do not like some one thing. Some do not like a thing and certainly that thing is a thing that some do like, that some are certain is a thing any one would like if one understood the meaning of that thing. Some do understand the meaning of that thing and certainly they do not like that thing, they completely do not like that thing. David Hersland was such a thing. Some certainly did not like him as a thing being existing. Some were certain that any one understanding the being in him would be ones liking that thing would be ones liking his being one being existing. Some were understanding the being in him, some were then, some of them, were ones not liking his being one being existing, were completely not liking that thing, were not at all liking his being one being existing.

Certainly some were certain that any one understanding the meaning in his being existing would be liking that thing. Some were certain and then later were certain that this was not what every one understanding the meaning of his being one being existing would be feeling. Some were certain that any one understanding the being in him would be liking his being one being existing. Some of such of them were learning in being ones going on being living that some could be understanding the being in him and would then be ones not liking that thing not liking his being one being existing.

He was one being existing and some were completely liking that thing. He was one being existing and certainly some were completely not liking that thing. He was one being existing and certainly some could be persuaded to be ones liking that thing. He was one being existing and some were almost persuaded to be ones liking that thing. He was one being existing and some were ones telling about liking that thing. He was one being existing and some were not liking that thing and were ones wanting some other ones to be persuaded to be ones liking that thing his being one being existing. He was one being existing and some were certainly not liking that thing not liking it that he was one being existing. He was one being existing and some were certain that any one coming to be one understanding the being would be ones liking his being one being existing. Some of such of them were certainly all their living certain of this thing, some of such of them were telling again and again about this thing about every one liking him being one being existing when they came to be ones understanding the being in him. Some were liking it all their living that he was being one being existing, were completely liking this thing, some of such of them were telling this thing again and again and were then ones learning that certainly some completely understanding the being in him were completely not liking his being one being existing, were completely not liking that thing.

David Hersland was all his living clearly feeling some of the things he was feeling. He was clearly thinking some of the things he was thinking. He was completely thinking some of the things he was thinking, he was almost completely needing completely thinking the things he was thinking. He was completely feeling some of the things he was feeling, he was not needing to be completely feeling the things he was feeling, he was not completely feeling some of the things he was feeling. He certainly was one thinking in being living. He was completely thinking about some of the things about which he was thinking. He was not completely thinking about some of the things he was thinking about in being one being living. He was completely thinking about some of the things he was thinking about in being living. He was not completely needing being one being one completely thinking in being one being living.

He was one completely thinking about some things in being one being living. He was not completely needing to be one completely thinking about anything. He was not completely needing this thing, not completely needing being one completely thinking about some thing. He was one completely thinking about some things. He was one not completely needing to be one completely thinking about some things.

He was one completely feeling some things. He was one clearly feeling some things. He was one completely clearly feeling some things. He was one wanting to be needing to be one completely clearly feeling some things. He was one not needing to be clearly feeling anything. He was one clearly feeling almost anything. He was one wanting to be needing to be clearly feeling to be completely feeling anything. He was not one needing to be clearly feeling anything, he was not one needing to be completely feeling anything. He was one clearly feeling everything. He was one not wanting to be completely feeling everything and he was one wanting to be completely clearly feeling everything. He was one wanting to be needing feeling completely, feeling everything completely, he was not wanting to be feeling everything completely, everything clearly, he was not wanting to be feeling everything clearly, everything completely. He was feeling everything clearly, he was not feeling everything completely, he was feeling everything completely clearly.

He was not wanting to be feeling everything completely clearly, he was not wanting to be feeling anything clearly, he was sometimes wanting to be feeling some thing completely, he was not wanting to be feeling anything completely clearly. He was one feeling everything completely clearly, he was not one feeling everything completely. He was one wanting to be needing feeling everything completely, some things completely. He was one sometimes wanting to be needing feeling everything completely clearly. He was sometimes wanting to be needing not feeling everything completely clearly. He was not needing to be one completely feeling anything, he was not one needing to be one feeling anything completely clearly. He was one feeling everything completely clearly. He was one needing to be thinking clearly about everything, he was one needing to be thinking almost completely about anything, he was one thinking clearly about anything, he was one thinking almost completely about something. He was one not completely wanting to be one needing being one thinking completely clearly about anything, he was one not completely wanting to be one needing being one thinking completely about something.

Some are not liking some one and are telling about that thing. Some other ones are not liking that one and are telling about that thing. Sometimes then very many are not liking some one and are telling about that thing.

Some are liking some one and are telling about that thing. Some other ones are liking that one and are telling about that thing. Very many are then liking that one and are telling about that thing.

Some are liking some one and are telling about that thing and some are not liking that one and are telling about that thing. Some who are liking some one are telling about that thing to some who are not liking that one. Some who are liking some one are telling about that thing to some who are liking that one. Some who are not liking some one are telling about that thing to some who are liking that one. Some who are not liking some one are telling about that thing to some who are not liking that one.

Sometimes some who are not liking some one do not mind that some who are liking that one are telling them about that thing. Some who are not liking some one sometimes do not mind that some who are not liking that one are telling them about this thing. Sometimes they do mind, some who are not liking some one, that some one liking that one is telling about that thing. Sometimes some who do not like some one do mind that some who do not like that one are telling about that thing. Sometimes some who do like some one do not mind if some one who likes that one is telling them about this thing about liking that one. Sometimes some who do like some one do not mind if some one who does not like that one tells about that thing about not liking that one. Sometime some one who likes some one does mind when some one who likes that one tells about that thing tells about liking that one. Sometimes some who do like some one do mind if some who do not like that one tell about that thing tell about not liking that one.

Certainly very many sometimes were telling about liking about not liking David Hersland while he was one being living and later then when he was not any longer being living. Very many were telling about liking about not liking David Hersland then when he was being a young one. Certainly some were sometimes telling about the feeling they had about him, about the feeling some others had about him, about liking about not liking him. Certainly some were certain about the meaning there was in any one being one liking, in any one being one not liking him. Certainly some were not certain about the meaning there was in any one being one liking, in any one being one not liking him. Some were certain about the meaning there was in liking, in not liking him and then they were not so certain about this thing about the meaning there was in liking in not liking him. Some were certain that they were completely understanding the meaning in being one liking, in being one not liking him. Some were always all their living certain in understanding this thing. Some were not certain all their living in understanding this thing. Some were ones sometime certain that there were different ways of liking of disliking him. Some were certain that there were not different ways of liking of disliking him. Some were certainly liking him, some certainly were not liking him. Some of them were telling about this thing. Some of them were telling about this thing again and again.

Some certainly know, some certainly do not know that they are liking, that they are not liking some one. Some do know, some do not know what meaning they are needing in anything being living. Some do know that they are liking, that they are not liking, some one. Some do not know that they are liking, that they are not liking some one. Some are clearly knowing this thing that they are liking, that they are not liking some one. Some completely clearly know this thing that they are liking that they are not liking some one. Some are knowing they are needing that anything being living has some meaning. Some are not knowing that they are needing that anything being living has some meaning. Some are knowing that they are needing that everything being living has some meaning. Some are knowing that they are not needing that anything being living has some meaning. Some are knowing that they are not needing that anything being living has any meaning. Some are knowing that they are liking something. Some are knowing that they are not liking something. Some are knowing that they are not liking that they are liking anything. Some are knowing that they are liking that they are not liking everything. Some are knowing that they are not liking everything. Some are knowing that they are liking everything. Certainly some are clearly completely clearly knowing that they are liking everything. Some are knowing completely clearly knowing that they are not liking anything. Some are knowing are completely clearly knowing that they are not liking everything.

Certainly very many are needing that everything being living is having meaning. Certainly very many are needing that something being living is having meaning. Some are not needing any such thing are not needing that everything being living is having meaning, that anything being living has meaning. Certainly David Hersland in being one being living was liking everything, was completely clearly knowing that he was liking everything. Certainly David Hersland sometime in

being one being living was liking anything, was completely clearly knowing that he was liking anything. Certainly David Hersland in being one
being living was sometimes not liking something, sometimes he was completely clearly knowing sometimes in his being one being living that he
was not liking something. Sometimes in his being living he was liking
something sometimes he was completely clearly knowing this thing sometimes when he was liking something.

Certainly each one being living is one then being one going on being
living. Sometimes some one in being one being living is one then not
then going on being living is one then not being one being living.

Certainly some are living and are being ones going on being living
and are needing for this thing being certain that being living is having
meaning and is being then existing. Certainly some are living and are
being ones going on being living and are not troubling and are needing
for this thing being certain that being living is having meaning and is
being then existing. Certainly some are living and are being ones going
on being living and are not troubling and are not needing for this thing
being certain that being living is having meaning and is being then existing. Certainly some are living and are going on being living and are
troubling and are needing for this thing that being living is having meaning and is being then existing. Certainly some are being living and are
going on being living and are troubling and are needing to be certain that
being living is not having meaning, that being living is not existing. Some
are being living and are going on being living and are troubling and they are
needing that being living is not having any meaning and that being living is existing.

Some are being living and are going on being living and are then not
going on being living, are then not being living. Some are being living
and are not troubling and are needing that being living is having meaning,
that being living is existing. Some are being living and are not troubling
and are not needing that being living is having meaning, is being existing. Some are being living and are going on then being living. Some are
being living and are then going on being living and are then not going
on being living and are then not being living. Some are being living and
are troubling and are needing that being living is not existing, that being
living is having meaning. Some are being living and are troubling and
are needing that being living is not having meaning, that being living is
existing. Some are being living and are not troubling and are needing
that being living is not having meaning, that being living is existing.

David Hersland was one being living and he was one going on being
living and he was one then not going on being living and he was one then
not being living. He was one troubling, he was one not troubling, he
was one needing that being living is having meaning, he was one needing
that being living is existing. He was one troubling, he was one not

troubling, he was one needing that being living has not any meaning, he was one needing that being living is not existing.

David Hersland when he was a boy was gentle enough and active enough and happy enough and earnest enough and quick enough and eager enough and strong enough and angry enough and glad enough and serious enough and lively enough and willing enough and quarrelsome enough and obstinate enough and quiet enough and enthusiastic enough and energetic enough and generous enough and selfish enough and talkative enough and hearing enough and remembering enough and forgetting enough and light enough and slow enough and foolish enough and silly enough and daring enough and weak enough and bashful enough and forward enough and careless enough and careful enough and easy enough and respectful enough and doing enough to be one being living then. He certainly was one being living then. He was sometimes then almost completely wanting to be needing being living then. Certainly some did what he was doing then. Certainly some heard what he was saying then, certainly some were wanting some others to be doing what he was doing then. Some did what he was doing then. He did what some were doing then. He listened to what some were saying then, he talked a good deal and quite often then, he listened some quite often then, he did what some were doing then, he wanted some to be doing what some others were doing then, he sometimes quite completely wanted some to be doing what some others were doing then. He did some things quite suddenly then. He did some things some others were doing and he did them quite suddenly then. He was sometimes talking very much and very often. He was sometimes listening some quite often. He was doing some things some others were doing. He was wanting some others to be doing things some others were doing. Some certainly were doing some things he was doing then. Some certainly did want some others to do what he was doing then. Certainly some of such of them did not do what he was doing then. Certainly sometimes some of them did do what he was doing. He was one being living and almost completely then sometimes wanting to be one being living then. He certainly was one being living. He certainly was doing then what some others were doing. Some were certainly then doing what he was doing. Some were certainly then wanting some others to be doing what he was doing then. He certainly wanted some to be doing what some others were doing then. He was doing what some others were doing, sometimes then. He certainly was sometimes wanting some others to be doing what some others were doing then.

He was being living when he was beginning in being one being living. He was doing what some others were doing. He was doing some things and some were doing these things with him. He was doing some things and he was not doing them with any one. He was doing some things when he was being one beginning living. He was being one then knowing some then. Some were knowing him then. He was having being in being living some inside in him then.

Some one sometimes ran after him. Some one sometimes ran after David Hersland when he was walking and that one ran quite breathless then and then said to him, how are you, and then that one did not really have anything to say to him. Sometimes that one ran after him to say how do you do to him and then had not any other thing to say to him just then. Sometimes he was wondering why that one ran after him when that one had not anything to say to him and was out of breath then from having been running and would then just ask him how he was and had not then just then any other thing to say to him. David Hersland had been a quite young one and then he was not a very young one he was coming then to the ending of the beginning being living. He was then knowing a good many men and women, some were then ones at the end of their beginning being living, some were then a little older, some of them were then a little younger, some were then a good deal older than he was then.

When some one ran after him and was quite breathless then and said how do you do, to him then and had not anything more to say just then, not anything more then to say to him he was quite certain that such a one was a silly one. He was certain then that that one was an affectionate one, one satisfied then with having been running, with having been saying how do you do, then, with having nothing more just then to say to him. He was certain that one being such a one was a silly one and one running after every one that one saw whom that one was knowing. He was certain that one running after him and being breathless then and saying how do you do to him then and having just then not any other thing to say to him was a completely silly one.

He was being one, David Hersland was being existing and sometimes some one ran after him and was breathless then and tired then and shook hands with him then and was more tired then and had not anything to say to him just then, certainly had not anything to say to him just then. He was certain that that one was a silly one, he was completely certain that that one was completely a silly one.

David Hersland was one certainly in a way needing to be certain that every woman was in a way a beautiful thing. Certainly not any woman was in a way a beautiful thing to him. He was completely needing that every woman is a beautiful thing. Certainly he was completely realising that affection is a thing that is in one wanting to be seeing another one. Certainly he was not completely wanting to be seeing any woman who is existing. Certainly he was one realising affection being in any woman completely wanting to be seeing some one. Certainly he was one completely needing realising that any woman is a beautiful thing. He was one realising, that affection being in some one, that one is one wanting to be seeing some one. He was one needing to be completely wanting to be seeing some one. Certainly some one sometimes ran after him and certainly asked him then how he was and was one not having any other thing just then to say to him. He certainly was one realising that affection is something making some one be one completely wanting to be seeing another one. Certainly this one was one running after him and being breathless then and saying how do you do to him and being tired then and not having anything just then to say to him. Certainly this one was one doing this quite often. Certainly this one was one doing this thing, running after them, after some men, after some women, and saying how do you do to them, and being breathless then and having just then not any other thing to say to any one of them.

David Hersland was certainly one knowing some men and some women while he was being one being living. Certainly some men and some women knew him while he was being living.

When he was quite a young one he knew some and some knew him, and when he was not such a young one he knew some and some knew him and when he was an older one he knew some and some knew him, and when he was a little older still he knew some and some knew him.

There are very many people being living. Certainly very many come together to see something, to hear something, to do something, to see some see something, to see some hear something, to see some do something, to hear some see something, to hear some do something, to hear some hear something, to feel something, to feel some feel something, to feel some hear something, to feel some see something, to see some one do something, to hear some one do something, to feel some one do something, to do something to some, to do something to some one, to feel some do something to some, to hear some do something to some one, to see some do something to some one, to feel some doing something to some, to hear some do something to some, to see some do something to some, to see some one do something to some, to feel some one do something to some, to hear some one do something to some, to feel some one do something to some one, to see some one do something to some one, to hear some one do something to some one, to believe something, to forget something, to remember something, to like something, to hate something, to believe some, to believe some one, to like some, to like some one, to remember some, to remember some one, to forget some, to forget some one, to hate some one, to hate some, to be happy, to be happy again, to be earnest, to be serious, to be serious again, to be quick, to be quick again, to be frightened, to be frightened again, to be quiet, to be angry, to be angry again, to be brave, to be brave again.

Certainly very many are being living. Very many are knowing that very many are being living. Very many are telling about this thing that very many are being living. Certainly very many are being living.

Certainly very many are very willing that very many be being living.

Very often very many who are being living come together and they are together then and very many are very willing that very many should be doing this thing should be coming together and very many are not very willing that very many should come together and very many are in some way telling about this thing about very many coming together and certainly very many are together and certainly very many very many are being living.

Certainly very many are living, certainly very many are together, certainly very many are telling about very many being together, about very many being living. Certainly very many are living, certainly very many are together, certainly very many are willing that very many are living, certainly very many are willing that very many are together, certainly very many are not very willing that so very many are living, certainly very many are not willing that very many are together.

Certainly very many are living. Certainly very many are together. Certainly very many are living. Certainly very many are telling about this thing about very many being living. Certainly very many are telling about very many being together when very many are together.

Certainly very many are being living. Certainly very many are very willing that very many be being living. Certainly very many are not so willing certainly very many are not at all willing that very many be living.

Certainly very many are being living and very many are telling about this thing about very many being living.

Certainly very many are together and very many are telling about this thing about very many being together and very many are willing that very many are telling about this thing about very many being together and very many are not very willing and very many are not at all willing that very many are telling about very many being together.

It certainly is in some ways a very nice thing very many being together, it certainly is in some ways not a very nice thing very many being together. It certainly is in some ways a cheerful thing very many being living, it certainly is in some ways not at all a cheerful thing very many being living.

David Hersland was certainly one who was all his living feeling something about this thing, about very many being living, feeling something about this thing about very many being together, he was one in a way all his living feeling something, thinking something, realising something about this thing about very many being together, about this thing about very many being living, pretty nearly all his living, very nearly in every part of his living he was feeling something, he was thinking something, he was realising something about very many being together, about very many being living.

Certainly very many are together. Certainly very many are living. Certainly very many are telling something about this thing about very many being living. Certainly very many are telling something about this thing about very many being together.

David Hersland was one being living and this is now a history of his being one being living, this is to be now a history of being living being in him, of his being one being living.

Certainly very many are being living, very many are dying, very many are commencing existing.

Very many are seriously living. Very many are not so seriously living. Very many are not so seriously living.

Very many are being living. Some are saying thank you to some one, some are not saying thank you to any one. In a way David Hers and was not saying thank you to any one, in a way David Hersland was not not saying thank you to any one.

Certainly very many are being existing, very many are dying, very many are commencing being existing.

Certainly David Hersland was being existing, certainly David Hersland was dying, certainly David Hersland was commencing being existing.

He was commencing being existing, he was going on being existing. He was going on being existing, he was not going on being existing.

If any one is sad enough then that one is certainly one wanting to be a sad one, is certainly one not wanting to be a sad one. If any one is not sad enough then that one is liking being a sad one, is not liking being a sad one.

David Hersland was not sad enough and he was liking being a sad one and he was not liking being a sad one. He was sad enough and he was certainly wanting then to be a sad one, he was certainly then not wanting to be one being a sad one.

All his living he was a sad enough one. All his living he was one wanting to be a sad enough one. All his living he was one wanting not to be a sad enough one. All his living he was not sad enough and he was not liking this thing not liking not being a sad enough one and all his living he was liking this thing liking being a not sad enough one.

Some are sad enough, certainly they are sad enough. Some are not sad enough, certainly they are not sad enough. Some certainly would be sad enough if they could be sad enough. Some certainly would be sad enough if they could be sad enough.

Some would be sad enough if they could be sad enough. Some of such of them are sad enough. Some of such of them are not sad enough.

David Hersland would not be sad enough if he could be sad enough. David Hersland was sad enough. David Hersland was not sad enough. David Hersland was pretty nearly sad enough. David Hersland could be sad enough. He could not be sad enough. He could be sad enough. He certainly was pretty nearly sad enough. He was sad enough. He was not really needing this thing, needing being sad enough. He could be sad enough. He was sad enough. He was not really needing this thing that is being sad enough. He was not sad enough. He was not needing that thing, he was not needing being one not being sad enough. He was not needing being one being sad enough, being not sad enough. He was not needing this thing. He was not needing being sad enough. He was not needing being not sad enough. He was sad enough. He was not sad enough.

Some are sad enough. Some are not sad enough. David Hersland knew very many who were being living while he was being living. Very many who were being living knew David Hersland.

Very many are being living. A very great many are always being living.

Sadness in himself and others was certainly interesting to him in being one being living. Sadness in himself was certainly interesting to him. David Hersland was certainly interested in sadness being existing, he was interested in sadness being in him, he was interested in sadness being in every one.

He was interested in sadness being existing. When he was a young one he was interested in sadness being existing, he was interested in sadness being in him. All his being living he was interested in sadness being existing, in sadness being in him, in sadness being in every one, in sadness being in any one.

All his living he was interested in not being certain that sadness is existing. All his living he was interested in not being certain that sadness was existing in him. All his living he was interested in not being certain that sadness is existing in every one. All his living he was interested in not being certain that sadness was existing in some one.

When he was a young one he was interested in being certain that sadness was existing in him. When he was being a young one he was interested in not being certain that sadness was existing in him. All his living he was interested in sadness being existing. All his living he was interested in sadness not being existing. All his living he was not certain that any sadness is existing. All his living he was certain that sadness is existing.

He was a young one and he was being living and he was quite completely living then, sometimes he was quite completely living, certainly he was sometimes quite completely living then. Certainly he was then, when he was a young one, not certain that sadness is being existing, certainly he was then when he was a young one certain that sadness is being existing.

He was not a sad one, in a way then when he was being a young one he was not a sad one, he was a sad one, in a way then when he was being a young one he was a sad one. Then when he was a young one he was interested in being not certain that sadness is existing. Then when he was a young one he was interested in being certain that sadness is existing.

Ways of being living is something some are knowing are existing and some are not knowing are existing. Some are knowing they are living in a way of being living. Some are not knowing they are living in a way of being living. Some are knowing they are living in a way of being living are knowing this thing when they are young ones, when they are beginning being ones being living. David Hersland was not one of such of them. Some are never in their being living are never knowing they are living in a way of being living. David Hersland was not one of such of them. Certainly very many being living are not ever knowing they are being living in a way of being living. Some are knowing they are living in a way of being living. Some when they are beginning being ones being living are ones knowing they are living in a way of being living. David Hersland when he was a young one was not one knowing then that he was living in a way of being living. He was one for sometime not interested in such a thing. He was one for sometime not interested in ways of being living. He was one certainly not ever completely interested in any such thing, in ways of being living. He was sometime almost interested in such a thing in ways of being living. He was not ever really completely interested in ways in being living. He was quite interested in being interested in ways of being living. Sometime he was quite interested in being interested in ways of being living. He was not one really knowing then when he was a young one about ways of being living. Certainly some are really knowing about this thing about ways of being living. Certainly some are not really knowing about this thing about ways of being living.

David Hersland was being living and sometimes he was with very many who were being living and sometimes he was not with very many. He knew some who really knew about ways of being living. He knew some who really did not know about ways of being living.

Little by little they are not so young those being young. Little by little they are not so young and they are then so young, they are then quite young. They are then young those who are young. Little by little they are not so young those being young.

Those being young little by little are not so young. They are young. They are not so young. They are then still quite young. Little by little they are not so young. They are still then quite young. Little by little then they are not so young. They are young then.

One is in the beginning of being living. One is then going on being living. Little by little each one is not so young. One is still then young.

Little by little one is not so young. Quickly one is not so young, quite quickly one is not so young. One is then still young. One is then not any longer young. One was young and then that one was older and then that one was not at all a very young one and then that one was not at all a young one and then that one was quite not a young one. If one had been beginning knowing that one when that one was this one one being quite not a young one that one would have been one to such a one one being quite a young one and then would have been for some time longer then quite a young one.

One is a young one a completely young one, one just beginning being living and this one little by little is not such a young one and is one then to one knowing that one not such a young one, and to one just beginning knowing that one a completely young one.

One was a young one and this one had been one being a young enough one so that some one could toss that one, toss up that one and one did toss up that one, did regularly toss up that one and then this one was one that that one could not toss up any longer and this one then the one that had been a tossed one had then to toss himself to earn a living and this one was then a quite young one and this one was then to the one that had tossed that one a completely not a young one, a young one was one that could be tossed by that one and this one could not be tossed by this one and this one did not toss himself enough to be another kind of a young one, a young one who tossed himself and he was not a young one because he could not toss himself again and again and certainly this one was to that one to himself inside him completely a young one, completely not a young one.

A young one is one tossing himself and not with a rhythm, not with a regular rhythm, one who is not a young one is one tossing himself with a rhythm, some rhythm, is tossing himself with a regularity that has meaning as a repeated thing and this is certainly the way one not being a young one is tossing himself and the way one being a young one is not tossing himself.

One who is tossing himself pretty nearly regularly would have been one who was not completely a young one but he was completely a young one and that was because there were older ones who had been ones tossing themselves regularly and this one knew then that this was the way that one should toss himself and that one then did not toss himself so then and always when this one was tossing himself as regularly as they had been tossing themselves they were tossing themselves more regularly, so that that one to himself then and to every one was a young one, a completely young one, quite a young one one who was not tossing himself with any regular rhythm, was then a quite completely young one.

Little by little they are not so young those being young. It is certainly steadily changing and certainly in each one they are each one a little and a little a different one that is one being an older one, one being not such a young one.

One is thinking and he is thinking quite the same thing he has been thinking since he commenced thinking and always and always it is a little older, a little different and a little different and it is a very pleasant thing to some to see in any one, to see in themselves little growing difference in them and then it is like a map of anything, one is finding that the real thing is like the description. That is very exciting and very depressing and very contenting and very disconcerting and very expected and very astonishing and some then are certain that it is not existing in every one and some are certain that it is existing in every one. And some in some part of their being living are seeing changing in men and women and in other parts of their living are not seeing changes happening.

Some one quite in the middle of the middle living in that one is meeting some one who is at the ending of the beginning living in that one and is then struck by the changing in that one and that one is then struck by the changing in the other one and each one is then knowing that every one is changing some.

Some are beginning seeing changing in every one when they are in the ending of the beginning of their middle living. Some who are in the ending of the beginning of their middle living are then seeing changing existing in every one who is being living. Some all their living are seeing changing in every one, are feeling changing to be existing in every one.

David Hersland was realising all his living that changing is existing in every one and he was not really feeling this thing, really seeing this thing until the middle of the beginning of his middle living and then he was loving this thing and looking at each one and thinking about this thing and living in this thing, and being a little frightened by this thing and being contented by this thing and being convinced of this thing and telling it to himself about each one he was knowing and being certain that being living was a thing being existing and being then almost completely certain of this thing. He was then one who came to be a dead one at the beginning of the middle of his middle living and he had been one who had been almost completely fully living in changing being existing in every one being living. He had been completely almost completely feeling each one being an older and an older one. He had been one almost completely seeing being a young one and being then a little and a little not such a young one. He was one certainly needing to be one realising changing being existing. He was one completely enjoying seeing changing being existing in each one. He was one almost completely being satisfied with being living in being one seeing changing happening in each one.

He was one being a young one and then he was knowing some who were young ones quite young ones and not such young ones and older ones and quite old ones and certainly he sometimes was feeling changing being existing but not very much then certainly not very much then because he was then being a young one and not going fast enough then in being living to be certain that anything was changing in the being in any one. He was knowing that changing is existing, any one could be knowing that thing, he was not living in that thing, not at all then living in that thing, not any one to him was then really living in that thing. He was a completely young one then, he knew quite a number who were living then.

David was a boy when he was a young one. That was a natural thing. He was a boy then, he was not a boy to himself then, he was a boy to himself then, he was one being existing to himself then, he was one not being existing to himself then. He was a boy to very many knowing him then. He was not a boy to some knowing him then. He was some one being existing to those knowing him then.

Certainly he was not certain not always certain then that he was one being one feeling something. He was quite often quite certain that some being existing are ones being existing in feeling something. He was quite often certain that very many who are being existing are then feeling something. He was one quite clearly feeling what he was feeling. He was one sometimes quite certain he was not one ever feeling and he was one who was quite certain that he was one who was one feeling enough to be a sad one and not feeling enough to have feeling being a thing that was being in him. He was one certainly quite clearly feeling feeling being existing. Certainly he was one quite clearly feeling something about some things and he was one almost being certain that feeling is existing in some who are existing, and then he came to be one going on being living and he came sometime to be quite certain he was very clearly feeling what he was feeling.

He was one beginning living and then he was one feeling something and he was then one not feeling anything and he was then a quite sad one and he was then not at all a sad one, a quite not sad one. He was then a troubled one and he was then troubled with this thing with being a troubled one and he was wondering then about any one being a troubled one and he was then not always certain about anything about this thing about being a trouble one. He was a troubled enough one, he was not then completely interested in this thing in being a troubled one, he was quite certain that he would be sometime interested in this thing in any one being a troubled one. He was in a way a troubled one and in a way he was one deciding then quite clearly deciding about any one whom he knew was a troubled one. He was one quite clearly deciding about each one who was a troubled one. He was a troubled one and in a way he was quite clearly deciding about himself then, about himself being a troubled one, and he was not then completely interested in this thing in any one being a troubled one, in he himself being a troubled one but he was certain that sometime he would be completely interested in this thing completely interested in being a troubled one, completely interested in every one being a troubled one. He was not ever completely interested in this thing, in any one being a troubled one, in himself being a troubled one, he was sometime and for quite sometime troubled by this thing, he was then not troubled by this thing for certainly then he was clearly certain that any one is a troubled one, that every one is a troubled one, that he himself was a troubled one and he was clearly feeling about this thing and he was clearly thinking about this thing and he was then not completely interested in this thing, not troubled by this thing, and he was certainly then being filled then with being certain that in some way he was one being existing and that sometime he would be one being a dead one and certainly every one would certainly sometime be a dead one and certainly every one would be one having been existing.

When he was a boy a young one if he had been a little different then he might have been troubled by being troubled by anybody being troubled, by everybody being troubled. He was one who was troubled then, he knew some were troubled then, he felt quite clearly about such a thing then about being troubled then, he was certain then that sometime he would be completely interested in this thing. He was sometime and for quite sometime troubled by this thing, he was not completely interested in this thing in any one being a troubled one.

He was then one beginning being living and he was one then being one who was one. He was being one then. He was in the beginning of being living. He had been living some time then. He was a boy then, certainly he was a boy then. He was one having been sometime being living, he was being one then being one being living. He was being one then.

He was one who had some feeling. He felt something when he was a young one. He always felt something. When he was a young one he was certain that he would not be one having feeling. When he was a young one he was certain that he would be one having some feeling. He was not then completely interested in this thing. Sometimes then he was almost completely interested in this thing. When he was one being a young one he could have been one writing it down every day that he was one not having feeling, that he was one not having any feeling. When he was a young one he could have been writing it down every day that he was wanting not going to be having feeling, not going to be having any feeling. When he was a young one he could have been writing it down every day that he was a troubled one. He could have been writing down every day, when he was a young one, that he was one doing everything, having complete living in doing everything. When he was a young one he could every day have been writing down that he was feeling clearly feeling something about everything, that he was feeling, clearly feeling something about every one.

He was quite clear in feeling what he was feeling and he was quite clear in deciding about being being existing. He was certainly then not completely interested in any one, in he himself then being a troubled one.

When he was a little older he was clearly feeling certainly clearly feeling something, he was clearly thinking then, he was almost then needing to be certain that sometime he would be clearly thinking about everything. He was not completely then needing to be clearly thinking about everything, he was clearly then clearly feeling something, he was then not clearly feeling something, he was not needing to be clearly feeling the thing he was not clearly feeling. He was clearly feeling something, he was almost completely living in clearly feeling that thing, the things he was clearly feeling. He was not completely living in the things he was clearly feeling. He was completely needing to be clearly thinking about the things about which he was clearly thinking. He was almost completely living in clearly thinking about the things he was clearly thinking, completely clearly thinking.

When he was a young one when he was beginning in being living he was a very little one, that is a natural thing, he was then quite completely a little one, he was then a very little one, that is a natural thing. When he was beginning being living he was a very little one. He was living then and then he was a little a bigger one and he was living then and he was still a little bigger then.

When he was beginning being living he was one who was one, who was of a kind of a one. He was living then. He was very well taken care of then as was a natural thing. He was not ever really interested in this thing, interested in having been a very little one, a completely little one. He was quite not interested in this thing in having been a quite little one. He was interested in having been one being a bigger one, he was not ever interested in having been a completely little one.

He was then in the beginning a completely little one and this interested some then, this did not ever interest him, this did not very much interest any one knowing him. He had been a very little one, certainly he had been, this was not a thing having meaning in the being in him and this is a thing not really needing mentioning that he had been a completely little one. He had been then in beginning being living a completely little one. He certainly was not ever remembering any such thing. He certainly was not really ever finding this thing interesting. He was then a little a bigger one and he a little remembered that thing and he did not interest himself ever very much in this thing in having been a very little bigger one. He was one quite remembering this thing having been a little bit a bigger one, he was not at all minding remembering this thing, he remembered quite clearly something of this thing, he was not ever interested in this thing, he certainly quite clearly remembered this thing remembered having been a little a bigger one and he certainly was not ever really interested in this thing in having been a little a bigger one. He was then a little more a bigger one and he remembered something of this thing, he even remembered feeling some little thing and it was a pleasant enough thing to him to remember something then but it did not interested him, it did not ever interest him. He quite clearly remembered having been living then, he was not interested in remembering having been living then, he remembered having been clearly feeling something then, he was not ever really interested in remembering having been clearly feeling something then.

He was then a little a bigger one then and he remembered somethings from then and he was not ever really very much interested in any of them, in remembering any of them. In a way he was not completely uninterested in having been living then but really he was not completely interested in having been living then, he went on being living then. He was interested in having been going on being living then. He always was interested in having been going on being living then. He want on living then. He remembered something of that thing. He was a little interested in remembering a little something of that thing.

He did sometimes write down something about having been just being living when he was a young one, when he was in the middle of his beginning living. He did then write down that he was a troubled one and really he was not then a troubled one in the sense of being interested in that thing, in the sense of remembering anything of such a thing. It was to him later a little later when he was reading what he had been writing surprising to be learning that he had been every day then, all day then completely a troubled one. Certainly he was not remembering any such a thing. Certainly he had not been living in any such thing. Certainly he had been being a troubled one, certainly he had not been completely interested in any such thing, certainly he had been writing down such a thing. This certainly did astonish him then. Anyway he was being living and he was then deciding somethings quite often and some asked him quite often then to decide something and certainly he was quite clearly thinking then and he was feeling something and feeling it clearly enough then and he was doing things with others who were doing something and it was a thing he did quite well, some things he did with them he did very well, some things he did with them he did very well.

Certainly he did some things he did with some then very well, very very well. Some of the others did some of these things very well, some did some of them very very well, some did not do them so very well. He did a good many things then and he did them with those he knew then, who knew him then who were doing them then. Certainly he did some of them very well, he did some of them quite well. He was clearly thinking then and clearly enough feeling then and he was with those he knew then and he did things together with them then and he did some of them very well and some of them extremely well and some of them quite well. He was living Hersland family living then. He was knowing then those who were living near the Hersland family then. He knew quite a number of ones being living then, a good many knew him then.

Certainly some when they are young ones are deciding some things. Certainly some when they are being living are deciding some things. Certainly some when they are not young ones are deciding some things. Some are deciding some things. Some are certain that any decision they are giving is a good one. Some are certain that not any decision is a good one. Some are certain that it is a good thing that there is not being any deciding. Some are deciding some things. Some when they are young ones are deciding some things. Certainly some are feeling when some one has decided some thing that some one should have decided something, that deciding should have been done. Certainly it is puzzling, certainly some are wondering if it is not puzzling that some are certain that some are deciding some things. Some are wondering if deciding some things is a thing that makes one one some one should be contradicting. Certainly some are deciding some things. Some are wondering if deciding some things is a thing that makes one one some one should be considering. Certainly some when they are young ones are deciding some things. Certainly some when they are not young ones are deciding some thing. Some are deciding something. Some are wondering if being certain that some thing is some thing some one will sometime be deciding is something that is a thing to be doing. Some are wondering if deciding something is something that makes one be some one who really is doing something. Some certainly are wondering if some things are being decided by those deciding some things. Some are certainly uncertain whether they should have a feeling of submission when some one has decided something. Some certainly are wondering if deciding anything is giving any meaning in being one being living. Some are certainly wondering if hoping something about something being decided sometime is a thing that is a feeling in them. Some are wondering if any one is not hoping that some time some things will be decided. Some are certain that sometime they will not be wondering about whether deciding anything has any meaning. Certainly some are deciding some things. Certainly some when they are young ones are deciding some things. Certainly some when they are not young ones are deciding some things. Certainly some are quite ready to have not anything be decided by any one. Some are quite ready to have it that every thing is not decided, that not any one is deciding anything. Some are certainly quite ready that no one should decide anything. Certainly some are quite ready for such a thing. Certainly some are quite ready that not any one should decide anything. Certainly some are deciding something. Certainly some when they are young ones are deciding something. David Hersland when he was a young one was deciding somethings. That certainly was a natural thing. David Hersland when he was not a young one was in a way deciding some things.

Some smell something. Some smell a good many things. Some have a very strong feeling when they are smelling something. Some smell themselves when they are smelling something. Some are certain that smelling something is something they are always doing. Some smell something more when they are young ones than when they are older ones. Some smell themselves when they smell something more when they are young ones than when they are older ones, some more when they are older ones than when they are young ones, some all of their living, all of their living are smelling something, are smelling themselves when they are smelling something. David Hersland was in a way not such a one. Certainly he did sometimes smell something, certainly he did sometimes smell himself when he smelled something, certainly some others he was knowing were very often smelling something, some of them were quite completely interested in this thing in smelling something, some were quite completely interested in smelling themselves when they were smelling something, some were not at all interested in smelling themselves when they were smelling something. David Hersland was sometimes smelling something, he was sometimes interested in smelling something, he was sometimes smelling himself when he was smelling something, he was not ever completely interested in smelling himself when he was smelling something.

Some are smelling something and then they are remembering something. Some are smelling something and are then completely remembering something. David Hersland was sometimes smelling something and then remembering something, he was interested enough in this thing. Some are very much interested in this thing in remembering something when they are smelling something. Some are not really interested in smelling anything. Some are interested in not smelling anything. David Hersland was not really interested in this thing, in not smelling anything.

David Hersland was a young one and he was living then and he was quite completely interested in this thing in being one being living then, almost completely interested in this thing in being one being living. He was being living and he was doing things then and he was remembering then that he was going to be doing some things and he was doing some of them and he was not doing some of them. He was doing a good many that he remembered he was going to be doing. He did not do all of them the things he remembered he was going to be doing. He did some things quite often as often as he was going to do them. He did not do some things very often not anywhere nearly as often as he was going to do them. He did a good many things quite often, really a great many things quite often, he did a good many things almost as often as he was going to be doing them.

He was a young one and he was being living then and he knew some then who were being ones being young then, he knew several of them every day then and he was sometimes very busy knowing everything he was knowing while he was being then being living. Sometimes he was very completely being one knowing some, sometimes he was not very completely being one knowing some who were being living then.

He knew some who were listening and he was telling something and these did not know they were listening and he was not then certain they were listening and he was then not feeling anything about this thing and then he was thinking about this thing thinking that he knew more than they did about everything and certainly they should have been listening and they were listening and certainly they were not remembering not ever remembering that they had been listening and he, he was remembering that they had been listening, that he had been telling something and they had been listening. Some of such of them were young ones then when they were listening. Some who had been listening were older ones who certainly were ones remembering that they had been ones teaching him something then and certainly they were ones remembering that they had been ones teaching then something.

He was a young one and he was being living and he was being living a long time that is to say he was being a young one all the time he was living when he was not an older one.

He was a young one and he was that all the time he was a young one, that is to say he was in the beginning of his being one being living, and was one being living then.

He was one almost completely clearly thinking when he was thinking. He was one almost completely clearly arranging something so that he could be completely clearly deciding something about that thing. He was such a one in being a young one. He was in a way such a one in being one being living. He was when he was a young one clearly thinking. He was when he was a young one arranging something and then clearly thinking about that thing.

When he was quite a young one he was quite often thinking. When he was quite a young one he was quite often almost completely clearly thinking about some thing. When he was quite a young one he was quite often arranging something and then clearly thinking about that thing.

He was, when he was quite a young one, quite often quite clearly deciding something. He was, when he was quite a young one, quite often enough clearly enough deciding something for some. He was, when he was quite a young one, quite often thinking about something.

He was, when he was quite a young one, quite often deciding some things for some one.

He was, when he was quite a young one, knowing some who were living then and some of them knew him then and some of them knew he was deciding some things quite clearly then and some did not know that he was deciding some things quite clearly then, some were almost certain that he was not deciding anything then. Some certainly did know some whom he knew then, did know that he was quite clearly deciding some things then. Some who knew him then knew he was thinking clearly then, some of such of them knew he was deciding some things then, some of such of them did not know he was deciding some things then.

He was one knowing, then when he was a young one, knowing some who were living then and some of them knew him then. He was living, being one being living and knowing some who were living then and having some who were living know him.

He was being living then when he was a young one, he was being living then, and he was being one being living then and being one doing some things and knowing some and having some know him.

He was one being living, then when he was quite a young one, and some knew him then and he knew some then. He was one being living then and he was being one and some knew he was that one the one he was then and some did not know then that he was that one the one he was then. He was being living then and some knowing some then did not know then that he was one of them one of those that one was knowing then. He was being living then and some knowing some then did know quite well that he was one of them one of those that one was knowing then.

He was being living then when he was a young one and certainly there were some being living then and some knew him then and knew him again when they saw him and some who knew he was one being living then did not know him again when they saw him again.

He was one being living and some whom he knew then were certain that they had not ever seen him and they had seen him but they had not remembered that he was that one the one they had seen. He was one being living and he knew some who were living then and he certainly did know then that some of them knew he was being living then. He was being living, then when he was quite a young one and some knew that he was being living then. He was being living then and some knew that some were being living there then and so they knew he was being living then. He was being living then and some knew that he was being living then and some of them knew some were being living then and certainly he was one of them one of those who were being living then.

He was being living, then when he was quite a young one, and he knew some then, some who were being living then, and some knew him then, and some knew he was being living then, and some knew some were being living then.

Some know some one is not another one and some do not know that some one is not another one. Some knew that David Hersland was not another one and some did not know that David Hersland was not another one. Some knew that some were being living then and some of them knew that David Hersland was one of such of them and some of them did not know that David Hersland was one of such of them.

David Hersland was being living then when he was a young one, he was being living then and some who were being living knew that thing knew that he was being living then.

She says go, go and I go, she says come, come and I come. She says come, come, and I come, she says go, go, and I go. David Hersland was almost wanting to be needing to be such a one, one coming and one going. When he was not any longer a completely young one he was one wanting to be needing to be such a one. He was not really wanting to be such a one, he was really not wanting, he was almost completely wanting to be such a one, one needing to be going and coming, one needing to be coming and going. He was one almost completely clearly thinking, he was one quite clearly feeling, he was not wanting to be such a one, one going and coming, one coming and going. He was almost completely wanting to be needing being such a one. In a way he was not ever coming and going, going and coming, in a way he was almost doing this thing, coming and going, going and coming. He was one clearly feeling in being living. He was one almost completely clearly thinking. He was one almost completely wanting to be needing being one coming and going, going and coming. He was one almost completely waiting to be needing this thing. He was one not needing this thing, he was almost completely wanting to be needing this thing. He was one clearly feeling in being living, he was one almost completely clearly thinking. He was not completely liking being living. He was clearly feeling in being living. He was quite completely clearly thinking in being one being living.

He was quite a young one and he was being one being living then. He was not such a very young one and he was one being living then.

He was one all his being living in a way wanting to be needing being one going and coming, coming and going. He was not really wanting needing this thing when he was quite a young one. He was then not wanting to be needing this thing. He was quite a young one and was being living then. He was an older one and was being living then.

Some are knowing that they are sorrowing when they are sorrowing. Some are showing this by gloominess being in them. Some are sorrowing when they are sorrowing and are ther quite certain that they would be always sorrowing if they were not ones certain that gloominess is not a cheerful way of being one being existing. Some are quite certain that sorrowing, that having gloominess in them is a thing that has meaning, is a thing that at any time there is a meaning in having, that always there is not any reason for not sorrowing and some of such of them could be ones being gloomy ones if they were not ones being cheerful ones. Some of such of them would be ones being gloomy ones if they were not ones not being gloomy ones. David Hersland was in a way such a one, he was one being certain that always there was reason enough for any one being one sorrowing and he might have been one being a gloomy one but he was not one being a gloomy one and really he was not ever sorrowing. He was not ever sorrowing when he was a young one, he was sometimes almost sorrowing when he was not any longer a young one. He was not a gloomy one and that was because he was not a gloomy one. He would have been almost a gloomy one if he had not been one not being a gloomy one. Certainly he was not a gloomy one. Certainly he was one who might have been a gloomy one if he had not been one not being a gloomy one. He was one clearly feeling what he was feeling. He was one clearly thinking, almost completely clearly thinking. He was one wanting to be needing to be feeling something and not be clearly feeling that thing, to be almost a complete one in feeling that thing.

He was one being living, he was clearly feeling what he was feeling, he was almost completely thinking about everything. He was one being living. He was one being living until he was not any longer a young one one beginning being living, and then he was not any longer being living.

Sometimes he was with one, sometimes he was with two, sometimes he was with three, sometimes he was with more than three. When he was a young one sometimes he was with one, sometimes he was with two, sometimes he was with three, sometimes he was with four, sometimes he was with more than four. Sometimes there was one and he was with that one, sometimes there were two and he was with one of the two of them, sometimes there were three and he was with two of them, sometimes there were three and he was with the three of them, sometimes there were four and he was with two of them, sometimes he was with the four of them, sometimes he was with three of them. Sometimes when he was a young one he was with one, sometimes he was with two, sometimes he was with more than one, sometimes he was with three, sometimes he was with more than three.

When he was not such a young one sometimes he was with one. Sometimes he was with six. Sometimes he was with more than six. Sometimes he was with two. Sometimes he was with three.

When he was not at all a very young one sometimes he was with one. Sometimes he was with more than one. Sometimes he was with two sometimes he was with more than two. Sometimes he was with three. Sometimes he was. with more than three. Sometimes he was with four. Sometimes he was with more than four. Sometimes he was with five. Sometimes he was with more than five.

When he was in between not being any longer a quite a young one and being one not being an older one, when he was at the ending of the beginning of being living he was sometimes with three. He was sometimes then with one. He was sometimes then with another one. He was often then with one. He was often then with three. He was often then with two. He was often then with one. He was often then with another one. He was often then with another one. He was often then with six. He was often then with ten. He was often then with one. He was often then with another one. He was often then with another one. He was often then with another one. He was often then with three. He was often then with two.

He was older then and he was often then not with any one. He was sometimes then with one. He was often then with more than one. He was often then with a good many more than one. He was sometimes then with one. He was sometimes then with another one. He was sometimes then with another one.

He was sometimes then with more than ten. He was sometimes then with more than one. He was sometimes then with three. He was sometimes then with one. He was sometimes then with not any one. He was sometimes then with more than one.

David Hersland was clearly thinking about some things about which he was thinking, David Hersland was thinking about some things. He was clearly thinking about them. He was clearly thinking about them.

David Hersland was thinking about things and clearly thinking about them about the things about which he was clearly thinking. He was clearly thinking about things about which he was thinking. He was thinking clearly about them. He was deciding to think about things and to clearly think about them. He certainly decided that some other ones would think about somethings would clearly think about the things about which they were thinking.

He was thinking about some things about very many things about anything and he was completely living in thinking clearly about the things about which he was thinking. He was thinking clearly and he was thinking about some things. He was thinking about anything. He was thinking about everything. He was thinking clearly about the things about which he was thinking. He was deciding about this thing about thinking clearly about the things about which he was thinking. He was deciding about thinking clearly about clearly thinking about the things about which he was thinking. He was deciding about some thinking clearly about things about which they were thinking. He was deciding about thinking clearly about things, about clearly thinking about the things about which thinking is being done as being existing. He was deciding that clearly thinking about the things about which there is thinking is something being existing. He was deciding this for some. He was one and there were some and there were more then and he was deciding that clearly thinking about things is being existing. He was deciding this for some.

He was not deciding, not really deciding for any one that they should not be ones sorrowing. He was not deciding for himself that he should not be one sorrowing. He was not deciding about sorrowing being existing. He was not deciding about this thing. He was not deciding for any one that any one should not smell everything. He was not deciding about smelling things, for any one. He was not deciding about smelling things, for himself. He was not deciding about his being about his not being one smelling everything. He was not one deciding for any one their smelling themselves in smelling anything. He was not really deciding this for any one. He was not thinking about deciding this thing for himself, he was not deciding about this thing about smelling oneself in smelling anything. He was really not deciding anything about this thing. He might have been one who could be one deciding something about smelling, about sorrowing, he was not one feeling anything of deciding about any such thing, about smelling, about sorrowing. He was smelling some in being living, he was not deciding anything about this thing. He was smelling himself in smelling something. He was not deciding anything about this thing. He was sorrowing some in being one being living, he was not deciding anything about this thing. Sometimes he was with one, sometimes he was with more than one. He was not then deciding anything about sorrowing, about smelling. He was sometimes with one. He was not then deciding anything about sorrowing, anything about smelling. He was sometimes with more than one. He was not then really deciding anything, about smelling, anything about sorrowing.

He was clearly feeling some things. He was very clearly feeling what he was feeling. He was wanting to be needing to be feeling some things and to be clearly thinking in not clearly feeling them. He was one really not deciding about smelling, about sorrowing.

A noise is something some one is hearing. Many are making noises and many are hearing noises. A noise is a great many things some one is hearing. A great deal of noise is something some one is hearing.

A good deal of noise, a very great deal of noise, noise, continued noise, more noise, always some noise, always a good deal of noise, noise is what some one is hearing. A good deal of noise, a great deal of noise, noise is something some one is not hearing. A great deal of noise, noise, continued noise, a good deal of noise is what some one would be hearing if there were any noise, if there were a great deal of noise, if there were any noise for that one to be hearing. Some one is sometime hearing very much noise. Sometimes that one is not hearing any noise. There is sometimes not any noise for that one to be hearing. A great deal of noise is something that one is sometimes hearing.

Some one is not certain that some one whom that one was certain was not a dull one is a dull one. Some one who was certain that some one was not a dull one is now certain that that one is a dull one. That one is asking if that one who was once not a dull one is not now a dull one. That one is not so certain that that one who was once not a dull one is now a dull one, is not so certain of this thing that that one can tell any one that that one is a dull one. That one is almost certain and that one can talk about this thing about the one who was not a dull one being now a dull one.

In a way it is a gentle thing to be one being not any longer living that is to say it is a gentle thing to be one having done something and doing that thing was not a gentle thing not at all a gentle thing. It is a gentle thing to be one being one not any more doing the thing that one was doing and it is a gentle thing to tell about that thing by some other one the thing that one was doing. Doing a thing is not quite a gentle thing, and having done the thing is almost a gentle thing, and some one telling about it when that one is not ever doing a thing is a gentle thing and discussing that thing the thing done is a very gentle thing.

There were times when certainly David Hersland made noises and others made noises and certainly there were times when he was interested in this thing in noises being existing, in some one hearing noises, in his being one listening to noises which were then being existing.

There were times when David Hersland was a noisy one. There were times when he was with one and he and that one were noisy ones then. There were times when he was with more than one and he and all of them were making noises then. There were times when he was hearing noises and there were times when he was liking this thing liking noises being existing. He was not ever completely needing that noises be existing. Some are completely needing that noises are existing. David Hersland was not completely needing noises being existing. David Hersland was one making noises sometime. David Hersland was hearing noises sometimes and very often he was not hearing any noise, not hearing very much noise. David Hersland was not completely needing that noise be existing. Certainly some are completely needing that noise is existing. Certainly some are needing this thing and some certainly are not needing this thing are not needing that noise is existing. David Hersland was not completely needing this thing not completely needing that noise is existing. David Hersland could know that he was not completely needing this thing thing not needing noise to be existing. Some are knowing that they are completely needing this thing needing that noises are existing. David Hersland was not completely needing that noises be existing.

All his living David Hersland was knowing this thing was knowing that noises were existing. This never made him a nervous one, this that noises are existing. This did not irritate him, this, that noises are existing. This did not disgust him, this, that noises are existing. This did not displease him, this did not arouse him, this, that noises are existing. He was not completely needing this thing, needing that noise is being existing. He could know this thing know that he was not completely needing this thing needing that noises are existing.

Sometimes in being living, all his living he was making noises and sometimes then he was with one and sometimes then he was with three and sometimes then he was with more than three and sometimes then he could know that he was not completely needing that noise is existing and sometimes then he was not knowing this thing knowing that he was not completely needing that noises are existing and sometimes then when he was not knowing it then knowing that he was not completely needing that noises are existing every one there then knew it that he was one not completely needing that noises be existing and sometimes then some one did not tell him that he was one not completely needing this thing needing that noises are existing and sometimes then some one talked about this thing to some other one and to him and certainly then he was not knowing then that he was not completely needing that noise be existing and certainly he was one who could be knowing that he was not completely needing that noise be existing. And all his being living he was one sometimes making noises and all his living he was one not completely needing that noises be existing and all his living he was one who could be knowing this thing knowing that he was one not completely needing that noises be existing and all his living some knew this thing knew that he was not completely needing that noises are existing and all his living he was sometimes making noises and sometimes then he was with one and sometimes then he was not with any one and sometimes then he was with more than one and sometimes then he was with a good many more than one. All his living he was not completely needing that noises be existing. He was making noises and he was then one making some noise and he heard then the noises that he was making and he could know then that he was not completely needing that noises be existing. He was sometimes liking this thing liking that sometimes noises were existing, he was not wanting to be completely needing that noises are existing. He could know that he was not completely needing that noises are existing. He was not interested in this thing in his not completely needing that noises are existing. He was all his living sometimes making noises sometimes with one, sometimes when alone, sometimes when with some, sometimes when there were a good many and he was with them. Certainly he was not needing that noises are existing, not completely needing that noises are existing. Certainly he was sometimes making noises, all his living he was sometimes making noises. Certainly he was not completely needing that noises are existing. Certainly he was making noises sometimes, all his living. Certainly any one was knowing that he was not completely needing that noises are existing. Certainly he could be knowing that he was not completely needing that noise is existing.

David Hersland certainly was not a dull one that is to say he was not one whom mostly every one was finding to be one who was not interesting. He was not a dull one sometimes, and mostly always he was not a dull one, that is to say mostly always most of those knowing him were interested when he was being one existing for them. He was then not a dull one. He was one certainly knowing that he was not a dull one. He was not completely interested in this thing in knowing that he was not a dull one. He was completely knowing this thing knowing that he was not a dull one. He was knowing that mostly every one knowing him were interested in him when he was being one being existing for them. Certainly all his living he was not a dull one. Certainly all his living he was one interesting some, interesting a good many when he was being existing to them. He was, all his living, not a dull one. He was completely knowing this thing, all his living he was completely knowing this thing, knowing that he was not a dull one. He was not completely interested in this thing in knowing that he was not a dull one. All his living he was not completely interested in this thing in knowing that he was not a dull one, that he was not dull to most who were knowing him, that he was interesting those who were knowing that he was being existing.

He was then not a dull one. Certainly some who were not dull ones are ones not being dull ones and then they are not interesting very many who are knowing that that one is being existing. Some are ones not being dull ones and they are ones then interesting mostly every one who is knowing that they are being existing and then they are not dull ones and they are then not interesting every one who are knowing they are being existing. Some are not being dull ones and they are interesting every one who is knowing they are being existing, mostly every, any one, and then they are not being dull ones and they are interesting then some who are knowing that they are being existing, and then they are not being dull ones and they are interesting some who are knowing they are being existing and they are then not really dull ones and they are then interesting some who are knowing they are being existing. They are then interesting some who are knowing they are being existing, they are not then really dull ones, they are then interesting some who are knowing they are being existing. In a way David Hersland was such a kind of one. David Hersland was interesting some who were knowing he was being living. He was not a dull one. He was interesting some who were knowing he was being existing. He was interesting some who were knowing he was being living, he was not then really a dull one, he was not then a dull one, he was then interesting some who were knowing that he was then being existing, he was then not really a dull one, he was then interesting to some who were knowing him then.

David Hersland was one who was finding some being dull ones, who was finding some not being dull ones when he was one being living. David Hersland was one not finding ones being dull ones, he was one finding some being stupid ones, he was one finding some being ones not finding any way to be ones knowing that they are the ones they are being in being living, he was one finding some being ones not ever coming to be certain that they are going on being living, he was one finding very many being ones not going to be ever beginning in keeping going in thinking, he was finding very many being living, he was finding some being not at all dull in being ones he was then knowing, he was finding very many being ones very likely to be ones not going to be interesting some time, he was one finding very many being quite stupid in being ones going on being living, he was one finding very many not being dull in being ones he was being knowing when they were being living, he was one finding some going to be ones beginning being ones thinking, he was one finding very many who were almost beginning being ones thinking, he was one finding very many who were not ones thinking what they were beginning to be thinking, he was one finding very many who were not thinking, he was one finding very many who were not clearly thinking, he was one finding some who were not interesting, he was one finding very many who were interesting when he was knowing them when they were being living.

Some one is doing something. Some have done something. What they have done they have done and they worked then and they did a thing and certainly it was a complete thing quite a complete thing and it was not so gently a complete thing as it is when some other ones are seeing it a completed thing. Some one has done something. It is a completed thing, a quite complete thing. It has a beginning, a middle and an end. It is all done. It is a complete thing. It was done by some one. The one that did that thing began it and went on with it and finished it. It is a complete thing. Any one can see it and every one is certain that it is a complete thing, and some are certain that it is a complete thing and some are feeling it to be a complete thing and they are telling about it as being existing, a complete thing, and certainly it is a complete thing, and certainly then it is in a way a gentle thing, that is to say a gently complete thing, that is to say a thing that is a complete thing and some are certain of this thing. A thing is a complete thing and then certainly if some come to know that of it it is a gentle thing for certainly if any one can come to be certain that a thing is a complete thing that thing is something that every one is gently seeing. Certainly then some are saying they are not looking at it and these then are not gently seeing anything, these are seeing a complete thing but certainly not every one can be seeing that as a complete thing. When any one, that is every one, that is some, that is mostly any one can see something as a complete thing, that thing has come to be a gently complete thing, a thing that can be gently seen as a complete thing and anything that is a complete thing will be sometime seen gently seen as a complete thing and certainly then some will then be looking at some other thing.

David Hersland was not gently seeing anything as a complete thing. He was looking at some things that mostly any one could see then as a complete thing and he was then not really seeing it as a complete thing and so he was not seeing it gently as a complete thing. Really he was not seeing the things which have been made by some one and are complete things. He certainly was looking at some of them, at a good many of them, and he was certain they were complete things, and he was almost seeing them gently, completely as gently complete things and he was almost not looking at them, he was almost looking at the things that are complete things, that some one was then making, as a complete thing, as complete things and he was not completely then seeing such a thing, seeing such things as complete things, really then in a way he was not completely seeing complete things as complete things, not really completely seeing complete things as complete things, not really seeing a complete thing as a complete thing and so he was almost seeing a complete thing, a thing any one then could gently be seeing as a complete thing, he was almost gently seeing that thing as a complete thing, and he was almost seeing a thing, a complete thing some one was then making, as a complete thing, he was almost then seeing such a thing as a complete thing.

David Hersland was being living and he was then not any longer being living. He was one being living and then being living and then he was not any longer one, he was not then being one being living.

Naturally some knew David Hersland had a brother and a sister and a father and a mother. Naturally some were certain that he was in Hersland family living. He was like them, of course he was like them, why should he be unlike them when he had been living with them and had come out of them and had heard them and had seen them. He did some things in the way they did things. He did some things in the way some of them did some things. Some do not like to do things in the way they do things that is in the way some other ones do things. Some are very earnest in this thing, some are very eager in this thing, some are often telling about this thing about not doing some things in the way some of the ones related to them by blood connection are doing such things. David Hersland was not one of such of them. He mostly was not thinking himself being one doing a thing in the way some other one was doing a thing. And sometimes it was a pleasant thing to him to be connected with every other one by such a thing by doing things in a way he was noticing other ones had been doing. Sometimes it was a pleasant thing to him to know then that everything means something, that he was a part of every one who was a part of him and sometimes he had very much family feeling in him, sometimes he had quite enough family feeling in him, very often he had not very much family feeling in him, very often he was naturally not having any family feeling.

Very naturally some were certain that he was not one interested in that thing in family feeling. Very naturally some were remembering that he was one not living in any family living. Naturally some were knowing that he was living in a family living. Naturally some were thinking of him as being in Hersland family living.

Some were understanding family living and were understanding that he was not in any family living. Some were understanding family living and were understanding that he was in a family living. Some were understanding the Hersland family living and were understanding that he was not living in the Hersland family living. Some were understanding the Hersland family living and were understanding that he was living in Hersland family living.

Some were understanding that he was liking his father and his mother and his brother and his sister. Some were understanding that he was admiring his mother and his father and his brother and his sister. He was understanding that he was liking his father and his mother and his brother and his sister. He was understanding that he was not liking his father and his mother and his sister and his brother. He was understanding that he was not admiring his father and his mother and his sister and his brother. He was understanding that he was admiring his father and his mother and his brother and his sister. Some were knowing that he had living a brother and a sister and a father and a mother. Some were not knowing that he had living a brother and a sister and a mother and a father.

He was being living every day. In a way he was needing to be certain that he was being living every day he was being living. He was being living every day he was being living. He was being living every day until he was not being living which was at the ending of the beginning of the middle of being living. He was being living every day. In a way he was needing knowing every day that he was being living every day. When he was beginning being living he was being living every day. In a way he was knowing then every day that he was being living. He was being living every day when he was beginning being living. In a way he was knowing that then. He was such a one. He went on being living and he was knowing this thing knowing he was being living every day. In a way he was knowing this thing every day all of his being living.

When he was beginning being living he was knowing this thing, knowing every day that he was being living. All his living he was knowing this thing, knowing every day that he was being living. In a way he was knowing this thing every day. He was, every day, knowing he was being living. He was being living every day. He was knowing it every day. He was knowing it all his living every day. He was knowing it when he was beginning being living, he was knowing it then in a way, every day.

It can be known, this thing, it can be known in a way every day, that one is being living. It can be known every day. It can be known all day. It can be known all of living every day. It can be known all of living all day every day that one is being living. David Hersland was knowing this thing every day, that he was being living. All of his living he was knowing this thing every day. In a way all his living he knew it every day. All his living, every day he knew he was being living.

He was being living every day. He knew it every day. All of his living he knew it every day.

He was being living every day. In a way he knew, every day, he knew he was being living. He was being living every day. He knew, every day, he knew he was being living, in a way he knew it every day. He was being living every day. Every day he knew, in a way, that he was being living. He knew every day that he was being living that day. He was being living every day all of his being living.

He was dead when he was at the ending of the beginning of being in middle living. He was dead by then. He was dead and buried by then. He was not being living beyond the ending of the beginning of being in the middle of being living. He was dead by then. He was not any longer living then.

He was living every day when he was being living. He was knowing every day that he was being living that day. He was not knowing all day that he was living that day, every day. He was not knowing it all day that he was being living that day. .He was knowing every day part of the day that he was being living then. He was not knowing every day mostly all day that he was being living that day. He was knowing part of the day, every day, that he was being living that day.

He was knowing that he was being living every day. He was being living every day. He was knowing he was being living every day. He was knowing it every day that he was being living that day.

He was being living every day. He was, and really he was not succeeding, he was knowing every day that he would know each day what he was meaning by being one being living that day. He was being living every day. He was knowing every day that he was being living that day. He was knowing every day that he would know that day what he was meaning by being living that day. He was being living every day. He would be knowing every day what he was meaning by being living that day and he was knowing every day that he was being living that day. Every day he was knowing he was being living that day.

He was being living every day. He was knowing every day that he was being living on that day. He was knowing every day that he was being living. He would know that he was meaning being one being living every day. He would be one being living every day and knowing every day he was being living that day and would be knowing every day the meaning in being living that day. He was being living every day. He was, every day, knowing he was being living. He was, every day knowing he was knowing the meaning of being living that day. He was not succeeding. He was being living. He was being living and that was being existing by knowing the meaning of being existing on that day. He was being living until the end of the beginning of middle living. He was succeeding in being living until the end of the beginning of being in middle living. He was being living every day. He was knowing every day that he was being living that day.

He was being living every day. He was knowing every day that he was being living that day. He was being living every day when he was in the beginning of being living. He was knowing then every day that he was being living that day. He was living every day when he was at the ending of the beginning of being living. He was knowing then every day that he was being living that day. He was being living every day when he was in the middle of the beginning of being living. He was knowing then every day that he was living that day.

He was living every day, all of his being living. He was knowing every day that he was being living that day, every day all of his being living. He was being living every day all of the beginning of being living. He was knowing every day that he was being living that day all of his beginning being living. He was being living every day all of his being living. He was knowing every day that he was being living, all of his living. He was being living every day through the beginning of the middle of being living. He was knowing then every day that he was being living that day. He was being living every day, all of his being living. He was knowing he was being living every day, all of his being living.

Sometime he was feeling something. Sometime he was eating something, sometime he was thinking something. In his daily living he was thinking, he was eating, he was feeling. Any one could be such a one. He was such a one. Not any one could be such a one. He was almost not eating anything, he was thinking something, he was feeling something. He had need of this thing of being one eating something, of being one almost not eating anything. He had need of these things of being one eating something, of being one almost not eating anything.

Eating one thing is a way of living for some. Deciding to be eating one thing is a way of living for some. Deciding anything about eating is a way of living for some. Eating one thing, deciding to eat one thing is all being living for some. David Hersland was one deciding about eating something. David Hersland was one sometimes deciding to be eating only one thing. Deciding about eating one thing, deciding about eating, eating one thing, eating some thing was not all of living for him.

He was then one living all his living that is to say until he was not any longer living, until he was one who had been living, who was then one not any longer living.

Every day that he was living he was one being himself inside him, he was one doing something, he was one going to be doing something, he was one knowing some, he was one some were knowing. Every day he was being living he was not being one being himself inside him to himself then as he was some other time in being living. Every day he was being living he was pretty nearly being to himself inside him what he was to himself inside him the other times in his being living. He was himself inside him, pretty nearly every day he was, was himself to himself inside him. Pretty nearly every day he was being himself inside him to himself then and being in a way different from being to himself inside him from the way he was any other day and being pretty nearly the same to himself inside him that day as every other day. He was, every day he was being living, he was being to himself inside him pretty nearly the same and quite not at all the same and certainly he was being pretty nearly the same. Certainly he was, certainly he was pretty nearly the same. Certainly he was not at all the same, quite not the same. Every day he was knowing some one, knowing some, and every day some one, some were knowing him. To some he was always pretty nearly the same, to some he was the same one day as another day. To some he was not the same not the same one day as another day. Some were certain he was the same every day. Some were certain he was not the same every day. He was the same every day, he was pretty nearly the same to himself inside him every day and this is not a description of him, this is certainly not a description of him, that he was the same every day, that he was to himself pretty nearly the same every day.

David Hersland lived as long as he was living and he certainly sometimes was quite certain that he needed to be completely expressing the feeling that certainly there was not any succeeding in being living, that certainly it was enough not to have been ever living, that it would have been enough to have not been one coming to be living, that having been living, being living had not in any way any meaning.

He certainly sometimes in being living was needing to have some way of completely feeling such a thing and certainly sometimes in being living he came almost completely to be feeling this thing, to be completely feeling that it would have been enough not to have come to be one being living. He certainly sometimes in being living came to be almost completely feeling, completely feeling that being living could not have in any way any meaning. He was sometimes needing to have some way of expressing such a thing and sometimes he did in some way express such a thing, he certainly did in some way sometimes express such a thing. He did sometimes almost completely feel such a thing. He did sometimes in some way express such a thing. He certainly did sometimes in some way express such a thing.

David Hersland was living and all the time he was not certain that he was not needing feeling something that certainly not any one and in a way he was certain of this thing, not any one was really feeling. And then he was not certain. Certainly some were really feeling something and that was then a thing that was completely making it that something is existing and some are being living in being doing something and that is making being living something that has in a way a possibility in meaning and in a way then it does not make any difference really of anything, does not make really everything in any complete way a different thing and certainly then there is not any way of having anything a different thing since the different thing if it is a different thing is completely a different thing and if it is not a different thing then it is not a completely different thing and certainly then David Hersland was not then feeling anything that was a completely different thing and certainly then he was completely interested and completely not interested in any such thing. He certainly was one almost completely interested in a different thing. He certainly was one almost completely not interested in a completely different thing. He was almost completely interested in feeling a different thing. He was pretty nearly not at all interested in feeling a different thing. He was almost completely interested in feeling any completely different thing. He certainly was almost completely interested in not having completely been feeling something. He certainly was almost completely interested in some having almost completely felt something. He went on living and not a very long time that is to say he was living to the ending of the beginning of middle living and certainly he was then such a one, having been such a one, one almost completely interested in feeling a completely different thing, one almost completely interested in not having been feeling a completely different thing, one almost completely interested in any one feeling a completely different thing, one almost not interested in feeling any different thing, one almost completely not interested in any one completely feeling any one thing, one almost completely interested in not completely feeling anything, one almost completely interested in not feeling any different thing.

In a way he was quite certain that not any one not coming to be loving him could be coming to be completely listening to him. In a way he was quite certain that not any one was coming to be loving him. In a way he was not certain of this thing. In a way some one was coming to be loving him and certainly then was listening to him and certainly then he was knowing this thing knowing that this one was listening to him and in a way then he was certain that this one in a way was coming to loving him and certainly then this one was not ever completely that thing and in a way he was certain of this thing certain that this one was not coming to be completely that thing one loving him. Certainly some were quite completely listening to him and certainly he was knowing this thing knowing they were quite completely listening to him and he knew too that some one coming to be loving him would be coming completely to listen to him and certainly in a way he was certain that not any one had been completely coming to be loving him and certainly some were almost completely doing this thing, loving him, and certainly some were quite completely listening to him certainly quite completely listening to him. In a way some one came to be loving him and certainly was listening to him and he certainly did know that if any one was coming completely to love him such a one would come to completely listen to him and in a way he was certain that not any one was doing any such thing coming to completely love him and he was not certain that some one would not come to be doing this thing coming to be completely loving him and certainly some one coming to be completely loving him would be completely listening to him, to all of him.

He was being living from the beginning of being living to the ending of the beginning of middle living. Certainly some were quite completely listening to him. Certainly some were quite completely listening to him.

David Hersland was certainly one thinking. He certainly was one knowing this thing. If he was thinking and knowing this thing, and he was thinking and knowing this thing knowing he was thinking, if he was thinking he was thinking about something, in a way he was thinking about anything. He was thinking and he was knowing this thing, he was knowing he was thinking. He was thinking about something, in a way he was thinking about anything Certainly if in a way he was thinking about anything and he was knowing this thing, he was knowing that he could be thinking about anything. He was thinking about anything, he was knowing this thing, he was knowing that he was thinking about anything. He was thinking about something. He was knowing this thing, knowing that he was thinking about something. He was knowing that he was thinking about something. He was knowing that he was thinking. He was knowing that he was thinking about anything. If he was thinking about something, really thinking about something and knowing this thing, knowing that he was thinking about something, he was knowing that he was thinking. He was one knowing about thinking. He was one completely thinking about thinking. Certainly then he was knowing that he was one thinking about anything. He was knowing that he was thinking about anything. He was one completely knowing about thinking. He was one knowing that he was one thinking. He was knowing that he was one thinking about anything and certainly he was doing this thing he was thinking about anything. He was certain of this thing that he was one thinking and certainly he was one thinking. He was one certain about this thing that he was thinking about something and certainly he was doing this thing he was thinking about something. He was one certain that he was thinking about anything and certainly he was doing this thing he was thinking about anything. In a way then he was one being completely interesting, one thinking about something, one thinking about anything. Certainly then he was one thinking, really thinking, he was one really thinking about something, he was one really thinking about anything. In a way then he was completely interesting, in a way then he was not completely interesting. He certainly was doing this thing, he certainly was really thinking. He certainly was knowing this thing, knowing that he was really thinking. He certainly was one completely knowing about thinking, about really thinking. In a way then he was not completely interesting in a way then he was not completely thinking, in a way he was completely thinking about something, in a way he was not completely thinking about anything. He was really thinking, he was really thinking about something, he was really thinking about anything, he was completely knowing about thinking. He was not completely interesting. He certainly was completely thinking about something, he certainly was really completely thinking, he certainly was not really completely thinking about anything. He was completely knowing about thinking. He was completely thinking. He was really completely thinking. He was completely thinking about something, he was completely thinking about anything. Certainly he was not completely interesting in being one completely thinking. He was one being living and certainly he was completely thinking and he was completely thinking about anything and he was completely thinking about something. Certainly he was completely thinking about anything, about that he was completely thinking. He was thinking about anything.

He was one and he was knowing that thing knowing that he was one. He was one wanting to be knowing that thing, that he was one. He was one and he was almost always knowing that thing knowing that he was one. He was needing this thing needing knowing that he was one and he certainly was one and he certainly was almost always knowing that thing knowing that he was one. He was needing this thing needing that he was knowing this thing knowing that he was one. He was not always knowing that he was needing this thing needing knowing that he was one.

He was very often knowing this thing knowing that he was needing knowing that he was one.

He was not often telling this thing telling that he was knowing he was one. He was sometimes telling this thing telling that he was knowing that he was one. He was quite certain of this thing, that he was one. He was sometimes telling this thing telling that he was one.

He was sometimes wanting to be needing another one. He was sometimes needing another one. He was often enough wanting to be needing another one. He was sometimes almost needing another one.

He was not often telling about this thing about almost needing another one. He was almost certain about this thing, sometimes he was almost certain about this thing about almost needing another one. He certainly was often enough wanting to be completely needing another one.

He was not completely needing this thing, needing another one. Sometimes he was almost needing another one. He was sometimes quite completely wanting to be needing another one.

He was quite a young one and then he was knowing this thing knowing that he was one. He was always knowing this thing knowing that he was one. He was at the ending of his being living knowing this thing knowing that he was one. He was then sometimes wanting to be needing another one. He was then not needing another one.

He certainly was sometimes almost completely wanting to be needing another one. He was sometimes almost needing another one. There were several of them and they were quite different each one from any other one of them and he was sometimes wanting to be needing one and he was sometimes almost needing one and he was not ever completely needing one, ever completely needing any one. He was one. He was very often not telling anything about that thing about being one. He was not ever telling any one he was almost needing telling about his being one. He was one. He was very often not telling about this thing. He was very often knowing this thing, he was almost always knowing this thing, that he was one, he was very often not telling about this thing, about being one, he was not telling about this thing, about being one, to any one he was almost needing, to any one he was wanting to be needing.

Some like to enjoy things the way they used to enjoy them. Some do not like to enjoy things the way they used to enjoy them. Some love to enjoy things the way they used to enjoy them. Some do not love to enjoy things the way they used to enjoy them. Some hate to enjoy things the way they used to enjoy them. Some like sometimes to enjoy things the way they used to enjoy them.

David Hersland sometimes liked to enjoy things the way he used to enjoy them. He enjoyed things and then sometimes he would like to enjoy things the way he used to enjoy them. He and some others sometimes enjoyed things. Some of them liked to enjoy things the way they used to enjoy them. He sometimes liked to enjoy things the way he used to enjoy them. Some and he was one of them enjoyed things. Some of them later would have liked to enjoy things the way they used to enjoy them. He sometimes would have liked to enjoy things the way he used to enjoy them. There were some and he was one who enjoyed things. They enjoyed them and they did them and they all did them and they all enjoyed them and they all told about this thing about enjoying them and they all later sometimes would have liked to enjoy things the way they had enjoyed them.

They all enjoyed things, they all of them enjoyed things and did them then. Some of them sometimes enjoyed them more than others of them. Some of them told about enjoying, more than others of them. David Hersland told about enjoying them about enjoying the things. He told about this after there were not so many of them enjoying them and he was then going on enjoying them and some were then going on enjoying them and some were then telling about enjoying them the way they used to be enjoying them. David Hersland was enjoying the things then and was telling then about enjoying them the way they used to be enjoying them and some of them then were wanting to be enjoying things the way they used to be enjoying them and some were then not wanting that they were, all of them, enjoying them, the things, the way they used to be enjoying them. David Hersland was sometimes then, and not with all of them, wanting to be enjoying the things the way they used to be enjoying them. Some of them were then telling about enjoying the things the way they used to be enjoying them. David Hersland was then sometimes telling about enjoying them the way they used to be enjoying and sometimes he was telling this to some of them, sometimes to one of them, sometimes to all of them.

He was when he was at the ending of beginning living he was with some and all of them were enjoying some things then. They were, all of them then going to be sometime wanting to be enjoying some things the way they were enjoying them then. They were all of them in a way living some in this thing in going to be sometime wanting to be enjoying some things in the way they were enjoying them then. David Hersland was not living in that thing in going to be wanting to be enjoying something in the way they all of them were enjoying it then. In a way he was not then with them in living some in this thing in going to be sometime wanting to be enjoying something in the way they were enjoying something then. In a way he was not enjoying then with them, he was being one then not living not at all living in going to be sometime wanting to be enjoying something in the way they were enjoying something then. And later he was wanting to be enjoying something the way they had been enjoying something then and he was sometimes telling about this thing, beginning this thing with one, with more than one who had been ones enjoying themselves then and in a way it was a different thing in him then as he had not been at all living,when they had been enjoying something, he had not been at all living in going to be sometimes wanting to be enjoying something the way they were enjoying it then.

He was then enjoying some things with them with some who were enjoying things, then when he was at the ending of beginning living, and he was then not enjoying with them living some in going to be ones sometime wanting to be enjoying things the way they were enjoying them then. In a way then he was not enjoying things then in being one being with some all of whom were enjoying things then. Certainly later he was telling one of them, some of them, that they would then be enjoying something and in a way then they were enjoying something and certainly then to him then they were enjoying something in the way they had been enjoying something when they had been enjoying something and to the other one then, and to the others then they were not doing that thing they were not enjoying that thing the way they had been enjoying something when they had been enjoying something. And not any of them were talking about that thing and David Hersland then sometimes was talking about that thing, talking about it to some one, sometimes talking about it to some. Later he was enjoying some things with another one who had not been then enjoying somethings when the others had been enjoying somethings. He was enjoying some things with this one. This one was enjoying some things with him then, he was not then enjoying things the way he had been enjoying them. He certainly then was not interested in that thing in enjoying things the way he had enjoyed them.

He was loving one then and he was in a way telling this thing, telling it to her and others were knowing it then and in a way it was not interesting to her and he was not really telling it to her then and certainly any one could be certain that he was telling then something about that thing about loving the one he was loving then and she could be certain of this thing that he was telling that thing, telling that he was loving. He certainly was loving one then and certainly some were then almost certain of that thing that he was loving that one and she was almost certain of that thing that he was loving her then and it was an interesting thing then to her and it was an interesting thing then to them and not any one not she not he not they were then completely interested in that thing and certainly they were not any of them not liking it then, some of them then were not liking it and they did not come to like it that he was loving and loving the one he was loving, and certainly then he went on and certainly then every one was telling something about this thing, every one of them, about his loving the one he was loving then and certainly any one could know that he and the one he was loving were ones who were not coming to be completely interested in that thing, in loving, in his loving her, and some were then certain of this thing and some were then not certain of this thing, and he was not then certain of this thing and she was not then certain of this thing.

When he was loving this one and this one was one he was loving he was showing this one this thing showing this one that he was loving this one. He went on showing this one this thing that he was loving this one and this one was one knowing he was showing this thing showing he was loving this one and they were then going on in this thing and this then was not completely interesting to any one.

David Hersland was one feeling something and certainly he was one clearly thinking completely clearly thinking and he was one clearly feeling and he was one not completely clearly feeling and he was clearly feeling and he was needing to be one completely clearly thinking and he was clearly feeling and he was not completely clearly feeling. He was living until the ending of the beginning of middle living.

Each one is one. David Hersland was completely remembering this thing, remembering that each one is one.

He was knowing some and he was almost completely remembering that each one is one, he was completely remembering this thing that each one is one. He was then loving one of them and he was then completely remembering that each one is one. He was always almost completely remembering that each one is one. He certainly was almost completely remembering that each one is one. Always, all his living, he was almost completely remembering this thing that each one is one.

Each one is one, he was, all his living, pretty nearly completely remembering this thing. He was certain of this thing that each one is one. He was, all his living completely certain of this thing that each one is one. He was, all his living, almost completely remembering this thing, remembering that each one is one. He was, very often completely remembering this thing, that each one is one.

He was loving one then at the ending of beginning being living and he was then almost completely remembering that each one is one. He was then always almost completely remembering this thing. Any one could be almost certain that he was almost completely remembering that each one is one, that he was always then almost completely remembering that each one is one.

He was one who could be certain that some one could do something for some one. Sometimes he was certain that he could do something for some one. Sometimes he was beginning to do something for some one. Sometimes he was certain that he could do something more for some one. Sometimes he was certain that he could not do anything more for that one. He was doing something for some one, he was giving advice to some one and he was giving it strongly enough to that one so that he was doing something for that one. He was certain that he could do something more for that one. He was doing something then for that one. He could come to be certain that he could not do anything more for that one. He could come to be certain that he could come to be doing something more for that one.

He certainly was interested in giving advice strongly enough to some one so that it would do something for that one. He certainly was interested in this thing. He was not interested in giving advice strongly enough to every one. He was interested in giving advice strongly enough to some. He was sometimes certain that he could do something more then for them. He was sometimes certain that he could again give advice strongly enough to do something for them. He was sometimes certain that he could not do anything more for them. He was sometimes certain that not any advice could be given strongly enough to do anything for them. He was sometimes certain that not any one could give advice strongly enough to any one. He was sometimes certain that not any one should give advice strongly enough to any one. He was very often certain that he had given advice strongly enough to some one and that he could do something more for that one. He was sometime certain that he would be giving advice strongly enough to some one and he was sometime certain then that he would do something more then for that one and he was sometime certain then giving advice strongly enough could be done.

He was not in any way wanting to give advice strongly enough to every one. He was not wanting to give advice strongly enough to some. He was wanting to give advice strongly enough to one and then he was not going on with this thing, he was not then going on with giving advice strongly enough to that one. He was then not wanting to give advice strongly enough to that one. He was giving advice strongly enough to some. He was giving advice strongly enough to any one he was advising. He was not needing to give advice strongly enough to every one. He was giving advice strongly enough to the one that he was for sometime wanting to give advice to strongly enough. He was not needing to give advice strongly enough to any one. He did give advice strongly enough to some. He did not need to do this thing to give advice strongly enough to some.

He was one certainly understanding something. He was one certainly having a way of understanding something. He was one using a way of understanding something in understanding anything. He was one in a way understanding any one. He was one using a way of understanding something in understanding any one. He was sometimes quite certain of this thing that he would be understanding any one. Some were quite certain of this thing that he would be understanding any one. In a way he came to be certain of this thing that he would be understanding any one and he came to be certain, in a way, that he was not understanding some. He was certain that he would be understanding any one in the way he was understanding something. And then certainly he was not going on in this thing, in understanding any one. He was then going on in understanding something. He certainly then would give advice strongly enough to some. He was not needing, to be one being living, he was not needing to be giving advice strongly enough to any one. He was needing, to be one being living, he was needing to be one understanding something, he was needing to be going to be using the way of understanding something to understanding anything. He was not completely needing, to be one being living, he was not completely needing to be one understanding everything. He was almost completely needing, to be one being living, he was almost completely needing to be going to be using the way he was understanding something to understand everything.

He was knowing some who were being ones at the end of the beginning of being living when he was at the end of the beginning being living. In a way he was one with them, in many ways he was not one with them. He was one with them in being one being one of them, in being one completely understanding something. He was one with some of them, in being one of them, in being one understanding something, in being one going to be using understanding something to understanding everything. He was one with some of them in being one being one of them, in being one understanding something, in being one using the way of understanding something to be understanding everything, in wanting to be one needing to be completely loving one. He was not of them, in being one toward whom each one of them had a completely different feeling and were telling some other one about such a thing, about the different feeling each one had about him. He was not one of them, in being one who was not completely interesting to any of them in being one wanting to be completely loving some one. He was almost completely one of them when there were not all of them being then them. He was completely one of them when there were some of them being then all of them. He was one almost completely wanting to be loving one then who would be then almost a completely beautiful one to him then. He was completely understanding something then. He was completely clearly thinking then, entirely completely clearly thinking then. He was clearly feeling then, quite completely clearly feeling then.

David Hersland was almost knowing which one of those with whom he was then being one being living, which ones were feeling that he was being one then who was one of them. He was then almost knowing that thing, he was then almost completely not certain that any of them of those he was knowing then were ones who would be knowing that he was almost knowing which ones were ones who were feeling that he was one of them then. When Hersland was at the ending of beginning being living he was then being with some who were ones being living then, almost completely being living then in being ones being living then, being some being living then. He was then almost knowing that some of them could come to be ones being certain that he was one of them. He was then one coming to be certain that some of them would come to be completely certain that he was one of them. He came then to be completely certain that one of them, that two of them were completely certain that he was one of them. He was knowing this thing then, he was not completely feeling this thing then, he was quite certain of this thing, he was wanting to be completely needing this thing then that one of them, that two of them were certain that he was one of them.

He was not being living in this thing in any of them being certain that he was one of them. He was not being living in this thing, he was almost completely wanting to be needing this thing that any of them, that one of them, that two of them, that some of them were quite certain that he was one of them. They were then, all of them, quite completely living in their being one of all of them. They were, all of them, living very well then in this thing, living quite well in this thing, going on living just then quite well in this thing.

They were, all of them, being ones at the ending of beginning living then. There were some then who were other ones and they were then knowing David Hersland and David Hersland was knowing them and they were each of them they and he, they were each of them being ones quite being living then.

They were all of them at the ending of beginning being living then. There were some of them who were being ones being living then and knowing David Hersland then and he was knowing them then and they were all of them being living then.

There were some then knowing evey one and every one was knowing them and these were not at the ending of their beginning living then, they were at the ending of the middle of their middle living then.

There were some, some of those who were being living in being ones being living then and in all of them being living, there were some who were being living then in being one knowing some other ones and one of the other ones then for such of them was David Hersland and David Hersland was knowing them then and sometimes then David Hersland was knowing that he was knowing them and they were all he and they being ones then living in being living then, in all being living there then, and sometimes then he was certain enough of this thing and sometimes then he was quite wanting to be completely wanting to be needing this thing, and sometimes then he was one being living and the others were being living then and they all, he and they were being living then and that was all there was to any such thing, that they were all being living then.

This was very often all there was to him in all of them being living then, this, that each one of them, they and he were being living then.

Some of those being living were needing to be completely expressing the feeling that there is a good deal of succeeding in being living. Some of those being living and who were being living then were not needing then to be expressing anything about succeeding in living being existing. Some of them of those being then all of them, at the ending of beginning living were needing to be expressing that succeeding in living is not being existing. Some of them were not then needing to be expressing this thing that succeeding in living is not existing. Some of them did not need then to be expressing that succeeding in living is existing. Some of them then were expressing that not succeeding in living is being existing, that there is existing not succeeding in living. Some were then expressing that there is existing succeeding in living. Some of them were then going to be expressing that succeeding in living is not existing, some of them were needing then to be going to be expressing that there is not existing, succeeding in living.

David Hersland was not expressing then that succeeding in living is not existing. David Hersland was not then needing to be going to be expressing that there is existing not succeeding in living. He was not expressing then that there is existing succeeding in living. He was not then completely not expressing that there is existing succeeding in living. He was almost needing then to be going to be expressing that there is existing succeeding in living. He was not completely needing then going to be expressing that there is existing succeeding in living. He was completely then clearly feeling anything, almost completely clearly feeling anything. He was then almost completely clearly feeling something, he was then almost completely clearly then feeling some things. He was not completely clearly feeling everything. He was almost completely clearly feeling anything. He was almost completely clearly feeling everything. He was almost completely clearly feeling something, he was almost completely clearly feeling some things. He was almost completely clearly feeling everything. He was completely clearly thinking. He was completely doing that thing. He was completely clearly thinking.

He was not completely needing being one going to be doing some other thing sometime. He was almost needing being one going to be doing some other thing sometime. When he was one being one at the ending of beginning being living he was almost needing being one going to be doing some other thing sometime. He was one then not really needing to be one wanting to be doing some other thing sometime. He was then not really interested in that thing in going to be doing some other thing sometime. He was not then really interested in any one being one going to be doing some other thing sometime. He was interested enough to be mentioning such a thing as going to be doing some other thing sometime.

He was enough interested to be mentioning that some are going to be doing some other thing sometime. He was almost really interested in some going to be doing some other thing sometime. He was not really interested in any one going to be doing some other thing sometime.

He was very often discussing such a thing, some one going to be doing some other thing sometime. He was quite interested in being one thinking clearly about this thing about his going to be sometime doing some other thing, about any one's sometime going to be doing some other thing, about some sometime going to be doing some other thing, about some one going to be sometime doing some other thing. He was almost completely clearly feeling something then, almost completely feeling something then.

He knew then that some were really completely interested in being one going to be doing some other thing sometime. He was quite interested then, quite really interested then. He was not really interested then. He was feeling, almost completely clearly feeling something then and he was then one almost really interested in any one being one going to be doing some other thing sometime. He was seriously enough interested in that thing then, almost completely seriously interested in that thing then, in any one going to be sometime doing some other thing.

He was not completely interested in that thing, in any one going to be doing some other thing sometime. He was quite clearly feeling then about himself being one going to be sometime doing some other thing. He was almost completely clearly feeling something about this thing about being one going to be sometime doing some thing, some other thing. They were all of them going on being living. He was going on being living then. He was not then completely interested in that thing in being one going on being living. He was completely interested in something then. He was completely interested then in being one being interested in something. He was completely feeling this then, completely feeling being one being living being interested in something, being interested in all being living. He was not completely interested in all living. He was completely interested in living being existing.

He could be certain that some one was one different from any other one. He could be certain that any one was different from any other one. He could be certain that some one was different from any other one. He could go on being certain that any one was different from any other one. He could go on being certain that some one was different from any other one. He was quite certain that some one was different from any other one. He mentioned that thing. He did not go on being certain that some one was different from any other one. He was not completely certain, he was not going on in being completely certain that some one was different from any other one. He was almost certain that any one was different from any other one. He was going on being almost certain that any one was different from any other one.

He was almost completely clearly feeling what he was feeling. He was extraordinarily completely clearly expressing what he was almost completely clearly feeling. He was one working in being one almost completely clearly feeling what he was feeling. He was one working, he was one needing to be clearly working, he was one needing to be completely clearly working. He was one needing to be certain that he was one being living. He was one needing to be completely clearly working to be certain that he was one being living. He was one needing to be working, clearly working, he was one needing to be clearly working and he was working to be certain that he was one being living. He was working at this thing, clearly working at this thing, completely clearly working at this thing, working at being certain that he was one being living. He was not really needing to be completely certain of this thing, certain that he was one being living. He was completely clearly working at this thing, working at being certain that he was one being living. He was not one needing this thing needing being certain that he was one being living. He was not one really needing to be certain of this thing certain of being one being living. He was not one completely needing to be certain of this thing, certain of being one being living.

He was almost completely feeling being one being living. He was almost completely clearly feeling being one being living.

He was almost completely feeling being one being living. He was almost completely clearly feeing being one being living. He was almost completely clearly feeling in being one being living. He was one almost completely clearly feeling about needing being one being living, about not needing being one being living, about knowing being one being living, about being certain of being one being living, about not being certain of being one being living. He was almost completely clearly feeling something, he was almost completely clearly feeling everything of any such thing.

He was almost completely clearly feeling that some one was different from any other one. He was almost completely clearly feeling such a thing. He was certainly mentioning this thing that some one was different from any other one. He was not completely certain of this thing that some one was different from any other one. He was mentioning being certain that some one was different from any other one. He was not completely certain of this thing that some one was different from any other one. He was almost completely clearly feeling something about this thing about some one being different from any other one. He went on being living until the ending of the beginning of middle living.

Some being living when David Hersland was being living were expecting that sometime he could be certain that something would be happening and that then that thing would be happening. Some who were living when David Hersland was living were not certain that when he came to be certain that something would be happening that it would not be happening.

When he came to be certain that something would be happening, sometimes something would be happening. He sometimes came to be certain that something would be happening and sometimes then something would be happening. He was not completely needing this thing needing being certain that something would be happening. He was not completely needing that thing, being certain that something would be happening and having then that thing happening. He was not completely needing this thing.

He was interested in this thing sometimes almost completely interested in this thing, he was sometimes almost completely interested in being certain that something would be happening, he was sometimes almost completely interested in being certain that something was going to be happening and then that thing was happening.

He was almost completely clearly feeling being one being living. He was almost completely clearly feeling being one going on being living. He was not completely needing this thing being one going on being living. He was almost completely needing the thing being one being living.

Some are ones needing being one succeeding in living. Some are ones not needing being one succeeding in living, David Hersland was such a one, he was one needing being one succeeding in living. He was one not needing being one succeeding in living. If he had gone on in being living he would not have been one succeeding in living, he would not have been one needing being one succeeding in living. If he had been one going on in being living he might have been succeeding in living. He might have been one succeeding in living if he had been one going on being living and then he would not have been needing being one succeeding in living. He was not going on being living after the ending of the beginning of middle living. He was not being living after the ending of the beginning of middle living.

He would not be one commencing again and again to be one being living. He would not be one commencing being living. He was one being living every day and always he was one needing to be understanding this thing, understanding being one being living. He was one completely clearly thinking, he was one completely clearly thinking about something. He was one almost completely clearly feeling.

He would not be one commencing again and again being one being living. He was not one commencing again and again being one being living. He was one being living. He was one almost completely needing to be understanding this thing, understanding being one being living. He was one being living every day. He was one understanding this thing understanding every day being living that day. He was one completely needing being one understanding every day being living that day.

He was one completely clearly thinking. He was one completely clearly thinking about something. He was one almost completely clearly thinking about anything. He was one completely clearly thinking about everything.

He could be certain that not any one would be thinking more completely about something than he was thinking about something. He could be certain that not any one could be thinking more completely clearly about something than he was thinking about something. He could be completely certain of this thing.

He was interested in any one thinking as completely, more completely about something than he was thinking about something. He was not completely interested in that thing. He could be certain that not any one was thinking more completely about something than he was thinking about something.

He was not needing being one coming to be certain that he was one needing some other one. He was not needing being one coming to be certain that he was not needing some other one. He was almost wanting to be one needing to be certain to be one needing another one. He was not needing to be one being certainly needing another one. He was not completely needing anything. He was completely clearly thinking. He was almost completly needing being certain that he was being living.

It was not any use being one going on being living for David Hersland when he was not being one needing to be being living. He was not completely needing being living. He was not completely wanting needing being living. He was almost completely deciding being living, he was almost completely deciding this thing. He was not feeling anything about this thing about not completely needing being living. He was not feeling anything at all about this thing. He was almost completely deciding something about this thing about being one being living. He was not completely deciding about this thing about being one being living, he was almost completely deciding about this thing about being one being living.

Being one being living is being one in a way being interested in that thing. Any one can be in a way such a one, one being living. Some are not in a way such a one one being interested in a way in being one being living. Some are being ones being living and are in a way not ones interested in being living. Some are being ones being living and are not interested in such a thing in being living and they are ones being living and they would not mention that thing to any one that any one should come to be one being living. Some are ones being living and they are not interested in that thing, in a way not at all interested in that thing and they are not mentioning that thing to any one that they are in a way not at all interested in being one being living. Some who are being living are not interested in that thing, in being one being living. They are, some of them, not mentioning anything about such a thing about any one being one being living. They are, some of them, not mentioning anything about their being not interested at all in that thing in being one being living.

In a way very many are being living and are being then not interested in that thing not quite interested in that thing, and they are not mentioning that thing, they are not mentioning being not quite interested in being one being living.

Very many are being living, very many are very often almost not quite interested in that thing, and they are almost not mentioning that thing not mentioning being almost not quite interested in that thing, in being one being living. There are very many being living. There are very many who are quite often not interested in that thing in being living and are not mentioning anything about being interested, about not being interested in that thing. There are very many being living and are not interested in that thing, in being living, and are not at all mentioning such a thing mentioning anything about being not interested in being one being living.

Some one can be certain that they have remembered something. Some one can come to be certain that they have remembered something and they are sure that they are not remembering what was really happening. Some can come to be certain of this thing can come to be certain that they are remembering something and that that thing was not the thing that happened the thing they are remembering. Some can come then to be not at all interested in that thing, they go on remembering and they go on being certain that the thing they are remembering is not a thing that happened and they are not at all interested in that thing and they certainly are going on being one being living.

David Hersland in being living was one living until the ending of the beginning of middle living. He was not interested in this thing in being one not living longer than the ending of the beginning of middle living. He was not really interested in this thing in being living only to the end of the beginning of middle living. He was not really interested in that thing.

Why should any one not be certain that David Hersland was being living? Why should any one not be certain of this thing? David Hersland was being living. Not every one was certain of this thing. Some are certain of this thing. Some were not certain of this thing. He was not completely living in any one being, in any one not being certain of this thing. He was being living and some were not certain of this thing, that he was being living, and some were certain of this thing, that he was being living. He was being living. Any one could almost be certain of this thing certain that he was being living. Some could be certain of this thing, certain that he was being living.

He was quietly enough doing that thing, being one being living. He was quietly enough being one being living. It was astonishing that he was so quietly doing that thing being one being living.

He was quite quietly doing that thing, being one being living. Certainly not every one was certain of this thing that he was quietly doing that thing, being one being living. Not every one was certain that he was one quietly doing being one being living. Some were certain that he was not so quietly doing this thing, being one being living. Some were certain that he was not quietly doing this thing, being one being living.

He was quietly doing this thing, quietly being one being living. This was a thing that might have been astonishing. That he was quietly doing the thing, quietly being one being living is a thing that might be astonishing to any one. Any one might be certain that he was not quietly doing that, not quietly being one being living. Some were certain that he was quietly doing this thing, doing being one being living.

A quite gentle one, a quite quiet one, any one was certain of this thing that this one was a quite quiet one, a quite gentle one, this one who was a quite quiet one was one whom he was knowing some and he was always being one, needing to be completely wanting to be certain that this one, that some one, that almost any one was one who was being existing and making something then be a thing leading to something which was then a thing failing being a complete thing, a whole one then and then not needing being anything not having been a beautiful thing.

He was a quietly enough one being one being living and he was then teaching any one any other thing. He was teaching some then. He was very nearly completely teaching some. He was being one then whom some who were quite quietly being living then were following then and all of them, any one of them were very quietly being one being living then, almost being one being living.

He was being one whom not any one of some was remembering being one being quietly enough one being living. He was certainly then telling about any one being one needing something and he was almost completely then being one who ought to have been one completely telling this thing and not being quietly doing this thing and he was not quietly doing this thing, he was almost doing this thing, he was one any one of some could be remembering as having been completely telling something to any one, as not having been at all quite quietly enough doing this thing, completely telling any one something.

He was one not quietly enough doing that thing being one being living to be satisfying some who were being living and these were then not needing that thing not completely needing that any one was one quite quietly being one being living. They were, these were not needing that any one, that every one was one being quietly doing that thing, quietly being one being living, these were quite not needing that thing needing that any one be one quite quietly be one being living. He was not satisfying these then, he was not then to them being one quite quietly being living. He was being one then not quite quietly being one being living, he was that to them.

There was one who was quite certain that he was not at all such a one one quietly doing this thing, quietly being one being living. This one knew him, knew David Hersland then and was quite certain that David Hersland never was and never could have been one quietly doing that thing quietly being one being living, and this one was always remembering this thing and he never forgot this thing and any one knowing David Hersland was completely liking this liking that this one never forgot that thing that David Hersland never was that David Hersland never could have been one quietly doing such a thing, quietly being one being living.

David Hersland was not quite quietly enough being one being living. That was certain. Some were almost completely certain of this thing. He was quite quietly being living. That was certain. Any one might have been almost certain of this thing. He was quite quietly enough being one being living. Not any one could be remembering this thing, not any one was ever remembering any such thing. Some were sometimes almost remembering this thing. He could not have been one quietly doing the thing, quietly being one being living. Some were always certain of this thing, always remembering this thing. He was almost quietly being one being living. Any one could be certain enough of this thing. Some were always certain enough of this thing, were remembering enough of this thing. He was quietly enough being one being living and not any one was completely certain of this thing. He was one who was almost not needing having been one at all being living in being one having been quietly enough, in having been not quietly enough being living. He was one whom almost not any one was really needing being remembering. Some were almost needing remembering his being one being living. Not any one was needing remembering any kind of living he ever had been doing, any quietness, any not quietness enough there could be in his having been one being living. He had been one being living. He was being living. He was living. He was being living and he was always being one then always being one being living then. He was always being one being living and any one could remember such a thing remember he was being living. Any one could have remembered that he had been one being living. Some remembered that he had been one being living. Any one could remember something of such a thing, of his being living.

He came to know every one Alfred Hersland was knowing. Alfred Hersland was married then. David came to know all of them all of those who were knowing Alfred then, almost all those who were knowing Alfred then. He had been knowing others, he was still knowing some of them. He was not then knowing some of them. He had been knowing very many whom Alfred would naturally not have been knowing. He was knowing some whom Mrs. Alfred Hersland came to be knowing. He was knowing George Dehning then. George Dehning was knowing him then. David Hersland had been knowing some whom George Dehning was not knowing. He was knowing some whom George Dehning was knowing. He was knowing very many whom George Dehning was knowing. He had been knowing some whom George Dehning had not been knowing.

He had known some whom George Dehning had not been knowing. He was still knowing some of them, he was not knowing all of them. He was knowing then very many that Alfred Hersland was knowing.

He went on then knowing some whom Alfred Hersland was not knowing, whom George Dehning was not knowing. He was not knowing then every one he had been knowing. He was knowing some of them then. Julia Hersland was knowing then very many he was knowing. He was knowing then every one she was knowing. He was knowing very many then. He had been knowing very many.

He did not ever completely forget that his sister and his father were living. He always remembered that they were living. In a way he was always remembering this thing. He did not forget that his brother Alfred was living. He did not really forget this thing. He remembered that his sister and his father were living. In a way he was always remembering this thing. In a way he did not at all forget this thing, that they were being living.

He had been knowing some and all of them had been knowing him. He had been knowing some who were all of them knowing each other then. He was knowing some who were not knowing any one who was knowing him. He was knowing some who were telling some other ones about knowing him. He was knowing some who were telling him about the thing, about knowing him.

He came to know almost any one who knew Julia Hersland. He came to know very many who were knowing Alfred Hersland. He came to know every one whom George Dehning was knowing. He was knowing quite a number then. He had been knowing quite a number and he was going on knowing some of them. Some of them were not going on knowing him. Some were and were not going on knowing him. Some were telling about knowing him, some who were not going on knowing him. Some were not telling about him, some who were not going on knowing him.

He had been knowing some, he had been knowing quite a number being living then. He had been knowing some who were all of them knowing other ones who were ones knowing him then. He was knowing some then who were not knowing any other ones who were knowing him then. He went on knowing some of such of them. He went on sometimes knowing some of such of them. He went on almost all his being living knowing some of them. He did not go on knowing some of them. George Dehning came to know a good many that David Hersland was knowing. He came to know something of almost all of them. David Hersland came to know all whom George Dehning was knowing. He did not come to know all who were and had been knowing George Dehning. David Hersland came to know almost every one Julia Hersland was knowing. He came to know very many whom Alfred Hersland was knowing and who were knowing him.

He had come to be not telling about enjoying things with those with whom he had been enjoying things. He had come not to tell any one about having been one enjoying things with some. He had come to be knowing others then others who were not hearing anything about his having been enjoying things with others. Those with whom he had been enjoying things were then being living. Some of them were quite certain that he had not been one enjoying things with them. Some of them were completely remembering that he had been one enjoying things with some of them. Some of them were not mentioning to others of them that he had been enjoying things with some of them. He had been enjoying things with some of them. He remembered with one of them that he had been enjoying things with some of them. He remembered with some of them that he had been enjoying things with all of them. Some of them remembered with him that he had been enjoying things with some of them.

He was not then telling any more, not any more thinking of telling anything about having been one enjoying things with some of them, he was not telling one any more anything about anything, he was not then thinking of mentioning anything to any one of them. He was then knowing one of them, two of them, a few of them. He was sometimes then meeting any of them. They were all then being living. He was then being living. He was then not thinking of telling any one anything about having been enjoying things with all of them, with any of them.

He was knowing some then. He was being living then and explaining that thing explaining being living, to one then, to a few then. He was being living then and almost completely then mentioning that thing, mentioning being living.

He was then interested in this thing, he was interested in almost completely mentioning that he was being living. He was completely explaining this thing to one and he was completely wondering then whether that one would be one coming to be completely needing that thing completely needing his completely telling that he was being living. He was completely wondering then whether that one was one who would go on being one completely needing that being living was a thing that one was having completely mentioned by him. He was almost completely wanting to be completely interested in this thing in that one coming to be one completely needing understanding living being existing. He was then knowing George Dehning. He was then later knowing very many he had not been knowing. He was then later not completely knowing any he had been pretty nearly completely knowing.

He was not a sad one. He was not at all a sad one. He had not been a sad one. He was not going to be a sad one. He was not a sad one. He was not at all a sad one. He never came to be a sad one.

He was not a sad one. He was not at all a sad one. He was one not interested in the thing, in being a sad one, in not being a sad one. He was not at all a sad one.

He was not a sad one. He came to know George Dehning and Julia Hersland and he came to know very many they were knowing. He came to know some who knew them. He was not at all a sad one. He went on knowing them and in a way he always knew them until he was one who was not being living. He was not at all a sad one.

He was not a sad one. He was not interested in this thing in being not a sad one. He was being living. He was remembering all the Hersland family who were being living then. He was remembering that his father and his sister were being living. He was then knowing Alfred Hersland and knowing some who knew him then and some whom he knew then. He was knowing Alfred Hersland very well then. He was always knowing him very well. He was always completely remembering all of him all of Alfred Hersland. He was remembering completely remembering that his sister and his father were being living. He was knowing Julia Hersland then and knowing almost every one she was knowing then. He was knowing George Dehning then and knowing every one George Dehning was knowing then. David Hersland was not a sad one. He was not at all a sad one.

He was always remembering all of Alfred Hersland. He was not remembering all of George Dehning. He came to remembering almost all of Julia Hersland. He was completely remembering that his sister and his father were being existing. He was not at all a sad one. He was not a sad one.

He was completely convincing Julia Hersland completely convincing every one of his being one being living and being one doing this thing and not being a sad one. He was completely convincing Julia Hersland and she was one feeling this thing feeling he was being living, feeling he was one and not at all a sad one.

George Dehning was living enough in David Hersland being one being living. He was living just enough in this thing. He was listening enough to this thing, to any one knowing that David Hersland was being living, was being one who was being living.

Alfred Hersland was not living in David Hersland being one being living. He was liking that David Hersland was being one being living, he was quite pleasantly liking this thing, almost completely pleasantly liking that David Hersland was being one being living.

David Hersland was knowing then every one that George Dehning was knowing then. He was knowing then mostly every one Julia Hersland was knowing then. There were a number then who knew Julia Hersland whom David Hersland was not remembering then. David Hersland knew some whom Alfred Hersland was knowing then.

David Hersland was convincing then Julia Hersland and he was coming to be completely doing this thing and she was being living then almost completely being living then being one understanding this thing understanding having David Hersland being completely convincing. He was one who could be completely convincing and he could be completely explaining this thing explaining that he was completely convincing, explaining that Julia Hersland was completely needing this thing, explaining this clearly, completely clearly to Julia Hersland then. He was completely then completely understanding needing to be completely convincing to Julia Hersland. He was completely understanding being completely convincing to Julia Hersland then. He and she were coming to be completely understanding this thing. He went on with the thing, he went on being completely convincing to her and it was a thing that they were almost pleasantly doing and he was one completely clearly understanding being completely convincing.

He was talking about something in being one being completely convincing, being completely convincing in being one completely clearly understanding thinking being existing. He was one doing this thing in anything, he was one almost completely clearly feeling, completely clearly understanding that thinking is existing. He was one doing this thing in everything, almost completely clearly feeling, he was doing this thing in everything, completely clearly understanding that thinking is existing. He was being completely convincing, he was telling something in being this thing in being completely convincing.

He was not determined in this thing, that thinking is existing. He was not determined in this thing. He was not repeating this thing, that thinking is existing, he was not repeating this thing. He was naturally completely certain of this thing, that thinking is existing. He was not telling that he was naturally certain of this thing, that thinking is existing. He was not completely using this thing, that he was completely understanding that thinking is existing, he was not completely using this thing. He was not stern in this thing, that thinking is existing. He was quick enough with this thing, that he was completely understanding that thinking is existing. He was steady enough with this thing, that thinking is existing. He was completely natural in this thing, that he was completely understanding that thinking is existing. He was almost completely using this thing, that thinking is existing. He was completely using that he was completely understanding that thinking is existing. He was naturally completely using this thing, that thinking is existing.

He was not repeating this thing, that thinking is existing. He was not repeating that he was understanding completely understanding that thinking is existing. He was naturally completely understanding that thinking is existing. He was entirely naturally completely understanding that thinking is existing. He was almost completely using this thing understanding that thinking is existing. He was naturally almost completely using this thing, that thinking is existing.

He was not completely using that thinking is existing. He was completely understanding that thinking is existing. He was completely clearly thinking. He was thinking of something. He was thinking of anything. He was thinking of everything. He was completely, naturally, he was naturally and completely understanding that thinking is existing. He was not entirely completely using this thing, using that thinking is existing. He was not repeating that thinking is existing, he was not repeating that he was completely clearly understanding that thinking is existing.

He was needing to be sometimes deciding that he would not be eating everything. And this was a natural thing. He was needing to be one being living. He was needing to be understanding that thing that he was one being living. He was being convincing in being one needing to be deciding not to be eating everything as he was one needing to be being living and understanding that thing. He was almost completely convincing Julia Hersland. George Dehning was one being living then with him and knowing every one who was knowing David Hersland then and whom David Hersland was knowing then.

David Hersland was then completely understanding something and completely then understanding any one else's understanding of that thing. Any one was certain of this thing that David Hersland was understanding something and understanding any one else's understanding and not understanding that thing. He was needing that any one understanding anything should be understanding that some are understanding the thing he, David Hersland was understanding. He was not completely needing this thing. He was telling something about such a thing and telling it very clearly to Mr. Dehning and Mr. Dehning was listening and David Hersland was not completely needing that Mr. Dehning should be listening and he was not completely needing that Mr. Dehning should be understanding this thing. David Hersland was understanding something and was understanding any one else's understanding of that thing. David Hersland was quite completely needing that any one understanding anything should be understanding any one else's understanding something. He was not completely needing this thing. Julia Hersland was completely needing this thing. David Hersland was completely convincing her of any one being one needing this thing. David Hersland was understanding something and was understanding any one else's understanding that thing. He was understanding something of any one else's not understanding that thing. He was almost needing to be completely understanding any one else's not understanding that thing the thing he was understanding.

He was completely understanding something and understanding any one else understanding that thing. He was completely convincing in this thing in understanding something, in understanding any one else understanding that thing.

He was sometimes urging this thing urging being one completely understanding something, understanding any one understanding this thing. He was sometimes urging this thing.

He was convincing to any one in being one understanding something, he was convincing to almost any one in being one understanding any one's understanding that thing. He was understanding something, he was understanding any one's understanding that thing.

He was completely clearly thinking, he was almost completely clearly feeling. He was feeling and he was thinking. He was completely clearly thinking, he was almost completely clearly feeling.

Completely clearly thinking, and giving advice strongly enough, and not completely clearly feeling, and being convincing is a different thing in different ones being living. It was in David Hersland being one almost wanting to be one needing to be succeeding in living. It was in David Hersland being one needing to be having something each day to be something meaning that being living is existing. It was in him being one not completely going on being living. It was in him being one who was definitely working. It was in him being one not quite succeeding in being one succeeding in living. It was in him being one telling something and having then that many who were then were not then entirely completely listening. It was in him being one deciding something and doing something and having then some who were with him not completely be going to be doing that thing. It was in him being one clearly telling something and not telling that thing again and again.

He was, to some, one clearly telling something and not telling it again and again. He was, to some, one not completely clearly telling something, and one going to be telling it again and again. He was, to some, one clearly telling something and one in some way going to be completely clearly telling it again and again. He was completely clearly telling something and then he was needing to be completely certain that living is being existing. He was needing, to be one being living to himself inside him, he was one needing being one eating, completely eating some one thing. He was then completely clearly telling something. He was then needing being one completely not eating some one thing. He was then completely clearly telling something and he was then not telling it again and again. He was needing then to be certain that being living is existing, that there is being existing, that there is existing being living. He was completely clearly telling something and not telling it again. He was then almost completing wanting to be needing succeeding in living. He was wanting to be one who was one needing to be succeeding in living. He was one who was clearly convincing. He was clearly telling something, he was not telling it again and again. He was convincing and he was with some and they were not then completely beginning anything. He was then clearly telling something. He was then needing being certain that he was completely eating one thing.

He could do something. He could completely understand doing that thing. He was understanding any one doing that thing. He was understanding what any one was understanding in doing that thing.

He was doing something and he was understanding that some one else was doing that thing. He could understand the way that one understood doing that thing. He was doing something. He was understanding some one else's doing that thing. He was not completely convincing as understanding any one's doing of that thing. He was almost completely convincing as understanding some other ones doing of that thing.

He was one working and clearly expressing that thing clearly expressing that he was working. He was one understanding that some one else was working and was almost clearly expressing that thing, expressing that working. He was understanding that some one was working and was not clearly expressing that thing working. He was clearly expressing any one's work at the thing at which he himself was working. He was doing something. He was clearly working at that thing.

He was not excited in understanding any one's working. He was not excited, he was feeling the thing feeling some one else's working and clearly expressing that thing that some else was working.

He was doing something, he was clearly working, he was clearly expressing this thing that he was clearly working. He could completely understand any one's work who was working at this thing and he could completely express this thing express his understanding.

He was not excited in understanding, he was not eager in understanding, he was not gay in understanding, he was not solemn in understanding, he was not persistent in understanding, he was not violent in understanding, he was not expository in understanding, he was continuous in understanding and clearer in understanding and he was almost firm in understanding and he was not repeating his understanding and he was strongly advising some to go on with his understanding. He might have been brilliant in understanding and he went on being understanding.

He was using understanding and he was not completing the using of understanding. He was steadily understanding and he was clearly understanding and he was clearly expressing understanding and he was strongly enough advising some to be going on using his understanding. He was not fighting with his understanding because not any one was meeting him to be fighting. He might have been fighting with his understanding. He might have been being one using his understanding in being one being fighting. He might have been fighting for his understanding. He was not ever really fighting and this was because not any one was needing really needing to be fighting him. He was clearly expressing being one understanding. He was clearly working. He was almost completely clearly feeling. He was understanding other one's being working and he was clearly expressing understanding this thing. He was not really repeating anything, he was clearly not repeating anything.

He was often almost quite alone with being one being living, and working, clearly working to be completely understanding this thing. He was often almost quite alone and he was not suffering, not at all suffering. He was clearly working, he was working and clearly working and he was clearly thinking and he was almost clearly feeling. He was almost completely clearly expressing that he was clearly working. He was clearly expressing that he was clearly thinking.

He was often enough alone and he had been going on being such a one, one who was often enough alone. He was not needing this thing, needing being often enough alone. He was naturally enough being such a one, one being often enough alone. He was not completely using this thing, being often enough alone. He was not completely needing being often enough alone. He was sometimes not at all using this thing using being often enough alone. He was often not being often enough alone. He was sometimes going on with this thing going on with not being often enough alone. He was not ever completely using being often enough alone. He was certainly very often alone. He was certainly often enough alone. He was not completely using this thing using being often enough alone.

He was often alone. He was often going on with this thing going on being often alone He was being one being living. He was not completely needing being certain of this thing, certain of being one being living. He was naturally thinking clearly about this thing about being living. He was completely clearly thinking about this thing about being living.

He was being living. He was using this thing then when he was beginning the beginning of middle living, he was using then being one being living. He was then almost completely using that thing then, he was not completely using that thing then not completly using then being one being living.

He was not one commencing again and again being one being living. He was completely clearly thinking about something. He was interested in any one's being one being thinking about something. He was not completely interested in that thing in any one's being one being thinking about something. He was completely clearly thinking. He was almost completely clearly feeling. He was not commencing again and again being one being living. He was almost understanding every day being one being living. He was almost needing understanding every day being being one being living. He was needing understanding that being living is existing. He was needing understanding that being living is existing. He was not completely needing to be certain that being living is existing. He was almost understanding every day being living that day. He was not commencing again and again being one being living. He was not commencing being one being living.

He was expressing something, he was completely clearly expressing something. He was not mentioning this thing again and again that he was completely clearly expressing something. He was telling something. He was quite often telling something. He was not quite completely telling something. He was certainly almost completely interested in completely telling something. He was completely clearly thinking. He was almost completely clearly feeling. He was completely clearly expressing something. He was completely clearly telling something. He was interested completely interested, almost completely interested in expressing, completely expressing something.

He was telling something. He was not mentioning again and again that he was telling something. He was telling something. He was completely clearly telling something. He was almost completely interested in any one's telling anything. He was not completely interested in any one's telling anything. He was expressing something, he was completely clearly expressing something and he was not completely telling that thing, completely telling that he was clearly expressing something. He was clearly expressing something and he was certainly completely interested in that thing in clearly expressing something. He was completely expressing something, he was almost completely clearly expressing everything. He was not completely clearly expressing everything. He was not completely expressing anything. He was almost completely expressing something. He was not beginning again and again being one being living.

He was going on being living. He was being living and he was understanding this thing understanding being living is being existing. He was going on being living, he was needing understanding this thing to be one completely understanding something, to be completely expressing something. He was needing being one understanding that going on being living is something being existing. He was not needing understanding going on being living. He was not understanding going on being living. He was understanding being living and he was not commencing again and again being living. He was understanding being living. He was being living. He was going on being living and he was not completely clearly thinking about going on being living, he was almost completely clearly feeling going on being living. He was not needing being one being going on being living.

He was not commencing again and again being one being living. He was being living. He was completely clearly thinking. He was completely clearly expressing something. He was going on being living. He was not needing that thing, not needing going on being living. He was completely understanding being living. He was needing every day to be understanding being living. He was not needing to be certain that any being living is existing. He was almost completely clearly feeling. He was feeling something. He was completely clearly expressing something. He was needing to be one clearly expressing complete thinking. He was going on being living. He was not commencing again and again being living. He was not commencing being living. He was not needing in his thinking being one going on being living. He was not needing in his feeling being completely certain that being living is existing. He was not commencing again and again being living. He was needing to be understanding something, to be understanding every day being living every day. He was understanding thinking. He was completely clearly expressing something. He was not commencing being living. He was not completely interested in completely expressing something. He was being living. He was not mentioning anything again and again. He was expressing something again and again, almost completely clearly expressing something again and again. He was clearly expressing something. He was not completely needing going on being living.

David Hersland was one not really needing something. Julia Hersland was one not really needing something. George Dehning was one not really needing something, Alfred Hersland was one not really needing something. Each one of them was one not really needing something. Each one of them was a very different one in being such a one in being one not really needing something.

David Hersland was one not really needing something. He was not needing being one succeeding in living. He was not needing being one needing another one. He was not needing being certain that being living is existing. He was not needing being one going on being living. He was not needing something.

He was not needing giving Julia Hersland anything. He was giving Julia Hersland something. He was giving it to her to be understanding that he was being one who was understanding every day being one being living. He was not needing to be giving her this thing. She was not needing to be having this thing. He was giving her advice strongly enough about her being one being living. He was not needing to be one doing this thing giving her advice strongly enough about her being one being living. She was using the advice he was giving strongly enough, she was not needing this thing not needing to be using the advice he was giving to her strongly enough. She was not really needing this thing not needing to be using the advice he was giving to her strongly enough. She was not really needing this thing needing the advice he was giving to her strongly enough. She was using this thing, she was using, could be using the advice he was giving to her strongly enough. He was not needing being one giving her advice strongly enough about being one being living. He was not needing being one bringing her to be understanding that he was understanding every day that he was being living.

He was not one really needing something. He was one not really needing something. Julia Hersland was one not really needing something. They were quite different the two of them in being such a one, one not really needing something.

George Dehning was one not really needing something. He was one succeeding in living. He was one completely admiring David Hersland. He was one being one completely in Dehning living. He was not one needing being such a one being one being completely in Dehning living, being one succeeding in living, being one entirely admiring David Hersland. David Hersland was telling him many things and David Hersland was not needing that thing was not needing being one telling him many things.

Alfred Hersland was not one needing something. Alfred Hersland was one not succeeding in living, Alfred Hersland was one not going on loving Julia Hersland, Alfred Hersland was one coming to know very many who came to know him and he was then almost succeeding in living. Alfred Hersland was one being proud enough in being one having David Hersland liking well enough being a brother to him. Alfred Hersland was not needing something. He was not needing being not going on loving Julia Hersland. He was not needing coming to know very many who came to know him. He was not needing not succeeding in living. He was not needing almost succeeding in living. He was not needing marrying again. He was not needing something. He was not needing having David Hersland being a brother to him. David Hersland was not needing something. He was not needing being a brother liking well enough having Alfred Hersland as a brother.

David Hersland was not being one needing something. He was one knowing completely well then and more and more then Julia Hersland and George Dehning and some who knew them and who came to know him.

Certainly he was not one needing anything. David Hersland was not one needing anything. He might have been one succeeding in living. He might not have been one succeeding in living. Certainly he was not really needing anything. He was not needing anything. He was not needing something. He was beginning succeeding in living. He was beginning not succeeding in living.

He was not needing something. He might have been one needing something if he had been one being one needing going on being living. He was not one needing going on being living and he might have been one needing going on being living if he had been one needing something, if he had been one needing being one succeeding in living. He was not one not needing succeeding in living. He was one not needing going on being living. He was one who might have been one needing going on being living if he had been one needing succeeding in living. He was not beginning being living. He was not beginning again and again being living. He was giving advice strongly enough to some. He was completely not eating somethings. He was understanding being one being living. He was wanting to be needing being certain that any one was completely a beautiful one. He was not completely wanting needing this thing. He was almost completely clearly feeling. He was strongly enough giving advice to some. He was completely not eating something He was being one being living. He was not needing being certain that there is being existing being living. He was strongly enough giving advice to some. He was certain of this thing of being one then giving advice strongly enough to some. He was completely not eating somethings.

He was not one really needing something. He was one being interesting. He was one knowing that he was keeping a mind open. He was doing something of this thing, he was keeping a mind open. He was doing something of this thing and Julia Hersland was needing feeling being one having something of this thing having a mind which was keeping open. He was knowing something of this thing of keeping a mind open and having then something more come in to make that one have it to be understanding something. He was knowing this thing, knowing that he was doing something in being one keeping some mind open. He was one completely clearly thinking. He was one completely not eating something. He was almost completely interested in being one keeping some mind open. He was beginning this thing beginning keeping some mind open. He was knowing this thing knowing that he was beginning this thing beginning keeping some mind open. He was almost completely interested in this thing, interested in keeping a mind open.

He was not succeeding in living in being one not being living after the ending of the beginning of middle living. He was being interesting. He was completely clearly thinking. He was completely not eating something. He was completely giving advice strongly enough. He was beginning being one keeping a mind open. He was clearly expressing something. He was completely clearly understanding any one expressing that thing.

Each one of the Dehning family came to know David Hersland and each one of them were sometimes telling him something of this thing, were telling him something of knowing him. Each one of the Dehning family came to tell him something of that one knowing him. Mr. Dehning and Mrs Dehning and Julia Hersland and George Dehning and Hortense Dehning each one of the Dehning family came to know David Hersland and told him something of this thing, told him something of their knowing him, of each one of them knowing him.

Mr. Dehning came to know him and he told him of this thing of knowing him. He told him that he liked it well enough knowing him, that he liked it very well knowing him and that he David Hersland was a man to understand something of such a thing of Mr. Dehning knowing him. Mr. Dehning told him something of being one knowing David Hersland and recognising David Hersland's in a way understanding that he was being one being living. Mr. Dehning was knowing David Hersland and knowing that he David Hersland could understand this thing and could not then be completely succeeding in living in being one not beginning again and again in being living, in being one not beginning in being living. Mr. Dehning was telling this thing to David Hersland and telling him that if there was any of way succeeding in living in being one not beginning being living, in being one not beginning again and again in being living, David Hersland would be succeeding in being living. Mr. Dehning was knowing David Hersland and telling him again and again something of this thing something of knowing him. Mr. Dehning was not completely certain that David Hersland would not be succeeding in living. Mr. Dehning was quite convincing in telling David Hersland that David Hersland was certainly in some way understanding that he was being living, that David Hersland was in some way understanding that being living is existing.

Mrs. Dehning was knowing David Hersland and was telling him something of this thing, was telling him something of knowing him. She was knowing him and not liking this thing and very often she was liking this thing and she could tell any one something of this thing and she was telling him of this thing of telling any one something of knowing him. She was knowing him and telling him very often telling him all the same thing about this thing, about knowing him. She was knowing him and knowing he was one having been living in Hersland family living. She was knowing him and knowing he was living in Dehning family living. She was telling him something of this thing, of her knowing him. She was knowing him in his being one completely not eating something and she was telling him that she was then completely knowing him. She was knowing him being one being interesting and she was telling him completely telling him almost everything of her being one knowing him being that thing. She was not needing him being one being certain that being living is existing and she was knowing him as being one she was needing being one knowing that being living is existing and she was telling him often telling him anything of this thing. She was liking this thing, knowing him, and certainly she was not needing this thing not needing liking this thing liking knowing him and she was knowing this thing, knowing that she was not needing liking him and she was knowing him and she was telling him sometimes and the same way something of this thing something of knowing him.

He knew Julia Hersland and she told him this thing, told him that she knew something in his being one understanding something. He knew something and was understanding any one understanding that thing. She knew this thing and was having then that thing having existing that he was understanding something and understanding any one who was understanding anything of that thing. She was certain enough that being living is existing. He was not really mentioning that thing, he was not mentioning anything of being living being existing. She was going on being living. She was not mentioning anything of any such thing, of going on being living.

He was knowing almost every one that she was knowing then. He was knowing some then and sometimes was not mentioning to her this thing, mentioning knowing some then. He was knowing some then and sometimes he was mentioning this thing, mentioning knowing some then.

They were, each one of them, knowing Alfred Hersland then. They were each one of them mentioning that thing, mentioning knowing him then. They were going then, each one of them was going on then mentioning that thing, mentioning knowing Alfred Hersland then. Each one of them was knowing Alfred Hersland then. David Hersland was telling Julia all of that thing all of his knowing Alfred Hersland. Julia Hersland was telling was completely telling David Hersland all of her knowing Alfred Hersland then. They were each one of them telling this thing, telling knowing Alfred Hersland. David Hersland was understanding this thing understanding knowing Alfred Hersland. Julia Hersland was understanding this thing, understanding knowing Alfred Hersland. David Hersland was knowing Julia Hersland and she was telling him enough about this thing.

He was knowing Julia Hersland. She was going on being living. He was being living. They were not then telling too much about those things about his being living, about her going on being living. They were telling something about these things, each of them was telling something about these things, about her being one going on being living, about his being one being living. She was telling about her being one going on being living, she was telling something about this thing. He was telling something about this thing about her being one going on being living.

He was giving her advice strongly enough and he was then not needing this thing, not needing being one giving her advice strongly enough. He was completely then doing that thing, giving her advice strongly enough. He was almost completely then interested in that thing in giving advice to her strongly enough. He was then being in the living the Dehning family were living. He was knowing then each one of them. Each one of them was telling him about this thing, about his knowing each one of them. He was then knowing Julia Hersland . He went on then knowing her. He was then not being one succeeding in living, not being one not suceeding in living.

He was knowing the Dehning family then, he went on knowing them then. He went on knowing Julia Hersland, he was almost completely interested in her being one going on being living. He was not completely interested in that thing being existing, in going on being living, being existing. He was interested in that thing, in going on being living, being existing.

David Hersland did go on being living until the ending of the beginning of middle living. He was then not really knowing Dehning family living. He was then knowing something of living being existing in George Dehning.

George Dehning was knowing David Hersland. He had been knowing him before David Hersland was knowing Dehning family living. David Hersland had been knowing George Dehning and George Dehning had been telling David Hersland something about this thing about his knowing him. George Dehning was going on being living, he was not completely doing this thing going on being living. He came later to be doing other things and he was succeeding then quite well then succeeding in being living. He was knowing then that David Hersland was not being living and he did not then quite completely forget that thing, forget that David Hersland was not then being living.

David Hersland was knowing George Dehning and George Dehning was saying something sometimes about this thing about David Hersland knowing him. George Dehning was content in having this thing as being existing that David Hersland was knowing him. He was knowing David Hersland then and David Hersland was knowing him then. They did not either of them quite completely mention this thing, mention knowing each other then. David Hersland did not completely mention knowing George Dehning. George Dehning did not completely mention knowing David Hersland. George Dehning was content in being one being living then, was almost content then. David Hersland was being living then and was not mentioning that thing much then, was not mentioning being living. George Dehning was later doing some other thing. He was remembering then that David Hersland had come to be a dead one. He was quite remembering that thing then, remembering that David Hersland had come to be a dead one.

David Hersland was being living and he was knowing the Dehning family living and each one of the Dehning family were knowing him then and each one of them were mentioning that thing to him mentioning knowing him.

Hortense Dehning mentioned to him this thing, mentioned to him knowing him then. She was quite needing then doing this thing, mentioning something to him then and perhaps then he would have been giving advice strongly enough to her and she was then mentioning to him again that she was knowing him then, that he was knowing her then.

Later she quite went on being living and very often then she gave advice quite strongly enough to some one and she did not then think anything of that thing that he, that David Hersland had come then to be a dead one. She was quite enough going on being living then. She was quite enough needing then being one going on living enough then.

He had come to quite completely not eating anything but one thing. He was strong then, he was strong in completely clearly thinking then. He was completely clearly thinking then. He was strong then in that thing, in completely clearly thinking. He was not then completely going on eating only one thing. He was completely strong then, almost completely strong then in completely clearly thinking. He was then beginning being one going to be succeeding in living. He was then not living in Dehning family living. He was then not living in Hersland living, almost not in any Hersland living. He was living then in being living. He was then not going on being living. He was then being living. He was not then beginning that thing, beginning that thing again. He was never beginning being living in being living, he was never beginning again being living in being living. He was then almost not at all living in any other Hersland living than in the living he was doing in being one then being living. He was not going on being living then. He was then going on in eating almost only one thing and he was always then completely being one completely clearly thinking and he was then being living, completely being living and he was then going on to being coming to be certain that being living is existing. He was then not going on commencing to begin to be one succeeding in living. He was then not commencing this thing not commencing beginning to be succeeding in living.

He was one who was not completely forgetting anything and he was one who did not remember everything. He was one who did not need that thing did not need being remembering. He did not need to remember anything. He did not need to remember everything. He did not need, to be one being living, he did not need to be remembering anything, he really did not need any such thing. He was not completely forgetting anything. He did not completely forget anything, he did not forget everything. He remembered everything. He did not need that thing, he did not at all need that thing to be one being living, he did not need to remember everything to be one being living. He did not need to remember anything to be one being living.

He was being living. He was not going on being living. He was not at all needing being one going on being living.

He did not need to be one being a dead one. He was not at all needing such a thing, needing being a dead one. He could be remembering that he could come to be a dead one. He was almost not needing that thing needing remembering that he could come to be a dead one. He was almost eating only one thing. He could be needing being such a one being one eating almost only one thing.

He was not really needing anything. He was not needing being certain that being living is existing. He was not needing being one going on being living. He was needing understanding that he was being living. He was almost completely needing being one completely clearly thinking. He was almost completely wanting to be feeling needing that any woman he was seeing was completely beautifully something. He was almost wanting to be giving advice strongly enough to some. He was almost being one coming to be beginning succeeding in living. He was completely clearly expressing something. He was completely understanding any one's understanding anything of that thing.

He was not really needing anything. He was not needing being one going on being living. He was almost completely needing being one completely clearly thinking. He was not needing being one remembering that any one can come to be a dead one. He was not needing being certain that being living is something that is existing. He was not needing to be remembering anything. He was not needing to be forgetting something. He was understanding that he was being living. He was almost needing to be one almost only eating one thing. He was being living. He was understanding that thing. He was clearly expressing something. He was not forgetting anything. He was not forgetting everything. He was not needing to be one remembering anything. He was not needing to be one remembering everything.

He was completely clearly expressing something. He could mention this thing, mention that he was completely clearly expressing something. He did sometimes mention that he was completely clearly expressing something. He was completely clearly expressing that thing, the thing he was clearly expressing. He could have been one being one clearly, completely clearly expressing that thing. He was such a one, he was one being one completely clearly expressing that thing the thing he was expressing. He was not completely filling anything in completely clearly expressing the thing he was completely clearly expressing. He could have been one completely filling something in being one completely clearly expressing what he was completely clearly expressing. He was completely clearly expressing something. He was completely clearly thinking. He was almost completely clearly feeling. He was almost completely being one eating only one thing. He was being living and he was not beginning that thing beginning being living. He was not ever beginning again and again.

He was completely clearly expressing one thing. He was understanding any one's understanding of that thing. He was understanding anything of any one's understanding of that thing. He was sometimes mentioning something of some one's understanding of that thing. He could go on mentioning some one's understanding of that thing. He was completely clearly expressing something. He was not being one going on being living. He was one being living. He was understanding that thing. He did sometimes mention that thing mention understanding being living. He did not mention anything again and again. He did not really mention anything again and again. He did completely clearly express something. He was being one who was completely clearly thinking. He did do that thing. He did completely clearly think about something. He did completely clearly think about anything. He did almost completely clearly think about everything. He did think completely clearly. He did completely clearly express something. He was being living. He did understand being one being living. He did understand any one else's understanding the thing he was completely clearly expressing.

He was not feeling being one being completely a different one from any other one. He was knowing something of this thing. He was knowing something of being one who was one who was completely a different one from any other one. He was feeling something and there was something in him to be feeling of being one who was completely a different one from any other one. He was feeling something. There was in him something to be feeling. There was in him knowing something of being one who was completely a different one from any other one. He was not feeling that thing feeling his being one being completely different from any other one. He came to be a dead one at the ending of the beginning of middle living. He was not feeling anything in being one being completely different from any other one. He was being this one one who was completely different from any other one. He was not feeling anything in being such a one. He was not living after the ending of the beginning of being living.

He was not completely forgetting knowing something of such a thing of being one being completely different from any other one. He was being living. He was one understanding being one being living. He was not living after the ending of the beginning of middle living. He came to be a dead one. He was completely forgetting something of being one knowing that he was a different one from any other one.

He was not feeling being one being a completely different one from any other one. He was knowing that he was being a completely differrent one from any other one. He was not forgetting knowing that he was a different one from any other one. He was not feeling being a different one from any other one.

He was not living after the ending of the beginning of middle living. He had come to be a dead one. He had been almost completely eating only one thing. He had been understanding being living. He had not been feeling being a different one from any other one. He had been understanding being one being living. He had been giving advice strongly enough to some. He had not been needing being one going on being living. He had not been needing being certain that being living is something existing. He had been coming and had then not come to be beginning succeeding in living. He had been knowing being a different one from any other one. He had been understanding something and understanding any one understanding that thing. He had been completely clearly expressing something. He had been almost completely clearly feeling. He had been completely clearly thinking.

He had come to be a dead one and he was then at the ending of beginning living. He had come to be a dead one and some then were knowing that thing knowing then that he was not any longer being living. Some were then knowing that he was a dead one.

He was not one who had been one being fighting. He had been one who had been completely eating only one thing. He was not one who had been one being fighting. He had been one coming to be beginning succeeding in living. He had not been one being fighting. He had been one choosing something and not then being one coming to be receiving any other thing to go with the thing he had been choosing. He had not been one being fighting. He had been one not doing another thing than the thing he had been choosing. He had been one coming to be beginning to be succeeding in living. He had been one who could be one completely urging that he was not one needing doing some other thing. He was completely clearly thinking. He was not coming to be one going on beginning to be succeeding in living and he was then not fighting and he was then almost urging being one not needing choosing some other thing and he was then completely clearly expressing something, and he was then going on being one almost completely eating only one thing and he was then one understanding any one's understanding something he was completely understanding.

He was not going on being living in being living. He was a dead one at the ending of the beginning of middle living. He was being living. He was understanding being living. He was not beginning being living. He was not beginning again and again in being living. He was almost needing being one coming to be beginning to be succeeding in living.

He was knowing he was understanding being one being living. He was almost completely knowing this thing. He was not completely knowing that he was not completely needing being certain that being living is something existing. He was almost completely clearly expressing being one not needing being one receiving doing some other thing. He was almost completely clearly expressing this thing. He was not completely clearly expressing being one almost needing to be coming to be beginning succeeding in living. He was not being one succeeding in living. He was not one failing in living. He was one not being living when he was at the end of the beginning of middle living. He was then a dead one. He was then not needing that thing not needing being then a dead one not at all needing that thing. He was then being eating only one thing. He came then to be a dead one. He had not been completely needing that thing needing being a dead one. He had not been one needing that thing really at all needing that thing needing being a dead one. He was then understanding something and understanding any one else who was understanding something of that thing. He was then eating only one thing. He was then not needing to be a dead one. He was then not living then when he was at the end of the beginning of middle living. He was then one who came to be a dead one and some were not knowing that thing before he was completely buried there were he had come to be a dead one. He had come to be a dead one. He certainly then had been eating only one thing. He certainly then had not been needing not really needing not at all needing being a dead one. He was a dead one and he had been then one being living and understanding that thing understanding being living in being one being then being living.

He came to be a dead one and not any one had been needing that thing had been at all needing that thing, had been wanting to be needing that he was a dead one. Not any one had been wanting to be needing that thing that he had come to be a dead one. Some did not know he had come to be a dead one before he had come to be buried there to be a buried one there where he had been a dead one.

He had come to be a dead one. He had not come to at all beginning this thing, beginning being a dead one. He had come to be a dead one. He had come to be a buried one and some then were coming to know this thing that he had come to be a dead and buried one.

Some knew he was a dead one after he had been buried there where he had come to be a dead one. Some knew it then and were earnest then in being certain that he could not have come to be a dead one and some of such of them were saying it again and again. Some knew it then knew that he was a dead one after he had been buried there where he had come to be a dead one and they regretted that he had come to be a dead one, they regretted that thing. Some of such of them were interested in any one's regretting that thing. Some of such of them could come to be wondering if he might have been one coming to be beginning succeeding in living. Some who regretted that he had come to be a dead one were wondering if any one would come to know anything about his being a dead one, some of such of them were interested in that thing in some one coming to know something about him as being a dead one.

Some did not know anything of his having come to be a dead one for sometime after he had come to be a dead one. Some of such of them were feeling it to be a strange thing that he had come to be a dead one. Some of such of them were hearing something about his being a dead one a long time after he had come to be a dead one.

He was not living after the ending of the beginning of middle living. He came to be a dead one and was buried there where he had come to be a dead one. This was a surprising thing to some that he had come to be buried there where he had come to be a dead one. Not any one was needing this thing that he should have come to be a dead one and to be buried there where he had come to be a dead one.

Not any one needed to be one expecting that he should come to be a dead one and be buried there where he had come to be a dead one. Not any one needed this thing, he had not needed this thing, it was not a needed thing. He had come to be a dead one and had come to be buried there where he had come to be a dead one. Some were indignant about this thing that he had come to be a dead one. Some were wondering about this thing that he had come to be a dead one. Some were remembering this thing, that he had come to be a dead one. Some were regretting this thing, that he had come to be a dead one. Some were hoping that there was not this thing, his having come to be a dead one. Some were vague about this thing about his having come to be a dead one and having been buried there where he had come to be a dead one. Some were interested in this thing, in his having come to be a dead one and some of such of them were wondering about coming to be knowing something about him as being then a dead one. Some were not remembering that he had come to be a dead one. Some were not certain that he would have been one coming to be beginning succeeding in living. Some were certain that he might then not have come to be a dead one. Some were quite certain about this thing. Some were not certain that there was any difference in anything in his being then a dead one. Some were certain that he was then a dead one and were certain that it was an important thing. Some were certain that he was then a dead one and were not certain that it was an important thing that he was then one not being a living one. Any one could be one not very constantly remembering his being a dead one, his having been a living one. Any one could remember this thing, his having been a dead one, his having been a living one.

HISTORY OF A FAMILY'S PROGRESS

Any one has come to be a dead one. Any one has not come to be such a one to be a dead one. Many who are living have not come yet to be a dead one. Many who were living have come to be a dead one. Any one has come not to be a dead one. Any one has come to be a dead one.

Any one has not come to be a dead one. Very many who have been living have not yet come to be dead ones. Very many are being living.

Very many who were being living are not being living, have come to be dead ones. Many who came to be old ones came then to be dead ones. Many who came to be almost old ones came then to be dead ones.

Very many who were being living are not being living, have come to be a dead one. Not every one has come to be one being an old one. Not every one has come to be one being almost an old one. Not every one has come to be a dead one. Some have come to be an old one and have' come to be a dead one. Some have come to be almost an old one and have come to be a dead one. Some have not come to be a dead one, they are being living. Some have come to be a dead one.

Some are not believing that any other one can really be only doing the thing that other one is doing. Some are not believing that some one can be coming to be doing every other thing than anything some other one would naturally be doing then. Some then come to be old ones. Some then come to be almost old ones. Any one then comes to be one who is going to be almost any old one. Any one is one not being a dead one. Any one is one coming to be an old one. Any one is one being a dead one. Any one is one being such a one. Any one is one coming to be almost an old one.

Any one is one only not needing to be understanding everything. Any one is one who might have been doing the things that one is doing. Any one is one who might do that thing, the thing that one is doing. Any one is one, whom some are knowing, that any one is not believing that that one might be doing what that one is doing. Any one is one whom any one might not be believing to be one who might be doing the things that one is doing. Any one might be one and some might be believing that that one is doing the things that one is doing. Any one might be one and some might be believing that that one has been doing what that one has been doing.

Any one might be one coming to be almost an old one. Any one might be one coming to be an old one. Any one might be one coming to be a dead one.

Some one is one whom some one is certain is one going to be doing some one thing. It is certain that all some one knows of some one is that that one will be doing some one thing when some thing has been happening. It is certain that what some one does when something is happening is the thing some one is certain that one will be doing when some thing is happening. All that some one knows about some one is what is true of that one as being one doing what that one is doing when something is happening. It is certain that some one is not believing that some one is going to be doing the thing that one is going to be doing when something is happening. It is certain that some one is not certain that some one could not be understanding something and be then doing something if that one was one being any one being living. Some one is certain that in a way some one is one understanding that any one could be doing something that that one has not been doing if any one is one being any one being living. Some one is certain that some one could not be doing something that that one has not been doing even if every one is one being any one being living. Some are certain that any one is one understanding something, could be one doing something if any one is one being living. Some are certain that not any one is one understanding something, is one doing something, some are certain that any one is one being living.

Some are certain that any one is one being living. Some are knowing only this thing about everything, that any one is one being living. Some are knowing that not any one is one being living. Some are knowing that any one who is one being living is one knowing something of this thing. Some are ones not understanding anything of any such thing, of any one knowing something of this thing that any one is being one being living. Some are knowing that any one could be understanding something of this thing, that any one is knowing something of any one being one being living. Some have been old ones and then are not any longer living. Some have been almost old ones and then have not been any longer living. Some are ones knowing what some are not coming to be understanding. Some are ones knowing what some are coming to be understanding. Some are saying something about any one understanding something. Some are saying something about any one not understanding something. Some are saying something about some not understanding anything. Some are saying something about some understanding everything. Some are not saying anything about any one being almost an old one. Some are saying something about any one being almost an old one. Some are saying something about any one being an old one. Some are not saying anything about any one being an old one. Some are certain about understanding something being a thing that is coming to be interesting in being something any one being one being living will be coming to be thinking about doing. Some are certain about understanding something, are certain that it is not coming to be interesting. Some are certainly knowing what some one who is doing something is doing when that one comes to be doing a thing when something has been happening. Some are not coming to be believing much of any such thing, of any one knowing any such thing. Some are coming to be believing such a thing of some one that that one is one knowing such a thing. Some are coming to be ones being dead ones. Any one is such a one. Any one can come to be a dead one. Any one is such a one. Any one can come to be almost an old one if they have not come to be dead by then. Any one can come to be an old one if they have not already come to be a dead one. Any one can come to be such a one one being a dead one, one being almost an old one, one being an old one, one not being almost an old one, one not being an old one. Some are knowing something about what some are going to be doing. Some are not believing that any one is knowing any such thing. Some are knowing something of some knowing such a thing, knowing that some are knowing something of what some are coming to be doing. Some are believing that some will be ones not believing any such thing. Some are ones not believing that some will be believing any such thing. Any one is one being living, some are knowing all of this thing, some are not knowing all of this thing. Some are almost old ones, some are old ones, some are not old ones. Some are ones coming to be almost old ones. Some are ones coming to be old ones.

It is certain that it can be interesting to some that any one can come to be almost an old one if that one has not come to be a dead one before that one has come to be almost an old one. It is certain that it can be interesting to some that any one can come to be an old one if that one has not come before that one has come to be an old one to be a dead one. It is certain that it can be interesting to some that there are kinds in men. It is certain that it can be interesting to some that each kind in men and women is different from the other kinds of them.

It is certain that some can be certain of some kinds in men and women being different from other kinds in men and women. It is certain that some one can realise something of this thing of kinds there are in men and women. It is certain that some will come to be certain that this is completely interesting that some one has been realising kinds in men and women. It is certain that some will come to be realising differences in kinds in men and women and will come to make lists of them and long lists of them and others will then copy some of them of the lists of kinds in men and women and some will then make more lists of them many more lists of kinds in men and women and some one then will tell something then about this thing about men and women, and some others will then tell that thing again and some will then tell that thing again and again and any one will then be one having heard something of some such thing and some then will tell some more about men and women and some will tell anything of such a thing again and again and some will then go on in this thing in telling something of the kinds that are being existing in men and women.

There are kinds in men and women. There are kinds of them. There can be lists of the kinds of them. There will be many lists of the kinds of them.

There are kinds of men and women. Many of each kind of them have been living. Many of each kind of them are living. Very many of each kind of them have come to be dead ones. Many of each kind of them are living. There will be lists of kinds of men and women. There will be many lists of them.

There is coming to be a list of kinds in men and women. There will be a list of them. There has been some description of a piece of a list of them. There will be a list of them.

Each one of them, each kind of them is one that can have a description. Each one of each kind of them can have a description. There can be very many descriptions being existing of each kind of them. Each kind of them, each kind of men and women can have a description. There are many kinds of them, each kind of them can have a description.

Some of each kind of them are being living. Some of each kind of them were being ones who were being living. Many of each kind of them have come to be dead ones. Some of each kind of them have come to be almost old ones. Some of each kind of them have come to be old ones. There can be a description of each kind there is in men and women and there can be a description of their being young ones very young ones and older ones still young ones and older ones and almost completely older ones and older ones and almost old ones and old ones. There can be descriptions of the kinds there are of men and women. There can be descriptions of each one of each kind there is in men and women.

Any one can be one coming to be almost an old one. Some can be then knowing that thing knowing that that one has come to be almost an old one. Any one can be one coming to be almost an old one. Some are then being the one they are being in living, they are then when they have come to be almost an old one, they are then the one they are being in living and it is then not a completely easy thing to be certain that they are the one that is of the kind of them that they are in being living. This is not then a completely easy thing because then they are ones being ones then not doing everything and not doing everything very often and certainly then it is not a completely easy thing to be certain that that one is being of a kind of a one completely of a kind of a one, that that one is completely that one of that kind of a one of kinds in men and women. Certainly any one could be one coming to be almost an old one. Certainly some have been doing this thing. Certainly some will be doing this thing. Certainly some have just been doing this thing coming to be almost an old one. Certainly some are doing this thing are coming to be almost an old one. Certainly some have come to be dead by then have come to be dead and have not come to be almost an old one.

Certainly some are forgetting that some have come to be dead and have then not come to be almost an old one. Certainly some have come to be almost an old one and are not telling enough of this thing, are certainly not telling enough about this thing. Certainly some have begun again coming to be almost an old one. Any one might be one coming to be almost an old one. In a way it is not a completely satisfying thing having come to be almost an old one. In a way it is a thing that is a finished thing having come to be almost an old one. Some one is coming to do that thing again and again coming to be almost an old one. Some one is almost completely doing this thing coming to be almost an old one. Some one could be one coming to be almost an old one and certainly then there is such a thing, there is being almost an old one. Certainly there is such a thing, there is being almost an old one. Some can know that there is such a thing, that there is being almost an old one, some can know that there is just enough of this thing, of there being that any one is almost an old one. Some one will be one going on enough to be such a one to be one being almost an old one. Some one is going on enough in being that one in being one being almost an old one. There can be enough of that thing of being almost an old one.

There is then coming to be almost an old one. There is then this thing, there is then coming to be almost an old one. Any one can be one coming to be almost an old one if they are not dead by then.

There were families of them families of men and women and children. They went on being ones being living, some of them went on being ones being living. All of them were ones being living. Some of them are ones being ones being living. These were families of them and there are some of them who are ones being living and are marrying some other one and there are families then of men and women and some children.

There were families and some of them are ones who are almost all of them being ones being living and some of them have died since then and are not being living and some of them are being living and these are marrying some one and are being living. There are some who have had some children and some of these children are being living and some of these children are going on being ones being living until they are ones marrying some other one and some of them then are ones having some children and some of them are ones who are dead by then.

There are some families and some of them are dead then very many of them are dead then when some of them are marrying some other one and are having some children and are not having children and are not marrying.

There are some families and the children are living and the mother is living and the father is dead and the children have married some one and they have had some children and the children are telling about any one being one marrying some one and having some children, and are telling about not marrying, and are telling about not having any children, and are going on doing then something.

There are some families and any one in them who has come to be almost an old one is then almost that thing, is then almost an old one. There are some families and any one in them who has come to be an old one is almost that thing is almost an old one. There are some families and any one in them who is not almost an old one is almost that thing is almost not an old one. There are some families and any ore in them who is a young one is almost that thing is almost a young one.

There are some families and this has been some description of some of them. There are some families and there has been a crowd then when all of them have been ones knowing that thing knowing that there are some families of them.

There are some families and some of them are ones going on being something of such a thing being a family of them.

There are some families and there are families and any one who has married another one is one who is being one, who has been one, who has been in a family of some one.

There are families and some of them have some children and some of them are dead then and some of them are not dead then and the father is dead then and the mother is almost dead then and the mother is living quite a long time longer then. There are families and the mother is dead and the father could be living then and any one in the family could be dead then and any one in the family could be living then.

There are some families and some of them are being living and some of them have been dead then and some of them are remembering this thing are remembering that some are dead then and that time has been passing very quickly all the time any one has been a dead one.

There are some families and any one can be married in them and some in them are not married and some in them are married and any one of them almost any one of them can have some children and some of them have some children and some of them do not have children and some of them do something, do anything again.

There are some families and some of them do again and again do such a thing do being such a one, do being such a family of them. There are some families and some in such of them are ones having been doing such a thing being such a family of them again and then not again.

There are some families and any one of them can almost remember having been doing being such a family again. There are families and some in such of them are completely doing having been a daughter and a son in such a family of them. There are families and some of them are being such a one and some in them can be being such ones and some in them do it again do again and again being such ones.

Any one might be one to do something, that is, what any family living is needing. No, not every one is doing something that any family living is needing. Very many are doing something that any family living is needing. Any family living is needing that some are doing something and doing it very often. Any family living is needing that some one is remembering that any family living is needing that some do something very often. There is family living. Some are remembering that there is family living. Any one can be one remembering something of this thing, that there is family living. Any one can be one knowing that some one in that family living is remembering that family living is needing that some are doing something often.

Some are remembering that some one is competely remembering that family living is needing that some are doing something often. Any one can be remembering that some one is completely remembering that family living is needing that some are doing something often.

Any one who has come to be almost an old one is one who was been one not being such a one being almost an old one. Any one who has been one being an old one is one who has been one not being an old one. Any one who has been one remembering that some one has been completely remembering that family living needs then that some do something often is one sometime remembering sometime almost remembering that some one is completely remembering that family living can be needing that some are doing something often.

Some are completely remembering something of the thing that some are completely remembering that family living has been needing that some are doing something often. Some are completely remembering and completely mentioning something of the thing that family living is going on needing some doing something often. Any one in family living can do something often. Some in family living do something very often. Some one in a family living does something often and does it again and again.

Some in family living are needing to be ones doing something often and doing it again and again. Some are remembering that some in family living are doing something often and doing it again and again and that that one is certain that some of any one in that family living can be one doing something often and doing it again and again. Any one can mention that some one in family living is being one going on doing something often and doing it again and again. Some can mention that some

one in family living is being one going on being such a one a one family
living is needing, being one going on doing something often and doing
it again.

They all do so well what they are doing. Any one does so well what
any one is doing. Any one does so well being one being living. Any one
does so well doing what any one is doing. They all do so well what they
are doing, any one being living. Any one does so well what any one is
doing.

Every one does so well what any one is doing. Every one is being
living. Every one does so well doing that thing doing being living.
Every one is being in family living. Any one is being in family living.
Any one is doing that thing so well, being living. Any one is living in
family living. Any one is living in any family living. Any one will be
doing what any one is doing that is living in any family living.

Any one can go on not doing something. Any one can go on not
doing being one living in any family living. Any one can go on not doing
this thing not living in any family living.

Any one can begin again doing anything, any one can begin again
not doing something. Any one can go on not doing something. Any one
can begin not doing something. Any one can have heard everything.
Any one can hear everything. Any one can not like anything. Any
one can know anything. Any one can go on hearing everything. Any
one can go on having been hearing everything. Any one can hear anything. Any one can hear everything. Every one is hearing anything.
Every one is hearing everything and every one has been hearing everything.

Any one has been hearing everything Every one has been hearing everything. Every one is doing very well being living. Any one can
be in any family living. Any one can be one beginning not being in any
family living. Any one can go on not being in any family living. Any
one can go on doing very well being one being living. Any one can be
one having been hearing everything.

Being one saying something is what any one is doing in being one
being living in any family living. Being one saying something is what
every one is doing in being one being living in being in family living.

Being one saying something is being one being that one is being one
being the one saying something saying that thing. Being one saying
something is what any one can be doing in being one being in any family
living.

Being one saying something, having been saying that thing is what
any one is doing in being one being living. Saying something, saying
anything, having been saying something is what any one is doing in being
in any family living. Saying it then, having said it again, having said
something, being one being in family living is what any one is doing

who is one being living and being living, having been being living, beginning not being living, beginning being living in any family living. Saying anything, saying anything again, saying something and not then saying it again, saying something again, going on saying anything again is what some are doing who are then not beginning being in any family living.

Saying anything again, saying something then, saying something again and then not saying anything is what some are doing, is what some are doing again and they are then not doing anything in being one having been in any family living.

Any one is one being one being living and any one is saying something and any one is saying anything again and any one is one having been in family living and any one is one not beginning anything of being in any family living and any one is one being one being in family living and being one then not beginning anything again and being one then saying anything again and having been saying something and being then not saying anything and being then again not saying something and being then again saying anything

Any one being one being in any family living is being one having been saying something. Any one being one being living is one having been saying something Any one being in any family living is one having been saying something again. Any one being living is one having been saying something again. Any one being in any family living is one saying something again. Any one being in any family living is one saying anything and saying anything again. Any one being living is one saying something again. Any one being living is one saying anything and saying anything again.

It is time and any one in any family living is one knowing something of some such thing, it is time that some in any family living are ones not forgetting that they are ones having been doing something, having been saying something. Any one in any family living is knowing something of its being time that some in any family living have not been saying something. Some in any family living are knowing that it is time that any one in any family living is doing something, is saying something. It is time and some in any family living are completely mentioning such a thing it is time and some in any family living are coming to be certain, it is time that any one in any family living is doing something again and doing it again and regularly doing it again. It is time that any one in any family living is doing something regularly again, any one in any family living can come to be quite certain of such a thing. Every one in any family living can come to be quite certain that every one could come to doing something regularly and to go on regularly doing some such thing.

Any one in any family living can come to be one not completely mentioning something. Every one in any family living can come to be one not completely mentioning everything. Every one in any family living can come to be one not completely hearing every one mentioning anything. Every one in any family living can be one completely remembering that any family living is existing. Any one in any family living can be one beginning not remembering that any family living is existing. Any one in any family living can be one being one having been remembering that any family living is existing.

There is no time to begin being in any family living for some being in family living. There is being in family living for some being in family living. There is no time for beginning being in any family living for some being in any family living. There is no time of beginning doing anything again for some being living in a family living. There is no time for being in any family living for some being in any family living. There is no time for not being in any family living for some being in any family living.

Some being in a family living are certain of some such thing as being in any family living. Some being in any family living are not certain of such a thing are not certain of being in any family living being then existing, in their being then being living. Some being in any family living are beginning some such thing are beginning being in any family living. Some beginning being in any family living are not going on beginning being in a family living. Some beginning being in any family living are going on beginning being in any family living. Some being in a family living are going on being being in a family living. Some being in a family living are not going on being in a family living. Some are not understanding any one undertanding any family living being existing. Some are not understanding any one not understanding something, some in any family living are not understanding every one not understanding something. Any one in any family living is doing something then and any one in any family living is understanding, is not understanding any one understanding, any one not understanding anything. Any one in any family living is one being in any family living. Any one in any family living is one not being in any family living. Any one not understanding something is any one not understanding anything of any such thing. Any one in any family living is not understanding everything. Every one being living is not understanding everything. Any one being living is not understanding anything of any one not understanding everything. Any one being is one being living. Any one being living in any family living is being one existing in family living. Any one being living is existing. Every one being living are not understanding everything. Every one being living is going on being living. Any one being living is not understanding any one not understanding everything. Any one being living is being living and is going on doing something in being such a one and is then understanding that every one is not understanding everything.

Any one in any family living is certainly not one liking everything. Any one in any family living is one not liking anything. Any one liking that something is being something and is then liking anything being anything and is then not liking everything being everything is one being in a family living and being one liking and not liking being in a family living.

Some are being one being in a family living and they are ones going on being such a one and they might not be ones going on being such a one and certainly they would be ones being such a one being ones going on being in a family living when they were ones being in the family living in which they were being. Certainly some being in any family living are ones going on being in the family living in which they are being and they are ones not going on being in the family living in which they are being and they have been being young ones and they are being ones not being young ones and they are being ones being young enough ones and they are being ones being almost young enough ones and they are being almost coming to be almost old ones and they are being coming to be almost old ones and they are being almost old ones and they are being old enough ones and they are being quite old enough ones and they are being old ones.

When some one has done something, that one might then do that thing again. When some one has done something and some other one has done something and both of them have not then been doing some other thing, both of them might do something and one of them might do that thing and tell the other one and the other one might then be one going on doing the same thing. When some one has done something that one might then do that thing again. When some one has done something and has then not done something that one might then do that thing again might then do something and then not do something. When some one has done something and some other one has then done something and it is a similar thing and they both then have not been doing something, they have similarly not been doing something then, they might be doing something and not doing something together. They might and some one may think that they will and they may and then they may not, they may and then they may not, and they may not at all do something and not do something together.

Certainly they may be in family living, they may be in any family living. Certainly they may not be in any family living. They may be in the family living they are then having. They may not be in the family living they are then having. One of the two of them may be in the family living that one is then having. One of the two of them may not be in the family living that one is then having. Any way they may be ones doing something together and one be one then telling the other. They may then not be ones doing something together, they may be ones then not telling anything either one to the other.

There may be family living and any one may be expecting something to be happening and something is happening. There may be happening what some one is expecting. There may not be happening what some one is expecting. There may be something happening and any one then knowing anything of any such thing will be expecting, will not be expecting something that is then going on happening. Any family living is existing and any one in any famliy living is one knowing something of family living being existing.

Any one doing anything is expecting to be one doing or not doing anything. Any one in any family living is one doing or not doing something and is one then expecting to be one then doing or not doing something.

Some one has been standing up and is then doing something. Some one is doing something standing. Any one will do something standing. Some one has been standing in doing something. Certainly any one is standing in doing something.

Some one was standing and doing something. He was doing that thing. He was standing and doing something. He was doing something and he was standing. He was one some one was seeing. Some were seeing him doing something and standing.

Some are doing something. Any one is doing something. Some one is doing something and standing. Some are doing something and standing. Any one is doing something and standing. Some one was doing something and standing.

Any one doing something and standing is one doing something and standing. Some one was doing something and was standing.

Any one doing something and standing is one doing something and standing. Any one doing something and standing is one who is standing and doing something. Some one was doing something and was standing. That one was doing something standing.

Any one doing something standing is doing something standing. Some one is doing something standing. Any one doing something standing is one doing something standing. Any one doing something and standing is one doing something and standing.

Some one was standing and doing something. That one was one standing and doing something. That one was doing something and was standing and doing that thing. That one was one doing something, that one was one doing something, standing. That one was one standing and doing something, that one was one doing something and standing.

Every one doing something and standing is one doing something and standing. Any one doing that thing is one doing such a thing. Any one doing such a thing is one doing something and standing.

Every one doing something and standing is one doing such a thing. Every one doing something and standing are all of them doing that thing.

Any one of them do that thing if they do that thing, any one of them, any of them standing and doing something are standing and are doing something.

Any one standing and doing something is one standing and doing something. All of them, all standing and doing something are standing and doing something. All of them all who are ones standing and doing something are all of them are all doing something and standing. Any one of them any one of them doing something and standing is one doing something standing. There are many of them, that is a natural thing as every one is one doing something standing. There are many of them, that is a natural thing.

There are many being living. There are many family livings being existing. There are many being one being living. There are many being one being in family living. Any one of them will do and there are many of them, any one of them will do for being one being existing, for being one being in a family living. Any one of them will do as every one of them is existing, as any one of them is in a family living.

Every one being in family living when they are no longer living have come to be a dead one. Any one having come to be a dead one is not then being living. Very many have come to be dead ones and are then not any longer living. Any one having come to be a dead one is not then any longer living.

Every one in any family living when they have come to be dead ones are then not any longer living. There are very many being living. There are very many living in family living.

Any one in any family living has been one who has been one being living. Any one in any family living who has come to be not any longer living has come to be a dead one.

There are very many who have been living. There are very many who have come to be dead ones, to be ones not any longer being living.

Any one in any family living coming to be a dead one is then later a dead one. Any one in any family living is sometime a dead one. There are very many who have come to be dead ones. There are very many who have been in family living who have come to be dead ones. There are very many living in family living.

Some are living in family living, any one is living in family living and family living is existing and every one is living who is not come to be a dead one.

Very many are living in family living. Very many have been living in family living. Very many are living. Very many who were living are not living.

Some living in family living are doing something and are coming again and again to be one doing that thing. Some living in family living have been doing something and have been coming again and again to do that thing.

How it is done the thing some one is doing in family living is a thing that every one in that family living is knowing. How it is done and how it is done again and again the thing that is done again and again, done by some one in some family living is a thing that every one in tnat family living is knowing. Some one in a family living does a thing and not any other one in that family living is doing enough of that thing to make it that thing the thing one in that family living is doing. Some one in a family living is doing something, and is doing it and every one in the family living is knowing that that one is the one who is doing that thing.

Some are doing something and in a way they are doing that thing to every one and there are very many of such of them, of ones doing that thing and each one doing that thing is one doing that thing and every one knows that thing knows that that one is doing the thing that one is doing. Every one can know that that one is doing that thing, that the one doing the thing is doing the thing because the one doing that thing is doing that thing. Any one can know this thing that the one doing the thing is doing the thing. Every one in the family living of the one doing the thing are knowing that that one is doing the thing and they know this thing they know that that one is doing that thing because that one is doing that thing and any one can go on knowing that that one is doing that thing because that one is doing that thing and all in the family living of that one are going on knowing that that one is doing that thing because that one is doing that thing.

Family living is being existing. There are very many knowing this thing, there are some completely knowing this thing

Everywhere something is done. Everywhere where that thing is done it is done by some one. Everywhere where the thing that is done by some one comes to be done it is done and done by some one. Certainly every where where something is done it is done and done by some one. Certainly some are doing something and it is done and done by each one of them.

Certainly in a family living where something is done by some one it is done and done by that one. Certainly where it is done and done by some one, the thing that is done and done by that one is done by that one in some family living. Every one doing that thing and there are many doing that thing, there are almost quite enough doing that thing, every one doing that thing, any one doing that thing is doing that thing in the way that one, the one doing that thing is naturally doing that thing. It is not always being completely done by that one, the thing that is done and done by that one, it is not completely done by that one in the way it is natural for that one to do that thing. Some doing the thing that is done and done by them in a family living are completely doing that thing in the way it is natural for them to do that thing. Some doing the thing that is done and done by them are not completely doing the thing in the way it is natural for them to do that thing. Some of such of them are completely doing the thing that is done and done by them in a family living, they are not completely doing the thing in the way it is natural for them to do that thing.

Some are doing the thing they are doing in a family living. It is done and done by them. There are enough of them doing some such thing, certainly not too many, certainly very many, certainly some and each one of them is some one by whom something is done and done. There are enough kinds of them. There are very many kinds of them doing something in a family living that is done and done and done by them.

Every one in any family living who does not come to be a dead one before coming to be almost an old one, comes to be almost an old one and any one coming to be almost an old one has it then to be as something existing that they are ones going on being living. Any one in any family living who does not come to be a dead one before coming to be an old one comes to be an old one and is then being one having it being as something being existing that they are ones going on being living. Certainly any one coming to be almost an old one is then having it being as something being existing that that one is then going on being living. Certainly any one coming to be an old one is one being one then having it as being something existing that that one is being then one going on being living. Almost any one coming to be almost an old one coming to be an old one is one having it then as being something existing being one going on being living. Almost every one coming to be almost an old one, coming to be an old one is one having it then as being something existing being one going on being living. Almost every one being one coming to be almost an old one is one having been being in some family living. Almost every one coming to be an old one is one having been being in some family living. Almost every one coming to being an old one is one having been being in some family living. Almost every one coming to be almost an old one is being in some family living. Almost every one coming to be an old one is being in some family living.

Some when they are being quite young ones are being ones doing something that is being done again and again by some one in a family living. Some when they are older ones are being ones doing something that is done and done and done again by some one in a family living. Some when they are almost old ones are being ones doing something that is something that is done and done in a family living. Some when they are being old ones are doing then something that is being something that is being done and done in a family living. Some all their living are doing what is being done and done in a family living.

When one has come to be one not going on being a living one, mostly every one has been one being in a family living. When any one has come to be one not going on being living, mostly any one is then being one being in a family living. When any one has come to be one not going on being living, any family living can be then being existing.

Any one can come to be one coming not to be going on being living. Any family living can be then being existing. Any one can come to be one coming not to be going on being living, in a family living, any family living can then have been something being existing. Any one can come to be one not going to be one going on being living. Any family can be one being existing. Any family living can be one having been existing.

Any family can be one having been existing. Any family living can be one being existing. Any one can come to be one not going on being living.

Any family living can have been being existing. Any family living can be existing. There are very many family livings being existing. There have been very many family livings being existing.

Some in any family living are older ones than any other one. Some in any family living are younger ones than any other one. Some in any family living are not so old and not so young as any other one in the family living.

Any one in a family living is younger than some other one in the family living, has been younger than some other one in the family living. Any one in a family living is older than some other one in the family living. Some in the family living have been older than any other one in the family living.

Some in the family living have come to be doing something again and again, something that is done and done in that family living. Some of such of them are older than very many then in the family living. Some of such of them are younger than some in the family living. Some in the family living who have come to be doing what is being done again and again in the family living are older than most of them in the family living. Some who have come to be doing what is being done and done in the family living are younger than most of them in that family living. Some who have come to be doing what is being done and done in the family living are older than some and younger than some of them living in that family living.

The way of doing what is done and done in a family living is a way that a family living is needing being one in a way existing. Sometimes then that family is going on in that way of existing. Sometimes that family living is going on into another way of being existing. Sometimes some one who has done and done what is done by some one in the family living of that one is coming to be an older one and is then going on doing what that one is doing and then it is a very different thing the thing that one is doing in the family living of that one.

Some in family living are doing what is done and done in family living in family living being existing.

Any one in a family living is one knowing any other one in the family living. Any one in a family living is one any other one in the family living is knowing. Any one in a family living is not knowing that another one in the family living is doing something and doing it again and again. Any one in a family living is doing something and doing it again and not any other one in the family living is knowing that thing is knowing that that one is doing something and is doing it again and again and again. Any one in a family living is knowing that any one in the family living is doing something and doing it again and again and again and again.

Any one in a family living is certain that some in the family living are not doing something. Any one in a family living is certain that any one in the family living has been doing something. Any one in a family living is certain that any one in the family living has been doing something.

Some one in a family living is needing that every one in the family living is certain that that one will go on being one being in the family living. Some in a family living are needing that any one is certain that they will go on being in the family living.

Some one in a family living is one needing that every one in the family living is not doing something. Some one in a family living is needing that any one in the family living is certain that that one is one needing that every one in the family living are not doing something.

Some one in a family living is needing that every one in the family living is doing something. Some one in a family living is needing that any one in the family living is certain that that one is needing that every one in the family living is doing something.

Any one in the family living is doing something. Any one in the family living is not doing something. Every one in the family living is knowing that any one in the family living is not doing something. Every one in the family living is knowing that any one in the family living is doing something.

Some one in a family living is needing to be certain that every one in the family living is not going to be doing something. Some one in a family living is needing to be certain that every one in the family living is going to be doing something.

Old ones come to be dead. Any one coming to be an old enough one comes to be a dead one. Old ones come to be dead ones. Any one not coming to be a dead one before coming to be an old one comes to be an old one and comes then to be a dead one as any old one comes to be a dead one.

Any one coming to be an old enough one comes then to be a dead one.

Every one coming to be an old enough one comes then to be a dead one. Certainly old ones come to be dead ones. Certainly any one not coming to be a dead one before coming to be an old enough one comes to be an old enough one to come to be a dead one. Old ones come to be dead. Any old one can come then to be a dead one. Old ones and how they come to be dead, they come to be old enough ones to come to be dead.

Any one coming to be an old one is coming then to, be a dead one. Every one not coming to be a dead one before coming to be an old one, is coming to be an old one and is then coming to be a dead one.

Old ones come to be dead. There are old ones in family living in some family livings and these when they come to be old enough ones come to be dead. Any one coming to be an old enough one comes then to be a dead one.

Doing something is done by some in family living. Some family living is existing. Some are doing something in family living. Some one in a family living is doing something and family living is existing and family living is going on being existing and that one is doing something in family living. That one has been doing something in family living, that one is doing something in family living, that one is going to be doing something in family living. That one has been doing something in family living and that one is doing that thing and any one in the family living is being one being in the family living and that one the one doing something in the family living is completely remembering that every one being in the family living is in the family living. That one is remembering something of this thing about every one being in the family living, is remembering something about each one being in the family living, is compeletely remembering something about each one being in the family living and any one in the family living can come to be remembering that that one the one completely remembering something about each one being in the family living is remembering something about each one in the family living being in the family living.

The one remembering completely remembering something about each one being in the family living has been completely remembering everything about any one being in the family living, is remembering completely remembering everything about some being in the family living, is completely remembering something about every one being in the family living, will be completely remembering everything about some being in the family living will completely remember something about every one being in the family living. Family living can be existing. Very many are remembering that family living can be existing.

Very many can go on living remembering that family living is existing. Very many are living and are remembering that family living can go on existing. Very many can go on living remembering that family living can go on existing.

Family living can go on existing. Very many are remembering this thing are remembering that family living living can go on existing. Very many are quite certain that family living can go on existing. Very many are remmbering that they are quite certain that family living can go on existing.

Any family living going on existing is going on and every one can come to be a dead one and there are then not any more living in that family living and that family is not then existing if there are not then any more having come to be living. Any family living is existing if there are some more being living when very many have come to be dead ones. Family living can be existing if not every one in the family living has come to be a dead one. Family living can be existing if there have come to be some existing who have not come to be dead ones. Family living can be existing and there can be some who are not completely remembering any such thing. Family living can be existing and there can be some who have been completely remembering such a thing. Family living can be existing and there can be some remembering something of such a thing. Family living can be existing and some can come to be old ones and then dead ones and some can have been then quite expecting some such thing. Family living can be existing and some can come to be old ones and not yet dead ones and some can be remembering something of some such thing. Family living can be existing and some one can come to be an old one and some can come to be a pretty old one and some can come to be completely expecting such a thing and completely remembering expecting such a thing. Family living can be existing and every one can come to be a dead one and not any one then is remembering any such thing. Family living can be existing and every one can come to be a dead one and some are remembering some such thing. Family living can be existing and any one can come to be a dead one and every one is then a dead one and there are then not any more being living. Any old one can come to be a dead one. Every old one can come to be a dead one. Any family being existing is one having some being then not having come to be a dead one. Any family living can be existing when not every one has come to be a dead one. Every one in a family living having come to be dead ones some are remembering something of some such thing. Some being living not having come to be dead ones can be ones being in a family living. Some being living and having come to be old ones can come then to be dead ones. Some being living and being in a family living and coming then to be old ones can come then to be dead ones. Any one can be certain that some can remember such a thing. Any family living can be one being existing and some can remember something of some such thing.

DALKEY ARCHIVE PAPERBACKS

FICTION: AMERICAN

BARNES, DJUNA. *Ladies Almanack*	9.95
BARNES, DJUNA. *Ryder*	11.95
BARTH, JOHN. *LETTERS*	14.95
CHARYN, JEROME. *The Tar Baby*	10.95
COOVER, ROBERT. *A Night at the Movies*	9.95
CRAWFORD, STANLEY. *Some Instructions to My Wife*	7.95
DOWELL, COLEMAN. *Too Much Flesh and Jabez*	9.95
DUCORNET, RIKKI. *The Fountains of Neptune*	10.95
DUCORNET, RIKKI. *The Jade Cabinet*	9.95
DUCORNET, RIKKI. *Phosphor in Dreamland*	12.95
DUCORNET, RIKKI. *The Stain*	11.95
FAIRBANKS, LAUREN. *Sister Carrie*	10.95
GASS, WILLIAM H. *Willie Masters' Lonesome Wife*	9.95
KURYLUK, EWA. *Century 21*	12.95
MARKSON, DAVID. *Springer's Progress*	9.95
MARKSON, DAVID. *Wittgenstein's Mistress*	11.95
MASO, CAROLE. *AVA*	12.95
MCELROY, JOSEPH. *Women and Men*	15.95
MERRILL, JAMES. *The (Diblos) Notebook*	9.95
NOLLEDO, WILFRIDO D. *But for the Lovers*	12.95
SEESE, JUNE AKERS. *Is This What Other Women Feel Too?*	9.95
SEESE, JUNE AKERS. *What Waiting Really Means*	7.95
SORRENTINO, GILBERT. *Aberration of Starlight*	9.95
SORRENTINO, GILBERT. *Imaginative Qualities of Actual Things*	11.95
SORRENTINO, GILBERT. *Mulligan Stew*	13.95
SORRENTINO, GILBERT. *Splendide-Hôtel*	5.95
SORRENTINO, GILBERT. *Steelwork*	9.95
SORRENTINO, GILBERT. *Under the Shadow*	9.95
STEIN, GERTRUDE. *The Making of Americans*	16.95
STEIN, GERTRUDE. *A Novel of Thank You*	9.95
STEPHENS, MICHAEL. *Season at Coole*	7.95
WOOLF, DOUGLAS. *Wall to Wall*	7.95
YOUNG, MARGUERITE. *Miss MacIntosh, My Darling*	2-vol. set, 30.00
ZUKOFSKY, LOUIS. *Collected Fiction*	9.95

DALKEY ARCHIVE PAPERBACKS

FICTION: BRITISH

BROOKE-ROSE, CHRISTINE. *Amalgamemnon*	9.95
CHARTERIS, HUGO. *The Tide Is Right*	9.95
FIRBANK, RONALD. *Complete Short Stories*	9.95
GALLOWAY, JANICE. *Foreign Parts*	12.95
GALLOWAY, JANICE. *The Trick Is to Keep Breathing*	11.95
MOSLEY, NICHOLAS. *Accident*	9.95
MOSLEY, NICHOLAS. *Impossible Object*	9.95
MOSLEY, NICHOLAS. *Judith*	10.95

FICTION: FRENCH

BUTOR, MICHEL. *Portrait of the Artist as a Young Ape*	10.95
CREVEL, RENÉ. *Putting My Foot in It*	9.95
ERNAUX, ANNIE. *Cleaned Out*	9.95
GRAINVILLE, PATRICK. *The Cave of Heaven*	10.95
NAVARRE, YVES. *Our Share of Time*	9.95
QUENEAU, RAYMOND. *The Last Days*	9.95
QUENEAU, RAYMOND. *Pierrot Mon Ami*	9.95
ROUBAUD, JACQUES. *The Great Fire of London*	12.95
ROUBAUD, JACQUES. *The Plurality of Worlds of Lewis*	9.95
ROUBAUD, JACQUES. *The Princess Hoppy*	9.95
SIMON, CLAUDE. *The Invitation*	9.95

FICTION: GERMAN

SCHMIDT, ARNO. *Nobodaddy's Children*	13.95

FICTION: IRISH

CUSACK, RALPH. *Cadenza*	7.95
MACLOCHLAINN, ALF. *Out of Focus*	5.95
O'BRIEN, FLANN. *The Dalkey Archive*	9.95
O'BRIEN, FLANN. *The Hard Life*	9.95

(continued on next page)

DALKEY ARCHIVE PAPERBACKS

FICTION: LATIN AMERICAN and SPANISH

CAMPOS, JULIETA. *The Fear of Losing Eurydice*	8.95
LINS, OSMAN. *The Queen of the Prisons of Greece*	12.95
SARDUY, SEVERO. *Cobra* and *Maitreya*	13.95
TUSQUETS, ESTHER. *Stranded*	9.95
VALENZUELA, LUISA. *He Who Searches*	8.00

POETRY

ANSEN, ALAN. *Contact Highs: Selected Poems 1957-1987*	11.95
BURNS, GERALD. *Shorter Poems*	9.95
FAIRBANKS, LAUREN. *Muzzle Thyself*	9.95
GISCOMBE, C. S. *Here*	9.95
MARKSON, DAVID. *Collected Poems*	9.95
THEROUX, ALEXANDER. *The Lollipop Trollops*	10.95

NONFICTION

FORD, FORD MADOX. *The March of Literature*	16.95
GREEN, GEOFFREY, ET AL. *The Vineland Papers*	14.95
MATHEWS, HARRY. *20 Lines a Day*	8.95
ROUDIEZ, LEON S. *French Fiction Revisited*	14.95
SHKLOVSKY, VIKTOR. *Theory of Prose*	14.95
WEST, PAUL. *Words for a Deaf Daughter* and *Gala*	12.95
YOUNG, MARGUERITE. *Angel in the Forest*	13.95

For a complete catalog of our titles, write to Dalkey Archive Press, Illinois State University, Campus Box 4241, Normal, IL 61790-4241, or fax (309) 438-7422.